THE WRITINGS OF HERMAN MELVILLE

*The Northwestern–Newberry Edition*

VOLUME SIX

# Moby-Dick

*This volume edited,*
*with Historical Note, by*
HARRISON HAYFORD
HERSHEL PARKER
G. THOMAS TANSELLE

*Editorial Coordinator*
ALMA A. MACDOUGALL

*Assistant Editor*
LYNN HORTH

*Associates*
RICHARD COLLES JOHNSON
BRIAN HIGGINS
ROBERT C. RYAN

*Contributing Scholars*
JOEL MYERSON
MARY K. BERCAW
MARK NIEMEYER

# Moby-Dick

*or*

*The Whale*

HERMAN MELVILLE

NORTHWESTERN UNIVERSITY PRESS
*and*
THE NEWBERRY LIBRARY
*Evanston and Chicago*
1988

PUBLICATION OF this edition of THE WRITINGS OF HERMAN MELVILLE *has been made possible through the financial support of Northwestern University and its Research Committee and The Newberry Library. The research necessary to establish the text was undertaken under the Cooperative Research Program of the Office of Education. Northwestern University Press produced and published this edition and reserves all rights.*

LIBRARY OF CONGRESS CATALOG CARD NUMBER 76–129499

PRINTED IN THE UNITED STATES OF AMERICA

Cloth Edition, ISBN 0–8101–0324–9
Paper Edition, ISBN 0–8101–0325–7

CENTER FOR EDITIONS OF
AMERICAN AUTHORS
*AN APPROVED TEXT*
MODERN LANGUAGE
ASSOCIATION OF AMERICA
®

IN TOKEN

OF MY ADMIRATION FOR HIS GENIUS,

This Book is Inscribed

TO

NATHANIEL HAWTHORNE

# Contents

CONTENTS

## EDITORIAL APPENDIX

# Etymology

*(Supplied by a Late Consumptive Usher to a Grammar School.)*

[The pale Usher—threadbare in coat, heart, body, and brain; I see him now. He was ever dusting his old lexicons and grammars, with a queer handker-chief, mockingly embellished with all the gay flags of all the known nations of the world. He loved to dust his old grammars; it somehow mildly reminded him of his mortality.]

## Etymology

"While you take in hand to school others, and to teach them by what name a whale-fish is to be called in our tongue, leaving out, through ignorance, the letter H, which almost alone maketh up the signification of the word, you deliver that which is not true."     *Hackluyt.*

"WHALE. * * * Sw. and Dan. *hval.* This animal is named from roundness or rolling; for in Dan. *hvalt* is arched or vaulted."
*Webster's Dictionary.*

"WHALE. * * *  It is more immediately from the Dut. and Ger. *Wallen;* A.S. *Walw-ian,* to roll, to wallow."     *Richardson's Dictionary.*

| | |
|---|---|
| ‏חן‎, | *Hebrew.* |
| κητος, | *Greek.* |
| CETUS, | *Latin.* |
| WHÆL, | *Anglo-Saxon.* |
| HVAL, | *Danish.* |
| WAL, | *Dutch.* |
| HWAL, | *Swedish.* |
| HVALUR, | *Icelandic.* |
| WHALE, | *English.* |
| BALEINE, | *French.* |
| BALLENA, | *Spanish.* |
| PEKEE-NUEE-NUEE, | *Fegee.* |
| PEHEE-NUEE-NUEE, | *Erromangoan.* |

# Extracts

*(Supplied by a Sub-Sub-Librarian.)*

[It will be seen that this mere painstaking burrower and grub-worm of a poor devil of a Sub-Sub appears to have gone through the long Vaticans and street-stalls of the earth, picking up whatever random allusions to whales he could anyways find in any book whatsoever, sacred or profane. Therefore you must not, in every case at least, take the higgledy-piggledy whale statements, however authentic, in these extracts, for veritable gospel cetology. Far from it. As touching the ancient authors generally, as well as the poets here appearing, these extracts are solely valuable or entertaining, as affording a glancing bird's eye view of what has been promiscuously said, thought, fancied, and sung of Leviathan, by many nations and generations, including our own.

So fare thee well, poor devil of a Sub-Sub, whose commentator I am. Thou belongest to that hopeless, sallow tribe which no wine of this world will ever warm; and for whom even Pale Sherry would be too rosy-strong; but with whom one sometimes loves to sit, and feel poor-devilish, too; and grow convivial upon tears; and say to them bluntly, with full eyes and empty glasses, and in not altogether unpleasant sadness—Give it up, Sub-Subs! For by how much the more pains ye take to please the world, by so much the more shall ye for ever go thankless! Would that I could clear out Hampton Court and the Tuileries for ye! But gulp down your tears and hie aloft to the royal-mast with your hearts; for your friends who have gone before are clearing out the seven-storied heavens, and making refugees of long-pampered Gabriel, Michael, and Raphael, against your coming. Here ye strike but splintered hearts together—there, ye shall strike unsplinterable glasses!]

## Extracts

"And God created great whales."
*Genesis.*

"Leviathan maketh a path to shine after him;
One would think the deep to be hoary."
*Job.*

"Now the Lord had prepared a great fish to swallow up Jonah."
*Jonah.*

"There go the ships; there is that Leviathan whom thou hast made to play therein."
*Psalms.*

"In that day, the Lord with his sore, and great, and strong sword, shall punish Leviathan the piercing serpent, even Leviathan that crooked serpent; and he shall slay the dragon that is in the sea."
*Isaiah.*

"And what thing soever besides cometh within the chaos of this monster's mouth, be it beast, boat, or stone, down it goes all incontinently that foul great swallow of his, and perisheth in the bottomless gulf of his paunch."
*Holland's Plutarch's Morals.*

"The Indian Sea breedeth the most and the biggest fishes that are: among which the Whales and Whirlpooles called Balænæ, take up as much in length as four acres or arpens of land."
*Holland's Pliny.*

"Scarcely had we proceeded two days on the sea, when about sunrise a great many Whales and other monsters of the sea, appeared. Among the former, one was of a most monstrous size. * * This came towards us, open-mouthed, raising the waves on all sides, and beating the sea before him into a foam."
*Tooke's Lucian.*
*"The True History."*

"He visited this country also with a view of catching horse-whales, which had bones of very great value for their teeth, of which he brought some to the king. \* \* \* The best whales were catched in his own country, of which some were forty-eight, some fifty yards long. He said that he was one of six who had killed sixty in two days."

*Other or Octher's verbal narrative taken down*
*from his mouth by King Alfred. A.D. 890.*

"And whereas all the other things, whether beast or vessel, that enter into the dreadful gulf of this monster's (whale's) mouth, are immediately lost and swallowed up, the sea-gudgeon retires into it in great security, and there sleeps." MONTAIGNE.—*Apology for Raimond Sebond.*

"Let us fly, let us fly! Old Nick take me if it is not Leviathan described by the noble prophet Moses in the life of patient Job." *Rabelais.*

"This whale's liver was two cart-loads." *Stowe's Annals.*

"The great Leviathan that maketh the seas to seethe like boiling pan."
*Lord Bacon's Version of the Psalms.*

"Touching that monstrous bulk of the whale or ork we have received nothing certain. They grow exceeding fat, insomuch that an incredible quantity of oil will be extracted out of one whale."
*Ibid. "History of Life and Death."*

"The sovereignest thing on earth is parmacetti for an inward bruise."
*King Henry.*

"Very like a whale." *Hamlet.*

"Which to recure, no skill of leach's art
Mote him availle, but to returne againe
To his wound's worker, that with lovely dart,
Dinting his breast, had bred his restless paine,
Like as the wounded whale to shore flies from the maine."
*The Fairie Queen.*

"Immense as whales, the motion of whose vast bodies can in a peaceful calm trouble the ocean till it boil."
*Sir William Davenant. Preface to Gondibert.*

"What spermacetti is, men might justly doubt, since the learned Hofmannus in his work of thirty years, saith plainly, *Nescio quid sit.*"

*Sir T. Browne. Of Sperma Ceti and the*
*Sperma Ceti Whale. Vide his V.E.*

"Like Spencer's Talus with his iron flail
He threatens ruin with his ponderous tail.
*     *     *     *     *
Their fixed jav'lins in his side he wears,
And on his back a grove of pikes appears."

*Waller's Battle of the Summer Islands.*

"By art is created that great Leviathan, called a Commonwealth or State—(in Latin, Civitas) which is but an artificial man."

*Opening sentence of Hobbes's Leviathan.*

"Silly Mansoul swallowed it without chewing, as if it had been a sprat in the mouth of a whale."                    *Holy War.*

"That sea beast
Leviathan, which God of all his works
Created hugest that swim the ocean stream."

*Paradise Lost.*

———"There Leviathan,
Hugest of living creatures, on the deep
Stretched like a promontory sleeps or swims,
And seems a moving land; and at his gills
Draws in, and at his trunk spouts out a sea."

*Ibid.*

"The mighty whales which swim in a sea of water, and have a sea of oil swimming in them."                    *Fuller's Profane and Holy State.*

"So close behind some promontory lie
The huge Leviathans to attend their prey,
And give no chace, but swallow in the fry,
Which through their gaping jaws mistake the way."

*Dryden's Annus Mirabilis.*

"While the whale is floating at the stern of the ship, they cut off his head, and tow it with a boat as near the shore as it will come; but it will be aground in twelve or thirteen foot water."

*Thomas Edge's Ten Voyages to Spitzbergen, in Purchass.*

"In their way they saw many whales sporting in the ocean, and in wantonness fuzzing up the water through their pipes and vents, which nature has placed on their shoulders."

*Sir T. Herbert's Voyages into Asia and Africa.*

*Harris Coll.*

"Here they saw such huge troops of whales, that they were forced to proceed with a great deal of caution for fear they should run their ship upon them."          *Schouten's Sixth Circumnavigation.*

"We set sail from the Elbe, wind N. E. in the ship called The Jonas-in-the-Whale. * * *

Some say the whale can't open his mouth, but that is a fable. * * *

They frequently climb up the masts to see whether they can see a whale, for the first discoverer has a ducat for his pains. * * *

I was told of a whale taken near Hitland, that had above a barrel of herrings in his belly. * * *

One of our harpooneers told me that he caught once a whale in Spitzbergen that was white all over."

*A Voyage to Greenland, A.D.* 1671.

*Harris Coll.*

"Several whales have come in upon this coast (Fife). Anno 1652, one eighty foot in length of the whale-bone kind came in, which, (as I was informed) beside a vast quantity of oil, did afford 500 weight of baleen. The jaws of it stand for a gate in the garden of Pitfirren."

*Sibbald's Fife and Kinross.*

"Myself have agreed to try whether I can master and kill this Spermaceti whale, for I could never hear of any of that sort that was killed by any man, such is his fierceness and swiftness."

*Richard Stafford's Letter from the Bermudas.*

*Phil. Trans. A.D.* 1668.

"Whales in the sea
God's voice obey."

*N. E. Primer.*

"We saw also abundance of large whales, there being more in these southern seas, as I may say, by a hundred to one; than we have to the northward of us."

*Captain Cowley's Voyage round the Globe. A.D.* 1729.

* * * * * "and the breath of the whale is frequently attended with such an insupportable smell, as to bring on a disorder of the brain."

*Ulloa's South America.*

"To fifty chosen sylphs of special note,
    We trust the important charge, the petticoat.
    Oft have we known that seven-fold fence to fail,
    Tho' stiff with hoops and armed with ribs of whale."

*Rape of the Lock.*

"If we compare land animals in respect to magnitude, with those that take up their abode in the deep, we shall find they will appear contemptible in the comparison. The whale is doubtless the largest animal in creation."

*Goldsmith, Nat. His.*

"If you should write a fable for little fishes, you would make them speak like great whales."                 *Goldsmith to Johnson.*

"In the afternoon we saw what was supposed to be a rock, but it was found to be a dead whale, which some Asiatics had killed, and were then towing ashore. They seemed to endeavor to conceal themselves behind the whale, in order to avoid being seen by us."                 *Cook's Voyages.*

"The larger whales, they seldom venture to attack. They stand in so great dread of some of them, that when out at sea they are afraid to mention even their names, and carry dung, brim-stone, juniper-wood, and some other articles of the same nature in their boats, in order to terrify and prevent their too near approach."

*Uno Von Troil's Letters on Banks's and*
*Solander's Voyage to Iceland in* 1772.

"The Spermacetti Whale found by the Nantuckois, is an active, fierce animal, and requires vast address and boldness in the fishermen."

*Thomas Jefferson's Whale Memorial to the*
*French minister in* 1788.

"And pray, sir, what in the world is equal to it?"
                              *Edmund Burke's reference in Parliament*
                              *to the Nantucket Whale-Fishery.*

"Spain——a great whale stranded on the shores of Europe."
                              *Edmund Burke. (somewhere.)*

"A tenth branch of the king's ordinary revenue, said to be grounded
on the consideration of his guarding and protecting the seas from pirates
and robbers, is the right to *royal* fish, which are whale and sturgeon. And
these, when either thrown ashore or caught near the coasts, are the property
of the king."
                              *Blackstone.*

"Soon to the sport of death the crews repair:
Rodmond unerring o'er his head suspends
The barbed steel, and every turn attends."
                              *Falconer's Shipwreck.*

"Bright shone the roofs, the domes, the spires,
    And rockets flew self driven,
To hang their momentary fires
    Amid the vault of heaven.

"So fire with water to compare,
    The ocean serves on high,
Up-spouted by a whale in air,
    To express unwieldy joy."
                              *Cowper, on the Queen's Visit to London.*

"Ten or fifteen gallons of blood are thrown out of the heart at a stroke,
with immense velocity."
                              *John Hunter's account of the dissection*
                              *of a whale. (A small sized one.)*

"The aorta of a whale is larger in the bore than the main pipe of the
water-works at London Bridge, and the water roaring in its passage through
that pipe is inferior in impetus and velocity to the blood gushing from the
whale's heart."
                              *Paley's Theology.*

"The whale is a mammiferous animal without hind feet."
                              *Baron Cuvier.*

"In 40 degrees south, we saw Spermacetti Whales, but did not take any till the first of May, the sea being then covered with them."

*Colnett's Voyage for the Purpose of*
*Extending the Spermacetti Whale Fishery.*

"In the free element beneath me swam,
Floundered and dived, in play, in chace, in battle,
Fishes of every color, form, and kind;
Which language cannot paint, and mariner
Had never seen; from dread Leviathan
To insect millions peopling every wave:
Gather'd in shoals immense, like floating islands,
Led by mysterious instinct through that waste
And trackless region, though on every side
Assaulted by voracious enemies,
Whales, sharks, and monsters, arm'd in front or jaw,
With swords, saws, spiral horns, or hooked fangs."

*Montgomery's World before the Flood.*

"Io! Pæan! Io! sing,
To the finny people's king.
Not a mightier whale than this
In the vast Atlantic is;
Not a fatter fish than he,
Flounders round the Polar Sea."

*Charles Lamb's Triumph of the Whale.*

"In the year 1690 some persons were on a high hill observing the whales spouting and sporting with each other, when one observed; there—pointing to the sea—is a green pasture where our children's grand-children will go for bread."          *Obed Macy's History of Nantucket.*

"I built a cottage for Susan and myself and made a gateway in the form of a Gothic Arch, by setting up a whale's jaw bones."

*Hawthorne's Twice Told Tales.*

"She came to bespeak a monument for her first love, who had been killed by a whale in the Pacific ocean, no less than forty years ago."

*Ibid.*

"No, Sir, 'tis a Right Whale," answered Tom; "I saw his spout; he threw up a pair of as pretty rainbows as a Christian would wish to look at. He's a raal oil-butt, that fellow!"
*Cooper's Pilot.*

"The papers were brought in, and we saw in the Berlin Gazette that whales had been introduced on the stage there."
*Eckermann's Conversations with Goethe.*

"My God! Mr. Chase, what is the matter?" I answered, "we have been stove by a whale."
*"Narrative of the Shipwreck of the Whale Ship Essex of Nantucket,
which was attacked and finally destroyed by a large Sperm Whale
in the Pacific Ocean." By Owen Chase of Nantucket, first mate
of said vessel. New York. 1821.*

"A mariner sat on the shrouds one night,
    The wind was piping free;
Now bright, now dimmed, was the moonlight pale,
And the phospher gleamed in the wake of the whale,
    As it floundered in the sea."
*Elizabeth Oakes Smith.*

"The quantity of line withdrawn from the different boats engaged in the capture of this one whale, amounted altogether to 10,440 yards or nearly six English miles." * * *

"Sometimes the whale shakes its tremendous tail in the air, which, cracking like a whip, resounds to the distance of three or four miles."
*Scoresby.*

"Mad with the agonies he endures from these fresh attacks, the infuriated Sperm Whale rolls over and over; he rears his enormous head, and with wide expanded jaw snaps at everything around him; he rushes at the boats with his head; they are propelled before him with vast swiftness, and sometimes utterly destroyed.

* * * It is a matter of great astonishment that the consideration of the habits of so interesting, and, in a commercial point of view, of so important an animal (as the Sperm Whale) should have been so entirely neglected, or should have excited so little curiosity among the numerous, and many of them competent observers, that of late years must have pos-

sessed the most abundant and the most convenient opportunities of witnessing their habitudes."

*Thomas Beale's History of the Sperm Whale*, 1839.

"The Cachalot" (Sperm Whale) "is not only better armed than the True Whale" (Greenland or Right Whale) "in possessing a formidable weapon at either extremity of its body, but also more frequently displays a disposition to employ those weapons offensively, and in a manner at once so artful, bold, and mischievous, as to lead to its being regarded as the most dangerous to attack of all the known species of the whale tribe."

*Frederick Debell Bennett's Whaling Voyage Round the Globe.* 1840.

October 13. "There she blows," was sung out from the mast-head.
"Where away?" demanded the captain.
"Three points off the lee bow, sir."
"Raise up your wheel. Steady!"
"Steady, sir."
"Mast-head ahoy! Do you see that whale now?"
"Ay ay, sir! A shoal of Sperm Whales! There she blows! There she breaches!"
"Sing out! sing out every time!"
"Ay ay, sir! There she blows! there—there—*thar* she blows—bowes—bo-o-o-s!"
"How far off?"
"Two miles and a half."
"Thunder and lightning! so near! Call all hands!"

*J. Ross Browne's Etchings of a Whaling Cruise.* 1846.

"The Whale-ship Globe, on board of which vessel occurred the horrid transactions we are about to relate, belonged to the island of Nantucket."

*"Narrative of the Globe Mutiny,"* by *Lay and Hussey, survivors. A.D.* 1828.

"Being once pursued by a whale which he had wounded, he parried the assault for some time with a lance; but the furious monster at length rushed on the boat; himself and comrades only being preserved by leaping into the water when they saw the onset was inevitable."

*Missionary Journal of Tyerman and Bennet.*

"Nantucket itself," said Mr. Webster, "is a very striking and peculiar portion of the National interest. There is a population of eight or nine thousand persons, living here in the sea, adding largely every year to the National wealth by the boldest and most persevering industry."

> *Report of Daniel Webster's Speech in the U. S. Senate, on the*
> *application for the Erection of a Breakwater at Nantucket.* 1828.

"The whale fell directly over him, and probably killed him in a moment."

> *"The Whale and his Captors, or The Whaleman's Adventures and*
> *the Whale's Biography, as gathered on the Homeward Cruise of*
> *the Commodore Preble." By Rev. Henry T. Cheever.*

"If you make the least damn bit of noise," replied Samuel, "I will send you to hell."

> *Life of Samuel Comstock (the mutineer), by his brother, William*
> *Comstock. Another Version of the whale-ship Globe narrative.*

"The voyages of the Dutch and English to the Northern Ocean, in order, if possible, to discover a passage through it to India, though they failed of their main object, laid open the haunts of the whale."

> *McCulloch's Commercial Dictionary.*

"These things are reciprocal; the ball rebounds, only to bound forward again; for now in laying open the haunts of the whale, the whalemen seem to have indirectly hit upon new clews to that same mystic North-West Passage."

> *From "Something" unpublished.*

"It is impossible to meet a whale-ship on the ocean without being struck by her mere appearance. The vessel under short sail, with look-outs at the mast-heads, eagerly scanning the wide expanse around them, has a totally different air from those engaged in a regular voyage."

> *Currents and Whaling. U.S. Ex. Ex.*

"Pedestrians in the vicinity of London and elsewhere may recollect having seen large curved bones set upright in the earth, either to form arches over gateways, or entrances to alcoves, and they may perhaps have been told that these were the ribs of whales."

> *Tales of a Whale Voyager*
> *to the Arctic Ocean.*

"It was not till the boats returned from the pursuit of these whales, that the whites saw their ship in bloody possession of the savages enrolled among the crew."

*Newspaper Account of the Taking and
Retaking of the Whale-ship Hobomock.*

"It is generally well known that out of the crews of Whaling vessels (American) few ever return in the ships on board of which they departed."

*Cruise in a Whale Boat.*

"Suddenly a mighty mass emerged from the water, and shot up perpendicularly into the air. It was the whale."

*Miriam Coffin or the Whale Fishermen.*

"The Whale is harpooned to be sure; but bethink you, how you would manage a powerful unbroken colt, with the mere appliance of a rope tied to the root of his tail."      *A Chapter on Whaling in Ribs and Trucks.*

"On one occasion I saw two of these monsters (whales) probably male and female, slowly swimming, one after the other, within less than a stone's throw of the shore" (Terra Del Fuego), "over which the beech tree extended its branches."                    *Darwin's Voyage of a Naturalist.*

"'Stern all!' exclaimed the mate, as upon turning his head, he saw the distended jaws of a large Sperm Whale close to the head of the boat, threatening it with instant destruction;—'Stern all, for your lives!'"

*Wharton the Whale Killer.*

"So be cheery, my lads, let your hearts never fail,
While the bold harpooneer is striking the whale!"

*Nantucket Song.*

"Oh, the rare old Whale, mid storm and gale
In his ocean home will be
A giant in might, where might is right,
And King of the boundless sea."

*Whale Song.*

# Moby-Dick

# Chapter 1

*Loomings*

C ALL me Ishmael. Some years ago—never mind how long
precisely—having little or no money in my purse, and nothing
particular to interest me on shore, I thought I would sail about a
little and see the watery part of the world. It is a way I have of driving off
the spleen, and regulating the circulation. Whenever I find myself growing
grim about the mouth; whenever it is a damp, drizzly November in my
soul; whenever I find myself involuntarily pausing before coffin warehouses,
and bringing up the rear of every funeral I meet; and especially whenever
my hypos get such an upper hand of me, that it requires a strong moral
principle to prevent me from deliberately stepping into the street, and
methodically knocking people's hats off—then, I account it high time to get
to sea as soon as I can. This is my substitute for pistol and ball. With a philosophical flourish Cato throws himself upon his sword; I quietly take to the
ship. There is nothing surprising in this. If they but knew it, almost all men
in their degree, some time or other, cherish very nearly the same feelings
towards the ocean with me.

There now is your insular city of the Manhattoes, belted round by
wharves as Indian isles by coral reefs—commerce surrounds it with her surf.
Right and left, the streets take you waterward. Its extreme down-town is
the Battery, where that noble mole is washed by waves, and cooled by

3

breezes, which a few hours previous were out of sight of land. Look at the
crowds of water-gazers there.

Circumambulate the city of a dreamy Sabbath afternoon. Go from
Corlears Hook to Coenties Slip, and from thence, by Whitehall, northward.
What do you see?—Posted like silent sentinels all around the town, stand
thousands upon thousands of mortal men fixed in ocean reveries. Some
leaning against the spiles; some seated upon the pier-heads; some looking
over the bulwarks of ships from China; some high aloft in the rigging, as
if striving to get a still better seaward peep. But these are all landsmen; of
week days pent up in lath and plaster—tied to counters, nailed to benches,
clinched to desks. How then is this? Are the green fields gone? What do
they here?

But look! here come more crowds, pacing straight for the water, and
seemingly bound for a dive. Strange! Nothing will content them but the
extremest limit of the land; loitering under the shady lee of yonder warehouses will not suffice. No. They must get just as nigh the water as they
possibly can without falling in. And there they stand—miles of them—
leagues. Inlanders all, they come from lanes and alleys, streets and avenues
—north, east, south, and west. Yet here they all unite. Tell me, does the
magnetic virtue of the needles of the compasses of all those ships attract
them thither?

Once more. Say, you are in the country; in some high land of lakes. Take
almost any path you please, and ten to one it carries you down in a dale, and
leaves you there by a pool in the stream. There is magic in it. Let the most
absent-minded of men be plunged in his deepest reveries—stand that man on
his legs, set his feet a-going, and he will infallibly lead you to water, if water
there be in all that region. Should you ever be athirst in the great American
desert, try this experiment, if your caravan happen to be supplied with a
metaphysical professor. Yes, as every one knows, meditation and water are
wedded for ever.

But here is an artist. He desires to paint you the dreamiest, shadiest,
quietest, most enchanting bit of romantic landscape in all the valley of the
Saco. What is the chief element he employs? There stand his trees, each with
a hollow trunk, as if a hermit and a crucifix were within; and here sleeps his
meadow, and there sleep his cattle; and up from yonder cottage goes a
sleepy smoke. Deep into distant woodlands winds a mazy way, reaching to
overlapping spurs of mountains bathed in their hill-side blue. But though
the picture lies thus tranced, and though this pine-tree shakes down its sighs
like leaves upon this shepherd's head, yet all were vain, unless the shepherd's

eye were fixed upon the magic stream before him. Go visit the Prairies in June, when for scores on scores of miles you wade knee-deep among Tiger-lilies—what is the one charm wanting?—Water—there is not a drop of water there! Were Niagara but a cataract of sand, would you travel your thousand miles to see it? Why did the poor poet of Tennessee, upon suddenly receiving two handfuls of silver, deliberate whether to buy him a coat, which he sadly needed, or invest his money in a pedestrian trip to Rockaway Beach? Why is almost every robust healthy boy with a robust healthy soul in him, at some time or other crazy to go to sea? Why upon your first voyage as a passenger, did you yourself feel such a mystical vibration, when first told that you and your ship were now out of sight of land? Why did the old Persians hold the sea holy? Why did the Greeks give it a separate deity, and make him the own brother of Jove? Surely all this is not without meaning. And still deeper the meaning of that story of Narcissus, who because he could not grasp the tormenting, mild image he saw in the fountain, plunged into it and was drowned. But that same image, we our-selves see in all rivers and oceans. It is the image of the ungraspable phantom of life; and this is the key to it all.

Now, when I say that I am in the habit of going to sea whenever I begin to grow hazy about the eyes, and begin to be over conscious of my lungs, I do not mean to have it inferred that I ever go to sea as a passenger. For to go as a passenger you must needs have a purse, and a purse is but a rag unless you have something in it. Besides, passengers get sea-sick—grow quarrel-some—don't sleep of nights—do not enjoy themselves much, as a general thing;—no, I never go as a passenger; nor, though I am something of a salt, do I ever go to sea as a Commodore, or a Captain, or a Cook. I abandon the glory and distinction of such offices to those who like them. For my part, I abominate all honorable respectable toils, trials, and tribulations of every kind whatsoever. It is quite as much as I can do to take care of myself, without taking care of ships, barques, brigs, schooners, and what not. And as for going as cook,—though I confess there is considerable glory in that, a cook being a sort of officer on ship-board—yet, somehow, I never fancied broiling fowls;—though once broiled, judiciously buttered, and judg-matically salted and peppered, there is no one who will speak more respect-fully, not to say reverentially, of a broiled fowl than I will. It is out of the idolatrous dotings of the old Egyptians upon broiled ibis and roasted river horse, that you see the mummies of those creatures in their huge bake-houses the pyramids.

No, when I go to sea, I go as a simple sailor, right before the mast, plumb

down into the forecastle, aloft there to the royal mast-head. True, they
rather order me about some, and make me jump from spar to spar, like a
grasshopper in a May meadow. And at first, this sort of thing is unpleasant
enough. It touches one's sense of honor, particularly if you come of an old
established family in the land, the Van Rensselaers, or Randolphs, or
Hardicanutes. And more than all, if just previous to putting your hand into
the tar-pot, you have been lording it as a country schoolmaster, making the
tallest boys stand in awe of you. The transition is a keen one, I assure you,
from a schoolmaster to a sailor, and requires a strong decoction of Seneca
and the Stoics to enable you to grin and bear it. But even this wears off in
time.

What of it, if some old hunks of a sea-captain orders me to get a broom
and sweep down the decks? What does that indignity amount to, weighed,
I mean, in the scales of the New Testament? Do you think the archangel
Gabriel thinks anything the less of me, because I promptly and respectfully
obey that old hunks in that particular instance? Who aint a slave? Tell me
that. Well, then, however the old sea-captains may order me about—however they may thump and punch me about, I have the satisfaction of knowing that it is all right; that everybody else is one way or other served in much
the same way—either in a physical or metaphysical point of view, that is;
and so the universal thump is passed round, and all hands should rub each
other's shoulder-blades, and be content.

Again, I always go to sea as a sailor, because they make a point of paying
me for my trouble, whereas they never pay passengers a single penny that
I ever heard of. On the contrary, passengers themselves must pay. And
there is all the difference in the world between paying and being paid. The
act of paying is perhaps the most uncomfortable infliction that the two
orchard thieves entailed upon us. But *being paid,*—what will compare with
it? The urbane activity with which a man receives money is really marvellous, considering that we so earnestly believe money to be the root of all
earthly ills, and that on no account can a monied man enter heaven. Ah!
how cheerfully we consign ourselves to perdition!

Finally, I always go to sea as a sailor, because of the wholesome exercise
and pure air of the forecastle deck. For as in this world, head winds are far
more prevalent than winds from astern (that is, if you never violate the
Pythagorean maxim), so for the most part the Commodore on the quarter-
deck gets his atmosphere at second hand from the sailors on the forecastle.
He thinks he breathes it first; but not so. In much the same way do the
commonalty lead their leaders in many other things, at the same time that

the leaders little suspect it. But wherefore it was that after having repeatedly smelt the sea as a merchant sailor, I should now take it into my head to go on a whaling voyage; this the invisible police officer of the Fates, who has the constant surveillance of me, and secretly dogs me, and influences me in some unaccountable way—he can better answer than any one else. And, doubtless, my going on this whaling voyage, formed part of the grand programme of Providence that was drawn up a long time ago. It came in as a sort of brief interlude and solo between more extensive performances. I take it that this part of the bill must have run something like this:

"*Grand Contested Election for the Presidency of the United States.*
"WHALING VOYAGE BY ONE ISHMAEL.
"BLOODY BATTLE IN AFFGHANISTAN."

Though I cannot tell why it was exactly that those stage managers, the Fates, put me down for this shabby part of a whaling voyage, when others were set down for magnificent parts in high tragedies, and short and easy parts in genteel comedies, and jolly parts in farces—though I cannot tell why this was exactly; yet, now that I recall all the circumstances, I think I can see a little into the springs and motives which being cunningly presented to me under various disguises, induced me to set about performing the part I did, besides cajoling me into the delusion that it was a choice resulting from my own unbiased freewill and discriminating judgment.

Chief among these motives was the overwhelming idea of the great whale himself. Such a portentous and mysterious monster roused all my curiosity. Then the wild and distant seas where he rolled his island bulk; the undeliverable, nameless perils of the whale; these, with all the attending marvels of a thousand Patagonian sights and sounds, helped to sway me to my wish. With other men, perhaps, such things would not have been inducements; but as for me, I am tormented with an everlasting itch for things remote. I love to sail forbidden seas, and land on barbarous coasts. Not ignoring what is good, I am quick to perceive a horror, and could still be social with it—would they let me—since it is but well to be on friendly terms with all the inmates of the place one lodges in.

By reason of these things, then, the whaling voyage was welcome; the great flood-gates of the wonder-world swung open, and in the wild conceits that swayed me to my purpose, two and two there floated into my inmost soul, endless processions of the whale, and, midmost of them all, one grand hooded phantom, like a snow hill in the air.

# Chapter 2

*The Carpet-Bag*

I STUFFED A SHIRT or two into my old carpet-bag, tucked it under my arm, and started for Cape Horn and the Pacific. Quitting the good city of old Manhatto, I duly arrived in New Bedford. It was on a Saturday night in December. Much was I disappointed upon learning that the little packet for Nantucket had already sailed, and that no way of reaching that place would offer, till the following Monday.

As most young candidates for the pains and penalties of whaling stop at this same New Bedford, thence to embark on their voyage, it may as well be related that I, for one, had no idea of so doing. For my mind was made up to sail in no other than a Nantucket craft, because there was a fine, boisterous something about everything connected with that famous old island, which amazingly pleased me. Besides though New Bedford has of late been gradually monopolizing the business of whaling, and though in this matter poor old Nantucket is now much behind her, yet Nantucket was her great original—the Tyre of this Carthage;—the place where the first dead American whale was stranded. Where else but from Nantucket did those aboriginal whalemen, the Red-Men, first sally out in canoes to give chase to the Leviathan? And where but from Nantucket, too, did that first adventurous little sloop put forth, partly laden with imported cobble-stones —so goes the story—to throw at the whales, in order to discover when they were nigh enough to risk a harpoon from the bowsprit?

Now having a night, a day, and still another night following before me in New Bedford, ere I could embark for my destined port, it became a matter of concernment where I was to eat and sleep meanwhile. It was a very dubious-looking, nay, a very dark and dismal night, bitingly cold and cheerless. I knew no one in the place. With anxious grapnels I had sounded my pocket, and only brought up a few pieces of silver,—So, wherever you go, Ishmael, said I to myself, as I stood in the middle of a dreary street shouldering my bag, and comparing the gloom towards the north with the darkness towards the south—wherever in your wisdom you may conclude to lodge for the night, my dear Ishmael, be sure to inquire the price, and don't be too particular.

With halting steps I paced the streets, and passed the sign of "The Crossed Harpoons"—but it looked too expensive and jolly there. Further on, from the bright red windows of the "Sword-Fish Inn," there came such fervent rays, that it seemed to have melted the packed snow and ice from before the house, for everywhere else the congealed frost lay ten inches thick in a hard, asphaltic pavement,—rather weary for me, when I struck my foot against the flinty projections, because from hard, remorseless service the soles of my boots were in a most miserable plight. Too expensive and jolly, again thought I, pausing one moment to watch the broad glare in the street, and hear the sounds of the tinkling glasses within. But go on, Ishmael, said I at last; don't you hear? get away from before the door; your patched boots are stopping the way. So on I went. I now by instinct followed the streets that took me waterward, for there, doubtless, were the cheapest, if not the cheeriest inns.

Such dreary streets! blocks of blackness, not houses, on either hand, and here and there a candle, like a candle moving about in a tomb. At this hour of the night, of the last day of the week, that quarter of the town proved all but deserted. But presently I came to a smoky light proceeding from a low, wide building, the door of which stood invitingly open. It had a careless look, as if it were meant for the uses of the public; so, entering, the first thing I did was to stumble over an ash-box in the porch. Ha! thought I, ha, as the flying particles almost choked me, are these ashes from that destroyed city, Gomorrah? But "The Crossed Harpoons," and "The Sword-Fish?" —this, then, must needs be the sign of "The Trap." However, I picked myself up and hearing a loud voice within, pushed on and opened a second, interior door.

It seemed the great Black Parliament sitting in Tophet. A hundred black faces turned round in their rows to peer; and beyond, a black Angel of Doom was beating a book in a pulpit. It was a negro church; and the preacher's text was about the blackness of darkness, and the weeping and wailing and teeth-gnashing there. 'Ha, Ishmael, muttered I, backing out, Wretched entertainment at the sign of "The Trap!"

Moving on, I at last came to a dim sort of out-hanging light not far from the docks, and heard a forlorn creaking in the air; and looking up, saw a swinging sign over the door with a white painting upon it, faintly representing a tall straight jet of misty spray, and these words underneath—"The Spouter-Inn:—Peter Coffin."

Coffin?—Spouter?—Rather ominous in that particular connexion, thought I. But it is a common name in Nantucket, they say, and I suppose this Peter here is an emigrant from there. As the light looked so dim, and the place, for the time, looked quiet enough, and the dilapidated little wooden house itself looked as if it might have been carted here from the ruins of some burnt district, and as the swinging sign had a poverty-stricken sort of creak to it, I thought that here was the very spot for cheap lodgings, and the best of pea coffee.

It was a queer sort of place—a gable-ended old house, one side palsied as it were, and leaning over sadly. It stood on a sharp bleak corner, where that tempestuous wind Euroclydon kept up a worse howling than ever it did about poor Paul's tossed craft. Euroclydon, nevertheless, is a mighty pleasant zephyr to any one in-doors, with his feet on the hob quietly toasting for bed. "In judging of that tempestuous wind called Euroclydon," says an old writer—of whose works I possess the only copy extant—"it maketh a marvellous difference, whether thou lookest out at it from a glass window where the frost is all on the outside, or whether thou observest it from that sashless window, where the frost is on both sides, and of which the wight Death is the only glazier." True enough, thought I, as this passage occurred to my mind—old black-letter, thou reasonest well. Yes, these eyes are windows, and this body of mine is the house. What a pity they didn't stop up the chinks and the crannies though, and thrust in a little lint here and there. But it's too late to make any improvements now. The universe is finished; the copestone is on, and the chips were carted off a million years ago. Poor Lazarus there, chattering his teeth against the curbstone for his pillow, and shaking off his tatters with his shiverings, he might plug up both ears with rags, and put a corn-cob into his mouth, and yet that would not keep out the tempestuous Euroclydon. Euroclydon! says old Dives, in his red silken wrapper (he had a redder one afterwards)—pooh, pooh! What a fine frosty night; how Orion glitters; what northern lights! Let them talk of their oriental summer climes of everlasting conservatories; give me the privilege of making my own summer with my own coals.

But what thinks Lazarus? Can he warm his blue hands by holding them up to the grand northern lights? Would not Lazarus rather be in Sumatra than here? Would he not far rather lay him down lengthwise along the line of the equator; yea, ye gods! go down to the fiery pit itself, in order to keep out this frost?

Now, that Lazarus should lie stranded there on the curbstone before the door of Dives, this is more wonderful than that an iceberg should be moored to one of the Moluccas. Yet Dives himself, he too lives like a Czar in an ice palace made of frozen sighs, and being a president of a temperance society, he only drinks the tepid tears of orphans.

But no more of this blubbering now, we are going a-whaling, and there is plenty of that yet to come. Let us scrape the ice from our frosted feet, and see what sort of a place this "Spouter" may be.

# Chapter 3

## *The Spouter-Inn*

NTERING that gable-ended Spouter-Inn, you found yourself in a wide, low, straggling entry with old-fashioned wain-
scots, reminding one of the bulwarks of some condemned old craft.
On one side hung a very large oil-painting so thoroughly besmoked, and
every way defaced, that in the unequal cross-lights by which you viewed it,
it was only by diligent study and a series of systematic visits to it, and careful
inquiry of the neighbors, that you could any way arrive at an understanding
of its purpose. Such unaccountable masses of shades and shadows, that at
first you almost thought some ambitious young artist, in the time of the
New England hags, had endeavored to delineate chaos bewitched. But by
dint of much and earnest contemplation, and oft repeated ponderings, and
especially by throwing open the little window towards the back of the
entry, you at last came to the conclusion that such an idea, however wild,
might not be altogether unwarranted.

But what most puzzled and confounded you was a long, limber, portentous, black mass of something hovering in the centre of the picture over
three blue, dim, perpendicular lines floating in a nameless yeast. A boggy,
soggy, squitchy picture truly, enough to drive a nervous man distracted.
Yet was there a sort of indefinite, half-attained, unimaginable sublimity
about it that fairly froze you to it, till you involuntarily took an oath with

yourself to find out what that marvellous painting meant. Ever and anon a bright, but, alas, deceptive idea would dart you through.—It's the Black Sea in a midnight gale.—It's the unnatural combat of the four primal elements.—It's a blasted heath.—It's a Hyperborean winter scene.—It's the breaking-up of the ice-bound stream of Time. But at last all these fancies yielded to that one portentous something in the picture's midst. *That* once found out, and all the rest were plain. But stop; does it not bear a faint resemblance to a gigantic fish? even the great leviathan himself?

In fact, the artist's design seemed this: a final theory of my own, partly based upon the aggregated opinions of many aged persons with whom I conversed upon the subject. The picture represents a Cape-Horner in a great hurricane; the half-foundered ship weltering there with its three dismantled masts alone visible; and an exasperated whale, purposing to spring clean over the craft, is in the enormous act of impaling himself upon the three mast-heads.

The opposite wall of this entry was hung all over with a heathenish array of monstrous clubs and spears. Some were thickly set with glittering teeth resembling ivory saws; others were tufted with knots of human hair; and one was sickle-shaped, with a vast handle, sweeping round like the segment made in the new-mown grass by a long-armed mower. You shuddered as you gazed, and wondered what monstrous cannibal and savage could ever have gone a death-harvesting with such a hacking, horrifying implement. Mixed with these were rusty old whaling lances and harpoons all broken and deformed. Some were storied weapons. With this once long lance, now wildly elbowed, fifty years ago did Nathan Swain kill fifteen whales between a sunrise and a sunset. And that harpoon—so like a corkscrew now —was flung in Javan seas, and run away with by a whale, years afterwards slain off the Cape of Blanco. The original iron entered nigh the tail, and, like a restless needle sojourning in the body of a man, travelled full forty feet, and at last was found imbedded in the hump.

Crossing this dusky entry, and on through yon low-arched way—cut through what in old times must have been a great central chimney with fire-places all round—you enter the public room. A still duskier place is this, with such low ponderous beams above, and such old wrinkled planks beneath, that you would almost fancy you trod some old craft's cockpits, especially of such a howling night, when this corner-anchored old ark rocked. so furiously. On one side stood a long, low, shelf-like table covered with cracked glass cases, filled with dusty rarities gathered from this wide world's remotest nooks. Projecting from the further angle of the room stands a dark-looking den—the bar—a rude attempt at a right whale's head. Be that how it may, there stands the vast arched bone of the whale's jaw, so wide, a coach might almost drive beneath it. Within are shabby shelves, ranged round with old decanters, bottles, flasks; and in those jaws of swift destruction, like another cursed Jonah (by which name indeed they called him), bustles a little withered old man, who, for their money, dearly sells the sailors deliriums and death.

Abominable are the tumblers into which he pours his poison. Though true cylinders without—within, the villanous green goggling glasses deceitfully tapered downwards to a cheating bottom. Parallel meridians rudely pecked into the glass, surround these footpads' goblets. Fill to *this* mark, and your charge is but a penny; to *this* a penny more; and so on to the full glass—the Cape Horn measure, which you may gulph down for a shilling.

Upon entering the place I found a number of young seamen gathered about a table, examining by a dim light divers specimens of *skrimshander*. I sought the landlord, and telling him I desired to be accommodated with a room, received for answer that his house was full—not a bed unoccupied. "But avast," he added, tapping his forehead, "you haint no objections to sharing a harpooneer's blanket, have ye? I s'pose you are goin' a whalin', so you'd better get used to that sort of thing."

I told him that I never liked to sleep two in a bed; that if I should ever do so, it would depend upon who the harpooneer might be, and that if he (the landlord) really had no other place for me, and the harpooneer was not decidedly objectionable, why rather than wander further about a strange town on so bitter a night, I would put up with the half of any decent man's blanket.

"I thought so. All right; take a seat. Supper?—you want supper? Supper 'll be ready directly."

I sat down on an old wooden settle, carved all over like a bench on the Battery. At one end a ruminating tar was still further adorning it with his jack-knife, stooping over and diligently working away at the space between his legs. He was trying his hand at a ship under full sail, but he didn't make much headway, I thought.

At last some four or five of us were summoned to our meal in an adjoining room. It was cold as Iceland—no fire at all—the landlord said he couldn't afford it. Nothing but two dismal tallow candles, each in a winding sheet. We were fain to button up our monkey jackets, and hold to our lips cups of scalding tea with our half frozen fingers. But the fare was of the most substantial kind—not only meat and potatoes, but dumplings; good heavens! dumplings for supper! One young fellow in a green box coat, addressed himself to these dumplings in a most direful manner.

"My boy," said the landlord, "you'll have the nightmare to a dead sartainty."

"Landlord," I whispered, "that aint the harpooneer, is it?"

"Oh, no," said he, looking a sort of diabolically funny, "the harpooner is a dark complexioned chap. He never eats dumplings, he don't—he eats nothing but steaks, and likes 'em rare."

"The devil he does," says I. "Where is that harpooneer? Is he here?"

"He'll be here afore long," was the answer.

I could not help it, but I began to feel suspicious of this "dark complexioned" harpooneer. At any rate, I made up my mind that if it so turned out that we should sleep together, he must undress and get into bed before I did.

Supper over, the company went back to the bar-room, when, knowing not what else to do with myself, I resolved to spend the rest of the evening as a looker on.

Presently a rioting noise was heard without. Starting up, the landlord cried, "That's the Grampus's crew. I seed her reported in the offing this morning; a four years' voyage, and a full ship. Hurrah, boys; now we'll have the latest news from the Feegees."

A tramping of sea boots was heard in the entry; the door was flung open, and in rolled a wild set of mariners enough. Enveloped in their shaggy watch coats, and with their heads muffled in woollen comforters, all bedarned and ragged, and their beards stiff with icicles, they seemed an eruption of bears from Labrador. They had just landed from their boat, and this was the first house they entered. No wonder, then, that they made a straight wake for the whale's mouth—the bar—when the wrinkled little old Jonah, there officiating, soon poured them out brimmers all round. One complained of a bad cold in his head, upon which Jonah mixed him a pitch-like potion of gin and molasses, which he swore was a sovereign cure for all colds and catarrhs whatsoever, never mind of how long standing, or whether caught off the coast of Labrador, or on the weather side of an ice-island.

The liquor soon mounted into their heads, as it generally does even with the arrantest topers newly landed from sea, and they began capering about most obstreperously.

I observed, however, that one of them held somewhat aloof, and though he seemed desirous not to spoil the hilarity of his shipmates by his own sober face, yet upon the whole he refrained from making as much noise as the rest. This man interested me at once; and since the sea-gods had ordained that he should soon become my shipmate (though but a sleeping-partner one, so far as this narrative is concerned), I will here venture upon a little description of him. He stood full six feet in height, with noble shoulders, and a chest like a coffer-dam. I have seldom seen such brawn in a man. His face was deeply brown and burnt, making his white teeth dazzling by the contrast; while in the deep shadows of his eyes floated some reminiscences that did not seem to give him much joy. His voice at once announced that he was a Southerner, and from his fine stature, I thought he must be one of those tall mountaineers from the Alleganian Ridge in Virginia. When the revelry of his companions had mounted to its height, this man slipped away unobserved, and I saw no more of him till he became my comrade on the sea. In a few minutes, however, he was missed by his shipmates, and being, it seems, for some reason a huge favorite with them, they raised a cry of "Bulkington! Bulkington! where's Bulkington?" and darted out of the house in pursuit of him.

It was now about nine o'clock, and the room seeming almost supernaturally quiet after these orgies, I began to congratulate myself upon a little plan that had occurred to me just previous to the entrance of the seamen.

No man prefers to sleep two in a bed. In fact, you would a good deal rather not sleep with your own brother. I don't know how it is, but people like to be private when they are sleeping. And when it comes to sleeping with an unknown stranger, in a strange inn, in a strange town, and that stranger a harpooneer, then your objections indefinitely multiply. Nor was there any earthly reason why I as a sailor should sleep two in a bed, more than anybody else; for sailors no more sleep two in a bed at sea, than bachelor Kings do ashore. To be sure they all sleep together in one apartment, but you have your own hammock, and cover yourself with your own blanket, and sleep in your own skin.

The more I pondered over this harpooneer, the more I abominated the thought of sleeping with him. It was fair to presume that being a harpooneer, his linen or woollen, as the case might be, would not be of the tidiest, certainly none of the finest. I began to twitch all over. Besides, it was getting late, and any decent harpooneer ought to be home and going bedwards. Suppose now, he should tumble in upon me at midnight—how could I tell from what vile hole he had been coming?

"Landlord! I've changed my mind about that harpooneer.—I shan't sleep with him. I'll try the bench here."

"Just as you please; I'm sorry I cant spare ye a table-cloth for a mattress, and it's a plaguy rough board here"—feeling of the knots and notches. "But wait a bit, Skrimshander; I've got a carpenter's plane there in the bar—wait, I say, and I'll make ye snug enough." So saying he procured the plane; and with his old silk handkerchief first dusting the bench, vigorously set to planing away at my bed, the while grinning like an ape. The shavings flew right and left; till at last the plane-iron came bump against an indestructible knot. The landlord was near spraining his wrist, and I told him for heaven's sake to quit—the bed was soft enough to suit me, and I did not know how all the planing in the world could make eider down of a pine plank. So gathering up the shavings with another grin, and throwing them into the great stove in the middle of the room, he went about his business, and left me in a brown study.

I now took the measure of the bench, and found that it was a foot too short; but that could be mended with a chair. But it was a foot too narrow, and the other bench in the room was about four inches higher than the planed one—so there was no yoking them. I then placed the first bench lengthwise along the only clear space against the wall, leaving a little interval between, for my back to settle down in. But I soon found that there came such a draught of cold air over me from under the sill of the window, that this plan would never do at all, especially as another current from the rickety door met the one from the window, and both together formed a series of small whirlwinds in the immediate vicinity of the spot where I had thought to spend the night.

The devil fetch that harpooneer, thought I, but stop, couldn't I steal a march on him—bolt his door inside, and jump into his bed, not to be wakened by the most violent knockings? It seemed no bad idea; but upon second thoughts I dismissed it. For who could tell but what the next morning, so soon as I popped out of the room, the harpooneer might be standing in the entry, all ready to knock me down!

Still, looking round me again, and seeing no possible chance of spending a sufferable night unless in some other person's bed, I began to think that after all I might be cherishing unwarrantable prejudices against this unknown harpooneer. Thinks I, I'll wait awhile; he must be dropping in before long. I'll have a good look at him then, and perhaps we may become jolly good bedfellows after all—there's no telling.

But though the other boarders kept coming in by ones, twos, and threes, and going to bed, yet no sign of my harpooneer.

"Landlord!" said I, "what sort of a chap is he—does he always keep such late hours?" It was now hard upon twelve o'clock.

The landlord chuckled again with his lean chuckle, and seemed to be mightily tickled at something beyond my comprehension. "No," he answered, "generally he's an airley bird—airley to bed and airley to rise— yes, he's the bird what catches the worm.—But to-night he went out a peddling, you see, and I don't see what on airth keeps him so late, unless, may be, he can't sell his head."

"Can't sell his head?—What sort of a bamboozling story is this you are telling me?" getting into a towering rage. "Do you pretend to say, landlord, that this harpooneer is actually engaged this blessed Saturday night, or rather Sunday morning, in peddling his head around this town?"

"That's precisely it," said the landlord, "and I told him he couldn't sell it here, the market's overstocked."

"With what?" shouted I.

"With heads to be sure; ain't there too many heads in the world?"

"I tell you what it is, landlord," said I, quite calmly, "you'd better stop spinning that yarn to me—I'm not green."

"May be not," taking out a stick and whittling a toothpick, "but I rayther guess you'll be done *brown* if that ere harpooneer hears you a slanderin' his head."

"I'll break it for him," said I, now flying into a passion again at this un-accountable farrago of the landlord's.

"It's broke a'ready," said he.

"Broke," said I—"*broke*, do you mean?"

"Sartain, and that's the very reason he can't sell it, I guess."

"Landlord," said I, going up to him as cool as Mt. Hecla in a snow storm,—"landlord, stop whittling. You and I must understand one another, and that too without delay. I come to your house and want a bed; you tell me you can only give me half a one; that the other half belongs to a certain harpooneer. And about this harpooneer, whom I have not yet seen, you persist in telling me the most mystifying and exasperating stories, tending to beget in me an uncomfortable feeling towards the man whom you design for my bedfellow—a sort of connexion, landlord, which is an intimate and confidential one in the highest degree. I now demand of you to speak out and tell me who and what this harpooneer is, and whether I shall be in all respects safe to spend the night with him. And in the first place, you will be so good as to unsay that story about selling his head, which if true I take to be good evidence that this har-pooneer is stark mad, and I've no idea of sleeping with a madman; and you, sir, *you* I mean, landlord, *you*, sir, by trying to induce me to do so knowingly, would thereby render yourself liable to a criminal prosecution."

"Wall," said the landlord, fetching a long breath, "that's a purty long sarmon for a chap that rips a little now and then. But be easy, be easy, this here harpooneer I have been tellin' you of has just arrived from the south seas, where he bought up a lot of 'balmed New Zealand heads (great curios, you know), and he's sold all on 'em but one, and that one he's trying to sell to-night, cause to-morrow's Sunday, and it would not do to be sellin' human heads about the streets when folks is goin' to churches. He wanted to, last Sunday, but I stopped him just as he was goin' out of the door with four heads strung on a string, for all the airth like a string of inions."

This account cleared up the otherwise unaccountable mystery, and showed that the landlord, after all, had had no idea of fooling me—but at the same time what could I think of a harpooneer who stayed out of a Saturday night clean into the holy Sabbath, engaged in such a cannibal business as selling the heads of dead idolators?

"Depend upon it, landlord, that harpooneer is a dangerous man."

"He pays reg'lar," was the rejoinder. "But come, it's getting dreadful late, you had better be turning flukes—it's a nice bed: Sal and me slept in that ere bed the night we were spliced. There's plenty room for two to kick about in that bed; it's an almighty big bed that. Why, afore we give it up, Sal used to put our Sam and little Johnny in the foot of it. But I got a dreaming and sprawling about one night, and somehow, Sam got pitched on the floor, and came near breaking his arm. Arter that, Sal said it wouldn't do. Come along here, I'll give ye a glim in a jiffy;" and so saying he lighted a candle and held it towards me, offering to lead the way. But I stood irresolute; when looking at a clock in the corner, he exclaimed "I vum it's Sunday—you won't see that harpooneer to-night; he's come to anchor somewhere—come along then; *do* come; *won't* ye come?"

I considered the matter a moment, and then up stairs we went, and I was ushered into a small room, cold as a clam, and furnished, sure enough, with a prodigious bed, almost big enough indeed for any four harpooneers to sleep abreast.

"There," said the landlord, placing the candle on a crazy old sea chest that did double duty as a wash-stand and centre table; "there, make yourself comfortable now, and good night to ye." I turned round from eyeing the bed, but he had disappeared.

Folding back the counterpane, I stooped over the bed. Though none of the most elegant, it yet stood the scrutiny tolerably well. I then glanced round the room; and besides the bedstead and centre table, could see no other furniture belonging to the place, but a rude shelf, the four walls, and a papered fireboard representing a man striking a whale. Of things not properly belonging to the room, there was a hammock lashed up, and thrown upon the floor in one corner; also a large seaman's bag, containing the harpooneer's wardrobe no doubt, in lieu of a land trunk. Likewise, there was a parcel of outlandish bone fish hooks on the shelf over the fire-place, and a tall harpoon standing at the head of the bed.

But what is this on the chest? I took it up, and held it close to the light, and felt it, and smelt it, and tried every way possible to arrive at some satisfactory conclusion concerning it. I can compare it to nothing but a large door mat, ornamented at the edges with little tinkling tags something like the stained porcupine quills round an Indian moccasin. There was a hole or slit in the middle of this mat, the same as in South American ponchos. But could it be possible that any sober harpooneer would get into a door mat, and parade the streets of any Christian town in that sort of guise? I put it on, to try it, and it weighed me down like a hamper, being uncommonly shaggy and thick, and I thought a little damp, as though this mysterious harpooneer had been wearing it of a rainy day. I went up in it to a bit of glass stuck against the wall, and I never saw such a sight in my life. I tore myself out of it in such a hurry that I gave myself a kink in the neck.

I sat down on the side of the bed, and commenced thinking about this head-peddling harpooneer, and his door mat. After thinking some time on the bed-side, I got up and took off my monkey jacket, and then stood in the middle of the room thinking. I then took off my coat, and thought a little more in my shirt sleeves. But beginning to feel very cold now, half undressed as I was, and remembering what the landlord said about the harpooneer's not coming home at all that night, it being so very late, I made no more ado, but jumped out of my pantaloons and boots, and then blowing out the light tumbled into bed, and commended myself to the care of heaven.

Whether that mattress was stuffed with corn-cobs or broken crockery, there is no telling, but I rolled about a good deal, and could not sleep for a long time. At last I slid off into a light doze, and had pretty nearly made a good offing towards the land of Nod, when I heard a heavy footfall in the passage, and saw a glimmer of light come into the room from under the door.

Lord save me, thinks I, that must be the harpooneer, the infernal head-peddler. But I lay perfectly still, and resolved not to say a word till spoken to. Holding a light in one hand, and that identical New Zealand head in the other, the stranger entered the room, and without looking towards the bed, placed his candle a good way off from me on the floor in one corner, and then began working away at the knotted cords of the large bag I before spoke of as being in the room. I was all eagerness to see his face, but he kept it averted for some time while employed in unlacing the bag's mouth. This accomplished, however, he turned round—when, good heavens! what a sight! Such a face! It was of a dark, purplish, yellow color, here and there stuck over with large, blackish looking squares. Yes, it's just as I thought, he's a terrible bedfellow; he's been in a fight, got dreadfully cut, and here he is, just from the surgeon. But at that moment he chanced to turn his face so towards the light, that I plainly saw they could not be sticking-plasters at all, those black squares on his cheeks. They were stains of some sort or other. At first I knew not what to make of this; but soon an inkling of the truth occurred to me. I remembered a story of a white man—a whaleman too—who, falling among the cannibals, had been tattooed by them. I concluded that this harpooneer, in the course of his distant voyages, must have met with a similar adventure. And what is it, thought I, after all! It's only his outside; a man can be honest in any sort of skin. But then, what to make of his unearthly complexion, that part of it, I mean, lying round about, and completely independent of the squares of tattooing. To be sure, it might be nothing but a good coat of tropical tanning; but I never heard of a hot sun's tanning a white man into a purplish yellow one. However, I had never been in the South Seas; and perhaps the sun there produced these extraordinary effects upon the skin. Now, while all these ideas were passing through me like lightning, this harpooneer never noticed me at all. But, after some difficulty having opened his bag, he commenced fumbling in it, and presently pulled out a sort of tomahawk, and a seal-skin wallet with the hair on. Placing these on the old chest in the middle of the room, he then took the New Zealand head—a ghastly thing enough—and crammed it down into the bag. He now took off his hat—a new beaver hat—when I came nigh singing out with fresh surprise. There was no hair on his head—none to speak of at least—nothing but a small scalp-knot twisted up on his forehead. His bald purplish head now looked for all the world like a mildewed skull. Had not the stranger stood between me and the door, I would have bolted out of it quicker than ever I bolted a dinner.

Even as it was, I thought something of slipping out of the window, but it was the second floor back. I am no coward, but what to make of this head-peddling purple rascal altogether passed my comprehension. Ignorance is the parent of fear, and being completely nonplussed and confounded

about the stranger. I confess I was now as much afraid of him as if it was the
devil himself who had thus broken into my room at the dead of night. In
fact, I was so afraid of him that I was not game enough just then to address
him, and demand a satisfactory answer concerning what seemed inexplicable in him.

Meanwhile, he continued the business of undressing, and at last showed
his chest and arms. As I live, these covered parts of him were checkered with
the same squares as his face; his back, too, was all over the same dark
squares; he seemed to have been in a Thirty Years' War, and just escaped
from it with a sticking-plaster shirt. Still more, his very legs were marked,
as if a parcel of dark green frogs were running up the trunks of young palms.
It was now quite plain that he must be some abominable savage or other
shipped aboard of a whaleman in the South Seas, and so landed in this
Christian country. I quaked to think of it. A peddler of heads too—perhaps
the heads of his own brothers. He might take a fancy to mine—heavens!
look at that tomahawk!

But there was no time for shuddering, for now the savage went about
something that completely fascinated my attention, and convinced me that
he must indeed be a heathen. Going to his heavy grego, or wrapall, or
dreadnaught, which he had previously hung on a chair, he fumbled in the
pockets, and produced at length a curious little deformed image with a
hunch on its back, and exactly the color of a three days' old Congo baby.
Remembering the embalmed head, at first I almost thought that this black
manikin was a real baby preserved in some similar manner. But seeing that
it was not at all limber, and that it glistened a good deal like polished ebony,
I concluded that it must be nothing but a wooden idol, which indeed it
proved to be. For now the savage goes up to the empty fire-place, and
removing the papered fire-board, sets up this little hunchbacked image, like
a tenpin, between the andirons. The chimney jambs and all the bricks inside
were very sooty, so that I thought this fire-place made a very appropriate
little shrine or chapel for his Congo idol.

I now screwed my eyes hard towards the half hidden image, feeling but
ill at ease meantime—to see what was next to follow. First he takes about
a double handful of shavings out of his grego pocket, and places them carefully before the idol; then laying a bit of ship biscuit on top and applying
the flame from the lamp, he kindled the shavings into a sacrificial blaze.
Presently, after many hasty snatches into the fire, and still hastier with-
drawals of his fingers (whereby he seemed to be scorching them badly), he
at last succeeded in drawing out the biscuit; then blowing off the heat and

ashes a little, he made a polite offer of it to the little negro. But the little devil did not seem to fancy such dry sort of fare at all; he never moved his lips. All these strange antics were accompanied by still stranger guttural noises from the devotee, who seemed to be praying in a sing-song or else singing some pagan psalmody or other, during which his face twitched about in the most unnatural manner. At last extinguishing the fire, he took the idol up very unceremoniously, and bagged it again in his grego pocket as carelessly as if he were a sportsman bagging a dead woodcock.

All these queer proceedings increased my uncomfortableness, and seeing him now exhibiting strong symptoms of concluding his business operations, and jumping into bed with me, I thought it was high time, now or never, before the light was put out, to break the spell in which I had so long been bound.

But the interval I spent in deliberating what to say, was a fatal one. Taking up his tomahawk from the table, he examined the head of it for an instant, and then holding it to the light, with his mouth at the handle, he puffed out great clouds of tobacco smoke. The next moment the light was extinguished, and this wild cannibal, tomahawk between his teeth, sprang into bed with me. I sang out, I could not help it now; and giving a sudden grunt of astonishment he began feeling me.

Stammering out something, I knew not what, I rolled away from him against the wall, and then conjured him, whoever or whatever he might be, to keep quiet, and let me get up and light the lamp again. But his guttural responses satisfied me at once that he but ill comprehended my meaning.

"Who-e debel you?"—he at last said—"you no speak-e, dam-me, I kill-e." And so saying the lighted tomahawk began flourishing about me in the dark.

"Landlord, for God's sake, Peter Coffin!" shouted I. "Landlord! Watch! Coffin! Angels! save me!"

"Speak-e! tell-ee me who-ee be, or dam-me, I kill-e!" again growled the cannibal, while his horrid flourishings of the tomahawk scattered the hot tobacco ashes about me till I thought my linen would get on fire. But thank heaven, at that moment the landlord came into the room light in hand, and leaping from the bed I ran up to him.

"Don't be afraid now," said he, grinning again. "Queequeg here wouldn't harm a hair of your head."

"Stop your grinning," shouted I, "and why didn't you tell me that that infernal harpooneer was a cannibal?"

"I thought ye know'd it;—didn't I tell ye, he was a peddlin' heads around town?—but turn flukes again and go to sleep. Queequeg, look here —you sabbee me, I sabbee you—this man sleepe you—you sabbee?"—

"Me sabbee plenty"—grunted Queequeg, puffing away at his pipe and sitting up in bed.

"You gettee in," he added, motioning to me with his tomahawk, and throwing the clothes to one side. He really did this in not only a civil but a really kind and charitable way. I stood looking at him a moment. For all his tattooings he was on the whole a clean, comely looking cannibal. What's all this fuss I have been making about, thought I to myself—the man's a human being just as I am: he has just as much reason to fear me, as I have to be afraid of him. Better sleep with a sober cannibal than a drunken Christian.

"Landlord," said I, "tell him to stash his tomahawk there, or pipe, or whatever you call it; tell him to stop smoking, in short, and I will turn in with him. But I don't fancy having a man smoking in bed with me. It's dangerous. Besides, I aint insured."

This being told to Queequeg, he at once complied, and again politely motioned me to get into bed—rolling over to one side as much as to say— I wont touch a leg of ye.

"Good night, landlord," said I, "you may go."

I turned in, and never slept better in my life.

# Chapter 4

*The Counterpane*

U PON WAKING NEXT MORNING about daylight, I found
Queequeg's arm thrown over me in the most loving and affectionate manner. You had almost thought I had been his wife. The
counterpane was of patchwork, full of odd little parti-colored squares and
triangles; and this arm of his tattooed all over with an interminable Cretan
labyrinth of a figure, no two parts of which were of one precise shade—
owing I suppose to his keeping his arm at sea unmethodically in sun and
shade, his shirt sleeves irregularly rolled up at various times—this same arm
of his, I say, looked for all the world like a strip of that same patchwork
quilt. Indeed, partly lying on it as the arm did when I first awoke, I could
hardly tell it from the quilt, they so blended their hues together; and it was
only by the sense of weight and pressure that I could tell that Queequeg was
hugging me.

My sensations were strange. Let me try to explain them. When I was a
child, I well remember a somewhat similar circumstance that befell me;
whether it was a reality or a dream, I never could entirely settle. The circumstance was this. I had been cutting up some caper or other—I think it was
trying to crawl up the chimney, as I had seen a little sweep do a few days
previous; and my stepmother who, somehow or other, was all the time
whipping me, or sending me to bed supperless,—my mother dragged me

by the legs out of the chimney and packed me off to bed, though it was only two o'clock in the afternoon of the 21st June, the longest day in the year in our hemisphere. I felt dreadfully. But there was no help for it, so up stairs I went to my little room in the third floor, undressed myself as slowly as possible so as to kill time, and with a bitter sigh got between the sheets.

I lay there dismally calculating that sixteen entire hours must elapse before I could hope for a resurrection. Sixteen hours in bed! the small of my back ached to think of it. And it was so light too; the sun shining in at the window, and a great rattling of coaches in the streets, and the sound of gay voices all over the house. I felt worse and worse—at last I got up, dressed, and softly going down in my stockinged feet, sought out my stepmother, and suddenly threw myself at her feet, beseeching her as a particular favor to give me a good slippering for my misbehavior; anything indeed but condemning me to lie abed such an unendurable length of time. But she was the best and most conscientious of stepmothers, and back I had to go to my room. For several hours I lay there broad awake, feeling a great deal worse than I have ever done since, even from the greatest subsequent misfortunes. At last I must have fallen into a troubled nightmare of a doze; and slowly waking from it—half steeped in dreams—I opened my eyes, and the before sun-lit room was now wrapped in outer darkness. Instantly I felt a shock running through all my frame; nothing was to be seen, and nothing was to be heard; but a supernatural hand seemed placed in mine. My arm hung over the counterpane, and the nameless, unimaginable, silent form or phantom, to which the hand belonged, seemed closely seated by my bedside. For what seemed ages piled on ages, I lay there, frozen with the most awful fears, not daring to drag away my hand; yet ever thinking that if I could but stir it one single inch, the horrid spell would be broken. I knew not how this consciousness at last glided away from me; but waking in the morning, I shudderingly remembered it all, and for days and weeks and months afterwards I lost myself in confounding attempts to explain the mystery. Nay, to this very hour, I often puzzle myself with it.

Now, take away the awful fear, and my sensations at feeling the supernatural hand in mine were very similar, in their strangeness, to those which I experienced on waking up and seeing Queequeg's pagan arm thrown round me. But at length all the past night's events soberly recurred, one by one, in fixed reality, and then I lay only alive to the comical predicament. For though I tried to move his arm—unlock his bridegroom clasp—yet, sleeping as he was, he still hugged me tightly, as though naught but death should part us twain. I now strove to rouse him—"Queequeg!"—but his only answer was a snore. I then rolled over, my neck feeling as if it were in a horse-collar; and suddenly felt a slight scratch. Throwing aside the counterpane, there lay the tomahawk sleeping by the savage's side, as if it were a hatchet-faced baby. A pretty pickle, truly, thought I; abed here in a strange house in the broad day, with a cannibal and a tomahawk! "Queequeg!— in the name of goodness, Queequeg, wake!" At length, by dint of much wriggling, and loud and incessant expostulations upon the unbecomingness of his hugging a fellow male in that matrimonial sort of style, I succeeded in extracting a grunt; and presently, he drew back his arm, shook himself all over like a Newfoundland dog just from the water, and sat up in bed, stiff as a pike-staff, looking at me, and rubbing his eyes as if he did not altogether remember how I came to be there, though a dim consciousness of knowing something about me seemed slowly dawning over him. Meanwhile, I lay quietly eyeing him, having no serious misgivings now, and bent upon narrowly observing so curious a creature. When, at last, his mind seemed made up touching the character of his bedfellow, and he became, as it were, reconciled to the fact; he jumped out upon the floor, and by certain signs and sounds gave me to understand that, if it pleased me, he would dress first and then leave me to dress afterwards, having the whole apartment to myself. Thinks I, Queequeg, under the circumstances, this is a very civilized overture; but, the truth is, these savages have an innate sense of delicacy, say what you will; it is marvellous how essentially polite they are. I pay this particular compliment to Queequeg, because he treated me with so much civility and consideration, while I was guilty of great rudeness; staring at him from the bed, and watching all his toilette motions; for the time my curiosity getting the better of my breeding. Nevertheless, a man like Queequeg you don't see every day, he and his ways were well worth unusual regarding.

He commenced dressing at top by donning his beaver hat, a very tall one, by the by, and then—still minus his trowsers—he hunted up his boots. What under the heavens he did it for, I cannot tell, but his next movement was to crush himself—boots in hand, and hat on—under the bed; when, from sundry violent gaspings and strainings, I inferred he was hard at work booting himself; though by no law of propriety that I ever heard of, is any man required to be private when putting on his boots. But Queequeg, do you see, was a creature in the transition state—neither caterpillar nor butterfly. He was just enough civilized to show off his outlandishness in the strangest possible manner. His education was not yet completed. He was an undergraduate. If he had not been a small degree civilized, he very probably would not have troubled himself with boots at all; but then, if he had not been still a savage, he never would have dreamt of getting under the bed to put them on. At last, he emerged with his hat very much dented and crushed down over his eyes, and began creaking and limping about the room, as if, not being much accustomed to boots, his pair of damp, wrinkled cowhide ones—probably not made to order either—rather pinched and tormented him at the first go off of a bitter cold morning.

Seeing, now, that there were no curtains to the window, and that the street being very narrow, the house opposite commanded a plain view into the room, and observing more and more the indecorous figure that Quee-queg made, staving about with little else but his hat and boots on; I begged him as well as I could, to accelerate his toilet somewhat, and particularly to get into his pantaloons as soon as possible. He complied, and then proceeded to wash himself. At that time in the morning any Christian would have washed his face; but Queequeg, to my amazement, contented himself with restricting his ablutions to his chest, arms, and hands. He then donned his waistcoat, and taking up a piece of hard soap on the wash-stand centre-table, dipped it into water and commenced lathering his face. I was watching to see where he kept his razor, when lo and behold, he takes the harpoon from the bed corner, slips out the long wooden stock, unsheathes the head, whets it a little on his boot, and striding up to the bit of mirror against the wall, begins a vigorous scraping, or rather harpooning of his cheeks. Thinks I, Queequeg, this is using Rogers's best cutlery with a vengeance. After-wards I wondered the less at this operation when I came to know of what fine steel the head of a harpoon is made, and how exceedingly sharp the long straight edges are always kept.

The rest of his toilet was soon achieved, and he proudly marched out of the room, wrapped up in his great pilot monkey jacket, and sporting his harpoon like a marshal's baton.

# Chapter 5

*Breakfast*

I QUICKLY FOLLOWED SUIT, and descending into the bar-room accosted the grinning landlord very pleasantly. I cherished no malice towards him, though he had been skylarking with me not a little in the matter of my bedfellow.

However, a good laugh is a mighty good thing, and rather too scarce a good thing; the more's the pity. So, if any one man, in his own proper person, afford stuff for a good joke to anybody, let him not be backward, but let him cheerfully allow himself to spend and be spent in that way. And the man that has anything bountifully laughable about him, be sure there is more in that man than you perhaps think for.

The bar-room was now full of the boarders who had been dropping in the night previous, and whom I had not as yet had a good look at. They were nearly all whalemen; chief mates, and second mates, and third mates, and sea carpenters, and sea coopers, and sea blacksmiths, and harpooneers, and ship keepers; a brown and brawny company, with bosky beards; an unshorn, shaggy set, all wearing monkey jackets for morning gowns.

You could pretty plainly tell how long each one had been ashore. This young fellow's healthy cheek is like a sun-toasted pear in hue, and would seem to smell almost as musky; he cannot have been three days landed from his Indian voyage. That man next him looks a few shades lighter; you might say a touch of satin wood is in him. In the complexion of a third still lingers a tropic tawn, but slightly bleached withal; *he* doubtless has tarried whole weeks ashore. But who could show a cheek like Queequeg? which, barred with various tints, seemed like the Andes' western slope, to show forth in one array, contrasting climates, zone by zone.

"Grub, ho!" now cried the landlord, flinging open a door, and in we went to breakfast.

They say that men who have seen the world, thereby become quite at ease in manner, quite self-possessed in company. Not always, though: Ledyard, the great New England traveller, and Mungo Park, the Scotch one; of all men, they possessed the least assurance in the parlor. But perhaps the mere crossing of Siberia in a sledge drawn by dogs as Ledyard did, or the taking a long solitary walk on an empty stomach, in the negro heart of Africa, which was the sum of poor Mungo's performances—this kind of travel, I say, may not be the very best mode of attaining a high social polish. Still, for the most part, that sort of thing is to be had anywhere.

These reflections just here are occasioned by the circumstance that after we were all seated at the table, and I was preparing to hear some good stories about whaling; to my no small surprise, nearly every man maintained a profound silence. And not only that, but they looked embarrassed. Yes, here were a set of sea-dogs, many of whom without the slightest bashfulness had boarded great whales on the high seas—entire strangers to them—and duelled them dead without winking; and yet, here they sat at a social breakfast table—all of the same calling, all of kindred tastes—looking round as sheepishly at each other as though they had never been out of sight of some sheepfold among the Green Mountains. A curious sight; these bashful bears, these timid warrior whalemen!

But as for Queequeg—why, Queequeg sat there among them—at the head of the table, too, it so chanced; as cool as an icicle. To be sure I cannot say much for his breeding. His greatest admirer could not have cordially justified his bringing his harpoon into breakfast with him, and using it there without ceremony; reaching over the table with it, to the imminent jeopardy of many heads, and grappling the beefsteaks towards him. But *that* was certainly very coolly done by him, and every one knows that in most people's estimation, to do anything coolly is to do it genteelly.

We will not speak of all Queequeg's peculiarities here; how he eschewed coffee and hot rolls, and applied his undivided attention to beefsteaks, done rare. Enough, that when breakfast was over he withdrew like the rest into the public room, lighted his tomahawk-pipe, and was sitting there quietly digesting and smoking with his inseparable hat on, when I sallied out for a stroll.

# Chapter 6

## *The Street*

IF I had been astonished at first catching a glimpse of so outlandish an individual as Queequeg circulating among the polite society of a civilized town, that astonishment soon departed upon taking my first daylight stroll through the streets of New Bedford.

In thoroughfares nigh the docks, any considerable seaport will frequently offer to view the queerest looking nondescripts from foreign parts. Even in Broadway and Chestnut streets, Mediterranean mariners will sometimes jostle the affrighted ladies. Regent street is not unknown to Lascars and Malays; and at Bombay, in the Apollo Green, live Yankees have often scared the natives. But New Bedford beats all Water street and Wapping. In these last-mentioned haunts you see only sailors; but in New Bedford, actual cannibals stand chatting at street corners; savages outright; many of whom yet carry on their bones unholy flesh. It makes a stranger stare.

But, besides the Feegeeans, Tongatabooans, Erromanggoans, Pannangians, and Brighggians, and, besides the wild specimens of the whaling-craft which unheeded reel about the streets, you will see other sights still more curious, certainly more comical. There weekly arrive in this town scores of green Vermonters and New Hampshire men, all athirst for gain and glory in the fishery. They are mostly young, of stalwart frames; fellows who have felled forests, and now seek to drop the axe and snatch the whale-lance.

Many are as green as the Green Mountains whence they came. In some things you would think them but a few hours old. Look there! that chap strutting round the corner. He wears a beaver hat and swallow-tailed coat, girdled with a sailor-belt and sheath-knife. Here comes another with a sou'-wester and a bombazine cloak.

No town-bred dandy will compare with a country-bred one—I mean a downright bumpkin dandy—a fellow that, in the dog-days, will mow his two acres in buckskin gloves for fear of tanning his hands. Now when a country dandy like this takes it into his head to make a distinguished reputation, and joins the great whale-fishery, you should see the comical things he does upon reaching the seaport. In bespeaking his sea-outfit, he orders bell-buttons to his waistcoats; straps to his canvas trowsers. Ah, poor Hay-Seed! how bitterly will burst those straps in the first howling gale, when thou art driven, straps, buttons, and all, down the throat of the tempest.

But think not that this famous town has only harpooneers, cannibals, and bumpkins to show her visitors. Not at all. Still New Bedford is a queer place. Had it not been for us whalemen, that tract of land would this day perhaps have been in as howling condition as the coast of Labrador. As it is, parts of her back country are enough to frighten one, they look so bony. The town itself is perhaps the dearest place to live in, in all New England. It is a land of oil, true enough: but not like Canaan; a land, also, of corn and wine. The streets do not run with milk; nor in the spring-time do they pave them with fresh eggs. Yet, in spite of this, nowhere in all America will you find more patrician-like houses; parks and gardens more opulent, than in New Bedford. Whence came they? how planted upon this once scraggy scoria of a country?

Go and gaze upon the iron emblematical harpoons round yonder lofty mansion, and your question will be answered. Yes; all these brave houses and flowery gardens came from the Atlantic, Pacific, and Indian oceans. One and all, they were harpooned and dragged up hither from the bottom of the sea. Can Herr Alexander perform a feat like that?

In New Bedford, fathers, they say, give whales for dowers to their daughters, and portion off their nieces with a few porpoises a-piece. You must go to New Bedford to see a brilliant wedding; for, they say, they have reservoirs of oil in every house, and every night recklessly burn their lengths in spermaceti candles.

In summer time, the town is sweet to see; full of fine maples—long avenues of green and gold. And in August, high in air, the beautiful and bountiful horse-chestnuts, candelabra-wise, proffer the passer-by their tapering upright cones of congregated blossoms. So omnipotent is art; which in many a district of New Bedford has superinduced bright terraces of flowers upon the barren refuse rocks thrown aside at creation's final day.

And the women of New Bedford, they bloom like their own red roses. But roses only bloom in summer; whereas the fine carnation of their cheeks is perennial as sunlight in the seventh heavens. Elsewhere match that bloom of theirs, ye cannot, save in Salem, where they tell me the young girls breathe such musk, their sailor sweethearts smell them miles off shore, as though they were drawing nigh the odorous Moluccas instead of the Puritanic sands.

# Chapter 7

## *The Chapel*

IN THIS SAME New Bedford there stands a Whaleman's Chapel, and few are the moody fishermen, shortly bound for the Indian Ocean or Pacific, who fail to make a Sunday visit to the spot. I am sure that I did not.

Returning from my first morning stroll, I again sallied out upon this special errand. The sky had changed from clear, sunny cold, to driving sleet and mist. Wrapping myself in my shaggy jacket of the cloth called bearskin, I fought my way against the stubborn storm. Entering, I found a small scattered congregation of sailors, and sailors' wives and widows. A muffled silence reigned, only broken at times by the shrieks of the storm. Each silent worshipper seemed purposely sitting apart from the other, as if each silent grief were insular and incommunicable. The chaplain had not yet arrived; and there these silent islands of men and women sat steadfastly eyeing several marble tablets, with black borders, masoned into the wall on either side the pulpit. Three of them ran something like the following, but I do not pretend to quote :—

SACRED
To the Memory
OF
JOHN TALBOT,
Who, at the age of eighteen, was lost overboard,
Near the Isle of Desolation, off Patagonia,
*November 1st, 1836.*
THIS TABLET
Is erected to his Memory
BY HIS SISTER.

SACRED
To the Memory
O F
ROBERT LONG, WILLIS ELLERY,
NATHAN COLEMAN, WALTER CANNY, SETH MACY,
AND SAMUEL GLEIG,
Forming one of the boats' crews
O F
THE SHIP ELIZA,
Who were towed out of sight by a Whale,
On the Off-shore Ground in the
PACIFIC,
*December 31st, 1839.*

THIS MARBLE
Is here placed by their surviving
**Shipmates.**

---

SACRED

To the Memory

OF

The late

CAPTAIN EZEKIEL HARDY,

Who in the bows of his boat was killed by a
Sperm Whale on the coast of Japan,

*August 3d, 1833.*

THIS  TABLET

Is erected to his Memory

BY

**HIS  WIDOW.**

---

Shaking off the sleet from my ice-glazed hat and jacket, I seated myself near the door, and turning sideways was surprised to see Queequeg near me. Affected by the solemnity of the scene, there was a wondering gaze of incredulous curiosity in his countenance. This savage was the only person present who seemed to notice my entrance; because he was the only one who could not read, and, therefore, was not reading those frigid inscriptions on the wall. Whether any of the relatives of the seamen whose names appeared there were now among the congregation, I knew not; but so many are the unrecorded accidents in the fishery, and so plainly did several women present wear the countenance if not the trappings of some unceasing grief, that I feel sure that here before me were assembled those, in whose unhealing hearts the sight of those bleak tablets sympathetically caused the old wounds to bleed afresh.

Oh! ye whose dead lie buried beneath the green grass; who standing among flowers can say—here, *here* lies my beloved; ye know not the desolation that broods in bosoms like these. What bitter blanks in those black-bordered marbles which cover no ashes! What despair in those immovable inscriptions! What deadly voids and unbidden infidelities in the lines that seem to gnaw upon all Faith, and refuse resurrections to the beings who have placelessly perished without a grave. As well might those tablets stand in the cave of Elephanta as here.

In what census of living creatures, the dead of mankind are included; why it is that a universal proverb says of them, that they tell no tales, though containing more secrets than the Goodwin Sands; how it is that to his name who yesterday departed for the other world, we prefix so significant and infidel a word, and yet do not thus entitle him, if he but embarks for the remotest Indies of this living earth; why the Life Insurance Companies pay death-forfeitures upon immortals; in what eternal, unstirring paralysis, and deadly, hopeless trance, yet lies antique Adam who died sixty round centuries ago; how it is that we still refuse to be comforted for those who we nevertheless maintain are dwelling in unspeakable bliss; why all the living so strive to hush all the dead; wherefore but the rumor of a knocking in a tomb will terrify a whole city. All these things are not without their meanings.

But Faith, like a jackal, feeds among the tombs, and even from these dead doubts she gathers her most vital hope.

It needs scarcely to be told, with what feelings, on the eve of a Nantucket voyage, I regarded those marble tablets, and by the murky light of that darkened, doleful day read the fate of the whalemen who had gone before me. Yes, Ishmael, the same fate may be thine. But somehow I grew merry again. Delightful inducements to embark, fine chance for promotion, it seems—aye, a stove boat will make me an immortal by brevet. Yes, there is death in this business of whaling—a speechlessly quick chaotic bundling of a man into Eternity. But what then? Methinks we have hugely mistaken this matter of Life and Death. Methinks that what they call my shadow here on earth is my true substance. Methinks that in looking at things spiritual, we are too much like oysters observing the sun through the water, and thinking that thick water the thinnest of air. Methinks my body is but the lees of my better being. In fact take my body who will, take it I say, it is not me. And therefore three cheers for Nantucket; and come a stove boat and stove body when they will, for stave my soul, Jove himself cannot.

# Chapter 8

*The Pulpit*

I HAD NOT been seated very long ere a man of a certain venerable robustness entered; immediately as the storm-pelted door flew back upon admitting him, a quick regardful eyeing of him by all the congregation, sufficiently attested that this fine old man was the chaplain. Yes, it was the famous Father Mapple, so called by the whalemen, among whom he was a very great favorite. He had been a sailor and a harpooneer in his youth, but for many years past had dedicated his life to the ministry. At the time I now write of, Father Mapple was in the hardy winter of a healthy old age; that sort of old age which seems merging into a second flowering youth, for among all the fissures of his wrinkles, there shone certain mild gleams of a newly developing bloom—the spring verdure peeping forth even beneath February's snow. No one having previously heard his history, could for the first time behold Father Mapple without the utmost interest, because there were certain engrafted clerical peculiarities about him, imputable to that adventurous maritime life he had led. When he entered I observed that he carried no umbrella, and certainly had not come in his carriage, for his tarpaulin hat ran down with melting sleet, and his great pilot cloth jacket seemed almost to drag him to the floor with the weight of the water it had absorbed. However, hat and coat and overshoes were one by one removed, and hung up in a little space in an adjacent corner; when, arrayed in a decent suit, he quietly approached the pulpit.

Like most old fashioned pulpits, it was a very lofty one, and since a regular stairs to such a height would, by its long angle with the floor, seriously contract the already small area of the chapel, the architect, it seemed, had acted upon the hint of Father Mapple, and finished the pulpit without a stairs, substituting a perpendicular side ladder, like those used in mounting a ship from a boat at sea. The wife of a whaling captain had provided the chapel with a handsome pair of red worsted man-ropes for this ladder, which, being itself nicely headed, and stained with a mahogany color, the whole contrivance, considering what manner of chapel it was, seemed by no means in bad taste. Halting for an instant at the foot of the ladder, and with both hands grasping the ornamental knobs of the man-ropes, Father Mapple cast a look upwards, and then with a truly sailor-like but still reverential dexterity, hand over hand, mounted the steps as if ascending the main-top of his vessel.

The perpendicular parts of this side ladder, as is usually the case with swinging ones, were of cloth-covered rope, only the rounds were of wood, so that at every step there was a joint. At my first glimpse of the pulpit, it had not escaped me that however convenient for a ship, these joints in the present instance seemed unnecessary. For I was not prepared to see Father Mapple after gaining the height, slowly turn round, and stooping over the pulpit, deliberately drag up the ladder step by step, till the whole was deposited within, leaving him impregnable in his little Quebec.

I pondered some time without fully comprehending the reason for this. Father Mapple enjoyed such a wide reputation for sincerity and sanctity, that I could not suspect him of courting notoriety by any mere tricks of the stage. No, thought I, there must be some sober reason for this thing; furthermore, it must symbolize something unseen. Can it be, then, that by that act of physical isolation, he signifies his spiritual withdrawal for the time, from all outward worldly ties and connexions? Yes, for replenished with the meat and wine of the word, to the faithful man of God, this pulpit, I see, is a self-containing stronghold—a lofty Ehrenbreitstein, with a perennial well of water within the walls.

But the side ladder was not the only strange feature of the place, borrowed from the chaplain's former sea-farings. Between the marble cenotaphs on either hand of the pulpit, the wall which formed its back was adorned with a large painting representing a gallant ship beating against a terrible storm off a lee coast of black rocks and snowy breakers. But high above the flying scud and dark-rolling clouds, there floated a little isle of sunlight, from which beamed forth an angel's face; and this bright face shed a distinct spot of radiance upon the ship's tossed deck, something like that silver plate now inserted into the Victory's plank where Nelson fell. "Ah, noble ship," the angel seemed to say, "beat on, beat on, thou noble ship, and bear a hardy helm; for lo! the sun is breaking through; the clouds are rolling off—serenest azure is at hand."

Nor was the pulpit itself without a trace of the same sea-taste that had achieved the ladder and the picture. Its panelled front was in the likeness of a ship's bluff bows, and the Holy Bible rested on a projecting piece of scroll work, fashioned after a ship's fiddle-headed beak.

What could be more full of meaning?—for the pulpit is ever this earth's foremost part; all the rest comes in its rear; the pulpit leads the world. From thence it is the storm of God's quick wrath is first descried, and the bow must bear the earliest brunt. From thence it is the God of breezes fair or foul is first invoked for favorable winds. Yes, the world's a ship on its passage out, and not a voyage complete; and the pulpit is its prow.

# Chapter 9

*The Sermon*

FATHER Mapple rose, and in a mild voice of unassuming authority ordered the scattered people to condense. "Starboard gangway, there! side away to larboard—larboard gangway to starboard! Midships! midships!"

There was a low rumbling of heavy sea-boots among the benches, and a still slighter shuffling of women's shoes, and all was quiet again, and every eye on the preacher.

He paused a little; then kneeling in the pulpit's bows, folded his large brown hands across his chest, uplifted his closed eyes, and offered a prayer so deeply devout that he seemed kneeling and praying at the bottom of the sea.

This ended, in prolonged solemn tones, like the continual tolling of a bell in a ship that is foundering at sea in a fog—in such tones he commenced reading the following hymn; but changing his manner towards the concluding stanzas, burst forth with a pealing exultation and joy—

"The ribs and terrors in the whale,
    Arched over me a dismal gloom,
While all God's sun-lit waves rolled by,
    And left me deepening down to doom.

"I saw the opening maw of hell,
    With endless pains and sorrows there;
Which none but they that feel can tell—
    Oh, I was plunging to despair.

"In black distress, I called my God,
    When I could scarce believe him mine,
He bowed his ear to my complaints—
    No more the whale did me confine.

"With speed he flew to my relief,
    As on a radiant dolphin borne;
Awful, yet bright, as lightning shone
    The face of my Deliverer God.

"My song for ever shall record
    That terrible, that joyful hour;
I give the glory to my God,
    His all the mercy and the power."

Nearly all joined in singing this hymn, which swelled high above the howling of the storm. A brief pause ensued; the preacher slowly turned over the leaves of the Bible, and at last, folding his hand down upon the proper page, said: "Beloved shipmates, clinch the last verse of the first chapter of Jonah—'And God had prepared a great fish to swallow up Jonah.'

"Shipmates, this book, containing only four chapters—four yarns—is one of the smallest strands in the mighty cable of the Scriptures. Yet what depths of the soul does Jonah's deep sea-line sound! what a pregnant lesson to us is this prophet! What a noble thing is that canticle in the fish's belly! How billow-like and boisterously grand! We feel the floods surging over us; we sound with him to the kelpy bottom of the waters; sea-weed and all the slime of the sea is about us! But *what* is this lesson that the book of Jonah teaches? Shipmates, it is a two-stranded lesson; a lesson to us all as sinful men, and a lesson to me as a pilot of the living God. As sinful men, it is a lesson to us all, because it is a story of the sin, hard-heartedness, suddenly awakened fears, the swift punishment, repentance, prayers, and finally the deliverance and joy of Jonah. As with all sinners among men, the sin of this son of Amittai was in his wilful disobedience of the command of God —never mind now what that command was, or how conveyed—which he found a hard command. But all the things that God would have us do are hard for us to do—remember that—and hence, he oftener commands us than endeavors to persuade. And if we obey God, we must disobey ourselves; and it is in this disobeying ourselves, wherein the hardness of obeying God consists.

"With this sin of disobedience in him, Jonah still further flouts at God, by seeking to flee from Him. He thinks that a ship made by men, will carry him into countries where God does not reign, but only the Captains of this earth. He skulks about the wharves of Joppa, and seeks a ship that's bound for Tarshish. There lurks, perhaps, a hitherto unheeded meaning here. By all accounts Tarshish could have been no other city than the modern Cadiz. That's the opinion of learned men. And where is Cadiz, shipmates? Cadiz is in Spain; as far by water, from Joppa, as Jonah could possibly have sailed in those ancient days, when the Atlantic was an almost unknown sea. Because Joppa, the modern Jaffa, shipmates, is on the most easterly coast of the Mediterranean, the Syrian; and Tarshish or Cadiz more than two thousand miles to the westward from that, just outside the Straits of Gibraltar. See ye not then, shipmates, that Jonah sought to flee world-wide from God? Miserable man! Oh! most contemptible and worthy of all scorn; with slouched hat and guilty eye, skulking from his God; prowling among the shipping like a vile burglar hastening to cross the seas. So disordered, self-condemning is his look, that had there been policemen in those days, Jonah, on the mere suspicion of something wrong, had been arrested ere he touched a deck. How plainly he's a fugitive! no baggage, not a hat-box, valise, or carpet-bag,—no friends accompany him to the wharf with their adieux. At last, after much dodging search, he finds the Tarshish ship receiving the last items of her cargo; and as he steps on board to see its Captain in the cabin, all the sailors for the moment desist from hoisting in the goods, to mark the stranger's evil eye. Jonah sees this; but in vain he tries to look all ease and confidence; in vain essays his wretched smile. Strong intuitions of the man assure the mariners he can be no innocent. In their gamesome but still serious way, one whispers to the other—'Jack, he's robbed a widow;' or, 'Joe, do you mark him; he's a bigamist;' or, 'Harry lad, I guess he's the adulterer that broke jail in old Gomorrah, or belike, one of the missing murderers from Sodom.' Another runs to read the bill that's stuck against the spile upon the wharf to which the ship is moored, offering five hundred gold coins for the apprehension of a parricide, and containing a description of his person. He reads, and looks from Jonah to the bill; while all his sympathetic shipmates now crowd round Jonah, prepared to lay their hands upon him. Frighted Jonah trembles, and summoning all his boldness to his face, only looks so much the more a coward. He will not confess himself suspected; but that itself is strong suspicion. So he makes the best of it; and when the sailors find him not to be the man that is advertised, they let him pass, and he descends into the cabin.

"'Who's there?' cries the Captain at his busy desk, hurriedly making out his papers for the Customs—'Who's there?' Oh! how that harmless question mangles Jonah! For the instant he almost turns to flee again. But he rallies. 'I seek a passage in this ship to Tarshish; how soon sail ye, sir?' Thus far the busy Captain had not looked up to Jonah, though the man now stands before him; but no sooner does he hear that hollow voice, than he darts a scrutinizing glance. 'We sail with the next coming tide,' at last he slowly answered, still intently eyeing him. 'No sooner, sir?'—'Soon enough for any honest man that goes a passenger.' Ha! Jonah, that's another stab. But he swiftly calls away the Captain from that scent. 'I'll sail with ye,' —he says,—'the passage money, how much is that?—I'll pay now.' For it is particularly written, shipmates, as if it were a thing not to be overlooked in this history, 'that he paid the fare thereof' ere the craft did sail. And taken with the context, this is full of meaning.

"Now Jonah's Captain, shipmates, was one whose discernment detects crime in any, but whose cupidity exposes it only in the penniless. In this world, shipmates, sin that pays its way can travel freely, and without a pass-port; whereas Virtue, if a pauper, is stopped at all frontiers. So Jonah's Captain prepares to test the length of Jonah's purse, ere he judge him openly. He charges him thrice the usual sum; and it's assented to. Then the Captain knows that Jonah is a fugitive; but at the same time resolves to help a flight that paves its rear with gold. Yet when Jonah fairly takes out his purse, prudent suspicions still molest the Captain. He rings every coin to find a counterfeit. Not a forger, any way, he mutters; and Jonah is put down for his passage. 'Point out my state-room, Sir,' says Jonah now, 'I'm travel-weary; I need sleep.' 'Thou look'st like it,' says the Captain, 'there's thy room.' Jonah enters, and would lock the door, but the lock contains no key. Hearing him foolishly fumbling there, the Captain laughs lowly to himself, and mutters something about the doors of convicts' cells being never allowed to be locked within. All dressed and dusty as he is, Jonah throws himself into his berth, and finds the little state-room ceiling almost resting on his forehead. The air is close, and Jonah gasps. Then, in that contracted hole, sunk, too, beneath the ship's water-line, Jonah feels the heralding presentiment of that stifling hour, when the whale shall hold him in the smallest of his bowel's wards.

"Screwed at its axis against the side, a swinging lamp slightly oscillates in Jonah's room; and the ship, heeling over towards the wharf with the weight of the last bales received, the lamp, flame and all, though in slight motion, still maintains a permanent obliquity with reference to the room; though, in truth, infallibly straight itself, it but made obvious the false, lying levels among which it hung. The lamp alarms and frightens Jonah; as lying in his berth his tormented eyes roll round the place, and this thus far successful fugitive finds no refuge for his restless glance. But that contradiction in the lamp more and more appals him. The floor, the ceiling, and the side, are all awry. 'Oh! so my conscience hangs in me!' he groans, 'straight upward, so it burns; but the chambers of my soul are all in crookedness!'

"Like one who after a night of drunken revelry hies to his bed, still reeling, but with conscience yet pricking him, as the plungings of the Roman race-horse but so much the more strike his steel tags into him; as one who in that miserable plight still turns and turns in giddy anguish, praying God for annihilation until the fit be passed; and at last amid the whirl of woe he feels, a deep stupor steals over him, as over the man who bleeds to death, for conscience is the wound, and there's naught to staunch it; so, after sore wrestlings in his berth, Jonah's prodigy of ponderous misery drags him drowning down to sleep.

"And now the time of tide has come; the ship casts off her cables; and from the deserted wharf the uncheered ship for Tarshish, all careening, glides to sea. That ship, my friends, was the first of recorded smugglers! the contraband was Jonah. But the sea rebels; he will not bear the wicked burden. A dreadful storm comes on, the ship is like to break. But now when the boatswain calls all hands to lighten her; when boxes, bales, and jars are clattering overboard; when the wind is shrieking, and the men are yelling, and every plank thunders with trampling feet right over Jonah's head; in all this raging tumult, Jonah sleeps his hideous sleep. He sees no black sky and raging sea, feels not the reeling timbers, and little hears he or heeds he the far rush of the mighty whale, which even now with open mouth is cleaving the seas after him. Aye, shipmates, Jonah was gone down into the sides of the ship—a berth in the cabin as I have taken it, and was fast asleep. But the frightened master comes to him, and shrieks in his dead ear, 'What meanest thou, O sleeper! arise!' Startled from his lethargy by that direful cry, Jonah staggers to his feet, and stumbling to the deck, grasps a shroud, to look out upon the sea. But at that moment he is sprung upon by a panther billow leaping over the bulwarks. Wave after wave thus leaps into the ship, and finding no speedy vent runs roaring fore and aft, till the mariners come

nigh to drowning while yet afloat. And ever, as the white moon shows her
affrighted face from the steep gullies in the blackness overhead, aghast
Jonah sees the rearing bowsprit pointing high upward, but soon beat downward again towards the tormented deep.

"Terrors upon terrors run shouting through his soul. In all his cringing
attitudes, the God-fugitive is now too plainly known. The sailors mark him;
more and more certain grow their suspicions of him, and at last, fully to
test the truth, by referring the whole matter to high Heaven, they fall to
casting lots, to see for whose cause this great tempest was upon them. The
lot is Jonah's; that discovered, then how furiously they mob him with their
questions. 'What is thine occupation? Whence comest thou? Thy country?
What people?' But mark now, my shipmates, the behavior of poor Jonah.
The eager mariners but ask him who he is, and where from; whereas, they
not only receive an answer to those questions, but likewise another answer
to a question not put by them, but the unsolicited answer is forced from
Jonah by the hard hand of God that is upon him.

"'I am a Hebrew,' he cries—and then—'I fear the Lord the God of
Heaven who hath made the sea and the dry land!' Fear him, O Jonah? Aye,
well mightest thou fear the Lord God *then!* Straightway, he now goes on to
make a full confession; whereupon the mariners become more and more
appalled, but still are pitiful. For when Jonah, not yet supplicating God for
mercy, since he but too well knew the darkness of his deserts,—when
wretched Jonah cries out to them to take him and cast him forth into the
sea, for he knew that for *his* sake this great tempest was upon them; they
mercifully turn from him, and seek by other means to save the ship. But
all in vain; the indignant gale howls louder; then, with one hand raised
invokingly to God, with the other they not unreluctantly lay hold of Jonah.

"And now behold Jonah taken up as an anchor and dropped into the sea;
when instantly an oily calmness floats out from the east, and the sea is still,
as Jonah carries down the gale with him, leaving smooth water behind. He
goes down in the whirling heart of such a masterless commotion that he
scarce heeds the moment when he drops seething into the yawning jaws
awaiting him; and the whale shoots-to all his ivory teeth, like so many
white bolts, upon his prison. Then Jonah prayed unto the Lord out of the
fish's belly. But observe his prayer, and learn a weighty lesson. For sinful
as he is, Jonah does not weep and wail for direct deliverance. He feels that
his dreadful punishment is just. He leaves all his deliverance to God, con-
tenting himself with this, that spite of all his pains and pangs, he will still
look towards His holy temple. And here, shipmates, is true and faithful

repentance; not clamorous for pardon, but grateful for punishment. And how pleasing to God was this conduct in Jonah, is shown in the eventual deliverance of him from the sea and the whale. Shipmates, I do not place Jonah before you to be copied for his sin but I do place him before you as a model for repentance. Sin not; but if you do, take heed to repent of it like Jonah."

While he was speaking these words, the howling of the shrieking, slanting storm without seemed to add new power to the preacher, who, when describing Jonah's sea-storm, seemed tossed by a storm himself. His deep chest heaved as with a ground-swell; his tossed arms seemed the warring elements at work; and the thunders that rolled away from off his swarthy brow, and the light leaping from his eye, made all his simple hearers look on him with a quick fear that was strange to them.

There now came a lull in his look, as he silently turned over the leaves of the Book once more; and, at last, standing motionless, with closed eyes, for the moment, seemed communing with God and himself.

But again he leaned over towards the people, and bowing his head lowly, with an aspect of the deepest yet manliest humility, he spake these words:

"Shipmates, God has laid but one hand upon you; both his hands press upon me. I have read ye by what murky light may be mine the lesson that Jonah teaches to all sinners; and therefore to ye, and still more to me, for I am a greater sinner than ye. And now how gladly would I come down from this mast-head and sit on the hatches there where you sit, and listen as you listen, while some one of you reads *me* that other and more awful lesson which Jonah teaches to *me*, as a pilot of the living God. How being an anointed pilot-prophet, or speaker of true things, and bidden by the Lord to sound those unwelcome truths in the ears of a wicked Nineveh, Jonah, appalled at the hostility he should raise, fled from his mission, and sought to escape his duty and his God by taking ship at Joppa. But God is everywhere; Tarshish he never reached. As we have seen, God came upon him in the whale, and swallowed him down to living gulfs of doom, and with swift slantings tore him along 'into the midst of the seas,' where the eddying depths sucked him ten thousand fathoms down, and 'the weeds were wrapped about his head,' and all the watery world of woe bowled over him. Yet even then beyond the reach of any plummet—'out of the belly of hell'—when the whale grounded upon the ocean's utmost bones, even then, God heard the engulphed, repenting prophet when he cried. Then God spake unto the fish; and from the shuddering cold and blackness of the sea, the whale came breeching up towards the warm and pleasant sun, and all the delights of air

and earth; and 'vomited out Jonah upon the dry land;' when the word of
the Lord came a second time; and Jonah, bruised and beaten—his ears, like
two sea-shells, still multitudinously murmuring of the ocean—Jonah did
the Almighty's bidding. And what was that, shipmates? To preach the
Truth to the face of Falsehood! That was it!

"This, shipmates, this is that other lesson; and woe to that pilot of the
living God who slights it. Woe to him whom this world charms from
Gospel duty! Woe to him who seeks to pour oil upon the waters when God
has brewed them into a gale! Woe to him who seeks to please rather than
to appal! Woe to him whose good name is more to him than goodness!
Woe to him who, in this world, courts not dishonor! Woe to him who
would not be true, even though to be false were salvation! Yea, woe to him
who, as the great Pilot Paul has it, while preaching to others is himself a
castaway!"

He drooped and fell away from himself for a moment; then lifting his
face to them again, showed a deep joy in his eyes, as he cried out with a
heavenly enthusiasm,—"But oh! shipmates! on the starboard hand of every
woe, there is a sure delight; and higher the top of that delight, than the
bottom of the woe is deep. Is not the main-truck higher than the kelson is
low? Delight is to him—a far, far upward, and inward delight—who against
the proud gods and commodores of this earth, ever stands forth his own
inexorable self. Delight is to him whose strong arms yet support him, when
the ship of this base treacherous world has gone down beneath him. Delight
is to him, who gives no quarter in the truth, and kills, burns, and destroys all
sin though he pluck it out from under the robes of Senators and Judges.
Delight,—top-gallant delight is to him, who acknowledges no law or lord,
but the Lord his God, and is only a patriot to heaven. Delight is to him,
whom all the waves of the billows of the seas of the boisterous mob can
never shake from this sure Keel of the Ages. And eternal delight and
deliciousness will be his, who coming to lay him down, can say with his
final breath—O Father!—chiefly known to me by Thy rod—mortal or
immortal, here I die. I have striven to be Thine, more than to be this world's,
or mine own. Yet this is nothing; I leave eternity to Thee; for what is man
that he should live out the lifetime of his God?"

He said no more, but slowly waving a benediction, covered his face
with his hands, and so remained, kneeling, till all the people had departed,
and he was left alone in the place.

# Chapter 10

*A Bosom Friend*

RETURNING to the Spouter-Inn from the Chapel, I found Queequeg there quite alone; he having left the Chapel before the benediction some time. He was sitting on a bench before the fire, with his feet on the stove hearth, and in one hand was holding close up to his face that little negro idol of his; peering hard into its face, and with a jack-knife gently whittling away at its nose, meanwhile humming to himself in his heathenish way.

But being now interrupted, he put up the image; and pretty soon, going to the table, took up a large book there, and placing it on his lap began counting the pages with deliberate regularity; at every fiftieth page—as I fancied—stopping a moment, looking vacantly around him, and giving utterance to a long-drawn gurgling whistle of astonishment. He would then begin again at the next fifty; seeming to commence at number one each time, as though he could not count more than fifty, and it was only by such a large number of fifties being found together, that his astonishment at the multitude of pages was excited.

With much interest I sat watching him. Savage though he was, and hideously marred about the face—at least to my taste—his countenance yet had a something in it which was by no means disagreeable. You cannot hide the soul. Through all his unearthly tattooings, I thought I saw the traces of a

simple honest heart; and in his large, deep eyes, fiery black and bold, there
seemed tokens of a spirit that would dare a thousand devils. And besides all
this, there was a certain lofty bearing about the Pagan, which even his
uncouthness could not altogether maim. He looked like a man who had
never cringed and never had had a creditor. Whether it was, too, that his
head being shaved, his forehead was drawn out in freer and brighter relief,
and looked more expansive than it otherwise would, this I will not venture
to decide; but certain it was his head was phrenologically an excellent one.
It may seem ridiculous, but it reminded me of General Washington's head,
as seen in the popular busts of him. It had the same long regularly graded
retreating slope from above the brows, which were likewise very projecting,
like two long promontories thickly wooded on top. Queequeg was George
Washington cannibalistically developed.

Whilst I was thus closely scanning him, half-pretending meanwhile to
be looking out at the storm from the casement, he never heeded my presence, never troubled himself with so much as a single glance; but appeared
wholly occupied with counting the pages of the marvellous book. Considering how sociably we had been sleeping together the night previous, and
especially considering the affectionate arm I had found thrown over me
upon waking in the morning, I thought this indifference of his very strange.
But savages are strange beings; at times you do not know exactly how to
take them. At first they are overawing; their calm self-collectedness of
simplicity seems a Socratic wisdom. I had noticed also that Queequeg never
consorted at all, or but very little, with the other seamen in the inn. He made
no advances whatever; appeared to have no desire to enlarge the circle of
his acquaintances. All this struck me as mighty singular; yet, upon second
thoughts, there was something almost sublime in it. Here was a man some
twenty thousand miles from home, by the way of Cape Horn, that is—
which was the only way he could get there—thrown among people as
strange to him as though he were in the planet Jupiter; and yet he seemed
entirely at his ease; preserving the utmost serenity; content with his own
companionship; always equal to himself. Surely this was a touch of fine
philosophy; though no doubt he had never heard there was such a thing
as that. But, perhaps, to be true philosophers, we mortals should not be
conscious of so living or so striving. So soon as I hear that such or such a man
gives himself out for a philosopher, I conclude that, like the dyspeptic old
woman, he must have "broken his digester."

As I sat there in that now lonely room; the fire burning low, in that mild
stage when, after its first intensity has warmed the air, it then only glows to

be looked at; the evening shades and phantoms gathering round the casements, and peering in upon us silent, solitary twain; the storm booming
without in solemn swells; I began to be sensible of strange feelings. I felt a
melting in me. No more my splintered heart and maddened hand were
turned against the wolfish world. This soothing savage had redeemed it.
There he sat, his very indifference speaking a nature in which there lurked
no civilized hypocrisies and bland deceits. Wild he was; a very sight of sights
to see; yet I began to feel myself mysteriously drawn towards him. And
those same things that would have repelled most others, they were the very
magnets that thus drew me. I'll try a pagan friend, thought I, since Christian
kindness has proved but hollow courtesy. I drew my bench near him, and
made some friendly signs and hints, doing my best to talk with him meanwhile. At first he little noticed these advances; but presently, upon my
referring to his last night's hospitalities, he made out to ask me whether we
were again to be bedfellows. I told him yes; whereat I thought he looked
pleased, perhaps a little complimented.

We then turned over the book together, and I endeavored to explain
to him the purpose of the printing, and the meaning of the few pictures that
were in it. Thus I soon engaged his interest; and from that we went to
jabbering the best we could about the various outer sights to be seen in this
famous town. Soon I proposed a social smoke; and, producing his pouch
and tomahawk, he quietly offered me a puff. And then we sat exchanging
puffs from that wild pipe of his, and keeping it regularly passing between us.

If there yet lurked any ice of indifference towards me in the Pagan's
breast, this pleasant, genial smoke we had, soon thawed it out, and left us
cronies. He seemed to take to me quite as naturally and unbiddenly as I to
him; and when our smoke was over, he pressed his forehead against mine,
clasped me round the waist, and said that henceforth we were married;
meaning, in his country's phrase, that we were bosom friends; he would
gladly die for me, if need should be. In a countryman, this sudden flame of
friendship would have seemed far too premature, a thing to be much distrusted; but in this simple savage those old rules would not apply.

After supper, and another social chat and smoke, we went to our room
together. He made me a present of his embalmed head; took out his enormous tobacco wallet, and groping under the tobacco, drew out some thirty
dollars in silver; then spreading them on the table, and mechanically dividing
them into two equal portions, pushed one of them towards me, and said it
was mine. I was going to remonstrate; but he silenced me by pouring them
into my trowsers' pockets. I let them stay. He then went about his evening

prayers, took out his idol, and removed the paper fireboard. By certain signs and symptoms, I thought he seemed anxious for me to join him; but well knowing what was to follow, I deliberated a moment whether, in case he invited me, I would comply or otherwise.

I was a good Christian; born and bred in the bosom of the infallible Presbyterian Church. How then could I unite with this wild idolator in worshipping his piece of wood? But what is worship? thought I. Do you suppose now, Ishmael, that the magnanimous God of heaven and earth— pagans and all included—can possibly be jealous of an insignificant bit of black wood? Impossible! But what is worship?—to do the will of God— *that* is worship. And what is the will of God?—to do to my fellow man what I would have my fellow man to do to me—*that* is the will of God. Now, Queequeg is my fellow man. And what do I wish that this Queequeg would do to me? Why, unite with me in my particular Presbyterian form of worship. Consequently, I must then unite with him in his; ergo, I must turn idolator. So I kindled the shavings; helped prop up the innocent little idol; offered him burnt biscuit with Queequeg; salamed before him twice or thrice; kissed his nose; and that done, we undressed and went to bed, at peace with our own consciences and all the world. But we did not go to sleep without some little chat.

How it is I know not; but there is no place like a bed for confidential disclosures between friends. Man and wife, they say, there open the very bottom of their souls to each other; and some old couples often lie and chat over old times till nearly morning. Thus, then, in our hearts' honeymoon, lay I and Queequeg—a cosy, loving pair.

# Chapter 11

## Nightgown

WE HAD LAIN thus in bed, chatting and napping at short intervals, and Queequeg now and then affectionately throwing his brown tattooed legs over mine, and then drawing them back; so entirely sociable and free and easy were we; when, at last, by reason of our confabulations, what little nappishness remained in us altogether departed, and we felt like getting up again, though day-break was yet some way down the future.

Yes, we became very wakeful; so much so that our recumbent position began to grow wearisome, and by little and little we found ourselves sitting up; the clothes well tucked around us, leaning against the head-board with our four knees drawn up close together, and our two noses bending over them, as if our knee-pans were warming-pans. We felt very nice and snug, the more so since it was so chilly out of doors; indeed out of bed-clothes too, seeing that there was no fire in the room. The more so, I say, because truly to enjoy bodily warmth, some small part of you must be cold, for there is no quality in this world that is not what it is merely by contrast. Nothing exists in itself. If you flatter yourself that you are all over comfortable, and have been so a long time, then you cannot be said to be comfortable any more. But if, like Queequeg and me in the bed, the tip of your nose or the crown of your head be slightly chilled, why then, indeed, in the general consciousness you feel most delightfully and unmistakably warm. For this reason a sleeping apartment should never be furnished with a fire, which is one of the luxurious discomforts of the rich. For the height of this sort of deliciousness is to have nothing but the blanket between you and your snugness and the cold of the outer air. Then there you lie like the one warm spark in the heart of an arctic crystal.

We had been sitting in this crouching manner for some time, when all at once I thought I would open my eyes; for when between sheets, whether by day or by night, and whether asleep or awake, I have a way of always keeping my eyes shut, in order the more to concentrate the snugness of being in bed. Because no man can ever feel his own identity aright except his eyes be closed; as if darkness were indeed the proper element of our essences, though light be more congenial to our clayey part. Upon opening my eyes then, and coming out of my own pleasant and self-created darkness into the imposed and coarse outer gloom of the unilluminated twelve-o'clock-at-night, I experienced a disagreeable revulsion. Nor did I at all object to the hint from Queequeg that perhaps it were best to strike a light, seeing that we were so wide awake; and besides he felt a strong desire to have a few quiet puffs from his Tomahawk. Be it said, that though I had felt such a strong repugnance to his smoking in the bed the night before, yet see how elastic our stiff prejudices grow when love once comes to bend them. For now I liked nothing better than to have Queequeg smoking by me, even in bed, because he seemed to be full of such serene household joy then. I no more felt unduly concerned for the landlord's policy of insurance. I was only alive to the condensed confidential comfortableness of sharing a pipe and a blanket with a real friend. With our shaggy jackets drawn about our shoulders, we now passed the Tomahawk from one to the other, till slowly there grew over us a blue hanging tester of smoke, illuminated by the flame of the new-lit lamp.

Whether it was that this undulating tester rolled the savage away to far distant scenes, I know not, but he now spoke of his native island; and, eager to hear his history, I begged him to go on and tell it. He gladly complied. Though at the time I but ill comprehended not a few of his words, yet subsequent disclosures, when I had become more familiar with his broken phraseology, now enable me to present the whole story such as it may prove in the mere skeleton I give.

# Chapter 12

*Biographical*

Q UEEQUEG WAS A NATIVE of Kokovoko, an island far away to
the West and South. It is not down in any map; true places never
are.

When a new-hatched savage running wild about his native woodlands
in a grass clout, followed by the nibbling goats, as if he were a green sapling;
even then, in Queequeg's ambitious soul, lurked a strong desire to see something more of Christendom than a specimen whaler or two. His father was
a High Chief, a King; his uncle a High Priest; and on the maternal side he
boasted aunts who were the wives of unconquerable warriors. There was
excellent blood in his veins—royal stuff; though sadly vitiated, I fear, by
the cannibal propensity he nourished in his untutored youth.

A Sag Harbor ship visited his father's bay, and Queequeg sought a
passage to Christian lands. But the ship, having her full complement of
seamen, spurned his suit; and not all the King his father's influence could
prevail. But Queequeg vowed a vow. Alone in his canoe, he paddled off
to a distant strait, which he knew the ship must pass through when she
quitted the island. On one side was a coral reef; on the other a low tongue
of land, covered with mangrove thickets that grew out into the water.
Hiding his canoe, still afloat, among these thickets, with its prow seaward,
he sat down in the stern, paddle low in hand; and when the ship was gliding

by, like a flash he darted out; gained her side; with one backward dash of his foot capsized and sank his canoe; climbed up the chains; and throwing himself at full length upon the deck, grappled a ring-bolt there, and swore not to let it go, though hacked in pieces.

In vain the captain threatened to throw him overboard; suspended a cutlass over his naked wrists; Queequeg was the son of a King, and Queequeg budged not. Struck by his desperate dauntlessness, and his wild desire to visit Christendom, the captain at last relented, and told him he might make himself at home. But this fine young savage—this sea Prince of Wales, never saw the captain's cabin. They put him down among the sailors, and made a whaleman of him. But like Czar Peter content to toil in the shipyards of foreign cities, Queequeg disdained no seeming ignominy, if thereby he might haply gain the power of enlightening his untutored countrymen. For at bottom—so he told me—he was actuated by a profound desire to learn among the Christians, the arts whereby to make his people still happier than they were; and more than that, still better than they were. But, alas! the practices of whalemen soon convinced him that even Christians could be both miserable and wicked; infinitely more so, than all his father's heathens. Arrived at last in old Sag Harbor; and seeing what the sailors did there; and then going on to Nantucket, and seeing how they spent their wages in *that* place also, poor Queequeg gave it up for lost. Thought he, it's a wicked world in all meridians; I'll die a pagan.

And thus an old idolator at heart, he yet lived among these Christians, wore their clothes, and tried to talk their gibberish. Hence the queer ways about him, though now some time from home.

By hints, I asked him whether he did not propose going back, and having a coronation; since he might now consider his father dead and gone, he being very old and feeble at the last accounts. He answered no, not yet; and added that he was fearful Christianity, or rather Christians, had unfitted him for ascending the pure and undefiled throne of thirty pagan Kings before him. But by and by, he said, he would return,—as soon as he felt himself baptized again. For the nonce, however, he proposed to sail about, and sow his wild oats in all four oceans. They had made a harpooneer of him, and that barbed iron was in lieu of a sceptre now.

I asked him what might be his immediate purpose, touching his future movements. He answered, to go to sea again, in his old vocation. Upon this, I told him that whaling was my own design, and informed him of my intention to sail out of Nantucket, as being the most promising port for an adventurous whaleman to embark from. He at once resolved to accompany me to that island, ship aboard the same vessel, get into the same watch, the same boat, the same mess with me, in short to share my every hap; with both my hands in his, boldly dip into the Potluck of both worlds. To all this I joyously assented; for besides the affection I now felt for Queequeg, he was an experienced harpooneer, and as such, could not fail to be of great usefulness to one, who, like me, was wholly ignorant of the mysteries of whaling, though well acquainted with the sea, as known to merchant seamen.

His story being ended with his pipe's last dying puff, Queequeg embraced me, pressed his forehead against mine, and blowing out the light, we rolled over from each other, this way and that, and very soon were sleeping.

# Chapter 13

*Wheelbarrow*

N EXT MORNING, Monday, after disposing of the embalmed head to a barber, for a block, I settled my own and comrade's bill; using, however, my comrade's money. The grinning landlord, as well as the boarders, seemed amazingly tickled at the sudden friendship which had sprung up between me and Queequeg—especially as Peter Coffin's cock and bull stories about him had previously so much alarmed me concerning the very person whom I now companied with.

We borrowed a wheelbarrow, and embarking our things, including my own poor carpet-bag, and Queequeg's canvas sack and hammock, away we went down to "the Moss," the little Nantucket packet schooner moored at the wharf. As we were going along the people stared; not at Queequeg so much—for they were used to seeing cannibals like him in their streets,—but at seeing him and me upon such confidential terms. But we heeded them not, going along wheeling the barrow by turns, and Queequeg now and then stopping to adjust the sheath on his harpoon barbs. I asked him why he carried such a troublesome thing with him ashore, and whether all whaling ships did not find their own harpoons. To this, in substance, he replied, that though what I hinted was true enough, yet he had a particular affection for his own harpoon, because it was of assured stuff, well tried in many a mortal combat, and deeply intimate with the hearts of whales. In

short, like many inland reapers and mowers, who go into the farmers' meadows armed with their own scythes—though in no wise obliged to furnish
them—even so, Queequeg, for his own private reasons, preferred his own
harpoon.

Shifting the barrow from my hands to his, he told me a funny story about
the first wheelbarrow he had ever seen. It was in Sag Harbor. The owners
of his ship, it seems, had lent him one, in which to carry his heavy chest to
his boarding house. Not to seem ignorant about the thing—though in truth
he was entirely so, concerning the precise way in which to manage the
barrow—Queequeg puts his chest upon it; lashes it fast; and then shoulders
the barrow and marches up the wharf. "Why," said I, "Queequeg, you
might have known better than that, one would think. Didn't the people
laugh?"

Upon this, he told me another story. The people of his island of Kokovoko, it seems, at their wedding feasts express the fragrant water of young
cocoanuts into a large stained calabash like a punchbowl; and this punch-
bowl always forms the great central ornament on the braided mat where the
feast is held. Now a certain grand merchant ship once touched at Kokovoko,
and its commander—from all accounts, a very stately punctilious gentleman,
at least for a sea captain—this commander was invited to the wedding feast
of Queequeg's sister, a pretty young princess just turned of ten. Well; when
all the wedding guests were assembled at the bride's bamboo cottage, this
Captain marches in, and being assigned the post of honor, placed himself
over against the punchbowl, and between the High Priest and his majesty
the King, Queequeg's father. Grace being said,—for those people have their
grace as well as we—though Queequeg told me that unlike us, who at such
times look downwards to our platters, they, on the contrary, copying the
ducks, glance upwards to the great Giver of all feasts—Grace, I say, being
said, the High Priest opens the banquet by the immemorial ceremony of the
island; that is, dipping his consecrated and consecrating fingers into the bowl
before the blessed beverage circulates. Seeing himself placed next the Priest,
and noting the ceremony, and thinking himself—being Captain of a ship—
as having plain precedence over a mere island King, especially in the King's
own house—the Captain coolly proceeds to wash his hands in the punch
bowl;—taking it I suppose for a huge finger-glass. "Now," said Queequeg,
"what you tink now?—Didn't our people laugh?"

At last, passage paid, and luggage safe, we stood on board the schooner.
Hoisting sail, it glided down the Acushnet river. On one side, New Bedford
rose in terraces of streets, their ice-covered trees all glittering in the clear,

cold air. Huge hills and mountains of casks on casks were piled upon her
wharves, and side by side the world-wandering whale ships lay silent and
safely moored at last; while from others came a sound of carpenters and
coopers, with blended noises of fires and forges to melt the pitch, all
betokening that new cruises were on the start; that one most perilous and
long voyage ended, only begins a second; and a second ended, only begins
a third, and so on, for ever and for aye. Such is the endlessness, yea, the
intolerableness of all earthly effort.

Gaining the more open water, the bracing breeze waxed fresh; the little
Moss tossed the quick foam from her bows, as a young colt his snortings.
How I snuffed that Tartar air!—how I spurned that turnpike earth!—that
common highway all over dented with the marks of slavish heels and hoofs;
and turned me to admire the magnanimity of the sea which will permit no
records.

At the same foam-fountain, Queequeg seemed to drink and reel with
me. His dusky nostrils swelled apart; he showed his filed and pointed teeth.
On, on we flew; and our offing gained, the Moss did homage to the blast;
ducked and dived her bows as a slave before the Sultan. Sideways leaning, we
sideways darted; every ropeyarn tingling like a wire; the two tall masts
buckling like Indian canes in land tornadoes. So full of this reeling scene
were we, as we stood by the plunging bowsprit, that for some time we did
not notice the jeering glances of the passengers, a lubber-like assembly, who
marvelled that two fellow beings should be so companionable; as though a
white man were anything more dignified than a whitewashed negro. But
there were some boobies and bumpkins there, who, by their intense greenness, must have come from the heart and centre of all verdure. Queequeg
caught one of these young saplings mimicking him behind his back. I
thought the bumpkin's hour of doom was come. Dropping his harpoon,
the brawny savage caught him in his arms, and by an almost miraculous
dexterity and strength, sent him high up bodily into the air; then slightly
tapping his stern in mid-somerset, the fellow landed with bursting lungs
upon his feet, while Queequeg, turning his back upon him, lighted his
tomahawk pipe and passed it to me for a puff.

"Capting! Capting!" yelled the bumpkin, running towards that officer;
"Capting, Capting, here's the devil."

"Hallo, *you* sir," cried the Captain, a gaunt rib of the sea, stalking up to
Queequeg, "what in thunder do you mean by that? Don't you know you
might have killed that chap?"

"What him say?" said Queequeg, as he mildly turned to me.

"He say," said I, "that you came near kill-e that man there," pointing to the still shivering greenhorn.

"Kill-e," cried Queequeg, twisting his tattooed face into an unearthly expression of disdain, "ah! him bery small-e fish-e; Queequeg no kill-e so small-e fish-e; Queequeg kill-e big whale!"

"Look you," roared the Captain, "I'll kill-e *you,* you cannibal, if you try any more of your tricks aboard here; so mind your eye."

But it so happened just then, that it was high time for the Captain to mind his own eye. The prodigious strain upon the main-sail had parted the weather-sheet, and the tremendous boom was now flying from side to side, completely sweeping the entire after part of the deck. The poor fellow whom Queequeg had handled so roughly, was swept overboard; all hands were in a panic; and to attempt snatching at the boom to stay it, seemed madness. It flew from right to left, and back again, almost in one ticking of a watch, and every instant seemed on the point of snapping into splinters. Nothing was done, and nothing seemed capable of being done; those on deck rushed towards the bows, and stood eyeing the boom as if it were the lower jaw of an exasperated whale. In the midst of this consternation, Queequeg dropped deftly to his knees, and crawling under the path of the boom, whipped hold of a rope, secured one end to the bulwarks, and then flinging the other like a lasso, caught it round the boom as it swept over his head, and at the next jerk, the spar was that way trapped, and all was safe. The schooner was run into the wind, and while the hands were clearing away the stern boat, Queequeg, stripped to the waist, darted from the side with a long living arc of a leap. For three minutes or more he was seen swimming like a dog, throwing his long arms straight out before him, and by turns revealing his brawny shoulders through the freezing foam. I looked at the grand and glorious fellow, but saw no one to be saved. The greenhorn had gone down. Shooting himself perpendicularly from the water, Queequeg now took an instant's glance around him, and seeming to see just how matters were, dived down and disappeared. A few minutes more, and he rose again, one arm still striking out, and with the other dragging a lifeless form. The boat soon picked them up. The poor bumpkin was restored. All hands voted Queequeg a noble trump; the captain begged his pardon. From that hour I clove to Queequeg like a barnacle; yea, till poor Queequeg took his last long dive.

Was there ever such unconsciousness? He did not seem to think that he at all deserved a medal from the Humane and Magnanimous Societies. He only asked for water—fresh water—something to wipe the brine off; that done, he put on dry clothes, lighted his pipe, and leaning against the bulwarks, and mildly eyeing those around him, seemed to be saying to himself—"It's a mutual, joint-stock world, in all meridians. We cannibals must help these Christians."

# Chapter 14

## Nantucket

NOTHING MORE HAPPENED on the passage worthy the mentioning; so, after a fine run, we safely arrived in Nantucket.

Nantucket! Take out your map and look at it. See what a real corner of the world it occupies; how it stands there, away off shore, more lonely than the Eddystone lighthouse. Look at it—a mere hillock, and elbow of sand; all beach, without a background. There is more sand there than you would use in twenty years as a substitute for blotting paper. Some gamesome wights will tell you that they have to plant weeds there, they don't grow naturally; that they import Canada thistles; that they have to send beyond seas for a spile to stop a leak in an oil cask; that pieces of wood in Nantucket are carried about like bits of the true cross in Rome; that people there plant toadstools before their houses, to get under the shade in summer time; that one blade of grass makes an oasis, three blades in a day's walk a prairie; that they wear quicksand shoes, something like Laplander snow-shoes; that they are so shut up, belted about, every way inclosed, surrounded, and made an utter island of by the ocean, that to their very chairs and tables small clams will sometimes be found adhering, as to the backs of sea turtles. But these extravaganzas only show that Nantucket is no Illinois.

Look now at the wondrous traditional story of how this island was settled by the red-men. Thus goes the legend. In olden times an eagle swooped down upon the New England coast, and carried off an infant

Indian in his talons. With loud lament the parents saw their child borne out
of sight over the wide waters. They resolved to follow in the same direction.
Setting out in their canoes, after a perilous passage they discovered the
island, and there they found an empty ivory casket,—the poor little Indian's
skeleton.

What wonder, then, that these Nantucketers, born on a beach, should
take to the sea for a livelihood! They first caught crabs and quohogs in the
sand; grown bolder, they waded out with nets for mackerel; more experienced, they pushed off in boats and captured cod; and at last, launching
a navy of great ships on the sea, explored this watery world; put an incessant
belt of circumnavigations round it; peeped in at Bhering's Straits; and in all
seasons and all oceans declared everlasting war with the mightiest animated
mass that has survived the flood; most monstrous and most mountainous!
That Himmalehan, salt-sea Mastodon, clothed with such portentousness
of unconscious power, that his very panics are more to be dreaded than his
most fearless and malicious assaults!

And thus have these naked Nantucketers, these sea hermits, issuing from
their ant-hill in the sea, overrun and conquered the watery world like so
many Alexanders; parcelling out among them the Atlantic, Pacific, and
Indian oceans, as the three pirate powers did Poland. Let America add
Mexico to Texas, and pile Cuba upon Canada; let the English overswarm
all India, and hang out their blazing banner from the sun; two thirds of this
terraqueous globe are the Nantucketer's. For the sea is his; he owns it, as
Emperors own empires; other seamen having but a right of way through it.
Merchant ships are but extension bridges; armed ones but floating forts;
even pirates and privateers, though following the sea as highwaymen the
road, they but plunder other ships, other fragments of the land like themselves, without seeking to draw their living from the bottomless deep itself.
The Nantucketer, he alone resides and rests on the sea; he alone, in Bible
language, goes down to it in ships; to and fro ploughing it as his own special
plantation. *There* is his home; *there* lies his business, which a Noah's flood
would not interrupt, though it overwhelmed all the millions in China. He
lives on the sea, as prairie cocks in the prairie; he hides among the waves,
he climbs them as chamois hunters climb the Alps. For years he knows not
the land; so that when he comes to it at last, it smells like another world,
more strangely than the moon would to an Earthsman. With the landless gull,
that at sunset folds her wings and is rocked to sleep between billows; so at
nightfall, the Nantucketer, out of sight of land, furls his sails, and lays him to
his rest, while under his very pillow rush herds of walruses and whales.

# Chapter 15

*Chowder*

IT WAS QUITE LATE in the evening when the little Moss came snugly
to anchor, and Queequeg and I went ashore; so we could attend to no
business that day, at least none but a supper and a bed. The landlord
of the Spouter-Inn had recommended us to his cousin Hosea Hussey of the
Try Pots, whom he asserted to be the proprietor of one of the best kept
hotels in all Nantucket, and moreover he had assured us that cousin Hosea,
as he called him, was famous for his chowders. In short, he plainly hinted
that we could not possibly do better than try pot-luck at the Try Pots. But
the directions he had given us about keeping a yellow warehouse on our
starboard hand till we opened a white church to the larboard, and then
keeping that on the larboard hand till we made a corner three points to the
starboard, and that done, then ask the first man we met where the place was:
these crooked directions of his very much puzzled us at first, especially as,
at the outset, Queequeg insisted that the yellow warehouse—our first point
of departure—must be left on the larboard hand, whereas I had understood
Peter Coffin to say it was on the starboard. However, by dint of beating
about a little in the dark, and now and then knocking up a peaceable
inhabitant to inquire the way, we at last came to something which there
was no mistaking.

Two enormous wooden pots painted black, and suspended by asses' ears, swung from the cross-trees of an old top-mast, planted in front of an old doorway. The horns of the cross-trees were sawed off on the other side, so that this old top-mast looked not a little like a gallows. Perhaps I was over sensitive to such impressions at the time, but I could not help staring at this gallows with a vague misgiving. A sort of crick was in my neck as I gazed up to the two remaining horns; yes, *two* of them, one for Queequeg, and one for me. It's ominous, thinks I. A Coffin my Innkeeper upon landing in my first whaling port; tombstones staring at me in the whalemen's chapel; and here a gallows! and a pair of prodigious black pots too! Are these last throwing out oblique hints touching Tophet?

I was called from these reflections by the sight of a freckled woman with yellow hair and a yellow gown, standing in the porch of the inn, under a dull red lamp swinging there, that looked much like an injured eye, and carrying on a brisk scolding with a man in a purple woollen shirt.

"Get along with ye," said she to the man, "or I'll be combing ye!"

"Come on, Queequeg," said I, "all right. There's Mrs. Hussey."

And so it turned out; Mr. Hosea Hussey being from home, but leaving Mrs. Hussey entirely competent to attend to all his affairs. Upon making known our desires for a supper and a bed, Mrs. Hussey, postponing further scolding for the present, ushered us into a little room, and seating us at a table spread with the relics of a recently concluded repast, turned round to us and said—"Clam or Cod?"

"What's that about Cods, ma'am?" said I, with much politeness.

"Clam or Cod?" she repeated.

"A clam for supper? a cold clam; is *that* what you mean, Mrs. Hussey?" says I; "but that's a rather cold and clammy reception in the winter time, ain't it, Mrs. Hussey?"

But being in a great hurry to resume scolding the man in the purple shirt, who was waiting for it in the entry, and seeming to hear nothing but the word "clam," Mrs. Hussey hurried towards an open door leading to the kitchen, and bawling out "clam for two," disappeared.

"Queequeg," said I, "do you think that we can make out a supper for us both on one clam?"

However, a warm savory steam from the kitchen served to belie the apparently cheerless prospect before us. But when that smoking chowder came in, the mystery was delightfully explained. Oh, sweet friends! hearken to me. It was made of small juicy clams, scarcely bigger than hazel nuts, mixed with pounded ship biscuit, and salted pork cut up into little flakes; the whole enriched with butter, and plentifully seasoned with pepper and salt. Our appetites being sharpened by the frosty voyage, and in particular, Queequeg seeing his favorite fishy food before him, and the chowder being surpassingly excellent, we despatched it with great' expedition: when leaning back a moment and bethinking me of Mrs. Hussey's clam and cod announcement, I thought I would try a little experiment. Stepping to the kitchen door, I uttered the word "cod" with great emphasis, and resumed my seat. In a few moments the savory steam came forth again, but with a different flavor, and in good time a fine cod-chowder was placed before us.

We resumed business; and while plying our spoons in the bowl, thinks I to myself, I wonder now if this here has any effect on the head? What's that stultifying saying about chowder-headed people? "But look, Queequeg, ain't that a live eel in your bowl? Where's your harpoon?"

Fishiest of all fishy places was the Try Pots, which well deserved its name; for the pots there were always boiling chowders. Chowder for breakfast, and chowder for dinner, and chowder for supper, till you began to look for fish-bones coming through your clothes. The area before the house was paved with clam-shells. Mrs. Hussey wore a polished necklace of codfish vertebra; and Hosea Hussey had his account books bound in superior old shark-skin. There was a fishy flavor to the milk, too, which I could not at all account for, till one morning happening to take a stroll along the beach among some fishermen's boats, I saw Hosea's brindled cow feeding on fish remnants, and marching along the sand with each foot in a cod's decapitated head, looking very slip-shod, I assure ye.

Supper concluded, we received a lamp, and directions from Mrs. Hussey concerning the nearest way to bed; but, as Queequeg was about to precede me up the stairs, the lady reached forth her arm, and demanded his harpoon; she allowed no harpoon in her chambers. "Why not?" said I; "every true whaleman sleeps with his harpoon—but why not?" "Because it's dangerous," says she. "Ever since young Stiggs coming from that unfort'nt v'y'ge of his, when he was gone four years and a half, with ony three barrels of *ile,* was found dead in my first floor back, with his harpoon in his side; ever since then I allow no boarders to take sich dangerous weepons in their rooms a-night. So, Mr. Queequeg" (for she had learned his name), "I will just take this here iron, and keep it for you till morning. But the chowder; clam or cod to-morrow for breakfast, men?"

"Both," says I; "and let's have a couple of smoked herring by way of variety."

# Chapter 16

## The Ship

IN BED we concocted our plans for the morrow. But to my surprise and
no small concern, Queequeg now gave me to understand, that he had
been diligently consulting Yojo—the name of his black little god—and
Yojo had told him two or three times over, and strongly insisted upon it
everyway, that instead of our going together among the whaling-fleet in
harbor, and in concert selecting our craft; instead of this, I say, Yojo
earnestly enjoined that the selection of the ship should rest wholly with me,
inasmuch as Yojo purposed befriending us; and, in order to do so, had
already pitched upon a vessel, which, if left to myself, I, Ishmael, should
infallibly light upon, for all the world as though it had turned out by chance;
and in that vessel I must immediately ship myself, for the present irrespective
of Queequeg.

I have forgotten to mention that, in many things, Queequeg placed
great confidence in the excellence of Yojo's judgment and surprising fore-
cast of things; and cherished Yojo with considerable esteem, as a rather good
sort of god, who perhaps meant well enough upon the whole, but in all
cases did not succeed in his benevolent designs.

Now, this plan of Queequeg's, or rather Yojo's, touching the selection
of our craft; I did not like that plan at all. I had not a little relied upon
Queequeg's sagacity to point out the whaler best fitted to carry us and our

fortunes securely. But as all my remonstrances produced no effect upon
Queequeg, I was obliged to acquiesce; and accordingly prepared to set
about this business with a determined rushing sort of energy and vigor, that
should quickly settle that trifling little affair. Next morning early, leaving
Queequeg shut up with Yojo in our little bedroom—for it seemed that it
was some sort of Lent or Ramadan, or day of fasting, humiliation, and
prayer with Queequeg and Yojo that day; *how* it was I never could find
out, for, though I applied myself to it several times, I never could master his
liturgies and XXXIX Articles—leaving Queequeg, then, fasting on his
tomahawk pipe, and Yojo warming himself at his sacrificial fire of shavings,
I sallied out among the shipping. After much prolonged sauntering and
many random inquiries, I learnt that there were three ships up for three-
years' voyages—The Devil-dam, the Tit-bit, and the Pequod. *Devil-Dam,*
I do not know the origin of; *Tit-bit* is obvious; *Pequod,* you will no doubt
remember, was the name of a celebrated tribe of Massachusetts Indians, now
extinct as the ancient Medes. I peered and pryed about the Devil-Dam;
from her, hopped over to the Tit-bit; and, finally, going on board the
Pequod, looked around her for a moment, and then decided that this was
the very ship for us.

You may have seen many a quaint craft in your day, for aught I know;
—square-toed luggers; mountainous Japanese junks; butter-box galliots,
and what not; but take my word for it, you never saw such a rare old craft
as this same rare old Pequod. She was a ship of the old school, rather small
if anything; with an old fashioned claw-footed look about her. Long
seasoned and weather-stained in the typhoons and calms of all four oceans,
her old hull's complexion was darkened like a French grenadier's, who has
alike fought in Egypt and Siberia. Her venerable bows looked bearded.
Her masts—cut somewhere on the coast of Japan, where her original ones
were lost overboard in a gale—her masts stood stiffly up like the spines of
the three old kings of Cologne. Her ancient decks were worn and wrinkled,
like the pilgrim-worshipped flag-stone in Canterbury Cathedral where
Becket bled. But to all these her old antiquities, were added new and marvellous features, pertaining to the wild business that for more than half a
century she had followed. Old Captain Peleg, many years her chief-mate,
before he commanded another vessel of his own, and now a retired seaman,
and one of the principal owners of the Pequod,—this old Peleg, during the
term of his chief-mateship, had built upon her original grotesqueness, and
inlaid it, all over, with a quaintness both of material and device, unmatched
by anything except it be Thorkill-Hake's carved buckler or bedstead. She

was apparelled like any barbaric Ethiopian emperor, his neck heavy with pendants of polished ivory. She was a thing of trophies. A cannibal of a craft, tricking herself forth in the chased bones of her enemies. All round, her unpanelled, open bulwarks were garnished like one continuous jaw, with the long sharp teeth of the sperm whale, inserted there for pins, to fasten her old hempen thews and tendons to. Those thews ran not through base blocks of land wood, but deftly travelled over sheaves of sea-ivory. Scorning a turnstile wheel at her reverend helm, she sported there a tiller; and that tiller was in one mass, curiously carved from the long narrow lower jaw of her hereditary foe. The helmsman who steered by that tiller in a tempest, felt like the Tartar, when he holds back his fiery steed by clutching its jaw. A noble craft, but somehow a most melancholy! All noble things are touched with that.

Now when I looked about the quarter-deck, for some one having authority, in order to propose myself as a candidate for the voyage, at first I saw nobody; but I could not well overlook a strange sort of tent, or rather wigwam, pitched a little behind the main-mast. It seemed only a temporary erection used in port. It was of a conical shape, some ten feet high; consisting of the long, huge slabs of limber black bone taken from the middle and highest part of the jaws of the right-whale. Planted with their broad ends on the deck, a circle of these slabs laced together, mutually sloped towards each other, and at the apex united in a tufted point, where the loose hairy fibres waved to and fro like the top-knot on some old Pottowottamie Sachem's head. A triangular opening faced towards the bows of the ship, so that the insider commanded a complete view forward.

And half concealed in this queer tenement, I at length found one who by his aspect seemed to have authority; and who, it being noon, and the ship's work suspended, was now enjoying respite from the burden of command. He was seated on an old-fashioned oaken chair, wriggling all over with curious carving; and the bottom of which was formed of a stout interlacing of the same elastic stuff of which the wigwam was constructed.

There was nothing so very particular, perhaps, about the appearance of the elderly man I saw; he was brown and brawny, like most old seamen, and heavily rolled up in blue pilot-cloth, cut in the Quaker style; only there was a fine and almost microscopic net-work of the minutest wrinkles interlacing round his eyes, which must have arisen from his continual sailings in many hard gales, and always looking to windward;—for this causes the muscles about the eyes to become pursed together. Such eye-wrinkles are very effectual in a scowl.

"Is this the Captain of the Pequod?" said I, advancing to the door of the tent.

"Supposing it be the Captain of the Pequod, what dost thou want of him?" he demanded.

"I was thinking of shipping."

"Thou wast, wast thou? I see thou art no Nantucketer—ever been in a stove boat?"

"No, Sir, I never have."

"Dost know nothing at all about whaling, I dare say—eh?"

"Nothing, Sir; but I have no doubt I shall soon learn. I've been several voyages in the merchant service, and I think that——"

"Marchant service be damned. Talk not that lingo to me. Dost see that leg?—I'll take that leg away from thy stern, if ever thou talkest of the marchant service to me again. Marchant service indeed! I suppose now ye feel considerable proud of having served in those marchant ships. But flukes! man, what makes thee want to go a whaling, eh?—it looks a little suspicious, don't it, eh?—Hast not been a pirate, hast thou?—Didst not rob thy last Captain, didst thou?—Dost not think of murdering the officers when thou gettest to sea?"

I protested my innocence of these things. I saw that under the mask of these half humorous inuendoes, this old seaman, as an insulated Quakerish Nantucketer, was full of his insular prejudices, and rather distrustful of all aliens, unless they hailed from Cape Cod or the Vineyard.

"But what takes thee a-whaling? I want to know that before I think of shipping ye."

"Well, sir, I want to see what whaling is. I want to see the world."

"Want to see what whaling is, eh? Have ye clapped eye on Captain Ahab?"

"Who is Captain Ahab, sir?"

"Aye, aye, I thought so. Captain Ahab is the Captain of this ship."

"I am mistaken then. I thought I was speaking to the Captain himself."

"Thou art speaking to Captain Peleg—that's who ye are speaking to, young man. It belongs to me and Captain Bildad to see the Pequod fitted out for the voyage, and supplied with all her needs, including crew. We are part owners and agents. But as I was going to say, if thou wantest to know what whaling is, as thou tellest ye do, I can put ye in a way of finding it out before ye bind yourself to it, past backing out. Clap eye on Captain Ahab, young man, and thou wilt find that he has only one leg."

"What do you mean, sir? Was the other one lost by a whale?"

"Lost by a whale! Young man, come nearer to me: it was devoured, chewed up, crunched by the monstrousest parmacetty that ever chipped a boat!—ah, ah!"

I was a little alarmed by his energy, perhaps also a little touched at the hearty grief in his concluding exclamation, but said as calmly as I could, "What you say is no doubt true enough, sir; but how could I know there was any peculiar ferocity in that particular whale, though indeed I might have inferred as much from the simple fact of the accident."

"Look ye now, young man, thy lungs are a sort of soft, d'ye see; thou dost not talk shark a bit. *Sure,* ye've been to sea before now; sure of that?"

"Sir," said I, "I thought I told you that I had been four voyages in the merchant——"

"Hard down out of that! Mind what I said about the marchant service —don't aggravate me—I won't have it. But let us understand each other. I have given thee a hint about what whaling is; do ye yet feel inclined for it?"

"I do, sir."

"Very good. Now, art thou the man to pitch a harpoon down a live whale's throat, and then jump after it? Answer, quick!"

"I am, sir, if it should be positively indispensable to do so; not to be got rid of, that is; which I don't take to be the fact."

"Good again. Now then, thou not only wantest to go a-whaling, to find out by experience what whaling is, but ye also want to go in order to see the world? Was not that what ye said? I thought so. Well then, just step forward there, and take a peep over the weather-bow, and then back to me and tell me what ye see there."

For a moment I stood a little puzzled by this curious request, not knowing exactly how to take it, whether humorously or in earnest. But concentrating all his crow's feet into one scowl, Captain Peleg started me on the errand.

Going forward and glancing over the weather bow, I perceived that the ship swinging to her anchor with the flood-tide, was now obliquely pointing towards the open ocean. The prospect was unlimited, but exceedingly monotonous and forbidding; not the slightest variety that I could see.

"Well, what's the report?" said Peleg when I came back; "what did ye see?"

"Not much," I replied—"nothing but water; considerable horizon though, and there's a squall coming up, I think."

"Well, what dost thou think then of seeing the world? Do ye wish to go round Cape Horn to see any more of it, eh? Can't ye see the world where you stand?"

I was a little staggered, but go a-whaling I must, and I would; and the Pequod was as good a ship as any—I thought the best—and all this I now repeated to Peleg. Seeing me so determined, he expressed his willingness to ship me.

"And thou mayest as well sign the papers right off," he added—"come along with ye." And so saying, he led the way below deck into the cabin.

Seated on the transom was what seemed to me a most uncommon and surprising figure. It turned out to be Captain Bildad, who along with Captain Peleg was one of the largest owners of the vessel; the other shares, as is sometimes the case in these ports, being held by a crowd of old annuitants; widows, fatherless children, and chancery wards; each owning about the value of a timber head, or a foot of plank, or a nail or two in the ship. People in Nantucket invest their money in whaling vessels, the same way that you do yours in approved state stocks bringing in good interest.

Now, Bildad, like Peleg, and indeed many other Nantucketers, was a Quaker, the island having been originally settled by that sect; and to this day its inhabitants in general retain in an uncommon measure the peculiarities of the Quaker, only variously and anomalously modified by things altogether alien and heterogeneous. For some of these same Quakers are the most sanguinary of all sailors and whale-hunters. They are fighting Quakers; they are Quakers with a vengeance.

So that there are instances among them of men, who, named with Scripture names—a singularly common fashion on the island—and in childhood naturally imbibing the stately dramatic thee and thou of the Quaker idiom; still, from the audacious, daring, and boundless adventure of their subsequent lives, strangely blend with these unoutgrown peculiarities, a thousand bold dashes of character, not unworthy a Scandinavian sea-king, or a poetical Pagan Roman. And when these things unite in a man of greatly superior natural force, with a globular brain and a ponderous heart; who has also by the stillness and seclusion of many long night-watches in the remotest waters, and beneath constellations never seen here at the north, been led to think untraditionally and independently; receiving all nature's sweet or savage impressions fresh from her own virgin, voluntary, and confiding breast, and thereby chiefly, but with some help from accidental advantages, to learn a bold and nervous lofty language—that man makes one in a whole nation's census—a mighty pageant creature, formed for noble tragedies. Nor will it at all detract from him, dramatically regarded,

if either by birth or other circumstances, he have what seems a half wilful
over-ruling morbidness at the bottom of his nature. For all men tragically
great are made so through a certain morbidness. Be sure of this, O young
ambition, all mortal greatness is but disease. But, as yet we have not to do
with such an one, but with quite another; and still a man, who, if indeed
peculiar, it only results again from another phase of the Quaker, modified
by individual circumstances.

Like Captain Peleg, Captain Bildad was a well-to-do, retired whaleman.
But unlike Captain Peleg—who cared not a rush for what are called serious
things, and indeed deemed those self-same serious things the veriest of all
trifles—Captain Bildad had not only been originally educated according to
the strictest sect of Nantucket Quakerism, but all his subsequent ocean life,
and the sight of many unclad, lovely island creatures, round the Horn—all
that had not moved this native born Quaker one single jot, had not so much
as altered one angle of his vest. Still, for all this immutableness, was there
some lack of common consistency about worthy Captain Bildad. Though
refusing, from conscientious scruples, to bear arms against land invaders,
yet himself had illimitably invaded the Atlantic and Pacific; and though
a sworn foe to human bloodshed, yet had he in his straight-bodied coat,
spilled tuns upon tuns of leviathan gore. How now in the contemplative
evening of his days, the pious Bildad reconciled these things in the reminiscence, I do not know; but it did not seem to concern him much, and very
probably he had long since come to the sage and sensible conclusion that
a man's religion is one thing, and this practical world quite another. This
world pays dividends. Rising from a little cabin-boy in short clothes of the
drabbest drab, to a harpooneer in a broad shad-bellied waistcoat; from that
becoming boat-header, chief-mate, and captain, and finally a ship-owner;
Bildad, as I hinted before, had concluded his adventurous career by wholly
retiring from active life at the goodly age of sixty, and dedicating his
remaining days to the quiet receiving of his well-earned income.

Now Bildad, I am sorry to say, had the reputation of being an incorri-
gible old hunks, and in his sea-going days, a bitter, hard task-master. They
told me in Nantucket, though it certainly seems a curious story, that when
he sailed the old Categut whaleman, his crew, upon arriving home, were
mostly all carried ashore to the hospital, sore exhausted and worn out. For
a pious man, especially for a Quaker, he was certainly rather hard-hearted,
to say the least. He never used to swear, though, at his men, they said; but
somehow he got an inordinate quantity of cruel, unmitigated hard work
out of them. When Bildad was a chief-mate, to have his drab-colored eye

intently looking at you, made you feel completely nervous, till you could clutch something—a hammer or a marling-spike, and go to work like mad, at something or other, never mind what. Indolence and idleness perished from before him. His own person was the exact embodiment of his utilitarian character. On his long, gaunt body, he carried no spare flesh, no superfluous beard, his chin having a soft, economical nap to it, like the worn nap of his broad-brimmed hat.

Such, then, was the person that I saw seated on the transom when I followed Captain Peleg down into the cabin. The space between the decks was small; and there, bolt-upright, sat old Bildad, who always sat so, and never leaned, and this to save his coat tails. His broad-brim was placed beside him; his legs were stiffly crossed; his drab vesture was buttoned up to his chin; and spectacles on nose, he seemed absorbed in reading from a ponderous volume.

"Bildad," cried Captain Peleg, "at it again, Bildad, eh? Ye have been studying those Scriptures, now, for the last thirty years, to my certain knowledge. How far ye got, Bildad?"

As if long habituated to such profane talk from his old shipmate, Bildad, without noticing his present irreverence, quietly looked up, and seeing me, glanced again inquiringly towards Peleg.

"He says he's our man, Bildad," said Peleg, "he wants to ship."

"Dost thee?" said Bildad, in a hollow tone, and turning round to me.

"I *dost*," said I unconsciously, he was so intense a Quaker.

"What do ye think of him, Bildad?" said Peleg.

"He'll do," said Bildad, eyeing me, and then went on spelling away at his book in a mumbling tone quite audible.

I thought him the queerest old Quaker I ever saw, especially as Peleg, his friend and old shipmate, seemed such a blusterer. But I said nothing, only looking round me sharply. Peleg now threw open a chest, and drawing forth the ship's articles, placed pen and ink before him, and seated himself at a little table. I began to think it was high time to settle with myself at what terms I would be willing to engage for the voyage. I was already aware that in the whaling business they paid no wages; but all hands, including the captain, received certain shares of the profits called *lays,* and that these lays were proportioned to the degree of importance pertaining to the respective duties of the ship's company. I was also aware that being a green hand at whaling, my own lay would not be very large; but considering that I was used to the sea, could steer a ship, splice a rope, and all that, I made no doubt that from all I had heard I should be offered at least the 275th lay—that is, the 275th part of the clear nett proceeds of the voyage, whatever that might eventually amount to. And though the 275th lay was what they call a rather *long lay,* yet it was better than nothing; and if we had a lucky voyage, might pretty nearly pay for the clothing I would wear out on it, not to speak of my three years' beef and board, for which I would not have to pay one stiver.

It might be thought that this was a poor way to accumulate a princely fortune—and so it was, a very poor way indeed. But I am one of those that never take on about princely fortunes, and am quite content if the world is ready to board and lodge me, while I am putting up at this grim sign of the Thunder Cloud. Upon the whole, I thought that the 275th lay would be about the fair thing, but would not have been surprised had I been offered the 200th, considering I was of a broad-shouldered make.

But one thing, nevertheless, that made me a little distrustful about receiving a generous share of the profits was this: Ashore, I had heard something of both Captain Peleg and his unaccountable old crony Bildad; how that they being the principal proprietors of the Pequod, therefore the other and more inconsiderable and scattered owners, left nearly the whole management of the ship's affairs to these two. And I did not know but what the stingy old Bildad might have a mighty deal to say about shipping hands, especially as I now found him on board the Pequod, quite at home there in the cabin, and reading his Bible as if at his own fireside. Now while Peleg was vainly trying to mend a pen with his jack-knife, old Bildad, to my no small surprise, considering that he was such an interested party in these proceedings; Bildad never heeded us, but went on mumbling to himself out of his book, "'*Lay* not up for yourselves treasures upon earth, where moth—'"

"Well, Captain Bildad," interrupted Peleg, "what d'ye say, what lay shall we give this young man?"

"Thou knowest best," was the sepulchral reply, "the seven hundred and seventy-seventh wouldn't be too much, would it?—'where moth and rust do corrupt, but *lay*—'"

*Lay,* indeed, thought I, and such a lay! the seven hundred and seventy-seventh! Well, old Bildad, you are determined that I, for one, shall not *lay* up many *lays* here below, where moth and rust do corrupt. It was an exceedingly *long lay* that, indeed; and though from the magnitude of the figure it might at first deceive a landsman, yet the slightest consideration. will show that though seven hundred and seventy-seven is a pretty large number, yet, when you come to make a *teenth* of it, you will then see, I say, that the seven hundred and seventy-seventh part of a farthing is a good deal less than seven hundred and seventy-seven gold doubloons; and so I thought at the time.

"Why, blast your eyes, Bildad," cried Peleg, "thou dost not want to swindle this young man! he must have more than that."

"Seven hundred and seventy-seventh," again said Bildad, without lifting his eyes; and then went on mumbling—"'for where your treasure is, there will your heart be also.'"

"I am going to put him down for the three hundredth," said Peleg, "do ye hear that, Bildad! The three hundredth lay, I say."

Bildad laid down his book, and turning solemnly towards him said, "Captain Peleg, thou hast a generous heart; but thou must consider the duty thou owest to the other owners of this ship—widows and orphans, many of them—and that if we too abundantly reward the labors of this young man, we may be taking the bread from those widows and those orphans. The seven hundred and seventy-seventh lay, Captain Peleg."

"Thou Bildad!" roared Peleg, starting up and clattering about the cabin. "Blast ye, Captain Bildad, if I had followed thy advice in these matters, I would afore now had a conscience to lug about that would be heavy enough to founder the largest ship that ever sailed round Cape Horn."

"Captain Peleg," said Bildad steadily, "thy conscience may be drawing ten inches of water, or ten fathoms, I can't tell; but as thou art still an impenitent man, Captain Peleg, I greatly fear lest thy conscience be but a leaky one; and will in the end sink thee foundering down to the fiery pit, Captain Peleg."

"Fiery pit! fiery pit! ye insult me, man; past all natural bearing, ye insult me. It's an all-fired outrage to tell any human creature that he's bound to hell. Flukes and flames! Bildad, say that again to me, and start my soul-bolts, but I'll—I'll—yes, I'll swallow a live goat with all his hair and horns on. Out of the cabin, ye canting, drab-colored son of a wooden gun—a straight wake with ye!"

As he thundered out this he made a rush at Bildad, but with a marvellous oblique, sliding celerity, Bildad for that time eluded him.

Alarmed at this terrible outburst between the two principal and responsible owners of the ship, and feeling half a mind to give up all idea of sailing in a vessel so questionably owned and temporarily commanded, I stepped aside from the door to give egress to Bildad, who, I made no doubt, was all eagerness to vanish from before the awakened wrath of Peleg. But to my astonishment, he sat down again on the transom very quietly, and seemed to have not the slightest intention of withdrawing. He seemed quite used to impenitent Peleg and his ways. As for Peleg, after letting off his rage as he had, there seemed no more left in him, and he, too, sat down like a lamb, though he twitched a little as if still nervously agitated. "Whew!" he whistled at last—"the squall's gone off to leeward, I think. Bildad, thou used to be good at sharpening a lance, mend that pen, will ye. My jack-knife here needs the grindstone. Thank ye; thank ye, Bildad. Now then, my young man, Ishmael's thy name, didn't ye say? Well then, down ye go here, Ishmael, for the three hundredth lay."

"Captain Peleg," said I, "I have a friend with me who wants to ship too—shall I bring him down to-morrow?"

"To be sure," said Peleg. "Fetch him along, and we'll look at him."

"What lay does *he* want?" groaned Bildad, glancing up from the book in which he had again been burying himself.

"Oh! never thee mind about that, Bildad," said Peleg. "Has he ever whaled it any?" turning to me.

"Killed more whales than I can count, Captain Peleg."

"Well, bring him along then."

And, after signing the papers, off I went; nothing doubting but that I had done a good morning's work, and that the Pequod was the identical ship that Yojo had provided to carry Queequeg and me round the Cape.

But I had not proceeded far, when I began to bethink me that the captain with whom I was to sail yet remained unseen by me; though, indeed, in many cases, a whale-ship will be completely fitted out, and receive all her crew on board, ere the captain makes himself visible by arriving to take command; for sometimes these voyages are so prolonged, and the shore intervals at home so exceedingly brief, that if the captain have a family, or any absorbing concernment of that sort, he does not trouble himself much about his ship in port, but leaves her to the owners till all is ready for sea. However, it is always as well to have a look at him before irrevocably committing yourself into his hands. Turning back I accosted Captain Peleg, inquiring where Captain Ahab was to be found.

"And what dost thou want of Captain Ahab? It's all right enough; thou art shipped."

"Yes, but I should like to see him."

"But I don't think thou wilt be able to at present. I don't know exactly what's the matter with him; but he keeps close inside the house; a sort of sick, and yet he don't look so. In fact, he ain't sick; but no, he isn't well either. Any how, young man, he won't always see me, so I don't suppose he will thee. He's a queer man, Captain Ahab—so some think—but a good one. Oh, thou'lt like him well enough; no fear, no fear. He's a grand, ungodly, god-like man, Captain Ahab; doesn't speak much; but, when he does speak, then you may well listen. Mark ye, be forewarned; Ahab's above the common; Ahab's been in colleges, as well as 'mong the cannibals; been used to deeper wonders than the waves; fixed his fiery lance in mightier, stranger foes than whales. His lance! aye, the keenest and the surest that, out of all our isle! Oh! he ain't Captain Bildad; no, and he ain't Captain Peleg; he's Ahab, boy; and Ahab of old, thou knowest, was a crowned king!"

"And a very vile one. When that wicked king was slain, the dogs, did they not lick his blood?"

"Come hither to me—hither, hither," said Peleg, with a significance in his eye that almost startled me. "Look ye, lad; never say that on board the Pequod. Never say it anywhere. Captain Ahab did not name himself. 'Twas a foolish, ignorant whim of his crazy, widowed mother, who died when he was only a twelvemonth old. And yet the old squaw Tistig, at Gay-head, said that the name would somehow prove prophetic. And, perhaps, other fools like her may tell thee the same. I wish to warn thee. It's a lie. I know Captain Ahab well; I've sailed with him as mate years ago; I know what he is—a good man—not a pious, good man, like Bildad, but a swearing good man—something like me—only there's a good deal more of him. Aye, aye, I know that he was never very jolly; and I know that on the passage home, he was a little out of his mind for a spell; but it was the sharp shooting pains in his bleeding stump that brought that about, as any one might see. I know, too, that ever since he lost his leg last voyage by that accursed whale, he's been a kind of moody—desperate moody, and savage sometimes; but that will all pass off. And once for all, let me tell thee and assure thee, young man, it's better to sail with a moody good captain than a laughing bad one. So good-bye to thee—and wrong not Captain Ahab, because he happens to have a wicked name. Besides, my boy, he has a wife —not three voyages wedded—a sweet, resigned girl. Think of that; by that sweet girl that old man has a child: hold ye then there can be any utter, hopeless harm in Ahab? No, no, my lad; stricken, blasted, if he be, Ahab has his humanities!"

As I walked away, I was full of thoughtfulness; what had been incidentally revealed to me of Captain Ahab, filled me with a certain wild vagueness of painfulness concerning him. And somehow, at the time, I felt a sympathy and a sorrow for him, but for I don't know what, unless it was the cruel loss of his leg. And yet I also felt a strange awe of him; but that sort of awe, which I cannot at all describe, was not exactly awe; I do not know what it was. But I felt it; and it did not disincline me towards him; though I felt impatience at what seemed like mystery in him, so imperfectly as he was known to me then. However, my thoughts were at length carried in other directions, so that for the present dark Ahab slipped my mind.

# Chapter 17

*The Ramadan*

AS Queequeg's Ramadan, or Fasting and Humiliation, was to continue all day, I did not choose to disturb him till towards night-fall; for I cherish the greatest respect towards everybody's religious obligations, never mind how comical, and could not find it in my heart to undervalue even a congregation of ants worshipping a toad-stool; or those other creatures in certain parts of our earth, who with a degree of footman-ism quite unprecedented in other planets, bow down before the torso of a deceased landed proprietor merely on account of the inordinate possessions yet owned and rented in his name.

I say, we good Presbyterian Christians should be charitable in these things, and not fancy ourselves so vastly superior to other mortals, pagans and what not, because of their half-crazy conceits on these subjects. There was Queequeg, now, certainly entertaining the most absurd notions about Yojo and his Ramadan;—but what of that? Queequeg thought he knew what he was about, I suppose; he seemed to be content; and there let him rest. All our arguing with him would not avail; let him be, I say: and Heaven have mercy on us all—Presbyterians and Pagans alike—for we are all some-how dreadfully cracked about the head, and sadly need mending.

Towards evening, when I felt assured that all his performances and rituals must be over, I went up to his room and knocked at the door; but no answer. I tried to open it, but it was fastened inside. "Queequeg," said I softly through the key-hole:—all silent. "I say, Queequeg! why don't you speak? It's I—Ishmael." But all remained still as before. I began to grow alarmed. I had allowed him such abundant time; I thought he might have had an apoplectic fit. I looked through the key-hole; but the door opening into an odd corner of the room, the key-hole prospect was but a crooked and sinister one. I could only see part of the foot-board of the bed and a line of the wall, but nothing more. I was surprised to behold resting against the wall the wooden shaft of Queequeg's harpoon, which the landlady the evening previous had taken from him, before our mounting to the chamber. That's strange, thought I; but at any rate, since the harpoon stands yonder, and he seldom or never goes abroad without it, therefore he must be inside here, and no possible mistake.

"Queequeg!—Queequeg!"—all still. Something must have happened. Apoplexy! I tried to burst open the door; but it stubbornly resisted. Running down stairs, I quickly stated my suspicions to the first person I met—the chamber-maid. "La! La!" she cried, "I thought something must be the matter. I went to make the bed after breakfast, and the door was locked; and not a mouse to be heard; and it's been just so silent ever since. But I thought, may be, you had both gone off and locked your baggage in for safe keeping. La! La, ma'am!—Mistress! murder! Mrs. Hussey! apoplexy!"—and with these cries, she ran towards the kitchen, I following.

Mrs. Hussey soon appeared, with a mustard-pot in one hand and a vinegar-cruet in the other, having just broken away from the occupation of attending to the castors, and scolding her little black boy meantime.

"Wood-house!" cried I, "which way to it? Run for God's sake, and fetch something to pry open the door—the axe!—the axe!—he's had a stroke; depend upon it!"—and so saying I was unmethodically rushing up stairs again empty-handed, when Mrs. Hussey interposed the mustard-pot and vinegar-cruet, and the entire castor of her countenance.

"What's the matter with you, young man?"

"Get the axe! For God's sake, run for the doctor, some one, while I pry it open!"

"Look here," said the landlady, quickly putting down the vinegar-cruet, so as to have one hand free; "look here; are you talking about prying open any of my doors?"—and with that she seized my arm. "What's the matter with you? What's the matter with you, shipmate?"

In as calm, but rapid a manner as possible, I gave her to understand the whole case. Unconsciously clapping the mustard-pot to one side of her nose, she ruminated for an instant; then exclaimed—"No! I haven't seen it since I put it there." Running to a little closet under the landing of the stairs, she glanced in, and returning, told me that Queequeg's harpoon was missing. "He's killed himself," she cried. "It's unfort'nate Stiggs done over again—there goes another counterpane—God pity his poor mother!—it will be the ruin of my house. Has the poor lad a sister? Where's that girl?—there, Betty, go to Snarles the Painter, and tell him to paint me a sign, with—'no suicides permitted here, and no smoking in the parlor;'—might as well kill both birds at once. Kill? The Lord be merciful to his ghost! What's that noise there? You, young man, avast there!"

And running up after me, she caught me as I was again trying to force open the door.

"I won't allow it; I won't have my premises spoiled. Go for the lock-smith, there's one about a mile from here. But avast!" putting her hand in her side-pocket, "here's a key that'll fit, I guess; let's see." And with that, she turned it in the lock; but, alas! Queequeg's supplemental bolt remained unwithdrawn within.

"Have to burst it open," said I, and was running down the entry a little, for a good start, when the landlady caught at me, again vowing I should not break down her premises; but I tore from her, and with a sudden bodily rush dashed myself full against the mark.

With a prodigious noise the door flew open, and the knob slamming against the wall, sent the plaster to the ceiling; and there, good heavens! there sat Queequeg, altogether cool and self-collected; right in the middle of the room; squatting on his hams, and holding Yojo on top of his head. He looked neither one way nor the other way, but sat like a carved image with scarce a sign of active life.

"Queequeg," said I, going up to him, "Queequeg, what's the matter with you?"

"He hain't been a sittin' so all day, has he?" said the landlady.

But all we said, not a word could we drag out of him; I almost felt like pushing him over, so as to change his position, for it was almost intolerable, it seemed so painfully and unnaturally constrained; especially, as in all probability he had been sitting so for upwards of eight or ten hours, going too without his regular meals.

"Mrs. Hussey," said I, "he's *alive* at all events; so leave us, if you please, and I will see to this strange affair myself."

Closing the door upon the landlady, I endeavored to prevail upon Queequeg to take a chair; but in vain. There he sat; and all I could do—

for all my polite arts and blandishments—he would not move a peg, nor say a single word, nor even look at me, nor notice my presence in any the slightest way.

I wonder, thought I, if this can possibly be a part of his Ramadan; do they fast on their hams that way in his native island. It must be so; yes, it's part of his creed, I suppose; well, then, let him rest; he'll get up sooner or later, no doubt. It can't last for ever, thank God, and his Ramadan only comes once a year; and I don't believe it's very punctual then.

I went down to supper. After sitting a long time listening to the long stories of some sailors who had just come from a plum-pudding voyage, as they called it (that is, a short whaling-voyage in a schooner or brig, confined to the north of the line, in the Atlantic Ocean only); after listening to these plum-puddingers till nearly eleven o'clock, I went up stairs to go to bed, feeling quite sure by this time Queequeg must certainly have brought his Ramadan to a termination. But no; there he was just where I had left him; he had not stirred an inch. I began to grow vexed with him; it seemed so downright senseless and insane to be sitting there all day and half the night on his hams in a cold room, holding a piece of wood on his head.

"For heaven's sake, Queequeg, get up and shake yourself; get up and have some supper. You'll starve; you'll kill yourself, Queequeg." But not a word did he reply.

Despairing of him, therefore, I determined to go to bed and to sleep; and no doubt, before a great while, he would follow me. But previous to turning in, I took my heavy bearskin jacket, and threw it over him, as it promised to be a very cold night; and he had nothing but his ordinary round jacket on. For some time, do all I would, I could not get into the faintest doze. I had blown out the candle; and the mere thought of Queequeg—not four feet off—sitting there in that uneasy position, stark alone in the cold and dark; this made me really wretched. Think of it; sleeping all night in the same room with a wide awake pagan on his hams in this dreary, un-accountable Ramadan!

But somehow I dropped off at last, and knew nothing more till break of day; when, looking over the bedside, there squatted Queequeg, as if he had been screwed down to the floor. But as soon as the first glimpse of sun entered the window, up he got, with stiff and grating joints, but with a cheerful look; limped towards me where I lay; pressed his forehead again against mine; and said his Ramadan was over.

Now, as I before hinted, I have no objection to any person's religion, be it what it may, so long as that person does not kill or insult any other person, because that other person don't believe it also. But when a man's religion becomes really frantic; when it is a positive torment to him; and, in fine, makes this earth of ours an uncomfortable inn to lodge in; then I think it high time to take that individual aside and argue the point with him.

And just so I now did with Queequeg. "Queequeg," said I, "get into bed now, and lie and listen to me." I then went on, beginning with the rise and progress of the primitive religions, and coming down to the various religions of the present time, during which time I labored to show Queequeg that all these Lents, Ramadans, and prolonged ham-squattings in cold, cheerless rooms were stark nonsense; bad for the health; useless for the soul; opposed, in short, to the obvious laws of Hygiene and common sense. I told him, too, that he being in other things such an extremely sensible and sagacious savage, it pained me, very badly pained me, to see him now so deplorably foolish about this ridiculous Ramadan of his. Besides, argued I, fasting makes the body cave in; hence the spirit caves in; and all thoughts born of a fast must necessarily be half-starved. This is the reason why most dyspeptic religionists cherish such melancholy notions about their hereafters. In one word, Queequeg, said I, rather digressively; hell is an idea first born on an undigested apple-dumpling; and since then perpetuated through the hereditary dyspepsias nurtured by Ramadans.

I then asked Queequeg whether he himself was ever troubled with dyspepsia; expressing the idea very plainly, so that he could take it in. He said no; only upon one memorable occasion. It was after a great feast given by his father the king, on the gaining of a great battle wherein fifty of the enemy had been killed by about two o'clock in the afternoon, and all cooked and eaten that very evening.

· "No more, Queequeg," said I, shuddering; "that will do;" for I knew the inferences without his further hinting them. I had seen a sailor who had visited that very island, and he told me that it was the custom, when a great battle had been gained there, to barbecue all the slain in the yard or garden of the victor; and then, one by one, they were placed in great wooden trenchers, and garnished round like a pilau, with breadfruit and cocoanuts; and with some parsley in their mouths, were sent round with the victor's compliments to all his friends, just as though these presents were so many Christmas turkeys.

After all, I do not think that my remarks about religion made much impression upon Queequeg. Because, in the first place, he somehow seemed dull of hearing on that important subject, unless considered from his own point of view; and, in the second place, he did not more than one third understand me, couch my ideas simply as I would; and, finally, he no doubt thought he knew a good deal more about the true religion than I did. He looked at me with a sort of condescending concern and compassion, as though he thought it a great pity that such a sensible young man should be so hopelessly lost to evangelical pagan piety.

At last we rose and dressed; and Queequeg, taking a prodigiously hearty breakfast of chowders of all sorts, so that the landlady should not make much profit by reason of his Ramadan, we sallied out to board the Pequod, sauntering along, and picking our teeth with halibut bones.

# Chapter 18

## *His Mark*

A S WE WERE WALKING down the end of the wharf towards the ship, Queequeg carrying his harpoon, Captain Peleg in his gruff voice loudly hailed us from his wigwam, saying he had not suspected my friend was a cannibal, and furthermore announcing that he let no cannibals on board that craft, unless they previously produced their papers.

"What do you mean by that, Captain Peleg?" said I, now jumping on the bulwarks, and leaving my comrade standing on the wharf.

"I mean," he replied, "he must show his papers."

"Yea," said Captain Bildad in his hollow voice, sticking his head from behind Peleg's, out of the wigwam. "He must show that he's converted. Son of darkness," he added, turning to Queequeg, "art thou at present in communion with any christian church?"

"Why," said I, "he's a member of the First Congregational Church." Here be it said, that many tattooed savages sailing in Nantucket ships at last come to be converted into the churches.

"First Congregational Church," cried Bildad, "what! that worships in Deacon Deuteronomy Coleman's meeting-house?" and so saying, taking out his spectacles, he rubbed them with his great yellow bandana handkerchief, and putting them on very carefully, came out of the wigwam, and leaning stiffly over the bulwarks, took a good long look at Queequeg.

"How long hath he been a member?" he then said, turning to me; "not very long, I rather guess, young man."

"No," said Peleg, "and he hasn't been baptized right either, or it would have washed some of that devil's blue off his face."

"Do tell, now," cried Bildad, "is this Philistine a regular member of Deacon Deuteronomy's meeting? I never saw him going there, and I pass it every Lord's day."

"I don't know anything about Deacon Deuteronomy or his meeting," said I, "all I know is, that Queequeg here is a born member of the First Congregational Church. He is a deacon himself, Queequeg is."

"Young man," said Bildad sternly, "thou art skylarking with me— explain thyself, thou young Hittite. What church dost thee mean? answer me."

Finding myself thus hard pushed, I replied, "I mean, sir, the same ancient Catholic Church to which you and I, and Captain Peleg there, and Quee-queg here, and all of us, and every mother's son and soul of us belong; the great and everlasting First Congregation of this whole worshipping world; we all belong to that; only some of us cherish some queer crotchets noways touching the grand belief; in *that* we all join hands."

"Splice, thou mean'st *splice* hands," cried Peleg, drawing nearer. "Young man, you'd better ship for a missionary, instead of a fore-mast hand; I never heard a better sermon. Deacon Deuteronomy—why Father Mapple himself couldn't beat it, and he's reckoned something. Come aboard, come aboard; never mind about the papers. I say, tell Quohog there—what's that you call him? tell Quohog to step along. By the great anchor, what a har-poon he's got there! looks like good stuff that; and he handles it about right. I say, Quohog, or whatever your name is, did you ever stand in the head of a whale-boat? did you ever strike a fish?"

Without saying a word, Queequeg, in his wild sort of way, jumped upon the bulwarks, from thence into the bows of one of the whale-boats hanging to the side; and then bracing his left knee, and poising his harpoon, cried out in some such way as this:—

"Cap'ain, you see him small drop tar on water dere? You see him? well, spose him one whale eye, well, den!" and taking sharp aim at it, he darted the iron right over old Bildad's broad brim, clean across the ship's decks, and struck the glistening tar spot out of sight.

"Now," said Queequeg, quietly hauling in the line, "spos-ee him whale-e eye; why, dad whale dead."

"Quick, Bildad," said Peleg, to his partner, who, aghast at the close vicinity of the flying harpoon, had retreated towards the cabin gangway. "Quick, I say, you Bildad, and get the ship's papers. We must have Hedge-hog there, I mean Quohog, in one of our boats. Look ye, Quohog, we'll give ye the ninetieth lay, and that's more than ever was given a harpooneer yet out of Nantucket."

So down we went into the cabin, and to my great joy Queequeg was soon enrolled among the same ship's company to which I myself belonged.

When all preliminaries were over and Peleg had got everything ready for signing, he turned to me and said, "I guess, Quohog there don't know how to write, does he? I say, Quohog, blast ye! dost thou sign thy name or make thy mark?"

But at this question, Queequeg, who had twice or thrice before taken part in similar ceremonies, looked no ways abashed; but taking the offered pen, copied upon the paper, in the proper place, an exact counterpart of a queer round figure which was tattooed upon his arm; so that through Captain Peleg's obstinate mistake touching his appellative, it stood some-thing like this:—

Quohog.<br>his ✠ mark.

Meanwhile Captain Bildad sat earnestly and steadfastly eyeing Quee-queg, and at last rising solemnly and fumbling in the huge pockets of his broad-skirted drab coat, took out a bundle of tracts, and selecting one entitled "The Latter Day Coming; or No Time to Lose," placed it in Queequeg's hands, and then grasping them and the book with both his, looked earnestly into his eyes, and said, "Son of darkness, I must do my duty by thee; I am part owner of this ship, and feel concerned for the souls of all its crew; if thou still clingest to thy Pagan ways, which I sadly fear, I beseech thee, remain not for aye a Belial bondsman. Spurn the idol Bel, and the hideous dragon; turn from the wrath to come; mind thine eye, I say; oh! goodness gracious! steer clear of the fiery pit!"

Something of the salt sea yet lingered in old Bildad's language, hetero-geneously mixed with Scriptural and domestic phrases.

"Avast there, avast there, Bildad, avast now spoiling our harpooneer," cried Peleg. "Pious harpooneers never make good voyagers—it takes the shark out of 'em; no harpooneer is worth a straw who aint pretty sharkish. There was young Nat Swaine, once the bravest boat-header out of all Nantucket and the Vineyard; he joined the meeting, and never came to good. He got so frightened about his plaguy soul, that he shrinked and sheered away from whales, for fear of after-claps, in case he got stove and went to Davy Jones."

"Peleg! Peleg!" said Bildad, lifting his eyes and hands, "thou thyself, as I myself, hast seen many a perilous time; thou knowest, Peleg, what it is to have the fear of death; how, then, can'st thou prate in this ungodly guise. Thou beliest thine own heart, Peleg. Tell me, when this same Pequod here had her three masts overboard in that typhoon on Japan, that same voyage when thou went mate with Captain Ahab, did'st thou not think of Death and the Judgment then?"

"Hear him, hear him now," cried Peleg, marching across the cabin, and thrusting his hands far down into his pockets,—"hear him, all of ye. Think of that! When every moment we thought the ship would sink! Death and the Judgment then? What? With all three masts making such an everlasting thundering against the side; and every sea breaking over us, fore and aft. Think of Death and the Judgment then? No! no time to think about Death then. Life was what Captain Ahab and I was thinking of; and how to save all hands—how to rig jury-masts—how to get into the nearest port; that was what I was thinking of."

Bildad said no more, but buttoning up his coat, stalked on deck, where we followed him. There he stood, very quietly overlooking some sail-makers who were mending a top-sail in the waist. Now and then he stooped to pick up a patch, or save an end of the tarred twine, which otherwise might have been wasted.

# Chapter 19

## *The Prophet*

SHIPMATES, have ye shipped in that ship?"
Queequeg and I had just left the Pequod, and were sauntering away
from the water, for the moment each occupied with his own thoughts,
when the above words were put to us by a stranger, who, pausing before us,
levelled his massive fore-finger at the vessel in question. He was but shabbily
apparelled in faded jacket and patched trowsers; a rag of a black handkerchief investing his neck. A confluent small-pox had in all directions flowed
over his face, and left it like the complicated ribbed bed of a torrent, when
the rushing waters have been dried up.

"Have ye shipped in her?" he repeated.

"You mean the ship Pequod, I suppose," said I, trying to gain a little
more time for an uninterrupted look at him.

"Aye, the Pequod—that ship there," he said, drawing back his whole
arm, and then rapidly shoving it straight out from him, with the fixed
bayonet of his pointed finger darted full at the object.

"Yes," said I, "we have just signed the articles."

"Anything down there about your souls?"

"About what?"

"Oh, perhaps you hav'n't got any," he said quickly. "No matter though,
I know many chaps that hav'n't got any,—good luck to 'em; and they are
all the better off for it. A soul's a sort of a fifth wheel to a wagon."

"What are you jabbering about, shipmate?" said I.

"*He's* got enough, though, to make up for all deficiencies of that sort in other chaps," abruptly said the stranger, placing a nervous emphasis upon the word *he*.

"Queequeg," said I, "let's go; this fellow has broken loose from somewhere; he's talking about something and somebody we don't know."

"Stop!" cried the stranger. "Ye said true—ye hav'n't seen Old Thunder yet, have ye?"

"Who's Old Thunder?" said I, again riveted with the insane earnestness of his manner.

"Captain Ahab."

"What! the captain of our ship, the Pequod?"

"Aye, among some of us old sailor chaps, he goes by that name. Ye hav'n't seen him yet, have ye?"

"No, we hav'n't. He's sick they say, but is getting better, and will be all right again before long."

"All right again before long!" laughed the stranger, with a solemnly derisive sort of laugh. "Look ye; when captain Ahab is all right, then this left arm of mine will be all right; not before."

"What do you know about him?"

"What did they *tell* you about him? Say that!"

"They didn't tell much of anything about him; only I've heard that he's a good whale-hunter, and a good captain to his crew."

"That's true, that's true—yes, both true enough. But you must jump when he gives an order. Step and growl; growl and go—that's the word with Captain Ahab. But nothing about that thing that happened to him off Cape Horn, long ago, when he lay like dead for three days and nights; nothing about that deadly skrimmage with the Spaniard afore the altar in Santa?—heard nothing about that, eh? Nothing about the silver calabash he spat into? And nothing about his losing his leg last voyage, according to the prophecy? Didn't ye hear a word about them matters and something more, eh? No, I don't think ye did; how could ye? Who knows it? Not all Nantucket, I guess. But hows'ever, mayhap, ye've heard tell about the leg, and how he lost it; aye, ye have heard of that, I dare say. Oh yes, *that* every one knows a'most—I mean they know he's only one leg; and that a parmacetti took the other off."

"My friend," said I, "what all this gibberish of yours is about, I don't know, and I don't much care; for it seems to me that you must be a little damaged in the head. But if you are speaking of Captain Ahab, of that ship there, the Pequod, then let me tell you, that I know all about the loss of his leg."

"*All* about it, eh—sure you do?—all?"

"Pretty sure."

With finger pointed and eye levelled at the Pequod, the beggar-like stranger stood a moment, as if in a troubled reverie; then starting a little, turned and said:—"Ye've shipped, have ye? Names down on the papers? Well, well, what's signed, is signed; and what's to be, will be; and then again, perhaps it wont be, after all. Any how, it's all fixed and arranged a'ready; and some sailors or other must go with him, I suppose; as well these as any other men, God pity 'em! Morning to ye, shipmates, morning; the ineffable heavens bless ye; I'm sorry I stopped ye."

"Look here, friend," said I, "if you have anything important to tell us, out with it; but if you are only trying to bamboozle us, you are mistaken in your game; that's all I have to say."

"And it's said very well, and I like to hear a chap talk up that way; you are just the man for him—the likes of ye. Morning to ye, shipmates, morning! Oh! when ye get there, tell 'em I've concluded not to make one of 'em."

"Ah, my dear fellow, you can't fool us that way—you can't fool us. It is the easiest thing in the world for a man to look as if he had a great secret in him."

"Morning to ye, shipmates, morning."

"Morning it is," said I. "Come along, Queequeg, let's leave this crazy man. But stop, tell me your name, will you?"

"Elijah."

Elijah! thought I, and we walked away, both commenting, after each other's fashion, upon this ragged old sailor; and agreed that he was nothing but a humbug, trying to be a bugbear. But we had not gone perhaps above a hundred yards, when chancing to turn a corner, and looking back as I did so, who should be seen but Elijah following us, though at a distance. Somehow, the sight of him struck me so, that I said nothing to Queequeg of his being behind, but passed on with my comrade, anxious to see whether the stranger would turn the same corner that we did. He did; and then it seemed to me that he was dogging us, but with what intent I could not for the life of me imagine. This circumstance, coupled with his ambiguous, half-hinting, half-revealing, shrouded sort of talk, now begat in me all kinds of vague wonderments and half-apprehensions, and all connected with the Pequod; and Captain Ahab; and the leg he had lost; and the Cape Horn fit; and the silver calabash; and what Captain Peleg had said of him, when I left the ship the day previous; and the prediction of the squaw Tistig; and the voyage we had bound ourselves to sail; and a hundred other shadowy things.

I was resolved to satisfy myself whether this ragged Elijah was really dogging us or not, and with that intent crossed the way with Queequeg, and on that side of it retraced our steps. But Elijah passed on, without seeming to notice us. This relieved me; and once more, and finally as it seemed to me, I pronounced him in my heart, a humbug.

# Chapter 20

## All Astir

A DAY OR TWO PASSED, and there was great activity aboard the Pequod. Not only were the old sails being mended, but new sails were coming on board, and bolts of canvas, and coils of rigging; in short, everything betokened that the ship's preparations were hurrying to a close. Captain Peleg seldom or never went ashore, but sat in his wigwam keeping a sharp look-out upon the hands: Bildad did all the purchasing and providing at the stores; and the men employed in the hold and on the rigging were working till long after night-fall.

On the day following Queequeg's signing the articles, word was given at all the inns where the ship's company were stopping, that their chests must be on board before night, for there was no telling how soon the vessel might be sailing. So Queequeg and I got down our traps, resolving, however, to sleep ashore till the last. But it seems they always give very long notice in these cases, and the ship did not sail for several days. But no wonder; there was a good deal to be done, and there is no telling how many things to be thought of, before the Pequod was fully equipped.

Every one knows what a multitude of things—beds, sauce-pans, knives and forks, shovels and tongs, napkins, nut-crackers, and what not, are indispensable to the business of housekeeping. Just so with whaling, which necessitates a three-years' housekeeping upon the wide ocean, far from all grocers, coster-mongers, doctors, bakers, and bankers. And though this also holds true of merchant vessels, yet not by any means to the same extent as with whalemen. For besides the great length of the whaling voyage, the numerous articles peculiar to the prosecution of the fishery, and the impossibility of replacing them at the remote harbors usually frequented, it must be remembered, that of all ships, whaling vessels are the most exposed to accidents of all kinds, and especially to the destruction and loss of the very things upon which the success of the voyage most depends. Hence, the spare boats, spare spars, and spare lines and harpoons, and spare everythings, almost, but a spare Captain and duplicate ship.

At the period of our arrival at the Island, the heaviest stowage of the Pequod had been almost completed; comprising her beef, bread, water, fuel, and iron hoops and staves. But, as before hinted, for some time there was a continual fetching and carrying on board of divers odds and ends of things, both large and small.

Chief among those who did this fetching and carrying was Captain Bildad's sister, a lean old lady of a most determined and indefatigable spirit, but withal very kindhearted, who seemed resolved that, if *she* could help it, nothing should be found wanting in the Pequod, after once fairly getting to sea. At one time she would come on board with a jar of pickles for the steward's pantry; another time with a bunch of quills for the chief mate's desk, where he kept his log; a third time with a roll of flannel for the small of some one's rheumatic back. Never did any woman better deserve her name, which was Charity—Aunt Charity, as everybody called her. And like a sister of charity did this charitable Aunt Charity bustle about hither and thither, ready to turn her hand and heart to anything that promised to yield safety, comfort, and consolation to all on board a ship in which her beloved brother Bildad was concerned, and in which she herself owned a score or two of well-saved dollars.

But it was startling to see this excellent hearted Quakeress coming on board, as she did the last day, with a long oil-ladle in one hand, and a still longer whaling lance in the other. Nor was Bildad himself nor Captain Peleg at all backward. As for Bildad, he carried about with him a long list of the articles needed, and at every fresh arrival, down went his mark opposite that article upon the paper. Every once and a while Peleg came running out of his whalebone den, roaring at the men down the hatchways, roaring up to the riggers at the mast-head, and then concluded by roaring back into his wigwam.

During these days of preparation, Queequeg and I often visited the craft, and as often I asked about Captain Ahab, and how he was, and when he was going to come on board his ship. To these questions they would answer, that he was getting better and better, and was expected aboard every day; meantime, the two Captains, Peleg and Bildad, could attend to everything necessary to fit the vessel for the voyage. If I had been downright honest with myself, I would have seen very plainly in my heart that I did but half fancy being committed this way to so long a voyage, without once laying my eyes on the man who was to be the absolute dictator of it, so soon as the ship sailed out upon the open sea. But when a man suspects any wrong, it sometimes happens that if he be already involved in the matter, he insensibly strives to cover up his suspicions even from himself. And much this way it was with me. I said nothing, and tried to think nothing.

At last it was given out that some time next day the ship would certainly sail. So next morning, Queequeg and I took a very early start.

# Chapter 21

*Going Aboard*

IT WAS NEARLY SIX O'CLOCK, but only grey imperfect misty dawn, when we drew nigh the wharf.

"There are some sailors running ahead there, if I see right," said I to Queequeg, "it can't be shadows; she's off by sunrise, I guess; come on!"

"Avast!" cried a voice, whose owner at the same time coming close behind us, laid a hand upon both our shoulders, and then insinuating himself between us, stood stooping forward a little, in the uncertain twilight, strangely peering from Queequeg to me. It was Elijah.

"Going aboard?"

"Hands off, will you," said I.

"Lookee here," said Queequeg, shaking himself, "go 'way!"

"Aint going aboard, then?"

"Yes, we are," said I, "but what business is that of yours? Do you know, Mr. Elijah, that I consider you a little impertinent?"

"No, no, no; I wasn't aware of that," said Elijah, slowly and wonderingly looking from me to Queequeg, with the most unaccountable glances.

"Elijah," said I, "you will oblige my friend and me by withdrawing. We are going to the Indian and Pacific Oceans, and would prefer not to be detained."

"Ye be, be ye? Coming back afore breakfast?"

"He's cracked, Queequeg," said I, "come on."

"Holloa!" cried stationary Elijah, hailing us when we had removed a few paces.

"Never mind him," said I, "Queequeg, come on."

But he stole up to us again, and suddenly clapping his hand on my shoulder, said—"Did ye see anything looking like men going towards that ship a while ago?"

Struck by this plain matter-of-fact question, I answered, saying "Yes, I thought I did see four or five men; but it was too dim to be sure."

"Very dim, very dim," said Elijah. "Morning to ye."

Once more we quitted him; but once more he came softly after us; and touching my shoulder again, said, "See if you can find 'em now, will ye?"

"Find who?"

"Morning to ye! morning to ye!" he rejoined, again moving off. "Oh! I was going to warn ye against—but never mind, never mind—it's all one, all in the family too;—sharp frost this morning, ain't it? Good bye to ye. Shan't see ye again very soon, I guess; unless it's before the Grand Jury." And with these cracked words he finally departed, leaving me, for the moment, in no small wonderment at his frantic impudence.

At last, stepping on board the Pequod, we found everything in profound quiet, not a soul moving. The cabin entrance was locked within; the hatches were all on, and lumbered with coils of rigging. Going forward to the forecastle, we found the slide of the scuttle open. Seeing a light, we went down, and found only an old rigger there, wrapped in a tattered pea-jacket. He was thrown at whole length upon two chests, his face downwards and inclosed in his folded arms. The profoundest slumber slept upon him.

"Those sailors we saw, Queequeg, where can they have gone to?" said I, looking dubiously at the sleeper. But it seemed that, when on the wharf, Queequeg had not at all noticed what I now alluded to; hence I would have thought myself to have been optically deceived in that matter, were it not for Elijah's otherwise inexplicable question. But I beat the thing down; and again marking the sleeper, jocularly hinted to Queequeg that perhaps we had best sit up with the body; telling him to establish himself accordingly. He put his hand upon the sleeper's rear, as though feeling if it was soft enough; and then, without more ado, sat quietly down there.

"Gracious! Queequeg, don't sit there," said I.

"Oh! perry dood seat," said Queequeg, "my country way; won't hurt him face."

"Face!" said I, "call that his face? very benevolent countenance then; but how hard he breathes, he's heaving himself; get off, Queequeg, you are heavy, it's grinding the face of the poor. Get off, Queequeg! Look, he'll twitch you off soon. I wonder he don't wake."

Queequeg removed himself to just beyond the head of the sleeper, and lighted his tomahawk pipe. I sat at the feet. We kept the pipe passing over the sleeper, from one to the other. Meanwhile, upon questioning him, in his broken fashion Queequeg gave me to understand that, in his land, owing to the absence of settees and sofas of all sorts, the king, chiefs, and great people generally, were in the custom of fattening some of the lower orders for ottomans; and to furnish a house comfortably in that respect, you had only to buy up eight or ten lazy fellows, and lay them round in the piers and alcoves. Besides, it was very convenient on an excursion; much better than those garden-chairs which are convertible into walking-sticks; upon occasion, a chief calling his attendant, and desiring him to make a settee of himself under a spreading tree, perhaps in some damp marshy place. ·

While narrating these things, every time Queequeg received the toma-hawk from me, he flourished the hatchet-side of it over the sleeper's head.

"What's that for, Queequeg?"

"Perry easy, kill-e; oh! perry easy!"

He was going on with some wild reminiscences about his tomahawk-pipe, which, it seemed, had in its two uses both brained his foes and soothed his soul, when we were directly attracted to the sleeping rigger. The strong vapor now completely filling the contracted hole, it began to tell upon him. He breathed with a sort of muffledness; then seemed troubled in the nose; then revolved over once or twice; then sat up and rubbed his eyes.

"Holloa!" he breathed at last, "who be ye smokers?"

"Shipped men," answered I, "when does she sail?"

"Aye, aye, ye are going in her, be ye? She sails to-day. The Captain came aboard last night."

"What Captain?—Ahab?"

"Who but him indeed?"

I was going to ask him some further questions concerning Ahab, when we heard a noise on deck.

"Holloa! Starbuck's astir," said the rigger. "He's a lively chief mate, that; good man, and a pious; but all alive now, I must turn to." And so saying he went on deck, and we followed.

It was now clear sunrise. Soon the crew came on board in twos and threes; the riggers bestirred themselves; the mates were actively engaged; and several of the shore people were busy in bringing various last things on board. Meanwhile Captain Ahab remained invisibly enshrined within his cabin.

# Chapter 22

*Merry Christmas*

A T LENGTH, towards noon, upon the final dismissal of the ship's riggers, and after the Pequod had been hauled out from the wharf, and after the ever-thoughtful Charity had come off in a whaleboat, with her last gifts—a night-cap for Stubb, the second mate, her brother-in-law, and a spare Bible for the steward—after all this, the two captains, Peleg and Bildad, issued from the cabin, and turning to the chief mate, Peleg said:

"Now, Mr. Starbuck, are you sure everything is right? Captain Ahab is all ready—just spoke to him—nothing more to be got from shore, eh? Well, call all hands, then. Muster 'em aft here—blast 'em!"

"No need of profane words, however great the hurry, Peleg," said Bildad, "but away with thee, friend Starbuck, and do our bidding."

How now! Here upon the very point of starting for the voyage, Captain Peleg and Captain Bildad were going it with a high hand on the quarter-deck, just as if they were to be joint-commanders at sea, as well as to all appearances in port. And, as for Captain Ahab, no sign of him was yet to be seen; only, they said he was in the cabin. But then, the idea was, that his presence was by no means necessary in getting the ship under weigh, and steering her well out to sea. Indeed, as that was not at all his proper business, but the pilot's; and as he was not yet completely recovered—so they said—

therefore, Captain Ahab stayed below. And all this seemed natural enough; especially as in the merchant service many captains never show themselves on deck for a considerable time after heaving up the anchor, but remain over the cabin table, having a farewell merry-making with their shore friends, before they quit the ship for good with the pilot.

But there was not much chance to think over the matter, for Captain Peleg was now all alive. He seemed to do most of the talking and commanding, and not Bildad.

"Aft here, ye sons of bachelors," he cried, as the sailors lingered at the main-mast. "Mr. Starbuck, drive 'em aft."

"Strike the tent there!"—was the next order. As I hinted before, this whalebone marquee was never pitched except in port; and on board the Pequod, for thirty years, the order to strike the tent was well known to be the next thing to heaving up the anchor.

"Man the capstan! Blood and thunder!—jump!"—was the next command, and the crew sprang for the handspikes.

Now, in getting under weigh, the station generally occupied by the pilot is the forward part of the ship. And here Bildad, who, with Peleg, be it known, in addition to his other offices, was one of the licensed pilots of the port—he being suspected to have got himself made a pilot in order to save the Nantucket pilot-fee to all the ships he was concerned in, for he never piloted any other craft—Bildad, I say, might now be seen actively engaged in looking over the bows for the approaching anchor, and at intervals singing what seemed a dismal stave of psalmody, to cheer the hands at the windlass, who roared forth some sort of a chorus about the girls in Booble Alley, with hearty good will. Nevertheless, not three days previous, Bildad had told them that no profane songs would be allowed on board the Pequod, particularly in getting under weigh; and Charity, his sister, had placed a small choice copy of Watts in each seaman's berth.

Meantime, overseeing the other part of the ship, Captain Peleg ripped and swore astern in the most frightful manner. I almost thought he would sink the ship before the anchor could be got up; involuntarily I paused on my handspike, and told Queequeg to do the same, thinking of the perils we both ran, in starting on the voyage with such a devil for a pilot. I was comforting myself, however, with the thought that in pious Bildad might be found some salvation, spite of his seven hundred and seventy-seventh lay; when I felt a sudden sharp poke in my rear, and turning round, was horrified at the apparition of Captain Peleg in the act of withdrawing his leg from my immediate vicinity. That was my first kick.

"Is that the way they heave in the marchant service?" he roared. "Spring, thou sheep-head; spring, and break thy backbone! Why don't ye spring, I say, all of ye—spring, Quohog! spring, thou chap with the red whiskers; spring there, Scotch-cap; spring, thou green pants. Spring, I say, all of ye, and spring your eyes out!" And so saying, he moved along the windlass, here and there using his leg very freely, while imperturbable Bildad kept leading off with his psalmody. Thinks I, Captain Peleg must have been drinking something to-day.

At last the anchor was up, the sails were set, and off we glided. It was a short, cold Christmas; and as the short northern day merged into night, we found ourselves almost broad upon the wintry ocean, whose freezing spray cased us in ice, as in polished armor. The long rows of teeth on the bulwarks glistened in the moonlight; and like the white ivory tusks of some huge elephant, vast curving icicles depended from the bows.

Lank Bildad, as pilot, headed the first watch, and ever and anon, as the old craft deep dived into the green seas, and sent the shivering frost all over her, and the winds howled, and the cordage rang, his steady notes were heard,—

> "Sweet fields beyond the swelling flood,
> Stand dressed in living green.
> So to the Jews old Canaan stood,
> While Jordan rolled between."

Never did those sweet words sound more sweetly to me than then. They were full of hope and fruition. Spite of this frigid winter night in the boisterous Atlantic, spite of my wet feet and wetter jacket, there was yet, it then seemed to me, many a pleasant haven in store; and meads and glades so eternally vernal, that the grass shot up by the spring, untrodden, unwilted, remains at midsummer.

At last we gained such an offing, that the two pilots were needed no longer. The stout sail-boat that had accompanied us began ranging alongside.

It was curious and not unpleasing, how Peleg and Bildad were affected at this juncture, especially Captain Bildad. For loath to depart, yet; very loath to leave, for good, a ship bound on so long and perilous a voyage—beyond both stormy Capes; a ship in which some thousands of his hard earned dollars were invested; a ship, in which an old shipmate sailed as captain; a man almost as old as he, once more starting to encounter all the terrors of the pitiless jaw; loath to say good-bye to a thing so every way

brimful of every interest to him,—poor old Bildad lingered long; paced
the deck with anxious strides; ran down into the cabin to speak another
farewell word there; again came on deck, and looked to windward; looked
towards the wide and endless waters, only bounded by the far-off unseen
Eastern Continents; looked towards the land; looked aloft; looked right
and left; looked everywhere and nowhere; and at last, mechanically coiling
a rope upon its pin, convulsively grasped stout Peleg by the hand, and
holding up a lantern, for a moment stood gazing heroically in his face, as
much as to say, "Nevertheless, friend Peleg, I can stand it; yes, I can."

As for Peleg himself, he took it more like a philosopher; but for all his
philosophy, there was a tear twinkling in his eye, when the lantern came
too near. And he, too, did not a little run from cabin to deck—now a word
below, and now a word with Starbuck, the chief mate.

But, at last, he turned to his comrade, with a final sort of look about
him,—"Captain Bildad—come, old shipmate, we must go. Back the main-
yard there! Boat ahoy! Stand by to come close alongside, now! Careful,
careful!—come, Bildad, boy—say your last. Luck to ye, Starbuck—luck to
ye, Mr. Stubb—luck to ye, Mr. Flask—good-bye, and good luck to ye
all—and this day three years I'll have a hot supper smoking for ye in old
Nantucket. Hurrah and away!"

"God bless ye, and have ye in His holy keeping, men," murmured old
Bildad, almost incoherently. "I hope ye'll have fine weather now, so that
Captain Ahab may soon be moving among ye—a pleasant sun is all he needs,
and ye'll have plenty of them in the tropic voyage ye go. Be careful in the
hunt, ye mates. Don't stave the boats needlessly, ye harpooneers; good
white cedar plank is raised full three per cent. within the year. Don't forget
your prayers, either. Mr. Starbuck, mind that cooper don't waste the spare
staves. Oh! the sail-needles are in the green locker! Don't whale it too much
a' Lord's days, men; but don't miss a fair chance either, that's rejecting
Heaven's good gifts. Have an eye to the molasses tierce, Mr. Stubb; it was
a little leaky, I thought. If ye touch at the islands, Mr. Flask, beware of
fornication. Good-bye, good-bye! Don't keep that cheese too long down
in the hold, Mr. Starbuck; it'll spoil. Be careful with the butter—twenty
cents the pound it was, and mind ye, if—"

"Come, come, Captain Bildad; stop palavering,—away!" and with
that, Peleg hurried him over the side, and both dropt into the boat.

Ship and boat diverged; the cold, damp night breeze blew between; a
screaming gull flew overhead; the two hulls wildly rolled; we gave three
heavy-hearted cheers, and blindly plunged like fate into the lone Atlantic.

# Chapter 23

### The Lee Shore

SOME CHAPTERS BACK, one Bulkington was spoken of, a tall, new-landed mariner, encountered in New Bedford at the inn.

When on that shivering winter's night, the Pequod thrust her vindictive bows into the cold malicious waves, who should I see standing at her helm but Bulkington! I looked with sympathetic awe and fearfulness upon the man, who in midwinter just landed from a four years' dangerous voyage, could so unrestingly push off again for still another tempestuous term. The land seemed scorching to his feet. Wonderfullest things are ever the unmentionable; deep memories yield no epitaphs; this six-inch chapter is the stoneless grave of Bulkington. Let me only say that it fared with him as with the storm-tossed ship, that miserably drives along the leeward land. The port would fain give succor; the port is pitiful; in the port is safety, comfort, hearthstone, supper, warm blankets, friends, all that's kind to our mortalities. But in that gale, the port, the land, is that ship's direst jeopardy; she must fly all hospitality; one touch of land, though it but graze the keel, would make her shudder through and through. With all her might she crowds all sail off shore; in so doing, fights 'gainst the very winds that fain would blow her homeward; seeks all the lashed sea's landlessness again; for refuge's sake forlornly rushing into peril; her only friend her bitterest foe!

Know ye, now, Bulkington? Glimpses do ye seem to see of that mortally intolerable truth; that all deep, earnest thinking is but the intrepid effort of the soul to keep the open independence of her sea; while the wildest winds of heaven and earth conspire to cast her on the treacherous, slavish shore?

But as in landlessness alone resides the highest truth, shoreless, indefinite as God—so, better is it to perish in that howling infinite, than be ingloriously dashed upon the lee, even if that were safety! For worm-like, then, oh! who would craven crawl to land! Terrors of the terrible! is all this agony so vain? Take heart, take heart, O Bulkington! Bear thee grimly, demigod! Up from the spray of thy ocean-perishing—straight up, leaps thy apotheosis!

# Chapter 24

*The Advocate*

A S Queequeg and I are now fairly embarked in this business of
whaling; and as this business of whaling has somehow come to be
regarded among landsmen as a rather unpoetical and disreputable
pursuit; therefore, I am all anxiety to convince ye, ye landsmen, of the
injustice hereby done to us hunters of whales.

In the first place, it may be deemed almost superfluous to establish the
fact, that among people at large, the business of whaling is not accounted
on a level with what are called the liberal professions. If a stranger were
introduced into any miscellaneous metropolitan society, it would but
slightly advance the general opinion of his merits, were he presented to the
company as a harpooneer, say; and if in emulation of the naval officers he
should append the initials S. W. F. (Sperm Whale Fishery) to his visiting
card, such a procedure would be deemed pre-eminently presuming and
ridiculous.

Doubtless one leading reason why the world declines honoring us
whalemen, is this: they think that, at best, our vocation amounts to a
butchering sort of business; and that when actively engaged therein, we are
surrounded by all manner of defilements. Butchers we are, that is true. But
butchers, also, and butchers of the bloodiest badge have been all Martial
Commanders whom the world invariably delights to honor. And as for the

matter of the alleged uncleanliness of our business, ye shall soon be initiated into certain facts hitherto pretty generally unknown, and which, upon the whole, will triumphantly plant the sperm whale-ship at least among the cleanliest things of this tidy earth. But even granting the charge in question to be true; what disordered slippery decks of a whale-ship are comparable to the unspeakable carrion of those battle-fields from which so many soldiers return to drink in all ladies' plaudits? And if the idea of peril so much enhances the popular conceit of the soldier's profession; let me assure ye that many a veteran who has freely marched up to a battery, would quickly recoil at the apparition of the sperm whale's vast tail, fanning into eddies the air over his head. For what are the comprehensible terrors of man compared with the interlinked terrors and wonders of God!

But, though the world scouts at us whale hunters, yet does it unwittingly pay us the profoundest homage; yea, an all-abounding adoration! for almost all the tapers, lamps, and candles that burn round the globe, burn, as before so many shrines, to our glory!

But look at this matter in other lights; weigh it in all sorts of scales; see what we whalemen are, and have been.

Why did the Dutch in De Witt's time have admirals of their whaling fleets? Why did Louis XVI. of France, at his own personal expense, fit out whaling ships from Dunkirk, and politely invite to that town some score or two of families from our own island of Nantucket? Why did Britain between the years 1750 and 1788 pay to her whalemen in bounties upwards of £1,000,000? And lastly, how comes it that we whalemen of America now outnumber all the rest of the banded whalemen in the world; sail a navy of upwards of seven hundred vessels; manned by eighteen thousand men; yearly consuming 4,000,000 of dollars; the ships worth, at the time of sailing, $20,000,000; and every year importing into our harbors a well reaped harvest of $7,000,000. How comes all this, if there be not something puissant in whaling?

But this is not the half; look again.

I freely assert, that the cosmopolite philosopher cannot, for his life, point out one single peaceful influence, which within the last sixty years has operated more potentially upon the whole broad world, taken in one aggregate, than the high and mighty business of whaling. One way and another, it has begotten events so remarkable in themselves, and so con-tinuously momentous in their sequential issues, that whaling may well be regarded as that Egyptian mother, who bore offspring themselves pregnant from her womb. It would be a hopeless, endless task to catalogue all these things. Let a handful suffice. For many years past the whale-ship has been the pioneer in ferreting out the remotest and least known parts of the earth. She has explored seas and archipelagoes which had no chart, where no Cook or Vancouver had ever sailed. If American and European men-of-war now peacefully ride in once savage harbors, let them fire salutes to the honor and the glory of the whale-ship, which originally showed them the way, and first interpreted between them and the savages. They may celebrate as they will the heroes of Exploring Expeditions, your Cooks, your Krusensterns; but I say that scores of anonymous Captains have sailed out of Nantucket, that were as great, and greater than your Cook and your Krusenstern. For in their succorless empty-handedness, they, in the heathenish sharked waters, and by the beaches of unrecorded, javelin islands, battled with virgin wonders and terrors that Cook with all his marines and muskets would not willingly have dared. All that is made such a flourish of in the old South Sea Voyages, those things were but the life-time commonplaces of our heroic Nantucketers. Often, adventures which Vancouver dedicates three chapters to, these men accounted unworthy of being set down in the ship's common log. Ah, the world! Oh, the world!

Until the whale fishery rounded Cape Horn, no commerce but colonial, scarcely any intercourse but colonial, was carried on between Europe and the long line of the opulent Spanish provinces on the Pacific coast. It was the whaleman who first broke through the jealous policy of the Spanish crown, touching those colonies; and, if space permitted, it might be distinctly shown how from those whalemen at last eventuated the liberation of Peru, Chili, and Bolivia from the yoke of Old Spain, and the establishment of the eternal democracy in those parts.

That great America on the other side of the sphere, Australia, was given to the enlightened world by the whaleman. After its first blunder-born discovery by a Dutchman, all other ships long shunned those shores as pestiferously barbarous; but the whale-ship touched there. The whale-ship is the true mother of that now mighty colony. Moreover, in the infancy of the first Australian settlement, the emigrants were several times saved from starvation by the benevolent biscuit of the whale-ship luckily dropping an anchor in their waters. The uncounted isles of all Polynesia confess the same truth, and do commercial homage to the whale-ship, that cleared the way for the missionary and the merchant, and in many cases carried the primitive missionaries to their first destinations. If that double-bolted land, Japan, is ever to become hospitable, it is the whale-ship alone to whom the credit will be due; for already she is on the threshold.

But if, in the face of all this, you still declare that whaling has no æstheti-cally noble associations connected with it, then am I ready to shiver fifty lances with you there, and unhorse you with a split helmet every time.

The whale has no famous author, and whaling no famous chronicler, you will say.

*The whale no famous author, and whaling no famous chronicler?* Who wrote the first account of our Leviathan? Who but mighty Job! And who com-posed the first narrative of a whaling-voyage? Who, but no less a prince than Alfred the Great, who, with his own royal pen, took down the words from Other, the Norwegian whale-hunter of those times! And who pronounced our glowing eulogy in Parliament? Who, but Edmund Burke!

True enough, but then whalemen themselves are poor devils; they have no good blood in their veins.

*No good blood in their veins?* They have something better than royal blood there. The grandmother of Benjamin Franklin was Mary Morrel; afterwards, by marriage, Mary Folger, one of the old settlers of Nantucket, and the ancestress to a long line of Folgers and harpooneers—all kith and kin to noble Benjamin—this day darting the barbed iron from one side of the world to the other.

Good again; but then all confess that somehow whaling is not respectable.

*Whaling not respectable?* Whaling is imperial! By old English statutory law, the whale is declared "a royal fish."*

Oh, that's only nominal! The whale himself has never figured in any grand imposing way.

*The whale never figured in any grand imposing way?* In one of the mighty triumphs given to a Roman general upon his entering the world's capital, the bones of a whale, brought all the way from the Syrian coast, were the most conspicuous object in the cymballed procession.*

Grant it, since you cite it; but, say what you will, there is no real dignity in whaling.

*No dignity in whaling?* The dignity of our calling the very heavens attest. Cetus is a constellation in the South! No more! Drive down your hat in presence of the Czar, and take it off to Queequeg! No more! I know a man that, in his lifetime, has taken three hundred and fifty whales. I account that man more honorable than that great captain of antiquity who boasted of taking as many walled towns.

And, as for me, if, by any possibility, there be any as yet undiscovered prime thing in me; if I shall ever deserve any real repute in that small

* See subsequent chapters for something more on this head.

but high hushed world which I might not be unreasonably ambitious of; if hereafter I shall do anything that, upon the whole, a man might rather have done than to have left undone; if, at my death, my executors, or more properly my creditors, find any precious MSS. in my desk, then here I prospectively ascribe all the honor and the glory to whaling; for a whale-ship was my Yale College and my Harvard.

# Chapter 25

## Postscript

IN BEHALF OF THE DIGNITY of whaling, I would fain advance naught but substantiated facts. But after embattling his facts, an advocate who should wholly suppress a not unreasonable surmise, which might tell eloquently upon his cause—such an advocate, would he not be blameworthy?

It is well known that at the coronation of kings and queens, even modern ones, a certain curious process of seasoning them for their functions is gone through. There is a saltcellar of state, so called, and there may be a caster of state. How they use the salt, precisely—who knows? Certain I am, however, that a king's head is solemnly oiled at his coronation, even as a head of salad. Can it be, though, that they anoint it with a view of making its interior run well, as they anoint machinery? Much might be ruminated here, concerning the essential dignity of this regal process, because in common life we esteem but meanly and contemptibly a fellow who anoints his hair, and palpably smells of that anointing. In truth, a mature man who uses hair-oil, unless medicinally, that man has probably got a quoggy spot in him somewhere. As a general rule, he can't amount to much in his totality.

But the only thing to be considered here, is this—what kind of oil is used at coronations? Certainly it cannot be olive oil, nor macassar oil, nor castor oil, nor bear's oil, nor train oil, nor cod-liver oil. What then can it possibly be, but sperm oil in its unmanufactured, unpolluted state, the sweetest of all oils?

Think of that, ye loyal Britons! we whalemen supply your kings and queens with coronation stuff!

# Chapter 26

*Knights and Squires*

THE CHIEF MATE of the Pequod was Starbuck, a native of Nantucket, and a Quaker by descent. He was a long, earnest man, and though born on an icy coast, seemed well adapted to endure hot latitudes, his flesh being hard as twice-baked biscuit. Transported to the Indies, his live blood would not spoil like bottled ale. He must have been born in some time of general drought and famine, or upon one of those fast days for which his state is famous. Only some thirty arid summers had he seen; those summers had dried up all his physical superfluousness. But this, his thinness, so to speak, seemed no more the token of wasting anxieties and cares, than it seemed the indication of any bodily blight. It was merely the condensation of the man. He was by no means ill-looking; quite the contrary. His pure tight skin was an excellent fit; and closely wrapped up in it, and embalmed with inner health and strength, like a revivified Egyptian, this Starbuck seemed prepared to endure for long ages to come, and to endure always, as now; for be it Polar snow or torrid sun, like a patent chronometer, his interior vitality was warranted to do well in all climates. Looking into his eyes, you seemed to see there the yet lingering images of those thousand-fold perils he had calmly confronted through life. A staid, steadfast man, whose life for the most part was a telling pantomime of action, and not a tame chapter of words. Yet, for all his hardy sobriety and fortitude, there were certain qualities in him which at times affected, and in some cases seemed well nigh to overbalance all the rest. Uncommonly conscientious for a seaman, and endued with a deep natural reverence, the wild watery loneliness of his life did therefore strongly incline him to superstition; but to that sort of superstition, which in some organizations seems rather to spring, somehow, from intelligence than from ignorance. Outward portents and inward presentiments were his. And if at times these things bent the welded iron of his soul, much more did his far-away domestic memories of his young Cape wife and child, tend to bend him still more from the original ruggedness of his nature, and open him still further to those latent influences which, in some honest-hearted men, restrain the gush of dare-devil daring, so often evinced by others in the more perilous vicissitudes of the fishery. "I will have no man in my boat," said Starbuck, "who is not afraid of a whale." By this, he seemed to mean, not only that the most reliable and useful courage was that which arises from the fair estimation of the encountered peril, but that an utterly fearless man is a far more dangerous comrade than a coward.

"Aye, aye," said Stubb, the second mate, "Starbuck, there, is as careful a man as you'll find anywhere in this fishery." But we shall ere long see what that word "careful" precisely means when used by a man like Stubb, or almost any other whale hunter.

Starbuck was no crusader after perils; in him courage was not a sentiment; but a thing simply useful to him, and always at hand upon all mortally practical occasions. Besides, he thought, perhaps, that in this business of whaling, courage was one of the great staple outfits of the ship, like her beef and her bread, and not to be foolishly wasted. Wherefore he had no fancy for lowering for whales after sun-down; nor for persisting in fighting a fish that too much persisted in fighting him. For, thought Starbuck, I am here in this critical ocean to kill whales for my living, and not to be killed by them for theirs; and that hundreds of men had been so killed Starbuck well knew. What doom was his own father's? Where, in the bottomless deeps, could he find the torn limbs of his brother?

With memories like these in him, and, moreover, given to a certain superstitiousness, as has been said; the courage of this Starbuck which could, nevertheless, still flourish, must indeed have been extreme. But it was not in reasonable nature that a man so organized, and with such terrible experiences and remembrances as he had; it was not in nature that these things should fail in latently engendering an element in him, which, under suitable circumstances, would break out from its confinement, and burn all his courage up. And brave as he might be, it was that sort of bravery, chiefly visible in some intrepid men, which, while generally abiding firm in the conflict with seas, or winds, or whales, or any of the ordinary irrational horrors of the world, yet cannot withstand those more terrific, because more spiritual terrors, which sometimes menace you from the concentrating brow of an enraged and mighty man.

But were the coming narrative to reveal, in any instance, the complete abasement of poor Starbuck's fortitude, scarce might I have the heart to write it; for it is a thing most sorrowful, nay shocking, to expose the fall of valor in the soul. Men may seem detestable as joint stock-companies and nations; knaves, fools, and murderers there may be; men may have mean and meagre faces; but man, in the ideal, is so noble and so sparkling, such a grand and glowing creature, that over any ignominious blemish in him all his fellows should run to throw their costliest robes. That immaculate manliness we feel within ourselves, so far within us, that it remains intact though all the outer character seem gone; bleeds with keenest anguish at the undraped spectacle of a valor-ruined man. Nor can piety itself, at such a shameful sight, completely stifle her upbraidings against the permitting stars. But this august dignity I treat of, is not the dignity of kings and robes, but that abounding dignity which has no robed investiture. Thou shalt see it shining in the arm that wields a pick or drives a spike; that democratic dignity which, on all hands, radiates without end from God; Himself! The great God absolute! The centre and circumference of all democracy! His omnipresence, our divine equality!

If, then, to meanest mariners, and renegades and castaways, I shall hereafter ascribe high qualities, though dark; weave round them tragic graces; if even the most mournful, perchance the most abased, among them all, shall at times lift himself to the exalted mounts; if I shall touch that workman's arm with some ethereal light; if I shall spread a rainbow over his disastrous set of sun; then against all mortal critics bear me out in it, thou just Spirit of Equality, which hast spread one royal mantle of humanity over all my kind! Bear me out in it, thou great democratic God! who didst not refuse to the swart convict, Bunyan, the pale, poetic pearl; Thou who didst clothe with doubly hammered leaves of finest gold, the stumped and paupered arm of old Cervantes; Thou who didst pick up Andrew Jackson from the pebbles; who didst hurl him upon a war-horse; who didst thunder him higher than a throne! Thou who, in all Thy mighty, earthly marchings, ever cullest Thy selectest champions from the kingly commons; bear me out in it, O God!

# Chapter 27

*Knights and Squires*

STUBB WAS THE SECOND MATE. He was a native of Cape Cod; and hence, according to local usage, was called a Cape-Cod-man. A happy-go-lucky; neither craven nor valiant; taking perils as they came with an indifferent air; and while engaged in the most imminent crisis of the chase, toiling away, calm and collected as a journeyman joiner engaged for the year. Good-humored, easy, and careless, he presided over his whale-boat as if the most deadly encounter were but a dinner, and his crew all invited guests. He was as particular about the comfortable arrangement of his part of the boat, as an old stage-driver is about the snugness of his box. When close to the whale, in the very death-lock of the fight, he handled his unpitying lance coolly and off-handedly, as a whistling tinker his hammer. He would hum over his old rigadig tunes while flank and flank with the most exasperated monster. Long usage had, for this Stubb, converted the jaws of death into an easy chair. What he thought of death itself, there is no telling. Whether he ever thought of it at all, might be a question; but, if he ever did chance to cast his mind that way after a comfortable dinner, no doubt, like a good sailor, he took it to be a sort of call of the watch to tumble aloft, and bestir themselves there, about something which he would find out when he obeyed the order, and not sooner.

What, perhaps, with other things, made Stubb such an easy-going, unfearing man, so cheerily trudging off with the burden of life in a world full of grave peddlers, all bowed to the ground with their packs; what helped to bring about that almost impious good-humor of his; that thing must have been his pipe. For, like his nose, his short, black little pipe was one of the regular features of his face. You would almost as soon have expected him to turn out of his bunk without his nose as without his pipe. He kept a whole row of pipes there ready loaded, stuck in a rack, within easy reach of his hand; and, whenever he turned in, he smoked them all out in succession, lighting one from the other to the end of the chapter; then loading them again to be in readiness anew. For, when Stubb dressed, instead of first putting his legs into his trowsers, he put his pipe into his mouth.

I say this continual smoking must have been one cause, at least, of his peculiar disposition; for every one knows that this earthly air, whether ashore or afloat, is terribly infected with the nameless miseries of the number-less mortals who have died exhaling it; and as in time of the cholera, some people go about with a camphorated handkerchief to their mouths; so, likewise, against all mortal tribulations, Stubb's tobacco smoke might have operated as a sort of disinfecting agent.

The third mate was Flask, a native of Tisbury, in Martha's Vineyard. A short, stout, ruddy young fellow, very pugnacious concerning whales, who somehow seemed to think that the great Leviathans had personally and hereditarily affronted him; and therefore it was a sort of point of honor with him, to destroy them whenever encountered. So utterly lost was he to all sense of reverence for the many marvels of their majestic bulk and mystic ways; and so dead to anything like an apprehension of any possible danger from encountering them; that in his poor opinion, the wondrous whale was but a species of magnified mouse, or at least water-rat, requiring only a little circumvention and some small application of time and trouble in order to kill and boil. This ignorant, unconscious fearlessness of his made him a little waggish in the matter of whales; he followed these fish for the fun of it; and a three years' voyage round Cape Horn was only a jolly joke that lasted that length of time. As a carpenter's nails are divided into wrought nails and cut nails; so mankind may be similarly divided. Little Flask was one of the wrought ones; made to clinch tight and last long. They called him King-Post on board of the Pequod; because, in form, he could be well likened to the short, square timber known by that name in Arctic whalers; and which by the means of many radiating side timbers inserted into it, serves to brace the ship against the icy concussions of those battering seas.

Now these three mates—Starbuck, Stubb, and Flask, were momentous men. They it was who by universal prescription commanded three of the Pequod's boats as headsmen. In that grand order of battle in which Captain Ahab would presently marshal his forces to descend on the whales, these three headsmen were as captains of companies. Or, being armed with their long keen whaling spears, they were as a picked trio of lancers; even as the harpooneers were flingers of javelins.

And since in this famous fishery, each mate or headsman, like a Gothic Knight of old, is always accompanied by his boat-steerer or harpooneer, who in certain conjunctures provides him with a fresh lance, when the former one has been badly twisted, or elbowed in the assault; and moreover, as there generally subsists between the two, a close intimacy and friendliness; it is therefore but meet, that in this place we set down who the Pequod's harpooneers were, and to what headsman each of them belonged.

First of all was Queequeg, whom Starbuck, the chief mate, had selected for his squire. But Queequeg is already known.

Next was Tashtego, an unmixed Indian from Gay Head, the most westerly promontory of Martha's Vineyard, where there still exists the last remnant of a village of red men, which has long supplied the neighboring island of Nantucket with many of her most daring harpooneers. In the fishery, they usually go by the generic name of Gay-Headers. Tashtego's long, lean, sable hair, his high cheek bones, and black rounding eyes—for an Indian, Oriental in their largeness, but Antarctic in their glittering expression—all this sufficiently proclaimed him an inheritor of the unvitiated blood of those proud warrior hunters, who, in quest of the great New England moose, had scoured, bow in hand, the aboriginal forests of the main. But no longer snuffing in the trail of the wild beasts of the woodland, Tashtego now hunted in the wake of the great whales of the sea; the unerring harpoon of the son fitly replacing the infallible arrow of the sires. To look at the tawny brawn of his lithe snaky limbs, you would almost have credited the superstitions of some of the earlier Puritans, and half believed this wild Indian to be a son of the Prince of the Powers of the Air. Tashtego was Stubb the second mate's squire.

Third among the harpooneers was Daggoo, a gigantic, coal-black negro-savage, with a lion-like tread—an Ahasuerus to behold. Suspended from his ears were two golden hoops, so large that the sailors called them ring-bolts, and would talk of securing the top-sail halyards to them. In his youth Daggoo had voluntarily shipped on board of a whaler, lying in a lonely bay on his native coast. And never having been anywhere in the world but in Africa, Nantucket, and the pagan harbors most frequented by whalemen; and having now led for many years the bold life of the fishery in the ships of owners uncommonly heedful of what manner of men they shipped; Daggoo retained all his barbaric virtues, and erect as a giraffe, moved about the decks in all the pomp of six feet five in his socks. There was a corporeal humility in looking up at him; and a white man standing before him seemed a white flag come to beg truce of a fortress. Curious to tell, this imperial negro, Ahasuerus Daggoo, was the Squire of little Flask, who looked like a chess-man beside him. As for the residue of the Pequod's company, be it said, that at the present day not one in two of the many thousand men before the mast employed in the American whale fishery, are Americans born, though pretty nearly all the officers are. Herein it is the same with the American whale fishery as with the American army and military and merchant navies, and the engineering forces employed in the construction of the American Canals and Railroads. The same, I say, because in all these cases the native American liberally provides the brains, the rest of the world as generously supplying the muscles. No small number of these whaling seamen belong to the Azores, where the outward bound Nantucket whalers frequently touch to augment their crews from the hardy peasants of those rocky shores. In like manner, the Greenland whalers sailing out of Hull or London, put in at the Shetland Islands, to receive the full complement of their crew. Upon the passage homewards, they drop them there again. How it is, there is no telling, but Islanders seem to make the best whalemen. They were nearly all Islanders in the Pequod, *Isolatoes* too, I call such, not acknowledging the common continent of men, but each *Isolato* living on a separate continent of his own. Yet now, federated along one keel, what a set these Isolatoes were! An Anacharsis Clootz deputation from all the isles of the sea, and all the ends of the earth, accompanying Old Ahab in the Pequod to lay the world's grievances before that bar from which not very many of them ever come back. Black Little Pip—he never did! Poor Alabama boy! On the grim Pequod's forecastle, ye shall ere long see him, beating his tambourine; prelusive of the eternal time, when sent for, to the great quarter-deck on high, he was bid strike in with angels, and beat his tambourine in glory; called a coward here, hailed a hero there!

# Chapter 28

## Ahab

FOR SEVERAL DAYS after leaving Nantucket, nothing above hatches was seen of Captain Ahab. The mates regularly relieved each other at the watches, and for aught that could be seen to the contrary, they seemed to be the only commanders of the ship; only they sometimes issued from the cabin with orders so sudden and peremptory, that after all it was plain they but commanded vicariously. Yes, their supreme lord and dictator was there, though hitherto unseen by any eyes not permitted to penetrate into the now sacred retreat of the cabin.

Every time I ascended to the deck from my watches below, I instantly gazed aft to mark if any strange face were visible; for my first vague disquietude touching the unknown captain, now in the seclusion of the sea, became almost a perturbation. This was strangely heightened at times by the ragged Elijah's diabolical incoherences uninvitedly recurring to me, with a subtle energy I could not have before conceived of. But poorly could I withstand them, much as in other moods I was almost ready to smile at the solemn whimsicalities of that outlandish prophet of the wharves. But whatever it was of apprehensiveness or uneasiness—to call it so—which I felt, yet whenever I came to look about me in the ship, it seemed against all warranty to cherish such emotions. For though the harpooneers, with the great body of the crew, were a far more barbaric, heathenish, and motley set than any of the tame merchant-ship companies which my previous experiences had made me acquainted with, still I ascribed this—and rightly ascribed it—to the fierce uniqueness of the very nature of that wild Scandinavian vocation in which I had so abandonedly embarked. But it was especially the aspect of the three chief officers of the ship, the mates, which was most forcibly calculated to allay these colorless misgivings, and induce confidence and cheerfulness in every presentment of the voyage. Three better, more likely sea-officers and men, each in his own different way, could not readily be found, and they were every one of them Americans; a Nantucketer, a Vineyarder, a Cape man. Now, it being Christmas when the ship shot from out her harbor, for a space we had biting Polar weather, though all the time running away from it to the southward; and by every degree and minute of latitude which we sailed, gradually leaving that merciless winter, and all its intolerable weather behind us. It was one of those less lowering, but still grey and gloomy enough mornings of the transition, when with a fair wind the ship was rushing through the water with a vindictive sort of leaping and melancholy rapidity, that as I mounted to the deck at the call of the forenoon watch, so soon as I levelled my glance towards the taffrail, foreboding shivers ran over me. Reality outran apprehension; Captain Ahab stood upon his quarter-deck.

There seemed no sign of common bodily illness about him, nor of the recovery from any. He looked like a man cut away from the stake, when the fire has overrunningly wasted all the limbs without consuming them, or taking away one particle from their compacted aged robustness. His whole high, broad form, seemed made of solid bronze, and shaped in an unalterable mould, like Cellini's cast Perseus. Threading its way out from among his grey hairs, and continuing right down one side of his tawny scorched face and neck, till it disappeared in his clothing, you saw a slender rod-like mark, lividly whitish. It resembled that perpendicular seam sometimes made in the straight, lofty trunk of a great tree, when the upper lightning tearingly darts down it, and without wrenching a single twig, peels and grooves out the bark from top to bottom, ere running off into the soil, leaving the tree still greenly alive, but branded. Whether that mark was born with him, or whether it was the scar left by some desperate wound, no one could certainly say. By some tacit consent, throughout the voyage little or no allusion was made to it, especially by the mates. But once Tashtego's senior, an old Gay-Head Indian among the crew, superstitiously asserted that not till he was full forty years old did Ahab become that way branded, and then it came upon him, not in the fury of any mortal fray, but

in an elemental strife at sea. Yet, this wild hint seemed inferentially nega-
tived, by what a grey Manxman insinuated, an old sepulchral man, who,
having never before sailed out of Nantucket, had never ere this laid eye
upon wild Ahab. Nevertheless, the old sea-traditions, the immemorial
credulities, popularly invested this old Manxman with preternatural
powers of discernment. So that no white sailor seriously contradicted him
when he said that if ever Captain Ahab should be tranquilly laid out—
which might hardly come to pass, so he muttered—then, whoever should
do that last office for the dead, would find a birth-mark on him from crown
to sole.

So powerfully did the whole grim aspect of Ahab affect me, and the livid
brand which streaked it, that for the first few moments I hardly noted that
not a little of this overbearing grimness was owing to the barbaric white leg
upon which he partly stood. It had previously come to me that this ivory
leg had at sea been fashioned from the polished bone of the sperm whale's
jaw. "Aye, he was dismasted off Japan," said the old Gay-Head Indian once;
"but like his dismasted craft, he shipped another mast without coming
home for it. He has a quiver of 'em."

I was struck with the singular posture he maintained. Upon each side of
the Pequod's quarter deck, and pretty close to the mizen shrouds, there was an
auger hole, bored about half an inch or so, into the plank. His bone leg
steadied in that hole; one arm elevated, and holding by a shroud; Captain
Ahab stood erect, looking straight out beyond the ship's ever-pitching
prow. There was an infinity of firmest fortitude, a determinate, unsur-
renderable wilfulness, in the fixed and fearless, forward dedication of that
glance. Not a word he spoke; nor did his officers say aught to him; though
by all their minutest gestures and expressions, they plainly showed the
uneasy, if not painful, consciousness of being under a troubled master-eye.
And not only that, but moody stricken Ahab stood before them with a
crucifixion in his face; in all the nameless regal overbearing dignity of some
mighty woe.

Ere long, from his first visit in the air, he withdrew into his cabin. But
after that morning, he was every day visible to the crew; either standing in
his pivot-hole, or seated upon an ivory stool he had; or heavily walking the
deck. As the sky grew less gloomy; indeed, began to grow a little genial, he
became still less and less a recluse; as if, when the ship had sailed from home,
nothing but the dead wintry bleakness of the sea had then kept him so
secluded. And, by and by, it came to pass, that he was almost continually
in the air; but, as yet, for all that he said, or perceptibly did, on the at last

sunny deck, he seemed as unnecessary there as another mast. But the Pequod was only making a passage now; not regularly cruising; nearly all whaling preparatives needing supervision the mates were fully competent to, so that there was little or nothing, out of himself, to employ or excite Ahab, now; and thus chase away, for that one interval, the clouds that layer upon layer were piled upon his brow, as ever all clouds choose the loftiest peaks to pile themselves upon.

Nevertheless, ere long, the warm, warbling persuasiveness of the pleasant, holiday weather we came to, seemed gradually to charm him from his mood. For, as when the red-cheeked, dancing girls, April and May, trip home to the wintry, misanthropic woods; even the barest, ruggedest, most thunder-cloven old oak will at least send forth some few green sprouts, to welcome such glad-hearted visitants; so Ahab did, in the end, a little respond to the playful allurings of that girlish air. More than once did he put forth the faint blossom of a look, which, in any other man, would have soon flowered out in a smile.

# Chapter 29

*Enter Ahab; to him, Stubb*

SOME DAYS ELAPSED, and ice and icebergs all astern, the Pequod now went rolling through the bright Quito spring, which, at sea, almost perpetually reigns on the threshold of the eternal August of the Tropic. The warmly cool, clear, ringing, perfumed, overflowing, redundant days, were as crystal goblets of Persian sherbet, heaped up—flaked up, with rose-water snow. The starred and stately nights seemed haughty dames in jewelled velvets, nursing at home in lonely pride, the memory of their absent conquering Earls, the golden helmeted suns! For sleeping man, 'twas hard to choose between such winsome days and such seducing nights. But all the witcheries of that unwaning weather did not merely lend new spells and potencies to the outward world. Inward they turned upon the soul, especially when the still mild hours of eve came on; then, memory shot her crystals as the clear ice most forms of noiseless twilights. And all these subtle agencies, more and more they wrought on Ahab's texture.

Old age is always wakeful; as if, the longer linked with life, the less man has to do with aught that looks like death. Among sea-commanders, the old greybeards will oftenest leave their berths to visit the night-cloaked deck. It was so with Ahab; only that now, of late, he seemed so much to live in the open air, that truly speaking, his visits were more to the cabin, than

from the cabin to the planks. "It feels like going down into one's tomb,"—
he would mutter to himself,—"for an old captain like me to be descending
this narrow scuttle, to go to my grave-dug berth."

So, almost every twenty-four hours, when the watches of the night
were set, and the band on deck sentinelled the slumbers of the band below;
and when if a rope was to be hauled upon the forecastle, the sailors flung it
not rudely down, as by day, but with some cautiousness dropt it to its place,
for fear of disturbing their slumbering shipmates; when this sort of steady
quietude would begin to prevail, habitually, the silent steersman would
watch the cabin-scuttle; and ere long the old man would emerge, griping
at the iron banister, to help his crippled way. Some considerating touch
of humanity was in him; for at times like these, he usually abstained from
patrolling the quarter-deck; because to his wearied mates, seeking repose
within six inches of his ivory heel, such would have been the reverberating
crack and din of that bony step, that their dreams would have been of the
crunching teeth of sharks. But once, the mood was on him too deep for
common regardings; and as with heavy, lumber-like pace he was measuring
the ship from taffrail to mainmast, Stubb, the odd second mate, came up
from below, and with a certain unassured, deprecating humorousness,
hinted that if Captain Ahab was pleased to walk the planks, then, no one
could say nay; but there might be some way of muffling the noise; hinting
something indistinctly and hesitatingly about a globe of tow, and the insertion into it, of the ivory heel. Ah! Stubb, thou did'st not know Ahab
then.

"Am I a cannon-ball, Stubb," said Ahab, "that thou wouldst wad me
that fashion? But go thy ways; I had forgot. Below to thy nightly grave;
where such as ye sleep between shrouds, to use ye to the filling one at last.—
Down, dog, and kennel!"

Starting at the unforeseen concluding exclamation of the so suddenly
scornful old man, Stubb was speechless a moment; then said excitedly, "I
am not used to be spoken to that way, sir; I do but less than half like it, sir."

"Avast!" gritted Ahab between his set teeth, and violently moving
away, as if to avoid some passionate temptation.

"No, sir; not yet," said Stubb, emboldened, "I will not tamely be called
a dog, sir."

"Then be called ten times a donkey, and a mule, and an ass, and begone,
or I'll clear the world of thee!"

As he said this, Ahab advanced upon him with such overbearing terrors
in his aspect, that Stubb involuntarily retreated.

"I was never servéd so before without giving a hard blow for it," muttered Stubb, as he found himself descending the cabin-scuttle. "It's very queer. Stop, Stubb; somehow, now, I don't well know whether to go back and strike him, or—what's that?—down here on my knees and pray for him? Yes, that was the thought coming up in me; but it would be the first time I ever *did* pray. It's queer; very queer; and he's queer too; aye, take him fore and aft, he's about the queerest old man Stubb ever sailed with. How he flashed at me!—his eyes like powder-pans! is he mad? Anyway there's something on his mind, as sure as there must be something on a deck when it cracks. He aint in his bed now, either, more than three hours out of the twenty-four; and he don't sleep then. Didn't that Dough-Boy, the steward, tell me that of a morning he always finds the old man's hammock clothes all rumpled and tumbled, and the sheets down at the foot, and the coverlid almost tied into knots, and the pillow a sort of frightful hot, as though a baked brick had been on it? A hot old man! I guess he's got what some folks ashore call a conscience; it's a kind of Tic-Dolly-row they say —worse nor a toothache. Well, well; I don't know what it is, but the Lord keep me from catching it. He's full of riddles; I wonder what he goes into the after hold for, every night, as Dough-Boy tells me he suspects; what's that for, I should like to know? Who's made appointments with him in the hold? Ain't that queer, now? But there's no telling, it's the old game— Here goes for a snooze. Damn me, it's worth a fellow's while to be born into the world, if only to fall right asleep. And now that I think of it, that's about the first thing babies do, and that's a sort of queer, too. Damn me, but all things are queer, come to think of 'em. But that's against my principles. Think not, is my eleventh commandment; and sleep when you can, is my twelfth—So here goes again. But how's that? didn't he call me a dog? blazes! he called me ten times a donkey, and piled a lot of jackasses on top of *that!* He might as well have kicked me, and done with it. Maybe he *did* kick me, and I didn't observe it, I was so taken all aback with his brow, somehow. It flashed like a bleached bone. What the devil's the matter with me? I don't stand right on my legs. Coming afoul of that old man has a sort of turned me wrong side out. By the Lord, I must have been dreaming, though—How? how? how?—but the only way's to stash it; so here goes to hammock again; and in the morning, I'll see how this plaguey juggling thinks over by daylight."

# Chapter 30

## *The Pipe*

WHEN Stubb had departed, Ahab stood for a while leaning over the bulwarks; and then, as had been usual with him of late, calling a sailor of the watch, he sent him below for his ivory stool, and also his pipe. Lighting the pipe at the binnacle lamp and planting the stool on the weather side of the deck, he sat and smoked.

In old Norse times, the thrones of the sea-loving Danish kings were fabricated, saith tradition, of the tusks of the narwhale. How could one look at Ahab then, seated on that tripod of bones, without bethinking him of the royalty it symbolized? For a Khan of the plank, and a king of the sea, and a great lord of Leviathans was Ahab.

Some moments passed, during which the thick vapor came from his mouth in quick and constant puffs, which blew back again into his face. "How now," he soliloquized at last, withdrawing the tube, "this smoking no longer soothes. Oh, my pipe! hard must it go with me if thy charm be gone! Here have I been unconsciously toiling, not pleasuring,—aye, and ignorantly smoking to windward all the while; to windward, and with such nervous whiffs, as if, like the dying whale, my final jets were the strongest and fullest of trouble. What business have I with this pipe? This thing that is meant for sereneness, to send up mild white vapors among mild white hairs, not among torn iron-grey locks like mine. I'll smoke no more—"

He tossed the still lighted pipe into the sea. The fire hissed in the waves; the same instant the ship shot by the bubble the sinking pipe made. With slouched hat, Ahab lurchingly paced the planks.

# Chapter 31

*Queen Mab*

NEXT MORNING Stubb accosted Flask.
"Such a queer dream, King-Post, I never had. You know the old man's ivory leg, well I dreamed he kicked me with it; and when I tried to kick back, upon my soul, my little man, I kicked my leg right off! And then, presto! Ahab seemed a pyramid, and I, like a blazing fool, kept kicking at it. But what was still more curious, Flask—you know how curious all dreams are—through all this rage that I was in, I somehow seemed to be thinking to myself, that after all, it was not much of an insult, that kick from Ahab. 'Why,' thinks I, 'what's the row? It's not a real leg, only a false leg.' And there's a mighty difference between a living thump and a dead thump. That's what makes a blow from the hand, Flask, fifty times more savage to bear than a blow from a cane. The living member— that makes the living insult, my little man. And thinks I to myself all the while, mind, while I was stubbing my silly toes against that cursed pyramid —so confoundedly contradictory was it all, all the while, I say, I was thinking to myself, 'what's his leg now, but a cane—a whalebone cane. Yes,' thinks I, 'it was only a playful cudgelling—in fact, only a whaleboning that he gave me—not a base kick. Besides,' thinks I, 'look at it once; why, the end of it—the foot part—what a small sort of end it is; whereas, if a broad footed farmer kicked me, *there's* a devilish broad insult. But this insult is

131

whittled down to a point only.' But now comes the greatest joke of the dream, Flask. While I was battering away at the pyramid, a sort of badger-haired old merman, with a hump on his back, takes me by the shoulders, and slews me round. 'What are you 'bout?' says he. 'Slid! man, but I was frightened. Such a phiz! But, somehow, next moment I was over the fright. 'What am I about?' says I at last. 'And what business is that of yours, I should like to know, Mr. Humpback? Do *you* want a kick?' By the lord, Flask, I had no sooner said that, than he turned round his stern to me, bent over, and dragging up a lot of sea-weed he had for a clout—what do you think, I saw?—why thunder alive, man, his stern was stuck full of marlin-spikes, with the points out. Says I, on second thoughts, 'I guess I won't kick you, old fellow.' 'Wise Stubb,' said he, 'wise Stubb;' and kept muttering it all the time, a sort of eating of his own gums like a chimney hag. Seeing he wasn't going to stop saying over his 'wise Stubb, wise Stubb,' I thought I might as well fall to kicking the pyramid again. But I had only just lifted my foot for it, when he roared out, 'Stop that kicking!' 'Halloa,' says I, 'what's the matter now, old fellow?' 'Look ye here,' says he; 'let's argue the insult. Captain Ahab kicked ye, didn't he?' 'Yes, he did,' says I—'right *here* it was.' 'Very good,' says he—'he used his ivory leg, didn't he?' 'Yes, he did,' says I. 'Well then,' says he, 'wise Stubb, what have you to complain of? Didn't he kick with right good will? it wasn't a common pitch pine leg he kicked with, was it? No, you were kicked by a great man, and with a beautiful ivory leg, Stubb. It's an honor; I consider it an honor. Listen, wise Stubb. In old England the greatest lords think it great glory to be slapped by a queen, and made garter-knights of; but, be *your* boast, Stubb, that ye were kicked by old Ahab, and made a wise man of. Remember what I say; *be* kicked by him; account his kicks honors; and on no account kick back; for you can't help yourself, wise Stubb. Don't you see that pyramid?' With that, he all of a sudden seemed somehow, in some queer fashion, to swim off into the air. I snored; rolled over; and there I was in my hammock! Now, what do you think of that dream, Flask?"

"I don't know; it seems a sort of foolish to me, tho'."

"May be; may be. But it's made a wise man of me, Flask. D'ye see Ahab standing there, sideways looking over the stern? Well, the best thing you can do, Flask, is to let that old man alone; never speak quick to him, what-ever he says. Halloa! what's that he shouts? Hark!"

"Mast-head, there! Look sharp, all of ye! There are whales hereabouts! If ye see a white one, split your lungs for him!"

"What d'ye think of that now, Flask? ain't there a small drop of something queer about that, eh? A white whale—did ye mark that, man? Look ye—there's something special in the wind. Stand by for it, Flask. Ahab has that that's bloody on his mind. But, mum; he comes this way."

# Chapter 32

## Cetology

ALREADY we are boldly launched upon the deep; but soon we shall be lost in its unshored, harborless immensities. Ere that come to pass; ere the Pequod's weedy hull rolls side by side with the barnacled hulls of the leviathan; at the outset it is but well to attend to a matter almost indispensable to a thorough appreciative understanding of the more special leviathanic revelations and allusions of all sorts which are to follow.

It is some systematized exhibition of the whale in his broad genera, that I would now fain put before you. Yet is it no easy task. The classification of the constituents of a chaos, nothing less is here essayed. Listen to what the best and latest authorities have laid down.

"No branch of Zoology is so much involved as that which is entitled Cetology," says Captain Scoresby, A. D. 1820.

"It is not my intention, were it in my power, to enter into the inquiry as to the true method of dividing the cetacea into groups and families. * * * Utter confusion exists among the historians of this animal" (sperm whale), says Surgeon Beale, A. D. 1839.

"Unfitness to pursue our research in the unfathomable waters." "Impenetrable veil covering our knowledge of the cetacea." "A field strewn with thorns." "All these incomplete indications but serve to torture us naturalists."

Thus speak of the whale, the great Cuvier, and John Hunter, and Lesson, those lights of zoology and anatomy. Nevertheless, though of real knowledge there be little, yet of books there are a plenty; and so in some small degree, with cetology, or the science of whales. Many are the men, small and great, old and new, landsmen and seamen, who have at large or in little, written of the whale. Run over a few:—The Authors of the Bible; Aristotle; Pliny; Aldrovandi; Sir Thomas Browne; Gesner; Ray; Linnæus; Rondeletius; Willoughby; Green; Artedi; Sibbald; Brisson; Marten; Lacépède; Bonnaterre; Desmarest; Baron Cuvier; Frederick Cuvier; John Hunter; Owen; Scoresby; Beale; Bennett; J. Ross Browne; the Author of Miriam Coffin; Olmsted; and the Rev. Henry T. Cheever. But to what ultimate generalizing purpose all these have written, the above cited extracts will show.

Of the names in this list of whale authors, only those following Owen ever saw living whales; and but one of them was a real professional harpooneer and whaleman. I mean Captain Scoresby. On the separate subject of the Greenland or right-whale, he is the best existing authority. But Scoresby knew nothing and says nothing of the great sperm whale, compared with which the Greenland whale is almost unworthy mentioning. And here be it said, that the Greenland whale is an usurper upon the throne of the seas. He is not even by any means the largest of the whales. Yet, owing to the long priority of his claims, and the profound ignorance which, till some seventy years back, invested the then fabulous or utterly unknown sperm-whale, and which ignorance to this present day still reigns in all but some few scientific retreats and whale-ports; this usurpation has been every way complete. Reference to nearly all the leviathanic allusions in the great poets of past days, will satisfy you that the Greenland whale, without one rival, was to them the monarch of the seas. But the time has at last come for a new proclamation. This is Charing Cross; hear ye! good people all,—the Greenland whale is deposed,—the great sperm whale now reigneth!

There are only two books in being which at all pretend to put the living sperm whale before you, and at the same time, in the remotest degree succeed in the attempt. Those books are Beale's and Bennett's; both in their time surgeons to English South-Sea whale-ships, and both exact and reliable men. The original matter touching the sperm whale to be found in their volumes is necessarily small; but so far as it goes, it is of excellent quality, though mostly confined to scientific description. As yet, however, the sperm whale, scientific or poetic, lives not complete in any literature. Far above all other hunted whales, his is an unwritten life.

Now the various species of whales need some sort of popular comprehensive classification, if only an easy outline one for the present, hereafter to be filled in all its departments by subsequent laborers. As no better man advances to take this matter in hand, I hereupon offer my own poor endeavors. I promise nothing complete; because any human thing supposed to be complete, must for that very reason infallibly be faulty. I shall not pretend to a minute anatomical description of the various species, or—in this place at least—to much of any description. My object here is simply to project the draught of a systematization of cetology. I am the architect, not the builder.

But it is a ponderous task; no ordinary letter-sorter in the Post-office is equal to it. To grope down into the bottom of the sea after them; to have one's hands among the unspeakable foundations, ribs, and very pelvis of the world; this is a fearful thing. What am I that I should essay to hook the nose of this leviathan! The awful tauntings in Job might well appal me. "Will he (the leviathan) make a covenant with thee? Behold the hope of him is vain!" But I have swam through libraries and sailed through oceans; I have had to do with whales with these visible hands; I am in earnest; and I will try. There are some preliminaries to settle.

First: The uncertain, unsettled condition of this science of Cetology is in the very vestibule attested by the fact, that in some quarters it still remains a moot point whether a whale be a fish. In his System of Nature, A.D. 1766, Linnæus declares, "I hereby separate the whales from the fish." But of my own knowledge, I know that down to the year 1850, sharks and shad, alewives and herring, against Linnæus's express edict, were still found dividing the possession of the same seas with the Leviathan.

The grounds upon which Linnæus would fain have banished the whales from the waters, he states as follows: "On account of their warm bilocular heart, their lungs, their movable eyelids, their hollow ears, penem intrantem feminam mammis lactantem," and finally, "ex lege naturæ jure meritoque." I submitted all this to my friends Simeon Macey and Charley Coffin, of Nantucket, both messmates of mine in a certain voyage, and they united in the opinion that the reasons set forth were altogether insufficient. Charley profanely hinted they were humbug.

Be it known that, waiving all argument, I take the good old fashioned ground that the whale is a fish, and call upon holy Jonah to back me. This fundamental thing settled, the next point is, in what internal respect does the whale differ from other fish. Above, Linnæus has given you those items.

But in brief, they are these: lungs and warm blood; whereas, all other fish are lungless and cold blooded.

Next: how shall we define the whale, by his obvious externals, so as conspicuously to label him for all time to come? To be short, then, a whale is *a spouting fish with a horizontal tail*. There you have him. However contracted, that definition is the result of expanded meditation. A walrus spouts much like a whale, but the walrus is not a fish, because he is amphibious. But the last term of the definition is still more cogent, as coupled with the first. Almost any one must have noticed that all the fish familiar to landsmen have not a flat, but a vertical, or up-and-down tail. Whereas, among spouting fish the tail, though it may be similarly shaped, invariably assumes a horizontal position.

By the above definition of what a whale is, I do by no means exclude from the leviathanic brotherhood any sea creature hitherto identified with the whale by the best informed Nantucketers; nor, on the other hand, link with it any fish hitherto authoritatively regarded as alien.\* Hence, all the smaller, spouting, and horizontal tailed fish must be included in this groundplan of Cetology. Now, then, come the grand divisions of the entire whale host.

First: According to magnitude I divide the whales into three primary BOOKS (subdivisible into CHAPTERS), and these shall comprehend them all, both small and large.

I. The FOLIO WHALE; II. the OCTAVO WHALE; III. the DUODECIMO WHALE.

As the type of the FOLIO I present the *Sperm Whale;* of the OCTAVO, the *Grampus;* of the DUODECIMO, the *Porpoise.*

FOLIOS. Among these I here include the following chapters:—I. The *Sperm Whale;* II. the *Right Whale;* III. the *Fin Back Whale;* IV. the *Humpbacked Whale;* V. the *Razor Back Whale;* VI. the *Sulphur Bottom Whale.*

BOOK I. (*Folio*), CHAPTER I. (*Sperm Whale*).—This whale, among the English of old vaguely known as the Trumpa whale, and the Physeter whale, and the Anvil Headed whale, is the present Cachalot of the French, and the Pottfisch of the Germans, and the Macrocephalus of the Long

---

\* I am aware that down to the present time, the fish styled Lamantins and Dugongs (Pig-fish and Sow-fish of the Coffins of Nantucket) are included by many naturalists among the whales. But as these pig-fish are a nosy, contemptible set, mostly lurking in the mouths of rivers, and feeding on wet hay, and especially as they do not spout, I deny their credentials as whales; and have presented them with their passports to quit the Kingdom of Cetology.

Words. He is, without doubt, the largest inhabitant of the globe; the most formidable of all whales to encounter; the most majestic in aspect; and lastly, by far the most valuable in commerce; he being the only creature from which that valuable substance, spermaceti, is obtained. All his peculiarities will, in many other places, be enlarged upon. It is chiefly with his name that I now have to do. Philologically considered, it is absurd. Some centuries ago, when the Sperm whale was almost wholly unknown in his own proper individuality, and when his oil was only accidentally obtained from the stranded fish; in those days spermaceti, it would seem, was popularly supposed to be derived from a creature identical with the one then known in England as the Greenland or Right Whale. It was the idea also, that this same spermaceti was that quickening humor of the Greenland Whale which the first syllable of the word literally expresses. In those times, also, spermaceti was exceedingly scarce, not being used for light, but only as an ointment and medicament. It was only to be had from the druggists as you nowadays buy an ounce of rhubarb. When, as I opine, in the course of time, the true nature of spermaceti became known, its original name was still retained by the dealers; no doubt to enhance its value by a notion so strangely significant of its scarcity. And so the appellation must at last have come to be bestowed upon the whale from which this spermaceti was really derived.

BOOK I. (*Folio*), CHAPTER II. (*Right Whale*).—In one respect this is the most venerable of the leviathans, being the one first regularly hunted by man. It yields the article commonly known as whalebone or baleen; and the oil specially known as "whale oil," an inferior article in commerce. Among the fishermen, he is indiscriminately designated by all the following titles: The Whale; the Greenland Whale; the Black Whale; the Great Whale; the True Whale; the Right Whale. There is a deal of obscurity concerning the identity of the species thus multitudinously baptized. What then is the whale, which I include in the second species of my Folios? It is the Great Mysticetus of the English naturalists; the Greenland Whale of the English whalemen; the Baleine Ordinaire of the French whalemen; the Gronlands Walfisk of the Swedes. It is the whale which for more than two centuries past has been hunted by the Dutch and English in the Arctic seas; it is the whale which the American fishermen have long pursued in the Indian ocean, on the Brazil Banks, on the Nor' West Coast, and various other parts of the world, designated by them Right Whale Cruising Grounds.

Some pretend to see a difference between the Greenland whale of the English and the right whale of the Americans. But they precisely agree in all their grand features; nor has there yet been presented a single determinate fact upon which to ground a radical distinction. It is by endless subdivisions based upon the most inconclusive differences, that some departments of natural history become so repellingly intricate. The right whale will be elsewhere treated of at some length, with reference to elucidating the sperm whale.

BOOK I. (*Folio*), CHAPTER III. (*Fin-Back*).—Under this head I reckon a monster which, by the various names of Fin-Back, Tall-Spout, and Long-John, has been seen almost in every sea and is commonly the whale whose distant jet is so often descried by passengers crossing the Atlantic, in the New York packet-tracks. In the length he attains, and in his baleen, the Fin-back resembles the right whale, but is of a less portly girth, and a lighter color, approaching to olive. His great lips present a cable-like aspect, formed by the intertwisting, slanting folds of large wrinkles. His grand distinguishing feature, the fin, from which he derives his name, is often a conspicuous object. This fin is some three or four feet long, growing vertically from the hinder part of the back, of an angular shape, and with a very sharp pointed end. Even if not the slightest other part of the creature be visible, this isolated fin will, at times, be seen plainly projecting from the surface. When the sea is moderately calm, and slightly marked with spherical ripples, and this gnomon-like fin stands up and casts shadows upon the wrinkled surface, it may well be supposed that the watery circle surrounding it somewhat resembles a dial, with its style and wavy hour-lines graved on it. On that Ahaz-dial the shadow often goes back. The Fin-Back is not gregarious. He seems a whale-hater, as some men are man-haters. Very shy; always going solitary; unexpectedly rising to the surface in the remotest and most sullen waters; his straight and single lofty jet rising like a tall misanthropic spear upon a barren plain; gifted with such wondrous power and velocity in swimming, as to defy all present pursuit from man; this leviathan seems the banished and unconquerable Cain of his race, bearing for his mark that style upon his back. From having the baleen in his mouth, the Fin-Back is sometimes included with the right whale, among a theoretic species denominated *Whalebone whales*, that is, whales with baleen. Of these so called Whalebone whales, there would seem to be several varieties, most of which, however, are little known. Broad-nosed whales and beaked whales; pike-headed whales; bunched whales; under-jawed whales and rostrated whales, are the fishermen's names for a few sorts.

In connexion with this appellative of "Whalebone whales," it is of great importance to mention, that however such a nomenclature may be convenient in facilitating allusions to some kind of whales, yet it is in vain to attempt a clear classification of the Leviathan, founded upon either his baleen, or hump, or fin, or teeth; notwithstanding that those marked parts or features very obviously seem better adapted to afford the basis for a regular system of Cetology than any other detached bodily distinctions, which the whale, in his kinds, presents. How then? The baleen, hump, back-fin, and teeth; these are things whose peculiarities are indiscriminately dispersed among all sorts of whales, without any regard to what may be the nature of their structure in other and more essential particulars. Thus, the sperm whale and the humpbacked whale, each has a hump; but there the similitude ceases. Then, this same humpbacked whale and the Greenland whale, each of these has baleen; but there again the similitude ceases. And it is just the same with the other parts above mentioned. In various sorts of whales, they form such irregular combinations; or, in the case of any one of them detached, such an irregular isolation; as utterly to defy all general methodization formed upon such a basis. On this rock every one of the whale-naturalists has split.

But it may possibly be conceived that, in the internal parts of the whale, in his anatomy—there, at least, we shall be able to hit the right classification. Nay; what thing, for example, is there in the Greenland whale's anatomy more striking than his baleen? Yet we have seen that by his baleen it is impossible correctly to classify the Greenland whale. And if you descend into the bowels of the various leviathans, why there you will not find distinctions a fiftieth part as available to the systematizer as those external ones already enumerated. What then remains? nothing but to take hold of the whales bodily, in their entire liberal volume, and boldly sort them that way. And this is the Bibliographical system here adopted; and it is the only 'one that can possibly succeed, for it alone is practicable. To proceed.

BOOK I. (*Folio*), CHAPTER IV. (*Hump Back*).—This whale is often seen on the northern American coast. He has been frequently captured there, and towed into harbor. He has a great pack on him like a peddler; or you might call him the Elephant and Castle whale. At any rate, the popular name for him does not sufficiently distinguish him, since the sperm whale also has a hump, though a smaller one. His oil is not very valuable. He has baleen. He is the most gamesome and light-hearted of all the whales, making more gay foam and white water generally than any other of them.

BOOK I. (*Folio*), CHAPTER V. (*Razor Back*).—Of this whale little is known but his name. I have seen him at a distance off Cape Horn. Of a retiring nature, he eludes both hunters and philosophers. Though no coward, he has never yet shown any part of him but his back, which rises in a long sharp ridge. Let him go. I know little more of him, nor does anybody else.

BOOK I. (*Folio*), CHAPTER VI. (*Sulphur Bottom*).—Another retiring gentleman, with a brimstone belly, doubtless got by scraping along the Tartarian tiles in some of his profounder divings. He is seldom seen; at least I have never seen him except in the remoter southern seas, and then always at too great a distance to study his countenance. He is never chased; he would run away with rope-walks of line. Prodigies are told of him. Adieu, Sulphur Bottom! I can say nothing more that is true of ye, nor can the oldest Nantucketer.

Thus ends BOOK I. (*Folio*), and now begins BOOK II. (*Octavo*).

OCTAVOES.* These embrace the whales of middling magnitude, among which at present may be numbered:—I., the *Grampus*; II., the *Black Fish*; III., the *Narwhale*; IV., the *Killer*; V., the *Thrasher*.

BOOK II. (*Octavo*), CHAPTER I. (*Grampus*).—Though this fish, whose loud sonorous breathing, or rather blowing, has furnished a proverb to landsmen, is so well known a denizen of the deep, yet is he not popularly classed among whales. But possessing all the grand distinctive features of the leviathan, most naturalists have recognised him for one. He is of moderate octavo size, varying from fifteen to twenty-five feet in length, and of corresponding dimensions round the waist. He swims in herds; he is never regularly hunted, though his oil is considerable in quantity, and pretty good for light. By some fishermen his approach is regarded as premonitory of the advance of the great sperm whale.

BOOK II. (*Octavo*), CHAPTER II. (*Black Fish*).—I give the popular fishermen's names for all these fish, for generally they are the best. Where any name happens to be vague or inexpressive, I shall say so, and suggest another. I do so now, touching the Black Fish, so called, because blackness is the rule among almost all whales. So, call him the Hyena Whale, if you please. His voracity is well known, and from the circumstance that the inner angles of his lips are curved upwards, he carries an everlasting Mephistophelean grin on his face. This whale averages some sixteen or eighteen feet in length. He is found in almost all latitudes. He has a peculiar way of showing his dorsal hooked fin in swimming, which looks something like a Roman

---

* Why this book of whales is not denominated the Quarto is very plain. Because, while the whales of this order, though smaller than those of the former order, nevertheless retain a proportionate likeness to them in figure, yet the bookbinder's Quarto volume in its diminished form does not preserve the shape of the Folio volume, but the Octavo volume does.

nose. When not more profitably employed, the sperm whale hunters sometimes capture the Hyena whale, to keep up the supply of cheap oil for
domestic employment—as some frugal housekeepers, in the absence of
company, and quite alone by themselves, burn unsavory tallow instead of
odorous wax. Though their blubber is very thin, some of these whales will
yield you upwards of thirty gallons of oil.

BOOK II. (*Octavo*), CHAPTER III. (*Narwhale*), that is, *Nostril whale*.—
Another instance of a curiously named whale, so named I suppose from his
peculiar horn being originally mistaken for a peaked nose. The creature is
some sixteen feet in length, while its horn averages five feet, though some
exceed ten, and even attain to fifteen feet. Strictly speaking, this horn is but
a lengthened tusk, growing out from the jaw in a line a little depressed from
the horizontal. But it is only found on the sinister side, which has an ill effect,
giving its owner something analogous to the aspect of a clumsy left-handed
man. What precise purpose this ivory horn or lance answers, it would be
hard to say. It does not seem to be used like the blade of the sword-fish and
bill-fish; though some sailors tell me that the Narwhale employs it for a
rake in turning over the bottom of the sea for food. Charley Coffin said it
was used for an ice-piercer; for the Narwhale, rising to the surface of the
Polar Sea, and finding it sheeted with ice, thrusts his horn up, and so breaks
through. But you cannot prove either of these surmises to be correct. My
own opinion is, that however this one-sided horn may really be used by the
Narwhale—however that may be—it would certainly be very convenient
to him for a folder in reading pamphlets. The Narwhale I have heard called
the Tusked whale, the Horned whale, and the Unicorn whale. He is certainly a curious example of the Unicornism to be found in almost every kingdom of animated nature. From certain cloistered old authors I have gathered
that this same sea-unicorn's horn was in ancient days regarded as the great
antidote against poison, and as such, preparations of it brought immense
prices. It was also distilled to a volatile salts for fainting ladies, the same way
that the horns of the male deer are manufactured into hartshorn. Originally
it was in itself accounted an object of great curiosity. Black Letter tells me
that Sir Martin Frobisher on his return from that voyage, when Queen
Bess did gallantly wave her jewelled hand to him from a window of Green-
wich Palace, as his bold ship sailed down the Thames; "when Sir Martin
returned from that voyage," saith Black Letter, "on bended knees he
presented to her highness a prodigious long horn of the Narwhale, which
for a long period after hung in the castle at Windsor." An Irish author
avers that the Earl of Leicester, on bended knees, did likewise present to

her highness another horn, pertaining to a land beast of the unicorn nature.

The Narwhale has a very picturesque, leopard-like look, being of a milk-white ground color, dotted with round and oblong spots of black. His oil is very superior, clear and fine; but there is little of it, and he is seldom hunted. He is mostly found in the circumpolar seas.

BOOK II. (*Octavo*), CHAPTER IV. (*Killer*).—Of this whale little is precisely known to the Nantucketer, and nothing at all to the professed naturalist. From what I have seen of him at a distance, I should say that he was about the bigness of a grampus. He is very savage—a sort of Feegee fish. He sometimes takes the great Folio whales by the lip, and hangs there like a leech, till the mighty brute is worried to death. The Killer is never hunted. I never heard what sort of oil he has. Exception might be taken to the name bestowed upon this whale, on the ground of its indistinctness. For we are all killers, on land and on sea; Bonapartes and Sharks included.

BOOK II. (*Octavo*), CHAPTER V. (*Thrasher*).—This gentleman is famous for his tail, which he uses for a ferule in thrashing his foes. He mounts the Folio whale's back, and as he swims, he works his passage by flogging him; as some schoolmasters get along in the world by a similar process. Still less is known of the Thrasher than of the Killer. Both are outlaws, even in the lawless seas.

Thus ends BOOK II. (*Octavo*), and begins BOOK III. (*Duodecimo*).

DUODECIMOES.—These include the smaller whales. I. The Huzza Porpoise. II. The Algerine Porpoise. III. The Mealy-mouthed Porpoise.

To those who have not chanced specially to study the subject, it may possibly seem strange, that fishes not commonly exceeding four or five feet should be marshalled among WHALES—a word, which, in the popular sense, always conveys an idea of hugeness. But the creatures set down above as Duodecimoes are infallibly whales, by the terms of my definition of what a whale is—i.e. a spouting fish, with a horizontal tail.

BOOK III. (*Duodecimo*), CHAPTER I. (*Huzza Porpoise*).—This is the common porpoise found almost all over the globe. The name is of my own bestowal; for there are more than one sort of porpoises, and something must be done to distinguish them. I call him thus, because he always swims in hilarious shoals, which upon the broad sea keep tossing themselves to heaven like caps in a Fourth-of-July crowd. Their appearance is generally hailed with delight by the mariner. Full of fine spirits, they invariably come from the breezy billows to windward. They are the lads that always live before the wind. They are accounted a lucky omen. If you yourself can withstand three cheers at beholding these vivacious fish, then heaven help

ye; the spirit of godly gamesomeness is not in ye. A well-fed, plump Huzza
Porpoise will yield you one good gallon of good oil. But the fine and delicate
fluid extracted from his jaws is exceedingly valuable. It is in request among
jewellers and watchmakers. Sailors put it on their hones. Porpoise meat is
good eating, you know. It may never have occurred to you that a porpoise
spouts. Indeed, his spout is so small that it is not very readily discernible.
But the next time you have a chance, watch him; and you will then see the
great Sperm whale himself in miniature.

   BOOK III. (*Duodecimo*), CHAPTER II. (*Algerine Porpoise*).—A pirate. Very
savage. He is only found, I think, in the Pacific. He is somewhat larger than
the Huzza Porpoise, but much of the same general make. Provoke him, and
he will buckle to a shark. I have lowered for him many times, but never yet
saw him captured.

   BOOK III. (*Duodecimo*), CHAPTER III. (*Mealy-mouthed Porpoise*).—The
largest kind of Porpoise; and only found in the Pacific, so far as it is known.
The only English name, by which he has hitherto been designated, is that
of the fishers—Right-Whale Porpoise, from the circumstance that he is
chiefly found in the vicinity of that Folio. In shape, he differs in some degree
from the Huzza Porpoise, being of a less rotund and jolly girth; indeed, he
is of quite a neat and gentlemanlike figure. He has no fins on his back (most
other porpoises have), he has a lovely tail, and sentimental Indian eyes of a
hazel hue. But his mealy-mouth spoils all. Though his entire back down to
his side fins is of a deep sable, yet a boundary line, distinct as the mark in a
ship's hull, called the "bright waist," that line streaks him from stem to
stern, with two separate colors, black above and white below. The white
comprises part of his head, and the whole of his mouth, which makes him
look as if he had just escaped from a felonious visit to a meal-bag. A most
mean and mealy aspect! His oil is much like that of the common porpoise.

                *         *         *         *         *
   Beyond the DUODECIMO, this system does not proceed, inasmuch as the
Porpoise is the smallest of the whales. Above, you have all the Leviathans
of note. But there are a rabble of uncertain, fugitive, half-fabulous whales,
which, as an American whaleman, I know by reputation, but not personally.
I shall enumerate them by their forecastle appellations; for possibly such a
list may be valuable to future investigators, who may complete what I have
here but begun. If any of the following whales, shall hereafter be caught
and marked, then he can readily be incorporated into this System, according to his Folio, Octavo, or Duodecimo magnitude:—The Bottle-Nose
Whale; the Junk Whale; the Pudding-Headed Whale; the Cape Whale;

the Leading Whale; the Cannon Whale; the Scragg Whale; the Coppered
Whale; the Elephant Whale; the Iceberg Whale; the Quog Whale; the
Blue Whale; &c. From Icelandic, Dutch, and old English authorities, there
might be quoted other lists of uncertain whales, blessed with all manner of
uncouth names. But I omit them as altogether obsolete; and can hardly
help suspecting them for mere sounds, full of Leviathanism, but signifying
nothing.

   Finally: It was stated at the outset, that this system would not be here,
and at once, perfected. You cannot but plainly see that I have kept my word.
But I now leave my cetological System standing thus unfinished, even as
the great Cathedral of Cologne was left, with the crane still standing upon
the top of the uncompleted tower. For small erections may be finished by
their first architects; grand ones, true ones, ever leave the copestone to
posterity. God keep me from ever completing anything. This whole book
is but a draught—nay, but the draught of a draught. Oh, Time, Strength,
Cash, and Patience!

# Chapter 33

*The Specksynder*

ONCERNING THE OFFICERS of the whale-craft, this seems as good a place as any to set down a little domestic peculiarity on shipboard, arising from the existence of the harpooneer class of officers, a class unknown of course in any other marine than the whale-fleet.

The large importance attached to the harpooneer's vocation is evinced by the fact, that originally in the old Dutch Fishery, two centuries and more ago, the command of a whale ship was not wholly lodged in the person now called the captain, but was divided between him and an officer called the Specksynder. Literally this word means Fat-Cutter; usage, however, in time made it equivalent to Chief Harpooneer. In those days, the captain's authority was restricted to the navigation and general management of the vessel: while over the whale-hunting department and all its concerns, the Specksynder or Chief Harpooneer reigned supreme. In the British Greenland Fishery, under the corrupted title of Specksioneer, this old Dutch official is still retained, but his former dignity is sadly abridged. At present he ranks simply as senior Harpooneer; and as such, is but one of the captain's more inferior subalterns. Nevertheless, as upon the good conduct of the harpooneers the success of a whaling voyage largely depends, and since in the American Fishery he is not only an important officer in the boat, but under certain circumstances (night watches on a whaling ground) the command of the ship's deck is also his; therefore the grand political maxim of the sea demands, that he should nominally live apart from the men before the mast, and be in some way distinguished as their professional superior; though always, by them, familiarly regarded as their social equal.

Now, the grand distinction drawn between officer and man at sea, is this—the first lives aft, the last forward. Hence, in whale-ships and merchantmen alike, the mates have their quarters with the captain; and so, too, in most of the American whalers the harpooneers are lodged in the after part of the ship. That is to say, they take their meals in the captain's cabin, and sleep in a place indirectly communicating with it.

Though the long period of a Southern whaling voyage (by far the longest of all voyages now or ever made by man), the peculiar perils of it, and the community of interest prevailing among a company, all of whom, high or low, depend for their profits, not upon fixed wages, but upon their common luck, together with their common vigilance, intrepidity, and hard work; though all these things do in some cases tend to beget a less rigorous discipline than in merchantmen generally; yet, never mind how much like an old Mesopotamian family these whalemen may, in some primitive instances, live together; for all that, the punctilious externals, at least, of the quarter-deck are seldom materially relaxed, and in no instance done away. Indeed, many are the Nantucket ships in which you will see the skipper parading his quarter-deck with an elated grandeur not surpassed in any military navy; nay, extorting almost as much outward homage as if he wore the imperial purple, and not the shabbiest of pilot-cloth.

And though of all men the moody captain of the Pequod was the least given to that sort of shallowest assumption; and though the only homage he ever exacted, was implicit, instantaneous obedience; though he required no man to remove the shoes from his feet ere stepping upon the quarter-deck; and though there were times when, owing to peculiar circumstances connected with events hereafter to be detailed, he addressed them in unusual terms, whether of condescension or *in terrorem,* or otherwise; yet even Captain Ahab was by no means unobservant of the paramount forms and usages of the sea.

Nor, perhaps, will it fail to be eventually perceived, that behind those forms and usages, as it were, he sometimes masked himself; incidentally making use of them for other and more private ends than they were legitimately intended to subserve. That certain sultanism of his brain, which had otherwise in a good degree remained unmanifested; through those forms that same sultanism became incarnate in an irresistible dictatorship. For be a man's intellectual superiority what it will, it can never assume the practical, available supremacy over other men, without the aid of some sort of external arts and entrenchments, always, in themselves, more or less paltry and base. This it is, that for ever keeps God's true princes of the Empire from the world's hustings; and leaves the highest honors that this air can give, to those men who become famous more through their infinite inferiority to the choice hidden handful of the Divine Inert, than through their undoubted superiority over the dead level of the mass. Such large virtue lurks in these small things when extreme political superstitions invest them, that in some royal instances even to idiot imbecility they have imparted potency. But when, as in the case of Nicholas the Czar, the ringed crown of geographical empire encircles an imperial brain; then, the plebeian herds crouch abased before the tremendous centralization. Nor, will the tragic dramatist who would depict mortal indomitableness in its fullest sweep and direst swing, ever forget a hint, incidentally so important in his art, as the one now alluded to.

But Ahab, my Captain, still moves before me in all his Nantucket grimness and shagginess; and in this episode touching Emperors and Kings, I must not conceal that I have only to do with a poor old whale-hunter like him; and, therefore, all outward majestical trappings and housings are denied me. Oh, Ahab! what shall be grand in thee, it must needs be plucked at from the skies, and dived for in the deep, and featured in the unbodied air!

# Chapter 34

### *The Cabin-Table*

I T IS NOON; and Dough-Boy, the steward, thrusting his pale loaf-of-bread face from the cabin-scuttle, announces dinner to his lord and master; who, sitting in the lee quarter-boat, has just been taking an observation of the sun; and is now mutely reckoning the latitude on the smooth, medallion-shaped tablet, reserved for that daily purpose on the upper part of his ivory leg. From his complete inattention to the tidings, you would think that moody Ahab had not heard his menial. But presently, catching hold of the mizen shrouds, he swings himself to the deck, and in an even, unexhilarated voice, saying, "Dinner, Mr. Starbuck," disappears into the cabin.

When the last echo of his sultan's step has died away, and Starbuck, the first Emir, has every reason to suppose that he is seated, then Starbuck rouses from his quietude, takes a few turns along the planks, and, after a grave peep into the binnacle, says, with some touch of pleasantness, "Dinner, Mr. Stubb," and descends the scuttle. The second Emir lounges about the rigging awhile, and then slightly shaking the main brace, to see whether it be all right with that important rope, he likewise takes up the old burden, and with a rapid "Dinner, Mr. Flask," follows after his predecessors.

But the third Emir, now seeing himself all alone on the quarter-deck, seems to feel relieved from some curious restraint; for, tipping all sorts of knowing winks in all sorts of directions, and kicking off his shoes, he strikes into a sharp but noiseless squall of a hornpipe right over the Grand Turk's head; and then, by a dexterous sleight, pitching his cap up into the mizentop for a shelf, he goes down rollicking, so far at least as he remains visible from the deck, reversing all other processions, by bringing up the rear with music. But ere stepping into the cabin doorway below, he pauses, ships a new face altogether, and, then, independent, hilarious little Flask enters King Ahab's presence, in the character of Abjectus, or the Slave.

It is not the least among the strange things bred by the intense artificialness of sea-usages, that while in the open air of the deck some officers will, upon provocation, bear themselves boldly and defyingly enough towards their commander; yet, ten to one, let those very officers the next moment go down to their customary dinner in that same commander's cabin, and straightway their inoffensive, not to say deprecatory and humble air towards him, as he sits at the head of the table; this is marvellous, sometimes most comical. Wherefore this difference? A problem? Perhaps not. To have been Belshazzar, King of Babylon; and to have been Belshazzar, not haughtily but courteously, therein certainly must have been some touch of mundane grandeur. But he who in the rightly regal and intelligent spirit presides over his own private dinner-table of invited guests, that man's unchallenged power and dominion of individual influence for the time; that man's royalty of state transcends Belshazzar's, for Belshazzar was not the greatest. Who has but once dined his friends, has tasted what it is to be Cæsar. It is a witchery of social czarship which there is no withstanding. Now, if to this consideration you superadd the official supremacy of a shipmaster, then, by inference, you will derive the cause of that peculiarity of sea-life just mentioned.

Over his ivory-inlaid table, Ahab presided like a mute, maned sea-lion on the white coral beach, surrounded by his war-like but still deferential cubs. In his own proper turn, each officer waited to be served. They were as little children before Ahab; and yet, in Ahab, there seemed not to lurk the smallest social arrogance. With one mind, their intent eyes all fastened upon the old man's knife, as he carved the chief dish before him. I do not suppose that for the world they would have profaned that moment with the slightest observation, even upon so neutral a topic as the weather. No! And when reaching out his knife and fork, between which the slice of beef was locked, Ahab thereby motioned Starbuck's plate towards him, the mate received his meat as though receiving alms; and cut it tenderly; and a little started if, perchance, the knife grazed against the plate; and chewed it noiselessly; and swallowed it, not without circumspection. For, like the Coronation banquet at Frankfort, where the German Emperor profoundly dines with the seven Imperial Electors, so these cabin meals were somehow solemn meals, eaten in awful silence; and yet at table old Ahab forbade not conversation; only he himself was dumb. What a relief it was to choking Stubb, when a rat made a sudden racket in the hold below. And poor little Flask, he was the youngest son, and little boy of this weary family party. His were the shinbones of the saline beef; his would have been the drumsticks. For Flask to have presumed to help himself, this must have seemed to him tantamount to larceny in the first degree. Had he helped himself at that table, doubtless, never more would he have been able to hold his head up in this honest world; nevertheless, strange to say, Ahab never forbade him. And had Flask helped himself, the chances were Ahab had never so much as noticed it. Least of all, did Flask presume to help himself to butter. Whether he thought the owners of the ship denied it to him, on account of its clotting his clear, sunny complexion; or whether he deemed that, on so long a voyage in such marketless waters, butter was at a premium, and therefore was not for him, a subaltern; however it was, Flask, alas! was a butterless man!

Another thing. Flask was the last person down at the dinner, and Flask is the first man up. Consider! For hereby Flask's dinner was badly jammed in point of time. Starbuck and Stubb both had the start of him; and yet they also have the privilege of lounging in the rear. If Stubb even, who is but a peg higher than Flask, happens to have but a small appetite, and soon shows symptoms of concluding his repast, then Flask must bestir himself, he will not get more than three mouthfuls that day; for it is against holy usage for Stubb to precede Flask to the deck. Therefore it was that Flask once admitted in private, that ever since he had arisen to the dignity of an officer, from that moment he had never known what it was to be otherwise than hungry, more or less. For what he ate did not so much relieve his hunger, as keep it immortal in him. Peace and satisfaction, thought Flask, have for ever departed from my stomach. I am an officer; but, how I wish I could fist a bit of old-fashioned beef in the forecastle, as I used to when I was before the mast. There's the fruits of promotion now; there's the vanity of glory: there's the insanity of life! Besides, if it were so that any mere sailor of the Pequod had a grudge against Flask in Flask's official capacity, all that sailor had to do, in order to obtain ample vengeance, was to go aft at dinnertime, and get a peep at Flask through the cabin sky-light, sitting silly and dumfoundered before awful Ahab.

Now, Ahab and his three mates formed what may be called the first table in the Pequod's cabin. After their departure, taking place in inverted order to their arrival, the canvas cloth was cleared, or rather was restored to some hurried order by the pallid steward. And then the three harpooneers were bidden to the feast, they being its residuary legatees. They made a sort of temporary servants' hall of the high and mighty cabin.

In strange contrast to the hardly tolerable constraint and nameless invisible domineerings of the captain's table, was the entire care-free license and ease, the almost frantic democracy of those inferior fellows the harpooneers. While their masters, the mates, seemed afraid of the sound of the hinges of their own jaws, the harpooneers chewed their food with such a relish that there was a report to it. They dined like lords; they filled their bellies like Indian ships all day loading with spices. Such portentous appetites had Queequeg and Tashtego, that to fill out the vacancies made by the previous repast, often the pale Dough-Boy was fain to bring on a great baron of salt-junk, seemingly quarried out of the solid ox. And if he were not lively about it, if he did not go with a nimble hop-skip-and-jump, then Tashtego had an ungentlemanly way of accelerating him by darting a fork at his back, harpoon-wise. And once Daggoo, seized with a sudden humor, assisted Dough-Boy's memory by snatching him up bodily, and thrusting his head into a great empty wooden trencher, while Tashtego, knife in hand, began laying out the circle preliminary to scalping him. He was naturally a very nervous, shuddering sort of little fellow, this bread-faced steward; the progeny of a bankrupt baker and a hospital nurse. And what with the standing spectacle of the black terrific Ahab, and the periodical tumultuous visitations of these three savages, Dough-Boy's whole life was one continual lip-quiver. Commonly, after seeing the harpooneers furnished with all things they demanded, he would escape from their clutches into his little pantry adjoining, and fearfully peep out at them through the blinds of its door, till all was over.

It was a sight to see Queequeg seated over against Tashtego, opposing his filed teeth to the Indian's: crosswise to them, Daggoo seated on the floor, for a bench would have brought his hearse-plumed head to the low carlines; at every motion of his colossal limbs, making the low cabin framework to shake, as when an African elephant goes passenger in a ship. But for all this, the great negro was wonderfully abstemious, not to say dainty. It seemed hardly possible that by such comparatively small mouthfuls he could keep up the vitality diffused through so broad, baronial, and superb a person. But, doubtless, this noble savage fed strong and drank deep of the abounding element of air; and through his dilated nostrils snuffed in the sublime life of the worlds. Not by beef or by bread, are giants made or nourished. But Queequeg, he had a mortal, barbaric smack of the lip in eating—an ugly sound enough—so much so, that the trembling Dough-Boy almost looked to see whether any marks of teeth lurked in his own lean arms. And when he would hear Tashtego singing out for him to produce himself, that his bones might be picked, the simple-witted Steward all but shattered the crockery hanging round him in the pantry, by his sudden fits of the palsy. Nor did the whetstones which the harpooneers carried in their pockets, for their lances and other weapons; and with which whetstones, at dinner, they would ostentatiously sharpen their knives; that grating sound did not at all tend to tranquillize poor Dough-Boy. How could he forget that in his Island days, Queequeg, for one, must certainly have been guilty of some murderous, convivial indiscretions. Alas! Dough-Boy! hard fares the white waiter who waits upon cannibals. Not a napkin should he carry on his arm, but a buckler. In good time, though, to his great delight, the three salt-sea warriors would rise and depart; to his credulous, fable-mongering ears, all their martial bones jingling in them at every step, like Moorish scimetars in scabbards.

But, though these barbarians dined in the cabin, and nominally lived there; still, being anything but sedentary in their habits, they were scarcely ever in it except at meal-times, and just before sleeping-time, when they passed through it to their own peculiar quarters.

In this one matter, Ahab seemed no exception to most American whale captains, who, as a set, rather incline to the opinion that by rights the ship's cabin belongs to them; and that it is by courtesy alone that anybody else is, at any time, permitted there. So that, in real truth, the mates and harpooneers of the Pequod might more properly be said to have lived out of the cabin than in it. For when they did enter it, it was something as a street-door enters a house; turning inwards for a moment, only to be turned out the next; and, as a permanent thing, residing in the open air. Nor did they lose much hereby; in the cabin was no companionship; socially, Ahab was inaccessible. Though nominally included in the census of Christendom, he was still an alien to it. He lived in the world, as the last of the Grisly Bears lived in settled Missouri. And as when Spring and Summer had departed, that wild Logan of the woods, burying himself in the hollow of a tree, lived out the winter there, sucking his own paws; so, in his inclement, howling old age, Ahab's soul, shut up in the caved trunk of his body, there fed upon the sullen paws of its gloom!

# Chapter 35

## The Mast-Head

I T was during the more pleasant weather, that in due rotation with the
other seamen my first mast-head came round.

In most American whalemen the mast-heads are manned almost
simultaneously with the vessel's leaving her port; even though she may have
fifteen thousand miles, and more, to sail ere reaching her proper cruising
ground. And if, after a three, four, or five years' voyage she is drawing nigh
home with anything empty in her—say, an empty vial even—then, her
mast-heads are kept manned to the last; and not till her skysail-poles sail in
among the spires of the port, does she altogether relinquish the hope of
capturing one whale more.

Now, as the business of standing mast-heads, ashore or afloat, is a very
ancient and interesting one, let us in some measure expatiate here. I take it,
that the earliest standers of mast-heads were the old Egyptians; because, in
all my researches, I find none prior to them. For though their progenitors,
the builders of Babel, must doubtless, by their tower, have intended to rear
the loftiest mast-head in all Asia, or Africa either; yet (ere the final truck was
put to it) as that great stone mast of theirs may be said to have gone by the
board, in the dread gale of God's wrath; therefore, we cannot give these
Babel builders priority over the Egyptians. And that the Egyptians were a

nation of mast-head standers, is an assertion based upon the general belief
among archæologists, that the first pyramids were founded for astronomical
purposes: a theory singularly supported by the peculiar stair-like formation
of all four sides of those edifices; whereby, with prodigious long upliftings
of their legs, those old astronomers were wont to mount to the apex, and
sing out for new stars; even as the look-outs of a modern ship sing out for a
sail, or a whale just bearing in sight. In Saint Stylites, the famous Christian
hermit of old times, who built him a lofty stone pillar in the desert and
spent the whole latter portion of his life on its summit, hoisting his food
from the ground with a tackle; in him we have a remarkable instance of a
dauntless stander-of-mast-heads; who was not to be driven from his place
by fogs or frosts, rain, hail, or sleet; but valiantly facing everything out to
the last, literally died at his post. Of modern standers-of-mast-heads we
have but a lifeless set; mere stone, iron, and bronze men; who, though well
capable of facing out a stiff gale, are still entirely incompetent to the business
of singing out upon discovering any strange sight. There is Napoleon;
who, upon the top of the column of Vendome, stands with arms folded,
some one hundred and fifty feet in the air; careless, now, who rules the
decks below; whether Louis Philippe, Louis Blanc, or Louis the Devil.
Great Washington, too, stands high aloft on his towering main-mast in
Baltimore, and like one of Hercules' pillars, his column marks that point of
human grandeur beyond which few mortals will go. Admiral Nelson,
also, on a capstan of gun-metal, stands his mast-head in Trafalgar Square;
and even when most obscured by that London smoke, token is yet given
that a hidden hero is there; for where there is smoke, must be fire. But
neither great Washington, nor Napoleon, nor Nelson, will answer a single
hail from below, however madly invoked to befriend by their counsels the
distracted decks upon which they gaze; however, it may be surmised, that
their spirits penetrate through the thick haze of the future, and descry what
shoals and what rocks must be shunned.

It may seem unwarrantable to couple in any respect the mast-head
standers of the land with those of the sea; but that in truth it is not so, is
plainly evinced by an item for which Obed Macy, the sole historian of
Nantucket, stands accountable. The worthy Obed tells us, that in the early
times of the whale fishery, ere ships were regularly launched in pursuit of
the game, the people of that island erected lofty spars along the sea-coast, to
which the look-outs ascended by means of nailed cleats, something as
fowls go upstairs in a hen-house. A few years ago this same plan was adopted
by the Bay whalemen of New Zealand, who, upon descrying the game, gave

notice to the ready-manned boats nigh the beach. But this custom has now become obsolete; turn we then to the one proper mast-head, that of a whale-ship at sea. The three mast-heads are kept manned from sun-rise to sun-set; the seamen taking their regular turns (as at the helm), and relieving each other every two hours. In the serene weather of the tropics it is exceedingly pleasant—the mast-head; nay, to a dreamy meditative man it is delightful. There you stand, a hundred feet above the silent decks, striding along the deep, as if the masts were gigantic stilts, while beneath you and between your legs, as it were, swim the hugest monsters of the sea, even as ships once sailed between the boots of the famous Colossus at old Rhodes. There you stand, lost in the infinite series of the sea, with nothing ruffled but the waves. The tranced ship indolently rolls; the drowsy trade winds blow; everything resolves you into languor. For the most part, in this tropic whaling life, a sublime unevent-fulness invests you; you hear no news; read no gazettes; extras with startling accounts of commonplaces never delude you into unneces-sary excitements; you hear of no domestic afflictions; bankrupt secur-ities; fall of stocks; are never troubled with the thought of what you shall have for dinner—for all your meals for three years and more are snugly stowed in casks, and your bill of fare is immutable.

In one of those southern whalemen, on a long three or four years' voyage, as often happens, the sum of the various hours you spend at the mast-head would amount to several entire months. And it is much to be deplored that the place to which you devote so considerable a portion of the whole term of your natural life, should be so sadly destitute of any-thing approaching to a cosy inhabitiveness, or adapted to breed a comfortable localness of feeling, such as pertains to a bed, a hammock, a hearse, a sentry box, a pulpit, a coach, or any other of those small and snug contrivances in which men temporarily isolate themselves. Your most usual point of perch is the head of the t' gallant-mast, where you stand upon two thin parallel sticks (almost peculiar to whalemen) called the t' gallant cross-trees. Here, tossed about by the sea, the beginner feels about as cosy as he would stand-ing on a bull's horns. To be sure, in coolish weather you may carry your house aloft with you, in the shape of a watch-coat; but properly speaking the thickest watch-coat is no more of a house than the unclad body; for as the soul is glued inside of its fleshly tabernacle, and cannot freely move about in it, nor even move out of it, without running great risk of perishing (like an ignorant pilgrim crossing the snowy Alps in winter); so a watch-coat is not so much of a house as it is a mere envelope, or additional skin encasing you. You cannot put a shelf or chest of drawers in your body, and no more can you make a convenient closet of your watch-coat.

Concerning all this, it is much to be deplored that the mast-heads of a southern whale ship are unprovided with those enviable little tents or pulpits, called *crow's-nests*, in which the look-outs of a Greenland whaler are protected from the inclement weather of the frozen seas. In the fire-side narrative of Captain Sleet, entitled "A Voyage among the Icebergs, in quest of the Greenland Whale, and incidentally for the re-discovery of the Lost Icelandic Colonies of Old Greenland;" in this admirable volume, all standers of mast-heads are furnished with a charmingly circumstantial account of the then recently invented *crow's-nest* of the Glacier, which was the name of Captain Sleet's good craft. He called it the *Sleet's crow's-nest*, in honor of himself; he being the original inventor and patentee, and free from all ridiculous false delicacy, and holding that if we call our own children after our own names (we fathers being the original inventors and patentees), so likewise should we denominate after ourselves any other apparatus we may beget. In shape, the Sleet's crow's-nest is something like a large tierce or pipe; it is open above, however, where it is furnished with a movable side-screen to keep to windward of your head in a hard gale. Being fixed on the summit of the mast, you ascend into it through a little trap-hatch in the bottom. On the after side, or side next the stern of the ship, is a comfortable seat, with a locker underneath for umbrellas, comforters, and coats. In front is a leather rack, in which to keep your speaking trumpet, pipe, telescope, and other nautical conveniences. When Captain Sleet in person stood his mast-head in this crow's nest of his, he tells us that he always had a rifle with him (also fixed in the rack), together with a powder flask and shot, for the purpose of popping off the stray narwhales, or vagrant sea unicorns infesting those waters; for you cannot successfully shoot at them from the deck owing to the resistance of the water, but to shoot down upon them is a very different thing. Now, it was plainly a labor of love for Captain Sleet to describe, as he does, all the little detailed conveniences of his crow's-nest; but though he so enlarges upon many of these, and though he treats us to a very scientific account of his experiments in this crow's-nest, with a small compass he kept there for the purpose of counter-acting the errors resulting from what is called the "local attraction" of all binnacle magnets; an error ascribable to the horizontal vicinity of the iron in the ship's planks, and in the Glacier's case, perhaps, to there having been so many broken-down blacksmiths among her crew; I say, that though the Captain is very discreet and scientific here, yet, for all his learned "binnacle deviations,"

"azimuth compass observations," and "approximate errors," he knows
very well, Captain Sleet, that he was not so much immersed in those profound magnetic meditations, as to fail being attracted occasionally towards
that well replenished little case-bottle, so nicely tucked in on one side of his
crow's nest, within easy reach of his hand. Though, upon the whole, I
greatly admire and even love the brave, the honest, and learned Captain;
yet I take it very ill of him that he should so utterly ignore that case-bottle,
seeing what a faithful friend and comforter it must have been, while with
mittened fingers and hooded head he was studying the mathematics aloft
there in that bird's nest within three or four perches of the pole.

But if we Southern whale-fishers are not so snugly housed aloft as
Captain Sleet and his Greenland-men were; yet that disadvantage is
greatly counterbalanced by the widely contrasting serenity of those seductive seas in which we Southern-fishers mostly float. For one, I used to
lounge up the rigging very leisurely, resting in the top to have a chat with
Queequeg, or any one else off duty whom I might find there; then ascending a little way further, and throwing a lazy leg over the top-sail yard, take
a preliminary view of the watery pastures, and so at last mount to my
ultimate destination.

Let me make a clean breast of it here, and frankly admit that I kept but
sorry guard. With the problem of the universe revolving in me, how could
I—being left completely to myself at such a thought-engendering altitude,
—how could I but lightly hold my obligations to observe all whale-ships'
standing orders, "Keep your weather eye open, and sing out every time."

And let me in this place movingly admonish you, ye ship-owners of
Nantucket! Beware of enlisting in your vigilant fisheries any lad with lean
brow and hollow eye; given to unseasonable meditativeness; and who
offers to ship with the Phædon instead of Bowditch in his head. Beware of
such an one, I say: your whales must be seen before they can be killed; and
this sunken-eyed young Platonist will tow you ten wakes round the world,
and never make you one pint of sperm the richer. Nor are these monitions
at all unneeded. For nowadays, the whale-fishery furnishes an asylum for
many romantic, melancholy, and absent-minded young men, disgusted
with the carking cares of earth, and seeking sentiment in tar and blubber.
Childe Harold not unfrequently perches himself upon the mast-head of
some luckless disappointed whale-ship, and in moody phrase ejaculates:—

"Roll on, thou deep and dark blue ocean, roll!
Ten thousand blubber-hunters sweep over thee in vain."

Very often do the captains of such ships take those absent-minded young philosophers to task, upbraiding them with not feeling sufficient "interest" in the voyage; half-hinting that they are so hopelessly lost to all honorable ambition, as that in their secret souls they would rather not see whales than otherwise. But all in vain; those young Platonists have a notion that their vision is imperfect; they are short-sighted; what use, then, to strain the visual nerve? They have left their opera-glasses at home.

"Why, thou monkey," said a harpooneer to one of these lads, "we've been cruising now hard upon three years, and thou hast not raised a whale yet. Whales are scarce as hen's teeth whenever thou art up here." Perhaps they were; or perhaps there might have been shoals of them in the far horizon; but lulled into such an opium-like listlessness of vacant, unconscious reverie is this absent-minded youth by the blending cadence of waves with thoughts, that at last he loses his identity; takes the mystic ocean at his feet for the visible image of that deep, blue, bottomless soul, pervading mankind and nature; and every strange, half-seen, gliding, beautiful thing that eludes him; every dimly-discovered, uprising fin of some undiscernible form, seems to him the embodiment of those elusive thoughts that only people the soul by continually flitting through it. In this enchanted mood, thy spirit ebbs away to whence it came; becomes diffused through time and space; like Wickliff's sprinkled Pantheistic ashes, forming at last a part of every shore the round globe over.

There is no life in thee, now, except that rocking life imparted by a gently rolling ship; by her, borrowed from the sea; by the sea, from the inscrutable tides of God. But while this sleep, this dream is on ye, move your foot or hand an inch, slip your hold at all; and your identity comes back in horror. Over Descartian vortices you hover. And perhaps, at mid-day, in the fairest weather, with one half-throttled shriek you drop through that transparent air into the summer sea, no more to rise for ever. Heed it well, ye Pantheists!

# Chapter 36

## The Quarter-Deck

*(Enter Ahab: Then, all.)*

IT WAS NOT a great while after the affair of the pipe, that one morning shortly after breakfast, Ahab, as was his wont, ascended the cabin-gangway to the deck. There most sea-captains usually walk at that hour, as country gentlemen, after the same meal, take a few turns in the garden.

Soon his steady, ivory stride was heard, as to and fro he paced his old rounds, upon planks so familiar to his tread, that they were all over dented, like geological stones, with the peculiar mark of his walk. Did you fixedly gaze, too, upon that ribbed and dented brow; there also, you would see still stranger foot-prints—the foot-prints of his one unsleeping, ever-pacing thought.

But on the occasion in question, those dents looked deeper, even as his nervous step that morning left a deeper mark. And, so full of his thought was Ahab, that at every uniform turn that he made, now at the main-mast and now at the binnacle, you could almost see that thought turn in him as he turned, and pace in him as he paced; so completely possessing him, indeed, that it all but seemed the inward mould of every outer movement.

"D'ye mark him, Flask?" whispered Stubb; "the chick that's in him pecks the shell. T'will soon be out."

The hours wore on;—Ahab now shut up within his cabin; anon, pacing the deck, with the same intense bigotry of purpose in his aspect.

It drew near the close of day. Suddenly he came to a halt by the bulwarks, and inserting his bone leg into the auger-hole there, and with one hand grasping a shroud, he ordered Starbuck to send everybody aft.

"Sir!" said the mate, astonished at an order seldom or never given on ship-board except in some extraordinary case.

"Send everybody aft," repeated Ahab. "Mast-heads, there! come down!"

When the entire ship's company were assembled, and with curious and not wholly unapprehensive faces, were eyeing him, for he looked not unlike the weather horizon when a storm is coming up, Ahab, after rapidly glancing over the bulwarks, and then darting his eyes among the crew, started from his stand-point; and as though not a soul were nigh him resumed his heavy turns upon the deck. With bent head and half-slouched hat he continued to pace, unmindful of the wondering whispering among the men; till Stubb cautiously whispered to Flask, that Ahab must have summoned them there for the purpose of witnessing a pedestrian feat. But this did not last long. Vehemently pausing, he cried:—

"What do ye do when ye see a whale, men?"

"Sing out for him!" was the impulsive rejoinder from a score of clubbed voices.

"Good!" cried Ahab, with a wild approval in his tones; observing the hearty animation into which his unexpected question had so magnetically thrown them.

"And what do ye next, men?"

"Lower away, and after him!"

"And what tune is it ye pull to, men?"

"A dead whale or a stove boat!"

More and more strangely and fiercely glad and approving, grew the countenance of the old man at every shout; while the mariners began to gaze curiously at each other, as if marvelling how it was that they themselves became so excited at such seemingly purposeless questions.

But, they were all eagerness again, as Ahab, now half-revolving in his pivot-hole, with one hand reaching high up a shroud, and tightly, almost convulsively grasping it, addressed them thus:—

"All ye mast-headers have before now heard me give orders about a white whale. Look ye! d'ye see this Spanish ounce of gold?"—holding up a broad bright coin to the sun—"it is a sixteen dollar piece, men,—a doubloon. D'ye see it? Mr. Starbuck, hand me yon top-maul."

While the mate was getting the hammer, Ahab, without speaking, was slowly rubbing the gold piece against the skirts of his jacket, as if to heighten its lustre, and without using any words was meanwhile lowly humming to himself, producing a sound so strangely muffled and inarticulate that it seemed the mechanical humming of the wheels of his vitality in him.

Receiving the top-maul from Starbuck, he advanced towards the main-mast with the hammer uplifted in one hand, exhibiting the gold with the other, and with a high raised voice exclaiming: "Whosoever of ye raises me a white-headed whale with a wrinkled brow and a crooked jaw; whosoever of ye raises me that white-headed whale, with three holes punctured in his starboard fluke—look ye, whosoever of ye raises me that same white whale, he shall have this gold ounce, my boys!"

"Huzza! huzza!" cried the seamen, as with swinging tarpaulins they hailed the act of nailing the gold to the mast.

"It's a white whale, I say," resumed Ahab, as he threw down the top-maul; "a white whale. Skin your eyes for him, men; look sharp for white water; if ye see but a bubble, sing out."

All this while Tashtego, Daggoo, and Queequeg had looked on with even more intense interest and surprise than the rest, and at the mention of the wrinkled brow and crooked jaw they had started as if each was separately touched by some specific recollection.

"Captain Ahab," said Tashtego, "that white whale must be the same that some call Moby Dick."

"Moby Dick?" shouted Ahab. "Do ye know the white whale then, Tash?"

"Does he fan-tail a little curious, sir, before he goes down?" said the Gay-Header deliberately.

"And has he a curious spout, too," said Daggoo, "very bushy, even for a parmacetty, and mighty quick, Captain Ahab?"

"And he have one, two, tree—oh! good many iron in him hide, too, Captain," cried Queequeg disjointedly, "all twiske-tee be-twisk, like him —him—" faltering hard for a word, and screwing his hand round and round as though uncorking a bottle—"like him—him—"

"Corkscrew!" cried Ahab, "aye, Queequeg, the harpoons lie all twisted and wrenched in him; aye, Daggoo, his spout is a big one, like a whole shock of wheat, and white as a pile of our Nantucket wool after the great annual sheep-shearing; aye, Tashtego, and he fan-tails like a split jib in a squall. Death and devils! men, it is Moby Dick ye have seen—Moby Dick—Moby Dick!"

"Captain Ahab," said Starbuck, who, with Stubb and Flask, had thus far been eyeing his superior with increasing surprise, but at last seemed struck with a thought which somewhat explained all the wonder. "Captain Ahab, I have heard of Moby Dick—but it was not Moby Dick that took off thy leg?"

"Who told thee that?" cried Ahab; then pausing, "Aye, Starbuck; aye, my hearties all round; it was Moby Dick that dismasted me; Moby Dick that brought me to this dead stump I stand on now. Aye, aye," he shouted with a terrific, loud, animal sob, like that of a heart-stricken moose; "Aye, aye! it was that accursed white whale that razeed me; made a poor pegging lubber of me for ever and a day!" Then tossing both arms, with measureless imprecations he shouted out: "Aye, aye! and I'll chase him round Good Hope, and round the Horn, and round the Norway Maelstrom, and round perdition's flames before I give him up. And this is what ye have shipped for, men! to chase that white whale on both sides of land, and over all sides of earth, till he spouts black blood and rolls fin out. What say ye, men, will ye splice hands on it, now? I think ye do look brave."

"Aye, aye!" shouted the harpooneers and seamen, running closer to the excited old man: "A sharp eye for the White Whale; a sharp lance for Moby Dick!"

"God bless ye," he seemed to half sob and half shout. "God bless ye, men. Steward! go draw the great measure of grog. But what's this long face about, Mr. Starbuck; wilt thou not chase the white whale? art not game for Moby Dick?"

"I am game for his crooked jaw, and for the jaws of Death too, Captain Ahab, if it fairly comes in the way of the business we follow; but I came here to hunt whales, not my commander's vengeance. How many barrels will thy vengeance yield thee even if thou gettest it, Captain Ahab? it will not fetch thee much in our Nantucket market."

"Nantucket market! Hoot! But come closer, Starbuck; thou requirest a little lower layer. If money's to be the measurer, man, and the accountants have computed their great counting-house the globe, by girdling it with guineas, one to every three parts of an inch; then, let me tell thee, that my vengeance will fetch a great premium *here!*"

"He smites his chest," whispered Stubb, "what's that for? methinks it rings most vast, but hollow."

"Vengeance on a dumb brute!" cried Starbuck, "that simply smote thee from blindest instinct! Madness! To be enraged with a dumb thing, Captain Ahab, seems blasphemous."

"Hark ye yet again,—the little lower layer. All visible objects, man, are but as pasteboard masks. But in each event—in the living act, the undoubted deed—there, some unknown but still reasoning thing puts forth the mouldings of its features from behind the unreasoning mask. If man will strike, strike through the mask! How can the prisoner reach outside except by thrusting through the wall? To me, the white whale is that wall, shoved near to me. Sometimes I think there's naught beyond. But 'tis enough. He tasks me; he heaps me; I see in him outrageous strength, with an inscrutable malice sinewing it. That inscrutable thing is chiefly what I hate; and be the white whale agent, or be the white whale principal, I will wreak that hate upon him. Talk not to me of blasphemy, man; I'd strike the sun if it insulted me. For could the sun do that, then could I do the other; since there is ever a sort of fair play herein, jealousy presiding over all creations. But not my master, man, is even that fair play. Who's over me? Truth hath no confines. Take off thine eye! more intolerable than fiends' glarings is a doltish stare! So, so; thou reddenest and palest; my heat has melted thee to anger-glow. But look ye, Starbuck, what is said in heat, that thing unsays itself. There are men from whom warm words are small indignity. I meant not to incense thee. Let it go. Look! see yonder Turkish cheeks of spotted tawn— living, breathing pictures painted by the sun. The Pagan leopards—the unrecking and unworshipping things, that live; and seek, and give no reasons for the torrid life they feel! The crew, man, the crew! Are they not one and all with Ahab, in this matter of the whale? See Stubb! he laughs! See yonder Chilian! he snorts to think of it. Stand up amid the general hurricane, thy one tost sapling cannot, Starbuck! And what is it? Reckon it. 'Tis but to help strike a fin; no wondrous feat for Starbuck. What is it more? From this one poor hunt, then, the best lance out of all Nantucket, surely he will not hang back, when every foremast-hand has clutched a whetstone? Ah! constrainings seize thee; I see! the billow lifts thee! Speak, but speak!—Aye, aye! thy silence, then, *that* voices thee. *(Aside)* Something shot from my dilated nostrils, he has inhaled it in his lungs. Starbuck now is mine; cannot oppose me now, without rebellion."

"God keep me!—keep us all!" murmured Starbuck, lowly.

But in his joy at the enchanted, tacit acquiescence of the mate, Ahab did not hear his foreboding invocation; nor yet the low laugh from the hold; nor yet the presaging vibrations of the winds in the cordage; nor yet the hollow flap of the sails against the masts, as for a moment their hearts sank in. For again Starbuck's downcast eyes lighted up with the stubbornness of life; the subterranean laugh died away; the winds blew on; the sails filled out; the ship heaved and rolled as before. Ah, ye admonitions and warnings! why stay ye not when ye come? But rather are ye predictions than warnings, ye shadows! Yet not so much predictions from without, as verifications of the foregoing things within. For with little external to constrain us, the innermost necessities in our being, these still drive us on.

"The measure! the measure!" cried Ahab.

Receiving the brimming pewter, and turning to the harpooneers, he ordered them to produce their weapons. Then ranging them before him near the capstan, with their harpoons in their hands, while his three mates stood at his side with their lances, and the rest of the ship's company formed a circle round the group; he stood for an instant searchingly eyeing every man of his crew. But those wild eyes met his, as the bloodshot eyes of the prairie wolves meet the eye of their leader, ere he rushes on at their head in the trail of the bison; but, alas! only to fall into the hidden snare of the Indian.

"Drink and pass!" he cried, handing the heavy charged flagon to the nearest seaman. "The crew alone now drink. Round with it, round! Short draughts—long swallows, men; 'tis hot as Satan's hoof. So, so; it goes round excellently. It spiralizes in ye; forks out at the serpent-snapping eye. Well done; almost drained. That way it went, this way it comes. Hand it me—here's a hollow! Men, ye seem the years; so brimming life is gulped and gone. Steward, refill!

"Attend now, my braves. I have mustered ye all round this capstan; and ye mates, flank me with your lances; and ye harpooneers, stand there with your irons; and ye, stout mariners, ring me in, that I may in some sort revive a noble custom of my fisherman fathers before me. O men, you will yet see that——Ha! boy, come back? bad pennies come not sooner. Hand it me. Why, now, this pewter had run brimming again, wert not thou St. Vitus' imp—away, thou ague!

"Advance, ye mates! Cross your lances full before me. Well done! Let me touch the axis." So saying, with extended arm, he grasped the three level, radiating lances at their crossed centre; while so doing, suddenly and nervously twitched them; meanwhile, glancing intently from Starbuck to Stubb; from Stubb to Flask. It seemed as though, by some nameless, interior volition, he would fain have shocked into them the same fiery emotion accumulated within the Leyden jar of his own magnetic life. The three mates quailed before his strong, sustained, and mystic aspect. Stubb and

Flask looked sideways from him; the honest eye of Starbuck fell downright.

"In vain!" cried Ahab; "but, maybe, 'tis well. For did ye three but once take the full-forced shock, then mine own electric thing, *that* had perhaps expired from out me. Perchance, too, it would have dropped ye dead. Perchance ye need it not. Down lances! And now, ye mates, I do appoint ye three cup-bearers to my three pagan kinsmen there—yon three most honorable gentlemen and noblemen, my valiant harpooneers. Disdain the task? What, when the great Pope washes the feet of beggars, using his tiara for ewer? Oh, my sweet cardinals! your own condescension, *that* shall bend ye to it. I do not order ye; ye will it. Cut your seizings and draw the poles, ye harpooneers!"

Silently obeying the order, the three harpooneers now stood with the detached iron part of their harpoons, some three feet long, held, barbs up, before him.

"Stab me not with that keen steel! Cant them; cant them over! know ye not the goblet end? Turn up the socket! So, so; now, ye cup-bearers, advance. The irons! take them; hold them while I fill!" Forthwith, slowly going from one officer to the other, he brimmed the harpoon sockets with the fiery waters from the pewter.

"Now, three to three, ye stand. Commend the murderous chalices! Bestow them, ye who are now made parties to this indissoluble league. Ha! Starbuck! but the deed is done! Yon ratifying sun now waits to sit upon it. Drink, ye harpooneers! drink and swear, ye men that man the deathful whaleboat's bow—Death to Moby Dick! God hunt us all, if we do not hunt Moby Dick to his death!" The long, barbed steel goblets were lifted; and to cries and maledictions against the white whale, the spirits were simultaneously quaffed down with a hiss. Starbuck paled, and turned, and shivered. Once more, and finally, the replenished pewter went the rounds among the frantic crew; when, waving his free hand to them, they all dispersed; and Ahab retired within his cabin.

# Chapter 37

## Sunset

*(The cabin; by the stern windows; Ahab sitting alone, and gazing out.)*

I LEAVE A WHITE AND TURBID WAKE; pale waters, paler cheeks, where'er I sail. The envious billows sidelong swell to whelm my track; let them; but first I pass.

Yonder, by the ever-brimming goblet's rim, the warm waves blush like wine. The gold brow plumbs the blue. The diver sun—slow dived from noon,—goes down; my soul mounts up! she wearies with her endless hill. Is, then, the crown too heavy that I wear? this Iron Crown of Lombardy. Yet is it bright with many a gem; I, the wearer, see not its far flashings; but darkly feel that I wear that, that dazzlingly confounds. 'Tis iron—that I know—not gold. 'Tis split, too—that I feel; the jagged edge galls me so, my brain seems to beat against the solid metal; aye, steel skull, mine; the sort that needs no helmet in the most brain-battering fight!

Dry heat upon my brow? Oh! time was, when as the sunrise nobly spurred me, so the sunset soothed. No more. This lovely light, it lights not me; all loveliness is anguish to me, since I can ne'er enjoy. Gifted with the high perception, I lack the low, enjoying power; damned, most subtly and most malignantly! damned in the midst of Paradise! Good night—good night! *(waving his hand, he moves from the window.)*

'Twas not so hard a task. I thought to find one stubborn, at the least; but my one cogged circle fits into all their various wheels, and they revolve.

Or, if you will, like so many ant-hills of powder, they all stand before me;
and I their match. Oh, hard! that to fire others, the match itself must needs
be wasting! What I've dared, I've willed; and what I've willed, I'll do!
They think me mad—Starbuck does; but I'm demoniac, I am madness
maddened! That wild madness that's only calm to comprehend itself! The
prophecy was that I should be dismembered; and—Aye! I lost this leg. I now
prophesy that I will dismember my dismemberer. Now, then, be the prophet
and the fulfiller one. That's more than ye, ye great gods, ever were. I
laugh and hoot at ye, ye cricket-players, ye pugilists, ye deaf Burkes and
blinded Bendigoes! I will not say as schoolboys do to bullies,—Take some
one of your own size; don't pommel *me!* No, ye've knocked me down,
and I am up again; but *ye* have run and hidden. Come forth from behind
your cotton bags! I have no long gun to reach ye. Come, Ahab's compliments to ye; come and see if ye can swerve me. Swerve me? ye cannot
swerve me, else ye swerve yourselves! man has ye there. Swerve me? The
path to my fixed purpose is laid with iron rails, whereon my soul is grooved
to run. Over unsounded gorges, through the rifled hearts of mountains,
under torrents' beds, unerringly I rush! Naught's an obstacle, naught's an
angle to the iron way!

# Chapter 38

## Dusk

*(By the Mainmast; Starbuck leaning against it.)*

M Y SOUL is more than matched; she's overmanned; and by a madman! Insufferable sting, that sanity should ground arms on such a field! But he drilled deep down, and blasted all my reason out of me! I think I see his impious end; but feel that I must help him to it. Will I, nill I, the ineffable thing has tied me to him; tows me with a cable I have no knife to cut. Horrible old man! Who's over him, he cries;—aye, he would be a democrat to all above; look, how he lords it over all below! Oh! I plainly see my miserable office,—to obey, rebelling; and worse yet, to hate with touch of pity! For in his eyes I read some lurid woe would shrivel me up, had I it. Yet is there hope. Time and tide flow wide. The hated whale has the round watery world to swim in, as the small gold-fish has its glassy globe. His heaven-insulting purpose, God may wedge aside. I would up heart, were it not like lead. But my whole clock's run down; my heart the all-controlling weight, I have no key to lift again.

*(A burst of revelry from the forecastle.)*

Oh, God! to sail with such a heathen crew that have small touch of human mothers in them! Whelped somewhere by the sharkish sea. The white whale is their demogorgon. Hark! the infernal orgies! that revelry is forward! mark the unfaltering silence aft! Methinks it pictures life. Foremost through the sparkling sea shoots on the gay, embattled, bantering bow, but only to drag dark Ahab after it, where he broods within his sternward cabin, builded over the dead water of the wake, and further on, hunted by its wolfish gurglings. The long howl thrills me through! Peace! ye revellers, and set the watch! Oh, life! 'tis in an hour like this, with soul beat down and held to knowledge,—as wild, untutored things are forced to feed—Oh, life! 'tis now that I do feel the latent horror in thee! but 'tis not me! that horror's out of me! and with the soft feeling of the human in me, yet will I try to fight ye, ye grim, phantom futures! Stand by me, hold me, bind me, O ye blessed influences!

# Chapter 39

*First Night-Watch*

FORE-TOP.
*(Stubb solus, and mending a brace.)*

HA! HA! HA! HA! HEM! clear my throat!—I've been thinking over it ever since, and that ha, ha's the final consequence. Why so? Because a laugh's the wisest, easiest answer to all that's queer; and come what will, one comfort's always left—that unfailing comfort is, it's all predestinated. I heard not all his talk with Starbuck; but to my poor eye Starbuck then looked something as I the other evening felt. Be sure the old Mogul has fixed him, too. I twigged it, knew it; had had the gift, might readily have prophesied it—for when I clapped my eye upon his skull I saw it. Well, Stubb, *wise* Stubb—that's my title—well, Stubb, what of it, Stubb? Here's a carcase. I know not all that may be coming, but be it what it will, I'll go to it laughing. Such a waggish leering as lurks in all your horribles! I feel funny. Fa, la! lirra, skirra! What's my juicy little pear at home doing now? Crying its eyes out?—Giving a party to the last arrived harpooneers, I dare say, gay as a frigate's pennant, and so am I—fa, la! lirra, skirra! Oh—

> We'll drink to-night with hearts as light,
>     To loves as gay and fleeting
> As bubbles that swim, on the beaker's brim,
>     And break on the lips while meeting.

171

A brave stave that—who calls? Mr. Starbuck? Aye, aye, sir— *(Aside)* he's my superior, he has his too, if I'm not mistaken.—Aye, aye, sir, just through with this job—coming.

# Chapter 40

*Midnight, Forecastle*

HARPOONEERS and SAILORS.
*(Foresail rises and discovers the watch standing, lounging, leaning, and lying in various attitudes, all singing in chorus.)*

Farewell and adieu to you, Spanish ladies!
Farewell and adieu to you, ladies of Spain!
Our captain's commanded—

1ST NANTUCKET SAILOR.

Oh, boys, don't be sentimental; it's bad for the digestion! Take a tonic, follow me!

*(Sings, and all follow.)*
Our captain stood upon the deck,
   A spy-glass in his hand,
A viewing of those gallant whales
   That blew at every strand.
Oh, your tubs in your boats, my boys,
   And by your braces stand,
And we'll have one of those fine whales,
   Hand, boys, over hand!
So, be cheery, my lads! may your hearts never fail!
While the bold harpooneer is striking the whale!

MATE'S VOICE FROM THE QUARTER-DECK.

Eight bells there, forward!

2D NANTUCKET SAILOR.

Avast the chorus! Eight bells there! d'ye hear, bell-boy? Strike the bell eight, thou Pip! thou blackling! and let me call the watch. I've the sort of mouth for that—the hogshead mouth. So, so, *(thrusts his head down the scuttle,)* Star—bo-Ļ-e-e-n-s, a-h-o-y! Eight bells there below! Tumble up!

DUTCH SAILOR.

Grand snoozing to-night, maty; fat night for that. I mark this in our old Mogul's wine; it's quite as deadening to some as filliping to others. We sing; they sleep—aye, lie down there, like ground-tier butts. At 'em again! There, take this copper-pump, and hail 'em through it. Tell 'em to avast dreaming of their lasses. Tell 'em it's the resurrection; they must kiss their last, and come to judgment. That's the way—*that's* it; thy throat ain't spoiled with eating Amsterdam butter.

FRENCH SAILOR.

Hist, boys! let's have a jig or two before we ride to anchor in Blanket Bay. What say ye? There comes the other watch. Stand by all legs! Pip! little Pip! hurrah with your tambourine!

PIP.

*(Sulky and sleepy.)*

Don't know where it is.

FRENCH SAILOR.

Beat thy belly, then, and wag thy ears. Jig it, men, I say; merry's the word; hurrah! Damn me, won't you dance? Form, now, Indian-file, and gallop into the double-shuffle? Throw yourselves! Legs! legs!

ICELAND SAILOR.

I don't like your floor, maty; it's too springy to my taste. I'm used to ice-floors. I'm sorry to throw cold water on the subject; but excuse me.

MALTESE SAILOR.

Me too; where's your girls? Who but a fool would take his left hand by his right, and say to himself, how d'ye do? Partners! I must have partners!

SICILIAN SAILOR.

Aye; girls and a green!—then I'll hop with ye; yea, turn grasshopper!

LONG-ISLAND SAILOR.

Well, well, ye sulkies, there's plenty more of us. Hoe corn when you may, say I. All legs go to harvest soon. Ah! here comes the music; now for it!

AZORES SAILOR.

*(Ascending, and pitching the tambourine up the scuttle.)*

Here you are, Pip; and there's the windlass-bitts; up you mount! Now, boys!

*(The half of them dance to the tambourine; some go below; some sleep or lie among the coils of rigging. Oaths a-plenty.)*

AZORES SAILOR.

*(Dancing.)*

Go it, Pip! Bang it, bell-boy! Rig it, dig it, stig it, quig it, bell-boy! Make fire-flies; break the jinglers!

PIP.

Jinglers, you say?—there goes another, dropped off; I pound it so.

CHINA SAILOR.

Rattle thy teeth, then, and pound away; make a pagoda of thyself.

FRENCH SAILOR.

Merry-mad! Hold up thy hoop, Pip, till I jump through it! Split jibs! tear yourselves!

TASHTEGO.

*(Quietly smoking.)*

That's a white man; he calls that fun: humph! I save my sweat.

OLD MANX SAILOR.

I wonder whether those jolly lads bethink them of what they are dancing over. I'll dance over your grave, I will—that's the bitterest threat of your night-women, that beat head-winds round corners. O Christ! to think of the green navies and the green-skulled crews! Well, well; belike the whole world's one ball, as your scholars have it; and so 'tis right to make one ball-room of it. Dance on, lads, you're young; I was once.

3D NANTUCKET SAILOR.

Spell oh!—whew! this is worse than pulling after whales in a calm— give us a whiff, Tash.

*(They cease dancing, and gather in clusters. Meantime the sky darkens—the wind rises.)*

LASCAR SAILOR.

By Brahma! boys, it'll be douse sail soon. The sky-born, high-tide Ganges turned to wind! Thou showest thy black brow, Seeva!

MALTESE SAILOR.

*(Reclining and shaking his cap.)*

It's the waves'—the snow-caps' turn to jig it now. They'll shake their tassels soon. Now would all the waves were women, then I'd go drown, and chassee with them evermore! There's naught so sweet on earth—heaven may not match it!—as those swift glances of warm, wild bosoms in the dance, when the over-arboring arms hide such ripe, bursting grapes.

SICILIAN SAILOR.

*(Reclining.)*

Tell me not of it! Hark ye, lad—fleet interlacings of the limbs—lithe swayings—coyings—flutterings! lip! heart! hip! all graze: unceasing touch and go! not taste, observe ye, else come satiety. Eh, Pagan? *(Nudging.)*

TAHITIAN SAILOR.

*(Reclining on a mat.)*

Hail, holy nakedness of our dancing girls!—the Heeva-Heeva! Ah! low valed, high palmed Tahiti! I still rest me on thy mat, but the soft soil has slid! I saw thee woven in the wood, my mat! green the first day I brought ye thence; now worn and wilted quite. Ah me!—not thou nor I can bear the change! How then, if so be transplanted to yon sky? Hear I the roaring streams from Pirohitee's peak of spears, when they leap down the crags and drown the villages?—The blast! the blast! Up, spine, and meet it! *(Leaps to his feet.)*

PORTUGUESE SAILOR.

How the sea rolls swashing 'gainst the side! Stand by for reefing, hearties! the winds are just crossing swords, pell-mell they'll go lunging presently.

DANISH SAILOR.

Crack, crack, old ship! so long as thou crackest, thou holdest! Well done! The mate there holds ye to it stiffly. He's no more afraid than the isle fort at Cattegat, put there to fight the Baltic with storm-lashed guns, on which the sea-salt cakes!

4TH NANTUCKET SAILOR.

He has his orders, mind ye that. I heard old Ahab tell him he must always kill a squall, something as they burst a water-spout with a pistol—fire your ship right into it!

ENGLISH SAILOR.

Blood! but that old man's a grand old cove! We are the lads to hunt him up his whale!

ALL.

Aye! aye!

OLD MANX SAILOR.

How the three pines shake! Pines are the hardest sort of tree to live when shifted to any other soil, and here there's none but the crew's cursed clay. Steady, helmsman! steady. This is the sort of weather when brave hearts snap ashore, and keeled hulls split at sea. Our captain has his birth-mark; look yonder, boys, there's another in the sky—lurid-like, ye see, all else pitch black.

DAGGOO.

What of that? Who's afraid of black's afraid of me! I'm quarried out of it!

SPANISH SAILOR.

(Aside.) He wants to bully, ah!—the old grudge makes me touchy. (Advancing.) Aye, harpooneer, thy race is the undeniable dark side of mankind—devilish dark at that. No offence.

DAGGOO.
(Grimly.)

None.

ST. JAGO'S SAILOR.

That Spaniard's mad or drunk. But that can't be, or else in his one case our old Mogul's fire-waters are somewhat long in working.

5TH NANTUCKET SAILOR.

What's that I saw—lightning? Yes.

SPANISH SAILOR.

No; Daggoo showing his teeth.

DAGGOO.
(Springing.)

Swallow thine, mannikin! White skin, white liver!

SPANISH SAILOR.
(Meeting him.)

Knife thee heartily! big frame, small spirit!

ALL.

A row! a row! a row!

TASHTEGO.

*(With a whiff.)*

A row a'low, and a row aloft—Gods and men—both brawlers! Humph!

BELFAST SAILOR.

A row! arrah a row! The Virgin be blessed, a row! Plunge in with ye!

ENGLISH SAILOR.

Fair play! Snatch the Spaniard's knife! A ring, a ring!

OLD MANX SAILOR.

Ready formed. There! the ringed horizon. In that ring Cain struck Abel. Sweet work, right work! No? Why then, God, mad'st thou the ring?

MATE'S VOICE FROM THE QUARTER DECK.

Hands by the halyards! in top-gallant sails! Stand by to reef topsails!

ALL.

The squall! the squall! jump, my jollies! *(They scatter.)*

PIP.

*(Shrinking under the windlass.)*

Jollies? Lord help such jollies! Crish, crash! there goes the jib-stay! Blang-whang! God! Duck lower, Pip, here comes the royal yard! It's worse than being in the whirled woods, the last day of the year! Who'd go climbing after chestnuts now? But there they go, all cursing, and here I don't. Fine prospects to 'em; they're on the road to heaven. Hold on hard! Jimmini, what a squall! But those chaps there are worse yet—they are your white squalls, they. White squalls? white whale, shirr! shirr! Here have I heard all their chat just now, and the white whale—shirr! shirr!—but spoken of once! and only this evening—it makes me jingle all over like my tambourine—that anaconda of an old man swore 'em in to hunt him! Oh, thou big white God aloft there somewhere in yon darkness, have mercy on this small black boy down here; preserve him from all men that have no bowels to feel fear!

\*       \*       \*       \*       \*

# Chapter 41

## Moby Dick

I, Ishmael, was one of that crew; my shouts had gone up with the rest; my oath had been welded with theirs; and stronger I shouted, and more did I hammer and clinch my oath, because of the dread in my soul. A wild, mystical, sympathetical feeling was in me; Ahab's quenchless feud seemed mine. With greedy ears I learned the history of that murderous monster against whom I and all the others had taken our oaths of violence and revenge.

For some time past, though at intervals only, the unaccompanied, secluded White Whale had haunted those uncivilized seas mostly frequented by the Sperm Whale fishermen. But not all of them knew of his existence; only a few of them, comparatively, had knowingly seen him; while the number who as yet had actually and knowingly given battle to him, was small indeed. For, owing to the large number of whale-cruisers; the disorderly way they were sprinkled over the entire watery circumference, many of them adventurously pushing their quest along solitary latitudes, so as seldom or never for a whole twelvemonth or more on a stretch, to encounter a single news-telling sail of any sort; the inordinate length of each separate voyage; the irregularity of the times of sailing from home; all these, with other circumstances, direct and indirect, long obstructed the spread through the whole world-wide whaling-fleet of the special individualizing tidings concerning Moby Dick. It was hardly to be doubted, that several vessels reported to have encountered, at such or such a time, or on such or such a meridian, a Sperm Whale of uncommon magnitude and malignity, which whale, after doing great mischief to his assailants, had completely escaped them; to some minds it was not an unfair presumption, I say, that the whale in question must have been no other than Moby Dick. Yet as of late the Sperm Whale fishery had been marked by various and not unfrequent instances of great ferocity, cunning, and malice in the monster attacked; therefore it was, that those who by accident ignorantly gave battle to Moby Dick; such hunters, perhaps, for the most part, were content to ascribe the peculiar terror he bred, more, as it were, to the perils of the Sperm Whale fishery at large, than to the individual cause. In that way, mostly, the disastrous encounter between Ahab and the whale had hitherto been popularly regarded.

And as for those who, previously hearing of the White Whale, by chance caught sight of him; in the beginning of the thing they had every one of them, almost, as boldly and fearlessly lowered for him, as for any other whale of that species. But at length, such calamities did ensue in these assaults—not restricted to sprained wrists and ancles, broken limbs, or devouring amputations—but fatal to the last degree of fatality; those repeated disastrous repulses, all accumulating and piling their terrors upon Moby Dick; those things had gone far to shake the fortitude of many brave hunters, to whom the story of the White Whale had eventually come.

Nor did wild rumors of all sorts fail to exaggerate, and still the more horrify the true histories of these deadly encounters. For not only do fabulous rumors naturally grow out of the very body of all surprising terrible events,—as the smitten tree gives birth to its fungi; but, in maritime life, far more than in that of terra firma, wild rumors abound, wherever there is any adequate reality for them to cling to. And as the sea surpasses the land in this matter, so the whale fishery surpasses every other sort of maritime life, in the wonderfulness and fearfulness of the rumors which sometimes circulate there. For not only are whalemen as a body unexempt from that ignorance and superstitiousness hereditary to all sailors; but of all sailors, they are by all odds the most directly brought into contact with whatever is appallingly astonishing in the sea; face to face they not only eye its greatest marvels, but, hand to jaw, give battle to them. Alone, in such remotest waters, that though you sailed a thousand miles, and passed a thousand shores, you would not come to any chiselled hearthstone, or aught hospitable beneath that part of the sun; in such latitudes and longitudes, pursuing too such a calling as he does, the whaleman is wrapped by influences all tending to make his fancy pregnant with many a mighty birth.

No wonder, then, that ever gathering volume from the mere transit over the widest watery spaces, the outblown rumors of the White Whale did in the end incorporate with themselves all manner of morbid hints, and half-formed fœtal suggestions of supernatural agencies, which eventually invested Moby Dick with new terrors unborrowed from anything that visibly appears. So that in many cases such a panic did he finally strike, that few who by those rumors, at least, had heard of the White Whale, few of those hunters were willing to encounter the perils of his jaw.

But there were still other and more vital practical influences at work. Not even at the present day has the original prestige of the Sperm Whale, as fearfully distinguished from all other species of the leviathan, died out of the minds of the whalemen as a body. There are those this day among them, who, though intelligent and courageous enough in offering battle to the Greenland or Right whale, would perhaps—either from professional inexperience, or incompetency, or timidity, decline a contest with the Sperm Whale; at any rate, there are plenty of whalemen, especially among those whaling nations not sailing under the American flag, who have never hostilely encountered the Sperm Whale, but whose sole knowledge of the leviathan is restricted to the ignoble monster primitively pursued in the North; seated on their hatches, these men will hearken with a childish fire-side interest and awe, to the wild, strange tales of Southern whaling. Nor is the pre-eminent tremendousness of the great Sperm Whale anywhere more feelingly comprehended, than on board of those prows which stem him.

And as if the now tested reality of his might had in former legendary times thrown its shadow before it; we find some book naturalists—Olassen and Povelsen—declaring the Sperm Whale not only to be a consternation to every other creature in the sea, but also to be so incredibly ferocious as continually to be athirst for human blood. Nor even down to so late a time as Cuvier's, were these or almost similar impressions effaced. For in his Natural History, the Baron himself affirms that at sight of the Sperm Whale, all fish (sharks included) are "struck with the most lively terror," and "often in the precipitancy of their flight dash themselves against the rocks with such violence as to cause instantaneous death." And however the general experiences in the fishery may amend such reports as these; yet in their full terribleness, even to the bloodthirsty item of Povelsen, the super-stitious belief in them is, in some vicissitudes of their vocation, revived in the minds of the hunters.

So that overawed by the rumors and portents concerning him, not
a few of the fishermen recalled, in reference to Moby Dick, the earlier days
of the Sperm Whale fishery, when it was oftentimes hard to induce long
practised Right whalemen to embark in the perils of this new and daring
warfare; such men protesting that although other leviathans might be
hopefully pursued, yet to chase and point lance at such an apparition as the
Sperm Whale was not for mortal man. That to attempt it, would be inevitably to be torn into a quick eternity. On this head, there are some
remarkable documents that may be consulted.

Nevertheless, some there were, who even in the face of these things were
ready to give chase to Moby Dick; and a still greater number who, chancing only to hear of him distantly and vaguely, without the specific details of
any certain calamity, and without superstitious accompaniments, were
sufficiently hardy not to flee from the battle if offered.

One of the wild suggestings referred to, as at last coming to be linked with
the White Whale in the minds of the superstitiously inclined, was the
unearthly conceit that Moby Dick was ubiquitous; that he had actually
been encountered in opposite latitudes at one and the same instant of time.

Nor, credulous as such minds must have been, was this conceit altogether
without some faint show of superstitious probability. For as the secrets of
the currents in the seas have never yet been divulged, even to the most
erudite research; so the hidden ways of the Sperm Whale when beneath the
surface remain, in great part, unaccountable to his pursuers; and from time
to time have originated the most curious and contradictory speculations
regarding them, especially concerning the mystic modes whereby, after
sounding to a great depth, he transports himself with such vast swiftness to
the most widely distant points.

It is a thing well known to both American and English whale-ships,
and as well a thing placed upon authoritative record years ago by Scoresby,
that some whales have been captured far north in the Pacific, in whose
bodies have been found the barbs of harpoons darted in the Greenland seas.
Nor is it to be gainsaid, that in some of these instances it has been declared
that the interval of time between the two assaults could not have exceeded
very many days. Hence, by inference, it has been believed by some whalemen, that the Nor' West Passage, so long a problem to man, was never a
problem to the whale. So that here, in the real living experience of living
men, the prodigies related in old times of the inland Strella mountain in
Portugal (near whose top there was said to be a lake in which the wrecks of
ships floated up to the surface); and that still more wonderful story of the

Arethusa fountain near Syracuse (whose waters were believed to have come from the Holy Land by an underground passage); these fabulous narrations are almost fully equalled by the realities of the whaleman.

Forced into familiarity, then, with such prodigies as these; and knowing that after repeated, intrepid assaults, the White Whale had escaped alive; it cannot be much matter of surprise that some whalemen should go still further in their superstitions; declaring Moby Dick not only ubiquitous, but immortal (for immortality is but ubiquity in time): that though groves of spears should be planted in his flanks, he would still swim away unharmed; or if indeed he should ever be made to spout thick blood, such a sight would be but a ghastly deception; for again in unensanguined billows hundreds of leagues away, his unsullied jet would once more be seen.

But even stripped of these supernatural surmisings, there was enough in the earthly make and incontestable character of the monster to strike the imagination with unwonted power. For, it was not so much his uncommon bulk that so much distinguished him from other sperm whales, but, as was elsewhere thrown out—a peculiar snow-white wrinkled forehead, and a high, pyramidical white hump. These were his prominent features; the tokens whereby, even in the limitless, uncharted seas, he revealed his identity, at a long distance, to those who knew him.

The rest of his body was so streaked, and spotted, and marbled with the same shrouded hue, that, in the end, he had gained his distinctive appellation of the White Whale; a name, indeed, literally justified by his vivid aspect, when seen gliding at high noon through a dark blue sea, leaving a milky-way wake of creamy foam, all spangled with golden gleamings.

Nor was it his unwonted magnitude, nor his remarkable hue, nor yet his deformed lower jaw, that so much invested the whale with natural terror, as that unexampled, intelligent malignity which, according to specific accounts, he had over and over again evinced in his assaults. More than all, his treacherous retreats struck more of dismay than perhaps aught else. For, when swimming before his exulting pursuers, with every apparent symptom of alarm, he had several times been known to turn round suddenly, and, bearing down upon them, either stave their boats to splinters, or drive them back in consternation to their ship.

Already several fatalities had attended his chase. But though similar disasters, however little bruited ashore, were by no means unusual in the fishery; yet, in most instances, such seemed the White Whale's infernal aforethought of ferocity, that every dismembering or death that he caused, was not wholly regarded as having been inflicted by an unintelligent agent.

Judge, then, to what pitches of inflamed, distracted fury the minds of his more desperate hunters were impelled, when amid the chips of chewed boats, and the sinking limbs of torn comrades, they swam out of the white curds of the whale's direful wrath into the serene, exasperating sunlight, that smiled on, as if at a birth or a bridal.

His three boats stove around him, and oars and men both whirling in the eddies; one captain, seizing the line-knife from his broken prow, had dashed at the whale, as an Arkansas duellist at his foe, blindly seeking with a six inch blade to reach the fathom-deep life of the whale. That captain was Ahab. And then it was, that suddenly sweeping his sickle-shaped lower jaw beneath him, Moby Dick had reaped away Ahab's leg, as a mower a blade of grass in the field. No turbaned Turk, no hired Venetian or Malay, could have smote him with more seeming malice. Small reason was there to doubt, then, that ever since that almost fatal encounter, Ahab had cherished a wild vindictiveness against the whale, all the more fell for that in his frantic morbidness he at last came to identify with him, not only all his bodily woes, but all his intellectual and spiritual exasperations. The White Whale swam before him as the monomaniac incarnation of all those malicious agencies which some deep men feel eating in them, till they are left living on with half a heart and half a lung. That intangible malignity which has been from the beginning; to whose dominion even the modern Christians ascribe one-half of the worlds; which the ancient Ophites of the east reverenced in their statue devil;—Ahab did not fall down and worship it like them; but deliriously transferring its idea to the abhorred white whale, he pitted himself, all mutilated, against it. All that most maddens and torments; all that stirs up the lees of things; all truth with malice in it; all that cracks the sinews and cakes the brain; all the subtle demonisms of life and thought; all evil, to crazy Ahab, were visibly personified, and made practically assailable in Moby Dick. He piled upon the whale's white hump the sum of all the general rage and hate felt by his whole race from Adam down; and then, as if his chest had been a mortar, he burst his hot heart's shell upon it.

It is not probable that this monomania in him took its instant rise at the precise time of his bodily dismemberment. Then, in darting at the monster, knife in hand, he had but given loose to a sudden, passionate, corporal animosity; and when he received the stroke that tore him, he probably but felt the agonizing bodily laceration, but nothing more. Yet, when by this collision forced to turn towards home, and for long months of days and

weeks, Ahab and anguish lay stretched together in one hammock, rounding
in mid winter that dreary, howling Patagonian Cape; then it was, that his
torn body and gashed soul bled into one another; and so interfusing, made
him mad. That it was only then, on the homeward voyage, after the encounter, that the final monomania seized him, seems all but certain from
the fact that, at intervals during the passage, he was a raving lunatic; and,
though unlimbed of a leg, yet such vital strength yet lurked in his Egyptian
chest, and was moreover intensified by his delirium, that his mates were
forced to lace him fast, even there, as he sailed, raving in his hammock. In a
strait-jacket, he swung to the mad rockings of the gales. And, when running
into more sufferable latitudes, the ship, with mild stun'sails spread, floated
across the tranquil tropics, and, to all appearances, the old man's delirium
seemed left behind him with the Cape Horn swells, and he came forth from
his dark den into the blessed light and air; even then, when he bore that
firm, collected front, however pale, and issued his calm orders once again;
and his mates thanked God the direful madness was now gone; even then,
Ahab, in his hidden self, raved on. Human madness is oftentimes a cunning
and most feline thing. When you think it fled, it may have but become trans-
figured into some still subtler form. Ahab's full lunacy subsided not, but
deepeningly contracted; like the unabated Hudson, when that noble
Northman flows narrowly, but unfathomably through the Highland gorge.
But, as in his narrow-flowing monomania, not one jot of Ahab's broad
madness had been left behind; so in that broad madness, not one jot of his
great natural intellect had perished. That before living agent, now became
the living instrument. If such a furious trope may stand, his special lunacy
stormed his general sanity, and carried it, and turned all its concentred
cannon upon its own mad mark; so that far from having lost his strength,
Ahab, to that one end, did now possess a thousand fold more potency than
ever he had sanely brought to bear upon any one reasonable object.

This is much; yet Ahab's larger, darker, deeper part remains unhinted.
But vain to popularize profundities, and all truth is profound. Winding far
down from within the very heart of this spiked Hotel de Cluny where we
here stand—however grand and wonderful, now quit it;—and take your
way, ye nobler, sadder souls, to those vast Roman halls of Thermes; where
far beneath the fantastic towers of man's upper earth, his root of grandeur,
his whole awful essence sits in bearded state; an antique buried beneath
antiquities, and throned on torsoes! So with a broken throne, the great gods
mock that captive king; so like a Caryatid, he patient sits, upholding on his
frozen·brow the piled entablatures of ages. Wind ye down there, ye prouder,

sadder souls! question that proud, sad king! A family likeness! aye, he did beget ye, ye young exiled royalties; and from your grim sire only will the old State-secret come.

Now, in his heart, Ahab had some glimpse of this, namely: all my means are sane, my motive and my object mad. Yet without power to kill, or change, or shun the fact; he likewise knew that to mankind he did long dissemble; in some sort, did still. But that thing of his dissembling was only subject to his perceptibility, not to his will determinate. Nevertheless, so well did he succeed in that dissembling, that when with ivory leg he stepped ashore at last, no Nantucketer thought him otherwise than but naturally grieved, and that to the quick, with the terrible casualty which had overtaken him.

The report of his undeniable delirium at sea was likewise popularly ascribed to a kindred cause. And so too, all the added moodiness which always afterwards, to the very day of sailing in the Pequod on the present voyage, sat brooding on his brow. Nor is it so very unlikely, that far from distrusting his fitness for another whaling voyage, on account of such dark symptoms, the calculating people of that prudent isle were inclined to harbor the conceit, that for those very reasons he was all the better qualified and set on edge, for a pursuit so full of rage and wildness as the bloody hunt of whales. Gnawed within and scorched without, with the infixed, un-relenting fangs of some incurable idea; such an one, could he be found, would seem the very man to dart his iron and lift his lance against the most appalling of all brutes. Or, if for any reason thought to be corporeally incapacitated for that, yet such an one would seem superlatively competent to cheer and howl on his underlings to the attack. But be all this as it may, certain it is, that with the mad secret of his unabated rage bolted up and keyed in him, Ahab had purposely sailed upon the present voyage with the one only and all-engrossing object of hunting the White Whale. Had any one of his old acquaintances on shore but half dreamed of what was lurking in him then, how soon would their aghast and righteous souls have wrenched the ship from such a fiendish man! They were bent on profitable cruises, the profit to be counted down in dollars from the mint. He was intent on an audacious, immitigable, and supernatural revenge.

Here, then, was this grey-headed, ungodly old man, chasing with curses a Job's whale round the world, at the head of a crew, too, chiefly made up of mongrel renegades, and castaways, and cannibals—morally enfeebled also, by the incompetence of mere unaided virtue or right-mindedness in Starbuck, the invulnerable jollity of indifference and recklessness in Stubb, and the pervading mediocrity in Flask. Such a crew, so officered, seemed specially picked and packed by some infernal fatality to help him to his monomaniac revenge. How it was that they so aboundingly responded to the old man's ire—by what evil magic their souls were possessed, that at times his hate seemed almost theirs; the White Whale as much their insufferable foe as his; how all this came to be—what the White Whale was to them, or how to their unconscious understandings, also, in some dim, unsuspected way, he might have seemed the gliding great demon of the seas of life,—all this to explain, would be to dive deeper than Ishmael can go. The subterranean miner that works in us all, how can one tell whither leads his shaft by the ever shifting, muffled sound of his pick? Who does not feel the irresistible arm drag? What skiff in tow of a seventy-four can stand still? For one, I gave myself up to the abandonment of the time and the place; but while yet all a-rush to encounter the whale, could see naught in that brute but the deadliest ill.

# Chapter 42

## The Whiteness of the Whale

W HAT the white whale was to Ahab, has been hinted; what, at times, he was to me, as yet remains unsaid.

Aside from those more obvious considerations touching Moby Dick, which could not but occasionally awaken in any man's soul some alarm, there was another thought, or rather vague, nameless horror concerning him, which at times by its intensity completely overpowered all the rest; and yet so mystical and well nigh ineffable was it, that I almost despair of putting it in a comprehensible form. It was the whiteness of the whale that above all things appalled me. But how can I hope to explain myself here; and yet, in some dim, random way, explain myself I must, else all these chapters might be naught.

Though in many natural objects, whiteness refiningly enhances beauty, as if imparting some special virtue of its own, as in marbles, japonicas, and pearls; and though various nations have in some way recognised a certain royal pre-eminence in this hue; even the barbaric, grand old kings of Pegu placing the title "Lord of the White Elephants" above all their other magniloquent ascriptions of dominion; and the modern kings of Siam unfurling the same snow-white quadruped in the royal standard; and the Hanoverian flag bearing the one figure of a snow-white charger; and the great Austrian Empire, Cæsarian heir to overlording Rome, having for the imperial color the same imperial hue; and though this pre-eminence in it applies to the human race itself, giving the white man ideal mastership over every dusky tribe; and though, besides all this, whiteness has been even made significant of gladness, for among the Romans a white stone marked a joyful day; and though in other mortal sympathies and symbolizings, this same hue is made the emblem of many touching, noble things—the innocence of brides, the benignity of age; though among the Red Men of America the giving of the white belt of wampum was the deepest pledge of honor; though in many climes, whiteness typifies the majesty of Justice in the ermine of the Judge, and contributes to the daily state of kings and queens drawn by milk-white steeds; though even in the higher mysteries of the most august religions it has been made the symbol of the divine spotlessness and power; by the Persian fire worshippers, the white forked flame being held the holiest on the altar; and in the Greek mythologies, Great Jove himself being made incarnate in a snow-white bull; and though to the noble Iroquois, the midwinter sacrifice of the sacred White Dog was by far the holiest festival of their theology, that spotless, faithful creature being held the purest envoy they could send to the Great Spirit with the annual tidings of their own fidelity; and though directly from the Latin word for white, all Christian priests derive the name of one part of their sacred vesture, the alb or tunic, worn beneath the cassock; and though among the holy pomps of the Romish faith, white is specially employed in the celebration of the Passion of our Lord; though in the Vision of St. John, white robes are given to the redeemed, and the four-and-twenty elders stand clothed in white before the great white throne, and the Holy One that sitteth there white like wool; yet for all these accumulated associations, with whatever is sweet, and honorable, and sublime, there yet lurks an elusive something in the innermost idea of this hue, which strikes more of panic to the soul than that redness which affrights in blood.

This elusive quality it is, which causes the thought of whiteness, when divorced from more kindly associations, and coupled with any object terrible in itself, to heighten that terror to the furthest bounds. Witness the white bear of the poles, and the white shark of the tropics; what but their smooth, flaky whiteness makes them the transcendent horrors they are? That ghastly whiteness it is which imparts such an abhorrent mildness, even more loathsome than terrific, to the dumb gloating of their aspect. So that not the fierce-fanged tiger in his heraldic coat can so stagger courage as the white-shrouded bear or shark.*

* With reference to the Polar bear, it may possibly be urged by him who would fain go still deeper into this matter, that it is not the whiteness, separately regarded, which

Bethink thee of the albatross: whence come those clouds of spiritual wonderment and pale dread, in which that white phantom sails in all imaginations? Not Coleridge first threw that spell; but God's great, unflattering laureate, Nature.*

---

heightens the intolerable hideousness of that brute; for, analysed, that heightened hideousness, it might be said, only arises from the circumstance, that the irresponsible ferociousness of the creature stands invested in the fleece of celestial innocence and love; and hence, by bringing together two such opposite emotions in our minds, the Polar bear frightens us with so unnatural a contrast. But even assuming all this to be true; yet, were it not for the whiteness, you would not have that intensified terror.

As for the white shark, the white gliding ghostliness of repose in that creature, when beheld in his ordinary moods, strangely tallies with the same quality in the Polar quadruped. This peculiarity is most vividly hit by the French in the name they bestow upon that fish. The Romish mass for the dead begins with "Requiem eternam" (eternal rest), whence Requiem denominating the mass itself, and any other funereal music. Now, in allusion to the white, silent stillness of death in this shark, and the mild deadliness of his habits, the French call him Requin.

* I remember the first albatross I ever saw. It was during a prolonged gale, in waters hard upon the Antarctic seas. From my forenoon watch below, I ascended to the over-clouded deck; and there, dashed upon the main hatches, I saw a regal, feathery thing of unspotted whiteness, and with a hooked, Roman bill sublime. At intervals, it arched forth its vast archangel wings, as if to embrace some holy ark. Wondrous flutterings and throbbings shook it. Though bodily unharmed, it uttered cries, as some king's ghost in supernatural distress. Through its inexpressible, strange eyes, methought I peeped to secrets which took hold of God. As Abraham before the angels, I bowed myself; the white thing was so white, its wings so wide, and in those for ever exiled waters, I had lost the miserable warping memories of traditions and of towns. Long I gazed at that prodigy of plumage. I cannot tell, can only hint, the things that darted through me then. But at last I awoke, and turning, asked a sailor what bird was this. A goney, he replied. Goney! I never had heard that name before; is it conceivable that this glorious thing is utterly unknown to men ashore! never! But some time after, I learned that goney was some seaman's name for albatross. So that by no possibility could Coleridge's wild Rhyme have had aught to do with those mystical impressions which were mine, when I saw that bird upon our deck. For neither had I then read the Rhyme, nor knew the bird to be an albatross. Yet, in saying this, I do but indirectly burnish a little brighter the noble merit of the poem and the poet.

I assert, then, that in the wondrous bodily whiteness of the bird chiefly lurks the secret of the spell; a truth the more evinced in this, that by a solecism of terms there are birds called grey albatrosses; and these I have frequently seen, but never with such emotions as when I beheld the Antarctic fowl.

But how had the mystic thing been caught? Whisper it not, and I will tell; with a treacherous hook and line, as the fowl floated on the sea. At last the Captain made a postman of it; tying a lettered, leathern tally round its neck, with the ship's time and place; and then letting it escape. But I doubt not, that leathern tally, meant for man, was taken off in Heaven, when the white fowl flew to join the wing-folding, the invoking, and adoring cherubim!

Most famous in our Western annals and Indian traditions is that of the White Steed of the Praries: a magnificent milk-white charger, large-eyed, small-headed, bluff-chested, and with the dignity of a thousand monarchs in his lofty, overscorning carriage. He was the elected Xerxes of vast herds of wild horses, whose pastures in those days were only fenced by the Rocky Mountains and the Alleghanies. At their flaming head he west-ward trooped it like that chosen star which every evening leads on the hosts of light. The flashing cascade of his mane, the curving comet of his tail, invested him with housings more resplendent than gold and silver-beaters could have furnished him. A most imperial and archangelical apparition of that unfallen, western world, which to the eyes of the old trappers and hunters revived the glories of those primeval times when Adam walked majestic as a god, bluff-bowed and fearless as this mighty steed. Whether marching amid his aides and marshals in the van of countless cohorts that endlessly streamed it over the plains, like an Ohio; or whether with his circumambient subjects browsing all around at the horizon, the White Steed gallopingly reviewed them with warm nostrils reddening through his cool milkiness; in whatever aspect he presented himself, always to the bravest Indians he was the object of trembling reverence and awe. Nor can it be questioned from what stands on legendary record of this noble horse, that it was his spiritual whiteness chiefly, which so clothed him with divine-ness; and that this divineness had that in it which, though commanding worship, at the same time enforced a certain nameless terror.

But there are other instances where this whiteness loses all that accessory and strange glory which invests it in the White Steed and Albatross.

What is it that in the Albino man so peculiarly repels and often shocks the eye, as that sometimes he is loathed by his own kith and kin? It is that whiteness which invests him, a thing expressed by the name he bears. The Albino is as well made as other men—has no substantive deformity—and yet this mere aspect of all-pervading whiteness makes him more strangely hideous than the ugliest abortion. Why should this be so?

Nor, in quite other aspects, does Nature in her least palpable but not the less malicious agencies, fail to enlist among her forces this crowning attribute of the terrible. From its snowy aspect, the gauntleted ghost of the Southern Seas has been denominated the White Squall. Nor, in some historic instances, has the art of human malice omitted so potent an auxiliary. How wildly it heightens the effect of that passage in Froissart, when, masked in the snowy symbol of their faction, the desperate White Hoods of Ghent murder their bailiff in the market-place!

Nor, in some things, does the common, hereditary experience of all mankind fail to bear witness to the supernaturalism of this hue. It cannot well be doubted, that the one visible quality in the aspect of the dead which most appals the gazer, is the marble pallor lingering there; as if indeed that pallor were as much the badge of consternation in the other world, as of mortal trepidation here. And from that pallor of the dead, we borrow the expressive hue of the shroud in which we wrap them. Nor even in our superstitions do we fail to throw the same snowy mantle round our phantoms; all ghosts rising in a milk-white fog—Yea, while these terrors seize us, let us add, that even the king of terrors, when personified by the evangelist, rides on his pallid horse.

Therefore, in his other moods, symbolize whatever grand or gracious thing he will by whiteness, no man can deny that in its profoundest idealized significance it calls up a peculiar apparition to the soul.

But though without dissent this point be fixed, how is mortal man to account for it? To analyse it, would seem impossible. Can we, then, by the citation of some of those instances wherein this thing of whiteness—though for the time either wholly or in great part stripped of all direct associations calculated to impart to it aught fearful, but, nevertheless, is found to exert over us the same sorcery, however modified;—can we thus hope to light upon some chance clue to conduct us to the hidden cause we seek?

Let us try. But in a matter like this, subtlety appeals to subtlety, and without imagination no man can follow another into these halls. And though, doubtless, some at least of the imaginative impressions about to be presented may have been shared by most men, yet few perhaps were entirely conscious of them at the time, and therefore may not be able to recall them now.

Why to the man of untutored ideality, who happens to be but loosely acquainted with the peculiar character of the day, does the bare mention of Whitsuntide marshal in the fancy such long, dreary, speechless processions of slow-pacing pilgrims, down-cast and hooded with new-fallen snow? Or, to the unread, unsophisticated Protestant of the Middle American States, why does the passing mention of a White Friar or a White Nun, evoke such an eyeless statue in the soul?

Or what is there apart from the traditions of dungeoned warriors and kings (which will not wholly account for it) that makes the White Tower of London tell so much more strongly on the imagination of an untravelled American, than those other storied structures, its neighbors—the Byward Tower, or even the Bloody? And those sublimer towers, the White Moun-

tains of New Hampshire, whence, in peculiar moods, comes that gigantic
ghostliness over the soul at the bare mention of that name, while the
thought of Virginia's Blue Ridge is full of a soft, dewy, distant dreaminess?
Or why, irrespective of all latitudes and longitudes, does the name of the
White Sea exert such a spectralness over the fancy, while that of the Yellow
Sea lulls us with mortal thoughts of long lacquered mild afternoons on the
waves, followed by the gaudiest and yet sleepiest of sunsets? Or, to choose a
wholly unsubstantial instance, purely addressed to the fancy, why, in
reading the old fairy tales of Central Europe, does "the tall pale man" of the
Hartz forests, whose changeless pallor unrustlingly glides through the
green of the groves—why is this phantom more terrible than all the whoop-
ing imps of the Blocksburg?

Nor is it, altogether, the remembrance of her cathedral-toppling earthquakes; nor the stampedoes of her frantic seas; nor the tearlessness of arid
skies that never rain; nor the sight of her wide field of leaning spires,
wrenched cope-stones, and crosses all adroop (like canted yards of anchored
fleets); and her suburban avenues of house-walls lying over upon each
other, as a tossed pack of cards;—it is not these things alone which make
tearless Lima, the strangest, saddest city thou can'st see. For Lima has taken
the white veil; and there is a higher horror in this whiteness of her woe. Old
as Pizarro, this whiteness keeps her ruins for ever new; admits not the
cheerful greenness of complete decay; spreads over her broken ramparts the
rigid pallor of an apoplexy that fixes its own distortions.

I know that, to the common apprehension, this phenomenon of whiteness is not confessed to be the prime agent in exaggerating the terror of
objects otherwise terrible; nor to the unimaginative mind is there aught of
terror in those appearances whose awfulness to another mind almost solely
consists in this one phenomenon, especially when exhibited under any form
at all approaching to muteness or universality. What I mean by these two
statements may perhaps be respectively elucidated by the following
examples.

First: The mariner, when drawing nigh the coasts of foreign lands, if by
night he hear the roar of breakers, starts to vigilance, and feels just enough of
trepidation to sharpen all his faculties; but under precisely similar circumstances, let him be called from his hammock to view his ship sailing through
a midnight sea of milky whiteness—as if from encircling headlands shoals
of combed white bears were swimming round him, then he feels a silent,
superstitious dread; the shrouded phantom of the whitened waters is
horrible to him as a real ghost; in vain the lead assures him he is still off

soundings; heart and helm they both go down; he never rests till blue water is under him again. Yet where is the mariner who will tell thee, "Sir, it was not so much the fear of striking hidden rocks, as the fear of that hideous whiteness that so stirred me?"

Second: To the native Indian of Peru, the continual sight of the snow-howdahed Andes conveys naught of dread, except, perhaps, in the mere fancying of the eternal frosted desolateness reigning at such vast altitudes, and the natural conceit of what a fearfulness it would be to lose oneself in such inhuman solitudes. Much the same is it with the backwoodsman of the West, who with comparative indifference views an unbounded prairie sheeted with driven snow, no shadow of tree or twig to break the fixed trance of whiteness. Not so the sailor, beholding the scenery of the Antarctic seas; where at times, by some infernal trick of legerdemain in the powers of frost and air, he, shivering and half shipwrecked, instead of rainbows speaking hope and solace to his misery, views what seems a boundless church-yard grinning upon him with its lean ice monuments and splintered crosses.

But thou sayest, methinks this white-lead chapter about whiteness is but a white flag hung out from a craven soul; thou surrenderest to a hypo, Ishmael.

Tell me, why this strong young colt, foaled in some peaceful valley of Vermont, far removed from all beasts of prey—why is it that upon the sunniest day, if you but shake a fresh buffalo robe behind him, so that he cannot even see it, but only smells its wild animal muskiness—why will he start, snort, and with bursting eyes paw the ground in phrensies of affright? There is no remembrance in him of any gorings of wild creatures in his green northern home, so that the strange muskiness he smells cannot recall to him anything associated with the experience of former perils; for what knows he, this New England colt, of the black bisons of distant Oregon?

No: but here thou beholdest even in a dumb brute, the instinct of the knowledge of the demonism in the world. Though thousands of miles from Oregon, still when he smells that savage musk, the rending, goring bison herds are as present as to the deserted wild foal of the prairies, which this instant they may be trampling into dust.

Thus, then, the muffled rollings of a milky sea; the bleak rustlings of the festooned frosts of mountains; the desolate shiftings of the windrowed snows of prairies; all these, to Ishmael, are as the shaking of that buffalo robe to the frightened colt!

Though neither knows where lie the nameless things of which the mystic sign gives forth such hints; yet with me, as with the colt, somewhere those things must exist. Though in many of its aspects this visible world seems formed in love, the invisible spheres were formed in fright.

But not yet have we solved the incantation of this whiteness, and learned why it appeals with such power to the soul; and more strange and far more portentous—why, as we have seen, it is at once the most meaning symbol of spiritual things, nay, the very veil of the Christian's Deity; and yet should be as it is, the intensifying agent in things the most appalling to mankind.

Is it that by its indefiniteness it shadows forth the heartless voids and immensities of the universe, and thus stabs us from behind with the thought of annihilation, when beholding the white depths of the milky way? Or is it, that as in essence whiteness is not so much a color as the visible absence of color, and at the same time the concrete of all colors; is it for these reasons that there is such a dumb blankness, full of meaning, in a wide landscape of snows—a colorless, all-color of atheism from which we shrink? And when we consider that other theory of the natural philosophers, that all other earthly hues—every stately or lovely emblazoning—the sweet tinges of sunset skies and woods; yea, and the gilded velvets of butterflies, and the butterfly cheeks of young girls; all these are but subtile deceits, not actually inherent in substances, but only laid on from without; so that all deified Nature absolutely paints like the harlot, whose allurements cover nothing but the charnel-house within; and when we proceed further, and consider that the mystical cosmetic which produces every one of her hues, the great principle of light, for ever remains white or colorless in itself, and if operating without medium upon matter, would touch all objects, even tulips and roses, with its own blank tinge—pondering all this, the palsied universe lies before us a leper; and like wilful travellers in Lapland, who refuse to wear colored and coloring glasses upon their eyes, so the wretched infidel gazes himself blind at the monumental white shroud that wraps all the prospect around him. And of all these things the Albino whale was the symbol. Wonder ye then at the fiery hunt?

# Chapter 43

*Hark!*

"HIST! Did you hear that noise, Cabaco?"

It was the middle-watch: a fair moonlight; the seamen were standing in a cordon, extending from one of the fresh-water butts in the waist, to the scuttle-butt near the taffrail. In this manner, they passed the buckets to fill the scuttle-butt. Standing, for the most part, on the hallowed precincts of the quarter-deck, they were careful not to speak or rustle their feet. From hand to hand, the buckets went in the deepest silence, only broken by the occasional flap of a sail, and the steady hum of the unceasingly advancing keel.

It was in the midst of this repose, that Archy, one of the cordon, whose post was near the after-hatches, whispered to his neighbor, a Cholo, the words above.

"Hist! did you hear that noise, Cabaco?"

"Take the bucket, will ye, Archy? what noise d'ye mean?"

"There it is again—under the hatches—don't you hear it—a cough—it sounded like a cough."

"Cough be damned! Pass along that return bucket."

"There again—there it is!—it sounds like two or three sleepers turning over, now!"

"Caramba! have done, shipmate, will ye? It's the three soaked biscuits ye eat for supper turning over inside of ye—nothing else. Look to the bucket!"

"Say what ye will, shipmate; I've sharp ears."

"Aye, you are the chap, ain't ye, that heard the hum of the old Quakeress's knitting-needles fifty miles at sea from Nantucket; you're the chap."

"Grin away; we'll see what turns up. Hark ye, Cabaco, there is somebody down in the after-hold that has not yet been seen on deck; and I suspect our old Mogul knows something of it too. I heard Stubb tell Flask, one morning watch, that there was something of that sort in the wind."

"Tish! the bucket!"

# Chapter 44

## The Chart

H AD YOU FOLLOWED Captain Ahab down into his cabin after the squall that took place on the night succeeding that wild ratification of his purpose with his crew, you would have seen him go to a locker in the transom, and bringing out a large wrinkled roll of yellowish sea charts, spread them before him on his screwed-down table. Then seating himself before it, you would have seen him intently study the various lines and shadings which there met his eye; and with slow but steady pencil trace additional courses over spaces that before were blank. At intervals, he would refer to piles of old log-books beside him, wherein were set down the seasons and places in which, on various former voyages of various ships, sperm whales had been captured or seen.

While thus employed, the heavy pewter lamp suspended in chains over his head, continually rocked with the motion of the ship, and for ever threw shifting gleams and shadows of lines upon his wrinkled brow, till it almost seemed that while he himself was marking out lines and courses on the wrinkled charts, some invisible pencil was also tracing lines and courses upon the deeply marked chart of his forehead.

But it was not this night in particular that, in the solitude of his cabin, Ahab thus pondered over his charts. Almost every night they were brought out; almost every night some pencil marks were effaced, and others were substituted. For with the charts of all four oceans before him, Ahab was threading a maze of currents and eddies, with a view to the more certain accomplishment of that monomaniac thought of his soul.

Now, to any one not fully acquainted with the ways of the leviathans, it might seem an absurdly hopeless task thus to seek out one solitary creature in the unhooped oceans of this planet. But not so did it seem to Ahab, who knew the sets of all tides and currents; and thereby calculating the driftings of the sperm whale's food; and, also, calling to mind the regular, ascertained seasons for hunting him in particular latitudes; could arrive at reasonable surmises, almost approaching to certainties, concerning the timeliest day to be upon this or that ground in search of his prey.

So assured, indeed, is the fact concerning the periodicalness of the sperm whale's resorting to given waters, that many hunters believe that, could he be closely observed and studied throughout the world; were the logs for one voyage of the entire whale fleet carefully collated, then the migrations of the sperm whale would be found to correspond in in-variability to those of the herring-shoals or the flights of swallows. On this hint, attempts have been made to construct elaborate migratory charts of the sperm whale.*

Besides, when making a passage from one feeding-ground to another, the sperm whales, guided by some infallible instinct—say, rather, secret intelligence from the Deity—mostly swim in *veins*, as they are called; continuing their way along a given ocean-line with such undeviating exactitude, that no ship ever sailed her course, by any chart, with one tithe of such marvellous precision. Though, in these cases, the direction taken by any one whale be straight as a surveyor's parallel, and though the line of advance be strictly confined to its own unavoidable, straight wake, yet the arbitrary *vein* in which at these times he is said to swim, generally embraces some few miles in width (more or less, as the vein is presumed to expand or contract); but never exceeds the visual sweep from the whale-ship's mast-heads, when circumspectly gliding along this magic zone. The sum is, that

* Since the above was written, the statement is happily borne out by an official circular, issued by Lieutenant Maury, of the National Observatory, Washington, April 16th, 1851. By that circular, it appears that precisely such a chart is in course of completion; and portions of it are presented in the circular. "This chart divides the ocean into districts of five degrees of latitude by five degrees of longitude; perpendicularly through each of which districts are twelve columns for the twelve months; and horizontally through each of which districts are three lines; one to show the number of days that have been spent in each month in every district, and the two others to show the number of days on which whales, sperm or right, have been seen."

at particular seasons within that breadth and along that path, migrating whales may with great confidence be looked for.

And hence not only at substantiated times, upon well known separate feeding-grounds, could Ahab hope to encounter his prey; but in crossing the widest expanses of water between those grounds he could, by his art, so place and time himself on his way, as even then not to be wholly without prospect of a meeting.

There was a circumstance which at first sight seemed to entangle his delirious but still methodical scheme. But not so in the reality, perhaps. Though the gregarious sperm whales have their regular seasons for particular grounds, yet in general you cannot conclude that the herds which haunted such and such a latitude or longitude this year, say, will turn out to be identically the same with those that were found there the preceding season; though there are peculiar and unquestionable instances where the contrary of this has proved true. In general, the same remark, only within a less wide limit, applies to the solitaries and hermits among the matured, aged sperm whales. So that though Moby Dick had in a former year been seen, for example, on what is called the Seychelle ground in the Indian ocean, or Volcano Bay on the Japanese Coast; yet it did not follow, that were the Pequod to visit either of those spots at any subsequent corresponding season, she would infallibly encounter him there. So, too, with some other feeding grounds, where he had at times revealed himself. But all these seemed only his casual stopping-places and ocean-inns, so to speak, not his places of prolonged abode. And where Ahab's chances of accomplishing his object have hitherto been spoken of, allusion has only been made to whatever way-side, antecedent, extra prospects were his, ere a particular set time and place were attained, when all possibilities would become probabilities, and, as Ahab fondly thought, every probability the next thing to a certainty. That particular set time and place were conjoined in the one technical phrase—the Season-on-the-Line. For there and then, for several consecutive years, Moby Dick had been periodically descried, lingering in those waters for awhile, as the sun, in its annual round, loiters for a predicted interval in any one sign of the Zodiac. There it was, too, that most of the deadly encounters with the white whale had taken place; there the waves were storied with his deeds; there also was that tragic spot where the monomaniac old man had found the awful motive to his vengeance. But in the cautious comprehensiveness and unloitering vigilance with which Ahab threw his brooding soul into this unfaltering hunt, he would not permit himself to rest all his hopes upon the one crowning fact above

mentioned, however flattering it might be to those hopes; nor in the sleep-
lessness of his vow could he so tranquillize his unquiet heart as to postpone
all intervening quest.

Now, the Pequod had sailed from Nantucket at the very beginning of
the Season-on-the-Line. No possible endeavor then could enable her
commander to make the great passage southwards, double Cape Horn, and
then running down sixty degrees of latitude arrive in the equatorial Pacific
in time to cruise there. Therefore, he must wait for the next ensuing season.
Yet the premature hour of the Pequod's sailing had, perhaps, been covertly
selected by Ahab, with a view to this very complexion of things. Because,
an interval of three hundred and sixty-five days and nights was before him;
an interval which, instead of impatiently enduring ashore, he would
spend in a miscellaneous hunt; if by chance the White Whale, spending his
vacation in seas far remote from his periodical feeding-grounds, should
turn up his wrinkled brow off the Persian Gulf, or in the Bengal Bay, or
China Seas, or in any other waters haunted by his race. So that Monsoons,
Pampas, Nor-Westers, Harmattans, Trades; any wind but the Levanter
and Simoom, might blow Moby Dick into the devious zig-zag world-
circle of the Pequod's circumnavigating wake.

But granting all this; yet, regarded discreetly and coolly, seems it not
but a mad idea, this; that in the broad boundless ocean, one solitary whale,
even if encountered, should be thought capable of individual recognition
from his hunter, even as a white-bearded Mufti in the thronged thoroughfares of Constantinople? No. For the peculiar snow-white brow of Moby
Dick, and his snow-white hump, could not but be unmistakable. And have
I not tallied the whale, Ahab would mutter to himself, as after poring over
his charts till long after midnight he would throw himself back in reveries—
tallied him, and shall he escape? His broad fins are bored, and scalloped out
like a lost sheep's ear! And here, his mad mind would run on in a breathless
race; till a weariness and faintness of pondering came over him; and in the
open air of the deck he would seek to recover his strength. Ah, God! what
trances of torments does that man endure who is consumed with one un-
achieved revengeful desire. He sleeps with clenched hands; and wakes with
his own bloody nails in his palms.

Often, when forced from his hammock by exhausting and intolerably
vivid dreams of the night, which, resuming his own intense thoughts
through the day, carried them on amid a clashing of phrensies, and whirled
them round and round in his blazing brain, till the very throbbing of his
life-spot became insufferable anguish; and when, as was sometimes the

case, these spiritual throes in him heaved his being up from its base, and a
chasm seemed opening in him, from which forked flames and lightnings
shot up, and accursed fiends beckoned him to leap down among them;
when this hell in himself yawned beneath him, a wild cry would be heard
through the ship; and with glaring eyes Ahab would burst from his state
room, as though escaping from a bed that was on fire. Yet these, perhaps,
instead of being the unsuppressable symptoms of some latent weakness, or
fright at his own resolve, were but the plainest tokens of its intensity. For,
at such times, crazy Ahab, the scheming, unappeasedly steadfast hunter of
the white whale; this Ahab that had gone to his hammock, was not the
agent that so caused him to burst from it in horror again. The latter was
the eternal, living principle or soul in him; and in sleep, being for the time
dissociated from the characterizing mind, which at other times employed
it for its outer vehicle or agent, it spontaneously sought escape from the
scorching contiguity of the frantic thing, of which, for the time, it was no
longer an integral. But as the mind does not exist unless leagued with the
soul, therefore it must have been that, in Ahab's case, yielding up all his
thoughts and fancies to his one supreme purpose; that purpose, by its own
sheer inveteracy of will, forced itself against gods and devils into a kind of
self-assumed, independent being of its own. Nay, could grimly live and
burn, while the common vitality to which it was conjoined, fled horror-
stricken from the unbidden and unfathered birth. Therefore, the tormented
spirit that glared out of bodily eyes, when what seemed Ahab rushed from
his room, was for the time but a vacated thing, a formless somnambulistic
being, a ray of living light, to be sure, but without an object to color, and
therefore a blankness in itself. God help thee, old man, thy thoughts have
created a creature in thee; and he whose intense thinking thus makes him
a Prometheus; a vulture feeds upon that heart for ever; that vulture the very
creature he creates.

# Chapter 45

### *The Affidavit*

SO FAR AS WHAT THERE MAY BE of a narrative in this book; and, indeed, as indirectly touching one or two very interesting and curious particulars in the habits of sperm whales, the foregoing chapter, in its earlier part, is as important a one as will be found in this volume; but the leading matter of it requires to be still further and more familiarly enlarged upon, in order to be adequately understood, and moreover to take away any incredulity which a profound ignorance of the entire subject may induce in some minds, as to the natural verity of the main points of this affair.

I care not to perform this part of my task methodically; but shall be content to produce the desired impression by separate citations of items, practically or reliably known to me as a whaleman; and from these citations, I take it—the conclusion aimed at will naturally follow of itself.

First: I have personally known three instances where a whale, after receiving a harpoon, has effected a complete escape; and, after an interval (in one instance of three years), has been again struck by the same hand, and slain; when the two irons, both marked by the same private cypher, have been taken from the body. In the instance where three years intervened between the flinging of the two harpoons; and I think it may have been something more than that; the man who darted them happening, in the interval, to go in a trading ship on a voyage to Africa, went ashore there, joined a discovery party, and penetrated far into the interior, where he travelled for a period of nearly two years, often endangered by serpents, savages, tigers, poisonous miasmas, with all the other common perils incident to wandering in the heart of unknown regions. Meanwhile, the whale he had struck must also have been on its travels; no doubt it had thrice circumnavigated the globe, brushing with its flanks all the coasts of Africa; but to no purpose. This man and this whale again came together, and the one vanquished the other. I say I, myself, have known three instances similar to this; that is in two of them I saw the whales struck; and, upon the second attack, saw the two irons with the respective marks cut in them, afterwards taken from the dead fish. In the three-year instance, it so fell out that I was in the boat both times, first and last, and the last time distinctly recognized a peculiar sort of huge mole under the whale's eye, which I had observed there three years previous. I say three years, but I am pretty sure it was more than that. Here are three instances, then, which I personally know the truth of; but I have heard of many other instances from persons whose veracity in the matter there is no good ground to impeach.

Secondly: It is well known in the Sperm Whale Fishery, however ignorant the world ashore may be of it, that there have been several memorable historical instances where a particular whale in the ocean has been at distant times and places popularly cognisable. Why such a whale became thus marked was not altogether and originally owing to his bodily peculiarities as distinguished from other whales; for however peculiar in that respect any chance whale may be, they soon put an end to his peculiarities by killing him, and boiling him down into a peculiarly valuable oil. No: the reason was this: that from the fatal experiences of the fishery there hung a terrible prestige of perilousness about such a whale as there did about Rinaldo Rinaldini, insomuch that most fishermen were content to recognise him by merely touching their tarpaulins when he would be discovered lounging by them on the sea, without seeking to cultivate a more intimate acquaintance. Like some poor devils ashore that happen to know an irascible great man, they make distant unobtrusive salutations to him in the street, lest if they pursued the acquaintance further, they might receive a summary thump for their presumption.

But not only did each of these famous whales enjoy great individual celebrity—nay, you may call it an ocean-wide renown; not only was he famous in life and now is immortal in forecastle stories after death, but he was admitted into all the rights, privileges, and distinctions of a name; had

as much a name indeed as Cambyses or Cæsar. Was it not so, O Timor Jack!
thou famed leviathan, scarred like an iceberg, who so long did'st lurk in the
Oriental straits of that name, whose spout was oft seen from the palmy
beach of Ombay? Was it not so, O New Zealand Tom! thou terror of all
cruisers that crossed their wakes in the vicinity of the Tattoo Land? Was it
not so, O Morquan! King of Japan, whose lofty jet they say at times
assumed the semblance of a snow-white cross against the sky? Was it not so,
O Don Miguel! thou Chilian whale, marked like an old tortoise with
mystic hieroglyphics upon the back! In plain prose, here are four whales as
well known to the students of Cetacean History as Marius or Sylla to the
classic scholar.

But this is not all. New Zealand Tom and Don Miguel, after at various
times creating great havoc among the boats of different vessels, were finally
gone in quest of, systematically hunted out, chased and killed by valiant
whaling captains, who heaved up their anchors with that express object as
much in view, as in setting out through the Narragansett Woods, Captain
Church of old had it in his mind to capture that notorious murderous
savage Annawon, the headmost warrior of the Indian King Philip.

I do not know where I can find a better place than just here, to make
mention of one or two other things, which to me seem important, as in
printed form establishing in all respects the reasonableness of the whole
story of the White Whale, more especially the catastrophe. For this is one of
those disheartening instances where truth requires full as much bolstering as
error. So ignorant are most landsmen of some of the plainest and most
palpable wonders of the world, that without some hints touching the plain
facts, historical and otherwise, of the fishery, they might scout at Moby
Dick as a monstrous fable, or still worse and more detestable, a hideous and
intolerable allegory.

First: Though most men have some vague flitting ideas of the general
perils of the grand fishery, yet they have nothing like a fixed, vivid conception of those perils, and the frequency with which they recur. One reason
perhaps is, that not one in fifty of the actual disasters and deaths by casualties
in the fishery, ever finds a public record at home, however transient and
immediately forgotten that record. Do you suppose that that poor fellow
there, who this moment perhaps caught by the whale-line off the coast of
New Guinea, is being carried down to the bottom of the sea by the sounding leviathan—do you suppose that that poor fellow's name will appear in
the newspaper obituary you will read to-morrow at your breakfast? No:
because the mails are very irregular between here and New Guinea. In fact,

did you ever hear what might be called regular news direct or indirect from New Guinea? Yet I tell you that upon one particular voyage which I made to the Pacific, among many others, we spoke thirty different ships, every one of which had had a death by a whale, some of them more than one, and three that had each lost a boat's crew. For God's sake, be economical with your lamps and candles! not a gallon you burn, but at least one drop of man's blood was spilled for it.

Secondly: People ashore have indeed some indefinite idea that a whale is an enormous creature of enormous power; but I have ever found that when narrating to them some specific example of this two-fold enormousness, they have significantly complimented me upon my facetiousness; when, I declare upon my soul, I had no more idea of being facetious than Moses, when he wrote the history of the plagues of Egypt.

But fortunately the special point I here seek can be established upon testimony entirely independent of my own. That point is this: The Sperm Whale is in some cases sufficiently powerful, knowing, and judiciously malicious, as with direct aforethought to stave in, utterly destroy, and sink a large ship; and what is more, the Sperm Whale *has* done it.

First: In the year 1820 the ship Essex, Captain Pollard, of Nantucket, was cruising in the Pacific Ocean. One day she saw spouts, lowered her boats, and gave chase to a shoal of sperm whales. Ere long, several of the whales were wounded; when, suddenly, a very large whale escaping from the boats, issued from the shoal, and bore directly down upon the ship. Dashing his forehead against her hull, he so stove her in, that in less than "ten minutes" she settled down and fell over. Not a surviving plank of her has been seen since. After the severest exposure, part of the crew reached the land in their boats. Being returned home at last, Captain Pollard once more sailed for the Pacific in command of another ship, but the gods shipwrecked him again upon unknown rocks and breakers; for the second time his ship was utterly lost, and forthwith forswearing the sea, he has never tempted it since. At this day Captain Pollard is a resident of Nantucket. I have seen Owen Chase, who was chief mate of the Essex at the time of the tragedy; I have read his plain and faithful narrative; I have conversed with his son; and all this within a few miles of the scene of the catastrophe.*

* The following are extracts from Chase's narrative: "Every fact seemed to warrant me in concluding that it was anything but chance which directed his operations; he made two several attacks upon the ship, at a short interval between them, both of which, according to their direction, were calculated to do us the most injury, by being made ahead, and thereby combining the speed of the two objects for the shock; to effect which, the exact

Secondly: The ship Union, also of Nantucket, was in the year 1807 totally lost off the Azores by a similar onset, but the authentic particulars of this catastrophe I have never chanced to encounter, though from the whale hunters I have now and then heard casual allusions to it.

Thirdly: Some eighteen or twenty years ago Commodore J—— then commanding an American sloop-of-war of the first class, happened to be dining with a party of whaling captains, on board a Nantucket ship in the harbor of Oahu, Sandwich Islands. Conversation turning upon whales, the Commodore was pleased to be sceptical touching the amazing strength ascribed to them by the professional gentlemen present. He peremptorily denied for example, that any whale could so smite his stout sloop-of-war as to cause her to leak so much as a thimbleful. Very good; but there is more coming. Some weeks after, the commodore set sail in this impregnable craft for Valparaiso. But he was stopped on the way by a portly sperm whale, that begged a few moments' confidential business with him. That business consisted in fetching the Commodore's craft such a thwack, that with all his pumps going he made straight for the nearest port to heave down and repair. I am not superstitious, but I consider the Commodore's interview with that whale as providential. Was not Saul of Tarsus converted from unbelief by a similar fright? I tell you, the sperm whale will stand no nonsense.

I will now refer you to Langsdorff's Voyages for a little circumstance in point, peculiarly interesting to the writer hereof. Langsdorff, you must know by the way, was attached to the Russian Admiral Krusenstern's

---

manœuvres which he made were necessary. His aspect was most horrible, and such as indicated resentment and fury. He came directly from the shoal which we had just before entered, and in which we had struck three of his companions, as if fired with revenge for their sufferings." Again: "At all events, the whole circumstances taken together, all happening before my own eyes, and producing, at the time, impressions in my mind of decided, calculating mischief, on the part of the whale (many of which impressions I cannot now recall), induce me to be satisfied that I am correct in my opinion."

Here are his reflections some time after quitting the ship, during a black night in an open boat, when almost despairing of reaching any hospitable shore. "The dark ocean and swelling waters were nothing; the fears of being swallowed up by some dreadful tempest, or dashed upon hidden rocks, with all the other ordinary subjects of fearful contemplation, seemed scarcely entitled to a moment's thought; the dismal looking wreck, and *the horrid aspect and revenge of the whale,* wholly engrossed my reflections, until day again made its appearance."

In another place—p. 45,—he speaks of *"the mysterious and mortal attack of the animal."*

\*    \*    \*    \*    \*    \*    \*    \*    \*    \*    \*
\*    \*    \*    \*    \*    \*    \*    \*    \*    \*    \*

famous Discovery Expedition in the beginning of the present century. Captain Langsdorff thus begins his seventeenth chapter.

"By the thirteenth of May our ship was ready to sail, and the next day we were out in the open sea, on our way to Ochotsk. The weather was very clear and fine, but so intolerably cold that we were obliged to keep on our fur clothing. For some days we had very little wind; it was not till the nineteenth that a brisk gale from the northwest sprang up. An uncommon large whale, the body of which was larger than the ship itself, lay almost at the surface of the water, but was not perceived by any one on board till the moment when the ship, which was in full sail, was almost upon him, so that it was impossible to prevent its striking against him. We were thus placed in the most imminent danger, as this gigantic creature, setting up its back, raised the ship three feet at least out of the water. The masts reeled, and the sails fell altogether, while we who were below all sprang instantly upon the deck, concluding that we had struck upon some rock; instead of this we saw the monster sailing off with the utmost gravity and solemnity. Captain D'Wolf applied immediately to the pumps to examine whether or not the vessel had received any damage from the shock, but we found that very happily it had escaped entirely uninjured."

Now, the Captain D'Wolf here alluded to as commanding the ship in question, is a New Englander, who, after a long life of unusual adventures as a sea-captain, this day resides in the village of Dorchester near Boston. I have the honor of being a nephew of his. I have particularly questioned him concerning this passage in Langsdorff. He substantiates every word. The ship, however, was by no means a large one: a Russian craft built on the Siberian coast, and purchased by my uncle after bartering away the vessel in which he sailed from home.

In that up and down manly book of old-fashioned adventure, so full, too, of honest wonders—the voyage of Lionel Wafer, one of ancient Dampier's old chums—I found a little matter set down so like that just quoted from Langsdorff, that I cannot forbear inserting it here for a corroborative example, if such be needed.

Lionel, it seems, was on his way to "John Ferdinando," as he calls the modern Juan Fernandes. "In our way thither," he says, "about four o'clock in the morning, when we were about one hundred and fifty leagues from the Main of America, our ship felt a terrible shock, which put our men in such consternation that they could hardly tell where they were or what to think; but every one began to prepare for death. And, indeed, the shock was so sudden and violent, that we took it for granted the ship had struck

against a rock; but when the amazement was a little over, we cast the lead, and sounded, but found no ground.         *       *       *       *       *       *
The suddenness of the shock made the guns leap in their carriages, and several of the men were shaken out of their hammocks. Captain Davis, who lay with his head over a gun, was thrown out of his cabin!" Lionel then goes on to impute the shock to an earthquake, and seems to substantiate the imputation by stating that a great earthquake, somewhere about that time, did actually do great mischief along the Spanish land. But I should not much wonder if, in the darkness of that early hour of the morning, the shock was after all caused by an unseen whale vertically bumping the hull from beneath.

I might proceed with several more examples, one way or another known to me, of the great power and malice at times of the sperm whale. In more than one instance, he has been known, not only to chase the assailing boats back to their ships, but to pursue the ship itself, and long withstand all the lances hurled at him from its decks. The English ship Pusie Hall can tell a story on that head; and, as for his strength, let me say, that there have been examples where the lines attached to a running sperm whale have, in a calm, been transferred to the ship, and secured there; the whale towing her great hull through the water, as a horse walks off with a cart. Again, it is very often observed that, if the sperm whale, once struck, is allowed time to rally, he then acts, not so often with blind rage, as with wilful, deliberate designs of destruction to his pursuers; nor is it without conveying some eloquent indication of his character, that upon being attacked he will frequently open his mouth, and retain it in that dread expansion for several consecutive minutes. But I must be content with only one more and a concluding illustration; a remarkable and most significant one, by which you will not fail to see, that not only is the most marvellous event in this book corroborated by plain facts of the present day, but that these marvels (like all marvels) are mere repetitions of the ages; so that for the millionth time we say amen with Solomon—Verily there is nothing new under the sun.

In the sixth Christian century lived Procopius, a Christian magistrate of Constantinople, in the days when Justinian was Emperor and Belisarius general. As many know, he wrote the history of his own times, a work every way of uncommon value. By the best authorities, he has always been considered a most trustworthy and unexaggerating historian, except in some one or two particulars, not at all affecting the matter presently to be mentioned.

Now, in this history of his, Procopius mentions that, during the term of his prefecture at Constantinople, a great sea-monster was captured in the neighboring Propontis, or Sea of Marmora, after having destroyed vessels at intervals in those waters for a period of more than fifty years. A fact thus set down in substantial history cannot easily be gainsaid. Nor is there any reason it should be. Of what precise species this sea-monster was, is not mentioned. But as he destroyed ships, as well as for other reasons, he must have been a whale; and I am strongly inclined to think a sperm whale. And I will tell you why. For a long time I fancied that the sperm whale had been always unknown in the Mediterranean and the deep waters connecting with it. Even now I am certain that those seas are not, and perhaps never can be, in the present constitution of things, a place for his habitual gregarious resort. But further investigations have recently proved to me, that in modern times there have been isolated instances of the presence of the sperm whale in the Mediterranean. I am told, on good authority, that on the Barbary coast, a Commander Davies of the British navy found the skeleton of a sperm whale. Now, as a vessel of war readily passes through the Dardanelles, hence a sperm whale could, by the same route, pass out of the Mediterranean into the Propontis.

In the Propontis, as far as I can learn, none of that peculiar substance called *brit* is to be found, the aliment of the right whale. But I have every reason to believe that the food of the sperm whale—squid or cuttle-fish— lurks at the bottom of that sea, because large creatures, but by no means the largest of that sort, have been found at its surface. If, then, you properly put these statements together, and reason upon them a bit, you will clearly perceive that, according to all human reasoning, Procopius's sea-monster, that for half a century stove the ships of a Roman Emperor, must in all probability have been a sperm whale.

# Chapter 46

*Surmises*

T HOUGH, consumed with the hot fire of his purpose, Ahab in all
his thoughts and actions ever had in view the ultimate capture of
Moby Dick; though he seemed ready to sacrifice all mortal
interests to that one passion; nevertheless it may have been that he was by
nature and long habituation far too wedded to a fiery whaleman's ways,
altogether to abandon the collateral prosecution of the voyage. Or at least
if this were otherwise, there were not wanting other motives much more
influential with him. It would be refining too much, perhaps, even considering his monomania, to hint that his vindictiveness towards the White
Whale might have possibly extended itself in some degree to all sperm
whales, and that the more monsters he slew by so much the more he multiplied the chances that each subsequently encountered whale would prove to
be the hated one he hunted. But if such an hypothesis be indeed exception-
able, there were still additional considerations which, though not so strictly
according with the wildness of his ruling passion, yet were by no means
incapable of swaying him.

To accomplish his object Ahab must use tools; and of all tools used in
the shadow of the moon, men are most apt to get out of order. He knew, for
example, that however magnetic his ascendency in some respects was over
Starbuck, yet that ascendency did not cover the complete spiritual man any

more than mere corporeal superiority involves intellectual mastership; for to the purely spiritual, the intellectual but stands in a sort of corporeal relation. Starbuck's body and Starbuck's coerced will were Ahab's, so long as Ahab kept his magnet at Starbuck's brain; still he knew that for all this the chief mate, in his soul, abhorred his captain's quest, and could he, would joyfully disintegrate himself from it, or even frustrate it. It might be that a long interval would elapse ere the White Whale was seen. During that long interval Starbuck would ever be apt to fall into open relapses of rebellion against his captain's leadership, unless some ordinary, prudential, circumstantial influences were brought to bear upon him. Not only that, but the subtle insanity of Ahab respecting Moby Dick was noways more significantly manifested than in his superlative sense and shrewdness in foreseeing that, for the present, the hunt should in some way be stripped of that strange imaginative impiousness which naturally invested it; that the full terror of the voyage must be kept withdrawn into the obscure background (for few men's courage is proof against protracted meditation unrelieved by action); that when they stood their long night watches, his officers and men must have some nearer things to think of than Moby Dick. For however eagerly and impetuously the savage crew had hailed the announcement of his quest; yet all sailors of all sorts are more or less capricious and unreliable— they live in the varying outer weather, and they inhale its fickleness—and when retained for any object remote and blank in the pursuit, however promissory of life and passion in the end, it is above all things requisite that temporary interests and employments should intervene and hold them healthily suspended for the final dash.

Nor was Ahab unmindful of another thing. In times of strong emotion mankind disdain all base considerations; but such times are evanescent. The permanent constitutional condition of the manufactured man, thought Ahab, is sordidness. Granting that the White Whale fully incites the hearts of this my savage crew, and playing round their savageness even breeds a certain generous knight-errantism in them, still, while for the love of it they give chase to Moby Dick, they must also have food for their more common, daily appetites. For even the high lifted and chivalric Crusaders of old times were not content to traverse two thousand miles of land to fight for their holy sepulchre, without committing burglaries, picking pockets, and gaining other pious perquisites by the way. Had they been strictly held to their one final and romantic object—that final and romantic object, too many would have turned from in disgust. I will not strip these men, thought Ahab, of all hopes of cash—aye, cash. They may scorn cash now; but let some months go by, and no perspective promise of it to them, and then this same quiescent cash all at once mutinying in them, this same cash would soon cashier Ahab.

Nor was there wanting still another precautionary motive more related to Ahab personally. Having impulsively, it is probable, and perhaps somewhat prematurely revealed the prime but private purpose of the Pequod's voyage, Ahab was now entirely conscious that, in so doing, he had indirectly laid himself open to the unanswerable charge of usurpation; and with perfect impunity, both moral and legal, his crew if so disposed, and to that end competent, could refuse all further obedience to him, and even violently wrest from him the command. From even the barely hinted imputation of usurpation, and the possible consequences of such a suppressed impression gaining ground, Ahab must of course have been most anxious to protect himself. That protection could only consist in his own predominating brain and heart and hand, backed by a heedful, closely calculating attention to every minute atmospheric influence which it was possible for his crew to be subjected to.

For all these reasons then, and others perhaps too analytic to be verbally developed here, Ahab plainly saw that he must still in a good degree continue true to the natural, nominal purpose of the Pequod's voyage; observe all customary usages; and not only that, but force himself to evince all his well known passionate interest in the general pursuit of his profession.

Be all this as it may, his voice was now often heard hailing the three mast-heads and admonishing them to keep a bright look-out, and not omit reporting even a porpoise. This vigilance was not long without reward.

# Chapter 47

*The Mat-Maker*

IT WAS A CLOUDY, SULTRY AFTERNOON; the seamen were lazily lounging about the decks, or vacantly gazing over into the lead-colored waters. Queequeg and I were mildly employed weaving what is called a sword-mat, for an additional lashing to our boat. So still and subdued and yet somehow preluding was all the scene, and such an incantation of revery lurked in the air, that each silent sailor seemed resolved into his own invisible self.

I was the attendant or page of Queequeg, while busy at the mat. As I kept passing and repassing the filling or woof of marline between the long yarns of the warp, using my own hand for the shuttle, and as Queequeg, standing sideways, ever and anon slid his heavy oaken sword between the threads, and idly looking off upon the water, carelessly and unthinkingly drove home every yarn: I say so strange a dreaminess did there then reign all over the ship and all over the sea, only broken by the intermitting dull sound of the sword, that it seemed as if this were the Loom of Time, and I myself were a shuttle mechanically weaving and weaving away at the Fates. There lay the fixed threads of the warp subject to but one single, ever returning, unchanging vibration, and that vibration merely enough to admit of the crosswise interblending of other threads with its own. This warp seemed necessity; and here, thought I, with my own hand I ply my own shuttle and weave my own destiny into these unalterable threads. Meantime, Queequeg's impulsive, indifferent sword, sometimes hitting the woof slantingly, or crookedly, or strongly, or weakly, as the case might be; and by this difference in the concluding blow producing a corresponding contrast in the final aspect of the completed fabric; this savage's sword, thought I, which thus finally shapes and fashions both warp and woof; this easy, indifferent sword must be chance—aye, chance, free will, and necessity —no wise incompatible—all interweavingly working together. The straight warp of necessity, not to be swerved from its ultimate course—its every alternating vibration, indeed, only tending to that; free will still free to ply her shuttle between given threads; and chance, though restrained in its play within the right lines of necessity, and sideways in its motions modified by free will, though thus prescribed to by both, chance by turns rules either, and has the last featuring blow at events.

       *          *          *          *          *

Thus we were weaving and weaving away when I started at a sound so strange, long drawn, and musically wild and unearthly, that the ball of free will dropped from my hand, and I stood gazing up at the clouds whence that voice dropped like a wing. High aloft in the cross-trees was that mad Gay-Header, Tashtego. His body was reaching eagerly forward, his hand stretched out like a wand, and at brief sudden intervals he continued his cries. To be sure the same sound was that very moment perhaps being heard all over the seas, from hundreds of whalemen's look-outs perched as high in the air; but from few of those lungs could that accustomed old cry have derived such a marvellous cadence as from Tashtego the Indian's.

As he stood hovering over you half suspended in air, so wildly and eagerly peering towards the horizon, you would have thought him some prophet or seer beholding the shadows of Fate, and by those wild cries announcing their coming.

"There she blows! there! there! there! she blows! she blows!"

"Where-away?"

"On the lee-beam, about two miles off! a school of them!"

Instantly all was commotion.

The Sperm Whale blows as a clock ticks, with the same undeviating and reliable uniformity. And thereby whalemen distinguish this fish from other tribes of his genus.

"There go flukes!" was now the cry from Tashtego; and the whales disappeared.

"Quick, steward!" cried Ahab. "Time! time!"

Dough-Boy hurried below, glanced at the watch, and reported the exact minute to Ahab.

The ship was now kept away from the wind, and she went gently rolling before it. Tashtego reporting that the whales had gone down heading to leeward, we confidently looked to see them again directly in advance of our bows. For that singular craft at times evinced by the Sperm Whale when, sounding with his head in one direction, he nevertheless, while concealed beneath the surface, mills round, and swiftly swims off in the opposite quarter—this deceitfulness of his could not now be in action; for there was no reason to suppose that the fish seen by Tashtego had been in any way alarmed, or indeed knew at all of our vicinity. One of the men selected for shipkeepers—that is, those not appointed to the boats, by this time relieved the Indian at the main-mast head. The sailors at the fore and mizzen had come down; the line tubs were fixed in their places; the cranes were thrust out; the mainyard was backed, and the three boats swung over the sea like three samphire baskets over high cliffs. Outside of the bulwarks their eager crews with one hand clung to the rail, while one foot was expectantly poised on the gunwale. So look the long line of man-of-war's men about to throw themselves on board an enemy's ship.

But at this critical instant a sudden exclamation was heard that took every eye from the whale. With a start all glared at dark Ahab, who was surrounded by five dusky phantoms that seemed fresh formed out of air.

# Chapter 48

*The First Lowering*

T HE PHANTOMS, for so they then seemed, were flitting on the other side of the deck, and, with a noiseless celerity, were casting loose the tackles and bands of the boat which swung there. This boat had always been deemed one of the spare boats, though technically called the captain's, on account of its hanging from the starboard quarter. The figure that now stood by its bows was tall and swart, with one white tooth evilly protruding from its steel-like lips. A rumpled Chinese jacket of black cotton funereally invested him, with wide black trowsers of the same dark stuff. But strangely crowning this ebonness was a glistening white plaited turban, the living hair braided and coiled round and round upon his head. Less swart in aspect, the companions of this figure were of that vivid, tiger-yellow complexion peculiar to some of the aboriginal natives of the Manillas;—a race notorious for a certain diabolism of subtilty, and by some honest white mariners supposed to be the paid spies and secret confidential agents on the water of the devil, their lord, whose counting-room they suppose to be elsewhere.

While yet the wondering ship's company were gazing upon these strangers, Ahab cried out to the white-turbaned old man at their head, "All ready there, Fedallah?"

"Ready," was the half-hissed reply.

"Lower away then; d'ye hear?" shouting across the deck. "Lower away there, I say."

Such was the thunder of his voice, that spite of their amazement the men sprang over the rail; the sheaves whirled round in the blocks; with a wallow, the three boats dropped into the sea; while, with a dexterous, off-handed daring, unknown in any other vocation, the sailors, goat-like, leaped down the rolling ship's side into the tossed boats below.

Hardly had they pulled out from under the ship's lee, when a fourth keel, coming from the windward side, pulled round under the stern, and showed the five strangers rowing Ahab, who, standing erect in the stern, loudly hailed Starbuck, Stubb, and Flask, to spread themselves widely, so as to cover a large expanse of water. But with all their eyes again riveted upon the swart Fedallah and his crew, the inmates of the other boats obeyed not the command.

"Captain Ahab?—" said Starbuck.

"Spread yourselves," cried Ahab; "give way, all four boats. Thou, Flask, pull out more to leeward!"

"Aye, aye, sir," cheerily cried little King-Post, sweeping round his great steering oar. "Lay back!" addressing his crew. "There!—there!—there again! There she blows right ahead, boys!—lay back!—Never heed yonder yellow boys, Archy."

"Oh, I don't mind 'em, sir," said Archy; "I knew it all before now. Didn't I hear 'em in the hold? And didn't I tell Cabaco here of it? What say ye, Cabaco? They are stowaways, Mr. Flask."

"Pull, pull, my fine hearts-alive; pull, my children; pull, my little ones," drawlingly and soothingly sighed Stubb to his crew, some of whom still showed signs of uneasiness. "Why don't you break your backbones, my boys? What is it you stare at? Those chaps in yonder boat? Tut! They are only five more hands come to help us—never mind from where—the more the merrier. Pull, then, do pull; never mind the brimstone—devils are good fellows enough. So, so; there you are now; that's the stroke for a thousand pounds; that's the stroke to sweep the stakes! Hurrah for the gold cup of sperm oil, my heroes! Three cheers, men—all hearts alive! Easy, easy; don't be in a hurry—don't be in a hurry. Why don't you snap your oars, you rascals? Bite something, you dogs! So, so, so, then;—softly, softly! That's it—that's it! long and strong. Give way there, give way! The devil fetch ye, ye ragamuffin rapscallions; ye are all asleep. Stop snoring, ye sleepers, and pull. Pull, will ye? pull, can't ye? pull, won't ye? Why in the name of gudgeons and ginger-cakes don't ye pull?—pull and break something!

pull, and start your eyes out! Here!" whipping out the sharp knife from his girdle; "every mother's son of ye draw his knife, and pull with the blade between his teeth. That's it—that's it. Now ye do something; that looks like it, my steel-bits. Start her—start her, my silver-spoons! Start her, marling-spikes!"

Stubb's exordium to his crew is given here at large, because he had rather a peculiar way of talking to them in general, and especially in inculcating the religion of rowing. But you must not suppose from this specimen of his sermonizings that he ever flew into downright passions with his congregation. Not at all; and therein consisted his chief peculiarity. He would say the most terrific things to his crew, in a tone so strangely compounded of fun and fury, and the fury seemed so calculated merely as a spice to the fun, that no oarsman could hear such queer invocations without pulling for dear life, and yet pulling for the mere joke of the thing. Besides he all the time looked so easy and indolent himself, so loungingly managed his steering-oar, and so broadly gaped—open-mouthed at times—that the mere sight of such a yawning commander, by sheer force of contrast, acted like a charm upon the crew. Then again, Stubb was one of those odd sort of humorists, whose jollity is sometimes so curiously ambiguous, as to put all inferiors on their guard in the matter of obeying them.

In obedience to a sign from Ahab, Starbuck was now pulling obliquely across Stubb's bow; and when for a minute or so the two boats were pretty near to each other, Stubb hailed the mate.

"Mr. Starbuck! larboard boat there, ahoy! a word with ye, sir, if ye please!"

"Halloa!" returned Starbuck, turning round not a single inch as he spoke; still earnestly but whisperingly urging his crew; his face set like a flint from Stubb's.

"What think ye of those yellow boys, sir!"

"Smuggled on board, somehow, before the ship sailed. (Strong, strong, boys!)" in a whisper to his crew, then speaking out loud again: "A sad business, Mr. Stubb! (seethe her, seethe her, my lads!) but never mind, Mr. Stubb, all for the best. Let all your crew pull strong, come what will. (Spring, my men, spring!) There's hogsheads of sperm ahead, Mr. Stubb, and that's what ye came for. (Pull, my boys!) Sperm, sperm's the play! This at least is duty; duty and profit hand in hand!"

"Aye, aye, I thought as much," soliloquized Stubb, when the boats diverged, "as soon as I clapt eye on 'em, I thought so. Aye, and that's what he went into the after hold for, so often, as Dough-Boy long suspected.

They were hidden down there. The White Whale's at the bottom of it. Well, well, so be it! Can't be helped! All right! Give way, men! It ain't the White Whale to-day! Give way!"

Now the advent of these outlandish strangers at such a critical instant as the lowering of the boats from the deck, this had not unreasonably awakened a sort of superstitious amazement in some of the ship's company; but Archy's fancied discovery having some time previous got abroad among them, though indeed not credited then, this had in some small measure prepared them for the event. It took off the extreme edge of their wonder; and so what with all this and Stubb's confident way of accounting for their appearance, they were for the time freed from superstitious surmisings; though the affair still left abundant room for all manner of wild conjectures as to dark Ahab's precise agency in the matter from the beginning. For me, I silently recalled the mysterious shadows I had seen creeping on board the Pequod during the dim Nantucket dawn, as well as the enigmatical hintings of the unaccountable Elijah.

Meantime, Ahab, out of hearing of his officers, having sided the furthest to windward, was still ranging ahead of the other boats; a circumstance bespeaking how potent a crew was pulling him. Those tiger yellow creatures of his seemed all steel and whalebone; like five trip-hammers they rose and fell with regular strokes of strength, which periodically started the boat along the water like a horizontal burst boiler out of a Mississippi steamer. As for Fedallah, who was seen pulling the harpooneer oar, he had thrown aside his black jacket, and displayed his naked chest with the whole part of his body above the gunwale, clearly cut against the alternating depressions of the watery horizon; while at the other end of the boat Ahab, with one arm, like a fencer's, thrown half backward into the air, as if to counter-balance any tendency to trip; Ahab was seen steadily managing his steering oar as in a thousand boat lowerings ere the White Whale had torn him. All at once the outstretched arm gave a peculiar motion and then remained fixed, while the boat's five oars were seen simultaneously peaked. Boat and crew sat motionless on the sea. Instantly the three spread boats in the rear paused on their way. The whales had irregularly settled bodily down into the blue, thus giving no distantly discernible token of the movement, though from his closer vicinity Ahab had observed it.

"Every man look out along his oar!" cried Starbuck. "Thou, Quee-queg, stand up!"

Nimbly springing up on the triangular raised box in the bow, the savage stood erect there, and with intensely eager eyes gazed off towards the

spot where the chase had last been descried. Likewise upon the extreme
stern of the boat where it was also triangularly platformed level with the
gunwale, Starbuck himself was seen coolly and adroitly balancing himself
to the jerking tossings of his chip of a craft, and silently eyeing the vast
blue eye of the sea.

Not very far distant Flask's boat was also lying breathlessly still; its
commander recklessly standing upon the top of the loggerhead, a stout sort
of post rooted in the keel, and rising some two feet above the level of the
stern platform. It is used for catching turns with the whale line. Its top is not
more spacious than the palm of a man's hand, and standing upon such a base
as that, Flask seemed perched at the mast-head of some ship which had
sunk to all but her trucks. But little King-Post was small and short, and at
the same time little King-Post was full of a large and tall ambition, so that
this loggerhead stand-point of his did by no means satisfy King-Post.

"I can't see three seas off; tip us up an oar there, and let me on to that."

Upon this, Daggoo, with either hand upon the gunwale to steady his
way, swiftly slid aft, and then erecting himself volunteered his lofty
shoulders for a pedestal.

"Good a mast-head as any, sir. Will you mount?"

"That I will, and thank ye very much, my fine fellow; only I wish you
fifty feet taller."

Whereupon planting his feet firmly against two opposite planks of the
boat, the gigantic negro, stooping a little, presented his flat palm to Flask's
foot, and then putting Flask's hand on his hearse-plumed head and bidding
him spring as he himself should toss, with one dexterous fling landed the
little man high and dry on his shoulders. And here was Flask now standing,
Daggoo with one lifted arm furnishing him with a breast-band to lean
against and steady himself by.

At any time it is a strange sight to the tyro to see with what wondrous
habitude of unconscious skill the whaleman will maintain an erect posture
in his boat, even when pitched about by the most riotously perverse and
cross-running seas. Still more strange to see him giddily perched upon the
loggerhead itself, under such circumstances. But the sight of little Flask
mounted upon gigantic Daggoo was yet more curious; for sustaining himself with a cool, indifferent, easy, unthought of, barbaric majesty, the noble
negro to every roll of the sea harmoniously rolled his fine form. On his
broad back, flaxen-haired Flask seemed a snow-flake. The bearer looked
nobler than the rider. Though, truly, vivacious, tumultuous, ostentatious
little Flask would now and then stamp with impatience; but not one added

heave did he thereby give to the negro's lordly chest. So have I seen
Passion and Vanity stamping the living magnanimous earth, but the earth
did not alter her tides and her seasons for that.

Meanwhile Stubb, the third mate, betrayed no such far-gazing solic-
itudes. The whales might have made one of their regular soundings,
not a temporary dive from mere fright; and if that were the case, Stubb, as
his wont in such cases, it seems, was resolved to solace the languishing
interval with his pipe. He withdrew it from his hatband, where he always
wore it aslant like a feather. He loaded it, and rammed home the loading
with his thumb-end; but hardly had he ignited his match across the rough
sand-paper of his hand, when Tashtego, his harpooneer, whose eyes had
been setting to windward like two fixed stars, suddenly dropped like
light from his erect attitude to his seat, crying out in a quick phrensy of
hurry, "Down, down all, and give way!—there they are!"

To a landsman, no whale, nor any sign of a herring, would have been
visible at that moment; nothing but a troubled bit of greenish white water,
and thin scattered puffs of vapor hovering over it, and suffusingly blowing
off to leeward, like the confused scud from white rolling billows. The air
around suddenly vibrated and tingled, as it were, like the air over intensely
heated plates of iron. Beneath this atmospheric waving and curling, and
partially beneath a thin layer of water, also, the whales were swimming.
Seen in advance of all the other indications, the puffs of vapor they spouted,
seemed their forerunning couriers and detached flying outriders.

All four boats were now in keen pursuit of that one spot of troubled
water and air. But it bade fair to outstrip them; it flew on and on, as a mass
of interblending bubbles borne down a rapid stream from the hills.

"Pull, pull, my good boys," said Starbuck, in the lowest possible but
intensest concentrated whisper to his men; while the sharp fixed glance from
his eyes, darted straight ahead of the bow, almost seemed as two visible
needles in two unerring binnacle compasses. He did not say much to his
crew, though, nor did his crew say anything to him. Only the silence of the
boat was at intervals startlingly pierced by one of his peculiar whispers,
now harsh with command, now soft with entreaty.

How different the loud little King-Post. "Sing out and say something,
my hearties. Roar and pull, my thunderbolts! Beach me, beach me on their
black backs, boys; only do that for me, and I'll sign over to you my
Martha's Vineyard plantation, boys; including wife and children, boys.
Lay me on—lay me on! O Lord, Lord! but I shall go stark, staring mad:
See! see that white water!" And so shouting, he pulled his hat from his head,

and stamped up and down on it; then picking it up, flirted it far off upon the sea; and finally fell to rearing and plunging in the boat's stern like a crazed colt from the prairie.

"Look at that chap now," philosophically drawled Stubb, who, with his unlighted short pipe, mechanically retained between his teeth, at a short distance, followed after—"He's got fits, that Flask has. Fits? yes, give him fits—that's the very word—pitch fits into 'em. Merrily, merrily, hearts-alive. Pudding for supper, you know;—merry's the word. Pull, babes —pull, sucklings—pull, all. But what the devil are you hurrying about? Softly, softly, and steadily, my men. Only pull, and keep pulling; nothing more. Crack all your backbones, and bite your knives in two—that's all. Take it easy—why don't ye take it easy, I say, and burst all your livers and lungs!"

But what it was that inscrutable Ahab said to that tiger-yellow crew of his—these were words best omitted here; for you live under the blessed light of the evangelical land. Only the infidel sharks in the audacious seas may give ear to such words, when, with tornado brow, and eyes of red murder, and foam-glued lips, Ahab leaped after his prey.

Meanwhile, all the boats tore on. The repeated specific allusions of Flask to "that whale," as he called the fictitious monster which he declared to be incessantly tantalizing his boat's bow with its tail—these allusions of his were at times so vivid and life-like, that they would cause some one or two of his men to snatch a fearful look over the shoulder. But this was against all rule; for the oarsmen must put out their eyes, and ram a skewer through their necks; usage pronouncing that they must have no organs but ears, and no limbs but arms, in these critical moments.

It was a sight full of quick wonder and awe! The vast swells of the omnipotent sea; the surging, hollow roar they made, as they rolled along the eight gunwales, like gigantic bowls in a boundless bowling-green; the brief suspended agony of the boat, as it would tip for an instant on the knife-like edge of the sharper waves, that almost seemed threatening to cut it in two; the sudden profound dip into the watery glens and hollows; the keen spurrings and goadings to gain the top of the opposite hill; the headlong, sled-like slide down its other side;—all these, with the cries of the headsmen and harpooneers, and the shuddering gasps of the oarsmen, with the wondrous sight of the ivory Pequod bearing down upon her boats with outstretched sails, like a wild hen after her screaming brood;—all this was thrilling. Not the raw recruit, marching from the bosom of his wife into the fever heat of his first battle; not the dead man's ghost encountering the

first unknown phantom in the other world;—neither of these can feel
stranger and stronger emotions than that man does, who for the first time
finds himself pulling into the charmed, churned circle of the hunted sperm
whale.

The dancing white water made by the chase was now becoming more
'and more visible, owing to the increasing darkness of the dun cloud-shadows
flung upon the sea. The jets of vapor no longer blended, but tilted everywhere to right and left; the whales seemed separating their wakes. The
boats were pulled more apart; Starbuck giving chase to three whales
running dead to leeward. Our sail was now set, and, with the still rising
wind, we rushed along; the boat going with such madness through the
water, that the lee oars could scarcely be worked rapidly enough to escape
being torn from the row-locks.

Soon we were running through a suffusing wide veil of mist; neither
ship nor boat to be seen.

"Give way, men," whispered Starbuck, drawing still further aft the
sheet of his sail; "there is time to kill a fish yet before the squall comes.
There's white water again!—close to! Spring!"

Soon after, two cries in quick succession on each side of us denoted that
the other boats had got fast; but hardly were they overheard, when with a
lightning-like hurtling whisper Starbuck said: "Stand up!" and Queequeg,
harpoon in hand, sprang to his feet.

Though not one of the oarsmen was then facing the life and death peril
so close to them ahead, yet with their eyes on the intense countenance of the
mate in the stern of the boat, they knew that the imminent instant had come;
they heard, too, an enormous wallowing sound as of fifty elephants stirring
in their litter. Meanwhile the boat was still booming through the mist, the
waves curling and hissing around us like the erected crests of enraged
serpents.

"That's his hump. There, there, give it to him!" whispered Starbuck.

A short rushing sound leaped out of the boat; it was the darted iron of
Queequeg. Then all in one welded commotion came an invisible push from
astern, while forward the boat seemed striking on a ledge; the sail collapsed
and exploded; a gush of scalding vapor shot up near by; something rolled
and tumbled like an earthquake beneath us. The whole crew were half
suffocated as they were tossed helter-skelter into the white curdling cream
of the squall. Squall, whale, and harpoon had all blended together; and the
whale, merely grazed by the iron, escaped.

Though completely swamped, the boat was nearly unharmed. Swimming round it we picked up the floating oars, and lashing them across the gunwale, tumbled back to our places. There we sat up to our knees in the sea, the water covering every rib and plank, so that to our downward gazing eyes the suspended craft seemed a coral boat grown up to us from the bottom of the ocean.

The wind increased to a howl; the waves dashed their bucklers together; the whole squall roared, forked, and crackled around us like a white fire upon the prairie, in which, unconsumed, we were burning; immortal in these jaws of death! In vain we hailed the other boats; as well roar to the live coals down the chimney of a flaming furnace as hail those boats in that storm. Meanwhile the driving scud, rack, and mist, grew darker with the shadows of night; no sign of the ship could be seen. The rising sea forbade all attempts to bale out the boat. The oars were useless as propellers, performing now the office of life-preservers. So, cutting the lashing of the waterproof match keg, after many failures Starbuck contrived to ignite the lamp in the lantern; then stretching it on a waif pole, handed it to Queequeg as the standard-bearer of this forlorn hope. There, then, he sat, holding up that imbecile candle in the heart of that almighty forlornness. There, then, he sat, the sign and symbol of a man without faith, hopelessly holding up hope in the midst of despair.

Wet, drenched through, and shivering cold, despairing of ship or boat, we lifted up our eyes as the dawn came on. The mist still spread over the sea, the empty lantern lay crushed in the bottom of the boat. Suddenly Queequeg started to his feet, hollowing his hand to his ear. We all heard a faint creaking, as of ropes and yards hitherto muffled by the storm. The sound came nearer and nearer; the thick mists were dimly parted by a huge, vague form. Affrighted, we all sprang into the sea as the ship at last loomed into view, bearing right down upon us within a distance of not much more than its length.

Floating on the waves we saw the abandoned boat, as for one instant it tossed and gaped beneath the ship's bows like a chip at the base of a cataract; and then the vast hull rolled over it, and it was seen no more till it came up weltering astern. Again we swam for it, were dashed against it by the seas, and were at last taken up and safely landed on board. Ere the squall came close to, the other boats had cut loose from their fish and returned to the ship in good time. The ship had given us up, but was still cruising, if haply it might light upon some token of our perishing,—an oar or a lance pole.

# Chapter 49

## The Hyena

THERE ARE CERTAIN QUEER TIMES and occasions in this strange mixed affair we call life when a man takes this whole universe for a vast practical joke, though the wit thereof he but dimly discerns, and more than suspects that the joke is at nobody's expense but his own. However, nothing dispirits, and nothing seems worth while disputing. He bolts down all events, all creeds, and beliefs, and persuasions, all hard things visible and invisible, never mind how knobby; as an ostrich of potent digestion gobbles down bullets and gun flints. And as for small difficulties and worryings, prospects of sudden disaster, peril of life and limb; all these, and death itself, seem to him only sly, good-natured hits, and jolly punches in the side bestowed by the unseen and unaccountable old joker. That odd sort of wayward mood I am speaking of, comes over a man only in some time of extreme tribulation; it comes in the very midst of his earnestness, so that what just before might have seemed to him a thing most momentous, now seems but a part of the general joke. There is nothing like the perils of whaling to breed this free and easy sort of genial, desperado philosophy; and with it I now regarded this whole voyage of the Pequod, and the great White Whale its object.

"Queequeg," said I, when they had dragged me, the last man, to the deck, and I was still shaking myself in my jacket to fling off the water;

226

"Queequeg, my fine friend, does this sort of thing often happen?" Without much emotion, though soaked through just like me, he gave me to understand that such things did often happen.

"Mr. Stubb," said I, turning to that worthy, who, buttoned up in his oil-jacket, was now calmly smoking his pipe in the rain; "Mr. Stubb, I think I have heard you say that of all whalemen you ever met, our chief mate, Mr. Starbuck, is by far the most careful and prudent. I suppose then, that going plump on a flying whale with your sail set in a foggy squall is the height of a whaleman's discretion?"

"Certain. I've lowered for whales from a leaking ship in a gale off Cape Horn."

"Mr. Flask," said I, turning to little King-Post, who was standing close by; "you are experienced in these things, and I am not. Will you tell me whether it is an unalterable law in this fishery, Mr. Flask, for an oarsman to break his own back pulling himself back-foremost into death's jaws?"

"Can't you twist that smaller?" said Flask. "Yes, that's the law. I should like to see a boat's crew backing water up to a whale face foremost. Ha, ha! the whale would give them squint for squint, mind that!"

Here then, from three impartial witnesses, I had a deliberate statement of the entire case. Considering, therefore, that squalls and capsizings in the water and consequent bivouacks on the deep, were matters of common occurrence in this kind of life; considering that at the superlatively critical instant of going on to the whale I must resign my life into the hands of him who steered the boat—oftentimes a fellow who at that very moment is in his impetuousness upon the point of scuttling the craft with his own frantic stampings; considering that the particular disaster to our own particular boat was chiefly to be imputed to Starbuck's driving on to his whale almost in the teeth of a squall, and considering that Starbuck, notwithstanding, was famous for his great heedfulness in the fishery; considering that I belonged to this uncommonly prudent Starbuck's boat; and finally considering in what a devil's chase I was implicated, touching the White Whale: taking all things together, I say, I thought I might as well go below and make a rough draft of my will. "Queequeg," said I, "come along, you shall be my lawyer, executor, and legatee."

It may seem strange that of all men sailors should be tinkering at their last wills and testaments, but there are no people in the world more fond of that diversion. This was the fourth time in my nautical life that I had done the same thing. After the ceremony was concluded upon the present occasion, I felt all the easier; a stone was rolled away from my heart. Besides, all the days I should now live would be as good as the days that Lazarus lived after his resurrection; a supplementary clean gain of so many months or weeks as the case might be. I survived myself; my death and burial were locked up in my chest. I looked round me tranquilly and contentedly, like a quiet ghost with a clean conscience sitting inside the bars of a snug family vault.

Now then, thought I, unconsciously rolling up the sleeves of my frock, here goes for a cool, collected dive at death and destruction, and the devil fetch the hindmost.

# Chapter 50

*Ahab's Boat and Crew · Fedallah*

W HO WOULD HAVE THOUGHT IT, Flask!" cried Stubb; "if I had but one leg you would not catch me in a boat, unless maybe to stop the plug-hole with my timber toe. Oh! he's a wonderful old man!"

"I don't think it so strange, after all, on that account," said Flask. "If his leg were off at the hip, now, it would be a different thing. That would disable him; but he has one knee, and good part of the other left, you know."

"I don't know that, my little man; I never yet saw him kneel."

\*      \*      \*      \*      \*

Among whale-wise people it has often been argued whether, considering the paramount importance of his life to the success of the voyage, it is right for a whaling captain to jeopardize that life in the active perils of the chase. So Tamerlane's soldiers often argued with tears in their eyes, whether that invaluable life of his ought to be carried into the thickest of the fight.

But with Ahab the question assumed a modified aspect. Considering that with two legs man is but a hobbling wight in all times of danger; considering that the pursuit of whales is always under great and extraordinary difficulties; that every individual moment, indeed, then comprises a peril; under these circumstances is it wise for any maimed man to enter a whale-boat in the hunt? As a general thing, the joint-owners of the Pequod must have plainly thought not.

Ahab well knew that although his friends at home would think little of his entering a boat in certain comparatively harmless vicissitudes of the chase, for the sake of being near the scene of action and giving his orders in person, yet for Captain Ahab to have a boat actually apportioned to him as a regular headsman in the hunt—above all for Captain Ahab to be supplied with five extra men, as that same boat's crew, he well knew that such generous conceits never entered the heads of the owners of the Pequod. Therefore he had not solicited a boat's crew from them, nor had he in any way hinted his desires on that head. Nevertheless he had taken private measures of his own touching all that matter. Until Archy's published discovery, the sailors had little foreseen it, though to be sure when, after being a little while out of port, all hands had concluded the customary business of fitting the whaleboats for service; when some time after this Ahab was now and then found bestirring himself in the matter of making thole-pins with his own hands for what was thought to be one of the spare boats, and even solicitously cutting the small wooden skewers, which when the line is running out are pinned over the groove in the bow: when all this was observed in him, and particularly his solicitude in having an extra coat of sheathing in the bottom of the boat, as if to make it better withstand the pointed pressure of his ivory limb; and also the anxiety he evinced in exactly shaping the thigh board, or clumsy cleat, as it is sometimes called, the horizontal piece in the boat's bow for bracing the knee against in darting or stabbing at the whale; when it was observed how often he stood up in that boat with his solitary knee fixed in the semi-circular depression in the cleat, and with the carpenter's chisel gouged out a little here and straightened it a little there; all these things, I say, had awakened much interest and curiosity at the time. But almost everybody supposed that this particular preparative heedfulness in Ahab must only be with a view to the ultimate chase of Moby Dick; for he had already revealed his intention to hunt that mortal monster in person. But such a supposition did by no means involve the remotest suspicion as to any boat's crew being assigned to that boat.

Now, with the subordinate phantoms, what wonder remained soon waned away; for in a whaler wonders soon wane. Besides, now and then such unaccountable odds and ends of strange nations come up from the unknown nooks and ash-holes of the earth to man these floating outlaws of whalers; and the ships themselves often pick up such queer castaway creatures found tossing about the open sea on planks, bits of wreck, oars,

whale-boats, canoes, blown-off Japanese junks, and what not; that Beelzebub himself might climb up the side and step down into the cabin to chat
with the captain, and it would not create any unsubduable excitement in the
forecastle.

But be all this as it may, certain it is that while the subordinate phantoms
soon found their place among the crew, though still as it were somehow
distinct from them, yet that hair-turbaned Fedallah remained a muffled
mystery to the last. Whence he came in a mannerly world like this, by what
sort of unaccountable tie he soon evinced himself to be linked with Ahab's
peculiar fortunes; nay, so far as to have some sort of a half-hinted influence;
Heaven knows, but it might have been even authority over him; all this
none knew. But one cannot sustain an indifferent air concerning Fedallah.
He was such a creature as civilized, domestic people in the temperate zone
only see in their dreams, and that but dimly; but the like of whom now and
then glide among the unchanging Asiatic communities, especially the
Oriental isles to the east of the continent—those insulated, immemorial,
unalterable countries, which even in these modern days still preserve much
of the ghostly aboriginalness of earth's primal generations, when the
memory of the first man was a distinct recollection, and all men his
descendants, **unknowing** whence he came, eyed each other as real phantoms,
and asked of the sun and the moon why they were created and to what end;
when though, according to Genesis, the angels indeed consorted with the
daughters of men, the devils also, add the uncanonical Rabbins, indulged in
mundane amours.

# Chapter 51

## *The Spirit-Spout*

DAYS, WEEKS PASSED, and under easy sail, the ivory Pequod had slowly swept across four several cruising-grounds; that off the Azores; off the Cape de Verdes; on the Plate (so called), being off the mouth of the Rio de la Plata; and the Carrol Ground, an unstaked, watery locality, southerly from St. Helena.

It was while gliding through these latter waters that one serene and moonlight night, when all the waves rolled by like scrolls of silver; and, by their soft, suffusing seethings, made what seemed a silvery silence, not a solitude: on such a silent night a silvery jet was seen far in advance of the white bubbles at the bow. Lit up by the moon, it looked celestial; seemed some plumed and glittering god uprising from the sea. Fedallah first descried this jet. For of these moonlight nights, it was his wont to mount to the main-mast head, and stand a look-out there, with the same precision as if it had been day. And yet, though herds of whales were seen by night, not one whaleman in a hundred would venture a lowering for them. You may think with what emotions, then, the seamen beheld this old Oriental perched aloft at such unusual hours; his turban and the moon, companions in one sky. But when, after spending his uniform interval there for several successive nights without uttering a single sound; when, after all this silence, his unearthly voice was heard announcing that silvery, moon-lit jet,

232

every reclining mariner started to his feet as if some winged spirit had lighted in the rigging, and hailed the mortal crew. "There she blows!" Had the trump of judgment blown, they could not have quivered more; yet still they felt no terror; rather pleasure. For though it was a most unwonted hour, yet so impressive was the cry, and so deliriously exciting, that almost every soul on board instinctively desired a lowering.

Walking the deck with quick, side-lunging strides, Ahab commanded the t'gallant sails and royals to be set, and every stunsail spread. The best man in the ship must take the helm. Then, with every mast-head manned, the piled-up craft rolled down before the wind. The strange, upheaving, lifting tendency of the taffrail breeze filling the hollows of so many sails, made the buoyant, hovering deck to feel like air beneath the feet; while still she rushed along, as if two antagonistic influences were struggling in her— one to mount direct to heaven, the other to drive yawingly to some horizontal goal. And had you watched Ahab's face that night, you would have thought that in him also two different things were warring. While his one live leg made lively echoes along the deck, every stroke of his dead limb sounded like a coffin-tap. On life and death this old man walked. But though the ship so swiftly sped, and though from every eye, like arrows, the eager glances shot, yet the silvery jet was no more seen that night. Every sailor swore he saw it once, but not a second time.

This midnight-spout had almost grown a forgotten thing, when, some days after, lo! at the same silent hour, it was again announced: again it was descried by all; but upon making sail to overtake it, once more it disappeared as if it had never been. And so it served us night after night, till no one heeded it but to wonder at it. Mysteriously jetted into the clear moonlight, or starlight, as the case might be; disappearing again for one whole day, or two days, or three; and somehow seeming at every distinct repetition to be advancing still further and further in our van, this solitary jet seemed for ever alluring us on.

Nor with the immemorial superstition of their race, and in accordance with the preternaturalness, as it seemed, which in many things invested the Pequod, were there wanting some of the seamen who swore that whenever and wherever descried; at however remote times, or in however far apart latitudes and longitudes, that unnearable spout was cast by one self-same whale; and that whale, Moby Dick. For a time, there reigned, too, a sense of peculiar dread at this flitting apparition, as if it were treacherously beckoning us on and on, in order that the monster might turn round upon us, and rend us at last in the remotest and most savage seas.

These temporary apprehensions, so vague but so awful, derived a wondrous potency from the contrasting serenity of the weather, in which, beneath all its blue blandness, some thought there lurked a devilish charm, as for days and days we voyaged along, through seas so wearily, lonesomely mild, that all space, in repugnance to our vengeful errand, seemed vacating itself of life before our urn-like prow.

But, at last, when turning to the eastward, the Cape winds began howling around us, and we rose and fell upon the long, troubled seas that are there; when the ivory-tusked Pequod sharply bowed to the blast, and gored the dark waves in her madness, till, like showers of silver chips, the foam-flakes flew over her bulwarks; then all this desolate vacuity of life went away, but gave place to sights more dismal than before.

Close to our bows, strange forms in the water darted hither and thither before us; while thick in our rear flew the inscrutable sea-ravens. And every morning, perched on our stays, rows of these birds were seen; and spite of our hootings, for a long time obstinately clung to the hemp, as though they deemed our ship some drifting, uninhabited craft; a thing appointed to desolation, and therefore fit roosting-place for their homeless selves. And heaved and heaved, still unrestingly heaved the black sea, as if its vast tides were a conscience; and the great mundane soul were in anguish and remorse for the long sin and suffering it had bred.

Cape of Good Hope, do they call ye? Rather Cape Tormentoso, as called of yore; for long allured by the perfidious silences that before had attended us, we found ourselves launched into this tormented sea, where guilty beings transformed into those fowls and these fish, seemed condemned to swim on everlastingly without any haven in store, or beat that black air without any horizon. But calm, snow-white, and unvarying; still directing its fountain of feathers to the sky; still beckoning us on from before, the solitary jet would at times be descried.

During all this blackness of the elements, Ahab, though assuming for the time the almost continual command of the drenched and dangerous deck, manifested the gloomiest reserve; and more seldom than ever addressed his mates. In tempestuous times like these, after everything above and aloft has been secured, nothing more can be done but passively to await the issue of the gale. Then Captain and crew become practical fatalists. So, with his ivory leg inserted into its accustomed hole, and with one hand firmly grasping a shroud, Ahab for hours and hours would stand gazing dead to windward, while an occasional squall of sleet or snow would all but congeal his very eyelashes together. Meantime, the crew driven from the forward part of the ship by the perilous seas that burstingly broke over its bows, stood in a line along the bulwarks in the waist; and the better to guard against the leaping waves, each man had slipped himself into a sort of bowline secured to the rail, in which he swung as in a loosened belt. Few or no words were spoken; and the silent ship, as if manned by painted sailors in wax, day after day tore on through all the swift madness and gladness of the demoniac waves. By night the same muteness of humanity before the shrieks of the ocean prevailed; still in silence the men swung in the bow-lines; still wordless Ahab stood up to the blast. Even when wearied nature seemed demanding repose he would not seek that repose in his hammock. Never could Starbuck forget the old man's aspect, when one night going down into the cabin to mark how the barometer stood, he saw him with closed eyes sitting straight in his floor-screwed chair; the rain and half-melted sleet of the storm from which he had some time before emerged, still slowly dripping from the unremoved hat and coat. On the table beside him lay unrolled one of those charts of tides and currents which have previously been spoken of. His lantern swung from his tightly clenched hand. Though the body was erect, the head was thrown back so that the closed eyes were pointed towards the needle of the tell-tale that swung from a beam in the ceiling.*

Terrible old man! thought Starbuck with a shudder, sleeping in this gale, still thou steadfastly eyest thy purpose.

* The cabin-compass is called the tell-tale, because without going to the compass at the helm, the Captain, while below, can inform himself of the course of the ship.

# Chapter 52

## The Albatross

SOUTH-EASTWARD from the Cape, off the distant Crozetts, a good cruising ground for Right Whalemen, a sail loomed ahead, the Goney (Albatross) by name. As she slowly drew nigh, from my lofty perch at the fore-mast-head, I had a good view of that sight so remarkable to a tyro in the far ocean fisheries—a whaler at sea, and long absent from home.

As if the waves had been fullers, this craft was bleached like the skeleton of a stranded walrus. All down her sides, this spectral appearance was traced with long channels of reddened rust, while all her spars and her rigging were like the thick branches of trees furred over with hoar-frost. Only her lower sails were set. A wild sight it was to see her long-bearded look-outs at those three mast-heads. They seemed clad in the skins of beasts, so torn and bepatched the raiment that had survived nearly four years of cruising. Standing in iron hoops nailed to the mast, they swayed and swung over a fathomless sea; and though, when the ship slowly glided close under our stern, we six men in the air came so nigh to each other that we might almost have leaped from the mast-heads of one ship to those of the other; yet, those forlorn-looking fishermen, mildly eyeing us as they passed, said not one word to our own look-outs, while the quarter-deck hail was being heard from below.

"Ship ahoy! Have ye seen the White Whale?"

But as the strange captain, leaning over the pallid bulwarks, was in the act of putting his trumpet to his mouth, it somehow fell from his hand into the sea; and the wind now rising amain, he in vain strove to make himself heard without it. Meantime his ship was still increasing the distance between. While in various silent ways the seamen of the Pequod were evincing their observance of this ominous incident at the first mere mention of the White Whale's name to another ship, Ahab for a moment paused; it almost seemed as though he would have lowered a boat to board the stranger, had not the threatening wind forbade. But taking advantage of his windward position, he again seized his trumpet, and knowing by her aspect that the stranger vessel was a Nantucketer and shortly bound home, he loudly hailed—"Ahoy there! This is the Pequod, bound round the world! Tell them to address all future letters to the Pacific ocean! and this time three years, if I am not at home, tell them to address them to————"

At that moment the two wakes were fairly crossed, and instantly, then, in accordance with their singular ways, shoals of small harmless fish, that for some days before had been placidly swimming by our side, darted away with what seemed shuddering fins, and ranged themselves fore and aft with the stranger's flanks. Though in the course of his continual voyagings Ahab must often before have noticed a similar sight, yet, to any monomaniac man, the veriest trifles capriciously carry meanings.

"Swim away from me, do ye?" murmured Ahab, gazing over into the water. There seemed but little in the words, but the tone conveyed more of deep helpless sadness than the insane old man had ever before evinced. But turning to the steersman, who thus far had been holding the ship in the wind to diminish her headway, he cried out in his old lion voice,—"Up helm! Keep her off round the world!"

Round the world! There is much in that sound to inspire proud feelings; but whereto does all that circumnavigation conduct? Only through numberless perils to the very point whence we started, where those that we left behind secure, were all the time before us.

Were this world an endless plain, and by sailing eastward we could for ever reach new distances, and discover sights more sweet and strange than any Cyclades or Islands of King Solomon, then there were promise in the voyage. But in pursuit of those far mysteries we dream of, or in tormented chase of that demon phantom that, some time or other, swims before all human hearts; while chasing such over this round globe, they either lead us on in barren mazes or midway leave us whelmed.

# Chapter 53

## *The Gam*

T HE OSTENSIBLE REASON why Ahab did not go on board of
the whaler we had spoken was this: the wind and sea betokened
storms. But even had this not been the case, he would not after all,
perhaps, have boarded her—judging by his subsequent conduct on similar
occasions—if so it had been that, by the process of hailing, he had obtained a
negative answer to the question he put. For, as it eventually turned out, he
cared not to consort, even for five minutes, with any stranger captain,
except he could contribute some of that information he so absorbingly
sought. But all this might remain inadequately estimated, were not something said here of the peculiar usages of whaling-vessels when meeting each
other in foreign seas, and especially on a common cruising-ground.

If two strangers crossing the Pine Barrens in New York State, or the
equally desolate Salisbury Plain in England; if casually encountering each
other in such inhospitable wilds, these twain, for the life of them, cannot
well avoid a mutual salutation; and stopping for a moment to interchange
the news; and, perhaps, sitting down for a while and resting in concert: then,
how much more natural that upon the illimitable Pine Barrens and Salisbury Plains of the sea, two whaling vessels descrying each other at the ends
of the earth—off lone Fanning's Island, or the far away King's Mills; how
much more natural, I say, that under such circumstances these ships should

not only interchange hails, but come into still closer, more friendly and sociable contact. And especially would this seem to be a matter of course, in the case of vessels owned in one seaport, and whose captains, officers, and not a few of the men are personally known to each other; and consequently, have all sorts of dear domestic things to talk about.

For the long absent ship, the outward-bounder, perhaps, has letters on board; at any rate, she will be sure to let her have some papers of a date a year or two later than the last one on her blurred and thumb-worn files. And in return for that courtesy, the outward-bound ship would receive the latest whaling intelligence from the cruising-ground to which she may be destined, a thing of the utmost importance to her. And in degree, all this will hold true concerning whaling vessels crossing each other's track on the cruising-ground itself, even though they are equally long absent from home. For one of them may have received a transfer of letters from some third, and now far remote vessel; and some of those letters may be for the people of the ship she now meets. Besides, they would exchange the whaling news, and have an agreeable chat. For not only would they meet with all the sympathies of sailors, but likewise with all the peculiar congenialities arising from a common pursuit and mutually shared privations and perils.

Nor would difference of country make any very essential difference; that is, so long as both parties speak one language, as is the case with Americans and English. Though, to be sure, from the small number of English whalers, such meetings do not very often occur, and when they do occur there is too apt to be a sort of shyness between them; for your Englishman is rather reserved, and your Yankee, he does not fancy that sort of thing in anybody but himself. Besides, the English whalers sometimes affect a kind of metropolitan superiority over the American whalers; regarding the long, lean Nantucketer, with his nondescript provincialisms, as a sort of sea-peasant. But where this superiority in the English whalemen does really consist, it would be hard to say, seeing that the Yankees in one day, collectively, kill more whales than all the English, collectively, in ten years. But this is a harmless little foible in the English whale-hunters, which the Nantucketer does not take much to heart; probably, because he knows that he has a few foibles himself.

So, then, we see that of all ships separately sailing the sea, the whalers have most reason to be sociable—and they are so. Whereas, some merchant ships crossing each other's wake in the mid-Atlantic, will oftentimes pass on without so much as a single word of recognition, mutually cutting each other on the high seas, like a brace of dandies in Broadway; and all the

time indulging, perhaps, in finical criticism upon each other's rig. As for
Men-of-War, when they chance to meet at sea, they first go through such a
string of silly bowings and scrapings, such a ducking of ensigns, that there
does not seem to be much right-down hearty good-will and brotherly love
about it at all. As touching Slave-ships meeting, why, they are in such a
prodigious hurry, they run away from each other as soon as possible. And as
for Pirates, when they chance to cross each other's cross-bones, the first hail
is—"How many skulls?"—the same way that whalers hail—"How many
barrels?" And that question once answered, pirates straightway steer
apart, for they are infernal villains on both sides, and don't like to see overmuch of each other's villanous likenesses.

But look at the godly, honest, unostentatious, hospitable, sociable, free-
and-easy whaler! What does the whaler do when she meets another whaler
in any sort of decent weather? She has a *"Gam,"* a thing so utterly unknown to all other ships that they never heard of the name even; and if by
chance they should hear of it, they only grin at it, and repeat gamesome stuff
about "spouters" and "blubber-boilers," and such like pretty exclamations.
Why it is that all Merchant-seamen, and also all Pirates and Man-of-War's
men, and Slave-ship sailors, cherish such a scornful feeling towards Whale-
ships; this is a question it would be hard to answer. Because, in the case of
pirates, say, I should like to know whether that profession of theirs has any
peculiar glory about it. It sometimes ends in uncommon elevation, indeed;
but only at the gallows. And besides, when a man is elevated in that odd
fashion, he has no proper foundation for his superior altitude. Hence, I
conclude, that in boasting himself to be high lifted above a whaleman, in
that assertion the pirate has no solid basis to stand on.

But what is a *Gam?* You might wear out your index-finger running up
and down the columns of dictionaries, and never find the word. Dr.
Johnson never attained to that erudition; Noah Webster's ark does not hold
it. Nevertheless, this same expressive word has now for many years been in
constant use among some fifteen thousand true born Yankees. Certainly, it
needs a definition, and should be incorporated into the Lexicon. With that
view, let me learnedly define it.

GAM. NOUN—*A social meeting of two (or more) Whale-ships, generally on
a cruising-ground; when, after exchanging hails, they exchange visits by boats'
crews: the two captains remaining, for the time, on board of one ship, and the two
chief mates on the other.*

There is another little item about Gamming which must not be forgotten here. All professions have their own little peculiarities of detail; so

has the whale fishery. In a pirate, man-of-war, or slave ship, when the captain is rowed anywhere in his boat, he always sits in the stern sheets on a comfortable, sometimes cushioned seat there, and often steers himself with a pretty little milliner's tiller decorated with gay cords and ribbons. But the whale-boat has no seat astern, no sofa of that sort whatever, and no tiller at all. High times indeed, if whaling captains were wheeled about the water on castors like gouty old aldermen in patent chairs. And as for a tiller, the whale-boat never admits of any such effeminacy; and therefore as in gamming a complete boat's crew must leave the ship, and hence as the boat steerer or harpooneer is of the number, that subordinate is the steersman upon the occasion, and the captain, having no place to sit in, is pulled off to his visit all standing like a pine tree. And often you will notice that being conscious of the eyes of the whole visible world resting on him from the sides of the two ships, this standing captain is all alive to the importance of sustaining his dignity by maintaining his legs. Nor is this any very easy matter; for in his rear is the immense projecting steering oar hitting him now and then in the small of his back, the after-oar reciprocating by rapping his knees in front. He is thus completely wedged before and behind, and can only expand himself sideways by settling down on his stretched legs; but a sudden, violent pitch of the boat will often go far to topple him, because length of foundation is nothing without corresponding breadth. Merely make a spread angle of two poles, and you cannot stand them up. Then, again, it would never do in plain sight of the world's riveted eyes, it would never do, I say, for this straddling captain to be seen steadying himself the slightest particle by catching hold of anything with his hands; indeed, as token of his entire, buoyant self-command, he generally carries his hands in his trowsers' pockets; but perhaps being generally very large, heavy hands, he carries them there for ballast. Nevertheless there have occurred instances, well authenticated ones too, where the captain has been known for an uncommonly critical moment or two, in a sudden squall say—to seize hold of the nearest oarsman's hair, and hold on there like grim death.

# Chapter 54

*The Town-Ho's Story*
*(As told at the Golden Inn.)*

THE Cape of Good Hope, and all the watery region round about there, is much like some noted four corners of a great highway, where you meet more travellers than in any other part. It was not very long after speaking the Goney that another homeward-bound whaleman, the Town-Ho,* was encountered. She was manned almost wholly by Polynesians. In the short gam that ensued she gave us strong news of Moby Dick. To some the general interest in the White Whale was now wildly heightened by a circumstance of the Town-Ho's story, which seemed obscurely to involve with the whale a certain wondrous, inverted visitation of one of those so called judgments of God which at times are said to overtake some men. This latter circumstance, with its own particular accompaniments, forming what may be called the secret part of the tragedy about to be narrated, never reached the ears of Captain Ahab or his mates. For that secret part of the story was unknown to the captain of the Town-Ho himself. It was the private property of three confederate white seamen of that ship, one of whom, it seems, communicated it to Tashtego with Romish injunctions of secrecy, but the following night Tashtego rambled in his sleep, and revealed so much of it in that way,

* The ancient whale-cry upon first sighting a whale from the mast-head, still used by whalemen in hunting the famous Gallipagos terrapin.

242

that when he was wakened he could not well withhold the rest. Nevertheless, so potent an influence did this thing have on those seamen in the
Pequod who came to the full knowledge of it, and by such a strange
delicacy, to call it so, were they governed in this matter, that they kept the
secret among themselves so that it never transpired abaft the Pequod's
main-mast. Interweaving in its proper place this darker thread with the
story as publicly narrated on the ship, the whole of this strange affair I now
proceed to put on lasting record.

For my humor's sake, I shall preserve the style in which I once narrated
it at Lima, to a lounging circle of my Spanish friends, one saint's eve,
smoking upon the thick-gilt tiled piazza of the Golden Inn. Of those fine
cavaliers, the young Dons, Pedro and Sebastian, were on the closer terms
with me; and hence the interluding questions they occasionally put, and
which are duly answered at the time.

"Some two years prior to my first learning the events which I am about
rehearsing to you, gentlemen, the Town-Ho, Sperm Whaler of Nantucket,
was cruising in your Pacific here, not very many days' sail westward from
the eaves of this good Golden Inn. She was somewhere to the northward of
the Line. One morning upon handling the pumps, according to daily
usage, it was observed that she made more water in her hold than common.
They supposed a sword-fish had stabbed her, gentlemen. But the captain,
having some unusual reason for believing that rare good luck awaited him
in those latitudes; and therefore being very averse to quit them, and the
leak not being then considered at all dangerous, though, indeed, they could
not find it after searching the hold as low down as was possible in rather
heavy weather, the ship still continued her cruisings, the mariners working
at the pumps at wide and easy intervals; but no good luck came; more days
went by, and not only was the leak yet undiscovered, but it sensibly increased. So much so, that now taking some alarm, the captain, making all
sail, stood away for the nearest harbor among the islands, there to have his
hull hove out and repaired.

"Though no small passage was before her, yet, if the commonest
chance favored, he did not at all fear that his ship would founder by the
way, because his pumps were of the best, and being periodically relieved at
them, those six-and-thirty men of his could easily keep the ship free; never
mind if the leak should double on her. In truth, well nigh the whole of this
passage being attended by very prosperous breezes, the Town-Ho had all
but certainly arrived in perfect safety at her port without the occurrence of
the least fatality, had it not been for the brutal overbearing of Radney, the

mate, a Nantucketer, and the bitterly provoked vengeance of Steelkilt, a Lakeman and desperado from Buffalo."

"Lakeman!—Buffalo! Pray, what is a Lakeman, and where is Buffalo?" said Don Sebastian, rising in his swinging mat of grass.

"On the eastern shore of our Lake Erie, Don; but—I crave your courtesy—may be, you shall soon hear further of all that. Now, gentlemen, in square-sail brigs and three-masted ships, well nigh as large and stout as any that ever sailed out of your old Callao to far Manilla; this Lakeman, in the land-locked heart of our America, had yet been nurtured by all those agrarian freebooting impressions popularly connected with the open ocean. For in their interflowing aggregate, those grand fresh-water seas of ours,—Erie, and Ontario, and Huron, and Superior, and Michigan,—possess an ocean-like expansiveness, with many of the ocean's noblest traits; with many of its rimmed varieties of races and of climes. They contain round archipelagoes of romantic isles, even as the Polynesian waters do; in large part, are shored by two great contrasting nations, as the Atlantic is; they furnish long maritime approaches to our numerous territorial colonies from the East, dotted all round their banks; here and there are frowned upon by batteries, and by the goat-like craggy guns of lofty Mackinaw; they have heard the fleet thunderings of naval victories; at intervals, they yield their beaches to wild barbarians, whose red painted faces flash from out their peltry wigwams; for leagues and leagues are flanked by ancient and un-entered forests, where the gaunt pines stand like serried lines of kings in Gothic genealogies; those same woods harboring wild Afric beasts of prey, and silken creatures whose exported furs give robes to Tartar Emperors; they mirror the paved capitals of Buffalo and Cleveland, as well as Winnebago villages; they float alike the full-rigged merchant ship, the armed cruiser of the State, the steamer, and the birch canoe; they are swept by Borean and dismasting blasts as direful as any that lash the salted wave; they know what shipwrecks are, for out of sight of land, however inland, they have drowned full many a midnight ship with all its shrieking crew. Thus, gentlemen, though an inlander, Steelkilt was wild-ocean born, and wild-ocean nurtured; as much of an audacious mariner as any. And for Radney, though in his infancy he may have laid him down on the lone Nantucket beach, to nurse at his maternal sea; though in after life he had long followed our austere Atlantic and your contemplative Pacific; yet was he quite as vengeful and full of social quarrel as the backwoods seaman, fresh from the latitudes of buck-horn handled Bowie-knives. Yet was this Nantucketer a man with some good-hearted traits; and this Lakeman, a mariner, who though a sort of devil indeed, might yet by inflexible firmness, only tempered by that common decency of human recognition which is the meanest slave's right; thus treated, this Steelkilt had long been retained harmless and docile. At all events, he had proved so thus far; but Radney was doomed and made mad, and Steelkilt—but, gentlemen, you shall hear.

"It was not more than a day or two at the furthest after pointing her prow for her island haven, that the Town-Ho's leak seemed again increasing, but only so as to require an hour or more at the pumps every day. You must know that in a settled and civilized ocean like our Atlantic, for example, some skippers think little of pumping their whole way across it; though of a still, sleepy night, should the officer of the deck happen to forget his duty in that respect, the probability would be that he and his shipmates would never again remember it, on account of all hands gently subsiding to the bottom. Nor in the solitary and savage seas far from you to the westward, gentlemen, is it altogether unusual for ships to keep clanging at their pump-handles in full chorus even for a voyage of considerable length; that is, if it lie along a tolerably accessible coast, or if any other reasonable retreat is afforded them. It is only when a leaky vessel is in some very out of the way part of those waters, some really landless latitude, that her captain begins to feel a little anxious.

"Much this way had it been with the Town-Ho; so when her leak was found gaining once more, there was in truth some small concern manifested by several of her company; especially by Radney the mate. He commanded the upper sails to be well hoisted, sheeted home anew, and every way expanded to the breeze. Now this Radney, I suppose, was as little of a coward, and as little inclined to any sort of nervous apprehensiveness touching his own person as any fearless, unthinking creature on land or on sea that you can conveniently imagine, gentlemen. Therefore when he betrayed this solicitude about the safety of the ship, some of the seamen declared that it was only on account of his being a part owner in her. So when they were working that evening at the pumps, there was on this head no small gamesomeness slily going on among them, as they stood with their feet continually overflowed by the rippling clear water; clear as any mountain spring, gentlemen—that bubbling from the pumps ran across the deck, and poured itself out in steady spouts at the lee scupper-holes.

"Now, as you well know, it is not seldom the case in this conventional world of ours—watery or otherwise; that when a person placed in command over his fellow-men finds one of them to be very significantly his superior in general pride of manhood, straightway against that man he

conceives an unconquerable dislike and bitterness; and if he have a chance
he will pull down and pulverize that subaltern's tower, and make a little
heap of dust of it. Be this conceit of mine as it may, gentlemen, at all events
Steelkilt was a tall and noble animal with a head like a Roman, and a flowing golden beard like the tasseled housings of your last viceroy's snorting
charger; and a brain, and a heart, and a soul in him, gentlemen, which had
made Steelkilt Charlemagne, had he been born son to Charlemagne's
father. But Radney, the mate, was ugly as a mule; yet as hardy, as stubborn,
as malicious. He did not love Steelkilt, and Steelkilt knew it.

"Espying the mate drawing near as he was toiling at the pump with the
rest, the Lakeman affected not to notice him, but unawed, went on with his
gay banterings.

"'Aye, aye, my merry lads, it's a lively leak this; hold a cannikin, one of
ye, and let's have a taste. By the Lord, it's worth bottling! I tell ye what,
men, old Rad's investment must go for it! he had best cut away his part of
the hull and tow it home. The fact is, boys, that sword-fish only began the
job; he's come back again with a gang of ship-carpenters, saw-fish, and file-
fish, and what not; and the whole posse of 'em are now hard at work cutting
and slashing at the bottom; making improvements, I suppose. If old Rad
were here now, I'd tell him to jump overboard and scatter 'em. They're
playing the devil with his estate, I can tell him. But he's a simple old soul,—
Rad, and a beauty too. Boys, they say the rest of his property is invested in
looking-glasses. I wonder if he'd give a poor devil like me the model of
his nose.'

"'Damn your eyes! what's that pump stopping for?' roared Radney,
pretending not to have heard the sailor's talk. 'Thunder away at it!'

"'Aye, aye, sir,' said Steelkilt, merry as a cricket. 'Lively, boys, lively,
now!' And with that the pump clanged like fifty fire-engines; the men
tossed their hats off to it, and ere long that peculiar gasping of the lungs was
heard which denotes the fullest tension of life's utmost energies.

"Quitting the pump at last, with the rest of his band, the Lakeman went
forward all panting, and sat himself down on the windlass; his face fiery red,
his eyes bloodshot, and wiping the profuse sweat from his brow. Now what
cozening fiend it was, gentlemen, that possessed Radney to meddle with
such a man in that corporeally exasperated state, I know not; but so
it happened. Intolerably striding along the deck, the mate commanded
him to get a broom and sweep down the planks, and also a shovel, and
remove some offensive matters consequent upon allowing a pig to run
at large.

"Now, gentlemen, sweeping a ship's deck at sea is a piece of household work which in all times but raging gales is regularly attended to every evening; it has been known to be done in the case of ships actually foundering at the time. Such, gentlemen, is the inflexibility of sea-usages and the instinctive love of neatness in seamen; some of whom would not willingly drown without first washing their faces. But in all vessels this broom business is the prescriptive province of the boys, if boys there be aboard. Besides, it was the stronger men in the Town-Ho that had been divided into gangs, taking turns at the pumps; and being the most athletic seaman of them all, Steelkilt had been regularly assigned captain of one of the gangs; consequently he should have been freed from any trivial business not connected with truly nautical duties, such being the case with his comrades. I mention all these particulars so that you may understand exactly how this affair stood between the two men.

"But there was more than this: the order about the shovel was almost as plainly meant to sting and insult Steelkilt, as though Radney had spat in his face. Any man who has gone sailor in a whale-ship will understand this; and all this and doubtless much more, the Lakeman fully comprehended when the mate uttered his command. But as he sat still for a moment, and as he steadfastly looked into the mate's malignant eye and perceived the stacks of powder-casks heaped up in him and the slow-match silently burning along towards them; as he instinctively saw all this, that strange forbearance and unwillingness to stir up the deeper passionateness in any already ireful being—a repugnance most felt, when felt at all, by really valiant men even when aggrieved—this nameless phantom feeling, gentlemen, stole over Steelkilt.

"Therefore, in his ordinary tone, only a little broken by the bodily exhaustion he was temporarily in, he answered him saying that sweeping the deck was not his business, and he would not do it. And then, without at all alluding to the shovel, he pointed to three lads as the customary sweepers; who, not being billeted at the pumps, had done little or nothing all day. To this, Radney replied with an oath, in a most domineering and outrageous manner unconditionally reiterating his command; meanwhile advancing upon the still seated Lakeman, with an uplifted cooper's club hammer which he had snatched from a cask near by.

"Heated and irritated as he was by his spasmodic toil at the pumps, for all his first nameless feeling of forbearance the sweating Steelkilt could but ill brook this bearing in the mate; but somehow still smothering the conflagration within him, without speaking he remained doggedly rooted to his seat, till at last the incensed Radney shook the hammer within a few inches of his face, furiously commanding him to do his bidding.

"Steelkilt rose, and slowly retreating round the windlass, steadily followed by the mate with his menacing hammer, deliberately repeated his intention not to obey. Seeing, however, that his forbearance had not the slightest effect, by an awful and unspeakable intimation with his twisted hand he warned off the foolish and infatuated man; but it was to no purpose. And in this way the two went once slowly round the windlass; when resolved at last no longer to retreat, bethinking him that he had now forborne as much as comported with his humor, the Lakeman paused on the hatches and thus spoke to the officer:

"'Mr. Radney, I will not obey you. Take that hammer away, or look to yourself.' But the predestinated mate coming still closer to him, where the Lakeman stood fixed, now shook the heavy hammer within an inch of his teeth; meanwhile repeating a string of insufferable maledictions. Retreating not the thousandth part of an inch; stabbing him in the eye with the unflinching poniard of his glance, Steelkilt, clenching his right hand behind him and creepingly drawing it back, told his persecutor that if the hammer but grazed his cheek he (Steelkilt) would murder him. But, gentlemen, the fool had been branded for the slaughter by the gods. Immediately the hammer touched the cheek; the next instant the lower jaw of the mate was stove in his head; he fell on the hatch spouting blood like a whale.

"Ere the cry could go aft Steelkilt was shaking one of the backstays leading far aloft to where two of his comrades were standing their mast-heads. They were both Canallers."

"Canallers!" cried Don Pedro. "We have seen many whale-ships in our harbors, but never heard of your Canallers. Pardon: who and what are they?"

"Canallers, Don, are the boatmen belonging to our grand Erie Canal. You must have heard of it."

"Nay, Senor; hereabouts in this dull, warm, most lazy, and hereditary land, we know but little of your vigorous North."

"Aye? Well then, Don, refill my cup. Your chicha's very fine; and ere proceeding further I will tell ye what our Canallers are; for such information may throw side-light upon my story.

"For three hundred and sixty miles, gentlemen, through the entire breadth of the state of New York; through numerous populous cities and most thriving villages; through long, dismal, uninhabited swamps, and affluent, cultivated fields, unrivalled for fertility; by billiard-room and bar-

room; through the holy-of-holies of great forests; on Roman arches over
Indian rivers; through sun and shade; by happy hearts or broken; through
all the wide contrasting scenery of those noble Mohawk counties; and
especially, by rows of snow-white chapels, whose spires stand almost like
milestones, flows one continual stream of Venetianly corrupt and often
lawless life. There's your true Ashantee, gentlemen; there howl your
pagans; where you ever find them, next door to you; under the long-flung
shadow, and the snug patronizing lee of churches. For by some curious
fatality, as it is often noted of your metropolitan freebooters that they ever
encamp around the halls of justice, so sinners, gentlemen, most abound in
holiest vicinities."

"Is that a friar passing?" said Don Pedro, looking downwards into the
crowded plaza, with humorous concern.

"Well for our northern friend, Dame Isabella's Inquisition wanes in
Lima," laughed Don Sebastian. "Proceed, Senor."

"A moment! Pardon!" cried another of the company. "In the name of
all us Limeese, I but desire to express to you, sir sailor, that we have by no
means overlooked your delicacy in not substituting present Lima for
distant Venice in your corrupt comparison. Oh! do not bow and look
surprised; you know the proverb all along this coast—'Corrupt as Lima.' It
but bears out your saying, too; churches more plentiful than billiard-tables,
and for ever open—and 'Corrupt as Lima.' So, too, Venice; I have been
there; the holy city of the blessed evangelist, St. Mark!—St. Dominic,
purge it! Your cup! Thanks: here I refill; now, you pour out again."

"Freely depicted in his own vocation, gentlemen, the Canaller would
make a fine dramatic hero, so abundantly and picturesquely wicked is he.
Like Mark Antony, for days and days along his green-turfed, flowery Nile,
he indolently floats, openly toying with his red-cheeked Cleopatra, ripening his apricot thigh upon the sunny deck. But ashore, all this effeminacy is
dashed. The brigandish guise which the Canaller so proudly sports; his
slouched and gaily-ribboned hat betoken his grand features. A terror to the
smiling innocence of the villages through which he floats; his swart visage
and bold swagger are not unshunned in cities. Once a vagabond on his own
canal, I have received good turns from one of these Canallers; I thank him
heartily; would fain be not ungrateful; but it is often one of the prime re-
deeming qualities of your man of violence, that at times he has as stiff an
arm to back a poor stranger in a strait, as to plunder a wealthy one. In sum,
gentlemen, what the wildness of this canal life is, is emphatically evinced
by this; that our wild whale-fishery contains so many of its most finished

graduates, and that scarce any race of mankind, except Sydney men, are so much distrusted by our whaling captains. Nor does it at all diminish the curiousness of this matter, that to many thousands of our rural boys and young men born along its line, the probationary life of the Grand Canal furnishes the sole transition between quietly reaping in a Christian corn-field, and recklessly ploughing the waters of the most barbaric seas."

"I see! I see!" impetuously exclaimed Don Pedro, spilling his chicha upon his silvery ruffles. "No need to travel! The world's one Lima. I had thought, now, that at your temperate North the generations were cold and holy as the hills.—But the story."

"I left off, gentlemen, where the Lakeman shook the backstay. Hardly had he done so, when he was surrounded by the three junior mates and the four harpooneers, who all crowded him to the deck. But sliding down the ropes like baleful comets, the two Canallers rushed into the uproar, and sought to drag their man out of it towards the forecastle. Others of the sailors joined with them in this attempt, and a twisted turmoil ensued; while standing out of harm's way, the valiant captain danced up and down with a whale-pike, calling upon his officers to manhandle that atrocious scoundrel, and smoke him along to the quarter-deck. At intervals, he ran close up to the revolving border of the confusion, and prying into the heart of it with his pike, sought to prick out the object of his resentment. But Steelkilt and his desperadoes were too much for them all; they succeeded in gaining the forecastle deck, where, hastily slewing about three or four large casks in a line with the windlass, these sea-Parisians entrenched themselves behind the barricade.

"'Come out of that, ye pirates!' roared the captain, now menacing them with a pistol in each hand, just brought to him by the steward. 'Come out of that, ye cut-throats!'

"Steelkilt leaped on the barricade, and striding up and down there, defied the worst the pistols could do; but gave the captain to understand distinctly, that his (Steelkilt's) death would be the signal for a murderous mutiny on the part of all hands. Fearing in his heart lest this might prove but too true, the captain a little desisted, but still commanded the insurgents instantly to return to their duty.

"'Will you promise not to touch us, if we do?' demanded their ring-leader.

"'Turn to! turn to!—I make no promise;—to your duty! Do you want to sink the ship, by knocking off at a time like this? Turn to!' and he once more raised a pistol.

"'Sink the ship?' cried Steelkilt. 'Aye, let her sink. Not a man of us turns to, unless you swear not to raise a rope-yarn against us. What say ye, men?' turning to his comrades. A fierce cheer was their response.

"The Lakeman now patrolled the barricade, all the while keeping his eye on the Captain, and jerking out such sentences as these:—'It's not our fault; we didn't want it; I told him to take his hammer away; it was boy's business; he might have known me before this; I told him not to prick the buffalo; I believe I have broken a finger here against his cursed jaw; ain't those mincing knives down in the forecastle there, men? look to those hand-spikes, my hearties. Captain, by God, look to yourself; say the word; don't be a fool; forget it all; we are ready to turn to; treat us decently, and we're your men; but we won't be flogged.'

"'Turn to! I make no promises, turn to, I say!'

"'Look ye, now,' cried the Lakeman, flinging out his arm towards him, 'there are a few of us here (and I am one of them) who have shipped for the cruise, d'ye see; now as you well know, sir, we can claim our discharge as soon as the anchor is down; so we don't want a row; it's not our interest; we want to be peaceable; we are ready to work, but we won't be flogged.'

"'Turn to!' roared the Captain.

"Steelkilt glanced round him a moment, and then said:—'I tell you what it is now, Captain, rather than kill ye, and be hung for such a shabby rascal, we won't lift a hand against ye unless ye attack us; but till you say the word about not flogging us, we don't do a hand's turn.'

"'Down into the forecastle then, down with ye, I'll keep ye there till ye're sick of it. Down ye go.'

"'Shall we?' cried the ringleader to his men. Most of them were against it; but at length, in obedience to Steelkilt, they preceded him down into their dark den, growlingly disappearing, like bears into a cave.

"As the Lakeman's bare head was just level with the planks, the Captain and his posse leaped the barricade, and rapidly drawing over the slide of the scuttle, planted their group of hands upon it, and loudly called for the steward to bring the heavy brass padlock belonging to the companion-way. Then opening the slide a little, the Captain whispered something down the crack, closed it, and turned the key upon them—ten in number—leaving on deck some twenty or more, who thus far had remained neutral.

"All night a wide-awake watch was kept by all the officers, forward and aft, especially about the forecastle scuttle and fore hatchway; at which last place it was feared the insurgents might emerge, after breaking through the bulkhead below. But the hours of darkness passed in peace; the men who still remained at their duty toiling hard at the pumps, whose clinking and clanking at intervals through the dreary night dismally resounded through the ship.

"At sunrise the Captain went forward, and knocking on the deck, summoned the prisoners to work; but with a yell they refused. Water was then lowered down to them, and a couple of handfuls of biscuit were tossed after it; when again turning the key upon them and pocketing it, the Captain returned to the quarter-deck. Twice every day for three days this was repeated; but on the fourth morning a confused wrangling, and then a scuffling was heard, as the customary summons was delivered; and suddenly four men burst up from the forecastle, saying they were ready to turn to. The fetid closeness of the air, and a famishing diet, united perhaps to some fears of ultimate retribution, had constrained them to surrender at discretion. Emboldened by this, the Captain reiterated his demand to the rest, but Steelkilt shouted up to him a terrific hint to stop his babbling and betake himself where he belonged. On the fifth morning three others of the mutineers bolted up into the air from the desperate arms below that sought to restrain them. Only three were left.

"'Better turn to, now!' said the Captain with a heartless jeer.

"'Shut us up again, will ye!' cried Steelkilt.

"'Oh! certainly,' said the Captain, and the key clicked.

"It was at this point, gentlemen, that enraged by the defection of seven of his former associates, and stung by the mocking voice that had last hailed him, and maddened by his long entombment in a place as black as the bowels of despair; it was then that Steelkilt proposed to the two Canallers, thus far apparently of one mind with him, to burst out of their hole at the next summoning of the garrison; and armed with their keen mincing knives (long, crescentic, heavy implements with a handle at each end) run a muck from the bowsprit to the taffrail; and if by any devilishness of desperation possible, seize the ship. For himself, he would do this, he said, whether they joined him or not. That was the last night he should spend in that den. But the scheme met with no opposition on the part of the other two; they swore they were ready for that, or for any other mad thing, for anything in short but a surrender. And what was more, they each insisted upon being the first man on deck, when the time to make the rush should come. But to this their leader as fiercely objected, reserving that priority for himself; particularly as his two comrades would not yield, the one to the other, in the matter; and both of them could not be first, for the ladder would but admit one man at a time. And here, gentlemen, the foul play of these miscreants must come out.

"Upon hearing the frantic project of their leader, each in his own separate soul had suddenly lighted, it would seem, upon the same piece of treachery, namely: to be foremost in breaking out, in order to be the first of the three, though the last of the ten, to surrender; and thereby secure whatever small chance of pardon such conduct might merit. But when Steelkilt made known his determination still to lead them to the last, they in some way, by some subtle chemistry of villany, mixed their before secret treacheries together; and when their leader fell into a doze, verbally opened their souls to each other in three sentences; and bound the sleeper with cords, and gagged him with cords; and shrieked out for the Captain at midnight.

"Thinking murder at hand, and smelling in the dark for the blood, he and all his armed mates and harpooneers rushed for the forecastle. In a few minutes the scuttle was opened, and, bound hand and foot, the still struggling ringleader was shoved up into the air by his perfidious allies, who at once claimed the honor of securing a man who had been fully ripe for murder. But all three were collared, and dragged along the deck like dead cattle; and, side by side, were seized up into the mizen rigging, like three quarters of meat, and there they hung till morning. 'Damn ye,' cried the Captain, pacing to and fro before them, 'the vultures would not touch ye, ye villains!'

"At sunrise he summoned all hands; and separating those who had rebelled from those who had taken no part in the mutiny, he told the former that he had a good mind to flog them all round—thought, upon the whole, he would do so—he ought to—justice demanded it; but for the present, considering their timely surrender, he would let them go with a reprimand, which he accordingly administered in the vernacular.

"'But as for you, ye carrion rogues,' turning to the three men in the rigging—'for you, I mean to mince ye up for the try-pots;' and, seizing a rope, he applied it with all his might to the backs of the two traitors, till they yelled no more, but lifelessly hung their heads sideways, as the two crucified thieves are drawn.

"'My wrist is sprained with ye!' he cried, at last; 'but there is still rope enough left for you, my fine bantam, that wouldn't give up. Take that gag from his mouth, and let us hear what he can say for himself.'

"For a moment the exhausted mutineer made a tremulous motion of his cramped jaws, and then painfully twisting round his head, said in a sort of hiss, 'What I say is this—and mind it well—if you flog me, I murder you!'

" 'Say ye so? then see how ye frighten me'—and the Captain drew off with the rope to strike.

" 'Best not,' hissed the Lakeman.

" 'But I must,'—and the rope was once more drawn back for the stroke.

"Steelkilt here hissed out something, inaudible to all but the Captain; who, to the amazement of all hands, started back, paced the deck rapidly two or three times, and then suddenly throwing down his rope, said, 'I won't do it—let him go—cut him down: d'ye hear?'

"But as the junior mates were hurrying to execute the order, a pale man, with a bandaged head, arrested them—Radney the chief mate. Ever since the blow, he had lain in his berth; but that morning, hearing the tumult on the deck, he had crept out, and thus far had watched the whole scene. Such was the state of his mouth, that he could hardly speak; but mumbling something about *his* being willing and able to do what the captain dared not attempt, he snatched the rope and advanced to his pinioned foe.

" 'You are a coward!' hissed the Lakeman.

" 'So I am, but take that.' The mate was in the very act of striking, when another hiss stayed his uplifted arm. He paused: and then pausing no more, made good his word, spite of Steelkilt's threat, whatever that might have been. The three men were then cut down, all hands were turned to, and, sullenly worked by the moody seamen, the iron pumps clanged as before.

"Just after dark that day, when one watch had retired below, a clamor was heard in the forecastle; and the two trembling traitors running up, besieged the cabin door, saying they durst not consort with the crew. Entreaties, cuffs, and kicks could not drive them back, so at their own instance they were put down in the ship's run for salvation. Still, no sign of mutiny reappeared among the rest. On the contrary, it seemed, that mainly at Steelkilt's instigation, they had resolved to maintain the strictest peacefulness, obey all orders to the last, and, when the ship reached port, desert her in a body. But in order to insure the speediest end to the voyage, they all agreed to another thing—namely, not to sing out for whales, in case any should be discovered. For, spite of her leak, and spite of all her other perils, the Town-Ho still maintained her mast-heads, and her captain was just as willing to lower for a fish that moment, as on the day his craft first struck the cruising ground; and Radney the mate was quite as ready to change his berth for a boat, and with his bandaged mouth seek to gag in death the vital jaw of the whale.

"But though the Lakeman had induced the seamen to adopt this sort of

passiveness in their conduct, he kept his own counsel (at least till all was
over) concerning his own proper and private revenge upon the man who
had stung him in the ventricles of his heart. He was in Radney the chief
mate's watch; and as if the infatuated man sought to run more than half way
to meet his doom, after the scene at the rigging, he insisted, against the
express counsel of the captain, upon resuming the head of his watch at
night. Upon this, and one or two other circumstances, Steelkilt systematically built the plan of his revenge.

"During the night, Radney had an unseamanlike way of sitting on the
bulwarks of the quarter-deck, and leaning his arm upon the gunwale of the
boat which was hoisted up there, a little above the ship's side. In this attitude,
it was well known, he sometimes dozed. There was a considerable vacancy
between the boat and the ship, and down beneath this was the sea. Steelkilt
calculated his time, and found that his next trick at the helm would come
round at two o'clock, in the morning of the third day from that in which he
had been betrayed. At his leisure, he employed the interval in braiding something very carefully in his watches below.

"'What are you making there?' said a shipmate.

"'What do you think? what does it look like?'

"'Like a lanyard for your bag; but it's an odd one, seems to me.'

"'Yes, rather oddish,' said the Lakeman, holding it at arm's length
before him; 'but I think it will answer. Shipmate, I haven't enough twine,—
have you any?'

"But there was none in the forecastle.

"'Then I must get some from old Rad;' and he rose to go aft.

"'You don't mean to go a begging to *him!*' said a sailor.

"'Why not? Do you think he won't do me a turn, when it's to help
himself in the end, shipmate?' and going to the mate, he looked at him
quietly, and asked him for some twine to mend his hammock. It was given
him—neither twine nor lanyard were seen again; but the next night an iron
ball, closely netted, partly rolled from the pocket of the Lakeman's monkey
jacket, as he was tucking the coat into his hammock for a pillow. Twenty-
four hours after, his trick at the silent helm—nigh to the man who was apt
to doze over the grave always ready dug to the seaman's hand—that fatal
hour was then to come; and in the fore-ordaining soul of Steelkilt, the mate
was already stark and stretched as a corpse, with his forehead crushed in.

"But, gentlemen, a fool saved the would-be murderer from the bloody
deed he had planned. Yet complete revenge he had, and without being the
avenger. For by a mysterious fatality, Heaven itself seemed to step in to take

out of his hands into its own the damning thing he would have done.

"It was just between daybreak and sunrise of the morning of the second day, when they were washing down the decks, that a stupid Teneriffe man, drawing water in the main-chains, all at once shouted out, 'There she rolls! there she rolls! Jesu, what a whale!' It was Moby Dick."

"'Moby Dick'!" cried Don Sebastian; "St. Dominic! Sir sailor, but do whales have christenings? Whom call you Moby Dick?"

"A very white, and famous, and most deadly immortal monster, Don; —but that would be too long a story."

"How? how?" cried all the young Spaniards, crowding.

"Nay, Dons, Dons—nay, nay! I cannot rehearse that now. Let me get more into the air, Sirs."

"The chicha! the chicha!" cried Don Pedro; "our vigorous friend looks faint;—fill up his empty glass!"

"No need, gentlemen; one moment, and I proceed.—Now, gentlemen, so suddenly perceiving the snowy whale within fifty yards of the ship— forgetful of the compact among the crew—in the excitement of the moment, the Teneriffe man had instinctively and involuntarily lifted his voice for the monster, though for some little time past it had been plainly beheld from the three sullen mast-heads. All was now a phrensy. 'The White Whale—the White ·Whale!' was the cry from captain, mates, and harpooneers, who, undeterred by fearful rumors, were all anxious to capture so famous and precious a fish; while the dogged crew eyed askance, and with curses, the appalling beauty of the vast milky mass, that lit up by a horizontal spangling sun, shifted and glistened like a living opal in the blue morning sea. Gentlemen, a strange fatality pervades the whole career of these events, as if verily mapped out before the world itself was charted. The mutineer was the bowsman of the mate, and when fast to a fish, it was his duty to sit next him, while Radney stood up with his lance in the prow, and haul in or slacken the line, at the word of command. Moreover, when the four boats were lowered, the mate's got the start; and none howled more fiercely with delight than did Steelkilt, as he strained at his oar. After a stiff pull, their harpooneer got fast, and, spear in hand, Radney sprang to the bow. He was always a furious man, it seems, in a boat. And now his ban-daged cry was, to beach him on the whale's topmost back. Nothing loath, his bowsman hauled him up and up, through a blinding foam that blent two whitenesses together; till of a sudden the boat struck as against a sunken ledge, and keeling over, spilled out the standing mate. That instant, as he fell on the whale's slippery back, the boat righted, and was dashed aside by the swell, while Radney was tossed over into the sea, on the other flank of the whale. He struck out through the spray, and, for an instant, was dimly seen through that veil, wildly seeking to remove himself from the eye of Moby Dick. But the whale rushed round in a sudden maelstrom; seized the swimmer between his jaws; and rearing high up with him, plunged head-long again, and went down.

"Meantime, at the first tap of the boat's bottom, the Lakeman had slackened the line, so as to drop astern from the whirlpool; calmly looking on, he thought his own thoughts. But a sudden, terrific, downward jerking of the boat, quickly brought his knife to the line. He cut it; and the whale was free. But, at some distance, Moby Dick rose again, with some tatters of Radney's red woollen shirt, caught in the teeth that had destroyed him. All four boats gave chase again; but the whale eluded them, and finally wholly disappeared.

"In good time, the Town-Ho reached her port—a savage, solitary place —where no civilized creature resided. There, headed by the Lakeman, all but five or six of the foremast-men deliberately deserted among the palms; eventually, as it turned out, seizing a large double war-canoe of the savages, and setting sail for some other harbor.

"The ship's company being reduced to but a handful, the captain called upon the Islanders to assist him in the laborious business of heaving down the ship to stop the leak. But to such unresting vigilance over their danger-ous allies was this small band of whites necessitated, both by night and by day, and so extreme was the hard work they underwent, that upon the vessel being ready again for sea, they were in such a weakened condition that the captain durst not put off with them in so heavy a vessel. After taking counsel with his officers, he anchored the ship as far off shore as possible; loaded and ran out his two cannon from the bows; stacked his muskets on the poop; and warning the Islanders not to approach the ship at their peril, took one man with him, and setting the sail of his best whaleboat, steered straight before the wind for Tahiti, five hundred miles distant, to procure a reinforcement to his crew.

"On the fourth day of the sail, a large canoe was descried, which seemed to have touched at a low isle of corals. He steered away from it; but the savage craft bore down on him; and soon the voice of Steelkilt hailed him to heave to, or he would run him under water. The captain presented a pistol. With one foot on each prow of the yoked war-canoes, the Lakeman laughed him to scorn; assuring him that if the pistol so much as clicked in the lock, he would bury him in bubbles and foam.

"'What do you want of me?' cried the captain.

"'Where are you bound? and for what are you bound?' demanded Steelkilt; 'no lies.'

"'I am bound to Tahiti for more men.'

"'Very good. Let me board you a moment—I come in peace.' With that he leaped from the canoe, swam to the boat; and climbing the gunwale, stood face to face with the captain.

"'Cross your arms, sir; throw back your head. Now, repeat after me. "As soon as Steelkilt leaves me, I swear to beach this boat on yonder island, and remain there six days. If I do not, may lightnings strike me!"'

"'A pretty scholar,' laughed the Lakeman. 'Adios, Senor!' and leaping into the sea, he swam back to his comrades.

"Watching the boat till it was fairly beached, and drawn up to the roots of the cocoa-nut trees, Steelkilt made sail again, and in due time arrived at Tahiti, his own place of destination. There, luck befriended him; two ships were about to sail for France, and were providentially in want of precisely that number of men which the sailor headed. They embarked; and so for ever got the start of their former captain, had he been at all minded to work them legal retribution.

"Some ten days after the French ships sailed, the whale-boat arrived, and the captain was forced to enlist some of the more civilized Tahitians, who had been somewhat used to the sea. Chartering a small native schooner, he returned with them to his vessel; and finding all right there, again resumed his cruisings.

"Where Steelkilt now is, gentlemen, none know; but upon the island of Nantucket, the widow of Radney still turns to the sea which refuses to give up its dead; still in dreams sees the awful white whale that destroyed him."     *     *     *     *

"Are you through?" said Don Sebastian, quietly.

"I am, Don."

"Then I entreat you, tell me if to the best of your own convictions, this your story is in substance really true? It is so passing wonderful! Did you get it from an unquestionable source? Bear with me if I seem to press."

"Also bear with all of us, sir sailor; for we all join in Don Sebastian's suit," cried the company, with exceeding interest.

"Is there a copy of the Holy Evangelists in the Golden Inn, gentlemen?"

"Nay," said Don Sebastian; "but I know a worthy priest near by, who will quickly procure one for me. I go for it; but are you well advised? this may grow too serious."

"Will you be so good as to bring the priest also, Don?"

"Though there are no Auto-da-Fés in Lima now," said one of the company to another; "I fear our sailor friend runs risk of the archiepiscopacy. Let us withdraw more out of the moonlight. I see no need of this."

"Excuse me for running after you, Don Sebastian; but may I also beg that you will be particular in procuring the largest sized Evangelists you can."

\* \* \* \* \*

"This is the priest, he brings you the Evangelists," said Don Sebastian, gravely, returning with a tall and solemn figure.

"Let me remove my hat. Now, venerable priest, further into the light, and hold the Holy Book before me that I may touch it.

"So help me Heaven, and on my honor, the story I have told ye, gentlemen, is in substance and its great items, true. I know it to be true; it happened on this ball; I trod the ship; I knew the crew; I have seen and talked with Steelkilt since the death of Radney."

# Chapter 55

## Of the Monstrous Pictures of Whales

I SHALL ERE LONG paint to you as well as one can without canvas, something like the true form of the whale as he actually appears to the eye of the whaleman when in his own absolute body the whale is moored alongside the whale-ship so that he can be fairly stepped upon there. It may be worth while, therefore, previously to advert to those curious imaginary portraits of him which even down to the present day confidently challenge the faith of the landsman. It is time to set the world right in this matter, by proving such pictures of the whale all wrong.

It may be that the primal source of all those pictorial delusions will be found among the oldest Hindoo, Egyptian, and Grecian sculptures. For ever since those inventive but unscrupulous times when on the marble panellings of temples, the pedestals of statues, and on shields, medallions, cups, and coins, the dolphin was drawn in scales of chain-armor like Saladin's, and a helmeted head like St. George's; ever since then has something of the same sort of license prevailed, not only in most popular pictures of the whale, but in many scientific presentations of him.

Now, by all odds, the most ancient extant portrait anyways purporting to be the whale's, is to be found in the famous cavern-pagoda of Elephanta, in India. The Brahmins maintain that in the almost endless sculptures of that immemorial pagoda, all the trades and pursuits, every conceivable avocation of man, were prefigured ages before any of them actually came into being. No wonder then, that in some sort our noble profession of whaling should have been there shadowed forth. The Hindoo whale referred to, occurs in a separate department of the wall, depicting the incarnation of Vishnu in the form of leviathan, learnedly known as the Matse Avatar. But though this sculpture is half man and half whale, so as only to give the tail of the latter, yet that small section of him is all wrong. It looks more like the tapering tail of an anaconda, than the broad palms of the true whale's majestic flukes.

But go to the old Galleries, and look now at a great Christian painter's portrait of this fish; for he succeeds no better than the antediluvian Hindoo. It is Guido's picture of Perseus rescuing Andromeda from the sea-monster or whale. Where did Guido get the model of such a strange creature as that? Nor does Hogarth, in painting the same scene in his own "Perseus Descending," make out one whit better. The huge corpulence of that Hogarthian monster undulates on the surface, scarcely drawing one inch of water. It has a sort of howdah on its back, and its distended tusked mouth into which the billows are rolling, might be taken for the Traitors' Gate leading from the Thames by water into the Tower. Then, there are the Prodromus whales of old Scotch Sibbald, and Jonah's whale, as depicted in the prints of old Bibles and the cuts of old primers. What shall be said of these? As for the book-binder's whale winding like a vine-stalk round the stock of a descending anchor—as stamped and gilded on the backs and title-pages of many books both old and new—that is a very picturesque but purely fabulous creature, imitated, I take it, from the like figures on antique vases. Though universally denominated a dolphin, I nevertheless call this book-binder's fish an attempt at a whale; because it was so intended when the device was first introduced. It was introduced by an old Italian publisher somewhere about the 15th century, during the Revival of Learning; and in those days, and even down to a comparatively late period, dolphins were popularly supposed to be a species of the Leviathan.

In the vignettes and other embellishments of some ancient books you will at times meet with very curious touches at the whale, where all manner of spouts, jets d'eau, hot springs and cold, Saratoga and Baden-Baden, come bubbling up from his unexhausted brain. In the title-page of the original edition of the "Advancement of Learning" you will find some curious whales.

But quitting all these unprofessional attempts, let us glance at those pictures of leviathan purporting to be sober, scientific delineations, by those who know. In old Harris's collection of voyages there are some plates of whales extracted from a Dutch book of voyages, A. D. 1671, entitled "A Whaling Voyage to Spitzbergen in the ship Jonas in the Whale, Peter Peterson of Friesland, master." In one of those plates the whales, like great rafts of logs, are represented lying among ice-isles, with white bears running over their living backs. In another plate, the prodigious blunder is made of representing the whale with perpendicular flukes.

Then again, there is an imposing quarto, written by one Captain Colnett, a Post Captain in the English navy, entitled "A Voyage round Cape Horn into the South Seas, for the purpose of extending the Spermaceti Whale Fisheries." In this book is an outline purporting to be a "Picture of a Physeter or Spermaceti whale, drawn by scale from one killed on the coast of Mexico, August, 1793, and hoisted on deck." I doubt not the captain had this veracious picture taken for the benefit of his marines. To mention but one thing about it, let me say that it has an eye which applied, according to the accompanying scale, to a full grown sperm whale, would make the eye of that whale a bow-window some five feet long. Ah, my gallant captain, why did ye not give us Jonah looking out of that eye!

Nor are the most conscientious compilations of Natural History for the benefit of the young and tender, free from the same heinousness of mistake. Look at that popular work "Goldsmith's Animated Nature." In the abridged London edition of 1807, there are plates of an alleged "whale" and a "narwhale." I do not wish to seem inelegant, but this unsightly whale looks much like an amputated sow; and, as for the narwhale, one glimpse at it is enough to amaze one, that in this nineteenth century such a hippogriff could be palmed for genuine upon any intelligent public of schoolboys.

Then, again, in 1825, Bernard Germain, Count de Lacépède, a great naturalist, published a scientific systemized whale book, wherein are several pictures of the different species of the Leviathan. All these are not only incorrect, but the picture of the Mysticetus or Greenland whale (that is to say, the Right whale), even Scoresby, a long experienced man as touching that species, declares not to have its counterpart in nature.

But the placing of the cap-sheaf to all this blundering business was reserved for the scientific Frederick Cuvier, brother to the famous Baron. In 1836, he published a Natural History of Whales, in which he gives what he calls a picture of the Sperm Whale. Before showing that picture to any Nantucketer, you had best provide for your summary retreat from Nantucket. In a word, Frederick Cuvier's Sperm Whale is not a Sperm Whale, but a squash. Of course, he never had the benefit of a whaling voyage (such men seldom have), but whence he derived that picture, who can tell? Perhaps he got it as his scientific predecessor in the same field, Desmarest, got one of his authentic abortions; that is, from a Chinese drawing. And what sort of lively lads with the pencil those Chinese are, many queer cups and saucers inform us.

As for the sign-painters' whales seen in the streets hanging over the shops of oil-dealers, what shall be said of them? They are generally Richard III. whales, with dromedary humps, and very savage; breakfasting on three or four sailor tarts, that is whaleboats full of mariners: their deformities floundering in seas of blood and blue paint.

But these manifold mistakes in depicting the whale are not so very surprising after all. Consider! Most of the scientific drawings have been taken from the stranded fish; and these are about as correct as a drawing of a wrecked ship, with broken back, would correctly represent the noble animal itself in all its undashed pride of hull and spars. Though elephants have stood for their full-lengths, the living Leviathan has never yet fairly floated himself for his portrait. The living whale, in his full majesty and significance, is only to be seen at sea in unfathomable waters; and afloat the vast bulk of him is out of sight, like a launched line-of-battle ship; and out of that element it is a thing eternally impossible for mortal man to hoist him bodily into the air, so as to preserve all his mighty swells and undulations. And, not to speak of the highly presumable difference of contour between a young sucking whale and a full-grown Platonian Leviathan; yet, even in the case of one of those young sucking whales hoisted to a ship's deck, such is then the outlandish, eel-like, limbered, varying shape of him, that his precise expression the devil himself could not catch.

But it may be fancied, that from the naked skeleton of the stranded whale, accurate hints may be derived touching his true form. Not at all. For it is one of the more curious things about this Leviathan, that his skeleton gives very little idea of his general shape. Though Jeremy Bentham's skeleton, which hangs for candelabra in the library of one of his executors, correctly conveys the idea of a burly-browed utilitarian old gentleman, with all Jeremy's other leading personal characteristics; yet nothing of this kind could be inferred from any leviathan's articulated bones. In fact, as the great Hunter says, the mere skeleton of the whale bears the same relation to the fully invested and padded animal as the insect does to the chrysalis that so roundingly envelopes it. This peculiarity is strikingly evinced in the head, as in some part of this book will be incidentally shown. It is also very curiously displayed in the side fin, the bones of which almost exactly answer to the bones of the human hand, minus only the thumb. This fin has four regular bone-fingers, the index, middle, ring, and little finger. But all these are permanently lodged in their fleshy covering, as the human fingers in an artificial covering. "However recklessly the whale may sometimes serve us," said humorous Stubb one day, "he can never be truly said to handle us without mittens."

For all these reasons, then, any way you may look at it, you must needs conclude that the great Leviathan is that one creature in the world which must remain unpainted to the last. True, one portrait may hit the mark much nearer than another, but none can hit it with any very considerable degree of exactness. So there is no earthly way of finding out precisely what the whale really looks like. And the only mode in which you can derive even a tolerable idea of his living contour, is by going a whaling yourself; but by so doing, you run no small risk of being eternally stove and sunk by him. Wherefore, it seems to me you had best not be too fastidious in your curiosity touching this Leviathan.

# Chapter 56

*Of the Less Erroneous Pictures of Whales, and the True Pictures of Whaling Scenes*

IN CONNEXION with the monstrous pictures of whales, I am strongly tempted here to enter upon those still more monstrous stories of them which are to be found in certain books, both ancient and modern, especially in Pliny, Purchas, Hackluyt, Harris, Cuvier, &c. But I pass that matter by.

I know of only four published outlines of the great Sperm Whale; Colnett's, Huggins's, Frederick Cuvier's, and Beale's. In the previous chapter Colnett and Cuvier have been referred to. Huggins's is far better than theirs; but, by great odds, Beale's is the best. All Beale's drawings of this whale are good, excepting the middle figure in the picture of three whales in various attitudes, capping his second chapter. His frontispiece, boats attacking Sperm Whales, though no doubt calculated to excite the civil scepticism of some parlor men, is admirably correct and life-like in its general effect. Some of the Sperm Whale drawings in J. Ross Browne are pretty correct in contour; but they are wretchedly engraved. That is not his fault though.

Of the Right Whale, the best outline pictures are in Scoresby; but they are drawn on too small a scale to convey a desirable impression. He has but one picture of whaling scenes, and this is a sad deficiency, because it is by such pictures only, when at all well done, that you can derive anything like a truthful idea of the living whale as seen by his living hunters.

But, taken for all in all, by far the finest, though in some details not the most correct, presentations of whales and whaling scenes to be anywhere found, are two large French engravings, well executed, and taken from paintings by one Garnery. Respectively, they represent attacks on the Sperm and Right Whale. In the first engraving a noble Sperm Whale is depicted in full majesty of might, just risen beneath the boat from the profundities of the ocean, and bearing high in the air upon his back the terrific wreck of the stoven planks. The prow of the boat is partially unbroken, and is drawn just balancing upon the monster's spine; and standing in that prow, for that one single incomputable flash of time, you behold an oarsman, half shrouded by the incensed boiling spout of the whale, and in the act of leaping, as if from a precipice. The action of the whole thing is wonderfully good and true. The half-emptied line-tub floats on the whitened sea; the wooden poles of the spilled harpoons obliquely bob in it; the heads of the swimming crew are scattered about the whale in contrasting expressions of affright; while in the black stormy distance the ship is bearing down upon the scene. Serious fault might be found with the anatomical details of this whale, but let that pass; since, for the life of me, I could not draw so good a one.

In the second engraving, the boat is in the act of drawing alongside the barnacled flank of a large running Right Whale, that rolls his black weedy bulk in the sea like some mossy rock-slide from the Patagonian cliffs. His jets are erect, full, and black like soot; so that from so abounding a smoke in the chimney, you would think there must be a brave supper cooking in the great bowels below. Sea fowls are pecking at the small crabs, shell-fish, and other sea candies and maccaroni, which the Right Whale sometimes carries on his pestilent back. And all the while the thick-lipped leviathan is rushing through the deep, leaving tons of tumultuous white curds in his wake, and causing the slight boat to rock in the swells like a skiff caught nigh the paddle-wheels of an ocean steamer. Thus, the foreground is all raging commotion; but behind, in admirable artistic contrast, is the glassy level of a sea becalmed, the drooping unstarched sails of the powerless ship, and the inert mass of a dead whale, a conquered fortress, with the flag of capture lazily hanging from the whale-pole inserted into his spout-hole.

Who Garnery the painter is, or was, I know not. But my life for it he was either practically conversant with his subject, or else marvellously tutored by some experienced whaleman. The French are the lads for paint-

ing action. Go and gaze upon all the paintings of Europe, and where will
you find such a gallery of living and breathing commotion on canvas, as in
that triumphal hall at Versailles; where the beholder fights his way, pell-
mell, through the consecutive great battles of France; where every sword
seems a flash of the Northern Lights, and the successive armed kings and
Emperors dash by, like a charge of crowned centaurs? Not wholly unworthy of a place in that gallery, are these sea battle-pieces of Garnery.

The natural aptitude of the French for seizing the picturesqueness of
things seems to be peculiarly evinced in what paintings and engravings they
have of their whaling scenes. With not one tenth of England's experience in
the fishery, and not the thousandth part of that of the Americans, they have
nevertheless furnished both nations with the only finished sketches at all
capable of conveying the real spirit of the whale hunt. For the most part, the
English and American whale draughtsmen seem entirely content with
presenting the mechanical outline of things, such as the vacant profile of the
whale; which, so far as picturesqueness of effect is concerned, is about tantamount to sketching the profile of a pyramid. Even Scoresby, the justly
renowned Right whaleman, after giving us a stiff full length of the Greenland whale, and three or four delicate miniatures of narwhales and porpoises, treats us to a series of classical engravings of boat hooks, chopping
knives, and grapnels; and with the microscopic diligence of a Leuwenhoeck
submits to the inspection of a shivering world ninety-six fac-similes of
magnified Arctic snow crystals. I mean no disparagement to the excellent
voyager (I honor him for a veteran), but in so important a matter it was
certainly an oversight not to have procured for every crystal a sworn affidavit
taken before a Greenland Justice of the Peace.

In addition to those fine engravings from Garnery, there are two other
French engravings worthy of note, by some one who subscribes himself
"H. Durand." One of them, though not precisely adapted to our present
purpose, nevertheless deserves mention on other accounts. It is a quiet
noon-scene among the isles of the Pacific; a French whaler anchored,
inshore, in a calm, and lazily taking water on board; the loosened sails of the
ship, and the long leaves of the palms in the background, both drooping
together in the breezeless air. The effect is very fine, when considered with
reference to its presenting the hardy fishermen under one of their few
aspects of oriental repose. The other engraving is quite a different affair: the
ship hove-to upon the open sea, and in the very heart of the Leviathanic
life, with a Right Whale alongside; the vessel (in the act of cutting-in) hove
over to the monster as if to a quay; and a boat, hurriedly pushing off from

this scene of activity, is about giving chase to whales in the distance. The harpoons and lances lie levelled for use; three oarsmen are just setting the mast in its hole; while from a sudden roll of the sea, the little craft stands half-erect out of the water, like a rearing horse. From the ship, the smoke of the torments of the boiling whale is going up like the smoke over a village of smithies; and to windward, a black cloud, rising up with earnest of squalls and rains, seems to quicken the activity of the excited seamen.

# Chapter 57

*Of Whales in Paint; in Teeth; in Wood; in Sheet-Iron;
in Stone; in Mountains; in Stars*

O N Tower-hill, as you go down to the London docks, you may
have seen a crippled beggar (or *kedger,* as the sailors say) holding a
painted board before him, representing the tragic scene in which
he lost his leg. There are three whales and three boats; and one of the boats
(presumed to contain the missing leg in all its original integrity) is being
crunched by the jaws of the foremost whale. Any time these ten years, they
tell me, has that man held up that picture, and exhibited that stump to an
incredulous world. But the time of his justification has now come. His three
whales are as good whales as were ever published in Wapping, at any rate;
and his stump as unquestionable a stump as any you will find in the western
clearings. But, though for ever mounted on that stump, never a stump-
speech does the poor whaleman make; but, with downcast eyes, stands
ruefully contemplating his own amputation.
Throughout the Pacific, and also in Nantucket, and New Bedford, and
Sag Harbor, you will come across lively sketches of whales and whaling-
scenes, graven by the fishermen themselves on Sperm Whale-teeth, or
ladies' busks wrought out of the Right Whale-bone, and other like skrimshander articles, as the whalemen call the numerous little ingenious
contrivances they elaborately carve out of the rough material, in their hours
of ocean leisure. Some of them have little boxes of dentistical-looking

implements, specially intended for the skrimshandering business. But, in general, they toil with their jack-knives alone; and, with that almost omnipotent tool of the sailor, they will turn you out anything you please, in the way of a mariner's fancy.

Long exile from Christendom and civilization inevitably restores a man to that condition in which God placed him, *i.e.* what is called savagery. Your true whale-hunter is as much a savage as an Iroquois. I myself am a savage, owning no allegiance but to the King of the Cannibals; and ready at any moment to rebel against him.

Now, one of the peculiar characteristics of the savage in his domestic hours, is his wonderful patience of industry. An ancient Hawaiian war-club or spear-paddle, in its full multiplicity and elaboration of carving, is as great a trophy of human perseverance as a Latin lexicon. For, with but a bit of broken sea-shell or a shark's tooth, that miraculous intricacy of wooden net-work has been achieved; and it has cost steady years of steady application.

As with the Hawaiian savage, so with the white sailor-savage. With the same marvellous patience, and with the same single shark's tooth, of his one poor jack-knife, he will carve you a bit of bone sculpture, not quite as workmanlike, but as close packed in its maziness of design, as the Greek savage, Achilles's shield; and full of barbaric spirit and suggestiveness, as the prints of that fine old Dutch savage, Albert Durer.

Wooden whales, or whales cut in profile out of the small dark slabs of the noble South Sea war-wood, are frequently met with in the forecastles of American whalers. Some of them are done with much accuracy.

At some old gable-roofed country houses you will see brass whales hung by the tail for knockers to the road-side door. When the porter is sleepy, the anvil-headed whale would be best. But these knocking whales are seldom remarkable as faithful essays. On the spires of some old-fashioned churches you will see sheet-iron whales placed there for weathercocks; but they are so elevated, and besides that are to all intents and purposes so labelled with "*Hands off!*" you cannot examine them closely enough to decide upon their merit.

In bony, ribby regions of the earth, where at the base of high broken cliffs masses of rock lie strewn in fantastic groupings upon the plain, you will often discover images as of the petrified forms of the Leviathan partly merged in grass, which of a windy day breaks against them in a surf of green surges.

Then, again, in mountainous countries where the traveller is continually girdled by amphitheatrical heights; here and there from some lucky point of view you will catch passing glimpses of the profiles of whales defined along the undulating ridges. But you must be a thorough whaleman, to see these sights; and not only that, but if you wish to return to such a sight again, you must be sure and take the exact intersecting latitude and longitude of your first stand-point, else—so chance-like are such observations of the hills—your precise, previous stand-point would require a laborious rediscovery; like the Solomon islands, which still remain incognita, though once high-ruffed Mendanna trod them and old Figueroa chronicled them.

Nor when expandingly lifted by your subject, can you fail to trace out great whales in the starry heavens, and boats in pursuit of them; as when long filled with thoughts of war the Eastern nations saw armies locked in battle among the clouds. Thus at the North have I chased Leviathan round and round the Pole with the revolutions of the bright points that first defined him to me. And beneath the effulgent Antarctic skies I have boarded the Argo-Navis, and joined the chase against the starry Cetus far beyond the utmost stretch of Hydrus and the Flying Fish.

With a frigate's anchors for my bridle-bitts and fasces of harpoons for spurs, would I could mount that whale and leap the topmost skies, to see whether the fabled heavens with all their countless tents really lie encamped beyond my mortal sight!

# Chapter 58

*Brit*

STEERING NORTH-EASTWARD from the Crozetts, we fell in with vast meadows of brit, the minute, yellow substance, upon which the Right Whale largely feeds. For leagues and leagues it undulated round us, so that we seemed to be sailing through boundless fields of ripe and golden wheat.

On the second day, numbers of Right Whales were seen, who, secure from the attack of a Sperm Whaler like the Pequod, with open jaws sluggishly swam through the brit, which, adhering to the fringing fibres of that wondrous Venetian blind in their mouths, was in that manner separated from the water that escaped at the lip.

As morning mowers, who side by side slowly and seethingly advance their scythes through the long wet grass of marshy meads; even so these monsters swam, making a strange, grassy, cutting sound; and leaving behind them endless swaths of blue upon the yellow sea.*

But it was only the sound they made as they parted the brit which at all reminded one of mowers. Seen from the mast-heads, especially when they

---

* That part of the sea known among whalemen as the "Brazil Banks" does not bear that name as the Banks of Newfoundland do, because of there being shallows and soundings there, but because of this remarkable meadow-like appearance, caused by the vast drifts of brit continually floating in those latitudes, where the Right Whale is often chased.

paused and were stationary for a while, their vast black forms looked more like lifeless masses of rock than anything else. And as in the great hunting countries of India, the stranger at a distance will sometimes pass on the plains recumbent elephants without knowing them to be such, taking them for bare, blackened elevations of the soil; even so, often, with him, who for the first time beholds this species of the leviathans of the sea. And even when recognised at last, their immense magnitude renders it very hard really to believe that such bulky masses of overgrowth can possibly be instinct, in all parts, with the same sort of life that lives in a dog or a horse.

Indeed, in other respects, you can hardly regard any creatures of the deep with the same feelings that you do those of the shore. For though some old naturalists have maintained that all creatures of the land are of their kind in the sea; and though taking a broad general view of the thing, this may very well be; yet coming to specialities, where, for example, does the ocean furnish any fish that in disposition answers to the sagacious kindness of the dog? The accursed shark alone can in any generic respect be said to bear comparative analogy to him.

But though, to landsmen in general, the native inhabitants of the seas have ever been regarded with emotions unspeakably unsocial and repelling; though we know the sea to be an everlasting terra incognita, so that Columbus sailed over numberless unknown worlds to discover his one superficial western one; though, by vast odds, the most terrific of all mortal disasters have immemorially and indiscriminately befallen tens and hundreds of thousands of those who have gone upon the waters; though but a moment's consideration will teach, that however baby man may brag of his science and skill, and however much, in a flattering future, that science and skill may augment; yet for ever and for ever, to the crack of doom, the sea will insult and murder him, and pulverize the stateliest, stiffest frigate he can make; nevertheless, by the continual repetition of these very impressions, man has lost that sense of the full awfulness of the sea which aboriginally belongs to it.

The first boat we read of, floated on an ocean, that with Portuguese vengeance had whelmed a whole world without leaving so much as a widow. That same ocean rolls now; that same ocean destroyed the wrecked ships of last year. Yea, foolish mortals, Noah's flood is not yet subsided; two thirds of the fair world it yet covers.

Wherein differ the sea and the land, that a miracle upon one is not a miracle upon the other? Preternatural terrors rested upon the Hebrews, when under the feet of Korah and his company the live ground opened and

swallowed them up for ever; yet not a modern sun ever sets, but in precisely
the same manner the live sea swallows up ships and crews.

But not only is the sea such a foe to man who is an alien to it, but it is also
a fiend to its own offspring; worse than the Persian host who murdered his
own guests; sparing not the creatures which itself hath spawned. Like a
savage tigress that tossing in the jungle overlays her own cubs, so the sea
dashes even the mightiest whales against the rocks, and leaves them there
side by side with the split wrecks of ships. No mercy, no power but its own
controls it. Panting and snorting like a mad battle steed that has lost its
rider, the masterless ocean overruns the globe.

Consider the subtleness of the sea; how its most dreaded creatures glide
under water, unapparent for the most part, and treacherously hidden
beneath the loveliest tints of azure. Consider also the devilish brilliance and
beauty of many of its most remorseless tribes, as the dainty embellished
shape of many species of sharks. Consider, once more, the universal cannibal-
ism of the sea; all whose creatures prey upon each other, carrying on eternal
war since the world began.

Consider all this; and then turn to this green, gentle, and most docile
earth; consider them both, the sea and the land; and do you not find a
strange analogy to something in yourself? For as this appalling ocean
surrounds the verdant land, so in the soul of man there lies one insular
Tahiti, full of peace and joy, but encompassed by all the horrors of the half
known life. God keep thee! Push not off from that isle, thou canst never
return!

# Chapter 59

## *Squid*

SLOWLY WADING through the meadows of brit, the Pequod still held on her way north-eastward towards the island of Java; a gentle air impelling her keel, so that in the surrounding serenity her three tall tapering masts mildly waved to that languid breeze, as three mild palms on a plain. And still, at wide intervals in the silvery night, the lonely, alluring jet would be seen.

But one transparent blue morning, when a stillness almost preternatural spread over the sea, however unattended with any stagnant calm; when the long burnished sun-glade on the waters seemed a golden finger laid across them, enjoining some secresy; when the slippered waves whispered together as they softly ran on; in this profound hush of the visible sphere a strange spectre was seen by Daggoo from the main-mast-head.

In the distance, a great white mass lazily rose, and rising higher and higher, and disentangling itself from the azure, at last gleamed before our prow like a snow-slide, new slid from the hills. Thus glistening for a moment, as slowly it subsided, and sank. Then once more arose, and silently gleamed. It seemed not a whale; and yet is this Moby Dick? thought Daggoo. Again the phantom went down, but on re-appearing once more, with a stiletto-like cry that startled every man from his nod, the negro yelled out— "There! there again! there she breaches! right ahead! The White Whale, the White Whale!"

Upon this, the seamen rushed to the yard-arms, as in swarming-time the bees rush to the boughs. Bare-headed in the sultry sun, Ahab stood on the bowsprit, and with one hand pushed far behind in readiness to wave his orders to the helmsman, cast his eager glance in the direction indicated aloft by the outstretched motionless arm of Daggoo.

Whether the flitting attendance of the one still and solitary jet had gradually worked upon Ahab, so that he was now prepared to connect the ideas of mildness and repose with the first sight of the particular whale he pursued; however this was, or whether his eagerness betrayed him; whichever way it might have been, no sooner did he distinctly perceive the white mass, than with a quick intensity he instantly gave orders for lowering.

The four boats were soon on the water; Ahab's in advance, and all swiftly pulling towards their prey. Soon it went down, and while, with oars suspended, we were awaiting its reappearance, lo! in the same spot where it sank, once more it slowly rose. Almost forgetting for the moment all thoughts of Moby Dick, we now gazed at the most wondrous phenomenon which the secret seas have hitherto revealed to mankind. A vast pulpy mass, furlongs in length and breadth, of a glancing cream-color, lay floating on the water, innumerable long arms radiating from its centre, and curling and twisting like a nest of anacondas, as if blindly to clutch at any hapless object within reach. No perceptible face or front did it have; no conceivable token of either sensation or instinct; but undulated there on the billows, an unearthly, formless, chance-like apparition of life.

As with a low sucking sound it slowly disappeared again, Starbuck still gazing at the agitated waters where it had sunk, with a wild voice exclaimed —"Almost rather had I seen Moby Dick and fought him, than to have seen thee, thou white ghost!"

"What was it, Sir?" said Flask.

"The great live squid, which, they say, few whale-ships ever beheld, and returned to their ports to tell of it."

But Ahab said nothing; turning his boat, he sailed back to the vessel; the rest as silently following.

Whatever superstitions the sperm whalemen in general have connected with the sight of this object, certain it is, that a glimpse of it being so very unusual, that circumstance has gone far to invest it with portentousness. So rarely is it beheld, that though one and all of them declare it to be the largest animated thing in the ocean, yet very few of them have any but the most vague ideas concerning its true nature and form; notwithstanding, they believe it to furnish to the sperm whale his only food. For though other species of whales find their food above water, and may be seen by man in the act of feeding, the spermaceti whale obtains his whole food in unknown zones below the surface; and only by inference is it that any one can tell of what, precisely, that food consists. At times, when closely pursued, he will disgorge what are supposed to be the detached arms of the squid; some of them thus exhibited exceeding twenty and thirty feet in length. They fancy that the monster to which these arms belonged ordinarily clings by them to the bed of the ocean; and that the sperm whale, unlike other species, is supplied with teeth in order to attack and tear it.

There seems some ground to imagine that the great Kraken of Bishop Pontoppidan may ultimately resolve itself into Squid. The manner in which the Bishop describes it, as alternately rising and sinking, with some other particulars he narrates, in all this the two correspond. But much abatement is necessary with respect to the incredible bulk he assigns it.

By some naturalists who have vaguely heard rumors of the mysterious creature, here spoken of, it is included among the class of cuttle-fish, to which, indeed, in certain external respects it would seem to belong, but only as the Anak of the tribe.

# Chapter 60

### The Line

WITH REFERENCE to the whaling scene shortly to be described, as well as for the better understanding of all similar scenes elsewhere presented, I have here to speak of the magical, sometimes horrible whale-line.

The line originally used in the fishery was of the best hemp, slightly vapored with tar, not impregnated with it, as in the case of ordinary ropes; for while tar, as ordinarily used, makes the hemp more pliable to the rope-maker, and also renders the rope itself more convenient to the sailor for common ship use; yet, not only would the ordinary quantity too much stiffen the whale-line for the close coiling to which it must be subjected; but as most seamen are beginning to learn, tar in general by no means adds to the rope's durability or strength, however much it may give it compactness and gloss.

Of late years the Manilla rope has in the American fishery almost entirely superseded hemp as a material for whale-lines; for, though not so durable as hemp, it is stronger, and far more soft and elastic; and I will add (since there is an æsthetics in all things), is much more handsome and becoming to the boat, than hemp. Hemp is a dusky, dark fellow, a sort of Indian; but Manilla is as a golden-haired Circassian to behold.

The whale line is only two thirds of an inch in thickness. At first sight,

278

you would not think it so strong as it really is. By experiment its one and fifty yarns will each suspend a weight of one hundred and twelve pounds; so that the whole rope will bear a strain nearly equal to three tons. In length, the common sperm whale-line measures something over two hundred fathoms. Towards the stern of the boat it is spirally coiled away in the tub, not like the worm-pipe of a still though, but so as to form one round, cheese-shaped mass of densely bedded "sheaves," or layers of concentric spiraliza-tions, without any hollow but the "heart," or minute vertical tube formed at the axis of the cheese. As the least tangle or kink in the coiling would, in running out, infallibly take somebody's arm, leg, or entire body off, the utmost precaution is used in stowing the line in its tub. Some harpooneers will consume almost an entire morning in this business, carrying the line high aloft and then reeving it downwards through a block towards the tub, so as in the act of coiling to free it from all possible wrinkles and twists.

In the English boats two tubs are used instead of one; the same line being continuously coiled in both tubs. There is some advantage in this; because these twin-tubs being so small they fit more readily into the boat, and do not strain it so much; whereas, the American tub, nearly three feet in diameter and of proportionate depth, makes a rather bulky freight for a craft whose planks are but one half-inch in thickness; for the bottom of the whale-boat is like critical ice, which will bear up a considerable distrib-uted weight, but not very much of a concentrated one. When the painted canvas cover is clapped on the American line-tub, the boat looks as if it were pulling off with a prodigious great wedding-cake to present to the whales.

Both ends of the line are exposed; the lower end terminating in an eye-splice or loop coming up from the bottom against the side of the tub, and hanging over its edge completely disengaged from everything. This arrangement of the lower end is necessary on two accounts. First: In order to facilitate the fastening to it of an additional line from a neighboring boat, in case the stricken whale should sound so deep as to threaten to carry off the entire line originally attached to the harpoon. In these instances, the whale of course is shifted like a mug of ale, as it were, from the one boat to the other; though the first boat always hovers at hand to assist its consort. Second: This arrangement is indispensable for common safety's sake; for were the lower end of the line in any way attached to the boat, and were the whale then to run the line out to the end almost in a single, smoking minute as he sometimes does, he would not stop there, for the doomed boat would infallibly be dragged down after him into the profundity of the sea; and in that case no town-crier would ever find her again.

Before lowering the boat for the chase, the upper end of the line is taken
aft from the tub, and passing round the loggerhead there, is again carried
forward the entire length of the boat, resting crosswise upon the loom or
handle of every man's oar, so that it jogs against his wrist in rowing; and also
passing between the men, as they alternately sit at the opposite gunwales, to
the leaded chocks or grooves in the extreme pointed prow of the boat, where
a wooden pin or skewer the size of a common quill, prevents it from slipping
out. From the chocks it hangs in a slight festoon over the bows, and is then
passed inside the boat again; and some ten or twenty fathoms (called box-
line) being coiled upon the box in the bows, it continues its way to the
gunwale still a little further aft, and is then attached to the short-warp—the
rope which is immediately connected with the harpoon; but previous to
that connexion, the short-warp goes through sundry mystifications too
tedious to detail.

Thus the whale-line folds the whole boat in its complicated coils, twisting and writhing around it in almost every direction. All the oarsmen are
involved in its perilous contortions; so that to the timid eye of the landsman,
they seem as Indian jugglers, with the deadliest snakes sportively festooning
their limbs. Nor can any son of mortal woman, for the first time, seat himself amid those hempen intricacies, and while straining his utmost at the
oar, bethink him that at any unknown instant the harpoon may be darted,
and all these horrible contortions be put in play like ringed lightnings; he
cannot be thus circumstanced without a shudder that makes the very
marrow in his bones to quiver in him like a shaken jelly. Yet habit—strange
thing! what cannot habit accomplish?—Gayer sallies, more merry mirth,
better jokes, and brighter repartees, you never heard over your mahogany,
than you will hear over the half-inch white cedar of the whale-boat, when
thus hung in hangman's nooses; and, like the six burghers of Calais before
King Edward, the six men composing the crew pull into the jaws of death,
with a halter around every neck, as you may say.

Perhaps a very little thought will now enable you to account for those
repeated whaling disasters—some few of which are casually chronicled—of
this man or that man being taken out of the boat by the line, and lost. For,
when the line is darting out, to be seated then in the boat, is like being seated
in the midst of the manifold whizzings of a steam-engine in full play, when
every flying beam, and shaft, and wheel, is grazing you. It is worse; for you
cannot sit motionless in the heart of these perils, because the boat is rocking
like a cradle, and you are pitched one way and the other, without the
slightest warning; and only by a certain self-adjusting buoyancy and simul-

taneousness of volition and action, can you escape being made a Mazeppa of, and run away with where the all-seeing sun himself could never pierce you out.

Again: as the profound calm which only apparently precedes and prophesies of the storm, is perhaps more awful than the storm itself; for, indeed, the calm is but the wrapper and envelope of the storm; and contains it in itself, as the seemingly harmless rifle holds the fatal powder, and the ball, and the explosion; so the graceful repose of the line, as it silently serpentines about the oarsmen before being brought into actual play—this is a thing which carries more of true terror than any other aspect of this dangerous affair. But why say more? All men live enveloped in whale-lines. All are born with halters round their necks; but it is only when caught in the swift, sudden turn of death, that mortals realize the silent, subtle, ever-present perils of life. And if you be a philosopher, though seated in the whale-boat, you would not at heart feel one whit more of terror, than though seated before your evening fire with a poker, and not a harpoon, by your side.

# Chapter 61

### Stubb kills a Whale

IF to Starbuck the apparition of the Squid was a thing of portents, to Queequeg it was quite a different object.

"When you see him 'quid," said the savage, honing his harpoon in the bow of his hoisted boat, "then you quick see him 'parm whale."

The next day was exceedingly still and sultry, and with nothing special to engage them, the Pequod's crew could hardly resist the spell of sleep induced by such a vacant sea. For this part of the Indian Ocean through which we then were voyaging is not what whalemen call a lively ground; that is, it affords fewer glimpses of porpoises, dolphins, flying-fish, and other vivacious denizens of more stirring waters, than those off the Rio de la Plata, or the in-shore ground off Peru.

It was my turn to stand at the foremast-head; and with my shoulders leaning against the slackened royal shrouds, to and fro I idly swayed in what seemed an enchanted air. No resolution could withstand it; in that dreamy mood losing all consciousness, at last my soul went out of my body; though my body still continued to sway as a pendulum will, long after the power which first moved it is withdrawn.

Ere forgetfulness altogether came over me, I had noticed that the seamen at the main and mizen mast-heads were already drowsy. So that at last all three of us lifelessly swung from the spars, and for every swing that we made there was a nod from below from the slumbering helmsman. The waves, too, nodded their indolent crests; and across the wide trance of the sea, east nodded to west, and the sun over all.

Suddenly bubbles seemed bursting beneath my closed eyes; like vices my hands grasped the shrouds; some invisible, gracious agency preserved me; with a shock I came back to life. And lo! close under our lee, not forty fathoms off, a gigantic Sperm Whale lay rolling in the water like the capsized hull of a frigate, his broad, glossy back, of an Ethiopian hue, glistening in the sun's rays like a mirror. But lazily undulating in the trough of the sea, and ever and anon tranquilly spouting his vapory jet, the whale looked like a portly burgher smoking his pipe of a warm afternoon. But that pipe, poor whale, was thy last. As if struck by some enchanter's wand, the sleepy ship and every sleeper in it all at once started into wakefulness; and more than a score of voices from all parts of the vessel, simultaneously with the three notes from aloft, shouted forth the accustomed cry, as the great fish slowly and regularly spouted the sparkling brine into the air.

"Clear away the boats! Luff!" cried Ahab. And obeying his own order, he dashed the helm down before the helmsman could handle the spokes.

The sudden exclamations of the crew must have alarmed the whale; and ere the boats were down, majestically turning, he swam away to the leeward, but with such a steady tranquillity, and making so few ripples as he swam, that thinking after all he might not as yet be alarmed, Ahab gave orders that not an oar should be used, and no man must speak but in whispers. So seated like Ontario Indians on the gunwales of the boats, we swiftly but silently paddled along; the calm not admitting of the noiseless sails being set. Presently, as we thus glided in chase, the monster perpendicularly flitted his tail forty feet into the air, and then sank out of sight like a tower swallowed up.

"There go flukes!" was the cry, an announcement immediately followed by Stubb's producing his match and igniting his pipe, for now a respite was granted. After the full interval of his sounding had elapsed, the whale rose again, and being now in advance of the smoker's boat, and much nearer to it than to any of the others, Stubb counted upon the honor of the capture. It was obvious, now, that the whale had at length become aware of his pursuers. All silence of cautiousness was therefore no longer of use. Paddles were dropped, and oars came loudly into play. And still puffing at his pipe, Stubb cheered on his crew to the assault.

Yes, a mighty change had come over the fish. All alive to his jeopardy, he was going "head out;" that part obliquely projecting from the mad yeast which he brewed.*

"Start her, start her, my men! Don't hurry yourselves; take plenty of time—but start her; start her like thunder-claps, that's all," cried Stubb, spluttering out the smoke as he spoke. "Start her, now; give 'em the long and strong stroke, Tashtego. Start her, Tash, my boy—start her, all; but keep cool, keep cool—cucumbers is the word—easy, easy—only start her like grim death and grinning devils, and raise the buried dead perpendicular out of their graves, boys—that's all. Start her!"

"Woo-hoo! Wa-hee!" screamed the Gay-Header in reply, raising some old war-whoop to the skies; as every oarsman in the strained boat involuntarily bounced forward with the one tremendous leading stroke which the eager Indian gave.

But his wild screams were answered by others quite as wild. "Kee-hee! Kee-hee!" yelled Daggoo, straining forwards and backwards on his seat, like a pacing tiger in his cage.

"Ka-la! Koo-loo!" howled Queequeg, as if smacking his lips over a mouthful of Grenadier's steak. And thus with oars and yells the keels cut the sea. Meanwhile, Stubb retaining his place in the van, still encouraged his men to the onset, all the while puffing the smoke from his mouth. Like desperadoes they tugged and they strained, till the welcome cry was heard— "Stand up, Tashtego!—give it to him!" The harpoon was hurled. "Stern all!" The oarsmen backed water; the same moment something went hot and hissing along every one of their wrists. It was the magical line. An instant before, Stubb had swiftly caught two additional turns with it round the loggerhead, whence, by reason of its increased rapid circlings, a hempen blue smoke now jetted up and mingled with the steady fumes from his pipe. As the line passed round and round the loggerhead; so also, just before reaching that point, it blisteringly passed through and through both of Stubb's hands, from which the hand-cloths, or squares of quilted canvas sometimes worn at these times, had accidentally dropped. It was like holding an enemy's sharp two-edged sword by the blade, and that enemy all the time striving to wrest it out of your clutch.

* It will be seen in some other place of what a very light substance the entire interior of the sperm whale's enormous head consists. Though apparently the most massive, it is by far the most buoyant part about him. So that with ease he elevates it in the air, and invariably does so when going at his utmost speed. Besides, such is the breadth of the upper part of the front of his head, and such the tapering cut-water formation of the lower part, that by obliquely elevating his head, he thereby may be said to transform himself from a bluff-bowed sluggish galliot into a sharp-pointed New York pilot-boat.

"Wet the line! wet the line!" cried Stubb to the tub oarsman (him seated by the tub) who, snatching off his hat, dashed the sea-water into it.* More turns were taken, so that the line began holding its place. The boat now flew through the boiling water like a shark all fins. Stubb and Tashtego here changed places—stem for stern—a staggering business truly in that rocking commotion.

From the vibrating line extending the entire length of the upper part of the boat, and from its now being more tight than a harpstring, you would have thought the craft had two keels—one cleaving the water, the other the air—as the boat churned on through both opposing elements at once. A continual cascade played at the bows; a ceaseless whirling eddy in her wake; and, at the slightest motion from within, even but of a little finger, the vibrating, cracking craft canted over her spasmodic gunwale into the sea. Thus they rushed; each man with might and main clinging to his seat, to prevent being tossed to the foam; and the tall form of Tashtego at the steering oar crouching almost double, in order to bring down his centre of gravity. Whole Atlantics and Pacifics seemed passed as they shot on their way, till at length the whale somewhat slackened his flight.

"Haul in—haul in!" cried Stubb to the bowsman; and, facing round towards the whale, all hands began pulling the boat up to him, while yet the boat was being towed on. Soon ranging up by his flank, Stubb, firmly planting his knee in the clumsy cleat, darted dart after dart into the flying fish; at the word of command, the boat alternately sterning out of the way of the whale's horrible wallow, and then ranging up for another fling.

The red tide now poured from all sides of the monster like brooks down a hill. His tormented body rolled not in brine but in blood, which bubbled and seethed for furlongs behind in their wake. The slanting sun playing upon this crimson pond in the sea, sent back its reflection into every face, so that they all glowed to each other like red men. And all the while, jet after jet of white smoke was agonizingly shot from the spiracle of the whale, and vehement puff after puff from the mouth of the excited headsman; as at every dart, hauling in upon his crooked lance (by the line attached to it), Stubb straightened it again and again, by a few rapid blows against the gunwale, then again and again sent it into the whale.

"Pull up—pull up!" he now cried to the bowsman, as the waning whale

* Partly to show the indispensableness of this act, it may here be stated, that, in the old Dutch fishery, a mop was used to dash the running line with water; in many other ships, a wooden piggin, or bailer, is set apart for that purpose. Your hat, however, is the most convenient.

relaxed in his wrath. "Pull up!—close to!" and the boat ranged along the fish's flank. When reaching far over the bow, Stubb slowly churned his long sharp lance into the fish, and kept it there, carefully churning and churning, as if cautiously seeking to feel after some gold watch that the whale might have swallowed, and which he was fearful of breaking ere he could hook it out. But that gold watch he sought was the innermost life of the fish. And now it is struck; for, starting from his trance into that unspeakable thing called his "flurry," the monster horribly wallowed in his blood, over-wrapped himself in impenetrable, mad, boiling spray, so that the im-perilled craft, instantly dropping astern, had much ado blindly to struggle out from that phrensied twilight into the clear air of the day.

And now abating in his flurry, the whale once more rolled out into view; surging from side to side; spasmodically dilating and contracting his spout-hole, with sharp, cracking, agonized respirations. At last, gush after gush of clotted red gore, as if it had been the purple lees of red wine, shot into the frighted air; and falling back again, ran dripping down his motion-less flanks into the sea. His heart had burst!

"He's dead, Mr. Stubb," said Tashtego.

"Yes; both pipes smoked out!" and withdrawing his own from his mouth, Stubb scattered the dead ashes over the water; and, for a moment, stood thoughtfully eyeing the vast corpse he had made.

# Chapter 62

### *The Dart*

**A** WORD CONCERNING AN INCIDENT in the last chapter. According to the invariable usage of the fishery, the whale-boat pushes off from the ship, with the headsman or whale-killer as temporary steersman, and the harpooneer or whale-fastener pulling the foremost oar, the one known as the harpooneer-oar. Now it needs a strong, nervous arm to strike the first iron into the fish; for often, in what is called a long dart, the heavy implement has to be flung to the distance of twenty or thirty feet. But however prolonged and exhausting the chase, the harpooneer is expected to pull his oar meanwhile to the uttermost; indeed, he is expected to set an example of superhuman activity to the rest, not only by incredible rowing, but by repeated loud and intrepid exclamations; and what it is to keep shouting at the top of one's compass, while all the other muscles are strained and half started—what that is none know but those who have tried it. For one, I cannot bawl very heartily and work very recklessly at one and the same time. In this straining, bawling state, then, with his back to the fish, all at once the exhausted harpooneer hears the exciting cry—"Stand up, and give it to him!" He now has to drop and secure his oar, turn round on his centre half way, seize his harpoon from the crotch, and with what little strength may remain, he essays to pitch it somehow into the whale. No wonder, taking the whole fleet of whalemen in a body, that out of

fifty fair chances for a dart, not five are successful; no wonder that so many
hapless harpooneers are madly cursed and disrated; no wonder that some of
them actually burst their blood-vessels in the boat; no wonder that some
sperm whalemen are absent four years with four barrels; no wonder that to
many ship owners, whaling is but a losing concern; for it is the harpooneer
that makes the voyage, and if you take the breath out of his body how can
you expect to find it there when most wanted!

Again, if the dart be successful, then at the second critical instant, that is,
when the whale starts to run, the boat-header and harpooneer likewise
start to running fore and aft, to the imminent jeopardy of themselves and
every one else. It is then they change places; and the headsman, the chief
officer of the little craft, takes his proper station in the bows of the boat.

Now, I care not who maintains the contrary, but all this is both foolish
and unnecessary. The headsman should stay in the bows from first to last;
he should both dart the harpoon and the lance, and no rowing whatever
should be expected of him, except under circumstances obvious to any
fisherman. I know that this would sometimes involve a slight loss of speed in
the chase; but long experience in various whalemen of more than one
nation has convinced me that in the vast majority of failures in the fishery, it
has not by any means been so much the speed of the whale as the before
described exhaustion of the harpooneer that has caused them.

To insure the greatest efficiency in the dart, the harpooneers of this
world must start to their feet from out of idleness, and not from out of toil.

# Chapter 63

## *The Crotch*

OUT OF THE TRUNK, the branches grow; out of them, the twigs. So, in productive subjects, grow the chapters.

The crotch alluded to on a previous page deserves independent mention. It is a notched stick of a peculiar form, some two feet in length, which is perpendicularly inserted into the starboard gunwale near the bow, for the purpose of furnishing a rest for the wooden extremity of the harpoon, whose other naked, barbed end slopingly projects from the prow. Thereby the weapon is instantly at hand to its hurler, who snatches it up as readily from its rest as a backwoodsman swings his rifle from the wall. It is customary to have two harpoons reposing in the crotch, respectively called the first and second irons.

But these two harpoons, each by its own cord, are both connected with the line; the object being this: to dart them both, if possible, one instantly after the other into the same whale; so that if, in the coming drag, one should draw out, the other may still retain a hold. It is a doubling of the chances. But it very often happens that owing to the instantaneous, violent, convulsive running of the whale upon receiving the first iron, it becomes impossible for the harpooneer, however lightning-like in his movements, to pitch the second iron into him. Nevertheless, as the second iron is already connected with the line, and the line is running, hence that weapon must, at

289

all events, be anticipatingly tossed out of the boat, somehow and some-where; else the most terrible jeopardy would involve all hands. Tumbled into the water, it accordingly is in such cases; the spare coils of box line (mentioned in a preceding chapter) making this feat, in most instances, prudently practicable. But this critical act is not always unattended with the saddest and most fatal casualties.

Furthermore: you must know that when the second iron is thrown over-board, it thenceforth becomes a dangling, sharp-edged terror, skittishly curvetting about both boat and whale, entangling the lines, or cutting them, and making a prodigious sensation in all directions. Nor, in general, is it possible to secure it again until the whale is fairly captured and a corpse.

Consider, now, how it must be in the case of four boats all engaging one unusually strong, active, and knowing whale; when owing to these qualities in him, as well as to the thousand concurring accidents of such an audacious enterprise, eight or ten loose second irons may be simultaneously dangling about him. For, of course, each boat is supplied with several harpoons to bend on to the line should the first one be ineffectually darted without recovery. All these particulars are faithfully narrated here, as they will not fail to elucidate several most important, however intricate passages, in scenes hereafter to be painted.

# Chapter 64

*Stubb's Supper*

STUBB'S WHALE had been killed some distance from the ship. It was a calm; so, forming a tandem of three boats, we commenced the slow business of towing the trophy to the Pequod. And now, as we eighteen men with our thirty-six arms, and one hundred and eighty thumbs and fingers, slowly toiled hour after hour upon that inert, sluggish corpse in the sea; and it seemed hardly to budge at all, except at long intervals; good evidence was hereby furnished of the enormousness of the mass we moved. For, upon the great canal of Hang-Ho, or whatever they call it, in China, four or five laborers on the foot-path will draw a bulky freighted junk at the rate of a mile an hour; but this grand argosy we towed heavily forged along, as if laden with pig-lead in bulk.

Darkness came on; but three lights up and down in the Pequod's main-rigging dimly guided our way; till drawing nearer we saw Ahab dropping one of several more lanterns over the bulwarks. Vacantly eyeing the heaving whale for a moment, he issued the usual orders for securing it for the night, and then handing his lantern to a seaman, went his way into the cabin, and did not come forward again until morning.

Though, in overseeing the pursuit of this whale, Captain Ahab had evinced his customary activity, to call it so; yet now that the creature was dead, some vague dissatisfaction, or impatience, or despair, seemed working

in him; as if the sight of that dead body reminded him that Moby Dick was
yet to be slain; and though a thousand other whales were brought to his
ship, all that would not one jot advance his grand, monomaniac object.
Very soon you would have thought from the sound on the Pequod's decks,
that all hands were preparing to cast anchor in the deep; for heavy chains are
being dragged along the deck, and thrust rattling out of the port-holes. But
by those clanking links, the vast corpse itself, not the ship, is to be moored.
Tied by the head to the stern, and by the tail to the bows, the whale now lies
with its black hull close to the vessel's, and seen through the darkness of the
night, which obscured the spars and rigging aloft, the two—ship and whale,
seemed yoked together like colossal bullocks, whereof one reclines while
the other remains standing.*

If moody Ahab was now all quiescence, at least so far as could be known
on deck, Stubb, his second mate, flushed with conquest, betrayed an
unusual but still good-natured excitement. Such an unwonted bustle was
he in that the staid Starbuck, his official superior, quietly resigned to him for
the time the sole management of affairs. One small, helping cause of all this
liveliness in Stubb, was soon made strangely manifest. Stubb was a high
liver; he was somewhat intemperately fond of the whale as a flavorish thing
to his palate.

"A steak, a steak, ere I sleep! You, Daggoo! overboard you go, and
cut me one from his small!"

Here be it known, that though these wild fishermen do not, as a general
thing, and according to the great military maxim, make the enemy defray
the current expenses of the war (at least before realizing the proceeds of the
voyage), yet now and then you find some of these Nantucketers who have
a genuine relish for that particular part of the Sperm Whale designated by
Stubb; comprising the tapering extremity of the body.

About midnight that steak was cut and cooked; and lighted by two

---

* A little item may as well be related here. The strongest and most reliable hold which
the ship has upon the whale when moored alongside, is by the flukes or tail; and as from
its greater density that part is relatively heavier than any other (excepting the side-fins), its
flexibility even in death, causes it to sink low beneath the surface; so that with the hand
you cannot get at it from the boat, in order to put the chain round it. But this difficulty is
ingeniously overcome: a small, strong line is prepared with a wooden float at its outer end,
and a weight in its middle, while the other end is secured to the ship. By adroit management
the wooden float is made to rise on the other side of the mass, so that now having girdled
the whale, the chain is readily made to follow suit; and being slipped along the body, is at
last locked fast round the smallest part of the tail, at the point of junction with its broad
flukes or lobes.

lanterns of sperm oil, Stubb stoutly stood up to his spermaceti supper at the capstan-head, as if that capstan were a sideboard. Nor was Stubb the only banqueter on whale's flesh that night. Mingling their mumblings with his own mastications, thousands on thousands of sharks, swarming round the dead leviathan, smackingly feasted on its fatness. The few sleepers below in their bunks were often startled by the sharp slapping of their tails against the hull, within a few inches of the sleepers' hearts. Peering over the side you could just see them (as before you heard them) wallowing in the sullen, black waters, and turning over on their backs as they scooped out huge globular pieces of the whale of the bigness of a human head. This particular feat of the shark seems all but miraculous. How, at such an apparently un-assailable surface, they contrive to gouge out such symmetrical mouthfuls, remains a part of the universal problem of all things. The mark they thus leave on the whale, may best be likened to the hollow made by a carpenter in countersinking for a screw.

Though amid all the smoking horror and diabolism of a sea-fight, sharks will be seen longingly gazing up to the ship's decks, like hungry dogs round a table where red meat is being carved, ready to bolt down every killed man that is tossed to them; and though, while the valiant butchers over the deck-table are thus cannibally carving each other's live meat with carving-knives all gilded and tasselled, the sharks, also, with their jewel-hilted mouths, are quarrelsomely carving away under the table at the dead meat; and though, were you to turn the whole affair upside down, it would still be pretty much the same thing, that is to say, a shocking sharkish business enough for all parties; and though sharks also are the invariable outriders of all slave ships crossing the Atlantic, systematically trotting alongside, to be handy in case a parcel is to be carried anywhere, or a dead slave to be decently buried; and though one or two other like instances might be set down, touching the set terms, places, and occasions, when sharks do most socially congregate, and most hilariously feast; yet is there no conceivable time or occasion when you will find them in such countless numbers, and in gayer or more jovial spirits, than around a dead sperm whale, moored by night to a whale-ship at sea. If you have never seen that sight, then suspend your decision about the propriety of devil-worship, and the expediency of conciliating the devil.

But, as yet, Stubb heeded not the mumblings of the banquet that was going on so nigh him, no more than the sharks heeded the smacking of his own epicurean lips.

"Cook, cook!—where's that old Fleece?" he cried at length, widening his legs still further, as if to form a more secure base for his supper; and, at the same time, darting his fork into the dish, as if stabbing with his lance; "cook, you cook!—sail this way, cook!"

The old black, not in any very high glee at having been previously roused from his warm hammock at a most unseasonable hour, came shambling along from his galley, for, like many old blacks, there was something the matter with his knee-pans, which he did not keep well scoured like his other pans; this old Fleece, as they called him, came shuffling and limping along, assisting his step with his tongs, which, after a clumsy fashion, were made of straightened iron hoops; this old Ebony floundered along, and in obedience to the word of command, came to a dead stop on the opposite side of Stubb's sideboard; when, with both hands folded before him, and resting on his two-legged cane, he bowed his arched back still further over, at the same time sideways inclining his head, so as to bring his best ear into play.

"Cook," said Stubb, rapidly lifting a rather reddish morsel to his mouth, "don't you think this steak is rather overdone? You've been beating this steak too much, cook; it's too tender. Don't I always say that to be good, a whale-steak must be tough? There are those sharks now over the side, don't you see they prefer it tough and rare? What a shindy they are kicking up! Cook, go and talk to 'em; tell 'em they are welcome to help themselves civilly, and in moderation, but they must keep quiet. Blast me, if I can hear my own voice. Away, cook, and deliver my message. Here, take this lantern," snatching one from his sideboard; "now then, go and preach to 'em!"

Sullenly taking the offered lantern, old Fleece limped across the deck to the bulwarks; and then, with one hand dropping his light low over the sea, so as to get a good view of his congregation, with the other hand he solemnly flourished his tongs, and leaning far over the side in a mumbling voice began addressing the sharks, while Stubb, softly crawling behind, overheard all that was said.

"Fellow-critters: I'se ordered here to say dat you must stop dat dam noise dare. You hear? Stop dat dam smackin' ob de lip! Massa Stubb say dat you can fill your dam bellies up to de hatchings, but by Gor! you must stop dat dam racket!"

"Cook," here interposed Stubb, accompanying the word with a sudden slap on the shoulder,—"Cook! why, damn your eyes, you mustn't swear that way when you're preaching. That's no way to convert sinners, Cook!"

"Who dat? Den preach to him yourself," sullenly turning to go.

"No, Cook; go on, go on."

"Well, den, Belubed fellow-critters:"—

"Right!" exclaimed Stubb, approvingly, "coax 'em to it; try that," and Fleece continued.

"Dough you is all sharks, and by natur wery woracious, yet I zay to you, fellow-critters, dat dat woraciousness—'top dat dam slappin' ob de tail! How you tink to hear, 'spose you keep up such a dam slappin' and bitin' dare?"

"Cook," cried Stubb, collaring him, "I wont have that swearing. Talk to 'em gentlemanly."

Once more the sermon proceeded.

"Your woraciousness, fellow-critters, I don't blame ye so much for; dat is natur, and can't be helped; but to gobern dat wicked natur, dat is de pint. You is sharks, sartin; but if you gobern de shark in you, why den you be angel; for all angel is not'ing more dan de shark well goberned. Now, look here, bred'ren, just try wonst to be cibil, a helping yourselbs from dat whale. Don't be tearin' de blubber out your neighbour's mout, I say. Is not one shark good right as toder to dat whale? And, by Gor, none on you has de right to dat whale; dat whale belong to some one else. I know some o' you has berry brig mout, brigger dan oders; but den de brig mouts sometimes has de small bellies; so dat de brigness ob de mout is not to swallar wid, but to bite off de blubber for de small fry ob sharks, dat can't get into de scrouge to help demselves."

"Well done, old Fleece!" cried Stubb, "that's Christianity; go on."

"No use goin' on; de dam willains will keep a scrougin' and slappin' each oder, Massa Stubb; dey don't hear one word; no use a-preachin' to such dam g'uttons as you call 'em, till dare bellies is full, and dare bellies is bottomless; and when dey do get em full, dey wont hear you den; for den dey sink in de sea, go fast to sleep on de coral, and can't hear not'ing at all, no more, for eber and eber."

"Upon my soul, I am about of the same opinion; so give the benediction, Fleece, and I'll away to my supper."

Upon this, Fleece, holding both hands over the fishy mob, raised his shrill voice, and cried—

"Cussed fellow-critters! Kick up de damndest row as ever you can; fill your dam' bellies 'till dey bust—and den die."

"Now, cook," said Stubb, resuming his supper at the capstan; "Stand just where you stood before, there, over against me, and pay particular attention."

"All dention," said Fleece, again stooping over upon his tongs in the desired position.

"Well," said Stubb, helping himself freely meanwhile; "I shall now go back to the subject of this steak. In the first place, how old are you, cook?"

"What dat do wid de 'teak," said the old black, testily.

"Silence! How old are you, cook?"

"'Bout ninety, dey say," he gloomily muttered.

"And have you lived in this world hard upon one hundred years, cook, and don't know yet how to cook a whale-steak?" rapidly bolting another mouthful at the last word, so that that morsel seemed a continuation of the question. "Where were you born, cook?"

"'Hind de hatchway, in ferry-boat, goin' ober de Roanoke."

"Born in a ferry-boat! That's queer, too. But I want to know what country you were born in, cook?"

"Didn't I say de Roanoke country?" he cried, sharply.

"No, you didn't, cook; but I'll tell you what I'm coming to, cook. You must go home and be born over again; you don't know how to cook a whale-steak yet."

"Bress my soul, if I cook noder one," he growled, angrily, turning round to depart.

"Come back, cook;—here, hand me those tongs;—now take that bit of steak there, and tell me if you think that steak cooked as it should be? Take it, I say"—holding the tongs towards him—"take it, and taste it."

Faintly smacking his withered lips over it for a moment, the old negro muttered, "Best cooked 'teak I eber taste; joosy, berry joosy."

"Cook," said Stubb, squaring himself once more; "do you belong to the church?"

"Passed one once in Cape-Down," said the old man sullenly.

"And you have once in your life passed a holy church in Cape-Town, where you doubtless overheard a holy parson addressing his hearers as his beloved fellow-creatures, have you, cook! And yet you come here, and tell me such a dreadful lie as you did just now, eh?" said Stubb. "Where do you expect to go to, cook?"

"Go to bed berry soon," he mumbled, half-turning as he spoke.

"Avast! heave to! I mean when you die, cook. It's an awful question. Now what's your answer?"

"When dis old brack man dies," said the negro slowly, changing his whole air and demeanor, "he hisself won't go nowhere; but some bressed angel will come and fetch him."

"Fetch him? How? In a coach and four, as they fetched Elijah? And fetch him where?"

"Up dere," said Fleece, holding his tongs straight over his head, and keeping it there very solemnly.

"So, then, you expect to go up into our main-top, do you, cook, when you are dead? But don't you know the higher you climb, the colder it gets? Main-top eh?"

"Didn't say dat t'all," said Fleece, again in the sulks.

"You said up there, didn't you? and now look yourself, and see where your tongs are pointing. But, perhaps you expect to get into heaven by crawling through the lubber's hole, cook; but, no, no, cook, you don't get there, except you go the regular way, round by the rigging. It's a ticklish business, but must be done, or else it's no go. But none of us are in heaven yet. Drop your tongs, cook, and hear my orders. Do ye hear? Hold your hat in one hand, and clap t'other a'top of your heart, when I'm giving my orders, cook. What! that your heart, there?—that's your gizzard! Aloft! aloft!— that's it—now you have it. Hold it there now, and pay attention."

"All 'dention," said the old black, with both hands placed as desired, vainly wriggling his grizzled head, as if to get both ears in front at one and the same time.

"Well then, cook, you see this whale-steak of yours was so very bad, that I have put it out of sight as soon as possible; you see that, don't you? Well, for the future, when you cook another whale-steak for my private table here, the capstan, I'll tell you what to do so as not to spoil it by over-doing. Hold the steak in one hand, and show a live coal to it with the other; that done, dish it; d'ye hear? And now to-morrow, cook, when we are cutting in the fish, be sure you stand by to get the tips of his fins; have them put in pickle. As for the ends of the flukes, have them soused, cook. There, now ye may go."

But Fleece had hardly got three paces off, when he was recalled.

"Cook, give me cutlets for supper to-morrow night in the mid-watch. D'ye hear? away you sail, then.—Halloa! stop! make a bow before you go. —Avast heaving again! Whale-balls for breakfast—don't forget."

"Wish, by gor! whale eat him, 'stead of him eat whale. I'm bressed if he ain't more of shark dan Massa Shark hisself," muttered the old man, limping away; with which sage ejaculation he went to his hammock.

# Chapter 65

## The Whale as a Dish

THAT MORTAL MAN should feed upon the creature that feeds his lamp, and, like Stubb, eat him by his own light, as you may say; this seems so outlandish a thing that one must needs go a little into the history and philosophy of it.

It is upon record, that three centuries ago the tongue of the Right Whale was esteemed a great delicacy in France, and commanded large prices there. Also, that in Henry VIIIth's time, a certain cook of the court obtained a handsome reward for inventing an admirable sauce to be eaten with barbacued porpoises, which, you remember, are a species of whale. Porpoises, indeed, are to this day considered fine eating. The meat is made into balls about the size of billiard balls, and being well seasoned and spiced might be taken for turtle-balls or veal balls. The old monks of Dunfermline were very fond of them. They had a great porpoise grant from the crown.

The fact is, that among his hunters at least, the whale would by all hands be considered a noble dish, were there not so much of him; but when you come to sit down before a meat-pie nearly one hundred feet long, it takes away your appetite. Only the most unprejudiced of men like Stubb, nowadays partake of cooked whales; but the Esquimaux are not so fastidious. We all know how they live upon whales, and have rare old vintages of prime old train oil. Zogranda, one of their most famous doctors, recommends strips of blubber for infants, as being exceedingly juicy and nourishing. And this reminds me that certain Englishmen, who long ago were accidentally left in Greenland by a whaling vessel—that these men actually lived for several months on the mouldy scraps of whales which had been left ashore after trying out the blubber. Among the Dutch whalemen these scraps are called "fritters;" which, indeed, they greatly resemble, being brown and crisp, and smelling something like old Amsterdam housewives' dough-nuts or oly-cooks, when fresh. They have such an eatable look that the most self-denying stranger can hardly keep his hands off.

But what further depreciates the whale as a civilized dish, is his exceeding richness. He is the great prize ox of the sea, too fat to be delicately good. Look at his hump, which would be as fine eating as the buffalo's (which is esteemed a rare dish), were it not such a solid pyramid of fat. But the spermaceti itself, how bland and creamy that is; like the transparent, half-jellied, white meat of a cocoanut in the third month of its growth, yet far too rich to supply a substitute for butter. Nevertheless, many whalemen have a method of absorbing it into some other substance, and then partaking of it. In the long try watches of the night it is a common thing for the seamen to dip their ship-biscuit into the huge oil-pots and let them fry there awhile. Many a good supper have I thus made.

In the case of a small Sperm Whale the brains are accounted a fine dish. The casket of the skull is broken into with an axe, and the two plump, whitish lobes being withdrawn (precisely resembling two large puddings), they are then mixed with flour, and cooked into a most delectable mess, in flavor somewhat resembling calves' head, which is quite a dish among some epicures; and every one knows that some young bucks among the epicures, by continually dining upon calves' brains, by and by get to have a little brains of their own, so as to be able to tell a calf's head from their own heads; which, indeed, requires uncommon discrimination. And that is the reason why a young buck with an intelligent looking calf's head before him, is somehow one of the saddest sights you can see. The head looks a sort of reproachfully at him, with an "Et tu Brute!" expression.

It is not, perhaps, entirely because the whale is so excessively unctuous that landsmen seem to regard the eating of him with abhorrence; that appears to result, in some way, from the consideration before mentioned: i.e. that a man should eat a newly murdered thing of the sea, and eat it too by its own light. But no doubt the first man that ever murdered an ox was regarded as a murderer; perhaps he was hung; and if he had been put on his trial by oxen, he certainly would have been; and he certainly deserved

it if any murderer does. Go to the meat-market of a Saturday night and
see the crowds of live bipeds staring up at the long rows of dead quadru-
peds. Does not that sight take a tooth out of the cannibal's jaw? Cannibals?
who is not a cannibal? I tell you it will be more tolerable for the Fejee that
salted down a lean missionary in his cellar against a coming famine; it will
be more tolerable for that provident Fejee, I say, in the day of judgment,
than for thee, civilized and enlightened gourmand, who nailest geese to
the ground and feastest on their bloated livers in thy paté-de-foie-gras.

But Stubb, he eats the whale by its own light, does he? and that is adding
insult to injury, is it? Look at your knife-handle, there, my civilized and
enlightened gourmand dining off that roast beef, what is that handle made
of?—what but the bones of the brother of the very ox you are eating? And
what do you pick your teeth with, after devouring that fat goose? With a
feather of the same fowl. And with what quill did the Secretary of the
Society for the Suppression of Cruelty to Ganders formerly indite his
circulars? It is only within the last month or two that that society passed a
resolution to patronize nothing but steel pens.

# Chapter 66

## *The Shark Massacre*

W HEN in the Southern Fishery, a captured Sperm Whale, after long and weary toil, is brought alongside late at night, it is not, as a general thing at least, customary to proceed at once to the business of cutting him in. For that business is an exceedingly laborious one; is not very soon completed; and requires all hands to set about it. Therefore, the common usage is to take in all sail; lash the helm a'lee; and then send every one below to his hammock till daylight, with the reservation that, until that time, anchor-watches shall be kept; that is, two and two, for an hour each couple, the crew in rotation shall mount the deck to see that all goes well.

But sometimes, especially upon the Line in the Pacific, this plan will not answer at all; because such incalculable hosts of sharks gather round the moored carcase, that were he left so for six hours, say, on a stretch, little more than the skeleton would be visible by morning. In most other parts of the ocean, however, where these fish do not so largely abound, their wondrous voracity can be at times considerably diminished, by vigorously stirring them up with sharp whaling-spades, a procedure notwithstanding, which, in some instances, only seems to tickle them into still greater activity. But it was not thus in the present case with the Pequod's sharks; though, to be sure, any man unaccustomed to such sights, to have looked over her side that night, would have almost thought the whole round sea was one huge cheese, and those sharks the maggots in it.

Nevertheless, upon Stubb setting the anchor-watch after his supper was concluded; and when, accordingly, Queequeg and a forecastle seaman came on deck, no small excitement was created among the sharks; for immediately suspending the cutting stages over the side, and lowering three lanterns, so that they cast long gleams of light over the turbid sea, these two mariners, darting their long whaling-spades, kept up an incessant murdering of the sharks,* by striking the keen steel deep into their skulls, seemingly their only vital part. But in the foamy confusion of their mixed and struggling hosts, the marksmen could not always hit their mark; and this brought about new revelations of the incredible ferocity of the foe. They viciously snapped, not only at each other's disembowelments, but like flexible bows, bent round, and bit their own; till those entrails seemed swallowed over and over again by the same mouth, to be oppositely voided by the gaping wound. Nor was this all. It was unsafe to meddle with the corpses and ghosts of these creatures. A sort of generic or Pantheistic vitality seemed to lurk in their very joints and bones, after what might be called the individual life had departed. Killed and hoisted on deck for the sake of his skin, one of these sharks almost took poor Queequeg's hand off, when he tried to shut down the dead lid of his murderous jaw.

"Queequeg no care what god made him shark," said the savage, agonizingly lifting his hand up and down; "wedder Fejee god or Nantucket god; but de god wat made shark must be one dam Ingin."

---

* The whaling-spade used for cutting-in is made of the very best steel; is about the bigness of a man's spread hand; and in general shape, corresponds to the garden implement after which it is named; only its sides are perfectly flat, and its upper end considerably narrower than the lower. This weapon is always kept as sharp as possible; and when being used is occasionally honed, just like a razor. In its socket, a stiff pole, from twenty to thirty feet long, is inserted for a handle.

# Chapter 67

## *Cutting In*

I T WAS a Saturday night, and such a Sabbath as followed! Ex officio professors of Sabbath breaking are all whalemen. The ivory Pequod was turned into what seemed a shamble; every sailor a butcher. You would have thought we were offering up ten thousand red oxen to the sea gods.

In the first place, the enormous cutting tackles, among other ponderous things comprising a cluster of blocks generally painted green, and which no single man can possibly lift—this vast bunch of grapes was swayed up to the main-top and firmly lashed to the lower mast-head, the strongest point anywhere above a ship's deck. The end of the hawser-like rope winding through these intricacies, was then conducted to the windlass, and the huge lower block of the tackles was swung over the whale; to this block the great blubber hook, weighing some one hundred pounds, was attached. And now suspended in stages over the side, Starbuck and Stubb, the mates, armed with their long spades, began cutting a hole in the body for the insertion of the hook just above the nearest of the two side-fins. This done, a broad, semicircular line is cut round the hole, the hook is inserted, and the main body of the crew striking up a wild chorus, now commence heaving in one dense crowd at the windlass. When instantly, the entire ship careens over on her side; every bolt in her starts like the nail-heads of an old house in

frosty weather; she trembles, quivers, and nods her frighted mast-heads
to the sky. More and more she leans over to the whale, while every gasping
heave of the windlass is answered by a helping heave from the billows; till
at last, a swift, startling snap is heard; with a great swash the ship rolls
upwards and backwards from the whale, and the triumphant tackle rises
into sight dragging after it the disengaged semicircular end of the first strip
of blubber. Now as the blubber envelopes the whale precisely as the rind
does an orange, so is it stripped off from the body precisely as an orange is
sometimes stripped by spiralizing it. For the strain constantly kept up by the
windlass continually keeps the whale rolling over and over in the water, and
as the blubber in one strip uniformly peels off along the line called the
"scarf," simultaneously cut by the spades of Starbuck and Stubb, the mates;
and just as fast as it is thus peeled off, and indeed by that very act itself, it is
all the time being hoisted higher and higher aloft till its upper end grazes the
main-top; the men at the windlass then cease heaving, and for a moment or
two the prodigious blood-dripping mass sways to and fro as if let down
from the sky, and every one present must take good heed to dodge it when
it swings, else it may box his ears and pitch him headlong overboard.

One of the attending harpooneers now advances with a long, keen
weapon called a boarding-sword, and watching his chance he dexterously
slices out a considerable hole in the lower part of the swaying mass. Into this
hole, the end of the second alternating great tackle is then hooked so as to
retain a hold upon the blubber, in order to prepare for what follows.
Whereupon, this accomplished swordsman, warning all hands to stand off,
once more makes a scientific dash at the mass, and with a few sidelong,
desperate, lunging slicings, severs it completely in twain; so that while the
short lower part is still fast, the long upper strip, called a blanket-piece,
swings clear, and is all ready for lowering. The heavers forward now resume
their song, and while the one tackle is peeling and hoisting a second strip
from the whale, the other is slowly slackened away, and down goes the
first strip through the main hatchway right beneath, into an unfurnished
parlor called the blubber-room. Into this twilight apartment sundry nimble
hands keep coiling away the long blanket-piece as if it were a great live mass
of plaited serpents. And thus the work proceeds; the two tackles hoisting
and lowering simultaneously; both whale and windlass heaving, the
heavers singing, the blubber-room gentlemen coiling, the mates scarfing,
the ship straining, and all hands swearing occasionally, by way of assuaging
the general friction.

# Chapter 68

*The Blanket*

I HAVE GIVEN no small attention to that not unvexed subject, the skin of the whale. I have had controversies about it with experienced whale-men afloat, and learned naturalists ashore. My original opinion remains unchanged; but it is only an opinion.

The question is, what and where is the skin of the whale? Already you know what his blubber is. That blubber is something of the consistence of firm, close-grained beef, but tougher, more elastic and compact, and ranges from eight or ten to twelve and fifteen inches in thickness.

Now, however preposterous it may at first seem to talk of any creature's skin as being of that sort of consistence and thickness, yet in point of fact these are no arguments against such a presumption; because you cannot raise any other dense enveloping layer from the whale's body but that same blubber; and the outermost enveloping layer of any animal, if reasonably dense, what can that be but the skin? True, from the unmarred dead body of the whale, you may scrape off with your hand an infinitely thin, transparent substance, somewhat resembling the thinnest shreds of isinglass, only it is almost as flexible and soft as satin; that is, previous to being dried, when it not only contracts and thickens, but becomes rather hard and brittle. I have several such dried bits, which I use for marks in my whale-books. It is transparent, as I said before; and being laid upon the printed page, I have sometimes pleased myself with fancying it exerted a magnifying influence. At any rate, it is pleasant to read about whales through their own spectacles, as you may say. But what I am driving at here is this. That same infinitely thin, isinglass substance, which, I admit, invests the entire body of the whale, is not so much to be regarded as the skin of the creature, as the skin of the skin, so to speak; for it were simply ridiculous to say, that the proper skin of the tremendous whale is thinner and more tender than the skin of a new-born child. But no more of this.

Assuming the blubber to be the skin of the whale; then, when this skin, as in the case of a very large Sperm Whale, will yield the bulk of one hundred barrels of oil; and, when it is considered that, in quantity, or rather weight, that oil, in its expressed state, is only three fourths, and not the entire substance of the coat; some idea may hence be had of the enormousness of that animated mass, a mere part of whose mere integument yields such a lake of liquid as that. Reckoning ten barrels to the ton, you have ten tons for the net weight of only three quarters of the stuff of the whale's skin.

In life, the visible surface of the Sperm Whale is not the least among the many marvels he presents. Almost invariably it is all over obliquely crossed and re-crossed with numberless straight marks in thick array, something like those in the finest Italian line engravings. But these marks do not seem to be impressed upon the isinglass substance above mentioned, but seem to be seen through it, as if they were engraved upon the body itself. Nor is this all. In some instances, to the quick, observant eye, those linear marks, as in a veritable engraving, but afford the ground for far other delineations. These are hieroglyphical; that is, if you call those mysterious cyphers on the walls of pyramids hieroglyphics, then that is the proper word to use in the present connexion. By my retentive memory of the hieroglyphics upon one Sperm Whale in particular, I was much struck with a plate representing the old Indian characters chiselled on the famous hieroglyphic palisades on the banks of the Upper Mississippi. Like those mystic rocks, too, the mystic-marked whale remains undecipherable. This allusion to the Indian rocks reminds me of another thing. Besides all the other phenomena which the exterior of the Sperm Whale presents, he not seldom displays the back, and more especially his flanks, effaced in great part of the regular linear appearance, by reason of numerous rude scratches, altogether of an irregular, random aspect. I should say that those New England rocks on the sea-coast, which Agassiz imagines to bear the marks of violent scraping contact with vast floating icebergs—I should say, that those rocks must not a little resemble the Sperm Whale in this particular. It also seems to me that such scratches in the whale are probably made by hostile contact with other whales; for I have most remarked them in the large, full-grown bulls of the species.

A word or two more concerning this matter of the skin or blubber of the whale. It has already been said, that it is stript from him in long pieces, called blanket-pieces. Like most sea-terms, this one is very happy and significant. For the whale is indeed wrapt up in his blubber as in a real blanket or counterpane; or, still better, an Indian poncho slipt over his head, and skirting his extremity. It is by reason of this cosy blanketing of his body, that the whale is enabled to keep himself comfortable in all weathers, in all seas, times, and tides. What would become of a Greenland whale, say, in those shuddering, icy seas of the North, if unsupplied with his cosy surtout? True, other fish are found exceedingly brisk in those Hyperborean waters; but these, be it observed, are your cold-blooded, lungless fish, whose very bellies are refrigerators; creatures, that warm themselves under the lee of an iceberg, as a traveller in winter would bask before an inn fire; whereas, like man, the whale has lungs and warm blood. Freeze his blood, and he dies. How wonderful is it then—except after explanation—that this great monster, to whom corporeal warmth is as indispensable as it is to man; how wonderful that he should be found at home, immersed to his lips for life in those Arctic waters! where, when seamen fall overboard, they are sometimes found, months afterwards, perpendicularly frozen into the hearts of fields of ice, as a fly is found glued in amber. But more surprising is it to know, as has been proved by experiment, that the blood of a Polar whale is warmer than that of a Borneo negro in summer.

It does seem to me, that herein we see the rare virtue of a strong individual vitality, and the rare virtue of thick walls, and the rare virtue of interior spaciousness. Oh, man! admire and model thyself after the whale! Do thou, too, remain warm among ice. Do thou, too, live in this world without being of it. Be cool at the equator; keep thy blood fluid at the Pole. Like the great dome of St. Peter's, and like the great whale, retain, O man! in all seasons a temperature of thine own.

But how easy and how hopeless to teach these fine things! Of erections, how few are domed like St. Peter's! of creatures, how few vast as the whale!

# Chapter 69

*The Funeral*

HAUL IN THE CHAINS! Let the carcase go astern!"
The vast tackles have now done their duty. The peeled white body of the beheaded whale flashes like a marble sepulchre; though changed in hue, it has not perceptibly lost anything in bulk. It is still colossal. Slowly it floats more and more away, the water round it torn and splashed by the insatiate sharks, and the air above vexed with rapacious flights of screaming fowls, whose beaks are like so many insulting poniards in the whale. The vast white headless phantom floats further and further from the ship, and every rod that it so floats, what seem square roods of sharks and cubic roods of fowls, augment the murderous din. For hours and hours from the almost stationary ship that hideous sight is seen. Beneath the unclouded and mild azure sky, upon the fair face of the pleasant sea, wafted by the joyous breezes, that great mass of death floats on and on, till lost in infinite perspectives.

There's a most doleful and most mocking funeral! The sea-vultures all in pious mourning, the air-sharks all punctiliously in black or speckled. In life but few of them would have helped the whale, I ween, if peradventure he had needed it; but upon the banquet of his funeral they most piously do pounce. Oh, horrible vulturism of earth! from which not the mightiest whale is free.

Nor is this the end. Desecrated as the body is, a vengeful ghost survives and hovers over it to scare. Espied by some timid man-of-war or blundering discovery-vessel from afar, when the distance obscuring the swarming fowls, nevertheless still shows the white mass floating in the sun, and the white spray heaving high against it; straightway the whale's unharming corpse, with trembling fingers is set down in the log—*shoals, rocks, and breakers hereabouts: beware!* And for years afterwards, perhaps, ships shun the place; leaping over it as silly sheep leap over a vacuum, because their leader originally leaped there when a stick was held. There's your law of precedents; there's your utility of traditions; there's the story of your obstinate survival of old beliefs never bottomed on the earth, and now not even hovering in the air! There's orthodoxy!

Thus, while in life the great whale's body may have been a real terror to his foes, in his death his ghost becomes a powerless panic to a world.

Are you a believer in ghosts, my friend? There are other ghosts than the Cock-Lane one, and far deeper men than Doctor Johnson who believe in them.

# Chapter 70

## The Sphynx

IT SHOULD NOT have been omitted that previous to completely stripping the body of the leviathan, he was beheaded. Now, the beheading of the Sperm Whale is a scientific anatomical feat, upon which experienced whale surgeons very much pride themselves: and not without reason.

Consider that the whale has nothing that can properly be called a neck; on the contrary, where his head and body seem to join, there, in that very place, is the thickest part of him. Remember, also, that the surgeon must operate from above, some eight or ten feet intervening between him and his subject, and that subject almost hidden in a discolored, rolling, and oftentimes tumultuous and bursting sea. Bear in mind, too, that under these untoward circumstances he has to cut many feet deep in the flesh; and in that subterraneous manner, without so much as getting one single peep into the ever-contracting gash thus made, he must skilfully steer clear of all adjacent, interdicted parts, and exactly divide the spine at a critical point hard by its insertion into the skull. Do you not marvel, then, at Stubb's boast, that he demanded but ten minutes to behead a sperm whale?

When first severed, the head is dropped astern and held there by a cable till the body is stripped. That done, if it belong to a small whale it is hoisted on deck to be deliberately disposed of. But, with a full grown leviathan this is impossible; for the sperm whale's head embraces nearly one third of his entire bulk, and completely to suspend such a burden as that, even by the immense tackles of a whaler, this were as vain a thing as to attempt weighing a Dutch barn in jewellers' scales.

The Pequod's whale being decapitated and the body stripped, the head was hoisted against the ship's side—about half way out of the sea, so that it might yet in great part be buoyed up by its native element. And there with the strained craft steeply leaning over to it, by reason of the enormous downward drag from the lower mast-head, and every yard-arm on that side projecting like a crane over the waves; there, that blood-dripping head hung to the Pequod's waist like the giant Holofernes's from the girdle of Judith.

When this last task was accomplished it was noon, and the seamen went below to their dinner. Silence reigned over the before tumultuous but now deserted deck. An intense copper calm, like a universal yellow lotus, was more and more unfolding its noiseless measureless leaves upon the sea.

A short space elapsed, and up into this noiselessness came Ahab alone from his cabin. Taking a few turns on the quarter-deck, he paused to gaze over the side, then slowly getting into the main-chains he took Stubb's long spade—still remaining there after the whale's decapitation—and striking it into the lower part of the half-suspended mass, placed its other end crutchwise under one arm, and so stood leaning over with eyes attentively fixed on this head.

It was a black and hooded head; and hanging there in the midst of so intense a calm, it seemed the Sphynx's in the desert. "Speak, thou vast and venerable head," muttered Ahab, "which, though ungarnished with a beard, yet here and there lookest hoary with mosses; speak, mighty head, and tell us the secret thing that is in thee. Of all divers, thou hast dived the deepest. That head upon which the upper sun now gleams, has moved amid this world's foundations. Where unrecorded names and navies rust, and untold hopes and anchors rot; where in her murderous hold this frigate earth is ballasted with bones of millions of the drowned; there, in that awful water-land, there was thy most familiar home. Thou hast been where bell or diver never went; hast slept by many a sailor's side, where sleepless mothers would give their lives to lay them down. Thou saw'st the locked lovers when leaping from their flaming ship; heart to heart they sank beneath the exulting wave; true to each other, when heaven seemed false to them. Thou saw'st the murdered mate when tossed by pirates from the midnight deck; for hours he fell into the deeper midnight of the insatiate maw; and his murderers still sailed on unharmed—while swift lightnings shivered the neighboring ship that would have borne a righteous husband to outstretched, longing arms. O head! thou hast seen enough to split the planets and make an infidel of Abraham, and not one syllable is thine!"

"Sail ho!" cried a triumphant voice from the main-mast-head.

"Aye? Well, now, that's cheering," cried Ahab, suddenly erecting himself, while whole thunder-clouds swept aside from his brow. "That lively cry upon this deadly calm might almost convert a better man.— Where away?"

"Three points on the starboard bow, sir, and bringing down her breeze to us!"

"Better and better, man. Would now St. Paul would come along that way, and to my breezelessness bring his breeze! O Nature, and O soul of man! how far beyond all utterance are your linked analogies! not the smallest atom stirs or lives in matter, but has its cunning duplicate in mind."

# Chapter 71

*The Jeroboam's Story*

H AND IN HAND, ship and breeze blew on; but the breeze came faster than the ship, and soon the Pequod began to rock.

By and by, through the glass the stranger's boats and manned mast-heads proved her a whale-ship. But as she was so far to windward, and shooting by, apparently making a passage to some other ground, the Pequod could not hope to reach her. So the signal was set to see what response would be made.

Here be it said, that like the vessels of military marines, the ships of the American Whale Fleet have each a private signal; all which signals being collected in a book with the names of the respective vessels attached, every captain is provided with it. Thereby, the whale commanders are enabled to recognise each other upon the ocean, even at considerable distances, and with no small facility.

The Pequod's signal was at last responded to by the stranger's setting her own; which proved the ship to be the Jeroboam of Nantucket. Squaring her yards, she bore down, ranged abeam under the Pequod's lee, and lowered a boat; it soon drew nigh; but, as the side-ladder was being rigged by Starbuck's order to accommodate the visiting captain, the stranger in question waved his hand from his boat's stern in token of that proceeding being entirely unnecessary. It turned out that the Jeroboam had a malignant epidemic on board, and that Mayhew, her captain, was fearful of infecting the Pequod's company. For, though himself and boat's crew remained untainted, and though his ship was half a rifle-shot off, and an incorruptible sea and air rolling and flowing between; yet conscientiously adhering to the timid quarantine of the land, he peremptorily refused to come into direct contact with the Pequod.

But this did by no means prevent all communication. Preserving an interval of some few yards between itself and the ship, the Jeroboam's boat by the occasional use of its oars contrived to keep parallel to the Pequod, as she heavily forged through the sea (for by this time it blew very fresh), with her main-top-sail aback; though, indeed, at times by the sudden onset of a large rolling wave, the boat would be pushed some way ahead; but would be soon skilfully brought to her proper bearings again. Subject to this, and other the like interruptions now and then, a conversation was sustained between the two parties; but at intervals not without still another interruption of a very different sort.

Pulling an oar in the Jeroboam's boat, was a man of a singular appearance, even in that wild whaling life where individual notabilities make up all totalities. He was a small, short, youngish man, sprinkled all over his face with freckles, and wearing redundant yellow hair. A long-skirted, cabalistically-cut coat of a faded walnut tinge enveloped him; the overlapping sleeves of which were rolled up on his wrists. A deep, settled, fanatic delirium was in his eyes.

So soon as this figure had been first descried, Stubb had exclaimed—"That's he! that's he!—the long-togged scaramouch the Town-Ho's company told us of!" Stubb here alluded to a strange story told of the Jeroboam, and a certain man among her crew, some time previous when the Pequod spoke the Town-Ho. According to this account and what was subsequently learned, it seemed that the scaramouch in question had gained a wonderful ascendency over almost everybody in the Jeroboam. His story was this:

He had been originally nurtured among the crazy society of Neskyeuna Shakers, where he had been a great prophet; in their cracked, secret meetings having several times descended from heaven by the way of a trap-door, announcing the speedy opening of the seventh vial, which he carried in his vest-pocket; but, which, instead of containing gunpowder, was supposed to be charged with laudanum. A strange, apostolic whim having seized him, he had left Neskyeuna for Nantucket, where, with that cunning peculiar to craziness, he assumed a steady, common sense exterior, and offered himself as a green-hand candidate for the Jeroboam's whaling voyage. They engaged him; but straightway upon the ship's getting out of sight of land, his insanity broke out in a freshet. He announced himself as the archangel Gabriel, and commanded the captain to jump overboard. He published his manifesto, whereby he set himself forth as the deliverer of the isles of the sea and vicar-general of all Oceanica. The unflinching earnestness with which he declared these things;—the dark, daring play of his sleepless, excited imagination, and all the preternatural terrors of real delirium, united to invest this Gabriel in the minds of the majority of the ignorant crew, with an atmosphere of sacredness. Moreover, they were afraid of him. As such a man, however, was not of much practical use in the ship, especially as he refused to work except when he pleased, the incredulous captain would fain have been rid of him; but apprised that that individual's intention was to land him in the first convenient port, the archangel forthwith opened all his seals and vials—devoting the ship and all hands to unconditional perdition, in case this intention was carried out. So strongly did he work upon his disciples among the crew, that at last in a body they went to the captain and told him if Gabriel was sent from the ship, not a man of them would remain. He was therefore forced to relinquish his plan. Nor would they permit Gabriel to be any way maltreated, say or do what he would; so that it came to pass that Gabriel had the complete freedom of the ship. The consequence of all this was, that the archangel cared little or nothing for the captain and mates; and since the epidemic had broken out, he carried a higher hand than ever; declaring that the plague, as he called it, was at his sole command; nor should it be stayed but according to his good pleasure. The sailors, mostly poor devils, cringed, and some of them fawned before him; in obedience to his instructions, sometimes rendering him personal homage, as to a god. Such things may seem incredible; but, however wondrous, they are true. Nor is the history of fanatics half so striking in respect to the measureless self-deception of the fanatic himself, as his measureless power of deceiving and bedevilling so many others. But it is time to return to the Pequod.

"I fear not thy epidemic, man," said Ahab from the bulwarks, to Captain Mayhew, who stood in the boat's stern; "come on board."

But now Gabriel started to his feet.

"Think, think of the fevers, yellow and bilious! Beware of the horrible plague!"

"Gabriel, Gabriel!" cried Captain Mayhew; "thou must either—" But that instant a headlong wave shot the boat far ahead, and its seethings drowned all **speech**.

"Hast thou seen the White Whale?" demanded Ahab, when the boat drifted back.

"Think, think of thy whale-boat, stoven and sunk! Beware of the horrible tail!"

"I tell thee again, Gabriel, that—" But again the boat tore ahead as if dragged by fiends. Nothing was said for some moments, while a succession of riotous waves rolled by, which by one of those occasional caprices of the seas were tumbling, not heaving it. Meantime, the hoisted sperm whale's head jogged about very violently, and Gabriel was seen eyeing it with rather more apprehensiveness than his archangel nature seemed to warrant.

When this interlude was over, Captain Mayhew began a dark story concerning Moby Dick; not, however, without frequent interruptions from Gabriel, whenever his name was mentioned, and the crazy sea that seemed leagued with him.

It seemed that the Jeroboam had not long left home, when upon speaking a whale-ship, her people were reliably apprised of the existence of Moby Dick, and the havoc he had made. Greedily sucking in this intelligence, Gabriel solemnly warned the captain against attacking the White Whale, in case the monster should be seen; in his gibbering insanity, pronouncing the White Whale to be no less a being than the Shaker God incarnated; the Shakers receiving the Bible. But when, some year or two afterwards, Moby Dick was fairly sighted from the mast-heads, Macey, the chief mate, burned with ardor to encounter him; and the captain himself being not unwilling to let him have the opportunity, despite all the archangel's denunciations and forewarnings, Macey succeeded in persuading five men to man his boat. With them he pushed off; and, after much weary pulling, and many perilous, unsuccessful onsets, he at last succeeded in getting one iron fast. Meantime, Gabriel, ascending to the main-royal mast-head, was tossing one arm in frantic gestures, and hurling forth prophecies of speedy doom to the sacrilegious assailants of his divinity. Now, while Macey, the mate, was standing up in his boat's bow, and with all the reckless energy of his tribe was venting his wild exclamations upon the whale, and essaying to get a fair chance for his poised lance, lo! a broad white shadow rose from the sea; by its quick, fanning motion, temporarily taking the breath out of the bodies of the oarsmen. Next instant, the luckless mate, so full of furious life, was smitten bodily into the air, and making a long arc in his descent, fell into the sea at the distance of about fifty yards. Not a chip of the boat was harmed, nor a hair of any oarsman's head; but the mate for ever sank.

It is well to parenthesize here, that of the fatal accidents in the Sperm-

Whale Fishery, this kind is perhaps almost as frequent as any. Sometimes, nothing is injured but the man who is thus annihilated; oftener the boat's bow is knocked off, or the thigh-board, in which the headsman stands, is torn from its place and accompanies the body. But strangest of all is the circumstance, that in more instances than one, when the body has been recovered, not a single mark of violence is discernible; the man being stark dead.

The whole calamity, with the falling form of Macey, was plainly descried from the ship. Raising a piercing shriek—"The vial! the vial!" Gabriel called off the terror-stricken crew from the further hunting of the whale. This terrible event clothed the archangel with added influence; because his credulous disciples believed that he had specifically fore-announced it, instead of only making a general prophecy, which any one might have done, and so have chanced to hit one of many marks in the wide margin allowed. He became a nameless terror to the ship.

Mayhew having concluded his narration, Ahab put such questions to him, that the stranger captain could not forbear inquiring whether he intended to hunt the White Whale, if opportunity should offer. To which Ahab answered—"Aye." Straightway, then, Gabriel once more started to his feet, glaring upon the old man, and vehemently exclaimed, with down-ward pointed finger—"Think, think of the blasphemer—dead, and down there!—beware of the blasphemer's end!"

Ahab stolidly turned aside; then said to Mayhew, "Captain, I have just bethought me of my letter-bag; there is a letter for one of thy officers, if I mistake not. Starbuck, look over the bag."

Every whale-ship takes out a goodly number of letters for various ships, whose delivery to the persons to whom they may be addressed, depends upon the mere chance of encountering them in the four oceans. Thus, most letters never reach their mark; and many are only received after attaining an age of two or three years or more.

Soon Starbuck returned with a letter in his hand. It was sorely tumbled, damp, and covered with a dull, spotted, green mould, in consequence of being kept in a dark locker of the cabin. Of such a letter, Death himself might well have been the post-boy.

"Can'st not read it?" cried Ahab. "Give it me, man. Aye, aye, it's but a dim scrawl;—what's this?" As he was studying it out, Starbuck took a long cutting-spade pole, and with his knife slightly split the end, to insert the letter there, and in that way, hand it to the boat, without its coming any closer to the ship.

Meantime, Ahab holding the letter, muttered, "Mr. Har—yes, Mr. Harry—(a woman's pinny hand,—the man's wife, I'll wager)—Aye—Mr. Harry Macey, Ship Jeroboam;—why it's Macey, and he's dead!"

"Poor fellow! poor fellow! and from his wife," sighed Mayhew; "but let me have it."

"Nay, keep it thyself," cried Gabriel to Ahab; "thou art soon going that way."

"Curses throttle thee!" yelled Ahab. "Captain Mayhew, stand by now to receive it;" and taking the fatal missive from Starbuck's hands, he caught it in the slit of the pole, and reached it over towards the boat. But as he did so, the oarsmen expectantly desisted from rowing; the boat drifted a little towards the ship's stern; so that, as if by magic, the letter suddenly ranged along with Gabriel's eager hand. He clutched it in an instant, seized the boat-knife, and impaling the letter on it, sent it thus loaded back into the ship. It fell at Ahab's feet. Then Gabriel shrieked out to his comrades to give way with their oars, and in that manner the mutinous boat rapidly shot away from the Pequod.

As, after this interlude, the seamen resumed their work upon the jacket of the whale, many strange things were hinted in reference to this wild affair.

# Chapter 72

### The Monkey-rope

IN THE TUMULTUOUS BUSINESS of cutting-in and attending to a whale, there is much running backwards and forwards among the crew. Now hands are wanted here, and then again hands are wanted there. There is no staying in any one place; for at one and the same time everything has to be done everywhere. It is much the same with him who endeavors the description of the scene. We must now retrace our way a little. It was mentioned that upon first breaking ground in the whale's back, the blubber-hook was inserted into the original hole there cut by the spades of the mates. But how did so clumsy and weighty a mass as that same hook get fixed in that hole? It was inserted there by my particular friend Queequeg, whose duty it was, as harpooneer, to descend upon the monster's back for the special purpose referred to. But in very many cases, circumstances require that the harpooneer shall remain on the whale till the whole flensing or stripping operation is concluded. The whale, be it observed, lies almost entirely submerged, excepting the immediate parts operated upon. So down there, some ten feet below the level of the deck, the poor harpooneer flounders about, half on the whale and half in the water, as the vast mass revolves like a tread-mill beneath him. On the occasion in question, Queequeg figured in the Highland costume—a skirt and socks—in which to my eyes, at least, he appeared to uncommon advantage; and no one had a better chance to observe him, as will presently be seen.

Being the savage's bowsman, that is, the person who pulled the bow-oar in his boat (the second one from forward), it was my cheerful duty to attend upon him while taking that hard-scrabble scramble upon the dead whale's back. You have seen Italian organ-boys holding a dancing-ape by a long cord. Just so, from the ship's steep side, did I hold Queequeg down there in the sea, by what is technically called in the fishery a monkey-rope, attached to a strong strip of canvas belted round his waist.

It was a humorously perilous business for both of us. For, before we proceed further, it must be said that the monkey-rope was fast at both ends; fast to Queequeg's broad canvas belt, and fast to my narrow leather one. So that for better or for worse, we two, for the time, were wedded; and should poor Queequeg sink to rise no more, then both usage and honor demanded, that instead of cutting the cord, it should drag me down in his wake. So, then, an elongated Siamese ligature united us. Queequeg was my own in-separable twin brother; nor could I any way get rid of the dangerous lia-bilities which the hempen bond entailed.

So strongly and metaphysically did I conceive of my situation then, that while earnestly watching his motions, I seemed distinctly to perceive that my own individuality was now merged in a joint stock company of two: that my free will had received a mortal wound; and that another's mistake or misfortune might plunge innocent me into unmerited disaster and death. Therefore, I saw that here was a sort of interregnum in Providence; for its even-handed equity never could have sanctioned so gross an injustice. And yet still further pondering—while I jerked him now and then from between the whale and the ship, which would threaten to jam him—still further pondering, I say, I saw that this situation of mine was the precise situation of every mortal that breathes; only, in most cases, he, one way or other, has this Siamese connexion with a plurality of other mortals. If your banker breaks, you snap; if your apothecary by mistake sends you poison in your pills, you die. True, you may say that, by exceeding caution, you may possibly escape these and the multitudinous other evil chances of life. But handle Queequeg's monkey-rope heedfully as I would, sometimes he jerked it so, that I came very near sliding overboard. Nor could I possibly forget that, do what I would, I only had the management of one end of it.*

* The monkey-rope is found in all whalers; but it was only in the Pequod that the monkey and his holder were ever tied together. This improvement upon the original usage was introduced by no less a man than Stubb, in order to afford to the imperilled harpooneer the strongest possible guarantee for the faithfulness and vigilance of his monkey-rope holder.

I have hinted that I would often jerk poor Queequeg from between the whale and the ship—where he would occasionally fall, from the incessant rolling and swaying of both. But this was not the only jamming jeopardy he was exposed to. Unappalled by the massacre made upon them during the night, the sharks now freshly and more keenly allured by the before pent blood which began to flow from the carcase—the rabid creatures swarmed round it like bees in a beehive.

And right in among those sharks was Queequeg; who often pushed them aside with his floundering feet. A thing altogether incredible were it not that attracted by such prey as a dead whale, the otherwise miscellaneously carnivorous shark will seldom touch a man.

Nevertheless, it may well be believed that since they have such a ravenous finger in the pie, it is deemed but wise to look sharp to them. Accordingly, besides the monkey-rope, with which I now and then jerked the poor fellow from too close a vicinity to the maw of what seemed a peculiarly ferocious shark—he was provided with still another protection. Suspended over the side in one of the stages, Tashtego and Daggoo continually flourished over his head a couple of keen whale-spades, wherewith they slaughtered as many sharks as they could reach. This procedure of theirs, to be sure, was very disinterested and benevolent of them. They meant Queequeg's best happiness, I admit; but in their hasty zeal to befriend him, and from the circumstance that both he and the sharks were at times half hidden by the blood-mudded water, those indiscreet spades of theirs would come nearer amputating a leg than a tail. But poor Queequeg, I suppose, straining and gasping there with that great iron hook—poor Queequeg, I suppose, only prayed to his Yojo, and gave up his life into the hands of his gods.

Well, well, my dear comrade and twin-brother, thought I, as I drew in and then slacked off the rope to every swell of the sea—what matters it, after all? Are you not the precious image of each and all of us men in this whaling world? That unsounded ocean you gasp in, is Life; those sharks, your foes; those spades, your friends; and what between sharks and spades you are in a sad pickle and peril, poor lad.

But courage! there is good cheer in store for you, Queequeg. For now, as with blue lips and bloodshot eyes the exhausted savage at last climbs up the chains and stands all dripping and involuntarily trembling over the side; the steward advances, and with a benevolent, consolatory glance hands him —what? Some hot Cogniac? No! hands him, ye gods! hands him a cup of tepid ginger and water!

"Ginger? Do I smell ginger?" suspiciously asked Stubb, coming near.

"Yes, this must be ginger," peering into the as yet untasted cup. Then standing as if incredulous for a while, he calmly walked towards the astonished steward slowly saying, "Ginger? ginger? and will you have the goodness to tell me, Mr. Dough-Boy, where lies the virtue of ginger? Ginger! is ginger the sort of fuel you use, Dough-Boy, to kindle a fire in this shivering cannibal? Ginger!—what the devil is ginger?—sea-coal?—firewood?—lucifer matches?—tinder?—gunpowder?—what the devil is ginger, I say, that you offer this cup to our poor Queequeg here?"

"There is some sneaking Temperance Society movement about this business," he suddenly added, now approaching Starbuck, who had just come from forward. "Will you look at that kannakin, sir: smell of it, if you please." Then watching the mate's countenance, he added: "The steward, Mr. Starbuck, had the face to offer that calomel and jalap to Queequeg, there, this instant off the whale. Is the steward an apothecary, sir? and may I ask whether this is the sort of bellows by which he blows back the breath into a half-drowned man?"

"I trust not," said Starbuck, "it is poor stuff enough."

"Aye, aye, steward," cried Stubb, "we'll teach you to drug a harpooneer; none of your apothecary's medicine here; you want to poison us, do ye? You have got out insurances on our lives and want to murder us all, and pocket the proceeds, do ye?"

"It was not me," cried Dough-Boy, "it was Aunt Charity that brought the ginger on board; and bade me never give the harpooneers any spirits, but only this ginger-jub—so she called it."

"Ginger-jub! you gingerly rascal! take that! and run along with ye to the lockers, and get something better. I hope I do no wrong, Mr. Starbuck. It is the captain's orders—grog for the harpooneer on a whale."

"Enough," replied Starbuck, "only don't hit him again, but—"

"Oh, I never hurt when I hit, except when I hit a whale or something of that sort; and this fellow's a weazel. What were you about saying, sir?"

"Only this: go down with him, and get what thou wantest thyself."

When Stubb reappeared, he came with a dark flask in one hand, and a sort of tea-caddy in the other. The first contained strong spirits, and was handed to Queequeg; the second was Aunt Charity's gift, and that was freely given to the waves.

# Chapter 73

*Stubb and Flask kill a Right Whale; and Then Have a Talk over Him*

IT MUST BE BORNE IN MIND that all this time we have a Sperm Whale's prodigious head hanging to the Pequod's side. But we must let it continue hanging there a while till we can get a chance to attend to it. For the present other matters press, and the best we can do now for the head, is to pray heaven the tackles may hold.

Now, during the past night and forenoon, the Pequod had gradually drifted into a sea, which, by its occasional patches of yellow brit, gave unusual tokens of the vicinity of Right Whales, a species of the Leviathan that but few supposed to be at this particular time lurking anywhere near. And though all hands commonly disdained the capture of those inferior creatures; and though the Pequod was not commissioned to cruise for them at all, and though she had passed numbers of them near the Crozetts without lowering a boat; yet now that a Sperm Whale had been brought alongside and beheaded, to the surprise of all, the announcement was made that a Right Whale should be captured that day, if opportunity offered.

Nor was this long wanting. Tall spouts were seen to leeward; and two boats, Stubb's and Flask's, were detached in pursuit. Pulling further and further away, they at last became almost invisible to the men at the mast-head. But suddenly in the distance, they saw a great heap of tumultuous

white water, and soon after news came from aloft that one or both the boats
must be fast. An interval passed and the boats were in plain sight, in the act
of being dragged right towards the ship by the towing whale. So close did
the monster come to the hull, that at first it seemed as if he meant it malice;
but suddenly going down in a maelstrom, within three rods of the planks,
he wholly disappeared from view, as if diving under the keel. "Cut, cut!"
was the cry from the ship to the boats, which, for one instant, seemed on the
point of being brought with a deadly dash against the vessel's side. But having plenty of line yet in the tubs, and the whale not sounding very rapidly,
they paid out abundance of rope, and at the same time pulled with all their
might so as to get ahead of the ship. For a few minutes the struggle was
intensely critical; for while they still slacked out the tightened line in
one direction, and still plied their oars in another, the contending strain
threatened to take them under. But it was only a few feet advance they
sought to gain. And they stuck to it till they did gain it; when instantly, a
swift tremor was felt running like lightning along the keel, as the strained
line, scraping beneath the ship, suddenly rose to view under her bows,
snapping and quivering; and so flinging off its drippings, that the drops
fell like bits of broken glass on the water, while the whale beyond also
rose to sight, and once more the boats were free to fly. But the fagged
whale abated his speed, and blindly altering his course, went round the
stern of the ship towing the two boats after him, so that they performed a
complete circuit.

Meantime, they hauled more and more upon their lines, till close flank-
ing him on both sides, Stubb answered Flask with lance for lance; and thus
round and round the Pequod the battle went, while the multitudes of
sharks that had before swum round the Sperm Whale's body, rushed to the
fresh blood that was spilled, thirstily drinking at every new gash, as the
eager Israelites did at the new bursting fountains that poured from the
smitten rock.

At last his spout grew thick, and with a frightful roll and vomit, he
turned upon his back a corpse.

While the two headsmen were engaged in making fast cords to his
flukes, and in other ways getting the mass in readiness for towing, some
conversation ensued between them.

"I wonder what the old man wants with this lump of foul lard," said
Stubb, not without some disgust at the thought of having to do with so
ignoble a leviathan.

"Wants with it?" said Flask, coiling some spare line in the boat's bow, "did you never hear that the ship which but once has a Sperm Whale's head hoisted on her starboard side, and at the same time a Right Whale's on the larboard; did you never hear, Stubb, that that ship can never afterwards capsize?"

"Why not?"

"I don't know, but I heard that gamboge ghost of a Fedallah saying so, and he seems to know all about ships' charms. But I sometimes think he'll charm the ship to no good at last. I don't half like that chap, Stubb. Did you ever notice how that tusk of his is a sort of carved into a snake's head, Stubb?"

"Sink him! I never look at him at all; but if ever I get a chance of a dark night, and he standing hard by the bulwarks, and no one by; look down there, Flask"—pointing into the sea with a peculiar motion of both hands— "Aye, will I! Flask, I take that Fedallah to be the devil in disguise. Do you believe that cock and bull story about his having been stowed away on board ship? He's the devil, I say. The reason why you don't see his tail, is because he tucks it up out of sight; he carries it coiled away in his pocket, I guess. Blast him! now that I think of it, he's always wanting oakum to stuff into the toes of his boots."

"He sleeps in his boots, don't he? He hasn't got any hammock; but I've seen him lay of nights in a coil of rigging."

"No doubt, and it's because of his cursed tail; he coils it down, do ye see, in the eye of the rigging."

"What's the old man have so much to do with him for?"

"Striking up a swap or a bargain, I suppose."

"Bargain?—about what?"

"Why, do ye see, the old man is hard bent after that White Whale, and the devil there is trying to come round him, and get him to swap away his silver watch, or his soul, or something of that sort, and then he'll surrender Moby Dick."

"Pooh! Stubb, you are skylarking; how can Fedallah do that?"

"I don't know, Flask, but the devil is a curious chap, and a wicked one, I tell ye. Why, they say as how he went a sauntering into the old flag-ship once, switching his tail about devilish easy and gentlemanlike, and inquiring if the old governor was at home. Well, he was at home, and asked the devil what he wanted. The devil, switching his hoofs, up and says, 'I want John.' 'What for?' says the old governor. 'What business is that of yours,' says the devil, getting mad,—'I want to use him.' 'Take him,' says the governor—and by the Lord, Flask, if the devil didn't give

John the Asiatic cholera before he got through with him, I'll eat this whale in one mouthful. But look sharp—aint you all ready there? Well, then, pull ahead, and let's get the whale alongside."

"I think I remember some such story as you were telling," said Flask, when at last the two boats were slowly advancing with their burden towards the ship, "but I can't remember where."

"Three Spaniards? Adventures of those three bloody-minded soldadoes? Did ye read it there, Flask? I guess ye did?"

"No: never saw such a book; heard of it, though. But now, tell me, Stubb, do you suppose that that devil you was speaking of just now, was the same you say is now on board the Pequod?"

"Am I the same man that helped kill this whale? Doesn't the devil live for ever; who ever heard that the devil was dead? Did you ever see any parson a wearing mourning for the devil? And if the devil has a latch-key to get into the admiral's cabin, don't you suppose he can crawl into a port-hole? Tell me that, Mr. Flask?"

"How old do you suppose Fedallah is, Stubb?"

"Do you see that mainmast there?" pointing to the ship; "well, that's the figure one; now take all the hoops in the Pequod's hold, and string 'em along in a row with that mast, for oughts, do you see; well, that wouldn't begin to be Fedallah's age. Nor all the coopers in creation couldn't show hoops enough to make oughts enough."

"But see here, Stubb, I thought you a little boasted just now, that you meant to give Fedallah a sea-toss, if you got a good chance. Now, if he's so old as all those hoops of yours come to, and if he is going to live for ever, what good will it do to pitch him overboard—tell me that?"

"Give him a good ducking, anyhow."

"But he'd crawl back."

"Duck him again; and keep ducking him."

"Suppose he should take it into his head to duck you, though—yes, and drown you—what then?"

"I should like to see him try it; I'd give him such a pair of black eyes that he wouldn't dare to show his face in the admiral's cabin again for a long while, let alone down in the orlop there, where he lives, and hereabouts on the upper decks where he sneaks so much. Damn the devil, Flask; do you suppose I'm afraid of the devil? Who's afraid of him, except the old governor who daresn't catch him and put him in double-darbies, as he deserves, but lets him go about kidnapping people; aye, and signed a bond with him, that all the people the devil kidnapped, he'd roast for him?

There's a governor!"

"Do you suppose Fedallah wants to kidnap Captain Ahab?"

"Do I suppose it? You'll know it before long, Flask. But I am going now to keep a sharp look-out on him; and if I see anything very suspicious going on, I'll just take him by the nape of his neck, and say—Look here, Beelzebub, you don't do it; and if he makes any fuss, by the Lord I'll make a grab into his pocket for his tail, take it to the capstan, and give him such a wrenching and heaving, that his tail will come short off at the stump—do you see; and then, I rather guess when he finds himself docked in that queer fashion, he'll sneak off without the poor satisfaction of feeling his tail between his legs."

"And what will you do with the tail, Stubb?"

"Do with it? Sell it for an ox whip when we get home;—what else?"

"Now, do you mean what you say, and have been saying all along, Stubb?"

"Mean or not mean, here we are at the ship."

The boats were here hailed, to tow the whale on the larboard side, where fluke chains and other necessaries were already prepared for securing him.

"Didn't I tell you so?" said Flask; "yes, you'll soon see this right whale's head hoisted up opposite that parmacetti's."

In good time, Flask's saying proved true. As before, the Pequod steeply leaned over towards the sperm whale's head, now, by the counterpoise of both heads, she regained her even keel; though sorely strained, you may well believe. So, when on one side you hoist in Locke's head, you go over that way; but now, on the other side, hoist in Kant's and you come back again; but in very poor plight. Thus, some minds for ever keep trimming boat. Oh, ye foolish! throw all these thunder-heads overboard, and then you will float light and right.

In disposing of the body of a right whale, when brought alongside the ship, the same preliminary proceedings commonly take place as in the case of a sperm whale; only, in the latter instance, the head is cut off whole, but in the former the lips and tongue are separately removed and hoisted on deck, with all the well known black bone attached to what is called the crown-piece. But nothing like this, in the present case, had been done. The carcases of both whales had dropped astern; and the head-laden ship not a little resembled a mule carrying a pair of overburdening panniers.

Meantime, Fedallah was calmly eyeing the right whale's head, and ever and anon glancing from the deep wrinkles there to the lines in his own hand.

And Ahab chanced so to stand, that the Parsee occupied his shadow; while, if the Parsee's shadow was there at all it seemed only to blend with, and lengthen Ahab's. As the crew toiled on, Laplandish speculations were bandied among them, concerning all these passing things.

# Chapter 74

## *The Sperm Whale's Head—Contrasted View*

HERE, NOW, are two great whales, laying their heads together; let us join them, and lay together our own.

Of the grand order of folio leviathans, the Sperm Whale and the Right Whale are by far the most noteworthy. They are the only whales regularly hunted by man. To the Nantucketer, they present the two extremes of all the known varieties of the whale. As the external difference between them is mainly observable in their heads; and as a head of each is this moment hanging from the Pequod's side; and as we may freely go from one to the other, by merely stepping across the deck:—where, I should like to know, will you obtain a better chance to study practical cetology than here?

In the first place, you are struck by the general contrast between these heads. Both are massive enough in all conscience; but there is a certain mathematical symmetry in the Sperm Whale's which the Right Whale's sadly lacks. There is more character in the Sperm Whale's head. As you behold it, you involuntarily yield the immense superiority to him, in point of pervading dignity. In the present instance, too, this dignity is heightened by the pepper and salt color of his head at the summit, giving token of advanced age and large experience. In short, he is what the fishermen technically call a "greyheaded whale."

329

Let us now note what is least dissimilar in these heads—namely, the two most important organs, the eye and the ear. Far back on the side of the head, and low down, near the angle of either whale's jaw, if you narrowly search, you will at last see a lashless eye, which you would fancy to be a young colt's eye; so out of all proportion is it to the magnitude of the head.

Now, from this peculiar sideway position of the whale's eyes, it is plain that he can never see an object which is exactly ahead, no more than he can one exactly astern. In a word, the position of the whale's eyes corresponds to that of a man's ears; and you may fancy, for yourself, how it would fare with you, did you sideways survey objects through your ears. You would find that you could only command some thirty degrees of vision in advance of the straight side-line of sight; and about thirty more behind it. If your bitterest foe were walking straight towards you, with dagger uplifted in broad day, you would not be able to see him, any more than if he were stealing upon you from behind. In a word, you would have two backs, so to speak; but, at the same time, also, two fronts (side fronts): for what is it that makes the front of a man—what, indeed, but his eyes?

Moreover, while in most other animals that I can now think of, the eyes are so planted as imperceptibly to blend their visual power, so as to produce one picture and not two to the brain; the peculiar position of the whale's eyes, effectually divided as they are by many cubic feet of solid head, which towers between them like a great mountain separating two lakes in valleys; this, of course, must wholly separate the impressions which each independent organ imparts. The whale, therefore, must see one distinct picture on this side, and another distinct picture on that side; while all between must be profound darkness and nothingness to him. Man may, in effect, be said to look out on the world from a sentry-box with two joined sashes for his window. But with the whale, these two sashes are separately inserted, making two distinct windows, but sadly impairing the view. This peculiarity of the whale's eyes is a thing always to be borne in mind in the fishery; and to be remembered by the reader in some subsequent scenes.

A curious and most puzzling question might be started concerning this visual matter as touching the Leviathan. But I must be content with a hint. So long as a man's eyes are open in the light, the act of seeing is involuntary; that is, he cannot then help mechanically seeing whatever objects are before him. Nevertheless, any one's experience will teach him, that though he can take in an undiscriminating sweep of things at one glance, it is quite impossible for him, attentively, and completely, to examine any two things—however large or however small—at one and the same instant of time;

never mind if they lie side by side and touch each other. But if you now come
to separate these two objects, and surround each by a circle of profound
darkness; then, in order to see one of them, in such a manner as to bring
your mind to bear on it, the other will be utterly excluded from your
contemporary consciousness. How is it, then, with the whale? True, both
his eyes, in themselves, must simultaneously act; but is his brain so much
more comprehensive, combining, and subtle than man's, that he can at the
same moment of time attentively examine two distinct prospects, one on
one side of him, and the other in an exactly opposite direction? If he can,
then is it as marvellous a thing in him, as if a man were able simultaneously
to go **through** the demonstrations of two distinct problems in Euclid. Nor,
strictly investigated, is there any incongruity in this comparison.

It may be but an idle whim, but it has always seemed to me, that the
extraordinary vacillations of movement displayed by some whales when
beset by three or four boats; the timidity and liability to queer frights, so
common to such whales; I think that all this indirectly proceeds from the
helpless perplexity of volition, in which their divided and diametrically
opposite powers of vision must involve them.

But the ear of the whale is full as curious as the eye. If you are an entire
stranger to their race, you might hunt over these two heads for hours, and
never discover that **organ**. The ear has no external leaf whatever; and into
the hole itself you can hardly insert a quill, so wondrously minute is it. It is
lodged a little behind the eye. With respect to their ears, this important difference is to be observed between the sperm whale and the right. While the
ear of the former has an external opening, that of the latter is entirely and
evenly covered over with a membrane, so as to be quite imperceptible from
without.

Is it not curious, that so vast a being as the whale should see the world
through so small an eye, and hear the thunder through an ear which is
smaller than a hare's? But if his eyes were broad as the lens of Herschel's
great telescope; and his ears capacious as the porches of cathedrals; would
that make him any longer of sight, or sharper of hearing? Not at all.—
Why then do you try to "enlarge" your mind? Subtilize it.

Let us now with whatever levers and steam-engines we have at hand,
cant over the sperm whale's head, so that it may lie bottom up; then,
ascending by a ladder to the summit, have a peep down the mouth; and
were it not that the body is now completely separated from it, with a
lantern we might descend into the great Kentucky Mammoth Cave of his
stomach. But let us hold on here by this tooth, and look about us where we

are. What a really beautiful and chaste-looking mouth! from floor to ceiling, lined, or rather papered with a glistening white membrane, glossy as bridal satins.

But come out now, and look at this portentous lower jaw, which seems like the long narrow lid of an immense snuff-box, with the hinge at one end, instead of one side. If you pry it up, so as to get it overhead, and expose its rows of teeth, it seems a terrific portcullis: and such, alas! it proves to many a poor wight in the fishery, upon whom these spikes fall with impaling force. But far more terrible is it to behold, when fathoms down in the sea, you see some sulky whale, floating there suspended, with his prodigious jaw, some fifteen feet long, hanging straight down at right-angles with his body, for all the world like a ship's jib-boom. This whale is not dead; he is only dispirited; out of sorts, perhaps; hypochondriac; and so supine, that the hinges of his jaw have relaxed, leaving him there in that ungainly sort of plight, a reproach to all his tribe, who must, no doubt, imprecate lock-jaws upon him.

In most cases this lower jaw—being easily unhinged by a practised artist—is disengaged and hoisted on deck for the purpose of extracting the ivory teeth, and furnishing a supply of that hard white whalebone with which the fishermen fashion all sorts of curious articles, including canes, umbrella-stocks, and handles to riding-whips.

With a long, weary hoist the jaw is dragged on board, as if it were an anchor; and when the proper time comes—some few days after the other work—Queequeg, Daggoo, and Tashtego, being all accomplished dentists, are set to drawing teeth. With a keen cutting-spade, Queequeg lances the gums; then the jaw is lashed down to ringbolts, and a tackle being rigged from aloft, they drag out these teeth, as Michigan oxen drag stumps of old oaks out of wild wood-lands. There are generally forty-two teeth in all; in old whales, much worn down, but undecayed; nor filled after our artificial fashion. The jaw is afterwards sawn into slabs, and piled away like joists for building houses.

# Chapter 75

*The Right Whale's Head—Contrasted View*

CROSSING THE DECK, let us now have a good long look at the Right Whale's head.

As in general shape the noble Sperm Whale's head may be compared to a Roman war-chariot (especially in front, where it is so broadly rounded); so, at a broad view, the Right Whale's head bears a rather inelegant resemblance to a gigantic galliot-toed shoe. Two hundred years ago an old Dutch voyager likened its shape to that of a shoemaker's last. And in this same last or shoe, that old woman of the nursery tale, with the swarming brood, might very comfortably be lodged, she and all her progeny.

But as you come nearer to this great head it begins to assume different aspects, according to your point of view. If you stand on its summit and look at these two *f*-shaped spout-holes, you would take the whole head for an enormous bass-viol, and these spiracles, the apertures in its sounding-board. Then, again, if you fix your eye upon this strange, crested, comb-like incrustation on the top of the mass—this green, barnacled thing, which the Greenlanders call the "crown," and the Southern fishers the "bonnet" of the Right Whale; fixing your eyes solely on this, you would take the head for the trunk of some huge oak, with a bird's nest in its crotch. At any rate, when you watch those live crabs that nestle here on this bonnet, such an idea will be almost sure to occur to you; unless, indeed, your fancy has been fixed

333

by the technical term "crown" also bestowed upon it; in which case you will take great interest in thinking how this mighty monster is actually a diademed king of the sea, whose green crown has been put together for him in this marvellous manner. But if this whale be a king, he is a very sulky looking fellow to grace a diadem. Look at that hanging lower lip! what a huge sulk and pout is there! a sulk and pout, by carpenter's measurement, about twenty feet long and five feet deep; a sulk and pout that will yield you some 500 gallons of oil and more.

A great pity, now, that this unfortunate whale should be hare-lipped. The fissure is about a foot across. Probably the mother during an important interval was sailing down the Peruvian coast, when earthquakes caused the beach to gape. Over this lip, as over a slippery threshold, we now slide into the mouth. Upon my word were I at Mackinaw, I should take this to be the inside of an Indian wigwam. Good Lord! is this the road that Jonah went? The roof is about twelve feet high, and runs to a pretty sharp angle, as if there were a regular ridge-pole there; while these ribbed, arched, hairy sides, present us with those wondrous, half vertical, scimetar-shaped slats of whalebone, say three hundred on a side, which depending from the upper part of the head or crown bone, form those Venetian blinds which have elsewhere been cursorily mentioned. The edges of these bones are fringed with hairy fibres, through which the Right Whale strains the water, and in whose intricacies he retains the small fish, when open-mouthed he goes through the seas of brit in feeding time. In the central blinds of bone, as they stand in their natural order, there are certain curious marks, curves, hollows, and ridges, whereby some whalemen calculate the creature's age, as the age of an oak by its circular rings. Though the certainty of this criterion is far from demonstrable, yet it has the savor of analogical probability. At any rate, if we yield to it, we must grant a far greater age to the Right Whale than at first glance will seem reasonable.

In old times, there seem to have prevailed the most curious fancies concerning these blinds. One voyager in Purchas calls them the wondrous "whiskers" inside of the whale's mouth;* another, "hogs' bristles;" a third old gentleman in Hackluyt uses the following elegant language: "There are about two hundred and fifty fins growing on each side of his upper *chop*, which arch over his tongue on each side of his mouth."

* This reminds us that the Right Whale really has a sort of whisker, or rather a moustache, consisting of a few scattered white hairs on the upper part of the outer end of the lower jaw. Sometimes these tufts impart a rather brigandish expression to his otherwise solemn countenance.

As every one knows, these same "hogs' bristles," "fins," "whiskers," "blinds," or whatever you please, furnish to the ladies their busks and other stiffening contrivances. But in this particular, the demand has long been on the decline. It was in Queen Anne's time that the bone was in its glory, the farthingale being then all the fashion. And as those ancient dames moved about gaily, though in the jaws of the whale, as you may say; even so, in a shower, with the like thoughtlessness, do we nowadays fly under the same jaws for protection; the umbrella being a tent spread over the same bone.

But now forget all about blinds and whiskers for a moment, and, standing in the Right Whale's mouth, look around you afresh. Seeing all these colonnades of bone so methodically ranged about, would you not think you were inside of the great Haarlem organ, and gazing upon its thousand pipes? For a carpet to the organ we have a rug of the softest Turkey—the tongue, which is glued, as it were, to the floor of the mouth. It is very fat and tender, and apt to tear in pieces in hoisting it on deck. This particular tongue now before us; at a passing glance I should say it was a six-barreler; that is, it will yield you about that amount of oil.

Ere this, you must have plainly seen the truth of what I started with—that the Sperm Whale and the Right Whale have almost entirely different heads. To sum up, then: in the Right Whale's there is no great well of sperm; no ivory teeth at all; no long, slender mandible of a lower jaw, like the Sperm Whale's. Nor in the Sperm Whale are there any of those blinds of bone; no huge lower lip; and scarcely anything of a tongue. Again, the Right Whale has two external spout-holes, the Sperm Whale only one.

Look your last, now, on these venerable hooded heads, while they yet lie together; for one will soon sink, unrecorded, in the sea; the other will not be very long in following.

Can you catch the expression of the Sperm Whale's there? It is the same he died with, only some of the longer wrinkles in the forehead seem now faded away. I think his broad brow to be full of a prairie-like placidity, born of a speculative indifference as to death. But mark the other head's expression. See that amazing lower lip, pressed by accident against the vessel's side, so as firmly to embrace the jaw. Does not this whole head seem to speak of an enormous practical resolution in facing death? This Right Whale I take to have been a Stoic; the Sperm Whale, a Platonian, who might have taken up Spinoza in his latter years.

# Chapter 76

## The Battering-Ram

E RE QUITTING, for the nonce, the Sperm Whale's head, I would have you, as a sensible physiologist, simply—particularly remark its front aspect, in all its compacted collectedness. I would have you investigate it now with the sole view of forming to yourself some unexaggerated, intelligent estimate of whatever battering-ram power may be lodged there. Here is a vital point; for you must either satisfactorily settle this matter with yourself, or for ever remain an infidel as to one of the most appalling, but not the less true events, perhaps anywhere to be found in all recorded history.

You observe that in the ordinary swimming position of the Sperm Whale, the front of his head presents an almost wholly vertical plane to the water; you observe that the lower part of that front slopes considerably backwards, so as to furnish more of a retreat for the long socket which receives the boom-like lower jaw; you observe that the mouth is entirely under the head, much in the same way, indeed, as though your own mouth were entirely under your chin. Moreover you observe that the whale has no external nose; and that what nose he has—his spout hole—is on the top of his head; you observe that his eyes and ears are at the sides of his head, nearly one third of his entire length from the front. Wherefore, you must now have perceived that the front of the Sperm Whale's head is a dead,

336

blind wall, without a single organ or tender prominence of any sort whatsoever. Furthermore, you are now to consider that only in the extreme,
lower, backward sloping part of the front of the head, is there the slightest
vestige of bone; and not till you get near twenty feet from the forehead do
you come to the full cranial development. So that this whole enormous
boneless mass is as one wad. Finally, though, as will soon be revealed, its
contents partly comprise the most delicate oil; yet, you are now to be apprised of the nature of the substance which so impregnably invests all that
apparent effeminacy. In some previous place I have described to you how the
blubber wraps the body of the whale, as the rind wraps an orange. Just so
with the head; but with this difference: about the head this envelope, though
not so thick, is of a boneless toughness, inestimable by any man who has not
handled it. The severest pointed harpoon, the sharpest lance darted by the
strongest human arm, impotently rebounds from it. It is as though the forehead of the Sperm Whale were paved with horses' hoofs. I do not think that
any sensation lurks in it.

Bethink yourself also of another thing. When two large, loaded India-
men chance to crowd and crush towards each other in the docks, what do
the sailors do? They do not suspend between them, at the point of coming
contact, any merely hard substance, like iron or wood. No, they hold there
a large, round wad of tow and cork, enveloped in the thickest and toughest
of ox-hide. That bravely and uninjured takes the jam which would have
snapped all their oaken handspikes and iron crow-bars. By itself this
sufficiently illustrates the obvious fact I drive at. But supplementary to this,
it has hypothetically occurred to me, that as ordinary fish possess what is
called a swimming bladder in them, capable, at will, of distension or
contraction; and as the Sperm Whale, as far as I know, has no such provision
in him; considering, too, the otherwise inexplicable manner in which he
now depresses his head altogether beneath the surface, and anon swims with
it high elevated out of the water; considering the unobstructed elasticity of
its envelop; considering the unique interior of his head; it has hypothetically
occurred to me, I say, that those mystical lung-celled honeycombs there
may possibly have some hitherto unknown and unsuspected connexion
with the outer air, so as to be susceptible to atmospheric distension and
contraction. If this be so, fancy the irresistibleness of that might, to which
the most impalpable and destructive of all elements contributes.

Now, mark. Unerringly impelling this dead, impregnable, uninjurable
wall, and this most buoyant thing within; there swims behind it all a mass of
tremendous life, only to be adequately estimated as piled wood is—by the

cord; and all obedient to one volition, as the smallest insect. So that when I shall hereafter detail to you all the specialities and concentrations of potency everywhere lurking in this expansive monster; when I shall show you some of his more inconsiderable braining feats; I trust you will have renounced all ignorant incredulity, and be ready to abide by this; that though the Sperm Whale stove a passage through the Isthmus of Darien, and mixed the Atlantic with the Pacific, you would not elevate one hair of your eye-brow. For unless you own the whale, you are but a provincial and sentimentalist in Truth. But clear Truth is a thing for salamander giants only to encounter; how small the chances for the provincials then? What befel the weakling youth lifting the dread goddess's veil at Sais?

# Chapter 77

## The Great Heidelburgh Tun

NOW COMES the Baling of the Case. But to comprehend it aright, you must know something of the curious internal structure of the thing operated upon.

Regarding the Sperm Whale's head as a solid oblong, you may, on an inclined plane, sideways divide it into two quoins,* whereof the lower is the bony structure, forming the cranium and jaws, and the upper an unctuous mass wholly free from bones; its broad forward end forming the expanded vertical apparent forehead of the whale. At the middle of the forehead horizontally subdivide this upper quoin, and then you have two almost equal parts, which before were naturally divided by an internal wall of a thick tendinous substance.

The lower subdivided part, called the junk, is one immense honeycomb of oil, formed by the crossing and re-crossing, into ten thousand infiltrated cells, of tough elastic white fibres throughout its whole extent. The upper part, known as the Case, may be regarded as the great Heidelburgh Tun of the Sperm Whale. And as that famous great tierce is mystically carved in

---

* Quoin is not a Euclidean term. It belongs to the pure nautical mathematics. I know not that it has been defined before. A quoin is a solid which differs from a wedge in having its sharp end formed by the steep inclination of one side, instead of the mutual tapering of both sides.

front, so the whale's vast plaited forehead forms innumerable strange devices for the emblematical adornment of his wondrous tun. Moreover, as
that of Heidelburgh was always replenished with the most excellent of the
wines of the Rhenish valleys, so the tun of the whale contains by far the
most precious of all his oily vintages; namely, the highly-prized spermaceti,
in its absolutely pure, limpid, and odoriferous state. Nor is this precious
substance found unalloyed in any other part of the creature. Though in life
it remains perfectly fluid, yet, upon exposure to the air, after death, it soon
begins to concrete; sending forth beautiful crystalline shoots, as when the
first thin delicate ice is just forming in water. A large whale's case generally
yields about five hundred gallons of sperm, though from unavoidable
circumstances, considerable of it is spilled, leaks, and dribbles away, or is
otherwise irrevocably lost in the ticklish business of securing what you can.

I know not with what fine and costly material the Heidelburgh Tun was
coated within, but in superlative richness that coating could not possibly
have compared with the silken pearl-colored membrane, like the lining of a
fine pelisse, forming the inner surface of the Sperm Whale's case.

It will have been seen that the Heidelburgh Tun of the Sperm Whale
embraces the entire length of the entire top of the head; and since—as has
been elsewhere set forth—the head embraces one third of the whole length
of the creature, then setting that length down at eighty feet for a good sized
whale, you have more than twenty-six feet for the depth of the tun, when it
is lengthwise hoisted up and down against a ship's side.

As in decapitating the whale, the operator's instrument is brought close
to the spot where an entrance is subsequently forced into the spermaceti
magazine; he has, therefore, to be uncommonly heedful, lest a careless,
untimely stroke should invade the sanctuary and wastingly let out its invaluable contents. It is this decapitated end of the head, also, which is at
last elevated out of the water, and retained in that position by the enormous
cutting tackles, whose hempen combinations, on one side, make quite a
wilderness of ropes in that quarter.

Thus much being said, attend now, I pray you, to that marvellous and—
in this particular instance—almost fatal operation whereby the Sperm
Whale's great Heidelburgh Tun is tapped.

# Chapter 78

*Cistern and Buckets*

NIMBLE AS A CAT, Tashtego mounts aloft; and without altering his erect posture, runs straight out upon the overhanging main-yard-arm, to the part where it exactly projects over the hoisted Tun. He has carried with him a light tackle called a whip, consisting of only two parts, travelling through a single-sheaved block. Securing this block, so that it hangs down from the yard-arm, he swings one end of the rope, till it is caught and firmly held by a hand on deck. Then, hand-over-hand, down the other part, the Indian drops through the air, till dexterously he lands on the summit of the head. There—still high elevated above the rest of the company, to whom he vivaciously cries—he seems some Turkish Muezzin calling the good people to prayers from the top of a tower. A short-handled sharp spade being sent up to him, he diligently searches for the proper place to begin breaking into the Tun. In this business he proceeds very heedfully, like a treasure-hunter in some old house, sounding the walls to find where the gold is masoned in. By the time this cautious search is over, a stout iron-bound bucket, precisely like a well-bucket, has been attached to one end of the whip; while the other end, being stretched across the deck, is there held by two or three alert hands. These last now hoist the bucket within grasp of the Indian, to whom another person has reached up a very long pole. Inserting this pole into the bucket, Tashtego downward guides the bucket into the Tun, till it entirely disappears; then giving the word to the seamen at the whip, up comes the bucket again, all bubbling like a dairy-maid's pail of new milk. Carefully lowered from its height, the full-freighted vessel is caught by an appointed hand, and quickly emptied into a large tub. Then re-mounting aloft, it again goes through the same round until the deep cistern will yield no more. Towards the end, Tashtego has to ram his long pole harder and harder, and deeper and deeper into the Tun, until some twenty feet of the pole have gone down.

Now, the people of the Pequod had been baling some time in this way; several tubs had been filled with the fragrant sperm; when all at once a queer accident happened. Whether it was that Tashtego, that wild Indian, was so heedless and reckless as to let go for a moment his one-handed hold on the great cabled tackles suspending the head; or whether the place where he stood was so treacherous and oozy; or whether the Evil One himself would have it to fall out so, without stating his particular reasons; how it was exactly, there is no telling now; but, on a sudden, as the eightieth or ninetieth bucket came suckingly up—my God! poor Tashtego—like the twin reciprocating bucket in a veritable well, dropped head-foremost down into this great Tun of Heidelburgh, and with a horrible oily gurgling, went clean out of sight!

"Man overboard!" cried Daggoo, who amid the general consternation first came to his senses. "Swing the bucket this way!" and putting one foot into it, so as the better to secure his slippery hand-hold on the whip itself, the hoisters ran him high up to the top of the head, almost before Tashtego could have reached its interior bottom. Meantime, there was a terrible tumult. Looking over the side, they saw the before lifeless head throbbing and heaving just below the surface of the sea, as if that moment seized with some momentous idea; whereas it was only the poor Indian unconsciously revealing by those struggles the perilous depth to which he had sunk.

At this instant, while Daggoo, on the summit of the head, was clearing the whip—which had somehow got foul of the great cutting tackles—a sharp cracking noise was heard; and to the unspeakable horror of all, one of the two enormous hooks suspending the head tore out, and with a vast vibration the enormous mass sideways swung, till the drunk ship reeled and shook as if smitten by an iceberg. The one remaining hook, upon which the entire strain now depended, seemed every. instant to be on the point of giving way; an event still more likely from the violent motions of the head.

"Come down, come down!" yelled the seamen to Daggoo, but with one hand holding on to the heavy tackles, so that if the head should drop, he would still remain suspended; the negro having cleared the foul line, rammed down the bucket into the now collapsed well, meaning that the buried harpooneer should grasp it, and so be hoisted out.

"In heaven's name, man," cried Stubb, "are you ramming home a cartridge there?—Avast! How will that help him; jamming that iron-bound bucket on top of his head? Avast, will ye!"

"Stand clear of the tackle!" cried a voice like the bursting of a rocket.

Almost in the same instant, with a thunder-boom, the enormous mass dropped into the sea, like Niagara's Table-Rock into the whirlpool; the suddenly relieved hull rolled away from it, to far down her glittering copper; and all caught their breath, as half swinging—now over the sailors' heads, and now over the water—Daggoo, through a thick mist of spray, was dimly beheld clinging to the pendulous tackles, while poor, buried-alive Tashtego was sinking utterly down to the bottom of the sea! But hardly had the blinding vapor cleared away, when a naked figure with a boarding-sword in its hand, was for one swift moment seen hovering over the bulwarks. The next, a loud splash announced that my brave Queequeg had dived to the rescue. One packed rush was made to the side, and every eye counted every ripple, as moment followed moment, and no sign of either the sinker or the diver could be seen. Some hands now jumped into a boat alongside, and pushed a little off from the ship.

"Ha! ha!" cried Daggoo, all at once, from his now quiet, swinging perch overhead; and looking further off from the side, we saw an arm thrust upright from the blue waves; a sight strange to see, as an arm thrust forth from the grass over a grave.

"Both! both!—it is both!"—cried Daggoo again with a joyful shout; and soon after, Queequeg was seen boldly striking out with one hand, and with the other clutching the long hair of the Indian. Drawn into the waiting boat, they were quickly brought to the deck; but Tashtego was long in coming to, and Queequeg did not look very brisk.

Now, how had this noble rescue been accomplished? Why, diving after the slowly descending head, Queequeg with his keen sword had made side lunges near its bottom, so as to scuttle a large hole there; then dropping his sword, had thrust his long arm far inwards and upwards, and so hauled out our poor Tash by the head. He averred, that upon first thrusting in for him, a leg was presented; but well knowing that that was not as it ought to be, and might occasion great trouble;—he had thrust back the leg, and by a dexterous heave and toss, had wrought a somerset upon the Indian; so that with the next trial, he came forth in the good old way—head foremost.

As for the great head itself, that was doing as well as could be expected.

And thus, through the courage and great skill in obstetrics of Queequeg, the deliverance, or rather, delivery of Tashtego, was successfully accomplished, in the teeth, too, of the most untoward and apparently hopeless impediments; which is a lesson by no means to be forgotten. Midwifery should be taught in the same course with fencing and boxing, riding and rowing.

I know that this queer adventure of the Gay-Header's will be sure to seem incredible to some landsmen, though they themselves may have either seen or heard of some one's falling into a cistern ashore; an accident which not seldom happens, and with much less reason too than the Indian's, considering the exceeding slipperiness of the curb of the Sperm Whale's well.

But, peradventure, it may be sagaciously urged, how is this? We thought the tissued, infiltrated head of the Sperm Whale, was the lightest and most corky part about him; and yet thou makest it sink in an element of a far greater specific gravity than itself. We have thee there. Not at all, but I have ye; for at the time poor Tash fell in, the case had been nearly emptied of its lighter contents, leaving little but the dense tendinous wall of the well —a double welded, hammered substance, as I have before said, much heavier than the sea water, and a lump of which sinks in it like lead almost. But the tendency to rapid sinking in this substance was in the present instance materially counteracted by the other parts of the head remaining undetached from it, so that it sank very slowly and deliberately indeed, affording Queequeg a fair chance for performing his agile obstetrics on the run, as you may say. Yes, it was a running delivery, so it was.

Now, had Tashtego perished in that head, it had been a very precious perishing; smothered in the very whitest and daintiest of fragrant spermaceti; coffined, hearsed, and tombed in the secret inner chamber and sanctum sanctorum of the whale. Only one sweeter end can readily be recalled—the delicious death of an Ohio honey-hunter, who seeking honey in the crotch of a hollow tree, found such exceeding store of it, that leaning too far over, it sucked him in, so that he died embalmed. How many, think ye, have likewise fallen into Plato's honey head, and sweetly perished there?

# Chapter 79

## *The Prairie*

TO SCAN THE LINES of his face, or feel the bumps on the head of this Leviathan; this is a thing which no Physiognomist or Phrenologist has as yet undertaken. Such an enterprise would seem almost as hopeful as for Lavater to have scrutinized the wrinkles on the Rock of Gibraltar, or for Gall to have mounted a ladder and manipulated the Dome of the Pantheon. Still, in that famous work of his, Lavater not only treats of the various faces of men, but also attentively studies the faces of horses, birds, serpents, and fish; and dwells in detail upon the modifications of expression discernible therein. Nor have Gall and his disciple Spurzheim failed to throw out some hints touching the phrenological characteristics of other beings than man. Therefore, though I am but ill qualified for a pioneer, in the application of these two semi-sciences to the whale, I will do my endeavor. I try all things; I achieve what I can.

Physiognomically regarded, the Sperm Whale is an anomalous creature. He has no proper nose. And since the nose is the central and most conspicuous of the features; and since it perhaps most modifies and finally controls their combined expression; hence it would seem that its entire absence, as an external appendage, must very largely affect the countenance of the whale. For as in landscape gardening, a spire, cupola, monument, or tower of some sort, is deemed almost indispensable to the completion of the scene; so no face can be physiognomically in keeping without the elevated open-work belfry of the nose. Dash the nose from Phidias's marble Jove, and what a sorry remainder! Nevertheless, Leviathan is of so mighty a magnitude, all his proportions are so stately, that the same deficiency which in the sculptured Jove were hideous, in him is no blemish at all. Nay, it is an added grandeur. A nose to the whale would have been impertinent. As on your physiognomical voyage you sail round his vast head in your jolly-boat, your noble conceptions of him are never insulted by the reflection that he has a nose to be pulled. A pestilent conceit, which so often will insist upon obtruding even when beholding the mightiest royal beadle on his throne.

In some particulars, perhaps the most imposing physiognomical view to be had of the Sperm Whale, is that of the full front of his head. This aspect is sublime.

In thought, a fine human brow is like the East when troubled with the morning. In the repose of the pasture, the curled brow of the bull has a touch of the grand in it. Pushing heavy cannon up mountain defiles, the elephant's brow is majestic. Human or animal, the mystical brow is as that great golden seal affixed by the German emperors to their decrees. It signifies—"God: done this day by my hand." But in most creatures, nay in man himself, very often the brow is but a mere strip of alpine land lying along the snow line. Few are the foreheads which like Shakspeare's or Melancthon's rise so high, and descend so low, that the eyes themselves seem clear, eternal, tideless mountain lakes; and all above them in the fore-head's wrinkles, you seem to track the antlered thoughts descending there to drink, as the Highland hunters track the snow prints of the deer. But in the great Sperm Whale, this high and mighty god-like dignity inherent in the brow is so immensely amplified, that gazing on it, in that full front view, you feel the Deity and the dread powers more forcibly than in beholding any other object in living nature. For you see no one point precisely; not one distinct feature is revealed; no nose, eyes, ears, or mouth; no face; he has none, proper; nothing but that one broad firmament of a forehead, pleated with riddles; dumbly lowering with the doom of boats, and ships, and men. Nor, in profile, does this wondrous brow diminish; though that way viewed, its grandeur does not domineer upon you so. In profile, you plainly perceive that horizontal, semi-crescentic depression in the forehead's middle, which, in man, is Lavater's mark of genius.

But how? Genius in the Sperm Whale? Has the Sperm Whale ever written a book, spoken a speech? No, his great genius is declared in his doing nothing particular to prove it. It is moreover declared in his pyramidical silence. And this reminds me that had the great Sperm Whale been known to the young Orient World, he would have been deified by their child-magian thoughts. They deified the crocodile of the Nile, because the crocodile is tongueless; and the Sperm Whale has no tongue, or at least it is so exceedingly small, as to be incapable of protrusion. If hereafter any highly cultured, poetical nation shall lure back to their birth-right, the merry May-day gods of old; and livingly enthrone them again in the now egotistical sky; in the now unhaunted hill; then be sure, exalted to Jove's high seat, the great Sperm Whale shall lord it.

Champollion deciphered the wrinkled granite hieroglyphics. But there is no Champollion to decipher the Egypt of every man's and every being's face. Physiognomy, like every other human science, is but a passing fable. If then, Sir William Jones, who read in thirty languages, could not read the simplest peasant's face in its profounder and more subtle meanings, how may unlettered Ishmael hope to read the awful Chaldee of the Sperm Whale's brow? I but put that brow before you. Read it if you can.

# Chapter 80

## The Nut

IF THE Sperm Whale be physiognomically a Sphinx, to the phrenologist his brain seems that geometrical circle which it is impossible to square.

In the full-grown creature the skull will measure at least twenty feet in length. Unhinge the lower jaw, and the side view of this skull is as the side view of a moderately inclined plane resting throughout on a level base. But in life—as we have elsewhere seen—this inclined plane is angularly filled up, and almost squared by the enormous superincumbent mass of the junk and sperm. At the high end the skull forms a crater to bed that part of the mass; while under the long floor of this crater—in another cavity seldom exceeding ten inches in length and as many in depth—reposes the mere handful of this monster's brain. The brain is at least twenty feet from his apparent forehead in life; it is hidden away behind its vast outworks, like the innermost citadel within the amplified fortifications of Quebec. So like a choice casket is it secreted in him, that I have known some whalemen who peremptorily deny that the Sperm Whale has any other brain than that palpable semblance of one formed by the cubic-yards of his sperm magazine. Lying in strange folds, courses, and convolutions, to their apprehensions, it seems more in keeping with the idea of his general might to regard that mystic part of him as the seat of his intelligence.

348

It is plain, then, that phrenologically the head of this Leviathan, in the creature's living intact state, is an entire delusion. As for his true brain, you can then see no indications of it, nor feel any. The whale, like all things that are mighty, wears a false brow to the common world.

If you unload his skull of its spermy heaps and then take a rear view of its rear end, which is the high end, you will be struck by its resemblance to the human skull, beheld in the same situation, and from the same point of view. Indeed, place this reversed skull (scaled down to the human magnitude) among a plate of men's skulls, and you would involuntarily confound it with them; and remarking the depressions on one part of its summit, in phrenological phrase you would say—This man had no self-esteem, and no veneration. And by those negations, considered along with the affirmative fact of his prodigious bulk and power, you can best form to yourself the truest, though not the most exhilarating conception of what the most exalted potency is.

But if from the comparative dimensions of the whale's proper brain, you deem it incapable of being adequately charted, then I have another idea for you. If you attentively regard almost any quadruped's spine, you will be struck with the resemblance of its vertebræ to a strung necklace of dwarfed skulls, all bearing rudimental resemblance to the skull proper. It is a German conceit, that the vertebræ are absolutely undeveloped skulls. But the curious external resemblance, I take it the Germans were not the first men to perceive. A foreign friend once pointed it out to me, in the skeleton of a foe he had slain, and with the vertebræ of which he was inlaying, in a sort of basso-relievo, the beaked prow of his canoe. Now, I consider that the phrenologists have omitted an important thing in not pushing their investigations from the cerebellum through the spinal canal. For I believe that much of a man's character will be found betokened in his backbone. I would rather feel your spine than your skull, whoever you are. A thin joist of a spine never yet upheld a full and noble soul. I rejoice in my spine, as in the firm audacious staff of that flag which I fling half out to the world.

Apply this spinal branch of phrenology to the Sperm Whale. His cranial cavity is continuous with the first neck-vertebra; and in that vertebra the bottom of the spinal canal will measure ten inches across, being eight in height, and of a triangular figure with the base downwards. As it passes through the remaining vertebræ the canal tapers in size, but for a considerable distance remains of large capacity. Now, of course, this canal is filled with much the same strangely fibrous substance—the spinal cord— as the brain; and directly communicates with the brain. And what is still more, for many feet after emerging from the brain's cavity, the spinal cord remains of an undecreasing girth, almost equal to that of the brain. Under all these circumstances, would it be unreasonable to survey and map out the whale's spine phrenologically? For, viewed in this light, the wonderful comparative smallness of his brain proper is more than compensated by the wonderful comparative magnitude of his spinal cord.

But leaving this hint to operate as it may with the phrenologists, I would merely assume the spinal theory for a moment, in reference to the Sperm Whale's hump. This august hump, if I mistake not, rises over one of the larger vertebræ, and is, therefore, in some sort, the outer convex mould of it. From its relative situation then, I should call this high hump the organ of firmness or indomitableness in the Sperm Whale. And that the great monster is indomitable, you will yet have reason to know.

# Chapter 81

*The Pequod meets the Virgin*

THE PREDESTINATED DAY ARRIVED, and we duly met the ship Jungfrau, Derick De Deer, master, of Bremen.

At one time the greatest whaling people in the world, the Dutch and Germans are now among the least; but here and there at very wide intervals of latitude and longitude, you still occasionally meet with their flag in the Pacific.

For some reason, the Jungfrau seemed quite eager to pay her respects. While yet some distance from the Pequod, she rounded to, and dropping a boat, her captain was impelled towards us, impatiently standing in the bows instead of the stern.

"What has he in his hand there?" cried Starbuck, pointing to something wavingly held by the German. "Impossible!—a lamp-feeder!"

"Not that," said Stubb, "no, no, it's a coffee-pot, Mr. Starbuck; he's coming off to make us our coffee, is the Yarman; don't you see that big tin can there alongside of him?—that's his boiling water. Oh! he's all right, is the Yarman."

"Go along with you," cried Flask, "it's a lamp-feeder and an oil-can. He's out of oil, and has come a-begging."

However curious it may seem for an oil-ship to be borrowing oil on the whale-ground, and however much it may invertedly contradict the old proverb about carrying coals to Newcastle, yet sometimes such a thing really happens; and in the present case Captain Derick De Deer did indubitably conduct a lamp-feeder as Flask did declare.

As he mounted the deck, Ahab abruptly accosted him, without at all heeding what he had in his hand; but in his broken lingo, the German soon evinced his complete ignorance of the White Whale; immediately turning the conversation to his lamp-feeder and oil can, with some remarks touching his having to turn into his hammock at night in profound darkness—his last drop of Bremen oil being gone, and not a single flying-fish yet captured to supply the deficiency; concluding by hinting that his ship was indeed what in the Fishery is technically called a *clean* one (that is, an empty one), well deserving the name of Jungfrau or the Virgin.

His necessities supplied, Derick departed; but he had not gained his ship's side, when whales were almost simultaneously raised from the mast-heads of both vessels; and so eager for the chase was Derick, that without pausing to put his oil-can and lamp-feeder aboard, he slewed round his boat and made after the leviathan lamp-feeders.

Now, the game having risen to leeward, he and the other three German boats that soon followed him, had considerably the start of the Pequod's keels. There were eight whales, an average pod. Aware of their danger, they were going all abreast with great speed straight before the wind, rubbing their flanks as closely as so many spans of horses in harness. They left a great, wide wake, as though continually unrolling a great wide parchment upon the sea.

Full in this rapid wake, and many fathoms in the rear, swam a huge, humped old bull, which by his comparatively slow progress, as well as by the unusual yellowish incrustations overgrowing him, seemed afflicted with the jaundice, or some other infirmity. Whether this whale belonged to the pod in advance, seemed questionable; for it is not customary for such venerable leviathans to be at all social. Nevertheless, he stuck to their wake, though indeed their back water must have retarded him, because the white-bone or swell at his broad muzzle was a dashed one, like the swell formed when two hostile currents meet. His spout was short, slow, and laborious; coming forth with a choking sort of gush, and spending itself in torn shreds, followed by strange subterranean commotions in him, which seemed to have egress at his other buried extremity, causing the waters behind him to upbubble.

"Who's got some paregoric?" said Stubb, "he has the stomach-ache, I'm afraid. Lord, think of having half an acre of stomach-ache! Adverse winds are holding mad Christmas in him, boys. It's the first foul wind I ever knew to blow from astern; but look, did ever whale yaw so before? it must be, he's lost his tiller."

As an overladen Indiaman bearing down the Hindostan coast with a deck load of frightened horses, careens, buries, rolls, and wallows on her way; so did this old whale heave his aged bulk, and now and then partly turning over on his cumbrous rib-ends, expose the cause of his devious wake in the unnatural stump of his starboard fin. Whether he had lost that fin in battle, or had been born without it, it were hard to say.

"Only wait a bit, old chap, and I'll give ye a sling for that wounded arm," cried cruel Flask, pointing to the whale-line near him.

"Mind he don't sling thee with it," cried Starbuck. "Give way, or the German will have him."

With one intent all the combined rival boats were pointed for this one fish, because not only was he the largest, and therefore the most valuable whale, but he was nearest to them, and the other whales were going with such great velocity, moreover, as almost to defy pursuit for the time. At this juncture, the Pequod's keels had shot by the three German boats last lowered; but from the great start he had had, Derick's boat still led the chase, though every moment neared by his foreign rivals. The only thing they feared, was, that from being already so nigh to his mark, he would be enabled to dart his iron before they could completely overtake and pass him. As for Derick, he seemed quite confident that this would be the case, and occasionally with a deriding gesture shook his lamp-feeder at the other boats.

"The ungracious and ungrateful dog!" cried Starbuck; "he mocks and dares me with the very poor-box I filled for him not five minutes ago!"— then in his old intense whisper—"give way, greyhounds! Dog to it!"

"I tell ye what it is, men"—cried Stubb to his crew—"It's against my religion to get mad; but I'd like to eat that villanous Yarman—Pull—wont ye? Are ye going to let that rascal beat ye? Do ye love brandy? A hogshead of brandy, then, to the best man. Come, why don't some of ye burst a blood-vessel? Who's that been dropping an anchor overboard—we don't budge an inch—we're becalmed. Halloo, here's grass growing in the boat's bottom—and by the Lord, the mast there's budding. This won't do, boys. Look at that Yarman! The short and long of it is, men, will ye spit fire or not?"

"Oh! see the suds he makes!" cried Flask, dancing up and down—"What a hump—Oh, *do* pile on the beef—lays like a log! Oh! my lads, *do* spring— slap-jacks and quohogs for supper, you know, my lads—baked clams and

muffins—oh, *do, do,* spring—he's a hundred barreler—don't lose him now
—don't, oh, *don't!*—see that Yarman—Oh! won't ye pull for your duff, my
lads—such a sog! such a sogger! Don't ye love sperm? There goes three
thousand dollars, men!—a bank!—a whole bank! The bank of England!—
Oh, *do, do, do!*—What's that Yarman about now?"

At this moment Derick was in the act of pitching his lamp-feeder at the
advancing boats, and also his oil-can; perhaps with the double view of
retarding his rivals' way, and at the same time economically accelerating his
own by the momentary impetus of the backward toss.

"The unmannerly Dutch dogger!" cried Stubb. "Pull now, men, like
fifty thousand line-of-battle-ship loads of red-haired devils. What d'ye say,
Tashtego; are you the man to snap your spine in two-and-twenty pieces
for the honor of old Gay-head? What d'ye say?"

"I say, pull like god-dam,"—cried the Indian.

Fiercely but evenly, incited by the taunts of the German, the Pequod's
three boats now began ranging almost abreast; and, so disposed, momentarily neared him. In that fine, loose, chivalrous attitude of the headsman
when drawing near to his prey, the three mates stood up proudly, occasionally backing the after oarsman with an exhilarating cry of, "There she slides,
now! Hurrah for the white-ash breeze! Down with the Yarman! Sail over
him!"

But so decided an original start had Derick had, that spite of all their
gallantry, he would have proved the victor in this race, had not a righteous
judgment descended upon him in a crab which caught the blade of his mid-
ship oarsman. While this clumsy lubber was striving to free his white-ash,
and while, in consequence, Derick's boat was nigh to capsizing, and he
thundering away at his men in a mighty rage;—that was a good time for
Starbuck, Stubb, and Flask. With a shout, they took a mortal start forwards,
and slantingly ranged up on the German's quarter. An instant more, and all
four boats were diagonally in the whale's immediate wake, while stretching
from them, on both sides, was the foaming swell that he made.

It was a terrific, most pitiable, and maddening sight. The whale was now
going head out, and sending his spout before him in a continual tormented
jet; while his one poor fin beat his side in an agony of fright. Now to this
hand, now to that, he yawed in his faltering flight, and still at every billow
that he broke, he spasmodically sank in the sea, or sideways rolled towards
the sky his one beating fin. So have I seen a bird with clipped wing, making
affrighted broken circles in the air, vainly striving to escape the piratical
hawks. But the bird has a voice, and with plaintive cries will make known

her fear; but the fear of this vast dumb brute of the sea, was chained up and enchanted in him; he had no voice, save that choking respiration through his spiracle, and this made the sight of him unspeakably pitiable; while still, in his amazing bulk, portcullis jaw, and omnipotent tail, there was enough to appal the stoutest man who so pitied.

Seeing now that but a very few moments more would give the Pequod's boats the advantage, and rather than be thus foiled of his game, Derick chose to hazard what to him must have seemed a most unusually long dart, ere the last chance would for ever escape.

But no sooner did his harpooneer stand up for the stroke, than all three tigers—Queequeg, Tashtego, Daggoo—instinctively sprang to their feet, and standing in a diagonal row, simultaneously pointed their barbs; and, darted over the head of the German harpooneer, their three Nantucket irons entered the whale. Blinding vapors of foam and white-fire! The three boats, in the first fury of the whale's headlong rush, bumped the German's aside with such force, that both Derick and his baffled harpooneer were spilled out, and sailed over by the three flying keels.

"Don't be afraid, my butter-boxes," cried Stubb, casting a passing glance upon them as he shot by; "ye'll be picked up presently—all right—I saw some sharks astern—St. Bernard's dogs, you know—relieve distressed travellers. Hurrah! this is the way to sail now. Every keel a sun-beam! Hurrah!—Here we go like three tin kettles at the tail of a mad cougar! This puts me in mind of fastening to an elephant in a tilbury on a plain—makes the wheel-spokes fly, boys, when you fasten to him that way; and there's danger of being pitched out too, when you strike a hill. Hurrah! this is the way a fellow feels when he's going to Davy Jones—all a rush down an endless inclined plane! Hurrah! this whale carries the everlasting mail!"

But the monster's run was a brief one. Giving a sudden gasp, he tumultuously sounded. With a grating rush, the three lines flew round the loggerheads with such a force as to gouge deep grooves in them; while so fearful were the harpooneers that this rapid sounding would soon exhaust the lines, that using all their dexterous might, they caught repeated smoking turns with the rope to hold on; till at last—owing to the perpendicular strain from the lead-lined chocks of the boats, whence the three ropes went straight down into the blue—the gunwales of the bows were almost even with the water, while the three sterns tilted high in the air. And the whale soon ceasing to sound, for some time they remained in that attitude, fearful of expending more line, though the position was a little ticklish. But though boats have been taken down and lost in this way, yet it is this "holding on," as it is called; this hooking up by the sharp barbs of his live flesh from the back; this it is that often torments the Leviathan into soon rising again to meet the sharp lance of his foes. Yet not to speak of the peril of the thing, it is to be doubted whether this course is always the best; for it is but reasonable to presume, that the longer the stricken whale stays under water, the more he is exhausted. Because, owing to the enormous surface of him—in a full grown sperm whale something less than 2000 square feet—the pressure of the water is immense. We all know what an astonishing atmospheric weight we ourselves stand up under; even here, above-ground, in the air; how vast, then, the burden of a whale, bearing on his back a column of two hundred fathoms of ocean! It must at least equal the weight of fifty atmospheres. One whaleman has estimated it at the weight of twenty line-of-battle ships, with all their guns, and stores, and men on board.

As the three boats lay there on that gently rolling sea, gazing down into its eternal blue noon; and as not a single groan or cry of any sort, nay, not so much as a ripple or a bubble came up from its depths; what landsman would have thought, that beneath all that silence and placidity, the utmost monster of the seas was writhing and wrenching in agony! Not eight inches of perpendicular rope were visible at the bows. Seems it credible that by three such thin threads the great Leviathan was suspended like the big weight to an eight day clock. Suspended? and to what? To three bits of board. Is this the creature of whom it was once so triumphantly said— "Canst thou fill his skin with barbed irons? or his head with fish-spears? The sword of him that layeth at him cannot hold, the spear, the dart, nor the habergeon: he esteemeth iron as straw; the arrow cannot make him flee; darts are counted as stubble; he laugheth at the shaking of a spear!" This the creature? this he? Oh! that unfulfilments should follow the prophets. For with the strength of a thousand thighs in his tail, Leviathan had run his head under the mountains of the sea, to hide him from the Pequod's fish-spears!

In that sloping afternoon sunlight, the shadows that the three boats sent down beneath the surface, must have been long enough and broad enough to shade half Xerxes' army. Who can tell how appalling to the wounded whale must have been such huge phantoms flitting over his head!

"Stand by, men; he stirs," cried Starbuck, as the three lines suddenly vibrated in the water, distinctly conducting upwards to them, as by magnetic wires, the life and death throbs of the whale, so that every oarsman felt them in his seat. The next moment, relieved in great part from the downward strain at the bows, the boats gave a sudden bounce upwards, as a

small ice-field will, when a dense herd of white bears are scared from it into
the sea.

"Haul in! Haul in!" cried Starbuck again; "he's rising."

The lines, of which, hardly an instant before, not one hand's breadth
could have been gained, were now in long quick coils flung back all dripping into the boats, and soon the whale broke water within two ship's
lengths of the hunters.

His motions plainly denoted his extreme exhaustion. In most land
animals there are certain valves or flood-gates in many of their veins,
whereby when wounded, the blood is in some degree at least instantly shut
off in certain directions. Not so with the whale; one of whose peculiarities
it is, to have an entire non-valvular structure of the blood-vessels, so that
when pierced even by so small a point as a harpoon, a deadly drain is at once
begun upon his whole arterial system; and when this is heightened by the
extraordinary pressure of water at a great distance below the surface, his life
may be said to pour from him in incessant streams. Yet so vast is the quantity
of blood in him, and so distant and numerous its interior fountains, that he
will keep thus bleeding and bleeding for a considerable period; even as in a
drought a river will flow, whose source is in the well-springs of far-off and
undiscernible hills. Even now, when the boats pulled upon this whale, and
perilously drew over his swaying flukes, and the lances were darted into
him, they were followed by steady jets from the new made wound, which
kept continually playing, while the natural spout-hole in his head was only
at intervals, however rapid, sending its affrighted moisture into the air.
From this last vent no blood yet came, because no vital part of him had thus
far been struck. His life, as they significantly call it, was untouched.

As the boats now more closely surrounded him, the whole upper part of
his form, with much of it that is ordinarily submerged, was plainly revealed. His eyes, or rather the places where his eyes had been, were beheld.
As strange misgrown masses gather in the knot-holes of the noblest oaks
when prostrate, so from the points which the whale's eyes had once occupied, now protruded blind bulbs, horribly pitiable to see. But pity there was
none. For all his old age, and his one arm, and his blind eyes, he must die the
death and be murdered, in order to light the gay bridals and other merry-
makings of men, and also to illuminate the solemn churches that preach
unconditional inoffensiveness by all to all. Still rolling in his blood, at last
he partially disclosed a strangely discolored bunch or protuberance, the
size of a bushel, low down on the flank.

"A nice spot," cried Flask; "just let me prick him there once."

"Avast!" cried Starbuck, "there's no need of that!"

But humane Starbuck was too late. At the instant of the dart an ulcerous jet shot from this cruel wound, and goaded by it into more than sufferable anguish, the whale now spouting thick blood, with swift fury blindly darted at the craft, bespattering them and their glorying crews all over with showers of gore, capsizing Flask's boat and marring the bows. It was his death stroke. For, by this time, so spent was he by loss of blood, that he helplessly rolled away from the wreck he had made; lay panting on his side, impotently flapped with his stumped fin, then over and over slowly revolved like a waning world; turned up the white secrets of his belly; lay like a log, and died. It was most piteous, that last expiring spout. As when by unseen hands the water is gradually drawn off from some mighty fountain, and with half-stifled melancholy gurglings the spray-column lowers and lowers to the ground—so the last long dying spout of the whale.

Soon, while the crews were awaiting the arrival of the ship, the body showed symptoms of sinking with all its treasures unrifled. Immediately, by Starbuck's orders, lines were secured to it at different points, so that ere long every boat was a buoy; the sunken whale being suspended a few inches beneath them by the cords. By very heedful management, when the ship drew nigh, the whale was transferred to her side, and was strongly secured there by the stiffest fluke-chains, for it was plain that unless artificially upheld, the body would at once sink to the bottom.

It so chanced that almost upon first cutting into him with the spade, the entire length of a corroded harpoon was found imbedded in his flesh, on the lower part of the bunch before described. But as the stumps of harpoons are frequently found in the dead bodies of captured whales, with the flesh perfectly healed around them, and no prominence of any kind to denote their place; therefore, there must needs have been some other unknown reason in the present case fully to account for the ulceration alluded to. But still more curious was the fact of a lance-head of stone being found in him, not far from the buried iron, the flesh perfectly firm about it. Who had darted that stone lance? And when? It might have been darted by some Nor' West Indian long before America was discovered.

What other marvels might have been rummaged out of this monstrous cabinet there is no telling. But a sudden stop was put to further discoveries, by the ship's being unprecedentedly dragged over sideways to the sea, owing to the body's immensely increasing tendency to sink. However, Starbuck, who had the ordering of affairs, hung on to it to the last; hung on to it so resolutely, indeed, that when at length the ship would have been capsized, if still persisting in locking arms with the body; then, when the command was given to break clear from it, such was the immovable strain upon the timber-heads to which the fluke-chains and cables were fastened, that it was impossible to cast them off. Meantime everything in the Pequod was aslant. To cross to the other side of the deck was like walking up the steep gabled roof of a house. The ship groaned and gasped. Many of the ivory inlayings of her bulwarks and cabins were started from their places, by the unnatural dislocation. In vain handspikes and crows were brought to bear upon the immovable fluke-chains, to pry them adrift from the timber-heads; and so low had the whale now settled that the submerged ends could not be at all approached, while every moment whole tons of ponderosity seemed added to the sinking bulk, and the ship seemed on the point of going over.

"Hold on, hold on, won't ye?" cried Stubb to the body, "don't be in such a devil of a hurry to sink! By thunder, men, we must do something or go for it. No use prying there; avast, I say with your handspikes, and run one of ye for a prayer book and a pen-knife, and cut the big chains."

"Knife? Aye, aye," cried Queequeg, and seizing the carpenter's heavy hatchet, he leaned out of a porthole, and steel to iron, began slashing at the largest fluke-chains. But a few strokes, full of sparks, were given, when the exceeding strain effected the rest. With a terrific snap, every fastening went adrift; the ship righted, the carcase sank.

Now, this occasional inevitable sinking of the recently killed Sperm Whale is a very curious thing; nor has any fisherman yet adequately accounted for it. Usually the dead Sperm Whale floats with great buoyancy, with its side or belly considerably elevated above the surface. If the only whales that thus sank were old, meagre, and broken-hearted creatures, their pads of lard diminished and all their bones heavy and rheumatic; then you might with some reason assert that this sinking is caused by an uncommon specific gravity in the fish so sinking, consequent upon this absence of buoyant matter in him. But it is not so. For young whales, in the highest health, and swelling with noble aspirations, prematurely cut off in the warm flush and May of life, with all their panting lard about them; even these brawny, buoyant heroes do sometimes sink.

Be it said, however, that the Sperm Whale is far less liable to this accident than any other species. Where one of that sort go down, twenty Right Whales do. This difference in the species is no doubt imputable in no small degree to the greater quantity of bone in the Right Whale; his Venetian blinds alone sometimes weighing more than a ton; from this incumbrance the Sperm Whale is wholly free. But there are instances where, after the lapse of many hours or several days, the sunken whale again rises, more buoyant than in life. But the reason of this is obvious. Gases are generated in him; he swells to a prodigious magnitude; becomes a sort of animal balloon. A line-of-battle ship could hardly keep him under then. In the Shore Whaling, on soundings, among the Bays of New Zealand, when a Right Whale gives token of sinking, they fasten buoys to him, with plenty of rope; so that when the body has gone down, they know where to look for it when it shall have ascended again.

It was not long after the sinking of the body that a cry was heard from the Pequod's mast-heads, announcing that the Jungfrau was again lowering her boats; though the only spout in sight was that of a Fin-Back, belonging to the species of uncapturable whales, because of its incredible power of swimming. Nevertheless, the Fin-Back's spout is so similar to the Sperm Whale's, that by unskilful fishermen it is often mistaken for it. And consequently Derick and all his host were now in valiant chase of this unnearable brute. The Virgin crowding all sail, made after her four young keels, and thus they all disappeared far to leeward, still in bold, hopeful chase.

Oh! many are the Fin-Backs, and many are the Dericks, my friend.

# Chapter 82

*The Honor and Glory of Whaling*

THERE ARE SOME ENTERPRISES in which a careful disorderliness is the true method.

The more I dive into this matter of whaling, and push my researches up to the very spring-head of it, so much the more am I impressed with its great honorableness and antiquity; and especially when I find so many great demi-gods and heroes, prophets of all sorts, who one way or other have shed distinction upon it, I am transported with the reflection that I myself belong, though but subordinately, to so emblazoned a fraternity.

The gallant Perseus, a son of Jupiter, was the first whaleman; and to the eternal honor of our calling be it said, that the first whale attacked by our brotherhood was not killed with any sordid intent. Those were the knightly days of our profession, when we only bore arms to succor the distressed, and not to fill men's lamp-feeders. Every one knows the fine story of Perseus and Andromeda; how the lovely Andromeda, the daughter of a king, was tied to a rock on the sea-coast, and as Leviathan was in the very act of carrying her off, Perseus, the prince of whalemen, intrepidly advancing, harpooned the monster, and delivered and married the maid. It was an admirable artistic exploit, rarely achieved by the best harpooneers of the present day; inasmuch as this Leviathan was slain at the very first dart. And let no man doubt this Arkite story; for in the ancient Joppa, now Jaffa, on the Syrian coast, in one of the Pagan temples, there stood for many ages the vast skeleton of a whale, which the city's legends and all the inhabitants asserted to be the identical bones of the monster that Perseus slew. When the Romans took Joppa, the same skeleton was carried to Italy in triumph. What seems most singular and suggestively important in this story, is this: it was from Joppa that Jonah set sail.

Akin to the adventure of Perseus and Andromeda—indeed, by some supposed to be indirectly derived from it—is that famous story of St. George and the Dragon; which dragon I maintain to have been a whale; for in many old chronicles whales and dragons are strangely jumbled together, and often stand for each other. "Thou art as a lion of the waters, and as a dragon of the sea," saith Ezekiel; hereby, plainly meaning a whale; in truth, some versions of the Bible use that word itself. Besides, it would much subtract from the glory of the exploit had St. George but encountered a crawling reptile of the land, instead of doing battle with the great monster of the deep. Any man may kill a snake, but only a Perseus, a St. George, a Coffin, have the heart in them to march boldly up to a whale.

Let not the modern paintings of this scene mislead us; for though the creature encountered by that valiant whaleman of old is vaguely represented of a griffin-like shape, and though the battle is depicted on land and the saint on horseback, yet considering the great ignorance of those times, when the true form of the whale was unknown to artists; and considering that as in Perseus' case, St. George's whale might have crawled up out of the sea on the beach; and considering that the animal ridden by St. George might have been only a large seal, or sea-horse; bearing all this in mind, it will not appear altogether incompatible with the sacred legend and the ancientest draughts of the scene, to hold this so-called dragon no other than the great Leviathan himself. In fact, placed before the strict and piercing truth, this whole story will fare like that fish, flesh, and fowl idol of the Philistines, Dagon by name; who being planted before the ark of Israel, his horse's head and both the palms of his hands fell off from him, and only the stump or fishy part of him remained. Thus, then, one of our own noble stamp, even a whaleman, is the tutelary guardian of England; and by good rights, we harpooneers of Nantucket should be enrolled in the most noble order of St. George. And therefore, let not the knights of that honorable company (none of whom, I venture to say, have ever had to do with a whale like their great patron), let them never eye a Nantucketer with disdain, since even in our woollen frocks and tarred trowsers we are much better entitled to St. George's decoration than they.

Whether to admit Hercules among us or not, concerning this I long remained dubious: for though according to the Greek mythologies, that antique Crockett and Kit Carson—that brawny doer of rejoicing good deeds, was swallowed down and thrown up by a whale; still, whether that strictly makes a whaleman of him, that might be mooted. It nowhere appears that he ever actually harpooned his fish, unless, indeed, from the inside. Nevertheless, he may be deemed a sort of involuntary whaleman; at any rate the whale caught him, if he did not the whale. I claim him for one of our clan.

But, by the best contradictory authorities, this Grecian story of Hercules and the whale is considered to be derived from the still more ancient Hebrew story of Jonah and the whale; and vice versâ; certainly they are very similar. If I claim the demi-god then, why not the prophet?

Nor do heroes, saints, demigods, and prophets alone comprise the whole roll of our order. Our grand master is still to be named; for like royal kings of old times, we find the head-waters of our fraternity in nothing short of the great gods themselves. That wondrous oriental story is now to be rehearsed from the Shaster, which gives us the dread Vishnoo, one of the three persons in the godhead of the Hindoos; gives us this divine Vishnoo himself for our Lord;—Vishnoo, who, by the first of his ten earthly incarnations, has for ever set apart and sanctified the whale. When Bramha, or the God of Gods, saith the Shaster, resolved to recreate the world after one of its periodical dissolutions, he gave birth to Vishnoo, to preside over the work; but the Vedas, or mystical books, whose perusal would seem to have been indispensable to Vishnoo before beginning the creation, and which therefore must have contained something in the shape of practical hints to young architects, these Vedas were lying at the bottom of the waters; so Vishnoo became incarnate in a whale, and sounding down in him to the uttermost depths, rescued the sacred volumes. Was not this Vishnoo a whaleman, then? even as a man who rides a horse is called a horseman?

Perseus, St. George, Hercules, Jonah, and Vishnoo! there's a member-roll for you! What club but the whaleman's can head off like that?

# Chapter 83

*Jonah Historically Regarded*

REFERENCE WAS MADE to the historical story of Jonah and the whale in the preceding chapter. Now some Nantucketers rather distrust this historical story of Jonah and the whale. But then there were some sceptical Greeks and Romans, who, standing out from the orthodox pagans of their times, equally doubted the story of Hercules and the whale, and Arion and the dolphin; and yet their doubting those traditions did not make those traditions one whit the less facts, for all that.

One old Sag-Harbor whaleman's chief reason for questioning the Hebrew story was this:—He had one of those quaint old-fashioned Bibles, embellished with curious, unscientific plates; one of which represented Jonah's whale with two spouts in his head—a peculiarity only true with respect to a species of the Leviathan (the Right Whale, and the varieties of that order), concerning which the fishermen have this saying, "A penny roll would choke him;" his swallow is so very small. But, to this, Bishop Jebb's anticipative answer is ready. It is not necessary, hints the Bishop, that we consider Jonah as tombed in the whale's belly, but as temporarily lodged in some part of his mouth. And this seems reasonable enough in the good Bishop. For truly, the Right Whale's mouth would accommodate a couple of whist-tables, and comfortably seat all the players. Possibly, too,

Jonah might have ensconced himself in a hollow tooth; but, on second thoughts, the Right Whale is toothless.

Another reason which Sag-Harbor (he went by that name) urged for his want of faith in this matter of the prophet, was something obscurely in reference to his incarcerated body and the whale's gastric juices. But this objection likewise falls to the ground, because a German exegetist supposes that Jonah must have taken refuge in the floating body of a *dead* whale— even as the French soldiers in the Russian campaign turned their dead horses into tents, and crawled into them. Besides, it has been divined by other continental commentators, that when Jonah was thrown overboard from the Joppa ship, he straightway effected his escape to another vessel near by, some vessel with a whale for a figure-head; and, I would add, possibly called "The Whale," as some craft are nowadays christened the "Shark," the "Gull," the "Eagle." Nor have there been wanting learned exegetists who have opined that the whale mentioned in the book of Jonah merely meant a life-preserver—an inflated bag of wind—which the en-dangered prophet swam to, and so was saved from a watery doom. Poor Sag-Harbor, therefore, seems worsted all round. But he had still another reason for his want of faith. It was this, if I remember right: Jonah was swallowed by the whale in the Mediterranean Sea, and after three days he was vomited up somewhere within three days' journey of Nineveh, a city on the Tigris, very much more than three days' journey across from the nearest point of the Mediterranean coast. How is that?

But was there no other way for the whale to land the prophet within that short distance of Nineveh? Yes. He might have carried him round by the way of the Cape of Good Hope. But not to speak of the passage through the whole length of the Mediterranean, and another passage up the Persian Gulf and Red Sea, such a supposition would involve the complete circum-navigation of all Africa in three days, not to speak of the Tigris waters, near the site of Nineveh, being too shallow for any whale to swim in. Besides, this idea of Jonah's weathering the Cape of Good Hope at so early a day would wrest the honor of the discovery of that great headland from Bartholomew Diaz, its reputed discoverer, and so make modern history a liar.

But all these foolish arguments of old Sag-Harbor only evinced his foolish pride of reason—a thing still more reprehensible in him, seeing that he had but little learning except what he had picked up from the sun and the sea. I say it only shows his foolish, impious pride, and abominable, devilish rebellion against the reverend clergy. For by a Portuguese Catholic priest, this very idea of Jonah's going to Nineveh viâ the Cape of Good Hope was advanced as a signal magnification of the general miracle. And so it was. Besides, to this day, the highly enlightened Turks devoutly believe in the historical story of Jonah. And some three centuries ago, an English traveller in old Harris's Voyages, speaks of a Turkish Mosque built in honor of Jonah, in which mosque was a miraculous lamp that burnt without any oil.

# Chapter 84

*Pitchpoling*

T O MAKE THEM run easily and swiftly, the axles of carriages are anointed; and for much the same purpose, some whalers perform an analogous operation upon their boat; they grease the bottom. Nor is it to be doubted that as such a procedure can do no harm, it may possibly be of no contemptible advantage; considering that oil and water are hostile; that oil is a sliding thing, and that the object in view is to make the boat slide bravely. Queequeg believed strongly in anointing his boat, and one morning not long after the German ship Jungfrau disappeared, took more than customary pains in that occupation; crawling under its bottom, where it hung over the side, and rubbing in the unctuousness as though diligently seeking to insure a crop of hair from the craft's bald keel. He seemed to be working in obedience to some particular presentiment. Nor did it remain unwarranted by the event.

Towards noon whales were raised; but so soon as the ship sailed down to them, they turned and fled with swift precipitancy; a disordered flight, as of Cleopatra's barges from Actium.

Nevertheless, the boats pursued, and Stubb's was foremost. By great exertion, Tashtego at last succeeded in planting one iron; but the stricken whale, without at all sounding, still continued his horizontal flight, with added fleetness. Such unintermitted strainings upon the planted iron must

367

sooner or later inevitably extract it. It became imperative to lance the flying whale, or be content to lose him. But to haul the boat up to his flank was impossible, he swam so fast and furious. What then remained?

Of all the wondrous devices and dexterities, the sleights of hand and countless subtleties, to which the veteran whaleman is so often forced, none exceed that fine manœuvre with the lance called pitchpoling. Small sword, or broad sword, in all its exercises boasts nothing like it. It is only indispensable with an inveterate running whale; its grand fact and feature is the wonderful distance to which the long lance is accurately darted from a violently rocking, jerking boat, under extreme headway. Steel and wood included, the entire spear is some ten or twelve feet in length; the staff is much slighter than that of the harpoon, and also of a lighter material—pine. It is furnished with a small rope called a warp, of considerable length, by which it can be hauled back to the hand after darting.

But before going further, it is important to mention here, that though the harpoon may be pitchpoled in the same way with the lance, yet it is seldom done; and when done, is still less frequently successful, on account of the greater weight and inferior length of the harpoon as compared with the lance, which in effect become serious drawbacks. As a general thing, therefore, you must first get fast to a whale, before any pitchpoling comes into play.

Look now at Stubb; a man who from his humorous, deliberate coolness and equanimity in the direst emergencies, was specially qualified to excel in pitchpoling. Look at him; he stands upright in the tossed bow of the flying boat; wrapt in fleecy foam, the towing whale is forty feet ahead. Handling the long lance lightly, glancing twice or thrice along its length to see if it be exactly straight, Stubb whistlingly gathers up the coil of the warp in one hand, so as to secure its free end in his grasp, leaving the rest unobstructed. Then holding the lance full before his waistband's middle, he levels it at the whale; when, covering him with it, he steadily depresses the butt-end in his hand, thereby elevating the point till the weapon stands fairly balanced upon his palm, fifteen feet in the air. He minds you somewhat of a juggler, balancing a long staff on his chin. Next moment with a rapid, nameless impulse, in a superb lofty arch the bright steel spans the foaming distance, and quivers in the life spot of the whale. Instead of sparkling water, he now spouts red blood.

"That drove the spigot out of him!" cries Stubb. "'Tis July's immortal Fourth; all fountains must run wine to-day! Would now, it were old Orleans whiskey, or old Ohio, or unspeakable old Monongahela! Then,

Tashtego, lad, I'd have ye hold a canakin to the jet, and we'd drink round it! Yea, verily, hearts alive, we'd brew choice punch in the spread of his spout-hole there, and from that live punch-bowl quaff the living stuff!"

Again and again to such gamesome talk, the dexterous dart is repeated, the spear returning to its master like a greyhound held in skilful leash. The agonized whale goes into his flurry; the tow-line is slackened, and the pitchpoler dropping astern, folds his hands, and mutely watches the monster die.

# Chapter 85

*The Fountain*

THAT FOR SIX THOUSAND YEARS—and no one knows how many millions of ages before—the great whales should have been spouting all over the sea, and sprinkling and mistifying the gardens of the deep, as with so many sprinkling or mistifying pots; and that for some centuries back, thousands of hunters should have been close by the fountain of the whale, watching these sprinklings and spoutings—that all this should be, and yet, that down to this blessed minute (fifteen and a quarter minutes past one o'clock P.M. of this sixteenth day of December, A.D. 1850), it should still remain a problem, whether these spoutings are, after all, really water, or nothing but vapor—this is surely a noteworthy thing.

Let us, then, look at this matter, along with some interesting items contingent. Every one knows that by the peculiar cunning of their gills, the finny tribes in general breathe the air which at all times is combined with the element in which they swim; hence, a herring or a cod might live a century, and never once raise its head above the surface. But owing to his marked internal structure which gives him regular lungs, like a human being's, the whale can only live by inhaling the disengaged air in the open atmosphere. Wherefore the necessity for his periodical visits to the upper world. But he cannot in any degree breathe through his mouth, for, in his ordinary attitude, the Sperm Whale's mouth is buried at least eight feet beneath the surface; and what is still more, his windpipe has no connexion with his mouth. No, he breathes through his spiracle alone; and this is on the top of his head.

If I say, that in any creature breathing is only a function indispensable to vitality, inasmuch as it withdraws from the air a certain element, which being subsequently brought into contact with the blood imparts to the blood its vivifying principle, I do not think I shall err; though I may possibly use some superfluous scientific words. Assume it, and it follows that if all the blood in a man could be aerated with one breath, he might then seal up his nostrils and not fetch another for a considerable time. That is to say, he would then live without breathing. Anomalous as it may seem, this is precisely the case with the whale, who systematically lives, by intervals, his full hour and more (when at the bottom) without drawing a single breath, or so much as in any way inhaling a particle of air; for, remember, he has no gills. How is this? Between his ribs and on each side of his spine he is supplied with a remarkable involved Cretan labyrinth of vermicelli-like vessels, which vessels, when he quits the surface, are completely distended with oxygenated blood. So that for an hour or more, a thousand fathoms in the sea, he carries a surplus stock of vitality in him, just as the camel crossing the waterless desert carries a surplus supply of drink for future use in its four supplementary stomachs. The anatomical fact of this labyrinth is indisputable; and that the supposition founded upon it is reasonable and true, seems the more cogent to me, when I consider the otherwise inexplicable obstinacy of that leviathan in *having his spoutings out,* as the fishermen phrase it. This is what I mean. If unmolested, upon rising to the surface, the Sperm Whale will continue there for a period of time exactly uniform with all his other unmolested risings. Say he stays eleven minutes, and jets seventy times, that is, respires seventy breaths; then whenever he rises again, he will be sure to have his seventy breaths over again, to a minute. Now, if after he fetches a few breaths you alarm him, so that he sounds, he will be always dodging up again to make good his regular allowance of air. And not till those seventy breaths are told, will he finally go down to stay out his full term below. Remark, however, that in different individuals these rates are different; but in any one they are alike. Now, why should the whale thus insist upon having his spoutings out, unless it be to replenish his reservoir of air, ere descending for good? How obvious is it, too, that this necessity for the whale's rising exposes him to all the fatal hazards of the chase. For not by hook or by net could this vast leviathan be caught, when sailing a thousand fathoms beneath the sunlight. Not so much thy skill, then, O hunter, as the great necessities, that strike the victory to thee!

In man, breathing is incessantly going on—one breath only serving for two or three pulsations; so that whatever other business he has to attend to, waking or sleeping, breathe he must, or die he will. But the Sperm Whale only breathes about one seventh or Sunday of his time.

It has been said that the whale only breathes through his spout-hole; if it could truthfully be added that his spouts are mixed with water, then I opine we should be furnished with the reason why his sense of smell seems obliterated in him; for the only thing about him that at all answers to his nose is that identical spout-hole; and being so clogged with two elements, it could not be expected to have the power of smelling. But owing to the mystery of the spout—whether it be water or whether it be vapor—no absolute certainty can as yet be arrived at on this head. Sure it is, nevertheless, that the Sperm Whale has no proper olfactories. But what does he want of them? No roses, no violets, no Cologne-water in the sea.

Furthermore, as his windpipe solely opens into the tube of his spouting canal, and as that long canal—like the grand Erie Canal—is furnished with a sort of locks (that open and shut) for the downward retention of air or the upward exclusion of water, therefore the whale has no voice; unless you insult him by saying, that when he so strangely rumbles, he talks through his nose. But then again, what has the whale to say? Seldom have I known any profound being that had anything to say to this world, unless forced to stammer out something by way of getting a living. Oh! happy that the world is such an excellent listener!

Now, the spouting canal of the Sperm Whale, chiefly intended as it is for the conveyance of air, and for several feet laid along, horizontally, just beneath the upper surface of his head, and a little to one side; this curious canal is very much like a gas-pipe laid down in a city on one side of a street. But the question returns whether this gas-pipe is also a water-pipe; in other words, whether the spout of the Sperm Whale is the mere vapor of the exhaled breath, or whether that exhaled breath is mixed with water taken in at the mouth, and discharged through the spiracle. It is certain that the mouth indirectly communicates with the spouting canal; but it cannot be proved that this is for the purpose of discharging water through the spiracle. Because the greatest necessity for so doing would seem to be, when in feeding he accidentally takes in water. But the Sperm Whale's food is far beneath the surface, and there he cannot spout even if he would. Besides, if you regard him very closely, and time him with your watch, you will find that when unmolested, there is an undeviating rhyme between the periods of his jets and the ordinary periods of respiration.

But why pester one with all this reasoning on the subject? Speak out! You have seen him spout; then declare what the spout is; can you not tell water from air? My dear sir, in this world it is not so easy to settle these plain things. I have ever found your plain things the knottiest of all. And as for this whale spout, you might almost stand in it, and yet be undecided as to what it is precisely.

The central body of it is hidden in the snowy sparkling mist enveloping it; and how can you certainly tell whether any water falls from it, when, always, when you are close enough to a whale to get a close view of his spout, he is in a prodigious commotion, the water cascading all around him. And if at such times you should think that you really perceived drops of moisture in the spout, how do you know that they are not merely condensed from its vapor; or how do you know that they are not those identical drops superficially lodged in the spout-hole fissure, which is countersunk into the summit of the whale's head? For even when tranquilly swimming through the mid-day sea in a calm, with his elevated hump sun-dried as a dromedary's in the desert; even then, the whale always carries a small basin of water on his head, as under a blazing sun you will sometimes see a cavity in a rock filled up with rain.

Nor is it at all prudent for the hunter to be over curious touching the precise nature of the whale spout. It will not do for him to be peering into it, and putting his face in it. You cannot go with your pitcher to this fountain and fill it, and bring it away. For even when coming into slight contact with the outer, vapory shreds of the jet, which will often happen, your skin will feverishly smart, from the acridness of the thing so touching it. And I know one, who coming into still closer contact with the spout, whether with some scientific object in view, or otherwise, I cannot say, the skin peeled off from his cheek and arm. Wherefore, among whalemen, the spout is deemed poisonous; they try to evade it. Another thing; I have heard it said, and I do not much doubt it, that if the jet is fairly spouted into your eyes, it will blind you. The wisest thing the investigator can do then, it seems to me, is to let this deadly spout alone.

Still, we can hypothesize, even if we cannot prove and establish. My hypothesis is this: that the spout is nothing but mist. And besides other reasons, to this conclusion I am impelled, by considerations touching the great inherent dignity and sublimity of the Sperm Whale; I account him no common, shallow being, inasmuch as it is an undisputed fact that he is never found on soundings, or near shores; all other whales sometimes are. He is both ponderous and profound. And I am convinced that from the heads of all ponderous profound beings, such as Plato, Pyrrho, the Devil, Jupiter, Dante, and so on, there always goes up a certain semi-visible steam, while in the act of thinking deep thoughts. While composing a little treatise on Eternity, I had the curiosity to place a mirror before me; and ere long saw reflected there, a curious involved worming and undulation in the atmosphere over my head. The invariable moisture of my hair, while plunged in deep thought, after six cups of hot tea in my thin shingled attic, of an August noon; this seems an additional argument for the above supposition.

And how nobly it raises our conceit of the mighty, misty monster, to behold him solemnly sailing through a calm tropical sea; his vast, mild head overhung by a canopy of vapor, engendered by his incommunicable contemplations, and that vapor—as you will sometimes see it—glorified by a rainbow, as if Heaven itself had put its seal upon his thoughts. For, d'ye see, rainbows do not visit the clear air; they only irradiate vapor. And so, through all the thick mists of the dim doubts in my mind, divine intuitions now and then shoot, enkindling my fog with a heavenly ray. And for this I thank God; for all have doubts; many deny; but doubts or denials, few along with them, have intuitions. Doubts of all things earthly, and intuitions of some things heavenly; this combination makes neither believer nor infidel, but makes a man who regards them both with equal eye.

# Chapter 86

## *The Tail*

OTHER POETS have warbled the praises of the soft eye of the antelope, and the lovely plumage of the bird that never alights; less celestial, I celebrate a tail.

Reckoning the largest sized Sperm Whale's tail to begin at that point of the trunk where it tapers to about the girth of a man, it comprises upon its upper surface alone, an area of at least fifty square feet. The compact round body of its root expands into two broad, firm, flat palms or flukes, gradually shoaling away to less than an inch in thickness. At the crotch or junction, these flukes slightly overlap, then sideways recede from each other like wings, leaving a wide vacancy between. In no living thing are the lines of beauty more exquisitely defined than in the crescentic borders of these flukes. At its utmost expansion in the full grown whale, the tail will considerably exceed twenty feet across.

The entire member seems a dense webbed bed of welded sinews; but cut into it, and you find that three distinct strata compose it:—upper, middle, and lower. The fibres in the upper and lower layers, are long and horizontal; those of the middle one, very short, and running crosswise between the outside layers. This triune structure, as much as anything else, imparts power to the tail. To the student of old Roman walls, the middle layer will furnish a curious parallel to the thin course of tiles always alternating with the stone in those wonderful relics of the antique, and which undoubtedly contribute so much to the great strength of the masonry.

But as if this vast local power in the tendinous tail were not enough, the whole bulk of the leviathan is knit over with a warp and woof of muscular fibres and filaments, which passing on either side the loins and running down into the flukes, insensibly blend with them, and largely contribute to their might; so that in the tail the confluent measureless force of the whole whale seems concentrated to a point. Could annihilation occur to matter, this were the thing to do it.

Nor does this—its amazing strength, at all tend to cripple the graceful flexion of its motions; where infantileness of ease undulates through a Titanism of power. On the contrary, those motions derive their most appalling beauty from it. Real strength never impairs beauty or harmony, but it often bestows it; and in everything imposingly beautiful, strength has much to do with the magic. Take away the tied tendons that all over seem bursting from the marble in the carved Hercules, and its charm would be gone. As devout Eckermann lifted the linen sheet from the naked corpse of Goethe, he was overwhelmed with the massive chest of the man, that seemed as a Roman triumphal arch. When Angelo paints even God the Father in human form, mark what robustness is there. And whatever they may reveal of the divine love in the Son, the soft, curled, hermaphroditical Italian pictures, in which his idea has been most successfully embodied; these pictures, so destitute as they are of all brawniness, hint nothing of any power, but the mere negative, feminine one of submission and endurance, which on all hands it is conceded, form the peculiar practical virtues of his teachings.

Such is the subtle elasticity of the organ I treat of, that whether wielded in sport, or in earnest, or in anger, whatever be the mood it be in, its flexions are invariably marked by exceeding grace. Therein no fairy's arm can transcend it.

Five great motions are peculiar to it. First, when used as a fin for progression; Second, when used as a mace in battle; Third, in sweeping; Fourth, in lobtailing; Fifth, in peaking flukes.

First: Being horizontal in its position, the Leviathan's tail acts in a different manner from the tails of all other sea creatures. It never wriggles. In man or fish, wriggling is a sign of inferiority. To the whale, his tail is the sole means of propulsion. Scroll-wise coiled forwards beneath the body, and then rapidly sprung backwards, it is this which gives that singular darting, leaping motion to the monster when furiously swimming. His side-fins only serve to steer by.

Second: It is a little significant, that while one sperm whale only fights another sperm whale with his head and jaw, nevertheless, in his conflicts with man, he chiefly and contemptuously uses his tail. In striking at a boat, he swiftly curves away his flukes from it, and the blow is only inflicted by the recoil. If it be made in the unobstructed air, especially if it descend to its mark, the stroke is then simply irresistible. No ribs of man or boat can withstand it. Your only salvation lies in eluding it; but if it comes sideways through the opposing water, then partly owing to the light buoyancy of the whale-boat, and the elasticity of its materials, a cracked rib or a dashed plank or two, a sort of stitch in the side, is generally the most serious result. These submerged side blows are so often received in the fishery, that they are accounted mere child's play. Some one strips off a frock, and the hole is stopped.

Third: I cannot demonstrate it, but it seems to me, that in the whale the sense of touch is concentrated in the tail; for in this respect there is a delicacy in it only equalled by the daintiness of the elephant's trunk. This delicacy is chiefly evinced in the action of sweeping, when in maidenly gentleness the whale with a certain soft slowness moves his immense flukes from side to side upon the surface of the sea; and if he feel but a sailor's whisker, woe to that sailor, whiskers and all. What tenderness there is in that preliminary touch! Had this tail any prehensile power, I should straightway bethink me of Darmonodes' elephant that so frequented the flower-market, and with low salutations presented nosegays to damsels, and then caressed their zones. On more accounts than one, a pity it is that the whale does not possess this prehensile virtue in his tail; for I have heard of yet another elephant, that when wounded in the fight, curved round his trunk and extracted the dart.

Fourth: Stealing unawares upon the whale in the fancied security of the middle of solitary seas, you find him unbent from the vast corpulence of his dignity, and kitten-like, he plays on the ocean as if it were a hearth. But still you see his power in his play. The broad palms of his tail are flirted high into the air; then smiting the surface, the thunderous concussion resounds for miles. You would almost think a great gun had been discharged; and if you noticed the light wreath of vapor from the spiracle at his other extremity, you would think that that was the smoke from the touch-hole.

Fifth: As in the ordinary floating posture of the leviathan the flukes lie considerably below the level of his back, they are then completely out of sight beneath the surface; but when he is about to plunge into the deeps, his entire flukes with at least thirty feet of his body are tossed erect in the air, and so remain vibrating a moment, till they downwards shoot out of view. Excepting the sublime *breach*—somewhere else to be described—this peaking of the whale's flukes is perhaps the grandest sight to be seen in all animated nature. Out of the bottomless profundities the gigantic tail seems spasmodically snatching at the highest heaven. So in dreams, have I seen majestic Satan thrusting forth his tormented colossal claw from the flame Baltic of Hell. But in gazing at such scenes, it is all in all what mood you are in; if in the Dantean, the devils will occur to you; if in that of Isaiah, the archangels. Standing at the mast-head of my ship during a sunrise that crimsoned sky and sea, I once saw a large herd of whales in the east, all heading towards the sun, and for a moment vibrating in concert with peaked flukes. As it seemed to me at the time, such a grand embodiment of adoration of the gods was never beheld, even in Persia, the home of the fire worshippers. As Ptolemy Philopater testified of the African elephant, I then testified of the whale, pronouncing him the most devout of all beings. For according to King Juba, the military elephants of antiquity often hailed the morning with their trunks uplifted in the profoundest silence.

The chance comparison in this chapter, between the whale and the elephant, so far as some aspects of the tail of the one and the trunk of the other are concerned, should not tend to place those two opposite organs on an equality, much less the creatures to which they respectively belong. For as the mightiest elephant is but a terrier to Leviathan, so, compared with Leviathan's tail, his trunk is but the stalk of a lily. The most direful blow from the elephant's trunk were as the playful tap of a fan, compared with the measureless crush and crash of the sperm whale's ponderous flukes, which in repeated instances have one after the other hurled entire boats with all their oars and crews into the air, very much as an Indian juggler tosses his balls.*

The more I consider this mighty tail, the more do I deplore my inability to express it. At times there are gestures in it, which, though they would well grace the hand of man, remain wholly inexplicable. In an extensive herd, so remarkable, occasionally, are these mystic gestures, that I have heard hunters who have declared them akin to Free-Mason signs and

---

* Though all comparison in the way of general bulk between the whale and the elephant is preposterous, inasmuch as in that particular the elephant stands in much the same respect to the whale that a dog does to the elephant; nevertheless, there are not wanting some points of curious similitude; among these is the spout. It is well known that the elephant will often draw up water or dust in his trunk, and then elevating it, jet it forth in a stream.

symbols; that the whale, indeed, by these methods intelligently conversed with the world. Nor are there wanting other motions of the whale in his general body, full of strangeness, and unaccountable to his most experienced assailant. Dissect him how I may, then, I but go skin deep; I know him not, and never will. But if I know not even the tail of this whale, how understand his head? much more, how comprehend his face, when face he has none? Thou shalt see my back parts, my tail, he seems to say, but my face shall not be seen. But I cannot completely make out his back parts; and hint what he will about his face, I say again he has no face.

# Chapter 87

*The Grand Armada*

THE LONG and narrow peninsula of Malacca, extending south-eastward from the territories of Birmah, forms the most southerly point of all Asia. In a continuous line from that peninsula stretch the long islands of Sumatra, Java, Bally, and Timor; which, with many others, form a vast mole, or rampart, lengthwise connecting Asia with Australia, and dividing the long unbroken Indian ocean from the thickly studded oriental archipelagoes. This rampart is pierced by several sally-ports for the convenience of ships and whales; conspicuous among which are the straits of Sunda and Malacca. By the straits of Sunda, chiefly, vessels bound to China from the west, emerge into the China seas.

Those narrow straits of Sunda divide Sumatra from Java; and standing midway in that vast rampart of islands, buttressed by that bold green promontory, known to seamen as Java Head; they not a little correspond to the central gateway opening into some vast walled empire: and considering the inexhaustible wealth of spices, and silks, and jewels, and gold, and ivory, with which the thousand islands of that oriental sea are enriched, it seems a significant provision of nature, that such treasures, by the very formation of the land, should at least bear the appearance, however ineffectual, of being guarded from the all-grasping western world. The shores of the Straits of Sunda are unsupplied with those domineering

fortresses which guard the entrances to the Mediterranean, the Baltic, and
the Propontis. Unlike the Danes, these Orientals do not demand the
obsequious homage of lowered top-sails from the endless procession of
ships before the wind, which for centuries past, by night and by day, have
passed between the islands of Sumatra and Java, freighted with the costliest
cargoes of the east. But while they freely waive a ceremonial like this, they do
by no means renounce their claim to more solid tribute.

Time out of mind the piratical proas of the Malays, lurking among the
low shaded coves and islets of Sumatra, have sallied out upon the vessels
sailing through the straits, fiercely demanding tribute at the point of their
spears. Though by the repeated bloody chastisements they have received at
the hands of European cruisers, the audacity of these corsairs has of late been
somewhat repressed; yet, even at the present day, we occasionally hear of
English and American vessels, which, in those waters, have been remorselessly boarded and pillaged.

With a fair, fresh wind, the Pequod was now drawing nigh to these
straits; Ahab purposing to pass through them into the Javan sea, and thence,
cruising northwards, over waters known to be frequented here and there
by the Sperm Whale, sweep inshore by the Philippine Islands, and gain the
far coast of Japan, in time for the great whaling season there. By these
means, the circumnavigating Pequod would sweep almost all the known
Sperm Whale cruising grounds of the world, previous to descending upon
the Line in the Pacific; where Ahab, though everywhere else foiled in his
pursuit, firmly counted upon giving battle to Moby Dick, in the sea he was
most known to frequent; and at a season when he might most reasonably
be presumed to be haunting it.

But how now? in this zoned quest, does Ahab touch no land? does his
crew drink air? Surely, he will stop for water. Nay. For a long time, now,
the circus-running sun has raced within his fiery ring, and needs no
sustenance but what's in himself. So Ahab. Mark this, too, in the whaler.
While other hulls are loaded down with alien stuff, to be transferred to
foreign wharves; the world-wandering whale-ship carries no cargo but
herself and crew, their weapons and their wants. She has a whole lake's
contents bottled in her ample hold. She is ballasted with utilities; not
altogether with unusable pig-lead and kentledge. She carries years' water in
her. Clear old prime Nantucket water; which, when three years afloat, the
Nantucketer, in the Pacific, prefers to drink before the brackish fluid, but
yesterday rafted off in casks, from the Peruvian or Indian streams. Hence it
is, that, while other ships may have gone to China from New York, and

back again, touching at a score of ports, the whale-ship, in all that interval, may not have sighted one grain of soil; her crew having seen no man but floating seamen like themselves. So that did you carry them the news that another flood had come; they would only answer—"Well, boys, here's the ark!"

Now, as many Sperm Whales had been captured off the western coast of Java, in the near vicinity of the Straits of Sunda; indeed, as most of the ground, roundabout, was generally recognised by the fishermen as an excellent spot for cruising; therefore, as the Pequod gained more and more upon Java Head, the look-outs were repeatedly hailed, and admonished to keep wide awake. But though the green palmy cliffs of the land soon loomed on the starboard bow, and with delighted nostrils the fresh cinnamon was snuffed in the air, yet not a single jet was descried. Almost renouncing all thought of falling in with any game hereabouts, the ship had well nigh entered the straits, when the customary cheering cry was heard from aloft, and ere long a spectacle of singular magnificence saluted us.

But here be it premised, that owing to the unwearied activity with which of late they have been hunted over all four oceans, the Sperm Whales, instead of almost invariably sailing in small detached companies, as in former times, are now frequently met with in extensive herds, sometimes embracing so great a multitude, that it would almost seem as if numerous nations of them had sworn solemn league and covenant for mutual assistance and protection. To this aggregation of the Sperm Whale into such immense caravans, may be imputed the circumstance that even in the best cruising grounds, you may now sometimes sail for weeks and months together, without being greeted by a single spout; and then be suddenly saluted by what sometimes seems thousands on thousands.

Broad on both bows, at the distance of some two or three miles, and forming a great semicircle, embracing one half of the level horizon, a continuous chain of whale-jets were up-playing and sparkling in the noon-day air. Unlike the straight perpendicular twin-jets of the Right Whale, which, dividing at top, fall over in two branches, like the cleft drooping boughs of a willow, the single forward-slanting spout of the Sperm Whale presents a thick curled bush of white mist, continually rising and falling away to leeward.

Seen from the Pequod's deck, then, as she would rise on a high hill of the sea, this host of vapory spouts, individually curling up into the air, and beheld through a blending atmosphere of bluish haze, showed like the thousand cheerful chimneys of some dense metropolis, descried of a balmy autumnal morning, by some horseman on a height.

As marching armies approaching an unfriendly defile in the mountains, accelerate their march, all eagerness to place that perilous passage in their rear, and once more expand in comparative security upon the plain; even so did this vast fleet of whales now seem hurrying forward through the straits; gradually contracting the wings of their semicircle, and swimming on, in one solid, but still crescentic centre.

Crowding all sail the Pequod pressed after them; the harpooneers handling their weapons, and loudly cheering from the heads of their yet suspended boats. If the wind only held, little doubt had they, that chased through these Straits of Sunda, the vast host would only deploy into the Oriental seas to witness the capture of not a few of their number. And who could tell whether, in that congregated caravan, Moby Dick himself might not temporarily be swimming, like the worshipped white-elephant in the coronation procession of the Siamese! So with stun-sail piled on stun-sail, we sailed along, driving these leviathans before us; when, of a sudden, the voice of Tashtego was heard, loudly directing attention to something in our wake.

Corresponding to the crescent in our van, we beheld another in our rear. It seemed formed of detached white vapors, rising and falling something like the spouts of the whales; only they did not so completely come and go; for they constantly hovered, without finally disappearing. Levelling his glass at this sight, Ahab quickly revolved in his pivot-hole, crying, "Aloft there, and rig whips and buckets to wet the sails;—Malays, sir, and after us!"

As if too long lurking behind the headlands, till the Pequod should fairly have entered the straits, these rascally Asiatics were now in hot pursuit, to make up for their over-cautious delay. But when the swift Pequod, with a fresh leading wind, was herself in hot chase; how very kind of these tawny philanthropists to assist in speeding her on to her own chosen pursuit,—mere riding-whips and rowels to her, that they were. As with glass under arm, Ahab to-and-fro paced the deck; in his forward turn beholding the monsters he chased, and in the after one the bloodthirsty pirates chasing *him;* some such fancy as the above seemed his. And when he glanced upon the green walls of the watery defile in which the ship was then sailing, and bethought him that through that gate lay the route to his vengeance, and beheld, how that through that same gate he was now both chasing and being chased . his deadly end; and not only that, but a herd of

remorseless wild pirates and inhuman atheistical devils were infernally
cheering him on with their curses;—when all these conceits had passed
through his brain, Ahab's brow was left gaunt and ribbed, like the black
sand beach after some stormy tide has been gnawing it, without being able
to drag the firm thing from its place.

But thoughts like these troubled very few of the reckless crew; and
when, after steadily dropping and dropping the pirates astern, the Pequod
at last shot by the vivid green Cockatoo Point on the Sumatra side, emerging at last upon the broad waters beyond; then, the harpooneers seemed
more to grieve that the swift whales had been gaining upon the ship, than to
rejoice that the ship had so victoriously gained upon the Malays. But still
driving on in the wake of the whales, at length they seemed abating their
speed; gradually the ship neared them; and the wind now dying away,
word was passed to spring to the boats. But no sooner did the herd, by some
presumed wonderful instinct of the Sperm Whale, become notified of the
three keels that were after them,—though as yet a mile in their rear,—than
they rallied again, and forming in close ranks and battalions, so that their
spouts all looked like flashing lines of stacked bayonets, moved on with
redoubled velocity.

Stripped to our shirts and drawers, we sprang to the white-ash, and
after several hours' pulling were almost disposed to renounce the chase,
when a general pausing commotion among the whales gave animating
token that they were now at last under the influence of that strange perplexity of inert irresolution, which, when the fishermen perceive it in the
whale, they say he is *gallied*.* The compact martial columns in which they
had been hitherto rapidly and steadily swimming, were now broken up in
one measureless rout; and like King Porus' elephants in the Indian battle

* To *gally*, or *gallow*, is to frighten excessively,—to confound with fright. It is an old
Saxon word. It occurs once in Shakspere:—

> "The wrathful skies
> *Gallow* the very wanderers of the dark,
> And make them keep their caves."

Lear, Act III. sc. ii.

To common land usages, the word is now completely obsolete. When the polite landsman first hears it from the gaunt Nantucketer, he is apt to set it down as one of the whaleman's self-derived savageries. Much the same is it with many other sinewy Saxonisms of
this sort, which emigrated to the New-England rocks with the noble brawn of the old
English emigrants in the time of the Commonwealth. Thus, some of the best and furthest-
descended English words—the etymological Howards and Percys—are now democratised,
nay, plebeianised—so to speak—in the New World.

with Alexander, they seemed going mad with consternation. In all directions expanding in vast irregular circles, and aimlessly swimming hither and thither, by their short thick spoutings, they plainly betrayed their distraction of panic. This was still more strangely evinced by those of their number, who, completely paralysed as it were, helplessly floated like water-logged dismantled ships on the sea. Had these leviathans been but a flock of simple sheep, pursued over the pasture by three fierce wolves, they could not possibly have evinced such excessive dismay. But this occasional timidity is characteristic of almost all herding creatures. Though banding together in tens of thousands, the lion-maned buffaloes of the West have fled before a solitary horseman. Witness, too, all human beings, how when herded together in the sheepfold of a theatre's pit, they will, at the slightest alarm of fire, rush helter-skelter for the outlets, crowding, trampling, jamming, and remorselessly dashing each other to death. Best, therefore, withhold any amazement at the strangely gallied whales before us, for there is no folly of the beasts of the earth which is not infinitely outdone by the madness of men.

Though many of the whales, as has been said, were in violent motion, yet it is to be observed that as a whole the herd neither advanced nor retreated, but collectively remained in one place. As is customary in those cases, the boats at once separated, each making for some one lone whale on the outskirts of the shoal. In about three minutes' time, Queequeg's harpoon was flung; the stricken fish darted blinding spray in our faces, and then running away with us like light, steered straight for the heart of the herd. Though such a movement on the part of the whale struck under such circumstances, is in no wise unprecedented; and indeed is almost always more or less anticipated; yet does it present one of the more perilous vicissitudes of the fishery. For as the swift monster drags you deeper and deeper into the frantic shoal, you bid adieu to circumspect life and only exist in a delirious throb.

As, blind and deaf, the whale plunged forward, as if by sheer power of speed to rid himself of the iron leech that had fastened to him; as we thus tore a white gash in the sea, on all sides menaced as we flew, by the crazed creatures to and fro rushing about us; our beset boat was like a ship mobbed by ice-isles in a tempest, and striving to steer through their complicated channels and straits, knowing not at what moment it may be locked in and crushed.

But not a bit daunted, Queequeg steered us manfully; now sheering off from this monster directly across our route in advance; now edging away from that, whose colossal flukes were suspended overhead, while all the time, Starbuck stood up in the bows, lance in hand, pricking out of our way whatever whales he could reach by short darts, for there was no time to make long ones. Nor were the oarsmen quite idle, though their wonted duty was now altogether dispensed with. They chiefly attended to the shouting part of the business. "Out of the way, Commodore!" cried one, to a great dromedary that of a sudden rose bodily to the surface, and for an instant threatened to swamp us. "Hard down with your tail, there!" cried a second to another, which, close to our gunwale, seemed calmly cooling himself with his own fan-like extremity.

All whaleboats carry certain curious contrivances, originally invented by the Nantucket Indians, called druggs. Two thick squares of wood of equal size are stoutly clenched together, so that they cross each other's grain at right angles; a line of considerable length is then attached to the middle of this block, and the other end of the line being looped, it can in a moment be fastened to a harpoon. It is chiefly among gallied whales that this drugg is used. For then, more whales are close round you than you can possibly chase at one time. But sperm whales are not every day encountered; while you may, then, you must kill all you can. And if you cannot kill them all at once, you must wing them, so that they can be afterwards killed at your leisure. Hence it is, that at times like these the drugg comes into requisition. Our boat was furnished with three of them. The first and second were successfully darted, and we saw the whales staggeringly running off, fettered by the enormous sidelong resistance of the towing drugg. They were cramped like malefactors with the chain and ball. But upon flinging the third, in the act of tossing overboard the clumsy wooden block, it caught under one of the seats of the boat, and in an instant tore it out and carried it away, dropping the oarsman in the boat's bottom as the seat slid from under him. On both sides the sea came in at the wounded planks, but we stuffed two or three drawers and shirts in, and so stopped the leaks for the time.

It had been next to impossible to dart these drugged-harpoons, were it not that as we advanced into the herd, our whale's way greatly diminished; moreover, that as we went still further and further from the circumference of commotion, the direful disorders seemed waning. So that when at last the jerking harpoon drew out, and the towing whale sideways vanished; then, with the tapering force of his parting momentum, we glided between two whales into the innermost heart of the shoal, as if from some mountain torrent we had slid into a serene valley lake. Here the storms in the roaring glens between the outermost whales, were heard but not felt. In this central expanse the sea presented that smooth satin-like surface, called a sleek, produced by the subtle moisture thrown off by the whale in his more quiet moods. Yes, we were now in that enchanted calm which they say lurks at the heart of every commotion. And still in the distracted distance we beheld the tumults of the outer concentric circles, and saw successive pods of whales, eight or ten in each, swiftly going round and round, like multiplied spans of horses in a ring; and so closely shoulder to shoulder, that a Titanic circus-rider might easily have overarched the middle ones, and so have gone round on their backs. Owing to the density of the crowd of reposing whales, more immediately surrounding the embayed axis of the herd, no possible chance of escape was at present afforded us. We must watch for a breach in the living wall that hemmed us in; the wall that had only admitted us in order to shut us up. Keeping at the centre of the lake, we were occasionally visited by small tame cows and calves; the women and children of this routed host.

Now, inclusive of the occasional wide intervals between the revolving outer circles, and inclusive of the spaces between the various pods in any one of those circles, the entire area at this juncture, embraced by the whole multitude, must have contained at least two or three square miles. At any rate—though indeed such a test at such a time might be deceptive—spoutings might be discovered from our low boat that seemed playing up almost from the rim of the horizon. I mention this circumstance, because, as if the cows and calves had been purposely locked up in this innermost fold; and as if the wide extent of the herd had hitherto prevented them from learning the precise cause of its stopping; or, possibly, being so young, unsophisticated, and every way innocent and inexperienced; however it may have been, these smaller whales—now and then visiting our becalmed boat from the margin of the lake—evinced a wondrous fearlessness and confidence, or else a still, becharmed panic which it was impossible not to marvel at. Like household dogs they came snuffling round us, right up to our gunwales, and touching them; till it almost seemed that some spell had suddenly domesticated them. Queequeg patted their foreheads; Starbuck scratched their backs with his lance; but fearful of the consequences, for the time refrained from darting it.

But far beneath this wondrous world upon the surface, another and still stranger world met our eyes as we gazed over the side. For, suspended in those watery vaults, floated the forms of the nursing mothers of the whales, and those that by their enormous girth seemed shortly to become mothers.

The lake, as I have hinted, was to a considerable depth exceedingly transparent; and as human infants while suckling will calmly and fixedly gaze
away from the breast, as if leading two different lives at the time; and while
yet drawing mortal nourishment, be still spiritually feasting upon some unearthly reminiscence;—even so did the young of these whales seem looking
up towards us, but not at us, as if we were but a bit of Gulf-weed in their
new-born sight. Floating on their sides, the mothers also seemed quietly
eyeing us. One of these little infants, that from certain queer tokens seemed
hardly a day old, might have measured some fourteen feet in length, and
some six feet in girth. He was a little frisky; though as yet his body seemed
scarce yet recovered from that irksome position it had so lately occupied in
the maternal reticule; where, tail to head, and all ready for the final spring,
the unborn whale lies bent like a Tartar's bow. The delicate side-fins, and
the palms of his flukes, still freshly retained the plaited crumpled appearance
of a baby's ears newly arrived from foreign parts.

"Line! line!" cried Queequeg, looking over the gunwale; "him fast!
him fast!—Who line him! Who struck?—Two whale; one big, one little!"

"What ails ye, man?"cried Starbuck.

"Look-e here," said Queequeg pointing down.

As when the stricken whale, that from the tub has reeled out hundreds of
fathoms of rope; as, after deep sounding, he floats up again, and shows the
slackened curling line buoyantly rising and spiralling towards the air; so
now, Starbuck saw long coils of the umbilical cord of Madame Leviathan,
by which the young cub seemed still tethered to its dam. Not seldom in the
rapid vicissitudes of the chase, this natural line, with the maternal end
loose, becomes entangled with the hempen one, so that the cub is thereby
trapped. Some of the subtlest secrets of the seas seemed divulged to us in this
enchanted pond. We saw young Leviathan amours in the deep.*

And thus, though surrounded by circle upon circle of consternations
and affrights, did these inscrutable creatures at the centre freely and fearlessly indulge in all peaceful concernments; yea, serenely revelled in

---

* The sperm whale, as with all other species of the Leviathan, but unlike most other
fish, breeds indifferently at all seasons; after a gestation which may probably be set down
at nine months, producing but one at a time; though in some few known instances giving
birth to an Esau and Jacob:—a contingency provided for in suckling by two teats, curiously
situated, one on each side of the anus; but the breasts themselves extend upwards from that.
When by chance these precious parts in a nursing whale are cut by the hunter's lance, the
mother's pouring milk and blood rivallingly discolor the sea for rods. The milk is very
sweet and rich; it has been tasted by man; it might do well with strawberries. When
overflowing with mutual esteem, the whales salute *more hominum*.

dalliance and delight. But even so, amid the tornadoed Atlantic of my being, do I myself still for ever centrally disport in mute calm; and while ponderous planets of unwaning woe revolve round me, deep down and deep inland there I still bathe me in eternal mildness of joy.

Meanwhile, as we thus lay entranced, the occasional sudden frantic spectacles in the distance evinced the activity of the other boats, still engaged in drugging the whales on the frontier of the host; or possibly carrying on the war within the first circle, where abundance of room and some convenient retreats were afforded them. But the sight of the enraged drugged whales now and then blindly darting to and fro across the circles, was nothing to what at last met our eyes. It is sometimes the custom when fast to a whale more than commonly powerful and alert, to seek to hamstring him, as it were, by sundering or maiming his gigantic tail-tendon. It is done by darting a short-handled cutting-spade, to which is attached a rope for hauling it back again. A whale wounded (as we afterwards learned) in this part, but not effectually, as it seemed, had broken away from the boat, carrying along with him half of the harpoon line; and in the extraordinary agony of the wound, he was now dashing among the revolving circles like the lone mounted desperado Arnold, at the battle of Saratoga, carrying dismay wherever he went.

But agonizing as was the wound of this whale, and an appalling spectacle enough, any way; yet the peculiar horror with which he seemed to inspire the rest of the herd, was owing to a cause which at first the intervening distance obscured from us. But at length we perceived that by one of the unimaginable accidents of the fishery, this whale had become entangled in the harpoon-line that he towed; he had also run away with the cutting-spade in him; and while the free end of the rope attached to that weapon, had permanently caught in the coils of the harpoon-line round his tail, the cutting-spade itself had worked loose from his flesh. So that tormented to madness, he was now churning through the water, violently flailing with his flexible tail, and tossing the keen spade about him, wounding and murdering his own comrades.

This terrific object seemed to recall the whole herd from their stationary fright. First, the whales forming the margin of our lake began to crowd a little, and tumble against each other, as if lifted by half spent billows from afar; then the lake itself began faintly to heave and swell; the submarine bridal-chambers and nurseries vanished; in more and more contracting orbits the whales in the more central circles began to swim in thickening clusters. Yes, the long calm was departing. A low advancing hum was soon heard; and then like to the tumultuous masses of block-ice when the great river Hudson breaks up in Spring, the entire host of whales came tumbling upon their inner centre, as if to pile themselves up in one common mountain. Instantly Starbuck and Queequeg changed places; Starbuck taking the stern.

"Oars! Oars!" he intensely whispered, seizing the helm—"gripe your oars, and clutch your souls, now! My God, men, stand by! Shove him off, you Queequeg—the whale there!—prick him!—hit him! Stand up—stand up, and stay so! Spring, men—pull, men; never mind their backs—scrape them!—scrape away!"

The boat was now all but jammed between two vast black bulks, leaving a narrow Dardanelles between their long lengths. But by desperate endeavor we at last shot into a temporary opening; then giving way rapidly, and at the same time earnestly watching for another outlet. After many similar hair-breadth escapes, we at last swiftly glided into what had just been one of the outer circles, but now crossed by random whales, all violently making for one centre. This lucky salvation was cheaply purchased by the loss of Queequeg's hat, who, while standing in the bows to prick the fugitive whales, had his hat taken clean from his head by the air-eddy made by the sudden tossing of a pair of broad flukes close by.

Riotous and disordered as the universal commotion now was, it soon resolved itself into what seemed a systematic movement; for having clumped together at last in one dense body, they then renewed their onward flight with augmented fleetness. Further pursuit was useless; but the boats still lingered in their wake to pick up what drugged whales might be dropped astern, and likewise to secure one which Flask had killed and waifed. The waif is a pennoned pole, two or three of which are carried by every boat; and which, when additional game is at hand, are inserted upright into the floating body of a dead whale, both to mark its place on the sea, and also as token of prior possession, should the boats of any other ship draw near.

The result of this lowering was somewhat illustrative of that sagacious saying in the Fishery,—the more whales the less fish. Of all the drugged whales only one was captured. The rest contrived to escape for the time, but only to be taken, as will hereafter be seen, by some other craft than the Pequod.

# Chapter 88

*Schools and Schoolmasters*

THE PREVIOUS CHAPTER gave account of an immense body or herd of Sperm Whales, and there was also then given the probable cause inducing those vast aggregations.

Now, though such great bodies are at times encountered, yet, as must have been seen, even at the present day, small detached bands are occasionally observed, embracing from twenty to fifty individuals each. Such bands are known as schools. They generally are of two sorts; those composed almost entirely of females, and those mustering none but young vigorous males, or bulls, as they are familiarly designated.

In cavalier attendance upon the school of females, you invariably see a male of full grown magnitude, but not old; who, upon any alarm, evinces his gallantry by falling in the rear and covering the flight of his ladies. In truth, this gentleman is a luxurious Ottoman, swimming about over the watery world, surroundingly accompanied by all the solaces and endearments of the harem. The contrast between this Ottoman and his concubines is striking; because, while he is always of the largest leviathanic proportions, the ladies, even at full growth, are not more than one third of the bulk of an average-sized male. They are comparatively delicate, indeed; I dare say, not to exceed half a dozen yards round the waist. Nevertheless, it cannot be denied, that upon the whole they are hereditarily entitled to *en bon point*.

It is very curious to watch this harem and its lord in their indolent ramblings. Like fashionables, they are for ever on the move in leisurely search of variety. You meet them on the Line in time for the full flower of the Equatorial feeding season, having just returned, perhaps, from spending the summer in the Northern seas, and so cheating summer of all unpleasant weariness and warmth. By the time they have lounged up and down the promenade of the Equator awhile, they start for the Oriental waters in anticipation of the cool season there, and so evade the other excessive temperature of the year.

When serenely advancing on one of these journeys, if any strange suspicious sights are seen, my lord whale keeps a wary eye on his interesting family. Should any unwarrantably pert young Leviathan coming that way, presume to draw confidentially close to one of the ladies, with what prodigious fury the Bashaw assails him, and chases him away! High times, indeed, if unprincipled young rakes like him are to be permitted to invade the sanctity of domestic bliss; though do what the Bashaw will, he cannot keep the most notorious Lothario out of his bed; for, alas! all fish bed in common. As ashore, the ladies often cause the most terrible duels among their rival admirers; just so with the whales, who sometimes come to deadly battle, and all for love. They fence with their long lower jaws, sometimes locking them together, and so striving for the supremacy like elks that warringly interweave their antlers. Not a few are captured having the deep scars of these encounters,—furrowed heads, broken teeth, scolloped fins; and in some instances, wrenched and dislocated mouths.

But supposing the invader of domestic bliss to betake himself away at the first rush of the harem's lord, then is it very diverting to watch that lord. Gently he insinuates his vast bulk among them again and revels there awhile, still in tantalizing vicinity to young Lothario, like pious Solomon devoutly worshipping among his thousand concubines. Granting other whales to be in sight, the fishermen will seldom give chase to one of these Grand Turks; for these Grand Turks are too lavish of their strength, and hence their unctuousness is small. As for the sons and the daughters they beget, why, those sons and daughters must take care of themselves; at least, with only the maternal help. For like certain other omnivorous roving lovers that might be named, my Lord Whale has no taste for the nursery, however much for the bower; and so, being a great traveller, he leaves his anonymous babies all over the world; every baby an exotic. In good time, nevertheless, as the ardor of youth declines; as years and dumps increase; as reflection lends her solemn pauses; in short, as a general lassitude overtakes the sated Turk; then a love of ease and virtue supplants the love for maidens; our Ottoman enters upon the impotent, repentant, admonitory stage of life, forswears, disbands the harem, and grown to an exemplary, sulky old soul, goes about all alone among the meridians and parallels saying his prayers, and warning each young Leviathan from his amorous errors.

Now, as the harem of whales is called by the fishermen a school, so is the lord and master of that school technically known as the schoolmaster. It is therefore not in strict character, however admirably satirical, that after going to school himself, he should then go abroad inculcating not what he learned there, but the folly of it. His title, schoolmaster, would very naturally seem derived from the name bestowed upon the harem itself, but some have surmised that the man who first thus entitled this sort of Ottoman whale, must have read the memoirs of Vidocq, and informed himself what sort of a country-schoolmaster that famous Frenchman was in his younger days, and what was the nature of those occult lessons he inculcated into some of his pupils.

The same secludedness and isolation to which the schoolmaster whale betakes himself in his advancing years, is true of all aged Sperm Whales. Almost universally, a lone whale—as a solitary Leviathan is called—proves an ancient one. Like venerable moss-bearded Daniel Boone, he will have no one near him but Nature herself; and her he takes to wife in the wilderness of waters, and the best of wives she is, though she keeps so many moody secrets.

The schools composing none but young and vigorous males, previously mentioned, offer a strong contrast to the harem schools. For while those female whales are characteristically timid, the young males, or forty-barrel-bulls, as they call them, are by far the most pugnacious of all Leviathans, and proverbially the most dangerous to encounter; excepting those wondrous greyheaded, grizzled whales, sometimes met, and these will fight you like grim fiends exasperated by a penal gout.

The Forty-barrel-bull schools are larger than the harem schools. Like a mob of young collegians, they are full of fight, fun, and wickedness, tumbling round the world at such a reckless, rollicking rate, that no prudent underwriter would insure them any more than he would a riotous lad at Yale or Harvard. They soon relinquish this turbulence though, and when about three fourths grown, break up, and separately go about in quest of settlements, that is, harems.

Another point of difference between the male and female schools is still more characteristic of the sexes. Say you strike a Forty-barrel-bull—

poor devil! all his comrades quit him. But strike a member of the harem school, and her companions swim around her with every token of concern, sometimes lingering so near her and so long, as themselves to fall a prey.

# Chapter 89

### Fast-Fish and Loose-Fish

T HE ALLUSION TO THE WAIFS and waif-poles in the last chapter
but one, necessitates some account of the laws and regulations of
the whale fishery, of which the waif may be deemed the grand
symbol and badge.

It frequently happens that when several ships are cruising in company, a
whale may be struck by one vessel, then escape, and be finally killed and
captured by another vessel; and herein are indirectly comprised many
minor contingencies, all partaking of this one grand feature. For example,—
after a weary and perilous chase and capture of a whale, the body may get
loose from the ship by reason of a violent storm; and drifting far away to
leeward, be retaken by a second whaler, who, in a calm, snugly tows it
alongside, without risk of life or line. Thus the most vexatious and violent
disputes would often arise between the fishermen, were there not some
written or unwritten, universal, undisputed law applicable to all cases.

Perhaps the only formal whaling code authorized by legislative enact-
ment, was that of Holland. It was decreed by the States-General in A.D.
1695. But though no other nation has ever had any written whaling law,
yet the American fishermen have been their own legislators and lawyers in
this matter. They have provided a system which for terse comprehensiveness surpasses Justinian's Pandects and the By-laws of the Chinese Society for

395

the Suppression of Meddling with other People's Business. Yes; these laws might be engraven on a Queen Anne's farthing, or the barb of a harpoon, and worn round the neck, so small are they.

I. A Fast-Fish belongs to the party fast to it.

II. A Loose-Fish is fair game for anybody who can soonest catch it.

But what plays the mischief with this masterly code is the admirable brevity of it, which necessitates a vast volume of commentaries to expound it.

First: What is a Fast-Fish? Alive or dead a fish is technically fast, when it is connected with an occupied ship or boat, by any medium at all controllable by the occupant or occupants,—a mast, an oar, a nine-inch cable, a telegraph wire, or a strand of cobweb, it is all the same. Likewise a fish is technically fast when it bears a waif, or any other recognised symbol of possession; so long as the party waifing it plainly evince their ability at any time to take it alongside, as well as their intention so to do.

These are scientific commentaries; but the commentaries of the whalemen themselves sometimes consist in hard words and harder knocks—the Coke-upon-Littleton of the fist. True, among the more upright and honorable whalemen allowances are always made for peculiar cases, where it would be an outrageous moral injustice for one party to claim possession of a whale previously chased or killed by another party. But others are by no means so scrupulous.

Some fifty years ago there was a curious case of whale-trover litigated in England, wherein the plaintiffs set forth that after a hard chase of a whale in the Northern seas, they (the plaintiffs) had succeeded in harpooning the fish; but at last, through peril of their lives, were obliged to forsake not only their lines, but their boat itself. Ultimately the defendants (the crew of another ship) came up with the whale, struck, killed, seized, and finally appropriated it before the very eyes of the plaintiffs. And when those defendants were remonstrated with, their captain snapped his fingers in the plaintiffs' teeth, and assured them that by way of doxology to the deed he had done, he would now retain their line, harpoons, and boat, which had remained attached to the whale at the time of the seizure. Wherefore the plaintiffs now sued for the recovery of the value of their whale, line, harpoons, and boat.

Mr. Erskine was counsel for the defendants; Lord Ellenborough was the judge. In the course of the defence, the witty Erskine went on to illustrate his position, by alluding to a recent crim. con. case, wherein a gentleman, after in vain trying to bridle his wife's viciousness, had at last abandoned her upon the seas of life; but in the course of years, repenting of that step, he instituted an action to recover possession of her. Erskine was on the other side; and he then supported it by saying, that though the gentleman had originally harpooned the lady, and had once had her fast, and only by reason of the great stress of her plunging viciousness, had at last abandoned her; yet abandon her he did, so that she became a loose-fish; and therefore when a subsequent gentleman re-harpooned her, the lady then became that subsequent gentleman's property, along with whatever harpoon might have been found sticking in her.

Now in the present case Erskine contended that the examples of the whale and the lady were reciprocally illustrative of each other.

These pleadings, and the counter pleadings, being duly heard, the very learned judge in set terms decided, to wit,—That as for the boat, he awarded it to the plaintiffs, because they had merely abandoned it to save their lives; but that with regard to the controverted whale, harpoons, and line, they belonged to the defendants; the whale, because it was a Loose-Fish at the time of the final capture; and the harpoons and line because when the fish made off with them, it (the fish) acquired a property in those articles; and hence anybody who afterwards took the fish had a right to them. Now the defendants afterwards took the fish; ergo, the aforesaid articles were theirs.

A common man looking at this decision of the very learned Judge, might possibly object to it. But ploughed up to the primary rock of the matter, the two great principles laid down in the twin whaling laws previously quoted, and applied and elucidated by Lord Ellenborough in the above cited case; these two laws touching Fast-Fish and Loose-Fish, I say, will, on reflection, be found the fundamentals of all human jurisprudence; for notwithstanding its complicated tracery of sculpture, the Temple of the Law, like the Temple of the Philistines, has but two props to stand on.

Is it not a saying in every one's mouth, Possession is half of the law: that is, regardless of how the thing came into possession? But often possession is the whole of the law. What are the sinews and souls of Russian serfs and Republican slaves but Fast-Fish, whereof possession is the whole of the law? What to the rapacious landlord is the widow's last mite but a Fast-Fish? What is yonder undetected villain's marble mansion with a door-plate for a waif; what is that but a Fast-Fish? What is the ruinous discount which Mordecai, the broker, gets from poor Woebegone, the bankrupt, on a loan to keep Woebegone's family from starvation; what is that ruinous discount but a Fast-Fish? What is the Archbishop of Savesoul's income of £100,000 seized from the scant bread and cheese of hundreds of thousands of broken-backed laborers (all sure of heaven without any of Savesoul's help) what is that globular 100,000 but a Fast-Fish? What are the Duke of Dunder's hereditary towns and hamlets but Fast-Fish? What to that redoubted harpooneer, John Bull, is poor Ireland, but a Fast-Fish? What to that apostolic lancer, Brother Jonathan, is Texas but a Fast-Fish? And concerning all these, is not Possession the whole of the law?

But if the doctrine of Fast-Fish be pretty generally applicable, the kindred doctrine of Loose-Fish is still more widely so. That is internationally and universally applicable.

What was America in 1492 but a Loose-Fish, in which Columbus struck the Spanish standard by way of waifing it for his royal master and mistress? What was Poland to the Czar? What Greece to the Turk? What India to England? What at last will Mexico be to the United States? All Loose-Fish.

What are the Rights of Man and the Liberties of the World but Loose-Fish? What all men's minds and opinions but Loose-Fish? What is the principle of religious belief in them but a Loose-Fish? What to the ostentatious smuggling verbalists are the thoughts of thinkers but Loose-Fish? What is the great globe itself but a Loose-Fish? And what are you, reader, but a Loose-Fish and a Fast-Fish, too?

# Chapter 90

### Heads or Tails

*"De balena vero sufficit, si rex habeat caput, et regina caudam."*
Bracton, l.3, c.3.

LATIN FROM THE BOOKS of the Laws of England, which taken along with the context, means, that of all whales captured by anybody on the coast of that land, the King, as Honorary Grand Harpooneer, must have the head, and the Queen be respectfully presented with the tail. A division which, in the whale, is much like halving an apple; there is no intermediate remainder. Now as this law, under a modified form, is to this day in force in England; and as it offers in various respects a strange anomaly touching the general law of Fast and Loose-Fish, it is here treated of in a separate chapter, on the same courteous principle that prompts the English railways to be at the expense of a separate car, specially reserved for the accommodation of royalty. In the first place, in curious proof of the fact that the above-mentioned law is still in force, I proceed to lay before you a circumstance that happened within the last two years.

It seems that some honest mariners of Dover, or Sandwich, or some one of the Cinque Ports, had after a hard chase succeeded in killing and beaching a fine whale which they had originally descried afar off from the shore. Now the Cinque Ports are partially or somehow under the jurisdiction of a sort of policeman or beadle, called a Lord Warden. Holding the office directly from the crown, I believe, all the royal emoluments incident to the

Cinque Port territories become by assignment his. By some writers this
office is called a sinecure. But not so. Because the Lord Warden is busily
employed at times in fobbing his perquisites; which are his chiefly by
virtue of that same fobbing of them.

Now when these poor sun-burnt mariners, bare-footed, and with their
trowsers rolled high up on their eely legs, had wearily hauled their fat fish
high and dry, promising themselves a good £150 from the precious oil and
bone; and in fantasy sipping rare tea with their wives, and good ale with
their cronies, upon the strength of their respective shares; up steps a very
learned and most Christian and charitable gentleman, with a copy of
Blackstone under his arm; and laying it upon the whale's head, he says—
"Hands off! this fish, my masters, is a Fast-Fish. I seize it as the Lord
Warden's." Upon this the poor mariners in their respectful consternation—
so truly English—knowing not what to say, fall to vigorously scratching
their heads all round; meanwhile ruefully glancing from the whale to the
stranger. But that did in nowise mend the matter, or at all soften the hard
heart of the learned gentleman with the copy of Blackstone. At length one
of them, after long scratching about for his ideas, made bold to speak.

"Please, sir, who is the Lord Warden?"

"The Duke."

"But the duke had nothing to do with taking this fish?"

"It is his."

"We have been at great trouble, and peril, and some expense, and is all
that to go to the Duke's benefit; we getting nothing at all for our pains but
our blisters?"

"It is his."

"Is the Duke so very poor as to be forced to this desperate mode of
getting a livelihood?"

"It is his."

"I thought to relieve my old bed-ridden mother by part of my share of
this whale."

"It is his."

"Won't the Duke be content with a quarter or a half?"

"It is his."

In a word, the whale was seized and sold, and his Grace the Duke of
Wellington received the money. Thinking that viewed in some particular
lights, the case might by a bare possibility in some small degree be deemed,
under the circumstances, a rather hard one, an honest clergyman of the
town respectfully addressed a note to his Grace, begging him to take the

case of those unfortunate mariners into full consideration. To which my Lord Duke in substance replied (both letters were published) that he had already done so, and received the money, and would be obliged to the reverend gentleman if for the future he (the reverend gentleman) would decline meddling with other people's business. Is this the still militant old man, standing at the corners of the three kingdoms, on all hands coercing alms of beggars?

It will readily be seen that in this case the alleged right of the Duke to the whale was a delegated one from the Sovereign. We must needs inquire then on what principle the Sovereign is originally invested with that right. The law itself has already been set forth. But Plowden gives us the reason for it. Says Plowden, the whale so caught belongs to the King and Queen, "because of its superior excellence." And by the soundest commentators this has ever been held a cogent argument in such matters.

But why should the King have the head, and the Queen the tail? A reason for that, ye lawyers!

In his treatise on "Queen-Gold," or Queen-pinmoney, an old King's Bench author, one William Prynne, thus discourseth: "Y$^e$ tail is y$^e$ Queen's, that y$^e$ Queen's wardrobe may be supplied with y$^e$ whalebone." Now this was written at a time when the black limber bone of the Greenland or Right whale was largely used in ladies' bodices. But this same bone is not in the tail; it is in the head, which is a sad mistake for a sagacious lawyer like Prynne. But is the Queen a mermaid, to be presented with a tail? An allegorical meaning may lurk here.

There are two royal fish so styled by the English law writers—the whale and the sturgeon; both royal property under certain limitations, and nominally supplying the tenth branch of the crown's ordinary revenue. I know not that any other author has hinted of the matter; but by inference it seems to me that the sturgeon must be divided in the same way as the whale, the King receiving the highly dense and elastic head peculiar to that fish, which, symbolically regarded, may possibly be humorously grounded upon some presumed congeniality. And thus there seems a reason in all things, even in law.

# Chapter 91

## The Pequod meets the Rose-bud

*"In vain it was to rake for Ambergriese in the paunch of this Leviathan, insufferable fetor denying that inquiry."*          Sir T. Browne, V.E.

I T WAS A WEEK OR TWO after the last whaling scene recounted, and when we were slowly sailing over a sleepy, vapory, mid-day sea, that the many noses on the Pequod's deck proved more vigilant discoverers than the three pairs of eyes aloft. A peculiar and not very pleasant smell was smelt in the sea.

"I will bet something now," said Stubb, "that somewhere hereabouts are some of those drugged whales we tickled the other day. I thought they would keel up before long."

Presently, the vapors in advance slid aside; and there in the distance lay a ship, whose furled sails betokened that some sort of whale must be alongside. As we glided nearer, the stranger showed French colors from his peak; and by the eddying cloud of vulture sea-fowl that circled, and hovered, and swooped around him, it was plain that the whale alongside must be what the fishermen call a blasted whale, that is, a whale that has died unmolested on the sea, and so floated an unappropriated corpse. It may well be conceived, what an unsavory odor such a mass must exhale; worse than an Assyrian city in the plague, when the living are incompetent to bury the departed. So intolerable indeed is it regarded by some, that no cupidity could persuade them to moor alongside of it. Yet are there those who will still do it; notwithstanding the fact that the oil obtained from such subjects is of a very inferior quality, and by no means of the nature of attar-of-rose.

Coming still nearer with the expiring breeze, we saw that the French-man had a second whale alongside; and this second whale seemed even more of a nosegay than the first. In truth, it turned out to be one of those problematical whales that seem to dry up and die with a sort of prodigious dyspepsia, or indigestion; leaving their defunct bodies almost entirely bankrupt of anything like oil. Nevertheless, in the proper place we shall see that no knowing fisherman will ever turn up his nose at such a whale as this, however much he may shun blasted whales in general.

The Pequod had now swept so nigh to the stranger, that Stubb vowed he recognised his cutting spade-pole entangled in the lines that were knotted round the tail of one of these whales.

"There's a pretty fellow, now," he banteringly laughed, standing in the ship's bows, "there's a jackal for ye! I well know that these Crappoes of Frenchmen are but poor devils in the fishery; sometimes lowering their boats for breakers, mistaking them for Sperm Whale spouts; yes, and sometimes sailing from their port with their hold full of boxes of tallow candles, and cases of snuffers, foreseeing that all the oil they will get won't be enough to dip the Captain's wick into; aye, we all know these things; but look ye, here's a Crappo that is content with our leavings, the drugged whale there, I mean; aye, and is content too with scraping the dry bones of that other precious fish he has there. Poor devil! I say, pass round a hat, some one, and let's make him a present of a little oil for dear charity's sake. For what oil he'll get from that drugged whale there, wouldn't be fit to burn in a jail; no, not in a condemned cell. And as for the other whale, why, I'll agree to get more oil by chopping up and trying out these three masts of ours, than he'll get from that bundle of bones; though, now that I think of it, it may contain something worth a good deal more than oil; yes, amber-gris. I wonder now if our old man has thought of that. It's worth trying. Yes, I'm in for it;" and so saying he started for the quarter-deck.

By this time the faint air had become a complete calm; so that whether or no, the Pequod was now fairly entrapped in the smell, with no hope of escaping except by its breezing up again. Issuing from the cabin, Stubb now called his boat's crew, and pulled off for the stranger. Drawing across her bow, he perceived that in accordance with the fanciful French taste, the upper part of her stem-piece was carved in the likeness of a huge drooping stalk, was painted green, and for thorns had copper spikes projecting from it here and there; the whole terminating in a symmetrical folded bulb of a bright red color. Upon her head boards, in large gilt letters, he read

"Bouton de Rose,"—Rose-button, or Rose-bud; and this was the romantic name of this aromatic ship.

Though Stubb did not understand the *Bouton* part of the inscription, yet the word *rose*, and the bulbous figure-head put together, sufficiently explained the whole to him.

"A wooden rose-bud, eh?" he cried with his hand to his nose, "that will do very well; but how like all creation it smells!"

Now in order to hold direct communication with the people on deck, he had to pull round the bows to the starboard side, and thus come close to the blasted whale; and so talk over it.

Arrived then at this spot, with one hand still to his nose, he bawled—"Bouton-de-Rose, ahoy! are there any of you Bouton-de-Roses that speak English?"

"Yes," rejoined a Guernsey-man from the bulwarks, who turned out to be the chief-mate.

"Well, then, my Bouton-de-Rose-bud, have you seen the White Whale?"

"*What* whale?"

"The *White* Whale—a Sperm Whale—Moby Dick, have ye seen him?"

"Never heard of such a whale. Cachalot Blanche! White Whale—no."

"Very good, then; good bye now, and I'll call again in a minute."

Then rapidly pulling back towards the Pequod, and seeing Ahab leaning over the quarter-deck rail awaiting his report, he moulded his two hands into a trumpet and shouted—"No, Sir! No!" Upon which Ahab retired, and Stubb returned to the Frenchman.

He now perceived that the Guernsey-man, who had just got into the chains, and was using a cutting-spade, had slung his nose in a sort of bag.

"What's the matter with your nose, there?" said Stubb. "Broke it?"

"I wish it was broken, or that I didn't have any nose at all!" answered the Guernsey-man, who did not seem to relish the job he was at very much. "But what are you holding *yours* for?"

"Oh, nothing! It's a wax nose; I have to hold it on. Fine day, aint it? Air rather gardenny, I should say; throw us a bunch of posies, will ye, Bouton-de-Rose?"

"What in the devil's name do you want here?" roared the Guernsey-man, flying into a sudden passion.

"Oh! keep cool—cool? yes, that's the word; why don't you pack those whales in ice while you're working at 'em? But joking aside, though; do you know, Rose-bud, that it's all nonsense trying to get any oil out of such whales? As for that dried up one, there, he hasn't a gill in his whole carcase."

"I know that well enough; but, d'ye see, the Captain here won't believe it; this is his first voyage; he was a Cologne manufacturer before. But come aboard, and mayhap he'll believe you, if he won't me; and so I'll get out of this dirty scrape."

"Anything to oblige ye, my sweet and pleasant fellow," rejoined Stubb, and with that he soon mounted to the deck. There a queer scene presented itself. The sailors, in tasselled caps of red worsted, were getting the heavy tackles in readiness for the whales. But they worked rather slow and talked very fast, and seemed in anything but a good humor. All their noses upwardly projected from their faces like so many jib-booms. Now and then pairs of them would drop their work, and run up to the mast-head to get some fresh air. Some thinking they would catch the plague, dipped oakum in coal-tar, and at intervals held it to their nostrils. Others having broken the stems of their pipes almost short off at the bowl, were vigorously puffing tobacco-smoke, so that it constantly filled their olfactories.

Stubb was struck by a shower of outcries and anathemas proceeding from the Captain's round-house abaft; and looking in that direction saw a fiery face thrust from behind the door, which was held ajar from within. This was the tormented surgeon, who, after in vain remonstrating against the proceedings of the day, had betaken himself to the Captain's round-house (*cabinet* he called it) to avoid the pest; but still, could not help yelling out his entreaties and indignations at times.

Marking all this, Stubb augured well for his scheme, and turning to the Guernsey-man had a little chat with him, during which the stranger mate expressed his detestation of his Captain as a conceited ignoramus, who had brought them all into so unsavory and unprofitable a pickle. Sounding him carefully, Stubb further perceived that the Guernsey-man had not the slightest suspicion concerning the ambergris. He therefore held his peace on that head, but otherwise was quite frank and confidential with him, so that the two quickly concocted a little plan for both circumventing and satirizing the Captain, without his at all dreaming of distrusting their sincerity. According to this little plan of theirs, the Guernsey-man, under cover of an interpreter's office, was to tell the Captain what he pleased, but as coming from Stubb; and as for Stubb, he was to utter any nonsense that should come uppermost in him during the interview.

By this time their destined victim appeared from his cabin. He was a small and dark, but rather delicate looking man for a sea-captain, with large whiskers and moustache, however; and wore a red cotton velvet vest with watch-seals at his side. To this gentleman, Stubb was now politely introduced by the Guernsey-man, who at once ostentatiously put on the aspect of interpreting between them.

"What shall I say to him first?" said he.

"Why," said Stubb, eyeing the velvet vest and the watch and seals, "you may as well begin by telling him that he looks a sort of babyish to me, though I don't pretend to be a judge."

"He says, Monsieur," said the Guernsey-man, in French, turning to his captain, "that only yesterday his ship spoke a vessel, whose captain and chief-mate, with six sailors, had all died of a fever caught from a blasted whale they had brought alongside."

Upon this the captain started, and eagerly desired to know more.

"What now?" said the Guernsey-man to Stubb.

"Why, since he takes it so easy, tell him that now I have eyed him carefully, I'm quite certain that he's no more fit to command a whale-ship than a St. Jago monkey. In fact, tell him from me he's a baboon."

"He vows and declares, Monsieur, that the other whale, the dried one, is far more deadly than the blasted one; in fine, Monsieur, he conjures us, as we value our lives, to cut loose from these fish."

Instantly the captain ran forward, and in a loud voice commanded his crew to desist from hoisting the cutting-tackles, and at once cast loose the cables and chains confining the whales to the ship.

"What now?" said the Guernsey-man, when the captain had returned to them.

"Why, let me see; yes, you may as well tell him now that—that—in fact, tell him I've diddled him, and (aside to himself) perhaps somebody else."

"He says, Monsieur, that he's very happy to have been of any service to us."

Hearing this, the captain vowed that they were the grateful parties (meaning himself and mate) and concluded by inviting Stubb down into his cabin to drink a bottle of Bordeaux.

"He wants you to take a glass of wine with him," said the interpreter.

"Thank him heartily; but tell him it's against my principles to drink with the man I've diddled. In fact, tell him I must go."

"He says, Monsieur, that his principles won't admit of his drinking; but that if Monsieur wants to live another day to drink, then Monsieur had best drop all four boats, and pull the ship away from these whales, for it's so calm they won't drift."

By this time Stubb was over the side, and getting into his boat, hailed the Guernsey-man to this effect,—that having a long tow-line in his boat, he would do what he could to help them, by pulling out the lighter whale of the two from the ship's side. While the Frenchman's boats, then, were engaged in towing the ship one way, Stubb benevolently towed away at his whale the other way, ostentatiously slacking out a most unusually long tow-line.

Presently a breeze sprang up; Stubb feigned to cast off from the whale; hoisting his boats, the Frenchman soon increased his distance, while the Pequod slid in between him and Stubb's whale. Whereupon Stubb quickly pulled to the floating body, and hailing the Pequod to give notice of his intentions, at once proceeded to reap the fruit of his unrighteous cunning. Seizing his sharp boat-spade, he commenced an excavation in the body, a little behind the side fin. You would almost have thought he was digging a cellar there in the sea; and when at length his spade struck against the gaunt ribs, it was like turning up old Roman tiles and pottery buried in fat English loam. His boat's crew were all in high excitement, eagerly helping their chief, and looking as anxious as gold-hunters.

And all the time numberless fowls were diving, and ducking, and screaming, and yelling, and fighting around them. Stubb was beginning to look disappointed, especially as the horrible nosegay increased, when suddenly from out the very heart of this plague, there stole a faint stream of perfume, which flowed through the tide of bad smells without being absorbed by it, as one river will flow into and then along with another, without at all blending with it for a time.

"I have it, I have it," cried Stubb, with delight, striking something in the subterranean regions, "a purse! a purse!"

Dropping his spade, he thrust both hands in, and drew out handfuls of something that looked like ripe Windsor soap, or rich mottled old cheese; very unctuous and savory withal. You might easily dent it with your thumb; it is of a hue between yellow and ash color. And this, good friends, is ambergris, worth a gold guinea an ounce to any druggist. Some six handfuls were obtained; but more was unavoidably lost in the sea, and still more, perhaps, might have been secured were it not for impatient Ahab's loud command to Stubb to desist, and come on board, else the ship would bid them good bye.

# Chapter 92

### *Ambergris*

NOW THIS AMBERGRIS is a very curious substance, and so important as an article of commerce, that in 1791 a certain Nantucket-born Captain Coffin was examined at the bar of the English House of Commons on that subject. For at that time, and indeed until a comparatively late day, the precise origin of ambergris remained, like amber itself, a problem to the learned. Though the word ambergris is but the French compound for grey amber, yet the two substances are quite distinct. For amber, though at times found on the sea-coast, is also dug up in some far inland soils, whereas ambergris is never found except upon the sea. Besides, amber is a hard, transparent, brittle, odorless substance, used for mouth-pieces to pipes, for beads and ornaments; but ambergris is soft, waxy, and so highly fragrant and spicy, that it is largely used in perfumery, in pastiles, precious candles, hair-powders, and pomatum. The Turks use it in cooking, and also carry it to Mecca, for the same purpose that frankincense is carried to St. Peter's in Rome. Some wine merchants drop a few grains into claret, to flavor it.

Who would think, then, that such fine ladies and gentlemen should regale themselves with an essence found in the inglorious bowels of a sick whale! Yet so it is. By some, ambergris is supposed to be the cause, and by others the effect, of the dyspepsia in the whale. How to cure such a dyspepsia

it were hard to say, unless by administering three or four boat loads of
Brandreth's pills, and then running out of harm's way, as laborers do in
blasting rocks.

I have forgotten to say that there were found in this ambergris, certain
hard, round, bony plates, which at first Stubb thought might be sailors'
trousers buttons; but it afterwards turned out that they were nothing more
than pieces of small squid bones embalmed in that manner.

Now that the incorruption of this most fragrant ambergris should be
found in the heart of such decay; is this nothing? Bethink thee of that
saying of St. Paul in Corinthians, about corruption and incorruption; how
that we are sown in dishonor, but raised in glory. And likewise call to mind
that saying of Paracelsus about what it is that maketh the best musk. Also
forget not the strange fact that of all things of ill-savor, Cologne-water, in
its rudimental manufacturing stages, is the worst.

I should like to conclude the chapter with the above appeal, but cannot,
owing to my anxiety to repel a charge often made against whalemen, and
which, in the estimation of some already biased minds, might be considered
as indirectly substantiated by what has been said of the Frenchman's two
whales. Elsewhere in this volume the slanderous aspersion has been dis-
proved, that the vocation of whaling is throughout a slatternly, untidy
business. But there is another thing to rebut. They hint that all whales
always smell bad. Now how did this odious stigma originate?

I opine, that it is plainly traceable to the first arrival of the Greenland
whaling ships in London, more than two centuries ago. Because those
whalemen did not then, and do not now, try out their oil at sea as the
Southern ships have always done; but cutting up the fresh blubber in small
bits, thrust it through the bung holes of large casks, and carry it home in
that manner; the shortness of the season in those Icy Seas, and the sudden
and violent storms to which they are exposed, forbidding any other course.
The consequence is, that upon breaking into the hold, and unloading one of
these whale cemeteries, in the Greenland dock, a savor is given forth
somewhat similar to that arising from excavating an old city grave-yard,
for the foundations of a Lying-in Hospital.

I partly surmise also, that this wicked charge against whalers may be
likewise imputed to the existence on the coast of Greenland, in former
times, of a Dutch village called Schmerenburgh or Smeerenberg, which
latter name is the one used by the learned Fogo Von Slack, in his great work
on Smells, a text-book on that subject. As its name imports (smeer, fat;
berg, to put up), this village was founded in order to afford a place for the

blubber of the Dutch whale fleet to be tried out, without being taken home to Holland for that purpose. It was a collection of furnaces, fat-kettles, and oil sheds; and when the works were in full operation certainly gave forth no very pleasant savor. But all this is quite different with a South Sea Sperm Whaler; which in a voyage of four years perhaps, after completely filling her hold with oil, does not, perhaps, consume fifty days in the business of boiling out; and in the state that it is casked, the oil is nearly scentless. The truth is, that living or dead, if but decently treated, whales as a species are by no means creatures of ill odor; nor can whalemen be recognised, as the people of the middle ages affected to detect a Jew in the company, by the nose. Nor indeed can the whale possibly be otherwise than fragrant, when, as a general thing, he enjoys such high health; taking abundance of exercise; always out of doors; though, it is true, seldom in the open air. I say, that the motion of a Sperm Whale's flukes above water dispenses a perfume, as when a musk-scented lady rustles her dress in a warm parlor. What then shall I liken the Sperm Whale to for fragrance, considering his magnitude? Must it not be to that famous elephant, with jewelled tusks, and redolent with myrrh, which was led out of an Indian town to do honor to Alexander the Great?

# Chapter 93

### *The Castaway*

I T WAS BUT SOME FEW DAYS after encountering the Frenchman, that a most significant event befell the most insignificant of the Pequod's crew; an event most lamentable; and which ended in providing the sometimes madly merry and predestinated craft with a living and ever accompanying prophecy of whatever shattered sequel might prove her own.

Now, in the whale ship, it is not every one that goes in the boats. Some few hands are reserved called ship-keepers, whose province it is to work the vessel while the boats are pursuing the whale. As a general thing, these ship-keepers are as hardy fellows as the men comprising the boats' crews. But if there happen to be an unduly slender, clumsy, or timorous wight in the ship, that wight is certain to be made a ship-keeper. It was so in the Pequod with the little negro Pippin by nick-name, Pip by abbreviation. Poor Pip! ye have heard of him before; ye must remember his tambourine on that dramatic midnight, so gloomy-jolly.

In outer aspect, Pip and Dough-Boy made a match, like a black pony and a white one, of equal developments, though of dissimilar color, driven in one eccentric span. But while hapless Dough-Boy was by nature dull and torpid in his intellects, Pip, though over tender-hearted, was at bottom very bright, with that pleasant, genial, jolly brightness peculiar to his tribe; a tribe, which ever enjoy all holidays and festivities with finer, freer relish than any other race. For blacks, the year's calendar should show naught but three hundred and sixty-five Fourth of Julys and New Year's Days. Nor smile so, while I write that this little black was brilliant, for even blackness has its brilliancy; behold yon lustrous ebony, panelled in king's cabinets. But Pip loved life, and all life's peaceable securities; so that the panic-striking business in which he had somehow unaccountably become entrapped, had most sadly blurred his brightness; though, as ere long will be seen, what was thus temporarily subdued in him, in the end was destined to be luridly illumined by strange wild fires, that fictitiously showed him off to ten times the natural lustre with which in his native Tolland County in Connecticut, he had once enlivened many a fiddler's frolic on the green; and at melodious even-tide, with his gay ha-ha! had turned the round horizon into one star-belled tambourine. So, though in the clear air of day, suspended against a blue-veined neck, the pure-watered diamond drop will healthful glow; yet, when the cunning jeweller would show you the diamond in its most impressive lustre, he lays it against a gloomy ground, and then lights it up, not by the sun, but by some unnatural gases. Then come out those fiery effulgences, infernally superb; then the evil-blazing diamond, once the divinest symbol of the crystal skies, looks like some crown-jewel stolen from the King of Hell. But let us to the story.

It came to pass, that in the ambergris affair Stubb's after-oarsman chanced so to sprain his hand, as for a time to become quite maimed; and, temporarily, Pip was put into his place.

The first time Stubb lowered with him, Pip evinced much nervousness; but happily, for that time, escaped close contact with the whale; and therefore came off not altogether discreditably; though Stubb observing him, took care, afterwards, to exhort him to cherish his courageousness to the utmost, for he might often find it needful.

Now upon the second lowering, the boat paddled upon the whale; and as the fish received the darted iron, it gave its customary rap, which happened, in this instance, to be right under poor Pip's seat. The involuntary consternation of the moment caused him to leap, paddle in hand, out of the boat; and in such a way, that part of the slack whale line coming against his chest, he breasted it overboard with him, so as to become entangled in it, when at last plumping into the water. That instant the stricken whale started on a fierce run, the line swiftly straightened; and presto! poor Pip came all foaming up to the chocks of the boat, remorselessly dragged there by the line, which had taken several turns around his chest and neck.

Tashtego stood in the bows. He was full of the fire of the hunt. He hated Pip for a poltroon. Snatching the boat-knife from its sheath, he suspended its sharp edge over the line, and turning towards Stubb, exclaimed interrogatively, "Cut?" Meantime Pip's blue, choked face plainly looked, Do, for God's sake! All passed in a flash. In less than half a minute, this entire thing happened.

"Damn him, cut!" roared Stubb; and so the whale was lost and Pip was saved.

So soon as he recovered himself, the poor little negro was assailed by yells and execrations from the crew. Tranquilly permitting these irregular cursings to evaporate, Stubb then in a plain, business-like, but still half humorous manner, cursed Pip officially; and that done, unofficially gave him much wholesome advice. The substance was, Never jump from a boat, Pip, except—but all the rest was indefinite, as the soundest advice ever is. Now, in general, *Stick to the boat*, is your true motto in whaling; but cases will sometimes happen when *Leap from the boat*, is still better. Moreover, as if perceiving at last that if he should give undiluted conscientious advice to Pip, he would be leaving him too wide a margin to jump in for the future; Stubb suddenly dropped all advice, and concluded with a peremptory command, "Stick to the boat, Pip, or by the Lord, I wont pick you up if you jump; mind that. We can't afford to lose whales by the likes of you; a whale would sell for thirty times what you would, Pip, in Alabama. Bear that in mind, and don't jump any more." Hereby perhaps Stubb indirectly hinted, that though man loves his fellow, yet man is a money-making animal, which propensity too often interferes with his benevolence.

But we are all in the hands of the Gods; and Pip jumped again. It was under very similar circumstances to the first performance; but this time he did not breast out the line; and hence, when the whale started to run, Pip was left behind on the sea, like a hurried traveller's trunk. Alas! Stubb was but too true to his word. It was a beautiful, bounteous, blue day; the spangled sea calm and cool, and flatly stretching away, all round, to the horizon, like gold-beater's skin hammered out to the extremest. Bobbing up and down in that sea, Pip's ebon head showed like a head of cloves. No boat-knife was lifted when he fell so rapidly astern. Stubb's inexorable back was turned upon him; and the whale was winged. In three minutes, a whole mile of shoreless ocean was between Pip and Stubb. Out from the centre of the sea, poor Pip turned his crisp, curling, black head to the sun, another lonely castaway, though the loftiest and the brightest.

Now, in calm weather, to swim in the open ocean is as easy to the practised swimmer as to ride in a spring-carriage ashore. But the awful lonesomeness is intolerable. The intense concentration of self in the middle of such a heartless immensity, my God! who can tell it? Mark, how when sailors in a dead calm bathe in the open sea—mark how closely they hug their ship and only coast along her sides.

But had Stubb really abandoned the poor little negro to his fate? No; he did not mean to, at least. Because there were two boats in his wake, and he supposed, no doubt, that they would of course come up to Pip very quickly, and pick him up; though, indeed, such considerateness towards oarsmen jeopardized through their own timidity, is not always manifested by the hunters in all similar instances; and such instances not unfrequently occur; almost invariably in the fishery, a coward, so called, is marked with the same ruthless detestation peculiar to military navies and armies.

But it so happened, that those boats, without seeing Pip, suddenly spying whales close to them on one side, turned, and gave chase; and Stubb's boat was now so far away, and he and all his crew so intent upon his fish, that Pip's ringed horizon began to expand around him miserably. By the merest chance the ship itself at last rescued him; but from that hour the little negro went about the deck an idiot; such, at least, they said he was. The sea had jeeringly kept his finite body up, but drowned the infinite of his soul. Not drowned entirely, though. Rather carried down alive to wondrous depths, where strange shapes of the unwarped primal world glided to and fro before his passive eyes; and the miser-merman, Wisdom, revealed his hoarded heaps; and among the joyous, heartless, ever-juvenile eternities, Pip saw the multitudinous, God-omnipresent, coral insects, that out of the firmament of waters heaved the colossal orbs. He saw God's foot upon the treadle of the loom, and spoke it; and therefore his shipmates called him mad. So man's insanity is heaven's sense; and wandering from all mortal reason, man comes at last to that celestial thought, which, to reason, is absurd and frantic; and weal or woe, feels then uncompromised, indifferent as his God.

For the rest, blame not Stubb too hardly. The thing is common in that fishery; and in the sequel of the narrative, it will then be seen what like abandonment befell myself.

# Chapter 94

## *A Squeeze of the Hand*

THAT WHALE of Stubb's, so dearly purchased, was duly brought to the Pequod's side, where all those cutting and hoisting operations previously detailed, were regularly gone through, even to the baling of the Heidelburgh Tun, or Case.

While some were occupied with this latter duty, others were employed in dragging away the larger tubs, so soon as filled with the sperm; and when the proper time arrived, this same sperm was carefully manipulated ere going to the try-works, of which anon.

It had cooled and crystallized to such a degree, that when, with several others, I sat down before a large Constantine's bath of it, I found it strangely concreted into lumps, here and there rolling about in the liquid part. It was our business to squeeze these lumps back into fluid. A sweet and unctuous duty! No wonder that in old times this sperm was such a favorite cosmetic. Such a clearer! such a sweetener! such a softener! such a delicious mollifier! After having my hands in it for only a few minutes, my fingers felt like eels, and began, as it were, to serpentine and spiralize.

As I sat there at my ease, cross-legged on the deck; after the bitter exertion at the windlass; under a blue tranquil sky; the ship under indolent sail, and gliding so serenely along; as I bathed my hands among those soft, gentle globules of infiltrated tissues, woven almost within the hour; as they richly broke to my fingers, and discharged all their opulence, like fully ripe grapes their wine; as I snuffed up that uncontaminated aroma,—literally and truly, like the smell of spring violets; I declare to you, that for the time I lived as in a musky meadow; I forgot all about our horrible oath; in that inexpressible sperm, I washed my hands and my heart of it; I almost began to credit the old Paracelsan superstition that sperm is of rare virtue in allaying the heat of anger: while bathing in that bath, I felt divinely free from all ill-will, or petulance, or malice, of any sort whatsoever.

Squeeze! squeeze! squeeze! all the morning long; I squeezed that sperm till I myself almost melted into it; I squeezed that sperm till a strange sort of insanity came over me; and I found myself unwittingly squeezing my co-laborers' hands in it, mistaking their hands for the gentle globules. Such an abounding, affectionate, friendly, loving feeling did this avocation beget; that at last I was continually squeezing their hands, and looking up into their eyes sentimentally; as much as to say,—Oh! my dear fellow beings, why should we longer cherish any social acerbities, or know the slightest ill-humor or envy! Come; let us squeeze hands all round; nay, let us all squeeze ourselves into each other; let us squeeze ourselves universally into the very milk and sperm of kindness.

Would that I could keep squeezing that sperm for ever! For now, since by many prolonged, repeated experiences, I have perceived that in all cases man must eventually lower, or at least shift, his conceit of attainable felicity; not placing it anywhere in the intellect or the fancy; but in the wife, the heart, the bed, the table, the saddle, the fire-side, the country; now that I have perceived all this, I am ready to squeeze case eternally. In thoughts of the visions of the night, I saw long rows of angels in paradise, each with his hands in a jar of spermaceti.

       *         *         *         *         *

Now, while discoursing of sperm, it behooves to speak of other things akin to it, in the business of preparing the sperm whale for the try-works.

First comes white-horse, so called, which is obtained from the tapering part of the fish, and also from the thicker portions of his flukes. It is tough with congealed tendons—a wad of muscle—but still contains some oil. After being severed from the whale, the white-horse is first cut into portable oblongs ere going to the mincer. They look much like blocks of Berkshire marble.

Plum-pudding is the term bestowed upon certain fragmentary parts of the whale's flesh, here and there adhering to the blanket of blubber, and often participating to a considerable degree in its unctuousness. It is a most refreshing, convivial, beautiful object to behold. As its name imports, it is of an exceedingly rich, mottled tint, with a bestreaked snowy and golden ground, dotted with spots of the deepest crimson and purple. It is plums of rubies, in pictures of citron. Spite of reason, it is hard to keep yourself from eating it. I confess, that once I stole behind the foremast to try it. It tasted something as I should conceive a royal cutlet from the thigh of Louis le Gros might have tasted, supposing him to have been killed the first day after the venison season, and that particular venison season contemporary with an unusually fine vintage of the vineyards of Champagne.

There is another substance, and a very singular one, which turns up in the course of this business, but which I feel it to be very puzzling adequately to describe. It is called slobgollion; an appellation original with the whalemen, and even so is the nature of the substance. It is an ineffably oozy, stringy affair, most frequently found in the tubs of sperm, after a prolonged squeezing, and subsequent decanting. I hold it to be the wondrously thin, ruptured membranes of the case, coalescing.

Gurry, so called, is a term properly belonging to right whalemen, but sometimes incidentally used by the sperm fishermen. It designates the dark, glutinous substance which is scraped off the back of the Greenland or right whale, and much of which covers the decks of those inferior souls who hunt that ignoble Leviathan.

Nippers. Strictly this word is not indigenous to the whale's vocabulary. But as applied by whalemen, it becomes so. A whaleman's nipper is a short firm strip of tendinous stuff cut from the tapering part of Leviathan's tail: it averages an inch in thickness, and for the rest, is about the size of the iron part of a hoe. Edgewise moved along the oily deck, it operates like a leathern squilgee; and by nameless blandishments, as of magic, allures along with it all impurities.

But to learn all about these recondite matters, your best way is at once to descend into the blubber-room, and have a long talk with its inmates. This place has previously been mentioned as the receptacle for the blanket-pieces, when stript and hoisted from the whale. When the proper time arrives for cutting up its contents, this apartment is a scene of terror to all tyros, especially by night. On one side, lit by a dull lantern, a space has been left clear for the workmen. They generally go in pairs,—a pike-and-gaff-man and a spade-man. The whaling-pike is similar to a frigate's boarding-weapon of the same name. The gaff is something like a boat-hook. With his gaff, the gaffman hooks on to a sheet of blubber, and strives to hold it from slipping, as the ship pitches and lurches about. Meanwhile, the spade-man stands on the sheet itself, perpendicularly chopping it into the portable horse-pieces. This spade is sharp as hone can make it; the spademan's feet are shoeless; the thing he stands on will sometimes irresistibly slide away from him, like a sledge. If he cuts off one of his own toes, or one of his assistant's, would you be very much astonished? Toes are scarce among veteran blubber-room men.

# Chapter 95

## The Cassock

HAD YOU STEPPED ON BOARD the Pequod at a certain juncture of this post-mortemizing of the whale; and had you strolled forward nigh the windlass, pretty sure am I that you would have scanned with no small curiosity a very strange, enigmatical object, which you would have seen there, lying along lengthwise in the lee scuppers. Not the wondrous cistern in the whale's huge head; not the prodigy of his unhinged lower jaw; not the miracle of his symmetrical tail; none of these would so surprise you, as half a glimpse of that unaccountable cone,—longer than a Kentuckian is tall, nigh a foot in diameter at the base, and jet-black as Yojo, the ebony idol of Queequeg. And an idol, indeed, it is; or, rather, in old times, its likeness was. Such an idol as that found in the secret groves of Queen Maachah in Judea; and for worshipping which, king Asa, her son, did depose her, and destroyed the idol, and burnt it for an abomination at the brook Kedron, as darkly set forth in the 15th chapter of the first book of Kings.

Look at the sailor, called the mincer, who now comes along, and assisted by two allies, heavily backs the grandissimus, as the mariners call it, and with bowed shoulders, staggers off with it as if he were a grenadier carrying a dead comrade from the field. Extending it upon the forecastle deck, he now proceeds cylindrically to remove its dark pelt, as an African hunter the

419

pelt of a boa. This done he turns the pelt inside out, like a pantaloon leg;
gives it a good stretching, so as almost to double its diameter; and at last
hangs it, well spread, in the rigging, to dry. Ere long, it is taken down; when
removing some three feet of it, towards the pointed extremity, and then
cutting two slits for arm-holes at the other end, he lengthwise slips himself
bodily into it. The mincer now stands before you invested in the full
canonicals of his calling. Immemorial to all his order, this investiture alone
will adequately protect him, while employed in the peculiar functions of his
office.

That office consists in mincing the horse-pieces of blubber for the pots;
an operation which is conducted at a curious wooden horse, planted endwise
against the bulwarks, and with a capacious tub beneath it, into which the
minced pieces drop, fast as the sheets from a rapt orator's desk. Arrayed in
decent black; occupying a conspicuous pulpit; intent on bible leaves; what
a candidate for an archbishoprick, what a lad for a Pope were this mincer!*

* Bible leaves! Bible leaves! This is the invariable cry from the mates to the mincer.
It enjoins him to be careful, and cut his work into as thin slices as possible, inasmuch as
by so doing the business of boiling out the oil is much accelerated, and its quantity considerably increased, besides perhaps improving it in quality.

# Chapter 96

## The Try-Works

BESIDES HER HOISTED BOATS, an American whaler is outwardly distinguished by her try-works. She presents the curious anomaly of the most solid masonry joining with oak and hemp in constituting the completed ship. It is as if from the open field a brick-kiln were transported to her planks.

The try-works are planted between the foremast and mainmast, the most roomy part of the deck. The timbers beneath are of a peculiar strength, fitted to sustain the weight of an almost solid mass of brick and mortar, some ten feet by eight square, and five in height. The foundation does not penetrate the deck, but the masonry is firmly secured to the surface by ponderous knees of iron bracing it on all sides, and screwing it down to the timbers. On the flanks it is cased with wood, and at top completely covered by a large, sloping, battened hatchway. Removing this hatch we expose the great try-pots, two in number, and each of several barrels' capacity. When not in use, they are kept remarkably clean. Sometimes they are polished with soapstone and sand, till they shine within like silver punch-bowls. During the night-watches some cynical old sailors will crawl into them and coil themselves away there for a nap. While employed in polishing them—one man in each pot, side by side—many confidential communications are carried on; over the iron lips. It is a place also for profound mathematical meditation. It was in the left hand try-pot of the Pequod, with the soapstone diligently circling round me, that I was first indirectly struck by the remarkable fact, that in geometry all bodies gliding along the cycloid, my soapstone for example, will descend from any point in precisely the same time.

Removing the fire-board from the front of the try-works, the bare masonry of that side is exposed, penetrated by the two iron mouths of the furnaces, directly underneath the pots. These mouths are fitted with heavy doors of iron. The intense heat of the fire is prevented from communicating itself to the deck, by means of a shallow reservoir extending under the entire inclosed surface of the works. By a tunnel inserted at the rear, this reservoir is kept replenished with water as fast as it evaporates. There are no external chimneys; they open direct from the rear wall. And here let us go back for a moment.

It was about nine o'clock at night that the Pequod's try-works were first started on this present voyage. It belonged to Stubb to oversee the business.

"All ready there? Off hatch, then, and start her. You cook, fire the works." This was an easy thing, for the carpenter had been thrusting his shavings into the furnace throughout the passage. Here be it said that in a whaling voyage the first fire in the try-works has to be fed for a time with wood. After that no wood is used, except as a means of quick ignition to the staple fuel. In a word, after being tried out, the crisp, shrivelled blubber, now called scraps or fritters, still contains considerable of its unctuous properties. These fritters feed the flames. Like a plethoric burning martyr, or a self-consuming misanthrope, once ignited, the whale supplies his own fuel and burns by his own body. Would that he consumed his own smoke! for his smoke is horrible to inhale, and inhale it you must, and not only that, but you must live in it for the time. It has an unspeakable, wild, Hindoo odor about it, such as may lurk in the vicinity of funereal pyres. It smells like the left wing of the day of judgment; it is an argument for the pit.

By midnight the works were in full operation. We were clear from the carcase; sail had been made; the wind was freshening; the wild ocean darkness was intense. But that darkness was licked up by the fierce flames, which at intervals forked forth from the sooty flues, and illuminated every lofty rope in the rigging, as with the famed Greek fire. The burning ship drove on, as if remorselessly commissioned to some vengeful deed. So the pitch and sulphur-freighted brigs of the bold Hydriote, Canaris, issuing from their midnight harbors, with broad sheets of flame for sails, bore down upon the Turkish frigates, and folded them in conflagrations.

The hatch, removed from the top of the works, now afforded a wide hearth in front of them. Standing on this were the Tartarean shapes of the pagan harpooneers, always the whale-ship's stokers. With huge pronged poles they pitched hissing masses of blubber into the scalding pots, or stirred up the fires beneath, till the snaky flames darted, curling, out of the doors to catch them by the feet. The smoke rolled away in sullen heaps. To every pitch of the ship there was a pitch of the boiling oil, which seemed all eagerness to leap into their faces. Opposite the mouth of the works, on the further side of the wide wooden hearth, was the windlass. This served for a sea-sofa. Here lounged the watch, when not otherwise employed, looking into the red heat of the fire, till their eyes felt scorched in their heads. Their tawny features, now all begrimed with smoke and sweat, their matted beards, and the contrasting barbaric brilliancy of their teeth, all these were strangely revealed in the capricious emblazonings of the works. As they narrated to each other their unholy adventures, their tales of terror told in words of mirth; as their uncivilized laughter forked upwards out of them, like the flames from the furnace; as to and fro, in their front, the harpooneers wildly gesticulated with their huge pronged forks and dippers; as the wind howled on, and the sea leaped, and the ship groaned and dived, and yet steadfastly shot her red hell further and further into the blackness of the sea and the night, and scornfully champed the white bone in her mouth, and viciously spat round her on all sides; then the rushing Pequod, freighted with savages, and laden with fire, and burning a corpse, and plunging into that blackness of darkness, seemed the material counterpart of her mono-maniac commander's soul.

So seemed it to me, as I stood at her helm, and for long hours silently guided the way of this fire-ship on the sea. Wrapped, for that interval, in darkness myself, I but the better saw the redness, the madness, the ghastliness of others. The continual sight of the fiend shapes before me, capering half in smoke and half in fire, these at last begat kindred visions in my soul, so soon as I began to yield to that unaccountable drowsiness which ever would come over me at a midnight helm.

But that night, in particular, a strange (and ever since inexplicable) thing occurred to me. Starting from a brief standing sleep, I was horribly conscious of something fatally wrong. The jaw-bone tiller smote my side, which leaned against it; in my ears was the low hum of sails, just beginning to shake in the wind; I thought my eyes were open; I was half conscious of putting my fingers to the lids and mechanically stretching them still further apart. But, spite of all this, I could see no compass before me to steer by; though it seemed but a minute since I had been watching the card, by the steady binnacle lamp illuminating it. Nothing seemed before me but a jet gloom, now and then made ghastly by flashes of redness. Uppermost was the impression, that whatever swift, rushing thing I stood on was not so much bound to any haven ahead as rushing from all havens astern. A stark, bewildered feeling, as of death, came over me. Convulsively my hands grasped the tiller, but with the crazy conceit that the tiller was, somehow, in some enchanted way, inverted. My God! what is the matter with me? thought I. Lo! in my brief sleep I had turned myself about, and was fronting the ship's stern, with my back to her prow and the compass. In an instant I faced back, just in time to prevent the vessel from flying up into the wind, and very probably capsizing her. How glad and how grateful the relief from this unnatural hallucination of the night, and the fatal contingency of being brought by the lee!

Look not too long in the face of the fire, O man! Never dream with thy hand on the helm! Turn not thy back to the compass; accept the first hint of the hitching tiller; believe not the artificial fire, when its redness makes all things look ghastly. To-morrow, in the natural sun, the skies will be bright; those who glared like devils in the forking flames, the morn will show in far other, at least gentler, relief; the glorious, golden, glad sun, the only true lamp—all others but liars!

Nevertheless the sun hides not Virginia's Dismal Swamp, nor Rome's accursed Campagna, nor wide Sahara, nor all the millions of miles of deserts and of griefs beneath the moon. The sun hides not the ocean, which is the dark side of this earth, and which is two thirds of this earth. So, therefore, that mortal man who hath more of joy than sorrow in him, that mortal man cannot be true—not true, or undeveloped. With books the same. The truest of all men was the Man of Sorrows, and the truest of all books is Solomon's, and Ecclesiastes is the fine hammered steel of woe. "All is vanity." ALL. This wilful world hath not got hold of un-christian Solomon's wisdom yet. But he who dodges hospitals and jails, and walks fast crossing grave-yards, and would rather talk of operas than hell; calls Cowper, Young, Pascal, Rousseau, poor devils all of sick men; and throughout a care-free lifetime swears by Rabelais as passing wise, and therefore jolly;—not that man is fitted to sit down on tomb-stones, and break the green damp mould with unfathomably wondrous Solomon.

But even Solomon, he says, "the man that wandereth out of the way of understanding shall remain" (*i.e.* even while living) "in the congregation of the dead." Give not thyself up, then, to fire, lest it invert thee, deaden thee; as for the time it did me. There is a wisdom that is woe; but there is a woe that is madness. And there is a Catskill eagle in some souls that can alike dive down into the blackest gorges, and soar out of them again and become invisible in the sunny spaces. And even if he for ever flies within the gorge, that gorge is in the mountains; so that even in his lowest swoop the mountain eagle is still higher than other birds upon the plain, even though they soar.

# Chapter 97

*The Lamp*

HAD YOU DESCENDED from the Pequod's try-works to the Pequod's forecastle, where the off duty watch were sleeping, for one single moment you would have almost thought you were standing in some illuminated shrine of canonized kings and counsellors. There they lay in their triangular oaken vaults, each mariner a chiselled muteness; a score of lamps flashing upon his hooded eyes.

In merchantmen, oil for the sailor is more scarce than the milk of queens. To dress in the dark, and eat in the dark, and stumble in darkness to his pallet, this is his usual lot. But the whaleman, as he seeks the food of light, so he lives in light. He makes his berth an Aladdin's lamp, and lays him down in it; so that in the pitchiest night the ship's black hull still houses an illumination.

See with what entire freedom the whaleman takes his handful of lamps —often but old bottles and vials, though—to the copper cooler at the try-works, and replenishes them there, as mugs of ale at a vat. He burns, too, the purest of oil, in its unmanufactured, and, therefore, unvitiated state; a fluid unknown to solar, lunar, or astral contrivances ashore. It is sweet as early grass butter in April. He goes and hunts for his oil, so as to be sure of its freshness and genuineness, even as the traveller on the prairie hunts up his own supper of game.

# Chapter 98

*Stowing Down and Clearing Up*

A LREADY HAS IT BEEN RELATED how the great leviathan is afar off descried from the mast-head; how he is chased over the watery moors, and slaughtered in the valleys of the deep; how he is then towed alongside and beheaded; and how (on the principle which entitled the headsman of old to the garments in which the beheaded was killed) his great padded surtout becomes the property of his executioner; how, in due time, he is condemned to the pots, and, like Shadrach, Meshach, and Abednego, his spermaceti, oil, and bone pass unscathed through the fire;—but now it remains to conclude the last chapter of this part of the description by rehearsing—singing, if I may—the romantic proceeding of decanting off his oil into the casks and striking them down into the hold, where once again leviathan returns to his native profundities, sliding along beneath the surface as before; but, alas! never more to rise and blow.

While still warm, the oil, like hot punch, is received into the six-barrel casks; and while, perhaps, the ship is pitching and rolling this way and that in the midnight sea, the enormous casks are slewed round and headed over, end for end, and sometimes perilously scoot across the slippery deck, like so many land slides, till at last man-handled and stayed in their course; and all round the hoops, rap, rap, go as many hammers as can play upon them, for now, *ex officio*, every sailor is a cooper.

At length, when the last pint is casked, and all is cool, then the great hatchways are unsealed, the bowels of the ship are thrown open, and down go the casks to their final rest in the sea. This done, the hatches are replaced, and hermetically closed, like a closet walled up.

In the sperm fishery, this is perhaps one of the most remarkable incidents in all the business of whaling. One day the planks stream with freshets of blood and oil; on the sacred quarter-deck enormous masses of the whale's head are profanely piled; great rusty casks lie about, as in a brewery yard; the smoke from the try-works has besooted all the bulwarks; the mariners go about suffused with unctuousness; the entire ship seems great leviathan himself; while on all hands the din is deafening.

But a day or two after, you look about you, and prick your ears in this self-same ship; and were it not for the tell-tale boats and try-works, you would all but swear you trod some silent merchant vessel, with a most scrupulously neat commander. The unmanufactured sperm oil possesses a singularly cleansing virtue. This is the reason why the decks never look so white as just after what they call an affair of oil. Besides, from the ashes of the burned scraps of the whale, a potent ley is readily made; and whenever any adhesiveness from the back of the whale remains clinging to the side, that ley quickly exterminates it. Hands go diligently along the bulwarks, and with buckets of water and rags restore them to their full tidiness. The soot is brushed from the lower rigging. All the numerous implements which have been in use are likewise faithfully cleansed and put away. The great hatch is scrubbed and placed upon the try-works, completely hiding the pots; every cask is out of sight; all tackles are coiled in unseen nooks; and when by the combined and simultaneous industry of almost the entire ship's company, the whole of this conscientious duty is at last concluded, then the crew themselves proceed to their own ablutions; shift themselves from top to toe; and finally issue to the immaculate deck, fresh and all aglow, as bridegrooms new-leaped from out the daintiest Holland.

Now, with elated step, they pace the planks in twos and threes, and humorously discourse of parlors, sofas, carpets, and fine cambrics; propose to mat the deck; think of having hangings to the top; object not to taking tea by moonlight on the piazza of the forecastle. To hint to such musked mariners of oil, and bone, and blubber, were little short of audacity. They know not the thing you distantly allude to. Away, and bring us napkins!

But mark: aloft there, at the three mast heads, stand three men intent on spying out more whales, which, if caught, infallibly will again soil the old oaken furniture, and drop at least one small grease-spot somewhere. Yes;

and many is the time, when, after the severest uninterrupted labors, which know no night; continuing straight through for ninety-six hours; when from the boat, where they have swelled their wrists with all day rowing on the Line,—they only step to the deck to carry vast chains, and heave the heavy windlass, and cut and slash, yea, and in their very sweatings to be smoked and burned anew by the combined fires of the equatorial sun and the equatorial try-works; when, on the heel of all this, they have finally bestirred themselves to cleanse the ship, and make a spotless dairy room of it; many is the time the poor fellows, just buttoning the necks of their clean frocks, are startled by the cry of "There she blows!" and away they fly to fight another whale, and go through the whole weary thing again. Oh! my friends, but this is man-killing! Yet this is life. For hardly have we mortals by long toilings extracted from this world's vast bulk its small but valuable sperm; and then, with weary patience, cleansed ourselves from its defilements, and learned to live here in clean tabernacles of the soul; hardly is this done, when—*There she blows!*—the ghost is spouted up, and away we sail to fight some other world, and go through young life's old routine again.

Oh! the metempsychosis! Oh! Pythagoras, that in bright Greece, two thousand years ago, did die, so good, so wise, so mild; I sailed with thee along the Peruvian coast last voyage—and, foolish as I am, taught thee, a green simple boy, how to splice a rope!

# Chapter 99

## The Doubloon

RE NOW IT HAS BEEN RELATED how Ahab was wont to pace his quarter-deck, taking regular turns at either limit, the binnacle and mainmast; but in the multiplicity of other things requiring narration it has not been added how that sometimes in these walks, when most plunged in his mood, he was wont to pause in turn at each spot, and stand there strangely eyeing the particular object before him. When he halted before the binnacle, with his glance fastened on the pointed needle in the compass, that glance shot like a javelin with the pointed intensity of his purpose; and when resuming his walk he again paused before the mainmast, then, as the same riveted glance fastened upon the riveted gold coin there, he still wore the same aspect of nailed firmness, only dashed with a certain wild longing, if not hopefulness.

But one morning, turning to pass the doubloon, he seemed to be newly attracted by the strange figures and inscriptions stamped on it, as though now for the first time beginning to interpret for himself in some monomaniac way whatever significance might lurk in them. And some certain significance lurks in all things, else all things are little worth, and the round world itself but an empty cipher, except to sell by the cart-load, as they do hills about Boston, to fill up some morass in the Milky Way.

Now this doubloon was of purest, virgin gold, raked somewhere out of the heart of gorgeous hills, whence, east and west, over golden sands, the head-waters of many a Pactolus flow. And though now nailed amidst all the rustiness of iron bolts and the verdigris of copper spikes, yet, untouchable and immaculate to any foulness, it still preserved its Quito glow. Nor, though placed amongst a ruthless crew and every hour passed by ruthless hands, and through the livelong nights shrouded with thick darkness which might cover any pilfering approach, nevertheless every sunrise found the doubloon where the sunset left it last. For it was set apart and sanctified to one awe-striking end; and however wanton in their sailor ways, one and all, the mariners revered it as the white whale's talisman. Sometimes they talked it over in the weary watch by night, wondering whose it was to be at last, and whether he would ever live to spend it.

Now those noble golden coins of South America are as medals of the sun and tropic token-pieces. Here palms, alpacas, and volcanoes; sun's disks and stars; ecliptics, horns-of-plenty, and rich banners waving, are in luxuriant profusion stamped; so that the precious gold seems almost to derive an added preciousness and enhancing glories, by passing through those fancy mints, so Spanishly poetic.

It so chanced that the doubloon of the Pequod was a most wealthy example of these things. On its round border it bore the letters, RE-PUBLICA DEL ECUADOR: QUITO. So this bright coin came from a country planted in the middle of the world, and beneath the great equator, and named after it; and it had been cast midway up the Andes, in the unwaning clime that knows no autumn. Zoned by those letters you saw the likeness of three Andes' summits; from one a flame; a tower on another; on the third a crowing cock; while arching over all was a segment of the partitioned zodiac, the signs all marked with their usual cabalistics, and the keystone sun entering the equinoctial point at Libra.

Before this equatorial coin, Ahab, not unobserved by others, was now pausing.

"There's something ever egotistical in mountain-tops and towers, and all other grand and lofty things; look here,—three peaks as proud as Lucifer. The firm tower, that is Ahab; the volcano, that is Ahab; the courageous, the undaunted, and victorious fowl, that, too, is Ahab; all are Ahab; and this round gold is but the image of the rounder globe, which, like a magician's glass, to each and every man in turn but mirrors back his own mysterious self. Great pains, small gains for those who ask the world to solve them; it cannot solve itself. Methinks now this coined sun wears a ruddy face; but see! aye, he enters the sign of storms, the equinox! and but six months before he wheeled out of a former equinox at Aries! From storm to storm! So be it, then. Born in throes, 'tis fit that man should live in pains and die in pangs! So be it, then! Here's stout stuff for woe to work on. So be it, then."

"No fairy fingers can have pressed the gold, but devil's claws must have left their mouldings there since yesterday," murmured Starbuck to himself, leaning against the bulwarks. "The old man seems to read Belshazzar's awful writing. I have never marked the coin inspectingly. He goes below; let me read. A dark valley between three mighty, heaven-abiding peaks, that almost seem the Trinity, in some faint earthly symbol. So in this vale of Death, God girds us round; and over all our gloom, the sun of Righteousness still shines a beacon and a hope. If we bend down our eyes, the dark vale shows her mouldy soil; but if we lift them, the bright sun meets our glance half way, to cheer. Yet, oh, the great sun is no fixture; and if, at midnight, we would fain snatch some sweet solace from him, we gaze for him in vain! This coin speaks wisely, mildly, truly, but still sadly to me. I will quit it, lest Truth shake me falsely."

"There now's the old Mogul," soliloquized Stubb by the try-works, "he's been twigging it; and there goes Starbuck from the same, and both with faces which I should say might be somewhere within nine fathoms long. And all from looking at a piece of gold, which did I have it now on Negro Hill or in Corlaer's Hook, I'd not look at it very long ere spending it. Humph! in my poor, insignificant opinion, I regard this as queer. I have seen doubloons before now in my voyagings; your doubloons of old Spain, your doubloons of Peru, your doubloons of Chili, your doubloons of Bolivia, your doubloons of Popayan; with plenty of gold moidores and pistoles, and joes, and half joes, and quarter joes. What then should there be in this doubloon of the Equator that is so killing wonderful? By Golconda! let me read it once. Halloa! here's signs and wonders truly! That, now, is what old Bowditch in his Epitome calls the zodiac, and what my almanack below calls ditto. I'll get the almanack; and as I have heard devils can be raised with Daboll's arithmetic, I'll try my hand at raising a meaning out of these queer curvicues here with the Massachusetts calendar. Here's the book. Let's see now. Signs and wonders; and the sun, he's always among 'em. Hem, hem, hem; here they are—here they go—all alive:—Aries, or the Ram; Taurus, or the Bull;—and Jimini! here's Gemini himself, or the Twins. Well; the sun he wheels among 'em. Aye, here on the coin he's just crossing the threshold between two of twelve sitting-rooms all in a ring. Book! you lie there; the fact is, you books must know your places. You'll do to give us the bare words and facts, but we come in to supply the thoughts. That's my small experience, so far as the Massachusetts calendar, and Bowditch's navigator, and Daboll's arithmetic go. Signs and wonders, eh? Pity if there is nothing wonderful in signs, and significant in wonders! There's a clue somewhere; wait a bit; hist—hark! By Jove, I have it! Look you, Doubloon, your zodiac here is the life of man in one round chapter; and now I'll read it off, straight out of the book. Come, Almanack! To begin: there's Aries, or the Ram—lecherous dog, he begets us; then, Taurus, or the Bull—he bumps us the first thing; then Gemini, or the Twins—that is, Virtue and Vice; we try to reach Virtue, when lo! comes Cancer the Crab, and drags us back; and here, going from Virtue, Leo, a roaring Lion, lies in the path—he gives a few fierce bites and surly dabs with his paw; we escape, and hail Virgo, the Virgin! that's our first love; we marry and think to be happy for aye, when pop comes Libra, or the Scales—happiness weighed and found wanting; and while we are very sad about that, Lord! how we suddenly jump, as Scorpio, or the Scorpion, stings us in rear; we are curing the wound, when whang come the arrows all round; Sagittarius, or the Archer, is amusing himself. As we pluck out the shafts, stand aside! here's the battering-ram, Capricornus, or the Goat; full tilt, he comes rushing, and headlong we are tossed; when Aquarius, or the Water-bearer, pours out his whole deluge and drowns us; and, to wind up, with Pisces, or the Fishes, we sleep. There's a sermon now, writ in high heaven, and the sun goes through it every year, and yet comes out of it all alive and hearty. Jollily he, aloft there, wheels through toil and trouble; and so, alow here, does jolly Stubb. Oh, jolly's the word for aye! Adieu, Doubloon! But stop; here comes little King-Post; dodge round the try-works, now, and let's hear what he'll have to say. There; he's before it; he'll out with something presently. So, so; he's beginning."

"I see nothing here, but a round thing made of gold, and whoever raises a certain whale, this round thing belongs to him. So, what's all this staring been about? It is worth sixteen dollars, that's true; and at two cents the cigar, that's nine hundred and sixty cigars. I wont smoke dirty pipes like Stubb, but I like cigars, and here's nine hundred and sixty of them; so here goes Flask aloft to spy 'em out."

"Shall I call that wise or foolish, now; if it be really wise it has a foolish look to it; yet, if it be really foolish, then has it a sort of wiseish look to it. But, avast; here comes our old Manxman—the old hearse-driver, he must have been, that is, before he took to the sea. He luffs up before the doubloon; halloa, and goes round on the other side of the mast; why, there's a horse-shoe nailed on that side; and now he's back again; what does that mean? Hark! he's muttering—voice like an old worn-out coffee-mill. Prick ears, and listen!"

"If the White Whale be raised, it must be in a month and a day, when the sun stands in some one of these signs. I've studied signs, and know their marks; they were taught me two score years ago, by the old witch in Copenhagen. Now, in what sign will the sun then be? The horse-shoe sign; for there it is, right opposite the gold. And what's the horse-shoe sign? The lion is the horse-shoe sign—the roaring and devouring lion. Ship, old ship! my old head shakes to think of thee."

"There's another rendering now; but still one text. All sorts of men in one kind of world, you see. Dodge again! here comes Queequeg—all tattooing—looks like the signs of the Zodiac himself. What says the Cannibal? As I live he's comparing notes; looking at his thigh bone; thinks the sun is in the thigh, or in the calf, or in the bowels, I suppose, as the old women talk Surgeon's Astronomy in the back country. And by Jove, he's found something there in the vicinity of his thigh—I guess it's Sagittarius, or the Archer. No: he don't know what to make of the doubloon; he takes it for an old button off some king's trowsers. But, aside again! here comes that ghost-devil, Fedallah; tail coiled out of sight as usual, oakum in the toes of his pumps as usual. What does he say, with that look of his? Ah, only makes a sign to the sign and bows himself; there is a sun on the coin—fire worshipper, depend upon it. Ho! more and more. This way comes Pip—poor boy! would he had died, or I; he's half horrible to me. He too has been watching all of these interpreters—myself included—and look now, he comes to read, with that unearthly idiot face. Stand away again and hear him. Hark!"

"I look, you look, he looks; we look, ye look, they look."

"Upon my soul, he's been studying Murray's Grammar! Improving his mind, poor fellow! But what's that he says now—hist!"

"I look, you look, he looks; we look, ye look, they look."

"Why, he's getting it by heart—hist! again."

"I look, you look, he looks; we look, ye look, they look."

"Well, that's funny."

"And I, you, and he; and we, ye, and they, are all bats; and I'm a crow, especially when I stand a'top of this pine tree here. Caw! caw! caw! caw! caw! caw! Ain't I a crow? And where's the scare-crow? There he stands;

two bones stuck into a pair of old trowsers, and two more poked into the sleeves of an old jacket."

"Wonder if he means me?—complimentary!—poor lad!—I could go hang myself. Any way, for the present, I'll quit Pip's vicinity. I can stand the rest, for they have plain wits; but he's too crazy-witty for my sanity. So, so, I leave him muttering."

"Here's the ship's navel, this doubloon here, and they are all on fire to unscrew it. But, unscrew your navel, and what's the consequence? Then again, if it stays here, that is ugly, too, for when aught's nailed to the mast it's a sign that things grow desperate. Ha, ha! old Ahab! the White Whale; he'll nail ye! This is a pine tree. My father, in old Tolland county, cut down a pine tree once, and found a silver ring grown over in it; some old darkey's wedding ring. How did it get there? And so they'll say in the resurrection, when they come to fish up this old mast, and find a doubloon lodged in it, with bedded oysters for the shaggy bark. Oh, the gold! the precious, precious gold!—the green miser 'll hoard ye soon! Hish! hish! God goes 'mong the worlds blackberrying. Cook! ho, cook! and cook us! Jenny! hey, hey, hey, hey, hey, Jenny, Jenny! and get your hoe-cake done!"

# Chapter 100

*Leg and Arm · The Pequod, of Nantucket, meets the Samuel Enderby, of London*

SHIP, AHOY! Hast seen the White Whale?"

So cried Ahab, once more hailing a ship showing English colors, bearing down under the stern. Trumpet to mouth, the old man was standing in his hoisted quarter-boat, his ivory leg plainly revealed to the stranger captain, who was carelessly reclining in his own boat's bow. He was a darkly-tanned, burly, good-natured, fine-looking man, of sixty or thereabouts, dressed in a spacious roundabout, that hung round him in festoons of blue pilot-cloth; and one empty arm of this jacket streamed behind him like the broidered arm of a huzzar's surcoat.

"Hast seen the White Whale?"

"See you this?" and withdrawing it from the folds that had hidden it, he held up a white arm of sperm whale bone, terminating in a wooden head like a mallet.

"Man my boat!" cried Ahab, impetuously, and tossing about the oars near him—"Stand by to lower!"

In less than a minute, without quitting his little craft, he and his crew were dropped to the water, and were soon alongside of the stranger. But here a curious difficulty presented itself. In the excitement of the moment, Ahab had forgotten that since the loss of his leg he had never once stepped on board of any vessel at sea but his own, and then it was always by an ingenious and very handy mechanical contrivance peculiar to the Pequod, and a thing not to be rigged and shipped in any other vessel at a moment's warning. Now, it is no very easy matter for anybody—except those who are almost hourly used to it, like whalemen—to clamber up a ship's side from a boat on the open sea; for the great swells now lift the boat high up towards the bulwarks, and then instantaneously drop it half way down to the kelson. So, deprived of one leg, and the strange ship of course being altogether unsupplied with the kindly invention, Ahab now found himself abjectly reduced to a clumsy landsman again; hopelessly eyeing the uncertain changeful height he could hardly hope to attain.

It has before been hinted, perhaps, that every little untoward circumstance that befel him, and which indirectly sprang from his luckless mishap, almost invariably irritated or exasperated Ahab. And in the present instance, all this was heightened by the sight of the two officers of the strange ship, leaning over the side, by the perpendicular ladder of nailed cleets there, and swinging towards him a pair of tastefully-ornamented man-ropes; for at first they did not seem to bethink them that a one-legged man must be too much of a cripple to use their sea bannisters. But this awkwardness only lasted a minute, because the strange captain, observing at a glance how affairs stood, cried out, "I see, I see!—avast heaving there! Jump, boys, and swing over the cutting-tackle."

As good luck would have it, they had had a whale alongside a day or two previous, and the great tackles were still aloft, and the massive curved blubber-hook, now clean and dry, was still attached to the end. This was quickly lowered to Ahab, who at once comprehending it all, slid his solitary thigh into the curve of the hook (it was like sitting in the fluke of an anchor, or the crotch of an apple tree), and then giving the word, held himself fast, and at the same time also helped to hoist his own weight, by pulling hand-over-hand upon one of the running parts of the tackle. Soon he was carefully swung inside the high bulwarks, and gently landed upon the capstan head. With his ivory arm frankly thrust forth in welcome, the other captain advanced, and Ahab, putting out his ivory leg, and crossing the ivory arm (like two sword-fish blades) cried out in his walrus way, "Aye, aye, hearty! let us shake bones together!—an arm and a leg!—an arm that never can shrink, d'ye see; and a leg that never can run. Where did'st thou see the White Whale?—how long ago?"

"The White Whale," said the Englishman, pointing his ivory arm towards the East, and taking a rueful sight along it, as if it had been a telescope; "There I saw him, on the Line, last season."

"And he took that arm off, did he?" asked Ahab, now sliding down from the capstan, and resting on the Englishman's shoulder, as he did so.

"Aye, he was the cause of it, at least; and that leg, too?"

"Spin me the yarn," said Ahab; "how was it?"

"It was the first time in my life that I ever cruised on the Line," began the Englishman. "I was ignorant of the White Whale at that time. Well, one day we lowered for a pod of four or five whales, and my boat fastened to one of them; a regular circus horse he was, too, that went milling and milling round so, that my boat's crew could only trim dish, by sitting all their sterns on the outer gunwale. Presently up breaches from the bottom of the sea a bouncing great whale, with a milky-white head and hump, all crows' feet and wrinkles."

"It was he, it was he!" cried Ahab, suddenly letting out his suspended breath.

"And harpoons sticking in near his starboard fin."

"Aye, aye—they were mine—*my* irons," cried Ahab, exultingly—"but on!"

"Give me a chance, then," said the Englishman, good-humoredly. "Well, this old great-grandfather, with the white head and hump, runs all afoam into the pod, and goes to snapping furiously at my fast-line."

"Aye, I see!—wanted to part it; free the fast-fish—an old trick—I know him."

"How it was exactly," continued the one-armed commander, "I do not know; but in biting the line, it got foul of his teeth, caught there somehow; but we didn't know it then; so that when we afterwards pulled on the line, bounce we came plump on to his hump! instead of the other whale's that went off to windward, all fluking. Seeing how matters stood, and what a noble great whale it was—the noblest and biggest I ever saw, sir, in my life —I resolved to capture him, spite of the boiling rage he seemed to be in. And thinking the hap-hazard line would get loose, or the tooth it was tangled to might draw (for I have a devil of a boat's crew for a pull on a whale-line); seeing all this, I say, I jumped into my first mate's boat—Mr. Mounttop's here (by the way, Captain—Mounttop; Mounttop—the captain);—as I was saying, I jumped into Mounttop's boat, which, d'ye see, was gunwale and gunwale with mine, then; and snatching the first harpoon, let this old great-grandfather have it. But, Lord, look you, sir—hearts and souls alive, man—the next instant, in a jiff, I was blind as a bat—both eyes out—all befogged and bedeadened with black foam—the whale's tail looming straight up out of it, perpendicular in the air, like a marble steeple. No use sterning all, then; but as I was groping at midday, with a blinding sun, all crown-jewels; as I was groping, I say, after the second iron, to toss it overboard—down comes the tail like a Lima tower, cutting my boat in two, leaving each half in splinters; and, flukes first, the white hump backed through the wreck, as though it was all chips. We all struck out. To escape his terrible flailings, I seized hold of my harpoon-pole sticking in him, and for a moment clung to that like a sucking fish. But a combing sea dashed me off, and at the same instant, the fish, taking one good dart for-wards, went down like a flash; and the barb of that cursed second iron towing along near me caught me here" (clapping his hand just below his shoulder); "yes, caught me just here, I say, and bore me down to Hell's flames, I was thinking; when, when, all of a sudden, thank the good God, the barb ript its way along the flesh—clear along the whole length of my arm—came out nigh my wrist, and up I floated;—and that gentleman there will tell you the rest (by the way, captain—Dr. Bunger, ship's surgeon: Bunger, my lad,—the captain). Now, Bunger boy, spin your part of the yarn."

The professional gentleman thus familiarly pointed out, had been all the time standing near them, with nothing specific visible, to denote his gentlemanly rank on board. His face was an exceedingly round but sober one; he was dressed in a faded blue woollen frock or shirt, and patched trowsers; and had thus far been dividing his attention between a marling-spike he held in one hand, and a pill-box held in the other, occasionally casting a critical glance at the ivory limbs of the two crippled captains. But, at his superior's introduction of him to Ahab, he politely bowed, and straightway went on to do his captain's bidding.

"It was a shocking bad wound," began the whale-surgeon; "and, taking my advice, Captain Boomer here, stood our old Sammy—"

"Samuel Enderby is the name of my ship," interrupted the one-armed captain, addressing Ahab; "go on, boy."

"Stood our old Sammy off to the northward, to get out of the blazing hot weather there on the Line. But it was no use—I did all I could; sat up with him nights; was very severe with him in the matter of diet—"

"Oh, very severe!" chimed in the patient himself; then suddenly alter-ing his voice, "Drinking hot rum toddies with me every night, till he couldn't see to put on the bandages; and sending me to bed, half seas over, about three o'clock in the morning. Oh, ye stars! he sat up with me indeed, and was very severe in my diet. Oh! a great watcher, and very dietetically severe, is Dr. Bunger. (Bunger, you dog, laugh out! why don't ye? You know you're a precious jolly rascal.) But, heave ahead, boy, I'd rather be killed by you than kept alive by any other man."

"My captain, you must have ere this perceived, respected sir"—said the imperturbable godly-looking Bunger, slightly bowing to Ahab—"is apt to be facetious at times; he spins us many clever things of that sort. But I may as well say—en passant, as the French remark—that I myself—that is to say, Jack Bunger, late of the reverend clergy—am a strict total abstinence man; I never drink—"

"Water!" cried the captain; "he never drinks it; it's a sort of fits to him; fresh water throws him into the hydrophobia; but go on—go on with the arm story."

"Yes, I may as well," said the surgeon, coolly. "I was about observing, sir, before Captain Boomer's facetious interruption, that spite of my best and severest endeavors, the wound kept getting worse and worse; the truth was, sir, it was as ugly gaping wound as surgeon ever saw; more than two feet and several inches long. I measured it with the lead line. In short, it grew black; I knew what was threatened, and off it came. But I had no hand in shipping that ivory arm there; that thing is against all rule"— pointing at it with the marlingspike—"that is the captain's work, not mine; he ordered the carpenter to make it; he had that club-hammer there put to the end, to knock some one's brains out with, I suppose, as he tried mine once. He flies into diabolical passions sometimes. Do ye see this dent, sir" —removing his hat, and brushing aside his hair, and exposing a bowl-like cavity in his skull, but which bore not the slightest scarry trace, or any token of ever having been a wound—"Well, the captain there will tell you how that came here; he knows."

"No, I don't," said the captain, "but his mother did; he was born with it. Oh, you solemn rogue, you—you Bunger! was there ever such another Bunger in the watery world? Bunger, when you die, you ought to die in pickle, you dog; you should be preserved to future ages, you rascal."

"What became of the White Whale?" now cried Ahab, who thus far had been impatiently listening to this bye-play between the two Englishmen.

"Oh!" cried the one-armed captain, "Oh, yes! Well; after he sounded, we didn't see him again for some time; in fact, as I before hinted, I didn't then know what whale it was that had served me such a trick, till some time afterwards, when coming back to the Line, we heard about Moby Dick—as some call him—and then I knew it was he."

"Did'st thou cross his wake again?"

"Twice."

"But could not fasten?"

"Didn't want to try to: ain't one limb enough? What should I do without this other arm? And I'm thinking Moby Dick doesn't bite so much as he swallows."

"Well, then," interrupted Bunger, "give him your left arm for bait to get the right. Do you know, gentlemen"—very gravely and mathematically bowing to each Captain in succession—"Do you know, gentlemen, that the digestive organs of the whale are so inscrutably constructed by Divine Providence, that it is quite impossible for him to completely digest even a man's arm? And he knows it too. So that what you take for the White Whale's malice is only his awkwardness. For he never means to swallow a single limb; he only thinks to terrify by feints. But sometimes he is like the old juggling fellow, formerly a patient of mine in Ceylon, that making believe swallow jack-knives, once upon a time let one drop into him in good earnest, and there it stayed for a twelvemonth or more; when I gave him an emetic, and he heaved it up in small tacks, d'ye see. No possible way for him to digest that jack-knife, and fully incorporate it into his general bodily system. Yes, Captain Boomer, if you are quick enough about it, and have a mind to pawn one arm for the sake of the privilege of giving decent burial to the other, why in that case the arm is yours; only let the whale have another chance at you shortly, that's all."

"No, thank ye, Bunger," said the English Captain, "he's welcome to the arm he has, since I can't help it, and didn't know him then; but not to another one. No more White Whales for me; I've lowered for him once, and that has satisfied me. There would be great glory in killing him, I know that; and there is a ship-load of precious sperm in him, but, hark ye, he's best let alone; don't you think so, Captain?"—glancing at the ivory leg.

"He is. But he will still be hunted, for all that. What is best let alone, that accursed thing is not always what least allures. He's all a magnet! How long since thou saw'st him last? Which way heading?"

"Bless my soul, and curse the foul fiend's," cried Bunger, stoopingly walking round Ahab, and like a dog, strangely snuffing; "this man's blood —bring the thermometer!—it's at the boiling point!—his pulse makes these planks beat!—sir!"—taking a lancet from his pocket, and drawing near to Ahab's arm.

"Avast!" roared Ahab, dashing him against the bulwarks—"Man the boat! Which way heading?"

"Good God!" cried the English Captain, to whom the question was put.

"What's the matter? He was heading east, I think.—Is your Captain crazy?" whispering Fedallah.

But Fedallah, putting a finger on his lip, slid over the bulwarks to take the boat's steering oar, and Ahab, swinging the cutting-tackle towards him, commanded the ship's sailors to stand by to lower.

In a moment he was standing in the boat's stern, and the Manilla men were springing to their oars. In vain the English Captain hailed him. With back to the stranger ship, and face set like a flint to his own, Ahab stood upright till alongside of the Pequod.

# Chapter 101

*The Decanter*

E RE THE English ship fades from sight, be it set down here, that
she hailed from London, and was named after the late Samuel
Enderby, merchant of that city, the original of the famous whaling
house of Enderby & Sons; a house which in my poor whaleman's opinion,
comes not far behind the united royal houses of the Tudors and Bourbons,
in point of real historical interest. How long, prior to the year of our Lord
1775, this great whaling house was in existence, my numerous fish-
documents do not make plain; but in that year (1775) it fitted out the first
English ships that ever regularly hunted the Sperm Whale; though for
some score of years previous (ever since 1726) our valiant Coffins and
Maceys of Nantucket and the Vineyard had in large fleets pursued that
Leviathan, but only in the North and South Atlantic: not elsewhere. Be it
distinctly recorded here, that the Nantucketers were the first among mankind to harpoon with civilized steel the great Sperm Whale; and that for
half a century they were the only people of the whole globe who so
harpooned him.

In 1788, a fine ship, the Amelia, fitted out for the express purpose, and
at the sole charge of the vigorous Enderbys, boldly rounded Cape Horn,
and was the first among the nations to lower a whale-boat of any sort in the
great South Sea. The voyage was a skilful and lucky one; and returning to

443

her berth with her hold full of the precious sperm, the Amelia's example was soon followed by other ships, English and American, and thus the vast Sperm Whale grounds of the Pacific were thrown open. But not content with this good deed, the indefatigable house again bestirred itself: Samuel and all his Sons—how many, their mother only knows—and under their immediate auspices, and partly, I think, at their expense, the British government was induced to send the sloop-of-war Rattler on a whaling voyage of discovery into the South Sea. Commanded by a naval Post-Captain, the Rattler made a rattling voyage of it, and did some service; how much does not appear. But this is not all. In 1819, the same house fitted out a discovery whale ship of their own, to go on a testing cruise to the remote waters of Japan. That ship—well called the "Syren"—made a noble experimental cruise; and it was thus that the great Japanese Whaling Ground first became generally known. The Syren in this famous voyage was commanded by a Captain Coffin, a Nantucketer.

All honor to the Enderbies, therefore, whose house, I think, exists to the present day; though doubtless the original Samuel must long ago have slipped his cable for the great South Sea of the other world.

The ship named after him was worthy of the honor, being a very fast sailer and a noble craft every way. I boarded her once at midnight somewhere off the Patagonian coast, and drank good flip down in the forecastle. It was a fine gam we had, and they were all trumps—every soul on board. A short life to them, and a jolly death. And that fine gam I had—long, very long after old Ahab touched her planks with his ivory heel—it minds me of the noble, solid, Saxon hospitality of that ship; and may my parson forget me, and the devil remember me, if I ever lose sight of it. Flip? Did I say we had flip? Yes, and we flipped it at the rate of ten gallons the hour; and when the squall came (for it's squally off there by Patagonia), and all hands—visitors and all—were called to reef topsails, we were so top-heavy that we had to swing each other aloft in bowlines; and we ignorantly furled the skirts of our jackets into the sails, so that we hung there, reefed fast in the howling gale, a warning example to all drunken tars. However, the masts did not go overboard; and by and bye we scrambled down, so sober, that we had to pass the flip again, though the savage salt spray bursting down the forecastle scuttle, rather too much diluted and pickled it to my taste.

The beef was fine—tough, but with body in it. They said it was bull-beef; others, that it was dromedary beef; but I do not know, for certain, how that was. They had dumplings too; small, but substantial, symmetrically globular, and indestructible dumplings. I fancied that you could feel them, and roll them about in you after they were swallowed. If you stooped over too far forward, you risked their pitching out of you like billiard-balls. The bread—but that couldn't be helped; besides, it was an anti-scorbutic; in short, the bread contained the only fresh fare they had. But the forecastle was not very light, and it was very easy to step over into a dark corner when you ate it. But all in all, taking her from truck to helm, considering the dimensions of the cook's boilers, including his own live parchment boilers; fore and aft, I say, the Samuel Enderby was a jolly ship; of good fare and plenty; fine flip and strong; crack fellows all, and capital from boot heels to hat-band.

But why was it, think ye, that the Samuel Enderby, and some other English whalers I know of—not all though—were such famous, hospitable ships; that passed round the beef, and the bread, and the can, and the joke; and were not soon weary of eating, and drinking, and laughing? I will tell you. The abounding good cheer of these English whalers is matter for historical research. Nor have I been at all sparing of historical whale research, when it has seemed needed.

The English were preceded in the whale fishery by the Hollanders, Zealanders, and Danes; from whom they derived many terms still extant in the fishery; and what is yet more, their fat old fashions, touching plenty to eat and drink. For, as a general thing, the English merchant-ship scrimps her crew; but not so the English whaler. Hence, in the English, this thing of whaling good cheer is not normal and natural, but incidental and particular; and, therefore, must have some special origin, which is here pointed out, and will be still further elucidated.

During my researches in the Leviathanic histories, I stumbled upon an ancient Dutch volume, which, by the musty whaling smell of it, I knew must be about whalers. The title was, "Dan Coopman," wherefore I concluded that this must be the invaluable memoirs of some Amsterdam cooper in the fishery, as every whale ship must carry its cooper. I was reinforced in this opinion by seeing that it was the production of one "Fitz Swackhammer." But my friend Dr. Snodhead, a very learned man, professor of Low Dutch and High German in the college of Santa Claus and St. Pott's, to whom I handed the work for translation, giving him a box of sperm candles for his trouble—this same Dr. Snodhead, so soon as he spied the book, assured me that "Dan Coopman" did not mean "The Cooper," but "The Merchant." In short, this ancient and learned Low Dutch book treated of the commerce of Holland; and, among other subjects, contained a very interesting account of its whale fishery. And in this chapter it was, headed "Smeer," or "Fat," that I found a long detailed list of the outfits for the larders and cellars of 180 sail of Dutch whalemen; from which list, as translated by Dr. Snodhead, I transcribe the following:

400,000 lbs. of beef.
 60,000 lbs. Friesland pork.
150,000 lbs. of stock fish.
550,000 lbs. of biscuit.
 72,000 lbs. of soft bread.
  2,800 firkins of butter.
 20,000 lbs. Texel & Leyden cheese.
144,000 lbs. cheese (probably an inferior article).
    550 ankers of Geneva.
 10,800 barrels of beer.

Most statistical tables are parchingly dry in the reading; not so in the present case, however, where the reader is flooded with whole pipes, barrels, quarts, and gills of good gin and good cheer.

At the time, I devoted three days to the studious digesting of all this beer, beef, and bread, during which many profound thoughts were incidentally suggested to me, capable of a transcendental and Platonic application; and, furthermore, I compiled supplementary tables of my own, touching the probable quantity of stock-fish, &c., consumed by every Low Dutch harpooneer in that ancient Greenland and Spitzbergen whale fishery. In the first place, the amount of butter, and Texel and Leyden cheese consumed, seems amazing. I impute it, though, to their naturally unctuous natures, being rendered still more unctuous by the nature of their vocation, and especially by their pursuing their game in those frigid Polar Seas, on the very coasts of that Esquimaux country where the convivial natives pledge each other in bumpers of train oil.

The quantity of beer, too, is very large, 10,800 barrels. Now, as those polar fisheries could only be prosecuted in the short summer of that climate, so that the whole cruise of one of these Dutch whalemen, including the short voyage to and from the Spitzbergen sea, did not much exceed three months, say, and reckoning 30 men to each of their fleet of 180 sail, we have 5,400 Low Dutch seamen in all; therefore, I say, we have precisely two barrels of beer per man, for a twelve weeks' allowance, exclusive of his fair proportion of that 550 ankers of gin. Now, whether these gin and beer harpooneers, so fuddled as one might fancy them to have been, were the right sort of men to stand up in a boat's head, and take good aim at flying whales; this would seem somewhat improbable. Yet they did aim at them, and hit them too. But this was very far North, be it remembered, where beer agrees well with the constitution; upon the Equator, in our southern fishery, beer would be apt to make the harpooneer sleepy at the mast-head and boozy in his boat; and grievous loss might ensue to Nantucket and New Bedford.

But no more; enough has been said to show that the old Dutch whalers of two or three centuries ago were high livers; and that the English whalers have not neglected so excellent an example. For, say they, when cruising in an empty ship, if you can get nothing better out of the world, get a good dinner out of it, at least. And this empties the decanter.

# Chapter 102

*A Bower in the Arsacides*

HITHERTO, in descriptively treating of the Sperm Whale, I have chiefly dwelt upon the marvels of his outer aspect; or separately and in detail upon some few interior structural features. But to a large and thorough sweeping comprehension of him, it behoves me now to unbutton him still further, and untagging the points of his hose, unbuckling his garters, and casting loose the hooks and the eyes of the joints of his innermost bones, set him before you in his ultimatum; that is to say, in his unconditional skeleton.

But how now, Ishmael? How is it, that you, a mere oarsman in the fishery, pretend to know aught about the subterranean parts of the whale? Did erudite Stubb, mounted upon your capstan, deliver lectures on the anatomy of the Cetacea; and by help of the windlass, hold up a specimen rib for exhibition? Explain thyself, Ishmael. Can you land a full-grown whale on your deck for examination, as a cook dishes a roast-pig? Surely not. A veritable witness have you hitherto been, Ishmael; but have a care how you seize the privilege of Jonah alone; the privilege of discoursing upon the joists and beams; the rafters, ridge-pole, sleepers, and underpinnings, making up the frame-work of leviathan; and belike of the tallowvats, dairy-rooms, butteries, and cheeseries in his bowels.

I confess, that since Jonah, few whalemen have penetrated very far beneath the skin of the adult whale; nevertheless, I have been blessed with an opportunity to dissect him in miniature. In a ship I belonged to, a small cub Sperm Whale was once bodily hoisted to the deck for his poke or bag, to make sheaths for the barbs of the harpoons, and for the heads of the lances. Think you I let that chance go, without using my boat-hatchet and jack-knife, and breaking the seal and reading all the contents of that young cub?

And as for my exact knowledge of the bones of the leviathan in their gigantic, full grown development, for that rare knowledge I am indebted to my late royal friend Tranquo, king of Tranque, one of the Arsacides. For being at Tranque, years ago, when attached to the trading-ship Dey of Algiers, I was invited to spend part of the Arsacidean holidays with the lord of Tranque, at his retired palm villa at Pupella; a sea-side glen not very far distant from what our sailors called Bamboo-Town, his capital.

Among many other fine qualities, my royal friend Tranquo, being gifted with a devout love for all matters of barbaric vertù, had brought together in Pupella whatever rare things the more ingenious of his people could invent; chiefly carved woods of wonderful devices, chiselled shells, inlaid spears, costly paddles, aromatic canoes; and all these distributed among whatever natural wonders, the wonder-freighted, tribute-rendering waves had cast upon his shores.

Chief among these latter was a great Sperm Whale, which, after an unusually long raging gale, had been found dead and stranded, with his head against a cocoa-nut tree, whose plumage-like, tufted droopings seemed his verdant jet. When the vast body had at last been stripped of its fathom-deep enfoldings, and the bones become dust dry in the sun, then the skeleton was carefully transported up the Pupella glen, where a grand temple of lordly palms now sheltered it.

The ribs were hung with trophies; the vertebræ were carved with Arsacidean annals, in strange hieroglyphics; in the skull, the priests kept up an unextinguished aromatic flame, so that the mystic head again sent forth its vapory spout; while, suspended from a bough, the terrific lower jaw vibrated over all the devotees, like the hair-hung sword that so affrighted Damocles.

It was a wondrous sight. The wood was green as mosses of the Icy Glen; the trees stood high and haughty, feeling their living sap; the industrious earth beneath was as a weaver's loom, with a gorgeous carpet on it, whereof the ground-vine tendrils formed the warp and woof, and the living flowers the figures. All the trees, with all their laden branches; all the shrubs, and ferns, and grasses; the message-carrying air; all these unceasingly were active. Through the lacings of the leaves, the great sun seemed a flying shuttle weaving the unwearied verdure. Oh, busy weaver! unseen weaver! —pause!—one word!—whither flows the fabric? what palace may it deck? wherefore all these ceaseless toilings? Speak, weaver!—stay thy hand!— but one single word with thee! Nay—the shuttle flies—the figures float from forth the loom; the freshet-rushing carpet for ever slides away. The weaver-god, he weaves; and by that weaving is he deafened, that he hears no mortal voice; and by that humming, we, too, who look on the loom are deafened; and only when we escape it shall we hear the thousand voices that speak through it. For even so it is in all material factories. The spoken words that are inaudible among the flying spindles; those same words are plainly heard without the walls, bursting from the opened casements. Thereby have villanies been detected. Ah, mortal! then, be heedful; for so, in all this din of the great world's loom, thy subtlest thinkings may be overheard afar.

Now, amid the green, life-restless loom of that Arsacidean wood, the great, white, worshipped skeleton lay lounging—a gigantic idler! Yet, as the ever-woven verdant warp and woof intermixed and hummed around him, the mighty idler seemed the cunning weaver; himself all woven over with the vines; every month assuming greener, fresher verdure; but himself a skeleton. Life folded Death; Death trellised Life; the grim god wived with youthful Life, and begat him curly-headed glories.

Now, when with royal Tranquo I visited this wondrous whale, and saw the skull an altar, and the artificial smoke ascending from where the real jet had issued, I marvelled that the king should regard a chapel as an object of vertù. He laughed. But more I marvelled that the priests should swear that smoky jet of his was genuine. To and fro I paced before this skeleton—brushed the vines aside—broke through the ribs—and with a ball of Arsacidean twine, wandered, eddied long amid its many winding, shaded colonnades and arbors. But soon my line was out; and following it back, I emerged from the opening where I entered. I saw no living thing within; naught was there but bones.

Cutting me a green measuring-rod, I once more dived within the skeleton. From their arrow-slit in the skull, the priests perceived me taking the altitude of the final rib. "How now!" they shouted; "Dar'st thou measure this our god! That's for us." "Aye, priests—well, how long do ye make him, then?" But hereupon a fierce contest rose among them, concerning feet and inches; they cracked each other's sconces with their yard-sticks—the great skull echoed—and seizing that lucky chance, I quickly concluded my own admeasurements.

These admeasurements I now propose to set before you. But first, be it recorded, that, in this matter, I am not free to utter any fancied measurement I please. Because there are skeleton authorities you can refer to, to test my accuracy. There is a Leviathanic Museum, they tell me, in Hull, England, one of the whaling ports of that country, where they have some fine specimens of fin-backs and other whales. Likewise, I have heard that in the museum of Manchester, in New Hampshire, they have what the proprietors call "the only perfect specimen of a Greenland or River Whale in the United States." Moreover, at a place in Yorkshire, England, Burton Constable by name, a certain Sir Clifford Constable has in his possession the skeleton of a Sperm Whale, but of moderate size, by no means of the full-grown magnitude of my friend King Tranquo's.

In both cases, the stranded whales to which these two skeletons belonged, were originally claimed by their proprietors upon similar grounds. King Tranquo seizing his because he wanted it; and Sir Clifford, because he was lord of the seignories of those parts. Sir Clifford's whale has been articulated throughout; so that, like a great chest of drawers, you can open and shut him, in all his bony cavities—spread out his ribs like a gigantic fan—and swing all day upon his lower jaw. Locks are to be put upon some of his trap-doors and shutters; and a footman will show round future visitors with a bunch of keys at his side. Sir Clifford thinks of charging twopence for a peep at the whispering gallery in the spinal column; threepence to hear the echo in the hollow of his cerebellum; and sixpence for the unrivalled view from his forehead.

The skeleton dimensions I shall now proceed to set down are copied verbatim from my right arm, where I had them tattooed; as in my wild wanderings at that period, there was no other secure way of preserving such valuable statistics. But as I was crowded for space, and wished the other parts of my body to remain a blank page for a poem I was then composing —at least, what untattooed parts might remain—I did not trouble myself with the odd inches; nor, indeed, should inches at all enter into a congenial admeasurement of the whale.

# Chapter 103

### Measurement of the Whale's Skeleton

IN THE FIRST PLACE, I wish to lay before you a particular, plain statement, touching the living bulk of this leviathan, whose skeleton we are briefly to exhibit. Such a statement may prove useful here.

According to a careful calculation I have made, and which I partly base upon Captain Scoresby's estimate, of seventy tons for the largest sized Greenland whale of sixty feet in length; according to my careful calculation, I say, a Sperm Whale of the largest magnitude, between eighty-five and ninety feet in length, and something less than forty feet in its fullest circumference, such a whale will weigh at least ninety tons; so that, reckoning thirteen men to a ton, he would considerably outweigh the combined population of a whole village of one thousand one hundred inhabitants.

Think you not then that brains, like yoked cattle, should be put to this leviathan, to make him at all budge to any landsman's imagination?

Having already in various ways put before you his skull, spout-hole, jaw, teeth, tail, forehead, fins, and divers other parts, I shall now simply point out what is most interesting in the general bulk of his unobstructed bones. But as the colossal skull embraces so very large a proportion of the entire extent of the skeleton; as it is by far the most complicated part; and as nothing is to be repeated concerning it in this chapter, you must not fail to carry it in your mind, or under your arm, as we proceed, otherwise you will not gain a complete notion of the general structure we are about to view.

In length, the Sperm Whale's skeleton at Tranque measured seventy-two feet; so that when fully invested and extended in life, he must have been ninety feet long; for in the whale, the skeleton loses about one fifth in length compared with the living body. Of this seventy-two feet, his skull and jaw comprised some twenty feet, leaving some fifty feet of plain back-bone. Attached to this back-bone, for something less than a third of its length, was the mighty circular basket of ribs which once enclosed his vitals.

To me this vast ivory-ribbed chest, with the long, unrelieved spine, extending far away from it in a straight line, not a little resembled the embryo hull of a great ship new-laid upon the stocks, when only some twenty of her naked bow-ribs are inserted, and the keel is otherwise, for the time, but a long, disconnected timber.

The ribs were ten on a side. The first, to begin from the neck, was nearly six feet long; the second, third, and fourth were each successively longer, till you came to the climax of the fifth, or one of the middle ribs, which measured eight feet and some inches. From that part, the remaining ribs diminished, till the tenth and last only spanned five feet and some inches. In general thickness, they all bore a seemly correspondence to their length. The middle ribs were the most arched. In some of the Arsacides they are used for beams whereon to lay foot-path bridges over small streams.

In considering these ribs, I could not but be struck anew with the circumstance, so variously repeated in this book, that the skeleton of the whale is by no means the mould of his invested form. The largest of the Tranque ribs, one of the middle ones, occupied that part of the fish which, in life, is greatest in depth. Now, the greatest depth of the invested body of this particular whale must have been at least sixteen feet; whereas, the corresponding rib measured but little more than eight feet. So that this rib only conveyed half of the true notion of the living magnitude of that part. Besides, for some way, where I now saw but a naked spine, all that had been once wrapped round with tons of added bulk in flesh, muscle, blood, and bowels. Still more, for the ample fins, I here saw but a few disordered joints; and in place of the weighty and majestic, but boneless flukes, an utter blank!

How vain and foolish, then, thought I, for timid untravelled man to try to comprehend aright this wondrous whale, by merely poring over his dead attenuated skeleton, stretched in this peaceful wood. No. Only in the heart of quickest perils; only when within the eddyings of his angry flukes; only on the profound unbounded sea, can the fully invested whale be truly and livingly found out.

But the spine. For that, the best way we can consider it is, with a crane, to pile its bones high up on end. No speedy enterprise. But now it's done, it looks much like Pompey's Pillar.

There are forty and odd vertebræ in all, which in the skeleton are not locked together. They mostly lie like the great knobbed blocks on a Gothic spire, forming solid courses of heavy masonry. The largest, a middle one, is in width something less than three feet, and in depth more than four. The smallest, where the spine tapers away into the tail, is only two inches in width, and looks something like a white billiard-ball. I was told that there were still smaller ones, but they had been lost by some little cannibal urchins, the priest's children, who had stolen them to play marbles with. Thus we see how that the spine of even the hugest of living things tapers off at last into simple child's play.

# Chapter 104

### The Fossil Whale

ROM HIS MIGHTY BULK the whale affords a most congenial theme whereon to enlarge, amplify, and generally expatiate. Would you, you could not compress him. By good rights he should only be treated of in imperial folio. Not to tell over again his furlongs from spiracle to tail, and the yards he measures about the waist; only think of the gigantic involutions of his intestines, where they lie in him like great cables and hausers coiled away in the subterranean orlop-deck of a line-of-battle-ship.

Since I have undertaken to manhandle this Leviathan, it behoves me to approve myself omnisciently exhaustive in the enterprise; not overlooking the minutest seminal germs of his blood, and spinning him out to the uttermost coil of his bowels. Having already described him in most of his present habitatory and anatomical peculiarities, it now remains to magnify him in an archæological, fossiliferous, and antediluvian point of view. Applied to any other creature than the Leviathan—to an ant or a flea—such portly terms might justly be deemed unwarrantably grandiloquent. But when Leviathan is the text, the case is altered. Fain am I to stagger to this emprise under the weightiest words of the dictionary. And here be it said, that whenever it has been convenient to consult one in the course of these dissertations, I have invariably used a huge quarto edition of Johnson, expressly purchased for that purpose; because that famous lexicographer's

uncommon personal bulk more fitted him to compile a lexicon to be used
by a whale author like me.

One often hears of writers that rise and swell with their subject, though
it may seem but an ordinary one. How, then, with me, writing of this
Leviathan? Unconsciously my chirography expands into placard capitals.
Give me a condor's quill! Give me Vesuvius' crater for an inkstand!
Friends, hold my arms! For in the mere act of penning my thoughts of this
Leviathan, they weary me, and make me faint with their outreaching
comprehensiveness of sweep, as if to include the whole circle of the sciences,
and all the generations of whales, and men, and mastodons, past, present,
and to come, with all the revolving panoramas of empire on earth, and
throughout the whole universe, not excluding its suburbs. Such, and so
magnifying, is the virtue of a large and liberal theme! We expand to its bulk.
To produce a mighty book, you must choose a mighty theme. No great
and enduring volume can ever be written on the flea, though many there be
who have tried it.

Ere entering upon the subject of Fossil Whales, I present my credentials
as a geologist, by stating that in my miscellaneous time I have been a stone-
mason, and also a great digger of ditches, canals and wells, wine-vaults,
cellars, and cisterns of all sorts. Likewise, by way of preliminary, I desire to
remind the reader, that while in the earlier geological strata there are found
the fossils of monsters now almost completely extinct; the subsequent relics
discovered in what are called the Tertiary formations seem the connecting,
or at any rate intercepted links, between the antechronical creatures, and
those whose remote posterity are said to have entered the Ark; all the Fossil
Whales hitherto discovered belong to the Tertiary period, which is the last
preceding the superficial formations. And though none of them precisely
answer to any known species of the present time, they are yet sufficiently
akin to them in general respects, to justify their taking rank as Cetacean
fossils.

Detached broken fossils of pre-adamite whales, fragments of their bones
and skeletons, have within thirty years past, at various intervals, been found
at the base of the Alps, in Lombardy, in France, in England, in Scotland, and
in the States of Louisiana, Mississippi, and Alabama. Among the more
curious of such remains is part of a skull, which in the year 1779 was disinterred in the Rue Dauphine in Paris, a short street opening almost directly
upon the palace of the Tuileries; and bones disinterred in excavating the
great docks of Antwerp, in Napoleon's time. Cuvier pronounced these
fragments to have belonged to some utterly unknown Leviathanic species.

But by far the most wonderful of all cetacean relics was the almost complete vast skeleton of an extinct monster, found in the year 1842, on the plantation of Judge Creagh, in Alabama. The awe-stricken credulous slaves in the vicinity took it for the bones of one of the fallen angels. The Alabama doctors declared it a huge reptile, and bestowed upon it the name of Basilosaurus. But some specimen bones of it being taken across the sea to Owen, the English Anatomist, it turned out that this alleged reptile was a whale, though of a departed species. A significant illustration of the fact, again and again repeated in this book, that the skeleton of the whale furnishes but little clue to the shape of his fully invested body. So Owen rechristened the monster Zeuglodon; and in his paper read before the London Geological Society, pronounced it, in substance, one of the most extraordinary creatures which the mutations of the globe have blotted out of existence.

When I stand among these mighty Leviathan skeletons, skulls, tusks, jaws, ribs, and vertebræ, all characterized by partial resemblances to the existing breeds of sea-monsters; but at the same time bearing on the other hand similar affinities to the annihilated antechronical Leviathans, their incalculable seniors; I am, by a flood, borne back to that wondrous period, ere time itself can be said to have begun; for time began with man. Here Saturn's grey chaos rolls over me, and I obtain dim, shuddering glimpses into those Polar eternities; when wedged bastions of ice pressed hard upon what are now the Tropics; and in all the 25,000 miles of this world's circumference, not an inhabitable hand's breadth of land was visible. Then the whole world was the whale's; and, king of creation, he left his wake along the present lines of the Andes and the Himmalehs. Who can show a pedigree like Leviathan? Ahab's harpoon had shed older blood than the Pharaohs'. Methuselah seems a schoolboy. I look round to shake hands with Shem. I am horror-struck at this antemosaic, unsourced existence of the unspeakable terrors of the whale, which, having been before all time, must needs exist after all humane ages are over.

But not alone has this Leviathan left his pre-adamite traces in the stereotype plates of nature, and in limestone and marl bequeathed his ancient bust; but upon Egyptian tablets, whose antiquity seems to claim for them an almost fossiliferous character, we find the unmistakable print of his fin. In an apartment of the great temple of Denderah, some fifty years ago, there was discovered upon the granite ceiling a sculptured and painted planisphere, abounding in centaurs, griffins, and dolphins, similar to the grotesque figures on the celestial globe of the moderns. Gliding among them, old Leviathan swam as of yore; was there swimming in that plani-sphere, centuries before Solomon was cradled.

Nor must there be omitted another strange attestation of the antiquity of the whale, in his own osseous post-diluvian reality, as set down by the venerable John Leo, the old Barbary traveller.

"Not far from the Sea-side, they have a Temple, the Rafters and Beams of which are made of Whale-Bones; for Whales of a monstrous size are oftentimes cast up dead upon that shore. The Common People imagine, that by a secret Power bestowed by God upon the Temple, no Whale can pass by it without immediate death. But the truth of the Matter is, that on either side of the Temple, there are Rocks that shoot two Miles into the Sea, and wound the Whales when they light upon 'em. They keep a Whale's Rib of an incredible length for a Miracle, which lying upon the Ground with its convex part uppermost, makes an Arch, the Head of which cannot be reached by a Man upon a Camel's Back. This Rib (says John Leo) is said to have layn there a hundred Years before I saw it. Their Historians affirm, that a Prophet who prophesy'd of Mahomet, came from this Temple, and some do not stand to assert, that the Prophet Jonas was cast forth by the Whale at the Base of the Temple."

In this Afric Temple of the Whale I leave you, reader, and if you be a Nantucketer, and a whaleman, you will silently worship there.

# Chapter 105

*Does the Whale's Magnitude Diminish?—Will He Perish?*

INASMUCH, THEN, as this Leviathan comes floundering down upon us from the head-waters of the Eternities, it may be fitly inquired, whether, in the long course of his generations, he has not degenerated from the original bulk of his sires.

But upon investigation we find, that not only are the whales of the present day superior in magnitude to those whose fossil remains are found in the Tertiary system (embracing a distinct geological period prior to man), but of the whales found in that Tertiary system, those belonging to its latter formations exceed in size those of its earlier ones.

Of all the pre-adamite whales yet exhumed, by far the largest is the Alabama one mentioned in the last chapter, and that was less than seventy feet in length in the skeleton. Whereas, we have already seen, that the tapemeasure gives seventy-two feet for the skeleton of a large sized modern whale. And I have heard, on whalemen's authority, that Sperm Whales have been captured near a hundred feet long at the time of capture.

But may it not be, that while the whales of the present hour are an advance in magnitude upon those of all previous geological periods; may it not be, that since Adam's time they have degenerated?

Assuredly, we must conclude so, if we are to credit the accounts of such gentlemen as Pliny, and the ancient naturalists generally. For Pliny tells us of whales that embraced acres of living bulk, and Aldrovandus of others which measured eight hundred feet in length—Rope Walks and Thames Tunnels of Whales! And even in the days of Banks and Solander, Cook's naturalists, we find a Swedish member of the Academy of Sciences setting down certain Iceland Whales (reydar-fiskur, or Wrinkled Bellies) at one hundred and twenty yards; that is, three hundred and sixty feet. And Lacépède, the French naturalist, in his elaborate history of whales, in the very beginning of his work (page 3), sets down the Right Whale at one hundred metres, three hundred and twenty-eight feet. And this work was published so late as A.D. 1825.

But will any whaleman believe these stories? No. The whale of to-day is as big as his ancestors in Pliny's time. And if ever I go where Pliny is, I, a whaleman (more than he was), will make bold to tell him so. Because I cannot understand how it is, that while the Egyptian mummies that were buried thousands of years before even Pliny was born, do not measure so much in their coffins as a modern Kentuckian in his socks; and while the cattle and other animals sculptured on the oldest Egyptian and Nineveh tablets, by the relative proportions in which they are drawn, just as plainly prove that the high-bred, stall-fed, prize cattle of Smithfield, not only equal, but far exceed in magnitude the fattest of Pharaoh's fat kine; in the face of all this, I will not admit that of all animals the whale alone should have degenerated.

But still another inquiry remains; one often agitated by the more recondite Nantucketers. Whether owing to the almost omniscient look-outs at the mast-heads of the whale-ships, now penetrating even through Behring's straits, and into the remotest secret drawers and lockers of the world; and the thousand harpoons and lances darted along all continental coasts; the moot point is, whether Leviathan can long endure so wide a chase, and so remorseless a havoc; whether he must not at last be extermi-nated from the waters, and the last whale, like the last man, smoke his last pipe, and then himself evaporate in the final puff.

Comparing the humped herds of whales with the humped herds of buffalo, which, not forty years ago, overspread by tens of thousands the prairies of Illinois and Missouri, and shook their iron manes and scowled with their thunder-clotted brows upon the sites of populous river-capitals, where now the polite broker sells you land at a dollar an inch; in such a comparison an irresistible argument would seem furnished, to show that the hunted whale cannot now escape speedy extinction.

But you must look at this matter in every light. Though so short a period ago—not a good life-time—the census of the buffalo in Illinois exceeded the census of men now in London, and though at the present day not one horn or hoof of them remains in all that region; and though the cause of this wondrous extermination was the spear of man; yet the far different nature of the whale-hunt peremptorily forbids so inglorious an end to the Leviathan. Forty men in one ship hunting the Sperm Whale for forty-eight months think they have done extremely well, and thank God, if at last they carry home the oil of forty fish. Whereas, in the days of the old Canadian and Indian hunters and trappers of the West, when the far west (in whose sunset suns still rise) was a wilderness and a virgin, the same number of moccasined men, for the same number of months, mounted on horse instead of sailing in ships, would have slain not forty, but forty thousand and more buffaloes; a fact that, if need were, could be statistically stated.

Nor, considered aright, does it seem any argument in favor of the gradual extinction of the Sperm Whale, for example, that in former years (the latter part of the last century, say) these Leviathans, in small pods, were encountered much oftener than at present, and, in consequence, the voyages were not so prolonged, and were also much more remunerative. Because, as has been elsewhere noticed, those whales, influenced by some views to safety, now swim the seas in immense caravans, so that to a large degree the scattered solitaries, yokes, and pods, and schools of other days are now aggregated into vast but widely separated, unfrequent armies. That is all. And equally fallacious seems the conceit, that because the so-called whale-bone whales no longer haunt many grounds in former years abounding with them, hence that species also is declining. For they are only being driven from promontory to cape; and if one coast is no longer enlivened with their jets, then, be sure, some other and remoter strand has been very recently startled by the unfamiliar spectacle.

Furthermore: concerning these last mentioned Leviathans, they have two firm fortresses, which, in all human probability, will for ever remain impregnable. And as upon the invasion of their valleys, the frosty Swiss have retreated to their mountains; so, hunted from the savannas and glades of the middle seas, the whale-bone whales can at last resort to their Polar citadels, and diving under the ultimate glassy barriers and walls there, come up among icy fields and floes; and in a charmed circle of everlasting December, bid defiance to all pursuit from man.

But as perhaps fifty of these whale-bone whales are harpooned for one cachalot, some philosophers of the forecastle have concluded that this positive havoc has already very seriously diminished their battalions. But though for some time past a number of these whales, not less than 13,000, have been annually slain on the nor' west coast by the Americans alone; yet there are considerations which render even this circumstance of little or no account as an opposing argument in this matter.

Natural as it is to be somewhat incredulous concerning the populousness of the more enormous creatures of the globe, yet what shall we say to Horto, the historian of Goa, when he tells us that at one hunting the King of Siam took 4000 elephants; that in those regions elephants are numerous as droves of cattle in the temperate climes. And there seems no reason to doubt that if these elephants, which have now been hunted for thousands of years, by Semiramis, by Porus, by Hannibal, and by all the successive monarchs of the East—if they still survive there in great numbers, much more may the great whale outlast all hunting, since he has a pasture to expatiate in, which is precisely twice as large as all Asia, both Americas, Europe and Africa, New Holland, and all the Isles of the sea combined.

Moreover: we are to consider, that from the presumed great longevity of whales, their probably attaining the age of a century and more, therefore at any one period of time, several distinct adult generations must be contemporary. And what that is, we may soon gain some idea of, by imagining all the grave-yards, cemeteries, and family vaults of creation yielding up the live bodies of all the men, women, and children who were alive seventy-five years ago; and adding this countless host to the present human population of the globe.

Wherefore, for all these things, we account the whale immortal in his species, however perishable in his individuality. He swam the seas before the continents broke water; he once swam over the site of the Tuileries, and Windsor Castle, and the Kremlin. In Noah's flood he despised Noah's Ark; and if ever the world is to be again flooded, like the Netherlands, to kill off its rats, then the eternal whale will still survive, and rearing upon the topmost crest of the equatorial flood, spout his frothed defiance to the skies.

# Chapter 106

### *Ahab's Leg*

THE PRECIPITATING MANNER in which Captain Ahab had quitted the Samuel Enderby of London, had not been unattended with some small violence to his own person. He had lighted with such energy upon a thwart of his boat that his ivory leg had received a half-splintering shock. And when after gaining his own deck, and his own pivot-hole there, he so vehemently wheeled round with an urgent command to the steersman (it was, as ever, something about his not steering inflexibly enough); then, the already shaken ivory received such an additional twist and wrench, that though it still remained entire, and to all appearances lusty, yet Ahab did not deem it entirely trustworthy.

And, indeed, it seemed small matter for wonder, that for all his pervading, mad recklessness, Ahab did at times give careful heed to the condition of that dead bone upon which he partly stood. For it had not been very long prior to the Pequod's sailing from Nantucket, that he had been found one night lying prone upon the ground, and insensible; by some unknown, and seemingly inexplicable, unimaginable casualty, his ivory limb having been so violently displaced, that it had stake-wise smitten, and all but pierced his groin; nor was it without extreme difficulty that the agonizing wound was entirely cured.

Nor, at the time, had it failed to enter his monomaniac mind, that all the anguish of that then present suffering was but the direct issue of a former woe; and he too plainly seemed to see, that as the most poisonous reptile of the marsh perpetuates his kind as inevitably as the sweetest songster of the grove; so, equally with every felicity, all miserable events do naturally beget their like. Yea, more than equally, thought Ahab; since both the ancestry and posterity of Grief go further than the ancestry and posterity of Joy. For, not to hint of this: that it is an inference from certain canonic teachings, that while some natural enjoyments here shall have no children born to them for the other world, but, on the contrary, shall be followed by the joy-childlessness of all hell's despair; whereas, some guilty mortal miseries shall still fertilely beget to themselves an eternally progressive progeny of griefs beyond the grave; not at all to hint of this, there still seems an inequality in the deeper analysis of the thing. For, thought Ahab, while even the highest earthly felicities ever have a certain unsignifying pettiness lurking in them, but, at bottom, all heart-woes, a mystic significance, and, in some men, an archangelic grandeur; so do their diligent tracings-out not belie the obvious deduction. To trail the genealogies of these high mortal miseries, carries us at last among the sourceless primogenitures of the gods; so that, in the face of all the glad, hay-making suns, and soft-cymballing, round harvest-moons, we must needs give in to this: that the gods themselves are not for ever glad. The ineffaceable, sad birth-mark in the brow of man, is but the stamp of sorrow in the signers.

Unwittingly here a secret has been divulged, which perhaps might more properly, in set way, have been disclosed before. With many other particulars concerning Ahab, always had it remained a mystery to some, why it was, that for a certain period, both before and after the sailing of the Pequod, he had hidden himself away with such Grand-Lama-like exclusiveness; and, for that one interval, sought speechless refuge, as it were, among the marble senate of the dead. Captain Peleg's bruited reason for this thing appeared by no means adequate; though, indeed, as touching all Ahab's deeper part, every revelation partook more of significant darkness than of explanatory light. But, in the end, it all came out; this one matter did, at least. That direful mishap was at the bottom of his temporary recluseness. And not only this, but to that ever-contracting, dropping circle ashore, who, for any reason, possessed the privilege of a less banned approach to him; to that timid circle the above hinted casualty—remaining, as it did, moodily unaccounted for by Ahab—invested itself with terrors, not entirely underived from the land of spirits and of wails. So that, through their zeal for him, they had all conspired, so far as in them lay, to muffle up the knowledge of this thing from others; and hence it was, that not till a considerable interval had elapsed, did it transpire upon the Pequod's decks.

But be all this as it may; let the unseen, ambiguous synod in the air, or the vindictive princes and potentates of fire, have to do or not with earthly Ahab, yet, in this present matter of his leg, he took plain practical procedures; —he called the carpenter.

And when that functionary appeared before him, he bade him without delay set about making a new leg, and directed the mates to see him supplied with all the studs and joists of jaw-ivory (Sperm Whale) which had thus far been accumulated on the voyage, in order that a careful selection of the stoutest, clearest-grained stuff might be secured. This done, the carpenter received orders to have the leg completed that night; and to provide all the fittings for it, independent of those pertaining to the distrusted one in use. Moreover, the ship's forge was ordered to be hoisted out of its temporary idleness in the hold; and, to accelerate the affair, the blacksmith was commanded to proceed at once to the forging of whatever iron contrivances might be needed.

# Chapter 107

## The Carpenter

SEAT THYSELF SULTANICALLY among the moons of Saturn, and take high abstracted man alone; and he seems a wonder, a grandeur, and a woe. But from the same point, take mankind in mass, and for the most part, they seem a mob of unnecessary duplicates, both contemporary and hereditary. But most humble though he was, and far from furnishing an example of the high, humane abstraction; the Pequod's carpenter was no duplicate; hence, he now comes in person on this stage.

Like all sea-going ship carpenters, and more especially those belonging to whaling vessels, he was, to a certain off-handed, practical extent, alike experienced in numerous trades and callings collateral to his own; the carpenter's pursuit being the ancient and outbranching trunk of all those numerous handicrafts which more or less have to do with wood as an auxiliary material. But, besides the application to him of the generic remark above, this carpenter of the Pequod was singularly efficient in those thousand nameless mechanical emergencies continually recurring in a large ship, upon a three or four years' voyage, in uncivilized and far-distant seas. For not to speak of his readiness in ordinary duties:—repairing stove boats, sprung spars, reforming the shape of clumsy-bladed oars, inserting bull's eyes in the deck, or new tree-nails in the side planks, and other miscellaneous matters more directly pertaining to his special business; he was moreover unhesitatingly expert in all manner of conflicting aptitudes, both useful and capricious.

The one grand stage where he enacted all his various parts so manifold, was his vice-bench; a long rude ponderous table furnished with several vices, of different sizes, and both of iron and of wood. At all times except when whales were alongside, this bench was securely lashed athwartships against the rear of the Try-works.

A belaying pin is found too large to be easily inserted into its hole: the carpenter claps it into one of his ever-ready vices, and straightway files it smaller. A lost land-bird of strange plumage strays on board, and is made a captive: out of clean shaved rods of right-whale bone, and cross-beams of sperm whale ivory, the carpenter makes a pagoda-looking cage for it. An oarsman sprains his wrist: the carpenter concocts a soothing lotion. Stubb longs for vermillion stars to be painted upon the blade of his every oar: screwing each oar in his big vice of wood, the carpenter symmetrically supplies the constellation. A sailor takes a fancy to wear shark-bone ear-rings: the carpenter drills his ears. Another has the toothache: the carpenter out pincers, and clapping one hand upon his bench bids him be seated there; but the poor fellow unmanageably winces under the unconcluded operation; whirling round the handle of his wooden vice, the carpenter signs him to clap his jaw in that, if he would have him draw the tooth.

Thus, this carpenter was prepared at all points, and alike indifferent and without respect in all. Teeth he accounted bits of ivory; heads he deemed but top-blocks; men themselves he lightly held for capstans. But while now upon so wide a field thus variously accomplished, and with such liveliness of expertness in him, too; all this would seem to argue some uncommon vivacity of intelligence. But not precisely so. For nothing was this man more remarkable, than for a certain impersonal stolidity as it were; impersonal, I say; for it so shaded off into the surrounding infinite of things, that it seemed one with the general stolidity discernible in the whole visible world; which while pauselessly active in uncounted modes, still eternally holds its peace, and ignores you, though you dig foundations for cathedrals. Yet was this half-horrible stolidity in him, involving, too, as it appeared, an all-ramifying heartlessness;—yet was it oddly dashed at times, with an old, crutch-like, antediluvian, wheezing humorousness, not unstreaked now and then with a certain grizzled wittiness; such as might have served to pass the time during the midnight watch on the bearded forecastle of Noah's ark. Was it that this old carpenter had been a life-long wanderer, whose much rolling, to and fro, not only had gathered no moss; but what is more, had

rubbed off whatever small outward clingings might have originally per-
tained to him? He was a stript abstract; an unfractioned integral; uncompromised as a new-born babe; living without premeditated reference to this
world or the next. You might almost say, that this strange uncompro-
misedness in him involved a sort of unintelligence; for in his numerous
trades, he did not seem to work so much by reason or by instinct, or simply
because he had been tutored to it, or by any intermixture of all these, even
or uneven; but merely by a kind of deaf and dumb, spontaneous literal
process. He was a pure manipulator; his brain, if he had ever had one, must
have early oozed along into the muscles of his fingers. He was like one of
those unreasoning but still highly useful, *multum in parvo*, Sheffield contrivances, assuming the exterior—though a little swelled—of a common
pocket knife; but containing, not only blades of various sizes, but also
screw-drivers, cork-screws, tweezers, awls, pens, rulers, nail-filers,
countersinkers. So, if his superiors wanted to use the carpenter for a screw-
driver, all they had to do was to open that part of him, and the screw was
fast: or if for tweezers, take him up by the legs, and there they were.

Yet, as previously hinted, this omnitooled, open-and-shut carpenter,
was, after all, no mere machine of an automaton. If he did not have a
common soul in him, he had a subtle something that somehow anomalously did its duty. What that was, whether essence of quicksilver, or a few drops
of hartshorn, there is no telling. But there it was; and there it had abided for
now some sixty years or more. And this it was, this same unaccountable,
cunning life-principle in him; this it was, that kept him a great part of the
time soliloquizing; but only like an unreasoning wheel, which also hum-
mingly soliloquizes; or rather, his body was a sentry-box and this solil-
oquizer on guard there, and talking all the time to keep himself awake.

# Chapter 108

*Ahab and the Carpenter*

THE DECK—FIRST NIGHT WATCH

*(Carpenter standing before his vice-bench, and by the light of two lanterns busily filing the ivory joist for the leg, which joist is firmly fixed in the vice. Slabs of ivory, leather straps, pads, screws, and various tools of all sorts lying about the bench. Forward, the red flame of the forge is seen, where the blacksmith is at work.)*

DRAT THE FILE, and drat the bone! That is hard which should be soft, and that is soft which should be hard. So we go, who file old jaws and shinbones. Let's try another. Aye, now, this works better *(sneezes)*. Halloa, this bone dust is *(sneezes)*—why it's *(sneezes)* — yes it's *(sneezes)*—bless my soul, it won't let me speak! This is what an old fellow gets now for working in dead lumber. Saw a live tree, and you don't get this dust; amputate a live bone, and you don't get it *(sneezes)*. Come, come, you old Smut, there, bear a hand, and let's have that ferule and buckle-screw; I'll be ready for them presently. Lucky now *(sneezes)* there's no knee-joint to make; that might puzzle a little; but a mere shin-bone—why it's easy as making hop-poles; only I should like to put a good finish on. Time, time; if I but only had the time, I could turn him out as neat a leg now as ever *(sneezes)* scraped to a lady in a parlor. Those buckskin legs and calves of legs I've seen in shop windows wouldn't compare at all. They soak water, they do; and of course get rheumatic, and have to be doctored *(sneezes)* with washes and lotions, just like live legs. There; before I saw it off, now, I must call his old Mogulship, and see whether the length will be all right; too short, if anything, I guess. Ha! that's the heel; we are in luck; here he comes, or it's somebody else, that's certain.

AHAB *(advancing).*

*(During the ensuing scene, the carpenter continues sneezing at times.)*
Well, manmaker!

Just in time, sir. If the captain pleases, I will now mark the length. Let me measure, sir.

Measured for a leg! good. Well, it's not the first time. About it! There; keep thy finger on it. This is a cogent vice thou hast here, carpenter; let me feel its grip once. So, so; it does pinch some.

Oh, sir, it will break bones—beware, beware!

No fear; I like a good grip; I like to feel something in this slippery world that can hold, man. What's Prometheus about there?—the blacksmith, I mean—what's he about?

He must be forging the buckle-screw, sir, now.

Right. It's a partnership; he supplies the muscle part. He makes a fierce red flame there!

Aye, sir; he must have the white heat for this kind of fine work.

Um-m. So he must. I do deem it now a most meaning thing, that that old Greek, Prometheus, who made men, they say, should have been a blacksmith, and animated them with fire; for what's made in fire must properly belong to fire; and so hell's probable. How the soot flies! This must be the remainder the Greek made the Africans of. Carpenter, when he's through with that buckle, tell him to forge a pair of steel shoulder-blades; there's a pedlar aboard with a crushing pack.

Sir?

Hold; while Prometheus is about it, I'll order a complete man after a desirable pattern. Imprimis, fifty feet high in his socks; then, chest modelled after the Thames Tunnel; then, legs with roots to 'em, to stay in one place; then, arms three feet through the wrist; no heart at all, brass forehead, and about a quarter of an acre of fine brains; and let me see—shall I order eyes to see outwards? No, but put a sky-light on top of his head to illuminate inwards. There, take the order, and away.

Now, what's he speaking about, and who's he speaking to, I should like to know? Shall I keep standing here? *(aside.)*

'Tis but indifferent architecture to make a blind dome; here's one. No, no, no; I must have a lantern.

Ho, ho! That's it, hey? Here are two, sir; one will serve my turn.

What art thou thrusting that thief-catcher into my face for, man? Thrusted light is worse than presented pistols.

I thought, sir, that you spoke to carpenter.

Carpenter? why that's—but no;—a very tidy, and, I may say, an extremely gentlemanlike sort of business thou art in here, carpenter;—or would'st thou rather work in clay?

Sir?—Clay? clay, sir? That's mud; we leave clay to ditchers, sir.

The fellow's impious! What art thou sneezing about?

Bone is rather dusty, sir.

Take the hint, then; and when thou art dead, never bury thyself under living people's noses.

Sir?—oh! ah!—I guess so;—yes—oh, dear!

Look ye, carpenter, I dare say thou callest thyself a right good workman-like workman, eh? Well, then, will it speak thoroughly well for thy work, if, when I come to mount this leg thou makest, I shall nevertheless feel another leg in the same identical place with it; that is, carpenter, my old lost leg; the flesh and blood one, I mean. Canst thou not drive that old Adam away?

Truly, sir, I begin to understand somewhat now. Yes, I have heard something curious on that score, sir; how that a dismasted man never entirely loses the feeling of his old spar, but it will be still pricking him at times. May I humbly ask if it be really so, sir?

It is, man. Look, put thy live leg here in the place where mine once was; so, now, here is only one distinct leg to the eye, yet two to the soul. Where thou feelest tingling life; there, exactly there, there to a hair, do I. Is't a riddle?

I should humbly call it a poser, sir.

Hist, then. How dost thou know that some entire, living, thinking thing may not be invisibly and uninterpenetratingly standing precisely where thou now standest; aye, and standing there in thy spite? In thy most solitary hours, then, dost thou not fear eavesdroppers? Hold, don't speak! And if I still feel the smart of my crushed leg, though it be now so long dissolved; then, why mayst not thou, carpenter, feel the fiery pains of hell for ever, and without a body? Hah!

Good Lord! Truly, sir, if it comes to that, I must calculate over again; I think I didn't carry a small figure, sir.

Look ye, pudding-heads should never grant premises.—How long before the leg is done?

Perhaps an hour, sir.

Bungle away at it then, and bring it to me *(turns to go)*. Oh, Life! Here I am, proud as a Greek god, and yet standing debtor to this blockhead for a bone to stand on! Cursed be that mortal inter-indebtedness which will not do away with ledgers. I would be free as air; and I'm down in the whole world's books. I am so rich, I could have given bid for bid with the wealthiest Prætorians at the auction of the Roman empire (which was the world's); and yet I owe for the flesh in the tongue I brag with. By heavens! I'll get a crucible, and into it, and dissolve myself down to one small, compendious vertebra. So.

CARPENTER.
*(Resuming his work.)*

Well, well, well! Stubb knows him best of all, and Stubb always says he's queer; says nothing but that one sufficient little word queer; he's queer, says Stubb; he's queer—queer, queer; and keeps dinning it into Mr. Starbuck all the time—queer, sir—queer, queer, very queer. And here's his leg! Yes, now that I think of it, here's his bedfellow! has a stick of whale's jaw-bone for a wife! And this is his leg; he'll stand on this. What was that now about one leg standing in three places, and all three places standing in one hell—how was that? Oh! I don't wonder he looked so scornful at me! I'm a sort of strange-thoughted sometimes, they say; but that's only haphazard-like. Then, a short, little old body like me, should never undertake to wade out into deep waters with tall, heron-built captains; the water chucks you under the chin pretty quick, and there's a great cry for life-boats. And here's the heron's leg! long and slim, sure enough! Now, for most folks one pair of legs lasts a lifetime, and that must be because they use them mercifully, as a tender-hearted old lady uses her roly-poly old coach-horses. But Ahab; oh he's a hard driver. Look, driven one leg to death, and spavined the other for life, and now wears out bone legs by the cord. Halloa, there, you Smut! bear a hand there with those screws, and let's finish it before the resurrection fellow comes a-calling with his horn for all legs, true or false, as brewery-men go round collecting old beer barrels, to fill 'em up again. What a leg this is! It looks like a real live leg, filed down to nothing but the core; he'll be standing on this to-morrow; he'll be taking altitudes on it. Halloa! I almost forgot the little oval slate, smoothed ivory, where he figures up the latitude. So, so; chisel, file, and sand-paper, now!

# Chapter 109

*Ahab and Starbuck in the Cabin*

ACCORDING TO USAGE they were pumping the ship next morning; and lo! no inconsiderable oil came up with the water; the casks below must have sprung a bad leak. Much concern was shown; and Starbuck went down into the cabin to report this unfavorable affair.*

Now, from the South and West the Pequod was drawing nigh to Formosa and the Bashee Isles, between which lies one of the tropical outlets from the China waters into the Pacific. And so Starbuck found Ahab with a general chart of the oriental archipelagoes spread before him; and another separate one representing the long eastern coasts of the Japanese islands—Niphon, Matsmai, and Sikoke. With his snow-white new ivory leg braced against the screwed leg of his table, and with a long pruning-hook of a jack-knife in his hand, the wondrous old man, with his back to the gangway door, was wrinkling his brow, and tracing his old courses again.

"Who's there?" hearing the footstep at the door, but not turning round to it. "On deck! Begone!"

* In Sperm-whalemen with any considerable quantity of oil on board, it is a regular semi-weekly duty to conduct a hose into the hold, and drench the casks with sea-water; which afterwards, at varying intervals, is removed by the ship's pumps. Hereby the casks are sought to be kept damply tight; while by the changed character of the withdrawn water, the mariners readily detect any serious leakage in the precious cargo.

473

"Captain Ahab mistakes; it is I. The oil in the hold is leaking, sir. We must up Burtons and break out."

"Up Burtons and break out? Now that we are nearing Japan; heave-to here for a week to tinker a parcel of old hoops?"

"Either do that, sir, or waste in one day more oil than we may make good in a year. What we come twenty thousand miles to get is worth saving, sir."

"So it is, so it is; if we get it."

"I was speaking of the oil in the hold, sir."

"And I was not speaking or thinking of that at all. Begone! Let it leak! I'm all aleak myself. Aye! leaks in leaks! not only full of leaky casks, but those leaky casks are in a leaky ship; and that's a far worse plight than the Pequod's, man. Yet I don't stop to plug my leak; for who can find it in the deep-loaded hull; or how hope to plug it, even if found, in this life's howling gale? Starbuck! I'll not have the Burtons hoisted."

"What will the owners say, sir?"

"Let the owners stand on Nantucket beach and outyell the Typhoons. What cares Ahab? Owners, owners? Thou art always prating to me, Starbuck, about those miserly owners, as if the owners were my conscience. But look ye, the only real owner of anything is its commander; and hark ye, my conscience is in this ship's keel.—On deck!"

"Captain Ahab," said the reddening mate, moving further into the cabin, with a daring so strangely respectful and cautious that it almost seemed not only every way seeking to avoid the slightest outward manifestation of itself, but within also seemed more than half distrustful of itself; "A better man than I might well pass over in thee what he would quickly enough resent in a younger man; aye, and in a happier, Captain Ahab."

"Devils! Dost thou then so much as dare to critically think of me?— On deck!"

"Nay, sir, not yet; I do entreat. And I do dare, sir—to be forbearing! Shall we not understand each other better than hitherto, Captain Ahab?"

Ahab seized a loaded musket from the rack (forming part of most South-Sea-men's cabin furniture), and pointing it towards Starbuck, exclaimed: "There is one God that is Lord over the earth, and one Captain that is lord over the Pequod.—On deck!"

For an instant in the flashing eyes of the mate, and his fiery cheeks, you would have almost thought that he had really received the blaze of the levelled tube. But, mastering his emotion, he half calmly rose, and as he quitted the cabin, paused for an instant and said: "Thou hast outraged, not insulted me, sir; but for that I ask thee not to beware of Starbuck; thou wouldst but laugh; but let Ahab beware of Ahab; beware of thyself, old man."

"He waxes brave, but nevertheless obeys; most careful bravery that!" murmured Ahab, as Starbuck disappeared. "What's that he said—Ahab beware of Ahab—there's something there!" Then unconsciously using the musket for a staff, with an iron brow he paced to and fro in the little cabin; but presently the thick plaits of his forehead relaxed, and returning the gun to the rack, he went to the deck.

"Thou art but too good a fellow, Starbuck," he said lowly to the mate; then raising his voice to the crew: "Furl the t'gallant-sails, and close-reef the top-sails, fore and aft; back the main-yard; up Burtons, and break out in the main-hold."

It were perhaps vain to surmise exactly why it was, that as respecting Starbuck, Ahab thus acted. It may have been a flash of honesty in him; or mere prudential policy which, under the circumstance, imperiously forbade the slightest symptom of open disaffection, however transient, in the important chief officer of his ship. However it was, his orders were executed; and the Burtons were hoisted.

# Chapter 110

## Queequeg in his Coffin

UPON SEARCHING, it was found that the casks last struck into the hold were perfectly sound, and that the leak must be further off. So, it being calm weather, they broke out deeper and deeper, disturbing the slumbers of the huge ground-tier butts; and from that black midnight sending those gigantic moles into the daylight above. So deep did they go; and so ancient, and corroded, and weedy the aspect of the lowermost puncheons, that you almost looked next for some mouldy corner-stone cask containing coins of Captain Noah, with copies of the posted placards, vainly warning the infatuated old world from the flood. Tierce after tierce, too, of water, and bread, and beef, and shooks of staves, and iron bundles of hoops, were hoisted out, till at last the piled decks were hard to get about; and the hollow hull echoed under foot, as if you were treading over empty catacombs, and reeled and rolled in the sea like an air-freighted demijohn. Top-heavy was the ship as a dinnerless student with all Aristotle in his head. Well was it that the Typhoons did not visit them then.

Now, at this time it was that my poor pagan companion, and fast bosom-friend, Queequeg, was seized with a fever, which brought him nigh to his endless end.

Be it said, that in this vocation of whaling, sinecures are unknown;

dignity and danger go hand in hand; till you get to be Captain, the higher you rise the harder you toil. So with poor Queequeg, who, as harpooneer, must not only face all the rage of the living whale, but—as we have elsewhere seen—mount his dead back in a rolling sea; and finally descend into the gloom of the hold, and bitterly sweating all day in that subterraneous confinement, resolutely manhandle the clumsiest casks and see to their stowage. To be short, among whalemen, the harpooneers are the holders, so called.

Poor Queequeg! when the ship was about half disembowelled, you should have stooped over the hatchway, and peered down upon him there; where, stripped to his woollen drawers, the tattooed savage was crawling about amid that dampness and slime, like a green spotted lizard at the bottom of a well. And a well, or an ice-house, it somehow proved to him, poor pagan; where, strange to say, for all the heat of his sweatings, he caught a terrible chill which lapsed into a fever; and at last, after some days' suffering, laid him in his hammock, close to the very sill of the door of death. How he wasted and wasted away in those few long-lingering days, till there seemed but little left of him but his frame and tattooing. But as all else in him thinned, and his cheek-bones grew sharper, his eyes, nevertheless, seemed growing fuller and fuller; they became of a strange softness of lustre; and mildly but deeply looked out at you there from his sickness, a wondrous testimony to that immortal health in him which could not die, or be weakened. And like circles on the water, which, as they grow fainter, expand; so his eyes seemed rounding and rounding, like the rings of Eternity. An awe that cannot be named would steal over you as you sat by the side of this waning savage, and saw as strange things in his face, as any beheld who were bystanders when Zoroaster died. For whatever is truly wondrous and fearful in man, never yet was put into words or books. And the drawing near of Death, which alike levels all, alike impresses all with a last revelation, which only an author from the dead could adequately tell. So that—let us say it again—no dying Chaldee or Greek had higher and holier thoughts than those, whose mysterious shades you saw creeping over the face of poor Queequeg, as he quietly lay in his swaying hammock, and the rolling sea seemed gently rocking him to his final rest, and the ocean's invisible flood-tide lifted him higher and higher towards his destined heaven.

Not a man of the crew but gave him up; and, as for Queequeg himself, what he thought of his case was forcibly shown by a curious favor he asked. He called one to him in the grey morning watch, when the day was just breaking, and taking his hand, said that while in Nantucket he had chanced to see certain little canoes of dark wood, like the rich war-wood of his native isle; and upon inquiry, he had learned that all whalemen who died in Nantucket, were laid in those same dark canoes, and that the fancy of being so laid had much pleased him; for it was not unlike the custom of his own race, who, after embalming a dead warrior, stretched him out in his canoe, and so left him to be floated away to the starry archipelagoes; for not only do they believe that the stars are isles, but that far beyond all visible horizons, their own mild, uncontinented seas, interflow with the blue heavens; and so form the white breakers of the milky way. He added, that he shuddered at the thought of being buried in his hammock, according to the usual sea-. custom, tossed like something vile to the death-devouring sharks. No: he desired a canoe like those of Nantucket, all the more congenial to him, being a whaleman, that like a whale-boat these coffin-canoes were without a keel; though that involved but uncertain steering, and much lee-way adown the dim ages.

Now, when this strange circumstance was made known aft, the carpenter was at once commanded to do Queequeg's bidding, whatever it might include. There was some heathenish, coffin-colored old lumber aboard, which, upon a long previous voyage, had been cut from the aboriginal groves of the Lackaday islands, and from these dark planks the coffin was recommended to be made. No sooner was the carpenter apprised of the order, than taking his rule, he forthwith with all the indifferent promptitude of his character, proceeded into the forecastle and took Queequeg's measure with great accuracy, regularly chalking Queequeg's person as he shifted the rule.

"Ah! poor fellow! he'll have to die now," ejaculated the Long Island sailor.

Going to his vice-bench, the carpenter for convenience sake and general reference, now transferringly measured on it the exact length the coffin was to be, and then made the transfer permanent by cutting two notches at its extremities. This done, he marshalled the planks and his tools, and to work.

When the last nail was driven, and the lid duly planed and fitted, he lightly shouldered the coffin and went forward with it, inquiring whether they were ready for it yet in that direction.

Overhearing the indignant but half-humorous cries with which the people on deck began to drive the coffin away, Queequeg, to every one's consternation, commanded that the thing should be instantly brought to him, nor was there any denying him; seeing that, of all mortals, some dying men are the most tyrannical; and certainly, since they will shortly trouble us so little for evermore, the poor fellows ought to be indulged.

Leaning over in his hammock, Queequeg long regarded the coffin with an attentive eye. He then called for his harpoon, had the wooden stock drawn from it, and then had the iron part placed in the coffin along with one of the paddles of his boat. All by his own request, also, biscuits were then ranged round the sides within: a flask of fresh water was placed at the head, and a small bag of woody earth scraped up in the hold at the foot; and a piece of sail-cloth being rolled up for a pillow, Queequeg now entreated to be lifted into his final bed, that he might make trial of its comforts, if any it had. He lay without moving a few minutes, then told one to go to his bag and bring out his little god, Yojo. Then crossing his arms on his breast with Yojo between, he called for the coffin lid (hatch he called it) to be placed over him. The head part turned over with a leather hinge, and there lay Queequeg in his coffin with little but his composed countenance in view. "Rarmai" (it will do; it is easy), he murmured at last, and signed to be replaced in his hammock.

But ere this was done, Pip, who had been slily hovering near by all this while, drew nigh to him where he lay, and with soft sobbings, took him by the hand; in the other, holding his tambourine.

"Poor rover! will ye never have done with all this weary roving? where go ye now? But if the currents carry ye to those sweet Antilles where the beaches are only beat with water-lilies, will ye do one little errand for me? Seek out one Pip, who's now been missing long: I think he's in those far Antilles. If ye find him, then comfort him; for he must be very sad; for look! he's left his tambourine behind;—I found it. Rig-a-dig, dig, dig! Now, Queequeg, die; and I'll beat ye your dying march."

"I have heard," murmured Starbuck, gazing down the scuttle, "that in violent fevers, men, all ignorance, have talked in ancient tongues; and that when the mystery is probed, it turns out always that in their wholly forgotten childhood those ancient tongues had been really spoken in their hearing by some lofty scholars. So, to my fond faith, poor Pip, in this strange sweetness of his lunacy, brings heavenly vouchers of all our heavenly homes. Where learned he that, but there?—Hark! he speaks again: but more wildly now."

"Form two and two! Let's make a General of him! Ho, where's his harpoon? Lay it across here.—Rig-a-dig, dig, dig! huzza! Oh for a game cock now to sit upon his head and crow! Queequeg dies game!—mind ye

that; Queequeg dies game!—take ye good heed of that; Queequeg dies
game! I say; game, game, game! but base little Pip, he died a coward; died
all a'shiver;—out upon Pip! Hark ye; if ye find Pip, tell all the Antilles he's
a runaway; a coward, a coward, a coward! Tell them he jumped from a
whale-boat! I'd never beat my tambourine over base Pip, and hail him
General, if he were once more dying here. No, no! shame upon all cowards
—shame upon them! Let 'em go drown like Pip, that jumped from a whale-
boat. Shame! shame!"

During all this, Queequeg lay with closed eyes, as if in a dream. Pip was
led away, and the sick man was replaced in his hammock.

But now that he had apparently made every preparation for death; now
that his coffin was proved a good fit, Queequeg suddenly rallied; soon there
seemed no need of the carpenter's box: and thereupon, when some expressed their delighted surprise, he, in substance, said, that the cause of his
sudden convalescence was this;—at a critical moment, he had just recalled a
little duty ashore, which he was leaving undone; and therefore had changed
his mind about dying: he could not die yet, he averred. They asked him,
then, whether to live or die was a matter of his own sovereign will and
pleasure. He answered, certainly. In a word, it was Queequeg's conceit, that
if a man made up his mind to live, mere sickness could not kill him:
nothing but a whale, or a gale, or some violent, ungovernable, unintelligent
destroyer of that sort.

Now, there is this noteworthy difference between savage and civilized;
that while a sick, civilized man may be six months convalescing, generally
speaking, a sick savage is almost half-well again in a day. So, in good time
my Queequeg gained strength; and at length after sitting on the windlass
for a few indolent days (but eating with a vigorous appetite) he suddenly
leaped to his feet, threw out arms and legs, gave himself a good stretching,
yawned a little bit, and then springing into the head of his hoisted boat, and
poising a harpoon, pronounced himself fit for a fight.

With a wild whimsiness, he now used his coffin for a sea-chest; and
emptying into it his canvas bag of clothes, set them in order there. Many
spare hours he spent, in carving the lid with all manner of grotesque figures
and drawings; and it seemed that hereby he was striving, in his rude way, to
copy parts of the twisted tattooing on his body. And this tattooing, had
been the work of a departed prophet and seer of his island, who, by those
hieroglyphic marks, had written out on his body a complete theory of the
heavens and the earth, and a mystical treatise on the art of attaining truth;
so that Queequeg in his own proper person was a riddle to unfold; a

wondrous work in one volume; but whose mysteries not even himself could read, though his own live heart beat against them; and these mysteries were therefore destined in the end to moulder away with the living parchment whereon they were inscribed, and so be unsolved to the last. And this thought it must have been which suggested to Ahab that wild exclamation of his, when one morning turning away from surveying poor Queequeg—"Oh, devilish tantalization of the gods!"

# Chapter 111

### The Pacific

WHEN GLIDING BY the Bashee isles we emerged at last upon the great South Sea; were it not for other things, I could have greeted my dear Pacific with uncounted thanks, for now the long supplication of my youth was answered; that serene ocean rolled eastwards from me a thousand leagues of blue.

There is, one knows not what sweet mystery about this sea, whose gently awful stirrings seem to speak of some hidden soul beneath; like those fabled undulations of the Ephesian sod over the buried Evangelist St. John. And meet it is, that over these sea-pastures, wide-rolling watery prairies and Potters' Fields of all four continents, the waves should rise and fall, and ebb and flow unceasingly; for here, millions of mixed shades and shadows, drowned dreams, somnambulisms, reveries; all that we call lives and souls, lie dreaming, dreaming, still; tossing like slumberers in their beds; the ever-rolling waves but made so by their restlessness.

To any meditative Magian rover, this serene Pacific, once beheld, must ever after be the sea of his adoption. It rolls the midmost waters of the world, the Indian ocean and Atlantic being but its arms. The same waves wash the moles of the new-built Californian towns, but yesterday planted by the recentest race of men, and lave the faded but still gorgeous skirts of Asiatic lands, older than Abraham; while all between float milky-ways of

coral isles, and low-lying, endless, unknown Archipelagoes, and impenetrable Japans. Thus this mysterious, divine Pacific zones the world's
whole bulk about; makes all coasts one bay to it; seems the tide-beating
heart of earth. Lifted by those eternal swells, you needs must own the
seductive god, bowing your head to Pan.

But few thoughts of Pan stirred Ahab's brain, as standing like an iron
statue at his accustomed place beside the mizen rigging, with one nostril he
unthinkingly snuffed the sugary musk from the Bashee isles (in whose
sweet woods mild lovers must be walking), and with the other consciously
inhaled the salt breath of the new found sea; that sea in which the hated
White Whale must even then be swimming. Launched at length upon these
almost final waters, and gliding towards the Japanese cruising-ground, the
old man's purpose intensified itself. His firm lips met like the lips of a vice;
the Delta of his forehead's veins swelled like overladen brooks; in his very
sleep, his ringing cry ran through the vaulted hull, "Stern all! the White
Whale spouts thick blood!"

# Chapter 112

### The Blacksmith

AVAILING HIMSELF of the mild, summer-cool weather that now reigned in these latitudes, and in preparation for the peculiarly active pursuits shortly to be anticipated, Perth, the begrimed, blistered old blacksmith, had not removed his portable forge to the hold again, after concluding his contributory work for Ahab's leg, but still retained it on deck, fast lashed to ringbolts by the foremast; being now almost incessantly invoked by the headsmen, and harpooneers, and bowsmen to do some little job for them; altering, or repairing, or new shaping their various weapons and boat furniture. Often he would be surrounded by an eager circle, all waiting to be served; holding boat-spades, pike-heads, harpoons, and lances, and jealously watching his every sooty movement, as he toiled. Nevertheless, this old man's was a patient hammer wielded by a patient arm. No murmur, no impatience, no petulance did come from him. Silent, slow, and solemn; bowing over still further his chronically broken back, he toiled away, as if toil were life itself, and the heavy beating of his hammer the heavy beating of his heart. And so it was.—Most miserable!

A peculiar walk in this old man, a certain slight but painful appearing yawing in his gait, had at an early period of the voyage excited the curiosity of the mariners. And to the importunity of their persisted questionings he had finally given in; and so it came to pass that every one now knew the shameful story of his wretched fate.

Belated, and not innocently, one bitter winter's midnight, on the road running between two country towns, the blacksmith half-stupidly felt the deadly numbness stealing over him, and sought refuge in a leaning, dilapidated barn. The issue was, the loss of the extremities of both feet. Out of this revelation, part by part, at last came out the four acts of the gladness, and the one long, and as yet uncatastrophied fifth act of the grief of his life's drama.

He was an old man, who, at the age of nearly sixty, had postponedly encountered that thing in sorrow's technicals called ruin. He had been an artisan of famed excellence, and with plenty to do; owned a house and garden; embraced a youthful, daughter-like, loving wife, and three blithe, ruddy children; every Sunday went to a cheerful-looking church, planted in a grove. But one night, under cover of darkness, and further concealed in a most cunning disguisement, a desperate burglar slid into his happy home, and robbed them all of everything. And darker yet to tell, the blacksmith himself did ignorantly conduct this burglar into his family's heart. It was the Bottle Conjuror! Upon the opening of that fatal cork, forth flew the fiend, and shrivelled up his home. Now, for prudent, most wise, and economic reasons, the blacksmith's shop was in the basement of his dwelling, but with a separate entrance to it; so that always had the young and loving healthy wife listened with no unhappy nervousness, but with vigorous pleasure, to the stout ringing of her young-armed old husband's hammer; whose reverberations, muffled by passing through the floors and walls, came up to her, not unsweetly, in her nursery; and so, to stout Labor's iron lullaby, the blacksmith's infants were rocked to slumber.

Oh, woe on woe! Oh, Death, why canst thou not sometimes be timely? Hadst thou taken this old blacksmith to thyself ere his full ruin came upon him, then had the young widow had a delicious grief, and her orphans a truly venerable, legendary sire to dream of in their after years; and all of them a care-killing competency. But Death plucked down some virtuous elder brother, on whose whistling daily toil solely hung the responsibilities of some other family, and left the worse than useless old man standing, till the hideous rot of life should make him easier to harvest.

Why tell the whole? The blows of the basement hammer every day grew more and more between; and each blow every day grew fainter than the last; the wife sat frozen at the window, with tearless eyes, glitteringly gazing into the weeping faces of her children; the bellows fell; the forge choked up with cinders; the house was sold; the mother dived down into the long church-yard grass; her children twice followed her thither; and the houseless, familyless old man staggered off a vagabond in crape; his every woe unreverenced; his grey head a scorn to flaxen curls!

Death seems the only desirable sequel for a career like this; but Death is only a launching into the region of the strange Untried; it is but the first salutation to the possibilities of the immense Remote, the Wild, the Watery, the Unshored; therefore, to the death-longing eyes of such men, who still have left in them some interior compunctions against suicide, does the all-contributed and all-receptive ocean alluringly spread forth his whole plain of unimaginable, taking terrors, and wonderful, new-life adventures; and from the hearts of infinite Pacifics, the thousand mermaids sing to them —"Come hither, broken-hearted; here is another life without the guilt of intermediate death; here are wonders supernatural, without dying for them. Come hither! bury thyself in a life which, to your now equally abhorred and abhorring, landed world, is more oblivious than death. Come hither! put up *thy* grave-stone, too, within the churchyard, and come hither, till we marry thee!"

Hearkening to these voices, East and West, by early sun-rise, and by fall of eve, the blacksmith's soul responded, Aye, I come! And so Perth went a-whaling.

# Chapter 113

*The Forge*

W ITH MATTED BEARD, and swathed in a bristling shark-skin apron, about mid-day, Perth was standing between his forge and anvil, the latter placed upon an iron-wood log, with one hand holding a pike-head in the coals, and with the other at his forge's lungs, when Captain Ahab came along, carrying in his hand a small rusty-looking leathern bag. While yet a little distance from the forge, moody Ahab paused; till at last, Perth, withdrawing his iron from the fire, began hammering it upon the anvil—the red mass sending off the sparks in thick hovering flights, some of which flew close to Ahab.

"Are these thy Mother Carey's chickens, Perth? they are always flying in thy wake; birds of good omen, too, but not to all;—look here, they burn; but thou—thou liv'st among them without a scorch."

"Because I am scorched all over, Captain Ahab," answered Perth, resting for a moment on his hammer; "I am past scorching; not easily can'st thou scorch a scar."

"Well, well; no more. Thy shrunk voice sounds too calmly, sanely woful to me. In no Paradise myself, I am impatient of all misery in others that is not mad. Thou should'st go mad, blacksmith; say, why dost thou not go mad? How can'st thou endure without being mad? Do the heavens yet hate thee, that thou can'st not go mad?—What wert thou making there?"

"Welding an old pike-head, sir; there were seams and dents in it."

"And can'st thou make it all smooth again, blacksmith, after such hard usage as it had?"

"I think so, sir."

"And I suppose thou can'st smoothe almost any seams and dents; never mind how hard the metal, blacksmith?"

"Aye, sir, I think I can; all seams and dents but one."

"Look ye here, then," cried Ahab, passionately advancing, and leaning with both hands on Perth's shoulders; "look ye here—*here*—can ye smoothe out a seam like this, blacksmith," sweeping one hand across his ribbed brow; "if thou could'st, blacksmith, glad enough would I lay my head upon thy anvil, and feel thy heaviest hammer between my eyes. Answer! Can'st thou smoothe this seam?"

"Oh! that is the one, sir! Said I not all seams and dents but one?"

"Aye, blacksmith, it is the one; aye, man, it is unsmoothable; for though thou only see'st it here in my flesh, it has worked down into the bone of my skull—*that* is all wrinkles! But, away with child's play; no more gaffs and pikes to-day. Look ye here!" jingling the leathern bag, as if it were full of gold coins. "I, too, want a harpoon made; one that a thousand yoke of fiends could not part, Perth; something that will stick in a whale like his own fin-bone. There's the stuff," flinging the pouch upon the anvil. "Look ye, black-smith, these are the gathered nail-stubs of the steel shoes of racing horses."

"Horse-shoe stubbs, sir? Why, Captain Ahab, thou hast here, then, the best and stubbornest stuff we blacksmiths ever work."

"I know it, old man; these stubbs will weld together like glue from the melted bones of murderers. Quick! forge me the harpoon. And forge me first, twelve rods for its shank; then wind, and twist, and hammer these twelve together like the yarns and strands of a tow-line. Quick! I'll blow the fire."

When at last the twelve rods were made, Ahab tried them, one by one, by spiralling them, with his own hand, round a long, heavy iron bolt. "A flaw!" rejecting the last one. "Work that over again, Perth."

This done, Perth was about to begin welding the twelve into one, when Ahab stayed his hand, and said he would weld his own iron. As, then, with regular, gasping hems, he hammered on the anvil, Perth passing to him the glowing rods, one after the other, and the hard pressed forge shooting up its intense straight flame, the Parsee passed silently, and bowing over his head towards the fire, seemed invoking some curse or some blessing on the toil. But, as Ahab looked up, he slid aside.

"What's that bunch of lucifers dodging about there for?" muttered Stubb, looking on from the forecastle. "That Parsee smells fire like a fusee; and smells of it himself, like a hot musket's powder-pan."

At last the shank, in one complete rod, received its final heat; and as Perth, to temper it, plunged it all hissing into the cask of water near by, the scalding steam shot up into Ahab's bent face.

"Would'st thou brand me, Perth?" wincing for a moment with the pain; "have I been but forging my own branding-iron, then?"

"Pray God, not that; yet I fear something, Captain Ahab. Is not this harpoon for the White Whale?"

"For the white fiend! But now for the barbs; thou must make them thyself, man. Here are my razors—the best of steel; here, and make the barbs sharp as the needle-sleet of the Icy Sea."

For a moment, the old blacksmith eyed the razors as though he would fain not use them.

"Take them, man, I have no need for them; for I now neither shave, sup, nor pray till——but here—to work!"

Fashioned at last into an arrowy shape, and welded by Perth to the shank, the steel soon pointed the end of the iron; and as the blacksmith was about giving the barbs their final heat, prior to tempering them, he cried to Ahab to place the water-cask near.

"No, no—no water for that; I want it of the true death-temper. Ahoy, there! Tashtego, Queequeg, Daggoo! What say ye, pagans! Will ye give me as much blood as will cover this barb?" holding it high up. A cluster of dark nods replied, Yes. Three punctures were made in the heathen flesh, and the White Whale's barbs were then tempered.

"Ego non baptizo te in nomine patris, sed in nomine diaboli!" deliriously howled Ahab, as the malignant iron scorchingly devoured the baptismal blood.

Now, mustering the spare poles from below, and selecting one of hickory, with the bark still investing it, Ahab fitted the end to the socket of the iron. A coil of new tow-line was then unwound, and some fathoms of it taken to the windlass, and stretched to a great tension. Pressing his foot upon it, till the rope hummed like a harp-string, then eagerly bending over it, and seeing no strandings, Ahab exclaimed, "Good! and now for the seizings."

At one extremity the rope was unstranded, and the separate spread yarns were all braided and woven round the socket of the harpoon; the pole was then driven hard up into the socket; from the lower end the rope was traced half way along the pole's length, and firmly secured so, with intertwistings of twine. This done, pole, iron, and rope—like the Three Fates—remained inseparable, and Ahab moodily stalked away with the weapon; the sound of his ivory leg, and the sound of the hickory pole, both hollowly ringing along every plank. But ere he entered his cabin, a light, unnatural, half-bantering, yet most piteous sound was heard. Oh, Pip! thy wretched laugh, thy idle but unresting eye; all thy strange mummeries not unmeaningly blended with the black tragedy of the melancholy ship, and mocked it!

# Chapter 114

### The Gilder

PENETRATING FURTHER AND FURTHER into the heart of the Japanese cruising ground, the Pequod was soon all astir in the fishery. Often, in mild, pleasant weather, for twelve, fifteen, eighteen, and twenty hours on the stretch, they were engaged in the boats, steadily pulling, or sailing, or paddling after the whales, or for an interlude of sixty or seventy minutes calmly awaiting their uprising; though with but small success for their pains.

At such times, under an abated sun; afloat all day upon smooth, slow heaving swells; seated in his boat, light as a birch canoe; and so sociably mixing with the soft waves themselves, that like hearth-stone cats they purr against the gunwale; these are the times of dreamy quietude, when beholding the tranquil beauty and brilliancy of the ocean's skin, one forgets the tiger heart that pants beneath it; and would not willingly remember, that this velvet paw but conceals a remorseless fang.

These are the times, when in his whale-boat the rover softly feels a certain filial, confident, land-like feeling towards the sea; that he regards it as so much flowery earth; and the distant ship revealing only the tops of her masts, seems struggling forward, not through high rolling waves, but through the tall grass of a rolling prairie: as when the western emigrants' horses only show their erected ears, while their hidden bodies widely wade through the amazing verdure.

491

The long-drawn virgin vales; the mild blue hill-sides; as over these there steals the hush, the hum; you almost swear that play-wearied children lie sleeping in these solitudes, in some glad May-time, when the flowers of the woods are plucked. And all this mixes with your most mystic mood; so that fact and fancy, half-way meeting, interpenetrate, and form one seamless whole.

Nor did such soothing scenes, however temporary, fail of at least as temporary an effect on Ahab. But if these secret golden keys did seem to open in him his own secret golden treasuries, yet did his breath upon them prove but tarnishing.

"Oh, grassy glades! oh, ever vernal endless landscapes in the soul; in ye, —though long parched by the dead drought of the earthy life,—in ye, men yet may roll, like young horses in new morning clover; and for some few fleeting moments, feel the cool dew of the life immortal on them. Would to God these blessed calms would last. But the mingled, mingling threads of life are woven by warp and woof: calms crossed by storms, a storm for every calm. There is no steady unretracing progress in this life; we do not advance through fixed gradations, and at the last one pause:—through infancy's unconscious spell, boyhood's thoughtless faith, adolescence' doubt (the common doom), then scepticism, then disbelief, resting at last in manhood's pondering repose of If. But once gone through, we trace the round again; and are infants, boys, and men, and Ifs eternally. Where lies the final harbor, whence we unmoor no more? In what rapt ether sails the world, of which the weariest will never weary? Where is the foundling's father hidden? Our souls are like those orphans whose unwedded mothers die in bearing them: the secret of our paternity lies in their grave, and we must there to learn it."

And that same day, too, gazing far down from his boat's side into that same golden sea, Starbuck lowly murmured:—

"Loveliness unfathomable, as ever lover saw in his young bride's eye!— Tell me not of thy teeth-tiered sharks, and thy kidnapping cannibal ways. Let faith oust fact; let fancy oust memory; I look deep down and do believe."

And Stubb, fish-like, with sparkling scales, leaped up in that same golden light:—

"I am Stubb, and Stubb has his history; but here Stubb takes oaths that he has always been jolly!"

# Chapter 115

### The Pequod meets the Bachelor

AND JOLLY ENOUGH were the sights and the sounds that came
bearing down before the wind, some few weeks after Ahab's
harpoon had been welded.

It was a Nantucket ship, the Bachelor, which had just wedged in her
last cask of oil, and bolted down her bursting hatches; and now, in glad
holiday apparel, was joyously, though somewhat vain-gloriously, sailing
round among the widely-separated ships on the ground, previous to pointing her prow for home.

The three men at her mast-head wore long streamers of narrow red
bunting at their hats; from the stern, a whale-boat was suspended, bottom
up; and hanging captive from the bowsprit was seen the long lower jaw
of the last whale they had slain. Signals, ensigns, and jacks of all colors were
flying from her rigging, on every side. Sideways lashed in each of her three
basketed tops were two barrels of sperm; above which, in her top-mast
cross-trees, you saw slender breakers of the same precious fluid; and nailed
to her main truck was a brazen lamp.

As was afterwards learned, the Bachelor had met with the most surprising success; all the more wonderful, for that while cruising in the same seas
numerous other vessels had gone entire months without securing a single
fish. Not only had barrels of beef and bread been given away to make room
for the far more valuable sperm, but additional supplemental casks had

493

been bartered for, from the ships she had met; and these were stowed along the deck, and in the captain's and officers' state-rooms. Even the cabin table itself had been knocked into kindling-wood; and the cabin mess dined off the broad head of an oil-butt, lashed down to the floor for a centrepiece. In the forecastle, the sailors had actually caulked and pitched their chests, and filled them; it was humorously added, that the cook had clapped a head on his largest boiler, and filled it; that the steward had plugged his spare coffee-pot and filled it; that the harpooneers had headed the sockets of their irons and filled them; that indeed everything was filled with sperm, except the captain's pantaloons pockets, and those he reserved to thrust his hands into, in self-complacent testimony of his entire satisfaction.

As this glad ship of good luck bore down upon the moody Pequod, the barbarian sound of enormous drums came from her forecastle; and drawing still nearer, a crowd of her men were seen standing round her huge try-pots, which, covered with the parchment-like *poke* or stomach skin of the black fish, gave forth a loud roar to every stroke of the clenched hands of the crew. On the quarter-deck, the mates and harpooneers were dancing with the olive-hued girls who had eloped with them from the Polynesian Isles; while suspended in an ornamented boat, firmly secured aloft between the foremast and mainmast, three Long Island negroes, with glittering fiddle-bows of whale ivory, were presiding over the hilarious jig. Meanwhile, others of the ship's company were tumultuously busy at the masonry of the try-works, from which the huge pots had been removed. You would have almost thought they were pulling down the cursed Bastile, such wild cries they raised, as the now useless brick and mortar were being hurled into the sea.

Lord and master over all this scene, the captain stood erect on the ship's elevated quarter-deck, so that the whole rejoicing drama was full before him, and seemed merely contrived for his own individual diversion.

And Ahab, he too was standing on his quarter-deck, shaggy and black, with a stubborn gloom; and as the two ships crossed each other's wakes— one all jubilations for things passed, the other all forebodings as to things to come—their two captains in themselves impersonated the whole striking contrast of the scene.

"Come aboard, come aboard!" cried the gay Bachelor's commander, lifting a glass and a bottle in the air.

"Hast seen the White Whale?" gritted Ahab in reply.

"No; only heard of him; but don't believe in him at all," said the other good-humoredly. "Come aboard!"

"Thou art too damned jolly. Sail on. Hast lost any men?"

"Not enough to speak of—two islanders, that's all;—but come aboard, old hearty, come along. I'll soon take that black from your brow. Come along, will ye (merry's the play); a full ship and homeward-bound."

"How wondrous familiar is a fool!" muttered Ahab; then aloud, "Thou art a full ship and homeward bound, thou sayst; well, then, call me an empty ship, and outward-bound. So go thy ways, and I will mine. Forward there! Set all sail, and keep her to the wind!"

And thus, while the one ship went cheerily before the breeze, the other stubbornly fought against it; and so the two vessels parted; the crew of the Pequod looking with grave, lingering glances towards the receding Bachelor; but the Bachelor's men never heeding their gaze for the lively revelry they were in. And as Ahab, leaning over the taffrail, eyed the homeward-bound craft, he took from his pocket a small vial of sand, and then looking from the ship to the vial, seemed thereby bringing two remote associations together, for that vial was filled with Nantucket soundings.

# Chapter 116

## The Dying Whale

NOT SELDOM in this life, when, on the right side, fortune's favorites sail close by us, we, though all adroop before, catch somewhat of the rushing breeze, and joyfully feel our bagging sails fill out. So seemed it with the Pequod. For next day after encountering the gay Bachelor, whales were seen and four were slain; and one of them by Ahab.

It was far down the afternoon; and when all the spearings of the crimson fight were done: and floating in the lovely sunset sea and sky, sun and whale both stilly died together; then, such a sweetness and such plaintiveness, such inwreathing orisons curled up in that rosy air, that it almost seemed as if far over from the deep green convent valleys of the Manilla isles, the Spanish land-breeze, wantonly turned sailor, had gone to sea, freighted with these vesper hymns.

Soothed again, but only soothed to deeper gloom, Ahab, who had sterned off from the whale, sat intently watching his final wanings from the now tranquil boat. For that strange spectacle observable in all sperm whales dying—the turning sunwards of the head, and so expiring—that strange spectacle, beheld of such a placid evening, somehow to Ahab conveyed a wondrousness unknown before.

"He turns and turns him to it,—how slowly, but how steadfastly, his

496

homage-rendering and invoking brow, with his last dying motions. He too worships fire; most faithful, broad, baronial vassal of the sun!—Oh that these too-favoring eyes should see these too-favoring sights. Look! here, far water-locked; beyond all hum of human weal or woe; in these most candid and impartial seas; where to traditions no rocks furnish tablets; where for long Chinese ages, the billows have still rolled on speechless and unspoken to, as stars that shine upon the Niger's unknown source; here, too, life dies sunwards full of faith; but see! no sooner dead, than death whirls round the corpse, and it heads some other way.—

"Oh, thou dark Hindoo half of nature, who of drowned bones hast builded thy separate throne somewhere in the heart of these unverdured seas; thou art an infidel, thou queen, and too truly speakest to me in the wide-slaughtering Typhoon, and the hushed burial of its after calm. Nor has this thy whale sunwards turned his dying head, and then gone round again, without a lesson to me.

"Oh, trebly hooped and welded hip of power! Oh, high aspiring, rainbowed jet!—that one striveth, this one jetteth all in vain! In vain, oh whale, dost thou seek intercedings with yon all-quickening sun, that only calls forth life, but gives it not again. Yet dost thou, darker half, rock me with a prouder, if a darker faith. All thy unnamable imminglings float beneath me here; I am buoyed by breaths of once living things, exhaled as air, but water now.

"Then hail, for ever hail, O sea, in whose eternal tossings the wild fowl finds his only rest. Born of earth, yet suckled by the sea; though hill and valley mothered me, ye billows are my foster-brothers!"

# Chapter 117

## *The Whale Watch*

THE FOUR WHALES slain that evening had died wide apart; one, far to windward; one, less distant, to leeward; one ahead; one astern. These last three were brought alongside ere nightfall; but the windward one could not be reached till morning; and the boat that had killed it lay by its side all night; and that boat was Ahab's.

The waif-pole was thrust upright into the dead whale's spout-hole; and the lantern hanging from its top, cast a troubled flickering glare upon the black, glossy back, and far out upon the midnight waves, which gently chafed the whale's broad flank, like soft surf upon a beach.

Ahab and all his boat's crew seemed asleep but the Parsee; who crouching in the bow, sat watching the sharks, that spectrally played round the whale, and tapped the light cedar planks with their tails. A sound like the moaning in squadrons over Asphaltites of unforgiven ghosts of Gomorrah, ran shuddering through the air.

Started from his slumbers, Ahab, face to face, saw the Parsee; and hooped round by the gloom of the night they seemed the last men in a flooded world. "I have dreamed it again," said he.

"Of the hearses? Have I not said, old man, that neither hearse nor coffin can be thine?"

"And who are hearsed that die on the sea?"

"But I said, old man, that ere thou couldst die on this voyage, two hearses must verily be seen by thee on the sea; the first not made by mortal hands; and the visible wood of the last one must be grown in America."

"Aye, aye! a strange sight that, Parsee:—a hearse and its plumes floating over the ocean with the waves for the pall-bearers. Ha! Such a sight we shall not soon see."

"Believe it or not, thou canst not die till it be seen, old man."

"And what was that saying about thyself?"

"Though it come to the last, I shall still go before thee thy pilot."

"And when thou art so gone before—if that ever befall—then ere I can follow, thou must still appear to me, to pilot me still?—Was it not so? Well, then, did I believe all ye say, oh my pilot! I have here two pledges that I shall yet slay Moby Dick and survive it."

"Take another pledge, old man," said the Parsee, as his eyes lighted up like fire-flies in the gloom—"Hemp only can kill thee."

"The gallows, ye mean.—I am immortal then, on land and on sea," cried Ahab, with a laugh of derision;—"Immortal on land and on sea!"

Both were silent again, as one man. The grey dawn came on, and the slumbering crew arose from the boat's bottom, and ere noon the dead whale was brought to the ship.

# Chapter 118

## The Quadrant

THE SEASON for the Line at length drew near; and every day when Ahab, coming from his cabin, cast his eyes aloft, the vigilant helmsman would ostentatiously handle his spokes, and the eager mariners quickly run to the braces, and would stand there with all their eyes centrally fixed on the nailed doubloon; impatient for the order to point the ship's prow for the equator. In good time the order came. It was hard upon high noon; and Ahab, seated in the bows of his high-hoisted boat, was about taking his wonted daily observation of the sun to determine his latitude.

Now, sometimes, in that Japanese sea, the days in summer are as freshets of effulgences. That unblinkingly vivid Japanese sun seems the blazing focus of the glassy ocean's immeasurable burning-glass. The sky looks lacquered; clouds there are none; the horizon floats; and this nakedness of unrelieved radiance is as the insufferable splendors of God's throne. Well that Ahab's quadrant was furnished with colored glasses, through which to take sight of that solar fire. So, swinging his seated form to the roll of the ship, and with his astrological-looking instrument placed to his eye, he remained in that posture for some moments to catch the precise instant when the sun should gain its precise meridian. Meantime while his whole attention was absorbed, the Parsee was kneeling beneath him on the ship's deck, and with face thrown up like Ahab's, was eyeing the same sun with him; only the lids of his eyes half hooded their orbs, and his wild face was subdued to an earthly passionlessness. At length the desired observation was taken; and with his pencil upon his ivory leg, Ahab soon calculated what his latitude must be at that precise instant. Then falling into a moment's revery, he again looked up towards the sun and murmured to himself: "Thou sea-mark! thou high and mighty Pilot! thou tellest me truly where I *am*—but canst thou cast the least hint where I *shall* be? Or canst thou tell where some other thing besides me is this·moment living? Where is Moby Dick? This instant thou must be eyeing him. These eyes of mine look into the very eye that is even now beholding him; aye, and into the eye that is even now equally beholding the objects on the unknown, thither side of thee, thou sun!"

Then gazing at his quadrant, and handling, one after the other, its numerous cabalistical contrivances, he pondered again, and muttered: "Foolish toy! babies' plaything of haughty Admirals, and Commodores, and Captains; the world brags of thee, of thy cunning and might; but what after all canst thou do, but tell the poor, pitiful point, where thou thyself happenest to be on this wide planet, and the hand that holds thee: no! not one jot more! Thou canst not tell where one drop of water or one grain of sand will be to-morrow noon; and yet with thy impotence thou insultest the sun! Science! Curse thee, thou vain toy; and cursed be all the things that cast man's eyes aloft to that heaven, whose live vividness but scorches him, as these old eyes are even now scorched with thy light, O sun! Level by nature to this earth's horizon are the glances of man's eyes; not shot from the crown of his head, as if God had meant him to gaze on his firmament. Curse thee, thou quadrant!" dashing it to the deck, "no longer will I guide my earthly way by thee; the level ship's compass, and the level dead-reckoning, by log and by line; *these* shall conduct me, and show me my place on the sea. Aye," lighting from the boat to the deck, "thus I trample on thee, thou paltry thing that feebly pointest on high; thus I split and destroy thee!"

As the frantic old man thus spoke and thus trampled with his live and dead feet, a sneering triumph that seemed meant for Ahab, and a fatalistic despair that seemed meant for himself—these passed over the mute, motion-less Parsee's face. Unobserved he rose and glided away; while, awestruck by the aspect of their commander, the seamen clustered together on the fore-castle, till Ahab, troubledly pacing the deck, shouted out—"To the braces! Up helm!—square in!"

In an instant the yards swung round; and as the ship half-wheeled upon her heel, her three firm-seated graceful masts erectly poised upon her long, ribbed hull, seemed as the three Horatii pirouetting on one sufficient steed.

Standing between the knight-heads, Starbuck watched the Pequod's tumultuous way, and Ahab's also, as he went lurching along the deck.

"I have sat before the dense coal fire and watched it all aglow, full of its tormented flaming life; and I have seen it wane at last, down, down, to dumbest dust. Old man of oceans! of all this fiery life of thine, what will at length remain but one little heap of ashes!"

"Aye," cried Stubb, "but sea-coal ashes—mind ye that, Mr. Starbuck—sea-coal, not your common charcoal. Well, well; I heard Ahab mutter, 'Here some one thrusts these cards into these old hands of mine; swears that I must play them, and no others.' And damn me, Ahab, but thou actest right; live in the game, and die in it!"

# Chapter 119

*The Candles*

WARMEST CLIMES but nurse the cruellest fangs: the tiger of Bengal crouches in spiced groves of ceaseless verdure. Skies the most effulgent but basket the deadliest thunders: gorgeous Cuba knows tornadoes that never swept tame northern lands. So, too, it is, that in these resplendent Japanese seas the mariner encounters the direst of all storms, the Typhoon. It will sometimes burst from out that cloudless sky, like an exploding bomb upon a dazed and sleepy town.

Towards evening of that day, the Pequod was torn of her canvas, and bare-poled was left to fight a Typhoon which had struck her directly ahead. When darkness came on, sky and sea roared and split with the thunder, and blazed with the lightning, that showed the disabled masts fluttering here and there with the rags which the first fury of the tempest had left for its after sport.

Holding by a shroud, Starbuck was standing on the quarter-deck; at every flash of the lightning glancing aloft, to see what additional disaster might have befallen the intricate hamper there; while Stubb and Flask were directing the men in the higher hoisting and firmer lashing of the boats. But all their pains seemed naught. Though lifted to the very top of the cranes, the windward quarter boat (Ahab's) did not escape. A great rolling sea, dashing high up against the reeling ship's high tetering side, stove in the boat's bottom at the stern, and left it again, all dripping through like a sieve.

"Bad work, bad work! Mr. Starbuck," said Stubb, regarding the wreck, "but the sea will have its way. Stubb, for one, can't fight it. You see, Mr. Starbuck, a wave has such a great long start before it leaps, all round the world it runs, and then comes the spring! But as for me, all the start I have to meet it, is just across the deck here. But never mind; it's all in fun: so the old song says;"—(sings.)

> Oh! jolly is the gale,
> And a joker is the whale,
> A' flourishin' his tail,—
> Such a funny, sporty, gamy, jesty, joky, hoky-poky lad, is the Ocean, oh!
>
> The scud all a flyin',
> That's his flip only foamin';
> When he stirs in the spicin',—
> Such a funny, sporty, gamy, jesty, joky, hoky-poky lad, is the Ocean, oh!
>
> Thunder splits the ships,
> But he only smacks his lips,
> A tastin' of this flip,—
> Such a funny, sporty, gamy, jesty, joky, hoky-poky lad, is the Ocean, oh!

"Avast Stubb," cried Starbuck, "let the Typhoon sing, and strike his harp here in our rigging; but if thou art a brave man thou wilt hold thy peace."

"But I am not a brave man; never said I was a brave man; I am a coward; and I sing to keep up my spirits. And I tell you what it is, Mr. Starbuck, there's no way to stop my singing in this world but to cut my throat. And when that's done, ten to one I sing ye the doxology for a wind-up."

"Madman! look through my eyes if thou hast none of thine own."

"What! how can you see better of a dark night than anybody else, never mind how foolish?"

"Here!" cried Starbuck, seizing Stubb by the shoulder, and pointing his hand towards the weather bow, "markest thou not that the gale comes from the eastward, the very course Ahab is to run for Moby Dick? the very course he swung to this day noon? now mark his boat there; where is that stove? In the stern-sheets, man; where he is wont to stand—his stand-point is stove, man! Now jump overboard, and sing away, if thou must!"

"I don't half understand ye: what's in the wind?"

"Yes, yes, round the Cape of Good Hope is the shortest way to Nantucket," soliloquized Starbuck suddenly, heedless of Stubb's question. "The gale that now hammers at us to stave us, we can turn it into a fair wind that will drive us towards home. Yonder, to windward, all is blackness of doom; but to leeward, homeward—I see it lightens up there; but not with the lightning."

At that moment in one of the intervals of profound darkness, following the flashes, a voice was heard at his side; and almost at the same instant a volley of thunder peals rolled overhead.

"Who's there?"

"Old Thunder!" said Ahab, groping his way along the bulwarks to his pivot-hole; but suddenly finding his path made plain to him by elbowed lances of fire.

Now, as the lightning rod to a spire on shore is intended to carry off the perilous fluid into the soil; so the kindred rod which at sea some ships carry to each mast, is intended to conduct it into the water. But as this conductor must descend to considerable depth, that its end may avoid all contact with the hull; and as moreover, if kept constantly towing there, it would be liable to many mishaps, besides interfering not a little with some of the rigging, and more or less impeding the vessel's way in the water; because of all this, the lower parts of a ship's lightning-rods are not always overboard; but are generally made in long slender links, so as to be the more readily hauled up into the chains outside, or thrown down into the sea, as occasion may require.

"The rods! the rods!" cried Starbuck to the crew, suddenly admonished to vigilance by the vivid lightning that had just been darting flambeaux, to light Ahab to his post. "Are they overboard? drop them over, fore and aft. Quick!"

"Avast!" cried Ahab; "let's have fair play here, though we be the weaker side. Yet I'll contribute to raise rods on the Himmalehs and Andes, that all the world may be secured; but out on privileges! Let them be, sir."

"Look aloft!" cried Starbuck. "The corpusants! the corpusants!"

All the yard-arms were tipped with a pallid fire; and touched at each tri-pointed lightning-rod-end with three tapering white flames, each of the three tall masts was silently burning in that sulphurous air, like three gigantic wax tapers before an altar.

"Blast the boat! let it go!" cried Stubb at this instant, as a swashing sea heaved up under his own little craft, so that its gunwale violently jammed his hand, as he was passing a lashing. "Blast it!"—but slipping backward on the deck, his uplifted eyes caught the flames; and immediately shifting his tone, he cried—"The corpusants have mercy on us all!"

To sailors, oaths are household words; they will swear in the trance of the calm, and in the teeth of the tempest; they will imprecate curses from the topsail-yard-arms, when most they teter over to a seething sea; but in all my voyagings, seldom have I heard a common oath when God's burning finger has been laid on the ship; when His "Mene, Mene, Tekel, Upharsin" has been woven into the shrouds and the cordage.

While this pallidness was burning aloft, few words were heard from the enchanted crew; who in one thick cluster stood on the forecastle, all their eyes gleaming in that pale phosphorescence, like a far away constellation of stars. Relieved against the ghostly light, the gigantic jet negro, Daggoo, loomed up to thrice his real stature, and seemed the black cloud from which the thunder had come. The parted mouth of Tashtego revealed his shark-white teeth, which strangely gleamed as if they too had been tipped by corpusants; while lit up by the preternatural light, Queequeg's tattooing burned like Satanic blue flames on his body.

The tableau all waned at last with the pallidness aloft; and once more the Pequod and every soul on her decks were wrapped in a pall. A moment or two passed, when Starbuck, going forward, pushed against some one. It was Stubb. "What thinkest thou now, man; I heard thy cry; it was not the same in the song."

"No, no, it wasn't; I said the corpusants have mercy on us all; and I hope they will, still. But do they only have mercy on long faces?—have they no bowels for a laugh? And look ye, Mr. Starbuck—but it's too dark to look. Hear me, then: I take that mast-head flame we saw for a sign of good luck; for those masts are rooted in a hold that is going to be chock a' block with sperm-oil, d'ye see; and so, all that sperm will work up into the masts, like sap in a tree. Yes, our three masts will yet be as three spermaceti candles—that's the good promise we saw."

At that moment Starbuck caught sight of Stubb's face slowly beginning to glimmer into sight. Glancing upwards, he cried: "See! see!" and once more the high tapering flames were beheld with what seemed redoubled supernaturalness in their pallor.

"The corpusants have mercy on us all," cried Stubb, again.

At the base of the mainmast, full beneath the doubloon and the flame, the Parsee was kneeling in Ahab's front, but with his head bowed away from him; while near by, from the arched and overhanging rigging, where they had just been engaged securing a spar, a number of the seamen, arrested by the glare, now cohered together, and hung pendulous, like a knot of numbed wasps from a drooping, orchard twig. In various enchanted attitudes, like the standing, or stepping, or running skeletons in Herculaneum, others remained rooted to the deck; but all their eyes upcast.

"Aye, aye, men!" cried Ahab. "Look up at it; mark it well; the white flame but lights the way to the White Whale! Hand me those main-mast links there; I would fain feel this pulse, and let mine beat against it; blood against fire! So."

Then turning—the last link held fast in his left hand, he put his foot upon the Parsee; and with fixed upward eye, and high-flung right arm, he stood erect before the lofty tri-pointed trinity of flames.

"Oh! thou clear spirit of clear fire, whom on these seas I as Persian once did worship, till in the sacramental act so burned by thee, that to this hour I bear the scar; I now know thee, thou clear spirit, and I now know that thy right worship is defiance. To neither love nor reverence wilt thou be kind; and e'en for hate thou canst but kill; and all are killed. No fearless fool now fronts thee. I own thy speechless, placeless power; but to the last gasp of my earthquake life will dispute its unconditional, unintegral mastery in me. In the midst of the personified impersonal, a personality stands here. Though but a point at best; whencesoe'er I came; wheresoe'er I go; yet while I earthly live, the queenly personality lives in me, and feels her royal rights. But war is pain, and hate is woe. Come in thy lowest form of love, and I will kneel and kiss thee; but at thy highest, come as mere supernal power; and though thou launchest navies of full-freighted worlds, there's that in here that still remains indifferent. Oh, thou clear spirit, of thy fire thou madest me, and like a true child of fire, I breathe it back to thee."

*(Sudden, repeated flashes of lightning; the nine flames leap lengthwise to thrice their previous height; Ahab, with the rest, closes his eyes, his right hand pressed hard upon them.)*

"I own thy speechless, placeless power; said I not so? Nor was it wrung from me; nor do I now drop these links. Thou canst blind; but I can then grope. Thou canst consume; but I can then be ashes. Take the homage of these poor eyes, and shutter-hands. I would not take it. The lightning flashes through my skull; mine eye-balls ache and ache; my whole beaten brain seems as beheaded, and rolling on some stunning ground. Oh, oh! Yet blindfold, yet will I talk to thee. Light though thou be, thou leapest out of darkness; but I am darkness leaping out of light, leaping out of thee! The javelins cease; open eyes; see, or not? There burn the flames! Oh, thou

magnanimous! now I do glory in my genealogy. But thou art but my fiery
father; my sweet mother, I know not. Oh, cruel! what hast thou done with
her? There lies my puzzle; but thine is greater. Thou knowest not how
came ye, hence callest thyself unbegotten; certainly knowest not thy
beginning, hence callest thyself unbegun. I know that of me, which thou
knowest not of thyself, oh, thou omnipotent. There is some unsuffusing
thing beyond thee, thou clear spirit, to whom all thy eternity is but time,
all thy creativeness mechanical. Through thee, thy flaming self, my scorched
eyes do dimly see it. Oh, thou foundling fire, thou hermit immemorial, thou
too hast thy incommunicable riddle, thy unparticipated grief. Here again
with haughty agony, I read my sire. Leap! leap up, and lick the sky! I leap
with thee; I burn with thee; would fain be welded with thee; defyingly I
worship thee!"

"The boat! the boat!" cried Starbuck, "look at thy boat, old man!"

Ahab's harpoon, the one forged at Perth's fire, remained firmly lashed
in its conspicuous crotch, so that it projected beyond his whale-boat's bow;
but the sea that had stove its bottom had caused the loose leather sheath to
drop off; and from the keen steel barb there now came a levelled flame of
pale, forked fire. As the silent harpoon burned there like a serpent's tongue,
Starbuck grasped Ahab by the arm—"God, God is against thee, old man;
forbear! t' is an ill voyage! ill begun, ill continued; let me square the yards,
while we may, old man, and make a fair wind of it homewards, to go on a
better voyage than this."

Overhearing Starbuck, the panic-stricken crew instantly ran to the
braces—though not a sail was left aloft. For the moment all the aghast
mate's thoughts seemed theirs; they raised a half mutinous cry. But dashing
the rattling lightning links to the deck, and snatching the burning harpoon,
Ahab waved it like a torch among them; swearing to transfix with it the
first sailor that but cast loose a rope's end. Petrified by his aspect, and still
more shrinking from the fiery dart that he held, the men fell back in dismay,
and Ahab again spoke:—

"All your oaths to hunt the White Whale are as binding as mine; and
heart, soul, and body, lungs and life, old Ahab is bound. And that ye may
know to what tune this heart beats: look ye here; thus I blow out the last
fear!" And with one blast of his breath he extinguished the flame.

As in the hurricane that sweeps the plain, men fly the neighborhood of
some lone, gigantic elm, whose very height and strength but render it so
much the more unsafe, because so much the more a mark for thunderbolts;
so at those last words of Ahab's many of the mariners did run from him in a
terror of dismay.

# Chapter 120

*The Deck towards the End of the First Night Watch*

*(Ahab standing by the helm. Starbuck approaching him.)*

WE must send down the main-top-sail yard, sir. The band is working loose, and the lee lift is half-stranded. Shall I strike it, sir?"

"Strike nothing; lash it. If I had sky-sail poles, I'd sway them up now."

"Sir?—in God's name!—sir?"

"Well."

"The anchors are working, sir. Shall I get them inboard?"

"Strike nothing, and stir nothing, but lash everything. The wind rises, but it has not got up to my table-lands yet. Quick, and see to it.—By masts and keels! he takes me for the hunchbacked skipper of some coasting smack. Send down my main-top-sail yard! Ho, gluepots! Loftiest trucks were made for wildest winds, and this brain-truck of mine now sails amid the cloud-scud. Shall I strike that? Oh, none but cowards send down their brain-trucks in tempest time. What a hooroosh aloft there! I would e'en take it for sublime, did I not know that the colic is a noisy malady. Oh, take medicine, take medicine!"

# Chapter 121

*Midnight—The Forecastle Bulwarks*

*(Stubb and Flask mounted on them, and passing additional lashings over the anchors there hanging.)*

NO, Stubb; you may pound that knot there as much as you please, but you will never pound into me what you were just now saying. And how long ago is it since you said the very contrary? Didn't you once say that whatever ship Ahab sails in, that ship should pay something extra on its insurance policy, just as though it were loaded with powder barrels aft and boxes of lucifers forward? Stop, now; didn't you say so?"

"Well, suppose I did? What then? I've part changed my flesh since that time, why not my mind? Besides, supposing we *are* loaded with powder barrels aft and lucifers forward; how the devil could the lucifers get afire in this drenching spray here? Why, my little man, you have pretty red hair, but you couldn't get afire now. Shake yourself; you're Aquarius, or the water-bearer, Flask; might fill pitchers at your coat collar. Don't you see, then, that for these extra risks the Marine Insurance companies have extra guarantees? Here are hydrants, Flask. But hark, again, and I'll answer ye the other thing. First take your leg off from the crown of the anchor here, though, so I can pass the rope; now listen. What's the mighty difference between holding a mast's lightning-rod in the storm, and standing close by a mast that hasn't got any lightning-rod at all in a storm? Don't you see, you timber-head, that no harm can come to the holder of the rod, unless the mast is first struck? What are you talking about, then? Not one ship in a hundred carries rods, and Ahab,—aye, man, and all of us,—were in no more danger then, in my poor opinion, than all the crews in ten thousand ships now sailing the seas. Why, you King-Post, you, I suppose you would have every man in the world go about with a small lightning-rod running up the corner of his hat, like a militia officer's skewered feather, and trailing behind like his sash. Why don't ye be sensible, Flask? it's easy to be sensible; why don't ye, then? any man with half an eye can be sensible."

"I don't know that, Stubb. You sometimes find it rather hard."

"Yes, when a fellow's soaked through, it's hard to be sensible, that's a fact. And I am about drenched with this spray. Never mind; catch the turn there, and pass it. Seems to me we are lashing down these anchors now as if they were never going to be used again. Tying these two anchors here, Flask, seems like tying a man's hands behind him. And what big generous hands they are, to be sure. These are your iron fists, hey? What a hold they have, too! I wonder, Flask, whether the world is anchored anywhere; if she is, she swings with an uncommon long cable, though. There, hammer that knot down, and we've done. So; next to touching land, lighting on deck is the most satisfactory. I say, just wring out my jacket skirts, will ye? Thank ye. They laugh at long-togs so, Flask; but seems to me, a long tailed coat ought always to be worn in all storms afloat. The tails tapering down that way, serve to carry off the water, d'ye see. Same with cocked hats; the cocks form gable-end eave-troughs, Flask. No more monkey-jackets and tarpaulins for me; I must mount a swallow-tail, and drive down a beaver; so. Halloa! whew! there goes my tarpaulin overboard; Lord, Lord, that the winds that come from heaven should be so unmannerly! This is a nasty night, lad."

# Chapter 122

*Midnight Aloft—Thunder and Lightning*

*(The Main-top-sail yard.—Tashtego passing new lashings
around it.)*

UM, UM, UM. Stop that thunder! Plenty too much thunder up here.
What's the use of thunder? Um, um, um. We don't want thunder;
we want rum; give us a glass of rum. Um, um, um!"

# Chapter 123

## *The Musket*

D URING THE MOST VIOLENT SHOCKS of the Typhoon, the man at the Pequod's jaw-bone tiller had several times been reelingly hurled to the deck by its spasmodic motions, even though preventer tackles had been attached to it—for they were slack—because some play to the tiller was indispensable.

In a severe gale like this, while the ship is but a tossed shuttle-cock to the blast, it is by no means uncommon to see the needles in the compasses, at intervals, go round and round. It was thus with the Pequod's; at almost every shock the helmsman had not failed to notice the whirling velocity with which they revolved upon the cards; it is a sight that hardly any one can behold without some sort of unwonted emotion.

Some hours after midnight, the Typhoon abated so much, that through the strenuous exertions of Starbuck and Stubb—one engaged forward and the other aft—the shivered remnants of the jib and fore and main-top-sails were cut adrift from the spars, and went eddying away to leeward, like the feathers of an albatross,. which sometimes are cast to the winds when that storm-tossed bird is on the wing.

The three corresponding new sails were now bent and reefed, and a storm-trysail was set further aft; so that the ship soon went through the water with some precision again; and the course—for the present, East-

south-east—which he was to steer, if practicable, was once more given to
the helmsman. For during the violence of the gale, he had only steered
according to its vicissitudes. But as he was now bringing the ship as near her
course as possible, watching the compass meanwhile, lo! a good sign! the
wind seemed coming round astern; aye, the foul breeze became fair!

Instantly the yards were squared, to the lively song of *"Ho! the fair wind!
oh-he-yo, cheerly, men!"* the crew singing for joy, that so promising an
event should so soon have falsified the evil portents preceding it.

In compliance with the standing order of his commander—to report
immediately, and at any one of the twenty-four hours, any decided change
in the affairs of the deck,—Starbuck had no sooner trimmed the yards to the
breeze—however reluctantly and gloomily,—than he mechanically went
below to apprise Captain Ahab of the circumstance.

Ere knocking at his state-room, he involuntarily paused before it a
moment. The cabin lamp—taking long swings this way and that—was
burning fitfully, and casting fitful shadows upon the old man's bolted
door,—a thin one, with fixed blinds inserted, in place of upper panels. The
isolated subterraneousness of the cabin made a certain humming silence to
reign there, though it was hooped round by all the roar of the elements. The
loaded muskets in the rack were shiningly revealed, as they stood upright
against the forward bulkhead. Starbuck was an honest, upright man; but
out of Starbuck's heart, at that instant when he saw the muskets, there
strangely evolved an evil thought; but so blent with its neutral or good
accompaniments that for the instant he hardly knew it for itself.

"He would have shot me once," he murmured, "yes, there's the very
musket that he pointed at me;—that one with the studded stock; let me
touch it—lift it. Strange, that I, who have handled so many deadly lances,
strange, that I should shake so now. Loaded? I must see. Aye, aye; and
powder in the pan;—that's not good. Best spill it?—wait. I'll cure myself of
this. I'll hold the musket boldly while I think.—I come to report a fair wind
to him. But how fair? Fair for death and doom,—*that's* fair for Moby Dick.
It's a fair wind that's only fair for that accursed fish.—The very tube he
pointed at me!—the very one; *this* one—I hold it here; he would have
killed me with the very thing I handle now.—Aye and he would fain kill all
his crew. Does he not say he will not strike his spars to any gale? Has he not
dashed his heavenly quadrant? and in these same perilous seas, gropes he not
his way by mere dead reckoning of the error-abounding log? and in this
very Typhoon, did he not swear that he would have no lightning-rods?
But shall this crazed old man be tamely suffered to drag a whole ship's

company down to doom with him?—Yes, it would make him the wilful
murderer of thirty men and more, if this ship come to any deadly harm; and
come to deadly harm, my soul swears this ship will, if Ahab have his way.
If, then, he were this instant—put aside, that crime would not be his. Ha! is
he muttering in his sleep? Yes, just there,—in there, he's sleeping. Sleeping?
aye, but still alive, and soon awake again. I can't withstand thee, then, old
man. Not reasoning; not remonstrance; not entreaty wilt thou hearken to;
all this thou scornest. Flat obedience to thy own flat commands, this is all
thou breathest. Aye, and say'st the men have vow'd thy vow; say'st all of us
are Ahabs. Great God forbid!—But is there no other way? no lawful way?
—Make him a prisoner to be taken home? What! hope to wrest this old
man's living power from his own living hands? Only a fool would try it.
Say he were pinioned even; knotted all over with ropes and hawsers;
chained down to ring-bolts on this cabin floor; he would be more hideous
than a caged tiger, then. I could not endure the sight; could not possibly fly
his howlings; all comfort, sleep itself, inestimable reason would leave me on
the long intolerable voyage. What, then, remains? The land is hundreds of
leagues away, and locked Japan the nearest. I stand alone here upon an
open sea, with two oceans and a whole continent between me and law.—
Aye, aye, 'tis so.—Is heaven a murderer when its lightning strikes a would-be
murderer in his bed, tindering sheets and skin together?—And would I be a
murderer, then, if"———and slowly, stealthily, and half sideways looking,
he placed the loaded musket's end against the door.

"On this level, Ahab's hammock swings within; his head this way. A
touch, and Starbuck may survive to hug his wife and child again.—Oh
Mary! Mary!—boy! boy! boy!—But if I wake thee not to death, old man,
who can tell to what unsounded deeps Starbuck's body this day week may
sink, with all the crew! Great God, where art thou? Shall I? shall I?———
The wind has gone down and shifted, sir; the fore and main topsails are
reefed and set; she heads her course."

"Stern all! Oh Moby Dick, I clutch thy heart at last!"

Such were the sounds that now came hurtling from out the old man's
tormented sleep, as if Starbuck's voice had caused the long dumb dream to
speak.

The yet levelled musket shook like a drunkard's arm against the panel;
Starbuck seemed wrestling with an angel; but turning from the door, he
placed the death-tube in its rack, and left the place.

"He's too sound asleep, Mr. Stubb; go thou down, and wake him, and
tell him. I must see to the deck here. Thou know'st what to say."

# Chapter 124

*The Needle*

NEXT MORNING the not-yet-subsided sea rolled in long slow billows of mighty bulk, and striving in the Pequod's gurgling track, pushed her on like giants' palms outspread. The strong, unstaggering breeze abounded so, that sky and air seemed vast outbellying sails; the whole world boomed before the wind. Muffled in the full morning light, the invisible sun was only known by the spread intensity of his place; where his bayonet rays moved on in stacks. Emblazonings, as of crowned Babylonian kings and queens, reigned over everything. The sea was as a crucible of molten gold, that bubblingly leaps with light and heat.

Long maintaining an enchanted silence, Ahab stood apart; and every time the tetering ship loweringly pitched down her bowsprit, he turned to eye the bright sun's rays produced ahead; and when she profoundly settled by the stern, he turned behind, and saw the sun's rearward place, and how the same yellow rays were blending with his undeviating wake.

"Ha, ha, my ship! thou mightest well be taken now for the sea-chariot of the sun. Ho, ho! all ye nations before my prow, I bring the sun to ye! Yoke on the further billows; hallo! a tandem, I drive the sea!"

But suddenly reined back by some counter thought, he hurried towards the helm, huskily demanding how the ship was heading.

"East-sou-east, sir," said the frightened steersman.

"Thou liest!" smiting him with his clenched fist. "Heading East at this hour in the morning, and the sun astern?"

Upon this every soul was confounded; for the phenomenon just then observed by Ahab had unaccountably escaped every one else; but its very blinding palpableness must have been the cause.

Thrusting his head half way into the binnacle, Ahab caught one glimpse of the compasses; his uplifted arm slowly fell; for a moment he almost seemed to stagger. Standing behind him Starbuck looked, and lo! the two compasses pointed East, and the Pequod was as infallibly going West.

But ere the first wild alarm could get out abroad among the crew, the old man with a rigid laugh exclaimed, "I have it! It has happened before. Mr. Starbuck, last night's thunder turned our compasses—that's all. Thou hast before now heard of such a thing, I take it."

"Aye; but never before has it happened to me, sir," said the pale mate, gloomily.

Here, it must needs be said, that accidents like this have in more than one case occurred to ships in violent storms. The magnetic energy, as developed in the mariner's needle, is, as all know, essentially one with the electricity beheld in heaven; hence it is not to be much marvelled at, that such things should be. In instances where the lightning has actually struck the vessel, so as to smite down some of the spars and rigging, the effect upon the needle has at times been still more fatal; all its loadstone virtue being annihilated, so that the before magnetic steel was of no more use than an old wife's knitting needle. But in either case, the needle never again, of itself, recovers the original virtue thus marred or lost; and if the binnacle compasses be affected, the same fate reaches all the others that may be in the ship; even were the lowermost one inserted into the kelson.

Deliberately standing before the binnacle, and eyeing the transpointed compasses, the old man, with the sharp of his extended hand, now took the precise bearing of the sun, and satisfied that the needles were exactly inverted, shouted out his orders for the ship's course to be changed accordingly. The yards were braced hard up; and once more the Pequod thrust her undaunted bows into the opposing wind, for the supposed fair one had only been juggling her.

Meanwhile, whatever were his own secret thoughts, Starbuck said nothing, but quietly he issued all requisite orders; while Stubb and Flask— who in some small degree seemed then to be sharing his feelings—likewise unmurmuringly acquiesced. As for the men, though some of them lowly rumbled, their fear of Ahab was greater than their fear of Fate. But as ever before, the pagan harpooneers remained almost wholly unimpressed; or if impressed, it was only with a certain magnetism shot into their congenial hearts from inflexible Ahab's.

For a space the old man walked the deck in rolling reveries. But chancing to slip with his ivory heel, he saw the crushed copper sight-tubes of the quadrant he had the day before dashed to the deck.

"Thou poor, proud heaven-gazer and sun's pilot! yesterday I wrecked thee, and to-day the compasses would feign have wrecked me. So, so. But Ahab is lord over the level loadstone yet. Mr. Starbuck—a lance without the pole; a top-maul, and the smallest of the sail-maker's needles. Quick!"

Accessory, perhaps, to the impulse dictating the thing he was now about to do, were certain prudential motives, whose object might have been to revive the spirits of his crew by a stroke of his subtile skill, in a matter so wondrous as that of the inverted compasses. Besides, the old man well knew that to steer by transpointed needles, though clumsily practicable, was not a thing to be passed over by superstitious sailors, without some shudderings and evil portents.

"Men," said he, steadily turning upon the crew, as the mate handed him the things he had demanded, "my men, the thunder turned old Ahab's needles; but out of this bit of steel Ahab can make one of his own, that will point as true as any."

Abashed glances of servile wonder were exchanged by the sailors, as this was said; and with fascinated eyes they awaited whatever magic might follow. But Starbuck looked away.

With a blow from the top-maul Ahab knocked off the steel head of the lance, and then handing to the mate the long iron rod remaining, bade him hold it upright, without its touching the deck. Then, with the maul, after repeatedly smiting the upper end of this iron rod, he placed the blunted needle endwise on the top of it, and less strongly hammered that, several times, the mate still holding the rod as before. Then going through some small strange motions with it—whether indispensable to the magnetizing of the steel, or merely intended to augment the awe of the crew, is uncertain—he called for linen thread; and moving to the binnacle, slipped out the two reversed needles there, and horizontally suspended the sail-needle by its middle, over one of the compass-cards. At first, the steel went round and round, quivering and vibrating at either end; but at last it settled to its place, when Ahab, who had been intently watching for this result, stepped frankly back from the binnacle, and pointing his stretched arm towards it, exclaimed,—"Look ye, for yourselves, if Ahab be not lord of the level loadstone! The sun is East, and that compass swears it!"

One after another they peered in, for nothing but their own eyes could persuade such ignorance as theirs, and one after another they slunk away.

In his fiery eyes of scorn and triumph, you then saw Ahab in all his fatal pride.

# Chapter 125

*The Log and Line*

WHILE NOW the fated Pequod had been so long afloat this voyage, the log and line had but very seldom been in use. Owing to a confident reliance upon other means of determining the vessel's place, some merchantmen, and many whalemen, especially when cruising, wholly neglect to heave the log; though at the same time, and frequently more for form's sake than anything else, regularly putting down upon the customary slate the course steered by the ship, as well as the presumed average rate of progression every hour. It had been thus with the Pequod. The wooden reel and angular log attached hung, long untouched, just beneath the railing of the after bulwarks. Rains and spray had damped it; sun and wind had warped it; all the elements had combined to rot a thing that hung so idly. But heedless of all this, his mood seized Ahab, as he happened to glance upon the reel, not many hours after the magnet scene, and he remembered how his quadrant was no more, and recalled his frantic oath about the level log and line. The ship was sailing plungingly; astern the billows rolled in riots.

"Forward, there! Heave the log!"

Two seamen came. The golden-hued Tahitian and the grizzly Manxman. "Take the reel, one of ye, I'll heave."

They went towards the extreme stern, on the ship's lee side, where the deck, with the oblique energy of the wind, was now almost dipping into the creamy, sidelong-rushing sea.

The Manxman took the reel, and holding it high up, by the projecting handle-ends of the spindle, round which the spool of line revolved, so stood with the angular log hanging downwards, till Ahab advanced to him.

Ahab stood before him, and was lightly unwinding some thirty or forty turns to form a preliminary hand-coil to toss overboard, when the old Manxman, who was intently eyeing both him and the line, made bold to speak.

"Sir, I mistrust it; this line looks far gone, long heat and wet have spoiled it."

"'Twill hold, old gentleman. Long heat and wet, have they spoiled thee? Thou seem'st to hold. Or, truer perhaps, life holds thee; not thou it."

"I hold the spool, sir. But just as my captain says. With these grey hairs of mine 'tis not worth while disputing, 'specially with a superior, who'll ne'er confess."

"What's that? There now's a patched professor in Queen Nature's granite-founded College; but methinks he's too subservient. Where wert thou born?"

"In the little rocky Isle of Man, sir."

"Excellent! Thou'st hit the world by that."

"I know not, sir, but I was born there."

"In the Isle of Man, hey? Well, the other way, it's good. Here's a man from Man; a man born in once independent Man, and now unmanned of Man; which is sucked in—by what? Up with the reel! The dead, blind wall butts all inquiring heads at last. Up with it! So."

The log was heaved. The loose coils rapidly straightened out in a long dragging line astern, and then, instantly, the reel began to whirl. In turn, jerkingly raised and lowered by the rolling billows, the towing resistance of the log caused the old reelman to stagger strangely.

"Hold hard!"

Snap! the overstrained line sagged down in one long festoon; the tugging log was gone.

"I crush the quadrant, the thunder turns the needles, and now the mad sea parts the log-line. But Ahab can mend all. Haul in here, Tahitian; reel up, Manxman. And look ye, let the carpenter make another log, and mend thou the line. See to it."

"There he goes now; to him nothing's happened; but to me, the skewer seems loosening out of the middle of the world. Haul in, haul in, Tahitian! These lines run whole, and whirling out: come in broken, and dragging slow. Ha, Pip? come to help; eh, Pip?"

"Pip? whom call ye Pip? Pip jumped from the whale-boat. Pip's missing. Let's see now if ye haven't fished him up here, fisherman. It drags hard; I guess he's holding on. Jerk him, Tahiti! Jerk him off; we haul in no cowards here. Ho! there's his arm just breaking water. A hatchet! a hatchet! cut it off—we haul in no cowards here. Captain Ahab! sir, sir! here's Pip, trying to get on board again."

"Peace, thou crazy loon," cried the Manxman, seizing him by the arm. "Away from the quarter-deck!"

"The greater idiot ever scolds the lesser," muttered Ahab, advancing. "Hands off from that holiness! Where sayest thou Pip was, boy?"

"Astern there, sir, astern! Lo, lo!"

"And who art thou, boy? I see not my reflection in the vacant pupils of thy eyes. Oh God! that man should be a thing for immortal souls to sieve through! Who art thou, boy?"

"Bell-boy, sir; ship's-crier; ding, dong, ding! Pip! Pip! Pip! Reward for Pip! One hundred pounds of clay—five feet high—looks cowardly—quickest known by that! Ding, dong, ding! Who's seen Pip the coward?"

"There can be no hearts above the snow-line. Oh, ye frozen heavens! look down here. Ye did beget this luckless child, and have abandoned him, ye creative libertines. Here, boy; Ahab's cabin shall be Pip's home henceforth, while Ahab lives. Thou touchest my inmost centre, boy; thou art tied to me by cords woven of my heart-strings. Come, let's down."

"What's this? here's velvet shark-skin," intently gazing at Ahab's hand, and feeling it. "Ah, now, had poor Pip but felt so kind a thing as this, perhaps he had ne'er been lost! This seems to me, sir, as a man-rope; something that weak souls may hold by. Oh, sir, let old Perth now come and rivet these two hands together; the black one with the white, for I will not let this go."

"Oh, boy, nor will I thee, unless I should thereby drag thee to worse horrors than are here. Come, then, to my cabin. Lo! ye believers in gods all goodness, and in man all ill, lo you! see the omniscient gods oblivious of suffering man; and man, though idiotic, and knowing not what he does, yet full of the sweet things of love and gratitude. Come! I feel prouder leading thee by thy black hand, than though I grasped an Emperor's!"

"There go two daft ones now," muttered the old Manxman. "One daft with strength, the other daft with weakness. But here's the end of the rotten line—all dripping, too. Mend it, eh? I think we had best have a new line altogether. I'll see Mr. Stubb about it."

# Chapter 126

## *The Life-Buoy*

STEERING NOW SOUTH-EASTWARD by Ahab's levelled steel, and her progress solely determined by Ahab's level log and line; the Pequod held on her path towards the Equator. Making so long a passage through such unfrequented waters, descrying no ships, and ere long, sideways impelled by unvarying trade winds, over waves monotonously mild; all these seemed the strange calm things preluding some riotous and desperate scene.

At last, when the ship drew near to the outskirts, as it were, of the Equatorial fishing-ground, and in the deep darkness that goes before the dawn, was sailing by a cluster of rocky islets; the watch—then headed by Flask—was startled by a cry so plaintively wild and unearthly—like half-articulated wailings of the ghosts of all Herod's murdered Innocents—that one and all, they started from their reveries, and for the space of some moments stood, or sat, or leaned all transfixedly listening, like the carved Roman slave, while that wild cry remained within hearing. The Christian or civilized part of the crew said it was mermaids, and shuddered; but the pagan harpooneers remained unappalled. Yet the grey Manxman—the oldest mariner of all—declared that the wild thrilling sounds that were heard, were the voices of newly drowned men in the sea.

Below in his hammock, Ahab did not hear of this till grey dawn, when

he came to the deck; it was then recounted to him by Flask, not unaccompanied with hinted dark meanings. He hollowly laughed, and thus
explained the wonder.

Those rocky islands the ship had passed were the resort of great numbers
of seals, and some young seals that had lost their dams, or some dams that
had lost their cubs, must have risen nigh the ship and kept company with
her, crying and sobbing with their human sort of wail. But this only the
more affected some of them, because most mariners cherish a very superstitious feeling about seals, arising not only from their peculiar tones when
in distress, but also from the human look of their round heads and semi-
intelligent faces, seen peeringly uprising from the water alongside. In the
sea, under certain circumstances, seals have more than once been mistaken
for men.

But the bodings of the crew were destined to receive a most plausible
confirmation in the fate of one of their number that morning. At sun-rise
this man went from his hammock to his mast-head at the fore; and whether
it was that he was not yet half waked from his sleep (for sailors sometimes
go aloft in a transition state), whether it was thus with the man, there is now
no telling; but, be that as it may, he had not been long at his perch, when a
cry was heard—a cry and a rushing—and looking up, they saw a falling
phantom in the air; and looking down, a little tossed heap of white bubbles
in the blue of the sea.

The life-buoy—a long slender cask—was dropped from the stern,
where it always hung obedient to a cunning spring; but no hand rose to
seize it, and the sun having long beat upon this cask it had shrunken, so that
it slowly filled, and the parched wood also filled at its every pore; and the
studded iron-bound cask followed the sailor to the bottom, as if to yield
him his pillow, though in sooth but a hard one.

And thus the first man of the Pequod that mounted the mast to look out
for the White Whale, on the White Whale's own peculiar ground; that
man was swallowed up in the deep. But few, perhaps, thought of that at the
time. Indeed, in some sort, they were not grieved at this event, at least as a
portent; for they regarded it, not as a foreshadowing of evil in the future,
but as the fulfilment of an evil already presaged. They declared that now
they knew the reason of those wild shrieks they had heard the night before.
But again the old Manxman said nay.

The lost life-buoy was now to be replaced; Starbuck was directed to see
to it; but as no cask of sufficient lightness could be found, and as in the
feverish eagerness of what seemed the approaching crisis of the voyage, all

hands were impatient of any toil but what was directly connected with its
final end, whatever that might prove to be; therefore, they were going to
leave the ship's stern unprovided with a buoy, when by certain strange signs
and inuendoes Queequeg hinted a hint concerning his coffin.

"A life-buoy of a coffin!" cried Starbuck, starting.

"Rather queer, that, I should say," said Stubb.

"It will make a good enough one," said Flask, "the carpenter here can
arrange it easily."

"Bring it up; there's nothing else for it," said Starbuck, after a melancholy pause. "Rig it, carpenter; do not look at me so—the coffin, I mean.
Dost thou hear me? Rig it."

"And shall I nail down the lid, sir?" moving his hand as with a hammer.

"Aye."

"And shall I caulk the seams, sir?" moving his hand as with a caulking-
iron.

"Aye."

"And shall I then pay over the same with pitch, sir?" moving his hands as
with a pitch-pot.

"Away! what possesses thee to this? Make a life-buoy of the coffin, and
no more.—Mr. Stubb, Mr. Flask, come forward with me."

"He goes off in a huff. The whole he can endure; at the parts he baulks.
Now I don't like this. I make a leg for Captain Ahab, and he wears it
like a gentleman; but I make a bandbox for Queequeg, and he wont put
his head into it. Are all my pains to go for nothing with that coffin? And
now I'm ordered to make a life-buoy of it. It's like turning an old coat;
going to bring the flesh on the other side now. I don't like this cobbling sort
of business—I don't like it at all; it's undignified; it's not my place. Let
tinkers' brats do tinkerings; we are their betters. I like to take in hand none
but clean, virgin, fair-and-square mathematical jobs, something that
regularly begins at the beginning, and is at the middle when midway, and
comes to an end at the conclusion; not a cobbler's job, that's at an end in the
middle, and at the beginning at the end. It's the old woman's tricks to be
giving cobbling jobs. Lord! what an affection all old women have for
tinkers. I know an old woman of sixty-five who ran away with a bald-headed
young tinker once. And that's the reason I never would work for lonely
widow old women ashore, when I kept my job-shop in the Vineyard; they
might have taken it into their lonely old heads to run off with me. But
heigh-ho! there are no caps at sea but snow-caps. Let me see. Nail down the
lid; caulk the seams; pay over the same with pitch; batten them down

tight, and hang it with the snap-spring over the ship's stern. Were ever such
things done before with a coffin? Some superstitious old carpenters, now,
would be tied up in the rigging, ere they would do the job. But I'm made of
knotty Aroostook hemlock; I don't budge. Cruppered with a coffin! Sailing
about with a grave-yard tray! But never mind. We workers in woods make
bridal-bedsteads and card-tables, as well as coffins and hearses. We work by
the month, or by the job, or by the profit; not for us to ask the why and
wherefore of our work, unless it be too confounded cobbling, and then we
stash it if we can. Hem! I'll do the job, now, tenderly. I'll have me—let's see
—how many in the ship's company, all told? But I've forgotten. Any way,
I'll have me thirty separate, Turk's-headed life-lines, each three feet long
hanging all round to the coffin. Then, if the hull go down, there'll be thirty
lively fellows all fighting for one coffin, a sight not seen very often beneath
the sun! Come hammer, calking-iron, pitch-pot, and marling-spike! Let's
to it."

# Chapter 127

## The Deck

*(The coffin laid upon two line-tubs, between the vice-bench and the open hatchway; the Carpenter calking its seams; the string of twisted oakum slowly unwinding from a large roll of it placed in the bosom of his frock.—Ahab comes slowly from the cabin-gangway, and hears Pip following him.)*

BACK, LAD; I will be with ye again presently. He goes! Not this hand complies with my humor more genially than that boy.— Middle aisle of a church! What's here?"

"Life-buoy, sir. Mr. Starbuck's orders. Oh, look, sir! Beware the hatchway!"

"Thank ye, man. Thy coffin lies handy to the vault."

"Sir? The hatchway? oh! So it does, sir, so it does."

"Art not thou the leg-maker? Look, did not this stump come from thy shop?"

"I believe it did, sir; does the ferrule stand, sir?"

"Well enough. But art thou not also the undertaker?"

"Aye, sir; I patched up this thing here as a coffin for Queequeg; but they've set me now to turning it into something else."

"Then tell me; art thou not an arrant, all-grasping, intermeddling, monopolizing, heathenish old scamp, to be one day making legs, and the next day coffins to clap them in, and yet again life-buoys out of those same coffins? Thou art as unprincipled as the gods, and as much of a jack-of-all-trades."

"But I do not mean anything, sir. I do as I do."

"The gods again. Hark ye, dost thou not ever sing working about a coffin? The Titans, they say, hummed snatches when chipping out the craters for volcanoes; and the grave-digger in the play sings, spade in hand. Dost thou never?"

"Sing, sir? Do I sing? Oh, I'm indifferent enough, sir, for that; but the reason why the grave-digger made music must have been because there was none in his spade, sir. But the calking mallet is full of it. Hark to it."

"Aye, and that's because the lid there's a sounding-board; and what in all things makes the sounding-board is this—there's naught beneath. And yet, a coffin with a body in it rings pretty much the same, Carpenter. Hast thou ever helped carry a bier, and heard the coffin knock against the church-yard gate, going in?"

"Faith, sir, I've ———"

"Faith? What's that?"

"Why, faith, sir, it's only a sort of exclamation-like—that's all, sir."

"Um, um; go on."

"I was about to say, sir, that ———"

"Art thou a silk-worm? Dost thou spin thy own shroud out of thyself? Look at thy bosom! Despatch! and get these traps out of sight."

"He goes aft. That was sudden, now; but squalls come sudden in hot latitudes. I've heard that the Isle of Albemarle, one of the Gallipagos, is cut by the Equator right in the middle. Seems to me some sort of Equator cuts yon old man, too, right in his middle. He's always under the Line—fiery hot, I tell ye! He's looking this way—come, oakum; quick. Here we go again. This wooden mallet is the cork, and I'm the professor of musical glasses—tap, tap!"

*(Ahab to himself.)*

"There's a sight! There's a sound! The greyheaded woodpecker tapping the hollow tree! Blind and deaf might well be envied now. See! that thing rests on two line-tubs, full of tow-lines. A most malicious wag, that fellow. Rat-tat! So man's seconds tick! Oh! how immaterial are all materials! What things real are there, but imponderable thoughts? Here now's the very dreaded symbol of grim death, by a mere hap, made the expressive sign of the help and hope of most endangered life. A life-buoy of a coffin! Does it go further? Can it be that in some spiritual sense the coffin is, after all, but an immortality-preserver! I'll think of that. But no. So far gone am I in the dark side of earth, that its other side, the theoretic bright one, seems but uncertain twilight to me. Will ye never have done, Carpenter, with that accursed sound? I go below; let me not see that thing here when I return again. Now, then, Pip, we'll talk this over; I do suck most wondrous philosophies from thee! Some unknown conduits from the unknown worlds must empty into thee!"

# Chapter 128

*The Pequod meets the Rachel*

NEXT DAY, a large ship, the Rachel, was descried, bearing directly down upon the Pequod, all her spars thickly clustering with men. At the time the Pequod was making good speed through the water; but as the broad-winged windward stranger shot nigh to her, the boastful sails all fell together as blank bladders that are burst, and all life fled from the smitten hull.

"Bad news; she brings bad news," muttered the old Manxman. But ere her commander, who, with trumpet to mouth, stood up in his boat; ere he could hopefully hail, Ahab's voice was heard.

"Hast seen the White Whale?"

"Aye, yesterday. Have ye seen a whale-boat adrift?"

Throttling his joy, Ahab negatively answered this unexpected question; and would then have fain boarded the stranger, when the stranger captain himself, having stopped his vessel's way, was seen descending her side. A few keen pulls, and his boat-hook soon clinched the Pequod's main-chains, and he sprang to the deck. Immediately he was recognised by Ahab for a Nantucketer he knew. But no formal salutation was exchanged.

"Where was he?—not killed!—not killed!" cried Ahab, closely advancing. "How was it?"

It seemed that somewhat late on the afternoon of the day previous, while three of the stranger's boats were engaged with a shoal of whales, which had led them some four or five miles from the ship; and while they were yet in swift chase to windward, the white hump and head of Moby Dick had suddenly loomed up out of the blue water, not very far to leeward; whereupon, the fourth rigged boat—a reserved one—had been instantly lowered in chase. After a keen sail before the wind, this fourth boat—the swiftest keeled of all—seemed to have succeeded in fastening—at least, as well as the man at the mast-head could tell anything about it. In the distance he saw the diminished dotted boat; and then a swift gleam of bubbling white water; and after that nothing more; whence it was concluded that the stricken whale must have indefinitely run away with his pursuers, as often happens. There was some apprehension, but no positive alarm, as yet. The recall signals were placed in the rigging; darkness came on; and forced to pick up her three far to windward boats—ere going in quest of the fourth one in the precisely opposite direction—the ship had not only been neces-sitated to leave that boat to its fate till near midnight, but, for the time, to increase her distance from it. But the rest of her crew being at last safe aboard, she crowded all sail—stunsail on stunsail—after the missing boat; kindling a fire in her try-pots for a beacon; and every other man aloft on the look-out. But though when she had thus sailed a sufficient distance to gain the presumed place of the absent ones when last seen; though she then paused to lower her spare boats to pull all around her; and not finding anything, had again dashed on; again paused, and lowered her boats; and though she had thus continued doing till day light; yet not the least glimpse of the missing keel had been seen.

The story told, the stranger Captain immediately went on to reveal his object in boarding the Pequod. He desired that ship to unite with his own in the search; by sailing over the sea some four or five miles apart, on parallel lines, and so sweeping a double horizon, as it were.

"I will wager something now," whispered Stubb to Flask, "that some one in that missing boat wore off that Captain's best coat; mayhap, his watch—he's so cursed anxious to get it back. Who ever heard of two pious whale-ships cruising after one missing whale-boat in the height of the whaling season? See, Flask, only see how pale he looks—pale in the very buttons of his eyes—look—it wasn't the coat—it must have been the—"

"My boy, my own boy is among them. For God's sake—I beg, I conjure"—here exclaimed the stranger Captain to Ahab, who thus far had but icily received his petition. "For eight-and-forty hours let me charter your ship—I will gladly pay for it, and roundly pay for it—if there be no other way—for eight-and-forty hours only—only that—you must, oh, you must, and you *shall* do this thing."

"His son!" cried Stubb, "oh, it's his son he's lost! I take back the coat and watch—what says Ahab? We must save that boy."

"He's drowned with the rest on 'em, last night," said the old Manx sailor standing behind them; "I heard; all of ye heard their spirits."

Now, as it shortly turned out, what made this incident of the Rachel's the more melancholy, was the circumstance, that not only was one of the Captain's sons among the number of the missing boat's crew; but among the number of the other boats' crews, at the same time, but on the other hand, separated from the ship during the dark vicissitudes of the chase, there had been still another son; as that for a time, the wretched father was plunged to the bottom of the cruellest perplexity; which was only solved for him by his chief mate's instinctively adopting the ordinary procedure of a whale-ship in such emergencies, that is, when placed between jeopardized but divided boats, always to pick up the majority first. But the captain, for some unknown constitutional reason, had refrained from mentioning all this, and not till forced to it by Ahab's iciness did he allude to his one yet missing boy; a little lad, but twelve years old, whose father with the earnest but unmisgiving hardihood of a Nantucketer's paternal love, had thus early sought to initiate him in the perils and wonders of a vocation almost immemorially the destiny of all his race. Nor does it unfrequently occur, that Nantucket captains will send a son of such tender age away from them, for a protracted three or four years' voyage in some other ship than their own; so that their first knowledge of a whaleman's career shall be un-enervated by any chance display of a father's natural but untimely partiality, or undue apprehensiveness and concern.

Meantime, now the stranger was still beseeching his poor boon of Ahab; and Ahab still stood like an anvil, receiving every shock, but without the least quivering of his own.

"I will not go," said the stranger, "till you say *aye* to me. Do to me as you would have me do to you in the like case. For *you* too have a boy, Captain Ahab—though but a child, and nestling safely at home now—a child of your old age too—Yes, yes, you relent; I see it—run, run, men, now, and stand by to square in the yards."

"Avast," cried Ahab—"touch not a rope-yarn;" then in a voice that prolongingly moulded every word—"Captain Gardiner, I will not do it. Even now I lose time. Good bye, good bye. God bless ye, man, and may I forgive myself, but I must go. Mr. Starbuck, look at the binnacle watch, and in three minutes from this present instant warn off all strangers: then brace forward again, and let the ship sail as before."

Hurriedly turning, with averted face, he descended into his cabin, leaving the strange captain transfixed at this unconditional and utter rejection of his so earnest suit. But starting from his enchantment, Gardiner silently hurried to the side; more fell than stepped into his boat, and returned to his ship.

Soon the two ships diverged their wakes; and long as the strange vessel was in view, she was seen to yaw hither and thither at every dark spot, however small, on the sea. This way and that her yards were swung round; starboard and larboard, she continued to tack; now she beat against a head sea; and again it pushed her before it; while all the while, her masts and yards were thickly clustered with men, as three tall cherry trees, when the boys are cherrying among the boughs.

But by her still halting course and winding, woful way, you plainly saw that this ship that so wept with spray, still remained without comfort. She was Rachel, weeping for her children, because they were not.

# Chapter 129

*The Cabin*

*(Ahab moving to go on deck; Pip catches him by the hand to follow.)*

LAD, LAD, I tell thee thou must not follow Ahab now. The hour is coming when Ahab would not scare thee from him, yet would not have thee by him. There is that in thee, poor lad, which I feel too curing to my malady. Like cures like; and for this hunt, my malady becomes my most desired health. Do thou abide below here, where they shall serve thee, as if thou wert the captain. Aye, lad, thou shalt sit here in my own screwed chair; another screw to it, thou must be."

"No, no, no! ye have not a whole body, sir; do ye but use poor me for your one lost leg; only tread upon me, sir; I ask no more, so I remain a part of ye."

"Oh! spite of million villains, this makes me a bigot in the fadeless fidelity of man!—and a black! and crazy!—but methinks like-cures-like applies to him too; he grows so sane again."

"They tell me, sir, that Stubb did once desert poor little Pip, whose drowned bones now show white, for all the blackness of his living skin. But I will never desert ye, sir, as Stubb did him. Sir, I must go with ye."

"If thou speakest thus to me much more, Ahab's purpose keels up in him. I tell thee no; it cannot be."

"Oh good master, master, master!"

"Weep so, and I will murder thee! have a care, for Ahab too is mad.

534

Listen, and thou wilt often hear my ivory foot upon the deck, and still know that I am there. And now I quit thee. Thy hand!—Met! True art thou, lad, as the circumference to its centre. So: God for ever bless thee; and if it come to that,—God for ever save thee, let what will befall."

*(Ahab goes; Pip steps one step forward.)*

"Here he this instant stood; I stand in his air,—but I'm alone. Now were even poor Pip here I could endure it, but he's missing. Pip! Pip! Ding, dong, ding! Who's seen Pip? He must be up here; let's try the door. What? neither lock, nor bolt, nor bar; and yet there's no opening it. It must be the spell; he told me to stay here: Aye, and told me this screwed chair was mine. Here, then, I'll seat me, against the transom, in the ship's full middle, all her keel and her three masts before me. Here, our old sailors say, in their black seventy-fours great admirals sometimes sit at table, and lord it over rows of captains and lieutenants. Ha! what's this? epaulets! epaulets! the epaulets all come crowding! Pass round the decanters; glad to see ye; fill up, monsieurs! What an odd feeling, now, when a black boy's host to white men with gold lace upon their coats!—Monsieurs, have ye seen one Pip?— a little negro lad, five feet high, hang-dog look, and cowardly! Jumped from a whale-boat once;—seen him? No! Well then, fill up again, captains, and let's drink shame upon all cowards! I name no names. Shame upon them! Put one foot upon the table. Shame upon all cowards.—Hist! above there, I hear ivory—Oh, master! master! I am indeed down-hearted when you walk over me. But here I'll stay, though this stern strikes rocks; and they bulge through; and oysters come to join me."

# Chapter 130

## *The Hat*

AND NOW that at the proper time and place, after so long and wide a preliminary cruise, Ahab,—all other whaling waters swept—seemed to have chased his foe into an ocean-fold, to slay him the more securely there; now, that he found himself hard by the very latitude and longitude where his tormenting wound had been inflicted; now that a vessel had been spoken which on the very day preceding had actually encountered Moby Dick;—and now that all his successive meetings with various ships contrastingly concurred to show the demoniac indifference with which the white whale tore his hunters, whether sinning or sinned against; now it was that there lurked a something in the old man's eyes, which it was hardly sufferable for feeble souls to see. As the unsetting polar star, which through the livelong, arctic, six months' night sustains its piercing, steady, central gaze; so Ahab's purpose now fixedly gleamed down upon the constant midnight of the gloomy crew. It domineered above them so, that all their bodings, doubts, misgivings, fears, were fain to hide beneath their souls, and not sprout forth a single spear or leaf.

In this foreshadowing interval too, all humor, forced or natural, vanished. Stubb no more strove to raise a smile; Starbuck no more strove to check one. Alike, joy and sorrow, hope and fear, seemed ground to finest dust, and powdered, for the time, in the clamped mortar of Ahab's iron soul. Like machines, they dumbly moved about the deck, ever conscious that the old man's despot eye was on them.

But did you deeply scan him in his more secret confidential hours; when he thought no glance but one was on him; then you would have seen that even as Ahab's eyes so awed the crew's, the inscrutable Parsee's glance awed his; or somehow, at least, in some wild way, at times affected it. Such an added, gliding strangeness began to invest the thin Fedallah now; such ceaseless shudderings shook him; that the men looked dubious at him; half uncertain, as it seemed, whether indeed he were a mortal substance, or else a tremulous shadow cast upon the deck by some unseen being's body. And that shadow was always hovering there. For not by night, even, had Fedallah ever certainly been known to slumber, or go below. He would stand still for hours: but never sat or leaned; his wan but wondrous eyes did plainly say—We two watchmen never rest.

Nor, at any time, by night or day could the mariners now step upon the deck, unless Ahab was before them; either standing in his pivot-hole, or exactly pacing the planks between two undeviating limits,—the main-mast and the mizen; or else they saw him standing in the cabin-scuttle,—his living foot advanced upon the deck, as if to step; his hat slouched heavily over his eyes; so that however motionless he stood, however the days and nights were added on, that he had not swung in his hammock; yet hidden beneath that slouching hat, they could never tell unerringly whether, for all this, his eyes were really closed at times: or whether he was still intently scanning them; no matter, though he stood so in the scuttle for a whole hour on the stretch, and the unheeded night-damp gathered in beads of dew upon that stone-carved coat and hat. The clothes that the night had wet, the next day's sunshine dried upon him; and so, day after day, and night after night; he went no more beneath the planks; whatever he wanted from the cabin that thing he sent for.

He ate in the same open air; that is, his two only meals,—breakfast and dinner: supper he never touched; nor reaped his beard; which darkly grew all gnarled, as unearthed roots of trees blown over, which still grow idly on at naked base, though perished in the upper verdure. But though his whole life was now become one watch on deck; and though the Parsee's mystic watch was without intermission as his own; yet these two never seemed to speak—one man to the other—unless at long intervals some passing un-momentous matter made it necessary. Though such a potent spell seemed secretly to join the twain; openly, and to the awe-struck crew, they seemed pole-like asunder. If by day they chanced to speak one word; by night, dumb men were both, so far as concerned the slightest verbal interchange. At times, for longest hours, without a single hail, they stood far parted in the starlight; Ahab in his scuttle, the Parsee by the mainmast; but still fixedly gazing upon each other; as if in the Parsee Ahab saw his forethrown shadow, in Ahab the Parsee his abandoned substance.

And yet, somehow, did Ahab—in his own proper self, as daily, hourly, and every instant, commandingly revealed to his subordinates,—Ahab seemed an independent lord; the Parsee but his slave. Still again both seemed yoked together, and an unseen tyrant driving them; the lean shade siding the solid rib. For be this Parsee what he may, all rib and keel was solid Ahab.

At the first faintest glimmering of the dawn, his iron voice was heard from aft—"Man the mast-heads!"—and all through the day, till after sunset and after twilight, the same voice every hour, at the striking of the helmsman's bell, was heard—"What d'ye see?—sharp! sharp!"

But when three or four days had slided by, after meeting the children-seeking Rachel; and no spout had yet been seen; the monomaniac old man seemed distrustful of his crew's fidelity; at least, of nearly all except the Pagan harpooneers; he seemed to doubt, even, whether Stubb and Flask might not willingly overlook the sight he sought. But if these suspicions were really his, he sagaciously refrained from verbally expressing them, however his actions might seem to hint them.

"I will have the first sight of the whale myself,"—he said. "Aye! Ahab must have the doubloon!" and with his own hands he rigged a nest of basketed bowlines; and sending a hand aloft, with a single sheaved block, to secure to the mainmast head, he received the two ends of the downward-reeved rope; and attaching one to his basket prepared a pin for the other end, in order to fasten it at the rail. This done, with that end yet in his hand and standing beside the pin, he looked round upon his crew, sweeping from one to the other; pausing his glance long upon Daggoo, Queequeg, Tashtego; but shunning Fedallah; and then settling his firm relying eye upon the chief mate, said,—"Take the rope, sir—I give it into thy hands, Starbuck." Then arranging his person in the basket, he gave the word for them to hoist him to his perch, Starbuck being the one who secured the rope at last; and afterwards stood near it. And thus, with one hand clinging round the royal mast, Ahab gazed abroad upon the sea for miles and miles,—ahead, astern, this side, and that,—within the wide expanded circle commanded at so great a height.

When in working with his hands at some lofty almost isolated place in the rigging, which chances to afford no foothold, the sailor at sea is hoisted up to that spot, and sustained there by the rope; under these circumstances, its fastened end on deck is always given in strict charge to some one man who has the special watch of it. Because in such a wilderness of running rigging, whose various different relations aloft cannot always be infallibly discerned by what is seen of them at the deck; and when the deck-ends of these ropes are being every few minutes cast down from the fastenings, it would be but a natural fatality, if, unprovided with a constant watchman, the hoisted sailor should by some carelessness of the crew be cast adrift and fall all swooping to the sea. So Ahab's proceedings in this matter were not unusual; the only strange thing about them seemed to be, that Starbuck, almost the one only man who had ever ventured to oppose him with anything in the slightest degree approaching to decision—one of those too, whose faithfulness on the look-out he had seemed to doubt somewhat;—it was strange, that this was the very man he should select for his watchman; freely giving his whole life into such an otherwise distrusted person's hands.

Now, the first time Ahab was perched aloft; ere he had been there ten minutes; one of those red-billed savage sea-hawks which so often fly incommodiously close round the manned mast-heads of whalemen in these latitudes; one of these birds came wheeling and screaming round his head in a maze of untrackably swift circlings. Then it darted a thousand feet straight up into the air; then spiralized downwards, and went eddying again round his head.

But with his gaze fixed upon the dim and distant horizon, Ahab seemed not to mark this wild bird; nor, indeed, would any one else have marked it much, it being no uncommon circumstance; only now almost the least heedful eye seemed to see some sort of cunning meaning in almost every sight.

"Your hat, your hat, sir!" suddenly cried the Sicilian seaman, who being posted at the mizen-mast-head, stood directly behind Ahab, though somewhat lower than his level, and with a deep gulf of air dividing them.

But already the sable wing was before the old man's eyes; the long hooked bill at his head: with a scream, the black hawk darted away with his prize.

An eagle flew thrice round Tarquin's head, removing his cap to replace it, and thereupon Tanaquil, his wife, declared that Tarquin would be king of Rome. But only by the replacing of the cap was that omen accounted good. Ahab's hat was never restored; the wild hawk flew on and on with it; far in advance of the prow: and at last disappeared; while from the point of that disappearance, a minute black spot was dimly discerned, falling from that vast height into the sea.

# Chapter 131

## *The Pequod meets the Delight*

THE INTENSE Pequod sailed on; the rolling waves and days went by; the life-buoy-coffin still lightly swung; and another ship, most miserably misnamed the Delight, was descried. As she drew nigh, all eyes were fixed upon her broad beams, called shears, which, in some whaling-ships, cross the quarter-deck at the height of eight or nine feet; serving to carry the spare, unrigged, or disabled boats.

Upon the stranger's shears were beheld the shattered, white ribs, and some few splintered planks, of what had once been a whale-boat; but you now saw through this wreck, as plainly as you see through the peeled, half-unhinged, and bleaching skeleton of a horse.

"Hast seen the White Whale?"

"Look!" replied the hollow-cheeked captain from his taffrail; and with his trumpet he pointed to the wreck.

"Hast killed him?"

"The harpoon is not yet forged that will ever do that," answered the other, sadly glancing upon a rounded hammock on the deck, whose gathered sides some noiseless sailors were busy in sewing together.

"Not forged!" and snatching Perth's levelled iron from the crotch, Ahab held it out, exclaiming—"Look ye, Nantucketer; here in this hand I hold his death! Tempered in blood, and tempered by lightning are these

540

barbs; and I swear to temper them triply in that hot place behind the fin, where the White Whale most feels his accursed life!"

"Then God keep thee, old man—see'st thou that"—pointing to the hammock—"I bury but one of five stout men, who were alive only yesterday; but were dead ere night. Only *that* one I bury; the rest were buried before they died; you sail upon their tomb." Then turning to his crew—"Are ye ready there? place the plank then on the rail, and lift the body; so, then—Oh! God"—advancing towards the hammock with up-lifted hands—"may the resurrection and the life——"

"Brace forward! Up helm!" cried Ahab like lightning to his men.

But the suddenly started Pequod was not quick enough to escape the sound of the splash that the corpse soon made as it struck the sea; not so quick, indeed, but that some of the flying bubbles might have sprinkled her hull with their ghostly baptism.

As Ahab now glided from the dejected Delight, the strange life-buoy hanging at the Pequod's stern came into conspicuous relief.

"Ha! yonder! look yonder, men!" cried a foreboding voice in her wake. "In vain, oh, ye strangers, ye fly our sad burial; ye but turn us your taffrail to show us your coffin!"

# Chapter 132

*The Symphony*

IT WAS a clear steel-blue day. The firmaments of air and sea were hardly separable in that all-pervading azure; only, the pensive air was transparently pure and soft, with a woman's look, and the robust and man-like sea heaved with long, strong, lingering swells, as Samson's chest in his sleep.

Hither, and thither, on high, glided the snow-white wings of small, unspeckled birds; these were the gentle thoughts of the feminine air; but to and fro in the deeps, far down in the bottomless blue, rushed mighty leviathans, sword-fish, and sharks; and these were the strong, troubled, murderous thinkings of the masculine sea.

But though thus contrasting within, the contrast was only in shades and shadows without; those two seemed one; it was only the sex, as it were, that distinguished them.

Aloft, like a royal czar and king, the sun seemed giving this gentle air to this bold and rolling sea; even as bride to groom. And at the girdling line of the horizon, a soft and tremulous motion—most seen here at the equator—denoted the fond, throbbing trust, the loving alarms, with which the poor bride gave her bosom away.

Tied up and twisted; gnarled and knotted with wrinkles; haggardly firm and unyielding; his eyes glowing like coals, that still glow in the ashes

542

of ruin; untottering Ahab stood forth in the clearness of the morn; lifting his splintered helmet of a brow to the fair girl's forehead of heaven.

Oh, immortal infancy, and innocency of the azure! Invisible winged creatures that frolic all round us! Sweet childhood of air and sky! how oblivious were ye of old Ahab's close-coiled woe! But so have I seen little Miriam and Martha, laughing-eyed elves, heedlessly gambol around their old sire; sporting with the circle of singed locks which grew on the marge of that burnt-out crater of his brain.

Slowly crossing the deck from the scuttle, Ahab leaned over the side, and watched how his shadow in the water sank and sank to his gaze, the more and the more that he strove to pierce the profundity. But the lovely aromas in that enchanted air did at last seem to dispel, for a moment, the cankerous thing in his soul. That glad, happy air, that winsome sky, did at last stroke and caress him; the step-mother world, so long cruel—forbidding—now threw affectionate arms round his stubborn neck, and did seem to joyously sob over him, as if over one, that however wilful and erring, she could yet find it in her heart to save and to bless. From beneath his slouched hat Ahab dropped a tear into the sea; nor did all the Pacific contain such wealth as that one wee drop.

Starbuck saw the old man; saw him, how he heavily leaned over the side; and he seemed to hear in his own true heart the measureless sobbing that stole out of the centre of the serenity around. Careful not to touch him, or be noticed by him, he yet drew near to him, and stood there.

Ahab turned.

"Starbuck!"

"Sir."

"Oh, Starbuck! it is a mild, mild wind, and a mild looking sky. On such a day—very much such a sweetness as this—I struck my first whale—a boy-harpooneer of eighteen! Forty—forty—forty years ago!—ago! Forty years of.continual whaling! forty years of privation, and peril, and storm-time! forty years on the pitiless sea! for forty years has Ahab forsaken the peaceful land, for forty years to make war on the horrors of the deep! Aye and yes, Starbuck, out of those forty years I have not spent three ashore. When I think of this life I have led; the desolation of solitude it has been; the masoned, walled-town of a Captain's exclusiveness, which admits but small entrance to any sympathy from the green country without—oh, weariness! heaviness! Guinea-coast slavery of solitary command!—when I think of all this; only half-suspected, not so keenly known to me before—and how for forty years I have fed upon dry salted fare—fit emblem of the dry nourishment of my soul!—when the poorest landsman has had fresh fruit to his daily hand, and broken the world's fresh bread, to my mouldy crusts—away, whole oceans away, from that young girl-wife I wedded past fifty, and sailed for Cape Horn the next day, leaving but one dent in my marriage pillow—wife? wife?—rather a widow with her husband alive! Aye, I widowed that poor girl when I married her, Starbuck; and then, the madness, the frenzy, the boiling blood and the smoking brow, with which, for a thousand lowerings old Ahab has furiously, foamingly chased his prey—more a demon than a man!—aye, aye! what a forty years' fool—fool —old fool, has old Ahab been! Why this strife of the chase? why weary, and palsy the arm at the oar, and the iron, and the lance? how the richer or better is Ahab now? Behold. Oh, Starbuck! is it not hard, that with this weary load I bear, one poor leg should have been snatched from under me? Here, brush this old hair aside; it blinds me, that I seem to weep. Locks so grey did never grow but from out some ashes! But do I look very old, so very, very old, Starbuck? I feel deadly faint, bowed, and humped, as though I were Adam, staggering beneath the piled centuries since Paradise. God! God! God!—crack my heart!—stave my brain!—mockery! mockery! bitter, biting mockery of grey hairs, have I lived enough joy to wear ye; and seem and feel thus intolerably old? Close! stand close to me, Starbuck; let me look into a human eye; it is better than to gaze into sea or sky; better than to gaze upon God. By the green land; by the bright hearth-stone! this is the magic glass, man; I see my wife and my child in thine eye. No, no; stay on board, on board!—lower not when I do; when branded Ahab gives chase to Moby Dick. That hazard shall not be thine. No, no! not with the far away home I see in that eye!"

"Oh, my Captain! my Captain! noble soul! grand old heart, after all! why should any one give chase to that hated fish! Away with me! let us fly these deadly waters! let us home! Wife and child, too, are Starbuck's—wife and child of his brotherly, sisterly, play-fellow youth; even as thine, sir, are the wife and child of thy loving, longing, paternal old age! Away! let us away!—this instant let me alter the course! How cheerily, how hilariously, O my Captain, would we bowl on our way to see old Nantucket again! I think, sir, they have some such mild blue days, even as this, in Nantucket."

"They have, they have. I have seen them—some summer days in the morning. About this time—yes, it is his noon nap now—the boy vivaciously wakes; sits up in bed; and his mother tells him of me, of cannibal old me; how I am abroad upon the deep, but will yet come back to dance him again."

"'Tis my Mary, my Mary herself! She promised that my boy, every morning, should be carried to the hill to catch the first glimpse of his father's sail! Yes, yes! no more! it is done! we head for Nantucket! Come, my Captain, study out the course, and let us away! See, see! the boy's face from the window! the boy's hand on the hill!"

But Ahab's glance was averted; like a blighted fruit tree he shook, and cast his last, cindered apple to the soil.

"What is it, what nameless, inscrutable, unearthly thing is it; what cozening, hidden lord and master, and cruel, remorseless emperor commands me; that against all natural lovings and longings, I so keep pushing, and crowding, and jamming myself on all the time; recklessly making me ready to do what in my own proper, natural heart, I durst not so much as dare? Is Ahab, Ahab? Is it I, God, or who, that lifts this arm? But if the great sun move not of himself; but is as an errand-boy in heaven; nor one single star can revolve, but by some invisible power; how then can this one small heart beat; this one small brain think thoughts; unless God does that beating, does that thinking, does that living, and not I. By heaven, man, we are turned round and round in this world, like yonder windlass, and Fate is the handspike. And all the time, lo! that smiling sky, and this unsounded sea! Look! see yon Albicore! who put it into him to chase and fang that flying-fish? Where do murderers go, man! Who's to doom, when the judge himself is dragged to the bar? But it is a mild, mild wind, and a mild looking sky; and the air smells now, as if it blew from a far-away meadow; they have been making hay somewhere under the slopes of the Andes, Starbuck, and the mowers are sleeping among the new-mown hay. Sleeping? Aye, toil we how we may, we all sleep at last on the field. Sleep? Aye, and rust amid greenness; as last year's scythes flung down, and left in the half-cut swaths— Starbuck!"

But blanched to a corpse's hue with despair, the Mate had stolen away.

Ahab crossed the deck to gaze over on the other side; but started at two reflected, fixed eyes in the water there. Fedallah was motionlessly leaning over the same rail.

# Chapter 133

*The Chase—First Day*

THAT NIGHT, in the mid-watch, when the old man—as his wont at intervals—stepped forth from the scuttle in which he leaned, and went to his pivot-hole, he suddenly thrust out his face fiercely, snuffing up the sea air as a sagacious ship's dog will, in drawing nigh to some barbarous isle. He declared that a whale must be near. Soon that peculiar odor, sometimes to a great distance given forth by the living sperm whale, was palpable to all the watch; nor was any mariner surprised when, after inspecting the compass, and then the dog-vane, and then ascertaining the precise bearing of the odor as nearly as possible, Ahab rapidly ordered the ship's course to be slightly altered, and the sail to be shortened.

The acute policy dictating these movements was sufficiently vindicated at daybreak, by the sight of a long sleek on the sea directly and lengthwise ahead, smooth as oil, and resembling in the pleated watery wrinkles bordering it, the polished metallic-like marks of some swift tide-rip, at the mouth of a deep, rapid stream.

"Man the mast-heads! Call all hands!"

Thundering with the butts of three clubbed handspikes on the forecastle deck, Daggoo roused the sleepers with such judgment claps that they seemed to exhale from the scuttle, so instantaneously did they appear with their clothes in their hands.

"What d'ye see?" cried Ahab, flattening his face to the sky.

"Nothing, nothing, sir!" was the sound hailing down in reply.

"T'gallant sails!—stunsails! alow and aloft, and on both sides!"

All sail being set, he now cast loose the life-line, reserved for swaying him to the main royal-mast head; and in a few moments they were hoisting him thither, when, while but two thirds of the way aloft, and while peering ahead through the horizontal vacancy between the main-top-sail and top-gallant-sail, he raised a gull-like cry in the air, "There she blows!—there she blows! A hump like a snow-hill! It is Moby Dick!"

Fired by the cry which seemed simultaneously taken up by the three look-outs, the men on deck rushed to the rigging to behold the famous whale they had so long been pursuing. Ahab had now gained his final perch, some feet above the other look-outs, Tashtego standing just beneath him on the cap of the top-gallant-mast, so that the Indian's head was almost on a level with Ahab's heel. From this height the whale was now seen some mile or so ahead, at every roll of the sea revealing his high sparkling hump, and regularly jetting his silent spout into the air. To the credulous mariners it seemed the same silent spout they had so long ago beheld in the moonlit Atlantic and Indian Oceans.

"And did none of ye see it before?" cried Ahab, hailing the perched men all around him.

"I saw him almost that same instant, sir, that Captain Ahab did, and I cried out," said Tashtego.

"Not the same instant; not the same—no, the doubloon is mine, Fate reserved the doubloon for me. *I* only; none of ye could have raised the White Whale first. There she blows! there she blows!—there she blows! There again!—there again!" he cried, in long-drawn, lingering, methodic tones, attuned to the gradual prolongings of the whale's visible jets. "He's going to sound! In stunsails! Down top-gallant-sails! Stand by three boats. Mr. Starbuck, remember, stay on board, and keep the ship. Helm there! Luff, luff a point! So; steady, man, steady! There go flukes! No, no; only black water! All ready the boats there? Stand by, stand by! Lower me, Mr. Starbuck; lower, lower,—quick, quicker!" and he slid through the air to the deck.

"He is heading straight to leeward, sir," cried Stubb, "right away from us; cannot have seen the ship yet."

"Be dumb, man! Stand by the braces! Hard down the helm!—brace up! Shiver her!—shiver her! So; well that! Boats, boats!"

Soon all the boats but Starbuck's were dropped; all the boat-sails set—all the paddles plying; with rippling swiftness, shooting to leeward; and

Ahab heading the onset. A pale, death-glimmer lit up Fedallah's sunken eyes; a hideous motion gnawed his mouth.

Like noiseless nautilus shells, their light prows sped through the sea; but only slowly they neared the foe. As they neared him, the ocean grew still more smooth; seemed drawing a carpet over its waves; seemed a noonmeadow, so serenely it spread. At length the breathless hunter came so nigh his seemingly unsuspecting prey, that his entire dazzling hump was distinctly visible, sliding along the sea as if an isolated thing, and continually set in a revolving ring of finest, fleecy, greenish foam. He saw the vast, involved wrinkles of the slightly projecting head beyond. Before it, far out on the soft Turkish-rugged waters, went the glistening white shadow from his broad, milky forehead, a musical rippling playfully accompanying the shade; and behind, the blue waters interchangeably flowed over into the moving valley of his steady wake; and on either hand bright bubbles arose and danced by his side. But these were broken again by the light toes of hundreds of gay fowl softly feathering the sea, alternate with their fitful flight; and like to some flag-staff rising from the painted hull of an argosy, the tall but shattered pole of a recent lance projected from the white whale's back; and at intervals one of the cloud of soft-toed fowls hovering, and to and fro skimming like a canopy over the fish, silently perched and rocked on this pole, the long tail feathers streaming like pennons.

A gentle joyousness—a mighty mildness of repose in swiftness, invested the gliding whale. Not the white bull Jupiter swimming away with ravished Europa clinging to his graceful horns; his lovely, leering eyes sideways intent upon the maid; with smooth bewitching fleetness, rippling straight for the nuptial bower in Crete; not Jove, not that great majesty Supreme! did surpass the glorified White Whale as he so divinely swam.

On each soft side—coincident with the parted swell, that but once laving him, then flowed so wide away—on each bright side, the whale shed off enticings. No wonder there had been some among the hunters who namelessly transported and allured by all this serenity, had ventured to assail it; but had fatally found that quietude but the vesture of tornadoes. Yet calm, enticing calm, oh, whale! thou glidest on, to all who for the first time eye thee, no matter how many in that same way thou may'st have bejuggled and destroyed before.

And thus, through the serene tranquillities of the tropical sea, among waves whose hand-clappings were suspended by exceeding rapture, Moby Dick moved on, still withholding from sight the full terrors of his submerged trunk, entirely hiding the wrenched hideousness of his jaw. But soon the fore part of him slowly rose from the water; for an instant his whole marbleized body formed a high arch, like Virginia's Natural Bridge, and warningly waving his bannered flukes in the air, the grand god revealed himself, sounded, and went out of sight. Hoveringly halting, and dipping on the wing, the white sea-fowls longingly lingered over the agitated pool that he left.

With oars apeak, and paddles down, the sheets of their sails adrift, the three boats now stilly floated, awaiting Moby Dick's reappearance.

"An hour," said Ahab, standing rooted in his boat's stern; and he gazed beyond the whale's place, towards the dim blue spaces and wide wooing vacancies to leeward. It was only an instant; for again his eyes seemed whirling round in his head as he swept the watery circle. The breeze now freshened; the sea began to swell.

"The birds!—the birds!" cried Tashtego.

In long Indian file, as when herons take wing, the white birds were now all flying towards Ahab's boat; and when within a few yards began fluttering over the water there, wheeling round and round, with joyous, expectant cries. Their vision was keener than man's; Ahab could discover no sign in the sea. But suddenly as he peered down and down into its depths, he profoundly saw a white living spot no bigger than a white weasel, with wonderful celerity uprising, and magnifying as it rose, till it turned, and then there were plainly revealed two long crooked rows of white, glistening teeth, floating up from the undiscoverable bottom. It was Moby Dick's open mouth and scrolled jaw; his vast, shadowed bulk still half blending with the blue of the sea. The glittering mouth yawned beneath the boat like an open-doored marble tomb; and giving one sidelong sweep with his steering oar, Ahab whirled the craft aside from this tremendous apparition. Then, calling upon Fedallah to change places with him, went forward to the bows, and seizing Perth's harpoon, commanded his crew to grasp their oars and stand by to stern.

Now, by reason of this timely spinning round the boat upon its axis, its bow, by anticipation, was made to face the whale's head while yet under water. But as if perceiving this stratagem, Moby Dick, with that malicious intelligence ascribed to him, sidelingly transplanted himself, as it were, in an instant, shooting his pleated head lengthwise beneath the boat.

Through and through; through every plank and each rib, it thrilled for an instant, the whale obliquely lying on his back, in the manner of a biting shark, slowly and feelingly taking its bows full within his mouth, so that the long, narrow, scrolled lower jaw curled high up into the open air, and one of the teeth caught in a row-lock. The bluish pearl-white of the inside of the jaw was within six inches of Ahab's head, and reached higher than that. In this attitude the White Whale now shook the slight cedar as a mildly cruel cat her mouse. With unastonished eyes Fedallah gazed, and crossed his arms; but the tiger-yellow crew were tumbling over each other's heads to gain the uttermost stern.

And now, while both elastic gunwales were springing in and out, as the whale dallied with the doomed craft in this devilish way; and from his body being submerged beneath the boat, he could not be darted at from the bows, for the bows were almost inside of him, as it were; and while the other boats involuntarily paused, as before a quick crisis impossible to withstand, then it was that monomaniac Ahab, furious with this tantalizing vicinity of his foe, which placed him all alive and helpless in the very jaws he hated; frenzied with all this, he seized the long bone with his naked hands, and wildly strove to wrench it from its gripe. As now he thus vainly strove, the jaw slipped from him; the frail gunwales bent in, collapsed, and snapped, as both jaws, like an enormous shears, sliding further aft, bit the craft completely in twain, and locked themselves fast again in the sea, midway between the two floating wrecks. These floated aside, the broken ends drooping, the crew at the stern-wreck clinging to the gunwales, and striving to hold fast to the oars to lash them across.

At that preluding moment, ere the boat was yet snapped, Ahab, the first to perceive the whale's intent, by the crafty upraising of his head, a movement that loosed his hold for the time; at that moment his hand had made one final effort to push the boat out of the bite. But only slipping further into the whale's mouth, and tilting over sideways as it slipped, the boat had shaken off his hold on the jaw; spilled him out of it, as he leaned to the push; and so he fell flat-faced upon the sea.

Ripplingly withdrawing from his prey, Moby Dick now lay at a little distance, vertically thrusting his oblong white head up and down in the billows; and at the same time slowly revolving his whole spindled body; so that when his vast wrinkled forehead rose—some twenty or more feet out of the water—the now rising swells, with all their confluent waves, dazzlingly broke against it; vindictively tossing their shivered spray still higher into the air.* So, in a gale, the but half baffled Channel billows only recoil from

---

* This motion is peculiar to the sperm whale. It receives its designation (pitchpoling) from its being likened to that preliminary up-and-down poise of the whale-lance, in the exercise called pitchpoling, previously described. By this motion the whale must best and most comprehensively view whatever objects may be encircling him.

the base of the Eddystone, triumphantly to overleap its summit with their scud.

But soon resuming his horizontal attitude, Moby Dick swam swiftly round and round the wrecked crew; sideways churning the water in his vengeful wake, as if lashing himself up to still another and more deadly assault. The sight of the splintered boat seemed to madden him, as the blood of grapes and mulberries cast before Antiochus's elephants in the book of Maccabees. Meanwhile Ahab half smothered in the foam of the whale's insolent tail, and too much of a cripple to swim,—though he could still keep afloat, even in the heart of such a whirlpool as that; helpless Ahab's head was seen, like a tossed bubble which the least chance shock might burst. From the boat's fragmentary stern, Fedallah incuriously and mildly eyed him; the clinging crew, at the other drifting end, could not succor him; more than enough was it for them to look to themselves. For so revolvingly appalling was the White Whale's aspect, and so planetarily swift the ever-contracting circles he made, that he seemed horizontally swooping upon them. And though the other boats, unharmed, still hovered hard by; still they dared not pull into the eddy to strike, lest that should be the signal for the instant destruction of the jeopardized castaways, Ahab and all; nor in that case could they themselves hope to escape. With straining eyes, then, they remained on the outer edge of the direful zone, whose centre had now become the old man's head.

Meantime, from the beginning all this had been descried from the ship's mast heads; and squaring her yards, she had borne down upon the scene; and was now so nigh, that Ahab in the water hailed her;—"Sail on the"—but that moment a breaking sea dashed on him from Moby Dick, and whelmed him for the time. But struggling out of it again, and chancing to rise on a towering crest, he shouted,—"Sail on the whale!—Drive him off!"

The Pequod's prow was pointed; and breaking up the charmed circle, she effectually parted the white whale from his victim. As he sullenly swam off, the boats flew to the rescue.

Dragged into Stubb's boat with blood-shot, blinded eyes, the white brine caking in his wrinkles; the long tension of Ahab's bodily strength did crack, and helplessly he yielded to his body's doom: for a time, lying all crushed in the bottom of Stubb's boat, like one trodden under foot of herds of elephants. Far inland, nameless wails came from him, as desolate sounds from out ravines.

But this intensity of his physical prostration did but so much the more abbreviate it. In an instant's compass, great hearts sometimes condense to one deep pang, the sum total of those shallow pains kindly diffused through feebler men's whole lives. And so, such hearts, though summary in each one suffering; still, if the gods decree it, in their life-time aggregate a whole age of woe, wholly made up of instantaneous intensities; for even in their pointless centres, those noble natures contain the entire circumferences of inferior souls.

"The harpoon," said Ahab, half way rising, and draggingly leaning on one bended arm—"is it safe?"

"Aye, sir, for it was not darted; this is it," said Stubb, showing it.

"Lay it before me;—any missing men?"

"One, two, three, four, five;—there were five oars, sir, and here are five men."

"That's good.—Help me, man; I wish to stand. So, so, I see him! there! there! going to leeward still; what a leaping spout!—Hands off from me! The eternal sap runs up in Ahab's bones again! Set the sail; out oars; the helm!"

It is often the case that when a boat is stove, its crew, being picked up by another boat, help to work that second boat; and the chase is thus continued with what is called double-banked oars. It was thus now. But the added power of the boat did not equal the added power of the whale, for he seemed to have treble-banked his every fin; swimming with a velocity which plainly showed, that if now, under these circumstances, pushed on, the chase would prove an indefinitely prolonged, if not a hopeless one; nor could any crew endure for so long a period, such an unintermitted, intense straining at the oar; a thing barely tolerable only in some one brief vicissitude. The ship itself, then, as it sometimes happens, offered the most promising intermediate means of overtaking the chase. Accordingly, the boats now made for her, and were soon swayed up to their cranes—the two parts of the wrecked boat having been previously secured by her—and then hoisting everything to her side, and stacking her canvas high up, and sideways outstretching it with stun-sails, like the double-jointed wings of an albatross; the Pequod bore down in the leeward wake of Moby Dick. At the well known, methodic intervals, the whale's glittering spout was regularly announced from the manned mast-heads; and when he would be reported as just gone down, Ahab would take the time, and then pacing the deck, binnacle-watch in hand, so soon as the last second of the allotted hour expired, his voice was heard.—"Whose is the doubloon now? D'ye see him?" and if the reply was, No, sir! straightway he commanded them to lift him to his perch. In this way the day wore on; Ahab, now aloft and motionless; anon, unrestingly pacing the planks.

As he was thus walking, uttering no sound, except to hail the men aloft, or to bid them hoist a sail still higher, or to spread one to a still greater breadth—thus to and fro pacing, beneath his slouched hat, at every turn he passed his own wrecked boat, which had been dropped upon the quarter-deck, and lay there reversed; broken bow to shattered stern. At last he paused before it; and as in an already over-clouded sky fresh troops of clouds will sometimes sail across, so over the old man's face there now stole some such added gloom as this.

Stubb saw him pause; and perhaps intending, not vainly, though, to evince his own unabated fortitude, and thus keep up a valiant place in his Captain's mind, he advanced, and eyeing the wreck exclaimed—"The thistle the ass refused; it pricked his mouth too keenly, sir; ha! ha!"

"What soulless thing is this that laughs before a wreck? Man, man! did I not know thee brave as fearless fire (and as mechanical) I could swear thou wert a poltroon. Groan nor laugh should be heard before a wreck."

"Aye, sir," said Starbuck drawing near, "'tis a solemn sight; an omen, and an ill one."

"Omen? omen?—the dictionary! If the gods think to speak outright to man, they will honorably speak outright; not shake their heads, and give an old wives' darkling hint.—Begone! Ye two are the opposite poles of one thing; Starbuck is Stubb reversed, and Stubb is Starbuck; and ye two are all mankind; and Ahab stands alone among the millions of the peopled earth, nor gods nor men his neighbors! Cold, cold—I shiver!—How now? Aloft there! D'ye see him? Sing out for every spout, though he spout ten times a second!"

The day was nearly done; only the hem of his golden robe was rustling. Soon, it was almost dark, but the look-out men still remained unset.

"Can't see the spout now, sir;—too dark"—cried a voice from the air.

"How heading when last seen?"

"As before, sir,—straight to leeward."

"Good! he will travel slower now 'tis night. Down royals and top-gallant stun-sails, Mr. Starbuck. We must not run over him before morning; he's making a passage now, and may heave-to a while. Helm there! keep her full before the wind!—Aloft! come down!—Mr. Stubb, send a fresh hand to the fore-mast head, and see it manned till morning."—Then advancing towards the doubloon in the main-mast—"Men, this gold is mine, for I earned it; but I shall let it abide here till the White Whale is dead; and then, whosoever of ye first raises him, upon the day he shall be killed, this gold is that man's; and if on that day I shall again raise him, then, ten times its sum shall be divided among all of ye! Away now!—the deck is thine, sir."

And so saying, he placed himself half way within the scuttle, and slouching his hat, stood there till dawn, except when at intervals rousing himself to see how the night wore on.

# Chapter 134

## The Chase—Second Day

AT DAY-BREAK, the three mast-heads were punctually manned afresh.

"D'ye see him?" cried Ahab, after allowing a little space for the light to spread.

"See nothing, sir."

"Turn up all hands and make sail! he travels faster than I thought for;— the top-gallant sails!—aye, they should have been kept on her all night. But no matter—'tis but resting for the rush."

Here be it said, that this pertinacious pursuit of one particular whale, continued through day into night, and through night into day, is a thing by no means unprecedented in the South sea fishery. For such is the wonderful skill, prescience of experience, and invincible confidence acquired by some great natural geniuses among the Nantucket commanders; that from the simple observation of a whale when last descried, they will, under certain given circumstances, pretty accurately foretell both the direction in which he will continue to swim for a time, while out of sight, as well as his probable rate of progression during that period. And, in these cases, somewhat as a pilot, when about losing sight of a coast, whose general trending he well knows, and which he desires shortly to return to again, but at some further point; like as this pilot stands by his compass, and takes the precise bearing of the cape at present visible, in order the more certainly to hit aright the remote, unseen headland, eventually to be visited: so does the fisherman, at his compass, with the whale; for after being chased, and diligently marked, through several hours of daylight, then, when night obscures the fish, the creature's future wake through the darkness is almost as established to the sagacious mind of the hunter, as the pilot's coast is to him. So that to this hunter's wondrous skill, the proverbial evanescence of a thing writ in water, a wake, is to all desired purposes well nigh as reliable as the steadfast land. And as the mighty iron Leviathan of the modern railway is so familiarly known in its every pace, that, with watches in their hands, men time his rate as doctors that of a baby's pulse; and lightly say of it, the up train or the down train will reach such or such a spot, at such or such an hour; even so, almost, there are occasions when these Nantucketers time that other Leviathan of the deep, according to the observed humor of his speed; and say to themselves, so many hours hence this whale will have gone two hundred miles, will have about reached this or that degree of latitude or longitude. But to render this acuteness at all successful in the end, the wind and the sea must be the whaleman's allies; for of what present avail to the becalmed or windbound mariner is the skill that assures him he is exactly ninety-three leagues and a quarter from his port? Inferable from these statements, are many collateral subtile matters touching the chase of whales.

The ship tore on; leaving such a furrow in the sea as when a cannon-ball, missent, becomes a plough-share and turns up the level field.

"By salt and hemp!" cried Stubb, "but this swift motion of the deck creeps up one's legs and tingles at the heart. This ship and I are two brave fellows!—Ha! ha! Some one take me up, and launch me, spine-wise, on the sea,—for by live-oaks! my spine's a keel. Ha, ha! we go the gait that leaves no dust behind!"

"There she blows—she blows!—she blows!—right ahead!" was now the mast-head cry.

"Aye, aye!" cried Stubb, "I knew it—ye can't escape—blow on and split your spout, O whale! the mad fiend himself is after ye! blow your trump—blister your lungs!—Ahab will dam off your blood, as a miller shuts his water-gate upon the stream!"

And Stubb did but speak out for well nigh all that crew. The frenzies of the chase had by this time worked them bubblingly up, like old wine worked anew. Whatever pale fears and forebodings some of them might have felt before; these were not only now kept out of sight through the

.growing awe of Ahab, but they were broken up, and on all sides routed, as timid prairie hares that scatter before the bounding bison. The hand of Fate had snatched all their souls; and by the stirring perils of the previous day; the rack of the past night's suspense; the fixed, unfearing, blind, reckless way in which their wild craft went plunging towards its flying mark; by all these things, their hearts were bowled along. The wind that made great bellies of their sails, and rushed the vessel on by arms invisible as irresistible; this seemed the symbol of that unseen agency which so enslaved them to the race.

They were one man, not thirty. For as the one ship that held them all; though it was put together of all contrasting things—oak, and maple, and pine wood; iron, and pitch, and hemp—yet all these ran into each other in the one concrete hull, which shot on its way, both balanced and directed by the long central keel; even so, all the individualities of the crew, this man's valor, that man's fear; guilt and guiltlessness, all varieties were welded into oneness, and were all directed to that fatal goal which Ahab their one lord and keel did point to.

The rigging lived. The mast-heads, like the tops of tall palms, were outspreadingly tufted with arms and legs. Clinging to a spar with one hand, some reached forth the other with impatient wavings; others, shading their eyes from the vivid sunlight, sat far out on the rocking yards; all the spars in full bearing of mortals, ready and ripe for their fate. Ah! how they still strove through that infinite blueness to seek out the thing that might destroy them!

"Why sing ye not out for him, if ye see him?" cried Ahab, when, after the lapse of some minutes since the first cry, no more had been heard. "Sway me up, men; ye have been deceived; not Moby Dick casts one odd jet that way, and then disappears."

It was even so; in their headlong eagerness, the men had mistaken some other thing for the whale-spout, as the event itself soon proved; for hardly had Ahab reached his perch; hardly was the rope belayed to its pin on deck, when he struck the key-note to an orchestra, that made the air vibrate as with the combined discharges of rifles. The triumphant halloo of thirty buckskin lungs was heard, as—much nearer to the ship than the place of the imaginary jet, less than a mile ahead—Moby Dick bodily burst into view! For not by any calm and indolent spoutings; not by the peaceable gush of that mystic fountain in his head, did the White Whale now reveal his vicinity; but by the far more wondrous phenomenon of breaching. Rising with his utmost velocity from the furthest depths, the Sperm Whale thus booms his entire bulk into the pure element of air, and piling up a mountain of dazzling foam, shows his place to the distance of seven miles and more. In those moments, the torn, enraged waves he shakes off, seem his mane; in some cases, this breaching is his act of defiance.

"There she breaches! there she breaches!" was the cry, as in his immeasurable bravadoes the White Whale tossed himself salmon-like to Heaven. So suddenly seen in the blue plain of the sea, and relieved against the still bluer margin of the sky, the spray that he raised, for the moment, intolerably glittered and glared like a glacier; and stood there gradually fading and fading away from its first sparkling intensity, to the dim mistiness of an advancing shower in a vale.

"Aye, breach your last to the sun, Moby Dick!" cried Ahab, "thy hour and thy harpoon are at hand!—Down! down all of ye, but one man at the fore. The boats!—stand by!"

Unmindful of the tedious rope-ladders of the shrouds, the men, like shooting stars, slid to the deck, by the isolated backstays and halyards; while Ahab, less dartingly, but still rapidly was dropped from his perch.

"Lower away," he cried, so soon as he had reached his boat—a spare one, rigged the afternoon previous. "Mr. Starbuck, the ship is thine—keep away from the boats, but keep near them. Lower, all!"

As if to strike a quick terror into them, by this time being the first assailant himself, Moby Dick had turned, and was now coming for the three crews. Ahab's boat was central; and cheering his men, he told them he would take the whale head-and-head,—that is, pull straight up to his forehead,—a not uncommon thing; for when within a certain limit, such a course excludes the coming onset from the whale's sidelong vision. But ere that close limit was gained, and while yet all three boats were plain as the ship's three masts to his eye; the White Whale churning himself into furious speed, almost in an instant as it were, rushing among the boats with open jaws, and a lashing tail, offered appalling battle on every side; and heedless of the irons darted at him from every boat, seemed only intent on annihilating each separate plank of which those boats were made. But skilfully manœuvred, incessantly wheeling like trained chargers in the field; the boats for a while eluded him; though, at times, but by a plank's breadth; while all the time, Ahab's unearthly slogan tore every other cry but his to shreds.

But at last in his untraceable evolutions, the White Whale so crossed and recrossed, and in a thousand ways entangled the slack of the three lines now fast to him, that they foreshortened, and, of themselves, warped the devoted boats towards the planted irons in him; though now for a moment the whale drew aside a little, as if to rally for a more tremendous charge. Seizing that opportunity, Ahab first paid out more line: and then was rapidly hauling and jerking in upon it again—hoping that way to disencumber it of some snarls—when lo!—a sight more savage than the embattled teeth of sharks!

Caught and twisted—corkscrewed in the mazes of the line, loose harpoons and lances, with all their bristling barbs and points, came flashing and dripping up to the chocks in the bows of Ahab's boat. Only one thing could be done. Seizing the boat-knife, he critically reached within—through—and then, without—the rays of steel; dragged in the line beyond, passed it, inboard, to the bowsman, and then, twice sundering the rope near the chocks—dropped the intercepted fagot of steel into the sea; and was all fast again. That instant, the White Whale made a sudden rush among the remaining tangles of the other lines; by so doing, irresistibly dragged the more involved boats of Stubb and Flask towards his flukes; dashed them together like two rolling husks on a surf-beaten beach, and then, diving down into the sea, disappeared in a boiling maelstrom, in which, for a space, the odorous cedar chips of the wrecks danced round and round, like the grated nutmeg in a swiftly stirred bowl of punch.

While the two crews were yet circling in the waters, reaching out after the revolving line-tubs, oars, and other floating furniture, while aslope little Flask bobbed up and down like an empty vial, twitching his legs upwards to escape the dreaded jaws of sharks; and Stubb was lustily singing out for some one to ladle him up; and while the old man's line—now parting—admitted of his pulling into the creamy pool to rescue whom he could; —in that wild simultaneousness of a thousand concreted perils,—Ahab's yet unstricken boat seemed drawn up towards Heaven by invisible wires,— as, arrow-like, shooting perpendicularly from the sea, the White Whale dashed his broad forehead against its bottom, and sent it, turning over and over, into the air; till it fell again—gunwale downwards—and Ahab and his men struggled out from under it, like seals from a sea-side cave.

The first uprising momentum of the whale—modifying its direction as he struck the surface—involuntarily launched him along it, to a little distance from the centre of the destruction he had made; and with his back to it, he now lay for a moment slowly feeling with his flukes from side to side; and whenever a stray oar, bit of plank, the least chip or crumb of the boats touched his skin, his tail swiftly drew back, and came sideways smiting the sea. But soon, as if satisfied that his work for that time was done, he pushed his pleated forehead through the ocean, and trailing after him the intertangled lines, continued his leeward way at a traveller's methodic pace.

As before, the attentive ship having descried the whole fight, again came bearing down to the rescue, and dropping a boat, picked up the floating mariners, tubs, oars, and whatever else could be caught at, and safely landed them on her decks. Some sprained shoulders, wrists, and ankles; livid contusions; wrenched harpoons and lances; inextricable intricacies of rope; shattered oars and planks; all these were there; but no fatal or even serious ill seemed to have befallen any one. As with Fedallah the day before, so Ahab was now found grimly clinging to his boat's broken half, which afforded a comparatively easy float; nor did it so exhaust him as the previous day's mishap.

But when he was helped to the deck, all eyes were fastened upon him; as instead of standing by himself he still half-hung upon the shoulder of Starbuck, who had thus far been the foremost to assist him. His ivory leg had been snapped off, leaving but one short sharp splinter.

"Aye aye, Starbuck, 'tis sweet to lean sometimes, be the leaner who he will; and would old Ahab had leaned oftener than he has."

"The ferrule has not stood, sir," said the carpenter, now coming up; "I put good work into that leg."

"But no bones broken, sir, I hope," said Stubb with true concern.

"Aye! and all splintered to pieces, Stubb!—d'ye see it.—But even with a broken bone, old Ahab is untouched; and I account no living bone of mine one jot more me, than this dead one that's lost. Nor white whale, nor man, nor fiend, can so much as graze old Ahab in his own proper and inaccessible being. Can any lead touch yonder floor, any mast scrape yonder roof?—Aloft there! which way?"

"Dead to leeward, sir."

"Up helm, then; pile on the sail again, ship keepers! down the rest of the spare boats and rig them—Mr. Starbuck away, and muster the boats' crews."

"Let me first help thee towards the bulwarks, sir."

"Oh, oh, oh! how this splinter gores me now! Accursed fate! that the unconquerable captain in the soul should have such a craven mate!"

"Sir?"

"My body, man, not thee. Give me something for a cane—there, that shivered lance will do. Muster the men. Surely I have not seen him yet. By heaven it cannot be!—missing?—quick! call them all."

The old man's hinted thought was true. Upon mustering the company, the Parsee was not there.

"The Parsee!" cried Stubb—"he must have been caught in——"

"The black vomit wrench thee!—run all of ye above, alow, cabin, forecastle—find him—not gone—not gone!"

But quickly they returned to him with the tidings that the Parsee was nowhere to be found.

"Aye, sir," said Stubb—"caught among the tangles of your line—I thought I saw him dragging under."

"*My* line! *my* line? Gone?—gone? What means that little word?—What death-knell rings in it, that old Ahab shakes as if he were the belfry. The harpoon, too!—toss over the litter there,—d'ye see it?—the forged iron, men, the white whale's—no, no, no,—blistered fool! this hand did dart it!—'tis in the fish!—Aloft there! Keep him nailed—Quick!—all hands to the rigging of the boats—collect the oars—harpooneers! the irons, the irons!—hoist the royals higher—a pull on all the sheets!—helm there! steady, steady for your life! I'll ten times girdle the unmeasured globe; yea and dive straight through it, but I'll slay him yet!"

"Great God! but for one single instant show thyself," cried Starbuck; "never, never wilt thou capture him, old man—In Jesus' name no more of this, that's worse than devil's madness. Two days chased; twice stove to splinters; thy very leg once more snatched from under thee; thy evil shadow gone—all good angels mobbing thee with warnings:—what more wouldst thou have?—Shall we keep chasing this murderous fish till he swamps the last man? Shall we be dragged by him to the bottom of the sea? Shall we be towed by him to the infernal world? Oh, oh,—Impiety and blasphemy to hunt him more!"

"Starbuck, of late I've felt strangely moved to thee; ever since that hour we both saw—thou know'st what, in one another's eyes. But in this matter of the whale, be the front of thy face to me as the palm of this hand—a lipless, unfeatured blank. Ahab is for ever Ahab, man. This whole act's immutably decreed. 'Twas rehearsed by thee and me a billion years before this ocean rolled. Fool! I am the Fates' lieutenant; I act under orders. Look thou, underling! that thou obeyest mine.—Stand round me, men. Ye see an old man cut down to the stump; leaning on a shivered lance; propped up on a lonely foot. 'Tis Ahab—his body's part; but Ahab's soul's a centipede, that moves upon a hundred legs. I feel strained, half stranded, as ropes that tow dismasted frigates in a gale; and I may look so. But ere I break, ye'll hear me crack; and till ye hear *that,* know that Ahab's hawser tows his purpose yet. Believe ye, men, in the things called omens? Then laugh aloud, and cry encore! For ere they drown, drowning things will twice rise to the surface; then rise again, to sink for evermore. So with Moby Dick—two days he's floated—to-morrow will be the third. Aye, men, he'll rise once more,—but only to spout his last! D'ye feel brave, men, brave?"

"As fearless fire," cried Stubb.

"And as mechanical," muttered Ahab. Then as the men went forward, he muttered on:—"The things called omens! And yesterday I talked the same to Starbuck there, concerning my broken boat. Oh! how valiantly I seek to drive out of others' hearts what's clinched so fast in mine!—The Parsee—the Parsee!—gone, gone? and he was to go before:—but still was to be seen again ere I could perish—How's that?—There's a riddle now might baffle all the lawyers backed by the ghosts of the whole line of judges:—like a hawk's beak it pecks my brain. *I'll, I'll* solve it, though!"

When dusk descended, the whale was still in sight to leeward.

So once more the sail was shortened, and everything passed nearly as on the previous night; only, the sound of hammers, and the hum of the grind-stone was heard till nearly daylight, as the men toiled by lanterns in the complete and careful rigging of the spare boats and sharpening their fresh weapons for the morrow. Meantime, of the broken keel of Ahab's wrecked craft the carpenter made him another leg; while still as on the night before, slouched Ahab stood fixed within his scuttle; his hid, heliotrope glance anticipatingly gone backward on its dial; set due eastward for the earliest sun.

# Chapter 135

## The Chase—Third Day

THE MORNING of the third day dawned fair and fresh, and once more the solitary night-man at the fore-mast-head was relieved by crowds of the daylight look-outs, who dotted every mast and almost every spar.

"D'ye see him?" cried Ahab; but the whale was not yet in sight.

"In his infallible wake, though; but follow that wake, that's all. Helm there; steady, as thou goest, and hast been going. What a lovely day again! were it a new-made world, and made for a summer-house to the angels, and this morning the first of its throwing open to them, a fairer day could not dawn upon that world. Here's food for thought, had Ahab time to think; but Ahab never thinks; he only feels, feels, feels; *that's* tingling enough for mortal man! to think's audacity. God only has that right and privilege. Thinking is, or ought to be, a coolness and a calmness; and our poor hearts throb, and our poor brains beat too much for that. And yet, I've sometimes thought my brain was very calm—frozen calm, this old skull cracks so, like a glass in which the contents turn to ice, and shiver it. And still this hair is growing now; this moment growing, and heat must breed it; but no, it's like that sort of common grass that will grow anywhere, between the earthy clefts of Greenland ice or in Vesuvius lava. How the wild winds blow it; they whip it about me as the torn shreds of split sails lash the tossed ship they cling to. A vile wind that has no doubt blown ere

this through prison corridors and cells, and wards of hospitals, and venti-
lated them, and now comes blowing hither as innocent as fleeces. Out
upon it!—it's tainted. Were I the wind, I'd blow no more on such a wicked,
miserable world. I'd crawl somewhere to a cave, and slink there. And yet,
'tis a noble and heroic thing, the wind! who ever conquered it? In every
fight it has the last and bitterest blow. Run tilting at it, and you but run
through it. Ha! a coward wind that strikes stark naked men, but will not
stand to receive a single blow. Even Ahab is a braver thing—a nobler thing
than *that*. Would now the wind but had a body; but all the things that most
exasperate and outrage mortal man, all these things are bodiless, but only
bodiless as objects, not as agents. There's a most special, a most cunning, oh,
a most malicious difference! And yet, I say again, and swear it now, that
there's something all glorious and gracious in the wind. These warm Trade
Winds, at least, that in the clear heavens blow straight on, in strong and
steadfast, vigorous mildness; and veer not from their mark, however the
baser currents of the sea may turn and tack, and mightiest Mississippies of
the land swift and swerve about, uncertain where to go at last. And by the
eternal Poles! these same Trades that so directly blow my good ship on;
these Trades, or something like them—something so unchangeable, and
full as strong, blow my keeled soul along! To it! Aloft there! What d'ye see?"

"Nothing, sir."

"Nothing! and noon at hand! The doubloon goes a-begging! See the
sun! Aye, aye, it must be so. I've oversailed him. How, got the start? Aye,
he's chasing *me* now; not I, *him*—that's bad; I might have known it, too.
Fool! the lines—the harpoons he's towing. Aye, aye, I have run him by last
night. About! about! Come down, all of ye, but the regular look outs!
Man the braces!"

Steering as she had done, the wind had been somewhat on the Pequod's
quarter, so that now being pointed in the reverse direction, the braced ship
sailed hard upon the breeze as she rechurned the cream in her own white
wake.

"Against the wind he now steers for the open jaw," murmured Starbuck
to himself, as he coiled the new-hauled main-brace upon the rail. "God keep
us, but already my bones feel damp within me, and from the inside wet my
flesh. I misdoubt me that I disobey my God in obeying him!"

"Stand by to sway me up!" cried Ahab, advancing to the hempen
basket. "We should meet him soon."

"Aye, aye, sir," and straightway Starbuck did Ahab's bidding, and once
more Ahab swung on high.

A whole hour now passed; gold-beaten out to ages. Time itself now held long breaths with keen suspense. But at last, some three points off the weather bow, Ahab descried the spout again, and instantly from the three mast-heads three shrieks went up as if the tongues of fire had voiced it.

"Forehead to forehead I meet thee, this third time, Moby Dick! On deck there!—brace sharper up; crowd her into the wind's eye. He's too far off to lower yet, Mr. Starbuck. The sails shake! Stand over that helmsman with a top-maul! So, so; he travels fast, and I must down. But let me have one more good round look aloft here at the sea; there's time for that. An old, old sight, and yet somehow so young; aye, and not changed a wink since I first saw it, a boy, from the sand-hills of Nantucket! The same!—the same! —the same to Noah as to me. There's a soft shower to leeward. Such lovely leewardings! They must lead somewhere—to something else than common land, more palmy than the palms. Leeward! the white whale goes that way; look to windward, then; the better if the bitterer quarter. But good bye, good bye, old mast-head! What's this?—green? aye, tiny mosses in these warped cracks. No such green weather stains on Ahab's head! There's the difference now between man's old age and matter's. But aye, old mast, we both grow old together; sound in our hulls, though, are we not, my ship? Aye, minus a leg, that's all. By heaven this dead wood has the better of my live flesh every way. I can't compare with it; and I've known some ships made of dead trees outlast the lives of men made of the most vital stuff of vital fathers. What's that he said? he should still go before me, my pilot; and yet to be seen again? But where? Will I have eyes at the bottom of the sea, supposing I descend those endless stairs? and all night I've been sailing from him, wherever he did sink to. Aye, aye, like many more thou told'st direful truth as touching thyself, O Parsee; but, Ahab, there thy shot fell short. Good by, mast-head—keep a good eye upon the whale, the while I'm gone. We'll talk to-morrow, nay, to-night, when the white whale lies down there, tied by head and tail."

He gave the word; and still gazing round him, was steadily lowered through the cloven blue air to the deck.

In due time the boats were lowered; but as standing in his shallop's stern, Ahab just hovered upon the point of the descent, he waved to the mate,—who held one of the tackle-ropes on deck—and bade him pause.

"Starbuck!"

"Sir?"

"For the third time my soul's ship starts upon this voyage, Starbuck."

"Aye, sir, thou wilt have it so."

"Some ships sail from their ports, and ever afterwards are missing, Starbuck!"

"Truth, sir: saddest truth."

"Some men die at ebb tide; some at low water; some at the full of the flood;—and I feel now like a billow that's all one crested comb, Starbuck. I am old;—shake hands with me, man."

Their hands met; their eyes fastened; Starbuck's tears the glue.

"Oh, my captain, my captain!—noble heart—go not—go not!—see, it's a brave man that weeps; how great the agony of the persuasion then!"

"Lower away!"—cried Ahab, tossing the mate's arm from him. "Stand by the crew!"

In an instant the boat was pulling round close under the stern.

"The sharks! the sharks!" cried a voice from the low cabin-window there; "O master, my master, come back!"

But Ahab heard nothing; for his own voice was high-lifted then; and the boat leaped on.

Yet the voice spake true; for scarce had he pushed from the ship, when numbers of sharks, seemingly rising from out the dark waters beneath the hull, maliciously snapped at the blades of the oars, every time they dipped in the water; and in this way accompanied the boat with their bites. It is a thing not uncommonly happening to the whale-boats in those swarming seas; the sharks at times apparently following them in the same prescient way that vultures hover over the banners of marching regiments in the east. But these were the first sharks that had been observed by the Pequod since the White Whale had been first descried; and whether it was that Ahab's crew were all such tiger-yellow barbarians, and therefore their flesh more musky to the senses of the sharks—a matter sometimes well known to affect them,—however it was, they seemed to follow that one boat without molesting the others.

"Heart of wrought steel!" murmured Starbuck gazing over the side, and following with his eyes the receding boat—"canst thou yet ring boldly to that sight?—lowering thy keel among ravening sharks, and followed by them, open-mouthed to the chase; and this the critical third day?—For when three days flow together in one continuous intense pursuit; be sure the first is the morning, the second the noon, and the third the evening and the end of that thing—be that end what it may. Oh! my God! what is this that shoots through me, and leaves me so deadly calm, yet expectant,—fixed at the top of a shudder! Future things swim before me, as in empty outlines and skeletons; all the past is somehow grown dim. Mary, girl!

thou fadest in pale glories behind me; boy! I seem to see but thy eyes grown wondrous blue. Strangest problems of life seem clearing; but clouds sweep between—Is my journey's end coming? My legs feel faint; like his who has footed it all day. Feel thy heart,—beats it yet?—Stir thyself, Starbuck!—stave it off—move, move! speak aloud!—Mast-head there! See ye my boy's hand on the hill?—Crazed;—aloft there!—keep thy keenest eye upon the boats:—mark well the whale!—Ho! again!—drive off that hawk! see! he pecks—he tears the vane"—pointing to the red flag flying at the main-truck—"Ha! he soars away with it!—Where's the old man now? sees't thou that sight, oh Ahab!—shudder, shudder!"

The boats had not gone very far, when by a signal from the mast-heads —a downward pointed arm, Ahab knew that the whale had sounded; but intending to be near him at the next rising, he held on his way a little sideways from the vessel; the becharmed crew maintaining the profoundest silence, as the head-beat waves hammered and hammered against the opposing bow.

"Drive, drive in your nails, oh ye waves! to their uttermost heads drive them in! ye but strike a thing without a lid; and no coffin and no hearse can be mine:—and hemp only can kill me! Ha! ha!"

Suddenly the waters around them slowly swelled in broad circles; then quickly upheaved, as if sideways sliding from a submerged berg of ice, swiftly rising to the surface. A low rumbling sound was heard; a subterraneous hum; and then all held their breaths; as bedraggled with trailing ropes, and harpoons, and lances, a vast form shot lengthwise, but obliquely from the sea. Shrouded in a thin drooping veil of mist, it hovered for a moment in the rainbowed air; and then fell swamping back into the deep. Crushed thirty feet upwards, the waters flashed for an instant like heaps of fountains, then brokenly sank in a shower of flakes, leaving the circling surface creamed like new milk round the marble trunk of the whale.

"Give way!" cried Ahab to the oarsmen, and the boats darted forward to the attack; but maddened by yesterday's fresh irons that corroded in him, Moby Dick seemed combinedly possessed by all the angels that fell from heaven. The wide tiers of welded tendons overspreading his broad white forehead, beneath the transparent skin, looked knitted together; as head on, he came churning his tail among the boats; and once more flailed them apart; spilling out the irons and lances from the two mates' boats, and dashing in one side of the upper part of their bows, but leaving Ahab's almost without a scar.

While Daggoo and Tashtego were stopping the strained planks; and as the whale swimming out from them, turned, and showed one entire flank as he shot by them again; at that moment a quick cry went up. Lashed round and round to the fish's back; pinioned in the turns upon turns in which, during the past night, the whale had reeled the involutions of the lines around him, the half torn body of the Parsee was seen; his sable raiment frayed to shreds; his distended eyes turned full upon old Ahab.

The harpoon dropped from his hand.

"Befooled, befooled!"—drawing in a long lean breath—"Aye, Parsee! I see thee again.—Aye, and thou goest before; and this, *this* then is the hearse that thou didst promise. But I hold thee to the last letter of thy word. Where is the second hearse? Away, mates, to the ship! those boats are useless now; repair them if ye can in time, and return to me; if not, Ahab is enough to die—Down, men! the first thing that but offers to jump from this boat I stand in, that thing I harpoon. Ye are not other men, but my arms and my legs; and so obey me.—Where's the whale? gone down again?"

But he looked too nigh the boat; for as if bent upon escaping with the corpse he bore, and as if the particular place of the last encounter had been but a stage in his leeward voyage, Moby Dick was now again steadily swimming forward; and had almost passed the ship,—which thus far had been sailing in the contrary direction to him, though for the present her headway had been stopped. He seemed swimming with his utmost velocity, and now only intent upon pursuing his own straight path in the sea.

"Oh! Ahab," cried Starbuck, "not too late is it, even now, the third day, to desist. See! Moby Dick seeks thee not. It is thou, thou, that madly seekest him!"

Setting sail to the rising wind, the lonely boat was swiftly impelled to leeward, by both oars and canvas. And at last when Ahab was sliding by the vessel, so near as plainly to distinguish Starbuck's face as he leaned over the rail, he hailed him to turn the vessel about, and follow him, not too swiftly, at a judicious interval. Glancing upwards, he saw Tashtego, Queequeg, and Daggoo, eagerly mounting to the three mast-heads; while the oarsmen were rocking in the two staved boats which had but just been hoisted to the side, and were busily at work in repairing them. One after the other, through the port-holes, as he sped, he also caught flying glimpses of Stubb and Flask, busying themselves on deck among bundles of new irons and lances. As he saw all this; as he heard the hammers in the broken boats; far other hammers seemed driving a nail into his heart. But he rallied. And now marking that the vane or flag was gone from the main-mast-head, he shouted to Tashtego, who had just gained that perch, to descend again for another flag, and a hammer and nails, and so nail it to the mast.

Whether fagged by the three days' running chase, and the resistance to his swimming in the knotted hamper he bore; or whether it was some latent deceitfulness and malice in him: whichever was true, the White Whale's way now began to abate, as it seemed, from the boat so rapidly nearing him once more; though indeed the whale's last start had not been so long a one as before. And still as Ahab glided over the waves the unpitying sharks accompanied him; and so pertinaciously stuck to the boat; and so continually bit at the plying oars, that the blades became jagged and crunched, and left small splinters in the sea, at almost every dip.

"Heed them not! those teeth but give new rowlocks to your oars. Pull on! 'tis the better rest, the shark's jaw than the yielding water."

"But at every bite, sir, the thin blades grow smaller and smaller!"

"They will last long enough! pull on!—But who can tell"—he muttered—"whether these sharks swim to feast on the whale or on Ahab? —But pull on! Aye, all alive, now—we near him. The helm! take the helm; let me pass,"—and so saying, two of the oarsmen helped him forward to the bows of the still flying boat.

At length as the craft was cast to one side, and ran ranging along with the White Whale's flank, he seemed strangely oblivious of its advance—as the whale sometimes will—and Ahab was fairly within the smoky mountain mist, which, thrown off from the whale's spout, curled round his great, Monadnock hump; he was even thus close to him; when, with body arched back, and both arms lengthwise high-lifted to the poise, he darted his fierce iron, and his far fiercer curse into the hated whale. As both steel and curse sank to the socket, as if sucked into a morass, Moby Dick sideways writhed; spasmodically rolled his nigh flank against the bow, and, without staving a hole in it, so suddenly canted the boat over, that had it not been for the elevated part of the gunwale to which he then clung, Ahab would once more have been tossed into the sea. As it was, three of the oarsmen—who foreknew not the precise instant of the dart, and were therefore unprepared for its effects—these were flung out; but so fell, that, in an instant two of them clutched the gunwale again, and rising to its level on a combing wave, hurled themselves bodily inboard again; the third man helplessly dropping astern, but still afloat and swimming.

Almost simultaneously, with a mighty volition of ungraduated, instantaneous swiftness, the White Whale darted through the weltering sea. But when Ahab cried out to the steersman to take new turns with the line, and hold it so; and commanded the crew to turn round on their seats, and tow the boat up to the mark; the moment the treacherous line felt that double strain and tug, it snapped in the empty air!

"What breaks in me? Some sinew cracks!—'tis whole again; oars! oars! Burst in upon him!"

Hearing the tremendous rush of the sea-crashing boat, the whale wheeled round to present his blank forehead at bay; but in that evolution, catching sight of the nearing black hull of the ship; seemingly seeing in it the source of all his persecutions; bethinking it—it may be—a larger and nobler foe; of a sudden, he bore down upon its advancing prow, smiting his jaws amid fiery showers of foam.

· Ahab staggered; his hand smote his forehead. "I grow blind; hands! stretch out before me that I may yet grope my way. Is't night?"

"The whale! The ship!" cried the cringing oarsmen.

"Oars! oars! Slope downwards to thy depths, O sea, that ere it be for ever too late, Ahab may slide this last, last time upon his mark! I see: the ship! the ship! Dash on, my men! Will ye not save my ship?"

But as the oarsmen violently forced their boat through the sledge-hammering seas, the before whale-smitten bow-ends of two planks burst through, and in an instant almost, the temporarily disabled boat lay nearly level with the waves; its half-wading, splashing crew, trying hard to stop the gap and bale out the pouring water.

Meantime, for that one beholding instant, Tashtego's mast-head hammer remained suspended in his hand; and the red flag, half-wrapping him as with a plaid, then streamed itself straight out from him, as his own forward-flowing heart; while Starbuck and Stubb, standing upon the bowsprit beneath, caught sight of the down-coming monster just as soon as he.

"The whale, the whale! Up helm, up helm! Oh, all ye sweet powers of air, now hug me close! Let not Starbuck die, if die he must, in a woman's fainting fit. Up helm, I say—ye fools, the jaw! the jaw! Is this the end of all my bursting prayers? all my life-long fidelities? Oh, Ahab, Ahab, lo, thy work. Steady! helmsman, steady. Nay, nay! Up helm again! He turns to meet us! Oh, his unappeasable brow drives on towards one, whose duty tells him he cannot depart. My God, stand by me now!"

"Stand not by me, but stand under me, whoever you are that will now help Stubb; for Stubb, too, sticks here. I grin at thee, thou grinning whale! Who ever helped Stubb, or kept Stubb awake, but Stubb's own unwinking eye? And now poor Stubb goes to bed upon a mattrass that is all too soft;

would it were stuffed with brushwood! I grin at thee, thou grinning whale!
Look ye, sun, moon, and stars! I call ye assassins of as good a fellow as ever
spouted up his ghost. For all that, I would yet ring glasses with ye, would
ye but hand the cup! Oh, oh! oh, oh! thou grinning whale, but there 'll be
plenty of gulping soon! Why fly ye not, O Ahab! For me, off shoes and
jacket to it; let Stubb die in his drawers! A most mouldy and over salted
death, though;—cherries! cherries! cherries! oh, Flask, for one red cherry
ere we die!"

"Cherries? I only wish that we were where they grow. Oh, Stubb, I
hope my poor mother's drawn my part-pay ere this; if not, few coppers will
now come to her, for the voyage is up."

From the ship's bows, nearly all the seamen now hung inactive;
hammers, bits of plank, lances, and harpoons, mechanically retained in their
hands, just as they had darted from their various employments; all their
enchanted eyes intent upon the whale, which from side to side strangely
vibrating his predestinating head, sent a broad band of overspreading semi-
circular foam before him as he rushed. Retribution, swift vengeance,
eternal malice were in his whole aspect, and spite of all that mortal man
could do, the solid white buttress of his forehead smote the ship's starboard
bow, till men and timbers reeled. Some fell flat upon their faces. Like dis-
lodged trucks, the heads of the harpooneers aloft shook on their bull-like
necks. Through the breach, they heard the waters pour, as mountain
torrents down a flume.

"The ship! The hearse!—the second hearse!" cried Ahab from the boat;
"its wood could only be American!"

Diving beneath the settling ship, the whale ran quivering along its keel;
but turning under water, swiftly shot to the surface again, far off the other
bow, but within a few yards of Ahab's boat, where, for a time, he lay
quiescent.

"I turn my body from the sun. What ho, Tashtego! let me hear thy
hammer. Oh! ye three unsurrendered spires of mine; thou uncracked keel;
and only god-bullied hull; thou firm deck, and haughty helm, and Pole-
pointed prow,—death-glorious ship! must ye then perish, and without me?
Am I cut off from the last fond pride of meanest shipwrecked captains?
Oh, lonely death on lonely life! Oh, now I feel my topmost greatness lies
in my topmost grief. Ho, ho! from all your furthest bounds, pour ye now in,
ye bold billows of my whole foregone life, and top this one piled comber of
my death! Towards thee I roll, thou all-destroying but unconquering
whale; to the last I grapple with thee; from hell's heart I stab at thee; for

hate's sake I spit my last breath at thee. Sink all coffins and all hearses to one common pool! and since neither can be mine, let me then tow to pieces, while still chasing thee, though tied to thee, thou damned whale! *Thus*, I give up the spear!"

The harpoon was darted; the stricken whale flew forward; with igniting velocity the line ran through the groove;—ran foul. Ahab stooped to clear it; he did clear it; but the flying turn caught him round the neck, and voicelessly as Turkish mutes bowstring their victim, he was shot out of the boat, ere the crew knew he was gone. Next instant, the heavy eye-splice in the rope's final end flew out of the stark-empty tub, knocked down an oarsman, and smiting the sea, disappeared in its depths.

For an instant, the tranced boat's crew stood still; then turned. "The ship? Great God, where is the ship?" Soon they through dim, bewildering mediums saw her sidelong fading phantom, as in the gaseous Fata Morgana; only the uppermost masts out of water; while fixed by infatuation, or fidelity, or fate, to their once lofty perches, the pagan harpooneers still maintained their sinking lookouts on the sea. And now, concentric circles seized the lone boat itself, and all its crew, and each floating oar, and every lance-pole, and spinning, animate and inanimate, all round and round in one vortex, carried the smallest chip of the Pequod out of sight.

But as the last whelmings intermixingly poured themselves over the sunken head of the Indian at the mainmast, leaving a few inches of the erect spar yet visible, together with long streaming yards of the flag, which calmly undulated, with ironical coincidings, over the destroying billows they almost touched;—at that instant, a red arm and a hammer hovered backwardly uplifted in the open air, in the act of nailing the flag faster and yet faster to the subsiding spar. A sky-hawk that tauntingly had followed the main-truck downwards from its natural home among the stars, pecking at the flag, and incommoding Tashtego there; this bird now chanced to intercept its broad fluttering wing between the hammer and the wood; and simultaneously feeling that etherial thrill, the submerged savage beneath, in his death-grasp, kept his hammer frozen there; and so the bird of heaven, with archangelic shrieks, and his imperial beak thrust upwards, and his whole captive form folded in the flag of Ahab, went down with his ship, which, like Satan, would not sink to hell till she had dragged a living part of heaven along with her, and helmeted herself with it.

Now small fowls flew screaming over the yet yawning gulf; a sullen white surf beat against its steep sides; then all collapsed, and the great shroud of the sea rolled on as it rolled five thousand years ago.

# Epilogue

"And I only am escaped alone to tell thee." *Job.*

THE *drama's done. Why then here does any one step forth?—Because one did survive the wreck.*

*It so chanced, that after the Parsee's disappearance, I was he whom the Fates ordained to take the place of Ahab's bowsman, when that bowsman assumed the vacant post; the same, who, when on the last day the three men were tossed from out the rocking boat, was dropped astern. So, floating on the margin of the ensuing scene, and in full sight of it, when the half-spent suction of the sunk ship reached me, I was then, but slowly, drawn towards the closing vortex. When I reached it, it had subsided to a creamy pool. Round and round, then, and ever contracting towards the button-like black bubble at the axis of that slowly wheeling circle, like another Ixion I did revolve. Till, gaining that vital centre, the black bubble upward burst; and now, liberated by reason of its cunning spring, and, owing to its great buoyancy, rising with great force, the coffin life-buoy shot lengthwise from the sea, fell over, and floated by my side. Buoyed up by that coffin, for almost one whole day and night, I floated on a soft and dirge-like main. The unharming sharks, they glided by as if with padlocks on their mouths; the savage sea-hawks sailed with sheathed beaks. On the second day, a sail drew near, nearer, and picked me up at last. It was the devious-cruising Rachel, that in her retracing search after her missing children, only found another orphan.*

FINIS

573

# Editorial Appendix

HISTORICAL NOTE

TEXTUAL RECORD

RELATED DOCUMENTS

*For*
WILLARD THORP
LEON HOWARD
*and*
JAY LEYDA

THE FIRST *of the three parts of this* APPENDIX *is a note on the background, composition, publication, reception, and later critical history of* Moby-Dick, *contributed by the three editors of the whole Northwestern-Newberry Edition, Harrison Hayford, Hershel Parker, and G. Thomas Tanselle. The second part, which records textual information, has also been prepared by these three editors. It consists of a note on the textual history of* Moby-Dick *and on the editorial principles of this edition, followed by discussions of certain problematical readings, a list of emendations, a report of line-end hyphenation, and a full list of substantive variants between the first American and the first English editions. The third part, prepared by Hayford, Lynn Horth, and Tanselle, presents related documents: (1) Melville's notes (1849–51) in a Shakespeare volume; (2) his memoranda in Owen Chase's* Narrative . . . *of the Whale-Ship Essex; (3) his memorandum about the crew of the* Acushnet; *(4) a discussion of the annotations in the copy of* The Whale *Melville presented in 1853 to his former* Acushnet *shipmate Henry F. Hubbard; and (5) a discussion of the copy of* Moby-Dick *acquired by Samuel Arthur Jones, in which was pasted a Harper* Whale *title page.*

*To insure uniform textual policy in all volumes of the edition, the same three editors, Harrison Hayford, Hershel Parker, and G. Thomas Tanselle, participate in the planning and establishment of textual policy for all volumes, except as otherwise noted; even when other editors are specifically named (as in the case of certain writings edited from manuscript) the final decisions still rest with one or more of these editors, as noted in individual volumes. Final responsibility for all aspects of every volume is exercised by the general editor, Harrison Hayford.*

*The editorial work on the Northwestern-Newberry* Moby-Dick *was carried on during the twenty-three years between 1965 and its publication date. Before this work was initiated, Hayford and Parker had undertaken the textual research reported in their Norton Critical Edition (1967). That research is incorporated herein, modified by changes in editorial policy and amplified by what they acknowledged (p. xi) was still needed—prolonged "intensive consideration of the range of possible emendations and of bibliographical problems"—and by new research into the publishing history. Tanselle's particular expertise in bibliography and publishing history, as well as Hayford and Parker's further research, has been brought to bear in a fully collaborative effort to make this edition more nearly what the Norton was avowedly not, an exhaustive treatment of the textual history and problems of* Moby-Dick.

*In the* HISTORICAL NOTE *many passages have been collaboratively reworked by two or all three of the editors, who have reviewed the facts and opinions expressed throughout. Citations, however, should be made to Hayford as author of Sections I and V; Tanselle as author of Section VI; and Parker as author of Sections II–IV and*

VII–IX. *Parker was responsible for reworking and harmonizing the* NOTE *as a whole.*

G. *Thomas Tanselle wrote the* NOTE ON THE TEXT, *following, where applicable, the basic pattern and wording set by the three editors in other volumes of the Northwestern-Newberry Edition. In addition, he was primarily responsible for overseeing the textual information presented there as well as in the other parts of the* TEXTUAL RECORD. *Among the* DISCUSSIONS OF ADOPTED READINGS, *those bearing on quotations from and paraphrases of other works (as in "Extracts") form the principal category that he wrote. Finally, the discussions of the Hubbard copy of* The Whale *and the Jones copy of* Moby-Dick *are slightly revised from his original publication of them in the* Book Collector.

*Harrison Hayford was the editor who took primary responsibility for identifying textual points requiring commentary and for drafting many of the* DISCUSSIONS OF ADOPTED READINGS. *He wrote most of the discussions bearing on emendable and unemendable discrepancies, and took primary charge of the selection and form of the* RELATED DOCUMENTS.

*Alma A. MacDougall, as editorial coordinator of the whole Northwestern-Newberry Edition since 1981, worked on this volume in unique collaboration both with its editors and with Northwestern University Press. She supervised its production and assisted indispensably in all its parts and procedures.*

*Lynn Horth, as assistant editor of the Northwestern-Newberry Edition since 1986, worked closely with the other editors in all aspects of the final preparation of the volume.*

*The editors were given help at crucial points throughout by the bibliographical associate, Richard Colles Johnson, by the editorial associate, Brian Higgins, and by the manuscript associate, Robert C. Ryan. They were also aided beyond the call of duty in the initial stage by the contributing scholar Joel Myerson, and in the later stages by the contributing scholars Mary K. Bercaw and Mark Niemeyer. In preparing the text indispensable assistance, particularly in collating and intensive proofreading, without which such an edition cannot succeed in its primary aims, was given by Ruth Adler, Alice Belair, Lynne Blumberg, Amy Puett Emmers, Cheryl Garnant, Josephine Wishart Hayford, Ralph Harrison Hayford, Alison Margaret Hayford, Virginia Heiserman, Sandra N. Herzog, William Holzberger, Roni Kaluza, Peter Roode, Geoffrey Rytell, Justine Smith, R. E. Steinhauer, and Pamela Thiele. In the final stages Hugh Campbell, Jennifer S. Johnson, Ann Larson, Kenneth Morrill, Moira Owens, and Carla Reiter all assisted materially.*

*Authorization to edit manuscript materials and permission to publish items and reproductions from their collections has been granted by (1) the Houghton Library, Harvard University; (2) the Newberry Library, Chicago (Melville Collection); (3) the New York Public Library, Astor, Lenox and Tilden Foundations (Duyckinck Collection and Melville Family Papers, Gansevoort-Lansing Collection, Rare Books and Manuscripts Division); (4) the University of Chicago Library; and (5)* the University of Illinois Library, Urbana-Champaign. The editors have also made use of manuscript materials, books, newspapers, and periodicals in the collections of the New York Public Library (Berg Collection), Northwestern University Library, Columbia University Library, Illinois State University (Normal) Library, Ohio State University Library, Morris Library of the University of Delaware, the New-York Historical Society, the Leicestershire Library and Information Service, the Boston Public Library, the Library of Congress, the Berkshire Athenaeum and Pittsfield Public Library, the Troy Public Library, New York State Library, the Lansingburgh Historical Society, the Albany Institute of History and Art, and the Philadelphia Free Library. They are indebted for information and assistance to Frederick Bassett, Warren Broderick, Barry Chernoff, Peter Christoph, James Corsaro, Susan Davis, Ruth T. Degenhardt, Karen T. Helm, Cara Jarowsky, Richard Leab, Miss H. Leach, Paul Mercer, Robert G. Newman, E. M. Reilly, Jr., Kathleen Reilly, and Lola L. Szladits.

The editors also extend thanks to Virginia Washburn Barden, Stewart Frank, Stanton Garner, Isaac Gewirtz, William M. Gibson, Glenn Gordiner, Gerald Graff, Thomas Heffernan, Wilson L. Heflin, Stan Hugill, W. A. Kenyon, Wayne R. Kime, Vera Brodsky Lawrence, John J. McCusker, Sanford E. Marovitz, Perry Miller, Martin Mueller, Laurence Nobles, Richard Ringler, Bernard Rosenthal, Merton M. Sealts, Jr., Robert Strotz, Lawrence W. Towner, David L. Vander Meulen, Jack B. Van Hooser, John Van Sickle, Kermit Vanderbilt, Howard P. Vincent, James M. Wells, and George Worth.

In addition to those just stated, acknowledgments are gratefully made to scholars and friends for scholarly and personal assistance rendered over the years to individual members of the Northwestern-Newberry editorial group. By Harrison Hayford to: Roger Asselineau, Richard S. Barnes, A. Robert Lee, Kubet Luchterhand, Leland Phelps, Walter B. Scott, Jr., and Viola Sachs and the members of her seminar (University of Paris VIII-Vincennes); and by Hershel Parker to: Frederick Crews, Robert H. Hirst, James B. Meriwether, Jane Millgate, Michael Millgate, Noel Polk, and Heddy-Ann Richter.

Finally, with admiration and gratitude for their contributions to the understanding of the genius of Herman Melville and the greatness of Moby-Dick, the editors dedicate their part of this volume to three Melville scholars: to Willard Thorp (1900–     ), who pioneered the Modern Language Association editions and who survives, and to two who went before, Leon Howard (1903–1982) and Jay Leyda (1910–1988).

The original bindings of the first English and American editions. By permission of The Newberry Library.

# Historical Note

I N WRITING *Moby-Dick* Melville attempted for the second time
to produce "a mighty book" on "a mighty theme." He avowed
that purpose in one of its late chapters (104) as he had openly
declared it in an earlier one (26) by invoking the "great democratic
God" to vindicate his effort to create a democratic tragic hero. Yet as
this book, his sixth, neared completion he wrote to Hawthorne early
in June, 1851, about the dilemma in which he found himself caught:
"What I feel most moved to write, that is banned,—it will not pay.
Yet, altogether, write the *other* way I cannot. So the product is a final
hash, and all my books are botches."[1] In another letter to Hawthorne
just after *Moby-Dick* was published, Melville recalled his "ditcher's
work with that book" and reiterated his sense of the inadequacy of its
"imperfect body" as the vehicle of "the pervading thought that impelled the book." Contemporary reviewers of *Moby-Dick* and of the
slightly earlier (and expurgated and truncated) London edition, *The
Whale,* while recognizing qualities of greatness in the book and qualities of genius in the author, found serious anomalies in its genre, plot,

1. In the section on "Sources" at the end of this NOTE (pp. 756ff.) its documentation is explained and its short citations are given in full.

581

characters, language, and thought. In the judgment of twentieth-century posterity, however, whatever faults Melville himself and his contemporaries saw in *Moby-Dick* and *The Whale* have faded from view. *Moby-Dick* is acclaimed as the mighty book that Melville had envisioned.

An article of faith for those who in the twentieth-century belatedly established the present high reputation of *Moby-Dick* came to be that even its formal anomalies go to constitute its own unique and successful form. But there is in fact no need to rationalize all of its aberrations thus or to attribute them all to Melville's principle, promulgated in *Moby-Dick*, that in some enterprises "a careful disorderliness is the true method" (chap. 82). The Shakespearean literary qualities of *Moby-Dick* have long been recognized, and now perhaps its text can be regarded as Shakespearean in a different sense: like his, this text is filled with discrepancies. However, as recent Shakespeare scholarship has shown, one cannot safely regard all such troublesome spots as involving corruption, since they may also consist of the author's own wording accurately preserved from different stages in the evolution of the text. In any case, only reliable textual knowledge places readers in a position to distinguish passages so problematic as to affect interpretation.

The editors of this critical text share the judgment that *Moby-Dick* is a masterpiece of American and world literature, yet they affirm its greatness despite actual imperfections. They must say at once that their examination of the textually imperfect body of *Moby-Dick* has revealed flaws that help to explain Melville's own sense that it was by his standards a hash or a botch. As a good literary workman who in writing it had become a great writer, he knew there were passages, large and small, that failed to meet his intentions. For months before the completion of *Moby-Dick* Melville had feared that he could not avoid leaving conceptual discrepancies, factual inconsistencies, patched-over flaws in transitions, lapses in technique, and stylistic lurches, and soon after he received his first copy he must have spotted some of the swarm of copyists' misreadings and typesetters' errors he had missed in his hasty proofreading.[2] These are all textual flaws of

---

2. By the time of his comments to Hawthorne (November 17, 1851) about the "imperfect body" of *Moby-Dick*, Melville may also have discovered that *The Whale* had been printed without the "Epilogue," to name only the grossest of the unauthorized ways in which the English edition departed from his intentions.

the kinds it has been the present editors' ungracious ditchers' work to locate, diagnose, and where possible emend in order to bring the text back to, or closer to, the author's thwarted intention.

Although Melville's confessions to Hawthorne about his struggles to make the imperfect body of *Moby-Dick* correspond to its perfect soul are now famous, they have never been taken as literally as he meant them and as editorial scrutiny of its text has now shown they should be understood. Many of the unemendable textual problems of *Moby-Dick* arose from Melville's shifting, expanding, and not altogether seamlessly blending conceptions of the work during the course of its year-and-a-half composition in varying circumstances at four domiciles in New York City and Pittsfield. As his ambition soared Melville built a kind of American tragedy with a Shakespearean hero out of what he seems to have begun as a simpler book intended to blend his own whaling experiences with wild stories and legends of Pacific whaling that he had heard and read. This development, along with others, led to defiant anomalies of genre, and it also left many textual loose ends. Sometimes, too, his conceptual changes left curious vestigial elements, particularly as to the changing roles of the central characters, such as the pattern of "unnecessary duplicates"[3] that offers clues to his writing process whether or not it creates actual contradictions in the text. Another cause of the textual problems lay in habits of research and composition that Melville had formed in writing his earlier books. As scholars have shown, he would use his own experiences and observations as he wrote narrative and expository sequences; then he would expand the sequences

---

3. This phrase, taken from a passage in *Moby-Dick* (chap. 20), is applied to textual duplications by Harrison Hayford in "Unnecessary Duplicates: A Key to the Writing of *Moby-Dick*" (see Section V and many of the DISCUSSIONS OF ADOPTED READINGS). The fullest critical consideration of textual anomalies in American fiction is Hershel Parker's *Flawed Texts and Verbal Icons*, where Chapter 5 uses the manuscript of *Pudd'nhead Wilson* to show the way many textual anomalies were inadvertently created. In its published text strong, late-written scenes, in which the villain had been made part black and a slave, were placed before more casual scenes, written early while he was still merely a white scamp, with the result that a reader could reasonably conclude that Mark Twain had lost interest in the race-slavery plot as he wrote. A striking number of anomalies in the familiar Mark Twain text demonstrably arose from compositional procedures like those about which Hayford, lacking any *Moby-Dick* manuscript for evidence, can only offer hypotheses that, however plausible, must be provisional, like all such inferential reconstructions.

here and there, often by interpolating passages rewritten from other people's experiences and observations which he had plundered from their works. In the letter of early June mentioned above Melville called this process of expansion "elaborating" his book. He referred to it metaphorically in another letter to Hawthorne on June 29, 1851: "Since you have been here, I have been building some shanties of houses (connected to the old one) and likewise some shanties of chapters and essays." In this way, all along, and even in the quite late stages of his work, Melville filled out and enriched his whaling manuscript, but in the process he sometimes introduced textual contradictions that he did not resolve, just as he had done from *Typee* (1846) onward. Still further textual discrepancies in *Moby-Dick* were generated by a strong characteristic bent of Melville's literary imagination, his greater concern for a scene's dramatic qualities than for its local consistency of realistic detail or its consistency with other parts of the manuscript. This propensity spawned numerous minor, and mostly unemendable, factual discrepancies in his text. A final, more mundane, cause brought about a myriad of textual errors in the book as first printed—the harassing circumstances under which Melville saw his still unfinished manuscript into type and distractedly read the proofs (or some of them) even while laboring to "finish" the book up "in some fashion or other."

The existence in *Moby-Dick* of so many textual problems, most of which are insoluble, is a fact that must be faced, along with any consequences for interpretation and evaluation. But one need not be led into disillusionment about the work as a whole. Shakespeare's plays remain masterpieces in spite of the textual problems that are observed in them; and the power of *Moby-Dick* is not diminished by the evidence of many signs that in its composition Melville wrestled with "the angel—Art," to use his much later formulation for the creative struggle (in the poem "Art"). In Emerson's phrase from "The Problem," Melville "builded better than he knew," though he also fully knew that he might have builded better still, granted more "Time, Strength, Cash, and Patience!" (chap. 32—a much-quoted phrase that is seldom taken literally enough as a cry from the stage in the creative process when the artist envisions an overarching goal but despairs of achieving it). Faulkner, the American novelist most akin to Melville in intensity of literary tragic ambition, regarded *Moby-Dick* as probably the greatest single book in American literature;

though it "was still an attempt that didn't quite come off, it was bigger than one human being could do." In no other work in the fifteen volumes of Melville's *Writings* in the Northwestern-Newberry Edition have the editors encountered such a plethora of textual problems as in *Moby-Dick* (not even in the unfinished *Billy Budd, Sailor*, with its very different problems of deciphering the words on the manuscript leaves and determining its genesis from the order in which the leaves or parts of leaves were inscribed). The most likely causes of these problems are developed in the course of this HISTORICAL NOTE.

Individual problems that the editors have noticed, whatever their causes and whether or not they are solvable, are reported, with the editors' decisions, in the DISCUSSIONS OF ADOPTED READINGS, as clues to the sorts of bafflements that Melville's imagination encountered (and often triumphed over) on its path to its goal. Most of them have never been, and need not be, noticed by readers, just as during dramatic productions most blunders, missed cues, improvised lines, and offstage commotions are unnoticed by a general audience carried along by the sustained illusion. But a thorough understanding, by critical readers, of Melville's mind and art and of their modes of manifestation in *Moby-Dick* must be grounded in detailed knowledge of the genesis of its textual characteristics and how those characteristics reached their published state in the English and American editions.

Section II of this HISTORICAL NOTE gives an account of Melville's life and career up to the time he began writing *Moby-Dick*, with emphasis upon the divided motivation that marked his work after *Mardi*, his first attempt to write a great book and his first failure to achieve popularity.

Section III is a survey of the working conditions under which Melville wrote *Moby-Dick* together with general notes on what is known, from his own and other contemporary letters, of the stages of his progress on the manuscript.

Section IV surveys some of the likely sources of *Moby-Dick* in whaling stories Melville heard and whaling information he encountered in printed form, and lists some of the discoveries and suggestions that have been made about the use of particular whaling sources in the writing of certain chapters, parts of chapters, or groups of chapters; it also glances at some of the more obvious major sources in great literature.

Section V traces the contributions of the scholars who have based theories of the genesis of *Moby-Dick* on the information about Melville's sources described in Section IV; it also summarizes Harrison Hayford's genetic theory inferred from internal anomalies.

Section VI details the circumstances of Melville's preparing the book for publication in New York and of his arranging for prior publication in London (where the publisher deliberately made many changes without consulting him and inadvertently made still others).

Section VII surveys the British reviews of *The Whale* and the American reviews of *Moby-Dick* (the last-minute substitution for the earlier title) and shows how Melville's reaction to the dual receptions affected both the composition of his next book, *Pierre*, and the subsequent reputation of *The Whale* and *Moby-Dick*.

Section VIII follows the discovery of *The Whale* (or *Moby-Dick*) by British literary people in the decades before Melville's death in 1891 and outlines much of the process by which it finally achieved fame during the "Melville revival," the greatest impetus for which was the centennial of his birth, in 1919.

Section IX is a coda on the present status of *Moby-Dick* as a great work of world literature.


The HISTORICAL NOTE in each previous Northwestern-Newberry edition aimed at reporting what has been discovered concerning four topics, the composition, publication, reception, and later critical history of the book; that is to say, for biographical information the authors of these previous NOTES relied very heavily on the documents gathered and published by the great generation of Melville researchers of the 1930's and 1940's, whose labors first significantly coalesced in 1938 in Willard Thorp's *Herman Melville: Representative Selections*, then culminated in 1951 in the first edition of Jay Leyda's *The Melville Log* and in Leon Howard's *Herman Melville: A Biography*. The debt to that generation of scholars remains deep, but this NOTE (the first to be written by the three editors) also benefits from a new stage of scholarship on Melville—a stage arrived at, in part, from the accumulation of biographical and textual knowledge incorporated into the volumes of the Northwestern-Newberry Edition published over two decades or still in preparation. Such information will be contained in new editions of some of the standard scholarly works on Melville that are being revised with the participation or supervision of one or more of the editors of this volume. *The New Melville Log*, by Jay Leyda and Hershel Parker, is forthcoming from Gordian Press, and new editions of the letters and of the journals of Melville are forthcoming in the Northwestern-Newberry Edition. (Parker is working on a new biography of Melville.) During the last years that this volume was in preparation the previously unknown Augusta Melville papers were acquired by the New York Public Library. This HISTORICAL NOTE is the first lengthy essay on this part of Melville's life to make full use of the documents in that new trove. It also derives from many discoveries by the editors and other scholars that bear directly on the four standard topics for these NOTES, discoveries not hitherto reported in print or else not yet interpreted in full biographical contexts. The editors hope that the presence in this volume of so much new information about Melville and about *Moby-Dick* will stimulate new research (for as Jay Leyda said, the study is endless), but the very abundance of new discoveries has led them to omit a summary (readily available elsewhere) of the course of criticism since 1930. Throughout the NOTE the editors have striven not to foreclose inquiry or to impose readings but to open up the book to scholars and critics, and also to students and general readers, who have always, even in some of the more minutely detailed portions of the EDITORIAL APPENDIX, been kept foremost in mind.

## II

Born August 1, 1819, of the union between Allan Melvill, of the Boston merchant Melvills who rejoiced in their close links to Scottish nobility, and Maria Gansevoort Melvill, of the Albany Gansevoorts who were complexly interrelated with all the powerful seventeenth-century Hudson River Valley Dutch families such as the Ten Eycks and Van Rensselaers, Melville was made keenly aware of his descent from two Revolutionary heroes (the paternal grandfather an "Indian" at the Tea Party, the maternal grandfather a hero of Fort Stanwix).[4]

---

4. In defiance of the norm he describes in *Flawed Texts and Verbal Icons*, Parker has adapted several paragraphs written by Hayford for his dissertation (1945) and for the HISTORICAL NOTE in the Northwestern-Newberry edition of *The Confidence-Man* (1984). Errors in documents quoted throughout occur in the originals.

He passed his childhood in New York City, then Albany, in a status about as near to patrician life as the young American republic afforded. That status was illusory, for his incorrigibly optimistic father, having recklessly overextended himself, died suddenly in early 1832, so deeply in debt that the effects were still felt in the family for half a century. Melville lived through his teens on or just over the edge of poverty. Soon after his father's death, his mother hired him out as a clerk at a bank in Albany where her brother Peter was an officer. In the summer of 1832 she fled the cholera epidemic to the Pittsfield farm of her brother-in-law, Major Thomas Melvill, Jr.—a paradisiacal refuge. Seven of her children stayed there with her in safety, but Herman was sent back into danger to protect his job. Two years later his older brother Gansevoort needed someone to wait on customers at his cap and fur store, so Herman was put to work there, under his brother's command. (In early September, 1834, a Pittsfield cousin wrote: "I was very much disapointed that *Hermans* business would not allow him to visit Pittsfield this year but *Gan* said he could not let him because he was wanted in the store.") After studying at the Albany Classical School in 1835–36, Melville attended the Albany Academy from the fall of 1836 until he was withdrawn early in 1837, just before his brother went bankrupt in the panic of 1837. (In due time Herman also fell victim to the family curse by overextending himself on borrowed money.) Out of school and jobless, nearing eighteen, in June of that year Melville became a farmhand and surrogate man of the house when his uncle left his wife and younger children on the farm at Pittsfield to try his fortune in Illinois. That fall and winter, following his cousin Robert's example, Melville taught school, in "a remote & secluded" area outside Pittsfield, boarding with a Yankee family who burrowed "together in the woods—like so many foxes" at the summit of a "savage and lonely" mountain. In the spring of 1838 as a drastic economy measure Melville's mother moved from Albany into exile in Lansingburgh, across the Hudson and a dozen miles north. That winter Herman took a course in surveying and engineering at the Lansingburgh Academy. The situation was such that on May 23, 1839, his mother said that he had gone off "for a few days on foot to see what he can find to do." Having found nothing, in June he shipped as a common sailor (rated "boy") on a merchantman bound for Liverpool and back. In the winter of 1839–

40 he taught a term at Greenbush, across the river from Albany, then in the summer went to Galena, Illinois, to see his uncle Thomas and his aunt and cousins.

Late in 1840, useless to his family, having come to manhood without a business or profession to satisfy the expectation early bred into him by family pride and tradition, he signed on the New Bedford (Fairhaven) whaleship *Acushnet* and set sail on January 3, 1841, for Cape Horn and the fisheries of the South Pacific. At the Marquesas he jumped ship with a companion and spent a month among the Typee cannibals. He escaped from there on a Sydney whaler, then joined her crew in refusing further duty at Tahiti, and lounged in and about a native calaboose at Papeete; he worked in the neighboring island, Eimeo, as a farmhand, and wandered about it as a beachcomber; he served aboard a third whaler on a five months' cruise to the Sandwich Islands, where he set pins in a Honolulu bowling alley and clerked and kept accounts for a merchant; there he joined the navy as an ordinary seaman and, after a year's cruise on the U.S. frigate *United States*, sailed home round the Horn on her and was discharged at Boston in October, 1844.

Within a year he had written his first book, mostly at the house his mother still rented in Lansingburgh. It is possible that one motivation behind Melville's signing on a whaler had been to gain experiences he could write about, much as a Bostonian of his own social class, Richard Henry Dana, Jr., had recently done in *Two Years Before the Mast* (1840), which Melville had read just before his voyage. Early in 1838 the Albany *Microscope* had printed a forensic free-for-all in which Melville proved that his training at debate had given him a ready command of the rhetoric of competitive invective and short-suffering indignation. Just before he went out job-hunting on foot in 1839 he had published at least two "Fragments from a Writing Desk" in a Lansingburgh newspaper (one of which was reprinted across the Hudson in West Troy), sketches which self-protectively spoofed Byronic attitudes. In 1844 four years at sea had left him less prepared than ever to earn his living ashore; even his brother Allan, four years his junior, had progressed from law clerk toward a career as a New York City lawyer, following the example of Gansevoort, who at the moment of Herman's return was winding down an extensive speaking tour on behalf of the candidacy of James K. Polk for president.

Melville's education largely consisted of his childhood schooling and what he had absorbed as the third child and second son in a literate family (in which the youngest children, growing up impoverished, had progressively less education, formal or informal); his catch-as-catch-can months of formal schooling in his teens seem to have counted for less in his education than the haphazard acquisitions of his alert mind. In his quieter way, however, he had his share of the family confidence that Gansevoort so histrionically displayed. By virtue of having a "rich and peculiar experience in life" (*Pierre*, bk. 18.i) to write about, and having nothing better to do ashore, Melville took up, perhaps for the nonce only, the profession of authorship. At Gansevoort's law office in New York City his brothers had paper, pen, and writing surface to spare, and later his mother and sisters made room for him to work on the book at Lansingburgh.

When Gansevoort Melville sailed on July 31, 1845, to become the American Secretary of Legation in London, he carried with him the supposedly complete manuscript of *Typee*, in which he promptly enough interested the London publisher John Murray, son of Byron's John Murray. In December Gansevoort had to interpolate some sections into the manuscript, Herman having decided to shore up his narrative with information from books such as Captain David Porter's *Journal of a Cruise Made to the Pacific Ocean, in the U.S. Frigate Essex, in the Years 1812, 1813, and 1814* (Philadelphia, 1815, or New York, 1822), Charles S. Stewart's *A Visit to the South Seas, in the U.S. Ship Vincennes, . . . 1829–1830* (New York, 1831), and William Ellis's *Polynesian Researches* (New York, 1833). Published in February, 1846, *Narrative of a Four Months' Residence among the Natives of a Valley of the Marquesas Islands; or, A Peep at Polynesian Life*, was in part an idyll based on Melville's brief stay among the Marquesans, fancifully woven from strands of his own memory (some strands already worked out at sea in tales for his fellows in whaleships and in a naval frigate) and the rope-yarn which he shamelessly raveled from his source books. Throughout the fabric, particularly in the latest patching, was a fairly conspicuous thread of social criticism. Without much formal education Melville had lived through a prolonged lessoning in the difference between an imperfect democracy ashore and varieties of perfected absolutism afloat, a hard schooling interspersed with a crash course in comparative anthropology, in which the lesson of cultural relativity provided him with an objective vantage point from

which to look at American society. Already in 1845 he was prepared
to suggest that in its own terms primitive society had some virtues
crowded out of a more complex, machine-driven civilization, that
perhaps evangelical Christianity brought some blights to the islands
along with blessings, ill news along with its gospel. Accepted in
London by the visiting G. P. Putnam, the book was promptly republished in the United States by Wiley & Putnam, under the title Melville preferred, *Typee*, in the firm's well-respected Library of American Books, a series supervised by Evert A. Duyckinck, a bookish
New York literary man who was to play a large and complex role in
Melville's career.

   *Typee* was rushed into print in New York before John Wiley quite
realized how critical of the missionaries some of its passages were (he
demanded that Melville prepare an expurgated edition, and the
young author complied, albeit grudgingly). In Great Britain and in
the United States the book was an immediate success, and it was soon
pirated in German and Dutch. Having launched his brother's career,
Gansevoort died suddenly in London, leaving the twenty-six-year-
old author the head of the family. In Lansingburgh, Melville came in
from hoeing in his mother's garden to answer a request for his autograph; he was inescapably reminded of Byron, for he had awakened
to find himself famous, or notorious, on both sides of the Atlantic, as
"a 'man who lived among the cannibals.' " *Omoo*, off the less-timid
Harpers' press in 1847, just over a year after *Typee*, took up the
semifictional autobiographical story where the first book left off, and
carried it through several drifting months afloat and ashore in Tahiti
and Eimeo. Memory supplied some narrative strands (and once again
parts of the material, such as the half-dangerous, half-comic-opera
revolt and imprisonment, may have been tried out as sea-yarns), but
this time Melville reinforced the narrative with a still greater proportion of borrowed or downright stolen rope-yarn, still more imagina-
tively interfused with his memories. His interweaving of criticism
now gave a more distinct stripe to the fabric, and of a hue far from
pleasing to eyes accustomed to screen out perturbing realities and see
the South Sea islands only in the light of Christian sweetness dispensed among the heathen by missionaries of a superior creed, society, and race.

   As narrator of these first books Melville showed something more
than a roving spirit, a zest for adventure, and a robust warm heart,

something besides an observant eye, an ingenuous gift for a moving story and lucid exposition, and a knack for hitting off shrewd thumbnail sketches of personalities. He showed an unorthodox, critical mind as well, a good mind, sharpened by the abrasive of hard experience in the world; and he had an independent tongue to speak this mind, though not yet in tones sufficiently loud or caustic to offend the sensibilities of many readers outside the circle of sober and exceedingly vocal supporters of the foreign missions, where even the relatively mild criticisms in *Typee* had raised hackles. Already, however, a penetrating reader could have detected, pervading the romantic adventures and underlying the disparagement of the missions, a certain independent disposition to find things wrong with the established order of society; to question and rebel against constituted authority—captains, consuls, bosses, priests; to take the side of the forecastle against the quarterdeck, of the simple native against the learned missionary; and to hint that some goodness and right reside in common men, who are imposed upon by the mighty and wealthy of organized society.

On August 4, 1847, three days after his twenty-eighth birthday, Melville married Elizabeth Shaw, daughter of his father's old friend Lemuel Shaw, the Chief Justice of the Supreme Judicial Court of Massachusetts. Melville's efforts earlier in the year to secure a Treasury clerkship or some other government post had failed, and with money Shaw had advanced against his daughter's inheritance Melville and his bride set up housekeeping in New York City, behind the new Grace Church, near Astor Place, together with his brother Allan and Allan's own new bride Sophia (of the wealthy Manhattan Thurstons) and their mother and four unmarried sisters. On the success of *Omoo* Melville had decided that he could support his family as a writer—a goal very few Americans of his generation had been able to accomplish.

Melville's next three books, *Mardi* (1849), *Redburn* (1849), and *White-Jacket* (1850), were written during the first two years of a three-year residence in New York City. During his work on these three books, as during the composition of *Omoo*, Melville for literary companionship relied most (as far as we know) on the man he met during the expurgation of *Typee*, Evert Duyckinck, who from 1845 to 1847 selected works for the Library of American Books, where *Typee* appeared along with titles by Nathaniel Hawthorne, Edgar Allan Poe, and William Gilmore Simms, with all of whom the New Yorker had ongoing editorial relations. In the course of his duties at Wiley & Putnam he had distributed review copies of *Typee*, with personal requests to Nathaniel Hawthorne, Margaret Fuller, and others.[5] Duyckinck played mentor to the slightly younger Melville, lent him books from his extensive library, and introduced him to the city's literary and artistic life. In Duyckinck's hospitable house on Clinton Place Melville enjoyed the literary talk of members of a coterie that included the novelist and propagandist for American literature Cornelius Mathews, and there, in the men-only basement, he partook of what passed for "Rabelaisian" companionship around a bountiful punch bowl. Early in 1847 Melville wrote a review of J. Ross Browne's *Etchings of a Whaling Cruise* for the New York *Literary World*, which the multifarious Duyckinck was editing. Just before his marriage that summer Melville wrote a few satiric pieces on the Whig hero of the Mexican War, Zachary Taylor, for *Yankee Doodle*, the comic weekly edited by Mathews with Duyckinck's assistance, one of their several short-lived editorial ventures. (In mid-century Manhattan literary circles an American *Punch* was a much-pursued will-o'-the-wisp.) Slow to adjust his image of Melville, Duyckinck wrote his younger brother George (then making a grand tour of Europe with his college friend William A. Butler) on March 18, 1848:

> By the way Melville reads old Books. He has borrowed Sir Thomas Browne of me and says finely of the speculations of the *Religio Medici* that Browne is a kind of "crack'd Archangel." Was ever any thing of this sort said before by a sailor?

After the revolutions of 1848 George Duyckinck and his companion returned, and the brothers became joint owners and editors of the *Literary World*. Duyckinck needed Melville as his in-basement expert on nautical affairs (his "Bunsby," he patronizingly said) and all-around travel expert, just the former adventurer who could be assigned early in 1849 to review Francis Parkman's new *The California and Oregon Trail*. For the *Literary World* from 1847 through 1850 Melville wrote four reviews besides the now-famous appreciative essay on Hawthorne's *Mosses from an Old Manse* (see below), a book four years old and not an obvious candidate for reviewing. (These were all

5. These details are from Davis (1952), p. 15.

printed anonymously, by custom.) Duyckinck also needed the popular young author Melville so he could review *him* as a prime example of the new democratic literature of "Young America" that he (and especially Mathews) had been more or less stridently calling for. Unquestionably, Melville for a time also needed the literary and general cultural encouragement of Duyckinck, but he began resenting his assigned role as early as November, 1848, when he refused to review Joseph C. Hart's *The Romance of Yachting*, the first of an increasingly difficult set of refusals to supply what Duyckinck wanted from him.

For his third book, *Mardi*, published in New York in March, 1849, two years after *Omoo*, Melville set out to continue his narrative of South Sea adventures, this time in the form of exciting nautical adventures where the hero was plainly a created character, not himself. A few months into the manuscript he was driven from the course of his proposed "sportive sail" by "a blast resistless" (chap. 169). His association with the Duyckinck circle, and his voracious reading (much of it in Duyckinck's books) in ancient and modern literature, and in history, science, and philosophy; later his reflections on contemporary political and social upheavals; his discovery, in short, of what in the chapter just cited he called "the world of mind"—all these brewed in him a ferment of ideas and aspirations that spilled over irrepressibly into the manuscript. The result was a bewildering and astonishing composite in form, substance, and style. Here the rope-yarn was borrowed far less from the books by or on South Sea explorers and missionaries than from such literary and philosophical adventurers as Rabelais, Browne, Burton, Seneca, and Plato. Rather than forging alliances with members of the New York literati he was fastening himself with hoops of steel to more durable associates: "my . . . friend Stanhope," "my old uncle Johnson," "my Right Reverend friend, Bishop Berkeley," "my fine frank friend, poor Mark [Antony]," "my. . . ancestor, Froissart," "my friend and correspondent, Edmund Burke," "my . . . friend Thucydides." In "Dreams" (chap. 119) he celebrated his belated intoxication with great literature:

> Like a grand, ground swell, Homer's old organ rolls its vast volumes under the light frothy wave-crests of Anacreon and Hafiz; and high over my ocean, sweet Shakespeare soars, like all the larks of the spring. Throned on my sea-side, like Canute, bearded Ossian

smites his hoar harp, wreathed with wild-flowers, in which warble my Wallers; blind Milton sings bass to my Petrarchs and Priors, and laureats crown me with bays.

In me, many worthies recline, and converse. I list to St. Paul who argues the doubts of Montaigne; Julian the Apostate cross-questions Augustine; and Thomas-a-Kempis unrolls his old black letters for all to decipher. Zeno murmurs maxims beneath the hoarse shout of Democritus; and though Democritus laugh loud and long, and the sneer of Pyrrho be seen; yet, divine Plato, and Proclus, and Verulam are of my counsel; and Zoroaster whispered me before I was born. I walk a world that is mine; and enter many nations, as Mungo Park rested in African cots; I am served like Bajazet: Bacchus my butler, Virgil my minstrel, Philip Sidney my page. My memory is a life beyond birth; my memory, my library of the Vatican, its alcoves all endless perspectives, eve-tinted by cross-lights from Middle-Age oriels.

The real islands and seas Melville had trodden and cruised past in the Pacific were all but forgotten, and the great bulk of the book was given over to an allegorical voyage through archipelagoes of ideas in quest of a vanished maiden.

If the allegory had any coherent pattern, it was confused by subordinate allegories, and piled heavy with the added cargo of essays, discussions, poems, legends, rhapsodies, episodes satirical of contemporary events in Manhattan and the world at large—the diverse products of sheer exuberant invention. The author's disposition toward social criticism and philosophy, intermittently evidenced in the two earlier books, now had full play in debate, satire, and direct exhortation. The hero and his four companions were mouthpieces through whom Melville projected speculations and opinions that were not so much statements of his own beliefs as headlong explorations of every available subject in this world or the next. The search for the vanished maiden, for some ideal happiness, became a search for truth, on various shifting levels, practical, political, philosophical, religious; and the conclusion of the book, wherein the hero resolved to pursue his quest into eternity, seemed to signify that none of the answers he had explored could satisfy him—that truth still eluded and allured him. The reviewers and the public, even when they grasped the none-too-subtle allegories, were far less interested in Yillah and the hero's quest for her and what she meant than they had been in Fayaway, the fanciful heroine of *Typee*, and in the picaresque characters in *Omoo*.

In the course of writing *Mardi* Melville had caught the vision of becoming a great writer, and taking a great theme in his immature hands, he had tried to write something more than a mere romantic narrative of adventure. He had tried to write, it seems clear, a genuinely Rabelaisian book, a book to stand on a shelf beside Burton's *The Anatomy of Melancholy* and Swift's *Gulliver's Travels*, or perhaps Jean-Paul Richter's *The Titan*, which he later compared to *Mardi*. Toward the end of his long struggle to make a great book of *Mardi*, Melville transparently described the process by which the great Lombardo created his masterwork, his *Koztanza*:

> When Lombardo set about his work, he knew not what it would become. He did not build himself in with plans; he wrote right on; and so doing, got deeper and deeper into himself; and like a resolute traveler, plunging through baffling woods, at last was rewarded for his toils. (chap. 180)

In this chapter Melville lashed out at the New York literati, represented by the judicious advisers to whom Lombardo showed the work: Zenzori "asked him where he picked up so much trash"; Hauto "bade him not be cast down, it was pretty good"; Lucree "desired to know how much he was going to get for it"; Roddi "offered a suggestion"—that he "had best make a faggot of the whole; and try again"; and Pollo took notes on the manuscript all night, then professed to have run through the sheets carelessly: "You might have done better; but then you might have done worse. Take them, my friend; I have put in some good things for you." With good reason did Lombardo despise the critics:

> Critics?—Asses! rather mules!—so emasculated, from vanity, they can not father a true thought. Like mules, too, from dunghills, they trample down gardens of roses: and deem that crushed fragrance their own. . . .Oh! that an eagle should be stabbed by a goose-quill! But at best, the greatest reviewers but prey on my leavings.

Here Melville had declared his literary independence from the New York literati, including the Duyckinck clique, but gaining it was another matter.

Early in 1849, while *Mardi* was in press, Melville took his wife to her father's home in Boston so their baby could be born there. With time suddenly on his hands, he listened to Emerson lecture, and to his surprise found the message not only intelligible but challenging. (Duyckinck so primly reproached him for his enthusiasm that he had to deny oscillating "in Emerson's rainbow.") While in Boston he fell in with a large-type edition of Shakespeare over which he could pore without hurting his sensitive eyes. His immediate delight was boundless as he found that in his present expanded mental state even familiar passages had become more significant, and the long-term consequences for his literary career were momentous.[6] (Despite knowing of Melville's fresh ecstatic reading of Shakespeare, Duyckinck seized him during his brief business trip to New York in early March to write a review of *The Oregon Trail* on the spot, before going back to Boston.) Already growing beyond *Mardi*, Melville wrote Duyckinck on April 5:

> Would that a man could do something & then say—It is finished.—not that one thing only, but all others—that he has reached his uttermost, & can never exceed it. But live & push—tho' we put one leg forward ten miles—its no reason the other must lag behind—no, *that* must again distance the other—& so we go till we get the cramp & die.

Brooding over still more ambitious literary projects, Melville envisioned a summer of thoughtful reading (in which he could go to sleep on the great folios of Pierre Bayle's dictionary he had just purchased, while holding "the Phaedon in one hand & Tom Brown in the other"). But on his return to New York, reality was not long in enforcing itself upon his private fantasies of literary grandeur.

The initial reviewers of *Mardi* were often hostile, and on April 23, 1849, Melville wrote defensively to his father-in-law:

> I see that Mardi has been cut into by the London Atheneum, and also burnt by the common hangman in the Boston Post. However the London Examiner & Literary Gazette; & other papers this side of the water have done differently. These attacks are matters of course, and are essential to the building up of any permanent reputation—if such should ever prove to be mine.

He did not mention the laudatory review in the *Literary World* (April 14 and 21, 1849), presumably by Evert Duyckinck. As a bellwether to later American reviewers of *Mardi* Duyckinck sensed and feared

---

6. So great was his delight that later that year he acquired a matching edition of Milton. See pp. 957–59 below.

the direction Melville's development might take, in its "romantic," reflective, satirical, and generally unorthodox tendencies. His review hailed Melville's growth as a writer and declared that "Mardi is a species of Utopia—or rather a satiric voyage—in which we discover human nature." But then it continued, "There is a world of poetical, thoughtful, ingenious moral writing in it which Emerson would not disclaim—gleams of high-raised fancy, quaint assemblages of facts in the learned spirit of Burton and [Southey's] the Doctor." After Duyckinck's recent agitation, Melville would have realized that the first part of this sentence was not meant as praise: the editor's limited tolerance for such things did not embrace Emerson's "ingenious moral writing" or extend to uncomfortable contemporary applications. Among conveniently opposable literary categories, Duyckinck regularly advocated not fancy but fact, not romance (which was foreign and going out of fashion, he hoped) but realism (which was soundly American, democratic, and on the rise); he disliked anything that savored of the morbid at the expense of the wholesome and the natural; and, as a good active Episcopalian, he bridled at whatever favored airy transcendentalisms or slighted organized Christianity.

Some other reviewers bent backwards to be tolerant toward Melville's strange new book, but the early reception prepared him for the grim news that came later from Richard Bentley, his new British publisher, and the Harpers. In acknowledgment that many reviewers of *Mardi* on both sides of the Atlantic preferred *Typee* to *Omoo*, and *Omoo* to *Mardi*, Melville buckled down to redeem his standing with his family, his publishers, and his reading audience, ready to do his duty as a literary craftsman just as if literary artists had no special exemptions from ordinary responsibility.

In a period of four months, toiling in New York City through the heat—and a cholera epidemic—of the summer, Melville pushed through to completion (a phrase like "dashed off" would minimize the labor) *Redburn* (a book about the size of *Omoo*) and *White-Jacket* (a book still longer), both designed for popularity. In the first, having cast about for unused segments of his experience which he could work up speedily and, perhaps he thought, painlessly, he seized on his voyage to Liverpool. Inventing a self-pitying boy (much younger than he had been in 1839) as the hero, and making the narrator that same character, older, sentimental, and sententious in the manner of Irving's bachelors, he appropriated family paraphernalia as well as his impoverished family condition in the late 1830's, and he filled out his description of Liverpool with borrowings from one main source-book, *The Picture of Liverpool; or Stranger's Guide*, and scrounged from a few lesser sources such as the *Penny Cyclopædia*. Melville in a period of rapid unfolding within himself could hardly have done something more dangerous than to disturb childhood memories, and by a little over two years later, in *Pierre* (bk. 21.i), he understood the consequences of *Redburn* well enough to note a temporary stage in his young hero's interior development: "Not yet had he dropped his angle into the well of his childhood, to find what fish might be there; for who dreams to find fish in a well?" In May and June of 1849 the plan worked, however, and the book was finished and accepted by the Harpers and by Bentley.

*White-Jacket* was also conceived as an easy book to write fast, and so it proved, although "easy" is relative: easier than *Mardi*, since it stirred up no frenzy of literary ambition; easier than *Redburn*, perhaps, since it loosely followed his passage home from the Pacific in the frigate *United States* and described life in a man-of-war in such a way that he could plunder a number of nautical source-books and the *Penny Cyclopædia* at his convenience rather than having to squeeze a single major source like *The Picture of Liverpool* for more than it could readily yield. Sure of himself, with one new manuscript triumphantly behind him already, in *White-Jacket* Melville often wrote prose not measurably inferior to many passages in *Moby-Dick*.

Both products of that summer's hard work testified to Melville's practical self-control, *Redburn* in the containment of dangerous self-pity and rage at memories of his victimized youth, *White-Jacket* in the containment of his fury at his prolonged vulnerability in a socially-sanctioned but sadistic institution. Each book, as Melville intended, presented a surface apparently unruffled by the intellectual, psychological, and literary turmoil that had surged up in *Mardi*. In both, Melville's critical temper found safe expression in attacks on social injustices: in *Redburn* the Liverpool slums and the plight of immigrants herded into filthy steerage quarters; in *White-Jacket* flogging and official brutality in the world of a man-of-war. In both books what he had witnessed of man's inhumanity to man moved him to aggressive protest, and in both he appealed from the way of the world to the ethics of the Sermon on the Mount. In each case the young author spoke for the oppressed, but he pitched his passages of

reformist rhetoric so as to persuade, not to offend, conservative readers such as Duyckinck; in the era of crusading reform, he had righ-
teously enlisted his pen in popular causes in the name of humanity,
democracy, and Christianity.

Through the spring of 1849, however, and long afterwards, Melville was defensive about *Mardi* and secretly hopeful that sooner or
later it would be recognized as a great book. "Time," (he said on
April 23, 1849) would "solve" *Mardi*, and on February 2, 1850, he
suggested two possibilities: it might "flower like the aloe, a hundred
years hence—or not flower at all, which is more likely by far, for
some aloes never flower." In a June 5, 1849, letter announcing the
realistic nature of *Redburn* ("no metaphysics, no conic-sections, nothing but cakes & ale") Melville excused himself to Bentley (with no
apparent sense that he was writing to a man who would lose money
on *Mardi*):

> You may think, in your own mind that a man is unwise,—indis-
> creet, to write a work of that kind, when he might have written one
> perhaps, calculated merely to please the general reader, & not provoke
> attack, however masqued in an affectation of indifference or contempt.
> But some of us scribblers, My Dear Sir, always have a certain some-
> thing unmanageable in us, that bids us do this or that, and be done it
> must—hit or miss.

This lurking impulse to behave recklessly broke out only once in the
manuscript of *Redburn*. Reviewing it in the *Literary World* on November 17, 1849, Duyckinck put his finger on that episode: "we are introduced to a fancy young gentleman who gets up with Redburn a hurried, romantic night visit to London, which is enveloped in the glare
of a splendid gambling establishment. The parties, however, soon
get back to duty, and find nothing whatever lurid or romantic in the
discipline under Captain Riga." In *White-Jacket* there was no such
recklessness, and for it in his review (March 16, 1850) Duyckinck had
no such reproach.

At another time—say, 1848—Melville's success in controlling his
reckless impulses might have been more lavishly rewarded. But on
June 5, 1849, the day that Melville described *Redburn* to Bentley, Sir
Frederick Pollock ruled in the case of *Boosey* v. *Purday* that no for-
eigner could gain a copyright in Great Britain by publishing a work
there before publishing it elsewhere: Melville's regular strategy for

gaining a British copyright had no standing. Bentley's magnanimous impulse was not to let Pollock's decision interfere with his "course of business," as he wrote James Fenimore Cooper on June 20, 1849; the failure of *Mardi* complicated his generous impulses, but on the same day he offered a hundred pounds for *Redburn*, on the basis of Melville's assurances about it. Keenly aware that he was risking attack "from any unprincipled persons who may choose to turn Pirate," and week by week ever more conscious that the initial sales of *Mardi* to admirers of Melville's first books had all but ceased once the reading public learned what it was like, Bentley grew more cautious. We do not possess a letter from Melville offering him *White-Jacket*, nor do we possess a letter from Bentley declining to purchase it. Just possibly such an exchange of letters took place before Melville made the momentous decision to go to London to negotiate a contract in person, with the hope of succeeding so well that he could then embark on eleven additional months of travel—not so much a vacation, presumably, as a source of experiences to be put into new literary works. He sailed on October 11, 1849, carrying a set of the Harper proof-sheets of *White-Jacket*.

Toward both hastily written books Melville at times took a detached attitude. While making his last preparations for the trip, on October 6, he wrote to his father-in-law:

> They are two *jobs*, which I have done for money—being forced to it, as other men are to sawing wood. And while I have felt obliged to refrain from writing the kind of book I would wish to; yet, in writing these two books, I have not repressed myself much—so far as *they* are concerned; but have spoken pretty much as I feel.—Being books, then, written in this way, my only desire for their "success" (as it is called) springs from my pocket, & not from my heart. So far as I am individually concerned, & independent of my pocket, it is my earnest desire to write those sort of books which are said to "fail."

On the same day, Melville wrote to thank Richard Henry Dana, Jr., for sending him a letter of introduction to Edward Moxon, who had published *Two Years Before the Mast* in London, possibly an indication that he expected to have to hunt for a publisher. Dana had taken the liberty of suggesting a literary topic: "Your hint concerning a man-of-war has, in anticipation, been acted on. A printed copy of the book is before me." Assuming that *White-Jacket* would be published while he was abroad, he diffidently suggested that Dana might defend at least its accuracy if it were "taken hold of in an unfair or ignorant way." In a postscript he made it clear that the second book of the summer ranked higher in his regard than the first: "A little nursery tale of mine (which, possibly, you may have seen advertised as in press) called 'Redburn' is not the book to which I refer above." As far as we know, Melville never spoke as contemptuously of *White-Jacket* as he did of *Redburn* in a letter to Duyckinck from London on December 14, 1849, explaining that Bentley's copies of the *Literary World* had been forwarded to the publisher in Brighton:

> so I did not see your say about the book Redburn, which to my surprise (somewhat) seems to have been favorably received. I am glad of it—for it puts money into an empty purse. But I hope I shall never write such a book again—Tho' when a poor devil writes with duns all round him, & looking over the back of his chair—& perching on his pen & diving in his inkstand—like the devils about St: Anthony—what can you expect of that poor devil?—What but a beggarly "Redburn!" And when he attempts anything higher—God help him & save him!

In his journal Melville had been equally contemptuous of *Redburn* as a book he wrote "to buy some tobacco with."

Although the voyage was probably not conceived as a therapeutic reward for a summer of forced labor, Melville's overconfidence began to burgeon once he got to sea. A friend of Duyckinck's was aboard, George Adler, a scholar of German philosophy and literature, a sort of adjunct professor of modern languages at New York University. Melville wrote in his journal that Adler was "full of the German metaphysics, & discourses of Kant, Swedenborg &c." Also aboard as ship's doctor was Frank Taylor, a former travel companion of his cousin Bayard Taylor, the young travel writer whom Melville had already met and whom he identified in the journal as "the pedestrian traveller." With Adler he had long talks on "Fixed Fate, Freewill, fore-knowledge absolute"—Milton's list of topics debated by the fallen angels, and Melville's favorite way of indicating the scope of any serious philosophical discussion he engaged in as well as his awareness of what opinion conventional society held of anyone willing to debate such topics. His journal entries show him as the novice learning from the professor (who happened to be two years his junior), making sure he gets philosophical niceties clearly in mind and clearly recorded; they also show him as what he called himself a few weeks later, a "pondering man." The consequences for *Moby-Dick* of these talks with Adler are hard either to define or to overestimate.

The early talks with Taylor were also momentous, particularly one (reported with characteristic misspellings) on October 15:

> This afternoon Dr Taylor & I sketched a plan for going down the Danube from Vienna to Constantinople; thence to Athens in the steamer; to Beyroot & Jerusalem—Alexandia & the Pyramids. From what I learn, I have no doubt this can be done at a comparitivly trifling expence. Taylor has had a good deal of experience in cheap European travel, & from his knowledge of German is well fitted for a travelling companion thro Austria & Turkey. I am full (just now) of this glorious *Eastern* jaunt. Think of it!—Jerusalem & the Pyramids—Constantinople, the Egean, & old Athens!

Adler was included in some of these travel plans, which shifted as bouts of " 'sober second thoughts' " gave way to revived enthusiasm. Melville could make no decision, he knew, until he found what price, if any, he could get for *White-Jacket*, but his longing to make the "grand Oriental & Spanish tour" (as one plan had it) was intense. Melville rarely put himself on record as wanting anything so much as he wanted this prolonged trip to eastern Europe, the Holy Land, and the entire Mediterranean region. He was careful to note that he was homesick for his wife and son, but he was wild to have his *Wanderjahr*.

Once in London, he had to stifle his hopes. On November 12 Bentley gave him his hundred pounds at sixty days for *Redburn* (although he had lost money on *Mardi*), and despite "the vexatious & uncertain state of the Copyright matter" the publisher made a generous offer for *White-Jacket*, two hundred pounds for the first thousand copies, but no advance. Needing an advance, Melville for several days made a fruitless canvass of publishers (John Murray, the man who still kept *Typee* and *Omoo* in print, then Colbourn, Longmans, Chapman, Bohn).⁷ "No go," his terse notation about the results of

7. Melville's ordeal prompted a newspaper brouhaha in the next months, after a correspondent of the *Times* in London (January 19, 1850) asked how it happened that Melville "wearily hawked this book from Piccadilly to Whitechapel, calling upon every publisher in his way, and could find no one rash enough to buy his 'protected right.' " The *Times* on January 25 printed Bentley's assurance that he had in fact bought what he "firmly" believed to "be the copyright, for a considerable sum." On

his calls on publishers, in effect became the epitaph for the trip with Taylor and Adler. On November 17, Melville had to renounce the larger trip: "Bad news enough—I shall not see Rome—I'm floored." On December 17 he and Bentley came to terms on *White-Jacket*, and the publisher gave him a promissory note at six months for two hundred pounds after Melville promised to reimburse him for any losses through piracy. This provision in the contract, proof of the publisher's magnanimity as much as of his caution, would at least allow Bentley to deduct such losses if he were to publish a subsequent book by Melville.

Melville had requested his father-in-law to ask Emerson for a letter of introduction to Carlyle, but he apparently had no such letter and did not try to call on him, and he did not meet Dickens, Thackeray, or Tennyson. He was much alone, and happy so—by day "victoriously" running "that painted gauntlet of the gods" in the art galleries (*Pierre*, bk. 26.i) and by day and by night striding the streets of London in quest of historical and literary sites and shrines (and also in quest of the perfect snuggery, the darker the better, best of all if there was a cozy inglenook where he could smoke while he drank). At the end of November and through early December he made a two-week side-trip to Paris, Belgium, and the Rhine. All in all, he was an elusive man to get to with an invitation, yet he found himself, surely to his gratified surprise, taken up by the most eminent American bookman of the century, Henry Stevens (who gave him a guided tour of "the library of the British Museum"), and received into very high English literary and artistic circles (which as always overlapped with commercial and political circles). The banker-poet and art collector Samuel Rogers twice had him to breakfast at his home in St. James's Place, where Melville saw displayed on the high walls many admirable and some very great works of art (including Turners in oil, watercolor, and pencil). (In "Sources" see Wallace, 1985.) Murray and Bentley were both hospitable, and dinners at Elm Court in the Temple (December 19) and at the Erechtheum Club, St. James's Square (December 22) were particularly memorable. "The Paradise of Batchelors," he noted of the first, and he had "a glorious time" at the

---

February 23 and March 2 Duyckinck gave this correspondence play in the *Literary World*, grim reminder to Melville of a miserable few days and of the fact that he was not in Vienna or Venice but in frigid New York.

second. Declining an invitation to spend Christmas with the painter Charles R. Leslie and a brother-in-law of Leslie, Samuel Stone, declining the Duke of Rutland's invitation to visit him at Belvoir Castle in January (although miserably aware of the opportunity he was forgoing), he started home. On June 27, 1850, he wrote Bentley that he had had "a prosperous passage across the water last winter; & embarking from Portsmouth on Christmas morning, carried the savor of the plumb-puddings & roast turkey all the way across the Atlantic."

He also carried many choice books, among them several folios of Elizabethan and Restoration writers, guidebooks, and an assortment of more recent books including "Ro[u]sseau Confessions," "Castle of Otranto," "Anastasius," "Calleb Williams," "Vathek," "Corinne," "Frankenstein," "Autobiography of Goethe," and "Confessions of an Opium Eater."[8] Having abandoned journal-keeping, he nevertheless made a few notes during the voyage, mainly about sailor-talk with the captain and about his reading in De Quincey, Sir Thomas Browne, Ben Jonson, and others; one note read "Indian (Gay-Head) Sweetheart flogged." He carried the thought of at least one literary project he had researched in London, the retelling of the story of Israel Potter. He had bought an old map of London on December 18, noting: "I want to use it in case I serve up the Revolutionary narrative of the beggar." The phrasing "serve up" suggests that Melville was thinking of doing another book to buy food and tobacco with, not another ambitious book like *Mardi*. Something happened, in London, on the ship, or soon after he returned; perhaps the voyage itself and his reading during it stirred his desire to outdo himself; perhaps his reflections on all he had seen and done whipped him into a new ambition; perhaps he simply felt he had been so good a husband, living cheaply, selling *White-Jacket* against all odds, renouncing his tour, that he deserved to write a book he wanted to write. Along with the savor of memories of what he had seen and done, he must have experienced irrepressible curiosity about what he might have seen and done. That "certain day in January" (after which he might any day have driven up to a cordial welcome at Belvoir Castle) can hardly

8. In the middle of December, in London, Melville was reading for the first time Laurence Sterne's *Tristram Shandy*; then he devoured that "most wondrous book," Thomas De Quincey's *Confessions of an English Opium Eater*, on December 22–23.

have passed on shipboard without a twinge for his renunciation of a chance of a lifetime. Small wonder that in the whaling book he wrote next he would treat domestic felicity ("the wife, the heart, the bed, the table, the saddle, the fire-side, the country") as irreconcilable with the life of "the intellect or the fancy," and preferable to it—but only if what one wanted was "attainable felicity" (chap. 94); small wonder that he contrasted the domestic values of the port ("safety, comfort, hearthstone, supper, warm blankets, friends, all that's kind to our mortalities") with landlessness where "alone resides the highest truth, shoreless, indefinite as God" (chap. 23).

On February 1, 1850, Melville disembarked and took up his life on Fourth Avenue, beginning work, before long, on what became *Moby-Dick*. (See Section III.) The household now consisted of the brothers and their wives, their mother and four sisters, Herman's son Malcolm (born February 16, 1849) and Allan's daughter Maria (born two days later). There was news. Sophia was pregnant again, so the family may have begun to think about making some change in living arrangements. And in the literary cliques of Manhattan, if all hell had not broken loose in Melville's absence, at least the petty local equivalent of the grand Miltonic outbreak had taken place. The English literary man Thomas Powell, fleeing charges of forgery, had arrived in New York the previous spring and had immediately charmed Duyckinck and his circle, including Melville, with his arsenal of anecdotes of British writers, as well as a gift to Duyckinck of a copy of Tennyson's poems purportedly containing a few trifling revisions in the poet's hand.[9] Duyckinck soon was paying for the stories and the gift, for Powell began asking for one small loan after another, invari-

9. Thomas Powell is not mentioned in Perry Miller's gamesome account of the Lewis Gaylord Clark / Duyckinck feuding, *The Raven and the Whale* (1956), although he ought to have been the marplot of a lurid climactic chapter or two. The account that follows is summarized from Hershel Parker's forthcoming *Herman Melville and the Powell Papers*, a study which Vera Brodsky Lawrence touched off by discovering and sending to G. Thomas Tanselle an anonymous essay on Melville in the New York *Figaro* which Parker recognized as being by Powell. Her *Resonances, 1836–1850* (New York: Oxford University Press, 1988), the first volume of *Strong on Music: The New York Music Scene in the Days of George Templeton Strong, 1836–1875*, features a throng of characters, some of whom overlap with the literary world of which Melville was a part. Parker's forthcoming book in effect continues Sidney P. Moss's *Poe's Major Crisis: His Libel Suit and New York's Literary World*, with a greatly overlapping cast of characters.

ably promising to repay each one promptly. Powell had given Melville sound parting advice to ask the price of anything alcoholic
before drinking it and had assured him that in England "he would
find no low press or publisher to abuse him, & no respectable persons
to believe them if they did"—a reference to Powell's arrest in New
York in September, an embarrassment he had lied himself out of. In
November a scandal had erupted over two parts of Powell's hastily
written *Living Authors of England.* The Transcendentalist George Ripley in Horace Greeley's *Tribune* (November 16) denounced Powell
for a casual slur against Washington Irving as " 'an agreeable essayist,
and a very successful imitator of the level style of Addison and
Pope,' " and for Powell's "outrageous calumny" of declaring Irving's new life of Goldsmith to be " 'so glaring an instance of unscrupulous appropriation of the labor of another, that it is utterly impossible to avoid arraigning the offender.' " To speak disparagingly of
Irving's manner of utilizing the work of other writers was simply not
acceptable behavior. Worse, the pre-publication printing of part of
the chapter on Charles Dickens in the New York *Evening Post* reached
the novelist, who fired off to his acquaintance Lewis Gaylord Clark,
the inveterate enemy of the Duyckinck-Mathews clique, a letter exposing Powell. Too impetuous to wait for the next issue of his *Knickerbocker,* Clark got Dickens's letter into the *Tribune* on November 20,
under the heading "A Scoundrel Branded." Powell brazened the situation out, even having one or two editors arrested for reprinting the
Dickens letter, while numerous enemies of Duyckinck and Mathews,
always on the ready, lambasted them as the Mutual Admiration Society. (Powell, in a part of the Dickens chapter the *Post* had not printed,
had compared Dickens and Mathews at length, not to Dickens's
favor.) In London, Dickens panicked, fearing a lawsuit for libel, and
hastily gathered affidavits and other proofs of his charges; there Melville got the news from Allan and went off to the Edinburgh Castle to
wash down the " 'Powell Papers,' " and later Henry Stevens told him
that "certain persons had called upon him denouncing Powell as a
rogue."

Duyckinck distanced himself from Powell, despite Powell's brazen flow of begging letters, and Powell took his revenge in an even
hastier book on *Living Authors of America.* In the chapter on Poe he
attacked Irving and Melville as two of the worst enemies of the
American mind:

It is a curious fact that the worst enemies of the national mind have been a few of her own sons. These are authors who till lately have entirely enjoyed the monopoly of the English market; now they will be obliged to join the body of native authors, and hurry to the rescue. So long as they could trespass on the mistaken courtesy of the British publishers, and get four thousand guineas for this Life of Columbus, and two hundred guineas for that Typee, there was no occasion for any interference; in fact, they were materially benefited by this crying injustice to the great body of authors. Now their own rights are in jeopardy, and they must join the ranks of International Copyright.

Nathaniel Parker Willis, about the time this appeared, unwittingly gave Powell more ammunition by a piece in the *Home Journal* on January 12, 1850, "Light Touchings" on the topic of international copyright:

—Our friend Herman Melville is one of the first and most signal realizers of the effect of the recent English repudiation of copyright. . . . Melville went abroad, about the time that this retaliatory system came first into action—but knowing nothing of it, and relying on the proceeds of the English editions of his books, for the means of prolonged travel. He writes us that he has abandoned his more extended plans, with this disappointment, and will return sooner than he expected.

With this he printed a portion of the letter of December 14, in which Melville doubts that "Gabriel enters the portals of Heaven without a fee to Peter the porter—so impossible is it to travel without money." Perhaps it was a mistake for Melville to write so incautiously to a newspaper editor, but this wonderful fragment is known only because Willis printed it. The short-term consequences were that Powell seized these "Light Touchings" and plotted a sufficiently malign distortion of them.

"Poor fellow—poor devel—poor Powell!" Melville had noted pityingly in his journal in mid-December. Now he stepped ashore to find Powell's slurring reference to him reprinted in the February 2, 1850, *Literary World*, headed facetiously: "ENEMIES OF THE NATIONAL MIND / (A dead lift for the copyright question.)"—Duyckinck having decided that the way to reestablish his credibility was to laugh Powell off. Powell was not finished. The egregious New York *Herald* on February 6 printed a very long article, unsigned but by Powell, which laid out specific charges of plagiarism against Irving and took incidental slaps at "the flippant, kaleidescope, polka-dancing Melville," who had hitherto "been enabled to line his pockets pretty substantially by the revenues accruing from his English editions."

> Mr. Melville started, we are told, some time ago, for England, with the early proof sheets of his last book, intending, on the avails of it, to make the fashionable tour over the continent, and luxuriate in the capitals of Europe, upon the fruit of his labors. The revulsion came on. He was coolly informed, by his former London publisher, that he could pay no more copyrights; and the aforesaid intellect quits the great metropolis in despair, with empty pockets, and turns his face once more towards his native land.

By this time, apparently, the New York literati of all camps had decided that the way to contain Powell was to ignore him, and his grosser attacks on Irving and Melville ceased, as far as we know.

There is no evidence as to how Melville responded to this inhospitable reception or to what followed—a period of unseemly sniping between Duyckinck in the *Literary World* and Nathaniel Parker Willis in the *Home Journal*. Duyckinck on March 23 condemned Willis's sketches as "occasionally disfigured by gross and inexcusable personality"; then Willis attacked the *Literary World* of March 23 as a "*journal of disappointed authors who have turned booksellers' hacks*" and fleered at "the Duyckin[c]k-dom of Envy," the "kingdom of those who die of envy." In the May *Knickerbocker* Clark scathingly reviewed Mathews's *The Adventures of Mr. Moneypenny*, treating Duyckinck as Mathews's "*Fidus Achates*," not the other way around, as modern literary historians usually see the pair. Gleefully quoting Willis's scornful description of the *Literary World*, Clark concluded piously, "These 'be cruel words!' " Nor do we know how Melville responded to newspaper coverage of the massively-built actor Edwin Forrest's attack on the frail dandy Willis in Washington Square on June 17 or to coverage of Willis's denials that he had committed adultery with Mrs. Forrest. These are only a sample of the lurid controversies involving the New York literati of which Melville had become a part. In London he had recognized that Allan and others would account him "a ninny" for not staying on to accept the Duke of Rutland's invitation, and that he would later "upbraid" himself "for neglecting such an opportunity of procuring '*material.*' " Now he must have felt he had returned, all too precipitously, to a discarded fragment of *Mardi*, a strange island teeming with hysterical pygmies.

The one saving grace in all the petty vituperation raging around (and emanating from) Duyckinck and Mathews in the newspapers and magazines is that their opponents (not all of whom have been named here) never, to our knowledge, attacked Melville personally because of his association with the *Literary World* clique and never reviewed one of his books hostilely because of that association. The proof lies in the reviews of *Redburn* in November and December, 1849, and of *White-Jacket* in March and April, 1850, the most opportune time for dragging down any associate of Duyckinck or Mathews or their " 'you-tickle-me-and-I'll-tickle-you-school' " (the sardonic insult in a November 24, 1849, article on the Powell affair in the New York *Metropolis*).[10]

All this is tenuous, but enough to suggest that during the spring of 1850, as he progressed on his whaling book, Melville had more and more reason to want to escape from Zenzori, Hauto, Lucree, Roddi, and Pollo. Yet after he went to vacation at the Melvill farm near Pittsfield that summer, he invited Duyckinck and Mathews to join him for a few days in early August. His motivations for inviting them are obscure. Certainly he felt a desire to play the host to Duyckinck in a grand fashion, as he could do on the Melvill farm, but he may also simply have felt sorry for their being trapped in the city while he had been rambling over the familiar terrain with his cousin Robert. Neither New Yorker had been to the Berkshires before. Once there Duyckinck guiltily wrote ecstatic descriptions of the air and scenery to his wife,[11] and the overtaxed Mathews was pathetical-

10. This is from a stray issue (at the New-York Historical Society) of a brilliantly edited newspaper never before used by Melville scholars and apparently not extant in any file substantial enough to have been reported—perfect evidence of how much scholars are at the mercy of what documents happen to have survived and to have been discovered.

11. He also wrote her the best description of the Melvill place: "The house where we live, Melville's is a rare place—an old family mansion, wainscoted and stately, with large halls & chimneys—quite a piece of mouldering rural grandeur—The family has gone down & this is their last season. The farm has been sold." He added: "Herman Melville knows every stone & tree & will probably make a book of its features." This is presumably something Melville said, not merely a fantasy of Duyckinck's. We know from Melville's letter to Duyckinck on December 13 (see Section III) that in the fall, while waiting to get back to work on his manuscript and

ly grateful for the bucolic respite. Inviting them was a generous thing for Melville to do.

To Melville himself the region was incalculably important, and it became incalculably important to *Moby-Dick*. Melville dedicated *Pierre* (1852) to Mount Greylock in gratitude for "his most bounteous and unstinted fertilizations." He might have done the same with the whaling book if he had not met a worthy human dedicatee there. During his first visit back as a married man, alone, his cousin Priscilla commented (April 3, 1848) on his manifesting "so much constancy toward the object of his *first love*, our *Berkshire* farm—as to *tear* himself from the idol of his heart to indulge again in the unfetter'd freedom of Batchelor ways." On that occasion the weather forbade any unfettered wandering, but the report that he and his wife passed their vacation there in the summer of 1848 may be true. Priscilla had a room in the village then, while Robert was trying to make the farm pay as a summer boarding house for a select clientele, the Berkshires having become fashionable as a summering place for artistic people such as the actress Fanny Kemble Butler. Among Robert's paying guests in 1848 were Henry Wadsworth Longfellow and his family. Oliver Wendell Holmes (who as a young whippersnapper had immortalized the Melvill-Melville cousins' grandfather and himself at the same time by writing "The Last Leaf") had a summer house nearby. In the early summer of 1850 Nathaniel Hawthorne and his wife Sophia and their two children had moved into a red cottage in Lenox overlooking the Stockbridge Bowl, and various other writers were in the neighborhood. A series of coincidental visits turned the Berkshires into something like a literary center for the first week of August, when New York and Boston luminaries met in the much-described Monument Mountain picnic of August 5, 1850. There Melville and Hawthorne were introduced to each other, in a company which included Duyckinck, Mathews, Holmes, Hawthorne's publisher James T. Fields, and the historian J. T. Headley. At Dudley Field's three-hour dinner after the picnic the Young America nationalists of New York and their skeptical Boston opponents collided, with Melville and Holmes as the respective champions. Field's Stock-

---

after getting back to work on it, he had thought of many literary projects. That he even spoke of writing a book about the farm suggests that Henry S. Salt (see Section VIII) was more right than one might think in wanting to include Melville in a book called *The Return to Nature*.

bridge house was not Elm Court or the Erechtheum Club, but it wasn't bad, and it afforded Melville a chance to drink and talk with literary men while his wife and son were safe, only a few miles away. Hawthorne, just turned forty-six, was still darkly handsome (Mathews called him "Mr. Noble Melancholy"). As a connoisseur of manly beauty from his sailing and island-hopping years and now almost frantic to validate his exalted new self-estimate by identifying another American fellow writer as comparably great, Melville beyond any doubt decided Hawthorne was the most fascinating American he had ever met.[12]

Melville's widowed aunt Mary, who had returned from Galena with some of the children to be with Robert, had thoughtfully given him a copy of *Mosses from an Old Manse* on July 18, knowing that Hawthorne was in the neighborhood. It seems that Melville did not read the book immediately, but two mornings after he met Hawthorne he apparently had time to dip into it. Duyckinck for years had promoted Hawthorne's reputation as assiduously as he had promoted Melville's, and he postponed his return to New York on the ninth because Melville had elected to spend the rainy morning writing an essay—nominally on the book his aunt had given him.[13] By his superficial praise of several of the pieces in *Mosses* Melville revealed that

---

12. That Melville had long needed male literary soul mates is clear from the depiction of Nord in *White-Jacket* (chap. 13). (Oliver Russ, on whom Nord was based, wrote Melville in 1859 that he had named a son Herman Melville Russ before Melville had become famous; and Melville's nonliterary companion in Nuku Hiva, Toby Greene, did the same. N. P. Willis plainly felt the same winning charm in Melville's personality. Dazzled by Gansevoort, the family tended to take Herman's character for granted.) In his May 1, 1850, letter he had cast Dana into the role of soul mate in recalling the "sort of Siamese link of affectionate sympathy" he had felt reading *Two Years Before the Mast* after his voyage to Liverpool in 1839. He even fantasized about Dana as the ideal audience of one (if only he did not need to get money for his books): "I almost think, I should hereafter—in the case of a sea book—get my M. S. S. neatly & legibly copied by a scrivener—send you that one copy—& deem such a procedure the best publication." This passage strikingly presages the rhapsodic language in his letter to Hawthorne on November 17, 1851: "I feel that the Godhead is broken up like the bread at the Supper, and that we are the pieces. Hence this infinite fraternity of feeling." (The comment about a scrivener may be merely part of the fantasy of what Melville would do if he had endless money, rather than an oblique slight at his actual copyists.)

13. As a result of Parker's work with recently acquired New York Public Library documents for the July–August, 1850, section of *The New Melville Log*, the dating is

he had started the essay without having read much of the book. He did not need to have read much of it, since he was writing about Shakespeare and himself and Hawthorne the man as much as he was writing about the book, and he surely had not read all of the pieces even when he finished the essay on the tenth. In the previous months, Melville had apparently been reading not only Shakespeare but some criticism, probably in the form of editorial introductions to Shakespeare, and was bursting to articulate a problem he had been considering as he worked on his "whaling voyage": how an American could write a democratic tragedy of Shakespearean heft without slavishly imitating archaic literary forms. Into the essay he poured out his aroused literary aspirations along with his delight upon discovering in *Mosses from an Old Manse* (and in its author) some of the repressed dark truths that were stirring in his own mind and that he had recently discerned "craftily" said or "insinuated" in Shakespeare's plays:

> For in this world of lies, Truth is forced to fly like a scared white doe in the woodlands; and only by cunning glimpses will she reveal herself, as in Shakespeare and other masters of the great Art of Telling the Truth,—even though it be covertly, and by snatches.

Hawthorne he found to be such a truth-teller, not greater than Shakespeare, or as great, though "the difference between the two men is by no means immeasurable," and though Shakespeare would yet be surpassed by an American. In his peroration for the part he wrote on the ninth (three-quarters of the final essay), Melville called upon his countrymen to join him in patriotically bestowing a "shock of recognition" upon America's native authors, and specifically Hawthorne, a living example of the American literary genius for whom Young America had been calling.[14]

In first writing the essay, Melville fictionalized his situation and declared he had never met Hawthorne, but he expressed the impact Hawthorne's book had had on him, and not until Elizabeth had cop-

---

offered here with more assurance than the same dating in the Northwestern-Newberry edition of THE PIAZZA TALES and Other Prose Pieces, 1839–1860, p. 655.

14. See p. 861, the discussion at 165.37–38, for correction of the common misinterpretation of "shock of recognition." Writing this much of the essay left Melville in a manic mood of aroused ambition and precipitous intimacy: first he kidnaped William Allen Butler's bride off a railway car (to her he was a bearded stranger, though one known to her husband), then hours later dressed as a Turk (turbaned, with a scimitar?) for the night's costume party (*not*, as Leon Howard thought, as a waiter!).

ied the draft for him did he ascribe the essay to "a Virginian spending July in Vermont" and adapt a few passages, in one replacing the word "me" with "the hot soil of my Southern soul":

> To what infinite height of loving wonder and admiration I may yet be borne, when by repeatedly banquetting on these Mosses, I shall have thoroughly incorporated their whole stuff into my being,—that, I can not tell. But already I feel that this Hawthorne has dropped germinous seeds into my soul. He expands and deepens down, the more I con-template him; and further and further, shoots his strong New-England roots into the hot soil of my Southern soul.

Such florid romantic rhetoric was not uncommon in reviews, and Duyckinck saw nothing in this language that required excision by his cautious editorial pen, although he did feel free to delete the names of American writers Melville had cited approvingly and to tone down some of Melville's extravagant literary nationalism.[15] Duyckinck was well pleased by the essay's praise of Hawthorne, and in particular by its promotion of *Mosses*, a book he had in 1845–46 solicited and pub-lished in the Library of American Books. At least one admirer of Hawthorne congratulated Duyckinck for publishing the essay and asked the name of the writer, and Longfellow took the practical step of sending it to Hawthorne to be sure he saw it.

The powerful impact on him of Hawthorne as man and writer may have affected Melville's apparently sudden decision to move to the Berkshires, though he must have known that the Hawthornes were merely renting the cottage and not planning to stay there indefi-nitely. The family farm had been sold, although the Melvills did not vacate it for several months; the selling price of $6,500 put it far out of Melville's range, even if he had known it was for sale before John Morewood bought it. In September, with a loan from his father-in-law, he bought an adjoining farm. Before he moved in he talked to the Hawthornes of building a new house on the property, one with a

15. The comment on Irving as "that graceful writer" who "owes his chief reputa-tion to the self-acknowledged imitation of a foreign model, and to the studied avoid-ance of all topics but smooth ones," although respectful, distressed Irving when the *Literary World* of August 24 reached Sunnyside, for the words seemed a delayed volley from the relentless attack by Thomas Powell. (The phrase "self-acknowl-edged" still rankled in Pierre M. Irving's mind years later as he prepared an outline [in the Berg Collection of the New York Public Library] from his now-lost diaries for his bland account of the episode in his biography of his uncle.)

writing-tower (Hawthorne built one later on his Concord house), so confident was he of the success of the whaling book he had given Duyckinck to understand in August was by now "mostly done." He already knew that one thing he had in common with Hawthorne was the need to reconcile family duties with the sacredness of a writing routine, and his admiration of the Hawthornes as "the loveliest family he ever met with, or anyone can possibly imagine" (as his sister Augusta quoted him on January 24, 1851) had much to do with his seeing how Sophia subordinated everything else to the needs of her husband, whom she quite literally worshiped. Early in September, 1850, while he was visiting the Hawthornes at Lenox, Sophia joined him "upon the Verandah of Chateau Brun in the golden light of evening twilight, when the lake was like glass of a rose tint," and in that idyllic setting he expressed himself freely:

> He said Mr Hawthorne was the first person whose physical being appeared to him wholly in harmony with the intellectual & spiritual. He said the sunny haze & the pensiveness, the symmetry of his face, the depth of eyes, "the gleam—the shadow—& the peace supreme" all were in exact response to the high calm intellect, the glowing, deep heart—the purity of actual & spiritual life.

Decades later Melville was able in *Clarel* (1876) to portray the homoerotic cast of feelings agitating his title character toward another character, Vine, who bears close resemblances to Hawthorne.[16] These feelings are very much like those that appear to have suffused Melville during his early meetings with Hawthorne, when he wrote and spoke impulsively, not inhibited by overmuch self-knowledge.

In the fall of 1850 and the first months of 1851 Melville's deepest feelings seem to have been engaged not with his family but with his manuscript and with the occasional meetings when he and Hawthorne companionably smoked cigars, drank brandy, and talked (at least Melville talked) "ontological heroics" (Melville's phrase from his letter to Hawthorne on June 29, 1851). Through the early months of 1851, Melville's literary ambitions were further stimulated by Hawthorne's success in the American literary marketplace, a success confirmed for him by *The House of the Seven Gables*. On April 16,

---

16. Walter E. Bezanson in the Hendricks House edition of *Clarel* (1960) made the case for Vine's being based on Hawthorne; Parker (1986) first argued for a comic reading of the characters' climactic encounter.

apparently, he sent Hawthorne a private criticism of the book, written for what he called the Pittsfield *Secret Review*. There he affirmed the value Hawthorne had for him simply by being a fine writer who was also an American and a neighbor: the book had "bred great exhilaration and exultation with the remembrance that the architect of the Gables resides only six miles off, and not three thousand miles away, in England, say." With Hawthorne only six miles off, Melville could stay reconciled to his having cut short his acquaintance with British writers and other good fellows a year and a half before, and in his present mood it was no hardship to have to do most of the talking when he was with his friend. Sophia Hawthorne in a letter to her sister, Elizabeth Peabody, on May 7, 1851, described Melville as speaking to Hawthorne "his innermost about GOD, the Devil & Life if so be he can get at the Truth—for he is a boy in opinion—having settled nothing as yet." She also described Melville in full monologue:

> Nothing pleases me better than to sit & hear this growing man dash his tumultuous waves of thought up against Mr Hawthorne's great, genial, comprehending silences—out of the profound of which a wonderful smile, or one powerful word sends back the foam & fury into a peaceful booming, calm—or perchance, not into a calm—but a murmuring expostulation—for there is never a "mush of concession" in him. Yet such a love & reverence & admiration for Mr Hawthorne as it is really beautiful to witness—& without doing any thing on his own part, except merely being, it is astonishing how people make him their innermost Father Confessor. Is it not?

Indisputably, Melville was often in a state of exaltation during the months that Sophia recorded her impressions of him.

Part of Melville's emotional state was due to the interaction between his present intense consciousness and the power of his memory, for everywhere in the region were traps for his "susceptible and peradventure feeble temperament," reminders of how his life had changed, and changed again—through death, impoverishment, bodily changes, seasonal changes, his own travels, his literary achievements, his marriage.[17] There, a boy tired from stage travel,

17. This paragraph is adapted from one written by Parker for a collaborative Higgins-Parker essay in *A Companion to Melville Studies* (where the intention to reuse it was signaled).

he had witnessed a meeting between his father and the uncle Thomas he did not remember seeing before: "It was in the larch-shaded porch of the mansion looking off, under urn-shaped road-side elms, across meadows to South Mountain." He recalled, de-cades later, their embracing "with the unaffectedness and warmth of boys—such boys as Van Dyck painted." As a fatherless adoles-cent on visits to the farm or later as an eighteen-year-old school-teacher, Melville had taken an outjutting of rock as a vantage point for brooding over the steeples of Pittsfield and the amphitheater dominated by Mount Greylock. He passed by that outcropping whenever he took the Old Lenox Road to see Hawthorne. Making a turn on a road, just as much as glancing about his uncle's old place, Melville in 1850 and 1851 collided with himself as a penniless and futureless boy, a sexually wondering and sexually excited youth, just as in 1849, a famous author stepping ashore in England, he had collided with his younger self, a crew "boy" of 1839. Small wonder that a turbulent state began flaring as soon as he arrived at Pittsfield, and that it blazed higher as soon as he met the only American writer he could even provisionally consider his equal.[18] The mere fact of staying for months in Pittsfield at such a time of psychological un-folding could have thrown Melville intermittently into states of febrile agitation; but, as it was, the excitement over being there, near Hawthorne, was infinitely compounded by the mind-body arousals, the anxieties, agitations, frustrations, and temporary tri-umphs of the aesthetic struggle he was waging, whenever he could find time to work, to shape out (in words Hawthorne wrote around the end of June, 1851) "the gigantic conception of his 'White Whale,' while the gigantic shape of Graylock" loomed "upon him from his study-window." Melville's imagination for many months had unrolled at will a panorama of Milton's dubious battle on the plains of heaven. The dubious battle being waged in his study was, as the months of 1851 went on, the most intense aesthetic struggle yet waged in the English language on this continent.

18. In a letter to Duyckinck on February 12, 1851, Melville modified his praise for his new friend judiciously: "I regard Hawthorne (in his books) as evincing a quality of genius, immensely loftier, & more profound, too, than any other American has shown hitherto in the printed form." Melville knew the quality of the unprinted work on his desk. For his further modification, see p. 965, below.

### III

The pages that follow lay out what is known about Melville's working conditions, beginning with the preparations for his work on *Mardi*, as documented by a hitherto unpublished letter (from the papers of Augusta Melville acquired by the New York Public Library in 1983), and ending with his completion of what he was calling *The Whale*. This letter (from their mother in Lansingburgh to Augusta on May 17, 1847) suggests that under optimum conditions the family might join in a ritualistic preparation not only of the proper chair, desk, and lighting but also the proper ambiance for their literary man:

> Herman just left the room & sends his love to you. We have been particularly busy to day in assisting him, in embellishing the small front room as a Library and Study. The walls have been colored the bed-sted removed a new carpet, and curtains, the library has been remove'd and placed before the door leading into the next room, a great box & two trunks have been unpacked filld with books, and handsomely disposed together with the Ship and miniature Anchor— his Desk &c together with three ancient mahogony Chairs from the attic, he looks, and his Study looks, ready to begin a new work, on the "South Seas"—of course . . . .

All that Melville had to do was to write.

The next piece of evidence is an account Elizabeth Melville (called Lizzie by the family) wrote on December 23, 1847, to her stepmother, Hope Savage Shaw, about the routine established soon after she and Herman had taken up housekeeping in New York City:

> We breakfast at 8 o'clock, then Herman goes to walk, and I fly up to put his room to rights, so that he can sit down to his desk immediately on his return. Then I bid him good bye, with many charges to be an industrious boy, and not upset the inkstand, and then flourish the duster, make the bed, &c in my own room. . . . This [luncheon] is half past 12 o'clock—by this time we must expect callers, and so must be dressed immediately after lunch. Then Herman insists upon my taking a walk every day of an hours length at least. . . . By the time I come home it is two o'clock and after, and then I must make myself look as bewitchingly as possible to meet Herman at dinner. . . . At four we dine, and after dinner is over, Herman and I come up to our room, and enjoy a cosy chat for an hour or so—or he reads me some of the chapters he has been writing in the day. Then he goes down town for a walk, looks at the papers in the reading-room &c, and returns about

half past seven or eight. Then my work or my book is laid aside, and as he does not use his eyes but very litle by candle light, I either read to him, or take a hand at whist for his amusement, or he listens to our reading or conversation, as best pleases him. For we all collect in the parlor in the evening, and generally one of us reads aloud for the benefit of the whole. Then we retire very early—at 10 o'clock we are all dispersed . . . . This is the general course of daily events . . . .

On May 5, 1848, Lizzie gave further details to her stepmother at a time she mistakenly thought that *Mardi* was finished:

I should write you a longer letter but I am very busy today copying and cannot spare the time so you must excuse it and all mistakes. I tore my sheet in two by mistake thinking it was my copying (for we only write on one side of the page) and if there is no punctuation marks you must make them yourself for when I copy I do not punctuate at all but leave it for a final revision for Herman. I have got so used to write without I cannot always think of it.

Even on June 6, 1848 (probably not knowing she was pregnant), she was reluctant to seek refuge from her allergies in Boston: "I don't know as I can make up my mind to go and leave him here—and besides I'm afraid to trust him to finish up the book without me!"

In the spring and summer of 1849 Melville probably resumed his well-established routine, with one major change. Regarding Malcolm as her primary daytime responsibility, his wife surely relinquished her duties as copyist to one of Melville's sisters. It is not known who copied *Redburn*. In the Northwestern-Newberry edition of *White-Jacket* the editors could not identify the copyist of the two draft preface pages, but comparison with his sister Helen Maria Melville's letters in the papers newly acquired by the New York Public Library indicates that the hand is hers. (By 1850 and 1851, Helen and Augusta were taking turns as Melville's copyist.)

On Melville's return from England in February of 1850 he probably settled rather soon into his accustomed work pattern in the house on Fourth Avenue, although Sophia's second pregnancy may have caused everyone to think ahead to the time they would have to break up the household. On March 6, 1850, Melville was unable to use tickets Duyckinck had sent him: "having been shut up all day, I could not stand being shut up all the evening—so I mounted my *green* jacket & strolled down to the Battery to study the stars." Possibly Melville had been shut up with final details for the Harper edition of *White-Jacket* (the title of which explains his emphasizing "green" in the letter), although in this month he may have done no more than write the short preface (dated March, 1850). Possibly also he could have been looking at, if not through, the new edition of Cooper's *The Red Rover* and writing the jeu d'esprit on the consonance of book content and book design that Duyckinck printed in the March 16 *Literary World* as "A Thought on Book-Binding." But he may have been "shut up all day" working on his whaling book.

On March 30, 1850, the New York *Albion* reviewed *White-Jacket*, in the main favorably, but with a particular objection to the emphasis on the horrors of flogging:

> In so able, so practical, and so large-minded an author as Herman Melville, we scarcely expected to find the "essential dignity of man" and "the spirit of our domestic intitutions" lugged in on such a question as this. Is it consistent with the "essential dignity," that one man should sweep the floor of Congress, and another make laws upon it which his democratic countrymen must obey?

The reviewer quoted Melville's diplomatic praise of British discipline on ships of war "as a little set-off against the 'democratic institutions.'" It is possible that now or later Melville wrote his reaction to this review into his manuscript in what became the end of the first "Knights and Squires" chapter (26) of *Moby-Dick*, for the paragraph is a plea that when he attributes high qualities to the men on the *Pequod* the "great democratic God" will bear him out "against all mortal critics," which is to say "all mortal reviewers."

Melville was well into the composition of the book when he wrote Richard Henry Dana, Jr., on May 1, 1850, his first surviving reference to what became *Moby-Dick*:

> About the "whaling voyage"—I am half way in the work, & am very glad that your suggestion so jumps with mine. It will be a strange sort of a book, tho', I fear; blubber is blubber you know; tho' you may get oil out of it, the poetry runs as hard as sap from a frozen maple tree;—& to cook the thing up, one must needs throw in a little fancy, which from the nature of the thing, must be ungainly as the gambols of the whales themselves. Yet I mean to give the truth of the thing, spite of this.

This passage directly follows his account of how Edward Moxon had spoken to him in London about the gratification *Two Years Before the Mast* had afforded certain people, among them the banker-poet Samuel Rogers, "who poetically appreciated the scenic sea passages, describing ice, storms, Cape Horn, & all that." To some extent, this use of "poetically" must condition Melville's use of "poetry."

The letter should be seen as the second of a pair. Dana had suggested that Melville write a book about his experiences on a man-of-war, and Melville on October 6, 1849, told him that his "hint" had, "in anticipation, been acted on," and that a printed copy of the book (the sheets) was before him. Once again, in April of 1850, Dana had made a suggestion—this time that Melville write a book based on his experiences as a whaleman. Once again the suggestion had jumped with (or a little later than) Melville's own. Yet there is a difference between the cases. The previous autumn Melville had made no qualifications at all: Dana had made a suggestion and could look forward to seeing just the sort of book he wanted to see. Now Dana had made a suggestion and had to be warned that the book would *not* be just the sort he had in mind. Rather, it would be "a strange sort of a book," probably less documentary than Melville thought Dana would have hoped, and more imaginative. Apparently the aesthetic problem as Melville defined it for himself was how to reconcile a realistic account of whaling processes with a poetic treatment of the subject: easy to get oil from blubber, harder to get poetry from blubber. Furthermore, in cooking the thing up, working it into literary form, "one must needs throw in a little fancy" (in the sense of "imagination"), ungainly though that fancy must be, given "the nature of the thing." Yet despite all difficulties Melville meant "to give the truth of the thing," presumably the sort of realistic depiction of whaling that Dana by literary example and temperament would be expected to prefer.

The next known document is the letter Melville wrote from New York on June 27, 1850, to Richard Bentley:

> In the latter part of the coming autumn I shall have ready a new work; and I write you now to propose its publication in England.
> The book is a romance of adventure, founded upon certain wild legends in the Southern Sperm Whale Fisheries, and illustrated by the author's own personal experience, of two years & more, as a harpooneer.

Having strained the Truth by claiming such service as a harpooneer, Melville went on to say that he thought the book would be worth two hundred pounds to Bentley, or more if he could be "positively put in possession of the copyright." This optimistic suggestion Melville justified in terms of the "great novelty" of the manuscript: "I do not know that the subject treated of has ever been worked up by a romancer; or, indeed, by any writer, in any adequate manner."

There seems no reason not to take seriously Melville's assurance that he expected to have the new work ready in the latter part of the next autumn—which would, at latest, have put the completion roughly between Thanksgiving and Christmas, a total of ten months or so for composition of a single book by a man who had written two books in four months the year before. For all we know, Melville worked steadily on the whaling book until mid-July, when he took Lizzie, Malcolm, and his mother to stay at the Melvill farm south of Pittsfield. Up to that point his sister Helen may have been his only copyist for the whaling book (as Augusta's letter of December 21 may imply). Melville was on an agricultural inspection tour with his cousin Robert for three days, and there is no indication whether he worked on the book at any other time before Duyckinck and Mathews came as his guests in the first week of August.

From Pittsfield on August 7, Duyckinck wrote to his brother George: "Melville has a new book mostly done—a romantic, fanciful & literal & most enjoyable presentment of the Whale Fishery—something quite new." The description of the book as "mostly done" is presumably based on Melville's own words, and considering the speed with which he wrote *Redburn* and *White-Jacket* seems a reasonable progression—from half done on May 1, to mostly done after another two and a half months in New York City. The specificity of the adjectives makes it sound as if Duyckinck had sampled the manuscript rather than merely having been told about it. If so, he had done so there at Pittsfield, or else he would surely have told his brother while they were all in New York City near each other. The most baffling implication of the letter is that Melville had given Duyckinck no hint during the preceding months that he was working on a whaling book.

On August 9, 1850, Melville dashed off three-quarters of an essay on Hawthorne's *Mosses from an Old Manse*, perhaps in the barn, and in some makeshift study Lizzie took up her old task as copyist. Always prone to put private references into his writings, Melville alluded to the whaling manuscript in this essay. Declaring that "imitation is often the first charge brought against real originality," he continued: "Why this is so, there is not space to set forth here. You must have plenty of sea-room to tell the Truth in." The "truth of the thing" in the May 1 letter to Dana seemed to refer to realistic depiction of American whaling; now "Truth" and truth-telling carry metaphysical dimensions.

Furthermore, the passage that precedes the reference to "sea-room" poses an aesthetic and cultural problem more complicated than the one implied in the letter to Dana—one Melville must have been brooding about for weeks if not months. The formidable question he had been facing as he worked on the whaling manuscript and now articulated is how an American, a democrat, could write a tragedy equal to Shakespeare's without decking it out "in the costume of Queen Elizabeth's day" or timidly accepting the status of "a writer of dramas founded upon old English history, or the tales of Boccaccio." (Some readers of *Moby-Dick* have judged that Melville never adequately solved that problem.) Another aspect of the problem is how the second generation of post-Revolutionary American writers was, without impiety, to break with the older, more imitative generation (a set consisting of only two looming figures, Irving and Cooper). For whatever reason, Melville was laboring under no anxiety of influence from Cooper, but in this essay he revealed his edginess about how to break away from Irving. (Six months later he wrote Duyckinck of Hawthorne's superiority: "Irving is a grasshopper to him— putting the *souls* of the two men together, I mean.")

After Duyckinck left, carrying the manuscript of the essay on *Mosses from an Old Manse*, Melville located a desk and put it in an appropriate spot, as he wrote the New Yorker on August 16:

> I write you this from the *garret-way*, seated at that little embrasure of a window (you must remember it) which commands so noble a view of Saddleback.—My desk is an odd one—an old thing of my Uncle the Major's, which for twelve years back has been packed away in the corn-loft over the carriage house. Upon dragging it out to day light, I found that it was covered with the marks of fowls—quite white with them—eggs had been laid in it—think of that!—Is it not typical of those other eggs that authors may be said to lay in their desks,— especially those with pigeon-holes?

Apparently Melville had written the essay on Hawthorne without the benefit of a desk, but now, still the stickler for proper equipment (whose first known fiction was published not as lines from a lapboard but as fragments from a writing desk) had set himself up with a memory-freighted heirloom, however soiled, and had appropriated a snug, quiet nook commanding an inspiring view. He was positioning himself to write greatly, although apparently with only Lizzie around to be his copyist.

How long Melville managed to continue any new routine is uncertain—hardly very far into September, for it was in the middle of that month that he bought a farm to the east of the Melvill place, and by the third week of September he was back in New York City preparing for the move. On October 6, from his new farm, which he named Arrowhead from its abundance of those Indian artifacts, Melville wrote to Duyckinck, making do with a table to write on:

> Until to day I have been as busy as man could be. Every thing to be done, & scarcely any one to help me do it. But I trust that before a great while we shall be all "to rights," and I shall take my ease on mine mountain. For a month to come, tho', I expect to be in the open air all day, except when assisting in lifting a bedstead or a bureau.

Melville wrote this letter at night, "an almost unexampled thing" because of his chronic inability to read or write by lamplight.

We do not know precisely how long it took for Melville to get back to work on the whaling book, but letters among Augusta Melville's papers show that it was longer than some scholars have thought. As he expected, Melville was involved in household duties for several weeks. By the middle of October (as Augusta wrote her friend Mary Blatchford in New York City) "locks & bolts" were going onto doors that had stood seventy years "guiltless of their sign." A month later Melville's need to return to, or turn steadily to, his manuscript became more intense, as signaled in a small rudeness toward his sister Helen as she left for a trip (Augusta wrote her, "Herman was in such haste to be on his way home again that I thought it would not do to ask him to wait until your train whirled out of sight"). That day, according to Augusta, Melville had been anxious to round up an elusive cabinet-maker while Lizzie waited "with bedstead upturned & room emptied in readiness to receive him" (he later showed up on his own and put castors on the bed);

presumably Melville had been anxious to get Helen to the train and get the artisan to Arrowhead so he could get in a little work on his manuscript, but it is not certain that he was even trying to write yet. He was making innumerable trips into Pittsfield—his own fault, to some extent, since he stubbornly would not trust any of the women to drive the horse (although in January his mother and Augusta proved their competence, no doubt to his secret relief). He may have established some sort of routine before November 25, when Lizzie left with Malcolm for Boston, the only town fit for celebrating a real New England Thanksgiving in. That day Augusta explained to Mary Blatchford why he had remained behind: "He being now engaged upon his new book, was not to be prevailed upon to leave it, even though a Boston Thanksgiving were held forth as an inducement." November 25 was a Monday, and in order to celebrate a Pittsfield sort of "grand Thanksgiving" with his aunt Mary Melvill's family Melville had not only to interrupt whatever work routine he had established but even to break up his work-room (Augusta wrote Helen, "Herman's Library is to be thrown open for their accommodation").

At last, with his wife and child away in Boston and his "Library" back in his possession, Melville established a schedule. On December 13, 1850, he wrote Duyckinck:

> Do you want to know how I pass my time?—I rise at eight—thereabouts—& go to my barn—say good-morning to the horse, & give him his breakfast. (It goes to my heart to give him a cold one, but it can't be helped) Then, pay a visit to my cow—cut up a pumpkin or two for her, & stand by to see her eat it—for it's a pleasant sight to see a cow move her jaws—she does it so mildly & with such a sanctity.—My own breakfast over, I go to my work-room & light my fire—then spread my M.S.S on the table—take one business squint at it, & fall to with a will. At 2 1/2 P.M. I hear a preconcerted knock at my door, which (by request) continues till I rise & go to the door, which serves to wean me effectively from my writing, however interested I may be. . . . My evenings I spend in a sort of mesmeric state in my room—not being able to read—only now & then skimming over some large-printed book.—Can you send me about fifty fast-writing youths, with an easy style & not averse to polishing their labors? If you can, I wish you would, because since I have been here I have planned about that number of future works & cant find enough time to think about them

separately.—But I dont know but a book in a man's brain is better off than a book bound in calf—at any rate it is safer from criticism. And taking a book off the brain, is akin to the ticklish & dangerous business of taking an old painting off a panel—you have to scrape off the whole brain in order to get at it with due safety—& even then, the painting may not be worth the trouble.

This was the routine Melville was following when he wrote the date December 16 and the time of day into what became "The Fountain" (chap. 85). Yet by December 21, 1850, he was still not writing at anything like top speed. That day Augusta wrote Helen: "As to Herman's M S. S. you need not hurry your return on that account, he gets on very slowly with it. As soon as he is ready for you, I will let you know."

In a brief biographical memorandum written toward the end of the century, some years after Melville's death, his widow recalled that he "Wrote White Whale or Moby Dick under unfavorable circumstances." What stuck in her mind for mention was a domestic vignette of his writing routine during the Pittsfield winter of 1850–51: "would sit at his desk all day not eating any thing till four or five o clock—then ride to the village after dark—Would be up early and out walking before breakfast—sometimes splitting wood for exercise" (Sealts, 1974, p. 169). In fact, she was in Boston from before Thanksgiving until New Year's Day, so her own memories of that winter are from 1851 only. With minor interruptions, the work routine established after Thanksgiving seems to have continued until time came for spring chores.

After if not before Thanksgiving another family pattern was reestablished in addition to Melville's work schedule: "The long evenings we have improved by reading aloud," Augusta wrote Mary Blatchford on January 4, 1851. After reading "several other interesting books" they had just finished reading Schiller's *The Ghost Seer* (which Melville had brought home from London bound in with *Frankenstein*), and had in store *David Copperfield* (which Lizzie had just brought home from Boston). In the January 4 letter to Mary Blatchford, Augusta must have described Melville as "busy writing," for in her reply (on January 9) Mary listed that as one of Augusta's news items: "Herman busy writing—Well, he has got that quiet place he longed for, and from your description of its glories, I think it must quite equal his expectations." Augusta answered her on January 16:

> As to time passing slowly with me here—why Mary it actually flies, I cannot believe that the winter is more than half over. We dine at 3 1/2 & after that drive up to the post office a distance of two & a half miles, for Herman is then at our disposal. Sometimes we extend our drive in different directions, & reach home just in time for tea at seven. Then there are the letters to be read, of which we generally have two or three, & the New York papers—& when those fail—we take up some interesting book. We have just begun "David Copperfield."—The morning I pass in copying Herman's M S, sewing & reading, & it is half past three before I know it.

It is not known whether or not Melville heard the Schiller or the Dickens or other books read aloud while he was working on *Moby-Dick*, or whether he remained unsociably in a mesmeric state in his room. Helen had been expected to continue the copying, but when she delayed her return from a visit to Lansingburgh Augusta took up the task. (An implication from two of Augusta's letters is that she and Helen did not always spend part of the morning copying what Melville had written the day before; when he was not writing at top speed they may have let pages pile up before they set to copying.)

Having returned to the manuscript for the months of December and January, Melville's smoldering knowledge that he was writing a great book burst out in a display of impatience with the limited literary horizons of his New York friends, who (like some of the women in his household) thought so little of his work or his work schedule that they renewed their customary trivial demands on his time. On February 12, 1851, he refused to contribute to the Duyckinck brothers' new enterprise, *Holden's Dollar Magazine*, or to supply a daguerreotype of himself so an engraving could be made for that magazine. Though in the humor, he said, to lend a hand to a friend, he was "not in the humor to write the kind of thing you need" (possibly a review, possibly something else). Tensions built about this episode when Melville's mother, on a trip to New York, connived with Duyckinck to keep pressuring him for a daguerreotype, which she thought any sensible man would supply, and all this flushed out Melville's lurking realization that he articulated to Hawthorne the next summer—that he did not think about Fame as he had done a year before.[19] The writing of the whaling book had changed him.

In these months Melville was surrounded by women who loved him but imperfectly understood his needs as a writer. (His sister Kate, it should be said, was not a regular part of the family group at Arrowhead, since Sophia and Allan strongly encouraged her to stay with them. His sister Fanny came and went, as all the sisters did, during this age of prolonged and almost ceremonial visits, but apparently never was conscripted as copyist.) Melville's mother saw no reason why he should not be at her "disposal" even before three-thirty in the afternoon, and devoted a good deal of energy to staying irritated at him when he did not cheerfully drop what he was doing to meet her reasonable requirements. When she returned to New York City in March of 1851 Melville grudgingly interrupted his work routine to take her to the depot. The gallant Gansevoort, had he lived to take her to a depot, would never have treated her as Herman did:

> Herman I hope returned home safe after dumping me & my trunks out so unceremoniously at the Depot—Altho we were there more than an hour before the time, he hurried off as if his life had depended upon his speed, a more ungallant man it would be difficult to find.

(Gansevoort, had he lived a little longer, would also have posed for any number of daguerreotypes.) When Melville left Helen at the depot in November, Augusta had apologized to her. Plainly Augusta was a little afraid of Herman's intensities, while his mother simply could not imagine that "his life"—his creative life—might really in some sense have "depended upon his speed." Chances are that his impatience meant that he had been summoned from his study at a crucial stage of composition—say something on the order of being a third of the way through "The Whiteness of the Whale" or halfway through "The Grand Armada."[20]

A letter to Duyckinck on March 26 showed that Melville's routine

19. Hawthorne's letters show he supplied Duyckinck a portrait; they need study for echoes of what he and Melville said or wrote to each other; see, for example, his letter to Horatio Bridge (March 15, 1851), on reputation.

20. Maria Melville liked her second son's being famous (as much as she hated his bringing public shame to the family with some of his writings), but she had no sympathy for the anxiety, arousal, and general moodiness which are an inescapable part of any great creative process; what she saw at this time was a slightly less upsetting version of what she described on April 20, 1853: "This constant working of

continued: "The Spring begins to open upon Pittsfield, but slowly. I only wish that I had more day-time to spend out *in the day*; but like an owl I steal about by twilight, owing to the twilight of my eyes."

On April 22, Mary Blatchford again wrote to Augusta: "So Herman has another book ready has he? Well I presume he has quiet enough, if that is all, to prepare his mind for literary meditations."

On April 25, anticipating its completion, Melville wrote the Harpers asking for an advance on *The Whale*. They refused, and on the first of May he borrowed $2,050 from a Lansingburgh friend, T. D. Stewart. Part of the money went immediately into "building the new kitchen, wood-house, piazza, making alterations, painting"—all efforts which Melville must have had to supervise.[21] In a major renunciation, he did not build on a writing tower to provide even more privacy than he had and an even more glorious view of Greylock.

On June 12, from Albany, when family members were pulled by different crises (including a death) in different directions, Augusta asked Helen (again the copyist), "How does Herman's book progress."

The early June, 1851, letter to Hawthorne already mentioned details the intense final phase of intermingled composition and proof-reading, toward the end of about three or four weeks when Melville was spending much of Stewart's money hiring work done while he was himself "building and patching and tinkering away in all directions," as well as planting his corn and potatoes and doing "many other things" that had to be done in spring or not at all. He wrote at such length because his new outdoor routine was disrupted: "It is a rainy morning; so I am indoors, and all work suspended. I feel cheerfully disposed, and therefore I write a little bluely." Now he foresaw no hope of laboring on the book in anything like ideal conditions. In New York, where he planned to finish work, he would be in unfamiliar surroundings, at Allan's new house on Thirty-First Street near

---

the brain, & excitement of the imagination, is wearing Herman out." By then it was also earning him opprobrium instead of money and fame.

21. Melville to Shaw, May 12, 1856, in Barber (1977). Parker suspects from fragmentary evidence that Stewart thought his lending Melville money would encourage Helen to marry him.

Lexington, much farther (and inconveniently) uptown, and in a room which by its location was almost sure to be stiflingly hot:[22]

> In a week or so, I go to New York, to bury myself in a third-story room, and work and slave on my "Whale" while it is driving through the press. *That* is the only way I can finish it now,—I am so pulled hither and thither by circumstances. The calm, the coolness, the silent grass-growing mood in which a man *ought* always to compose,—that, I fear, can seldom be mine. Dollars damn me; and the malicious Devil is forever grinning in upon me, holding the door ajar. . . . What I feel most moved to write, that is banned,—it will not pay. Yet, altogether, write the *other* way I cannot. So the product is a final hash, and all my books are botches. . . .
>
> But I was talking about the "Whale." As the fishermen say, "he's in his flurry" when I left him some three weeks ago. I'm going to take him by his jaw, however, before long, and finish him up in some fashion or other. What's the use of elaborating what, in its very essence, is so short-lived as a modern book? Though I wrote the Gospels in this century, I should die in the gutter.

Melville's language here, the "final hash," the "botches," resembles that he employed a few months later in his next novel (*Pierre*, bk. 22.iv), where the hero "immaturely attempts a mature book":

> Two books are being writ; of which the world shall only see one, and that the bungled one. The larger book, and the infinitely better, is for Pierre's own private shelf. That it is, whose unfathomable cravings drink his blood; the other only demands his ink. But circumstances have so decreed, that the one can not be composed on the paper, but only as the other is writ down in his soul. . . .
>
> Who shall tell all the thoughts and feelings of Pierre in that desolate and shivering room, when at last the idea obtruded, that the wiser and

22. In *Pierre* Melville placed his hero in a wintry room, one worse than Allan would have provided: "A rickety chair, two hollow barrels, a plank, paper, pens, and infernally black ink, four leprously dingy white walls, no carpet, a cup of water, and a dry biscuit or two" (bk. 22.ii). At best, Melville did not like to work in unfamiliar situations and at makeshift writing surfaces, and in the summer of 1851 his working conditions in New York City may have seemed more onerous than any since 1844 or early 1845, when he scrounged space from Gansevoort and Allan before finishing *Typee* in Lansingburgh. For all we know, he may have been working without one of his usual copyists or even without *any* copyist. (The "Devil" in this letter is not Satan but the printer's errand-boy, waiting to carry new pages of manuscript to the compositor.)

the profounder he should grow, the more and the more he lessened the chances for bread; that could he now hurl his deep book out of the window, and fall to on some shallow nothing of a novel, composable in a month at the longest, then could he reasonably hope for both appreciation and cash. But the devouring profundities, now opened up in him, consume all his vigor; would he, he could not now be entertainingly and profitably shallow in some pellucid and merry romance.

In turning Pierre into an author who "directly plagiarized from his own experiences" (bk. 22.iii), Melville was plagiarizing, at least indirectly, from his own.

In the next letter to Hawthorne, June 29, 1851, Melville returned to the topic of the conflicting demands on his time:

> I have been building some shanties of houses (connected with the old one) and likewise some shanties of chapters and essays. I have been plowing and sowing and raising and painting and printing and praying,—and now begin to come out upon a less bustling time, and to enjoy the calm prospect of things from a fair piazza at the north of the old farm house here.
>
> Not entirely yet, though, am I without something to be urgent with. The "Whale" is only half through the press; for, wearied with the long delay of the printers, and disgusted with the heat and dust of the babylonish brick-kiln of New York, I came back to the country to feel the grass—and end the book reclining on it, if I may. . . . Shall I send you a fin of the *Whale* by way of a specimen mouthful? The tail is not yet cooked—though the hell-fire in which the whole book is broiled might not unreasonably have cooked it all ere this. This is the book's motto (the secret one),—Ego non baptizo te in nomine—but make out the rest yourself.

This is the last of the letters to Hawthorne during the actual composition of the book.

On July 20, 1851, Melville wrote to Richard Bentley:

> I am now passing thro' the press, the closing sheets of my new work; so that I shall be able to forward it to you in the course of two or three weeks—perhaps a little longer.

(This letter is discussed in more detail in Section VI.)

On September 12?, in the aftermath of his labors, Melville wrote to Sarah Morewood, now the mistress of the former Melvill place:

> Concerning my own forthcoming book—it is off my hands, but must cross the sea before publication here. Dont you buy it—dont you read it, when it does come out, because it is by no means the sort of book for you. It is not a peice of fine feminine Spitalfields silk—but is of the horrible texture of a fabric that should be woven of ships' cables & hausers. A Polar wind blows through it, & birds of prey hover over it. Warn all gentle fastidious people from so much as peeping into the book—on risk of a lumbago & sciatics.

Then on November 7 Melville acknowledged Duyckinck's clipping about the sinking of the *Ann Alexander* by a whale with an explicit comment on how thoroughly behind him the long creative process had been left: "the Whale had almost completely slipped me for the time (& I was the merrier for it) when Crash! comes Moby Dick himself (as you justly say) & reminds me of what I have been about for part of the last year or two." (See p. 1040, footnote 35, below.)

The last letter to Hawthorne in this wonderful sequence, like the others difficult to excerpt, was written (November 17?) a few days after the American publication, the day after Melville had been handed a letter of praise from Hawthorne on the road going to the old Melvill place. Melville had opened it there, and read it outdoors. He responded:

> People think that if a man has undergone any hardship, he should have a reward; but for my part, if I have done the hardest possible day's work, and then come to sit down in a corner and eat my supper comfortably—why, then I don't think I deserve any reward for my hard day's work—for am I not now at peace? Is not my supper good? My peace and my supper are my reward, my dear Hawthorne. So your joy-giving and exultation-breeding letter is not my reward for my ditcher's work with that book, but is the good goddess's bonus over and above what was stipulated for—for not one man in five cycles, who is wise, will expect appreciative recognition from his fellows, or any one of them. Appreciation! Recognition! Is Jove appreciated? Why, ever since Adam, who has got to the meaning of his great allegory—the world? Then we pygmies must be content to have our paper allegories but ill comprehended. I say your appreciation is my glorious gratuity. In my proud, humble way,—a shepherd-king,—I was lord of a little vale in the solitary Crimea; but you have now given me the crown of India. But on trying it on my head, I found it fell down on my ears, notwithstanding their asinine length—for it's only such ears that sustain such crowns.

This is the letter in which Melville declared that as Hawthorne read he "understood the pervading thought that impelled the book," and that it was the impelling thought that Hawthorne praised: "You were archangel enough to despise the imperfect body, and embrace the soul." In this letter also he asked Hawthorne not to rob him of his "miserly delight" by reviewing *Moby-Dick* (a decision that ranks high among the worst mistakes he ever made) and declared his again-expanded ambition: "Lord, when shall we be done growing? As long as we have anything more to do, we have done nothing. So, now, let us add Moby Dick to our blessing, and step from that. Leviathan is not the biggest fish;—I have heard of Krakens."

At just this time Hawthorne was making good his flight back to eastern Massachusetts from the Berkshire winter, which he loathed, and also from a tenant-landlord contretemps over rights to pick fruit on the rented property, so Melville's tone is literally that of a benediction, delivered not from a secure vantage point like his rocky outjutting of land nearby but from pell-mell emotional, intellectual, and aesthetic change, a fluid state when "the very fingers that now guide this pen are not precisely the same that just took it up and put it on this paper." In a letter which expresses a whirlwind of feelings, Melville isolated one moment to stand on record as the feeling of a great artist after triumphant creativity, one of absolute distance from the created object and absolute security in the knowledge that the one ideal reader had understood it:

> A sense of unspeakable security is in me this moment, on account of your having understood the book. I have written a wicked book, and feel spotless as the lamb. Ineffable socialities are in me. I would sit down and dine with you and all the gods in old Rome's Pantheon. It is a strange feeling—no hopefulness is in it, no despair. Content—that is it; and irresponsibility; but without licentious inclination.

He added, freezing the onrush of moods: "I speak now of my profoundest sense of being, not of an incidental feeling."

From New York City Melville wrote to Sophia Hawthorne on January 8, 1852, in reply to her "highly flattering letter" about *Moby-Dick*:

> It really amazed me that you should find any satisfaction in that book. It is true that some *men* have said they were pleased with it, but you are the only *woman*—for as a general thing, women have small taste for the

sea. But, then, since you, with your spiritualizing nature, see more things than other people, and by the same process, refine all you see, so that they are not the same things that other people see, but things which while you think you but humbly discover them, you do in fact create them for yourself—Therefore, upon the whole, I do not so much marvel at your expressions concerning Moby Dick. At any rate, your allusion for example to the "Spirit Spout" first showed to me that there was a subtile significance in that thing—but I did not, in that case, *mean* it. I had some vague idea while writing it, that the whole book was susceptible of an allegoric construction, & also that *parts* of it were—but the speciality of many of the particular subordinate allegories, were first revealed to me, after reading M^r Hawthorne's letter, which, without citing any particular examples, yet intimated the part-&-parcel allegoricalness of the whole.

He added that he would not again send her "a bowl of salt water"; the next chalice he would commend would be "a rural bowl of milk"—a complexly ironic reference to *Pierre*.

The letters that have been quoted here document some of the stages of progress on the manuscript ("half way," "mostly done") and some of the rhythms of intense application and deliberate respite (and the tensions that grew from enforced, over-prolonged, and ill-timed interruptions). We can, even on the basis of the fragmentary information, understand something of Melville's working conditions: his need for physical exercise (walking, chopping wood, driving);[23] his demand for late mornings and early afternoons as his private work time; his absolute demand for a copyist; his availability for family duties in the late afternoon; his ways of passing the evening hours, when he could barely read (unless a book was in very large print) but might listen as one or another of the women read aloud; then the harried months he endured at the end, when he most needed to concentrate. We even divine something, more than some people might think seemly, about the relation of his creative intensities to his

23. A still-youngish man of thirty and thirty-one when he wrote *Moby-Dick*, Melville had not lost all of the sailor's agility he returned home with in 1844. But he knew that health of the body was, under his circumstances, incompatible with fullest development of the creative mind: "Yoke the body to the soul, and put both to the plough, and the one or the other must in the end assuredly drop in the furrow. Keep, then, thy body effeminate for labor, and thy soul laboriously robust; or else thy soul effeminate for labor, and thy body laboriously robust. Elect! the two will not lastingly abide in one yoke" (*Pierre*, bk. 18.ii).

sexual needs.[24] Since he described the ideal state for writing, Melville must have experienced, at times, that "silent grass-growing mood in which a man *ought* always to compose." He also knew the stages between that and the mood in which he could see only "the endlessness, yea, the intolerableness of all earthly effort" (chap. 13).

## IV

It seems most likely that Melville started to write *Moby-Dick*, on the pattern of his five earlier books, as a sailor-voyager's firsthand account of his experiences and observations, ashore and aship, amid ways of life strange at first to him and still strange to his stay-at-home readers. Beginning with Charles R. Anderson in the 1930's,[25] scholars have established that, as in the earlier books, some of the materials in *Moby-Dick* were autobiographical, some borrowed and reshaped from other works, and some invented. For *Typee, Omoo, Redburn,*

24. Before Thanksgiving Melville needed his privacy, but before New Year's he needed his wife back; she conceived Stanwix (born October 22, 1851) almost as soon as she returned to Arrowhead. A study which at many points sheds light on this account of the writing of *Moby-Dick* (including the place of sexual arousal in literary creativity) is Albert Rothenberg's *The Emerging Goddess: The Creative Process in Art, Science, and Other Fields*, especially Chapter 13, "Goddess Emergent: Creative Process and Created Product."

25. From the late 1920's into the 1930's, forerunning any inquiry about how *Moby-Dick* was written, pioneering Melville scholars conducted overlapping biographical researches, fragmentary, mostly solitary, and too often secretive (as individualistic academic usage seems to require). Active then were Henry A. Murray, John H. Birss, Robert S. Forsythe, and Charles Olson, who all projected larger works on Melville which proved abortive, along with Charles R. Anderson, Luther S. Mansfield, and Willard Thorp, who completed important studies. They all published findings that proved relevant to the composition of *Moby-Dick*, but did not focus their discoveries on genetic questions. Their work that has proved most relevant to genetic study of *Moby-Dick* was the documentation of Melville's extensive reading, and their discovery of his surprising uses of his reading. While this section is in part indebted to their initial discoveries, and their work underlies the theories reported in the first part of Section V, it draws most heavily on several later contributions: Wilbur S. Scott, Jr.'s Princeton Ph.D. dissertation on "Melville's Originality" (1943), directed by Willard Thorp; Howard P. Vincent's *The Trying-Out of MOBY-DICK* (1949); Sumner W. D. Scott's Chicago Ph.D. dissertation, "The Whale in *Moby Dick*" (1950); the Luther S. Mansfield and Howard P. Vincent edition of *Moby-Dick* (1952); and James Barbour's UCLA Ph.D. dissertation, "The Writing of *Moby-Dick*" (1970).

and *White-Jacket* many documents of several kinds permit a check upon what parts of the books are fictional and what are autobiographical, but the evidence about what is autobiographical in *Moby-Dick* is very slight. The shipmate, Henry F. Hubbard, to whom Melville gave one of his textually flawed but nevertheless precious sets of *The Whale*, in his one marginal comment identified Pip as Backus, a crew member on the *Acushnet* (though not one who sailed from Fairhaven), and recalled Backus's leap overboard from a whaleboat headed by the second mate, John Hall. (See pp. 1006-7, 1012-13.) Aside from Hubbard's tantalizing notation there is little evidence to prove that any of the characters on shore or on the *Pequod* were based on real people. (The only convincing exception is Father Mapple, for whom Father Edward Taylor of Boston supplied more than a hint.) To be sure, Melville used many of his own experiences in characterizing his narrator, implying that Ishmael came as he did from an old-established family in the land and had been a country schoolmaster, and giving Ishmael (or himself in his narrative voice) allusions to the same range of European travel he had made in 1849—London, Paris, the Rhine. Melville truthfully (if discreetly) referred to an "acquaintance" of his as "Commodore J——" (the real Commodore Jones) and truthfully named the real John D'Wolf of Dorchester, Massachusetts, as his uncle. The similarities (and differences) could be extended. While it appears that in the June 27, 1850, letter to Richard Bentley (see p. 621) Melville misrepresented his years of service as a harpooneer, if not also the degree to which he would recount his own experiences in the book, he had at least served on whaleships that, in fact, hunted whales, lost whales, caught whales, cut whales up and tried them out, cleaned up the bloody and greasy decks (which had been heaped with parts of whale heads and other recently living debris), stowed away the signs of trying out, lost men to desertion and death, and met and gammed with other ships.

Even before he went whaling Melville had in all likelihood read and heard many facts and stories about the whale fishery, mainly from newspaper and magazine items devoted to what was, after all, a major part of the national economy as well as a regular source of newsworthy events. Just before he sailed to Liverpool the popular New York magazine, the *Knickerbocker* (May, 1839), printed J. N. Reynolds's "Mocha Dick: or the White Whale of the Pacific: A Leaf from a Manuscript Journal," an account that readers found both enthralling and memorable. (The magazine was available nationally; Melville's uncle in Albany, Peter Gansevoort, seems to have kept up a subscription to it.) Reynolds presented the somber story of an obsessive hunt in a classic "frame story" situation, where a witness to the wild events told it to the writer afterwards, when the danger was over—an oceanic equivalent of the technique T. B. Thorpe used a few years later in his comic-mythic hunt story, "The Big Bear of Arkansas," and Melville himself was to use in "The Town-Ho's Story" (chap. 54 of *Moby-Dick*). Mocha Dick was real, "an old bull whale, of prodigious size and strength," "*white as wool*," and he shared other attributes with Moby Dick:

> From the period of Dick's first appearance, his celebrity continued to increase, until his name seemed naturally to mingle with the salutations which whalemen were in the habit of exchanging, in their encounters upon the broad Pacific; the customary interrogatories almost always closing with, 'Any news from Mocha Dick?'

The mate who narrates the story within the frame closes with the death of Mocha Dick, the longest whale he had ever seen, and profitable to the killers, yielding an extraordinary "one hundred barrels of clear oil." Significantly, the battle-scarred Mocha Dick was a near-legendary beast as well as profitable: "not less than twenty harpoons did we draw from his back; the rusted mementos of many a desperate rencounter." Even more significant for Melville's uses, he was reported as sighted in the years following his death, and after the publication of Reynolds's story. A reviewer of *Moby-Dick* recalled that every "old 'Jack-tar' " knew the story in one form or another, and in 1839–43 the young jack-tar Herman Melville had good chances to know it, or part of it, from print or from sailors' yarns, and perhaps even then had chances to retell it. As a whaleman Melville had participated in one of the most remarkable literary phenomena of his time, the frontier-training of writers, in which ordinary Americans confronted natural horrors and wonders, far from home, and came back, when they were lucky, to tell tall tales about their experiences, or truthful tales so extraordinary that stay-at-home people would take them as false. Melville said he had based the narrative in *Moby-Dick* on certain wild legends of the whale fishery, but he could as well have based it on tales that his own careful inquiries had established as true stories, however wild. Some such stories, to be sure, were passing into legendary status, among them, recent scholars are finding, a good number of stories of hunting great white whales in the Pacific.[26]

Simply by being months at a time on a whaleship Melville heard (along with sailor songs, jokes, proverbs, and miscellaneous tall tales) a range of whaling stories from the other members of the crew, some stories surely more than once, and—starved for news—avidly heard fresh stories or fresh versions of old stories from crews of other whaling ships encountered in the open waters or ports of the Pacific. Such an assertion would be true of any whaleman, but it happens that Melville in "What I know of Owen Chace &c" (see pp. 979–83) put on record how he learned that a whale had sunk Chase's ship, the *Essex*:

> When I was on board the ship Acushnet of Fairhaven, on the passage to the Pacific cruising-grounds, among other matters of forecastle conversation at times was the story of the Essex. It was then that I first became acquainted with her history and her truly astounding fate.

The *Acushnet*'s second mate, Mr. Hall, had served with Chase on another ship, and was a source of information, and in the Pacific the *Acushnet* gammed with a ship on which Melville met a teenage son of Chase who let him read a copy of his father's *Narrative of the Most Extraordinary and Distressing Shipwreck of the Whale-Ship Essex, of Nantucket; Which Was Attacked and Finally Destroyed by a Large Spermaceti-Whale, in the Pacific Ocean; with an Account of the Unparalleled Sufferings of the Captain and Crew during a Space of Ninety-Three Days at Sea, in Open Boats; in the Years 1819 & 1820* (New York: Gilley, 1821). A decade afterwards he recalled the special qualities of the experience: "The reading of this wondrous story upon the landless sea, & close to the very latitude of the shipwreck had a surprising effect upon me."

A constant of Melville's mind was that a book he read remained associated with the time and the place he read it. It would have been one thing to read "Mocha Dick" ashore in New York state, another

26. In his journal on February 19, 1834, Ralph Waldo Emerson recorded that a seaman, a fellow-passenger in a stagecoach, had told "the story of an old sperm whale which he called a white whale which was known for many years by the whalemen as Old Tom & who rushed upon the boats which attacked him & crushed the boats to small chips in his jaws, the men generally escaping by jumping overboard & being picked up. A vessel was fitted out at New Bedford, he said, to take him. And he was finally taken somewhere off Payta head by the Winslow or the Essex." In "Sources" see Janez Stanonik, F. De Wolfe Miller, and Joel Myerson.

to hear the story on the ocean. Similarly, stories he heard ashore in Tahiti and Honolulu may have produced surprisingly different effects from those he experienced as he read whaling books in Manhattan in the spring of 1850. Cases in point are the real sailor adventures, analogues to "The Town-Ho's Story" (chap. 54), which Wilson L. Heflin discovered could readily have come to Melville's attention, either at sea or in Honolulu. Melville must have heard excited versions of the sensational story of a one-man rebellion on the New Bedford whaler *Nassau*, in 1843, during which Luther Fox fatally wounded the mate by all but severing his leg with a mincing knife, for he was in Honolulu when the *Nassau* entered the harbor, and full news accounts were printed there. Quoting *Omoo* on the custom of hanging around jails in the islands for companionship and news, Heflin reasonably suggests that Melville may have gone to the jail at the fort and talked to Fox, who was from Rensselaerville, near Albany, and no cold-blooded murderer to be shunned but a self-appalled naif who had committed a hotheaded manslaughter because no one had ever taught him that he would not lose his pride of manhood if he backed down after he had boldly taken his stand. Melville may well have known other real-life stories Heflin discovered (one involves a fact that sounds like tall talk in "The Town-Ho's Story": a swordfish could stab a ship and cause a leak), and chances are that he heard whaling stories on the frigate *United States* as well.

Melville's reading of his whaling sources for *Moby-Dick* may have gone at least as far back as May 27, 1839, when the Albany *Argus* printed "Method of Taking the Whale" from the British surgeon Thomas Beale's *The Natural History of the Sperm Whale to Which Is Added a Sketch of a South-Sea Whaling Voyage in Which the Author Was Personally Engaged* (London: Van Voorst, 1839), including the powerful passage about the death flurry of the immense creature, mad with his agonies. If Melville missed that sample of Beale, he had another chance to read it when the West Troy *Advocate* devoted two columns to "Method of Taking the Whale" on October 23, 1839 (a few months after it reprinted one of his own "Fragments"). As far back as 1840 he read *Two Years Before the Mast*, a minor source. More than two columns (taken from the New Hampshire *Courier*) were devoted to Dana's book in the West Troy *Advocate* on December 16, 1840—about the time he was making his decision to sign on a whaler. His first reading of Owen Chase's *Narrative* (under the evocative circumstances already described) took place in July or August of 1841.

Melville's subsequent reading in his frigate's library and in libraries ashore had exposed him to more whaling information, and well before he started writing his own whaling voyage he owned some of the source-books or at least was already familiar with them. Around the first of February, 1847, he got a copy of J. Ross Browne's *Etchings of a Whaling Cruise, with Notes of a Sojourn on the Island of Zanzibar. To Which Is Appended a Brief History of the Whale Fishery; Its Past and Present Condition* (New York: Harper & Brothers, 1846) in order to review it in the *Literary World* (March 6, 1847). During the early stages of his work on *Mardi* he had a copy of Frederick Debell Bennett's *Narrative of a Whaling Voyage round the Globe, from the Year 1833 to 1836. Comprising Sketches of Polynesia, California, the Indian Archipelago, etc. with an Account of Southern Whales, the Sperm Whale Fishery, and the Natural History of the Climates Visited* (London: Bentley, 1840). By April 28, 1849, he knew at least one of William Scoresby, Jr.'s works on the North Atlantic fishery, the *Journal of a Voyage to the Northern Whale Fishery; Including Researches and Discoveries on the Eastern Coast of West Greenland . . . in . . . 1822* (Edinburgh: Constable, 1823), the source for the "level lodestone" passage in "The Needle" (chap. 124), since he made offhand mention of it in his *Literary World* review of Cooper's *The Red Rover*. In that review he also referred to Charles Wilkes's *United States Exploring Expedition. During the Years 1838 . . . 1842. Under the Command of Charles Wilkes, U.S.N.* (Philadelphia: Sherman, 1844–46), another source for *Moby-Dick*, which he had bought in April, 1847, for work on *Mardi*.[27] Early in 1850 Melville also had at hand in his working library some information about the natural history of whales, including the *Penny Cyclopædia of the Society for the Diffusion of Useful Knowledge* (London: Charles Knight, 1843), with its long article "Whales" which cited and paraphrased whole passages from the standard work by Thomas Beale (in "Sources," see Kendra Gaines). We know only a sample of the works Melville had access to, and new sources are still turning up.

A striking fact is that Melville did not seek out whaling sources

27. We use full or nearly full titles at a first or an early naming of Melville's whaling sources because each subtitle is (by definition) a more succinct guide to the nature and scope of the book than we could provide in another way.

during his sojourn in London, not proof but certainly a good indication that while he was there and at the time he left he had no idea of writing a whaling book any time soon. Very likely the return voyage itself so stirred his memories that he decided then, or soon after he reached New York, that his next book would be based on the most adventurous episodes left from his sea-going years, his whaling experiences. Although he could start writing from his memories and his imagination, he needed every source he could lay hands on, for even when writing about events he had lived through he habitually relied on printed works as prompt books to remind him of things worth writing about and to suggest ways they might be served up to readers. At the outset Browne was useful for "the story pattern, the scenes employed, the structure in the presentation of whaling information," important borrowings even though Melville often supplemented these parts from other books.[28] With his own memories and with Browne open before him, Melville could have gotten under weigh. Because he had lived by whaling routines far longer than he experienced the naval routines he had described in *White-Jacket*, he could infuse those experiences and observations into his work and even tardily transform a particular section of the manuscript which was based upon some printed source.

To the books already in his library he added others, such as the Rev. Henry T. Cheever's *The Whale and His Captors; or, The Whaleman's Adventures, and the Whale's Biography, as Gathered on the Homeward Cruise of the "Commodore Preble"* (New York: Harper & Brothers, 1849), which became a major source. Some of Cheever's chapter titles advertised useful passages for Melville's borrowing: "Authentic Tragedies and Perils of the Whaling Service" and "Yarns from the Experience of Old Whalemen." James Barbour names the following chapters as being derived at least in part from Cheever: 45 ("The Affidavit"); 48 ("The First Lowering"); 59 ("Squid"); 61 ("Stubb

---

28. See Barbour (1970), p. 90; also Vincent (1949) and Howard (1951 and 1987). These chapters have been cited as deriving at least in part from J. Ross Browne's *Etchings*: 1 ("Loomings"); 3 ("The Spouter-Inn"); 16 ("The Ship"); 22 ("Merry Christmas"); 24 ("The Advocate"); 29 ("Enter Ahab; to him, Stubb"); 31 ("Queen Mab"); 35 ("The Mast-Head"); 36 ("The Quarter-Deck"); 40 ("Midnight, Forecastle"); 48 ("The First Lowering"); 53 ("The Gam"); 54 ("The Town-Ho's Story"); 65 ("The Whale as a Dish"); 69 ("The Funeral"); 73 ("Stubb and Flask kill a Right Whale"); 81 ("The Pequod meets the Virgin"); and 96 ("The Try-Works").

kills a Whale"); 73 ("Stubb and Flask kill a Right Whale"); 78 ("Cistern and Buckets"); 81 ("The Pequod meets the Virgin"); 87 ("The Grand Armada"); and 91 ("The Pequod meets the Rose-bud"). In "The Affidavit" Melville took from Cheever evidence for two basic points: that a whaling captain seeking a particular whale would have a chance of finding it and that a whale could sink a ship. In other words, the purpose of the chapter, which seems to date initially from an early stage of the composition, before the stage of writing about the natural history of the whale, was to establish the plausibility of someone's (presumably an officer's) quest for a particular whale and to establish as well the plausibility of a catastrophe like that which befell the *Essex*—the sinking of a ship by a whale, in all likelihood by the particular whale being sought. Howard P. Vincent (1949) thought that perhaps Cheever's book was published too late for Melville to make much use of it, but Barbour pointed out that it was copyrighted in 1849; it was in fact published late in 1849 and reviewed along with *Redburn* while Melville was abroad.

Bennett's *A Whaling Voyage round the Globe* is another source Melville used extensively in both the whaling chapters and the chapters on the natural history of whales. Melville used Bennett in "The Affidavit" to supplement Cheever, drawing from him names of legendary whales. In that chapter, first writing before he received his own copy of Chase's *Narrative* but after seeing many "stupedly abbreviated" accounts of it, Melville used Cheever for the account of the sinking of the *Essex*, but supplemented him with Bennett. Barbour believes that in "The Grand Armada" Melville also combined information from Cheever and Bennett, taking the "harrowing ride" from Cheever and the observations of the "boudoir and nursery scenes" from Bennett. Some other sources include: Francis Allyn Olmsted, *Incidents of a Whaling Voyage. To Which Are Added Observations on the Scenery, Manners and Customs, and Missionary Stations, of the Sandwich and Society Islands* (New York, 1841); J. C. Hart, *Miriam Coffin, or the Whale-Fishermen: A Tale* (New York, 1834)[29]; Obed Macy, *The History of Nantucket; Being a Compendious Account of the First Settlement of the Island by the English; Together with the Rise and Progress of the Whale Fishery; and Other Historical Facts Relative to Said*

---

29. *Miriam Coffin* was the subject of "A Predecessor of *Moby-Dick*" (1934), the first article Leon Howard wrote on Melville.

*Island and Its Inhabitants* (Boston: Hilliard, Gray, 1835); W. A. G., *Ribs and Trucks, from Davy's Locker; Being Magazine Matter Broke Loose, and Fragments of Sundry Things In-edited* (Boston: Charles D. Strong, 1842); Captain James Colnett, *A Voyage to the South Atlantic and round Cape Horn into the Pacific Ocean, for the Purpose of Extending the Spermaceti Whale Fisheries, and Other Objects of Commerce, by Ascertaining the Ports, Bays, Harbours, and Anchoring Births, in Certain Islands and Coasts in Those Seas at Which the Ships of the British Merchants Might Be Refitted* (London, 1798); Pierre Bayle, *An Historical and Critical Dictionary* (London, 1710); John Kitto, *A Cyclopædia of Biblical Literature* (Edinburgh, 1845). Some chronology of the use Melville made of some of these sources can be established; for instance, the fact that he says in "The Affidavit" that he had not yet learned particulars of the destruction of the *Union* by a whale must mean that he had not yet acquired (or read through) Macy's book, where (as Anderson pointed out) they do occur.

The consensus of scholars is that Melville wrote for some two or three months without having ready access to the basic books about whales—as opposed to whaling—although he had access to passages from Thomas Beale's standard work, as quoted or subsumed in other sources, among them Browne's *Etchings*, Cheever's *The Whale and His Captors*, and one of his hard-worked reference tools, the *Penny Cyclopædia*. From the New York Society Library on April 29, 1850, he borrowed the two volumes of Scoresby's *An Account of the Arctic Regions, with a History and Description of the Northern Whale Fishery* (Edinburgh: Constable, 1820), two days before he wrote Dana that he was "half way" in the whaling voyage (and kept them out for over a year, until June 14, 1851). Much of Scoresby's book was of little use to Melville because it dealt with the Northern (Atlantic) fishery for the right whale and from a British point of view, but he took from it incidental information on topics such as the head and spiracle of the right whale, the narwhale's use of its tusk, and the way ships in the Holland fishery are fitted out. Furthermore, Scoresby's stuffy and pious tone proved so irritating or amusing that Melville treated him as a stooge whenever he plundered him (as he had mocked the good missionary William Ellis while plundering his *Polynesian Researches* in *Omoo*), repeatedly contriving comic names for the imaginary authorities to whom he attributed particular bits of poor Scoresby's information. As Leon Howard says, Melville probably ordered Beale about the time he borrowed Scoresby, judging from the fact that on July 10, 1850, he received the copy that Putnam had imported for him from London. The week before he left for Pittsfield, therefore, Melville had books to quarry both for whaling and for whales, although, as Sections II and III have shown, he did not immediately settle into using those books.

Beale's scholarly volume was only a decade old, but long quotations from it had already made their way into encyclopedias and into books on whaling, as well as into newspapers and magazines; Melville was far from the first to recognize Beale as the standard source on the natural history of the whale, and to some extent on whaling. As Melville expected when he ordered the book, he found Beale useful for information which he could quote and assimilate into his manuscript.[30] After he received his copy, if not before, he realized that Beale would also give him such an abundance of materials that he could give the impression of having read far more reference books than had in fact come his way. Howard P. Vincent instances "Cetology" (chap. 32), where Melville quotes "four cetological experts all alluding to the mystery of whale groupings" (Scoresby, Cuvier, Hunter, and Lesson):

30. Vincent, Howard, Barbour, and others have cited these as the chapters most influenced by Beale: 24 ("The Advocate")—for a long account, quoted by Beale, on the "importance of the southern whale fishery"; 32 ("Cetology"), discussed below; 41 ("Moby Dick"); 42 ("The Whiteness of the Whale"); 44 ("The Chart"); 45 ("The Affidavit"); 47 ("The Mat-Maker"); 51 ("The Spirit-Spout"); 52 (The Albatross"); 55 ("Of the Monstrous Pictures of Whales"); 56 ("Of the Less Erroneous Pictures of Whales"); 57 ("Of Whales in Paint; in Teeth; . . ."); 59 ("Squid"); 60 ("The Line"); 61 ("Stubb kills a Whale"); 65 ("The Whale as a Dish"); 68 ("The Blanket"); 71 ("The Jeroboam's Story"); 74 ("The Sperm Whale's Head"); 76 ("The Battering-Ram"); 77 ("The Great Heidelburgh Tun"); 78 ("Cistern and Buckets"); 79 ("The Prairie"); 80 ("The Nut"); 82 ("The Honor and Glory of Whaling"); 83 ("Jonah Historically Regarded"); 85 ("The Fountain"); 86 ("The Tail"); 88 ("Schools and Schoolmasters"); 89 ("Fast-Fish and Loose-Fish"); 90 ("Heads or Tails"); 91 ("The Pequod meets the Rose-bud"); 92 ("Ambergris"); 95 ("The Cassock"); 99 ("The Doubloon"); 101 ("The Decanter"); 102 ("A Bower in the Arsacides"); 103 ("Measurement of the Whale's Skeleton"); 104 ("The Fossil Whale"); and 105 ("Does the Whale's Magnitude Diminish?"). Melville (see Vincent) used Beale for learned information in the chapters on the pictures of whales (55–57) and the fossils and skeletons (102–105). Howard (1987) concluded that only three chapters show the influence of both Browne and Beale: Chapters 48 ("The First Lowering"), 65 ("The Whale as a Dish"), 81 ("The Pequod meets the Virgin").

although they sound as though Melville had surgically removed them directly from their original contexts, they had actually been quoted together on an unnumbered page in the front part of Beale's *Natural History of the Sperm Whale*; instead of ransacking a large whaling library, Melville had merely lifted his authorities from Beale's convenient cache of quotations.

Four experts from one page is over and above what a plunderer should expect, but otherwise this example of Melville at work is as characteristic as it is vivid. Yet Melville's claim in this chapter to having "swam through libraries" in his quest for whaling authorities is followed by a list of authorities taken from the *Penny Cyclopædia*, not from Beale. Little about Melville's use of sources in *Moby-Dick* can be described simply.

Melville's working methods have complicated all attempts to chart his progress on his manuscript by the evidence of his use of sources. The problem is that in a given chapter he might use a single source, and in widely differing ways, as simple as using it only as a "prompt book" to jog his memory, to remind him of a topic, scene, or process from which to take off on his own without identifiable borrowing, or perhaps as complicated as cannibalizing a little or a lot of its pattern, matter, or wording.[31] In another chapter he might use only one source at first then come back and use further sources, then use the first source again. In a third chapter he might use two or more sources from the start, and he might well use Beale (for instance) at second or third hand, or in a now unknown copy, so that it becomes incautious, and possibly fallacious, for a scholar to date all of Melville's uses of Beale after July 10, 1850. Furthermore, in the course of Melville's writing what started as a patch of one or two sentences or a paragraph may have ended up either pretty much at their original length, or expanded but kept in the same location, or expanded and spread through a chapter, or spread into one or more other chapters, placed earlier or later.[32] Failure to take this process into consideration

---

31. In the introduction to the Hendricks House *Omoo* Harrison Hayford was the first to work out Melville's use of sources in this genetic way.

32. An extant manuscript example of the whole course of one of Melville's expansion processes, where the material remained in a single place, may be found in the growth of Chapter 14 of *The Confidence-Man* from a single sentence into the forty-sentence chapter. See the Northwestern-Newberry edition, pp. 413–68.

has led some scholars to sort the information about Melville's use of whaling sources into too rigid a schematization.

Most reviewers did not recognize the whaling sources, but they did see the main literary sources. It was plain to the British reviewers of *Mardi* and *The Whale* (and to the best American reviewers of *Mardi* and *Moby-Dick*) that Melville was a remarkably literary sea-writer. (See Section VII.) The books these well-educated reviewers were reminded of were precisely the "old Books" that Melville had borrowed from Duyckinck and had commented on with such surprising intelligence. By the count of Mary K. Bercaw in *Melville's Sources*, critics (from reviewers through present academic critics) have named more than a hundred and sixty works as Melville's sources for *Moby-Dick*, more than a source for every chapter, if that had been the way Melville worked. A value of Bercaw's historical recapitulation is that it allows one to restate obvious propositions, some of which tend to be shuffled aside. By general agreement, the literary works most important to Melville in *Moby-Dick* include the Bible and classics of English literature (along with some European classics, in translation), but they also include some of "the books that prove most agreeable, grateful, and companionable" because they are picked up "by chance here and there": "those which seem put into our hands by Providence; those which pretend to little, but abound in much" (*White-Jacket*, chap. 41). Yet Melville had a way of taking hold of even the classics providentially, as when he discovered a large-print edition of Shakespeare just when he was both intellectually ready to grapple with the plays and had days and days when he did not have to do much else besides look in at his wife and newborn son, and read.

For Melville nothing fell into the category of required reading, and any attempt to systematize the sometimes routine and other times idiosyncratic twists he made of his literary sources risks ending up in fatuous reductiveness. With that gesture toward mitigating the critical sin of oversimplification, we report in this paragraph some of what the best authorities have concluded about literary influences on *Moby-Dick*. It was pervasively influenced by the Bible (in particular the Book of Job, providing an analogue for Ahab's quarrel with God, and the Book of Jonah, providing an analogue for Ishmael's less defiant method of coming to terms with the universe); by Shakespeare's plays (where King Lear and other tragic heroes provided models for Ahab); by Milton's *Paradise Lost* (from which Melville took some of

Ahab's qualities as satanic opponent); by Marlowe's *Doctor Faustus* and Goethe's *Faust* (for analogues of demonic temptation and heroic obsession); by Robert Burton, whose *Anatomy of Melancholy* served as this pondering-man's textbook on morbid psychology; by Sir Thomas Browne, that cracked archangel (for seductive prose rhythm serving a dumbfoundingly self-possessed idiosyncrasy); by Thomas Hope's *Anastasius; or, Memoirs of a Greek* (for hints at Ishmael's twists of mind and actions, not least for a ceremonial marriage between men); by Mary Shelley's *Frankenstein* (for a prolonged revenge pursuit); by Dante (for an anatomy of human sinfulness); by Pierre Bayle's dictionary and Montaigne's essays (for their worldly-wise skepticism which braced him against superficial pieties); by Coleridge's lecture on *Hamlet* (for the crucial definition of the Shakespearean hero that he worked into "The Ship" [chap. 16]); by Carlyle, especially *Sartor Resartus* but also *Heroes and Hero-Worship* (for a sardonic verbal playfulness and a depiction of the physical universe as emblematical, but also hints for Ahab from the depiction of Cromwell); by Sterne's *Tristram Shandy* (for liberating gamesomeness toward the lofty task of bookmaking); by De Quincey's *Confessions* (for the Malay whose Asiatic associations were infused into Fedallah and his boat's crew, and for the apparently inimitable prose style which to Melville was as natural as his own breath). Any such list has at least the virtue of reminding readers of the obvious—that in Melville's own resolve (*Pierre*, bk. 21.i) "to give the world a book, which the world should hail with surprise and delight," his reading—from Shakespeare to Scoresby, from Milton to Macy, from Bayle to Beale—flowed into a "contributary stream":

> A varied scope of reading, little suspected by his friends, and randomly acquired by a random but lynx-eyed mind, in the course of the multifarious, incidental, bibliographic encounterings of almost any civilized young inquirer after Truth; this poured one considerable contributary stream into that bottomless spring of original thought which the occasion and time had caused to burst out in himself.

We have dealt in this section with only a few of the books that formed the "considerable contributary stream" pouring into Melville's "bottomless spring of original thought" which burst out in him as he worked on *Moby-Dick*.

The evidence now at hand about how *Moby-Dick* was written, as laid out in Sections II–IV, took many years to recognize and assemble. Most of it was unknown to the British and American men and women of letters of the Melville revival whose enthusiastic essays established *Moby-Dick* as a world masterpiece (see Section VIII). Little of the external evidence was found, or applied to this problem, by Melville's first full-length biographers, Raymond Weaver (1923) and Lewis Mumford (1929), though much of it was not far off, still in the hands of Melville's surviving daughter, Frances Thomas (or passed from her to her daughters, particularly to Eleanor Melville Metcalf), or his grandnieces, or else in the Gansevoort-Lansing and Duyckinck Collections of the New York Public Library, while other documents were in the less readily accessible archives of the American and British publishers, the Harper and Bentley firms, and (at this period) the still-substantial Putnam archives. Not until the 1930's did scholars take on the job of assembling the scattered documentary records of Melville's whole life and literary career. Over the ensuing two decades, during which academic study of American literature became a profession, the efforts of these scholars were the more difficult because the early collapse of Melville's literary reputation had meant that no nineteenth-century full-scale biography had been written, not even of the filio-pietistic life-and-letters sort compiled, for example, for Hawthorne.

Charles R. Anderson's Columbia Ph.D. dissertation (1935) and his *Melville in the South Seas* (1939), a book epochal for Melville scholarship, first systematically demonstrated one of Melville's practices in writing his South Sea books. Through study of archival documents he had located, and through examination of books on the South Seas which he determined Melville had used as sources, Anderson distinguished components of autobiography, borrowings, and invention in *Typee*, *Omoo*, and *White-Jacket*, on which he concentrated more than on *Moby-Dick*. (His discovery of Melville's habit of mingling personal observations with information from printed sources, confirmed by Harrison Hayford's study of *Omoo* [1969] and by other work, has passed into general knowledge, and is reported as such in Section II of this NOTE.) Anderson did not attempt, in his analyses of any of the four books just named, to identify the time-order in which

Melville used his source-books, and therefore did not contribute directly to study of the sequence in which Melville wrote the parts of *Moby-Dick*.

After Anderson, up to mid-century only five scholars addressed the problem of the genesis of *Moby-Dick*, perhaps because the prevailing academic attitude through the 1940's (as to the present) made historical questioning about the genesis of literary works seem uninteresting or even illegitimate, or else interesting only in terms of the author's milieu rather than his creative processes. These five were Leon Howard (1938, 1940, 1951), Charles Olson (1938, 1947), Harrison Hayford (1944, 1945), Howard P. Vincent (1949), and George Stewart (1954). After the middle of the century only one more scholar, James Barbour (1970, 1975, 1976), joined the inquiry seriously, while Hayford once (1978) and Howard himself several times (most significantly, in his posthumous pamphlet, 1987) returned to it; only one critic, Robert Milder (1977), has seriously attempted to evaluate the inquiry.

Charles Olson's work on Melville first appeared in his 1933 Wesleyan M.A. essay, then was carried further in a seminar paper under F. O. Matthiessen at Harvard. In the 1930's Olson was more assiduous and successful than any other scholar in locating books that survived from Melville's library. With assistance from Edward Dahlberg he shaped his Harvard paper into "*Lear* and *Moby-Dick*" (in *Twice a Year*, 1938), becoming the first to develop a major literary component of later genetic theories, the influence of Shakespeare: "I propose a Melville whose masterpiece, *Moby-Dick*, was actually precipitated by Shakespeare." Olson's claim for the catalytic force of Shakespeare upon *Moby-Dick* was derived from his conviction that he had discovered the very moment of conception:

> It is beautifully right to find what seem to be rough jottings for *Moby-Dick* in the Shakespeare set itself. With dramatic aptness, they are written upon the last fly-leaf of the last volume, the one containing *Lear*,— *Othello* and *Hamlet*.

(See pp. 955–70.) The notes contained, as Olson said, a "longer form of what Melville told Hawthorne to be the secret motto of *Moby-Dick*": "Ego non baptizo te in nomine patris, sed in nomine diaboli"; they contained "Filii et Spiritus Sancti." Olson proclaimed the significance:

In that change we witness the process of creation going on before our eyes, for the removal of Christ and the Holy Ghost . . . is the mechanical act mirroring the imaginative one. Of necessity, from Ahab's world, both Christ and the Holy Ghost are absent.

This rich essay also made the first attempt since Evert Duyckinck's review to distinguish Melville the author, Ishmael the narrator, and Ahab the hero. A dazzling tour de force, it was neglected for nearly a decade, being subsumed in Matthiessen's treatment of the Shakespearean influence in *American Renaissance* (1941, pp. 457–58).

In a 1938 MLA paper and a 1940 article on the limits of Melville's craftsmanship ("Struggle"), Leon Howard called attention to an apparent contradiction as to the date *Moby-Dick* reached completion. The first date was set by Duyckinck's August 7, 1850, letter (for which Howard had only the month) reporting Melville's "romantic, fanciful & literal & most enjoyable presentment of the Whale Fishery" as being "mostly done." The second date was set by Melville's letter to Hawthorne on June 1?, 1851 (again Howard had only the month) indicating that it was still unfinished. He spelled out the difficulty in reconciling the dates and his recourse to Luther S. Mansfield, who had published Duyckinck's letter for the first time:[33]

> Since all the available correspondence recording Melville's labors on the book is from the year *following* August, 1850, I considered the

33. Howard saw it in Mansfield's article in *American Literature* (March, 1937) on Melville in Pittsfield during 1850–51. He had not read Mansfield's 1936 Chicago dissertation, "Herman Melville: Author and New Yorker, 1844–1851," or the pamphlet of the same title (consisting only of the eighth chapter of the dissertation, on Melville's reading during 1844–1851, based partly on Duyckinck's record of "Books Lent"), which the University of Chicago Libraries distributed privately in 1938. By 1940 Howard also knew Olson's article, and was troubled by his unconsciously inconsistent transcription of one phrase in Melville's notes in the Shakespeare volume, first as "right reasons" but later as "right reason" (see p. 970, below), and also by the whole interpretation he developed from the latter. As Howard reflected on Olson's transcription, he decided to check the volume for himself. Many of Melville's books and papers were by then in the Houghton Library, but "were restricted for a period of ten years to the exclusive use of a graduate student named Charles Olson." (He had been largely instrumental in getting them there.) How this restriction was circumvented is told in Howard's "The Case of the Left-Out Letter" (1976). The difference between Olson's initial and correct "right reasons" and his alternative incorrect "right reason" was highly significant in Howard's lasting view, though fleeting in Olson's (see Sealts, *Pursuing Melville* [1982], pp. 148 and 367, n. 15).

statement that it was "mostly done" by that time sufficiently arresting to justify a query. Mr. Mansfield, however, assures me that it is accurate.

Reflecting on the discrepancy between the description of the book as "mostly done" and the publication date of October, 1851 (London), and November, 1851 (New York), and reflecting further on possible causes for both the delay and the difference between the tragic story of Ahab and what Duyckinck had described, Howard focused on August of 1850, which Mansfield had documented in much detail, as the time when Melville had changed direction with his manuscript. There had been two versions of *Moby-Dick*, the "original version," to which Duyckinck's adjectives would have applied, and the later "finished novel."

Having studied Melville's essay on Hawthorne, which Willard Thorp had printed in his *Representative Selections* (1938), as well as Olson's 1938 article on the precipitating influence of Shakespeare on *Moby-Dick*, Howard added two new elements, first the idea that Melville had "learned—or thought he learned—from Shakespeare a specific creative method that filled a large vacancy in his artistic bag of tricks." Melville had "looked at Shakespeare through the medium of Samuel Taylor Coleridge":

> *Moby-Dick* itself indicated that Coleridge's lecture on *Hamlet* came into Melville's mind whenever he stopped to comment on Captain Ahab as an artistic creation. Remembering the dictum that "one of Shakespeare's modes of creating characters is to conceive any one intellectual or moral faculty in *morbid* excess, and then to place himself . . . thus *mutilated* or *diseased*, under given circumstances," Melville prepared for the introduction of his own hero as "a mighty page[a]nt creature, formed for noble tragedies," by explaining that it would not "at all detract from him, dramatically regarded, if either by birth or other circumstances, he have what seems a half-wilful *over-ruling morbidness* at the bottom of his nature."

Howard felt assured not only that Melville had read Coleridge but that the reading had rescued him from a period in which he was delayed in his progress on the book by "new technical problems" for which Coleridge's theory of Shakespearean tragedy provided the solution. In that summer of 1850 Melville's "problem of narrative invention had become acute," Howard decided, so acute that he required a second rescue, this time by his reading of *Mosses from an Old Manse;* the essay on it that Melville dashed off "shows all the enthusiasm of a struggling young author who had discovered the man who could teach him his art," or at least could teach him the "narrative technique" he needed if he were to get on with his book.[34] Howard summed up the advance in Melville's writing as "an art learned from Shakespeare under the tutelage of Coleridge and adjusted to Melville's own peculiar temperament and to the requirements of the novel according to the example set by Hawthorne."

Howard's argument was taken up and elaborated by Harrison Hayford in a 1944 article reporting his discovery of two of Melville's letters to Dana, the second of which, written on May 1, 1850, is still the earliest known reference to the book. This letter (discussed above in Section III) was enough to lead Hayford to offer this hypothesis:

> is it not possible that the "whaling voyage" book Melville wrote between February and August, 1850, was another *Redburn* or *White-Jacket*, with Ishmael as its narrator and protagonist and the whale fishery as its real subject, and that what occupied him so painfully for nearly a year thereafter was the creation of the whole drama and allegory of Ahab and the revision of the earlier narrative to incorporate the Ahab theme?

In his 1945 Yale dissertation Hayford printed for the first time a portion of Melville's letter to Bentley on June 27, 1850 (a copy of which John H. Birss had provided him). Hayford saw his new evidence as confirmation and elaboration of Howard's conclusions, although he dealt much more extensively than Howard with the personal relationship between Melville and Hawthorne.

Shortly after this 1944 article appeared, Howard P. Vincent got in touch with Hayford, and was directed to Howard's 1940 article. Stirred up, Vincent immediately began to try to work the new information and theorizing into the nearly finished manuscript of his *The Trying-Out of MOBY-DICK*. The best he could do, under the circumstances, was to add a section on the genesis of *Moby-Dick* (pp. 22–56) to his chapters on whaling sources of the book. Before his book went to press, he unwarily told Charles Olson about Howard's argument and its elaboration by Hayford. He also told him the name (Perc S.

---

34. Howard did not focus on the now-famous picnic and the impact on Melville of Hawthorne the man; he did so in his biography (1951).

Brown) of the owner of Melville's copy of Owen Chase's *Narrative*
with bound-in leaves of Melville's manuscript memoranda about the
*Essex*. (See pp. 971–95.) Engaged now in refashioning his earlier
manuscript study of Melville, Olson with no ado and with no apparent lucubrations scooped Vincent. Calling on the collector, he obtained Melville's memoranda and rushed into print with them in his
elliptical *Call Me Ishmael* (1947), where he also proclaimed the compositional theory much as Vincent had reported it to him: "*Moby-
Dick* was two books written between February, 1850 and August,
1851. The first book did not contain Ahab. It may not, except incidentally, have contained Moby-Dick." In his now vatic role Olson
identified with the Melville who had no need to acknowledge his
plunderings:

> He was a skald, and knew how to appropriate the work of others. He
> read to write. Highborn stealth, Edward Dahlberg calls originality,
> the act of a cutpurse Autolycus who makes his thefts as invisible as
> possible. Melville's books batten on other men's books.

In *Call Me Ishmael* the notion of *Moby-Dick* as two books reached the
general reading public as it had not done in the articles Howard and
Hayford had published in learned journals.

Vincent's *Trying-Out* (1949) accepted the Howard-Hayford theory and introduced another class of evidence. Vincent dated Melville's
borrowing of Scoresby's book and his purchase of Beale (see Section
IV) and hypothesized that Melville acquired them with the purpose of
working "a large mass of cetological and whaling data" into "a story
already well developed." He also introduced a new element into the
speculation about the form of the book Melville had described as a
"whaling voyage": the "original or first plot" was that of "The
Town-Ho's Story"—"a conflict between two men, an officer and a
common sailor." Even with some thunder stolen from his book,
Vincent like Olson reached a general audience few academics ever
touch.

In 1951, in his biography of Melville, Leon Howard carried his
earlier speculations into much greater detail. He now could use information gathered by various scholars since his 1940 article, including
the biographical detail in Jay Leyda's *Log* (available to him before
publication), Hayford's 1944 article and 1945 Yale dissertation, Vincent's *Trying-Out*, and one other dissertation, by Wilbur S. Scott

(Princeton, 1943). Closely scrutinizing dates in Melville's biography, including the borrowing of Scoresby and the purchase of Beale, Howard still hypothesized two main phases in the composition of *Moby-Dick*. Now, taking books Melville brought home from London as evidence that he was thinking of writing a gothic romance of whaling, he decided that Melville had progressed on that romance for several months. After August, 1850, Melville had begun to revise his romantic narrative of the whale fishery at a time when his reading of Hawthorne's stories and his meeting with their author had just served as a catalytic agent for the precipitation in words of a new attitude toward human nature which his mind had held in increasingly strong solution for some years. In this view, Melville "planned to make his new story a dramatic romance that combined the characteristics of a romantic novel with those of a Shakespearean tragedy." Howard also began the process of mustering references within the book to datable events that really happened, and to the apparent inclusion of the actual date Melville wrote one passage in "The Fountain."[35]

In 1954 George R. Stewart became the first to discuss the genesis of *Moby-Dick* primarily on the basis of internal evidence. He was struck by the large number of details which "imply certain actions to follow"—actions which do not exist in the text as published.[36] Then

35. Howard and later scholars have pointed to the following passages as being more or less closely tied to datable contemporary events mentioned in them or journalistic items Melville drew on: at least part of Chapter 26, as probably written after the *Albion* reviewed *White-Jacket* on March 30, 1850; Chapter 45, "The Affidavit," as apt to be contemporaneous with the June 27 letter to Bentley; Chapter 71, "The Jeroboam's Story," as later than mid-August, 1850, when Melville refreshed his memory of the Shakers; Chapter 76, "The Battering-Ram," as unlikely to have been written until after Melville had access to both Cheever and Chase, apparently April, 1851; at least part of Chapter 78, "Cistern and Buckets," as after the collapse of Table Rock into Niagara Falls on June 25, 1850; Chapter 85, "The Fountain" (declared to have been written on December 16, 1851—an error for 1850); Chapter 90, "Heads and Tails," as later than June 29, 1850, when the *Literary World* printed an item on which it is based; Chapter 92, "Ambergris," as probably later than September 9, 1850; at least part of Chapter 102, as later than August 5, 1850. (A complication, mentioned in Section IV, is that even if Melville wrote one part of a chapter after a certain time, another part may have been written earlier.)

36. The more persuasive of these problematic details (for example, does the *Pequod* have "a turnstile wheel" or a tiller?) are cited in the DISCUSSIONS OF ADOPTED READINGS.

he listed other categories of inconsistencies of which the most striking was "Shifts in conception and function of characters." Here Stewart saw Bulkington as a character meant for the original narrative, but unnecessary in the final version: "His description, however, was already written, and Melville liked it as such. Moreover, like most professional authors, he was reluctant to throw away something he had already written." Stewart attempted to describe, in more detail than anyone had done before, what the hypothetical original narrative (the "Ur-*Moby-Dick*") had been like:

> Sailing to the Pacific by way of Cape Horn, Ishmael and Queequeg experienced many adventures of whaling. Their ship, the *Pequod*, was a conventional whaling ship, steered by a wheel and carrying a normal crew of about thirty officers and men. One of the seamen was named Bulkington; he figured in various incidents and was remarkable for his physical strength. The one-legged captain was nicknamed "Old Thunder," and his word was "growl and go." From him Ishmael, a greenhorn at whaling, received many kicks, but Ishmael respected and got along well with the somewhat eccentric third mate, named Stubb, in whose boat he served for a time at least. Meanwhile Queequeg was the hero. Unfortunately, in the pursuit of a large and vicious whale (which may have been a white one) Queequeg was entangled with the line and jerked out of the boat headforemost in "his last long dive." Shortly afterward, the objectionable features of the ship overbalanced the agreeable ones for Ishmael, and he deserted at a tropical island.

Stewart's article gave such currency to the term "two *Moby-Dicks*" that later writers often either accepted the idea of "twoness" as an established fact or rejected it as the only theory about the book's genesis.

James Barbour's 1970 UCLA Ph.D. dissertation, written under the direction of Leon Howard, extended the previous work of Howard, Hayford, Vincent, Stewart, and others. Barbour's was the first attempt (and remains the only completed effort) to accumulate and systematize external evidence and datable internal evidence. His main new conclusion was that *Moby-Dick* was produced in "three distinct stages of composition." Rather than changing his conception in mid-August under the stimulus of Shakespeare and Hawthorne, as Howard and others had suggested, Melville during the fall had continued to write chapters on whaling or on whales, but now under the powerful influence of Carlyle, which blended with that of Shakespeare during the "revision" or "rewriting" of "the whaling novel" "in the early months of 1851." Barbour's 1975 article succinctly summarizes much of the dissertation (although leaving out most of his evidence from Melville's use of whaling sources), and it reiterates his theory that there were three, not two, major phases in the composition of *Moby-Dick*, the first ending in August, 1850, the second extending till about the end of the year, the third begun early in 1851.

In the 1970's, while working on the present edition of *Moby-Dick*, Hayford found a "curious pattern of duplicates" in the book. The pattern offered "evidence for a major hypothesis . . . about Melville's shifting intentions for some of the central characters in *Moby-Dick* as it developed through several phases during the year and a half he was writing it."[37] Hayford's evidence, like and including some of Stewart's, was altogether internal. The pattern, as he interpreted it, was the layered result of Melville's revisions and additions as he went back over passages he had already written at earlier composition stages. Chapter by chapter (1–22) Hayford pointed out and summarized the accumulating duplicates:

> At long last chapter 22 gets the *Pequod* hauled out from the Nantucket wharf. The twenty-one shore chapters have already taken up about a fifth of the book—surely a disproportionate share—before the whaling voyage begins, before Ishmael sees anything of the watery part of the world, before the book's tragic protagonist appears, and before its plot and Ahab's mighty antagonist are revealed. There have been two narrative starts, two whaling ports, two inns (and two chowders), two innkeepers, two beds and goings-to-bed, two comrades (one dismissed already), two signings-aboard, two Quaker captain-owners and a third Quaker captain-in-command, four (of an eventual seven) prophets, four hide-outs, and an extra boat-crew. No wonder it has taken so much space, with so much duplication already! Did Melville think the book itself had to be stocked with duplicates just as the *Pequod* had to be provided with 'spare boats, spare spars, and spare lines and harpoons, and spare everythings, almost, but a spare Captain and duplicate ship'? (chap. 20)

37. In "Sources" see Hayford, "Unnecessary Duplicates: A Key to the Writing of *Moby-Dick*" (1978). This summary and many of the notes in the DISCUSSIONS OF ADOPTED READINGS use wording from the essay, which was written from materials developed for this edition. The phrase "unnecessary duplicates" (from chap. 107) applies only in the sense that finding two's or three's so many times, where only one would be normally expected, reveals a pattern that needs explanation.

By "hide-outs" in this summary, Hayford meant characters who by normal expectation should be present in one or more scenes but are kept out of sight until later. He interpreted this recurrent peculiarity as evidence of two or more stages of composition. "Duplicate" characters (ones who somehow overlap in their roles in a peculiar way) are also a major category of such evidence. The two chief pairs of duplicates are Bulkington and Queequeg, and Peleg and Ahab. The key one of the four characters is Bulkington. In "The Spouter-Inn" (chap. 3) he is introduced to be Ishmael's "comrade," but at once he is hustled offstage (a "hide-out") not to be seen by Ishmael for many chapters, and then dismissed from the book (chap. 21). Back at the Spouter Inn, Queequeg takes over Bulkington's vacated role as comrade; but only after being a hide-out for much of the chapter—while Ishmael goes to bed twice, first on a cold bench downstairs, then in Queequeg's room upstairs, where Queequeg finally shows up. But Queequeg soon hides out again, for his Ramadan (chap. 17), whereas in his role of experienced whaleman mentor, one would expect him to go with Ishmael and take the lead in choosing their ship.

Hayford accounts for these "hide-outs" as the way Melville avoided at later stages the job of writing new characters into or old characters out of scenes he had written earlier. Sometimes this meant he had to do that job by adding new (and hence duplicate) scenes or chapters. According to this hypothesis, in Chapter 16 Ishmael signs aboard the *Pequod* in a scene Melville had already written, without Queequeg in it; and Melville had to write a second scene in which Queequeg belatedly signs aboard after his Ramadan. In that earlier-written scene, whose details back up this theory, Ishmael encounters two (duplicate) captains, but not the third one, Ahab, who will command her—he is a hide-out. The explanation Hayford deduced from the pattern of hide-outs, duplicates, and other anomalous details in the text is that Peleg was earlier the captain for the voyage, until Melville displaced him from that role at a later compositional stage by the newly conceived hero—Ahab. Making Ahab a hide-out until the ship is at sea was the way Melville avoided having to write him into scenes written earlier, such as this one. By changing a few words in it, Melville demoted Peleg from captain to stay-at-home joint-owner, thereby duplicating that role, which Bildad already occupied. Hayford theorized that perhaps when Melville gave Peleg's captaincy to Ahab he also gave him a whalebone leg that was earlier Peleg's.

About this time, too, Melville probably added the passage in which Ishmael goes back to ask Peleg about Ahab, and inserted the eloquent digression on a Quaker tragic hero—one nowhere in sight. Hayford was convinced that these compositional procedures wonderfully enriched the shore chapters, and also that they explain why those chapters take up one-fifth of the book.

Those internal clues led Hayford to his "major hypothesis": Melville was engaged in "a multiple reassignment of roles" (partly written, partly projected) "among four of his central characters." Ahab displaced both Peleg as captain and Bulkington as the book's projected heroic quester. Perhaps Bulkington had developed such stature that, renamed, he "became" Ahab. Concurrently, Queequeg took over Bulkington's vacated role as Ishmael's companion. In sea-chapters, already written, he had been only one of the three pagan harpooneers—maybe only a crewman. Earlier he had not been Ishmael's companion, as shown by such anomalies as Ishmael's "hiding out" from the scene where Queequeg seems to be dying—dying in the forecastle, where a harpooneer does not belong. Ishmael is "hiding out" from the scene for the good reason (Hayford argued) that when Melville wrote the chapter Queequeg was not his friend yet— Melville had not yet assigned him that role—that came later, at the stage which eliminated Bulkington. At the end of his article Hayford confessed the tentative state of his interpretation of the peculiar features within the text of *Moby-Dick* but also expressed his confidence that he had added a new key to the keys already used by the earlier theorizers whose work is reviewed here.

Leon Howard pursued his admittedly obsessive concern with the genesis of *Moby-Dick* from 1938 until his death in 1982, when he was engaged on a new, and only partly-written, formulation, which was published in 1987, as a fragment. He had come to accept Barbour's theory of three instead of two major phases for the composition of *Moby-Dick*, the second a phase in which Melville, under the stylistic influence of Carlyle, sardonically expanded his cetological chapters. Eager to tie Melville to a particular book in which he read Coleridge's lecture on *Hamlet*, Howard had, with uncharacteristic rashness, come to believe that Melville had gained access to that book at the Boston Athenaeum on December 30, 1850, although no record of his presence there survives. The fact is, as documents in the Augusta Melville papers show, that Melville did not go to Boston that December: his wife was there but he was in Pittsfield (see pp. 625–26 above). This unfortunate error mars but does not vitally affect Howard's tightly argued but tantalizingly incomplete reworking of the now-familiar evidence and arguments about Melville's progress on the book.

Perhaps the most lasting value of the pamphlet is Howard's treatment of a topic only Barbour had considered in such detail—which chapters in *Moby-Dick* are derived from which of the whaling sources Vincent and others identified. But Howard was plainly intrigued by, and meant to engage, Hayford's hypothesis about the "multiple reassignment of roles among four of his central characters":

> These are, to say the least, startling suggestions; and they provide a challenging opportunity to explore the ways in which textual evidence and such scholarly evidence as sources and influences can contradict, modify, or confirm each other. Such a combination of evidence may also solve problems created by or left unsolved by the use of more restrictive evidence.

Just after this point the text breaks off, before Howard could show how far he was able to to reconcile Hayford's hypothesis with the sorts of external evidence he had carefully reexamined. This outlined but unfinished piece ends Howard's pursuit of a satisfactory theory of the composition of *Moby-Dick*—a pursuit that lasted longer than Ahab pursued whales. Howard saw the challenge plainly: to reconcile theories based on internal discrepancies with theories based on external evidence. The challenge remains, to be taken up, perhaps in new ways, by scholars of a new generation.

# VI

As early as June 27, 1850, Melville had begun to give thought to the publishing arrangements for his new book. On that day he wrote to Richard Bentley, the English publisher of *Mardi, Redburn,* and *White-Jacket,* proposing publication of a "new work" that would be "ready" by "the latter part of the coming autumn." Stressing his use of personal experience and his treatment of "certain wild legends" in the whaling industry, he suggested a payment of £200, since that was the sum paid for *White-Jacket,* a book which Melville wrongly assumed "must have been, in some degree, profitable" to Bentley. In fact, he thought the whaling book might be worth more: "I do not know," he said, "that the subject treated of has ever been worked up by a romancer; or, indeed, by any writer, in any adequate manner." At this stage Melville expected Harper & Brothers to be his American publishers, for they had published his four preceding books and had taken over the distribution of his first book. The usual arrangement was that proof sheets of the American edition were sent to the English publisher and that American publication was held up until after the work had been set in type and published in England. Given the uncertain legal status of the English copyright for an American work, this procedure was generally regarded as providing the strongest claims for such a copyright; and it is clear that Melville anticipated no difference in the handling of this book and hoped to reach a prompt agreement with Bentley "so as to lose no time, when the book has passed thro' the Harpers' press," in putting Bentley "in early & certain possession of the proof sheets, as in previous cases."

As matters turned out, Melville's protracted work on the book, extending a year beyond the date he had announced, resulted in some alteration of these plans. Deprived of the expected income from a new book in the winter of 1850–51, he wrote to the Harpers in the spring of 1851 asking for an advance; but their sixth statement of account with him, dated April 29, 1851, showed that he was already indebted to his publishers for $695.65, and the advance was denied. One result was that Melville had to borrow from T. D. Stewart— $2,050 at nine percent for five years (see p. 629)—for current expenses, building improvements, and such previous obligations as his note to John M. Brewster the preceding September in connection with the purchase of Arrowhead. But another result apparently was that Melville no longer considered the Harpers his automatic choice as publishers for the new book. Whether or not their failure to make the advance was responsible, two pieces of evidence suggest that Melville was considering other publishing arrangements in the summer of 1851. One is a letter Evert Duyckinck wrote to his wife on August 7, during his visit to Pittsfield. He reported, "Harpers are to publish Melville's whale book. I have said a great deal for Redfield but it appears to have been concluded." There would have been no point in suggesting Justus Redfield as publisher if the Harpers had already been firmly settled on, and Duyckinck's speaking of him "a great deal" suggests that there may have been considerable, and perhaps repeated, discussion of the matter. The second piece of evidence is a clause in the Harper contract as it was finally signed on September 12, specifying that the publishers agreed "to publish said work from the stereotype plates now in the possession of R. Craighead." In each of the contracts for the four preceding books the Harpers referred to a "manuscript" rather than a "work"[38] and agreed to "stereotype, publish, and sell" the resulting book. The change of wording shows that in this instance the typesetting and stereotyping had been completed before a publisher was secured, and it reinforces the possibility that Melville may have been hesitant at first to place the book with the Harpers (or that they may have been reluctant to take it).

Although it had not been Melville's previous custom to arrange for the plating of his books, the practice was not uncommon in the nineteenth century, particularly among prominent authors with considerable sales. For example, William Prescott owned the plates of his works from the beginning of his career, and Longfellow bought the plates of his earlier books when he decided to switch to this system. There were several reasons why authors might want to own their plates. For one thing, their net profits were likely to be higher, especially on works that sold well—whether they leased the plates to their publisher or received royalties at the time of publication. In addition, they would have closer control over the texts and the typography of their works; they would not be faced with the suggestions or alterations of publishers' readers or with house styling, and they could see to it that the layout of pages and the typesetting satisfied them. Closer control over the manufacture of the plates also meant closer control over the expenses of production, and the suspicious author would have fewer and less complicated figures from the publisher to worry about. Any of these reasons might have appealed to Melville. Certainly he had had experience with publishers' demands for alterations, and he would have welcomed any means of increasing his rate of profit. It may be, however, that he was thinking principally of saving time. If the book could be set in type and plated while the choice of publisher was still undecided, there would be less delay after an agreement was reached. That Melville did not mean to retain ownership of the plates or alter in a basic way his previous manner of

---

38. In the case of the only previous book of Melville's for which Harpers was not the originating publisher—*Typee,* published by Wiley & Putnam—the agreement by which Harpers took over the distribution of the book also referred to a "work."

dealing with publishers is suggested by another clause in the Harper contract, providing that the Harpers would pay "said Craighead for the cost of said plates." It would appear that Melville arranged for the plating as a way of getting the production of the book under way sooner than would otherwise be possible; but the exact nature of the difficulties that prevented an earlier agreement with a publisher is not clear from the available evidence.

At any rate, when Melville referred, in his letters of June and July of 1851, to the fact that his book was going "through the press," he was presumably speaking of the press of Robert Craighead. The choice of Craighead—whose shop, at 112 Fulton Street in New York, seems somewhat inconveniently located for an author living in Pittsfield—was not surprising: Craighead was the printer whom Wiley & Putnam had employed to print *Typee* (and he was thus the only American printer besides the Harpers who had printed any of Melville's books up to that time); in addition, Duyckinck may have recommended him, since he was the printer of the *Literary World*.[39] Mel-

39. For *Typee,* Craighead performed only the actual printing, from stereotype plates made by Thomas B. Smith; indeed, it was common at this period for the jobs of typesetting, stereotyping, and printing to be divided, one printer doing the typesetting and plating and another the presswork. Craighead did not advertise himself in the *Literary World* as a stereotyper until after his disastrous fire early on January 23, 1852 (described in the New York *Times* that day and the following day and in the *Literary World* on January 31, pp. 87–88), but it is likely that he had facilities for stereotyping earlier, for the accounts of the fire reveal what a well-equipped and prosperous shop he ran. The cost of the plates—$512.76, unpaid until the Harpers took over—was an appropriate figure to cover both the typesetting and plating of some 650 pages, judging from the fact that earlier the same year a Boston stereotyper had charged $270 for the typesetting and plating of the 344 pages of Hawthorne's *The House of the Seven Gables* (see William Charvat's note in the Centenary Edition [Columbus: Ohio State University Press, 1965], p. lxiii). Besides, if someone else had manufactured the *Moby-Dick* plates, Craighead's ownership of them at the time of the Harper contract would have to be explained by the implausible assumption that he was planning to print and publish the work. Craighead's name did occasionally appear on title pages as publisher, but probably only when the author was underwriting the expenses; it is unlikely that he would have undertaken *Moby-Dick* as publisher and unlikely that Melville—in view of the later agreement with the Harpers—had asked him to. Frances Jane Crosby's *Monterey and Other Poems,* printed a few months before *Moby-Dick* and bearing Craighead's title-page imprint, exhibits a number of typographical similarities to *Moby-Dick* (the same diamond-center rules and question marks, the same system of signatures, the same policy about display capitalization at chapter and poem openings) but not enough to demonstrate by themselves that

ville was in New York for one day late in May, and it is possible that
he made arrangements with Craighead at that time. In June he went
to New York again, "to bury myself in a third-story room, and work
and slave on my 'Whale' while it is driving through the press," as he
wrote Hawthorne in early June. Nevertheless, by the end of the
month he had again returned to Pittsfield, reporting to Hawthorne,
"The 'Whale' is only half through the press; for, wearied with the
long delay of the printers, and disgusted with the heat and dust of the
babylonish brick-kiln of New York, I came back to the country to
feel the grass—and end the book reclining on it, if I may." What
caused the delay at the printer's is not known, but three weeks later,
on July 20, the typesetting had not yet been finished: in a letter to
Richard Bentley he reported, "I am now passing thro' the press, the
closing sheets of my new work." By this time the fact that the book
was in press had been announced in at least two periodicals: the July 1
number of the *International Magazine* reported that Melville would
"soon be again before the public in a romance," and the *Literary
World* on July 5 predicted the new book for "early in the season."

The process of overseeing the plating of his own work thus did
not turn out to be the satisfying kind of experience for Melville that it
was for some authors. Since he was still working on the book at the
time it was being set in type, his attention was divided between writing and proofreading; and since the earlier parts of the book would
have been not only in type but probably plated as well when he was
revising later parts, he undoubtedly felt restricted in the kinds of
revision that were feasible. When, in writing his next book the following winter, he described Pierre's problems as an author, he must
have been thinking of his own experiences in his New York room:

> At length, domestic matters—rent and bread—had come to such a
> pass with him, that whether or no, the first pages must go to the
> printer; and thus was added still another tribulation; because the
> printed pages now dictated to the following manuscript, and said to all
> subsequent thoughts and inventions of Pierre—*Thus and thus; so and so;
> else an ill match.* Therefore, was his book already limited, bound over,
> and committed to imperfection, even before it had come to any con-

---

*Moby-Dick* was set by Craighead. Nevertheless, all the available evidence taken together supports the idea that Craighead had the plates in his possession because the
typesetting and plating had been done in his shop.

firmed form or conclusion at all. Oh, who shall reveal the horrors of poverty in authorship that is high? (bk. 25.iii)

The famous passage describing Pierre's proofreading may also reflect something of Melville's feelings at the time of *Moby-Dick:*

> As every evening, after his day's writing was done, the proofs of the beginning of his work came home for correction, Isabel would read them to him. They were replete with errors; but preoccupied by the thronging, and undiluted, pure imaginings of things, he became impatient of such minute, gnat-like torments; he randomly corrected the worst, and let the rest go; jeering with himself at the rich harvest thus furnished to the entomological critics. (bk. 25.iii)

In any event, it seems clear that the one time in Melville's career when he was in a position to see a full-length book through the press without the intervention of a publisher's editor turned into a situation in which he was trying to do too many things at once and was discouraged about doing any of them satisfactorily.

Meanwhile negotiations were going forward for the English publication of the book. Apparently Melville had written to Bentley in late spring or early summer, before his session in New York, describing his book once again, but whether he repeated his request of a year before for a payment of £200 is not now known. At any rate, on July 3 Bentley wrote, "I am ready to give you £150 on account of half profits for your new work in my notes at three & six months." The slow sales of the previous three books were clearly in Bentley's mind, for he went on to say, "I think that, as we shall be in the same boat, this mode of publication is the most suitable to meet all the contingencies of the case." Melville replied on July 20, accepting Bentley's offer and going on to discuss the vexed copyright question, expressing the hope that, if more English publishers would protect their American authors, American publishers might begin to reciprocate. His prevailing mood of frustration during these weeks, stimulated by his difficulties with the Harpers and his exhausting trip to New York, was reflected in the letter: "This country is at present engaged in furnishing material for future authors; not in encouraging its living ones." That Melville was grateful to Bentley is further suggested by a letter that his wife wrote to her stepmother on August 3: "Mr Bentley is to give Herman £150 and half profits after, for his new book—a much smaller sum than before to be sure, but certainly worth waiting for—and quite generous on Mr Bentleys part considering the unsettled state of things." It is not quite true that £150 was "a much smaller sum than before," since Bentley's payment for *Redburn* had been only £100; but it is true that the payments for both *Mardi* (£210) and *White-Jacket* (£200) were higher.

After receiving Melville's July 20 letter of acceptance, Bentley drew up and signed, on August 13, the official agreement—one of his standard printed forms for a half-profits arrangement. Under this system the author was to receive half the profits that remained after deducting all the expenses of production and advertising (including "the Allowance of Ten per Cent. on the gross amount of the Sale, for Commission and risk of Bad Debts"). The gross income was to be reckoned in terms of the trade sale price, counting twenty-five copies as twenty-four (unless Bentley decided to sell some copies at a lower price). There are five blank lines in the form for a description of the book, filled in as follows: "an original work written by the said Herman Melville, descriptive of an American Whaling Voyage with its accompanying Adventures, more particularly described in a letter of the said Herman Melville to the said Richard Bentley"—presumably the unlocated letter of late spring. At the end of the form is inserted a handwritten paragraph explaining that the sum of £150 was to be advanced against the half-profits, that no part of this advance need be refunded if half-profits never reached £150, and that English publication was to precede American by at least fourteen days. These terms were essentially the same (except for the amount of the advance) as those under which Bentley published *Mardi* and *Redburn;* for *White-Jacket,* however, the advance payment purchased the copyright for the first impression, and the half-profits arrangement was to take effect with the second printing. It is true that Bentley frequently turned to the half-profits system when he had doubts about the commercial success of a book or when its copyright was questionable, as with American books; but his switch to a different plan for *White-Jacket* and his return to half-profits for *Moby-Dick* is of little significance in judging his evaluations of these books, since half-profits were to apply even to *White-Jacket* in printings after the first. Normally an outright purchase of copyright included no provision for later payments, but the *White-Jacket* agreement, with such a provision, was in effect little different from a regular half-profits contract.[40] What is of more significance is the fact that Bentley continued to make advance payments to Melville. Such advances were not a routine part of half-profits agreements (there was no provision for them in Bentley's printed forms), and the sales of Melville's previous books did not inspire confidence. It is no wonder that Melville, in need of money and without a contract for publication in his own country, was grateful for Bentley's offer and readily accepted it.

Bentley's August 13 contract would have reached Melville near the end of the month or in the first days of September, and he added his signature to it, asking his friend and neighbor John R. Morewood and his wife's cousin Samuel H. Savage to serve as witnesses. He probably sent Bentley's copy back, with an accompanying letter, on September 5; and he probably went to New York at about this same time to turn the proof sheets over to his brother Allan for shipment abroad. At any rate, on September 10 Allan dispatched them from New York, aboard the *Asia,* to J. C. B. Davis, the American Secretary of Legation in London. Although Melville wasted no time in getting the proofs on their way after the contract was signed, the fact remains that they must have been in his possession for several weeks before that. In his earlier letter to Bentley, on July 20, he had said that, since the "closing sheets" were then "passing thro' the press,", he could forward the complete work "in the course of two or three weeks—perhaps a little longer." If the typesetting and proofreading were completed soon after July 20—as they should have been unless the reference to "closing sheets" was an optimistic exaggeration— Melville would have had a full set of the proofs in his possession for at least a month, and possibly as much as six weeks, before giving them to Allan in early September. Yet he had estimated on July 20 that several weeks would elapse before he could send the sheets to Bentley, and one wonders what reason he had in mind. Although he might have wanted to wait until the actual contract arrived before dispatching the sheets, the "two or three weeks" he spoke of seem, in the context of his letter, to be more directly related to the process of getting the proofs ready to send. If so, one explanation is that he

40. Of course, if Bentley had ordered a large first printing of *White-Jacket* and had managed to sell it, he would have received more profit than under the half-profits system; but the fact that he had no more copies printed than in the case of *Mardi* (one thousand copies) and made a similar initial payment suggests that the slightly differing terms of his offer were not based on very different expectations.

expected to spend several weeks proofreading the "closing sheets" that were just then being set in type; but it seems unlikely—since he had presumably read proofs for most of the book in slightly over a month, while he was still writing parts of it—that he would have anticipated spending several weeks on the last sheets at a time when he would not be distracted by writing. Another possibility is that he desired to have several weeks' time in which to go over Bentley's set of proofs, making alterations to be incorporated in the English edition. He might well have wanted to make further revisions if, as seems likely, he had not been able to give his full attention to proofreading earlier and had been thwarted in some of his revision by the fact that previous parts of the book were already in type. Knowing that the book would be reset in England, he had an opportunity for making revisions freely—revisions that could not be introduced into the American edition without additional expense. And since American publication had not yet been arranged, there was not the usual urgency about getting the sheets abroad so that English publication could precede American. Whichever of these explanations is closer to the truth, Melville did have time to make revisions in the proofs for Bentley, and it seems certain that he had the motive for doing so as well.

In the absence of the marked proof sheets it is impossible to determine conclusively just what revisions Melville did in fact make at this stage. The only evidence available is the published text of the English edition, which of course includes changes made in Bentley's office as well as those made by Melville. A comparison of the English and American editions reveals an enormous number of differences—over seven hundred in wording and several thousand in punctuation and spelling. It is a safe working assumption that at each point of variance in the main body of the text the English reading is the later one. While there is the theoretical possibility that Melville requested certain changes in the American edition after the proofs went to England—in which cases the English readings would be earlier—the fact that the American edition was not only in type but almost certainly plated as well would have acted as a deterrent to making alterations in it. If any such alterations were made, they were surely very few and would therefore constitute only a minute fraction of the large number of differences between the two editions.

An examination of these differences shows that Melville did indeed devote some attention to the proofs for Bentley before sending them on September 10. Perhaps the most unmistakable evidence is his addition of a footnote on the word "gally" (384.28–40), which does not appear in the American edition. It is characteristically Melvillean, with its quotation from *King Lear* and its description of the "best and furthest-descended English words" as the "etymological Howards and Percys." Perhaps it was written with the English audience in mind; but there can be no doubt that Melville wrote it, and the possibility is thus strengthened that other changes in the English edition are his as well. A good example occurs in Chapter 33 in the sentence about "the tragic dramatist who would depict mortal indomitableness in its fullest sweep and direst swing" (148.13–15). In the American edition "direst" appears as "direct," which is an obvious enough typographical error, once the right word is known—but, because it makes sense, not an obvious error that would call itself to the attention of even a careful editor or reader. Bentley's editorial reader certainly was careful when it came to grammar and religious or sexual allusions; but there is nothing about "direct" that would have stimulated his zeal, and the alteration to "direst" must have been Melville's. The same can be said of the change from "leaving" to "laving" (548.28) in the description of the sea washing against Moby Dick on the first day of the chase ("coincident with the parted swell, that but once laving him, then flowed so wide away"). Other changes fall into the same class. The alteration of "directed" to "modified" (215.13) in the description of the Loom of Time in "The Mat-Maker" is not a mere "correction" but a revision of the kind that no one but the author would be likely to undertake ("chance, though restrained in its play within the right lines of necessity, and sideways in its motions modified by free will, though thus prescribed to by both, chance by turns rules either . . ."). In Chapter 57 the simple expedient of inserting a pair of dashes and removing the word "that" (271.6–7) clears up the sentence structure by making parenthetical a clause that previously seemed to be introducing a comparison; yet this revision would be difficult for a publisher's reader to see, since a revision that would probably suggest itself first is the omission of "else" (the sentence, revised with the dashes, reads, " . . . you must be sure and take the exact intersecting latitude and longitude of your first stand-point, else—so chance-like are such observations of the hills—your precise, previous stand-point would require a laborious re-discovery"). Again, the italicizing of "he" in Chapter 16 in Bildad's question "What lay does *he* want?" (78.13) emphasizes the point of the question; but the passage reads well enough without the italics that Bentley's reader would not have been likely to think of altering it. Another simple alteration—the move of a comma— changes the meaning of a sentence in Chapter 21 to what was obviously intended: in the sentence beginning, "Meanwhile, upon questioning him, in his broken fashion Queequeg gave me to understand ..." (100.9–10), the deletion of a comma after "fashion" and the insertion of one after "him" shifts the sense to "upon my questioning him" and thus the identity of the questioner from Queequeg to Ishmael.[41] It is conceivable, of course, that some changes of this kind, taken individually, could have been hit upon by Bentley's reader; but since a pattern of them emerges, the chances seem overwhelming that Melville was responsible.

The proofs, thus revised, having been sent off on September 10, Melville's principal remaining business in regard to the book was to secure a contract for American publication. Presumably he had by this time reached an understanding with the Harpers, since Duyckinck had referred to the matter as "concluded" a month earlier. Perhaps Melville made final arrangements on a visit to New York to deliver Bentley's set of proofs to Allan; in any event, on September 12, only two days after those proofs were shipped, Allan, acting as Melville's attorney, signed an agreement with Harper & Brothers for the publication of "a certain work entitled '*The Whale.*' " This contract, though handwritten (like Melville's other Harper contracts), contained several standard provisions: that the copyright belonged to Melville; that the Harpers were to be the exclusive publishers in the United States (and that the contract referred only to American publication); that the agreement would be in effect for seven years; that at any time after the seven years Melville could take possession of the plates for half their original cost (less depreciation for damage) and the publisher could sell any remaining copies of the book; and that the publisher would render semiannual accounts, with any balance due

41. Small changes of this kind provide additional assurance that the English variants are later than the American: one cannot conceive of the American readings being the revised ones in these cases; and, if any late changes were incorporated into the American edition, one would expect them to be exactly like these—small alterations that would not be difficult to make in type or plates but that are of some significance.

Melville payable in notes at three months. The basis for payment was to be a half-profits system, as it had been for the previous books (except that *Typee* was taken over by the Harpers on a royalty basis), and Melville was given the option, after the cost of the plates had been covered, of switching to a payment based on "a sum certain per copy for all copies sold." The most unusual aspect of the contract was its reference to "the stereotype plates now in the possession of R. Craighead." Under normal circumstances, the fact that the Harpers were publishing the book "at their own cost and expence" would mean that the outlay for plating should be understood as one of the routine costs; but since the plating had already been done (and not paid for), the payment to Craighead for the plates was specifically mentioned. Three features were missing from this contract that had been present in previous ones: for the three preceding books Melville was given an advance against half-profits (five hundred dollars for *Mardi* and *White-Jacket,* three hundred dollars for *Redburn),* but no advance was offered in this case; for all the preceding books some arrangement was made for review copies (including the provision, for *Redburn* and *White-Jacket,* that twenty-five were to be given to Melville for distribution), but review copies were not mentioned in this contract; and for the preceding books there was a clause stipulating that Melville be provided with an extra set of proofs and that American publication be deferred for a specified period (so that those proofs could be used as copy for an English edition), but for this book no reference to proofs was made. This last omission was to be expected, since the proofs had already been sent to England; but the other two may reflect a decreasing confidence in Melville's work and a growing dissatisfaction with his perennial indebtedness and uninspiring sales.

If Melville had hesitated, because of the expense, to have his numerous revisions for Bentley incorporated into the American edition while the plates were under his direct control, the Harpers would have been no more likely to encourage such expenditure after they took ownership of the plates. Nevertheless, Melville's alterations to the book did not stop at the moment when he relinquished Bentley's proofs to Allan. Some time after the proofs were shipped—probably later in September—Allan enclosed two more pages of proof in a letter to Bentley (the undated draft of which survives in the Harvard collection):

Since sending proofs of my brothers new work by the Asia on the 10th he has determined upon a new title & dedication—Enclosed you have proof of both—It is thought here that the new title will be a better *selling* title—It is to be hoped that this letter may reach New Burlington Street before it is too late to adopt these new pages.

Moby-Dick is a legitimate title for the book. being the name given to a particular whale who if I may so express myself is the hero of the volume—My brother will draw upon you by the next steamber two drafts at 3 & 6 months from Sept 22 the supposed date of your receipt of the proofs

I will add that the earliest opportunity has been taken to acquaint you with this change the proof was only recᵈ by me yesterday & in the absence of my brother from the city I have been necessitated to communicate it[.]

The change in title from *The Whale* to *Moby-Dick* may have come about in discussions with the Harpers, since Allan emphasized that the shift was motivated, at least in part, by commercial considerations. (Perhaps the Harpers thought it unwise to publish another book with "Whale" in the title so soon after publishing Henry T. Cheever's *The Whale and His Captors* [1849].) The Harpers, even if they wished to, could not make suggestions for altering the text to increase its salability, since it was in plates. But there was no problem about changing the title. After all, the title page would not have been plated until after an agreement with a publisher was signed, since the publisher's name would have to appear in the imprint; and the running heads throughout the book used only chapter titles, so that there was nothing in the already plated text to prevent a change of title. The exact time of this change is not now known, but the book was still referred to as *"The Whale"* in the October number of *Harper's New Monthly Magazine*. In that issue "The Town-Ho's Story" was published, with a footnote citing its source: "From 'THE WHALE.' The title of a new work by Mr. Melville, in the press of Harper and Brothers, and now publishing in London by Mr. Bentley." Although each issue of *Harper's* normally went to press about the tenth of the preceding month,[42] this October issue contained news dating as late as September 14, for in the "Monthly Record of Current Events" the

42. *Harper's New Monthly Magazine*, VIII (January, 1854), 145. The decision to include "The Town-Ho's Story" in the October issue was therefore likely to have been made before the contract for the book was signed on September 12.

death of James Fenimore Cooper was noted. Although this news section was probably one of the last parts of the magazine to be put in final shape, one would expect any mention of a Harper book to be up-to-date, in order to maximize the advertising value of the reference. Therefore the change probably took place after September 14— which is to say, it did not occur in the first day or two after the signing of the Harper contract.[43] These observations are in line with the only known surviving piece of printed proof for the volume: a leaf that appears to be a "trial" title page bearing the title "The Whale" and the Harper imprint. Such a title page would presumably not have been produced until after the Harpers had agreed to publish the book, and this document therefore shows that at some point thereafter (how early or late is impossible to say) the title as stated in the contract was still the accepted one.[44]

Whether or not Allan's letter reached Bentley in time to produce any alterations in the English edition is difficult to determine. In any case *The Whale* was retained as title. However, it is curious that only the first volume has a half title and that it reads, "The Whale; or, Moby Dick." It is unusual for a book to have a longer title on the half-title page than on the title page, and one is tempted to speculate that the inclusion of "Moby Dick" at this spot was Bentley's attempt to make some accommodation of Allan's request, at a time when it was impractical to alter the main title. Since the English edition is in three volumes, changing the title at a late stage would not have been quite as simple a task as in the case of the American edition, for three

43. When the *Literary World* first referred to the book on July 5, it reported, "The title is not yet given." Because of the connections among Duyckinck, Craighead, and Melville, such statements may carry more weight than would otherwise be the case (though Melville had referred to the book as "my 'Whale'" a month before). However, the *Literary World* for October 4 was probably printing out-of-date information when it said, "Herman Melville's forthcoming book is announced by the Harpers. Its title is simply 'The Whale.'" Even allowing for the fact that copy for this issue would have been sent to the printer about a week earlier, the decision to change the title must have been made before that; if not, Allan's letter about the change could not have reached Bentley before the English publication date, and there is some reason, as explained below, to believe that it did. A title page with the new title was deposited for copyright on October 15, but the change in the title must surely have been made well before that time.

44. For further discussion of this title page and a reproduction of it, see the RELATED DOCUMENTS, pp. 1021–43.

title pages were involved—though to alter standing type should not have been a difficult chore, either. But the title also appears on the opening page of text in each volume, making three more occurrences that would have to be altered, and it is possible that the sheets of text (or some of them) were already printed at the time Allan's letter arrived. Even if Allan sent it very soon after September 14, it would not have reached Bentley until early October, after some of Bentley's advertisements using the earlier title were already in press—for *"The Whale"* appeared in Bentley's notices of forthcoming books in both the *Athenæum* and the *Spectator* of October 4 and 11. It is understandable that Bentley would have found it awkward to change the title at this time.

The other change that Allan mentioned—involving the dedication—raises somewhat different questions. In Allan's phrase "a new title & dedication," it is probable that "new" modifies only "title" and that the dedication was being supplied for the first time. But whether the dedication Allan enclosed was the first and only one or a replacement for an earlier one, the dedication as printed is identical in the two editions (except for the change from "this book is" to "these volumes are" in the English): "In token of my admiration for his genius, this book is inscribed to Nathaniel Hawthorne." Since Allan implied that the dedication, like the title, was to be used in the American edition (he was sending "proof" of both pages), the fact that the English agrees with the American suggests that Bentley was able to fulfill Allan's request. The preliminaries were normally printed last, anyway; and, if this dedication replaced an earlier one, the switch would not have involved the problems that a change of title entailed. If, on the other hand, there was no previous dedication, Bentley could have inserted the dedication page along with the half-title page (to include the new subtitle), making a preliminary gathering of four leaves rather than two[45] and neatly accommodating, to the best of his

45. Bentley apparently followed no standard procedure about the inclusion of half titles and seemed sometimes to use them merely to occupy an otherwise blank page. In the first volume of *The Whale,* if there had been no dedication, there would probably have been no half title either, with the result that the preliminary gathering would be only two leaves (the title leaf and the contents leaf), as in the second and third volumes. In Bentley's edition of *Mardi* (3 vols.), there are half titles only in volumes 2 and 3; in *Redburn* (2 vols.), there is one in volume 2; and in *White-Jacket* (2 vols.), there are none.

ability at the time, both the requested changes. One might even regard the extremely crowded (double-column) table of contents in the American edition as evidence that a four-page table of contents had been condensed to two to make room for a dedication page (with a blank verso) where none had existed before.[46] But such a theory is not very convincing when one recalls that all Melville's books had had dedications, and it would be surprising if the idea of having one in this instance were an afterthought. Nevertheless, if the dedication page, like the title page, were not part of the material set by Craighead, some maneuvering might have been required at Harpers to make the new parts of the preliminaries mesh with any that had already been set, and the dedication would not have been in the sheets sent to Bentley. There remains, of course, the possibility that the dedication forwarded by Allan was meant for the English edition only and that the two editions agree merely because Bentley was not able to insert the new copy. In this case, however, there would have been no need to set the material in type in New York, for handwritten copy would have done as well; yet Allan sent Bentley "proof" of the dedication. The effect of all this speculation is to diminish the possibility that Melville may have reconsidered his dedication to Hawthorne. That dedication may have replaced one to somebody else, but it does not seem likely that the dedication Allan sent Bentley was one that removed Hawthorne's name.

If changes involving the title and dedication were made in the American edition after the proofs had been sent to Bentley, other changes in material not already plated might have been made as well. The table of contents, for example, differs between the American and English editions. In the English edition, the chapter titles as reported in the table of contents generally correspond (apart from occasional differences in punctuation) to the actual chapter titles, with two interesting exceptions:[47] the title of Chapter 70 in the table of contents contains the spelling "Sphynx," whereas at the chapter head it is "Sphinx"; and for Chapter 122 the phrase "Thunder and Lightning" in the table of contents appears as "Lightning and Thunder" at the chapter head. In both cases the reading of the table of contents corre-

---

46. The Harpers had made no effort to compress the still longer table of contents for *Mardi*.

47. A third exception, the omission of "in Stone" from the title of Chapter 57 in the table of contents, appears to be nothing more than an oversight.

sponds to the reading at the chapter head in the American edition. Therefore printer's copy for the English table of contents—whether supplied to Bentley or made up by someone on his staff—must have been prepared from the proof sheets of the American edition before the two changes were made in the English edition; otherwise one would have to explain two failures to follow copy that happened to produce the American readings. In the American edition, on the other hand, nineteen titles in the table of contents vary in wording from the corresponding titles at chapter heads. Since this table of contents is squeezed onto two double-column pages, it is natural that some titles would have required shortening, and if all the variants were simply instances of compression they would be of little significance. Only nine, however, involve a routine shortening of the title (Chapters 55, 56, 57, 73, 74, 75, 105, 120, 122); leaving aside one (40) that is merely a transposition of two words, the remaining nine variants in the table of contents are either longer (36, 52, 71, 108, 127, 129) or are altered in an unexpected way (100, 109, 121). Why would anyone who was shortening titles to make them fit a crowded page change "The Albatross" (Chapter 52) to "The Pequod meets the Albatross"? Or "The Jeroboam's Story" (71) to "The Pequod meets the Jeroboam. Her Story"? And why would "Leg and Arm. The Pequod, of Nantucket, meets the Samuel Enderby, of London" (100) not become simply "Leg and Arm" instead of "The Pequod meets the Samuel Enderby of London"? It is difficult to see what motive, other than shortening, anyone at Harpers would have had for producing inconsistent chapter titles; therefore it would appear that the printer's copy for the American table of contents was, in all probability, some document that reflected Melville's own alternative wording for these titles.

If the tables of contents in the two editions were set from different printer's copy, it follows that the American table of contents was probably another addition made after the proofs were sent to Bentley—for if it had been in type earlier, it would have been included in those proofs and presumably used as copy by Bentley. Tables of contents, for obvious reasons, are normally set in type after the bulk of the text, and it is likely that no table of contents was yet in type at the time the proofs went to England.[48] Perhaps someone—Melville's

48. The running title on the second (and final) page of the American table of

wife or Allan or Melville himself—copied the chapter titles from the proof sheets to form a table of contents for Bentley, but more probably the sheets went abroad without such a table, and Bentley had one made from those sheets by a clerk in his office. In the United States the Harpers needed copy for the table of contents and perhaps asked Melville if he could supply it. If so, what he gave them was either a new list made up for this purpose, in which he incorporated various revisions, or else an old list (or a copy of an old list), which represented earlier forms of certain titles.[49] In the table of contents all the chapters describing encounters with other ships, with the exception of "The Town-Ho's Story," are parallel in form, beginning "The Pequod meets the . . . "; in the text three of them vary—each in a different way—from that form (52, 71, 100). Melville might have decided, in the act of copying down the titles, to stress the parallelism of these chapters; but it could also be that the parallel forms were present in an earlier outline and altered in later stages of composition ("Leg and Arm," for example, might have emerged as a title during the course of composition, while the more prosaic and indicative title naming the *Enderby* might more plausibly have served in an earlier outline as a reminder of the subject). Similarly, "The Deck" (127) could have been changed to "Ahab and the Carpenter" in the act of writing out a new list because the title of Chapter 120 ("The Deck towards the End of the First Night Watch") had already been shortened to "The Deck" (and the words "The Deck," in turn, added to "Ahab and the Carpenter" in Chapter 108 so that 108 would not be identical with 127); on the other hand, "Ahab and the Carpenter" may have been a more descriptive outline entry, changed in the course of composition to "The Deck," supplemented by a long stage direction. Whatever the nature of the document, someone at Harpers probably abbreviated some of the titles in it; nevertheless, the printed table of contents in the American edition seems to preserve some of Melville's own wording that does not appear in the text, and it could be wording from a period earlier than September or October of 1851, when the "Contents" was being set in type.

---

contents is in a different typographical style from all the other running titles in the book.

49. Surviving manuscript fragments for *The Confidence-Man* show Melville drafting a list of chapter titles in several stages—see the Northwestern-Newberry edition, pp. 468–82.

Another difference between the American and English editions that may point to a late alteration is the position of the "Etymology" and "Extracts"—as part of the preliminaries (with roman-numeral pagination) in the American edition and at the end (headed "Appendix") of the English edition. If these sections were furnished to Bentley after the bulk of the proofs, Bentley might have regarded them, unless otherwise instructed, as an appendix. Of course, if page proofs were sent, the page numbers should have revealed their intended location, but if manuscript copy were supplied, their position might not be so obvious. It is clear, however, that the English "Extracts" were not set from a manuscript—for the English edition agrees with the American in more than a dozen erroneous readings (such as "secure" for "recure" in the passage from *The Faerie Queene* or "breath" for "trunk" in the second quotation from *Paradise Lost*), and it would be unreasonable to assume that the English compositor repeatedly misread a manuscript (or that the copyist of the manuscript repeatedly misread an earlier manuscript) in exactly the same way that the American compositor did. Instead, the English "Extracts" must have been set from the American proof sheets as corrected by Melville—corrected, because the English edition does contain the correct words at several points where Bentley's reader could not have been expected to check the source quoted and correct the American proofs (the citation of *Holy War* instead of *Pilgrim's Progress,* for example, or the presence of "mere" for "near" in the quotation from *Currents and Whaling).* It is unlikely, therefore, if proof rather than manuscript was furnished, that Bentley would not have known of the position of this material in the American edition. Even if it were a late addition, there would seem to be no technical reason why Bentley could not have included the extracts among the preliminaries: they fill exactly eight leaves in his edition and, in combination with the present four leaves of preliminaries in the first volume, would have formed a regular twelve-leaf gathering, like the others throughout the book. If the extracts were not a late addition—that is, were sent to Bentley along with the other proofs—the same could of course be said, for there would obviously be no technical reason why they could not have been planned from the beginning as preliminaries. Therefore, barring the remote possibility that Bentley did not know where these sections belonged and concluded that they were intended as an appendix, his treatment of them must either reflect his own judgment that they were somehow inappropriate for the opening pages of a novel, and would adversely affect its sales and reception in that position, or else indicate that they actually stood at the end in the proofs he received (or were marked to be moved there).

The epigraph from *Paradise Lost* that appears on each of the three Bentley title pages but not on the Harper title page may offer some related evidence. One might at first think of its presence as supporting the idea that the extracts were a late addition. One might argue, in other words, that this one extract was all that Melville originally intended and that, when he later decided on a whole section of extracts, he removed this one (which is, after all, included in the longer section as the second of two quotations from *Paradise Lost*) from the American title page but failed to inform Bentley of the change. The trouble with this theory is that Bentley probably had no title-page proofs to follow in the first place; and it is likely that an added section of extracts would have been accompanied by instructions to remove the single quotation. Unless Melville provided Bentley with a manuscript title page that contained the lines from Milton (along with "The Whale" as title),[50] one must presume that Bentley selected that passage from among the extracts and placed it on the title page as a gesture (like the subtitle) toward meeting Melville's wishes, when he knew that he was not fully complying with them. It is difficult, in other words, to explain the position of the extracts and the presence of the epigraph simply by holding that the "Extracts" were a late addition. If they were present at the beginning of the proofs all along, there remains the possibility that the shift, like some other changes on Bentley's set of proofs, was called for by Melville himself; but since this alteration, unlike the addition of the "gally" footnote, is not obviously authorial, one cannot be certain. All that can be said is that the American title page as published, without the epigraph, probably represents Melville's final decision, since it must have been set after the proofs went abroad (whether it is identical with the one Allan sent Bentley or is a subsequent version).

One final significant difference between the two editions is the presence of the "Epilogue" in the American and its absence in the English. How Bentley's reader could have found anything objection-

---

50. The Harpers' "trial" title page with "The Whale" as title (see p. 672 above) does not contain the quotation, but neither does it include Melville's name.

able in it or why it would be excluded is difficult to imagine; to have eliminated it on aesthetic grounds—regarding the ending as more effective without it—would have been a drastic revision even for one of Bentley's readers. The possibility is strengthened, then, that Bentley did not receive it—or, if he did, that it was simply lost or misplaced. Of course, there is the theoretical possibility that Melville had not yet written it at the time the proofs were shipped and that it was a late addition; but there is no clear evidence to work with. The epilogue page has no page number or running title—as pages that begin chapters (except for page 1) do—but since it is a special case one cannot conclude that another printer set it. Even so, it is conceivable that Bentley was following accurately the proofs that he received— that there was no epilogue at that time and that the etymology and extracts formed an "Appendix." If that were the case, one could then say that Melville subsequently moved the etymology and extracts to the beginning when he decided to add an epilogue. Such a move might provide an explanation for some of the difficulties that the printer evidently had with the preliminaries (suggested by the odd position of signature "A*" and, indeed, by the use of "A" at all, since the signatures through the rest of the book are numbers);[51] and the fact that the move would have necessitated the alteration of twelve page numbers (and possibly the removal of four others and of "Finis." or an equivalent phrase from the last page of extracts) would not have made a great deal of difference, since the insertion of the epilogue would have thrown off the succeeding page numbers anyway. Such an explanation, however, is only a theoretical speculation, occasioned by the need to try to account for the absence of the epilogue in the English edition. It is not an inherently probable explanation, for the body of the book gives evidence that the epilogue was not an afterthought: Ishmael says, at the end of "The Castaway," that "in the sequel of the narrative, it will then be seen what like abandonment befell myself" (414.33–34)—information actually presented not in the final chapter but in the epilogue. And the reference in the final

---

51. The text begins, it is true, with signature "1", so that some other kind of designation would have been called for; but the choice of "A" could suggest work done at the Harper office rather than Craighead's, since all of Melville's other Harper books have letter signatures, and both *Omoo* and *Redburn* have preliminaries signed "A". For further discussion of the typographical peculiarities of the preliminary gathering, see the Note on the Text, p. 767, footnote 12.

chapter to "the third man helplessly dropping astern, but still afloat
and swimming" (569.35–36) is an anticipation of what is taken up in
the epilogue. Similarly, one could say that the description of the "Extracts"—in the headnote about the sub-sub-librarian—as a "glancing
bird's eye view" suggests a preliminary, not a concluding, position
and weakens the possibility that the extracts at some point stood at
the end in the American proofs or that the shift of them in the English
edition could have been indicated by Melville himself on the proofs.
The most reasonable explanation would therefore seem to be that the
"Etymology" and "Extracts" were moved to the end on the authority of someone at Bentley's and that the "Epilogue" was somehow
lost in the course of the shift, if indeed it had not been misplaced or
overlooked at an earlier stage in the process of getting the proofs
from New York to Bentley's reader.

There are just too many variables involved to permit a definite
conclusion about possible late adjustments made to the proofs. What
can be said is that the new title and the dedication reached Bentley in
the early days of October; that any other alterations made after the
proofs were shipped would have arrived still later, since Allan's letter
does not imply that any previous revisions had been sent; and that
any instructions arriving after early October would have been too
late, since the London edition was published on the eighteenth, only
about two weeks after the receipt of Allan's letter regarding the title.
It does not seem likely that the extracts could have been sent later and
still have been included at all. Beyond that, it is impossible to say
definitely either that Bentley's reader relocated the extracts after receiving the proofs or that Melville did so after sending them; nor can
one say absolutely whether Bentley's reader deleted the epilogue, or
misplaced it, before publication or whether Melville added it in late
September or October. Whatever the course of events, the available
evidence leans toward the American edition as representing Melville's final (and probably first) intention about the arrangement of
the preliminaries and the epilogue.

The American proof sheets—probably including the sections of
etymology and extracts but not the table of contents and possibly not
the epilogue—marked with some corrections and revisions by Melville, arrived in Bentley's hands on September 24 (on the twenty-fifth
he wrote that he had received Melville's "packet yesterday from the
Secretary of Legation"). He must have turned it over to one of his

readers immediately, for he intended to make the book one of his October publications, inserting its title in his list of new books for the month in the October 4 number of the *Athenæum* and of the *Spectator*. Probably Melville's lost letter of late spring describing the book to Bentley had given some indication of its length, so that Bentley would have known that it could be issued as a "three-decker"; the proofs confirmed this assumption, in good measure, and his October 4 advertisement contained the familiar description, "3 vols. post 8vo." Bentley's reader must have set to work with great efficiency, because in the short time available (the book was published in slightly more than three weeks after the arrival of the proofs) he managed to go over the book thoroughly and make a remarkably large number of alterations (even assuming that many routine variations were compositorial). Like other English publishers of the time, Bentley had working arrangements with a number of persons who would serve as "readers" for him, both advising him on the merits of manuscripts and revising or "editing" accepted works. When Melville the following April submitted *Pierre* to Bentley, he was told that a "judicious literary friend" would have to make alterations if the work were to be "properly appreciated" in England. For obvious reasons, an effort was made to keep the names of such readers confidential, and it is not now known who went over Melville's proofs in late September of 1851; that a "literary friend" did go over them is unquestionable.

One of the reviser's principal concerns was to purge the book of material that might give offense for any reason. Passages that seemed sacrilegious were his special target, and he removed enough of them to total more than 1200 words. For example, a passage of nearly 150 words had to be stricken because it connected the diet with spiritual concerns and concluded that "hell is an idea first born on an undigested apple-dumpling" (85.9–20). References to God were altered, when not omitted entirely, and it is not surprising that Queequeg was prohibited from saying, "de god wat made shark must be one dam Ingin" (302.22–24). Even single words that had a religious association could not be used figuratively or without reverence. When Ishmael, recalling his childhood, says, "I lay there dismally calculating that sixteen entire hours must elapse before I could hope for a resurrection," the final prepositional phrase became "to get out of bed again" (26.7); when Ahab stands with "a crucifixion in his face," the English reader supplied him with "an apparently eternal anguish"

(124.29–30); when two members of the *Town-Ho*'s crew are put below for "salvation," the reader substituted "security" (254.27); or when the bird fastened to the sinking *Pequod*'s mast gives forth "archangelic shrieks," the adjective became "unearthly" (572.33). Similarly, "the Devil" could not be allowed to remain in a list of "ponderous profound beings" (374.3), nor could "hermaphroditical" be one of the characteristics of Italian paintings of Jesus (376.22). Biblical figures could not be alluded to flippantly or used as the objects of unfavorable comparisons, and to associate them with sexual activity was unthinkable: Bentley's reader did not need to pause before expunging the reference to "pious Solomon devoutly worshipping among his thousand concubines" (392.28–29). Indeed, he was constantly alert for comments relating to sexual matters, even when applied to whales. Thus an old whale could not go about "warning each young Leviathan from his amorous errors" but instead must warn about his "own juvenile" errors (393.5). Even Ishmael's worried anticipation of the nature of Queequeg's underwear was too daring to retain (16.31–33). Obviously remarks belittling royalty or implying a criticism of the British could not be allowed either, and as a result all of Chapter 25 was omitted. (A few of these expurgations—like some of those in Bentley's edition of *White-Jacket*—are so skillful or witty as to suggest that Melville himself, perhaps attempting to anticipate Bentley's reader, may have been responsible for them; but even if such speculation were correct, one could not argue that the revisions truly represent Melville's intention, since they would have been motivated by the expectation of outside pressure.)

All these concerns did not prevent Bentley's energetic, if not always judicious, friend from keeping a sharp watch for what he regarded as grammatical or stylistic solecisms. At dozens of places he changed a singular to a plural, a present to a past, an objective to a nominative, in a highly conservative interpretation of rules of "correctness"; to speak of "a mighty deal" (76.20) or to say "this here" (67.11) was to be too colloquial, and one could not use the title "Czar" without the article "the" (56.11) nor "minds" instead of "reminds" (368.32). In addition, he may have made a great many other kinds of small changes, but a large number of the variants in wording (about a fourth of the total) seem to make so little difference that it is difficult to think why they were made or who made them; some may have been compositors' slips and some perhaps Melville's own revisions, but, judging from the concern with small details shown by Bentley's reader, some must be his as well. At times other revisions tend to make a statement more cautious and less assertive; some of these, too, may be Melville's, but they seem characteristic of the reader's general conservatism. Not all such revisions therefore can be attributed to him with certainty; but, of the seven hundred differences in wording between the two editions, one can with good reason regard him as responsible for at least half. As for punctuation and spelling, there is even less way of knowing just what he did, since some of the differences in punctuation in the printed text were undoubtedly inadvertent (and compositorial) and most of the shifts to English spelling would have been routine; but hundreds of the changes must reflect his disapproval of the American punctuation, just as it was probably he who insisted on "fœtid" for "fetid" (252.13) and "frenzied" for "phrensied" (286.11).[52]

The proofs that were turned over to Richard Clay, the London printer whom Bentley employed for the job of typesetting and printing, thus contained numerous alterations in addition to those Melville had made before shipping them. Probably the proofs were supplied to Clay in batches, so that he and the reader could be working simultaneously. More alterations to the text occurred at that stage, in the form of compositors' oversights and casual substitutions; although the English edition corrected many of the obvious typographical errors of the American, it produced an even larger number of its own. The job was pushed through with great dispatch, because the printing and binding were completed in time for the book to be published on October 18. Bentley's manuscript publication record (and later published *List*) cites this as the publication date, and his advertisements in the October 18 number of the *Athenæum* and of the *Spectator* labeled *The Whale* as *"Now ready."* That the first copies of the book were actually ready at this time is suggested by the fact that the earliest known review appeared in the London *Morning Herald* on October 20. Bentley ordered only five hundred copies printed, just half the number that had been printed of *Mardi* and *White-Jacket,* and two-thirds the figure for *Redburn;* the slow sales of the previous books had

---

52. A more detailed analysis of the variant readings between the two editions is provided in the NOTE ON THE TEXT, pp. 783–91.

obviously convinced him that a smaller edition would be more realistic.

The Whale, like Mardi, was published in three volumes; although it sold for the usual three-decker price of a guinea and a half, in several respects it was not a characteristic three-decker. By this time the tradition of the three-decker, as the dominant form for the publication of prose fiction in England, was at least a quarter of a century old, and the product that had developed was for the most part rigidly standardized. The Whale did not fit the pattern, first of all, by its very appearance. The cloth binding, or casing, of most three-deckers was attractive enough, but not elaborate, usually decorated with a conventional pattern blind-stamped on the front and back covers and lettered in gold on the spine. The Whale, by contrast, as bound by the prominent firm of Remnant & Edmonds, used two kinds of cloth, deep blue for the covers and white for the spines; the covers were blind-stamped in the usual way, but the spines, decorated in gold, showed a whale moving downward, with enough room for the title, author, and volume number above it and the city and publisher below. (See the reproduction, p. 580 above.) One is tempted to think that the idea came from Melville's description of the "book-binder's fish" in Chapter 55; asserting that what is usually called a dolphin in the familiar publisher's device introduced by Aldus is actually a whale, Melville describes "the book-binder's whale winding like a vine-stalk round the stock of a descending anchor—as stamped and gilded on the back and title-pages of many books both old and new" (261.21–24). With the anchor left out, this statement could serve as a description of the spine of each volume of The Whale. But ironically—as the reviewer for the London Literary Gazette (December 6) noticed—the whale depicted is a right whale, not a sperm whale like Moby Dick, and Melville, when he saw it, probably classified it among his "monstrous pictures of whales" (particularly in view of his belief that bindings should be suitable for the books they cover, as expressed in his review of Cooper's The Red Rover). The book has of course become one of the most desirable items for any collection of three-decker fiction, not only because of its importance as literature but also because of its place as a showpiece of Victorian binding, foreshadowing the style to become prominent in the 1890's. (John Carter, the historian of publishers' bindings, called it "the most stunning and successful piece of bravura treatment on any mid-century three-decker of my experience.'') Bentley's reason for dressing the work in an undoubtedly more expensive casing is not clear—and probably he did not bind more than a third of the edition (or perhaps two hundred copies) in this fashion, since some of the remaining sheets were later bound in ordinary cloth, and there were still sheets on hand to be bound up as one volume in 1853.

Another way in which *The Whale* was an unusual three-decker was in its typographical layout, which was, in turn, related to its length. Novels frequently had to be stretched out to fill three volumes by such devices as extra leading between lines, short type pages, wide margins, and mid-page chapter openings. Publishers preferred issuing a novel in three volumes rather than one or two because they could charge more for it; and the higher price did not decrease sales, since the principal buyers were the circulating librar- ies, which stood to take in more from lending three volumes than one or two. In the case of *The Whale,* however, there was no problem about making the text fill three volumes; at well over two hundred thousand words, it was much longer than the average three-decker. As a result, its margins were made somewhat less generous; it was laid out with twenty-nine lines on most pages (some three-deckers had as few as nineteen); and, most telling of all, each chapter was started on the same page where the previous one ended rather than on the next page. Even by three-decker standards, Melville's 135 chapter divisions were excessive, for relatively few of these novels had more than 60 or 70 chapters; if the book had required padding the numer- ous chapter breaks would have been a great boon to the compositor, but, as it was, they were probably something of a complication. Even so, the finished product was made to appear about the normal size— the average three-decker ran approximately 850 to 950 pages, and *The Whale,* excluding the preliminaries and extracts, came to 927. But achieving this goal meant that the usual devices of expansion had to be reversed.

Still another difference between *The Whale* and the conventional three-decker was the content and tone of the work itself. The three- decker was standardized not only in physical form but also in intellec- tual content. Since the circulating libraries bought most of the copies, the works had to have an appeal for the customers of those libraries— not exclusively women, though novels by women writers about do- mestic and matrimonial concerns were certainly among the most popular items. A three-decker was normally expected to contain, somewhere among its many pages, a love plot, as well as episodes demonstrating the virtues of middle-class values; any questioning of accepted religious or social standards had no place. The inappropriateness of Melville's book in such a context is obvious; Melville himself had warned Sarah Morewood in September not to buy the book because it was "not a peice of fine feminine Spitalfields silk," and he was later surprised at Sophia Hawthorne's appreciation of it. Yet Bentley's reader clearly went over the book with a three-decker point of view in mind. Bentley himself, of course, must have recognized that the book would have little appeal to the circulating-library audience when he ordered only five hundred copies to be printed, for the number of copies of a popular work that he sold to a single library sometimes surpassed this figure (Mudie's, for example, subscribed to one thousand copies of Mrs. Henry Wood's *The Channings* in 1862). Why Bentley, an astute businessman, undertook this kind of work from a writer whose three previous books had lost money can only be explained by assuming that he was genuinely interested in Melville (he was certainly interested in American literature). Perhaps his personal acquaintance with Melville (dating from 1849) had something to do with it; at any rate more than politeness seems to have prompted his comment in a letter to Melville written the following May "with real admiration": "Everybody must admit the genius displayed in your writings."

In New York the Harpers published the book, under the title *Moby-Dick,* about a month later than the English edition, rather than merely the fourteen days that were required by the Bentley contract. The official publication date was probably November 14, the date that William H. Demarest, a Harper employee, entered in his record book. In any event, the book was advertised on November 12 as available at E. H. Pease's bookstore in Albany and at Ticknor's in Boston and on November 14 at Evans & Brittan's in New York; it was reviewed on November 14 in the Albany *Argus* and in the *Morning Courier and New-York Enquirer;* the Harper advertisement in the *Literary World* of November 15 announced it as "just published"; and the copy deposited for copyright purposes was received in Washington on November 19.[53] The first printing consisted of 2,915 copies—

---

53. The Duyckincks had announced in the October 25 *Literary World* that the

only 133 fewer copies than the first printing of *Mardi,* but smaller by over a thousand than the first printings of Melville's other three previous Harper books. Unlike Bentley, the Harpers did not provide the book with a distinctive casing; except for an unusual life-preserver device (containing the publisher's name) blind-stamped in the center of the front and back covers, the casing was typical of the Harper style, with blind-stamped frames around the covers and a gold-stamped spine displaying (between the rules at the top and bottom) the title and the author's and publisher's names. Bound in varying colors of cloth (red, blue, green, purple, and brown or black), the book in outward appearance was hardly different, except for the greater width of its spine, from most of the books coming from the Harpers at this time. (Unbound sheets of the first printing were later—probably about mid-1852—put in casings like those used at the same time for *Pierre,* with a blind-stamped arabesque pattern on the front and back covers.) Since the vogue of the three-decker had not spread to the United States, the text had been set with continuous pagination (running to 635 pages, excluding the preliminaries and extracts); the amount of type on the page was about the same as in other Harper novels, so that the Harpers were able to print the book on the usual paper (which did not allow a very spacious margin) and have a resulting page size of about seven and one-half by five inches. With its nearly two-inch thickness rather out of proportion to the other dimensions, the book was somewhat ungainly; indeed, on November 18 the New Bedford *Daily Mercury* noted, "This is a bulky, queer looking volume, in some respects 'very like a whale' even in outward appearance." Certainly it did not have the elegance of the Bentley edition, but then—priced at $1.50—it sold for only about a fifth as much.[54]

---

book "is now very nearly ready"; two weeks later, in a letter of November 7, George Duyckinck had reported that he was reading the opening pages of *Moby-Dick* "in sheets" and that the book "is not yet published," and he mistakenly conjectured that it "will not be for a fortnight." The November 1 number of the *International Magazine* had erroneously stated that "Mr. Melville's new novel, *The Whale,* will be published in a few days, simultaneously, by the Harpers and by Bentley of London."

54. In the list of books published during November, 1851, as provided in *Norton's Literary Advertiser,* I (December 15, 1851), 93, the entry for *Moby-Dick* specifies an issue in paper wrappers for $1.00 as well as the one in cloth casing for $1.50; but there is no evidence in the Harper records suggesting that paper-covered copies were issued, and none is known to survive today.

Although the Harper contract had said nothing about review copies, a considerable number must have been sent out. In fact, 169 copies were unaccounted for in the Harpers' statement of November 25, and it is likely that most of these were given out for review; if so, the number of review copies would have surpassed the standard 125 that had been distributed for Melville's other Harper books. By the date of that statement, eleven days after publication, the Harpers had sold 1,535 copies, or slightly more than half the edition—though of course many of those copies would still have been in the hands of booksellers. In the next two and a half months, 471 more copies were sold; but from that point on the sales fell off sharply, for in the next year only an additional 294 copies were disposed of. By the time of the Harpers' statement of October 6, 1854, roughly three years after the appearance of the book, 2,390 copies had been sold (not enough, that is, to exhaust the original printing), and Melville's half-share of the profits amounted to only $363.92. In England the sales were still less encouraging. On March 3, 1852—four and a half months after the English publication date—Bentley still had on hand 217 of the 500 copies printed, and the following day he reported to Melville (who had written to propose the publication of *Pierre)* that his deficit on *The Whale* then stood at £135. Even after binding some sheets in cheaper single-colored casings of brown and of purple (with simple gold lettering on the spine and without the whale), there were still enough sheets remaining in 1853 for Bentley to have cancel title pages printed bearing the current date, which he inserted in those sheets before issuing them as a very thick one-volume work in red cloth. In the end Bentley failed by £74 to recover the £150 that he had advanced Melville (since his payment-book entry designating Melville's "actual share" as £38 implies a total profit of £76), and he had no incentive for considering a new edition of the book.

The Harpers, on the other hand, did find a second printing (of 250 copies) justified in 1855, because their fire on December 10, 1853, had destroyed 287 copies; if the fire had not occurred, a new printing would not have been required for another nine years. In 1863, when the supply on hand had dwindled to about 50 copies, a third printing (of 253 copies) was ordered, and it took eight more years for the stock again to fall below 50, necessitating a fourth printing (277 copies). This time thirteen years passed before the bulk of the new printing was sold, and the Harpers did not order a fifth printing. By the date of the Harpers' last statement to Melville, on March 4, 1887, no copies remained, and the book was out of print during the last four years of Melville's life. Over a period of thirty-five years the Harpers had managed to sell a total of 3,215 copies, but 2,300 of those copies had been sold within the first sixteen months after publication, and for nearly thirty-four years interest in the book was sufficient only to sustain an average sale of about 27 copies a year. Melville's total earnings from the Harpers for *Moby-Dick* amounted to $556.37, a smaller sum (by over a hundred dollars) than for any of his earlier books. Bentley's single payment of £150 (equivalent to more than $700)[55] was therefore larger than the amount Melville earned in America from the sale of seven times as many copies as the English edition over three and a half decades. His total lifetime earnings from the book thus came to about $1,260; and the book produced only an additional $81.06 for his widow during the nineteenth century, from sales of 1,787 copies of the United States Book Company's edition between 1892 and 1898. During the first half-century of its existence, then, the book sold about 5,500 copies, and another quarter century was to elapse before sales and the production of new editions would reflect any kind of general awareness of the distinctive qualities of the work, which had in fact been suggested by some of the earliest reviewers.

## VII

When Melville wrote Hawthorne on November 17, 1851—and for some weeks to come—he seems to have thought that in *Pierre* he was composing a book as much greater than *Moby-Dick* as Krakens are greater than whales. He must have thought that *Pierre* was less a botch, so far, than he had once felt the whaling book was becoming. For instance, in the narration through the first half of the book, presumably the first half he wrote, narratorial-authorial thought is explicitly dissociated from the thoughts of the young hero, a sudden gain in aesthetic control for the Melville who had just completed a book in which his own uncle John D'Wolf seemed to be identified as the uncle of the Ishmael who sailed on the *Pequod*. He must have believed that the greatness in *Pierre* would be tightly compressed, for

55. In the synopsis of Melville's English earnings in Harvard MS Am 188–470, the £150 payment is recorded as converting to $703.08.

at the start of the new year he had ready for the publisher a short book which he wrote in the last two or three or four months of 1851 after taking a year and a half on *Moby-Dick* (just as he had written both *Redburn* and *White-Jacket* in the summer of 1849 after taking more than a year and a half on *Mardi*). All along during the intense composition of *Pierre* he may have persuaded himself that it could succeed as a romance even while it embodied more profound psychological analysis than any fiction he had ever read, and he may have been right about what he had written by then.

From late November, however, something of the defensive mood he later ascribed in "The Fiddler" (1854) to the author of a failed tragedy probably began to build up in him. When his copies of *The Whale* arrived from London, probably in November, Melville had cause for deep chagrin, since Bentley had not made the last-minute substitution of *Moby-Dick* as the title, and the handsome whale on the spines was a humble right whale, not a spermaceti whale. When he looked through the volumes he had further cause in the many textual alterations. He can only have been heartsick when he focused on the absence of the "Epilogue." Yet he apparently made no complaint to Bentley about these vexatious matters. He treated his now known presentation copies of *The Whale* as gifts for favored recipients, and inscribed them elaborately without supplying or even signaling the absence of the epilogue from the third volume. At some point in the fall, before or after he received his copies, he realized that the condemnation of the catastrophe by English reviewers (who could not know of the missing epilogue) was unjust and that American reprintings of such British reviews were doubly so: he was not only being castigated in England for a literary sin of which he as author was innocent but was also being punished for it in the United States, where that sin had not been committed. Having proudly rejected the sort of publicity tactics Evert Duyckinck thought were necessary for promoting and sustaining a reputation, he probably scorned the thought of trying to register or arrange a public protest in either country. The irony is that he probably saw very little of the extravagant praise *The Whale* often received in London, simply because much of that praise appeared in newspapers that seldom crossed the Atlantic, while the English criticism most often reprinted in the United States happened to be some of the most hostile. We can be sure that Melville saw much that was published about *Moby-Dick* in the United States, and the evidence seems clear that he was less gratified or consoled by the best than devastated by the worst.

What Duyckinck said about *Moby-Dick* in the *Literary World* will be discussed below in the sequence of important American reviews, but it needs to be mentioned here in relation to Melville's mounting anger over it, as displayed in *Pierre* and in his cancellation of his subscription to the *Literary World*. This patron and close friend of Melville's, in his journal that only a year before had exultantly printed Melville's essay on Hawthorne, now displayed in a carefully impersonal review his enduring myopia. Melville had begun as a sea-writer and in Duyckinck's mind Melville had stayed a sea-writer. Duyckinck commenced the first installment of his review with avid interest—*not* in what his friend had spent the better part of two years creating (possibly he had in fact not read it all). Instead, he evinced inordinate interest in the startling news he had already reported to Melville—that the *Ann Alexander* had been sunk by a whale in the Pacific. He retold her story in fascinated detail, relating it to the book under review only when almost halfway through the part of the installment that he did not fill up with extracts from Chapter 91 (headed "The Rose-Bud") and Chapter 81 (headed "Death Scenes of the Whale"). A dozen or two small papers around the Northeast had already reached the same offhand conclusion as Duyckinck, and had used almost the same cliché he did: "This is no everyday writing, and in Herman Melville's best manner." For a crucial week in the reception of *Moby-Dick*, this banality stood as the authoritative verdict of the influential *Literary World*.

Duyckinck's second installment was both more respectfully attentive and in effect more damning. The tone was that of a determinedly fair-minded man, who in the last short paragraph takes genuine relief in making "an end of what we have been reluctantly compelled to object to in this volume." It is not hard to imagine Melville's feelings as he mulled over this review. He might reasonably have expected Duyckinck to see that it was, in all equity, his turn to be promoted in the *Literary World* as he had generously and extravagantly promoted Hawthorne the year before. But Duyckinck was righteous as well as fair-minded, and he believed that Melville did not deserve such praise as Hawthorne had merited and received. No wonder Hawthorne reproved Duyckinck on December 1, 1851: "What a book Melville has written! It gives me an idea of much greater power than his preceding ones. It hardly seemed to me that the review of it, in the Literary World, did justice to its best points."

In late November and in December, as the accumulating American reviews reached the winter wastes of Pittsfield, Melville toiled onward with the brief tragic life of his hero Pierre. He must have cringed intermittently under well-meant perfunctory comments on his whaling book almost as much as under lacerating personal assaults such as that by an inveterate enemy in the Boston *Post*. Phrases of high praise abounded in many reviews, but unjust, obtuse, libelous, and barely endurable phrases (exceedingly memorable phrases) were strewn thickly in highly accessible reviews. At Christmas his mother described him as angered by village gossip that his book was "more than Blasphemous"—opinion neighbors unwilling to buy the book or too busy to read it could have picked up and passed along from any number of reviews. An accusation of blasphemy was painful to the religious women in Melville's household, more particularly because his wife's father in 1838 had become the last judge in America to sentence a man to jail for blasphemy, defined as "speaking evil of the Deity with an impious purpose to derogate from the divine majesty," and "a wilful and malicious attempt to lessen men's reverence of God." Whatever Melville had meant when he told Hawthorne he had written a wicked book, he had not meant what his neighbors meant by calling it more than blasphemous, and the gossip itself, compounded by the way the women in his family dealt with it, shook his briefly cherished emotional and aesthetic security. In that state he made two rapid-fire mistakes: he left home and then he wrote his troubles into his manuscript.

On or soon after New Year's Day of 1852 Melville went to New York City to offer the manuscript of *Pierre* to the Harpers. His brother Allan probably showed him a file of reviews of *Moby-Dick* he had been saving, among them, very possibly, some that modern scholars have not seen (important reviewing organs for these years have disappeared, and only stray issues of others survive). For a week either side of the first, the January issues of magazines were appearing, some with reviews of *Moby-Dick*, including the scathing personal attack in the New York *United States Magazine and Democratic Review*, and by mid-month the scornful review in William Gilmore Simms's belated January *Southern Quarterly Review* (Charleston) had reached New York. From the city on January 8 Melville replied to Sophia Hawthorne's letter of serious praise for *Moby-Dick* with the comment that she was the only woman who had liked *Moby-Dick*, though some men had "said they were pleased with it." That was diplomatically phrased, since by then he must have heard and read his fill of criticisms, by men or women pleased and displeased.

Melville's comment to Mrs. Hawthorne on what he had "heard" about *Moby-Dick* was understated, but on or around the day he wrote her he had begun to express elsewhere his agonized reactions to the reviews—in the manuscript of *Pierre*. To reconstruct the circumstances under which Melville began to write his reactions and then pursued them through unforeseen final compositional stages of *Pierre* will require several paragraphs. These may at first seem digressive, but they are necessary here because the story reveals much about Melville's otherwise unknown view of the reception of *Moby-Dick* and much about why *Moby-Dick* and *The Whale* were all but ignored during the next decades.

When Melville showed the manuscript of *Pierre* to the Harpers, probably not on New Year's Day, which was set aside for social calls, but perhaps on Friday, the second, both he and the publishers estimated that it would make about 360 pages—a very short book beside three of his last four. The Harpers readily enough agreed to publish it, but not on "the old basis—half-profits" (as Melville put it late in 1853). Instead, they offered him a new basis, the most conspicuous feature of which was that he was to receive one-fifth of the retail price (after the first 1190 copies, from which the Harpers were to recoup their costs). The Harpers' reasons for reducing Melville's share of profits are not known. They may have been disappointed at the sales of his books so far, or concerned that *Moby-Dick* had occasioned attacks on the firm as well as himself, or simply determined to tighten their purse-strings as they had done the previous spring when they denied him an advance.[56] Quite aside from any strain in the negotiations, the terms meant that *Pierre* (if priced at one dollar as expected) would have to sell two and a half times as many copies as *Redburn* or *White-Jacket* merely to keep Melville at roughly the same shaky financial level.

---

56. The Harpers were famous for the aggressive marketing strategies they pioneered, but they were also notorious for sharp dealing. (Richard Henry Dana, Jr., left an account of the ruthless way they got the copyright to *Two Years Before the Mast.*)

Whether on the spot or after a day or two of brooding with Allan over the terms and perhaps coming to recognize that he had no other options, Melville accepted the offer. The prudent thing then was to let the Harpers publish the book just as it stood, after whatever tidying up was required, and go on to another literary project or else find some better means of supporting his family. Instead, what Melville did in early January was reckless. Almost at once after accepting the contract, while still in New York, he fell to expanding the manuscript. (A comment in his letter to Mrs. Hawthorne suggests that Augusta was also in New York, so he may have had a copyist there rather than having to carry home a mass of uncopied new pages.) Clearly, he was not just adding more in order to reach the estimated 360 pages, for he so far overshot that estimate that Allan felt obliged on January 21 to inform the Harpers because they might need to change the projected price and adjust other details. Quite aside from the chance he was taking that he might wreck any success the book might have had, expanding the book was against his immediate financial interests, since under the terms of the contract if the book ran, say, half again longer than estimated the Harpers could sell 1785 copies before starting to pay him his pittance per copy. Even as he wrote the first of the additions his sense of "unspeakable security" at Hawthorne's understanding *Moby-Dick* was dissipating, for the prospect of drastic reduction in his already insufficient earnings meant that his career might be ending—and ending, he knew, just as he had become a great writer.

One acute reviewer of *Pierre* saw what had happened. The critic in the *American Whig Review* (November, 1852) raged that halfway through "it comes out suddenly that Pierre is an author, a fact not even once hinted at in the preceding pages." That section was "nothing more than an afterthought of Mr. Melville's, and not contemplated in the original plan of the book, if it ever had a plan." This shrewd inference from the palpable evidence of the text is supported by surviving documents—Allan's drafts of parts of the contract with the Harpers, the contract itself, and Melville's correspondence: in fact Melville added some 150 pages after the book was completed or all but completed. Modern scholars have concluded that (allowing for some scrapping, revising, and salvaging) those 150 pages are represented by the section on Pierre as an author. No one has argued that any other group of 150 pages could be the ones Melville added to the manuscript.

Whatever he felt as he read the first installment of Duyckinck's review of *Moby-Dick*, or during the week of waiting for the second part then responding to it, Melville's feelings had undergone further changes from the first of the year until around the beginning of the second week of January, after he had accepted the Harpers' terms and while he was lingering in New York. He had focused on Duyckinck as an obstacle to his succeeding with the kind of ambitious books he wanted to write, for very likely the first new passage he dashed off, enlarging the book he had shown the Harpers, was the first of two sections on Pierre as a juvenile writer, "Young America in Literature" (bk. 17). There he portrayed an officious joint editor of the *Captain Kidd Monthly* who, insistently demanding a daguerreotype, is Evert Duyckinck to the life (see pp. 627–28)—satire unmistakable to its target, since it drew upon their private correspondence and embodied Melville's profound sense that to yield to Duyckinck's pressures to publicize him was unworthy of anyone striving for enduring fame.

The available evidence does not identify what precipitated Melville's anger. On a Friday afternoon that month in Allan's office on Wall Street he wrote Duyckinck a note thanking him for some nutcrackers (a New Year's gift, in the Dutch fashion?) but declining an invitation because he had to be out of town all day. However, he said he would be glad to call "at some other time—not very remote in the future, either." Although he had nursed his resentment for a month and a half, he could write to Duyckinck politely because there had been no open break. Probably the note was written on January 2 (not the ninth, as Davis and Gilman conjectured, since by then Melville most likely had written Duyckinck into the manuscript and would have been hypocritical in writing in such a friendly fashion). Melville may have been slightly vague about the day he could see Duyckinck because the Harpers had the manuscript and he wanted to be free to meet them at their convenience, around Monday the fifth. Meanwhile, the January 3 issue of the *Literary World* contained a bit of gossip salted with a private message from Duyckinck written before Melville came to town:

Nathaniel Hawthorne, who has just drawn off a third or fourth series

of his Twice Told Tales from his nutty old vintage, has exchanged the
ice and snows of Lenox for a village shelter near Boston, at Newton;
while Herman Melville, close-reefed in his library at Pittsfield, is
doubling old Saddleback and winter, with a thermometer below zero,
it is rumored on a new literary tack for the public when he next
emerges in Cliff street.

The thermometer was Duyckinck's own bread-and-butter gift for
the previous summer's hospitality, as few but Melville would know;
most subscribers would know the Harpers' establishment was on
Cliff Street. Perhaps Mrs. Morewood had passed the accurate rumor
to the Duyckinck brothers.

Once the cautious brothers on Cliff Street had told him their
terms, Melville had an obvious recourse. Since only five months earlier Duyckinck had "said a great deal" to persuade Melville to let
Redfield publish the whaling book instead of the Harpers, he may
have gone straight to his friend with the new manuscript, perhaps
waiting while Duyckinck looked at it, perhaps dropping it off and
coming back to hear the verdict on it. But he may not have consulted
Duyckinck at all. The next thing we know is that by the third week of
January Melville had added a great deal to the manuscript, almost
surely including the satire of Duyckinck, and after that the first document to survive is Melville's terse cancellation of his subscription to
the *Literary World* on February 14.

Whatever the precipitating cause, when Melville set about writing
new pages for his manuscript (probably ensconced once again in Allan's "third-story room," where he had buried himself to finish
*Moby-Dick*, hot in summer then, cold in winter now), he likely
thought he would write only long enough for him to disburden himself of his anger at Duyckinck and the other reviewers and of his
contempt for the publishing world as he had come to know it. What
stands first in the sections on Pierre as an author, in any case, is
"Young America in Literature" (bk. 17). Melville's larger target was
the reviewers of *Moby-Dick* as a group, and his satiric method was to
reverse or sardonically twist phrases they had just written about
*Moby-Dick* into the praise asinine critics lavished upon the bland,
inoffensive, tasteful effusions he had abruptly attributed to his young
hero. Melville may have meant to stop there but probably was drawn
on to add the section on "Pierre as a Juvenile Author, Reconsidered"
(bk. 18). In it he wrote an objective analysis attributing the success of

a book very like his own *Typee* to "some rich and peculiar experience in life, embodied in a book," rather than genuine originality. There too he traced Pierre's delusive notion that he "could live on himself" by becoming a writer, ignorant that the world operates on the system "of giving to him who already hath more than enough, still more of the superfluous article, and taking away from him who hath nothing at all, even that which he hath." He still may have thought he could stop his additions there, having openly vented his wrath at Duyck-inck for playing first the domineering, then the betraying patron and having less obviously jibed at the Harpers for "taking away" what he must have counted on, half-profits. These sections on Pierre's surprising authorship and on the New York publishing scene would have made a relatively small bulge in the outline of the book as it stood, and Melville could still have told himself, however speciously, that he was enriching his manuscript with spicy truth-telling satire.

What most concerns *Moby-Dick* in all this is still to be said. Melville did not stop his additions with those two "books," XVII and XVIII. While he was still in New York, by the middle of January, he was led on into much longer sections that reflected not his reaction to the reception of *Moby-Dick* and not the irony of the success of *Typee* but instead explored his struggles (perhaps recollected from writing *Mardi*, and surely from phases of writing *Moby-Dick*) to transform himself (to "force" himself, as one would force a plant) into a great writer and thinker—a struggle that had brought him, momentarily, the Crown of India from Hawthorne's hands but that had left him publicly flayed and deprived of the future earnings he needed to support his family. After returning to Pittsfield around the end of the third week of January, Melville continued to elaborate the account of Pierre as an author, under a compulsion which probably had little to do, day by day, with Duyckinck and the Harpers.[57] But his feelings

---

57. The late passages on Isabel's sexual jealousy may possibly reflect his own pain at the agony his friend Nathaniel Parker Willis was enduring daily in the luridly reported trial in which the actor Edwin Forrest was suing his wife for divorce on grounds of adultery with Willis and others. Newspaper reports of the case supplanted those on the American tour of the Hungarian patriot Louis Kossuth and monopolized the papers from the second half of December through much of January; then the case was hawked to the greedy public in competing instant books. While he was in New York expanding *Pierre* Melville undoubtedly saw or heard much of the sordid testimony.

continued to change, and after he had enlarged the original manuscript by a third or so he marked some sort of turning point on February 14, when having the *Literary World* at Arrowhead became too painful. Perhaps he simply was near enough to the end of the book to face the consequences of publishing his satire on Duyckinck. Perhaps he reacted to some straw in one of the issues of the magazine, such as the insensitive praise (February 7) of Simms's *Southern Quarterly Review* as motivated not by pecuniary profit but by "a disinterested zeal for good scholarship." (Insultingly, Duyckinck kept sending the magazine, although Melville did not want free copies; he wanted the magazine stopped, as he wrote Duyckinck in a still terser note on April 16.) Very late in the composition, probably, toward the end of the weeks between early January and February 20, when the contract was signed (in the form drawn up in early January), he recklessly worked out his feelings toward the Harpers (and his fear of how they would react to his additions) in a letter addressed to Pierre by his prospective publishers (bk. 26.iv):

> SIR:—You are a swindler. Upon the pretense of writing a popular novel for us, you have been receiving cash advances from us, while passing through our press the sheets of a blasphemous rhapsody, filched from the vile Atheists, Lucian and Voltaire. Our great press of publication has hitherto prevented our slightest inspection of our reader's proofs of your book. Send not another sheet to us. Our bill for printing thus far, and also for our cash advances, swindled out of us by you, is now in the hands of our lawyer, who is instructed to proceed with instant rigor.
>
> *(Signed)* STEEL, FLINT, & ASBESTOS.

This frantic letter, like the new mass of pages in which it was embedded, can only have appalled the Harpers. The wonder is that they honored the contract.

Probably as soon as *Pierre* was finished (seven or eight weeks after he first thought it was finished), Melville offered it to Bentley again (having already approached him about the short version). Bentley replied promptly, on March 4, declining his request for an advance but offering to publish on half-profits. When a set of the proofs for *Pierre* was ready on April 16, Melville sent it to Bentley along with a long, cajoling, wishful, and sometimes downright pleading letter which must have caused him much bruised pride to write.[58] But Bentley had taken losses on all four of Melville's books he had published, and there were obstacles in the way of achieving legal copyright. Bentley had not taken heart from reviews of *The Whale* that were brilliant and extravagant even when not wholly laudatory. In his letter to Melville on May 5, 1852, he stressed, in pained sincerity, that if Melville had revised his books more and had written in a more accessible style and further if he "had not sometimes offended the feelings of many sensitive readers" he "would have succeeded in England." Nevertheless, rather than rejecting *Pierre*, Bentley accepted it on the condition that Melville would allow him to have some "judicious literary friend" expurgate it (presumably more thoroughly than *The Whale* had been expurgated) and would take his chances on half-profits. Whether or not he thought for a moment that, as Melville had assured him, it was really "calculated for popularity" or that it could be accepted as "a regular romance," we do not know, but he saw what it was like, was neither shocked nor outraged, and apparently decided that even in its final form it could be made publishable, and perhaps profitable, as an American gothic romance. In any case, he was willing to take his chances on the book because of his respect for Melville's genius and for Melville personally. If Melville had accepted that help, the English reviewers still might not have liked *Pierre*: the *Athenæum* received a copy and ridiculed it in the only known English review. But that was the Harper edition, not the book it would have been if Bentley had made it more acceptable for a British audience. And we know just how judicious Bentley's expurgations could be, for although the "feelings" of many readers of Melville's last four books had been offended in various ways, only one of the London reviewers complained of irreverence in *The Whale*, while

---

58. "And more especially am I impelled to decline those overtures [the offer of half-profits without an advance] upon the ground that my new book possessing unquestionable novelty, as regards my former ones,—treating of utterly new scenes & characters;—and, as I beleive, very much more calculated for popularity than anything you have yet published of mine—being a regular romance, with a mysterious plot to it, & stirring passions at work, and withall, representing a new & elevated aspect of American life . . . . I trust that our connection will thus be made to continue, and that on the new field of productions, upon which I embark in the present work, you & I shall hereafter participate in many not unprofitable business adventures."

many American reviewers complained about the unexpurgated Harper edition. In view of all the circumstances, including the intermittent threat of piracy, Bentley's offer was a great tribute to Melville. The pity is that Melville did not recognize it as such. His mistake in failing to authorize the publication of *Pierre* in England on Bentley's terms had profound implications for the British reputation of *The Whale* during the rest of the century, as this NOTE will show, after a survey of the critical reception.

Readers of this HISTORICAL NOTE must now be warned that the critical reception of *The Whale* and *Moby-Dick* as pieced together and reported here must not be mistaken for the reception as Melville and his publishers perceived it. We know much more than they could have known about the whole range of the commentary (although some reviews are not extant or are unlocated). Still, we can only guess at which specific reviews hurt him most. No correspondence, diary entries, or other privately written reactions to *The Whale* are known to survive from 1851, and only a few are known about *Moby-Dick*. The evidence about the reception lies almost wholly in the reviews of *The Whale* and *Moby-Dick* that twentieth-century scholars have located.

*The Whale* received extraordinary attention in London, where professional literary men and women—experienced critics and trenchant prose stylists—wrote for daily newspapers as well as the prominent monthlies and quarterlies. The twenty-one known London reviews (another came later, in Dublin) are all competent, and many are brilliant responses to what was plainly perceived as a remarkable book. Bentley gathered some of the best phrases from the early ones in a large advertisement in the London *Morning Post* (November 14) quoting the *Athenæum*, *John Bull*, the *Spectator*, the *Morning Advertiser*, the *Britannia*, and a still-unidentified "Evening paper" that called the work "the raciest thing of the kind that was ever produced." In the United States for their review copies the Harpers got a good numerical return of eighty or so (counting the known brief notices of publication as well as reviews). Most reviews were written by newspaper staffers with their minds on partisan politics or else by amateur contributors more noted for religious piety than critical acumen. Only a handful were written by professional or semi-professional critics, simply because almost no editor besides Horace Greeley paid his literary critics anything like enough to live on. Even the exceptional reviewers tended to be governed more by moral than aesthetic principles. As bad luck had it, the curmudgeonly reviews in the *Athenæum* and the *Spectator* were the only two so widely reprinted or quoted in the United States as to become part of the American reception. In January *Harper's* commented on the London reception (quoting from the *Atlas*) and in April belatedly extracted the opening of the review in George H. Lewes's *Leader*. Perhaps the Harpers passed the review on to Allan Melville, who at the beginning of Chapter 42 in a copy of *Moby-Dick* wrote out the praise of "The Whiteness of the Whale"—which *Harper's* had not printed (see pp. 1038–39). Melville presumably saw at least this extravagant praise, but the American reading public had scant reason to think *The Whale* had received much attention, let alone favorable attention, in London.[59]

A further warning: readers of this NOTE should not think simply of "*the* critical reception." The considerable differences between the British and American texts (as much as the differences between British and American reviewers) brought about two distinct critical receptions. One strong reason for thinking so is that there seems to have been only one complaint—the restrained one in *John Bull*—about "heathenish talk" and "thrusts against revealed religion" in *The Whale*. As we have said, Bentley showed good business sense in expurgating the text, or more likely having a "judicious literary friend" do it for him; the less cautious Harper edition (where expurgation would have required changing the plates) was frequently attacked on both scores. Bentley also made his edition more palatable to his readers by altering some of the Americanisms. *John Bull* on October 25 defended all "that is idiomatically American" in the tone of Melville's sentiments and "in the slang which runs through his

---

59. All the reviews of *The Whale* and *Moby-Dick* known in 1970 are reprinted in *MOBY-DICK as Doubloon*. Only a few reviewers have been plausibly identified, notably Evert Duyckinck in the *Literary World*, George Ripley in the New York *Tribune*, and William Allen Butler in the Washington *National Intelligencer*. Hugh W. Hetherington and sometimes Jay Leyda assumed that editors of periodicals wrote their own reviews, and indeed some did, and others probably made sure that the reviews reflected their own judgments. The present discussion will err on the side of caution by naming reviewers only with good cause. Since only one known review of *The Whale* was published outside London, belatedly, in Dublin, and only two known reviews of *Moby-Dick* were published outside the United States, in Canada, this NOTE will sometimes refer to "London" reviewers and "American" reviewers.

discourse" (maybe what was left was just enough to spice it) but the *Britannia* (November 8) thought the language was "appropriate and impressive" except for "a few Americanisms, which sometimes mar the perspicuity and the purity of the style." Bentley's burying the garner of "Extracts" with the "Etymology" at the end of the third volume (see pp. 677–78) destroyed any chance that it could provide an initial bird's-eye view of whaling, a loss to the English reader, though one not measurable in the reviews. The crucial difference in the texts, for the London reception and for its reverberations in America, was the omission of the "Epilogue" from *The Whale:* British reviewers read a book in which the first-person narrator seemed to perish at the end. Consequently the urge to remark upon Melville's failure to include any news of Ishmael's survival skewed what the London reviewers said, not just about the catastrophe but also about such other aspects as characterization (not a topic easy to treat with comprehensive sympathy when so major a character as the narrator seems to perish with the rest of the crew, especially not for the few reviewers who talked of the narrator as if he were Melville himself). Even when British and American reviewers were praising parts of the text common to both editions, they were talking on the basis of somewhat different reading experiences. Therefore in this NOTE the reception of *The Whale* is discussed separately from that of *Moby-Dick*. This is a distinction not made in earlier reports; it is a distinction with a difference.

By and large, British reviewers were concerned with *The Whale* as a phenomenal literary work, a philosophical, metaphysical, and poetic romance, not primarily as a source of practical information about the whale fisheries—a high concern with many American reviewers. The *Morning Advertiser* (October 24) praised Melville's learning (as evinced in "Cetology"), his "dramatic ability for producing a prose poem" (evinced in "The Whiteness of the Whale" and "The Quarter-Deck"), as well as the "whale adventures wild as dreams, and powerful in their cumulated horrors." *John Bull*, amazed to find "philosophy in whales" and "poetry in blubber," asserted that "few books which professedly deal in metaphysics, or claim the parentage of the muses, contain as much true philosophy and as much genuine poetry as the tale of the *Pequod's* whaling expedition." The *Morning Post* (November 14) declared: "There is a wild and wonderful fascination in the story against which no man may hope to secure himself into whose intellectual composition the faculty called fancy has in any degree entered." Reviewers said that no work had been "more honourable to American literature" (*Morning Advertiser*), that *The Whale* was "far beyond the level of an ordinary work of fiction" (*John Bull*), that it was "a book of extraordinary merit, and one which will do great things for the literary reputation of its author" and was "one of the cleverest, wittiest, and most amusing of modern books" (*Morning Post*), and "certainly one of the most remarkable books that has appeared many years past" (*Bentley's*, January, 1852).

The pity is that Melville never knew that readers of the current London papers were repeatedly told that the prolific and interesting young sea-writer had now written his most ambitious and most successful book. If he had known, he would have been better armed against the provinciality of Duyckinck and the personal savagery of other reviewers. It is not too much to say that there has been no period in American literature when so much stood in the balance as in the months between November of 1851 and May of 1852, and during that time Melville had about all the bad luck he could have and made about all the mistakes he could make. The bitter irony is that the British reception was all he could possibly have hoped for, short of a few conspicuous proclamations that the distance between him and Shakespeare was by no means immeasurable.

Wasting no time on comparisons to writers of nautical fiction, the London reviewers described the affinities of *The Whale* to works by masters of English style. The *Morning Advertiser* said that the "whalers' hostelrie and its inmates" (chap. 3) were "pencilled with the mastery and minuteness of Washington Irving." Furthermore, Ishmael's reflection that a "good laugh is a mighty good thing, and rather too scarce a good thing" (chap. 5) was reminiscent of Charles Lamb, while through the middle of the book one could find now "a Carlylism of phrase," then a quaintness suggestive of Sir Thomas Browne, "and anon a heap of curious out-of-the-way learning after the fashion of the Burton who 'anatomised' 'melancholy.'" With distaste the reviewer in the *Athenæum* saw that the Appendix (that is, the "Extracts") contained "such an assortment of curious quotations as Southey might have wrought up into a whale-chapter for 'The Doctor,'" but for all his hostility he admitted pleasure in passages which recalled gothic fiction:

There is a wild humorous poetry in some of his terrors which distinguishes him from the vulgar herd of fustian-weavers. For instance, his interchapter on "The Whiteness of the Whale" is full of ghostly suggestions for which a Maturin or a Monk Lewis would have been thankful.

As "a fit prelude to the thrilling pages of Melville's *Whale*," the reviewer in the *Leader* (possibly Lewes) printed "a splendid passage from our greatest prose writer, descriptive of the superstitious nature of sailors—(you divine that we are to quote from De Quincey)." The reviewer did not spell out what he must have felt was obvious—that the passage from the greatest prose writer of contemporary England could well have been lifted from *The Whale*, not only because of the coincidence of subject matter but also because some of Melville's greatest prose was patently—and brilliantly—De Quinceyan. The writer in the *Leader* and his fellow London reviewers most often acted as if *The Whale*, whatever its faults, belonged in the finest literary company.

Yet to express such praise the reviewers had to overcome their expectations for any piece of fiction that came from Bentley in three volumes, as *The Whale* did. As the *Britannia* tartly said, Bentley was "*par excellence*" the "publisher of the novels of the fashionable world," love stories. Thus the reviewers as they worked their way into the first volume confronted subject matter, or mixtures of subject matter, which belied the format. The *Athenæum*, which called *The Whale* an "ill-compounded mixture of romance and matter-of-fact," complained of its patchiness, in which ravings and "scraps of useful knowledge" were "flung together salad-wise." The *Spectator* saw it as "a singular medley of naval observation, magazine article writing, satiric reflection upon the conventionalisms of civilized life, and rhapsody run mad." Ahab was "the high hero of romance," but the groundwork—the plot—was "hardly natural enough for a regular-built novel, though it might form a tale, if properly managed." The London *Illustrated News* (while plagiarizing from the London *Atlas*) contrasted the "controversial novel" *Cecile* with "Mr. Melville's romance." The *Britannia* complained that *The Whale* was "certainly neither a novel nor a romance," for no one "ever heard of novel or romance without a heroine or a single love scene." Besides, the plot was "meagre beyond comparison, as the whole of the incident might very conveniently have been comprised in half of one of these three interminable volumes." The *Leader* said it was "not a romance, nor a treatise on Cetology," but "something of both: a strange, wild work with the tangled overgrowth and luxuriant vegetation of American forests, not the trim orderliness of an English park." The London *Literary Gazette* (December 6) said the Bentley edition professed "to be a novel" although the "story of this novel scarcely deserves the name." The London *New Quarterly Review* (First Quarter, 1852) threw up the matter:

> Many, doubtless, will cavil at the application of the term "novel" to such a production as this, seeing that no tale of love is interwoven with the strange ana of which it is compounded. Still we cannot trouble ourselves to devise for it a happier term.

There was striking agreement that the book was (in the phrase in the London *Morning Chronicle* on December 20) *sui generis*. The uniqueness was a problem, but few reviewers denied out of hand Melville's right to mix genres, if only he managed the mixture tactfully.

For London reviewers it was still harder to deal with Melville's mixture of styles, particularly his indulging in rhapsodic writing appropriate perhaps for one inferior sort of work, an extravaganza, but not for a novel. The *Spectator* sorted out some varieties: "The rhapsody belongs to wordmongering where ideas are the staple; where it takes the shape of narrative or dramatic fiction, it is phantasmal—an attempted description of what is impossible in nature and without probability in art." Though praising Melville for showing in *The Whale* his most thorough "command over the strength and the beauties of our language," the London *Atlas* (November 1) lamented his "besetting sin of extravagance":

> Extravagance is the bane of the book, and the stumbling block of the author. He allows his fancy not only to run riot, but absolutely to run amuck, in which poor defenceless Common Sense is hustled and belaboured in a manner melancholy to contemplate. Mr. Melville is endowed with a fatal facility for the writing of rhapsodies. Once embarked on a flourishing topic, he knows not when or how to stop.

As a random example of Melville's "maundering with the pen in the hand," the reviewer cited Stubb's long soliloquy in "The Doubloon." The London *Weekly News and Chronicle* (November 29) said that the "blemish of the book is its occasional extravagance and exaggeration—faults which mar the effect they were intended to heighten, and here and there, as in the character of Captain Ahab, make a melodramatic caricature of what, with a little more simplicity, might have been a striking and original picture." Borrowing from the first part of the review in the *Atlas* but improving what he took, the reviewer in the London *Morning Chronicle* said that lurking in all Melville's works was the "tendency to rhapsody—the constant leaning towards wild and aimless extravagance." In *The Whale* Melville came "in all his pristine powers" but "alas! too, with the old extravagance, running a perfect muck throughout the three volumes, raving and rhapsodising in chapter after chapter," until it seemed the writing could hardly be "anything other than sheer moonstruck lunacy." More than to anything else, the reviewers applied the term "rhapsody" to Ahab's longer speeches—what the London *New Quarterly Review* (First Quarter, 1852) called "wild rhapsodies from the crack-brained captain" or the *Atlas* labeled "the constant rigmarole rhapsodies placed in the monomaniac's mouth." (Genuinely ambivalent, the *Atlas* noted that "a little of this sort of thing would be well in character, and might be made very effective.") The *Examiner* (November 8) spoke for many reviewers in its lament: "Mr Melville is a man of too real an imagination, and a writer with too singular a mastery over language and its resources, to have satisfied our expectations by such an extravaganza as this."

The London reviewers expected characters to behave like characters in other fiction, and were not wholly disappointed. The *Spectator* thought that the "strongest point of the book is its 'characters,' " except for Ahab ("a melodramatic exaggeration") and Ishmael ("little more than a mouthpiece" for the author). The harpooneers, mates, and several of the seamen were "truthful portraitures of the sailor as modified by the whaling service," while the "persons ashore" were "equally good." Struck by Melville's "hit at the religious hypocrisies" through the two Quaker owners, the reviewer quoted a long conversation from Chapter 16. The London *Atlas* took the opposite view, recognizing "no flesh and blood" aboard the *Pequod*:

> The sailors might have voyaged with the "Ancient Mariner," or have been borne on the hooks of the "Flying Dutchman." The three mates are mere phantoms—stupid, characterless phantoms, too. The black

cook is a caricature. Pip, the negro boy, is a clumsy monstrosity. Queequeg and his fellow-harpooneers, both savages, one of them a Red Indian from the lakes, the other a coal-black man from Africa, are the happiest, because the most fanciful of the minor sketches. Nor is the forecastle more happily painted. Most of the conversation allotted to the seamen is in the wild, rhapsodic vein to which we have alluded—destitute either of sense, appropriateness, or character.

Worst of all were Fedallah ("a semi-supernatural sage"—this in the November 8 installment) and his mystic boat's crew of "theatrical demons." The *Britannia*, however, devoted much space to praise of the characters, declaring that in them Melville had "evinced acuteness of observation and powers of discrimination, which would alone render his work a valuable addition to the literature of the day." Despite the exciting interest of the concluding sixth of the book, the original sketches of "all these different castes of men" constituted "the principal merit of the work."

About narrative conventions some of the British reviewers displayed a degree of naivete or laxness, but others demanded respect for the rules governing the narration of a novel, or romance, or tale, or whatever. Melville had presented special problems to reviewers from *Typee* on, where much that he wrote under the label of true experience looked suspiciously like fiction; the difficulty of satisfactorily separating Melville from his first-person narrators or identifying him with them had persisted through *Redburn* and *White-Jacket*, which were generally regarded as fully autobiographical. Therefore the reviewer in the London *Atlas* quite understandably was referring to Melville, not Ishmael, when he said the author ("a fore-mast man on . . . the Old Peequod, of New Bedford") tells the story "*in propria persona.*" He thought, in accordance with his expectations about a book by Melville, that the scene in which "the harpooneer and Melville pay adoration to Yojo" was a strange specimen "of powerfully imaginative writing." The brilliant plagiarist (or two-time reviewer?) in the *Morning Chronicle* echoed the *Atlas* in this judgment. A few other reviewers treated Ishmael as merely a narrative convenience rather than a realized character. Some comments were so vaguely couched that it is hard to decide whether the writers had distinguished between Melville and Ishmael. The most interesting of these is John Francis Waller's attempt in the *Dublin University Magazine* (February, 1852) to characterize the author-hero as "a gentleman and a person of education, or he never could have described the scenes as he does." Edginess informs some comments by reviewers who first took Ishmael as the narrator then decided that many passages, particularly the cetological chapters, were in Melville's voice. When they finished the third volume (and perhaps flipped in bafflement through the Appendix), reviewers had to deal not merely with the seeming disappearance of Ishmael from the final episode but with the apparent death of the narrator before he could have told the tale.

Many assumed from the catastrophe that Melville was either ignorant of basic narrative conventions or else willfully reckless of literary proprieties. The reviewer in the *Spectator* certainly did:

> It is a canon with some critics that nothing should be introduced into a novel which it is physically impossible for the writer to have known: thus, he must not describe the conversation of miners in a pit if they *all* perish. Mr. Melville hardly steers clear of this rule, and he continually violates another, by beginning in the autobiographical form and changing ad libitum into the narrative. His catastrophe overrides all rule: not only is Ahab, with his boat's-crew, destroyed in his last desperate attack upon the white whale, but the Pequod herself sinks with all on board into the depths of the illimitable ocean. Such is the go-ahead method.

In a tone of baffled fascination Waller in the *Dublin University Magazine* complained that all "the rules which have been hitherto understood to regulate the composition of works of fiction are despised and set at naught"; one of those rules was that narrators should survive to tell the tale:

> he [Ishmael] was present at those scenes which he so vividly described, or else he could not have described them at all; he must also necessarily have been present, too, at the final catastrophe, or how could he have known anything about it?—and if he was present when the whale smashed the ship to pieces, capsized the boats, and drowned every mother's son among the crew, how does it happen that the author is alive to tell the story? Eh! Mr. Melville, answer that question, if you please.

Other British critics made sport of the situation, as the *Literary Gazette* did: "How the imaginary writer, who appears to have been drowned with the rest, communicated his notes for publication to Mr. Bentley is not explained." The damage caused by the loss of the

"Epilogue" was insidious, for some critics who did not specifically condemn the defective catastrophe seem to have had it in mind when pointing out violations of rules of fiction elsewhere in *The Whale*.

Several London reviewers applauded Melville's triumph in bringing unlikely and recalcitrant materials and dangerous styles under firm literary control. *John Bull* said that praise was "the more abundantly due, because the artist has succeeded in investing objects apparently the most unattractive with an absorbing fascination." Observing that if "Captain Ahab was bewitched by Moby Dick, Mr. Melville is not the less spell-bound by Leviathan in general," the London *Atlas* declared that the "mass of knowledge touching the whale" was all "written in a tone of exaltation and poetic sentiment which has a strange effect upon the reader's mind in refining and elevating the subject of discourse, and at last making him look upon the whale as a sort of awful and unsoluble mystery." The *Morning Post* triumphed over its own uneasiness:

> Judgment is occasionally shocked by the improbable character of the incidents narrated—and even reason is not always treated with that punctilious deference she has a right to expect—but imagination is banqueted on celestial fare, and delight, top-gallant delight, is the sensation with which the reader is most frequently familiar.

Others besides *John Bull* cheerfully acknowledged the charm of what "may not fall within the ordinary canons of beauty." As the *Leader* said, "Criticism may pick many holes in this work; but no criticism will thwart its fascination." For so many of the London reviewers to praise the work in the form in which it was offered to them was a triumph of their own—a triumph of acute literary sensibility and human decency over a masterpiece slightly botched by the author and then mangled in the process of being sent to England or published there (see pp. 678–80).

That *The Whale* was one of the notable works of the London publishing season in 1851 is proved by several explicit comments, such as the willingness of the *Morning Advertiser* to put "Loomings" "against the same amount of prose in any book of fiction for the last dozen years, with a couple of exceptions, which we shall keep to ourselves." Testimony from decades later suggests that it occasioned much ardent discussion, but neither the initial printed commentary nor whatever conversations the volumes inspired among literary-

minded Londoners was sufficient to establish it in the public record as
a book of *more* than one season. During the six years of Melville's
career London critics had repeatedly weighed his newest book against
its predecessor from a year or so before, or made summary comparative comments on two or more of the earlier books. In evaluating *The
Whale*, for instance, the reviewer in the *Morning Chronicle* devoted a
long, perceptive section to *Mardi*. Had this pattern continued, many
British critics would have written about *The Whale* the next year if
*Pierre* had appeared in a London edition. (Some sets of Harper sheets
were imported and issued with a new title page by the London firm of
Sampson Low, the Harpers' agent, late in 1852, and, as we have said,
one of these copies was reviewed by the *Athenæum*.) Melville's failure
to let Bentley modify *Pierre* for the British audience therefore lost him
more than any possible profits from the book and the chance to have
great British critics consider *Pierre* in the light of *The Whale*. The
importance of this episode for the future fortunes of *The Whale*, we
reemphasize, is that Melville also lost the chance to have British critics reconsider *The Whale* in the light of *Pierre*.

The next slight occasion for recollecting *The Whale* came in 1855,
when some sheets of *Israel Potter* were bound for distribution by
Low, Son & Co., and George Routledge pirated it. Neither imprint
was promoted as vigorously as Bentley had promoted *The Whale*,
and in any case the nature of the new narrative did not lend itself to
fruitful comparison to the metaphysical romance of whaling. The
three known London reviews of *Israel Potter* do not mention any of
Melville's earlier works by name, not even *Typee*, nor did the single
known London review of *The Piazza Tales* the next year. In 1857 *The
Confidence-Man* was published in London by Longman, the first of
Melville's books since *The Whale* to be printed there in a new edition
with his approval. Its known reviews evoked one vivid recollection
of *The Whale* and of *Pierre*: the *Literary Gazette* defended "the conception of *The Whale*, ghostly and grand as the great grey sweep of the
ridged and rolling sea" and declared that the wild beauties were introduced with "a congruity of outward accompaniment" ("Captain
Ahab did not chase Moby Dick in a Mississippi Steamboat"); the
reviewer then recalled *Pierre* as having been ruined "by a strained
effort after excessive originality." Thus while every literate Britisher
could have followed the course of Melville's career through *The
Whale*, very few had a chance to follow it thereafter, mainly because

*Pierre* was not widely available but also because most of the magazine stories he wrote in the following years were not available in Great Britain until the 1920's.

As it was, printed comments on *The Whale* in the next years after 1851 occurred mainly in retrospective essays on Melville's literary career (as far as the British knew that career) or in routine encyclopedia entries. "Sir Nathaniel" (Francis Jacox) in the London *New Monthly Magazine* (July, 1853) gave a zestful survey of Melville's career as known in England—lacking *Pierre*. In *The Whale* Melville had been "a Doppelganger—a dual number incarnate," the one half "sensible, sagacious, observant, graphic, and producing admirable matter—the other maundering, drivelling, subject to paroxysms, cramps, and total collapse, and penning exceedingly many pages of unaccountable 'bosh.'" Jacox had all his pronouncements ready. The style of the book was "maniacal—mad as a March hare—mowing, gibbering, screaming, like an incurable Bedlamite, reckless of keeper or strait-waistcoat." The Yankeeisms were "plentiful as blackberries." The story was "a strange, wild, furibund thing." Ahab's ravings were in "a lingo borrowed from Rabelais, Carlyle, Emerson, newspapers transcendental and transatlantic, and the magnificent proems of our Christmas pantomimes." The ending was a mixed affair: the "climax of the three days' chase after Moby Dick is highly wrought and sternly exciting—but the catastrophe, in its whirl of waters and fancies, resembles one of Turner's later nebulous transgressions in gamboge." Jacox was responding in 1853 as intensely as the best reviewers had responded.

"A Trio of American Sailor-Authors" (January, 1856) in the *Dublin University Magazine* also seems more a slightly delayed printing of characteristic responses from 1846 to 1851 than the product of a new phase in Melville's reputation. And like the survey by "Sir Nathaniel," this anonymous one (by William Hurton, who himself was a writer on the sperm whale) was unwittingly truncated, since it included neither *Pierre* nor Melville's recent stories. Hurton saw that beyond the eccentricities and extravagancies that linked it to *Mardi*, *The Whale* was "a very valuable book, on account of the unparalleled mass of information it contains on the subject of the history and capture of the great and terrible cachalot, or sperm-whale." He summed up the "merits and demerits of Herman Melville" with a paragraph that was destined to be echoed repeatedly in both the nineteenth and the twentieth centuries:

> Such is Herman Melville! a man of whom America has reason to be proud, with all his faults; and if he does not eventually rank as one of her greatest giants in literature, it will be owing not to any lack of innate genius, but solely to his own incorrigible perversion of his rare and lofty gifts.

The commentary on *The Whale* in this essay was the longest as well as the most vigorous to be printed in Great Britain during the next three decades. The faltering trajectory of Melville's literary career was accurately reflected in the dwindling mention of his name in the British press after he ceased publishing fiction with *The Confidence-Man* in 1857.

Unlike the British reviewers, the sixty-odd known American reviewers[60] read the book as Melville wrote it except for copyists' and compositors' errors. They had only a week to form their opinions unaffected by the British reception, for as early as November 20 the Boston *Post*, edited by Charles Gordon Greene, scorned the book while claiming to have read nearly half of it and quoted the *Athenæum* as a way of finishing Melville off with an ultimate authority. The reviewer was out to trash the book and vilify Melville (just possibly from years-old personal-political reasons involving Melville's brother Gansevoort or Lemuel Shaw, for Greene, the likely reviewer, was a friend of Abner Kneeland, the man Shaw sent to prison for blasphemy), but he probably had not looked at either the book or the *Athenæum* review closely enough to realize that the complaint about the ending of *The Whale* did not apply to *Moby-Dick*. (This vicious review cannot have escaped the attention of Melville's Boston relatives.) The December New York *Eclectic Magazine* briefly objected to the *Athenæum* for not writing with "its accustomed candor" (meaning "fairness"), but plainly did not understand why the London paper was so scornful of the ending. The December New York *North American Miscellany* simply spread the bad report: "Melville's new work,

---

60. Here "reviewers" will be used of anyone who made critical comments about *Moby-Dick* in a periodical beyond a line or two introducing extracts (long quotations) from the book; it does not include those who merely announced in a book column that it had been published and was for sale in a local bookstore.

'The Whale, or Moby Dick,' is pronounced by the Athenaeum an absurd book. Its catastrophe, it says, is hastily, weakly, and obscurely managed, and the style in places disfigured by mad (rather than bad) English." In the same month, the New York *International Magazine* reprinted from the *Spectator* its attack on *The Whale*, spreading the influence of a second hostile London review. In January *Harper's New Monthly Magazine* apparently tried to save the situation by announcing that Melville's latest work "has excited a general interest among the critical journals of London." Admitting that the "bold and impulsive style of some portions of the book, seems to shock John Bull's fastidious sense of propriety," *Harper's* went on to quote a passage from the London *Atlas*, one of the "most discriminating reviewals." Still trying in April, long after sales had dwindled, *Harper's* quoted the highly complimentary opening of the review in "a late number" of the *Leader*, an indication that this ammunition may have been slow coming to the Harper brothers. As far as we know, this set of comments is all the news about the reception of *The Whale* that a reader of the American papers would have encountered. Half a century passed before anyone commented in public on the most obvious textual differences between the two editions, other than the two titles.

A few American papers merely listed the publication of *Moby-Dick*, sometimes identifying the local bookstore which had copies for sale, sometimes making an offhand comment. A couple of dozen of the notices that ran to several lines of a newspaper column were based on a predisposition toward Melville (normally favorable) but not on more than a glance at some pages of the book. On November 12, for instance, the Albany *Evening Journal* had a copy and looked forward to reading it, and the Boston *Daily Evening Transcript* had a copy and had opened it far enough to see the dedication to Hawthorne. The next day the Troy *Daily Whig* had glanced through it and felt justified in predicting that it would "be universally regarded as 'Melville's best,' " good news for acquaintances and relatives of the Melvilles in nearby Lansingburgh and Albany as well as in Troy. Even warmer praise, extended through a dozen or so lines of type, may be based more on wishful thinking than on actual reading, as when on November 14 the Troy *Daily Budget* (like the *Whig* keeping up with the local boy) said that the book was "written in the author's happiest vein" and the *Morning Courier and New-York Enquirer* said that Melville wrote with "the gusto of true genius." By November 15 the

Hartford *Daily Courant* had looked through some of *Moby-Dick*, and the Philadelphia *Dollar Newspaper* had not read it but flipped through and selected an extract from Chapter 80, "The Nut." Two days later the New York *Morning Express* had not read it but wanted to publish a review, so it disingenuously quoted from the *Courier and Enquirer*, attributing the praise only to "one" who had read it. (The Boston *Littell's Living Age* openly reprinted the *Courier and Enquirer* review on January 17.) Others who bluffed through a few lines of commentary without having read much or any of the book were the Worcester *Palladium* (November 19); the Boston *Daily Atlas*, the New York *Christian Intelligencer*, the New York *Observer*, the New York *Sun*, and the Washington *National Era* (all November 20); the Baltimore *American and Commercial Daily Advertiser* (November 25); the Providence *Daily Journal* and the Toronto *Globe* (November 29); and the Philadelphia *Graham's Magazine* (February). The anti-slavery *National Era*, going by memory of *White-Jacket*—"good to read, and good for use"—assumed the new book was a comparable introduction "to the hard, eventful life of a whaleman." Local pride called forth a couple of comments. The New Bedford *Daily Mercury* (November 18) devoted half its comments to the role the home town and Nantucket played in the plot, then advised dubiously that the adventures of "our author" in New Bedford "are extended through several pages, and are followed by others of greater importance," and the New Bedford *Daily Evening Standard* (December 11) quoted with glee Melville's spoofing comparison (chap. 6) of the women of New Bedford to the odorous young girls of Salem (Melville's private joke for Hawthorne's eye?) but professed itself "sorry Herman 'piles on the agony' to so great an extent, as it may make the dear creatures proud."

Aside from these brief reviews, there were several other items more or less openly based on other reviews: The Albany *Daily State Register* (November 17) picked up from the *Literary World* the coincidence of the book's appearing so soon after news of the sinking of the *Ann Alexander* by a whale; the Boston *Bee* derived a piece on November 19 and 20 from the *Literary World*. Furthermore, a dozen or more papers around New England printed lengthy extracts (that is, quotations from chapters in *Moby-Dick*, not from the section Melville called "Extracts"), usually deriving them from the first installment of the *Literary World* review (Chapter 81, "Death Scene of the Whale") or the *Tribune* (part of Chapter 61, usually printed as "Killing a Whale" or "Stubb Kills a Whale") or from other papers that had already copied from one or the other. Sometimes the papers bothered to name the paper they were taking the extract from, sometimes not: after a short splicing of criticism derived without acknowledgment from the New York *Evening Post* and the New York *Tribune*, the Boston *Daily Commonwealth* reprinted the extract "Killing a Whale" from the *Tribune*. The following list of papers which did not really review the book but picked up from other papers substantial extracts from *Moby-Dick* indicates the range of publicity Melville received: the New Bedford *Daily Mercury* and the New York *Evening Mirror* (November 20); the Boston *Daily Mail* (November 24); the Hartford *Daily Courant* (November 29); the New York *Evening Post*, the New Bedford *Daily Evening Standard* (December 1); the Portland *Eclectic* (December 6); the North Adams *Greylock Sentinel* (December 13). In addition, the *Harper's New Monthly Magazine* pre-publication printing of "The Town-Ho's Story" was reprinted in the Baltimore *Weekly Sun* (November 8) and the Cincinnati *Daily Gazette* (November 29 and December 6). The publicity these extracts gave the book should have helped sales and was undoubtedly good for Melville's reputation: better a column and more of Melville's prose, noncommittally or favorably offered, than a perfunctory review.

Most reviewers who made an effort to read *Moby-Dick* could not rise to many of its challenges, as this brief review in the New Haven *Daily Palladium* (November 17) suggests:

> Herman Melville has long ago made his name current among men of taste and letters. His "Typee," "Omoo," and "White Jacket," have all afforded pleasure to thousands of readers, and his lively, roving story of Moby-Dick, we presume will be as popular as any other work that bears his name. It has numerous thrilling sketches of sea life, whale captures, shark massacres, &c.—but in some of the colloquies between old weatherbeaten Jacks, there is a little more irreverence and profane jesting than was needful to publish, however true to the life the conversation may be. The work possesses all the interest of the most exciting fiction, while, at the same time, it conveys much valuable information in regard to things pertaining to natural history, commerce, life on ship board, &c.

Given a point or two of emphasis, this is almost interchangeable with what reviewers said in the Albany *Argus* (November 14), the Boston

*Daily Evening Traveller* (November 15), the Springfield *Republican* (November 17), the Utica *Daily Gazette* (November 19), the St. John, New Brunswick, *News* (December 10), the New York *Methodist Quarterly Review* (January), and the Philadelphia *Peterson's Magazine* (January). The evidence is clear that many reviewers had made their minds up about Melville: they enjoyed him, despite some reservations, but they certainly did not expect him to write great works of literature.

Several authors of moderate-sized reviews, usually two or three times as long as the one quoted in the previous paragraph, took pretty much the same line as the perfunctory reviewers mentioned earlier, but with an intensity or individuality of response which set them apart. The reviewer in the New York *Evangelist* (November 20) had read the book, had thought about the course of Melville's career, had decided that *Moby-Dick* represented Melville's "very limbo of eccentricity," but liked it, and did not complain about irreverence. *Parker's* on November 22 said unhappily that Melville ran "into the grave error of giving us altogether too much for our money" when he added fiction to the information which had made *Typee* "just perfect." Yet the reviewer was ambivalent about Melville:

> He spreads his subject out beyond all reasonable bounds; until the scene becomes altogether too long for the motive, and the finest writing will not prevent it from being tiresome. If any writer of the present day could play with his subject, after this fashion, with impunity, it would be Melville; for his style is a rare mixture of power and sweetness, and, indeed, under the influence of the least excitement becomes as truly poetry as if every line were measured for verse, and the fine madness of his soul poured out in lyric flow instead of straightened into prose. But, even his power of expression, and elegance of style, will not redeem a book from being prosy after the natural interest of its subject has been exhausted. More than five acts of the best tragedy would be too much for mere mortal to bear.

The reviewer in the Philadelphia *American Saturday Courier* (November 22) seized the reader at once:

> Who is Herman Melville? There, dear reader, you puzzle us. We only know just what you and all other general readers know, that he is one of the most spirited, vigorous, good-natured writers in existence; as sparkling and racy as old wine and sweet as nuts, with a constant

flow of animating description and thrilling incident, picked up all
along shore, or in the polished drawing-room—on land or upon the
far-off ocean.

The intelligent voice in the short notice in the New York *Home Journal* (November 29) seems distinctively that of Melville's friend Nathaniel Parker Willis, but because of the scandalous trial in which he
was involved (see footnote 57) his heart could not have been in the
little he said about Melville's resolving to combine in *Moby-Dick* "all
his popular characteristics, and so fully justify his fame." The reviewer in the Washington *Daily Union* (November 30, one of the few
Sunday papers) named all five of Melville's earlier and "admirable"
works, then demonstrated that he had given thought to *Moby-Dick*.
Anticipating the *Albion*, he said the hunt for Moby Dick was "not
really so Quixotic as would at first appear, for experience had taught
Ahab, what Lieutenant Maury has since partially demonstrated by his
charts, that whales have regular migratory habits." Considerately he
did not spoil the ending: "One of the combatants, at least, lived, and
has told the tale, and to him we refer those who may have become
interested therein." His choice of "The Pulpit" for an extract had
nothing to do with the day of the week or with its having "any
peculiar merit" over the rest; it was the only fair sample of Melville's
style he could find which would fit in the space at his disposal without
having to be condensed. The Newark *Daily Advertiser* (December 5),
the paper edited by the father of Melville's friend Dr. Augustus K.
Gardner, offered standard praise in good spirits but worried at the
end about the offensiveness of what he cautiously called "the metaphysical discussions." The New York *Churchman* (December 6)
thought it was "pitiable to see so much talent perverted to sneers at
revealed religion and the burlesquing of sacred passages of Holy
Writ." In January the reviewer in the New Haven *Church Review and
Ecclesiastical Register*, who had long been interested in the white whale
"Mocha-Dick," challenged anyone who doubted the existence of the
"imaginary hero of the seas":

> Ask any old "Jack-tar," and he will meet you with as pitiable or indig-
> nant stare, as an old soldier would hear questioned the valor of the raw
> troops at Lexington. We remember, years ago, to have started the
> subject of "*Mocha*-Dick," (for that was the name then,) with an old

"Whale-man," and at once the old soldier "shouldered his crutch to show how fields were won."

He also gave exuberant praise to Melville's comic power: "Those persons who believe in *laughing*, not the ceaseless school-girl titter, but the right-hearty, side-splitting explosion of genuine mirth, may be referred to 'Moby-Dick.' " Only at the end did he acknowledge that Melville's orthodoxy was in doubt and that his irreverence was undeniable. The Philadelphia *Peterson's* (January) judged that "had the story been compressed one-half, and all the transcendental chapters omitted," *Moby-Dick* "would have been decidedly the best sea-novel in the English language." Even as it was, the concluding chapters were "really beyond rivalry." Another personal, and deeply ambivalent, response was in *To-day: A Boston Literary Journal* (January 10): Melville's career had declined after *Typee*, yet *Moby-Dick* possessed "the charming accessory of apparent reality" that characterizes writing in which the hero "tells his story in the first person." The latest good statistics about whaling were in Mr. Grinnell's 1844 report to Congress, but Melville in his "loose way" of handling facts "gives a sort of summary of these same numbers apparently without date or authority, on page 120, as representing the present state of things." The book would be "dangerous" to many readers because of Melville's making light of sacred things, as in the "wretched sophistry" by which Ishmael justified his worshiping an idol, yet the book after all had many "fine and valuable passages." In February *Graham's Magazine* (Philadelphia) declared that the seeming helter-skelter movement was guided with real judgment.

Lurid indignation or invective marked a few other reviews. Having used the *Athenæum* to carry much of his attack on the "crazy sort of affair" Melville had written, the reviewer in the Boston *Post* (November 20) concluded with a bitter complaint about the price of the American edition:

> The production under notice is now issued by the Harpers in a handsome bound volume for *one dollar and fifty cents*—no mean sum, in these days. It seems to us that our publishers have gone from one extreme to the other, and that instead of publishing good books in too cheap a form, they are issuing poor books, in far too costly apparel. "The Whale" is not worth the money asked for it, either as a literary work or as a mass of printed paper. Few people would read it more

than once, and yet it is issued at the usual cost of a standard volume. Published at *twenty five cents*, it might do to buy, but at any higher price, we think it a poor speculation.

A passionate voice was that of "H," the author of the review in the New York *Independent* (November 20)—not a regular reviewer for the paper but someone who had special qualifications for writing about *Moby-Dick*, possibly a former missionary to the South Seas. Borrowing from a favorite of Melville's, Robert Burton, he jibed at the "fantastical title" and at "harlequin writers" like Melville, "as ready as in Burton's time to make themselves Merry-andrews and Zanies, in order to raise the wind of curiosity about their literary wares." (The title was printed throughout as *Moly-Dick*, probably a misreading of the reviewer's handwriting.) In Melville "H" saw talent that was misused because of something foul inherent in his nature: "there is a primitive formation of profanity and indecency that is ever and anon shooting up through all the strata of his writings; and it is this which makes it impossible for a religious journal heartily to commend any of the works of this author which we have ever perused." Melville and the Harpers were risking eternal damnation:

> The Judgment day will hold him liable for not turning his talents to better account, when, too, both authors and publishers of injurious books will be conjointly answerable for the influence of those books upon the wide circle of immortal minds on which they have written their mark. The book-maker and the book-publisher had better do their work with a view to the trial it must undergo at the bar of God.

January brought two brutally personal attacks. From Charleston the *Southern Quarterly Review* charged that Ahab's "ravings, and the ravings of some of the tributary characters, and the ravings of Mr. Melville himself, meant for eloquent declamation, are such as would justify a writ *de lunatico* against all the parties." From New York the *United States Magazine and Democratic Review* began in full fury: "Mr. Melville is evidently trying to ascertain how far the public will consent to be imposed upon. He is gauging, at once, our gullibility and our patience." The savagery was unabated:

> The truth is, Mr. Melville has survived his reputation. If he had been contented with writing one or two books, he might have been famous, but his vanity has destroyed all his chances of immortality, or even of a good name with his own generation. For, in sober truth, Mr.

Melville's vanity is immeasurable. He will either be first among the book-making tribe, or he will be nowhere. He will centre all attention upon himself, or he will abandon the field of literature at once. From this morbid self-esteem, coupled with a most unbounded love of notoriety, spring all Mr. Melville's efforts, all his rhetorical contortions, all his declamatory abuse of society, all his inflated sentiment, and all his insinuating licentiousness.

Such was the fresh welcome for Melville when he came to New York City to sell the original 360-page *Pierre* to the Harpers.

This survey has cleared the way for discussing the American reviews that bear comparison with the London ones. Five are in New York periodicals: the *Literary World* (November 15 and 22), attributed here to Evert Duyckinck; the *Tribune* (attributed to George Ripley) and the *Albion* (both November 22); *Harper's* (December), also attributed here to Ripley; and the *Spirit of the Times* (December 6). One (attributed to William Allen Butler) is in a Washington paper, the *National Intelligencer* (December 16). Two or three of them were intended almost as much for Melville's eyes as for those of the general readership, and they all would have come promptly to his attention.

The November 15 installment of Duyckinck's review has been summarized above. On November 22 he turned earnestly to his primary duty to warn the public against irreligious tendencies in *Moby-Dick* even while guiding his unmanageable friend toward truer literary practice. As in *Mardi*, Melville had made reviewing difficult by writing a book with a "double character," in one light romantic fiction, in another absolute fact, then had further complicated the task of the reviewer by making the romance into a veiled allegorical "vehicle of opinion and satire." A reviewer therefore was helpless to classify the book "as fact, fiction, or essay," but Duyckinck recognized precedents:

Something of a parallel may be found in Jean Paul's German tales, with an admixture of Southey's Doctor. Under these combined influences of personal observation, actual fidelity to local truthfulness in description, a taste for reading and sentiment, a fondness for fanciful analogies, near and remote, a rash daring in speculation, reckless at times of taste and propriety, again refined and eloquent, this volume of Moby Dick may be pronounced a most remarkable sea-dish—an intellectual chowder of romance, philosophy, natural history, fine writing, good feeling, bad sayings—but over which, in spite of all uncertainties, and in spite of the author himself, predominates his keen perceptive faculties exhibited in vivid narration.

This was to say that Melville deserved blame for his faults but did not quite deserve credit for his virtues—which emerged "in spite of" himself.

Taking the tone of a disapproving judge straining to be fair, Duyckinck proceeded to divide the work into three books. "Book No. 1," the "thorough exhaustive account" of the great sperm whale, pleased him altogether, so he devoted little space to it. "Book No. 2," the "romance of Captain Ahab, Queequeg, Tashtego, Pip & Co.," pleased him much less. These characters, he wrote, in a tone of bluff humor he perhaps adopted to palliate his obvious distaste, "are more or less spiritual personages talking and acting differently from the general business run of the conversation on the decks of whalers":

> They are for the most part very serious people, and seem to be concerned a great deal about the problem of the universe. They are striking characters withal, of the romantic spiritual cast of the German drama; realities of some kinds at bottom, but veiled in all sorts of poetical incidents and expressions. As a bit of German melodrama, with Captain Ahab for the Faust of the quarter-deck, and Queequeg with the crew, for Walpurgis night revellers in the forecastle, it has its strong points, though here the limits as to space and treatment of the stage would improve it.

This was to say that the characters were unrealistic and, worse still, were made vehicles for inappropriate religious concerns. Having been given to understand that the book would be "a romantic, fanciful & literal & most enjoyable presentment of the Whale Fishery," Duyckinck felt betrayed, and the best he could do for Melville was to "caution the reader against a light or hasty condemnation of this part of the work." (Expressing the joint feelings of the joint editors, George Duyckinck wrote a friend on November 28, 1851, that he felt "out of all patience with Melville for almost wilfully spoiling his book.")

About the third part of *Moby-Dick* Duyckinck offered no such caution against condemnation:

> Book III, appropriating perhaps a fourth of the volume, is a vein of moralizing, half essay, half rhapsody, in which much refinement and

subtlety, and no little poetical feeling, are mingled with quaint conceit and extravagant daring speculation. This is to be taken as in some sense dramatic, the narrator throughout among the personages of the Pequod being one Ishmael, whose wit may be allowed to be against everything on land, as his hand is against everything at sea. This piratical running down of creeds and opinions, the conceited indifferentism of Emerson, or the run-a-muck style of Carlyle is, we will not say dangerous in such cases, for there are various forces at work to meet more powerful onslaught, but it is out of place and uncomfortable. We do not like to see what, under any view, must be to the world the most sacred associations of life violated and defaced.

Two more paragraphs on this order called for "fair play" toward the Christian religion. Ishmael's worshiping a wooden idol with a cannibal "may be all very well in its way; but why dislodge from heaven, with contumely, 'long-pampered Gabriel, Michael and Raphael.' Surely Ishmael, who is a scholar, might have spoken respectfully of the Archangel Gabriel, out of consideration, if not for the Bible (which might be asking too much of the school), at least for one John Milton, who wrote Paradise Lost." Melville had also played unfairly in inveighing "against the terrors of priestcraft," which "at least seeks to provide a remedy for the evils of the world," while he was "petrifying us with imaginary horrors, and all sorts of gloomy suggestions, all the world through." Duyckinck indulged in a personal slap at Melville: "It is a curious fact that there are no more bilious people in the world, more completely filled with megrims and head shakings, than some of these very people who are constantly inveighing against the religious melancholy of priestcraft."

Outraged as he was by the irreligious tone he encountered in parts of the second "Book" and found throughout the third, Duyckinck was diplomatic enough and perceptive enough to give his friend an aesthetic escape hatch by deflecting some of his indignation onto the narrator rather than the author, although he knew how close Ishmael's views were to Melville's and was not to be bamboozled by such ventriloquism:

> So much for the consistency of Ishmael—who, if it is the author's object to exhibit the painful contradictions of this self-dependent, self-torturing agency of a mind driven hither and thither as a flame in a whirlwind, is, in a degree, a successful embodiment of opinions, without securing from us, however, much admiration for the result.

Straining for a strategy that would allow him to condemn much of the book without wholly repudiating his friend, Duyckinck had elaborated a distinction between author and narrator which as a critical perception stood unrivaled (and neglected) for almost a century. Then in ending the review with renewed conciliatory praise for Melville's wrestling with "strong powers," Duyckinck still withheld from him an accolade for subduing them "to the highest uses of fiction." (Charles Olson in 1938 next attempted to distinguish among Melville, Ishmael, and Ahab—a critical strategy which rapidly became received opinion. See Section V.)

The writer in the *Tribune* on November 22 was surely the regular reviewer of Melville, the Transcendentalist George Ripley, although his customary "R." is not present at the end of the review, for he declared that the narrative, "in Herman Melville's best manner," combined "the various features which form the chief attractions of his style," and was "commendably free from the faults" that the reviewer had earlier "had occasion to specify in this powerful writer." In the *Tribune* on May 10, 1849, Ripley had wearied of the "huge allegory" bits of which peeped out "here and there" through *Mardi* and had deplored the "mystic speculation and wizard fancies" ungrounded in "graphic, poetical narration." Now he wrote:

> We have occasional touches of the subtle mysticism, which is carried to such an inconvenient excess in Mardi, but it is here mixed up with so many tangible and odorous realities, that we always safely alight from the excursions through mid-air upon the solid deck of the whaler. We are recalled to this world by the fumes of "oil and blubber," and are made to think more of the contents of barrels than of allegories.

Ripley loved the " 'Whaliad,' or the Epic of that veritable old leviathan" who was the traditional hero of stories among "the old salts of Nantucket and New-Bedford." After quoting extensively from "the honeymoon of friendship" in Chapter 10, some "quaint moralizings" on rope in Chapter 60, and two extracts on "Killing a Whale" from Chapter 61 and "The Chase—First Day" from Chapter 133, the writer parted reluctantly with "the adventurous philosophical Ishmael" (whom he blurred with Melville):

> We think it the best production which has yet come from that seething brain, and in spite of its lawless flights, which put all regular criticism at defiance, it gives us a higher opinion of the author's originality and

power than even the favorite and fragrant first-fruits of his genius, the never-to-be-forgotten Typee.

Ripley's praise of *Moby-Dick* was spread throughout the East and beyond, thanks to Horace Greeley's superb distribution system, swamping what Duyckinck had to say, at least for the day.

On the same day the New York *Albion*, edited for British expatriates by the English-born William Young, published a substantial review, if not by him, then surely (the continuity of reviews indicates) by a staff member educated in Great Britain—the only chance such a person had to review *Moby-Dick* in 1851 (so far as we know), and our only glimpse of how London reviewers of *The Whale* might have responded to a text with more irreverence throughout—toward God and even toward British royalty—but with the satisfying catastrophe. He found that it was "not lacking much of being a great work," and he was the man to show just how "it falls short of this." He was so thrown by the manner of narration that he made no distinction between Melville and Ishmael: "The writer uses the first person in narrating his tale, without however any attempt at making himself its hero. He was (or says he was, which is the same thing) but a seaman on board the vessel whose voyage he relates, and a consequent eyewitness of the strange characters on board her." Recovering with an extensive description of the developing plot, the reviewer paused to deflect skepticism:

> The idea of even a nautical Don Quixote chasing a particular fish from ocean to ocean, running down the line of the Equator, or rushing from Torrid to Temperate zones—this may seem intolerably absurd. But the author clearly shows the *possibility* of such a search being successful, which is more than sufficient motive.

The reviewer said the "*dramatis personae*" were "all vivid sketches done in the author's best style" and that it "is only when Mr. Melville puts words into the mouths of these living and moving beings, that his cunning fails him, and the illusion passes away," for from "the Captain to the Cabin-boy, not a soul amongst them talks pure seaman's lingo." He substantiated that charge by quotations from Starbuck, Stubb, and Flask before concluding:

> But there is no pleasure in making these extracts; still less would there be in quoting anything of the stuff and nonsense spouted forth by

the crazy Captain; for so indeed must nine-tenths of his dialogue be considered, even though one bears in mind that it has been compounded in a maniac's brain from the queer mixture of New England conventicle phraseology with the devilish profanity too common on board South-Sea Whalers.

Despite the reviewer's irritation, this was a clear attempt to acknowledge a dramatic justification for Ahab's speech, and throughout he revealed genuine delight in aspects of the book, such as a passage from "The Hyena" that he offered as a "peep into a particular mood of mind" in which Melville had blended truth and satire.

As Melville might have expected, the review in *Harper's* was extremely favorable. It has been attributed to George Ripley, on the grounds that he had helped organize the magazine and was writing much of its criticism, and it may well be that he wrote it as well as the review in the *Tribune*, omitting the customary "R." in the newspaper so as not to call attention to his double reviewing. Certainly the remarkably capable reviewer sounds suspiciously like Ripley:

> On this slight framework [of Ahab's pursuit of Moby Dick], the author has constructed a romance, a tragedy, and a natural history, not without numerous gratuitous suggestions on psychology, ethics, and theology. Beneath the whole story, the subtle, imaginative reader may perhaps find a pregnant allegory, intended to illustrate the mystery of human life. Certain it is that the rapid, pointed hints which are often thrown out, with the keenness and velocity of a harpoon, penetrate deep into the heart of things, showing that the genius of the author for moral analysis is scarcely surpassed by his wizard power of description.

Seeing that the processes of procuring oil contrasted "strangely with the weird, phantom-like character of the plot, and of some of the leading personages, who present a no less unearthly appearance than the witches in Macbeth," the reviewer declared his admiration:

> These sudden and decided transitions form a striking feature of the volume. Difficult of management, in the highest degree, they are wrought with consummate skill. To a less gifted author, they would inevitably have proved fatal. He has not only deftly avoided their dangers, but made them an element of great power.

The reviewer observed shrewdly that many readers would be most interested in the "succession of portraitures, in which the lineaments of nature shine forth, through a good deal of perverse, intentional exaggeration," and then pursued the topic to the point of declaring that the members of the ship's company "all stand before us in the strongest individual relief, presenting a unique picture gallery, which every artist must despair of rivaling."

The review of *Moby-Dick* in the *Spirit of the Times* may be by the editor, William T. Porter, the indefatigable encourager of the Big Bear school of literature. His paper had long evinced a fondness for Melville's works, and indeed the opening sentence of this review ("Our friend Melville's books begin to accumulate") may well indicate personal acquaintanceship, since in the tiny publishing center in lower Manhattan Melville would have had plenty of opportunities to get to know Porter or members of his staff. The reviewer called all five of Melville's earlier books the "results of the youthful experience on the ocean of a man who is at once philosopher, painter, and poet." He went on to make the remarkable point that Melville's painful early experiences had become "infinitely valuable to the world" simply because "the humanities of the world" had been quickened by his first five books:

> Taken as matters of art these books are amongst the largest and freshest contributions of original thought and observation which have been presented in many years. Take the majority of modern writers, and it will be admitted that however much they may elaborate and rearrange the stock of ideas pre-existant, there is little added to the "common fund." Philosophers bark at each other—poets sing stereotyped phrases—John Miltons re-appear in innumerable "Pollock's Courses of Time"—novelists and romances [romancers?] stick to the same overdone incidents, careless of the memories of defunct Scotts and Radcliffs, and it is only now and then when genius, by some lucky chance of youth, ploughs deeper into the soil of humanity and nature, that fresher experiences—perhaps at the cost of much individual pain and sorrow—are obtained; and the results are books, such as those of Herman Melville and Charles Dickens. Books which are living pictures, at once of the practical truth, and the ideal amendment: books which mark epochs in literature and art.

As for the title (which the *Independent* had scorned), "*Moby-Dick*" was one of the "taking titles" at which no man was more felicitous than Melville. The reviewer knew the book was too good to be praised by everyone: "As a romance its characters are so new and unusual that we doubt not it will excite the ire of critics. It is not tame enough to pass this ordeal safely." Apologizing for not giving sufficient quotations to justify his praise, the reviewer quoted amply from Chapter 91, "The Pequod meets the Rose-bud," "in which a whaling scene is described with infinite humor"—a tale which seemed at home in the exuberant sporting magazine. Had space permitted, he would have reprinted "the fine little episode, contained in the chapter called 'The Castaway,' " but he contented himself with recommending the book "to all who can appreciate a work of exceeding power, beauty, and genius."

The review in the Washington *National Intelligencer* is almost surely by William Allen Butler, the friend of Evert Duyckinck's younger brother George from their years at the College of the City of New York and his companion on their grand tour of Europe in the late 1840's. Preening himself, he spent the first two-thirds of the very long article on an essay about the reviewer as devil's advocate whose role is to object to canonizing the "presentation copies" authors and publishers furnish to reviewers. One such candidate for canonization, he finally admitted, was *Moby-Dick*. While conceding Melville "a palm of high praise for his literary excellencies," Butler entered a "decided protest against the querulous and cavilling innuendoes," which Melville "so much loves to discharge, like barbed and poisoned arrows, against objects that should be shielded from his irreverent wit." In all his books, including this one, Melville had written many passages "which 'dying he would wish to blot.' " He had an example at hand:

> Neither good taste nor good morals can approve the "forecastle scene," with its maudlin and ribald orgies, as contained in the 40th chapter of "Moby Dick." It has all that is disgusting in Goethe's "Witches' Kitchen," without its genius.

After this obligatory moral caveat, Butler made a nod toward Melville's earlier indebtedness to Defoe and then toward his similarities with his present rival "in this species of romance-writing, founded on personal adventure in foreign and unknown lands." This was William Starbuck Mayo, whose *Kaloolah* (1849) had capitalized on the vogue *Typee* had created. Still, Butler thought that Melville's "delineation of character" was "actually Shakespearean" and that the "humor of Mr. Melville is of that subdued yet unquenchable nature

which spreads such a charm over the pages of Sterne," while the
" 'wild imagining' " was reminiscent of Coleridge's "Ancient Mariner." Butler was after all too good a critic not to say some words that
needed saying:

> Language in the hands of this master becomes like a magician's wand,
> evoking at will "thick-coming fancies," and peopling the "chambers
> of imagery" with hideous shapes of terror or winning forms of beauty
> and loveliness. Mr. Melville has a strange power to reach the sinuosi-
> ties of a thought, if we may so express ourselves; he touches with his
> lead and line depths of pathos that few can fathom, and by a single
> word can set a whole chime of sweet or wild emotions into a pealing
> concert.

(Having called attention to his striking phrase "the sinuosities of a
thought," Butler saved it for a worthy occasion—his review of Whitman's *Leaves of Grass* four years later.) Melville probably had been
told the year before that the editors of the *National Intelligencer* had
accepted Butler's account of the Berkshire idyll of August, 1850,
although complaining stiffly "that the great mass of their readers
could not feel much interest in the private pursuits habits & whereabouts of writers in the North of whom they have scarcely heard." If
Melville saw the review, he realized who wrote it.

The reviews of *Moby-Dick* did not stimulate sales, which were
considerably lower than the initial sales of *Redburn* and *White-Jacket*.
Nor did they significantly affect the subsequent course of Melville's
career, because only a few months later, at the end of July, *Pierre* was
widely distributed, then promptly reviewed—reviewed so hostilely
that it all but crowded *Moby-Dick* from public awareness. *Pierre* confirmed for many hostile or merely uneasy reviewers their conviction
that Melville was a dangerous writer. He was so irreverent that he
was liable to eternal damnation and, worse, so depraved that he was
capable of violating in print the sanctity of family relationships. Reviewers with any sympathy for Melville tended to look back past
*Moby-Dick* to his two early successes, *Typee* and *Omoo*, as the pinna-
cle from which he had steadily fallen. For most of the American
literary world the debacle of *Pierre* obliterated *Moby-Dick*.

G. P. Putnam had been the right man (an American publisher) in
the right place (London) at the right time (January, 1846) to listen to
his prize author Washington Irving's advice that he help launch

young Gansevoort Melville's still younger brother's literary career with *Typee*. He was privy to Irving's abrupt retrenchment once the American minister Louis McLane had expressed his views on Gansevoort's incendiary behavior in London, and undoubtedly knew why Irving, the consummate old boy of the political and literary establishment, simply stopped mentioning Herman Melville's name. Putnam's partner John Wiley stepped in with an expurgated text to control the damage *Typee* might cause in America, and in December of 1869 Putnam recorded in *Putnam's Magazine* an anecdote about how dangerous Gansevoort Melville's temperament had been when loosed on the real world of international politics. In the aftermath of *Pierre* he knew how dangerous Herman Melville's share of the family temperament was, yet he admired his achievements and in the fall of 1852 invited him to contribute to the planned *Putnam's Monthly* and, going further, in the second issue of the magazine featured Fitz-James O'Brien's retrospective survey of Melville's career (February, 1853). In it O'Brien merely glanced at *Moby-Dick*: "Typee, his first book, was healthy; Omoo nearly so; after that came Mardi, with its excusable wildness; then came Moby Dick, and Pierre with its inexcusable insanity." In still another *Putnam's* essay on Melville's career (April, 1857) O'Brien devoted more space to *Moby-Dick*:

> What, for instance, did Mr. Melville mean when he wrote "Moby Dick?" We have a right to know; for he carried us floundering on with him after his great white whale, through all manner of scenes, and all kinds of company—now perfectly exhausted with fatigue and deafened with many words whereof we understand no syllable, and then suddenly refreshed with a brisk sea breeze and a touch of nature kindling as the dawn.

Melville had "indulged himself in a trick of metaphysical and morbid meditations" until he had "almost perverted his fine mind from its healthy productive tendencies." Within him the commands of nature ("You shall be as true as Teniers or Defoe, without the coarseness of the Fleming or the bluntness of the Englishman") were warring with those of obstinate cultivation ("you shall be as grotesquely terrible as Callot, as subtly profound as Balzac, as formidably satirical as Rabelais"). These two essays (by an Irish-born writer) were the last serious American surveys of Melville's career in his lifetime.

The nadir of the reputation of *Moby-Dick* (in the United States) was from the mid-1850's through the 1870's. In their *Cyclopædia of American Literature* (1855) the Duyckincks briefly recalled *Moby-Dick* as "the most dramatic and imaginative of Melville's books":

> In the character of Captain Ahab and his contest with the whale, he [Melville] has opposed the metaphysical energy of despair to the physical sublime of the ocean. In this encounter the whale becomes a representative of moral evil in the world. In the purely descriptive passages, the details of the fishery, and the natural history of the animal, are narrated with constant brilliancy of illustration from the fertile mind of the author.

In a footnote almost as long as these comments they recounted yet again the curious coincidence of the sinking of the *Ann Alexander* just before the publication of *Moby-Dick*. The one other significant comment yet found (from 1863) is by the critic Henry T. Tuckerman, an acquaintance of Melville's:

> "Moby Dick," indeed, has the rare fault of redundant power; the story is wild and wonderful enough without being interwoven with such a thorough, scientific, and economical treatise on the whale; it is a fine contribution to natural history and to political economy, united to an original and powerful romance of the sea.

Other known mentions from these decades are almost totally restricted to routine encyclopedia entries, at the time when new anthologies and handbooks of American literature, meant for use in academies, were defining a canon where Melville was excluded or barely noticed and where promoting Hawthorne's stature, in particular, seemed equivalent to promoting the United States' claims to have produced great literature.

As recent critics have suggested, the exaltation of Hawthorne was to an extent the product of well-designed institutional hype—the shrewd packaging and marketing strategies of his publishers, Ticknor & Fields, and their successors. (A kind of fame, Melville wrote an English admirer in 1885, "can be manufactured to order, and sometimes is so manufactured thro the agency of a certain house.") Ironically, in view of the significance the Hawthornes attached to Melville's being the first to say the "right word" about him, the Hawthorne family in their turn brought Melville before the public—merely in the process of abetting Hawthorne's apotheosis. Sophia printed partial entries about Melville from Hawthorne's notebooks (which Melville must have found tantalizing), and after her death in 1871 her children began printing Melville's letters to Hawthorne because they formed a large part of their documentary evidence for the Berkshire interlude. From the 1890's onward through his very long life, Julian perceived rising interest in Melville as a threat to his father's supremacy and tried to scotch it. Lacking vociferous disciples such as Whitman had gained, and having a publisher who had suffered a little in reputation by printing *Moby-Dick* and had been humiliated by printing *Pierre*, Melville was easy to ignore, and for some decades American textbook and handbook makers, and later the earliest historians of American literature, simply did not know how strongly interested in Melville the British were becoming. Then in the first two decades of the twentieth century, some American academic writers seemed to resent the pressure that the British periodicals (and many individual British admirers of Melville) were putting on them to acknowledge his greatness.

Between 1851 and 1919 there reached print in North America only two pieces on *Moby-Dick* fit to rank with the best reviews. The New York *Critic* in 1893 published a review of the new edition prepared by Arthur Stedman which in brilliance of language and scope of literary knowledge was a throwback to the best of the ones in 1851 and 1852:

> In this story Melville is as fantastically poetical as Coleridge in the "Ancient Mariner," and yet, while we swim spellbound over the golden rhythms of Coleridge feeling at every stroke their beautiful improbability, everything in "Moby-Dick" might have happened. . . . Even the recondite information about whales and sea-fisheries sprinkled plentifully over the pages does not interfere seriously with the intended effect; they are the paraphernalia of the journey. The author's extraordinary vocabulary, its wonderful coinages and vivid turnings and twistings of worn-out words, are comparable only to Chapman's translations of Homer. The language fairly shrieks under the intensity of his treatment, and the reader is under an excitement which is hardly controllable. The only wonder is that Melville is so little known and so poorly appreciated.

This was extraordinary praise, isolated except for the Canadian professor Archibald MacMechan's brave attempt in *Queen's Quarterly* (October, 1899) to rescue from neglect "The Best Sea Story Ever Written." His opening is stunning evidence of the depth to which

Melville's reputation had declined in this continent: "Anyone who undertakes to reverse some judgment in history or criticism, or to set the public right regarding some neglected man or work, becomes at once an object of suspicion." Most academic writers on American literature continued to scorn Melville or ignore him. Even Carl Van Doren, who read several of Melville's books with relish in 1914, treated him in the *Cambridge History of American Literature* (1917) as one of the "Contemporaries of Cooper," ending his pages on Melville with this comment: "Of late his fame has shown a tendency to revive." It needs to be stressed: the revival of Melville's reputation was almost exclusively a British phenomenon until after all the hard work had been done.

## VIII

In London after the mid-1850's Melville's achievement in *The Whale* seemed to be forgotten, but the book began to lead an underground life, away from the literary columns of the magazines and newspapers. Perhaps people who read the book in 1851 cherished it and brought it to the attention of their friends during the next decade (perhaps some of the remarkable artists, literary men, and travelers who dined with Melville so jovially in 1849 did so), but our best proof that any such continuity existed is the 1922 recollection of J. St. Loe Strachey that in 1893, during the "boom" following Melville's death, a "lady of letters" expressed her delight that people were reading Melville again, and added: "I can't tell you how enthusiastic we all were, young and old, at the end of the 'forties and beginning of the 'fifties, over *Typee*, *Omoo*, and *Moby-Dick*. There was quite a furore over Melville in those days. All the young people worshipped him."

For the decade and a half following 1853 there was (as far as we know) near-total silence about *The Whale* in the London periodicals, yet a change in British attitudes toward American literature was in process. There had been previous changes since 1820, when Sydney Smith posed his scornful rhetorical question, "In the four quarters of the globe, who reads an American book?" The height of the new mid-century respect for American literature is well represented by the concluding compliment the London *Morning Advertiser* paid to *The Whale*: three volumes "more honourable to American literature, albeit issued in London, have not yet reflected credit on the country of Washington Irving, Fenimore Cooper, Dana, Sigourney, Bryant, Longfellow, and Prescott." In the next phase, beginning around the mid-century and overlapping with the previous one, some British critics concluded that Irving and Cooper were not validly American in spirit but imitation English writers (precisely the conclusion Melville had come to about Irving, at least, in his essay on Hawthorne). This phase is well represented by the way the *Leader* cleared away the field before commencing to talk about *The Whale*:

> Want of originality has long been the just and standing reproach to American literature; the best of its writers were but second-hand Englishmen. Of late some have given evidence of originality; not *absolute* originality, but such genuine outcoming of the American intellect as can be safely called national. Edgar Poe, Nathaniel Hawthorne, Herman Melville are assuredly no British offshoots; nor is Emerson—the *German* American that he is!

George H. Lewes may have written these words; possibly the author was the young Scottish sailor James Hannay, then just crashing into London life as a bohemian and professional critic and novelist. Hannay wrote for the *Leader* (July 3, 1852) a review of James Russell Lowell's *Poems* in which he paid tribute to the "breath of genius" that swept through all of Melville's books, and the same distinction between generations of American writers as promulgated in the *Leader* informs Hannay's brief preface to his edition of Poe's poems (1853, published in December, 1852). There Hannay spoke kindly of Irving and Cooper as essentially British, both founding their work "on our own classical models." Now, however, the British public was getting "acquainted with writers amongst the Americans who are really national"—Emerson, Lowell, Hawthorne, Poe—and Melville, whom he extolled for *The Whale*, "such a fresh, daring book—wild, and yet true,—with its quaint, spiritual portraits looking ancient and also fresh,—Puritanism, I may say, *kept fresh* in the salt water over there and looking out living upon us once more!" Even though the attitude of the *Morning Advertiser* continued to be dominant, a new attitude was forming.

While the effects of *The Whale* were still reverberating in London, then, a few readers (mainly young people) were pondering their way toward a further stage in their sense of what was of value in American literature. Their rankings did not jibe with the opinions of the British reading public and the British literary establishment, in whose view Henry Wadsworth Longfellow was a poet almost if not quite the equal of Alfred Tennyson and in whose view Nathaniel Hawthorne was the equal of most living British novelists, one of whom, George Eliot (less radical than her companion Lewes), in 1856 praised *Hiawatha* and *The Scarlet Letter* as the "two most indigenous and masterly productions in American literature." In *American Literature: An Historical Sketch 1620–1880* (1882) John Nichol, a professor of English literature at the University of Glasgow, praised *The Scarlet Letter* as the most important romance written in the English language during the century. To most English readers Hawthorne felt, as Irving had felt, unthreatening, indeed, downright *English*. It took time for an anti-establishment evaluation of American writers to crystallize—it took the publication of *Walden* in 1854 and *Leaves of Grass* in 1855, then more years, for only a few copies of each reached England in the mid-fifties. (George Eliot is thought to have reviewed *Walden* early in 1856—without its impressing her greatly.) *Walden* was first published there in 1884 and first actually printed there in 1886, while part of *Leaves of Grass* was first printed there, without "Song of Myself" and otherwise sanitized, in W. M. Rossetti's *Poems of Walt Whitman* of 1868. It took time for the young radical writers to have the evidence with which to conduct their shakedown of the American canon, but by the 1860's and 1870's a remarkable number of the brightest, most vigorous young British lovers of literature and art, men (the available evidence is almost exclusively about men) who shared idealistic and iconoclastic social views as well as aesthetic values, were deciding that great literature had come from one or another of three American writers (or perhaps two of them or all three) who at the time were practically unknown in Great Britain and were marginal figures in their own country: Melville, Whitman, Thoreau.

Although it is clear that a third of a century or so after the publication of *The Whale* a number of British artists and writers saw Melville in a new way, how the change occurred has not been documented in any detail. What follows here is a suggestive, impressionistic survey of some connections among Melville's admirers and the admirers of Whitman and Thoreau. The best evidence for how Melville's reputation grew in Great Britain during this period may ultimately be found by searching out published comments on Melville and evidence still ignored in archives and then correlating that information with study of who attended the same public schools and the universities together, who lived near each other (or shared quarters with each other), who belonged to the same clubs, who wrote for the same newspapers and magazines, who shared a publisher, who were bound by mutual acquaintances, by family connections, and by personal affection for each other. This much can be ventured now: the younger members of the British literary world who constituted the admirers of Melville, Whitman, and Thoreau belonged for the most part to three or four overlapping groups. They were members of the Pre-Raphaelite Brotherhood of artist-writers or their associates; they were adherents of the working-men's movement (datable from 1854, when F. D. Maurice, the Christian Socialist, founded the Working Men's College in London); they were (a little later) Fabian Socialists; or they were themselves sea-writers or writers about remote countries. To belong in any of the first three of these groups was to be politically and socially radical, never far from the revolutionary spirit of Shelley (or from the aging but still formidable physical shapes of men and women who had seen "Shelley plain," including Trelawney and Peacock); to belong to the last group almost always meant to have done one's own fieldwork in comparative anthropology and to have learned (often under Southern constellations) to think untraditionally and independently and therefore to look at European society unconventionally.[61]

One link between these writers and the *Leader* of the early 1850's was James Hannay, who made an almost instant transition from sailor to London journalist connected with Lewes's paper, which was especially influential (as Francis Espinasse recalled) "among the younger and more thoughtful members of the 'advanced' party in politics and religion"—and in literature. From unpublished entries in

---

61. The starting point for research on this section was Brian Higgins's *Herman Melville: An Annotated Bibliography*; Higgins long helped piece together the story and provided some articles from *Transactions of the Leicestershire Archæological Society* and the Leicester *Wyvern*. George Worth very generously shared his microfilm of James Hannay's diaries. Books on Pre-Raphaelites, Fabian Socialists, and others which were scanned for this section would require many pages to list, and any such listing would thwart the purpose of encouraging others to elaborate or challenge the hypotheses advanced here. Kenneth Morrill at Parker's request looked through Edward Carpenter's books for references to Melville and readily found *Iölaus: An Anthology of Friendship* (1902), discussed below.

Hannay's diaries we learn that in late 1852 he began a conscientious reading or rereading of Melville, who was already "a favourite writer" of his. While he was reading Melville he was also seeing the Rossettis, although he moved in a faster, "bohemian" set and drank a great deal more alcohol (W. M. Rossetti remembered) than most members of the Pre-Raphaelite Brotherhood did. Between reading *White-Jacket* and *Mardi* he spent Sunday evening, December 5, at Dante Gabriel Rossetti's, slept over, and breakfasted the next morning with "Gabriel" (the name the family used). The evidence stops there: Hannay does not record that he discussed Melville with D. G. or his brother W. M. (who earlier in the year read a little Tacitus with Hannay and spent the night at his place). Hannay was still intimate with the Rossettis in the 1860's when W. M. Rossetti was preparing his selection from *Leaves of Grass*. (In the preface Rossetti recalled that one of the few reviews which did not sneer at the 1855 *Leaves of Grass* had appeared in the *Leader*, and in his *Recollections* he made it clear that he assumed the reviewer was Lewes.) On Christmas Day of 1870 D. G. Rossetti put *Pierre* on his list of "high-class" book orders, saying, with offhand authority, that he believed it "is not easily met with like others of his [Melville's], as it has not been republished in England."

The Hannay-Rossetti connection is suggestive but not conclusive, and other links are also tenuous. We know that in 1855 the painter William Bell Scott, master of a school of design in Newcastle on Tyne, sent a copy of the first American edition of *Leaves of Grass* to W. M. Rossetti, who was powerfully drawn toward the American and toward others, including Algernon Swinburne, who shared his sense of the importance of the American poet. (Swinburne lived with D. G. Rossetti for a time in the mid-1860's at Cheyne Walk.) W. M. Rossetti was affected by the burgeoning literary-social workingmen's movement centered in the Working Men's College, at which D. G. Rossetti was a part-time staff member. The poet James Thomson ("B. V."—the "B." for Bysshe, in tribute to Shelley), who displayed his knowledge of *Mardi* in 1865 in the scruffily radical *National Reformer* edited by his friend the freethinker Charles Bradlaugh, became a friend of W. M. Rossetti's in 1871 and in a second article on Whitman in Bradlaugh's journal in 1874 became the first, as far as we know, to compare Melville and Whitman in print, describing Melville as the only living American writer who approached Whitman "in his sympathy with all ordinary life and vulgar occupations, in his feeling of brotherhood for all rough workers." This claim could have been made from a reading of Melville's early books or even from the Bentley edition of *The Whale*, which omitted from Chapter 26 "The great God absolute! The centre and circumference of all democracy! His omnipresence, our divine equality!" and tamed "thou great democratic God!" to "thou great God!"; but had Thomson brought a copy of *Moby-Dick* home from his trip to America in 1873?

Early in 1881 Thomson went to Leicester for the opening of a new Secularist hall and formed a friendship with J. W. Barrs, who lived nearby. During his visits that year he introduced some of Melville's works to Barrs and (directly or through Barrs) to James Billson, a young solicitor who for years regularly taught classes in Latin and Greek at the Working Men's College there. In class Billson gave rein to "his strong and racy sense of humour" as he taught artisans "enough Greek to enjoy Aristophanes." Two years after Thomson's death in 1882 from dipsomania, young Billson, spurred by the enthusiasm he now shared with Barrs and other friends, wrote Melville an admiring letter (August 21, 1884) in which he made clear that in his experience (unlike D. G. Rossetti's) Melville's books were scarce, and "in great request." Billson added: "as soon as one is discovered (for that is what it really is with us) it is eagerly read & passed round a rapidly increasing knot of 'Melville readers.' " Barrs, who in 1886 sent gifts of Thomson's books to Melville, introduced Thomson's friend the blind poet Philip Bourke Marston to *Mardi* in the 1880's (Thomson seems not to have done so himself, although he is the link between Barrs and Marston, and his last alcoholic collapse was in Marston's room in D. G. Rossetti's house in Cheyne Walk). Marston subsequently obtained all of Melville's books that were "accessible to him"—presumably to have read aloud to him. Marston knew the Pre-Raphaelites Madox Brown and the short-lived Oliver Madox Brown as well as Swinburne; he was especially intimate with W. M. Rossetti (who in 1874 married Lucy Brown, Madox Brown's daughter) and with D. G. Rossetti. In the 1870's the Rossettis and Swinburne knew John Payne, who in 1903 published a sonnet on "Herman Melville" in which he praised the five earlier books but valued *The Whale* over Melville's "idylls of the life afloat."

Older than and apparently independent of the circle of the Pre-Raphaelites and friends of "B. V.," the playwright and novelist

Charles Reade not only read *The Whale* (perhaps after encountering it at the publisher's, for he became a Bentley novelist late in 1852) but annotated it in a way that suggested to Michael Sadleir (who saw his copy decades later) that he had thought of making an abridgment of it. In 1885, the year after Reade's death, his friend the dramatist and poet Robert Buchanan visited Whitman while staging one of his own plays in Philadelphia and on his return to London published in *The Academy* (August 15, 1885) "Socrates in Camden, with a Look Round," a poem on Whitman that included a tribute to the power of Melville as the

> sea-compelling man,
> Before whose wand Leviathan
> Rose hoary white upon the Deep,
> With awful sounds that stirred its sleep.

Melville, he continued, "Sits all forgotten or ignored, / While haberdashers are adored!" In a footnote Buchanan said he had "sought everywhere for this Triton, who is still living somewhere in New York. No one seemed to know anything of the one great imaginative writer fit to stand shoulder to shoulder with Whitman on that continent." The praise of Melville was extraordinary, but the other comment is puzzling. In New York City Buchanan had visited E. C. Stedman, a neighbor of Melville's, who in corresponding with British writers while preparing his book on Victorian poetry had formed a notable Swinburne archive, and who then was or soon afterwards became an adherent of *Moby-Dick*, "its tale often on his lips, and the recommendation by all odds to read it at once to nearly every young writer who sought his counsel." (See Sealts, 1974.) Whatever the reason Buchanan did not locate Melville, his footnote may have roused Stedman to make polite overtures to Melville, for Stedman's son Arthur soon made Melville's acquaintance and became in effect his literary executor, in consultation with Mrs. Melville. Buchanan's fascination with Melville grew, and his *The Outcast*, a poem that went on sale in New York just before Melville died in 1891, was a strange homage to him through a mixing of the Flying Dutchman legend with a *Typee*-like romance. The volume concluded with an open letter on the state of his own career and the deplorable state of English publishing, part confessional, part apologia, addressed to an American he had never met, Charles Warren Stoddard, the homosexual writer (fascinated by Kory-Kory in *Typee*) who corresponded with both Whitman and Melville, and who introduced Melville's works to Robert Louis Stevenson. Buchanan's connection with the Pre-Raphaelites was intense but adversarial, for his "The Fleshly School of Poetry," first published in the *Contemporary Review* (October, 1871), so grieved D. G. Rossetti that W. M. Rossetti recalled it as precipitating his breakdown and early death. In so small a literary society mutual enthusiasms among enemies are perhaps inevitable, and no one has shown that there was anything like two sets of rival Whitman or Melville admirers in London.

Some time before 1889 Henry S. Salt, all-round humanitarian as well as Fabian Socialist, learned of Melville from the bookseller and publisher Bertram Dobell, the friend of Thomson's who arranged the book publication of *The City of Dreadful Night* (1880); Salt in turn brought *The Whale* to the notice of William Morris, and a week or two afterwards heard Morris quoting it "with huge gusto and delight." Writing his biography of Thomson apparently led Salt into acquaintance with the Leicester admirers of both Thomson and Melville, then into writing an essay on Melville in 1889 and another in 1892. In the second essay Salt said he had been told "of instances in which English working-men became his [Melville's] hearty admirers"—perhaps Billson had communicated to his artisan students a love of Melville as well as of Aristophanes. In 1889, Salt wrote to Melville just after his essay on him appeared in the *Scottish Art Review*. Knowing that Barrs was sending Melville a copy of the essay, he sent Melville his own recent book on Thomson, thereby reaffirming the confluence of interests he and the Leicester admirers shared.

Born at mid-century (in India), Salt could not remember Melville's reception in the 1840's and 1850's, so he pulled down old periodicals to see what contemporary reviewers had said—an act that makes him the first recorded "Melville scholar," as distinguished from reviewer or simple enthusiast. Always high-minded, he looked hard through Melville's early books for signs of "direct ethical teaching" and had to settle for praising Melville's "strong and genuine feeling" on the rather vague subject of humanity as well as a few specific positions such as his opposition to modern warfare. In 1892, after Melville's death, Salt's second Melville article, in *Gentleman's Magazine*, showed that he had come to delight in Melville's language, especially in *The Whale*, which he now praised as a work of "ambitious conception and colossal proportions," the "crown and glory" of Melville's later phase. Here he made good use of Melville's private letters to Billson, and in a footnote listed some competent judges who numbered among Melville admirers: William Morris, Theodore Watts, R. L. Stevenson, Robert Buchanan, and W. Clark Russell. The least well remembered of these admirers, the solicitor Walter Theodore Watts, had become intimate with D. G. Rossetti and helped W. M. with legal matters after his brother's death. Later, as Theodore Watts-Dunton, he was Swinburne's protector for three decades, and on one occasion talked to George Bernard Shaw and Salt about George Meredith and Melville on the way to see Swinburne, "taking it for granted that they had never heard of them, though Salt was a friend of both." Shaw himself recorded in a posthumously published preface to *Salt and His Circle* (1951) that he agreed with Salt on the subject of *Moby-Dick*. Among more radical British literary people interest in Whitman, Melville, and Thoreau converged, so that in 1894 Salt could write scathingly not only of a "recent unhappy defamation of Walt Whitman" but specifically of "Lowell's malicious misrepresentations of Thoreau"—the efforts of a member of the American literary establishment to suppress a better writer—and better man—than himself. Salt and his friends stood ready to defend the writers they felt were not properly estimated at home but were known in England among a widening circle of devotees.

And unquestionably Salt was at the center of that circle. In the 1880's and 1890's he initiated correspondence not only with Melville but other Americans, among them Thoreau acquaintances and the early Thoreau collector Dr. Samuel A. Jones, and John Burroughs, the admirer of both Whitman and Thoreau, and in 1890 he published his biography of Thoreau, the product of intense and judicious research by transatlantic correspondence. Soon after Melville's death he began a correspondence with Arthur Stedman and was kept informed of the slow progress toward a selected edition of Melville's works. He wrote Dr. Jones on June 9, 1892, after his second article on Melville had been reprinted in the United States: "Did you see my art. on Melville in the *Eclectic* for April? I wonder whether you are a Melville enthusiast? You *ought* to be. He was one of the very greatest of American writers." Jones's failure to act evoked a further recommendation on November 11, 1892:

I can't help thinking that you would greatly enjoy Herman Melville's works, if you once got started off on them, especially *Typee* and *The Whale*. They are so full of profound reflection & earnest humanity—I do not know any literature I more heartily enjoy reading. He is undoubtedly one of the great brotherhood of nature-writers.

Dr. Jones had in fact seen Melville years before in a Manhattan bookstore without knowing who he was and without knowing his writings. After Salt's insistence he looked for Melville's books and had the good fortune to become the first major Melville collector we know of outside of the Melville family. (See pp. 1021–43.) Extended comments on Thoreau and on Whitman run through many of Salt's writings, such as his 1894 *Richard Jefferies: His Life and Ideals*, in which Salt quoted from a manuscript on Jefferies by Dr. Jones, whom he identified as "a well-known student of Thoreau." In the months before and after Melville's death in September, 1891, Salt found that the "literateurs" of the British publishing world, aloof from issues of human nature and society, were threatened by his proposed collection of essays on "the whole *Nature* subject," to be called *The Return to Nature* and to consist of his articles on "Jefferies, Carpenter, Burroughs, Thoreau, Melville, &c, &c." Had Salt found a publisher for *The Return to Nature*, or had he set himself to write a biography of Melville instead of Thoreau, the course of Melville's reputation would have been incalculably but powerfully altered. As it was, he promoted Melville's reputation for decades more, living long enough to give Arthur Stedman's letters to Willard Thorp, one of the major earliest Melville scholars.

Chances are that the Socialist and champion of homosexual love Edward Carpenter knew *The Whale*, for several of his close acquaintances, notably Salt, were Melville admirers, and he clearly knew *Typee* and *Omoo*. (Carpenter had been F. D. Maurice's curate before breaking with the church.) Upon reading W. M. Rossetti's edition of Whitman he initiated a correspondence with the American poet and made a pilgrimage in 1877 to see Whitman at Camden (he "stayed in the house with him for a week"), then went to Concord to learn about Thoreau. Emerson put him up. Having bathed in Walden Pond, Carpenter on his return sent a copy of *Walden* to William Morris, who thought it presented a one-sided view of life; more important for Thoreau's reputation, he also introduced *Walden* to his Socialist friend Salt. Carpenter's *Towards Democracy* was a Whitmanesque plea for equality of mankind infused with his ideal of love, which he specified elsewhere as "a powerful, strongly built man, of my own age or rather younger—preferably of the working class." There is no reason to question Chushichi Tsuzuki's observation that an "element of sexual attraction" was present for Carpenter and others "in the fellowship of Socialism, and sustained its moral fervour." Such a sexual element infused the earlier working-men's movement as well. Carpenter, who soon became a spokesman for an idealized notion of homosexuality in works such as *Homogenic Love* (1895), was in the thick of Melville admirers (Havelock Ellis asked Melville for information about his ancestry at about the time he was using Carpenter as a major case-study of homosexuality; his intimate friend Salt resorted to Chapter 3 of *Moby-Dick* in describing an occasion when Carpenter was left looking "a sort of diabolically funny"; Augustine Birrell, cited below, was a friend from his Cambridge years). In *Iölaus* (1902) he used Melville's "reliable" first two books to illustrate male friendship-customs in the pagan world, quoting first the account of the Polynesian habit "of making bosom friends at the shortest possible notice" (from *Omoo*, chap. 39) then the description of the "Polynesian Apollo" Marnoo (from *Typee*, chap. 18).[62] Carpenter had enormous influence not only on his contemporaries at home and abroad but also on at least two younger writers who were also profoundly influenced by Melville—D. H. Lawrence and E. M. Forster.

Undeniably, for many readers, male or female, the appeal of *The Whale* or *Moby-Dick* during its gradual discovery was grounded in part on the fact that by style and subject matter it could nurture a class-bridging philanthropic idealism not without an element of seductive eroticism. The late-nineteenth-century British admirers of Whitman, Melville, and Thoreau were driven by industrialization, urban poverty, and repressive moral codes to look afresh at all human

---

62. Melville endured many jests in the press about his fickleness in abandoning the charming Fayaway and marrying the daughter of Judge Shaw. Later the young Californian Charles Warren Stoddard, mentioned above, found erotic pleasure in the treatment of Kory-Kory, the narrator's special male companion in *Typee*. Jonathan Katz in *Gay American History* (1976) describes Stoddard's debt to Melville in "A South Sea Idyl," published in the *Overland Monthly* (1869). In *Gay/Lesbian Almanac* (1983) Katz shows that Carpenter's *Homogenic Love* was read in the canyons of Northern California in the 1890's by men who were corresponding with Carpenter.

institutions (conspicuously including Christianity) and at man's relationship with nature. Hawthorne in *The Scarlet Letter* (chap. 18) had made his position clear on the lawless thoughts that visited Hester Prynne. When she looked from an "estranged point of view at human institutions" she showed that in her suffering she had been taught "much amiss." That conservatism marked Hawthorne as irrelevant to most of the early British admirers of Melville, Whitman, and Thoreau. In their social idealism they were willing to experiment with ways of establishing on a surer ground of mutual happiness not only what Hawthorne called "the whole relation between man and woman" but also the whole relation between man and man. To be true to their principled radicalism these British admirers excluded no aspect of life from idealistic experimentation: being social idealists led logically to their being sexual idealists and sexual explorers. There was not a libertine among them (although one was court-martialed for a tantalizingly vague offense which apparently occurred while swimming with other men), but they included some celibates (temporary or long-term), some male homosexuals and bisexuals, apparently a fetishist or two, and more than one man who though heterosexual (or possibly either homosexual or celibate by preference) married a lesbian. (Carpenter gave Kate Salt a name for her sexual status—"an Urning," thereby arming her in her refusal to consummate her marriage.) Some of them strained or violated social and sexual conventions in various ways (tolerating a ménage à trois out of respect for the principle of another's freedom, living more or less communally for extended periods, displaying an unusual intensity in male-male relationships, keeping a mistress or living so as to be suspected of keeping one, cohabiting with a divorced woman, marrying a divorced woman).

Concurrently with the enthusiasm about Melville among survivors of or connections of the Pre-Raphaelite writer-artists and adherents of the working-men's movement and Fabian Socialism, and in part independently, a reevaluation of Melville was going on among other British writers—travelers and out-of-doors men, men who had been to the far reaches of the Empire, where *Typee* and *Omoo*, standard works in John Murray's Colonial and Home Library, had also penetrated decade after decade. (Rudyard Kipling, a nephew of the wife of the Pre-Raphaelite Edward Burne-Jones, appropriately put some books by Melville on his reading list for the Empire League.) In regions remote from London *The Whale* was sometimes passed hand to hand under strange circumstances, as when in the early 1870's "a sweet, dainty little English lady" came aboard a small trading schooner in Apea, in the Samoas, and gave the "grizzled old captain" some books, offering the three volumes of *The Whale* as "the strangest, wildest, and saddest story I have ever read." The captain read the entire three volumes aloud to the crew, which included the sea-writer-to-be Louis Becke, who told the story as the introduction to Putnam's 1901 London issue of *Moby-Dick*. Most important among this group of outdoor literary men are the nautical writers, of whom W. Clark Russell was most earnest in establishing the reputation of *Moby-Dick*. In the London *Contemporary Review* (September, 1884) Russell claimed first rank for Melville among "the poets of the deep":

> Whoever has read the writings of Melville must I think feel disposed to consider "Moby Dick" as his finest work. It is indeed all about the sea, whilst "Typee" and "Omoo," are chiefly famous for their lovely descriptions of the South Sea Islands, and of the wild and curious inhabitants of those coral strands; but though the action of the story is altogether on shipboard, the narrative is not in the least degree nautical in the sense that Cooper's and Marryat's novels are. . . . "Moby Dick" is not a sea-story—one could not read it as such—it is a medley of noble impassioned thoughts born of the deep, pervaded by a grotesque human interest, owing to the contrast it suggests between the rough realities of the cabin and the forecastle, and the phantasms of men conversing in rich poetry, and strangely moving and acting in that dim weather-worn Nantucket whaler.

The speeches in "Midnight, Forecastle" (Chapter 40—which William Allen Butler had found so disgusting) "might truly be thought to have come down to us from some giant mind of the Shakespearean era." *Moby-Dick* as a whole was "like a drawing by William Blake" or "of the 'Ancient Mariner' pattern." Russell was early in preferring *Moby-Dick* to Melville's other works and also early in admiring it not simply as a superb nautical tale but as a work of poetic imagination set in a nautical frame.

By the 1890's Hannay was dead, but Russell and the young Becke were far from the only living voyager-authors or authors-to-be who cherished a love of *Moby-Dick*. In the summer of 1896, as a teenage laborer in a Yonkers carpet mill, John Masefield made up a short list of sea authors he had not read and bought some Melvilles (including *Moby-Dick*) from a Sixth Avenue bookdealer. He appreciated the "masterly account" of New Bedford, and his love of Melville grew. During the 1890's W. H. Hudson introduced Morley Roberts to *Moby-Dick* (and they also talked together about Richard Jefferies). Afterwards Roberts recalled that he and Hudson often "wondered how it was that the Americans still looked forward to some great American book when all they had to do was to cast their eyes backward and find it." By the first years of the twentieth century Hudson had also talked about the book with Joseph Conrad, whose fulminations against *The Whale* on January 15, 1907 ("a rather strained rhapsody with whaling for a subject and not a single sincere line in the 3 vols of it") are so excessive as to arouse suspicions that he was denying a rival he saw as powerful, if not denying an influence on his own work. The American artist Peter Toft (whom Melville dispatched in 1886 with greetings to Russell, who had not been sure that he was still alive) introduced *Moby-Dick* to the sea-novelist Frank T. Bullen; later Bullen in turn talked about the book with J. St. Loe Strachey (whose cousin John Addington Symonds was obsessed with the poetry and the life-example of Walt Whitman). Hudson in 1917 predicted that when Thoreau's bicentenary came around he would be regarded as "one without master or mate," in the "foremost ranks of the prophets"—evidence that some of these travel-writer and nautical-writer admirers of Melville shared either Buchanan's dual enthusiasm for Whitman and Melville or the frequent enthusiasm of the Pre-Raphaelites and the supporters of the working men's movement and the Fabian Socialists for Whitman or Thoreau (or both) as well as Melville.

These lovers of *The Whale* or *Moby-Dick* in the decades before the centennial of Melville's birth sometimes declared their love for it publicly, and sometimes treated it as a self-identifying and other-identifying token. A writer in the *Nation and Athenæum* in 1922 (perhaps H. M. Tomlinson, or John Middleton Murry—whose own most intense relationship was probably with D. H. Lawrence) reported what he had learned about the use of the work as a talisman:

> That book, indeed, appears to have been a wonder treasured as a sort of secret for years by some select readers who had chanced upon it. They said little about it. We gather that they had been in the habit of

hinting the book to friends they could trust, so that "Moby Dick" became a sort of cunning test by which genuineness of another man's response to literature could be proved. If he was not startled by "Moby Dick," then his opinion on literature was of little account. It should be observed, however, that the victim was never told this, because this test was made by those who seemed scared by the intensity of their own feelings aroused by the strange, subliminal potency of the monster called the White Whale.

Some lovers of the book had taken greater risks than handing someone else a book: in the year of Melville's death a young teacher in Baltimore, Edward Lucas White, invited another young man, Frank Jewett Mather, to his rooms and read to him from *Moby-Dick*, thereby initiating one of the most important American enthusiasms for Melville. (If Houghton Mifflin had not refused in 1906 to give him the $500 advance he needed, Mather would have proceeded with a biography of Melville, with the cooperation of Melville's daughter Bessie.) Such sharing of the book, even between heterosexual men, was not without the component of ritual bonding, for reading aloud usually occurred in companionable seclusion and required from the uninitiate the intense intimacy of becoming alive to Melville's words not through his own eyes but through the voice of the reader. Sometimes, in this sort of sharing more was at stake than the possible validation of the reader's own advanced literary judgment. And in discussing the appeal of Melville to the British admirers from the last decades of his life through the 1920's it is essential also to remember the way William Morris read the book and immediately began quoting it with "huge gusto and delight." The "bold and nervous lofty language" that Melville had created in the book, and the humbler but equally memorable quaintnesses of phrasings, took rank in his admirers' minds with phrases from Shakespeare and Wordsworth, and were irresistibly sharable.

In the next generation Melville's most famous admirers would include men (D. H. Lawrence and Lawrence of Arabia are obvious examples) who devoted about as much passionate writing to male-male relationships as to male-female relationships, as well as bisexual females, most notably Virginia Woolf. Even though Melville did not come, as Whitman and Thoreau did, with social programme in hand, the British admirers saw him as having learned to think the way they wanted to think, "untraditionally and independently." Equally appealing to these writers was his intense awareness of his own "moods of thought," his phrase in *Pierre* (bk. 24.i), and his capacity for analyzing and evoking even more complicated moods of body-and-mind, often in relationship to the physical universe and to the fellowship of all human beings (among whom, as many of his admirers were keenly aware, were well-muscled men whose appeal was not diminished by their not always being of the white race and not always being altogether fluent in the English language). Part of Melville's special appeal to his British admirers came from specific scenes of male bonding as well as from his more general underlying feeling of brotherhood with all men. One needs to acknowledge that a substantial set of Melvilleans from his own time to the present has consisted of male (and some female) homosexuals or bisexuals, men and women who often become influential out of proportion to their absolute numbers (however high those numbers are) in artistic and literary circles—journalistic critics, academic critics, editors, bibliographers, rare book dealers, publishers, and writers as diverse as Carl Van Vechten, Lawrence of Arabia, W. H. Auden, Malcolm Lowry, and Angus Wilson. Little enough is known about the topic of the relationship between sexual orientation and the cherishing and sharing of literary works (certainly not in relation to Melville). Little was said until recently about the much larger topic of the relationship between aesthetic responses, sexual stimulation, and social and cosmic questionings—a topic that must form a part of any history of the reputation of *The Whale* and *Moby-Dick*.[63]

The "Melville revival" which began in nineteenth-century London simmered there until the centennial of Melville's birth, 1919. The term was justifiably used in the New York *Times Saturday Review of Books* on July 22, 1899, where "T. B. F." reported in "Book News in London" on "a conspicuous revival of interest in America's sea author," the result of W. Clark Russell's "repeated glowing tributes." Russell deserves such credit, but it took dozens of men and

---

63. In the supercharged psychological, aesthetic, and intellectual unfolding which culminated in 1851 and early 1852, Melville recognized something very like what in modern French literary theory is called the pleasures of the text and devised a style which he thought would allow him to write about such a forbidden topic. Very likely the first literary writing he did after finishing *Moby-Dick* was the opening of *Pierre* as we know it, where we learn that Pierre had thrilled from the simultaneous effects of puberty and of imaginative eroticism in literature.

women over the course of four decades to bring about the rediscovery of Melville and *Moby-Dick*. In the first two decades of the
twentieth century John Masefield repeatedly praised *Moby-Dick* in his
books and in interviews. Not all his early tributes to Melville have
been located, but in *A Mainsail Haul* (1905) he put an evocative prose
fantasy into the mouth of an old sailor named Blair. In this "Port of
Many Ships" "the great white whale, old Moby Dick, the king of all
the whales," leads all the other whales of the world in raising all the
sunken ships and drowned sailors and towing them "to where the sun
is." Then "the red ball will swing open like a door, and Moby Dick,
and all the whales, and all the ships will rush through it into a grand
anchorage in Kingdom Come." During this time W. H. Hudson was
as loyal an admirer as Masefield, and Melville's influence was plain in
the writings of James Barrie. Many of the admirers from the 1890's
survived for decades—G. B. Shaw, H. S. Salt, and other Fabians
spanned literary generations—but did they talk much about Melville
to younger friends in the 1910's? There were living links between the
Pre-Raphaelite admirers of Melville and the Bloomsbury crowd
(around 1915 Ford Madox Hueffer encouraged D. H. Lawrence and
introduced him to Edward Garnett, who had corresponded with
Melville—but did they mention Melville to each other?). Evidence is
scant, but a surprising number of Lady Ottoline Morrell's friends
came to know *The Whale* or *Moby-Dick*. Among them were Augustine Birrell (born like Salt in mid-century) and younger literary people—Walter de la Mare, D. H. Lawrence, J. D. Beresford (in whose
Cornwall cottage Lawrence first read *The Whale*, in 1916), later Virginia Woolf, Leonard Woolf, Lytton Strachey, Aldous Huxley. De la
Mare knew Alice Meynell (mother of Viola Meynell, whose role is
discussed below) and John Freeman, who in 1926 became the first
Englishman to write a book on Melville. We know that some of these
people were among the secret sharers of *The Whale* or *Moby-Dick* in
the 1910's, but the proof is fragmentary and elusive.

Therefore the following discussion of the canonization of *Moby-
Dick*, like the foregoing discussion of its gradual discovery, cannot be
exhaustive but only suggestive, a glimpse of the unpredictable
rhythms in interest, the missed opportunities, the near-
breakthroughs, the happy confluence of enthusiasm, occasion, and
forum. Some of the most glowing tributes had no obvious immediate
effect because they were written by little-known writers and pub-

lished in more or less obscure journals. The first explicit plea for canonizing *Moby-Dick*, Archibald MacMechan's 1899 essay already referred to, was published not in the *Atlantic Monthly* or *Harper's* but in *Queen's Quarterly*, a provincial journal of limited circulation (then reprinted in a minor London journal and, much later, in book form). William Livingston Alden, the London correspondent for the New York *Times Saturday Review of Books,* in 1899 declared that "Melville was perhaps the most original genius that America has produced" and suggested that a Melville Society be formed. From 1899 for the next decade the New York *Times* (often spurred by a letter from London) repeatedly praised Melville and offered factual information (including a list of Melville's books submitted by his widow). A review of a sea-novel would contain a comparison to Melville's works that would provoke correspondence, then a letter to the newspaper would provoke a flurry of comments (sometimes one by a new and excited discoverer of *Moby-Dick*), until discussion subsided (for the time). The institutional power of the press was such that an anonymous long-time staff member could give the book repeated tributes. Just as such British periodicals as the *National Reformer*, the *Academy*, and the *Pall Mall Gazette* were important in the rediscovery of the 1860's through the 1880's, during the next decades the *Athenæum* and the *Spectator* (both of which had scorned *The Whale* in 1851) repeatedly recalled Melville in favorable terms when they reviewed the latest sea-fiction. Ultimately the single great occasion for reviving Melville's reputation was simply the centennial of his birth. The significance of the year 1919 as precipitating the Melville revival may sometimes seem overstated, given the interest already manifested in the preceding decades, but as a public focus for diverse manifestations of interest it was incalculably important.

Before the process of canonizing *Moby-Dick* could be completed, the book had to become readily available. The "Melville boom" of the late 1880's and early 1890's, fueled first by the surprising news that Melville was not only alive but could be written to, then by news of his death, gained momentum from word that a collected edition was forthcoming. The four books that Arthur Stedman eventually got into print evoked some important comment on Melville after the London branch of Putnam's imported 270 copies of the Stedman edition of *Moby-Dick* in 1893, the first time the American text had been for sale there. The Putnam London issue of 1901 consisted of

another 270 sets of sheets from the Stedman plates and contained
Louis Becke's introduction, the first ever written for an edition of
*Moby-Dick* and arguably still the best—simply because much of it
consists of one of the most wonderfully evocative stories about *The
Whale* anyone has ever told. (No one is on record as having been
moved by Becke's account until the present editors sought it out in
the 1970's.) The Everyman's Library text (1907), based on the Bentley edition and with a brief note by Ernest Rhys, by contrast was
frequently reprinted and widely available, but did not add the "Epilogue" until the Melville revival was over. In 1920 Oxford based its
World's Classics edition on the Harper text, the first time it had been
printed in England, and accompanied it with Viola Meynell's appreciative introduction. Precisely which of the variant passages of Melville's text an English edition contained was for decades extremely
chancy, and remains so. Even carelessly prepared and poorly promoted editions by lesser publishers were reviewed, and therefore
could occasion astonishing commentary which otherwise might never have been written: was the amazing review of the Stedman edition
in the New York *Critic* in 1893 written by a long-time lover of Melville who never expressed himself or herself in print elsewhere? was it
written by some staffer who was casually handed the book to review?
One could write a reasonably adequate history of the book's reputation by studying introductions to new editions and reviews of those
editions.

The Oxford World's Classics edition lost nothing by just missing
the centennial, for Meynell's introduction (brief and inexact as it was)
pushed the vogue of the book out from the Bloomsburyites into
public view. A copy caused such consternating ecstasy in the office of
*The Nation* that two years later the sea-novelist H. M. Tomlinson
dated the Melville revival from its publication. Tomlinson was recalling that early in 1921, as a staff member of the *Nation* just before its
merger with the *Athenæum*, he had bought a copy of the World's
Classics edition and written about it, "incoherently indeed, but with
signs of emotion as intense and as pleasingly uncouth as Man Friday
betrayed at the sight of his long-lost father." While the editor, John
Middleton Murry, was "struggling" with Tomlinson's article, "and
wondering what the deuce it could mean," there arrived from Augustine Birrell, an enthusiast for many years (put on to Melville by
Sir Alfred Lyall), a review of the World's Classics edition "marked on

the outside 'Urgent,' and on the inner scroll of the MS. itself, 'A Rhapsody.' " Having read Birrell's tribute ("The two striking features of this book, after allowing for the fact that it is a work of genius and therefore *sui generis*, are, as it appears to me, its most amazing eloquence, and its mingling of an ever-present romanticism of style with an almost savage reality of narrative"), Murry himself read the book and reported: "I hereby declare, being of sane intellect, that since letters began there never was such a book, and that the mind of man is not constructed so as to produce such another; that I put its author with Rabelais, Swift, Shakespeare, and other minor and disputable worthies; and that I advise any adventurer of the soul to go at once into the morose and prolonged retreat necessary for its deglutition." From this time Tomlinson and Murry used the columns of the *Nation and Athenæum* in promoting the reputation of Melville and his masterpiece.[64]

That reputation culminated in London in the early 1920's as statesmen, scientists, men of commerce, and literary people—many classically trained, able to recognize Melville's wide-ranging allusions—shared an astonished enthusiasm for *Moby-Dick*. In *Gifts of*

---

64. Gradually those defining the stature Melville ought to hold began to compare *Moby-Dick* to classics of world literature (often in terms which suggested exclusively male readership). Carl Van Vechten (a distant cousin of Melville's) in the New York *Literary Review* (1921) said it far surpassed every American work from *The Scarlet Letter* to *The Golden Bowl* and stood with the great classics of all time—the Greek tragedies, *Don Quixote*, the *Inferno*, and *Hamlet*. In 1922 J. C. Squire, (a friend of John Freeman) said simply that there is no greater work of prose fiction in English than *Moby-Dick*. On August 22, 1922, Freeman reported to John Haines that Conrad Aiken "said that if he had to decide on five novels for himself, he would choose *Karamazov*, *The Idiot*, *Crime and Punishment*, *Moby Dick*, and *The Wings of a [the] Dove*; a sixth would certainly be *The Brook Kerith*." Freeman added: "So far as novels in English are concerned I should assuredly choose the last three." The most avid ranker was T. E. Lawrence, who on August 26, 1922, reminded Edward Garnett of his assembling "a shelf of 'Titanic' books (those distinguished by greatness of spirit, 'sublimity,' as Longinus would call it)"—*The Brothers Karamazov*, *Zarathustra*, and *Moby-Dick*. His ambition, he added "was to make an English fourth." In March, 1923, he named a slightly different group of " 'big' " books—*Leaves of Grass*, *War and Peace*, *The Brothers Karamazov*, *Moby-Dick*, Rabelais, *Don Quixote*. More than mere whimsical confessions of taste, these rankings, whether in public or private, consolidated the climate of opinion about *Moby-Dick* in the 1920's, even while they worked to refine the special sensibility of a Melville-lover: the reader who cherished *Moby-Dick* would cherish *The Seven Pillars of Wisdom*.

*Fortune* (1926) Tomlinson recalled that a year or two before he was in a drawing-room in a London suburb where a group of neighbors, men of commerce, discussed *Moby-Dick* with animation and the symptoms of wonder. He thought the war somehow had freed such non-literary men to talk about such a book. In the same period *Moby-Dick* was cherished by some workingmen, as it had been near the time of Melville's death; Harold Laski met an English bargeman who regarded it "as the greatest piece of literature ever produced by man." This near-magical moment never came again in England, since one essential element in it was fresh mutual discovery of a masterpiece. Nothing like that moment ever occurred in the United States, where even in the 1920's politicians, scientists, men of commerce, and literary people rarely shared the classical education and deep knowledge of English literature such as many Melville lovers in the English drawing-room had in common. And nothing like that moment came in America because the wrong man wrote the first full-scale biography. Carl Van Doren, enthusiastic about Melville since 1914 but always overcommitted to many projects, impulsively assigned the "great old boy" to a student at Columbia, Raymond Weaver. Remembered by Melville's great-grandson Paul Metcalf as a "sweet" man, Weaver was not a gifted researcher or critic. *Herman Melville: Mariner and Mystic* (1921), the product of an absolute minimum of original research, was clumsily proportioned (overloaded toward the early years), stuffed with unassimilated data about the South Seas, laced with quotations badly transcribed from manuscripts or misquoted from writers on Melville (and often not attributed to other writers at all), and relentlessly faddish in psychological analysis of Melville and of all too many members of Melville's family. Weaver relied on assertion to establish the significance of Melville's masterpiece ("Born in hell-fire, and baptised in an unspeakable name, *Moby-Dick* is, with *The Scarlet Letter*, among the few very notable literary achievements of American literature") and strung other people's critical judgments together to pad out his analysis. In 1922 J. St. Loe Strachey rightly saw that Weaver's book was inadequate and complained, with much justice, that Weaver did not realize how "strong the feeling about Melville has always been in England"—how long, and how earnestly, some remarkable people had cherished the book. Tomlinson, who had called for an American to write a biography of Melville while it was possible to interview people who had known him, ruefully assessed the discrepancy between an ideal biography and the poor actuality of Weaver's book.

To a great extent, as far as the American reading public and literary people were concerned, Weaver's biography preempted more intelligent consideration of Melville, blocking research into his life and the history of the composition and publication of *Moby-Dick*. Once the biography had been done, there was no longer a strong impetus to gather the facts, even though many people still living had known Melville. John Freeman's critical biography (1926), like Lewis Mumford's three years later, was damaged by reliance on Weaver for most factual information. Biographical research on Melville took years in beginning to recover from the obstacle of Weaver's book. Not the least of the damage Weaver did was to distress Melville's surviving daughter, Frances Thomas, to the point that she absolutely refused to cooperate with later biographical researchers. There were other reasons, besides the deficiencies of Weaver's book and the diverse educational backgrounds of political, commercial, and literary leaders, for the fact that *Moby-Dick* never achieved in the United States the sort of culmination of cultural and literary significance that it had in England in the early 1920's—the power of a hostile and entrenched academic establishment; the absence of Melville lovers among the dominant poets, fiction writers, and literary critics; the often brief, erratic, and insignificant existence of literary periodicals; and perhaps even a visceral chauvinistic resentment at being repeatedly told by the British what American writers Americans should admire.

The years around 1930 marked a quiet turning point in England. By then *Moby-Dick* had been so thoroughly absorbed into the English literary consciousness that even today Melville turns up in the *Times Literary Supplement* in lists of British writers. In the natural course of things there was less need for public commentary on *Moby-Dick* from anyone except a very late comer indeed. After admirers had succeeded in exalting its reputation, a new enthusiast would no longer find an editor eager to print a rhapsodic appreciation of the book. Furthermore, there seems to have been an irritated if not hostile response to the belated (and in British eyes inadequate) American praise of Melville and his masterpiece. Perhaps also British enthusiasts liked it better when Americans had not caught up with the fact that they had a great writer they did not recognize. Whatever the congeries of reasons, the British continued to read Melville but wrote about him less frequently, and they did not turn to the task of finding what could be found about Melville in England while documentary evidence was still available. They did not, for instance, seek out the papers of men Weaver said Melville met in London to see if any of them recorded their dinners and conversations with him. They did not go to files of newspapers to recover evidence of Melville's contemporary reception—this before German bombs damaged or destroyed many newspaper files. They did not seek out the Bentley papers or ask the help of the current John Murray in researching the sales (and the overseas distribution) of Melville's books. Even after many British colleges and universities began hiring specialists in American literature, there emerged no British scholar of Melville of the rank Salt still holds as scholar of Thoreau. The British revived Melville and left him for the Americans to study.

## IX

Even decades after the Melville revival it would be wrong to dismiss what Frank Swinnerton said in 1921 as he reflected that while *Moby-Dick* would never be wholly forgotten again, it would not be long before it would be half forgotten: "For one thing, it is not everybody's book. It is too fervid." *Moby-Dick* was never everybody's book, nor Melville everybody's author. For many people it is too long, too burdened down with whaling information, and worst of all it contains no romance between a hero and a heroine. In fact, critics— mainly male—who have tried to define the special qualities of a Melvillean have regularly excluded women from consideration. The reviewer in the London *News of the World* (November 2, 1851) offered this flattering definition: "There are people who delight in mulligatawny. They love curry at its warmest point. Ginger cannot be too hot in the mouth for them. Such people, we should think, constitute the admirers of Herman Melville." In all likelihood he was thinking of male readers when he added: "If you love heroics and horrors he is your man." The London *Weekly News and Chronicle* (November 29, 1851) also defined the potential readership of *The Whale*:

> The poetry of the great South Seas, the rude lawless adventure of the rough mariners who for years of continuous voyaging peril themselves on its waters; the excitement and the danger of the fishery for the

sperm whale, the fiercest and hugest monster "of all who swim the ocean stream," combine to make these pages attractive and interesting to many different classes of readers. Artists and sportsmen, the lovers of scenery, and the lovers of excitement, will alike find in them ample material of gratification.

In concluding, the reviewer recommended the volumes to "the artist, the naturalist and the general reader." It was in much this spirit that H. S. Salt recommended Melville as "one of the great brotherhood of nature-lovers." Archibald MacMechan went so far as to describe the small, select audience *Moby-Dick* ought to have: "To the class of gentleman-adventurer, to those who love both books and free life under the wide and open sky, it must always appeal. Melville takes rank with Borrow, and Jefferies, and Thoreau, and Sir Richard Burton; and his place in this brotherhood of notables is not the lowest."

As the praise of later Melville lovers from D. H. Lawrence to Lawrence of Arabia suggests, response to Melville in his *Moby-Dick* during the revival was still largely a response to a man who wrote about men living their most intense physical, emotional, and intellectual experiences away from women, out of doors, in places remote from civilization and familiar domesticity. (The significance of the fact that Melville wrote most of the book in a household of women has hardly been noticed.) To some extent *Moby-Dick* has remained a cult book, even among highly domesticated and perhaps overcivilized male and female academicians, if only because (however large and motley a crew they have become) they are wont to fancy themselves, with more or less weighty facetiousness, as comprising a special breed of readers. What kind of reader that might be has become harder to define than it was when many lovers of *Moby-Dick* shared the sense that Melville belonged to the great brotherhood of nature-lovers and the great band of high hushed aspirants who will always find cause and occasion to champion, as he did, not only the company of intellectuals and metaphysicians but also the company of "meanest mariners, and renegades and castaways."

To rephrase Swinnerton in terms of gender, *Moby-Dick* is not every man's book and not every woman's book. Yet *Moby-Dick* has passed into world literature, a book every person literate in European languages must know about, if only at second or third hand. So far the book has survived the strenuous tributes of being abridged, translated, staged, danced, filmed, taped, radiothoned, painted, and sculpted. It has survived the compliment of innumerable cartoons that rely on the instant recognizability of the phrases "Call me" and "Hast seen" as tags from *Moby-Dick*. It has outlived many a fast-food Moby Dock and similar earnest tributes that only a consumer economy can afford. So far *Moby-Dick* has survived being assigned to tens of thousands of students, even though listing a good book for compulsory reading is the lowest form of sharing. It has survived the compiling of collections of essays about it, the compiling of bibliographies of essays on it, and has even survived being edited and having accounts written about its composition, publication, contemporary reception, and subsequent critical history. But it would be wrong to slight the tributes in mass culture, the value of classroom teaching, and even the value of academic articles, bibliographies, and editions as sincere forms of sharing. If many professors, those whom Melville sardonically would have included among the best contradictory authorities, have cast their harpoons at phantoms rather than the actual *The Whale* or *Moby-Dick*; if some have saved themselves by sharkishly tearing at hunks from a majestic body; if most have been as solipsistic as Ahab (or even as solipsistic as Ishmael), at worst they have trivialized only criticism or scholarship, and at best they too have become sharers of the great book, which though "nailed amidst all the rustiness of iron bolts and the verdigris of copper spikes," though "placed amongst a ruthless crew and every hour passed by ruthless hands," still preserves its Quito glow.

## SOURCES

R EFERENCES TO DATES, events, and documents that are not footnoted or otherwise documented in the NOTE are based upon the following printed sources: *The Letters of Herman Melville*, ed. Merrell R. Davis and William H. Gilman (New Haven: Yale University Press, 1960), of which a revised edition will appear as Volume 14 of the Northwestern-Newberry Edition of *The Writings of Herman Melville*; Herman Melville, *Journal of a Visit to Europe and the Levant, October 11, 1865–May 6, 1857*, ed. Howard C. Horsford (Princeton: Princeton University Press, 1955), of which a revised edition, quoted from in this work, will appear in Volume 15 of the *Writings*; Mary K. Bercaw, *Melville's Sources* (Evanston, Ill.: Northwestern University

Press, 1987); John Bryant, ed., *A Companion to Melville Studies* (New York: Greenwood Press, 1986); Brian Higgins, *Herman Melville: An Annotated Bibliography, . . . 1846–1930* and *Herman Melville: A Reference Guide, 1931–1960* (Boston: G. K. Hall, 1979, 1987); Jay Leyda, *The Melville Log* (New York: Harcourt Brace, 1951; enl. ed., New York: Gordian Press, 1969); Jay Leyda and Hershel Parker, *The New Melville Log* (New York: Gordian Press, forthcoming); Eleanor Melville Metcalf, *Herman Melville: Cycle and Epicycle* (Cambridge: Harvard University Press, 1953); Merton M. Sealts, Jr., *Melville's Reading: A Check-List of Books Owned and Borrowed* (Madison: University of Wisconsin Press, 1966; rev. and enl. ed., Columbia: University of South Carolina Press, 1988); and previously published volumes of the Northwestern-Newberry Edition. Several documents not covered by these sources are among the Augusta Melville papers at the New York Public Library (quoted here with permission), parts of which will be included in *The New Melville Log*. All documents are quoted *literatim* (except for silent correction of several typographical errors in reviews); any variation in readings or in dating between a document as transcribed in these sources and as printed in this NOTE is based on an examination of the original or on further research. Quotations from Melville's works follow the already published or forthcoming Northwestern-Newberry texts (except when there is reason for quoting a passage in some other form). Parenthetical references to the text of *Moby-Dick* are by page and line.

Despite many new discoveries, most references to documents pertinent to *Moby-Dick* can be checked in the *Log*, which is arranged chronologically, and many other documents, especially passages from books Melville used as sources, are quoted in Luther S. Mansfield and Howard P. Vincent's Hendricks House edition of *Moby-Dick* (New York, 1952). The present edition, like most volumes in the Northwestern-Newberry Edition, annotates only items bearing on textual decisions (and does so in the DISCUSSIONS OF ADOPTED READINGS). The Hendricks House *Moby-Dick* provides copious annotation to the full range of Melville's allusions and to his sources in reading, art, and experience. The Penguin edition (London, 1973), edited by Harold Beaver, largely incorporates the Mansfield-Vincent annotations and supplements them with interpretive glosses of what are taken as interlinked ("coded") allusions.

Since literary source studies have long been out of fashion, investigation of such sources for *Moby-Dick*, summarized in Section IV, are still well surveyed in two long-published essays: Stanley T. Williams's chapter on Melville in *Eight American Authors* (New York: Modern Language Association, 1956), pp. 207–70, and Nathalia Wright's chapter in *Eight American Authors: Revised Edition* (New York: W. W. Norton, 1971), pp. 173–224. For each year since 1963 these surveys may be supplemented by the chapter on Melville in *American Literary Scholarship: An Annual* (Durham: Duke University Press).

Some of the central studies of the composition of *Moby-Dick*, not all of which could be discussed in Section V, are listed here chronologically (along with a few important studies of its whaling sources): Charles Roberts Anderson, "With Melville in the South Seas" (Ph.D. dissertation, Columbia University, 1935); Luther S. Mansfield, "Herman Melville: Author and New Yorker, 1844–51" (Ph.D. dissertation, University of Chicago, 1936); Mansfield, "Glimpses of Herman Melville's Life in Pittsfield, 1850–51," *American Literature*, IX (March, 1937), 26–48; Mansfield, *Herman Melville: Author and New Yorker, 1844–51* (Chicago: University of Chicago Libraries, 1938); Charles Olson, "*Lear* and *Moby-Dick*," *Twice a Year*, I (Fall–Winter, 1938), 165–189; Charles Roberts Anderson, *Melville in the South Seas* (New York: Columbia University Press, 1939); Leon Howard, "Melville's Struggle with the Angel," *Modern Language Quarterly*, I (June, 1940), 195–206; Wilbur S. Scott, "Melville's Originality: A Study of Some of the Sources of *Moby-Dick*" (Ph.D. dissertation, Princeton University, 1943); Harrison Hayford, "Two New Letters of Herman Melville," *ELH: A Journal of English Literary History*, II (March, 1944), 76–83; Charles Olson, *Call Me Ishmael* (New York: Reynal & Hitchcock, 1947); Howard P. Vincent, *The Trying-Out of MOBY-DICK* (Boston: Houghton Mifflin, 1949); Sumner W. D. Scott, "The Whale in *Moby Dick*" (Ph.D. dissertation, University of Chicago, 1950); George R. Stewart, "The Two *Moby-Dick*s," *American Literature*, XXV (January, 1954), 414–48; Janez Stanonik, *MOBY-DICK: The Myth and the Symbol. A Study in Folklore and Literature* (Ljubljana: Ljubljana University Press, 1962); F. De Wolfe Miller, "Another Chapter in the History of the Great White Whale," in *Melville and Hawthorne in the Berkshires*, ed. Howard P. Vincent (Kent: Kent State University Press, 1968), pp. 109–17; James Barbour, "The Writing of *Moby-Dick*" (Ph.D. dissertation, UCLA,

1970); Barbour, "The *Town-Ho*'s Story: Melville's Original Whale," *ESQ*, XXI (Second Quarter, 1975), 111–15; Barbour, "The Composition of *Moby-Dick*," *American Literature*, XLVII (November, 1975), 343–60; Joel Myerson, "Comstock's White Whale and *Moby-Dick*," *American Transcendental Quarterly*, XXIX, Part 1 (Winter, 1976), 8–9; Wilson L. Heflin, "Sources from the Whale-Fishery and the 'The Town-Ho's Story'," in *Artful Thunder: Versions of the Romantic Tradition in American Literature in Honor of Howard P. Vincent*, ed. Robert J. DeMott and Sanford E. Marovitz (Kent: Kent State University Press, 1976), pp. 163–76; Leon Howard, "Melville and the American Tragic Hero," in *Four Makers of the American Mind: Emerson, Thoreau, Whitman, and Melville, A Bicentennial Tribute*, ed. Thomas Edward Crawley (Durham: Duke University Press, 1976), pp. 65–82; James Barbour and Leon Howard, "Carlyle and the Conclusion of *Moby-Dick*," *New England Quarterly*, XLIX (June, 1976), 214–24; Howard, "The Case of the Left-Out Letter," in *Mysteries and Manuscripts* (Albuquerque: Leon Howard, 1976), pp. 17–26; Kendra F. Gaines, "A Consideration of an Additional Source for Melville's *Moby-Dick*," *Melville Society Extracts*, No. 29 (January, 1977), 6–12; Robert Milder, "The Composition of *Moby-Dick*: A Review and a Prospect," *ESQ*, XXIII (Fourth Quarter, 1977), 203–16; Harrison Hayford, "Unnecessary Duplicates: A Key to the Writing of *Moby-Dick*," in *New Perspectives on Melville*, ed. Faith Pullin (Edinburgh: Edinburgh University Press, 1978), pp. 128–61; James Barbour and Harrison Hayford, "The Composition of *Moby-Dick*," *Melville Society Extracts*, No. 43 (September, 1980), 2–4; Tom Quirk, "More on the Composition of *Moby-Dick*: Leon Howard Shows Us Ahab's Leg," *Melville Society Extracts*, No. 46 (May, 1981), 6–7; and Leon Howard, *The Unfolding of MOBY-DICK*, ed. James Barbour and Thomas Quirk (Glassboro: The Melville Society, 1987).

For Section VI, many of the details regarding the American publication and sales of *Moby-Dick* are derived from Melville's copies of the Harper contract and statements of account, now in the Melville Collection of the Houghton Library of Harvard University; many details from these records are available in G. Thomas Tanselle, "The Sales of Melville's Books," *Harvard Library Bulletin*, XVII (April, 1969), 195–215, and in Harrison Hayford, "Contract: *Moby-Dick*, by Herman Melville," *Proof*, I (1971), 1–7. Information regarding British publication comes from the Richard Bentley papers at the British

Library and Bentley's *A List of the Principal Publications Issued from New Burlington Street during the Year 1851* (London: Bentley, 1902); see also J. H. Birss, " 'A Mere Sale to Effect' with Letters of Herman Melville," *New Colophon,* I (July, 1948), 239–55; Bernard R. Jerman, " 'With Real Admiration': More Correspondence between Melville and Bentley," *American Literature,* XXV (November, 1953), 307–13; Royal A. Gettmann, *A Victorian Publisher* (Cambridge: Cambridge University Press, 1960); and the Hayford article just cited.

All reviews of *The Whale* and *Moby-Dick* known in 1970 are reprinted in *MOBY-DICK as Doubloon,* ed. Hershel Parker and Harrison Hayford (New York: Norton, 1970). Steven Mailloux and Hershel Parker, *Checklist of Melville Reviews* (Los Angeles: The Melville Society, 1975) needs to be updated but is still useful, pending the publication of the forthcoming G. K. Hall collection, *Critical Essays on Herman Melville's MOBY-DICK,* edited by Brian Higgins and Hershel Parker, which is to include all the reviews known at the time of its publication.

Given the abundance of critical works on *Moby-Dick* the following list focuses only on works beyond those listed above that are quoted in the NOTE without full bibliographical information, that have added new scholarly knowledge, or that are auxiliary to topics discussed: Jonathan Arac, *Commissioned Spirits* (New Brunswick: Rutgers University Press, 1979); Patricia Barber, "Two New Melville Letters," *American Literature,* XLIX (November, 1977), 418–21; G. J. Barker-Benfield, *The Horrors of the Half-Known Life: Male Attitudes Toward Women and Sexuality in Nineteenth-Century America* (New York: Harper & Row, 1976); Walter E. Bezanson, ed., *Clarel* (New York: Hendricks House, 1960); Bezanson, "*Moby-Dick*: Work of Art," in *MOBY-DICK: Centennial Essays,* ed. Tyrus Hillway and Luther S. Mansfield (Dallas: Southern Methodist University Press, 1953), pp. 31–58; Bezanson, "*Moby-Dick*: Document, Drama, and Dream," in Bryant, *Companion,* pp. 169–210; Walter Blair and Harrison Hayford, eds., *Omoo* (New York: Hendricks House, 1969); Merrell R. Davis, *Melville's MARDI: A Chartless Voyage* (New Haven: Yale University Press, 1952); Douglas C. Ewing, "The Three-Volume Novel," *Papers of the Bibliographical Society of America,* LXI (Third Quarter, 1967), 201–7; John Freeman, *Herman Melville* (London: Macmillan, 1926); Nathaniel Hawthorne, *The Letters, 1843–1853,* ed. Thomas Woodson, L. Neal Smith, and Norman Holmes

Pearson (Columbus: Ohio State University Press, 1985); Harrison Hayford, "Melville and Hawthorne: A Biographical and Critical Study" (Ph.D. dissertation, Yale University, 1945); Hayford, "Loomings," in *Artful Thunder: Versions of the Romantic Tradition in American Literature in Honor of Howard P. Vincent*, ed. Robert J. DeMott and Sanford E. Marovitz (Kent: Kent State University Press, 1975), pp. 119–37; Hugh W. Hetherington, *Melville's Reviewers* (Chapel Hill: University of North Carolina Press, 1961); Brian Higgins and Hershel Parker, "Reading *Pierre*," in Bryant, *Companion*, pp. 211–39; Leon Howard, "A Predecessor of *Moby-Dick*," *Modern Language Notes*, XLIX (May, 1934), 310–11; Howard, *Herman Melville: A Biography* (Berkeley: University of California Press, 1951); Jonathan Katz, *Gay American History* (New York: Thomas Y. Crowell, 1976); Katz, *Gay/Lesbian Almanac* (New York: Harper & Row, 1983); Charles E. Lauterbach and Edward S. Lauterbach, "The Nineteenth Century Three-Volume Novel," *Papers of the Bibliographical Society of America*, LI (Fourth Quarter, 1957), 263–302; Sanford E. Marovitz, "More Chartless Voyaging: Melville and Adler at Sea," *Studies in the American Renaissance*, 1986, 373–84; F. O. Matthiessen, *American Renaissance: Art and Expression in the Age of Emerson and Whitman* (New York: Oxford University Press, 1941); Perry Miller, *The Raven and the Whale: The War of Words and Wits in the Era of Poe and Melville* (New York: Harcourt, Brace, 1956); Sidney P. Moss, *Poe's Major Crisis: His Libel Suit and New York's Literary World* (Durham: Duke University Press, 1970); Lewis Mumford, *Herman Melville* (New York: Harcourt, Brace, 1929); Henry A. Murray, "In Nomine Diaboli," *New England Quarterly*, XXIV (December, 1951), 435–52; Murray, "Introduction," *Pierre* (New York: Hendricks House, 1949), xiii–ciii; Hershel Parker, "The Character of Vine in Melville's *Clarel*," *Essays in Arts and Sciences*, XV (June, 1986), 91–113; Parker, "Contract: *Pierre*, by Herman Melville," *Proof*, V (1977), 27–45; Parker, *Flawed Texts and Verbal Icons* (Evanston: Northwestern University Press, 1984); Albert Rothenberg, *The Emerging Goddess: The Creative Process in Art, Science, and Other Fields* (Chicago: University of Chicago Press, 1979); Henry S. Salt, *Toward the Making of Thoreau's Modern Reputation: Selected Correspondence of S. A. Jones, A. W. Hosmer, H. S. Salt, H. G. O. Blake, and D. Ricketson*, ed. Fritz Oehlschlaeger and George Hendrick (Urbana: University of Illinois Press, 1979); Merton M. Sealts, Jr., *The Early Lives of Melville*

(Madison: University of Wisconsin Press, 1974); Sealts, *Pursuing Melville, 1940–1980* (Madison: University of Wisconsin Press, 1982); G. Thomas Tanselle, "Bibliographical Problems in Melville," *Studies in American Fiction*, II (Spring, 1974), 57–74; Tanselle, *A Checklist of Editions of MOBY-DICK, 1851–1976* (Evanston and Chicago: Northwestern University Press and The Newberry Library, 1976); Tanselle, "Two Melville Association Copies: The Hubbard *Whale* and the Jones *Moby-Dick*," *Book Collector*, XXXI (Summer–Autumn, 1982), 170–86, 309–30; Tanselle, "Melville and the World of Books," in Bryant, *Companion*, pp. 781–835; Willard Thorp, ed., *Herman Melville: Representative Selections* (New York: American Book Co., 1938); Chushichi Tzusuki, *Edward Carpenter: Eighteen-Forty-Four to Nineteen-Twenty-Nine* (Cambridge: Cambridge University Press, 1980); Robert K. Wallace, "The 'Sultry Creator of Captain Ahab': Herman Melville and J. M. W. Turner," *Turner Studies*, V (Winter, 1985), 2–20; Wallace, "Melville's Prints and Engravings at the Berkshire Athenaeum," *Essays in Arts and Sciences*, XV (June, 1986), 59–90; Raymond M. Weaver, *Herman Melville: Mariner and Mystic* (New York: Doran, 1921).

Several works in progress should also be mentioned because in one way or another research on them has gone into this edition: Harrison Hayford, "The Genesis of *Moby-Dick*," *Melville's Prisoners*, "The Shock of Recognition"; Lynn Horth, "*Frankenstein* and *Moby-Dick*," "Melville's Devil Figures," "The 'Devil as a Quaker' Problem"; R. D. Madison, *MOBY-DICK: Genetic Theories Reexamined*; Hershel Parker, *Herman Melville and the Powell Papers* and a full-scale biography of Melville; G. Thomas Tanselle, a full-scale descriptive bibliography of Melville's works.

# Note on the Text

T HIS EDITION of *Moby-Dick* presents an unmodernized critical text, prepared according to the theory of copy-text for-
mulated by Sir Walter Greg.[1] Central to that theory is the
distinction between substantives (the words of a text) and accidentals
(spelling and punctuation). Persons involved in the printing and publishing of texts have often taken it upon themselves to alter accidentals; and authors, when examining or revising printed forms of
their work, have often been relatively unconcerned with accidentals.[2]

1. "The Rationale of Copy-Text," *Studies in Bibliography*, III (1950–51), 19–36,
reprinted in his *Collected Papers*, ed. J. C. Maxwell (Oxford: Clarendon Press, 1966),
pp. 374–91. For an application of this method to the period of Melville, see the
Center for Editions of American Authors, *Statement of Editorial Principles and Procedures* (rev. ed.; New York: Modern Language Association of America, 1972) and the
various discussions recorded in *The Center for Scholarly Editions: An Introductory Statement* (New York: Modern Language Association of America, 1977; also printed in
*PMLA*, XCII [1977], 586–97).

2. Accidentals can affect the meaning (or substance) of a text, and Greg's distinction is not meant to suggest otherwise; rather, its purpose is to emphasize the fact that
those involved in the transmission of texts have habitually behaved differently in
regard to the two categories.

An author's failure to change certain accidentals altered by a copyist, publisher, or compositor does not amount to an endorsement of those accidentals. When the aim of a critical edition, as here, is to establish a text that represents as nearly as possible the author's intentions, it follows that—in the absence of contrary evidence—the formal texture of the work will be most accurately reproduced by adopting as copy-text[3] either the fair-copy manuscript or the first printing based on it. The printed form is chosen if the manuscript does not exist or if the author worked in such a way that corrected proof became in effect the final form of the manuscript. This basic text may then be emended with any later authorial alterations (whether substantive or accidental) and with other obvious corrections. Following this procedure maximizes the probability of keeping authorial readings when evidence is inconclusive as to the source of an alteration in a later authorized edition. The resulting text is *critical* in that it does not correspond exactly to any single authorized edition, but it is closer to the author's intentions—insofar as they are recoverable—than any such edition.

As the preceding HISTORICAL NOTE has shown, the first English edition of *Moby-Dick* (entitled *The Whale),* though it was published earlier than the first American, was set from the American proof sheets. The American edition was the one set directly from the manuscript Melville furnished the printer, and, in the absence of that manuscript, the text of the first impression of the American edition becomes the copy-text for the present edition.[4] Any impressions or editions published during Melville's lifetime are a potential source for emendations in this copy-text, since theoretically it would have been possible for Melville to make corrections or changes in them.[5] The two authorized editions—those of Harper & Brothers in the United States and Richard Bentley in England—have been fully collated in the following pattern:

---

3. "Copy-text" is the text accepted as the basis for an edition.

4. The particular copy of the first American impression that served (in the form of a marked Xerox reproduction of a Copyflo print) as printer's copy is Harvard *AC85M4977.851ma(D) (see footnote 7).

5. Excerpts from *Moby-Dick* (aside from extracts in reviews) appeared in at least five publications during Melville's lifetime; these texts are commented on in more detail below, pp. 772–74.

1. American against English Editions
   a. One complete sight collation[6] of the first American impression (1851) against the first issue of the English impression (1851)
   b. One substantive sight collation of the first American impression (1851) against the first issue of the English impression (1851)
   c. One complete sight collation of the first American impression (1851) against the second issue of the English impression (1853)
   d. One substantive sight collation of the first American impression (1851) against the second issue of the English impression (1853)
2. Impressions of the American Edition
   a. Two machine collations of the first impression of this edition (1851)—with sheet A in the earlier state—against the last impression (1871)
   b. Two machine collations of the first impression of this edition (1851)—with sheet A in the later state—against the last impression (1871)
3. Issues of the English Edition
   a. One machine collation of two copies of the first issue of this edition (1851) against each other
   b. Two machine collations of the first issue of this edition (1851) against the last (1853)[7]

---

6. Collations between two *editions,* which (because they are printed from different settings of type) cannot be performed on the Hinman Collator, are "sight collations." Those between *impressions* of the same edition are "machine collations"—so called because the Hinman Collator, by superimposing page images, enables the human collator's eye to see differences, including minute changes not otherwise easily detected, such as resettings and type damage. A "complete sight collation" is one in which both substantive and accidental variants are recorded; a "substantive sight collation" is one in which only substantive variants are recorded. The terms *edition, impression (printing), issue,* and *state,* as used here, follow the definitions of Fredson Bowers in *Principles of Bibliographical Description* (Princeton: Princeton University Press, 1949), pp. 379–426, supplemented by G. Thomas Tanselle, "The Bibliographical Concepts of *Issue* and *State," Papers of the Bibliographical Society of America,* LXIX (1975), 17–66.

7. The English edition of *Moby-Dick* is in three volumes, the American edition in one. Since each volume of any multivolume work is a separate entity, no biblio-

The text was thus collated for record eleven times.[8] In addition, routine procedures in the process of compiling, checking, and preparing the information for publication have resulted in a larger total number of collations.[9]

Analysis of the variants (in both substantives and accidentals) disclosed by these collations has resulted in the adoption of 185 emendations in the copy-text; and 237 other emendations, not taken from English variants, have been made by the present editors. In order to make clear the evidence and rationale on which these decisions rest, an account of the textual history of the work is given below, followed by a discussion of the treatment in this text of substantives and accidentals, and an explanation of the editorial apparatus through which the evidence is presented.

---

graphical significance attaches to any particular combination of volumes. In these collations, therefore, no attempt was made to treat presently constituted sets as units, although no set was in fact separated for collation. The copies used for these collations are here recorded by identification number (for those books in the Melville Collection of The Newberry Library) or by library name and call number (for books not in the Melville Collection): (1a) M68–2711 vs. Newberry Case Y255M5131; (1b) Gift M66–103a (Harrison Hayford copy) vs. University of Illinois x813M49mo1851a; (1c) photocopy of Harvard *AC85M4977.851ma(D) vs. M75–18801 (M. Douglas Sackman copy); (1d) photocopy of Harvard *AC85M4977.851ma(D) vs. M75–18801; (2a) Gift M66–103a vs. M67–3243 and Illinois State University (Normal) copy; (2b) M66–2717 vs. M67–3243, twice; (3a) Newberry Case Y255M5131 vs. M67–747–4; (3b) University of Chicago PS2384M7.1851a vs. M75–18801; Ohio State University PS2384M6.1851a vs. Illinois State University (Normal) copy.

8. The number of collations that must be performed in order to detect all significant variations in a given text can never be prescribed with certainty, since chance determines, at least to some extent, the particular copies available for collation. Whether or not variant states of a first impression are detected, for example, depends largely upon whether or not at least one copy of an earlier state is present in the collection of copies assembled for collation; regardless of the size of this collection, there is always the chance that an unknown earlier state is missing. To reduce the element of chance somewhat, the present editors have checked many points in every copy of Moby-Dick in the Melville Collection of The Newberry Library and have examined numerous copies in other collections. For making copies of Moby-Dick available, the editors are indebted to M. Douglas Sackman and the late Howard P. Vincent.

9. Proofreading provided the chief opportunity for making these additional collations. Six proofreadings were made of the page proofs against copies of the first American edition, and one was made against a copy of the first English edition.

## THE TEXTS

N O MANUSCRIPT of *Moby-Dick* is known to survive, and the closest text to the missing manuscript is not the one published first. Although the English edition was published on October 18, 1851, about a month earlier than the American, it was set from proofs of the American edition that were mailed to England on September 10. What is technically the second edition of the book (New York: Harper & Brothers, 1851), therefore, is the one set directly from the manuscript supplied by Melville. Copies of this American edition dated 1851 on the title page exist in various states, produced by two kinds of differences. One is the reversal in the position of two pages: in one state, the page of the "Extracts" section (in sheet A) that includes in its heading the phrase "Supplied by a Sub-Sub-Librarian" appears as the second page of extracts (p. [xi] of the Harper edition), while in the other it appears as the first page of extracts (p. [x]). Second is plate damage: in some copies, for example, the word "then" at 99.38[10] (sheet 5) is perfect, while in others the first letter does not print; in some the word "is" at 139.2 (sheet 7) is perfect, while in others the first letter does not print; in some a comma (or a damaged comma) appears after "time" at 294.2 (sheet 14), while in others it is missing; and in some a comma (or a damaged comma) appears after "head" at 297.3 (sheet 14), while in others it is missing.[11] The reversal of the two pages was a deliberate change effected to correct the erroneous earlier arrangement,[12] whereas the

10. Reference numbers with prefixed letters refer to page and line of the American edition (A) or to volume, page, and line of the English edition (E); when these letters do not appear, reference is to the Northwestern-Newberry Edition.

11. Although there are more than a dozen other instances of plate damage or defective inking that varies among copies of the 1851 impression (such as that along the right margin of A101.13–14 or in the middle of A165.32–33), the examination of numerous copies suggests that only these four result in the complete obliteration of a letter or a mark of punctuation and are thus of textual interest.

12. The existence of the erroneously imposed sheet A, in conjunction with a peculiarity in the signature and pagination of the sheet in all copies examined, leads one to speculate that a still earlier state of the text of this sheet may once have existed. In the corrected version of the sheet, p. [x] (the introductory page to the "Extracts" section) is signed "A*" and in addition bears the small numerals "9–10" in the lower right corner; p. [xi] (the first page of actual extracts) bears the small numeral "11" (the later pages of the sheet are numbered with roman numerals). Since the signature "A*" properly belongs on p. [ix] (the recto of the fifth leaf of the gathering), one may surmise that the

loss of the two letters and two commas simply resulted from damage to the plates or defective inking.[13] The reimposition required to alter

"9–10" notation was meant as some sort of indication that the page originally intended to be the ninth was now to be the tenth and that it was not to be imposed in the position where a page with an asterisked signature would normally go. (Why it would not have been simpler, even in a plate, to remove the signature is not clear.) The erroneously imposed version of the sheet can then be explained through a failure on the part of the shopman doing the imposing to interpret the "9–10" properly; seeing the "A*" and assuming the page to be a recto, he placed it where the eleventh page would regularly go (the ninth would be in the other forme), and he placed p. "11" at the opposite corner of the inner forme, where the tenth page should go.

It is not difficult to see why two tries should have been required to get the pages in the correct order after the "9–10" and the "11" had been inserted; the question is why they were needed in the first place and why the signature fell on the wrong page. One can only speculate, and a possibility that suggests itself is that the "Etymology" section (pp. [viii–ix]) may have been inserted after the rest of the pages of this sheet had been set in type or plated (either because it was an afterthought of Melville's or because it was inadvertently omitted during composition in the printing shop). Without the "Etymology" section, the verso (p. [viii]) of the divisional title would be blank (as one might expect it to be), and the introductory page to the "Extracts" section would fall on p. [ix], the correct page for the signature that it carries; then the pages of extracts would end on p. [xxii], leaving an entire blank leaf before the beginning of the text. (This leaf could have been used for a divisional title, with a blank verso, although divisional titles do not occur at corresponding points in the Harper editions of Melville's other books.) Another possible arrangement, which would again allow the "A*" to appear on the recto of the fifth leaf, would place the blank leaf first (before the title leaf), begin the "Extracts" section immediately after the table of contents, and shift the divisional title to the last leaf. If either of these arrangements had been the original one, however, the insertion of two pages of "Etymology"—and the consequent pushing of the entire "Extracts" section forward one page—would have necessitated altering twelve page numbers in the "Extracts" section; and if this alteration could be performed, one wonders why the "A*" could not have been altered as well. Of course, the page numbers could have been altered in type, while the signature was overlooked until after plating—but such speculation is endless. For that matter, the misplaced "A*" may be of no significance whatever; it may have been a mistake from the beginning. Nevertheless, the misplaced signature, the small arabic numerals, and the two known stages of imposition, taken together, seem to be a vestigial record of some earlier arrangement. (Additional discussion of the possibilities involved appears above in the HISTORICAL NOTE, pp. 679–80.)

13. Although some damage to the plates is probably involved in each instance, variations in inking result in the reappearance of these letters and commas in some copies of later printings. Thus the "i" of "is" does appear, but in a damaged condition, in some copies of the 1871 printing; the comma after "time" is visible in some copies of the later printings; and the comma after "head" is quite legible in the later printings.

the position of two pages in the inner forme of sheet A possibly means that two impressions of sheet A are involved; but there is no evidence to suggest that the plate damage or the variations in inking are indicative of separate impressions of other sheets, since a mixture of perfect and defective states can be found in the same copies (and defective states occur with the earlier state of sheet A). While this situation could result from the binding up of mixed sheets from two impressions, the simpler and more likely explanation is that the plate damage or variations in inking occurred during a single press run.[14]

Since these variations exist among copies of the 1851 impression, the copy-text for a critical edition of *Moby-Dick* must be defined in terms of the variations. Because they obviously involve errors resulting simply from the mechanical process of imposing and printing and because the correct text in each instance does appear in some copies, it seems sensible to regard the correct state of the text as the copy-text. (Otherwise one would have to regard as editorial emendations the correct readings that actually are present in some copies.) Therefore the copy-text for the present edition can be defined as the text of a copy of the 1851 impression that has the corrected (and thus later) state of sheet A, as well as the undamaged states of sheets 5, 7, and 14 (which contain the two letters and the two commas that do not always show up).[15] The Harper edition was printed three more times from these plates, in 1855, 1863, and 1871, with no deliberate changes in the text; since all of the more than 170 slight variations resulted from plate damage, none has any textual authority.[16]

14. Facts about the dates, sizes, and backgrounds of the various printings and editions are given in the HISTORICAL NOTE; precise physical descriptions will appear in the full-scale bibliography to be published in conjunction with the Northwestern-Newberry Edition. The present discussion is not concerned with bibliographical details discovered in the process of collation unless they bear on textual questions. Type or plate damage, for example, that may distinguish the states within an impression or the impressions within a given year is not reported here if it does not create a textual variant (as defined at the end of footnote 16) and if the states or impressions involved are not otherwise of textual significance.

15. The particular copy that served as printer's copy (see footnote 4) for this edition did in fact contain these correct states—though, if it had not, bringing it into conformity with the copy-text as here defined would obviously not have constituted emendation (but rather the correction of a defective example of the copy-text).

16. In the 1855 printing, although there were at least sixty instances of damage to the plates in addition to those already mentioned, only seven could conceivably

The English edition *(The Whale)*, unlike the American, was printed only once but was issued at two different times, two years apart. The first issue (3 vols.; London: Richard Bentley, 1851) exists in various states, distinguishable by the relative positions or inking of certain pieces of type in at least twenty places. Since the book was printed from type rather than from plates, the shifting (or failure to print) of individual types does not furnish evidence of an irreversible progression. For example, the absence of certain letters in five words (in "But" at 270.28, "laughed" at 403.13, "rascal" at 440.1, "grow" at 563.20, and "faces" at 571.20) and the failure of letters to print along the left margin of E3.93.14–19 are probably indications of later states, though it is possible that the states in which these types print properly are later. The other variations are usually matters of spacing (as when "monomaniac" at 463.22 appears as "m onomaniac" or "was heading" at 516.21 as "wa sheading") and do not occur at points where they create substantive differences. In 1853 Bentley issued the sheets remaining from the 1851 edition in one-volume form with new title pages (dated 1853); many of the variations present in

---

create a textual ambiguity: the loss of commas after "it" at 3.16, "coolly" at 201.20, and "was" at 445.28, of a semicolon after "hieroglyphical" at 306.25, and of the final letter in "your" at 320.29, as well as two damaged semicolons, one printing like a colon (after "girdle" at 219.2) and the other like a comma (after "water" at 245.33). The 1863 printing, with at least forty additional damaged spots, contained five more examples of this kind: a missing single quotation mark before "Stern" at xxviii.21, missing line-end hyphens in "dark-looking" at 14.1 and "blood-vessels" at 288.3, a missing "a" at 279.32, and a double quotation mark that printed as a single one after "ahead!" at 556.30. The only deliberate alteration made in the 1863 printing was a resetting of the copyright page. Finally, at least seventy instances of damage appeared in the 1871 printing, but only seven came at places where they might affect one's reading of the text: one semicolon (after "noon" at 149.3) disappeared entirely, while two other semicolons (after "gloomy" at 124.35 and "head" at 316.38) printed so that only the top members were visible, the double quotation mark before "I" at 42.1 appeared to be a single one, and the line-end hyphen in "vinegar-cruet" at 82.30, one semicolon (after "herself" at 393.21), and one comma (after "this" at 403.8) were barely visible. In this NOTE, when changes are listed within either the American or the English edition, the many instances of damaged type or plates are not included when it is clear what letter is intended, nor is missing end-punctuation mentioned when the absent mark is a period; and missing hyphens at the ends of lines are not reported when the divided word is not a compound. Missing commas, however, are listed, since they might pass unnoticed. In other words, type or plate wear is noted only when it could pass unnoticed or be mistaken for intentional revision.

copies with 1851 title pages have been discovered in the same states in copies with the 1853 title pages. None of these differences between copies of the English edition gives any evidence of editorial intervention during the course of printing.

The text of the English edition differs substantively from the American edition at 711 points (there are literally thousands of other differences in spelling and punctuation). Four dozen or so of these English variants are obviously the result of careless typesetting and proofreading,[17] but nearly three dozen are corrections of obvious substantive errors in the American edition.[18] Most of the variant readings, however, are neither obvious errors nor corrections of obvious errors. Of these, an important category consists of omissions and additions of whole passages. The English text lacks 38 passages of one complete sentence or more, amounting to some 2,000 words (as well as various other phrases totaling more than 250 words). The largest of these missing passages are the entire Chapter 25 (pp. 113–14) and the epilogue (p. 573), along with three omissions of more than 100 words each (11.3–15, 85.9–20, 87.16–88.19).[19] Additions to

17. Among such errors in the English edition are "others'" for "other's" (6.22), "he" for "we" (99.3), "afternoon" for "forenoon" (123.18), "afforded" for "afford" (140.4), "tune" for "turn" (150.31), "unsound" for "unsounded" (168.17), "leek" for "leak" (254.33), "an" for "and" (327.9), "fishing" for "flashing" (384.18), "blubber-book" for "blubber-hook" (437.24), and "moon" for "morn" (543.1); several of the errors involve the number of nouns (as "whale" for "whales" at 220.33) or duplication of words ("man man" at 299.37, "to to" at 383.20, "a a" at 443.21, and "not not" at 560.20).

18. For example, "mid most" is corrected to "midmost" (7.36; cf. 482.18), "brows" to "bows" (60.18), "Peleg" to "Bildad" (74.16), "he" to "I" (83.39), "XVII" to "XVIII" (87.1), "up up" to "up" (256.14), "let's" to "lets" (326.38), "plaintiffs" to "defendants" (397.20), "too" to "to" (506.25), and "intenting" to "intently" (522.23). One large category of these corrections, amounting to about a quarter of the whole, involves the number of nouns and verbs (153.9, 212.2, 280.22, 313.5, 431.3, 457.28, 545.22, 551.29, 560.31)—often reflecting the difficulty of a copyist or the American compositors in reading Melville's final *s*.

19. It may be convenient for reference to have a listing of the remaining 33 passages referred to here; they are those recorded in the LIST OF SUBSTANTIVE VARIANTS at 6.14–16, 6.26–29, 7.5–8, 10.32–38, 16.31–33, 32.31, 52.7–10, 105.31–32, 117.22–24, 174.11–12, 178.13, 190.43–45, 207.19–20, 259.5–6, 297.1, 297.6–7, 297.10–13, 300.4–8, 302.22–24, 312.3–4, 344.5–7, 344.26, 356.27, 379.7–9, 388.28, 388.39–40, 401.5–7, 422.30–32, 435.16–18, 451.23–26, 539.32–38, 542.16–20, and 543.3–8. Of the omissions of less than a sentence, the longest are those at 53.4–6, 167.15–16, 195.20–22, 392.30–32, and 472.26–28.

the English text, on the other hand, consist of one footnote of 139 words (384.28–40), clearly written by Melville, and approximately five dozen single words (plus half a dozen short phrases). Of the remaining variants—that is, about three-fourths of the total number—some are routine compositorial substitutions and casual anglicizations, but many must be the work either of Melville himself or of a careful house stylist. Distinguishing between these categories is of course one of the central tasks an editor faces.[20]

No other edition of *Moby-Dick* as a complete book was published during Melville's lifetime, but several excerpts from it appeared. Aside from the extracts that were included in reviews,[21] five such appearances are known. The first was the publication of "The Town-Ho's Story" (chap. 54) in *Harper's New Monthly Magazine* for Octo-

20. Of these variants, nearly a hundred involve the forms of nouns and verbs (number and tense)—such differences as "has" for "have" (74.1, 78.27), "have" for "has" (140.17), "honour" for "honors" (148.5), "men" for "man" (164.13), "ate" for "eat" (197.1), "ships'" for "ship's" (357.6), "perceive" for "perceived" (373.13), or "had not" for "did not have" (468.19). About twice that number have to do with the choice of individual words: for example, "tumbling" for "clattering" (45.27), "consent" for "prescription" (120.1), "security" for "salvation" (254.27), "nameless" for "unnamable" (497.20), "perceive" for "discover" (549.18), and "instantaneously" for "simultaneously" (569.37). Transposed words account for about a dozen variants (as "previous night" for "night previous" at 50.18 or "swims swiftly" for "swiftly swims" at 216.8), and most of the remaining two hundred are revised expressions requiring the alteration of several words (such as those at 26.7, 37.26, 47.16, 124.29–30, 147.5, 263.31, 392.17–18, and 435.13, for example) or the elimination of a word or two (such as those at 40.12, 217.10, and 368.39). Analysis of the authority of certain classes of readings is made below, pp. 784–91, and further comment on individual readings will be found in the DISCUSSIONS OF ADOPTED READINGS.

21. These extracts were normally taken from the published book under review, without consulting the author, and are of no textual significance, but the two extracts from *Moby-Dick* that appeared in the *Literary World* on November 15, 1851 (IX, 382–83), are worth somewhat closer examination, since Melville was a friend of the editor, Evert A. Duyckinck, and could conceivably have made revisions in the copy furnished. The two extracts consist of three pages from Chapter 81 (355.28–358.14) and three from Chapter 91 (403.31–406.39). A complete collation of the *Literary World* text of these passages with the Harper edition indicates that Melville did not in fact make any alterations, since the only differences—aside from the erroneous substitution of "roses" for "posies" at 404.33 and the adjustment of quotation marks necessitated by the fact that each passage was regarded as quoted—are a dozen or so changes in accidentals (particularly in hyphens and commas), which are of the kind that could easily have resulted from compositorial carelessness. (Copies collated: M67–1301–1 *vs.* M67–722–108.)

ber, 1851 (III, 658–65). Since this number of *Harper's* was issued before the publication of the book and since Harper & Brothers were the publishers of the book, the magazine text might theoretically incorporate authorial readings not found elsewhere. As the HISTORICAL NOTE has shown, proof sheets of the book were ready in August, and it seems unlikely that the magazine compositors would have been furnished a manuscript when proof sheets were available—but those proof sheets could have been annotated by Melville. As it turns out, a collation of the book and magazine texts does not provide unmistakable evidence of authorial revision, but it does suggest that the author may have given his attention to certain individual spots. The inconsistent use of single and double quotation marks found in the book is generally followed; the few stray instances in which the pointing is improved in this respect seem to be the result of inadvertent failure to follow copy rather than any conscious attempt at correction. Aside from these changes and the omission of the subtitle and the footnote, there are some 125 differences, mostly in punctuation and spelling, of the kind that an editor[22] or a compositor might be expected to make (and that—like the change from "harpooneer" to "harpooner" at 253.15, 256.22, and 256.33—Melville would certainly not have made). The only variants in the magazine that produce superior readings are the substitution of "three" for "these" at 253.19 and the shift in the position of a quotation mark at 256.5. Although a careful editor could conceivably have made these changes, it seems more likely that Melville was responsible for them; but there is no evidence to suggest that any of the other variants result from his attention to this chapter.[23]

The other four appearances of excerpts, in various anthologies,

22. Someone on the editorial staff of the magazine probably would have gone over all extracts, even when taken from Harper books, since certain allusions to other parts of a book might have to be eliminated, regardless of whether styling was in need of change; in this case the editors were dealing with a text that had been set and plated before it became a Harper book.

23. Further examples of the kinds of substantive differences found in the magazine are such alterations for the sake of supposed correctness as "awakened" for "wakened" (243.1) and "was" for "were" (255.30) and such outright errors as "separated" for "separating" (253.24) and "arm" for "arms" (258.8). (Copies collated: M68–2295 *vs.* Newberry A5.391. No differences have been noted between one copy of the magazine and another, in a collation of Northwestern Lo51H295 *vs.* University of Chicago AP2H3, copy 2.)

have less claim to consideration. Nine years after *Moby-Dick* was published, Captain E. C. Williams included parts of "The Line" and "The Symphony" (chaps. 60 and 132), along with fifteen of the "Extracts," in *Life in the South Seas* (New York: Polhemus & De Vries, 1860). Then, eleven years later, a passage from "The First Lowering" (chap. 48) appeared in *Choice Specimens of American Literature,* edited by Benjamin N. Martin (New York: Sheldon, 1871); a longer passage from the same chapter appeared in an 1874 edition. In 1887, Charles Morris's *Half-Hours with the Best American Authors* (Philadelphia: Lippincott, 1887) contained "The Death of the Whale" (most of chap. 61). And in 1889 most of "Stubb kills a Whale" (chap. 61) was again offered, under the title "Whale Fishing in the Indian Ocean," in *Harper's Fifth Reader,* edited by James Baldwin. Aside from omissions within the selections (designed to make the text more appropriate for a particular occasion or audience), practically all the variants in these texts are in spelling, capitalization, or punctuation; none of the changes introduced can be attributed to Melville, and none of these editions is of textual importance.[24]

24. The passages in Williams (on pp. 10–11, 21–22) correspond to all of Chapter 60 except 278.7–21, 279.15–24, and 281.11–16 (with lesser omissions at 279.32, 279.38–39, 280.27–30, 280.39–281.3), and to the middle part of Chapter 132 (543.27–545.6, omitting 544.17–26); of roughly one hundred variants, nearly all (except for two new paragraph divisions) involve punctuation or capitalization, when they are not simple typographical errors. (Copies collated: M67–2129 *vs.* Newberry Case R739.976.) The brief passage in the first edition of Martin (on pp. 163–64) corresponds to one paragraph of Chapter 48 (223.27–224.4); in 1874 the enlarged edition of Martin included (on pp. 371–72) a passage about three times as long, beginning with the same paragraph (223.27–225.5, omitting 224.5–13 and 224.19–22). Except for the spelling of "harpooneers" as "harpooners", the dozen variants in this passage are all in punctuation (especially the omission of dashes); the first paragraph, containing about half the variants, repeats the text from Martin's first edition, except that it includes the "his" (223.39) that had been omitted earlier. (Copies collated: M66–2717 *vs.* Harvard AL398.71 and M67–1599–42.) Morris's excerpt amounts to all of Chapter 61 except the first two sentences (282.3–6) and the footnotes; its three dozen variants are almost entirely in punctuation, half of them added commas. (Copies collated: Newberry Case Y255M5132 *vs.* M67–3213–9 [1896 printing].) The selection in *Harper's Fifth Reader* (on pp. 99–104) corresponds to all of Chapter 61 except the opening and closing lines (282.3–6, 286.20–21), the footnotes, and a few short passages evidently considered inappropriate for schoolchildren (such as Stubb's chant referring to "grinning devils" at 284.6–9, or the description of the whale "spasmodically dilating and contracting his spout-hole" at 286.13–14); aside from these and a few other brief omissions, the five dozen variants are mostly in punctua-

The first edition to appear after Melville's death was published in New York in 1892 by the United States Book Company. Although no editor's name appeared on the volume, it was part of a series of new editions of Melville supervised by Arthur Stedman. In his introduction to *Typee*, Stedman pointed out that he had some written instructions about that book from Melville himself; and a document in Mrs. Melville's hand, recording directives such as those Stedman was presumably referring to, is presently among Stedman's papers in the Columbia University Library.[25] Although there is no hint of any such instructions in the case of *Moby-Dick*, the fact that Stedman had direct contact with the Melville family makes his edition worth examining in more detail than a posthumous edition would normally require. However, although collation of the Stedman text against the first American impression reveals more than two hundred variants in substantives alone, there is nothing about any of these alterations to suggest that Stedman was following instructions from Melville.[26]

---

tion. (Copies collated: M66–2717 *vs.* M69–316–11.) The wide use of the Harper readers (later distributed by the American Book Company) meant that the plates of this *Fifth Reader* eventually became so damaged that a new edition was required, and in the resetting several further compositorial errors crept into the Melville selection. (The later edition cannot easily be recognized by the title page, but the reading "of the" instead of "off the" at 99.19 in the *Reader* can be used to identify the later edition. Copies collated: M69–316–11 *vs.* M67–3213–8.)

25. For further discussion of this document, see the NOTE ON THE TEXT in the Northwestern-Newberry edition of *Typee*, p. 312.

26. Although Stedman was obviously using the American edition as his copytext, he placed the "Etymology" and "Extracts" sections at the end, as the English edition did. His edition corrects a number of the obvious errors in the American edition (such as "bows" for "brows" at 60.18, "XVIII" for "XVII" at 87.1, and "stranger's" for "strangers'" at 313.5, as well as some not caught in the English edition, such as "fair" for "far" at 222.25), but it makes a number of other errors (such as "who" for "whom" at 18.32, "world" for "word" at 39.30, "posing" for "poising" at 88.31, "stop" for "top" at 221.9, "scourgin'" for "scrougin'" at 295.25, and "tears" for "tiers" at 567.34). There are no extensive omissions, as there were in Stedman's *White-Jacket*, but there are many changes clearly intended to "correct" the grammar (such as "everything" for "everythings" at 96.9, "in" for "and" at 96.35, the omission of "a" at 135.3, "farther and farther" for "further and further" at 308.10, and "killingly" for "killing" at 432.29). Of all the new readings introduced in Stedman's edition, only a few deserve serious consideration (such as "places" for "placed" at 59.23 and "or" for "of" in "of cautiousness" at 283.36), and there is no reason to suppose that they stem from Melville's instructions rather than from the

The chief significance of Stedman's United States Book Company edition is that its plates have been used by a long succession of publishers, and a great many people have read *Moby-Dick* in this edition. Impressions bearing the imprints of G. P. Putnam's Sons, Tait, Sons & Co., American Publishers Corp., Dana Estes & Co., L. C. Page, the St. Botolph Society, Jonathan Cape, and D. D. Nickerson all use these plates. Since this edition of 1892, *Moby-Dick* has been set in type at least sixty times[27] (not counting abridgments and adaptations, of which there have been over sixty), and many of these editions have been published by more than one firm. For example, the Doubleday, Doran edition of 1928 reappeared under the Kennerley imprint the next year; the Random House edition of 1930 was published in England by Cassell and later in the United States by Garden City Publishing Co. and as a Modern Library Giant; and the "Fairmount Classics" edition of George W. Jacobs (1924) and Macrae Smith (1925) later appeared under the imprints of Grosset & Dunlap and Library Publications and in the Harper's Modern Classics series. Only six of these presently known editions are based on the Bentley edition (Everyman, 1907; Dodd, Mead, 1922; Sears, 1928; Consolidated Book Publishers [Spencer Press], 1937; Macmillan, 1962, 1963), and even they include the epilogue from the Harper edition (although the Everyman and the Dodd, Mead did not include it in their early impressions). Only two new editions appeared between 1892 and 1920 (Scribner, 1899; Everyman, 1907), but eleven came out in the 1920's and eleven more by the time of the centennial in 1951;

---

careful reading that produced most of Stedman's other changes. (Copies collated: photocopy of Harvard *AC85M4977.851ma(D) *vs.* M66–2757–135.)

27. The number cannot be stated with assurance, since further editions—which have not been discovered in an extensive search of catalogues, libraries, and bookstores—occasionally still turn up. Details of all located editions will be included in the forthcoming descriptive bibliography. A provisional list to 1976 is provided by G. Thomas Tanselle's *A Checklist of Editions of MOBY-DICK, 1851–1976* (Evanston and Chicago: Northwestern University Press and The Newberry Library, 1976). The Melville Collection of The Newberry Library, assembled in connection with the preparation of the Northwestern-Newberry Edition, contains these later editions. Charles Roberts Anderson, in *Melville in the South Seas* (New York: Columbia University Press, 1939), states that 72 "editions" of *Moby-Dick* had been published by 1938 (p. 439); but he is not using "edition" in the sense employed here and in the Tanselle checklist, as a technical bibliographical term that encompasses all the impressions from a given setting of type.

the rest of the 1950's saw the production of ten new editions, the 1960's a dozen, and the 1970's and 1980's together at least another ten. Most of these editions give no attention whatever to textual matters, and only a few require any comment here. The Constable edition of *Moby-Dick* (1922)—in the collected *Works*—is the most significant of the editions that appeared during the Melville "revival" of the 1920's because it is part of the only complete set of Melville's work that has been available to scholars in the past and is therefore often cited as standard.[28] Its text generally follows the Harper edition but departs from it occasionally in substantive readings (introducing such errors as "broad" for "bread" in "bread-faced" at 152.23 and "revelry" for "revery" at 214.8) and frequently in punctuation and spelling (especially through the substitution of British forms and changes in capitalization and hyphenation), and it offers no explanation of its editorial policy.[29]

Of the editions published since that time, eight deserve notice for providing some discussion of their editorial procedure. Four of them include a general statement of policy, without furnishing a listing of emendations. In 1947 Willard Thorp, editing the book for Oxford University Press (New York), pointed out (p. xvii) that his text followed the Harper edition, except that typographical errors and "undeniable misspellings" were "silently corrected." Thorp was careful, however, not to modernize words "which seem to be misspelled" but are "actually older forms," and he did not try to regularize or modernize punctuation and capitalization, recognizing that Melville "punctuated rhetorically as well as logically, and some of his meaning would be lost if his freedom in this respect were taken from him."

28. Another edition of the 1920's, published by Albert & Charles Boni in 1925, is of more than routine interest because it was part of what was announced as an "Authorized Uniform Edition" (also called the "Pequod Edition") and because it was edited and contained an introduction by Raymond Weaver. Its text was not reliable, however; William S. Ament, who judged in 1932 that it was "probably as good a reprint as there is," mentioned some examples of its typographical errors in his "Bowdler and the Whale: Some Notes on the First English and American Editions of *Moby-Dick*," *American Literature*, IV (November, 1932), 39–46.

29. This generalization is based on a partial collation of a copy of the 1851 American edition (Newberry Case Y255M5132) with a copy of the Constable *Moby-Dick* in the Russell & Russell reprinting (New York, 1963; M67–722–123). For some background relating to the Constable texts, see Philip Durham, "Prelude to the Constable Edition of Melville," *Huntington Library Quarterly*, XXI (1957–58), 285–89.

The following year Newton Arvin, in his Rinehart edition, also stated (p. x) that his text followed that of the first American edition and that "some obvious typographical errors" were "silently corrected"; but he took more freedom than Thorp in attempting to remove inconsistencies, especially in modernizing inconsistent spellings ("it has seemed unnecessarily literal to preserve a too conspicuous archaic spelling to which Melville himself did not adhere"), and one student of his text has pointed out that he "introduces as many as a dozen emendations in a single chapter."[30] In 1956 Alfred Kazin provided "A Note on the Text" (p. xv) in Houghton Mifflin's Riverside edition, identifying the original Harper edition as the one followed "very closely indeed" and calling attention to his correction of a few substantive mistakes as well as "trifling printer's errors," explaining at the same time that he retained "Melville's nineteenth-century or idiosyncratically personal usages" in cases that "would not cause total confusion to a contemporary reader." In fact, however, his text was based on the Hendricks House edition (discussed below) and contained inadvertent departures from it. Charles Feidelson, Jr., in his 1964 Bobbs-Merrill edition, also noted (p. viii) his adherence to the Harper edition and his silent correction of "minor typographical errors" but not of "Melville's extremely erratic spelling and punctuation"; in cases of "obvious slips of the pen," the text was corrected and the changes recorded in footnotes, while possible emendations for other "dubious readings" were only suggested in footnotes, without alteration to the text. Like Kazin, Feidelson used the Hendricks House edition as printer's copy.[31]

Although these four editions show concern for textual matters, they do not provide a record of adopted changes that would enable readers to evaluate these textual decisions for themselves; three other editions, however, do furnish such information. Luther S. Mansfield and Howard P. Vincent edited the book for Hendricks House in 1952 as one of the volumes in a proposed complete edition of Melville's works. Their "Textual Notes" (pp. 833–38) contained four parts: (1) a listing of twenty emendations made in the text of the Harper edi-

30. William H. Hutchinson, in a footnote to his discussion of the Hendricks House edition—"A Definitive Edition of *Moby-Dick*," *American Literature*, XXV (January, 1954), 475.

31. See Hershel Parker, "Practical Editions: Herman Melville's *Moby-Dick*," *Proof*, III (1973), 371–78.

tion; (2) a discussion of certain other troublesome readings that an editor might be tempted to alter (though such temptation "must be strenuously resisted"); (3) a record of "the verbal changes made in the first English edition"; and (4) a discussion of the wording of the table of contents in the American edition. Although the list of substantive variants this edition presents is not complete and although it contains more emendations than are recorded and a considerable number of typographical errors,[32] it provided the first extensive published listing of the English variants, and it served for fifteen years as the most reliable and fully documented text available.[33] In 1967 Harrison Hayford and Hershel Parker published their Norton Critical Edition of *Moby-Dick,* which contained still more extensive textual discussion and lists. The section called "The Text: History, Variants, and Emendations" (pp. 471–98) presented a concise but detailed discussion of the composition and publication of the book, followed by a list of "Substantive Variants between *Moby-Dick* and *The Whale*" and lists of substantive emendations (99 from the English edition and 36 others), substantive readings considered but rejected, and emendations of accidentals (110 from the English edition and 100 others, aside from corrections of 14 typographical errors and one unitemized group of quotation marks). Besides reporting more textual data than had previously been available, this edition was the first to recognize that some of the variants in the English edition (in addition to the added footnote on the word "gally") were authorial and to incorporate them into the American text. The information in this edition was appropriated five years later by Harold Beaver in his edition for the Penguin English Library; though it did not include a list of substantive differences between the American and English editions, its other lists copied the pattern employed in the Norton edition.

The text of the Northwestern-Newberry edition, based on the rationale set forth in the pages to follow, differs at some 200 points from the present Norton text, as a result of newly discovered information, particularly concerning the texts from which Melville de-

32. Hutchinson (pp. 472–78) discusses and records what he classifies as 20 additional emendations and 108 typographical errors; further departures from the American edition have since been located.

33. The explanatory notes in this edition, treating sources and allusions, are obviously still of great usefulness; the concern here is solely with the text of the edition and the textual apparatus.

rived his "Extracts" and other quotations. (Future Norton printings will incorporate these differences.) Earlier versions of the Northwestern-Newberry text have appeared in two editions: the Arion Press edition (reprinted, with a few alterations, by the University of California Press), which had as its aim the printing of the Northwestern-Newberry text as it stood in 1978 but in fact did not offer a reliable setting of that text; and the Library of America edition, which did accurately provide the Northwestern-Newberry text as it stood in 1983 and contained a brief discussion by G. Thomas Tanselle of textual principles and selected textual cruxes. Since 1983 the present editors have made 27 changes in the text, and these alterations are to be incorporated in future Library of America printings.

## TREATMENT OF SUBSTANTIVES

T HE TEXTUAL HISTORY of *Moby-Dick* is somewhat different from that of Melville's previous books. As in the case of all the earlier books except *Typee,* proof sheets of the American edition became printer's copy for the English edition; but the circumstances surrounding Melville's preparation of the proofs of *Moby-Dick* did not repeat those for any of the other books. Since it was considered necessary, as a way of attempting to secure an English copyright, for the English publication of an American book to precede the American publication, the proofs of *Omoo, Mardi,* and *Redburn* had been shipped to England as quickly as possible; Melville had not been able to spend much time going over them, and as a result there are not a great many differences in wording between the American and English texts. The proofs of *White-Jacket,* in contrast, were taken abroad by Melville himself, and he had time, both on shipboard and after he arrived in London, to make revisions; when he returned to the United States, he had the opportunity, though there is no proof that he took advantage of it, to duplicate those revisions or make new ones in the American edition. The considerable differences between the published texts, though they are undoubtedly due in part to a house reader for Bentley, must also be in some part the result of Melville's revision; and it is theoretically possible that the English readings are later in some instances and the American in others. The publishing history of *Moby-Dick* is closer to that of *White-Jacket* than to the earlier books, since Melville again had access to the proofs for several weeks before they went to Bentley; but the details of the situation are significantly different.

The central difference is that Melville had the text of *Moby-Dick* set in type and plated before an agreement had been reached with a publisher. As the HISTORICAL NOTE has shown, during the spring and summer of 1851 the choice of the Harpers as publishers was not certain, and a contract with them was not signed until September 12. Yet Melville referred in letters of June 29 and July 20 to the fact that his work was "passing thro' the press," and the Harper contract spoke of "stereotype plates now in the possession of R. Craighead." In contrast to the pattern followed with all of Melville's other books, in which the original publisher contracted to publish a "manuscript" and made the arrangements for setting and plating, Melville in this instance had the book set and plated himself. By this means he had proof sheets to send to England so that publication there would not be delayed, regardless of the time it took to secure an American publisher; and when an agreement for American publication was reached, the plates would be ready for printing at the earliest opportunity.

This arrangement has three principal implications for the study of the text. First, since the plating was completed before American publication was arranged, there was not the same urgency about getting proof sheets to England that there would have been if American publication were already scheduled. Melville did in fact keep the final proofs at hand for over a month: he finished the proofreading for the plating near the end of July but did not dispatch a set of sheets to Bentley until September 10. Second, there is particular reason to believe that he would have wanted to make changes in that set of sheets; since he had been completing the writing of the book at the same time that he was proofreading earlier parts, he probably did not give full attention to the proofreading, and the fact that some of the earlier parts in all likelihood were plated before his work was finished placed further restrictions on his freedom in writing and revising. Third, he knew that the book had to be reset in England, and he could feel free to make more extensive alterations than were practical at this late stage in the American edition—for the text of the American edition was probably already completely plated or, if not, at least in type, and either way could not be altered without additional expense. As a result, variant readings in the English text almost certainly are later readings: those made by someone at Bentley's are obviously later, but all those resulting from a change by Melville are probably later as well, since there is no evidence to support the unlikely possibility that Melville incurred the expense of ordering further changes in the American edition. The Harper records for *White-Jacket* do show a charge for alterations; but for *Moby-Dick* there is no record of such a charge after the Harpers took over the plates, and before that time, without a publisher established, Melville would probably have been even more reluctant to add to his expenses.

It is possible, of course, that some of the material outside the main body of the text may have been supplied to the American edition at a late stage, and in such cases the English edition may in fact preserve an earlier version. It is known, for example, from his brother's letter to Bentley (see the HISTORICAL NOTE, p. 671), that Melville altered the title from *The Whale* and supplied a dedication after the proofs had already been sent to England; since the dedication is essentially the same in the two editions, this information must have reached Bentley in time, yet the English title page retains the earlier title. Similarly, the "Epilogue," not present in the English edition, could have been added to the American without disturbing previously set pages, as could the "Etymology" and "Extracts" sections, which appear at the end, rather than the beginning, of the English edition. Indeed, the epigraph from Milton on the three English title pages may represent Melville's earlier intention, before he decided to supply a whole section of epigraphs; it could have been removed from the American at the time when the Harpers set up a "trial" title page, though a more reasonable supposition is that no American title page existed before the Harpers took over, since the name of the publisher would not have been known earlier. Even the American table of contents, which differs from the English and from the actual chapter titles and which shows some signs of being Melville's, may have been given to the compositor late—especially since the English table of contents, repeating the chapter titles accurately, could easily have been constructed in routine fashion at Bentley's office, if no copy had been supplied.[34] It is possible, therefore, that the preliminaries (or

34. Of course it is possible that the document furnished to the American composi-tor may still have contained earlier versions of chapter titles; the fact that it may have been set in type late does not necessarily mean that its readings are late. A more detailed discussion of the possible revisions involved in the preliminaries is given in the HISTORICAL NOTE, pp. 672–80.

some of them)—and theoretically the epilogue as well—may be late additions to the American version (though it does not seem likely that the "Etymology" and "Extracts" could have been very late, since Bentley was able to include them, or that the epilogue, anticipated in the body of the text, could be an afterthought). Even if the "Etymology" and "Extracts" were present in the proofs all along, there is no evidence to suggest that Melville wished to place them at the end; and it is inconceivable that he would have ordered the deletion of the epilogue from the proofs. Whether the American edition in these respects represents a later or an earlier stage than the English, therefore, the American title page, table of contents, arrangement of preliminaries, and inclusion of the epilogue would seem to reflect Melville's final intention.

An editor must choose the American edition as the copy-text, since it was set directly from Melville's manuscript. After adopting the obvious corrections from the English substantive variants and rejecting the English treatment of the preliminaries and omission of the epilogue, the editor faces two problems. The first is to determine which of the remaining English variants are authorial and should therefore be adopted as Melville's revisions. The second is to find and correct any readings that are erroneous in both editions—readings, that is, where the English text follows the American in printing words that cannot be the ones Melville intended.

About three dozen of the English substantive variants are corrections obviously called for by the context (see p. 771, footnote 18). Whether compositors' errors or slips of the author's pen, the American readings can hardly have been intended by Melville, and whether the correction was made by Melville or by someone at Bentley's is immaterial. (Similarly, an even larger number of equally obvious errors in the English edition can automatically be rejected.) As for the preliminaries and the epilogue, the discussion in the HISTORICAL NOTE (summarized above) has shown that the chances of reproducing Melville's intended wording and arrangement are stronger if the American edition is followed than if it is emended from the English.

Once these decisions are made, an editor must consider the large category of variants in the body of the book—about 600—in which both the American and the English readings make sense in the context. Although many of these English variants are the kinds of differences that can be expected whenever a text is reset in type, they require scrutiny since they could theoretically be Melville's revisions; indeed, a number seem unquestionably to be the sort of change that only Melville could have made. These variants can be divided into seven groups, ranging from those that are almost certainly not Melville's to those that can confidently be attributed to him. The size of each group, of course, bears no relation to its place in this continuum, for the largest number of individual differences falls into the fourth category and the largest total number of affected words into the first.

(1) A large category of variant readings in the English edition—and the one that involves the greatest alteration in the tone of the book—consists of changes that may be called expurgations. By far the largest number of these has to do with religion and consists of the elimination of whole passages or the revision of shorter phrases that might be considered sacrilegious. Of the 38 omitted passages of a sentence or more (enumerated above, p. 771), about three-fourths fit this description, and an additional four dozen smaller changes are of this type as well. Thus the last part of Chapter 2, referring to Dives and Lazarus in too unreverential a tone, is eliminated (10.32–38, 11.3–15; cf. 228.1–2); so is the long passage in Chapter 18 in which Ishmael plays on the phrase "First Congregational Church" (87.16–88.19), as well as passages that express unfavorable opinions of missionaries (300.4–8) or that refer to heaven in unconventional ways (190.43–45, 297.6–7, 297.10–13)—or to creation (33.3), the devil (184.22–23), the prophets (356.27), salvation (398.1–2), martyrs (422.25), the day of judgment (422.30–32), or God (435.16–18, 472.26–28). Any insufficiently solemn references to such biblical figures as Gabriel (6.14–16), Saul of Tarsus (207.19–20), Elijah (297.1), Abraham (312.3–4), or Shadrach, Meshach, and Abednego (427.9–10) are omitted—particularly if they involve an unflattering application of biblical names, as when "Jonah" is changed to "fellow" in the phrase "the wrinkled little old Jonah" (15.28; cf. 14.5, 15.30). When unworthy human traits are attributed to God (52.7–10), or when there is a suggestion that God's power may be limited (37.26), the offending phrases are stricken, while curses must be weakened or eliminated (294.22, 294.37, 325.18), along with other individual words, such as "archangel" (190.22) or "trinity" (507.11).

The next largest group of expurgations (about a third as many) concerns references to sex or parts of the body. The longest single passage removed for this reason is the description of the sun and the sea in "The Symphony" in terms of bride and groom (542.16–20), but several lines about Queequeg's legs lying over Ishmael's (53.4–6), about whales' "amours" (388.28, 388.39–40), and about the "back parts" of whales (379.7–9) are deleted, as well as all references to Queequeg's rescue of Tashtego in terms of obstetrics (344.2, 344.5–7, 344.25, 344.26). Individual words like "bridegroom" (26.37), "matrimonial" (27.8), and "impotent" (393.2) are omitted, as are allusions to fornication (105.31–32) and harlots (195.20–22) and the phrases "in our hearts' honeymoon" (in reference to Queequeg and Ishmael, 52.24) and "ripening his apricot thigh" (in reference to the Canaller, 249.28–29). A third (and much smaller) group of expurgations consists, not surprisingly, of passages that are sarcastic about royalty or are anti-British. The principal instance is the omission of all of Chapter 25, which cites the use of whale oil in coronations, but a sentence critical of British aristocracy (401.5–7) and two instances of linking God with democracy (117.22–24, 117.32) are also removed. All these expurgations, which shorten the book by some two thousand words and alter its phrasing at many points, are clearly the work of a reader at Bentley's who was making a systematic effort to remove anything that might be regarded as offensive. An editor can safely reject these variants.

(2) Nearly seven dozen of the variants in the English edition are small alterations or omissions that may have been intended as stylistic improvements or may, in some instances, be nothing more than compositors' errors. At any rate, they produce inferior (though not impossible) readings; and, while Melville could have made some changes for the worse, one can hardly attribute to him so many alterations that repeatedly misunderstand a particular passage or actually spoil it. For example, the word "yaw" was apparently troublesome to Bentley's reader or compositor, for it was changed twice to "yawn" (233.14, 353.2) and twice to "yawl" (354.35, 533.9), just as the "try" of "try-pots" was altered four times to "twy" (65.7, 65.10, 67.14, 253.31); and the shift from "powerless" to "powerful" at 309.14, probably meant as a correction, destroys the intended meaning, as does the substitution of "sore" for "scorched" at 186.21. A number of changes replace unusual or distinctive expressions with more regular ones, leveling or dulling a passage in the process: thus "slept" becomes "was" in "The profoundest slumber slept upon him" (99.28–29); the second noun in "difficulties and worryings" is,

with the elimination of the comma that followed it, made into the adjective "worrying" (226.11); "slicings" is changed to "slices" (304.26); "iron" is omitted from "stout Labor's iron lullaby" (485.24); and "unnamable" is replaced with "nameless" (497.20) and "wrenched" with "wretched" (548.39). Many of the omissions of single words—of "down" (26.11), "very" (111.31), "other" (116.21), "mortally" (116.23), "out" (420.18), or "grimly" (560.11), for example—may be additional instances of the same process, though they could be merely compositors' oversights. And most of the substitutions of words that resemble one another are more likely such oversights than attempted revisions: "you" for "yon" (166.6), "own" for "one" (177.24), "concentrated" for "concentred" (185.26), "rocky" for "rocking" (285.6), or "air" for "hair" (449.33). Similarly, changes that produce repetition (as "at" for "in" at 142.38 and "instantaneously" for "simultaneously" at 569.37) are probably simple errors. Several changes in tense (as at 191.12, 231.21, and 422.27) and number (as at 140.17, 552.5, and 559.12) fall into this general category, too—but it is clear, without multiplying examples, that this type of variant cannot realistically be attributed to Melville.

(3) About 125 of the changes are apparently intended to correct grammar or usage, often pedantically following schoolbook notions of correctness. For example, "-ly" is regularly added to adverbs that lacked it in the American edition, such as "previous" (204.15, 220.7), "scarce" (250.1), "high" (341.11), and "new" (357.22), and even to one adjective ("painful" at 484.19), altering the meaning. Subordinate clauses are sometimes supplied with an introductory "that" (as at 40.12 and 40.13), possessive nouns are made singular or plural according to logic (as in the change from "boy's" to "boys'" at 251.6 and from "ship's" to 'ships'" at 357.6),[35] "ye" is changed to

---

35. The change in the English edition from "Pharaoh's" to "Pharaohs'" (457.28) is a different matter; because the meaning of the sentence requires the change, an editor would have to make it whether or not it appeared in the English edition. But the singular in "boy's business" and "two ship's lengths" (or in "king's cabinets" at 412.5–6, not altered in the English edition) can be regarded as idiomatic, if not necessarily logical, and an editor has no reason to change it, unless there is strong evidence that the author wanted it altered. Such distributive constructions are allowed to remain, therefore, as they appear in the copy-text. Similarly, the change from "vertebra" to "vertebræ" (67.19) in the English edition is probably the result of concern for "correctness" on the part of Bentley's reader; the plural is not necessary

"you" (as at 248.34, 297.29, 353.28, 440.22, and 541.7), and cases of pronouns are corrected ("I" for "me" at 170.8). Verb forms are frequently shifted, such as "shall" for "will" (379.5, 565.24) and "should" for "would" (99.32), "swum" for "swam" (136.17) and "sprung" for "sprang" (224.22), "cracked" for "did crack" (551.33–34) and "pointed" for "did point" (557.17), and "to" is inserted before infinitives (as at 325.28, 326.12, and 528.11). In general, phraseology that might seem colloquial is made more formal: "but what" becomes "but that" (17.27, 76.19), "on" becomes "upon" (67.11), and "all at once" becomes "at once" (283.13). A whole category of this sort involves Melville's use of "of" in such expressions as "Circumambulate the city of a dreamy Sabbath afternoon"; repeatedly the "of" is replaced by "on" (4.3, 13.36, 20.19, 232.14). Similarly, the "of" is deleted or altered when the American edition reads "feeling of the knots" (17.1) or "lay hold of Jonah" (46.27). In one respect, the English edition seems to move in the opposite direction and introduce a less formal construction: almost invariably the subjunctive—as in "if this ship come to any deadly harm"—is replaced by the indicative (74.1, 336.18, 377.7, 515.2). Any of these "pedantic" changes could possibly be Melville's; but it is not characteristic of him to engage in this kind of revision, and the changes are more likely to be the work of Bentley's reader.

(4) More than a fourth of the changes (roughly 175) seem to make so little difference that it is difficult to see why Melville or anyone else went to the trouble of making them. There are a number of transpositions, for instance: "so long been" becomes "been so long" (23.12), "night previous" becomes "previous night" (50.18), "into them" becomes "them into" (165.37), "swiftly swims" becomes "swims swiftly" (216.8), and so on (282.10, 379.4, 434.10, 450.8, 512.2, 564.9). Other substitutions of adverbs, pronouns, or articles, though they may change the meaning slightly, do not produce noticeably superior or inferior readings: "there" for "then" (51.22), for example, or "these" for "those" (110.23), "his" for "its" (152.30), "the" for "our" (190.33), "a" for "the" (365.20), "the" for "these" (460.11), and "the" for "its" (500.21). The same could be said of many omissions (of "they" at 64.4, "most" at 248.38, or "the" at

---

for the sense (in the singular the word refers to the material in general rather than to individual pieces), and an editor has no compelling reason for changing it.

500.5) and additions (of "ever" at 206.25, "a" at 352.34, or "he" at 538.29). Melville could of course have made any of these changes, but they could also—and more probably—be compositors' slips or alterations made by Bentley's reader. Indeed, such shifts as replacing "accustomed" with "customary" (234.36) or certain revisions to avoid repetition (152.4, 449.39) may be regarded as further examples of "pedantic" changes. There is no strong reason, in other words, to believe that such alterations are particularly characteristic of Melville; the safest course for an editor, then, is to retain the American readings in these indifferent cases.

(5) A small group of changes (two dozen or so) results in toning down certain statements, making them less emphatic or definite. They range from the substitution of "scarcely" for "not" (64.32) to the deletion of the first two words in the phrase "wilful and erring" (543.16). It is hard to think that Melville would have changed "Louis the Devil" to "Louis Napoleon" (155.19) or altered "hangs for candelabra" to "is preserved" in his reference to Jeremy Bentham's skeleton (263.31); such changes constitute a kind of expurgation. On the other hand, the statement in the American edition that "the grand distinction drawn between officer and man at sea, is this—the first lives aft, the last forward" (147.5–6) may have been changed by Melville to read, more accurately, "one of the grand distinctions". Melville, of course, could have had second thoughts about any exaggerated or extreme statement and decided to make it more temperate or unexceptionable; at the same time, caution was one of the characteristics exhibited by Bentley's reader, and such changes are consistent with his general approach. While some of these revisions may have been Melville's, therefore, it is unlikely that the group as a whole can be his; and without further basis for choosing, a conservative editor must reject this class of changes. Once in a while, however, the editor does have a further basis for choosing: thus when the English edition prints "coolish weather" for "cold weather" (156.33), the statement is made more cautious, to be sure, but not in a way stylistically characteristic of Bentley's reader; it is difficult to conceive of his inserting such a word as "coolish," when "cool" would have been the more formal way of changing the sense. In rare instances, then, alterations of this class may be accepted, even though the general policy must be to reject them.

(6) About three dozen changes produce genuine improvements

(as opposed to mere corrections) of diction or style. In many of these cases, the problem apparently began either with a slip of the pen on Melville's part or a misreading of Melville's frequently difficult handwriting by a copyist or by the American compositors, producing a word that superficially seemed to fit but that was not quite appropriate and not the word Melville originally wrote or intended to write. Some of the restorations of Melville's intended wording are not beyond the powers of a careful reader at Bentley's—the change from "antichronical" to "ante-chronical" (456.24, 457.18), for example. But the number of instances in which the alteration of a few letters produces a much more appropriate word is so large that it is difficult to conceive of even a careful reader locating them all in the limited time at his disposal, especially in view of the fact that the words involved are innocuous and would not have been likely to catch his attention. Where the American edition, for instance, says that "the premature hour of the Pequod's sailing had, perhaps, been correctly selected", the English edition alters the adverb to "covertly" (201.9); similarly, the adverb in "might happily gain the power" becomes "haply" (56.13), the second adjective in "fullest sweep and direct swing" becomes "direst" (148.15), the first noun in "such considerations towards oarsmen" becomes "considerateness" (414.9), and the present participle in "the parted swell, that but once leaving him, then flowed so wide away" becomes "laving" (548.28). Other less imaginative revisions are indicative of characteristic difficulties in Melville's handwriting: "you scholars" is restored to "your scholars" (175.26), "oars" to "oar" (220.36), "on matter" to "in matter" (312.15), and "death-gasp" to "death-grasp" (572.32). Melville may not have made every one of the changes in this category, but it seems certain that he was responsible for the great majority of them; and, since each produces what must have been his intended reading, all are adopted here despite the small risk of including a few nonauthorial changes.

The evidence of Melville's own hand in these revisions is strengthened by examining some related groups, in which the problem in the American edition stems not from a misreading of copy but apparently from the accurate setting of copy that was faulty. For example, several English changes produce improvements in the rendering of dialect: "early" is altered to "airley" (18.3), "only" to "ony" (67.31), "at night" to "a-night" (67.34), and "Do" (meaning

"Though") to "Dough" (295.5). While Bentley's reader could conceivably have made these alterations, it is hard to imagine him introducing such forms (except perhaps "airley", for consistency in the passage), when his revisions normally moved in the other direction. Corrections of fact or of quotation, too, are more than one could reasonably expect even of a literary man like the publisher's reader: "Cranmer's sprinkled Pantheistic ashes" is corrected to "Wickliff's" (159.21), and, in the epigraph to Chapter 91, Thomas Browne's statement is corrected from "denying not inquiry" to "denying that inquiry" (402.4). Certain alterations of diction involve more than rectifying a misreading; rather, they supply a more appropriate word that bears little, if any, physical resemblance to the original word. Good examples are the shift of the verb in "directed by free will" to "modified" (215.13) and the substitution of "breath" for "life" (322.15). In addition, there are places where the syntax is confused (probably because of an incomplete manuscript revision in which Melville forgot to mark out all of a superseded phrase or failed to complete all of a new phrase), and sometimes these are skillfully clarified in the English edition. One of the best examples is the insertion of two dashes and the deletion of the word "that" to emphasize the parenthetical nature of a clause (271.6–7)—a simple, but by no means obvious, way of untangling a syntactical snarl. Again, "as you see the same in" becomes "the same as in" (20.14); the "like" is omitted from "as much like the badge" (192.5); and a whole clause—"oh, no! he went before"—is deleted from the reference to Pip at the end of the second "Knights and Squires" chapter (121.30). This last example offers particularly strong evidence that Bentley's reader was not involved, for he would not have known at this point that Pip does not die before the others (and would hardly have remembered to return to this passage later).

Taken together, these changes provide convincing testimony that Melville himself worked over the American proofs before sending them to Bentley. Many of the revisions, regarded individually, could be assigned to Bentley's reader; but the pattern they form as a group clearly suggests authorial intervention. In accepting alterations of this kind as emendations, an editor may be taking the risk of incorporating into the text a few nonauthorial changes; but the assurance that most of the changes are Melville's is strong enough to make that risk worth taking.

(7) A final category consists of additions that either extend a discussion (at one point) or clarify an individual sentence (in half a dozen instances). The one passage that was added is the 139-word footnote defining "gally" (384.28–40). In style and approach to its subject, with its quotation from Shakespeare and its generalization about etymology, it is unquestionably Melville's. Even if the original motivation for writing it was to explain an unfamiliar word to the English audience, its final form goes beyond that intention; the word is said to be unfamiliar to the "landsman" in general, not just the English, and the contribution that the passage makes—both in information and flavor—is equally great for American readers. One can feel certain, in other words, that the passage was written by Melville and that it should be included in any text representing his final intention. The presence of this passage in the English edition strengthens the argument that other additions and revisions are his as well. Although it is more difficult to judge the authority of single-word insertions, there are several that would seem to be attributable only to the author. For example, in the description of Ishmael coming "to a dim sort of out-hanging light not far from the docks" (10.5–6), the word "outhanging" was not present in the American edition; yet its insertion is not necessary for the sense, and it is hard to conceive of anyone besides Melville deciding to add such a word here. In another place an inserted word drastically alters the meaning and produces a much more likely statement: Stubb's advice to Flask regarding Ahab read, in the American edition, "never speak to him, whatever he says"; in the English the word "quick" is added after "speak" (132.35). And the addition of "a doubloon" in apposition to "a sixteen dollar piece" (162.1–2) seems clearly to be an afterthought of Melville's to make a more explicit connection with Chapter 99, "The Doubloon." Similarly, the insertions of "embryo" at 453.13, of "sometimes," at 500.12, and of "braced" at 517.32 seem hardly possible as the work of anyone other than the author. All these additions must have been entered by Melville on the proofs he sent to England, and the American text, therefore, can safely be emended with the English variants at these points.

Besides the emendations taken from the English edition, there is a further class of emendations, involving readings in which the American and English texts concur but which are clearly erroneous and demand correction. There are two principal groups of such readings. The first group consists of roughly two dozen errors that can be explained either as mistakes in typesetting or as compositorial or scribal misreadings of Melville's manuscript —if they were not slips of the pen in the manuscript itself. For example, the American and English readings "bade far" should undoubtedly be "bade fair" (222.25), "false bow" should be "false brow" (349.4), "argued well" should be "augured well" (405.24), and "tasting cruise" should be "testing cruise" (444.11). The context makes clear that "That's he" should be "Thank ye" (78.7), "formally" should be "formerly" (300.15), and "guiltiness" should be "guiltlessness" (557.15). The use of "between" for "beneath" at 255.13 must have been influenced by the earlier occurrence of "between" in the sentence; and necessary prepositions were omitted at two places—"to" at 88.39 and "in" at 502.14. Several errors in tense and number could have resulted from the difficulty of reading certain letters in Melville's hand, especially $o$, $a$, and $s$ (see the errors in tense at 12.15, 413.25, and 467.14, and those in number at 102.6 and 171.21);[36] errors in number involving a misplaced apostrophe may stem from either Melville's or a copyist's or compositor's carelessness (see 246.26, 418.6, and 532.10). In all these instances, the emendations restore what Melville must originally have written, or at least intended to write.[37]

The second group of errors not caught in the English edition consists of slightly over a dozen factual errors or other slips probably made by Melville in his manuscript. It is unlikely, for example, that a compositor or copyist made the error that resulted in mistaking Cabaco for Archy at one point; probably Melville inadvertently wrote "Cabaco's", but in any case the word must now be emended to

36. The plural reading "circumferences" at 552.5, changed to the singular in the English edition, may be another example, but because the plural makes sense it is not emended here. Some occurrences of "in" or "on" where the other preposition might now seem more idiomatic may also be the result of Melville's handwriting (see "in the third floor" at 26.4 and "on her . . . files" at 239.8); but the argument is not convincing enough to justify emendation.

37. Such changes are of course made only when the copy-text reading is unsatisfactory. The emendation must produce wording that Melville would have used in the context (judging from his literary practice); it must improve the sense and fit the tone of the context; and, if a substitution, it must be a word that in Melville's hand could have been misread as the word in the copy-text (or that Melville himself could mistakenly have written).

"Archy's" (230.12). Similarly, "vinegar-cruet" must be changed to "mustard-pot" (82.39), "eastward" to "westward" (243.17), "Vineyarder" to "Nantucketer" (244.1), and "Daggoo" to "Tashtego" in one spot (286.18) and "Queequeg" to "Tashtego" in another (568.1). Such matters of external fact as dates, names, and figures are occasionally wrong also: the date of Linnæus's work must be changed from 1776 to 1766 (136.23) and that of the *Amelia*'s voyage from 1778 to 1788 (443.19); "Captain Butler" should be "Captain Church" (205.17) and "Commodore Davis" should be "Commander Davies" (210.15); and the weight that each yarn of the whale line can bear should be "one hundred and twelve", rather than "one hundred and twenty", pounds (279.2), as Melville's source indicates. In other places Melville gets mixed up in what he is saying, as when he answers "Yes" to a rhetorical question that should be answered "No" (201.24)[38] or confuses "Timor Jack" and "New Zealand Tom" (205.1, 205.4).[39] A few errors of this kind had been corrected in the English edition, probably by Melville himself (see 159.21, 370.11, 397.20), but a larger number evidently passed unnoticed; and when a simple substitution will correct them, the necessary emendation is made.

38. There is a cluster of problematical readings that involve possible mix-ups in the use of negatives, but they are not always as easily settled as this one. The copy-text reading is allowed to stand if it can possibly be construed in a sense that fits the context: thus "clerical peculiarities" is retained (rather than "unclerical") at 38.16 and "earthly passionlessness" (rather than the English reading "unearthly") at 501.3, and the "not" is allowed to remain in "not to approach the ship at their peril" (257.29). Related awkward readings are "but, nevertheless" at 192.19 (which should perhaps be simply "nevertheless") and "than though seated" at 281.15 (which should perhaps be "than seated").

39. Grammatical solecisms, too, are corrected when they can only be regarded as slips on Melville's part, not intentional constructions. Thus when Melville has Ahab, in one of the soliloquies, say, "that one strivest, this one jettest" (497.17), he has merely made a blunder in the use of an obsolete form, and the verbs should be corrected to "striveth" and "jetteth". But when Bildad and Peleg use "thee" for "thou" (75.22, 78.15, 88.12), Melville is attempting to reproduce Quaker speech and the forms should be retained. Melville's use of second-person pronouns is discussed—though without reference to these "errors"—by Merrel D. Clubb, Jr., in "The Second Personal Pronoun in *Moby-Dick*," *American Speech*, XXXV (1960), 252–60. However, awkwardness of syntax, as opposed to simple grammatical error, is not altered: "to learn" at 73.37 does not fit the syntax as well as "learning", and "her" at 424.14 is unnecessary, but the copy-text readings are retained.

In many instances, however, the inconsistencies or anomalies are of such a nature that only considerable rewriting would correct them, and in such cases there is no alternative but to let them stand. Sometimes, for example, Melville's description of physical actions has not been completely visualized, as when Ishmael reports that Queequeg, holding "both my hands in his", dips into the Potluck (57.3), or when Starbuck is said to rise when he had not been sitting (474.37). (For some other instances, see the DISCUSSIONS OF ADOPTED READINGS at 416.26, 442.6, and 551.13.) Melville, in other words, often loses track of realistic detail in the process of thinking about literary effect, as when he mixes references to hammocks and bunks (see the discussion at 16.28) or when he names many more crew members than the specified total of thirty (see the discussion at 121.8–9). The largest category of unemendable discrepancies consists of those that seem to reflect incomplete revision of earlier stages of composition. At one point the *Pequod* has open bulwarks and at another closed bulwarks (70.4, 234.39–235.4), sometimes a tiller and at other times a wheel (see the discussions at 70.8 and 283.18–19); Pip's birthplace is named as Alabama at one point (121.30), as Connecticut at another (412.11–12); and in a single episode (chap. 48) Ishmael seems first to be in Stubb's boat, then in Starbuck's. (For some further examples of the many similar instances, see the discussions at 56.39, 61.35–36, 72.31, 95.11, 120.10–12, 123.4–10, 124.16, 146.2, 161.7, 173.3, 179.7, 216.22, 217.21, 242.21, 243.12, 292.21, 302.4, 320.11, 437.26, 441.5, 478.17, and 543.17.) Such discrepancies are so frequent that they become in fact a prominent characteristic of *Moby-Dick;* although they may spoil the effect of certain passages, they do not lessen the power of the book as a whole, and in any case a scholarly editor cannot engage in the kind of rewriting that their repair would necessitate.

Finally, it should be noted that more than two dozen emendations of substantives have been made in the "Extracts" section. Since this section and the opening part of "Etymology" (as well as about two dozen passages in the body of the book) consist of quotations from other works, they present a different situation from the rest of the text, for the accuracy of the quotations can be checked against the cited sources. Three errors in the "Extracts" were corrected in the English edition, almost certainly by Melville (since Bentley's reader would not have been likely to check the sources): *"Pilgrim's Progress"* was altered to *"Holy War"* (xx.15), "stuffed" to "stiff" in the passage from Pope (xxii.11), and "near appearance" to "mere appearance" in the extract from *Currents and Whaling* (xxvii.24). But many errors remained, most of them apparently the result of a misreading of the manuscript. In the quotation from Spenser, for example, there are three errors in both the American and English editions: "secure" for "recure" (xix.24), "lowly" for "lovely" (xix.26), and "thro' " for "from" (xix.28). In the passage from *Paradise Lost* (repeated in the English edition on each of its three title pages) both editions make two substantive errors: "in" for "on" (xx.21) and "breath" for "trunk" (xx.24). Or in the extract from Cowper, "blew" was printed for "flew" (xxiii.16), "fire" for "fires" (xxiii.17), and "Around" for "Amid" (xxiii.18). And such serious misreadings as "modern" for "iron" (xx.5) and "lime-stone" for "brim-stone" (xxii.25) occur in other quotations. In each case the correct word is one that might have looked like the erroneous one in Melville's handwriting, and there is no reason to suppose in these instances that Melville was purposely altering his extract; it seems proper, therefore, to make the emendations.

There are other places, however, in which it does not seem proper to emend the printed extract, even though it does not conform to the cited source. Given the nineteenth-century custom of approximate quotation or paraphrase, Melville would have felt no obligation to indicate just which passages were summarized, conflated, or revised rather than quoted directly and would have seen no objection to labeling them all as "Extracts." Thus whenever a passage is obviously an adaptation of its source (involving either altered wording or unmarked ellipsis) and direct quotation is not intended, no attempt is made here to restore the precise wording of the original. Examples of such adapted or conflated passages are those from Bacon (xix.17–19) and Goldsmith (xxii.13–15).[40] For the same reason certain minor misquotations or omissions are not rectified even in passages that for the

---

40. The other extracts involving adapted wording, paraphrase, or rearrangement are those beginning at xix.14, xxii.5, xxii.17, xxii.19, xxii.23, xxiii.4, and xxiii.32; those involving an unmarked ellipsis of more than two words begin at xx.14, xxi.10, xxi.29, xxii.1, xxii.30, xxiii.11, xxiv.1, xxiv.25, xxv.25, xxvi.32, and xxviii.9. Quoted passages within the body of the text are treated in the same way as the "Extracts"; for those that involve adaptation or ellipsis, see the discussions at 41.21, 136.16–17, 142.35–38, 209.5, 262.2–4, 334.33, 356.23–26, 362.11–12, and 401.18–19.

most part are faithful quotations. Whenever a misquotation in the Harper text of a passage, for example, does not seem a likely misreading for the correct reading, it is conceivable that the change was an intentional one on Melville's part. He may have revised Scoresby's "two or three" to "three or four" (xxv.23) for exaggeration and shifted Bacon's "exceedingly" to "exceeding" (xix.18) to increase the archaic effect; certainly he made some alterations so that passages would be clear when taken out of context, as when "Leviathan" is substituted for "He" in the extract from Job (xviii.9) or when "this Sperma-ceti whale" replaces "them" in the Stafford passage (xxi.29–30). Whereas the shift from "those weapons" to "these weapons" in the Bennett extract (xxvi.7) serves no purpose and could easily have resulted from a misinterpretation of Melville's handwriting or from his own miscopying, the reading "monsters of the sea" for "monsters of the deep" in the Lucian quotation (xviii.27) alters the flavor of the sentence and does not seem a likely handwriting error; the first is therefore corrected and the second is not. Minor omissions present somewhat more difficult cases, since they can always be inadvertent; but when an omitted word (or short phrase) is not essential to the sense of the passage, it is normally not restored, for Melville may have intentionally omitted it, either to change the effect (an instance is perhaps the omission of "other" at xviii.19) or to eliminate what he considered unnecessary for his purpose (an example is probably the omission of "from" at xv.15).[41] Citations of sources, too, are allowed

41. Similarly, in the Browne passage, "shoal" (xxvi.18) is not corrected to "school", though a misreading may possibly have occurred, since the meaning is not affected and since an earlier quotation establishes the usage "shoals" of whales (xxiv.11); and the omitted words "amount of" are not restored before "National" (xxvii.4) in the Webster extract, since they are not essential to the meaning and could represent an intentional abridgment. For further examples of uncorrected minor misquotations, see the entries for xviii.24–25, xix.10, xix.15, xix.21, xx.8, xxii.13–15, xxiii.24–25, xxiv.5–17, xxiv.32–33, xxv.4–5, xxv.13, xxv.25–xxvi.2, xxvi.4–9, xxvi.28, xxvii.25, xxvii.32, xxviii.12, xxviii.15–18, xxviii.19–22, xxviii.23–25, 42.21, 76.32, 134.13–22, 136.16–17, 136.23–31, 173.13–22, 199.39, 208.3–19, 262.11–13, 399.3, and 401.13 in the DISCUSSIONS OF ADOPTED READINGS. It should be emphasized that the concern here is solely with substantives; no attempt has been made to bring the accidentals of the extracts or other quotations into conformity with those of any given printings of the source passages (though, of course, undeniable errors in accidentals—such as the spelling of Owen Chase's name as "Chace" at xxv.7 and xxv.11 or the presence of a period in mid-sentence at xxiv.15—are corrected).

to stand, even when they do not report the exact wording of a title, if they can be regarded as examples of the nineteenth-century practice of allusive citation; thus *"Darwin's Voyage of a Naturalist"* (xxviii. 18) is not emended. When Melville follows a source that is erroneous, the error in the source is not corrected, for Melville obviously accepted the source reading; thus Melville's citation of *"World before the Flood"* (xxiv. 17) is not altered to *"Pelican Island"*, because Melville was accurately reproducing the mistaken attribution made by Cheever.[42] The aim, in other words, is not factual accuracy but fidelity to Melville's intended forms of his quotations and citations.

## TREATMENT OF ACCIDENTALS

IN THE ABSENCE of a final manuscript, the degree to which the author was responsible for the accidentals—the punctuation and spelling—of a printed text is a matter impossible to settle conclusively. Greg's theory of copy-text provides a method for playing the odds to advantage: adhering to the printed text closest to the manuscript will allow a maximum number of characteristic authorial usages to be retained, since each successive impression or edition offers further opportunities for corruption, in the form of publishers' changes, compositors' errors, or plate damage. Even though changes in the spelling and punctuation of *Moby-Dick* were undoubtedly made by the compositors in Craighead's shop, the American edition was nevertheless set directly from Melville's manuscript and inevitably preserves more of its accidentals than the English edition, another step removed, could possibly do. Of course, some of the variants in ac-

---

42. In some cases the citation provided by Melville is adequate for locating the original with little difficulty; but in many instances additional information is necessary if the passage is to be found without considerable effort. The Discussions of Adopted Readings that comment on the relation of Melville's quotations to their sources also provide precise references to those sources—occasionally supplementing the pioneer listing of sources in Mansfield and Vincent's edition of *Moby-Dick*, pp. 582–86. (In addition to those mentioned in the two preceding footnotes, discussions dealing with quotations in the body of the text are entered for 171.20–23, 173.6–8, 181.33, 206.35–39, 207.25–39, 334.33–35, 384.33, 402.4, 424.39–425.2, 458.6–19, 504.8–19, and 573.2.) Further discussion of the allusions to factual matters in *Moby-Dick* is provided in G. Thomas Tanselle, "External Fact as an Editorial Problem," *Studies in Bibliography*, XXXII (1979), 1–47 (reprinted in *Selected Studies in Bibliography* [Charlottesville: University Press of Virginia, 1979], pp. 355–401.)

cidentals in the English edition must be changes that Melville made in the proofs he sent to Bentley, but it is impossible in most cases to determine just which ones; to accept all the English variants that appear to be improvements would be to risk adopting many instances of nonauthorial spelling and punctuation on the chance of acquiring some authorial alterations—and to defeat the purpose of selecting a copy-text on Greg's principles.[43]

Accordingly, the accidentals of the first American impression of *Moby-Dick* have been retained in the present edition, except in the instances outlined below, even when the spelling and punctuation may appear incorrect or inconsistent by late-twentieth-century standards. Certainly the American edition was full of inconsistencies. Many of them were no doubt present in the manuscript, and, although Melville may not have been aware of them, they constitute a suggestive part of his total expression, since patterns of accidentals do affect the texture of a literary work. Some of the inconsistencies in accidentals were probably occasioned by the practice Melville asked his wife and sisters to follow in copying his manuscripts: to omit the punctuation, so that he could insert it later (see the HISTORICAL NOTE, p. 619). On the other hand, further inconsistencies may of course have resulted from changes (either intentional or inadvertent) introduced in the printing shop. To regularize the punctuation and spelling would be to risk choosing nonauthorial forms.[44] Indeed, since the printer's copy of *Moby-Dick* presumably never passed through the

43. Among the variants in accidentals in the English edition, aside from the predictable classes of differences in pointing and in spelling, are two groups of more than usual interest. One is the use of dashes to replace the middle letters of such words as "damned" (71.12) and "blast" (77.4)—further evidence of the squeamishness of Bentley's reader. The other is the introduction of seven new paragraph openings (at the sentences beginning in 16.4, 69.4, 156.3, 166.25, 209.5, 244.31, and 324.2) and the elimination of two paragraph breaks (at the second sentence in 218.20 and at 538.9); these alterations (or some of them) could conceivably be Melville's, but they could just as well reflect the subjective decisions of Bentley's reader as to what constitutes proper paragraphing, and (except for the one change—at 218.20—which makes a necessary correction in the paragraphing of direct discourse) they are not adopted here.

44. Melville's habits in the extant manuscripts and letters are not definite enough to offer grounds to emend for consistency (and in any case the letters, not intended for publication, do not provide a parallel situation). Nor is enough known about the procedures of Craighead's shop to be helpful in determining precisely what elements of the spelling and punctuation of *Moby-Dick* resulted from them.

hands of a publisher's editor, the American edition, with its large number of inconsistencies, may actually reflect Melville's manuscript more closely than does the original edition of any other of his prose works published in his lifetime. Completely to regularize the accidentals would involve making thousands of changes, inevitably taking one farther away from Melville's manuscript and, in effect, producing a modernization. Therefore, no attempt has been made in this edition to impose general consistency on either spelling or punctuation,[45] and changes have been made sparingly, according to the following guidelines:

SPELLING. The general rule adopted here is to retain any spellings (even when inconsistent) that were acceptable by the standards of 1851, as well as any obsolete variants that may have been intended by

45. For example, no emendations are made to secure consistency in the use (or nonuse) of capital letters; of apostrophes in contractions; of hyphens in compounds; of hyphens or apostrophes in words prefixed with "a"; and of italics or of quotation marks (or both at once) for such items as foreign words, the first occurrence of special terms (nautical terminology, slang, and the like), names of ships, and titles of books.

Thus such titles as "captain," "commodore," "king," "queen," and "squire," both when attached to proper names and when used separately to refer to specific individuals, are capitalized in some instances (see 92.26, 120.2, 121.7, 207.5, 419.14) and not capitalized in others (see 92.18, 120.15, 207.13, 419.15). Contractions have apostrophes in varying positions or no apostrophe at all (see "T'will" at 160.22, "'Twill" at 521.10, "'Tis" at 544.39, and "'em" and "em" only a line apart, at 295.27 and 295.28), and the copy-text spacings of contractions are retained (see "miser 'll" at 435.16 and "t' is" at 508.21); of course, when the copy-text placing or omission of an apostrophe produces the wrong meaning, it must be corrected (see the correction of "Slid" at 132.4, "wer't" at 165.30, "let's" at 326.38, and "its" at 525.27), but oddly placed apostrophes that do not affect the sense are not altered (as in "unfort'nt" at 67.31 or "'till" at 295.36). Similarly, the inconsistent use of hyphens in such terms as "right whale" (compare 135.17 with 139.4) is not changed; nor is any attempt made to regularize the form of words like "a-whaling" (71.24, 72.21, 73.3), "a-begging" (564.22), "A viewing" (173.15), "a flyin'" (504.12), and "A' flourishin'" (504.10), or of "a-plenty" (175.6), "a-rush" (187.14), "alow" (433.26), and "a'top" (434.38). Finally, quotation marks are sometimes used in the copy-text to set off words cited as words (for example, "the word 'clam'" at 66.30, or "the word 'cod'" at 67.6), but at other times italics are used for this purpose (as in "what they call a rather long lay" at 76.2–3, or in "kedger, as the sailors say" at 269.5), while ship names and other titles now conventionally italicized are usually not set off in any way; again, such irregularities, as long as they do not distort the meaning, are allowed to stand. (The same principles apply to the accidentals of the "Extracts" as to the accidentals of the rest of the text; see footnote 41 above.)

Melville or reflect his reading in earlier material; spellings are corrected only when they do not fall into these categories. One available guide for decisions about spelling is the 1847 revision of Webster's *American Dictionary of the English Language* (Springfield, Mass., 1848). Webster's was the dictionary used by Harper & Brothers at the time, for Melville remarked, in his letter to John Murray, his first English publisher, on January 28, 1849, that "my printers here 'go for' Webster." The Harper accounts show that Melville ordered at least three copies of Webster's (on April 10 and November 15, 1847, and on November 16, 1848), the third of which could have been the 1848 edition. In any case, the 1848 Webster's can be taken as a generally accepted standard in use when Melville was writing *Moby-Dick*. Recourse to it and to other contemporary dictionaries, such as Worcester's *A Universal and Critical Dictionary of the English Language* (Boston, 1847), to editions of American novels and other works published in the 1840's and 1850's, as well as to such sources for the historical study of spelling as the *Oxford English Dictionary* and the *Dictionary of American English,* has resulted in the retention of some anomalous-appearing copy-text forms, such as "Bastile" (494.24), "Bhering" (64.11), "bitts" (271.18), "Blocksburg" (193.10), "Bramha" (363.21), "calking" (526.14, 527.4—along with "caulk", 525.39), "christian" (87.14), "Cogniac" (321.37), "Corlaer's" (432.23) and "Corlears" (4.4), "Crozetts" (236.3, 272.3, 323.16), "D'Wolf" (208.17, 208.20), "Fernandes" (208.34), "Garnery" (266.6, 266.37, 267.7, 267.27), "gulph" (14.13), "Hackluyt" (xv.13, 265.7, 334.33), "Heidelburgh" (339–40, 342.19, 415.6), "inuendoes" (71.21, 525.4), "Leuwenhoeck" (267.21), "Melancthon" (346.23), "Mendanna" (271.9), "Morrel" (111.15), "Neskyeuna" (314.32, 314.38), "nett" (76.1), "Olassen" (181.27), "pastiles" (408.15), "Praries" (191.2), "salamed" (52.17), "scimetar" (153.18, 334.17), "smoothe" (488.5, 488.10, 488.13), "Specksynder" (x.17, 146.2, 146.11, 146.15), and a group of adjective forms of proper names, including "Alleganian" (16.10), "Chilian" (164.26, 205.8), "Descartian" (159.27), and "Tartarian" (141.5).[46]

A number of other forms, not found in reliable parallels in such

46. Since contemporary practice did not demand accuracy in the use of diacritical marks on foreign words (indeed, contemporary dictionaries sometimes listed them without these marks), such forms as "Durer" (270.22) and "Vendome" (155.17) are also allowed to stand as they appear in the copy-text.

contemporary sources, have been corrected; but any changes to bring spelling into conformity with an 1851 standard have been made cautiously so as to preserve the wide latitude allowed in contemporary usage, especially for proper names. Several of these errors were caught in the English edition: "Baliene" (138.32), "Beckett" (69.32), "Bell" (in "the idol Bel" at 89.28), "Cooke" (110.8, 110.10, 110.13, 460.3), "cozzening" (545.8), "Cruize" (xxvi.27), "demigorgon" (169.21), "diagonically" (354.30), "fowels" (548.19), "petulence" (416.8, 484.15), "praire" (xi.29, 345.2), "Quohag" (104.3), "Rokovoko" (59.14–15, 59.18), "Tahitan" (176.13), "Tongatabooarrs" (31.16), "vicisitudes" (388.25), and "vultureism" (308.21). But several more also require correcting: "Azore" (175.1, 175.7), "Bennett" (xxvi.36), "Bonneterre" (135.9), "Chace" (xxv.7, xxv.11, 206.32, 206.35), "Eckerman" (376.18), "Figuera" (271.9), "Growlands Walfish" (138.32), "Harto" (462.7), "Hosmannus" (xx.2), "Lais" (338.11), "Lamatins" (137.34), "Ochotsh" (208.4), "Olmstead" (135.11), "Pitferren" (xxi.27), "plazza" (249.13), "Plowdon" (401.11, 401.12), "Pontoppodan" (277.11), "Pottsfich" (137.33), "Povelson" (181.28, 181.37), "Soloma" (271.8), "Strafford" (xxi.32), "Strello" (182.37), and "Tormentoto" (234.22). In addition, two capitalizations made in the English edition (of "Battery" at 3.22 and "First" at 87.15) are accepted here, because the sense might not be clear otherwise.[47] Any emendations in spelling made in the English edition and adopted here are necessary emendations that would have been made regardless of who was first responsible for them; but it does appear that most of them are corrections that Melville would have been more likely than Bentley's reader to make.

PUNCTUATION. Emendations in punctuation are made only to correct obvious typographical errors and evidently incorrect pointing; but when punctuation is not manifestly wrong no alterations are made to bring it into conformity with some presumed standard. Most of the obvious errors, which have been emended, fall into three categories: (1) The largest category consists of errors in the use of quotation marks, 82 of them in "The Town-Ho's Story" (chap. 54) alone. In that chapter the conversation set at the Golden Inn should be

---

47. Corrections in the English edition of obvious typographical errors are of course accepted also—such errors as "auy" for "any" (27.33) or "Stbub" for "Stubb" (116.20).

punctuated with the usual double quotation marks, and comments that Ishmael reports as having been said on the *Town-Ho,* being quotations within quotations, should be further enclosed in single quotation marks. The American edition becomes hopelessly mixed up in its use of these marks, and neither the *Harper's New Monthly Magazine* printing of this chapter nor the English edition is much better, though at a few scattered spots each has the correct punctuation where the American edition has it wrong—more likely the result of mistakes in following copy than any attempt to correct faulty punctuation. (One change in a quotation mark in the *Harper's* text—falling into a different category because it involves a shift in the position of the mark—does suggest, however, that some careful attention—by the editor or even by Melville himself—was given to punctuation, at least at this one spot: a misplaced quotation mark in the American edition, which attributes to Ishmael part of the Teneriffe man's exclamation at 256.5, is placed correctly in *Harper's*—and in the English edition.) Other, much smaller, clusters of errors in marking quotations, some of them again involving quotations within quotations, occur in Father Mapple's sermon (at 42.21, 44.4, 44.18, and 46.28) and in Bildad's conversation (at 76.26, 76.27, 77.7, and 77.8). And scattered through the book are instances of the inadvertent omission of individual quotation marks (93.25, 132.16, 215.39, 434.29, 505.1). No attempt is made in the Northwestern-Newberry Edition to bring about consistency in the placing of quotation marks in relation to other marks of punctuation (or in the use of other marks in conjunction with quotation marks); all these emendations of quotation marks are for the purpose of correcting outright and obvious errors in the designation of what is being spoken.[48] (2) Another group of errors involves end punctuation: typographical errors resulting in the absence of periods at the ends of sentences (560.27, 570.31) or in what is clearly the wrong punctuation (a period instead of a question mark

48. In none of these instances, however, does the emendation involve a decision affecting the meaning, since in none does the misuse or omission of quotation marks seriously call into question who is speaking or what is said. For some examples in which the meaning is affected, see the next paragraph. (Within quoted passages, Melville sometimes places words in parentheses to show that they are not part of the quotation—in the way we would now use square brackets—and this practice is not altered here, since the meaning in each case is clear; examples are at xix.9, xxi.24, xxv.32, xxviii.7, xxviii.15, 136.16, and 458.15–16.)

after "prophecy" at 92.31, a comma instead of a period after "say" at 123.35, or a question mark instead of an exclamation point after "power" at 497.16). (3) A third small group is made up of errors in the use of commas, either the absence of commas where they are obviously required (as after *"Hussey"* at xxvi.31, "eyes" at 222.29, "honor" at 259.12, "Tekel" at 506.7, and "bread" at 544.2) or the placing of a comma in the wrong position (as after "hour" instead of "two" at 301.10–11).[49] The English edition occasionally makes some of the corrections in all these categories, but the errors are of a kind that would have to be corrected here in any case.

Besides the emendations to rectify obvious slips in punctuation, the Northwestern-Newberry Edition emends punctuation at about a dozen and a half other places, where the copy-text punctuation seems to distort the intended meaning sufficiently that a reader might have difficulty with the passage or be misled by it. Most of these emendations involve commas, generally their insertion but sometimes their removal or shift. For instance, in the description of Father Mapple at the end of his sermon, the American edition says that he "remained kneeling, till all the people had departed" (48.36); but the context surely demands that a comma be inserted after "remained", since he had not previously been described as kneeling after the sermon. Similarly, a comma is required after "others" at 206.3 if "others" is to refer to "voyages" rather than "ships": "upon one particular voyage which I made to the Pacific, among many others, we spoke thirty different ships". In the phrase that reads "still becharmed panic" (387.30) in the copy-text, the context makes clear that "still" is not to be regarded as an adverb but is rather one of two adjectives modifying "panic"; therefore a comma must be added after "still". And clearly the meaning of Ahab's question which appears in the American edition as "D'ye feel brave men, brave?" (562.5) is distorted if a comma is not added after the first "brave". This last emendation was made in the English edition, which also made several others of the same kind (see, in particular, 73.35, 79.8, 100.9–10, 117.1, 188.22, 190.1, and 221.38), suggesting once again the sort of careful reading

49. In addition to these categories, there are a few miscellaneous typographical errors that demand correction, such as missing apostrophes (as in "Slid" at 132.4), incorrect apostrophes (as in "wer't" at 165.30 or "come's" at 174.35), missing semicolons (as after "Bull" at 432.37), incorrect semicolons (as after "oar" at 467.14), or incorrect colons (as after "seas" at 193.14).

of the proof sheets that can more readily be attributed to the author than to the publisher's reader. In any event, these emendations must be made, along with a number of additional ones not caught in the English edition (see, besides those already cited, 13.19, 20.7, 104.3, 155.28, 354.15, 355.12, 372.2, and 433.23). The only emendations in punctuation that affect meaning besides these changes in commas are three emendations in quotation marks. In "The First Lowering" one of Flask's speeches, as printed in the American edition, is divided into two paragraphs, with ending quotation marks for each, making it appear that someone else is speaking the second part; a simple correction is to join both parts in the same paragraph, as in the English edition (218.20). Then in "The Town-Ho's Story," the exclamation of the Teneriffe man upon seeing Moby Dick is cut off too soon, seeming to give four words of his speech to Ishmael (256.5), and again the proper placing of the quotation mark was made in the English edition (and earlier in the *Harper's Magazine* text, as noted above). Finally, in "The Gilder," a long paragraph that seems intended to be a soliloquy of Ahab's is not placed within quotation marks and thus appears to be a further reflection on Ishmael's part (492.11–26); the quotation marks are inserted for the first time in this edition. All the emendations of this class, whether of commas or of quotation marks, are actually substantive in their effect, since they involve a shift of meaning or the imposition of a single meaning on a possibly ambiguous construction; in each instance, however, the resulting reading seems clearly to be the one required by the context.

## EDITORIAL APPARATUS

T HE BASIC EVIDENCE for textual decisions in the present edition is given in the preceding sections of this NOTE and in the four lists that follow it and complete the TEXTUAL RECORD:[50]

DISCUSSIONS OF ADOPTED READINGS. These discussions take up any reading (whether a copy-text reading or an emendation) adopted

---

50. On file in the Melville Collection at The Newberry Library is a complete list of variants between the American and English editions, including both substantives (which are reported in the LIST OF SUBSTANTIVE VARIANTS) and accidentals (which are reported in the LIST OF EMENDATIONS only when English variants are adopted). Also on file is the evidence for the decisions in the first list of the REPORT OF LINE-END HYPHENATION.

in the Northwestern-Newberry text that seems to require discussion or explanation beyond the general guidelines already stated. Certain instances of decisions not to emend, as well as some actual emendations, are commented upon. In addition, references are included here to some of the comments on individual readings made in the NOTE ON THE TEXT.

LIST OF EMENDATIONS. This list records every change made in the copy-text for the present edition, accidentals as well as substantives. The left column gives the Northwestern-Newberry readings, the right column the rejected copy-text readings. Each emendation is followed by a symbol to indicate whether the source is the English edition (E), the *Harper's New Monthly Magazine* printing of "The Town-Ho's Story" (H), or the present editors (NN).[51] Items marked with an asterisk are commented on in the DISCUSSIONS OF ADOPTED READINGS.

Aside from the 82 emendations of quotation marks in "The Town-Ho's Story" (recorded separately in 80 entries at the end of the list), 175 emendations have been made in accidentals, 165 in substantives (recorded in 337 entries). Of the emendations in accidentals, 101 are corrections made in the English edition, one comes from the *Harper's* printing of "The Town-Ho's Story," and the other 73 have been made by the present editors; of the substantives, 79 come from the English edition, one is from *Harper's*, and 85 have been made by the present editors. No emendations of any sort have been made silently; using the LIST OF EMENDATIONS and the REPORT OF LINE-END HYPHENATION, one can reconstruct the copy-text in every detail.[52]

---

51. The presence of an NN symbol signifies only that the reading does not occur in the authorized texts; it does not imply that no one has ever thought of it before.

52. That is, every *textual* detail: features of the styling or design of the edition containing the copy-text are of course not recoverable from these lists. The following are regarded as features of styling and therefore nontextual: the form and content of the title page, half-title page, and running titles; the typography and punctuation of the dedication; the typography and punctuation of chapter numbers and chapter titles, both in the table of contents and at chapter heads (as well as the typography and punctuation of other headings or closings, such as "Extracts" or "Finis"); the inclusion of additional entries in the table of contents; the typography of epigraphs, both in the "Extracts" section and at chapter heads (as well as their position on the page relative to chapter openings); the display capitalization of chapter openings; the length of the lines of type; the number of asterisks used to indicate a break, an ellipsis, or the passage of time; the typography and position of stage directions; the setting off

REPORT OF LINE-END HYPHENATION. Since some compound words are hyphenated at the ends of lines in the copy-text, the intended forms of these words become a matter for editorial decision. When such a

---

of the tablet inscriptions on pp. 35–36 (each one is now enclosed in a frame, whereas the copy-text had only a rule separating the first two, which fell on the same page); the typography of the punctuation following italic letters; and the typography of the roman numerals and the terminal punctuation of the headings in Chapter 32, "Cetology" (now made consistent, with large numerals referring to books and small to chapters, and with a period and a dash at the ends of headings).

Although the chapter titles in the copy-text were set in capitals at the heads of chapters, they are set in upper and lower case here in conformity with the styling of the Northwestern-Newberry Edition; the capitalization of these titles has been derived from that in the table of contents of the copy-text. Even though it does not always correspond to the wording or punctuation of the titles at chapter heads, the wording and punctuation of the table of contents has been retained from the copy-text (except that entries for "Etymology" and "Extracts" have been added). In both positions chapter numbers have been switched from roman to arabic, and periods within chapter titles are replaced with centered dots (except in period-dash combinations, where only the dash is used). Whenever running titles use a shortened form of a chapter title, that shortened form has, for convenience, been made to correspond to the one that appears in the copy-text. As for the display capitalization of chapter openings, it at no time obscures a capitalized word; that is to say, all display capitals (except of course the first one) at chapter openings can be transcribed as lowercase letters in quotations from this text. By typographical convention, opening quotation marks are omitted before the display capitals at the beginning of Chapters 19 (p. 91), 43 (p. 196), 50 (p. 229), 69 (p. 308), 100 (p. 436), 120 (p. 509), 121 (p. 510), 122 (p. 512), 127 (p. 527), and 129 (p. 534).

It may further be pointed out that, while the precise number of asterisks on pp. 134, 178, 207, 209, 215, 229, 258, 259, and 416 is a nontextual matter, the extent of them in each case is made to approximate the copy-text usage, which seems to have a suggestive value; thus there are two rows of asterisks on p. 207 and only a partial line of them on pp. 134, 209, and 258 (and at several points in the "Etymology" and the "Extracts"). Similarly, the lengths of dashes appear to serve a purpose (the longer dashes often marking interruptions); thus the copy-text practice is followed, resulting in varying lengths of dashes, for example, in 237.13 and 237.15 or in 541.9. The discrepancy in the formal presentation of stage directions in the copy-text, on the other hand, seems only distracting, not functional, and stage directions not attached to particular sentences are now consistently styled in italics, centered and enclosed in parentheses, with the first word capitalized (except that those attached to characters' names are not centered or capitalized when a second stage direction immediately follows, as at 470.1). To illustrate the confusion in the copy-text, one notes that the direction at 169.18 was printed at the right side of the page, with a bracket at the beginning, while the one at 507.27–29 was centered, with brackets at beginning and end; the directions at 169.3, 509.3, 510.3–4, and 512.3–4

word appears elsewhere in the copy-text in only one form, that form is followed; when its treatment is not consistent (and the inconsistency is an acceptable one, to be retained in the present text), the form that occurs more times in analogous situations is followed. If the word does not occur elsewhere in the copy-text, the form is determined by a survey of similar words, by the usage in the 1847 Worcester's and the 1848 Webster's, and by any relevant evidence in a Melville manuscript. The first list in the REPORT OF LINE-END HYPHENATION records these decisions, by listing the adopted Northwestern-Newberry forms of compounds that are hyphenated at the ends of lines in the copy-text. The second list is a guide to the established copy-text forms of compounds that are hyphenated at the ends of lines in the Northwestern-Newberry Edition. No editorial decisions are involved in this second list,[53] but the information recorded is essential for reconstructing the copy-text and making exact quotations from the present edition.

LIST OF SUBSTANTIVE VARIANTS. This list is a record of all variant substantive readings in the two editions authorized by Melville.[54] The

---

were centered, without parentheses, while the ones at 160.3, 171.4, 528.27, 535.5, and other places were centered, with parentheses; the directions at 167.3–4 and 527.3–7 (without parentheses) and 469.4–9 (with parentheses) were printed with the lines after the first indented, while those at 173.4–5, 175.5–6, and 175.31–32 (with parentheses) had the first line indented; and the directions at 177.21, 177.31, 177.34, 178.4, 178.19, and 472.8 (with the first letter uncapitalized) were attached to the characters' names, while those at 174.19, 175.2, 175.8, 175.19, 176.2, 176.9, 176.14, and other places (with the first letter capitalized) were printed separately below the names. Since no attempt is made in this edition to impose consistency on the accidentals of the text, the accidentals within the stage directions are not altered; but the formal presentation of the stage directions (including, besides the italic type and the centered position, the initial capital letter, the final period, and the enclosing parentheses), being nontextual, is regularized.

53. Except in the cases of words hyphenated at the ends of lines in the copy-text as well. These words, which also appear in the first list and are marked with daggers, are given in the forms which the present editors adopted but which are obscured by hyphenation at the ends of lines in this edition.

54. Such variants as "phrensied"/"frenzied" (286.11) or "calking"/"caulking" (526.14, 527.4) are considered accidentals whenever the 1848 Webster's or other contemporary dictionaries classify them as interchangeable forms of the same word—as are such equivalent forms as "Damn"/"D—n" (128.22). (However, spelling variants in the rendering of dialect are regarded as substantive and are listed; and such variants as "leach"/"leech" at xix.24 or "feign"/"fain" at 518.8, though actually only spelling variants, are included in this list because of the substantive differences that these spellings now signify.) Treated as a nontextual feature is the fact that the

left column gives the readings of the first American impression (preceded by Northwestern-Newberry readings when they emend those of the copy-text). The right column lists the English substantive readings that are at variance with the copy-text. Editions are designated by three symbols: A (American), E (English), and NN (Northwestern-Newberry). (Entries for pages 242–59 have a fourth symbol, H, referring to the *Harper's New Monthly Magazine* printing of "The Town-Ho's Story"; this symbol may appear in either column, depending on whether the magazine text agrees with the American or the English edition. In one instance—253.19—the magazine text differs from the reading of both editions.)

In these four lists readers have before them all the copy-text readings and all the substantive variations from those readings in the only other authorized edition. With the lists they can examine and reconsider for themselves the textual decisions for the present edition and in the process see more clearly the relationships between the texts of *Moby-Dick* available during Melville's lifetime and the one that is offered here as a more faithful representation of the author's intentions.

---

American edition numbered the chapters I–CXXXV and listed them in a single table of contents, whereas the English edition, in three volumes, numbered them I–XLI in the first, I–XLIV in the second, and I–XLIX in the third, with a separate table of contents in each volume. Furthermore, since the twenty-fifth chapter of the American edition was omitted in the English, each of the roman numerals in the first volume of the English edition from "XXV" on is one less than the numeral attached to the corresponding chapter in the American edition; the omission of Chapter 25 is of course reported in this list, but the resulting discrepancy in chapter numbers between the two editions is regarded as nontextual and is not recorded there.

# Discussions of Adopted Readings

I
N THESE COMMENTS on emendations and on decisions not
to emend, the following symbols are employed:

A   American Edition (1851)
E   English Edition (1851)
H   *Harper's New Monthly Magazine* (October, 1851)
NN  Northwestern-Newberry Edition

For commentary on special classes of textual decisions, see the NOTE
ON THE TEXT, pp. 780–804. Because *Moby-Dick* involves a large
number of problematical readings and because many of them are
touched on in the more general discussion in the NOTE ON THE TEXT,
the present section can also usefully serve as a kind of selective index
to that discussion; a number of references to the NOTE ON THE TEXT
are therefore included here. In these discussions, allusions to any pre-
1852 books that are listed in Merton M. Sealts, Jr., *Melville's Reading:
A Check-List of Books Owned and Borrowed* (Madison: University of
Wisconsin Press, 1966; rev. ed., Columbia: University of South Carolina Press, 1988) are provided with citations of Sealts numbers, and
discussions of Melville's sources are provided with reference num-

bers from Mary K. Bercaw, *Melville's Sources* (Evanston, Ill.: Northwestern University Press, 1987).

v.1  Moby-Dick]  The title of the book, as it appeared on the title page (and divisional title page) of A, contained the hyphen; but the name of the whale, in its many appearances within the body of the book, was not hyphenated in A (except once, commented on below). The title in E, of course, was *"The Whale,"* but the subtitle *"or, Moby Dick"* appeared on the half-title page, and the name had no hyphen there, or anywhere else in E. The question whether the hyphen should be retained in the title is not an easy one. The numerous occurrences of the unhyphenated "Moby Dick" within the text would seem to offer conclusive evidence that the name of the whale was not hyphenated in the manuscript and that Melville did not intend it to be hyphenated; but that fact does not automatically answer the question about the *title* of the book. As the HISTORICAL NOTE explains, the title page and divisional title page in A were set in type at a late stage, since the title was altered from *"The Whale"* only after the American proof sheets had already been sent to the English publisher; if it could be shown that the hyphenation of titles was a common practice among American publishers at this time, one would have a conceivable explanation for the presence of the hyphen and would have an additional factor to take into account in thinking about the form of the title. Certainly Melville's own writings provide examples of hyphenated titles—*White-Jacket, The Confidence-Man,* "The Bell-Tower"— though these other instances, because they are consistently hyphenated, do not present the same problem about whether or not to retain the hyphen. The hyphenated form of *"Moby-Dick"* does in fact exist in Melville's own hand, written on the back of his copy of the Bentley contract (it is reproduced in Harrison Hayford, "Contract: *Moby-Dick,* by Herman Melville," *Proof,* I [1971], 1–7); but the date of that inscription is not known and could be after the publication of the American edition, in which case the hyphenated form might simply be a reference to the title as published. Another possibility is that Melville's use of the hyphen was almost automatic, reflecting a tradition of hyphenated titles. It may be that Allan Melville (acting as his brother Herman's agent) was influenced by such a tradition when he gave the hyphenated form as the new title, in writing to the English publisher about the change; on the other hand, he may have been copying the form that appeared on the special title-page proof he was enclosing, but, if so, he was also giving tacit approval to the hyphenated title. (Whether or not Melville had actually seen that proof before Allan sent it off is not known.) One can easily find numerous books of this period with hyphenated titles, both in the Harpers' and other publishers' lists. Besides Hawthorne's *The Snow-Image* (1852), which springs immediately to mind, a few examples out of many are Joseph H. Ingraham's *The Clipper-Yacht* (1845), E. Z. C. Judson's *The Ice-King* (1848), Charles E. Averill's *The Cholera-Fiend* (1850), John H. Robinson's *Silver-Knife* (1850), Benjamin F. Tefft's *The Shoulder-Knot* (Harper, 1850), T. S. Arthur's *Heart-Histories and Life-Pictures* (1853), Orestes Brownson's *The Spirit-Rapper* (1854), George P. Burnham's *The Rag-Picker* (1855), Mary Jane Holmes's *Meadow-Brook* (1857), and Cornelia Huntington's *Sea-Spray* (1857). Of course, many similar titles were not hyphenated: the point is not that such hyphenation was invariable but simply that it occurred widely enough to represent a common and recognizable pattern. One should hesitate, in other words, to assume that the hyphenation of *"Moby-Dick"* resulted merely from carelessness on the part of a compositor (even though it is likely that the compositor was not one who had worked on the text, since the text was set at Craighead's and the title page— and some other preliminary pages—probably at the Harpers').

Taking all these matters into account, an editor has at least three reasons for retaining the hyphen in the title, despite the fact that it does not appear in the name "Moby Dick" in the text: (1) in the absence of a document revealing Melville's intention directly, the most authoritative documents are Allan's letter to Bentley, which contained the hyphenated form and enclosed the title-page proof, presumably with that form, and Melville's notation on the Bentley contract, which used the hyphenated form; (2) although the exact course of events that resulted in differences between the preliminaries in A and E cannot be reconstructed from the evidence now available, it seems clear—as the HISTORICAL NOTE shows—that the preliminaries in the American edition do represent Melville's intention and that the A readings should therefore be retained (as in the rest of the text) unless there is overwhelming evidence to the contrary; and (3) the practice of hyphenating titles was common enough that Melville may have intended the hyphenated form in the title in deference to this convention. NN, therefore, retains the hyphen in the title.

Certain practical consequences follow from this decision. One is obviously the fact that the title of the book can be distinguished from the name of the whale, even when the former is not italicized, by the presence or absence of the hyphen. The usefulness of this distinction can be illustrated by an often-cited sentence in "The Affidavit," in which the reader is told that landsmen "might scout at Moby Dick as a monstrous fable, or still worse and more detestable, a hideous and intolerable allegory" (205.26–28). If the name of the book and of the whale are not formally distinguishable (and book titles are not italicized in this text), this sentence is ambiguous. It is a fact, however, that Melville is speaking here only of the whale, not the book, for the book was not yet entitled *"Moby-Dick"* when this passage was written and set in type; retaining the hyphen in the title, leaving the unhyphenated form to denote the whale, resolves this ambiguity.

Another consequence of the decision to keep the hyphen in the title is that the one occurrence of that form within the A text must be emended to remove the hyphen, since the reference is to the whale itself. In the statement that the *Pequod* "bore down in the leeward wake of Moby Dick" (552.31), the whale's name was hyphenated in A (but not in E); possibly the compositor was somehow led to insert the hyphen because "Moby" fell at the end of a line, although in other such situations no hyphen was included (for example, the occurrences of "Moby Dick" at ·565.5 and 568.19 fell in A so that the two words were split by the end of the line). Although it is not the policy of NN to regularize accidentals when more than one form is acceptable, the interpretation of the hyphenated form as referring to the book makes the question in effect a substantive one: "Moby Dick" would mean the wrong thing here if the hyphen were allowed to remain. Besides, given the inconsistencies in punctuation that pervade the book, the lack of a hyphen in all the occurrences of "Moby Dick" except this one is a remarkable instance of regularity, which makes it all the more certain that this one hyphen is merely a slip.

A consideration of the general question of consistency in mid-nineteenth-century works, however, forces one to recognize, finally, that the hyphen on the title page and divisional title page in A—but not in the text—may mean nothing more than that consistency in such punctuation was not a matter of concern. The general NN policy of allowing inconsistent accidentals to stand (when they are not unquestionably in error) rests on the view that regularization often amounts to modernization. If the three occurrences in A of hyphens between the words "Moby Dick" (in the two titles and at 552.31) are regarded in this light—if, that is, it was a matter of no concern to Melville or anyone else whether the hyphens were present or not—then an unmodernized edition should leave them all as they are in the copy-text, and NN would be correct in leaving the hyphen in the titles and incorrect in deleting the one at 552.31. The whole matter is uncertain, but the unusually high degree of regularity in the form of "Moby Dick" in the text and the prominence of the hyphenated occurrence in the titles offer strong support for the distinction between book and whale that NN adopts. In any case, it follows that, if NN has erred, it has done so in deleting the hyphen at 552.31, not in retaining it in the title; and the prominence of the title inevitably makes an editor's decision about it of wider significance than that about any one particular spot in the text. Both practical and theoretical considerations, then, have converged in the NN decision to retain the hyphen in the title.

v.4  MELVILLE]  Beneath Melville's name on the title page (and beneath the listing—present in both A and E—of his five previous books, omitted in NN as a matter of design), E includes a five-line epigraph from *Paradise Lost,* whereas A has no epigraph. Since (as pointed out in the preceding discussion and explained more fully in the HISTORICAL NOTE) the preliminaries in A are more likely to represent Melville's intention than those in E, NN follows A in printing no title-page epigraph (this quotation from Milton appears in any case as the twenty-fourth of the "Extracts," xx.20–24). The presence of the epigraph in E could reflect either an earlier intention of Melville's or an attempt on Bentley's part to offer some kind of epigraph at the beginning of his edition as a compensation for moving the "Extracts" to the end.

vii.1–5   In token '... HAWTHORNE.]   See the HISTORICAL NOTE, pp. 673–74.

ix.1   *Contents*]   See the HISTORICAL NOTE, pp. 674–77.

x.17   *Specksynder*]   The A and E spelling "Specksynder", here and at 146.2, 146.11, and 146.15, no doubt results from Melville's use of William Scoresby, Jr., *An Account of the Arctic Regions* (Edinburgh, 1820), since Scoresby gives the same spelling. Although, as Leon T. Dickinson has pointed out (in *Melville Society Newsletter,* Spring, 1956), that spelling is an erroneous anglicization of the Dutch "speksnijder," NN retains it as an established English form. (Cf. Bercaw 616.)

xi.29   *Prairie*]   NN follows E in altering the A spelling "Praire" (here and at 345.2) to "Prairie" (it is also made italic to conform with NN style). Although a number of variant spellings of this word were current in the nineteenth century, "praire" does not appear to be one of them. Elsewhere in *Moby-Dick* the spelling "prairie" occurs sixteen times and "Praries" once (191.2)—the latter an acceptable variant that also appears in Melville's manuscript of his 1849 review of Francis Parkman's *The California and Oregon Trail* (see the NN *Piazza Tales* volume, p. 641, the discussion at 232.20).

xv.4–8   [The ... mortality.]]   The square brackets—present in E but not in A—around the introductory paragraphs to "Etymology" here and "Extracts" (xvii.3–xviii.5) are adopted not because of any particular authority that attaches to E in this respect but simply because some means needs to be found for making clear that these paragraphs are parenthetical comments on the Usher and the Sub-Sub-Librarian and not part of the actual contents of these sections. The solution in A, smaller type, might not be reproduced in future typesettings based on NN; the square brackets are another contemporary solution—whether Melville's or not—and seem a preferable way of solving the problem.

xv.10–13   "While ... Hackluyt.]   This passage accurately follows the wording of the quotation in Charles Richardson's entry for "whale" in *A New Dictionary of the English Language* (London, 1836–37; Philadelphia, 1846; also in *Encyclopædia Metropolitana),* the work cited just below, at xv.18

(where the quotation is also accurate in wording). Melville drew two further quotations from Richardson: those from Pliny (xviii.24–25) and from Spenser (xix.24–28).

xv.15　or rolling] In the 1848 Webster's the definition reads "or from rolling" at this point; but the copy-text omission of "from", whether intentional or not, is consistent with Melville's habit of abbreviated quotation and is not rectified.

xvi.1　תן ] The A and E reading, in which the Hebrew character on the right side is *he*, is almost certainly not what Melville wrote or intended to write. If Melville wrote only two Hebrew characters, he presumably meant the one on the right to be *tav*, forming (with *nun* in its terminal form on the left) the word that can be represented in roman characters as "tan," because this word was thought to mean "whale" by C. Hamilton Smith, author of the article on "Whale" (II, 947) in *A Cyclopædia of Biblical Literature*, ed. John Kitto (Edinburgh, 1845; New York, 1846), a book that Melville used. (Howard P. Vincent, in *The Trying-Out of MOBY-DICK* [Boston: Houghton Mifflin, 1949], says, "We need have no question that he knew the work fairly well" [p. 271].) The *tav* and *he* are similarly formed characters that could easily be confused by anyone unfamiliar with Hebrew. Therefore NN (following its policy of retaining forms and details that appear in Melville's sources) emends the Hebrew to the form cited in Kitto, assuming that Melville accepted it as the word for "whale" and meant it to appear here. (In fact, "tan" is not the word for "whale" but is the singular of "tanim," a word appearing in Scripture only in the plural and meaning "jackals." The error in Kitto perhaps resulted from a confusion of this plural "tanim" with the singular "tanim" or "tanin," which does refer to a beast that lives in water. In Ezekiel 29:3 and 32:2, the latter cited by Melville at 362.11–12, "tanim" is clearly a singular and is translated in the first instance as "dragon" ["that lieth in the midst of his rivers"] and in the second as "whale" ["in the seas"] in the King James Version; the plural "taninim" appears in Genesis 1:21, the first of Melville's "Extracts," and is translated as "whales" in the King James Version. Despite the ambiguity of "tanim" out of context, it would seem difficult for anyone familiar with the passages in Genesis and Ezekiel to conclude that "tan" is the singular of the words used there; to do so would require thinking that the occurrences in Ezekiel were plurals, despite the singular contexts, and that the word in Genesis contained an erroneously duplicated plural suffix. Hebrew dictionaries of the early nineteenth century regularly give "tanim" or "tanin," not "tan," as the singular for "whale"; see also the historical citations in the Ben Yehuda dictionary. Nevertheless, the Kitto volume was a standard reference in the nineteenth century, and many people besides Melville must have accepted unquestioningly its equation of "tan" with "whale.") Dorothee Metlitzki, in "The Letter 'H' in Melville's Whale" (*Melville Society Extracts*, No. 47 [September, 1981], 9) has suggested that Melville may have intended the *he* because he wished to emphasize the letter "H," which is commented on in the quotation from Hakluyt just above and which is traditionally used to stand for "Yahweh." (The resulting word, made up of *he* and *nun*, means "whether," "behold," "yes," or "them" or "those" [feminine], depending on the context.) It seems more likely, given the similar shapes of *tav* and *he* and the presence of *tav* in Kitto, that Melville meant to reproduce the two-character word (*tav* and *nun*) equated with "whale" in Kitto. (For another use of Kitto, see the discussion at 210.15.)

xvi.2 κητος] In A this word appears in a Greek typeface that has misled some readers. A number of commentators on *Moby-Dick* have believed that in A the first character is *chi* and that it therefore requires correction to *kappa*. The A reading in fact does begin with *kappa*—in a type design that is no longer conventional but that nevertheless has appeared in such standard editions as the Teubner series. Actually the third character has a much more unconventional design in A; yet it can represent no letter other than *tau*, the required one. NN prints this word in a more standard Greek typeface; but this shift is only a matter of typography, not an emendation, for the letters represented are still the same ones. (In E the second character, *eta*, is appropriately supplied with a circumflex; but given the frequent indifference to accents in nineteenth-century American nonscholarly usage [see the NOTE ON THE TEXT, p. 800, footnote 46], NN does not adopt it.)

xvi.4 WHÆL] The ligature in the A and E reading "WHŒL" is clearly in error and must be emended. Whether the first two letters should be reversed to produce the conventional Old English form "hwæl" is another matter, however: because Richardson's *Dictionary*—which Melville used (see the discussion at xv. 10–13)—contains the "whæl" spelling, it is kept here. (Similarly, at xvi.7, the "hwal" spelling is retained because it appears in Richardson, though the 1848 Webster's has "hval".)

xvi.5 HVAL] The erroneous A and E reading "HVALT" could have resulted from a slip of Melville's in copying from the 1848 Webster's, where Danish "hvalt" (meaning "arched" or "vaulted") is cited; but Webster's clearly shows "hval" as the Swedish and Danish word for "whale".

xvi.6 *Dutch*] I.e., "German", in then-current American (and earlier English) usage, as at 270.22 and 354.10. (At 351.6, however, the distinction is made between "the Dutch and Germans".) "Wal" is the German but not Dutch (Netherlandish) word for "whale".

xvi.8 HVALUR] The A and E reading "WHALE", which is not a possible Icelandic form, perhaps results from a slip by the A compositor, whose eye may have skipped to the next line of his copy, where "WHALE" properly appears. Conceivably Melville did think that "whale" was Icelandic, because the form "illwhale" appears on the same page (p. 130) of Uno von Troil's *Letters on Iceland* (London, 1780) as the passage quoted in the "Extracts" (xxii.23–27)—though this erroneous form was altered to "Illhwele" in the second (1780) and third (1783) editions of Troil, one of which Melville might have used instead of the first edition. There is no way to conjecture what form appeared in Melville's manuscript, but it seems unlikely that the form was "WHALE" (Melville apparently wished, after all, to represent a variety of words in this list). Under the circumstances, the best course seems to be to emend with the modern Icelandic word "hvalur".

xvi.12–13   PEKEE-NUEE-NUEE . . . *Erromangoan*.] Although "pekee-nuee-nuee" and "pehee-nuee-nuee" are not the terms for "whale" in the languages indicated, they are not emended since they are apparently Traders' Pidgin (or possibly Melville's own invention), obviously based on the Polynesian words usually transcribed "pihi" ("fish") and "nui" ("big")—but consistently spelled "pehee" and "nuee" in *Typee* and *Omoo*. Cf. Boniface Mosblech, *Vocabulaire océanien-français et français-océanien: Des dialectes parlés aux iles Marquises, Sandwich, Gambier, etc.* (Paris, 1843) and Captain Barnacle (i.e., Charles Martin Newell), *Leaves from an Old Log: Péhe Nú-e, the Tiger Whale of the Pacific* (Boston, 1877). (Since "pekee" is not the Polynesian equivalent of "pihi" and does not mean "fish," the question arises whether the "k" is a compositorial error; however, the likelihood that Melville wished to show two different words for these languages seems strong enough to warrant retaining the copy-text spelling.)

xviii.5   glasses!]]   Although the square bracket is supplied from E, the exclamation mark is retained from A (at this point E has a period). For comment on the brackets, see the discussion at xv.4–8.

xviii.9   Leviathan]   The substitution of "Leviathan" for "He" (the reading of the King James Bible at Job 41:32) can scarcely be regarded as a copyist's or compositor's error and must certainly be Melville's intentional change. (The other four quotations from the Bible correspond exactly to the wording of the King James Version at Genesis 1:21, Jonah 1:17, Psalms 104:26, and Isaiah 27:1. Cf. Sealts 60–62.)

xviii.19   And what thing]   In Philemon Holland's edition of Plutarch (London, 1603), the passage begins "and look what other thing" (p. 975; p. 799 of the revised edition of 1657); the omission in A and E of "look" and "other" does not alter the sense and is probably Melville's deliberate change to make the quotation less awkward when taken out of context. (Cf. Bercaw 559.)

xviii.24–25   as much in length]   As quoted in Melville's source, Charles

Richardson's *A New Dictionary of the English Language* (London, 1836–37; Philadelphia, 1846; also in *Encyclopædia Metropolitana*), the phrase in Pliny reads "in length as much"; the A and E reading "as much in length" does not change the meaning and is allowed to stand as an instance of Melville's approximate quotation (whereas the A and E reading "Balæne" in the same line is an outright error and is corrected to "Balænæ" to conform with the source). For other uses of Richardson, see the discussion at xv.10–13. (Cf. Bercaw 201, 229.)

xviii.26–30 "Scarcely . . . foam."] Melville's quotation exactly follows the wording of William Tooke's edition of Lucian (London, 1820), II, 94, except for two substitutions: "sea" for "deep" in "monsters of the sea", and "monstrous" for "enormous" in "a most monstrous size." Although the second could possibly have resulted from a misreading of Melville's manuscript, both could be intentional alterations on Melville's part; therefore both are retained. (Cf. Bercaw 458a.)

xix.1 this country] Robert Henry's *The History of Great Britain,* Volume II (London, 1774), reads "these parts" (p. 464). No correction is made, however, because "this country" appears in the quotation of this passage (p. 512) in J. Ross Browne's *Etchings of a Whaling Cruise* (New York, 1846), a work that Melville quotes from elsewhere (e.g., xxvi.12–25, xxviii.23–24). Browne's quotation refers to "Octher" and "Ochter" (Melville's "Other" is another permissible form) and states that Octher's "relation" was "written down from his mouth by King Alfred with his own hand." That Browne was in fact the source is also suggested by Melville's citation of the date 890, which does not occur in Henry but does appear in Browne, who derives it from Hakluyt (where the account is differently worded). (Cf. Sealts 88, Bercaw 82.)

xix.10 the sea-gudgeon] The substitution of "the sea-gudgeon" for "this little fish"—the reading at this point (p. 219) in William Hazlitt's *The Complete Works of Michel de Montaigne* (London, 1842)—cannot be inadvertent and was apparently made by Melville ("sea-gudgeon" occurs earlier in Montaigne's sentence), as was the addition of the opening "And". The insertion of "(whale's)" at xix.9 follows Melville's usual custom of employing parentheses where square brackets are now conventional. (Cf. Sealts 366, Bercaw 502.)

xix.12–13 "Let . . . Job."] In wording but not in punctuation, this extract accurately reproduces the sentence in Book IV, Chapter 33 (III, 312), in the John Miller edition of Rabelais (London, 1844), which is probably the one Melville used. (Cf. Sealts 417, Bercaw 574.)

xix.14 "This . . . loads."] Either Melville is paraphrasing the actual words that appear (on p. 1158) in John Stow's *Annales* (London, 1592) or he is quoting from a secondary source that paraphrased Stow. (Bercaw 201.)

xix.15    "The . . . pan."]    Melville's quotation accurately reproduces the wording from lines 91–92 of Bacon's version of Psalms 104:26 in *The Translation of Certaine Psalmes* (London, 1625), p. 15, except that it gives "maketh" for "makes" (perhaps an intentional change to produce an archaic effect). The quotation makes Bacon's verse appear to be prose by beginning with the fifth word of a couplet and not indicating the line break (after "Leviathan").

xix.18    exceeding]    In Bacon's *History Naturall and Experimentall of Life and Death* (London, 1638), this word appears as "exceedingly" (p. 69); Melville may have intentionally altered it to add to the archaic flavor (as with the shift from "makes" to "maketh" in the previous quotation, also from Bacon). Furthermore, Melville is joining together sentences from two places: the first sentence here is Item 48, the second Item 41, in the section entitled "Length, and Shortnesse of Life in living Creatures."

xix.21    is]    In Shakespeare's *1 Henry IV*, I.iii.58, the word is "Was" (it begins a new line). (The following quotation, from *Hamlet*, III.ii.382, is accurate. Cf. Sealts 460, Bercaw 634.)

xix.24–28    "Which . . . maine."]    In A and E, there are three substantive errors ("secure" for "recure"—an error that also occurs in the epigraph to "Sketch First" of "The Encantadas," NN *Piazza Tales* volume, 125.16— "lowly" for "lovely", and "thro'" for "from") in this passage from Spenser (VI.X.xxxi.5–9), which is quoted accurately in Melville's source, Charles Richardson's *A New Dictionary of the English Language* (London, 1836–37; Philadelphia, 1846; also in *Encyclopædia Metropolitana*); because these readings are not likely to have resulted from intentional changes on Melville's part, NN corrects them. (For other uses of Richardson, see the discussion at xv.10–13. Also see the NOTE ON THE TEXT, p. 795.)

xix.30–31    "Immense . . . boil."]    This quotation, from D'Avenant's *Works* (London, 1673), p. 16, is accurate in wording, though it is only a middle portion of a long sentence that runs eleven lines. (Cf. Sealts 176, Bercaw 192.)

xx.2    Hofmannus]    Since Melville's source was probably his own copy of the 1686 London edition of Browne's *Works,* containing *Pseudodoxia Epidemica* (p. 139)—the *"V.E."* (*"Vulgar Errors"*) of his citation—it is conceivable that he misread the *f* as a long *s* and wrote "Hosmannus", which appears in A and E. In any case, the man referred to is Caspar Hofmann, author of *De medicamentis officinalibus* (Paris, 1646). (Cf. Sealts 90, Bercaw 83.)

xx.5 iron] Apparently Edmund Waller's "iron" *(Poems,* London, 1664, p. 66) got changed to "modern" (the A and E reading) by a copyist or compositor: Melville's awareness—at least by 1855—that Spenser's Talus had threshed out falsehood with "an yron flale" *(Faerie Queene,* V.I.xii.9) is clear in his reference to Talus as an "iron slave" in "The Bell-Tower" (NN *Piazza Tales* volume, 184.10). It seems unlikely, therefore, that Melville was responsible for the misreading. (The 1664 edition of Waller's *Poems* is the first to contain the reading "Spenser's"; the original 1645 edition reads "fairy".)

xx.8 his] Melville changes Waller's feminine pronoun *(Poems,* London, 1664, p. 69) to masculine (here and in the two succeeding instances) so that it will agree with the pronouns in the first two lines quoted (in the original, forty lines intervene between these two couplets).

xx.13 *Opening*] Although this sentence (which in the original begins "For by art") is actually the fifth in Hobbes's "Introduction" to *Leviathan* (London, 1651), *"Opening"* is obviously the word Melville wrote and presumably meant (in the sense of "early" rather than "first"). (Cf. Bercaw 358.)

xx.14–15 "Silly . . . whale."] The wording here, except for an unmarked ellipsis (sixteen words) after "Mansoul", is an accurate quotation of the paraphrase of a passage from Bunyan's *The Holy War* (London, 1682), p. 42, made by Henry T. Cheever in *The Whale and His Captors* (New York, 1849), p. 70 (Bercaw 136). (In A, the citation is given incorrectly as *"Pilgrim's Progress";* the correct reference, *"Holy War",* which appears in E, was presumably marked on the proofs by Melville.)

xx.20–24 "There . . . sea."] In A and E, there are two substantive errors ("in" for "on" in the second line and "breath" for "trunk" in the fifth) in this passage from Milton (VII, 412–16), here corrected; see the NOTE ON THE TEXT, p. 795. The errors do not occur in the Hilliard, Gray edition of *The Poetical Works* (Boston, 1836), which Melville owned and annotated (his copy, with an 1849 signature, was in a New York Phillips auction on March 27, 1984 [see pp. 957–59 below], Sealts 358b); nor do they occur in the quotation of this passage in Henry T. Cheever's *The Whale and His Captors* (New York, 1849), p. 52, a book that may also have been Melville's source; cf. Bercaw 136. The previous quotation (I, 200–202) is accurate.

xx.26 which] The wording here agrees with that in the London 1841 edition of Thomas Fuller's *The Holy State, and the Profane State* (bk. 2, chap. 21, p. 123)—which is the edition cited by Sealts (221) as having been borrowed by Melville from Evert A. Duyckinck—although the first edition (Cambridge, 1642; bk. 2, chap. 20, p. 130) and the "second edition enlarged" (Cambridge, 1648; bk. 2, chap. 21, p. 122) read "who". (Cf. Bercaw 283.)

xx.28–31 "So . . . way."] This quotation of stanza 203 accurately follows the wording of the original (London, 1667), p. 52; the shift from
"t' attend" to "to attend", however, makes the meter less regular.

xxi.1–23 "While . . . *Coll.*] Although the citation in A and E for the first
(xxi.1–3) of these four extracts is *"Purchass"*, Melville's direct source was
obviously the Harris collection referred to in the citation for the next extract:
the wording of the extract does not correspond, except for a few phrases,
with that of the passage occurring in the London 1625 edition of *Purchas His
Pilgrimes* (III, 471), but it does correspond exactly (except that "feet" appears
in place of "foot") with the wording of the passage in John Harris's *Navigantium atque Itinerantium Bibliotheca; or, a Compleat Collection of Voyages and
Travels: Consisting of above Four Hundred of the Most Authentick Writers; Beginning with Hackluit, Purchass, &c. in English* . . . (London, 1705), I, 574 (Bercaw 323). The second (xxi.5–7) of these extracts exactly follows the wording
in Harris, I, 406 (the corresponding passage in Book I of the revised edition
of Thomas Herbert's *Some Yeares Travels into Divers Parts of Asia and Afrique*
[London, 1638], p. 13, is considerably different). The third extract (xxi.10–
12) also comes from Harris, though Melville's reference is only to William
Cornelius Schouten's circumnavigation; the quotation accurately reproduces the wording in Harris, I, 38, except that six words—"an incredible
number of Penguins, and"—are omitted following "saw". The fourth extract (xxi.13–21) from Harris consists of five sentences from different points
in the account of Friedrich Martens's voyage to Greenland (respectively,
from Harris, I, 617, 632, 631, 630, 629); all are accurate in wording except
that A and E replace "he" with "the whale" in the second sentence and
"Hitland" with "Shetland" in the fourth, and in the fifth they insert "that"
after "me" and alter "at" to "in". (Despite these differences, Melville is
following Harris, as his citation indicates, and not Martens's "Voyage into
Spitzbergen and Greenland . . . Anno 1671" in *An Account of Several Late
Voyages & Discoveries to the South and North* [London, 1694], compiled by
Tancred Robinson, because the corresponding sentences in the Robinson
volume—on pp. 1, 165, 158, 142, and 135—are substantially different from
the sentences Melville quotes.) Of the variations between these extracts and
Harris, there are only two that are difficult to regard as possibly intentional
alterations by Melville. One is the A and E reading "feet"; if Melville had
changed "foot" to "feet", he would presumably have added "of" as well,
since it is not idiomatic to say "twelve or thirteen feet water". The other is
the A and E reading "Shetland" for "Hitland"; there is no change of meaning involved, and it seems more likely that "Shetland" resulted from a misreading of handwriting (Melville's looped *H* resembles *Sh*) than that Melville deliberately altered the word to the more familiar form. NN thus
restores "foot" and "Hitland". (For Melville's other uses or citations of

Harris's book that raise textual questions, see the discussions at 262.2–4, 339.2, 366.5, and 458.6–19; in fact, Melville made use of all but three of the eleven page-references to whales in Harris's index. Cf. Bercaw 323 and John M. J. Gretchko, "New Evidence for Melville's Use of John Harris in *Moby-Dick*," *Studies in the American Renaissance*, 1983, 303–11.)

xxi.24–27 "Several . . . Pitfirren."] The word "(Fife)" does not appear in Robert Sibbald's *The History, Ancient and Modern, of the Sheriffdoms of Fife and Kinross* (Edinburgh, 1710), Part IV, Chapter 1, p. 119, and is another example (cf. xix.9, xxviii.15) of Melville's insertion of an explanatory word within parentheses. Otherwise the extract in A and E is accurate in wording. Three probably inadvertent differences in spelling—"feet" for "foot", "besides" for "beside", and "Pitferren" for "Pitfirren"—are here corrected to the forms found in the original. (Cf. Bercaw 642.)

xxi.29–33 "Myself . . . 1668.] Melville's text differs at several points from "An Extract of a Letter. Written to the Publisher from the Bermudas by Mr. Richard Stafford," dated July 16, 1668, and published in the October 19, 1668, number of the *Philosophical Transactions* of the Royal Society (III, 792–95): aside from an omission ("with about 20 more") after "Myself", these differences consist of "I" (in the first line) for "we", "this Sperma-ceti whale" for "them", "was" for "were", and "his" for "their". Melville's source was probably Thomas Beale's *The Natural History of the Sperm Whale* (London, 1839)—where this passage is quoted as it appears in the original, except that Beale gives "and about twenty others" for "with about 20 more" and "was" for "were" (p. 137)—or J. Ross Browne's *Etchings of a Whaling Cruise* (New York, 1846), which quotes it (p. 521) from Beale. (Cf. Sealts 52, 88, and Bercaw 51, 82.) The misspelling of Stafford's name as "Strafford" in A and E is here corrected.

xxi.34–35 "Whales . . . obey."] This extract is an accurate quotation from page 13 of Melville's own copy of the *New England Primer* (Worcester, [183–?]), in which his signature is dated March 6, 1851. (Cf. Sealts 384, Bercaw 517.)

xxii.1–3 "We . . . us."] After the A and E reading "those" in the first line is corrected to "these", this passage corresponds exactly in substantives (except for an omission of eighteen words after "also") to the passage in the section on William Ambrosia Cowley's voyage (1683–86) in William Hacke's *A Collection of Voyages* (London, 1729), p. 6—included in William Dampier's *A Collection of Voyages*, Volume IV, section 2. (These collections originally appeared in 1699, but Melville's citation of 1729 indicates that he used the 1729 edition. Cf. Bercaw 187a.)

xxii.5–6 "and . . . brain."] Melville's passage appears to be his own construction based on the phrase "an insupportable smell" (referring to a fish called "cope"), which occurs on page 332 of the second volume of the English translation of Antonio de Ulloa's *A Voyage to South-America* (London, 1758). (Cf. the discussion at 401.18–19 and Bercaw 725.)

xxii.11   stiff]   The A reading "stuffed" is erroneous; NN follows E in restoring Pope's original reading of line 120 in Canto 2 (London, 1714, p. 17). See the NOTE ON THE TEXT, p. 795.

xxii.13–15   "If . . . creation."]   Apart from one substitution (the third "in" for "by"), this extract is an accurate quotation of the openings of the first and fourth paragraphs in the section "Of the Whale" in *Goldsmith's History of the Earth and Animated Nature, Abridged . . . by Mrs. Pilkington* (London: Vernor, Hood, & Sharpe, 1807), pp. 293–94. For Melville's reference to "the abridged London edition of 1807", see the discussion at 262.22. (The section on whales is not included in the other London abridgment of 1807, *An Abridgment of Dr. Goldsmith's Natural History of Beasts and Birds*, published by Scatcherd & Letterman.)

xxii.17–18   "If . . . whales."]   This statement is a paraphrase of the comment reported by Boswell in the April, 1773, section of *The Life of Samuel Johnson, LL.D.* (London, 1835), III, 274. (Cf. Sealts 84, Bercaw 72.)

xxii.19–22   "In . . . us."]   The wording here is not an exact quotation from James Cook's entry for September 3, 1778, in *A Voyage to the Pacific Ocean* (London, 1784), II, 473, but is another example of Melville's use of paraphrase: for example, "supposed to be" is substituted for "first taken for", "was found" for "proved", and "were then towing" for "were dragging".

xxii.23–27   "The . . . approach."]   The second sentence, after "limestone" is emended to "brim-stone", follows the wording of Uno von Troil's Letter XII in his *Letters on Iceland* (London, 1780), p. 130; but the first sentence is a rearrangement of the earlier part of the preceding sentence in Troil.

xxii.30–33   "The . . . 1788.]   The wording of the extract follows exactly—except for an omission of fifty-one words after "Nantuckois"—the text in *Memoir, Correspondence, and Miscellanies from the Papers of Thomas Jefferson,* ed. Thomas Jefferson Randolph (Charlottesville, 1829; also 2d ed., Boston, 1830), II, 398 (and II, 401, in the 1829 London edition). The date, erroneously given in A and E as 1778, is corrected in NN.

xxiii.1   "And . . . it?"]   This sentence follows accurately the wording of *The Speech of Edmund Burke, Esq; on Moving His Resolutions for Conciliation with the Colonies, March 22, 1775* (London, 1775), p. 13. But the fact that Melville's quotation does not capitalize "sir" suggests that his source was either Thomas Beale's reprinting of a passage from this speech in *The Natu-*

*ral History of the Sperm Whale* (London, 1839), p. 142, or J. Ross Browne's excerpt from Beale in *Etchings of a Whaling Cruise* (New York, 1846), p. 524 (both of which wrongly assign the speech to 1774). (Cf. Sealts 52, 88, Bercaw 51, 82.)

xxiii.4 "Spain . . . Europe."] Melville's wording does not exactly correspond to that in either (1) the translated reminiscences of the Duc de Lévis, *England at the Beginning of the Nineteenth Century* (London, 1815), which describes Burke as saying, in a debate on the French Revolution, "Spain is like a whale cast on the sea shore" (p. 310), or (2) James Prior's quotation from Lévis in his *Memoir of the Life and Character of the Right Hon. Edmund Burke* (London, 1824), where Burke's description of Spain ends with the words "a whale stranded upon the sea-shore of Europe" (p. 529; enlarged edition, London, 1826, II, 471). (This speech has not been identified with any of Burke's printed speeches.) If Melville drew directly on either of these sources, he is paraphrasing or remembering inexactly; Prior is the more likely possibility because he uses the verb "stranded" and specifies "Europe". Melville may, of course, be quoting exactly from still another source—one that may have been even less precise in identifying the speech, as his vague citation ("somewhere") suggests.

xxiii.9 coasts] The A and E reading "coast", if not a slip on Melville's part, is probably a compositorial misreading of his handwriting, because "coasts" is what appears in William Blackstone's *Commentaries on the Laws of England*, Book I (Oxford, 1765), p. 280 (chap. 8, sec. X), and later editions. For other uses of Blackstone, see the discussions at 399.3, 401.13, and 401.18–19.

xxiii.11–13 "Soon . . . attends."] These lines correspond in wording to lines 71 and 75–76 in Canto 2 of William Falconer's *The Shipwreck* (London, 1762); the same three lines are quoted by Joseph C. Hart in *Miriam Coffin* (New York, 1834), II, 78, presumably Melville's source in one of its editions; see the discussion at 135.10.

xxiii.15–22 "Bright . . . joy."] In A and E, there are three substantive errors ("blew" for "flew", "fire" for "fires", and "Around" for "Amid"— all emended in NN) in these stanzas (lines 13–20) from Cowper's "On the Queen's Visit to London, the Night of the 17th March, 1789," first published in William Hayley's *The Life, and Posthumous Writings, of William Cowper* (London, 1803), pp. 326–27. See also the NOTE ON THE TEXT, p. 795. (Cf. Sealts 161 for an unidentified edition of Cowper; Bercaw 177.)

xxiii.24–25 "Ten . . . velocity."] In John Hunter's "Observations on the Structure and Oeconomy of Whales," *Philosophical Transactions* of the Royal Society, LXXVII (1787), 371–450, the sentence reads "thrown out at one stroke, and moved with an immense velocity" (p. 416). The extract, however, exactly reproduces the wording in William Paley's account in Chapter 10 of his *Natural Theology* (London, 1802), p. 166, except that "an" appears in Paley after "with". Since the next extract comes from the same passage in Paley (pp. 165–66), it seems certain that Paley was Melville's source for this extract also. (Cf. Bercaw 537.)

xxiii.32  "The . . . feet."]  This statement may be a paraphrase of the statement in Georges Cuvier's *The Animal Kingdom*, Volume IV, *The Class Mammalia* (London, 1827): "The Cetacea are mammiferous animals without hind feet" (p. 429), or it may paraphrase the one in the *Penny Cyclopædia* (London, 1843), in its article on "Whales" (see the discussion at 136.23–31), which reads, "Cuvier defines the Cetaceans to be mammiferous animals without posterior feet" (XXVII, 273). (Cf. Sealts 171, Bercaw 186, 544.)

xxiv.1–2  "In . . . them."]  This sentence, from James Colnett's entry for May 1, 1793, in his *A Voyage to the South Atlantic* (London, 1798), pp. 28–29, is quoted exactly, except that five words ("when we made the Isle") are omitted following "May". (Cf. Bercaw 154.)

xxiv.5–17  "In . . . Flood.]  This extract in A and E corresponds in wording to Canto 2, lines 22–24, 26–28, 37–42, of the title poem of James Montgomery's *The Pelican Island and Other Poems* (London, 1827), pp. 17–18, except for three differences: "Had" for "Hath", "Gather'd" for "Others", and "instincts" for "instinct". The first two of these readings are not emended, since they are obviously intentional and appear in Melville's source, Henry T. Cheever's *The Whale and His Captors* (New York, 1849), p. 128, where precisely the same lines from Montgomery are quoted. In the third instance, however, the original reading "instinct" is restored, since Cheever quotes it accurately and since the *s* probably resulted from a slip of Melville's pen or a misreading of his handwriting. The citation in A and E, "*World before the Flood*", is incorrect, but the same citation appears in Cheever. Because Melville accepted Cheever's attribution (and perhaps was influenced in his selection of this extract by the suggestiveness of the title), it is retained here. (Cf. Bercaw 136.) See also the NOTE ON THE TEXT, p. 797.

xxiv.18–23  "Io . . . Sea."]  These lines, the opening six lines of Lamb's "The Triumph of the Whale," correspond in wording to the text as first published in the *Examiner* for March 15, 1812 (No. 220, p. 173) and reprinted in *The Poetical Recreations of The Champion,* ed. John Thelwall (London, 1822), p. 197. (Cf. Sealts 315, 316, Bercaw 430, 431.)

xxiv.25–28  "In . . . bread."]  Except for omissions following "1690" and "hill", Melville's extract accurately follows the wording of this sentence as it appears in Obed Macy's *The History of Nantucket* (Boston, 1835), p. 33, and as it is quoted in J. Ross Browne's *Etchings of a Whaling Cruise* (New York, 1846), p. 518. (Cf. Sealts 88, 345, Bercaw 82, 469.)

xxiv.32–33 "She . . . ago."] This quotation corresponds to the sentence in Hawthorne's "Chippings with a Chisel," in the second volume of *Twice-Told Tales* (Boston, 1842), p. 245, except that "She" has been substituted for "An elderly lady" and "ago" for "before". (The preceding quotation, from Hawthorne's "The Village Uncle" in the same volume, p. 112, is accurate in wording. Cf. Sealts 258–60, Bercaw 341.)

xxv.1–3 "No . . . fellow!"] Except for the capitalizing of "Sir" and "Right Whale", this passage is accurately quoted from Chapter 17 of James Fenimore Cooper's *The Pilot* (New York, 1823), I, 230. (Cf. Bercaw 167.)

xxv.4–5 "The . . . there."] The entry for January 31, 1830, in J. P. Eckermann's *Conversations with Goethe,* as translated by Margaret Fuller (Boston, 1839), p. 336, agrees with Melville's wording, except that "papers" reads "newspapers" and "whales" reads "whales and sea-monsters". Cf. Bercaw 235 and Harrison Hayford, "Melville's German Streak," in *A Conversation in the Life of Leland R. Phelps,* ed. Frank L. Borchardt and Marion C. Salinger (Durham, N.C.: Duke University Center for International Studies, 1987), pp. 11–12.

xxv.10 *Sperm Whale*] The title of the original reads "Spermaceti-Whale" at this point, but Melville apparently shortened the phrase, and no emendation is made. Otherwise the title quoted here corresponds exactly in wording to the first ten lines of the original title page, except that the words "Most Extraordinary and Distressing" are omitted before "Shipwreck". (The extract itself is also identical in wording to the corresponding passage in Chase, p. 25.) Cf. Sealts 134, Bercaw 130, and the discussions at 206.31–32, 206.35–39, 569.8–11, and pp. 971–95, below.

xxv.13 on] In Elizabeth Oakes Smith's *Poetical Writings* (New York, 1845), the opening line of "The Drowned Mariner" (p. 186) reads "on the shrouds" rather than "in the shrouds" (the A and E reading); although it is possible that Melville changed the wording, the confusion of "in" and "on" in his handwriting was common enough that he may well have quoted exactly at this point, and "in" is here emended to "on". (In the last line, however, there is no reason to suppose that a misreading of the handwriting accounts for the shift from "he" to "it", and the "it" is retained as an intentional change of Melville's.)

xxv.19–23 "The . . . miles."] As the asterisks suggest, the two statements are taken from different parts of William Scoresby, Jr., *An Account of the Arctic Regions with a History and Description of the Northern Whale-Fishery* (Edinburgh, 1820)—the first from Volume II (pp. 281–82), the second from Volume I (p. 468). The wording of both is accurate, except that for "of this one whale" the original reads "was singularly great. It", and for "three or four" the original reads "two or three". As remarked by Wilbur S. Scott,

Jr., "Melville, in the interest of impressing the reader, exaggerates the figures" ("Melville's Originality: A Study of Some of the Sources of *Moby-Dick*," Ph.D. dissertation, Princeton University, 1943, p. 3). (Cf. Sealts 450, Bercaw 615.)

xxv.25–xxvi.2 "Mad . . . habitudes."] The wording of the first sentence—from page 165 of Beale's *The Natural History of the Sperm Whale* (London, 1839)—is accurate, except that "agonies" originally read "agony which", "Sperm Whale" read " 'sea beast' ", "jaws" read "jaw", an unmarked ellipsis occurs after "over", and "around him" read simply "around"; the second sentence (from page 33) is accurate, except for the insertion of the parenthetical phrase "(as the Sperm Whale)". Of these differences, the only one that appears to be unintentional is "jaws", which is therefore corrected to "jaw". (Cf. Sealts 52, Bercaw 51.)

xxvi.4–9 "The . . . tribe."] In this instance Melville places his explanatory phrases (in parentheses) outside the quotation marks (cf. xix.9, xxi.24, xxviii.15–17, 425.1); the quoted material, as printed in A and E, follows accurately the wording of Bennett's *Narrative of a Whaling Voyage round the Globe* (London, 1840), II, 213, except that "on the other hand" (obviously inappropriate when the passage is taken out of context) is omitted after "Cachalot", "enormous" is omitted in the phrase "of its enormous body", and "those weapons" appears as "these weapons". The last of these differences probably resulted from a misreading of Melville's handwriting, and "these" is here emended to "those". (Cf. Bercaw 60.)

xxvi.18 shoal] The word at this point in the original is "school"; while "shoal" could possibly be a misreading of Melville's handwriting, "shoal" was an established expression in connection with whales (used by Melville at 206.21 and 386.38, for instance) and may be his intentional substitution. In other respects the wording of this passage follows the source (New York, 1846), p. 115. (See also the NOTE ON THE TEXT, p. 796. Cf. Sealts 88, Bercaw 82.)

xxvi.28 Whale-ship] The word is simply "ship" in William Lay and Cyrus M. Hussey's *A Narrative of the Mutiny, on Board the Ship Globe* (New London, Conn., 1828), p. 11. On the title page the authors are described as "The only Survivors from the Massacre of the Ship's Company by the Natives." NN clarifies the A reading "*Lay and Hussey survivors*" (xxvi.31) by following E in supplying a comma after "*Hussey*". (Cf. Sealts 323, Bercaw 437.)

xxvi.32–35 "Being . . . inevitable."] This extract follows the wording of the *Journal of Voyages and Travels by the Rev. Daniel Tyerman and George Bennet, Esq.,* ed. James Montgomery (London, 1831, p. 4; Boston, 1832, p. 3), except for the unmarked omission of eleven words after "boat" ("and with one crash of its jaws bit it in two") and of "his" before "comrades". (Cf. Bercaw 724.)

xxvii.1–4 "Nantucket . . . industry."] The only discrepancy in wording between the extract and the original printing of the report of Webster's speech of May 2, 1828, in *Speeches and Forensic Arguments* (Boston, 1830), p. 435, is that the extract omits "amount of" before "National" at xxvii.4.

xxvii.9 *as*] The lengthy title citation of Cheever's book (New York, 1849) is precise except for the omission of *"as"* before *"gathered"*. (Cf. Bercaw 136.) Such precision is unusual enough in Melville's citations to suggest that an exact transcription was intended in this instance; hence *"as"* is restored here. (The extract itself is an exact quotation from page 151 of Cheever.)

xxvii.11–12 "If . . . hell."] This quotation accurately reproduces the statement on page 80 of *The Life of Samuel Comstock* (Boston, 1840) and on page 21 of the abridged edition (Boston, 1845); the 1840 edition was probably Melville's source since its title page names William Comstock as the author and identifies him as Samuel's brother. Cf. Bercaw 156c, 157, and F. DeWolfe Miller, "Another Chapter in the History of the Great White Whale," in *Melville and Hawthorne in the Berkshires,* ed. Howard P. Vincent (Kent, Ohio: Kent State University Press, 1968), pp. 109–17. See also Joel Myerson, "Comstock's White Whale and *Moby-Dick*," *American Transcendental Quarterly*, No. 29 (Winter, 1976), 8–27.

xxvii.15–17 "The . . . whale."] The extract corresponds exactly to the passage in John Ramsay McCulloch's *A Dictionary, Practical, Theoretical, and Historical, of Commerce and Commercial Navigation* (London, 1832), p. 1110— and to the quotation from this work in J. Ross Browne's *Etchings of a Whaling Cruise* (New York, 1846), p. 514, Melville's probable source. (Cf. Sealts 88, Bercaw 82.)

xxvii.19–22 "These . . . Passage."] The structure and phrasing of this passage show that it is a direct extension of the preceding quotation. But it does not appear in McCulloch following that earlier quotation, and presumably—as is hinted by the citation *"From 'Something' unpublished"*—it was written by Melville himself to develop a point suggested by McCulloch's statement. Establishing a critical text of this "extract," therefore—in contrast to the situation with all the other extracts except possibly one (xxviii.1–5)—does not involve comparison with a source beyond the A and E texts, which in this case are identical. For similar instances of Melville's citing passages of his own composition, see the discussions at xxviii.5, 10.23–28, 142.35–38, and 401.18–19 and in *Billy Budd, Sailor,* ed. Harrison Hayford and Merton M. Sealts, Jr. (Chicago: University of Chicago Press, 1962), note to leaf 127 (p. 161).

xxvii.25   mast-heads]   In the chapter "Currents and Whaling" in Charles Wilkes's *Narrative of the United States Exploring Expedition* (Philadelphia, 1844, V, 526; 1845, V, 496) and in one of Melville's source books, J. Ross Browne's *Etchings of a Whaling Cruise* (New York, 1846), p. 559, this word is singular. But the plural form, present in A and E, may have been Melville's alteration to make the expression more idiomatic (in Chapter 35 he repeatedly refers to "mast-heads"); and there is strong evidence that he gave attention to this extract in proof (the correction at xxvii.24 of "near" to "mere" in E). (Cf. Sealts 88, 532, Bercaw 759, 82.)

xxvii.32   *Whale*]   The actual title of Robert P. Gillies's book (London, 1826) does not include the word "Whale", which was evidently inserted by Melville to emphasize the relevance of the book to whaling. (The quoted passage, from II, 316, is accurate in wording.) (Cf. Bercaw 292.)

xxviii.5   *Hobomock*]   The A and E reading *"Hobomack"* is apparently a reference to the Falmouth ship *Hobomok*, but no such mutiny took place on board that ship. Wilson L. Heflin, in "Herman Melville's Whaling Years" (Ph.D. dissertation, Vanderbilt University, 1952), p. 224, suggests that Melville's mistaken allusion here and in *Typee* (NN27.9)—where the name is spelled "Hobomak"—can be explained as "a hazy recollection in later years which resulted in the unwitting synthesis of elements in two very similar narratives" that Melville must have known about: (1) the fight on October 5, 1835, between some Namorik Island natives and the crew of the Falmouth ship *Awashonks*, on which Silas Jones (captain of the *Hobomok* in 1841 when Melville's ship, the *Acushnet*, met it) served as third mate (see Heflin, pp. 210–18); (2) the fight on November 6, 1842, between some Kingsmill Islanders among the crew of the Fairhaven ship *Sharon* and the crew members who returned in the boats to find those natives in control of the ship (see Heflin, pp. 218–24). Heflin, after a thorough investigation of the problem, concludes that the *"Newspaper Account"* must therefore be "a piece of Melville's invention" (p. 224). As such, it need not be factually accurate (cf. the discussion at xxvii.19–22), and there would seem to be insufficient reason for altering *"Hobomack"* to *"Awashonks"* or *"Sharon"* (both of which Melville may have had in mind). The spelling "Hobomack" is a different matter, however. Because Melville is referring to a real ship, the *Hobomok*, and because his *o* and *a* are sometimes indistinguishable, he may well have written "Hobomock" (which would have the same pronunciation as "Hobomok"), not "Hobomack". NN emends the *a* to *o* but retains the *c*, which is presumably what Melville wrote and which produces what may be considered an acceptable variant spelling of the ship's name. (If Melville's reference were to the evil deity of the Indians rather than to the ship named for it, one could argue that "Hobomack" would be an allowable spelling, because the deity's name was rendered in a great variety of ways, including "Hobomoko", "Hobbamock", and "Abamacho", according to the *Dictionary of American English*. These renderings actually form a family of related names, not simply variant spellings; but there is no question what the ship's name is, and there is accordingly less latitude in acceptable variant spellings of it.)

xxviii.7 (American)] In the opening sentence of James A. Rhodes's *A Cruise in a Whale Boat* (New York, 1848), the word "American" does not appear; the A and E reading is an example of Melville's practice of enclosing insertions in parentheses.

xxviii.9–10 "Suddenly . . . whale."] The wording of this quotation accurately follows Joseph C. Hart's novel, II, 156 (1834 edition), except for an unindicated ellipsis of three words ("with inconceivable velocity") following "perpendicularly". *("Fisherman" in the citation in A and E is corrected to "Fishermen".)* (Cf. Bercaw 325.) The wording is the same in each of the three editions (New York, 1834; New York and London, 1835; and New York, 1835). See the discussion at 135.10.

xxviii.12 Whale] The word in Melville's source—"A Chapter on Whaling" in *Ribs and Trucks, from Davy's Locker . . . by W.A.G.* (Boston, 1842), p. 13—is "prize", and his substitution of "Whale" was obviously intended to make the passage clearer when taken out of context. (Cf. Bercaw 752b.)

xxviii.15–18 "On . . . branches."] The wording of this passage accurately follows that in the New York 1846 printing of Darwin's *Journal of Researches into the Natural History and Geology of the Countries Visited during the Voyage of H.M.S. Beagle round the World* (I, 288), except for Melville's two explanatory insertions—which illustrate two of the ways he handled such insertions: both are in parentheses, but one, "(whales)", is placed within the quoted passage, while the other, "(Terra Del Fuego)", is placed outside the quotation marks. His citation matches the wording on the binding of the 1846 printing ("*Voyage of a Naturalist Round the World*"). (Cf. Sealts 175, Bercaw 191.)

xxviii.19–22 " 'Stern . . . *Killer.*] In this quotation from Harry Halyard's *Wharton the Whale-Killer!* (Boston, 1848), p. 40, the wording is accurate, except that the exclamation in the third line begins " 'Stern all hands" in the original. While the omission of "hands" in A and E may have been inadvertent (prompted by the occurrence of "Stern all" two lines earlier), it is also conceivable that Melville intentionally left the word out, so the A and E reading is retained. From the title Melville himself also probably omitted the hyphen and exclamation mark.

xxviii.23–25 "So . . . *Song.*] As quoted in J. Ross Browne's *Etchings of a*

*Whaling Cruise* (New York, 1846), p. 17, these lines do not begin with "So", "may" appears instead of "let", and the couplet is called a "toast" and not attributed to a *"Nantucket Song"*; on page 78 of that volume, however, in a longer quotation from "Captain Bunker," the first of these lines has the same wording as A and E, but the second reads "a striking of" for "striking". Each of these lines, therefore, corresponds in wording to one of the quotations in Browne. (See also the discussion at 173.13–22 and Stuart M. Frank, " 'The King of the Southern Sea' and 'Captain Bunker': Two Songs in *Moby-Dick,"* *Melville Society Extracts,* No. 63 [September, 1985], 4–7. Cf. Sealts 88, Bercaw 82.)

xxviii.26–30  "Oh . . . *Song.*]  Like the preceding extract, this quotation occurs in a book Melville drew on frequently; this one is from Henry T. Cheever's *The Whale and His Captors* (New York, 1849). (Cf. Bercaw 136.) Except for three differences in punctuation and capitalization, it exactly corresponds to the passage quoted on Cheever's title page; but Cheever provides no such identification as *"Whale Song".* It also corresponds in wording to the refrain of "The King of the Southern Sea" as printed in *The Sailors' Magazine,* XVI (December, 1843), 129—a source that Melville may have been familiar with, as Stuart M. Frank has pointed out (see his article cited in the preceding discussion).

5.13  own brother]  NN follows E in supplying "make him the" before "own", judging the revision to be Melville's. However, the use of "own" as in A, without a preceding article or possessive, is reported by the *Oxford English Dictionary*. Cf. "as if she were own daughter of Nebuchadnezzar," in "I and My Chimney" (NN *Piazza Tales* volume, 362.1).

6.35–36  winds from astern . . . Pythagorean]  The low pun in this sailor/ officer context, referring to the high-minded philosopher's injunction to his disciples not to use beans (because of a body/soul effect), is an early occurrence in *Moby-Dick* of Melville's more or less covert peppering of its text fore-and-aft with often indecorous word-play that switches valuation of the topic in hand back and forth, between the "low" and "high" verbal, social, or conceptual levels (or all three). Sometimes the effect is deflation, as here; sometimes elevation, as in "Rose-bud" at 402.2 (see the discussion); and sometimes conflation, as in "archbishoprick" at 420.15. See the discussion of *"Roast beef . . . over spiritual man",* p. 965 below. See also the note at 5.10 in the Hendricks House edition of *Moby-Dick* (New York, 1952), and Harrison Hayford, " 'Loomings': Yarns and Figures in the Fabric," in *Artful Thunder: Versions of the Romantic Tradition in American Literature in Honor of Howard P. Vincent,* ed. Robert J. DeMott and Sanford E. Marovitz (Kent, Ohio: Kent State University Press, 1975), pp. 119–37. Study of esoteric tissues of meaning in *Moby-Dick,* including Pythagorean and many other interwoven strands, has been carried furthest and most suggestively by Viola Sachs and members (especially Janine Dove and Dominique Marçais) of her ongoing seminars in structures of the American imagination. Her earlier publications are subsumed in *The Game of Creation: The Primeval Unlettered Language of MOBY-DICK; OR, THE WHALE* (Paris: Editions de la Maison des sciences de l'homme, 1982).

7.1  But wherefore]  Probably through oversight, there is no paragraph break at this point in A or E, although a new topic begins: Ishmael has given his final reason for always going to sea as a common sailor and turns here to consider why this time he went not on a merchantman but on a whaling ship. The normally expected paragraph break is not supplied by NN because its omission does not alter the sense, though it obscures the structure of the chapter. See the discussions at 42.30, 121.8, 123.10, 137.18, 284.19, and 365.18.

7.14  shabby part]  This is a misleading cue: the whaling voyage in *Moby-Dick,* as George Stewart points out, "is notable for its lack of shabbiness and for its approach to both epic and tragic grandeur." He conjectures that this passage was part of the "Ur-*Moby-Dick*" before the "transformation of a whaling voyage from something shabby into something magnificent" ("The Two *Moby-Dicks,*" *American Literature,* XXV [January, 1954], 425).

10.5  out-hanging]  See the NOTE ON THE TEXT, p. 791. (The hyphen fell at the end of a line in E and is retained in NN.)

10.23–28  "In . . . glazier."]  This "quotation," which Melville attributes to "an old writer" (10.23–24)—"old black-letter" (10.29)—is presumably altogether his own invention, as indicated by the words "of whose works I possess the only copy extant", and its text therefore cannot be verified by any source outside the A and E readings, which are identical. (Cf. the discussions at xxvii.19–22, xxviii.5, 142.35–38, and 401.18–19.)

13.19  handle,]  NN supplies the comma (absent in A and E) necessary to make clear that the participial phrase introduced by "sweeping" does not modify "handle" but "one"—i.e., the "sickle-shaped" weapon, not just its vast handle.

14.13  gulph]  This unusual form (emended to "gulp" in E) is recorded in the *Oxford English Dictionary* and occurs in Thomas Beale's *The Natural History of the Sperm Whale* (London, 1839), p. 391, one of Melville's most frequently used source books. (Cf. Sealts 52, Bercaw 51.) The word "engulphed" occurs below at 47.36–37 and also in a comic piece "The New Planet," in *Yankee Doodle* (1847), attributed to Melville in the NN *Piazza Tales* volume, at 446.4.

15.1  green box coat]  Labeled obsolete by the *Dictionary of American Eng-*

*lish*, "box coat" is defined as "a heavy overcoat, or one with a cape, formerly worn by coachmen on the box." The color green here suggests that this inconsequent detail is an instance of the private allusions characteristic of Melville's writing (see the discussion at 33.7–10 and others cited there). His own "*green* jacket"—evidently shorter and lighter—is mentioned (with "green" underlined in reference to his newly published *White-Jacket*) in a letter to Evert A. Duyckinck, March 7, 1850; the reference is annotated by Merrell R. Davis and William H. Gilman in *The Letters of Herman Melville* (New Haven and London: Yale University Press, 1960), p. 106: "Melville had taken the jacket to England with him in 1849 and worn it regularly, but even before he left the *Southampton* to go to London someone dropped him a 'mysterious hint . . . about [his] green coat.' Two days later, as he walked along London Streets, 'the green coat attracted attention.' But though he called on the publisher John Murray in the '*green* jacket,' he later found it expedient to buy 'a Paletot in the Strand, so as to look decent—for I find my green coat plays the devil with my respectability here' " (see Eleanor Melville Metcalf, *Journal of a Visit to London and the Continent by Herman Melville, 1849–50* [Cambridge: Harvard University Press, 1948], pp. 18, 23, 32, and 69).

15.20    four]    Three years (not four) are assigned here in both A and E as the length of the *Grampus*'s voyage; the emendation is made on the grounds that the four years assigned in both editions in Chapter 23 (106.8) must represent Melville's later intention (to heighten the effect), since he must have written the passage in Chapter 23 dismissing Bulkington later than this one introducing him. Melville evidently overlooked the discrepancy. (George Stewart noted it in "The Two *Moby-Dick*s," *American Literature*, XXV [January, 1954], 422.)

16.2    sleeping-partner]    A major unemendable textual anomaly is presented by the two passages (15.37–16.16 and all of Chapter 23) where Bulkington is each time brought into the narrative but at once dismissed—here in parentheses. Bulkington seems best explained as a vestigial character from an earlier stage in the book's composition, in which he was to be Ishmael's "comrade" (16.12), a role subsequently reassigned to Queequeg, who was thereupon introduced in this same chapter and is the only other shipmate to whom the word "comrade" is applied (58.4, 5, 87.9, 321.27). See the HIS-TORICAL NOTE, pp. 656–58, for the pattern of "unneccessary duplicates" in *Moby-Dick* pointed out by Harrison Hayford, and the discussions at 71.1, 106.3, 146.2. and 302.4.

16.28    hammock]    This is the first of numerous references in which Melville—unless he uses "hammock" as a loose synonym for "bed" and "berth"—seems to forget that men on whaleships and merchant ships regularly slept in berths, not hammocks as in warships (see *White-Jacket*, chap.

20, NN79–81). (In a letter of January 24, 1978, to Harrison Hayford, Wilson L. Heflin reported Edouard Stackpole's telling him that it was not uncommon in the heat of the tropics for whalemen to use hammocks; but such heat seems not to explain the repeated references in *Moby-Dick*. Heflin added, "Certainly in the extreme cold of Chapter 51 [NN235.10], Ahab had no need for the comfort of a hammock. With his peg-leg, he would have had a hell of a time getting into and out of one when the seas were as violent as those in Chapter 51.") Although Melville accurately specifies berths for the *Pequod*'s crew at 103.29 and 426.3–13, he gives sailors in general a "hammock" here and the whaleman Queequeg his own hammock at 20.5 and 58.11 as well as at 477.16ff. (see below). Other examples follow throughout. Ahab has a "grave-dug berth" at 127.3, a "bed" at 128.10, but "hammock clothes" (apparently in a berth) at 128.12–15 and a "hammock" at 185.9 (on his previous ship), 201.35, 235.10, and 515.24. Stubb has a "bunk" at 119.6 but a "hammock" at 128.35 and 132.30. Old Fleece has a "hammock" at 294.5 and 297.36. Steelkilt has a "hammock" on the *Town-Ho* at 255.29 and 255.32. These mixed references may indicate a loose synonymous usage by Melville, but they also show his greater interest, as at other points, in immediate literary effect than in realistic detail (see, for examples, the discussions at 72.31, 102.12, 103.15, 119.8, 161.7, 163.8, 179.7, 489.9–10, 523.18–19, 543.17, 551.13, and 569.14). The only instance of probable genetic significance as to hammocks is the placing of the dying Queequeg in a hammock in the forecastle (see the discussion at 477.16). Tashtego is likewise misplaced as sleeping forward (see the discussion at 242.21).

18.3   airley]   See the NOTE ON THE TEXT, p. 789.

18.25   Mt. Hecla]   Possible questions arise whether "Hecla" is a misspelling for Mt. Hekla in Iceland, or designates Mt. Hecla in the Hebrides, or confuses the two. However, both "Hecla" and "Hekla" were current variant spellings for the Iceland mountain (see John Ramsay McCulloch's *Universal Gazetteer* [New York, 1843–44]). That Melville means the well-known Iceland volcano (which had erupted again in 1845) is obvious from the tenor: Ishmael is hot within (lines 8–21) but outwardly cool, like the volcano "in a snow storm". Probably Melville had in mind here (as at xxii.23–29, 69.39, and 460.3–6) Uno von Troil's *Letters on Iceland* (London, 1780), where Letter XX (pp. 239ff.) tells "Of Mount Heckla" and Letter I reports its "burning inwardly" while "covered over with four or five inches deep of snow" (p. 7).

20.6   wardrobe no doubt,]   Since the phrase "no doubt" must refer to Ishmael's conjecture as to the sea bag's contents, not to its patently serving "in lieu of a land trunk", NN removes the A and E comma after "wardrobe" and supplies one (not in A and E) after "doubt".

20.14 the same as in] See the NOTE ON THE TEXT, p. 790.

26.4 in the third floor] See the NOTE ON THE TEXT, p. 792, footnote 36.

27.19 having] The A and E reading "leaving" seems less likely than "having" in view of the reflexive "myself" construction.

31.17 specimens of] Possibly Melville wrote "off" rather than "of", since whaling-craft are the vessels "off" which the reeling sailors come, not "of" which they are "specimens". The emendation is not made, however, since, more loosely, "of" may be taken to mean "belonging to" the ships.

32.1 came] In E this word appears as "come", which one might regard as a correction that Melville entered on the proofs for Bentley, recognizing that his intended word had been misread ("came" and "come" are often indistinguishable in his hand) and that he had not caught the mistake in his proof-reading for the American edition. However, since the A reading makes satisfactory sense and since the E reading could easily have resulted from a compositorial error, NN does not emend.

32.21 Canaan;] Removal of the A and E semicolon after this word would clarify the syntax (obstructed by the rhetorical punctuation) by making clear that the second phrase "a land", paralleling the first, refers to "It" not to "Canaan", as the semicolon makes it appear to do. See the discussion at 311.35–312.3.

32.35–36 burn their lengths] Although the purport of this phrase is clear, its precise meaning is not. Possibly either a textual corruption or an obsolete proverbial expression, in this passage of Nantucket folklore, is involved (cf. "to burn to the socket" and "to burn one's candle at both ends").

33.7–10 Salem . . . sands.] This reference to the odorous musk-breathing young girls of Salem may have been intended as a private joke for Hawthorne's eye, like those pointed out in the discussions at 83.8 and 402.2. Cf. the discussions at 15.1 and 567.9. The New Bedford reviewer of the book was amused; see p. 714 above.

36.33 cave of Elephanta] Possibly Melville wrote "caves" since his reference in Mardi to "the great grottos of Elephanta" (chap. 75, NN229.17–18) shows he knew then that there is more than one rock-cave temple there; but his reference at 260.20–22, to "the famous cavern-pagoda of Elephanta . . . that immemorial pagoda", suggests that in both passages in Moby-Dick he was thinking of the single major cave. The loose usage was common in Melville's sources (cf. the article on "Elephanta" in the Penny Cyclopædia [London, 1837], IX, 354, which discusses only one "cave, or temple" there); and in any case emendation (from singular to plural) is not feasible because in both Moby-Dick passages the meaning requires a single cave. See the discussion by Howard P. Vincent in The Trying-Out of MOBY-DICK (Boston:

Houghton Mifflin, 1949), pp. 278–80, and by Luther S. Mansfield and Vincent in their Hendricks House edition of *Moby-Dick* (New York, 1952), p. 613, of this point and of Melville's unemendable error at 261.4–6 in locating a representation of the Matse Avatar of Vishnu there.

38.16 clerical] The intended sense ("mannerisms peculiar in a cleric") would be made clearer by emendation to "unclerical"; however, the rest of the sentence insures the right interpretation. In any case, analogous constructions, in which a negative prefix might seem called for, appear elsewhere in the book—for example, "earthly passionlessness" at 501.3. See also the NOTE ON THE TEXT, p. 793, footnote 38.

41.21 left] Although Melville adapts and rewrites parts of his source (an eight-stanza rhymed version of the First Part of Psalm 18, first included in *The Psalms and Hymns* . . . *of the Reformed Dutch Church in North America* in the first of the New York 1814 editions, pp. 34–35), it is clear that the E reading "left" more accurately reflects the past tense of the source than the A reading "lift" (which is probably a scribal or compositorial error). However, the shift in E from "opening" to "open" (42.1) is not confirmed by the source (which reads "I saw the opening gates of hell"). For further discussion, see David H. Battenfeld, "The Source for the Hymn in *Moby-Dick*," *American Literature*, XXVII (November, 1955), 393–96 (the 1854 text that Battenfeld prints is identical in wording to the 1814 text except for the reading "wings" instead of "wing" in line 18 of the poem). Cf. Bercaw 569.

42.21 And God] In Jonah 1:17 (King James Version) this sentence begins "Now the Lord". In certain other quotations from Jonah in the sermon Melville also makes minor alterations. At 44.16, the first word of the quoted clause ("that") reads "so" in Jonah 1:3. At 46.11–12, the questions appear in Jonah 1:8 as "What is thine occupation? and whence comest thou? what is thy country? and of what people art thou?" For "who" at 46.18, the reading in Jonah 1:9 is "which"; for "into" at 47.32, the reading in Jonah 2:3 is "In"; and for "his" at 47.33, the reading in Jonah 2:5 is "my". But in none of these cases is it reasonable to suppose that the A and E reading represents a misinterpretation of Melville's handwriting. The other quotations, at 45.34–35 (Jonah 1:6), 47.35 (2:2), and 48.1 (2:10) are accurate.

42.30 As sinful men] A paragraph break would normally be required at this major transition point in the sermon. Its omission in A and E obscures the structural pattern. Father Mapple has just distinguished in the Book of Jonah "a two-stranded lesson"—(1) "to us all", (2) "to me". At this point (42.30) he begins his development of the first, its application to us all "As sinful men", an application that occupies the main body of his sermon (42.30–47.6) restating the story of Jonah through the seven stages of "sin, hard-heartedness, suddenly awakened fears, the swift punishment, repentance, prayers, and finally the deliverance and joy of Jonah" (42.31–33). After the three-paragraph interlude in which Ishmael describes the scene in the chapel (47.7–18), Father Mapple opens his development of the second lesson, its application to himself as, like Jonah, "an anointed pilot-prophet" (47.25–26; see the discussion at 168.6). However, emendation to secure greater clarity through normalization of punctuation and paragraphing is not NN policy except where meaning is altered, not simply obscured. (See the discussions at 7.1, 121.8, 123.10, 137.18, 284.19, and 365.18.)

44.10   tide]   "Father Mapple or Melville twice makes a slip when he mentions the tide" (here and at 45.21), so George Stewart points out ("The Two *Moby-Dick*s," *American Literature,* XXV [January, 1954], 425n.). However, the slip—like the anachronistic printed "Man Wanted" bill (43.33–36)— seems of a piece with Father Mapple's simple sailor reconstruction of Jonah's story (neither he nor his whalemen auditors need be supposed to know that the Mediterranean is tideless), and in any case emendation is not in order since it is not the intention of the passage to convey fact.

48.36   remained, kneeling,]   The A and E reading, which has a comma only after "kneeling", implies that Father Mapple has already been depicted as kneeling; but in the last description of his position he is "standing motionless" (47.15). While it is true that Melville in this chapter is not interested in detailing Father Mapple's actions precisely—near the beginning Father Mapple is "kneeling" (41.10), but he is not said to rise after the prayer—the use of the word "remained" here, without any punctuation following it, produces an actual discrepancy, since it implies the reader's previous knowledge of something that has not in fact been stated. NN therefore eliminates the discrepancy by the insertion of a comma after "remained", which shifts the meaning so that "remained" now refers to his remaining in the pulpit with his hands covering his face.

50.28   Cape Horn]   See the discussion at 73.1.

56.13   haply]   See the NOTE ON THE TEXT, p. 789.

56.39   resolved]   Several unemendable discrepancies are involved in the fact that neither Queequeg's resolutions here nor the evident narrative plan Melville projected in the following passage are completely realized in the book. Though Queequeg does accompany Ishmael to Nantucket, "ship aboard the same vessel, get into the same watch, the same boat" (see the discussions at 161.7 and 220.13), he is not—and, as a harpooneer, could not be—in "the same mess" because as a harpooneer he messes in the captain's cabin, as stated in Chapter 33, "The Specksynder" (147.9–10), and shown in Chapter 34, "The Cabin-Table" (pp. 152–53). Nor is he shown "to share" Ishmael's "every hap" in more than a couple of chapters, "The First Lowering" (48) and "The Monkey-rope" (72). Elsewhere they are shown together at sea only incidentally, as in Chapters 24 and 35, for example. Melville's narrative plan at this point is indicated by Ishmael's welcoming Queequeg's companionship as "an experienced harpooneer" who would be "of great usefulness to one, who, like me, was wholly ignorant of the mysteries of whaling" (60.5–7). But the book does not show Queequeg as Ishmael's mentor teaching him about whales and whaling, though such a function would be appropriate in Chapters 47 (214.3ff.), 49 (226.21–227.3), and 61 (282.4–6). Ishmael's knowledge of whales and whaling is never represented as imparted to him by Queequeg or, indeed, as cumulating from the *Pequod*'s voyage, but is presented from his point of view as an experienced whaleman who has sailed on later voyages, conducted researches, and "swam through libraries" (136.17).

57.3  both my hands in his]  As in some other passages, Melville overlooks the impossible, and unemendable, literal meaning of his wording—here perhaps mixed metaphors: Queequeg could not, while holding both of Ishmael's hands in both of his own, "dip into the Potluck . . .". See also the discussions at 59.5, 93.27–28, and 119.8.

59.5  hands]  The A and E reading "hand" makes Ishmael and Queequeg each impossibly able to manage a (two-handled) wheelbarrow with a single hand. This may be an instance of Melville's failure to visualize an operation precisely (the operation is not figurative); but NN emends to the plural on the assumption that more likely he wrote "hands" and that his often indistinct terminal *s* was not seen by his copyist (for other examples see the NOTE ON THE TEXT, p. 794).

61.35–36  clove . . . dive]  Two unemendable discrepancies (probably due to Melville's shifting conceptions in the course of composition) seem evident between this passage and what comes about in the book. First, as discussed at 56.39, Ishmael is not in fact shown "to cleave to Queequeg"; he is not present even when Queequeg is supposedly dying in Chapter 110 (see the discussion at 477.39); nor does he mention in the epilogue that the coffin lifebuoy that saved him had been Queequeg's. Second, the phrase "his last long dive" (61.36) does not literally fit the manner of Queequeg's actual death—that is, his going down on the *Pequod* together with her crew (a scene in which Tashtego's, not Queequeg's, final moments are played up), though the ship's sinking may of course be taken figuratively as a "dive" (cf. "the mother dived down into the long church-yard grass" at 485.38–39). George Stewart lists the phrase "his last long dive" among the inconsistencies he takes as clues to Melville's rewriting of the book ("The Two *Moby-Dicks*," *American Literature*, XXV [January, 1954], 421–22) and conjectures that "it looks as if in the manner of his death Ahab had taken over the part which had originally been Queequeg's." Preparations for Queequeg's death in still another manner, from a fever, are elaborated then abruptly dropped in Chapter 110, "Queequeg in his Coffin"; if at some stage of composition this fever was meant to issue in his actual death, he would not have been parted from Ishmael in a "last long dive" but would have been "floated away to the starry archipelagoes" in his coffin-canoe (478.7). See the discussions at 56.39 and 478.17.

64.29  rests]  The A and E reading "riots" is emended as a misreading: the verbs "resides and rests" introduce a word pattern developed in the ensuing passage ("resides", lines 13–30, in "plantation", "home", and "lives"; and "rests", in the concluding sentence, lines 36–39, where like the landless gull the Nantucketer "lays him to his rest"). Although "riots", in the sense of "revels", also can be taken to generalize the activities named, it does not start a pattern, whereas the whole last sentence develops, and includes, the word "rests". (This emendation was advocated by William H. Gilman in a letter to the NN editors, June 26, 1969.) In the two sources discussed by Howard P. Vincent for this passage, the idea of "resides" is played up, but not those of either "riots" or "rests"; see *The Trying-Out of MOBY-DICK* (Boston: Houghton Mifflin, 1949), pp. 84–85.

67.2  fishy]  NN emends the A reading "fishing" to the E reading "fishy"—which seems more likely Melville's own correction (on the proofs he sent to Bentley) than a misreading by the English compositor. See "Fishiest of all fishy places" at 67.14.

67.19  vertebra]  The E reading "vertebræ" was a correction to plural number; but the singular in A is an acceptable idiom if the reference is to the material (cf. "a necklace of bone"). Similar uses of the singular are retained at 251.6, 357.6, and 412.5.

67.31  ony]  See the NOTE ON THE TEXT, p. 789.

67.34  a-night]  See the NOTE ON THE TEXT, p. 789.

68.21–69.1  I . . . securely]  Here Ishmael again (unemendably) touches on the mentor's function Queequeg was set up to serve for Ishmael but does not perform in the book (see the discussion at 56.39). The reason for the anomaly of his not doing so by choosing the ship may be that Melville introduced him into the shore sequence as Ishmael's companion, supplanting Bulkington (see the discussion at 16.2), after he had already written the scene in which Ishmael alone signs aboard the ship (chap. 16), and instead of revising it to include Queequeg chose to invent the Ramadan episode (chap. 17) to supply a reason why Queequeg could not appear in that scene, and to write an added chapter (18) in which he signs aboard.

69.13  Devil-dam]  In only the first of the three occurrences (twice in this line and once at 69.16) of this ship's name was its second word not capitalized in A and E; NN does not supply the capital, since it is not NN policy to regularize such inconsistencies when Melville's intention is indeterminable. No conjecture of textual corruption is needed to account for Ishmael's professed not knowing the origin of this term (mother of a devil)—than which "Tit-bit" (a variant of "tid-bit", a choice morsel) is no more "obvious". What is obvious is the innuendo that a devil's mother gets her teat bitten. Not yet obvious at this point is the third ship's devilish affiliation—the *Pequod*'s imminent devil-driven, hell-bound career. See Harrison Hayford, "Unnecessary Duplicates: A Key to the Writing of *Moby-Dick*," in *New Perspectives on Melville*, ed. Faith Pullin (Edinburgh: Edinburgh University Press, 1978), pp. 132–34, 146. The word "tit-bit" also occurs in Chapter 40 of *Mardi* (NN40.31), and in a comic verse about the Chinese Junk in *Yankee Doodle* (1847), attributed to Melville in the NN *Piazza Tales* volume, 438.16: " 'Salt junk's' a tit-bit, in old Neptune's muzzle".

69.15 Massachusetts Indians] The Pequods were Connecticut Indians. The misassignment is unemendable because it involves Melville's intentions in associating the tribe and the ship's name with Massachusetts and her Nantucket ownership. Luther S. Mansfield and Howard P. Vincent speculate as to sources of Melville's error, and his spelling of the word, in their Hendricks House edition of *Moby-Dick* (New York, 1952), pp. 631–33.

69.39 buckler or bedstead] Melville possibly wrote the two nouns as manuscript alternatives but neglected in revision to resolve the choice by checking his uncertainly remembered source. This was evidently Letter XIV in *Letters on Iceland* (London, 1780), where Uno von Troil reports that though Icelanders probably did not cut Runic characters on stones before 1000, "they used, however, to scratch them on bucklers, and sometimes on their cielings and walls: and the *Laxdaela Saga* makes mention of one Olof of Hiardarhult, who had a large house built, on the beams and rafters of which remarkable stories are said to have been marked, in the same manner as Thorkil Hake cut an account of his own deeds on his bedstead and chair" (pp. 158–59). No reference to deeds being cut on a buckler (only on a bed and stool) occurs in the *Njalssaga*, which was first translated into English in 1861 (by Sir George Dasent, *The Story of Burnt Njal*), as pointed out by Luther S. Mansfield and Howard P. Vincent in their Hendricks House edition of *Moby-Dick* (New York, 1952), p. 634. For further notes on Troil, see the discussions at xxii.23–27, 18.25, 460.4, and 460.5.

70.4 open bulwarks] There is an unemendable discrepancy between this descriptive detail of the *Pequod*'s build and the account at 234.39–235.4 of how off the Cape of Good Hope the crew "stood in a line along the bulwarks" as the best place to guard against the leaping waves—which "open bulwarks" would scarcely be (cf. *White-Jacket*, chap. 26, NN106.2.) Possibly Melville simply nods here, but possibly the open—or the closed—bulwarks, like the ivory jawbone tiller in place of "a turnstile wheel", are vestiges of his earlier conception of the ship (see the following discussion). In the letter cited in the discussion at 16.28, Wilson L. Heflin wrote: "I think you are right in taking 'panelled' as you do. . . .[Edouard] Stackpole says this kind of construction was altogether unconventional, that solid and panelled bulwarks were needed to protect the crew and the structures on the weather (exposed) deck and to support the boat davits. (I take it that Melville erred in favor of the striking imagery of a rail that looked like a toothed-whale's jaw rather than having conventional belaying pins fixed in the holes of interior pin-rails.)"

70.8   a tiller]   This detail about the *Pequod* (see also 423.37, 424.9, 424.19, 513.4, and 513.7) is glaringly discrepant with two later references to her having a wheel with spokes (283.18–19, 500.5); it may reflect either an earlier or a later conception on Melville's part. See the discussions at 70.4 and 283.18–19.

71.1   the Captain]   As part of the pattern of anomalous, sometimes discrepant, duplications in *Moby-Dick* that suggest stages in its composition, Harrison Hayford points out: "Besides . . . minor duplications in the ship's details, there are at once major duplicates among characters associated with her, notably in her having not one but three 'captains'. For as Ishmael first goes aboard the *Pequod,* who's in charge? Not, as might be expected, just one agent, owner, or captain to sign him on, but two—both retired Quaker captains who are also the two chief owners, Peleg and Bildad. And—though it's old Captain Peleg who has served for years on the Indian-named ship, who sits in a 'wigwam' of whalebone on her deck, and who has, we're told, done the curious whalebone carving work that dresses her in 'barbaric' apparel—it turns out to be not Peleg but still a third duplicate old Quaker captain, Ahab, who is to be her actual captain in command on the upcoming voyage and who (not Peleg) possesses the most striking piece of whalebone carving, a 'barbaric white leg' which 'had at sea been fashioned from the polished bone of the sperm whale's jaw' (ch. 28). But this third duplicate captain is not to be seen until days after the ship sails; he's said to be sick (like Bulkington and Queequeg he 'hides out'), and so his appearance will require a later separate chapter (ch. 28). The two old Quaker captains who do appear in chapter 16, Peleg and Bildad, so overlap in fictional uses that they may seem to be duplicates as indistinguishable as Rosenkrantz and Guildenstern, though they are given individualizing peculiarities. Peleg is a profane 'blusterer' while Bildad is a quiet, pious canter who solemnly declares his fear that impenitent Peleg's leaky conscience will sink him 'foundering down to the fiery pit'. Peleg angrily rejects Bildad's prophecy, rephrasing it in plain

English: 'Fiery pit! fiery pit! ye insult me, man; past all natural bearing, ye insult me. It's an all-fired outrage to tell any human creature that he's bound to hell'. But, as it turns out, it is not the first captain, Peleg, with his mild everyday profanities, but the third captain, Ahab, with his outraged sense of the insults and indignities heaped upon the human creature, and with his major blasphemies, who is the one indeed 'bound to hell' and who drives the *Pequod* and all her crew (save one) to 'sink to hell' (ch. 135)" ("Unnecessary Duplicates: A Key to the Writing of *Moby-Dick*," in *New Perspectives on Melville*, ed. Faith Pullin [Edinburgh: Edinburgh University Press, 1978], pp. 131–32).

71.12–13 that leg] Peleg's reason for calling attention to the leg with which he will kick Ishmael (as he later does, 103.37–39) can be taken as just Yankee humor; possibly, however, as Harrison Hayford suggests (in the article cited in the preceding discussion, pp. 131, 136, 146–47), his question is a discrepant vestige from a composition stage before the invention of Ahab, when it was Peleg (possibly then named "Pegleg") who had a whale-bone leg to replace one lost to a whale, and when his subsequent speeches (71.37–72.8) referred to his own loss (but were later revised to refer to Ahab's). See the discussions at 92.18, 96.35, 103.39, and 441.5.

72.31 anchor] An unemendable discrepancy occurs between Chapter 16 and Chapters 18 and 21, as well as within Chapter 22, as to whether the *Pequod* was initially at anchor in the harbor or tied up at the wharf. Here in Chapter 16, with no account of just how Ishmael got aboard (69.17), she is at anchor and moves with the tide, giving Ishmael an "unlimited" prospect of the open ocean (not possible, incidentally, in the Nantucket harbor, which Melville had never seen). But, in Chapter 18, on the next day she is at the wharf, from which Ishmael and Queequeg jump aboard (87.8–9, 88.29–30), and she is evidently still there in Chapter 20, as she is in Chapter 21 when they again step aboard from it (99.22). Then in Chapter 22 she is "hauled out from the wharf" about noon (102.3–4) but is once more discrepantly presented as anchored (unaccountably as an ensuing maneuver), for at once her anchor has to be laboriously heaved up (103.15ff.). The discrepancy may have arisen during separate stages of composition. It may also be due to Melville's greater attention to local literary effect than to consistent narrative realism, as shown in other passages (see, for examples, the discussions at 102.12, 119.8, 161.7, 163.8, 179.7, 489.9–10, 523.18–19, 543.17, 551.13, and 569.14; also the NOTE ON THE TEXT, p. 794).

73.1 Cape Horn] Unless Captain Peleg is to be taken as speaking figuratively, not as indicating the *Pequod*'s prospective course (via the Cape of Good Hope, chaps. 51–52), this reference, like the one at 50.28, may be either an authorial slip or a compositional vestige. George Stewart (in "The

Two *Moby-Dicks*," *American Literature*, XXV [January, 1954], 421, 445) takes it as the latter, along with further references at 8.4, 74.13, 77.20, 78.21, and 201.4–19; he posits "Sailing to the Pacific by way of Cape Horn" in the synopsis of his conjectural "Ur-*Moby-Dick*." However, no emendation (to "Cape of Good Hope") seems needed here or at any of the other points just cited; as they stand, all the references can be taken figuratively, even if Melville originally meant them literally.

73.35–36 virgin, voluntary, and confiding] The commas, not present in A, were supplied in E. NN, construing the three words as adjectives in series, all modifying "breast", also supplies the commas, on the assumption that they were probably omitted by Melville's copyist (see p. 798) and inadvertently not supplied by him when he punctuated the printer's-copy manuscript. Possibly it was Melville himself who added the commas to E, for he entered on the proofs for Bentley a number of other changes that reflect his close attention to some details. (An alternative explanation, in which the phrase "virgin voluntary" is taken as a compound adjective, seems less likely.)

73.37 to learn] See the NOTE ON THE TEXT, p. 793, footnote 39.

74.34 Categut] This name is probably a textual error: the closest name located is "Cattegat" (the arm of the North Sea between Sweden and Denmark), an unlikely one for this Nantucket ship. The allusion at 176.29–30 to "the isle fort at Cattegat" does not seem to increase the likelihood. Conceivably, what Melville wrote was "Pequod".

75.22 thee] On the use of "thee" for "thou" here and at 78.15 and 88.12, see the NOTE ON THE TEXT, p. 793, footnote 39.

75.27 queerest] This word presents a textual difficulty: the sentence's third clause (beginning "especially as") implies a preceding reference in its first clause to Bildad's *quietness* rather than to his immutable Quaker *peculiarity* (in dress, speech, piety, hypocrisy). These are two of Bildad's principal traits that Ishmael develops in contrast to his apparently ill-assorted crony Peleg's choleric and profane bluster and "anomalously modified" Quakerism. Bildad's "most uncommon and surprising" *peculiarity* is announced at once at 73.9–10; its not being "modified" like Peleg's and other Nantucketers' general Quaker peculiarity (73.17–21) is explained at 74.9–15; he is "unaccountable" at 76.16. Bildad's *quietness* in manner and behavior is noted with the words "contemplative" (74.20), "quiet" (74.30), "absorbed in reading" (75.13), "quietly" (75.19), "very quietly" (77.39, 90.20), and "imperturbable" (104.6). However, while emendation from "queerest" to "quietest" is needed here to set right the sense of this sentence's juxtaposed clauses (by opposing quiet—not queerness—to bluster), retention of "queerest" is also needed to summarize Ishmael's impression of Bildad's general demeanor in the whole context. Neither word will serve both needs; one fits the sentence, the other the larger context. The difficulty is beyond repair by allowable emendation.

76.32 do] In the King James Version, Matthew 6:19 reads "doth" at this point; but since "do" is not a likely misreading of "doth" in Melville's handwriting, "do" is retained as the word Melville must have written. Bildad's quotation (beginning six lines earlier) consists of Matthew 6:19 (omitting the last seven words, following "corrupt") and the first two words of 6:20. His other quotation from Matthew (6:21), at 77.7–8, is accurate.

76.39 *teenth*] Of course the actual suffix added to seventy-seven to indicate the fraction 1/77 is "-th" (whereas "-teenth" means "tenth"); but Ishmael's *"teenth"* seems clearly enough to be what Melville intended him to use, as a humorously effective nonce word (or possibly a colloquialism) for the "teeny" fraction.

78.7 Thank ye] See the NOTE ON THE TEXT, p. 792.

83.8 no smoking in the parlor] This placing the parlor off-limits, common at the time, and here a comic thrifty afterthought of Mrs. Hussey's, is possibly Melville's private joke for Hawthorne's eye, alluding to the evident rule against indulging their mutual addiction to cigars either in the parlor at Arrowhead (where they did so in Melville's upstairs room or in the barn) or in that of the Hawthornes' little red farmhouse in Lenox. Hawthorne confessed their commission of this offense during Sophia Hawthorne's absence, in his journal entry for August 1, 1851 (Melville's thirty-second birthday), about a long evening visit from Melville: ". . . and if the truth must be told, we smoked cigars even within the sacred precincts of the sitting room." (See Harrison Hayford's 1945 dissertation, p. 238, cited above on p. 761, where the passage was first reported, as newly recovered under special light by Randall Stewart from the original journal, one of the many passages inked out by Mrs. Hawthorne in editing its first publication in 1868; Sealts 250). See the discussions at 33.7–10 and 402.2.

83.23 sent] The reading may be corrupt, since plaster when struck, however hard, by a doorknob would not in fact be "sent" to the ceiling—a fact Melville may be supposed to have realized. The plausible emendation "rent" does not supply a more likely actual effect of the impact. If not the reading, Melville's visualization is at fault.

84.36 again] This word collides so awkwardly with the next word, "against", as to suggest the possibility that "again" should be excluded as a manuscript or compositorial anticipation. However, since at 57.10 Queequeg has already pressed his forehead against Ishmael's, the A and E reading is retained.

87.1 18] The correction of the chapter number (from the erroneous "XVII" in A) is made in E; the roman numeral of E is changed to arabic to conform with NN styling.

88.39 to his partner] The A and E reading "his partner" makes Peleg retreat for safety toward the cabin gangway. NN supplies the "to", thereby making Bildad the cautious partner who has retreated from "the close vicinity of the flying harpoon". Peleg has been characterized as anything but timid in both speech and action, and the words attributed to him in the A and E reading are hardly those spoken by a man just after the act of cowardly retreat. On the contrary, Melville must have meant Peleg to be reproaching Bildad for waste of valuable time by his flight and his subsequent hesitation: " 'Quick, I say, you Bildad, and get the ship's papers.' " Besides, in the A and E version "his partner" merely identifies Peleg, and there would seem to be no reason at this point for Melville to repeat identifying information that the reader already knows.

89.19 mark] The formée cross (which appears in both A and E) cannot be what Melville's manuscript called for, since the mark is described just above as "an exact counterpart of a queer round figure" tattooed on Queequeg's arm. Probably the cross was an available stock piece of type substituted by the printer. A number of twentieth-century editors, noting the discrepancy, have substituted other "round" figures; the figure (probably drawn by the illustrator, Rockwell Kent) in the 1931 Lakeside Press edition (later followed by the Random House and Modern Library Giant edition and by others) resembles an infinity sign and has thus misled some critics.

89.28–29 Bel . . . dragon] The A spelling "Bell" was corrected in E to "Bel". Peleg warns Queequeg to forsake pagan worship, as a "Belial bondsman" or servant of Satan, and to reject the Babylonian idol Bel, whose priests Daniel exposed, along with the dragon of Babylon whom he destroyed, as told in the story of Bel and the Dragon in the Apocrypha, from the end of the Book of Daniel.

90.7 on Japan] Harrison Hayford and Hershel Parker emended "on" to "off" in the Norton Critical Edition (New York, 1967), p. 85, identifying this idiom with "off Japan" (NN124.16). But as Keith Huntress pointed out with a contemporary citation, by "on Japan" whalemen did not necessarily mean near ("off") the Japanese islands but more generally all the North Pacific Ocean eastward of them ("A Note on the Text of Moby Dick," American Notes and Queries Supplement, I [1978], 283–84).

92.7, 9 Old Thunder] An unemendable anomaly about this nickname is pointed out by George Stewart: while here "Ahab is called 'Old Thunder,' and it is implied that this is his nickname," in the later parts of the book "he is called Old Thunder only once, and that when the actual occurrence of thunder seems to suggest the name" (chap. 119; 505.11); instead, he is twice called "the old Mogul" by Stubb (171.10–11, 432.19), three times "our old Mogul" by different crew members (174.7–8, 177.24, 197.9), and once "his old Mogulship" by the Carpenter (469.26). Stewart sees this anomaly as indicating earlier and later composition stages. He takes Chapter 19 in general as part of the "Ur-*Moby-Dick*": "On the whole . . . the characterization of Ahab here presented is more in common with that of an ordinary brutal, even murderous, mad sea captain, than with the tragic hero with which Ahab is later absorbed. The previous details of Ahab's life, moreover, though twice mentioned in this chapter, are never afterwards explained to us" ("The Two *Moby-Dicks*," *American Literature*, XXV [January, 1954], 421, 437).

92.19 left arm] Since nothing wrong about Elijah's arm is specified, the speech is puzzling. A quibble on a left arm never being "all right" seems an inadequate explanation. Possibly at an earlier composition stage Elijah (or a corresponding character differently named) was represented as lacking his left arm, though at 98.7–8 he has his two hands to lay on Ishmael's and Queequeg's shoulders. See the discussions at 71.12–13 and 441.5.

93.27–28 after each other's fashion] Since the intended meaning ("each after his own fashion") is clear, no emendation is made, even though the garbled A and E wording—no doubt Melville's own—says literally that each was commenting after the other's fashion. For similarly garbled idioms, see the discussions at 57.3, 191.26–27, 192.19, and 219.18–19.

95.11 On the day following] A discrepancy appears between this phrase and the clause introducing the previous paragraph, "A day or two passed". The awkward handling of time-sequence in the whole chapter possibly reflects separate stages in its composition. See the discussion at 102.6–7 for a further possible inconsistency and the one at 422.15–16 for Melville's more deft handling of a displacement in time-sequence, possibly by the same cause.

96.35 running] The A reading "hobbling" is impossible, since Peleg is regularly characterized as quick of limb (see, for instance, 77.32, 90.10, 103.37–39). E alters the word to "running", which is clearly an improvement. But one could argue that the authorial word is "roaring", on the grounds that the later expression "roaring back into his wigwam"—along with two more parallel instances of "roaring"—may suggest that Melville meant the opening element in the series to be "roaring out of his whalebone den". In order to support that argument on anything more than stylistic grounds, however, one would have to postulate two stages of blundering: (1) If "hobbling" actually appeared at this point in Melville's manuscript, it could have been an oversight at the time of inscription or could be an un-canceled vestige of an earlier conception of the character (see the discussion at 71.12–13); or if "roaring" was the word in the manuscript, Melville's peaked r could possibly have made a copyist or the American compositor misread "roaring" as "hobbling". (2) However "hobbling" got into the American edition, Melville might have corrected it to "roaring" on the proofs for Bentley, only to have the English compositor in turn misread his correction as "running"; or Bentley's reader, noticing that "hobbling" must have been an error, might possibly have supplied "running", which could be thought to correct the inconsistency without restoring Melville's intend-ed wording. NN, however, adopts the E reading "running", which corrects the sense adequately, requires no complicated theory, and may in fact be Melville's own correction made on the proofs.

102.6–7 brother-in-law] If Stubb is the brother-in-law of Aunt Charity (Captain Bildad's sister, 96.17), he is also Bildad's; and either she is married to his brother, or, more likely, Stubb is married to their sister, who must be considerably younger than this "old lady" and this retired old captain. (He calls his wife—presumably—"my juicy little pear" at 171.16.) Since no such family relationships are again referred to in the book, some discrepancy seems to be involved here.

102.7 the two captains] In Chapter 22 the peculiar "duplication" of func-tion by Peleg and Bildad as two owners continues as two "joint com-manders" and two licensed pilots (see the discussions at 71.1 and 103.39); and textual anomalies also support Harrison Hayford's hypothesis (in the article cited at 71.1) that at an earlier composition stage Peleg may have sailed as the *Pequod*'s captain while only Bildad remained behind. The devel-opment, at a later stage, of Ahab as captain, with the demotion of Peleg, may have called for only a few simple revisions in this chapter. Ahab's not existing at the earlier stage may account for his not appearing in the scene or before Chapter 28 (his "hiding out," now explained by his moody sickness); the three direct references to him in this chapter (102.10–11, 102.18–103.6, 105.22–24) could have been easily inserted, and the one indirect reference to him would originally have applied just as well to Peleg ("in which an old shipmate sailed as captain; a man almost as old as he", 104.36–37). The part Peleg now plays in the chapter may have been written when he was in fact the actual captain: he issues the orders (102.9–12, 103.7–16, 103.30–104.8, 105.15–17). The few words confining him to a shore-role may be simple revisions ("with Peleg", 103.18; "the two pilots", 104.29; possibly "And he . . . mate", 105.12–13; "we", 105.15; the farewells, which could have been

Bildad's, 105.17–20; and "both dropt", 105.36). The textual anomalies both relate to Bildad: first, the syntactical awkwardness of the passage "And here Bildad, who, with Peleg, . . . was one of the licensed pilots . . . " suggests that "with Peleg" may be an insertion (103.18–19). More strikingly, the paragraph about the time for the pilot(s) to leave the ship is so written that the scene would make better sense (apart from the possibly revised phrases just noted) if Bildad alone, not both he and Peleg, were leaving. The paragraph's first sentence couples them, but immediately it narrows to Bildad alone: "It was curious . . . how Peleg and Bildad were affected at this juncture, especially Captain Bildad" (104.32–33). Bildad behaves as if he were giving Peleg a goodbye handshake and taking a last long look at him: " . . . poor old Bildad lingered long; . . . convulsively grasped stout Peleg by the hand, and holding up a lantern, for a moment stood gazing heroically in his face . . . " (105.1–8). Why does he do that if they are not separating? "As for Peleg himself"—why "himself"?—his less emotional behavior fits that of a person going on the voyage, though "there was a tear twinkling in his eye, when the lantern came too near" (105.10–12). Apart from the easily adjustable farewells to the mates, the rest of Peleg's words and actions fit perfectly the situation of his urging Bildad to stop talking and leave them: " 'Come, come, Captain Bildad; stop palavering,—away!' and with that, Peleg hurried him over the side, and both dropt into the boat." Only the words "both dropt" would need to have been supplied.

102.12 Muster] The evident discrepancies with ordinary whaleship routine as to this command, repeated at 103.9–10, and as to the one at 103.15ff. are pointed out in the discussions at 72.31 and 161.7.

103.15 capstan] Although a capstan (usually on a large ship) stands and turns vertically and a windlass (usually on a smaller ship) horizontally, Melville either uses the terms interchangeably (as in this chapter and Chapter 103, 448.13–14) or is inconsistent in his conception of which one the *Pequod* is equipped with. Only a windlass is used in Chapter 67. In the letter cited in the discussion at 16.28, Wilson L. Heflin wrote: "The windlass, not a capstan, was the 'standard machine [in whaleships] for heaving the anchors and raising heavy weights for over a hundred years,' according to Reginald Hegarty's authoritative *Birth of a Whaleship* (New Bedford: Reynolds Printing, 1964, p. 59). With tryworks, skids, large hatch for lowering blubber, etc., there was scant room on the weather deck for a capstan but sufficient room at the broad bows for a windlass. This could be operated by as few as three men. . . . The *Pequod*'s capstan was evidently a Melville original, probably based on the anchor-raiser of the *Neversink*." That is, of the frigate in *White-Jacket*, drawn from the frigate *United States*, upon which Melville served in 1843–44; Chapter 2 begins with the command "All hands up anchor! Man the capstan!" and continues, "When that order was given, how we sprang to the bars, and heaved round that capstan; every man a Goliath, every tendon a hawser! . . . " (NN6.3, 7.11–12). Melville was apparently recalling his naval experience when he wrote this whaleship scene, with more concern for literary effect than for authenticity, as in some other scenes and perhaps in his references to hammocks rather than bunks or berths. See the discussion at 16.28 with further citations.

103.39  my first kick]  Emendation of the A and E reading "first" to "only" might be defended, since "first" implies one or more further kicks, but none follows, and at sea the only abuse of the crew by captain or mates is Stubb's hitting Dough-Boy once in Chapter 72. (The captain kicks only in Stubb's fancy, 128.29–30, and in his dream, 131.4ff.) George Stewart considers this discrepancy among the vestiges of his conjectural "Ur-*Moby-Dick*," in which Ishmael "received many kicks" from a harsh pre-Ahab captain ("The Two *Moby-Dicks*," *American Literature*, XXV [January, 1954], 421, 445). See the discussions at 71.1 and 71.12–13. The HISTORICAL NOTE (pp. 656–58) reports Harrison Hayford's conjecture that Peleg may have been that original captain (see the discussion at 102.7 and p. 136 of "Unnecessary Duplicates," cited in the discussion at 71.1); in that case, Stubb's Queen Mab dream (chap. 31) was perhaps originally Ishmael's own, after the kick from Peleg: it follows his pattern of rationalizing a captain's blows in Chapter 1 (6.17–22), and its pyramid image links to his pyramid reference in that chapter (5.38); its reference to garter-knights seems a bit beyond Stubb's range elsewhere but typical of Ishmael's (e.g., in Chapter 25, on coronation anointment); and its vein of jocularly specious but practical reasoning is characteristic of Ishmael all along.

104.3  ye—spring,]  NN substitutes a comma for the exclamation point after "spring" in A and E, so that this word of command is clearly addressed to "Quohog" (not to the preceding "all of ye"), as it is to the person(s) after it in its six other parallel uses in the passage.

104.3  Quohog]  The A reading "Quohag" (E has "Quohog") is emended on the assumption that the *a* spelling is a copyist's or compositor's error. Presumably Melville did not mean Peleg to garble the familiar word "Quohog" (the round or hard clam), which he has eight times substituted for the unfamiliar word "Queequeg" (88.24, 25, 27, 89.3, 9, 10, 18).

104.19–22  "Sweet . . . between."]  This quotation, comprising the third stanza of Isaac Watts's hymn (entitled "A Prospect of Heaven Makes Death Easy") beginning "There is a Land of pure Delight", accurately follows the wording of the original in *Hymns and Spiritual Songs* (London, 1707), Book II, hymn 66 (p. 139).

104.36  old shipmate]  Applied to Ahab, as here, this phrase is discrepant, since he and Bildad are nowhere else made old shipmates. It fits Peleg, however, who has been presented as Bildad's old shipmate (75.28) and who calls him that just below (105.15). Harrison Hayford points to this phrase at 104.36 as one of several vestigial anomalies indicating that when Chapter 22 was written Peleg was to sail on this voyage as captain of the *Pequod* (and that Ahab was substituted later and given a previous voyage with Peleg as mate, 79.20, 90.8–18). See "Unnecessary Duplicates: A Key to the Writing of *Moby-Dick*," in *New Perspectives on Melville*, ed. Faith Pullin (Edinburgh: Edinburgh University Press, 1978), pp. 157–59.

106.3 Bulkington] Melville's reason for anomalously including Bulkington in two passages even while excluding him from the ensuing narrative is conjectural, whether or not he is a vestigial character (see the discussion at 16.2).

109.26–29 navy . . . $7,000,000] One reviewer of *Moby-Dick* (see above, p. 718) objected to Melville's "loose way" of stating statistics here, citing those in an 1844 report to Congress by a Mr. Grinnell of which Melville "gives a sort of summary . . . as representing the present state of things." Melville reported Grinnell's 1844 statistics quite accurately from J. Ross Browne's *Etchings of a Whaling Cruise* (New York, 1846), p. 539; emendation to correct them to the "present state of things" in 1851 is of course out of the question.

110.15 Voyages] The intended sense of this word as books about voyages, or compendia such as those of Purchas, Hakluyt, and Harris, is obscured by its not being italicized or placed in quotation marks to designate it as a generic title, though the capitalization is indicative and the sense emerges from the reference just below to Vancouver's dedicating "three chapters" to an adventure. Styling in the Harper *Moby-Dick* was inconsistent in this matter and is left unregularized in NN. See the NOTE ON THE TEXT, p. 799, footnote 45; also the discussions at 205.26–27, 261.19–20, 326.7, and 366.5.

111.15 Morrel] A variant spelling of Franklin's grandmother's name (Melville's source is not known), which also appears as "Morrell", "Morrill", "Morrils", and "Morriel" (the last in Chapter 1 of Hart's *Miriam Coffin*, where she is erroneously named as Franklin's great-grandmother; see the discussion at xxviii.9–10).

115.22 words] The A and E reading "sounds" is emended because it does not complete the contrast between a "pantomime" and a "chapter"; as the first involves action, the second involves words. That is, in "pantomime of action" and "chapter of words" each phrasal modifier indicates what its noun is made up of: a pantomime consists of actions; a chapter consists of words (not sounds). Thus the intended epitome of Starbuck's life embodies the proverbial contrast of "deeds" and "words". In Melville's handwriting "words" could be misread as "sounds"; see its occurrence at 17.8 in the manuscript reproduction on p. 987 below.

117.17–18   itself . . . her]   The shift from neuter to feminine pronoun for the antecedent "piety" is better seen as carrying the developing feeling of the passage than as an emendable authorial aberration.

117.34–35   stumped . . . arm]   See the discussion at 437.26.

119.8   turned in]   Emendation of this A and E reading to "turned out" would clarify the confused matter of whether Stubb smoked his whole row of pipes while in his bunk, beginning "whenever he turned in" (line 8), or, as seems more plausible, while out of it, beginning as soon as he would "turn out" (line 6). Either alternative offers obvious practical difficulties: if while in it, did that leave him any time to sleep? If while out of it, did that require him to return to it for each successive ready-filled pipe? And are the alternatives exclusive? As in some other passages Melville seems more concerned with general effect than with realistic detail (see, for examples, the discussions at 83.23, 416.26, 543.17, and 551.13).

119.34–35   King-Post]   This nickname and a short, stout stature (119.20), so George Stewart points out, are anomalous for Flask and would better fit Stubb, whose own name suggests such a stature and whose physical build (alone of the mates) is not described, whereas Flask's name suggests a toper, though he is not so presented. Stewart conjectures, "On revision the two may have had their names exchanged for some reason and have had their characters somewhat mixed up" ("The Two *Moby-Dicks*," *American Literature,* XXV [January, 1954], 430–31).

120.1–2   three of the Pequod's boats]   This phrasing implies that she had more than three. A common number for a whaleship was four, and the number repeatedly given for the *Pequod*'s crew, some thirty (see the discussion at 121.8–9), would man four boats with the usual six men each (five oarsmen, including the harpooneer-boatsteerer, plus the officer-headsman), leaving an ample six as shipkeepers. Thus, the *Pequod* should have had four boats. Yet any implication in the next sentence (120.2–3) that Ahab would himself command a fourth in the "grand order of battle" would be a discrepancy here, since his in fact doing so is a surprise reserved for the first lowering, in Chapter 48. See the further discussions of the discrepant number of the *Pequod*'s men and boats at 121.8–9 and of her "missing whaleboat" at 230.6–8.

120.3   presently]   The A and E reading "probably" does not fit: that Ahab will so marshal (if not join) his forces is not *probable* but *certain,* as both the immediate and larger contexts make clear by detailing the relationships and duties of individual officers in terms of established whaling usages. A temporal rather than conditional adverb is called for; "presently" fits well and in Melville's hand could be misread as "probably" (see his manuscript "?pleasurably"/"?pleasantly" at 5.12 on p. 981 below).

120.10–12 and . . . friendliness] Since no "close intimacy and friendliness" between any of the three pairs of mates and harpooneers is in fact developed later, this clause given as the second reason for introducing the harpooneers is a superfluous oddity. Even so, the clause makes sense enough as a generalization, and editorial excision is unwarranted. See the discussions at 121.8, 122.21, 146.2, 173.3, 242.21, 286.18, 292.21, and 568.1.

120.16 Tashtego] See the discussion at 242.21.

121.8 As for] A paragraph break would be normal at this point to signal the major transition from the chapter's first topic, the mates and harpooneers (a topic itself subdivided into paragraphs), to its second topic, the crew—"the residue of the Pequod's company". Emendation is not made by NN, however, since what is affected by the probable oversight in paragraphing is structural clarity, not altered sense. The oversight was perhaps incidental to revisions in the presentation of the Pequod's officers and men that left various unemendable structural anomalies and conceptual vestiges not only in this chapter but in the sequence of Chapters 23 and 26 through 29. (See the discussions at 7.1, 42.30, 123.4–10, 161.7, and 284.19.) Melville's offhand and nonrealistic treatment of the crew here, where some detailed commentary and introductions in one or more dramatized scenes would be in order, constitutes a major discrepancy with his apparent program up to this point of using Ishmael's voyage to document whalers and whaling from a greenhand crewman's point of view. From here on very little attention is paid to the crew's shipboard life and lot. (Contrast the presentation of the crew in greenhand Redburn's introduction to the merchant sailor's forecastle life in Redburn, chaps. 8–12, NN38–62.) The most likely explanation is a marked change in Melville's program between separate composition stages. Now no individual crewmen are introduced for some while; curiously, there are no scenes in the forecastle until Chapters 97 and 110, and no further kicks or other abusive treatment of men by officers (see the discussion at 103.39). Instead the focus moves to the heroic Captain Ahab, whose ensuing tyrannical clash (chaps. 29–31) is not with a crewman but with the second mate, Stubb. This shift in focus coincides with the shift in point of view away from close first-person detailing of Ishmael's (and Queequeg's) experiences.

121.8–9 residue . . . company] The unemendable inconsistency that develops in the course of the book over the number of men in the Pequod's crew is noted by George Stewart: "Melville apparently kept the number thirty in mind for the crew, about the average for a whaler. He mentions this number three times [515.2, 557.10, 557.33]. Actually, however, apparently in trying to establish the atmosphere of *Moby-Dick* [in contrast to his originally planned whaling voyage] in the grand manner, he dealt out characters with such liberality that forty-four of them can be distinguished" ("The Two *Moby-Dicks*," *American Literature*, XXV [January, 1954], 426). Starbuck, at 515.2, speaks of "thirty men and more", and (as if speaking for Melville) the Carpenter, at 526.10–13, asks, "how many in the ship's company, all told? But I've forgotten. Anyway, I'll have me thirty separate . . . life-lines. . . . Then, if the hull go down, there'll be thirty lively fellows all fighting for one coffin". See the discussions at 120.1–2 and 230.6–8.

121.29   come]   The A and E reading, retained in NN, may be a copyist's or compositor's misreading of "came" in Melville's hand. The context in some ways would better support the use of the past tense. Previous lines in the paragraph have generalized about American use of foreign nationals in canal and railroad building and in whaling; after defining such men as Isolatoes, Ishmael focuses on the particular set of Isolatoes on the *Pequod*. In the sentence itself, the "Anacharsis Clootz deputation" is specifically the Isolatoes on the *Pequod,* the ones "accompanying Old Ahab in the Pequod to lay the world's grievances before that bar from which not very many of them ever come back." It is difficult to account for the words "of them" except as a reference to the crew of the *Pequod*. One might expect a sentence dealing so particularly with the mission and the fate of this crew to carry the past tense: "that bar from which not very many of them ever came back." The present tense makes the meaning general—that not many men in such deputations ever do return, even though other deputations have not been mentioned. Still, the A and E reading receives a degree of corroboration, first from the fact that the implied form of the verb called for by the words "he never did" in the next sentence must be "come" ("he never did come back"), and second from the probability that Melville himself looked over the passage in the American proofs and deleted "—oh, no! he went before" (and therefore had a good chance for seeing an error in the previous sentence). Since none of these arguments is conclusive, the copy-text reading is allowed to stand.

121.30   did! Poor]   In A "did" is followed by "—oh, no! he went before." In E those five words are omitted, presumably canceled by Melville himself on the proofs he sent to England, and an exclamation point follows "did". As Leon Howard, in *Herman Melville: A Biography* (Berkeley: University of California Press, 1951), p. 166, points out, Pip does not in fact precede anyone before the heavenly throne, though he goes mad. Probably Melville removed this phrase as a vestige of an earlier stage of composition. If so, what happened to Pip at that earlier stage may have provided a more literal motivation for the apparently discrepant reference just below to his being "hailed a hero" in heaven than does anything in the experience described in Chapter 93, "The Castaway," 414.20–31, or in his subsequent behavior. On the other hand the meaning of "he went before" may not be the literal one that Pip drowned and went to heaven before the others but the figurative one (indicated in the cited passage in Chapter 93 and in Pip's own belief, voiced in Chapter 110, 479.25–27, 480.2–8) that he "died a coward" and went to heaven ("those sweet Antilles") at the time he was left a castaway by Stubb. But Melville may have found such a figurative sense of Pip's death unmanageably incompatible with his literal survival and possession of his tambourine. Eliminating the phrase "he went before" postpones his death to the time of the *Pequod*'s sinking and defers his summons to heaven and his beating his tambourine in glory there to some subsequent "eternal time."

121.30 Alabama] There seems to be an unemendable discrepancy as to where Pip comes from. Here Alabama is named as the place (unless a native Connecticut Negro can be called figuratively an "Alabama boy"), and in Chapter 93 it is likewise implied as the place in Stubb's choice of Alabama as the appropriate slave state where a whale would sell for thirty times what Pip would (413.21–22). But two specific references in Chapters 93 and 99 name "his native Tolland County in Connecticut" (412.11–12) and have Pip tell of his father "in old Tolland county" (435.11). If Melville needed Alabama (as a Deep South state) to make the point both here and in the later chapters, whereas Connecticut would destroy the point in both, what made him bring in Tolland County at all? Perhaps the answer may lie in Pip's original source-character—James Backus, according to the notation ("Pip — Backus — his real name.") made by Melville's "old Shipmate" Henry Hubbard in a copy of *The Whale* presented to him by Melville in 1853. (See the account of this volume below, pp. 1005–20.) In an unpublished paper, Maria Mootry has reported an actual Negro community in Tolland County and looked into the possibility that Backus may have come from there.

122.11 my watches below] As the voyage begins, this important detail of shipboard routine is taken into account here (and at 122.4–5 and 123.17–18) in placing characters in a scene, particularly Ishmael as a witness (cf. 122.9–10). Later, however, it is repeatedly ignored, so that characters belonging to different watches (and whaleboats) are discrepantly placed. Examples are pointed out in numerous ensuing discussions.

122.21 harpooneers] An unemendable discrepancy seems evident here in the lumping of Queequeg (unnamed) with the other harpooneers as simply "barbaric, heathenish, and motley", while saying nothing about his humane qualities and friendship as matters that would allay Ishmael's "apprehensions and uneasiness" and "induce confidence and cheerfulness" about the voyage. And indeed the discrepancy introduced here persists and broadens, in that no passage associates Ishmael and Queequeg closely between Chapter 21 ("Going Aboard") and Chapter 47 ("The Mat-Maker"). For a possible genetic explanation, see the discussions at 56.39, 61.35–36, and others cited there.

123.4–10  But . . . Cape man]  These two sentences (like the preceding sentence, 122.21–123.4) seem not to take account of matters already laid before the reader. Here the minor but perhaps revealing discrepancy is that the geographical epithets (besides being unnecessary glosses to "Americans") do not list the three mates in order of rank—the order in which they have just pointedly been treated in Chapters 26 and 27: Starbuck, first mate, is the Nantucketer; but Stubb, second mate, is the Cape man; while Flask, third mate, is the Vineyarder. This discrepancy and the similar slight one above (122.21), of overlooking Queequeg's friendship, when taken together with the chapter's shift back to narrative mode, suggest that the passage was written at a different stage from the expository chapters (23–27) standing just before it (i.e., without having clearly in mind matters laid out in them). See the discussion at 244.1 for a possibly related discrepancy.

123.10  Now,]  A paragraph break would be normal at this point, where the topic shifts from Ishmael's thoughts about the voyage and ship's company back to the ship's progress, the weather, and Ahab. Emendation is not made by NN because the absence of the paragraph break does not alter the sense of the passage, simply the clarity of its structure. The oversight may be associated with other anomalies in the paragraph, pointed out in the discussions at 122.21 and 123.4–10. See also discussions of paragraphing at 7.1, 42.30, 121.8, 123.10, 284.19, and 365.18.

124.16–18  "Aye . . . 'em."]  This direct quotation attributed to the old Gay-Head Indian seems inappropriate in its non-dialectal forms and its rhetorical balance of the dismasted Ahab and the dismasted craft, though the last sentence ("He has a quiver of 'em") fits him as an Indian speaker. But Melville was inconsistent (as in other matters) as to realistic rendition of speech, not only of the officers but of the pagan harpooneers and the crew. Tashtego speaks at times in standard English (162.24–25, 28; 175.20; 178.5–6; 286.18; 547.21–22), at times in "Indian" dialect (354.14, 512.5–7). Queequeg speaks only in a kind of pidgin (23.25ff.; 54.35, a "broken phraseology"; 88.33–38; 98.13; 162.32–35). Daggoo speaks only non-dialectal English (162.30–31; 177.14–15, 22, 32; 221.19), as does Pip (434.30–435.18; 479.22–480.8; 522.1–6, 11, 15–17); but Fleece speaks a comic black dialect (chap. 64).

124.16  dismasted off Japan]  An unemendable discrepancy occurs in the book as to where Ahab lost his leg: here the old Gay-Header, who is represented as knowing Ahab's history from birth (unlike the old Manxman who has "never ere this laid eye upon wild Ahab", 124.3–4), says he lost it off Japan (and does not say how); but at two later points the location is specifically said to have been on the equatorial line (200.35–36, 536.6–7). The Gay-Header's version, like that old Indian himself, may be a vestige of an earlier composition stage (see the discussion at 242.21); the other version is appropriate to Ahab's management of the ship's whole course as it is finally represented. See the discussion at 465.5–6.

132.4  'Slid]  NN emendation of the A and E form without the apostrophe makes Stubb's interjection more immediately recognizable as the oath (contraction of "God's lid [i.e., eyelid]") listed by the *Oxford English Dictionary*, s.v. "'Slid", as common in the seventeenth century, and obsolete, citing both forms. The one OED citation from Shakespeare, in *The Merry Wives of Windsor*, III.iv.25, occurs without the apostrophe in Melville's set of *The Dramatic Works* (Boston, 1837), I, 208 (Sealts 460, Bercaw 634). Inconsistently, however, the other occurrence of the word in Shakespeare has the apostrophe in Melville's set, in *Twelfth Night*, III.iv.370, a passage that Melville scored in the margins. His making Stubb use this obsolete oath is a literary, probably Shakespearean, touch, not a realistic one; his reading in this set, acquired in 1849, was among the major influences on the language of *Moby-Dick*.

132.35  quick]  See the NOTE ON THE TEXT, p. 791.

134.13–22  "No . . . naturalists."]  The first quotation (134.13–14) in these lines, from William Scoresby, Jr., accurately follows the wording of the third of four epigraphs to Thomas Beale's *The Natural History of the Sperm Whale* (London, 1839), the book Melville cites in the following paragraph. Beale was obviously Melville's source, because the four quotations just below at 134.19–22 come from Beale's three other epigraphs: the first one comes from Beale's first epigraph and corresponds to the last part of a long sentence credited to John Hunter (except that "researches" appears there in place of "research"); the second and third are phrases from Beale's second epigraph, attributed to René Primevère Lesson (except that "covers" appears there in place of "covering" and no "the" appears before "cetacea"); and the fourth is a translation of Beale's fourth epigraph, from Baron Georges Cuvier (except that a literal translation would omit "us": "Toutes ces indications incompletes ne servent qu'à mettre les naturalists à la torture"). (When Melville names these writers, at 135.1, he does not list them in the order quoted, placing Cuvier first.) Although Beale provides no date for Scoresby, Melville apparently added "1820" because he was familiar with Scoresby's *An Account of the Arctic Regions* (Edinburgh, 1820) and mistakenly assumed that the quotation came from it (cf. Sealts 450, Bercaw 616). The quotation (134.15–17) from the body of Beale's work is accurate in wording, except that for "groups and families" the original reads "groups, families, genera, or species"; the original has "which" after "confusion"; and the second of the quoted sentences comes earlier in Beale (pp. 9–10) than the first (p. 12). All these changes were probably made deliberately by Melville. (Cf. Sealts 52, Bercaw 51.)

135.10   the Author]   Probably Melville cited "the Author" of *Miriam Coffin*, the historical novel of early Nantucket, because no author's name was on the title page of any of the three separate editions (New York, 1834; New York and London, 1835; New York, 1835); which one Melville used has not been determined. Apparently he did not know it was by Joseph C. Hart, whose curious book *The Romance of Yachting* (New York, 1848) he had declined to review, in a facetiously condemnatory letter to Evert A. Duyckinck (see *The Letters of Herman Melville*, ed. Merrell R. Davis and William H. Gilman [New Haven and London: Yale University Press, 1960], pp. 73–75). For *Moby-Dick*, Melville took from *Miriam Coffin* an extract from its own text (xxviii.9–10), its quotation from Falconer (xxiii.11–13), and possibly several details of characters and plot. See discussions at the points just cited.

135.11   Henry T. Cheever]   The A and E reading "T. Cheever" (omitting "Henry") is taken to be a copyist's or compositor's error, not Melville's; he used Cheever's *The Whale and His Captors* (New York, 1849) as a source book for *Moby-Dick,* crediting one extract to it correctly as *"By Rev. Henry T. Cheever"* (see the discussion at xxvii.9). The other names listed, 135.6–11, are given in acceptable spellings in A, except Bonnaterre, given as "Bonneterre" (135.9), and Olmsted, given as "Olmstead" (135.11), both corrected in NN. Both were evidently copying errors, since Melville's presumable sources presented correct spellings: for Pierre Joseph Bonnaterre, Thomas Beale, *The Natural History of the Sperm Whale* (London, 1839), p. 10; and for Francis Allyn Olmsted, the title page of that author's own book, *Incidents of a Whaling Voyage* (New York, 1841), which Melville used extensively.

136.16–17   "Will . . . vain!"]   These two sentences, from Job 41:4 and 41:9, correspond in wording to the King James Version, except that Melville has inserted "the leviathan" parenthetically to explain the reference and has omitted "in" before "vain".

136.23–31   In . . . meritoque."]   In wording, Melville's quotations correspond to his source—the article on "Whales" in the *Penny Cyclopædia,* Volume XXVII (London, 1843)—except that the opening "I hereby" is not part of the wording attributed to Linnæus (p. 272). The date of Linnæus's work, given as "1776" in A and E, is emended here to "1766", since this date appears in the *Penny Cyclopædia* and no 1776 edition has been located. (Cf. Bercaw 544.)

137.18   Now]   A paragraph break before this word would clarify the transition here. See other discussions of paragraphing at 7.1, 42.30, 121.8, 123.10, 284.19, and 365.18.

137.31 Trumpa] There is the possibility that the spelling here should be "Trumpo", since some standard nineteenth-century discussions—such as those in the article on whales in the fourth edition of the *Encyclopædia Britannica* (Edinburgh, 1810) or in the first American edition of the *Edinburgh Encyclopædia* (Philadelphia, 1832)—employ the spelling "Trumpo" and since *o* and *a* were not always easily distinguishable in Melville's hand (cf. the emendations at 12.15, 104.3, and 462.7). However, "Trumpa" was indeed used, as Melville points out, "among the English of old", for it occurs several times in the account of Thomas Edge's voyages in John Harris's *Navigantium atque Itinerantium Bibliotheca* (London, 1705), I, 574—on the same page from which Melville took one of the extracts (see the discussion at xxi.1–23); it also occurs in *Purchas His Pilgrimes* ("The Third Part"; London, 1625), p. 471 (cf. the discussion at 334.33).

138.32 Gronlands Walfisk] The corrupt A and E form "Growlands Walfish", probably a misreading of Melville's hand, is emended from his apparent direct source, the *Penny Cyclopædia* (London, 1843), s.v. "Whales", XXVII, 296.

140.27 Bibliographical system] The delayed announcement of this system, several paragraphs after classification according to it has begun, seems anomalous enough to suggest the possibility of some error in the copying or typesetting, especially since the classification is begun so abruptly, at 137.20, with no comment on this humorous bookish basis for determining "the grand divisions", beyond the phrase "According to magnitude". The paragraph starting at 139.38 contains the discussion of possible bases of classification (actually used by naturalists) that leads up to announcement of the bibliographical system at 140.25–28; this paragraph might be expected to be followed by the paragraph beginning "First: According to magnitude", which actually precedes it by two pages, at 137.20. Possibly this illogical order resulted from Melville's writing the chapter in several stages, employing different source books. But that he finally intended the present ordering is clear, because no group of sentences forms a detachable unit (one that could have been on a single displaced manuscript leaf) that by emendation could be transposed to achieve the more logical order. The two-paragraph passage (139.38–140.28) is integral and as it stands is tied to the preceding paragraph on finback whales and is introduced as a digression, "In connexion with . . . ", and similarly ended with "To proceed."—Melville's frequent phrase for returning to his main line of discussion after an inserted passage. In any case, no emendation is possible, and the literary effect of the illogical displacement is to enhance Melville's intention in willfully imposing the "Bibliographical system"—that is, questioning the adequacy of scientific taxonomy to encompass reality.

141.14   *Killer . . . Thrasher*]   In A and E the order of these two names does not correspond with the order in which they are actually discussed (143.6–20). That the proper switch is of the two names here rather than of the two paragraphs later is made clear by the next to the last sentence of the "Thrasher" paragraph ("Still less is known of the Thrasher than of the Killer"), which implies the previous discussion of the "Killer".

142.35–38   "when . . . Windsor."]   These words are not a direct quotation from the accounts of Frobisher's voyages included in the third volume of Hakluyt's *Principal Navigations* (London, 1600)—which, as the main source for these voyages, is the obvious candidate for Melville's "Black Letter". Indeed, there is only a brief reference in Hakluyt (III, 65) to the "horne . . . in her [Queen Elizabeth's] Wardrope of Robes" (the statement appears in George Best's account, originally published—in black letter—in 1578). Queen Elizabeth's waving, credited to "Black Letter" in the earlier part of this sentence, is also briefly described in Hakluyt (III, 29); but it is associated there with the beginning of Frobisher's first voyage, whereas the display of the horn follows his second voyage. The statement that the horn hung in Windsor Castle "for a long period after" suggests that the quotation does not in fact come from one of the contemporary accounts; possibly the wording is Melville's own, as it presumably is in the other quotation attributed to "old black-letter" (10.23–28).

143.29   i.e.]   The necessary period following "e" was supplied by E, but NN retains the unitalicized form of A.

146.2   *Specksynder*]   Chapter 33, on close reading, is so incoherent in its shifting focus that one suspects textual corruption of the sort that might result from a misplacement of manuscript leaves, but no emendation on that basis seems possible. Harrison Hayford conjectures, "Such questions [raised by this chapter] suggest a genetic phase of *Moby-Dick* when Melville was projecting a book that would focus both its narrative line and its whaling activities on the harpooneers. And even, it could be, on a harpooneer hero— on Bulkington, whom he intended to be Ishmael's comrade at sea, before he substituted the harpooneer Queequeg. In the opening three paragraphs of 'The Specksynder' (ch. 33), Melville carefully established the harpooneer class of officers as intermediary between crewmen and officers; the harpooneer is in a sense both and thus provides a social bridge between them. Fictionally, in these three paragraphs Melville was preparing the way for some narrative situation that was to follow. But nothing does follow from it. The chapter in its fourth paragraph drops the harpooneers altogether and with a shaky transition via the topic of officer-crew relations is soon discussing Ahab's relations with his crew, in highly exalted terms. Some ill-spliced genetic seam divides the chapter into two ill-matched parts. The Specksynder-harpooneer is displaced by the captain: perhaps Bulkington by Ahab? Its first part is the one passage . . . that I can now identify as one I think Melville wrote for Bulkington. My suspicion is that these opening paragraphs were setting up Bulkington, Ishmael's comrade-to-be, for a role which involved his harpooneer status between officers and men. If so, several inferences follow. If Bulkington as harpooneer was to be the book's heroic figure, Ishmael as his comrade would have been personally close to the action and the main actor, whereas now he has no plausible close access to Ahab—one reason for the book's curious hiatus in point-of-view, and for the veteran-narrator's (putatively Ishmael's) reporting various matters he could know nothing about. . . . Bulkington, in Melville's mind, outgrew his station, 'becoming', in his heroic role, Ahab. For if Bulkington was a heroic harpooneer, at what was his harpoon, in more than a routine whaleman's way, to be pointed? At the White Whale some call Moby Dick?" ("Unnecessary Duplicates: A Key to the Writing of *Moby-Dick,*" in *New Perspectives on Melville,* ed. Faith Pullin [Edinburgh: Edinburgh University Press, 1978], p. 156.) See the discussion at 16.2. For the spelling of the title of this chapter, see the discussion at x.17.

147.5 the grand distinction] See the NOTE ON THE TEXT, p. 788.

148.3 entrenchments] The possibility that Melville wrote "entrancements" is suggested by Ahab's use elsewhere of arts to entrance the minds of his officers and crew, notably in Chapter 36 by several dramatic devices and in Chapter 124 by creating his own compass-needle (518.8ff.). However, this whole passage (147.34ff.) develops a point paralleling the figure of "entrenchments": that "behind . . . forms and usages" Ahab sometimes "masked himself".

148.15 direst] See the NOTE ON THE TEXT, p. 789.

155.7 Saint Stylites] The solecism in so designating St. Simeon Stylites by his epithet alone is unemendable, since Melville no doubt wrote it thus, whether or not he recognized its impropriety. See the discussions at 243.12 and 376.20.

156.33 coolish] See the NOTE ON THE TEXT, p. 788.

157.7–9 "A . . . Greenland;"] The quoted title is Melville's humorous creation and not the title of an actual book. The travestied discussion of the invention of the crow's nest (157.11) actually occurs in *An Account of the Arctic Regions* (Edinburgh, 1820), by William Scoresby, Jr.; Scoresby there attributes its invention to his father (on the ship *Resolution)* and makes only brief reference to his own use of it (II, 203–5). In his own "Captain Sleet"

Melville merges the two Scoresbys, making the inventor of the crow's nest and the author of the account of its invention the same person. See the discussions at 298.22, 409.36, and 445.28.

158.16 Queequeg . . . off duty] This casual detail poses an unemendable discrepancy since it would mean that Queequeg is not in the same watch with Ishmael, who is here on duty to stand lookout at the masthead. But although the fact has not yet been stated (and indeed never is narrated), they are both later consistently though casually placed in Starbuck's boat. See the discussions at 161.7 and 214.10.

158.37–38 "Roll . . . vain."] Melville has of course substituted "blubber-hunters" for "fleets" in this quotation from Byron's *Childe Harold's Pilgrimage* (London, 1818), Canto 4, stanza 179, in which "ocean" is capitalized.

159.21 Wickliff's] See the NOTE ON THE TEXT, p. 790.

161.7 an order] Another instance of odd "duplication" occurs here. True, once a whaling ship had settled into sea routine an order to muster all hands aft would be unusual, but it was an order regularly given early in a whaler's cruise, and therefore such a scene would be expected about here or a bit earlier in this fictional voyage. In J. N. Reynolds's "Mocha Dick," *Knickerbocker*, XIII (May, 1839), 377–92, a source for *Moby-Dick* (reprinted in the Norton Critical Edition [New York, 1967], pp. 571–90), it is related that "soon after a whale-ship . . . is fairly at sea, the men are summoned aft; then boats' crews are selected by the captain and first mate . . . " (p. 576). Similarly, Albert Cook Church, in *Whale Ships and Whaling* (New York: W. W. Norton, 1938), states, "Once fairly offshore no time is lost making preparations for the business of the voyage. The captain calls all hands aft, reads the rules governing the ship, explains the objects of the voyage and the necessity for co-operation. Officers and crew receive their instructions, watches and boat crews are chosen, the ship's routine is established and masthead lookouts posted in the 'crow's nest' from sunrise to sunset" (p. 29). It is an oddity of *Moby-Dick* that Melville presents no muster scene as part of the ship's routine. By the oddity of "duplication," such a scene begins in Chapter 22 (102.12; see the discussion), where Captain Peleg orders the first mate to "call all hands, then. Muster 'em aft here . . . " and reiterates it (103.9–10) as the crew, amidships, delay coming aft. But then, instead of the muster and the order of business as outlined by Reynolds and Church, the next orders are to strike the tent and man the capstan, and the ship gets under way. Conjecturally, Melville had written a normal mustering scene (as begun in Chapter 22) but then reworked it when he introduced Ahab (supplanting the original captain) and put it here in Chapter 36 where Ahab "explains the objects of the voyage" not as the regular whale-hunting business the owners expect (see 186.29–34) and Starbuck declares (163.28–29) but as the special quest for Moby Dick. The routine of choosing watches and boat crews is never accounted for in this book beyond the introductory pairing of mates and harpooneers, with no dramatic or even summarized scene. As pointed out in the discussion at 121.8, no mention is anywhere made of the crew's assignment to particular watches. Ishmael's assignment to Starbuck's watch and boat, and as Queequeg's bowsman, is mentioned only incidentally (214.10, 224.9ff., 320.1).

162.1–2 a doubloon] See the NOTE ON THE TEXT, p. 791.

163.8 "Who . . . that?"] Ahab's question, like Starbuck's, entails a breach of narrative realism; see the discussion at 179.7.

165.37–38 shocked into them . . . Leyden jar] The transposed E reading "shocked them into" foreshadowed the now universal twentieth-century misapplication of Melville's Leyden-jar metaphor in the phrase "shock of recognition" in his essay "Hawthorne and His Mosses." The crux of the misunderstanding of this now-famous but misapplied phrase is that in it Melville (like Ahab here) *gives* a "shock of recognition" to Hawthorne, not *gets* one from him or upon meeting him and reading his *Mosses from an Old Manse*. The tenor of Melville's metaphor is clear in the present passage because its vehicle, the Leyden jar, is named, whereas in the essay Melville's intended meaning became lost because the Leyden jar, then a well known laboratory apparatus, is not mentioned and was later generally forgotten. (See "The Lightning-Rod Man" in the NN *Piazza Tales* volume, 124.10.) From the late eighteenth century onward it figured (usually illustrated) in elementary science textbooks to demonstrate the conductivity of the static electricity accumulated in the Leyden jar (as in this passage "in Ahab"). In a favorite application the demonstrator holding the Leyden jar administers a shock from it to the first person in a circle of people holding hands (in illustrations often attractive women in a parlor)—as Melville's essay puts it, "one shock . . . runs the circle round". Thus in his "Mosses" essay Melville puts American critics in the place of the demonstrator and exhorts them to administer "one shock" of critical "recognition" to one American writer, for by doing so they will energize them all—as Ahab here strives to energize his mates—"for genius, all over the world, stands hand in hand, and one shock of recognition runs the whole circle round" (see the NN *Piazza Tales* volume, pp. 248–49). In the "Mosses" passage Melville was bestowing such a "shock of recognition" on one insufficiently recognized American writer whom his essay proclaims most worthy of it—Nathaniel Hawthorne. Thereby, Melville believed, other American writers would be encouraged. Melville was not, as critics have thought ever since Edmund Wilson popularized the phrase, in his *Shock of Recognition* (New York: Doubleday, 1943), himself experiencing a "shock of recognition" in the quite different sense

Wilson took it to stand for, that is, one transmitted to him upon his encounter with Hawthorne and his *Mosses*. By now, however, Melville's thus misinterpreted metaphor has become a critical commonplace. Harrison Hayford clarifies Melville's original meaning in a forthcoming publication based on his paper "Melville's Missed Metaphor," delivered at "A Melville Seminar in Honor of Nathalia Wright," University of Tennessee, Knoxville, October 2–3, 1981.

166.22    sit]    Since in normal idiom the sun would "set" not "sit" (as in the following chapter title, "Sunset"), the possibility occurs that this A and E reading is wrong. But it can be explained: the adjective "ratifying" introduces a characteristic metaphorical word play by Ahab in which the sun waits to "sit" as in official session to ratify the deed—i.e., declare it history.

168.6    prophecy]    It may be discrepant that Ahab here alludes to a prophecy of his dismemberment that is elsewhere reported only by Elijah (92.30–31) and, though true (in the loss of his leg), is not one of his parallels to the wicked biblical King Ahab, who was killed by a man who "drew a bow at a venture," and whose blood, as Ishmael remembered, "the dogs licked up" (I Kings 22:34, 38; see 79.11–12). Even so, Ahab's name did otherwise "somehow prove prophetic", as the old squaw Tistig at Gay Head predicted (79.17–18), and just as King Ahab had both true and false prophets, so Captain Ahab has his true Elijah and false Fedallah, among various others. On the possible textual implications of the book's having seven prophets (besides Father Mapple—see the discussion at 42.30) of the profane captain's hell-bound career, see Harrison Hayford, "Unnecessary Duplicates: A Key to the Writing of *Moby-Dick*," in *New Perspectives on Melville*, ed. Faith Pullin (Edinburgh: Edinburgh University Press, 1978), pp. 132–34, and the discussions at 42.30, 71.1, and 242.21.

170.7    feed]    The A and E reading "feed" is possibly an error for "feel". The sense with "feed" contrasts Starbuck, whose soul is forced to *knowledge,* with wild things (untutored, without knowledge), which are forced merely to *feed.* The sense with "feel" parallels Starbuck with wild untutored things—just as they are forced to *feel,* so, too, his soul (held to knowledge) does now *feel* the latent horror in life. In the second reading Starbuck is expressing the same idea that Ishmael develops four chapters later in "The Whiteness of the Whale" (chap. 42, 194.21–195.5), when he argues that he and the Vermont colt share the same intuitive knowledge of the world's demonism: " . . . thou beholdest even in a dumb brute, the instinct of the knowledge of the demonism in the world." As whiteness in various things "appeals with such power to the soul" of Ishmael, so the smell of "wild animal muskiness" from a shaken buffalo robe frightens the colt: "Though neither knows where lie the nameless things of which the mystic sign gives forth such hints; yet with me, as with the colt, somewhere those things must exist." Cf. also Ahab's statement that "Pagan leopards . . . give no reasons for the torrid life they feel!" (164.22–24). However, since "feed" does make sense, it is not emended.

171.21  loves]  The concluding lines of each stanza of Charles Fenno Hoffman's "Sparkling and Bright," as printed in the *New-Yorker* for March 21, 1840 (p. 8), and in *Love's Calendar, Lays of the Hudson, and Other Poems* (New York, 1847), pp. 117–18, contain the word "loves" at this point, with no punctuation. The A and E reading "love," (i.e., with a comma) produces a different, and less satisfactory, meaning. Given the difficulty of final *s* in Melville's handwriting, it is more likely that his *s* here was misread as a comma (or that he was simply misquoting) than that he was purposely shifting the word to the singular. Therefore Hoffman's wording is restored. Cf. the emendations at xxiii.9, xxiii.17, 59.5, 102.6, 153.9, 175.1, 175.7, 212.2, and 280.22.

173.3  HARPOONEERS]  Two of the three harpooneers, Tashtego and Daggoo, appear in the ensuing scene, but—oddly for a major character—not Queequeg. Possibly Melville omitted him by oversight; possibly, however, he wrote the scene at a stage so early that he had not yet made Queequeg a harpooneer—a conjecture consistent with further discrepancies involving Queequeg. See the discussions at 61.35–36, 477.39, and 478.17.

173.6–8  Farewell . . . commanded—]  The first two lines are quoted from a popular sea song—variously called "Spanish Ladies" or "Farewell and Adieu" or "Farewell to You, Ye Fine Spanish Ladies." The song has been often reprinted, with some variation in wording. Although Melville probably knew the song well and needed no printed source for it (in Chapter 74 of *White-Jacket* he calls it "a favorite thing with British man-of-war's men" [NN311.17–18]), the wording of these two lines in A and E corresponds with that in Chapter 17 of Frederick Marryat's *Poor Jack* (London, 1840), p. 116 (cf. Bercaw 482). The third line here, however, is at variance with the third line of the song, which traditionally begins "For we've received orders". The shift to "Our captain's commanded" is possibly a deliberate alteration to emphasize Ahab's effect on the crew, as Agnes Dicken Cannon suggests in "Melville's Use of Sea Ballads and Songs," *Western Folklore,* XXIII (1964), 1–16. Certainly Melville knew the usual wording of the line, for in his poem "Tom Deadlight," which follows the pattern of this "famous old sea-ditty", the third line begins "For I've received orders".

173.13–22  Our . . . whale!]  The version of "Captain Bunker" that appears in a book Melville frequently drew upon, J. Ross Browne's *Etchings of a Whaling Cruise* (New York, 1846), pp. 77–78, differs in wording from the quotation in A and E at five points: it reads "blowed" for "blew", "Get" for

"Oh," "gallant" for "fine", "let" for "may", and "a striking of" for "striking". Although "Get" seems a distinctly better reading than "Oh," no emendation is made because the number of differences, not attributable to a misreading of handwriting, suggests that Melville may have intentionally altered the wording or that he was quoting from a different source altogether. (The last two lines correspond to the wording quoted on page 17 of Browne; see the discussion at xxviii.23–25. Cf. Sealts 88, Bercaw 82.)

175.1   AZORES]   The A and E reading "AZORE" (here and at 175.7) has not been located elsewhere as either a noun or an adjectival form (usually "Azorean") for "Azores", which is not a plural. NN emends on the assumption that the copyist or the compositor misread Melville's frequently unclear final s (for further examples see the discussions at 59.5 and 171.21 and the NOTE ON THE TEXT, p. 792). At three points in Moby-Dick "the Azores" are mentioned: 121.17, 207.2, 232.4–5.

175.26   your scholars]   See the NOTE ON THE TEXT, p. 789.

176.16   valed]   The E spelling is adopted rather than the A "veiled", as required by the sense; but the hyphenated form, "low-valed" (as well as "high-palmed" immediately following), employed in E, is not required.

176.20   Pirohitee's]   This spelling of the peak's name (now known as La Diadème) has not been located elsewhere except in Omoo (chap. 18, NN65.18) and Mardi (chap. 152, NN492.9). It may be Melville's own idiosyncratic rendition of the native name given as "Pito-hito" by William Ellis in his Polynesian Researches (New York, 1833), I, 28–29, a work that was one of Melville's main sources for those books.

177.23   ST. JAGO'S]   NN retains this anomalous A and E anglicized variant of "São Tiago" or "Santiago," the largest of the Cape Verde Islands. Cf. the reference to "a St. Jago monkey" at 406.16.

179.7   I learned]   An unemendable discrepancy emerges (despite the attempt to conceal it in the ensuing paragraph) as to who does and does not know that Moby Dick was the whale that took off Ahab's leg. On shore, Peleg has told Ishmael "the monstrousest [not "a"] parmacetty" did it (72.1–3), and Elijah concedes that "every one knows a'most . . . that a parmacetti" did it (92.33–36); but though Peleg may and Elijah must know that the whale was Moby Dick, neither has named him. In the "Quarter-Deck" chapter, Starbuck (who like all three harpooneers has heard of Moby Dick, 162.20ff.) gets his first glimmer of it, as apparently do Stubb and Flask, and Ahab is angry that someone has told Starbuck (163.3–8). All this ignorance of the facts, presented in dramatized scenes, is consistent enough, though implausible—why did the crew on that voyage not know and tell "all Nantucket"? But such general ignorance is discrepant with Melville's representing Ishmael as able to learn with "greedy ears" (from whom?) "the history of that murderous monster" and to summarize it, starting off with Moby Dick's having become widely known, even legendary, among whalemen (179.10–180.1), and implying even while concealing that he was "popularly" known to be the whale involved in Ahab's disastrous encounter (180.12–14). As the book stands, the discrepancy between those dramatic scenes and this expository chapter serves Melville's purpose of mystification, though it may have arisen from different conceptions he held at separate stages of composition. See the discussions at 163.8, 489.9–10, 523.18–19, 543.17, 551.13, and 569.14.

180.17 them, almost,] As punctuated in A and E (set off by commas) "almost" modifies "every one of them". Possibly, however, Melville meant it rather to modify what follows ("almost as boldly and fearlessly"), and it would do so were the second comma (or both commas) removed, as added mistakenly by Melville, the copyist, or the compositor. The emendation is not made because the present reading also makes an acceptable sense.

181.27–28 Olassen . . . Povelsen] Melville derived these names from Thomas Beale's *The Natural History of the Sperm Whale* (London, 1839), p. 4, where they are linked as "Olassen and Povelsen". In A and E the first name appears in this same form, the second as "Povelson". "Olassen" is in fact an error for "Olafsen", but because it is the form that Melville accurately reproduced from his source, NN does not alter it; "Povelson" (here and at 181.37), on the other hand, probably resulted from a misreading of handwriting or from Melville's own slip in copying from Beale, and it is emended.

181.33 terror] The A and E reading "terrors" is emended to the singular form from Melville's direct source, Thomas Beale's *The Natural History of the Sperm Whale* (London, 1839), p. 5, because the rest of the direct quotation follows Beale's wording so exactly (though reordering the portions quoted) that the plural form does not seem intentional on Melville's part. Beale attributes the quotation to Cuvier, but it in fact occurs in one of the supplements—by Edward Griffith, Charles Hamilton Smith, and Edward Pidgeon, not "the Baron himself" (181.32)—to Baron Georges Cuvier's *The Animal Kingdom*, Volume IV, *The Class Mammalia* (London, 1827), p. 464. (Cf. Sealts 171, Bercaw 186.)

182.37 Strella] The emended A and E reading "Strello" may have come from a misreading of Melville's terminal *a* as *o;* the mountain referred to is Serra da Estrella. Willard Thorp *(Moby-Dick* [New York: Oxford University Press, 1947], p. 170n.) cites Marie, Comtesse d'Aulnoy's *Relation du voyage d'Espagne* (The Hague, 1691), II, 106–7, where the legend of "le Lac de la Montagne de Strella" is recounted.

186.8   perceptibility]   I.e., "perceptivity". The *Oxford English Dictionary* definition "capacity or faculty of perceiving; perceptivity" is labeled obsolete, with citations in 1642 and 1662. This is apparently an example of Melville's common use of older word forms and senses. See the discussions at 213.1 and 250.19.

191.2   Praries]   See the discussion at xi.29.

191.26–27   so . . . as that]   The A and E reading, in which "as" seems superfluous, is retained by NN because it was possibly idiomatic (it passed the finicky Bentley editor—see pp. 786–87) and was almost certainly written by Melville—who, however, sometimes lost track of syntax (see the discussions at 93.27–28, 192.5, and 192.19).

192.5   as much the badge]   See the NOTE ON THE TEXT, p. 790.

192.19   but, nevertheless]   Here "but," is superfluous. See the discussion at 191.26–27 and the NOTE ON THE TEXT, p. 793, footnote 38.

199.32   circular]   Although neither Sumner W. D. Scott nor Luther S. Mansfield and Howard P. Vincent (see their Hendricks House edition of *Moby-Dick* [New York, 1952], pp. 717–18) could locate a copy of this circular, Scott pointed out that "A 'Notice to Whalemen,' dated May 1, 1851, which conforms in every respect to the circular described in *Moby Dick* is reproduced in Lieut. M. F. Maury's *Explanations and Sailing Directions to Accompany the Wind and Current Charts* (Washington, 1851), pp. 207–216, with the explanation that it had been 'published in the newspapers of the day' " (see Scott's "The Whale in *Moby Dick*," Ph.D. dissertation, University of Chicago, 1950, p. 10).

199.39   on]   Matthew Fontaine Maury's statement (dated May, 1851), on page 207 of his *Explanations and Sailing Directions* (Washington, 1851), reads at this point "the number of days on which . . ."; the less idiomatic A and E reading "in which" probably resulted from a misreading of Melville's handwriting rather than an intentional alteration on his part, and it is therefore emended. The rest of the quotation from Maury is accurate in wording, except for the insertion of "of" before both "latitude" and "longitude" and the deletion of "one" before both occurrences of "of which".

200.18   Seychelle]   This A and E variant of "Seychelles" occurs in three of Melville's prime sources: Thomas Beale's *The Natural History of the Sperm Whale* (London, 1839), p. 20; J. Ross Browne's *Etchings of a Whaling Cruise* (New York, 1846), p. 528; and the *Penny Cyclopædia*, s.v. "Seychelles". The word (cf. "AZORES", emended at 175.1, 7) is not a plural; the archipelago in the Indian Ocean north of Madagascar was named (1756) for Moreau de Seychelles.

200.28   probability]   The NN emendation of the A and E reading "possibility" is clearly required by the logic of progression in the terms: from "possibilities" to "probabilities", then from "probability" (not "possibility") to "certainty".

201.9   covertly]   See the NOTE ON THE TEXT, p. 789.

201.24   No]   See the NOTE ON THE TEXT, p. 793.

204.9–10   three instances similar to this]   Melville loses sight of the construction: three similar ones plus this one would make four in all, whereas only three instances are involved in the paragraph, whose repetitive development is one of several anomalies in the chapter that may have resulted from separate stages in its composition.

205.1   Timor Jack]   In A this whale is called "Timor Tom" and the whale three lines later "New Zealand Jack"; but when the name "New Zealand Tom" appears in the first line of the next paragraph, it becomes clear that a mix-up has occurred. E, in an attempt to correct the error, makes the simplest change that will produce consistency—changing "Tom" to "Jack" in the third instance. However, two books Melville used as sources settle the matter: the whales are "New Zealand Tom" and a nameless Timor whale in Frederick Debell Bennett, *Narrative of a Whaling Voyage* (London, 1840), II, 220, and both "Timor Jack" and "New Zealand Tom" in Thomas Beale, *The Natural History of the Sperm Whale* (London, 1839), p. 183, in his copy of which (Sealts 52) Melville marked this passage and underlined "Timor Jack". These sources are pointed out by Howard P. Vincent in *The Trying-Out of MOBY-DICK* (Boston: Houghton Mifflin, 1949), pp. 188–89, and in the Hendricks House edition of *Moby-Dick* (New York, 1952), p. 720, note 202.20. Cf. Bercaw 51.

205.17   Church]   The A and E reading "Butler" is a factual error, for it was Captain Benjamin Church who pursued Annawon in Rhode Island in 1676; Lieutenant Colonel William Butler led an expedition in upstate New York a century later (1778) against the Mohawk Indian leader Brant. The error is probably a simple slip, for Melville was acquainted with the story of Brant, who is mentioned in *Pierre* (NN6.3–9) as a wartime opponent and later dinner companion of Pierre's grandfather general, as he in fact was of Melville's own maternal grandfather, General Peter Gansevoort (see the Hendricks House edition of *Pierre* [New York, 1949], pp. 432–33, note 4.23). Melville also knew William Leete Stone's *Life of Joseph Brant— Thayendanegea* (New York, 1838—cf. Sealts 491a), which discusses Butler at I, 355–56, 367–68. Since the context of this passage—a chapter entitled "The Affidavit"—is one that stresses facts, it seems unlikely that Melville made the change intentionally; hence NN emends to correct the error.

205.26–27   Moby Dick]   See the discussion at v.1 concerning the hyphenation of the title, especially the third paragraph, touching on the point that "hideous and intolerable allegory" here refers to the white whale, not to the title of the book. Many commentators have misconstrued it, presumably because "allegory" now usually refers to a whole work, not (as an archaic synonym for "symbol") to a single part of it—in this instance to the white whale—and also because the inconsistent styling of this book, in which titles are not always italicized or placed in quotation marks, allows the words "Moby Dick" to be taken as meaning the book's title. See also the discussions at 110.15, 261.19–20, 326.7, and 366.5, and the NOTE ON THE TEXT, p. 799, footnote 45.

206.3   others,]   A and E have no comma after "others", thereby making the construction seem to mean that on one particular voyage Ishmael's ship spoke many ships (far more than thirty), among which thirty different ships had had at least one sailor killed by a whale. That meaning is far less emphatic than the one demanded by the context—that "every one" of the ships encountered had sustained such loss of life: otherwise "different" makes no sense. Adding the comma makes the sentence more emphatic, but it also makes clear that Ishmael is claiming to have made "many" voyages to the Pacific—a claim not explicitly made elsewhere, though it is supported by various passages, such as 288.18–19, 444.23–24, and 449.11–14.

206.31–32   I have seen Owen Chase]   This is an unemendable factual error: although Melville wrote the statement (and the rest of the sentence) as his own true experience, not Ishmael's fictional one, he was mistaken in the belief that he had met Owen Chase, who was not at sea when the supposed meeting took place. It is true, however, that at sea he conversed with Chase's son and read Chase's narrative (borrowed there from the son). See Melville's manuscript account "What I know of Owen Chace &c", reproduced and transcribed below, pp. 979–83.

206.35–39, 207.25–39   "Every . . . animal."]   These four quotations from Owen Chase's Narrative of the . . . Shipwreck of the Whale-Ship Essex of Nantucket (New York, 1821), pp. 37–38, 38–39, 52, and 45, are accurate in wording, but the italics in 207.37 and 207.39 do not appear in the original. (Cf. Sealts 134, Bercaw 130.) See the discussion at xxv.10.

208.3–19   "By . . . uninjured."]   This quotation from the beginning (pp. 328–29) of Chapter 17 in the second volume of Georg Heinrich von Langsdorff's Voyages and Travels in Various Parts of the World (London, 1813–14) is accurate in wording, except that "sprang" appears instead of "sprung" at 208.7. While "sprang" could have resulted from a misreading of handwriting, it is also possible that Melville intentionally altered the spelling to agree with the form of the past tense used later in the quotation (208.14), and it is allowed to stand. However, the A and E spelling "Ochotsh" (208.4) is clearly a mistake—probably deriving from a misreading of handwriting—for the spelling in Langsdorff, "Ochotsk", which is here restored (cf. the spelling "Okotsk" in *Redburn*, NN35.12). (Cf. Bercaw 433.)

209.5 over] The A and E reading "on" does not make sense; Melville's source, Lionel Wafer's *A New Voyage and Description of the Isthmus of America* (London, 1699), reveals the obviously correct word, for it reads "over" at this point (p. 212). The other differences in wording between Melville's quotation and Wafer's original seem likely to be intentional changes introduced by Melville, and they are allowed to remain: there is an unmarked ellipsis of ten words (giving the latitude) after "were" at 208.35, one of two words ("and Bark") after "ship" at 208.36, and one of three words ("of the Ship") after "guns" at 209.3; and "in such" at 208.36–37 was originally "into such a", "against" at 209.1 was "upon", and "the shock" at 209.3 was "this Shock".

210.15 Commander Davies] The A and E reading "Commodore Davis" is emended from Melville's source, the article on "Whale" by C. Hamilton Smith in John Kitto's standard *Cyclopædia of Biblical Literature* (first published in Edinburgh in 1845), II, 947. Melville's knowledge of Kitto is discussed by Howard P. Vincent in *The Trying-Out of MOBY-DICK* (Boston: Houghton Mifflin, 1949), pp. 271–74. (Cf. Bercaw 421 and the discussion at xvi.1.)

212.28 manufactured] This word is conceivably a textual corruption. Neither in generalized reference to all mankind (212.27) nor in particular reference to Ahab's savage crew (212.29–33) or the Crusaders (212.33–38) does it seem to mean industrialized products (as in "oil in its manufactured state"). The word "manufactured" does make sense in the context (1) as conveying Ahab's contempt for factitious men, and (2) as hinting his blasphemous view of the implied maker of mass-produced men—both are attitudes of Ahab amply paralleled elsewhere. However, neither attitude is otherwise brought into this paragraph, and both intrude extraneous elements upon its otherwise consistently integral restatements of the two contrasting elements in Ahab's thought here about men: their capacity for temporary idealism versus their native permanent bent to materialism. Further, the word "manufactured" is redundant, since the topic of native bent is already carried by the phrase "constitutional condition". A further intrusion, of a grammatical order, by this sentence upon the paragraph's consistency is its shift to the singular (in "the manufactured man") from the otherwise regular use of plurals for men (as shown in the inflected forms of nouns, pronouns, and verbs) in the other sentences (after the first): "mankind" (212.27); "crew", "their", "them", "they", "they", "their" (212.30–32); "Crusaders", "their" (212.33–35); "they", "their" (212.36–37); "these men"

(212.38–39); and "They", "them", "them" (212.39–213.2). To meet these objections would require emendation of both "manufactured" and "man". A somewhat daring three-word emendation for "manufactured" seems possible: "mass of actual", which entails the secondary emendation of "man" to "men". This double emendation would assume that a copyist misread in Melville's manuscript the words "mass of actual" (scrawled closely together) as "manufactured" and consequently also misread the word "men" as "man"—and further that in his proofreading Melville did not catch the misreading. The resulting phrase would render the sentence consistent (in the sense set forth above) with the rest of the paragraph. Parallel phrasing elsewhere may be adduced. The first paragraph of Chapter 107 (466.3–9) furnishes a close parallel to both the high ideal and the low materialistic aspects that Ahab sees here in men, particularly in these words, " . . . high abstracted man . . . seems a wonder, a grandeur, and a woe" and " . . . take mankind in mass, and . . . they seem a mob of unnecessary duplicates". Similarly, Melville in a letter to Hawthorne asserted an "unconditional democracy in all things" while confessing "a dislike to all mankind—in the mass" (June 1?, 1851, in Merrell R. Davis and William H. Gilman, eds., *The Letters of Herman Melville* [New Haven and London: Yale University Press, 1960], p. 127); and in Chapter 42 of *The Confidence-Man* the Cosmopolitan uses the phrase "the mass of mankind" and repeats it, telling the Barber, "you are no Timon to hold the mass of mankind untrustworthy" (NN229.38–230.1). However, since there is a sense in which "manufactured" is appropriate, no emendation is ventured here.

213.1   perspective]   NN retains the A and E reading, an adjective questioned by the *Oxford English Dictionary* as misused for "prospective" but with examples from 1709 and 1796 and as a noun ("a churchwarden in perspective") by Charlotte Brontë in 1849. Cf. the discussions at 186.8 and 250.19. Melville's accurate use of "prospectively" at 112.5, however, suggests that he may have written "prospective" here, miscopied as "perspective".

214.10   attendant . . . Queequeg]   No account has been given either of Ishmael's choice by Starbuck as a member of the first mate's watch or of his assignment as bowsman in that mate's boat. See the discussions at 158.16, 161.7, 220.13, and 320.1.

215.13   modified]   See the NOTE ON THE TEXT, p. 790.

215.19   mad]   Possibly a misreading for "wild": Tashtego is nowhere before (or after) characterized as "mad", as the demonstrative "that" would imply; but he is introduced with the epithet "this wild Indian" (120.31), in the present passage "wild" and "wildly" describe his cries and manner (215.17, 26, 28), and later he gives wild screams (284.14) and is again called "that wild Indian" (342.11). "Wild Indian" was an established epithet for "primitive, savage, or roving rather than settled" ones (see the entry in the *Dictionary of American English;* cf. the *Oxford English Dictionary,* "Wild man"); Melville used it elsewhere, e.g., *Pierre,* NN307.4, and in his 1849 journal, Friday, December 14.

216.22   five dusky phantoms]   An unemendable discrepancy emerges and persists concerning Fedallah: all five of these men are repeatedly grouped as "yellow" (217.13–14, 219.29, 220.19–20, 223.14–15), even though Fedallah (while repeatedly included in the count of five and called a "gamboge ghost" at 325.6) is individualized (220.23–26) and distinguished from these "subordinate" Manilla Islands natives as "swart" and of separate origin (217.8–13 and 230.34–231.24). Five has to be the maximum number in Ahab's crew in any case because that was the regular number of oarsmen in a whaleboat, plus an officer as headsman—in this case Ahab himself, first here in Chapter 28 and regularly thereafter to the end (see the discussions at 230.6–7 and 230.6–8). The apparent dilemma posed that Fedallah must be either yellow or a sixth oarsman (he turns out to be neither) suggests two compositional stages: an early one in which he was not yet individualized among the five dusky phantoms, then a later one in which he became swart, a "devil" figure (325.14ff.), a prophet, Ahab's shadow, and a Parsee (see the discussions at 168.6 and 217.21)—all without Melville's having made revisions to reduce the number of unnamed yellow oarsmen from five to four.

217.21   Fedallah]   That this Arabic name would be an impossible one for a Parsee is asserted by Luther S. Mansfield and Howard P. Vincent in their Hendricks House edition of *Moby-Dick* (New York, 1952), p. 732; their assertion is refuted by Dorothee Metlitsky Finkelstein, in *Melville's Orienda* (New Haven and London: Yale University Press, 1961), p. 288. The anomaly is also discussed by George Stewart as possibly "another example of Melville's carelessness in details of which there are so many," but possibly also as having "something to do with the fact that Fedallah is not declared to be a Parsee" until Chapter 73 (328.1). "Quite possibly Melville had the original idea that Fedallah was simply another of the 'Manilla-men' (who might well be Mohammedans), and only later had the idea of making him a Parsee, in order to bring in the idea of the fire-worshiper. In this case the name might be some further evidence of the fact of a change of plan between earlier and later parts of the book" ("The Two *Moby-Dicks*," *American Literature,* XXV [January, 1954], 426–27). See the discussion at 216.22.

217.22   half-hissed]   See the discussion at 254.17.

218.20   back!—Never]   See the NOTE ON THE TEXT, p. 798, footnote 43.

219.18–19   those odd sort of humorists]   NN policy does not call for "correction" of this sort of grammatically objectionable but idiomatically common constructions when they are presumably authorial. See the NOTE ON THE TEXT, p. 793, footnote 39.

220.13   For me]   A serious but unemendable confusion arises from the unusually inconsistent handling of point of view in Chapter 48. First-person reference by Ishmael, dropped near the end of Chapter 47 at 216.5, is taken up here momentarily but again dropped, to be resumed only at 224.10, with "Our sail . . . ". As George Stewart remarks, ". . . the question is: 'In which boat is Ishmael?' He is certainly not in Ahab's or in Flask's. In the latter part of the chapter [224.10ff.] he is certainly in Starbuck's. But in the earlier part he seems to be in Stubb's. Note that when Stubb's and Starbuck's boats diverge, Starbuck goes out of the picture, and we are given the words of Stubb. Later we have mention of Tashtego, Stubb's harpooneer, 'whose eyes had been setting to windward like two fixed stars' [222.11–12]. This is surely too intimate a detail to be observed from another boat, and in any case the discovery of the whale might just as well have been made from Starbuck's boat. Only later is Ishmael surely in Starbuck's boat. Then Melville definitely establishes the point of view by writing 'our sail,' and after that Stubb is absent" ("The Two *Moby-Dick*s," *American Literature*, XXV [January, 1954], 442). From such anomalies Stewart infers compositional vestiges and suggests that in the conjectural "Ur-*Moby-Dick*" Ishmael "served for a time at least" (445) in Stubb's boat.

220.36   oar]   See the NOTE ON THE TEXT, p. 789.

222.4   third]   The A and E reading "third" may at first appear to be an error, since Stubb is the second mate. More likely, however, Melville is not referring to Stubb's rank here but identifying him as the third of the mates to be taken up in this passage. Starbuck and Flask have previously been discussed (beginning at 220.36) without any mention of their rank, and there would be no point in Melville's reminding the reader here of Stubb's. NN therefore retains "third" as Melville's intended transitional word. This interpretation of "third mate" removes the basis for (1) the Norton Critical Edition's emendation (New York, 1967) to "second" (p. 191) and (2) for George Stewart's conjecture that Stubb was the third, not second, mate in the "Ur-*Moby-Dick*" (see "The Two *Moby-Dick*s," *American Literature*, XXV [January, 1954], 431, 445).

230.6–7   Ahab . . . regular headsman]   The headsman serves at the stern in the chase as temporary boatsteerer until the whale has been harpooned and then changes places with the forward oarsman-harpooneer, who is permanent boatsteerer, to wield darts and lances in killing the whale (see Chapter 62, "The Dart"). To enhance Ahab's literary role, Melville makes him in the final three-day fray with Moby Dick play first the headsman's role of temporary boatsteerer, then (nonrealistically) that of harpooneer, then again that of headsman as lancer. See the discussions at 442.6 and 489.9–10.

230.6–8   a boat actually apportioned . . . five extra men]   As pointed out in the discussions at 120.1–2 and 121.8–9, the *Pequod* was in fact supplied by her Quaker owners with enough crew, some thirty, to man four whaleboats (five oarsmen and an officer in each), as common in the whale fishery. Thus if, as this passage states, the owners did not mean Ahab to act as the "regular headsman" of the fourth boat (while the three mates were headsmen of the other three), it would appear that the *Pequod* has a "missing whaleboat" to be accounted for. Two explanations of this major discrepancy may be conjectured. A first, genetic explanation may be that at an earlier composition stage Melville actually gave the *Pequod* four boats, the now "missing" fourth then manned by the five now unassigned crewmen and officered either by the captain (perhaps Ahab, perhaps a less-developed version of him, for example Peleg) or by a now missing officer (perhaps Bulkington, perhaps Radney, now of the *Town-Ho*). In any scenario of this explanation, that "missing whaleboat," with her officer and crew, may at a later stage have been revised out of the manuscript as one too many for compositional management, especially in whaling scenes, when, otherwise making five, Ahab's secret "boat and crew" of five "yellow boys" were introduced (see the discussion at 216.22). This genetic line of conjecture might also offer explanations for various anomalies in the handling of the crew, the point of view in whaling scenes, and occasional misassignment of harpooneers and mates throughout the book. A second, alternative explanation might be that Melville, as repeatedly shown in the book, was too concerned with literary scene and effect to be attentive to such routine practical details of whaling as those involved in these discrepancies as to numbers of men and boats. This literary explanation, however, leaves many anomalies only loosely accounted for and is called into question by Melville's consistent specification of four as the number of whaleboats belonging to ships that the *Pequod* encounters (the *Town-Ho* at 256.31, with her mate Radney plus "three junior mates and the four harpooneers" at 250.12–13; the *Jungfrau* at 353.18–19; the *Rose-bud* at 406.38; and the *Rachel* at 531.1, 5, 6); in *Mardi* Melville refers to "thirty men—captain, mates, and crew" and to "the boats of a South Seaman" as "generally four in number, spare ones omitted" (chap. 5, NN19.5–6, 9–10). The *Acushnet*, however, was a small ship, with only three boats, as indicated by her having only three boatsteerers (i.e., harpooneers): two men so designated on her official crew list, plus a third designated there as a seaman but promoted during the voyage, as shown by Melville's memorandum of her crew (see Wilson L. Heflin's dissertation, as cited on p. 999, below). If Melville was drawing on the three-boat *Acushnet*, with the captain and twenty-five men, as the model for his three-boat *Pequod*, his supplying her with a crew of thirty (at the least) still overmans her by one boat's crew. See the RELATED DOCUMENTS, pp. 997–1004, below.

230.12    Archy's]    The reading "Cabaco's" in A and E is emended, since at 218.22–24 it is Archy who claims the discovery.

230.26    solitary knee]    See the discussion at 437.26.

238.14    Pine Barrens in New York State]    Although some annotators of *Moby-Dick* have questioned whether these were in that state (the seemingly better known ones being in New Jersey), the *Dictionary of American English* gives citations placing such a "tract of sandy or peaty land upon which the prevailing native growth is pine" in New York as well as in several southern states.

239.8    on . . . files]    See the NOTE ON THE TEXT, p. 792, footnote 36.

242.21    Tashtego . . . sleep]    Melville blunders unemendably here in representing Tashtego, a harpooneer, as sleeping forward (evidently in the forecastle), where his ramblings were heard by common seamen, rather than "abaft the Pequod's main-mast" (243.5–6) near the captain's cabin where the harpooneers were quartered (147.8–10). (For the same discrepancy with respect to Queequeg, see the discussion at 478.17.) Furthermore, Tashtego the Indian harpooneer seems so unlikely (and unnecessary) a choice of confidant for the *Town-Ho*'s white seaman in communicating "the secret part of the tragedy . . . with Romish injunctions of secrecy" that speculation seems in order whether both the blunder and the unlikely choice may reflect a stage of composition at which Melville had not yet cast the Indian as a harpooneer but only in the crewman role of soothsayer-prophet now assigned to "Tashtego's senior, an old Gay-Head Indian among the crew" (123.37). This old Indian crewman (contradicted by the Manxman) "superstitiously asserted" that Ahab was branded at full forty years old and "not in the fury of any mortal fray, but in an elemental strife at sea" (123.37–124.1). But while this Indian never appears again after furnishing this "wild hint" and the information (later contradicted) that Ahab was "dismasted off Japan" and shipped his whalebone leg there (see the discussion at 124.16–18), the Gay-Header Tashtego is repeatedly associated elsewhere with a secular prophet-seer role—though nothing in his formal introduction except probably the imputation of his being "a son of the Prince of the Powers of the Air" (120.31) forecasts him for this role. As he sights the first whale (215.26–29) he is aloft like "some prophet or seer beholding the shadows of Fate, and by those wild cries announcing their coming"; as he mounts aloft on the whale's head to bale the case, he "seems some Turkish Muezzin calling the good people to prayers" (341.12–13); on the first day of the chase, aloft as lookout, he sights Moby Dick and cries out at almost the same instant as Ahab (547.12–23); and at the end he is aloft nailing Ahab's pennant to the masthead as the ship sinks to hell. Perhaps Melville's original wild Gay-Head Indian was intended to play these parts, and was a soothsaying old crewman, diabolical according to the Puritan "superstition" (120.30), old enough to have followed Ahab's whole career, and associated with that other soothsaying Gay-Head Indian "the old squaw Tistig", who said Ahab's name "would somehow prove prophetic" (79.17–18). Harrison Hayford asks, "Wasn't Tashtego, the wild Indian harpooneer, generated (by adding the possessive and the word 'senior' to the name 'Tashtego' in his epithet 'Tashtego's senior'? [123.37]) from the 'old Gay-Head Indian' prophet, who thus became vestigial in his one appearance while the thus-created Tashtego took over his name and Indian-devil role as Ahab's (Peleg's?) original accompanying prophet and his original series of masthead prophetic assignments . . . ?" ("Unnecessary Duplicates: A Key to the Writing of *Moby-Dick*," in *New Perspectives on Melville,* ed. Faith Pullin [Edinburgh: Edinburgh University Press, 1978], p. 159). See the following discussion.

243.12 closer terms] An unemendable discrepancy appears between this statement of the "closer terms" of two of the Dons, Pedro and Sebastian, among the circle of Ishmael's Spanish friends and the fact that these interlocutors in their five sets of "interluding questions" never call him by name or seem to know it. (Don Pedro addresses him once as "Senor", 248.31, once with no vocative, 250.7–10; Don Sebastian calls him "Sir sailor" once, 256.6, and speaks to him twice with no vocative, 244.3, 258.29ff.; others of the company twice call him "sir sailor", 249.17, 258.34.) Nor does Ishmael address either Pedro or Sebastian by name, but only as "Don" (without a given name—an unwitting gaffe or deliberate democratic presumption on Melville's and perhaps Ishmael's part; see the discussions at 155.7 and 376.20). This inconsequential discrepancy may have a genetic origin. One possible inference is that Melville composed the story at a stage when he had not distinguished its first-person narrator as "Ishmael"—nothing in the chapter so identifies him. Cf. the discussion at 242.21, on the peculiarity of Tashtego's selection as confidant of the *Town-Ho*'s seaman, and the discussion at 244.1.

243.17 westward] See the NOTE ON THE TEXT, p. 793.

244.1 Nantucketer] The A and E reading "Vineyarder" conflicts with three ensuing references that place Radney as a Nantucketer, at 244.34, 244.38, and 258.25–26. Since nothing in the story and no conjectural explanation of the discrepancy indicates which island was Melville's later choice, NN makes the emendation that requires the change of only one word. See the discussion at 123.4–10.

244.10 agrarian] Grammatically, the words "popularly connected with the open ocean" modify "agrarian freebooting impressions", though the sense demands that they modify only "freebooting impressions". What Melville means, in rough paraphrase, is "agrarian freebooting impressions", (attitudes that are piratical in nature, even though they are formed in the interior of a country) similar to the "freebooting impressions popularly connected with the open ocean". That is, in the process of reading the sentence, the reader must take the words "freebooting impressions" in two senses, one when they are construed with the preceding word "agrarian" and the other when they are construed with the succeeding six words. Somewhat elliptical though it is, the construction is explained by another reference in the chapter: Melville is extending the term "freebooting" (ocean piracy) to include agrarian (inland and rural) freebooting as well as "metropolitan" freebooting (249.9). Between 1839 and 1854 "agrarian" farmers were involved in the Anti-Rent War against feudal landlords in New York state, a war unsympathetically chronicled in Cooper's Littlepage Manuscripts trilogy, culminating in *The Redskins* (1846).

244.25 furs . . . Emperors] Melville nods here. The verb tense is questioned by Charles Feidelson (ed., *Moby-Dick* [Indianapolis: Bobbs-Merrill, 1964], p. 325n.) "since there had been no Tartar emperors since the fifteenth century"; but his conjectured reading "gave" does not help, because in that century America did not furnish them furs. Melville's conception rather than his word seems somehow askew.

248.29 "Canallers] At this point H happens to have the correct quotation mark (where A and E have double and single quotation marks), but there is no reason to adopt H's habitual spelling "Canalers".

248.33 "Aye] The erroneous double and single quotation marks in A and E are emended with the correct double quotation mark in H; but the spelling "Ay" in H is not accepted.

249.13 plaza] The A and E reading "plazza" is corrected to "plaza", the reading in H. That the intended word was not "piazza" is indicated by the fact that "piazza" is used at 243.11 to refer to the place where the story is being told ("the thick-gilt tiled piazza of the Golden Inn"); the reference here, in contrast, is to the adjacent public ("crowded") square.

250.19 smoke] The intended reading may be "snake": the use of "smoke" in the sense required by the context, "to urge at high speed," is labeled obsolete by the *Oxford English Dictionary*, with no example after 1658, whereas s.v. "snake" (II, 5) it gives the definition "to drag or pull forcibly or quickly" with relevant nineteenth-century examples, including "snaked those monsters along" from Frank Bullen's *The Cruise of the "Cachelot" round the World after Sperm Whales* (London, 1898). However,

Melville's repeated use of old words, word senses, and spellings warns against hasty emendation (cf. the discussions at 186.8 and 213.1).

251.6 boy's] See the NOTE ON THE TEXT, p. 786, footnote 35.

254.17 hissed] Since no sibilant sounds (fricatives or spirants) occur in Steelkilt's sentence, this verb seems questionable here; but its insistent use to designate his five other speeches in this scene (which do have such words) establishes that it is not a misreading, as Bernard Mosher (accepting "half-hissed" at 217.22) has suggested in "Barnwell, Ekdal, and the Melville World," *Peristalsis* (Winter–Summer, 1947), 31–45 (cited by W. B. Scott, *Parodies, Etcetera & So Forth* [Evanston: Northwestern University Press, 1985], p. 7).

255.13 beneath] See the NOTE ON THE TEXT, p. 792.

256.5 rolls . . . whale!'] See the NOTE ON THE TEXT, pp. 802, 804.

257.29 not] See the NOTE ON THE TEXT, p. 793, footnote 38.

258.11 A pretty scholar] This speech implies that the captain has repeated the sworn promise just dictated to him by Steelkilt. Possibly Melville's manuscript called for a word-for-word repetition and the copyist or compositor omitted it as unintended. But Melville may well have left the repeated words for the reader's inference, and no emendation is required. For portions of text omitted by oversight see the discussions in the NN *Israel Potter* at 15.23 and the NN *Piazza Tales* volume at 140.3.

259.12 honor,] The comma is accepted from both H and E but the American spelling—rather than the E spelling "honour"—is retained.

260.20 cavern-pagoda] See the discussion at 36.33.

261.19–20 Prodromus . . . Sibbald] The word "Prodromus" in A and E simply means "introduction"; it is not a type of whale designated by Robert Sibbald in his book on whales, *Phalainologia nova sive Observationes de rarioribus quibusdam balænis in Scotiæ littus nuper ejectis* (Edinburgh, 1692)—which does include two plates showing whales. However, Sibbald's earlier book on the natural history of Scotland, *Scotia illustrata sive Prodromus historiæ naturalis* (Edinburgh, 1684), contains the word in its title and includes a brief outline of *"Balæna, the Common Whale"* (pt. II, bk. III, sec. 4, chap. 2, p. 23) but no pictures of whales. Perhaps Melville, confusing the two books, means here "the kind of whale illustrated in Sibbald's *Prodromus*" (in which case the use of italics or quotation marks for short-title citation would make the meaning clearer—see the NOTE ON THE TEXT, p. 799, footnote 45, and the discussions at 110.15, 205.26–27, and 366.5); or perhaps he is playing a learned joke on the reader. In either case, "Prodromus" is clearly the word he wanted at this point.

261.29   15th]   The right century would be the sixteenth, since Aldus Manutius and his family used the anchor and dolphin as their printer's mark
from 1502 to 1546; but emendation is not called for because Melville's loose
phrase "somewhere about" indicates that, appropriately to the context, he
did not mean to be precise.

261.30–31   dolphins . . . Leviathan]   Melville seems entangled in an
unemendable error here in treating dolphins of the sort in question as not
properly whales; naturalists have regularly classified them as such, as did his
own chief sources for cetological information, e.g., the article on "Whales"
in the *Penny Cyclopædia* (London, 1843), XXVII, 277–78, 291–92; William
Scoresby's *An Account of the Arctic Regions* (Edinburgh, 1820), I, 448, 496ff.;
and Frederick Debell Bennett's *Narrative of a Whaling Voyage* (London,
1840), II, 152, 237. (Cf. Bercaw 544, 616, 60.) Likewise, Sir Thomas
Browne, in *Pseudodoxia Epidemica* (*"Vulgar Errors"*), Book V, "Of many
things questionable as they are commonly described in Pictures"—possibly
Melville's source for the idea of Chapters 55–57—treats them in Chapter 2
("Of the Pictures of Dolphins") in a way that recognizes them as cetaceans.
(Cf. Sealts 90, Bercaw 83.) Melville's apparent error may come from an
effort to avoid the common confusion between two quite different creatures
both called dolphins—the cetacean mammal *(Delphinus)* and the dolphin fish
or dorado *(Coryphaena),* whose beautiful iridescent colors (especially when
it is out of water or dying) are celebrated by poets. He may have thought of
"dolphins" solely as the latter fish and have used the name "porpoises" for
the cetacean dolphins, as he does in the "Cetology" chapter (32), where he
devotes Book III (143.22–144.28) to precisely this family of whales without
calling any of them dolphins, and also in Chapter 65, "The Whale as a Dish"
(298.9–11). In Chapter 61 (282.11) he lists "porpoises, dolphins" as different. Apparently sailor usage was to call cetacean dolphins "common
porpoises" (see Bennett, II, 237n.); but Melville's sources cited above treat
porpoises and dolphins as closely related whales whose names are sometimes
loosely interchanged. The dolphin of the bookbinders and publishers was
indeed intended to represent the cetacean dolphin, not the dolphin fish, and
was rendered a "fabulous creature" by incorporating anatomical characteristics of fish, such as gills (or the lack of a blowhole), scales, or a vertical tail.

262.2–4   "A . . . master."]   As Melville's citation of Harris (262.1) indicates, the reference here is to the account of Friedrich Martens's voyage to
Spitzbergen and Greenland in John Harris's *Navigantium atque Itinerantium
Bibliotheca* (London, 1705), the work Melville also used for the four extracts
at xxi.1–23. The quoted title is not an exact transcription either of the title
(on I, 617) of the relevant chapter of Harris or of the caption to the first of the
plates mentioned (facing I, 617); presumably Melville constructed this title

by combining information from that chapter title (beginning *"The first Part of the Voyage to* Spitzbergen *and* Greenland") and from the first paragraph of the chapter (which consists of the words quoted in the "Extracts" at xxi.13–14, followed by *"Peter Peterson* of *Frieseland* Master"). (Melville's description of the two plates—262.4–7—does accurately describe the plates in Harris facing I, 617 and 629. These are reproduced among the plates following page 532 in Willard Thorp's edition of *Moby-Dick* [New York: Oxford University Press, 1947], by John M. J. Gretchko in "New Evidence for Melville's Use of John Harris in *Moby-Dick,*" *Studies in the American Renaissance,* 1983, 305–6, and by Stuart M. Frank in *Herman Melville's Picture Gallery* [Fairhaven, Mass.: Edward J. Lefkowicz, 1986], pp. 24–25.)

262.11–13 "Picture . . . deck."] The wording of this caption is quoted accurately from James Colnett's *Voyage* (London, 1798), except that the caption actually begins with the word "Physeter" and ends with the words "in on Deck." (Melville's rendering of the title of Colnett's work is another example—like many of the titles in the "Extracts"—of the nineteenth-century practice of allusive citation, and it is not emended; Colnett's title in fact has the words "to the South Atlantic and" following "Voyage" and reads "Pacific Ocean" instead of "South Seas".)

262.22 plates] Both the whale and the narwhale are in fact depicted on the same plate in the 1807 Pilkington abridgment from which Melville drew the extract at xxii.13–15. His reference cannot be to the other London abridgment of that year—*An Abridgment of Dr. Goldsmith's Natural History of Beasts and Birds,* published by Scatcherd & Letterman—because it contains no section on whales or plates illustrating them.

262.27 1825] This date, though it is also given with a page citation at 460.7–10, is apparently in error. No 1825 edition of Lacépède's "systemized whale book" could be located either by the NN editors or by Sumner W. D. Scott, in "The Whale in *Moby Dick*" (Ph.D. dissertation, University of Chicago, 1950), p. 57. The book in question is Etienne de Lacépède's *Histoire naturelle des cétacées* (Paris, l'an xii de la République [1804]). Because William Scoresby, Jr., in *An Account of the Arctic Regions* (Edinburgh, 1820), I, 447, cites this work—indeed, cites page 3 (I, 449), as does Melville—it seems likely that Scoresby was Melville's source, as he was at other places. If so, Melville could not have thought that the date of Lacépède was 1825 (since Scoresby's book came out in 1820). The "1825" in A and E may have resulted from a misreading of Melville's handwriting; but because "1825" does not seem a likely misreading for "1804", possibly Melville wrote some other date, having figured differently what the twelfth year of the French Republic would be. On the other hand, the appearance of "1825" in both citations, two hundred pages apart, and the wording "so late as A.D. 1825" (in the second instance) suggests that Melville may have intended this later date. The matter is uncertain, and no emendation is made.

266.6 Garnery] The name of this well-known marine painter is normally given as Ambrose Louis Garneray. But the A and E spelling "Garnery", here and at 266.37, 267.7, and 267.27, appears on one state of the two engravings to which Melville refers, and it is therefore not emended. (See Sumner W. D. Scott, "The Whale in *Moby Dick*" [Ph.D. dissertation, University of Chicago, 1950], p. 81, and the Hendricks House edition of *Moby-Dick* [New York, 1952], p. 749, note 267.2.)

267.29 H. Durand] Melville's phrasing indicates that he knew this name was a pseudonym commonly used by French engravers—as pointed out by Sumner W. D. Scott in "The Whale in *Moby Dick*" (Ph.D. dissertation, University of Chicago, 1950), p. 42, and by Luther S. Mansfield and Howard P. Vincent in their Hendricks House edition of *Moby-Dick* (New York, 1952), p. 750, note 268.38. Neither Scott nor Mansfield and Vincent could locate the two engravings to which Melville refers, but Stuart M. Frank, in *Herman Melville's Picture Gallery: Sources and Types of the "Pictorial" Chapters of MOBY-DICK* (Fairhaven, Mass.: Edward J. Lefkowicz, 1986), pp. 80–83, identifies the artist as Henri Durand-Brager (1814–79) and reproduces "Oriental Repose" and "In the Very Heart of the Leviathanic Life" (both ca. 1844–45) as the "two other French engravings worthy of note" (267.27–28). Frank also reproduces many of the other works to which Melville refers in this chapter.

270.22 Dutch] The A reading, though literally incorrect, and corrected to "German" in E, is retained since "Dutch" is colloquial American usage for "German." Further, the E alteration was less likely Melville's than the Bentley reader's. For other instances of this usage, see xvi.6 and 354.10.

271.6–7 else . . . hills—] See the NOTE ON THE TEXT, p. 790.

273.21 his] The A and E reference to the world discovered by Columbus as "his one superficial Western one" makes sense, but possibly Melville intended not "his" but "this". In his hand the two words might be mistaken.

279.2 twelve] The A and E reading "twenty" is in error. It is emended from Melville's source, Frederick Debell Bennett's *Narrative of a Whaling Voyage* (London, 1840), which states the weight sustained as "one hundred and twelve pounds" (II, 198). That Melville did not mean to alter this figure is shown by his computing the total weight borne (not given by Bennett) as "nearly equal to three tons" instead of *more* than three tons (51 x 112 is somewhat less than three tons—of 2000 pounds each—whereas 51 x 120 is somewhat more).

281.15 than though seated] See the NOTE ON THE TEXT, p. 793, footnote 38.

283.18–19 helm . . . spokes] Many readers have noted the inconsistency that here (as at 500.5) the *Pequod* is given a wheel helm, whereas in the first description of her it is stated that "Scorning a turnstile wheel at her reverend helm, she sported there a tiller . . ." (70.8). The inconsistency, which cannot have been intended by Melville, is unemendable.

284.19 Meanwhile] A paragraph break is needed here (or possibly before "And" in the line above) to make clear that the scene shifts from Starbuck's boat to Stubb's. However, NN does not make the emendation, because clarity not sense is at issue. (See the discussions of similar cases at 7.1, 42.30, 121.8, 123.10, 137.18, and 365.18.)

286.18 Tashtego] The A and E reading "Daggoo" is either an authorial slip or a compositional vestige, since Tashtego, not Daggoo, is Stubb's harpooner (cf. 120.31–32 and 284.22).

291.10 Hang-Ho] "Yün-ho" is the name of the canal referred to; but "Hang-Ho" approximates "Huang Ho" or "Hwang ho," the Yellow River, and a part of the canal followed an old bed of the river, so no emendation is called for, especially since the appositive "or whatever they call it" indicates that Ishmael means his form as a humorous stab at an outlandish name (much as Peleg gives up on "Queequeg" and calls him "Quohog, or whatever your name is" and "Hedgehog there, I mean Quohog" in Chapter 18, 88.27–28, 89.2–3). The spellings "Hoang Ho" and "Ho-hang-ho" occur in two of the humorous items on the Chinese Junk in *Yankee Doodle* (1847) that are attributed to Melville (see the NN *Piazza Tales* volume, pp. 436, 442). In Chapter 2 of *The Confidence-Man* the canal is given a more fanciful name, "the great shipping canal of Ving-King-Ching" (NN8.7).

292.21 Daggoo] One would expect Stubb, to whom command of the watch has been given over by Starbuck (292.16–17), to issue this order to his own harpooner, Tashtego, not to Daggoo, who is Flask's harpooner and who therefore should be off-watch below. Probably Melville was paying no attention to such protocol in writing this scene (any more than to the question how Ishmael, who should also be off-watch below, witnessed it). On the other hand, the same mismatching of Stubb and Daggoo occurs just above at 286.18, even though they are correctly matched earlier in the same chapter (284.6, 22; 285.4–5). Possibly these as well as some other anomalies about the harpooneers may be vestiges of earlier stages in the composition of the book. (See the discussion at 120.10–12.)

294.5 hammock] Melville nods again: whaleships had no hammocks, only wooden berths; he makes the same slip repeatedly elsewhere (see the discussions at 16.28 and 477.16).

295.5  Dough]  See the NOTE ON THE TEXT, pp. 789–90, and the discussion at 124.16–18. (Cf. also Melville's use of "Dough" for "Though" in Black Guinea's dialect in Chapter 3 of *The Confidence-Man,* NN11.2.)

295.18  good]  The A and E reading "dood" is apparently an error for "good", because the Cook has no difficulty with initial *g* in other words (such as "gobern", "Gor", "goin' ", and "g'uttons") and uses *d* in place of *t* or *th* (as in "dat", "dention", and "Cape-Down"). (In Chapter 3 of *The Confidence-Man,* Black Guinea—whose dialect is represented in the same way as the Cook's here—says "good" several times.)

298.22  Zogranda]  This name is likely a humorous intentional distortion of the Zorgdrager cited by William Scoresby, Jr., as "the writer of an account of the whale-fishery, and one of the earliest superintendents of the Dutch northern fisheries," a few pages from the passage where Melville found Scoresby's report of the Eskimos' whale-eating habits that Ishmael is recounting. See *An Account of the Arctic Regions* (Edinburgh, 1820), I, 452, 475–76; also II, 150, 152. See also the discussions at 157.7–9, 409.36, and 445.28.

300.15  formerly]  See the NOTE ON THE TEXT, p. 792.

302.4  forecastle seaman]  An unemendable discrepancy: this "forecastle seaman" with Queequeg is apparently not Ishmael, though novelistically he should be, both as Queequeg's companion and as the observer who saw and heard what is reported here. But in fact the chapter is not presented in first-person narration, possibly because Melville wrote it at a stage so early that he had neither joined Ishmael and Queequeg as companions nor established the narrator as "Ishmael," though apparently he had already made Queequeg a harpooneer, quartered not in the forecastle but aft with the officers. See the discussions at 16.2 and 56.39 and the HISTORICAL NOTE, p. 658.

304.1  frighted]  Possibly Melville wrote "freighted": emphasis is placed upon the ponderous weight of the tackles "lashed to the lower mast-head" of the mainmast (303.8–12) and upon the severe strain the mast takes as the men heave at the windlass to lift the strip of blubber. Also, if "frighted" is the correct reading it is the only "gothic" or extraneously literary touch (beyond the personification it extends) in Chapter 67, which Howard P. Vincent remarks upon as "almost unique in *Moby-Dick* as a chapter of pure exposition unaccompanied by humorous or metaphysical ornamentation" (*The Trying-Out of MOBY-DICK* [Boston: Houghton Mifflin, 1949], p. 237). However, since not all three masts but only the mainmast would in fact be "freighted" (see 311.8–9), the plural form "mast-heads" casts doubt on the possible emendation—even though the weight might be thought of as distributed to them all. (There is some uncertainty at several points in the book whether Melville intended the singular or plural form for this word. See 96.37, 353.21–22, 493.11, and the discussion at xxvii.25.)

308.16 perspectives] The fact that the whale's carcass could not literally be lost to the observer's sight at more than one vanishing point suggests a misreading. But emendation to the singular, as Melville's intended form, would not give a satisfactory literal sense and would shut out the imaginative dimensions of the "infinite perspectives" into which the "great mass of death" floats as the paragraph closes.

311.35–312.3 Thou saw'st . . . arms.] The syntax and sense of these two sentences might emerge more readily to twentieth-century readers if their punctuation were emended thus: "Thou saw'st . . . when, . . . ship, . . . wave, . . . them."; and "Thou . . . when, . . . deck, . . . maw and . . . arms." But the rhetorical punctuation in A (and E) is, or is close to, Melville's own, and it is retained here.

312.15 lives in matter] See the NOTE ON THE TEXT, p. 789.

314.32, 38 Neskyeuna] NN retains this A and E form as a possible variant spelling, since none had yet been standardized (now "Niskayuna"). Perhaps, however, it is Melville's idiosyncratic spelling or a copyist's or compositor's misreading (transposing "ey" to "ye"): variant forms, all ending "una", commonly combined "Nesk" or "Nisk" with "ey" or "ay", but none with "ye" has been located. "Niskeyuna" is given as the name of this Shaker community (near Albany, New York) in *A Summary View of the Millennial Church, or United Society of Believers, Commonly Called Shakers . . .* (Albany, 1848), p. 8. Melville marked this passage in the copy he purchased on July 21, 1850, at the Shaker village of Hancock, Massachusetts, a few miles from Pittsfield, and used as a source for other details in this chapter of *Moby-Dick*. See Sealts 459a, Bercaw 680.

316.21 Shakers . . . Bible] Following Willard Thorp, in his edition of *Moby-Dick* (New York: Oxford University Press, 1947), p. 297n., editors have suspected textual corruption in this elliptical phrase but have advanced no convincing emendation.

318.15 Ahab's feet] Taken literally, this is a factual discrepancy, since Ahab has only one foot. Leon Howard took it so and suggested that the passage was written at an earlier stage when Melville had not yet given Ahab one whalebone leg (see *Melville Society Extracts*, No. 46 [May, 1981], 6, and Howard, *The Unfolding of MOBY-DICK* [Glassboro, N.J., 1987], pp. 55–56).

319.21 skirt] NN emends the A and E reading "shirt" as a misreading for "skirt", since not a shirt but a skirt and socks are the two articles of Scottish dress that make Ishmael see Queequeg as if in "the Highland costume". Skirt and socks correspond to "tartans" (i.e., the kilt) and "leggings" in Melville's description of the ship *Highlander*'s painted figurehead with "bright tartans, bare knees, barred leggings, and blue bonnet" in Chapter 24 of *Redburn* (NN116.12–13). Whereas the skirt is a lower garment, a shirt is always an upper one (whether inner or outer, short or long). For more secure foothold, harpooneers customarily stood on the whale's slippery back shoeless but in woolen socks. To conserve their usual clothes during this wet and bloody job, they often donned old articles of dress, such as old trousers. While the idiom "in one's shirt," or "in one's shirttails," may mean "with one's pants off," it is unclear here what item of Queequeg's dress (or undress)—surely neither a short nor long shirt—would resemble a skirt, but perhaps in effect a short wraparound "butcher's apron", leaving his bare knees visible. In any case, the way Queequeg appeared is suggested by a citation from Scott's *Waverley* in the *Oxford English Dictionary*, s.v. "Kilt": "The short kilt, or petticoat, showed his sinewy and clean-made limbs."

320.1   the savage's bowsman]   This phrase implies, discrepantly, that Ishmael's assignment to this post has already been told. See the discussions at 161.7, 214.10, and 220.13.

320.8   humorously perilous]   The A and E adverb may be a misreading. On the one hand, humor is present in the preceding three sentences (entailing Ishmael's special view of Queequeg in his skirt and as a monkey on a rope), and the phrase "humorously perilous" is a characteristic paradox. Edward H. Rosenberry in *Melville and the Comic Spirit* (Cambridge: Harvard University Press, 1955), p. 125, quotes the phrase and includes the episode with others in which "the reaction of man" is both laughter and tears. The paradox is explicitly developed, for example, in Chapter 49, "The Hyena," with reference in cosmic terms to "That odd sort of wayward mood" that "comes over a man only in some time of extreme tribulation . . . in the very midst of his earnestness, so that what just before might have seemed to him a thing most momentous, now seems but a part of the general joke. There is nothing like the perils of whaling to breed this free and easy sort of genial, desperado philosophy . . . " (226.14–19). On the other hand, in this chapter (72) no humor is brought out in what follows. After the declaration "It was a humorously perilous business for both of us", the conjunction "For"—indicating that what follows will show why—introduces six paragraphs that develop its perils for Ishmael and for Queequeg but nothing humorous that Ishmael saw—or sees—about those perils for either of them (320.8–321.32). Indeed, he declares that he conceived of his situation "strongly and metaphysically" while "earnestly" watching Queequeg's motions (320.17–18).

Perhaps Melville wrote the word "humorously" but did not develop the humor in what follows. Or perhaps he wrote it in an earlier composition stage and in a later one let it stand although developing only the serious implications of the monkey-rope. Perhaps, however, Melville wrote some other word: "tumultuously", echoing "tumultuous business" from the opening line of the chapter (319.3); or "numerously" (easily misread as "humorously" and parallel in idea to "multitudinous" at 320.31). The six paragraphs develop the number of perils (to the first of which alone is Ishmael exposed): of their drowning together (320.12–13); of Queequeg's being jammed between the whale and the ship (320.24–25, 321.1–2); of Queequeg's being bitten by sharks (321.3–16); of Queequeg's amputation by the harpooneers' whale-spades (321.16–24). The concluding comic scene, in any case, is humorous, as the tone of an earlier version of the chapter may have been, with the phrase "humorously perilous".

320.11  for the time]  A surprising unemendable discrepancy: Ishmael and Queequeg have already been metaphorically "wedded" in friendship since Chapter 10 (51.28), where Queequeg declares "henceforth we were married"—a metaphor Ishmael has anticipated some pages earlier (25.5, 26.37–39) and repeats a page later (52.24–25) as the friends lie abed making confidential disclosures like "Man and wife, . . . in our hearts' honeymoon . . . a cosy, loving pair." To write here of the pair (already thus "wed" by bosom friendship) that "for better or for worse, we two, *for the time* [italics supplied], were wedded" by an external tie, the monkey-rope, is more than awkward (as is the sequential metaphor by which the "Siamese ligature" makes the wedded friends also into twin brothers). One possible explanation (developed by Harrison Hayford in "Unnecessary Duplicates," pp. 152–53—cited in the discussion at 71.1), has broad genetic implications: that Melville in fact wrote this monkey-rope passage at an earlier stage than the one in which he worked the Ishmael-Queequeg friendship into the shore chapters. If so, he nodded when he failed in later revisions to notice the discrepancy just pointed out here and to excise it as a vestigial metaphor superseded by its fuller and deeper dramatic development in Chapters 4, 10, and 11.

322.15  breath]  See the NOTE ON THE TEXT, p. 790.

326.7  Three Spaniards]  This is indeed the title of a book, as Flask's response to Stubb's question shows he is aware—a gothic novel, *The Three Spaniards* by George Walker, first published in London in 1800. It is alluded to, italicized, in Chapter 17 of *Redburn* (NN83.23). Emendation of the title here into italics would make the fact that it is a book more immediately clear to the reader, but it would be inconsistent with the NN policy of following

A in not regularly setting book titles in italics or quotation marks (see the NOTE ON THE TEXT, p. 799, footnote 45).

328.1  Parsee]  Here, anomalously, Fedallah is casually first called "the Parsee" many chapters after his first introduction in Chapter 48. See the discussion at 217.21.

334.33  Hackluyt]  The quotation attributed to "Hackluyt" is actually a paraphrase of a statement in *Purchas His Pilgrimes* ("The Third Part"; London, 1625), p. 470 (the "old gentleman" is therefore Thomas Edge). If "Purchas" were substituted for "Hackluyt", however, the effect of the sentence would be altered, because Purchas would then be named twice, and Melville apparently wanted to refer to three different sources. (Cf. Bercaw 570.) (The middle quotation, "hogs' bristles", is a translation from Aristotle, which Melville could have taken from the article on "Whales" in the *Penny Cyclopædia* [London, 1843], XXVII, 283: "the whole concavity of the palate appearing to be beset with coarse rigid hairs or bristles, which explains the passage in Aristotle . . . , who, speaking of the Great Whale . . . , says, 'The Mysticete has no teeth in its mouth, but hairs like hog's bristles.' ") It is possible that the earlier reference to Purchas (at 334.31) is in error, since "whiskers" has not been located in Purchas; but it has not been found in Hakluyt, either, and there is thus no basis for emending "Purchas". Under the circumstances, then, it is better to let "Hackluyt" stand also, even though it is a factual error.

338.11  Sais]  The A and E reading "Lais" offers a clear example of the kinds of misreadings induced by peculiarities of Melville's letter-formation, in this case his capital *S*, which resembles *L*. See the word "Sequel" in the first line of the reproduction on p. 989 (transcribed "Legend" in the book cited on p. 977).

339.2  *Heidelburgh*]  This unusual spelling (which appears in this passage five more times, on this page and the next, and at xi.27, 342.19, and 415.6) is not emended to the conventional form "Heidelberg" because it occurs in this way on page 645 and on the plate facing that page in the second volume of John Harris's *Navigantium atque Itinerantium Bibliotheca* (London, 1705), a book that Melville made much use of elsewhere (see the discussions at xxi.1–23, 262.2–4, 366.5, and 458.6–19).

345.2  *Prairie*]  The spelling "PRAIRE" in A was altered to "PRAIRIE" in E; NN follows the spelling of E but makes the typography conform with the styling of NN. For comment on this emendation, see the discussion at xi.29.

349.31  half]  The meaning of Ishmael's flinging his flag "half out" (rather than "straight out", like Ahab's red flag at 570.25) is unclear enough to suggest that a misreading may be involved.

356.23–26 "Canst . . . spear!"] The wording of these lines from Job is accurate, except for three unmarked ellipses: 356.23 corresponds to Job 41:7; the next line jumps to Job 41:26; and the rest of the quotation runs through Job 41:29, except that five words are omitted after "straw" and eight after "flee".

357.6 ship's] See the NOTE ON THE TEXT, p. 786, footnote 35.

362.11–12 "Thou . . . sea,"] Apart from three substitutions (the first "as" for "like", "waters" for "nations", and the second "of" for "in") and one omission ("art" after "and"), this passage is an accurate quotation of part of Ezekiel 32:2 as quoted in the article on "Whales" in the *Penny Cyclopædia* (London, 1843), XXVII, 272, from "Barker's Bible" (i.e., the Geneva Version). As Melville says, other versions (including the King James, according to the encyclopedia) use the word "whale" for "dragon". Although "waters" is conceivably a misreading of Melville's hand for the original reading, "nations" (cf. the confusion of "nations" and "matrons" in *Typee*, NN215.10), he may well have wanted this additional marine reference, and it is allowed to stand. (Cf. the discussions of Melville's use of this encyclopedia at 136.23–31 and 457.13.)

365.18 But] A paragraph break is needed here, with none at 365.24, to keep the pattern already set at 364.11 and 365.3 that gives each of old Sag-Harbor's reasons in a separate paragraph together with its refutations. Inconsistency alone, however, does not call for NN emendation. See the discussions at 7.1, 42.30, 121.8, 123.10, 137.18, and 284.19.

366.5 Harris's] Melville's citation of Harris's compendium is incorrect. (The sense of the word "Voyages" as a short-title citation would be more immediately clear if it were italicized or placed in quotation marks. See the NOTE ON THE TEXT, p. 167, footnote 45; also the discussions at 110.15, 205.26–27, 261.19–20, and 326.7.) The relevant passages assembled by Luther S. Mansfield and Howard P. Vincent in their Hendricks House edition of *Moby-Dick* (New York, 1952), p. 782, show that Melville's source was the article on "Jonas" in Pierre Bayle's *An Historical and Critical Dictionary* (cf. Sealts 51, Bercaw 50), which mentions the English traveler and miraculous lamp, whereas the account in John Harris's *Navigantium atque Itinerantium Bibliotheca* (London, 1705) does not. (More recently James Duban has identified the particular translation of Bayle that Melville used: the four-volume London edition of 1710, in which the source passage appears at III, 1766—see "The Translation of Pierre Bayle's *An Historical and Critical Dictionary* Owned by Melville," *Papers of the Bibliographical Society of America*, LXXI [Third Quarter, 1977], 347–51.) Because the evocative quality of "old Harris's Voyages" would be altered if the wording were emended to "old Bayle's Dictionary", this error is one of those—like the use of "Hackluyt" at

334.33—that a conservative editor must regard as unemendable; as in the earlier instance, making the correction would mean changing the stylistic or rhetorical effect of the sentence as Melville apparently left it.

370.11   1850] Since the book was in print over a month before December 16, 1851, the date given in A, the E reading "1850" is adopted on the assumption that "1851" is a compositorial slip (made during 1851).

376.20   Angelo] Melville's reference to Michelangelo (or Michael Angelo) Buonarroti by this name is not traditional, but it is characteristic enough of Melville's handling of names to be unemendable (cf. the discussions of "Saint Stylites" at 155.7 and "Don" at 243.12).

377.24   Darmonodes'] Apparently a misreading as the name for the elephant's owner. The editors of the Hendricks House *Moby-Dick* (New York, 1952), p. 785, point out that it does not occur in Melville's source passages and that its form is an impossible one in Greek. The NN editors have no explanation or emendation to offer.

384.28–40   *To . . . World.] See the NOTE ON THE TEXT, p. 791.

384.33   Act III. sc. ii.] The citation in E (the footnote containing it does not occur in A) is "Act iii. sc. 11." Although "11" was obviously meant to refer to the second scene, it is an awkward (and possibly misleading) usage; therefore NN restyles the reference to "Act III. sc. ii." (The quotation itself, from lines 43–45 of that scene, is accurate in wording.)

387.30   still,] See the NOTE ON THE TEXT, p. 803.

396.23–27   Some . . . itself.] This sentence, as it appears in A, is confused in its syntax, perhaps as a result of a manuscript revision in which Melville failed to cancel part of the superseded wording; the three alterations made in E (deleting "and when indeed" after "seas", substituting "but" for "they were", and inserting "were" after "lives") could be the work either of Melville or of Bentley's reader, but they constitute a skillful revision of a sentence that cannot be allowed to stand unchanged and are therefore adopted in NN. This whole passage, running on through 397.9, is awkward in its syntax and evidently gave trouble either to Melville (in the proofs he sent to Bentley) or to Bentley's reader, perhaps indeed to both, for a considerable number of differences appear in E. Though some or all were conceivably made by Melville, these further changes in the rest of the passage resemble the "pedantic" alterations made elsewhere by the publisher's reader. Since they are by no means required to make the meaning clear, they are not adopted in NN.

397.6   she became a loose-fish] No use Melville makes in Chapter 89 of the term "loose-fish" seems equivocal in a way that would show that he knew that in British slang it then meant "prostitute," as the witty Erskine and the court presumably did, but apparently not the pious Scotsman William Scoresby, Jr., who must have stretched a point even to include this illustrative anecdote along with the law case, in the humorless pages of his *An Account of the Arctic Regions* (Edinburgh, 1820), II, 518–21. This was Melville's source for the whaling laws and the "fast" and "loose" terms he expounds in the chapter. His "greedy ears" (179.7) may well have picked up the term "loose-fish" derivatively used in the course of his London street rovings and convivial conversations with journalists, lawyers, and lively young literary men, as suggested by entries in his 1849 London journal and in the first part of "The Paradise of Bachelors and the Tartarus of Maids" (see the NN *Piazza Tales* volume, pp. 316–23). For the meaning "common prostitute" see the *Oxford English Dictionary*, s.v. "loose."

399.3 *"De . . . caudam."*] This statement, though grammatically correct, is a shortened form of the one in Henry de Bracton's *De legibus & consuetudinibus Angliæ* (London, 1569), Liber III, Tractatus secundus ("De corona"), Cap. 3, paragraph 5, which includes two additional words ("secundum quosdam") after "sufficit" and reads "inde habuerit" instead of "habeat". However, precisely the same shortened wording appears in Chapter 4 of William Blackstone's *Commentaries on the Laws of England*, Book I (Oxford, 1765), p. 216 (where the citation of Bracton also appears in identical form to that in A and E). Melville obviously took this quotation from Blackstone's work, which also supplied the references to Plowden and Prynne in this chapter (see the next two discussions).

401.13 "because . . . excellence."] Melville undoubtedly derived this phrase (like the quotation at the head of the chapter—see the preceding discussion) from William Blackstone's *Commentaries on the Laws of England*, Book I (Oxford, 1765), p. 280 (chap. 4, sec. X), which says (citing Plowden) that whales and sturgeon "are the property of the king, on account of their superior excellence." Indeed, these words of Blackstone's form the ending of the same sentence that Melville used the earlier part of for one of his "Extracts" (see the discussion at xxiii.9). Melville's version, focusing only on the whale, changes "on account of their" to "because of its"; but the matching phrase "superior excellence" provides the link to Blackstone, for these words apparently originate with Blackstone's paraphrase. They are not an exact translation from Edmund Plowden's *Les commentaries, ou reportes* (London, 1578, 1588), leaf 315 verso, or an exact quotation from either Fabian Hicks's *An Exact Abridgment of the Commentaries, or Reports* (London, 1659), p. 181, or the full translation, *The Commentaries, or Reports* (London, 1761), p. 315. Melville would have had no way to know from Blackstone that Plowden is here reporting the argument of the Queen's Solicitor, not the court's decision or his own judgment. (The A and E spelling

"Plowdon", corrected by NN to "Plowden", could have resulted from a misreading of Melville's hand or from Melville's own incorrect expansion of the abbreviation "Plowd." in Blackstone.)

401.18–19  "Yᵉ . . . whalebone."] After the typographical error in A ("warbrobe") is corrected (as it was in E), this statement is an accurate paraphrase, though not an exact quotation, of a passage on page 127 of William Prynne's *Aurum Reginæ* (London, 1668). William Blackstone's *Commentaries on the Laws of England*, Book I (Oxford, 1765), refers to this same passage of Prynne, and does so in the next sentence following the one from which Melville took the Bracton epigraph for this chapter (see the discussion at 399.3). Blackstone does not quote Prynne but paraphrases him thus: "The reason of this whimsical division, as assigned by our antient records, was, to furnish the queen's wardrobe with whalebone" (p. 216). The sentence that Melville places in quotation marks, with its ostentatious archaism, is therefore probably one that he constructed himself, following Blackstone's paraphrase. (For other instances of purported quotations presumably written by Melville, see the discussions at xxvii.19–22, xxviii.5, 10.23–28, and 142.35–38.) What edition of Blackstone Melville used has not been established, but two points suggest that it might have had annotations by Edward Christian, whose commentary first appeared in the twelfth edition (London, 1793): (1) Christian's footnote on Blackstone's statement (about Prynne's judgment being "whimsical") reads, "The reason is more whimsical than the division, for the whalebone lies entirely in the head" (p. 221), and Melville also points out Prynne's error in this regard at 401.21–23; (2) earlier in this chapter (400.10) Melville calls the man carrying a copy of Blackstone a "most Christian and charitable gentleman". Of course Melville did not need Christian's note to tell him that whalebone is in the whale's head, and his description of the gentleman as "Christian" does not necessarily involve an allusion to Edward Christian. Still, Christian's notes were normally included in the printings of Blackstone in the first half of the nineteenth century, such as those published in New York by the senior Evert Duyckinck in the 1820's and by the Harpers in the 1840's. Melville might well have found one of these printings in his brother Allan's law office; and Allan might also have expanded for him Blackstone's reference to "Pryn. *Aur. Reg.* 127", for Melville mentions "William Prynne" by name (401.18) and calls his treatise " 'Queen-Gold' " (401.17). Melville's anecdote about the Cinque Ports mariners was perhaps (as the Hendricks House edition of *Moby-Dick* suggests [New York, 1952, note 397.21]) a reworking of the version of the story that appeared in the *Literary World*, VI (June 29, 1850), 642, which he would have been likely to see; but the use of Blackstone as an authority does not occur in that version.

402.2 *Rose-bud*] It seems likely that the name (and perhaps naming) of this aromatic ship involved a private joke, shared by Melville and Hawthorne, that associated mingled odors of the diaper and the rose with the Hawthornes' baby daughter Rose, who was born May 20, 1851, and at once nicknamed "Rosebud." Cf. the discussion at 83.8. Melville's letter to Hawthorne of July 17, 1852, closes with " 'compliments' & perfumes of the season to the 'Rose-bud' " (see *The Letters of Herman Melville*, ed. Merrell R. Davis and William H. Gilman [New Haven and London: Yale University Press, 1960], p. 153).

402.4 *that*] The correction of the A reading "not" was made in E; it is italicized here to conform to the styling of NN. Otherwise the quotation accurately follows the 1686 London edition of Sir Thomas Browne's *Pseudodoxia Epidemica* (p. 138), except for the omission of eighteen words after "Leviathan". (Cf. the discussion at xx.2; Sealts 90, Bercaw 83.)

402.19 unmolested] There is an evident discrepancy in the identification (402.10–11, 403.10–12, 403.20–21, 24) of this first-described of the *Rose-bud*'s two whales as the one drugged and wounded (not specifically by Stubb) in Chapter 88 (389.15–32, 390.32–35), since "it was plain" that this first whale was a "blasted whale, that is, a whale that has died unmolested on the sea". The explanation may be that this chapter (91) with its two whales offers still another instance of the pattern pointed out by Harrison Hayford of "unnecessary duplicates" generated in *Moby-Dick* by separate stages of composition (see the HISTORICAL NOTE, pp. 656–58). The textual evidence suggests that at an earlier stage the French ship had secured only a single whale, a "dried" one, dead of natural causes, entailing ambergris that Yankee Stubb tricks away from her captain. Later, it appears, in order to link Chapter 88 with Chapter 91, Melville made use of the drugged whale there, adding to 88 the final lines (390.32–35) and to 91 the opening lines (402.5, 10–12, along with the others cited above that now identify the whale as Stubb's). In so doing, he realized that such a healthy whale, dying of wounds inflicted by Stubb, would not supply ambergris and so had to give it to the *Rose-bud* as a "duplicate," an additional and otherwise "unnecessary" one. The present description of it as the first ("blasted") whale (402.17–403.1) overlaps with that of the original ("dried") second one (403.3–9), in that both died of natural causes; it appears that in the earlier stage all these lines together comprised the description of a single such whale, the present ("dried") second, ambergris-bearing one, and that in the later stage Melville detached the first part of it to describe the newly introduced drugged whale, now identified as Stubb's, but without noticing that the retained definition of it as "blasted" and characterization of its death as "unmolested" are discrepancies. The newly introduced whale, while linking the two chapters, is strictly "unnecessary" to the ambergris episode but like other such "duplicates" enriches it—in this instance by doubling the motif of the French captain's incompetence (as well as the odor).

409.36  Smeerenberg]  The spelling and etymology (with "-berg" for "-bergen") are those given by William Scoresby, Jr., in *An Account of the Arctic Regions* (Edinburgh, 1820), II, 52; but "Schmerenburgh", "Fogo Von Slack", and the great textbook work on smells (cf. Scoresby, II, 410–11) are examples of Melville's Carlylean humor at Scoresby's expense, as elsewhere, e.g., 157.7–9, 298.22, and 445.28. Perhaps by association with his home town of Lansingburgh, New York, such shaggy terminations as "-burgh" (in comparison with "-berg") carried more resonance for Melville than etymological accuracy; see the discussion at 339.2.

411.7  prophecy . . . sequel]  This prophecy, if not very loose, may be a vestige of an earlier intention for the catastrophe, since it seems to foretell that the *Pequod,* like Pip, will be shattered but will survive—perhaps that its "soul" will be gone but its broken body will be left behind, as "the sea jeeringly kept his [Pip's] finite body up, but drowned the infinite of his soul" (414.20–21). Similarly, in the last sentence of the chapter, the clause "what like abandonment befell myself" (414.33–34) may reflect some shift in Melville's intentions. The obvious general likeness is that Ishmael, like Pip, was left alone in the ocean; but the ship, unlike the abandoned person, goes down, and Ishmael, unlike Pip, survives with soul and body integral. (Other passages can also be taken as vestigial evidence that Melville did not at all stages of composition intend the ship to be sunk. George Stewart cites as foreshadowings "three small matters: that Queequeg is to take 'his last long dive,' that Ishmael likes to 'land on barbarous coasts,' and that on leaving Nantucket he seems to see ahead 'meads and glades so eternally vernal' " (61.36, 7.29, 104.26–27). He adds, "The suggestion that the voyage was to end on such a coast and amid such greenery recalls the actual ending of Melville's voyage on the *Acushnet*"—i.e., on a South Sea island. See "The Two *Moby-Dicks*," *American Literature*, XXV [January, 1954], 445.)

412.5  king's]  See the NOTE ON THE TEXT, p. 786, footnote 35.

412.10  fictitiously]  As remarked by Wilson Carey McWilliams in *The Idea of Fraternity in America* (Berkeley and Los Angeles: University of California Press, 1973), p. 359, "fictitiously" is a "curious" word here. Since it can be made to yield some sense (though McWilliams's own reading seems doubtful), the tempting emendation to "factitiously" is not made by NN.

414.9  considerateness]  See the NOTE ON THE TEXT, p. 789.

416.25–26  thoughts . . . visions]  The editors of the Norton Critical Edition, Harrison Hayford and Hershel Parker, blundered in emending the A and E phrase "In thoughts of the visions" to "In visions", assuming "that Melville first wrote 'In thoughts of' and then changed it to 'In visions of' without adequately marking the first phrase for deletion" (New York, 1967, p. 493). The late Marjorie Dew repeatedly, on "intuition," protested the emendation, then found conclusive grounds in a motel Gideon Bible: "In thoughts from the visions of the night " (Job 4:13). The editors confessed, with Dr. Johnson, "Ignorance, madam, pure ignorance."

416.26 rows] This vision entails another of Melville's inexactly detailed (or visualized) operations, if he meant the angels' situation to match that of Ishmael and his "co-laborers" sitting before (or around) a single "Constantine bath" squeezing sperm and hands in it. For if there are "long rows" of angels "each with his hands in a jar of spermaceti", it would seem that there must also be long rows of jars as well (one to each angel?), not just a single "bath" as on the *Pequod,* and that the angels consequently cannot "squeeze hands all round".

422.15–16 try-works were first started] George Stewart points out the anomaly that after much whaling this process (which routinely followed the cutting-in) has so long been delayed. The whale Stubb kills in Chapter 61 (p. 282) is kept in focus, with interruptions, up through Chapter 80. But with Chapter 81 (p. 351) this whale, cut up and ready for trying-out, is lost sight of. In Chapter 81, another whale is killed, but no account is given of its being tried out. In Chapter 87 another whale is killed. Only in Chapter 94—which takes place many days later—is the account of processing resumed. Stewart's suggestion is that the awkward delay—or presentation of a scene after another that happened later—is a vestige of Melville's rewriting the "Ur-*Moby-Dick*" into the present *Moby-Dick,* a process in which the present chapter, and account of trying-out, stood earlier in the work. See "The Two *Moby-Dick*s," *American Literature,* XXV (January, 1954), 441.

424.14 her] See the NOTE ON THE TEXT, p. 793, footnote 39.

424.39–425.2 "the . . . dead."] This quotation accurately reproduces Proverbs 21:16 in the King James Version and illustrates Melville's interpolation of an explanatory phrase outside the quotation marks (as in xxvi.4–5 and xxviii.17, and in contrast to xix.9, xxi.24, and xxviii.15).

433.34 nine hundred and sixty] This A and E reading (here and in the next line) may at first appear to be an error in arithmetic that ought to be corrected by emendation. But the figure could be correct if Flask is using "dollar" to mean a Spanish-American "dollar," even though such dollars and United States dollars were of the same weight. At this time Spanish-American "dollars" generally circulated as the equivalent of a British crown—that is, five shillings or sixty pence. And since a British penny was regularly equal to two American cents ($£1 = \$4.80$), sixty cigars that would sell for two cents apiece in the United States could have been purchased for each of these "dollars" from someone who was following the British exchange practice. It is possible that Melville meant "dollar" to be taken in this sense, because Spanish coins were in common use among American seamen (and in the United States as well) and "dollar" was colloquially used (as the *Oxford English Dictionary* indicates) to mean "five-shilling-piece." Flask might realistically be expected, therefore, to calculate in these terms. The possibility that Melville made a miscalculation, or attributed one to Flask, seems less likely than that he regarded the value of Spanish-American "dollars"—and this usage of "dollar"—as common knowledge. The figure would also be correct, of course, if Flask were—more simply—assuming a quantity price of twenty cents a dozen. (For a clear example of confusion in arithmetic, see the discussion at 279.2. See also the discussion of a similar crux at 44.26 in the NN *Israel Potter*.)

435.17–18   Jenny! . . . done!]   These words are an adaptation of part of a traditional minstrel song, "Old King Crow." In the version published by Elias Howe in *The Ethiopian Glee Book* (Boston, 1849), p. 67, Sambo's lines go "Caw! Caw! Caw! / Jenny get de hoe-cake, / Fetch along de hoe-cake, / Will you bring de hoe-cake! / fotch along de hoe-cake / Soon it am done."

436.2–3   *Leg . . . London*]   In both A and E the second of the two elements in the heading for Chapter 100 is printed below the first (beginning a new line). It is possible that the second element was intended as a kind of subtitle, and E in fact treated it in this way by setting it in smaller type. In NN, however, the two elements are regarded as parts of a single chapter title because in A they are printed in the same size type. Conceivably, the two elements were in fact alternative titles, one of which was meant to supplant the other, but the superseded one was not canceled in the manuscript. (As the HISTORICAL NOTE, pp. 675–77, suggests, the table of contents in A may reproduce a document that preserves the earlier titles for some chapters. For Chapter 100, the table of contents reads "The Pequod meets the Samuel Enderby of London", not the more expected [because shorter] "Leg and Arm"; it may be, therefore, that "Leg and Arm" was added later to the manuscript and written above the original title.)

437.26   solitary thigh]   The assertion that Ahab has only one thigh (and at 230.26 a "solitary knee") reveals an unemendable discrepancy in Melville's notion of just where Ahab's leg was bitten off: at 229.7–10 Stubb says that if Ahab's "leg were off at the hip", "That would disable him; but he has one knee, and a good part of the other left . . . ". This report is confirmed by the Carpenter's comment at 469.18–20 that "there's no knee-joint to make" for Ahab "but a mere shinbone". For the prolonged (but unconsummated) critical engagement over the question of which (and how much) leg Ahab lacks, and the entailed problem of his castration, consult *passim* the indispensable work of Brian Higgins, the first volume titled *Herman Melville: An Annotated Bibliography, . . . 1846–1930*, the second titled *Herman Melville: A Reference Guide, 1931–1960* (Boston: G. K. Hall, 1979, 1987), with a third volume pending. While the uncertainty about the extent of Ahab's dismemberment probably reflects a shifting conception on Melville's part, it may also reflect his willingness to concoct a "COCK and a BULL" story analogous to the mystery about Uncle Toby's groin wound (cf. Ahab's groin wound, 463.15–21). A passage in *Tristram Shandy* (IX.24) was the direct source for the invocation at the end of Chapter 26 that refers to "the stumped and paupered arm of old Cervantes" (117.34–35). See the allusion to the Widow Wadman in "Cock-A-Doodle-Doo!", with a discussion at 273.11–12 in the NN *Piazza Tales* volume, and discussions about missing arms and legs in *Moby-Dick* at 71.12–13, 92.19, 124.16, 168.6, and 441.5. Such real or apparent bodily impairment is a motif throughout Melville's works, beginning with the "once gay and dapper young cock . . . moping all day on that everlasting one leg of his" who awaits decapitation and devouring by the captain in Chapter 1 of *Typee* (NN4.6–26).

441.5  swallows]  The discrepancy (lines 5–25) between Bunger's statement that the white whale swallowed Captain Boomer's arm and his account above (440.16–17) that he himself amputated it fits well enough with his other straightfaced fantasies; however, in the composition of the book this lost right arm may be somehow linked to the left arm that the prophet Elijah (perhaps differently named) may have been missing at one stage, though in the final stage what is wrong with it is not specified. It seems possible that this character at one stage had lost an arm to Moby Dick, replaced at the captain's orders with an ivory one, as the captain lost a leg he replaced with an ivory one. The captain who fancied ivory-work was not Ahab but Peleg (69.36–70.10). See the discussions at 71.12–13, 92.19, and 103.39.

442.6  standing]  There is a discrepancy in Ahab's standing as the captain does at 241.7–12 (and perhaps Captain Mayhew at 315.34) because he has no place to sit in a boat already fully manned by its five oarsmen and regular boatsteerer. Unless Ahab stands simply for dignity's sake (or as a literary flourish by Melville), he might more realistically either take the steering oar himself (as he always does at first as the boat's headsman in the chase), or else occupy Fedallah's harpooneer-oar bow position (as he always does in harpooning and lancing), which on this occasion is vacant since Fedallah, with no whale in prospect, is performing his job as Ahab's regular boat-steerer. See the discussion at 230.6–7.

443.19    1788]    NN emends the incorrect A and E reading "1778". The correct date is given in Thomas Beale's *The Natural History of the Sperm Whale* (London, 1839), p. 148, Melville's direct source for most of the information in the first three paragraphs of Chapter 101, as shown by Howard P. Vincent in *The Trying-Out of MOBY-DICK* (Boston: Houghton Mifflin, 1949), pp. 342–44, and also in the Hendricks House edition of *Moby-Dick* (New York, 1952), p. 807, note 440.14, which explains the error as Melville's miscopying and cites his markings of the source passage in his own copy of Beale (Sealts 52), pp. 148–50.

444.11    testing]    NN emends the A and E adjective "tasting" in light of the purpose assigned the voyage in the phrase Melville is paraphrasing—"an experimental voyage"—from his source in Thomas Beale's *The Natural History of the Sperm Whale* (London, 1839), p. 150 (see the preceding discussion).

445.19    Zealanders]    The exact reference (and correct spelling) of "Zealanders" may be in question. But Melville's source for the "historical whale research" in this and the following paragraph was William Scoresby, Jr., *An Account of the Arctic Regions* (Edinburgh, 1820), where "Zealanders" (so spelled) and "Hollanders" are both called "Dutch" (II, 32ff., *passim*) and no allusion is made to the Danish island of Zealand. The reference here, therefore, is to men from Zealand (a variant of "Zeeland"), now a province of the Netherlands. Whether deliberately or by misunderstanding, Melville's statement, 445.18–19, that "The English were preceded in the whale fishery by the Hollanders, Zealanders, and Danes," reverses Scoresby's contention (II, 18ff.).

445.28    Dan Coopman]    Although Melville's source, Scoresby, has "Den Koopman", the two spelling changes are both intentional, as the repetition and the play on terms indicate. Melville also confuses (probably willfully) two separate works named by Scoresby, attributing to "Dan Coopman" the statistics Scoresby cites from another work—statistics that Melville tabulates selectively but accurately, 446.4–13, as from "Dan Coopman's" chapter headed "Smeer" or "Fat". See William Scoresby, Jr., *An Account of the Arctic Regions* (Edinburgh, 1820), II, 151–52, and discussions at 157.7–9, 298.22, and 409.36.

449.10    Tranque . . . Arsacides]    Tranque is not one of the Arsacides (which are near the Solomon Islands in the Pacific) but an island off the coast of Chile. Presumably Melville mislocated it deliberately. From references at 7.29 ("land on barbarous coasts") and 104.26 ("many a pleasant haven in store") George Stewart conjectures that in the "Ur-*Moby-Dick*" Ishmael jumped ship at a tropical island (see "The Two *Moby-Dicks*," *American Literature*, XXV [January, 1954], 422, 445). If so, perhaps Tranque was it.

453.13 embryo] See the NOTE ON THE TEXT, p. 791.

456.24 antechronical] Here and at 457.18 the obviously intended sense of the passages calls for adoption of the prefix "ante" from the E reading "antechronical"; but the unhyphenated form of the A reading "antichronical" is retained. (Cf. "antemosaic" at 457.29.)

457.2 1842] Possibly the date Melville wrote, or meant to write, was 1832, the year in which Judge Creagh sent some fossil bones to the American Philosophical Society. These were indeed the bones Melville describes in the rest of the paragraph, first declared (by Richard Harlan of Philadelphia, not the "Alabama doctors") to be those of a reptile and later (1838) examined in London by Richard Owen, who identified them as cetacean and delivered a paper on them in January, 1839, to the Geological Society of London *(Transactions,* 2d ser., VI [1842], 69–79). They were not, however, part of the "almost complete vast skeleton" collected from Judge Creagh's property in 1842 by Samuel B. Buckley, who reported his find in the *American Journal of Science* in April, 1843 (XXXV, 77–79). Melville is thus merging two fossil discoveries: the first sentence of this paragraph deals with the discovery of a nearly complete skeleton, and the date 1842 is correct for it; but the rest of the paragraph, claiming to continue the discussion of the same discovery, actually relates to an earlier discovery (of a fossil vertebra, not a skeleton), and for it the correct date is 1832. Melville's principal source for this passage, the article on "Whales" in the *Penny Cyclopædia* (London, 1843), XXVII, 297, mentions both discoveries and quotes from both Owen's and Buckley's papers; but the dates it provides are those of the two papers (1839 and 1843), not of the two discoveries (1832 and 1842). Melville may therefore have used another source as well. In any case, because the date 1842 is correct for one of the two discoveries alluded to, no emendation is made.

457.13 mutations] Perhaps Melville intended the word "revolutions" (misread by a copyist or compositor): the exact quotation from Richard Owen's 1839 paper (cited in the preceding discussion) that Melville presents "in substance" is "we cannot hesitate in pronouncing the colossal *Zeuglodon* to have been one of the most extraordinary of the Mammalia which the revolutions of the globe have blotted out of the number of existing things." Melville's direct source was the quotation from Owen in the article on "Whales" in the *Penny Cyclopædia* (London, 1843), XXVII, 297.

457.28 Pharaohs'] See the NOTE ON THE TEXT, p. 786, footnote 35.

457.36 Denderah] The spelling is that of Melville's source, the *Penny Cyclopædia* (London, 1843), XXVII, 794 (s.v. "Zodiac").

458.6–19  "Not . . . Temple."]  This passage, as Melville indicates, is based upon John Leo (Johannes Leo Africanus); however, Melville did not take it directly from John Pory's translation of Leo's *A Geographical Historie of Africa* (London, 1600), pp. 59–60, but instead from John Harris's version of Leo's account in his *Navigantium atque Itinerantium Bibliotheca* (London, 1705), the book Melville also used for the four extracts at xxi.1–23. The passage as quoted in A and E corresponds exactly in wording—and in most of the accidentals as well—with the passage in Harris, I, 318, except for the omission of "by" after "pass" at 458.10 and the substitution of "at the Base of the Temple" for "upon the Shoar of *Messa*" at 458.19. The high degree of accuracy of this extract indicates that the omission of "by" was inadvertent, and NN restores it. Although the parenthetical "(says John Leo)" at 458.15–16 is similar to Melville's interpolations in quotations elsewhere (as at xix.9, xxi.24, and xxviii.15), in this case the parenthesis is in his source, for Harris is paraphrasing Leo; the "is said" which follows is not an erroneous duplication, because Leo, in the original passage of 1600, is citing what "a certaine gentleman" had reported.

460.4  Swedish]  The A and E reading "Danish" (presumably Melville's own error) identifies Uno von Troil incorrectly: the title page of his *Letters on Iceland* (London, 1780) identifies him as a "Member of the Academy of Sciences at Stockholm"; he is further identified as "a Swede by birth, and descended of a noble family" (p. xiv); and he writes of "us Swedes" (p. 32).

460.5  reydar-fiskur]  The A and E reading "reydan-siskur" is a misreading (probably Melville's own, mistaking the *f* as an initial long *s*) of these words ("*reydar fiskur, or wrinkle-bellied*") in his source, Letter XII in Uno von Troil's *Letters on Iceland* (London, 1780), p. 129. Changes from these phrases in A and E that are retained by NN as intended by Melville are the hyphen added between the first two words as well as the added capitals, omitted hyphen, and grammatical change to "Wrinkled Bellies" (the latter made to fit the grammatical context—see pp. 795–96). Melville cited this work at xxii.23–29. The names of Banks and Solander (460.3) appear on its title page.

460.10  1825]  See the discussion at 262.27.

462.7  Horto]  The A and E reading "Harto" is emended as probably a copyist's or compositor's misreading; Melville was drawing on Sir Thomas Browne's *Pseudodoxia Epidemica* (in his 1686 London *Works)*, Book VI, Chapter 6, p. 245, where Browne cites "*Gurcias ab Horto*, Physician to the Viceroy at Goa". (Cf. Sealts 90, Bercaw 83.)

465.5–6  leg . . . carpenter]  For the discrepancy between Ahab's needing the Carpenter to make him a new leg (Chapters 106–7) and the statement by the old Gay-Head Indian (who knows Ahab's history from birth) that "he has a quiver of 'em", see the discussions at 124.16–18 and 124.16.

473.12  Niphon, Matsmai, and Sikoke]  The apparent error in naming "Matsmai" (a town) as one of "the Japanese islands" may be explained by the fact that certain "Japanese dependencies" were then collectively called "the government of Matsmai," as in the tabulation of "Islands, and their Provinces," which also listed "Niphon" and "Sikokf" among the islands, in John Ramsay McCulloch's *Universal Gazetteer* (New York, 1843–44), s.v. "Japan." Melville's spellings of all three names were acceptable variants.

474.37  rose]  Unless a textual corruption has occurred here, it would appear that Starbuck's rising at this point is another instance of Melville's not always recognizing an inconsistency in his assignment of a name or action. Starbuck is not said to have taken a sitting position (his last action, at 474.21–22, was "moving further into the cabin"), and surely Melville would not deliberately have had him sit in Ahab's presence in such a scene.

477.16  hammock]  Melville nods in assigning Queequeg a hammock in this forecastle scene (also at 477.33, 478.11, 479.18, and 480.10), since whaleship forecastles had only wooden berths. See the discussion at 16.28. As to the misplacement of Queequeg, a harpooneer, in the forecastle, see the discussion at 478.17.

477.39  one]  The possibility that "one" is a misreading for "me" is suggested by the certainty that the appropriate shipmate for Queequeg to call at such a moment would be his bosom friend Ishmael; but that possibility is removed by the third-person pronoun "his" at 478.1 and by repetition of the same impersonal construction in "told one to go" at 479.12. The fact that at both points Queequeg is said to address an indefinite shipmate rather than his companion Ishmael, taken together with the fact that Ishmael is not dramatically present at all in the scene, amounts to a striking discrepancy; it strongly suggests that Melville wrote the episode before he wrote those in the opening chapters where he established the close relationship between Ishmael and Queequeg. The suggestion is supported by two further matters in the narrative technique: the repeated use all through the chapter and elsewhere of the epithet "poor" for Queequeg rather than any more personal terms, and the description of the dying Queequeg (477.21–36) as seen by an impersonal "you" rather than by the first-person Ishmael. (Contrast the first-person account of Shenly's death scene in *White-Jacket,* chap. 79.) In the present chapter, the special friendship of Queequeg and Ishmael is recognized at only two points: in a phrase at the beginning, "my poor pagan companion, and fast bosom-friend" (476.19), and by the pronoun in the phrase "my Queequeg" near the end (480.26); both of these could easily have been inserted after the episode was written. See the HISTORICAL NOTE, pp. 656–58 and the Hayford article cited there, and the discussions at 56.39, 61.35–36, and 478.17.

478.17 aft] There is a major unemendable discrepancy between the statement in Chapter 33 ("The Specksynder") that "harpooneers are lodged in the after part of the ship" where they "sleep in a place indirectly communicating" with the captain's cabin (147.8–10) and Queequeg's being quartered throughout this chapter in the forecastle with the crew: in order to visit him at 478.24, the Carpenter "proceeded into the forecastle", and at 478.35 "went forward"; at 479.29 Starbuck looked "down the scuttle" at Queequeg in his coffin. One possible (and simple) explanation is that in writing the scene Melville simply nodded and forgot "the grand distinction drawn between officer and man at sea"—that "the first lives aft, the last forward" (147.5–6). The blunder is so glaring, however, that another and genetically more complex explanation seems likely—that at the stage when Melville first wrote Queequeg's "death" scene he had not yet made him one of the harpooneers and that after doing so he neglected to make the appropriate revision relocating the scene aft. (See the discussion of the same discrepancy involving Tashtego's sleeping forward with the crew in Chapter 54, "The Town-Ho's Story," at 242.21.) Such a genetic explanation is strengthened by the further discrepancy discussed at 477.39. See also the discussions at 56.39, 61.35–36, 302.4, and 320.11.

478.21 Lackaday islands] Possibly a reference to the Laccadives off the southeast coast of India, as suggested by Willard Thorp in his edition of *Moby-Dick* (New York: Oxford University Press, 1947), p. 448n. The reading is unverifiable but seems intended, in Ishmael's—and Melville's—frequent jocular vein, as a play on the obsolete interjection of regret or deprecation, "lackaday." (Compare, for example, "Buggerry Island" in Chapter 4 of *Typee* [NN23.6], a name that he directed to be changed to "Desolate Island" in the 1892 edition; see the NN edition, p. 312.)

486.8 all-contributed] Emendation to "all-contributing" would seem to supply a better complement to the second adjectival term "all-receptive" because the two would then designate balancing characteristics of the ocean—its giving all and receiving all. The sense of the retained A and E reading is less clear, but in any case it involves, like "all-receptive", some idea of the ocean's *taking,* rather than the idea actually developed in what follows, of what it alluringly *offers.*

488.23 stubbs] NN does not emend as incorrect the thrice-repeated A and E spelling with the double consonant because the *Oxford English Dictionary* lists it as a variant of "stub", the only form for which the OED supplies citations in reference to horseshoe nails, and the spelling occurs in Melville's source passage in William Scoresby's *An Account of the Arctic Regions* (Edinburgh, 1820), II, 225–26, as pointed out by Luther S. Mansfield and Howard P. Vincent in their Hendricks House edition of *Moby-Dick* (New York, 1952), p. 816, note 483.15.

489.9–10 this harpoon] Departing from whaling usage for Ahab's literary enhancement, Melville makes him all along plan to harpoon Moby Dick (the boatsteerer's job) and to lance and kill him (the headsman's job). In the final three-day chase Ahab attempts both roles. See the discussion at 230.6–7. At several points (e.g., in Chapter 131, 540.17ff.) Melville, who glorifies the harpooneer's role all along, unrealistically makes Ahab and other characters speak as if the harpoon, not the lance, is the whale's death instrument. See the discussion at 179.7.

492.11–26 "Oh . . . it."] A and E print this paragraph without initial and final quotation marks, thereby making it one of Ishmael's long reflections. The structure of the chapter conclusively shows that the paragraph should be spoken by Ahab, for the chapter moves from Ishmael's definition of the effect of "times of dreamy quietude" (491.13) in the Pacific upon a rover like himself, to the effect of such scenes upon Ahab, upon Starbuck, and finally upon Stubb. The fifth paragraph sets up a comparison and a contrast between the effect of "such soothing scenes" (492.7) upon Ishmael and upon Ahab. While Ahab at first responds much as Ishmael does, his breath upon the "secret golden keys" of these scenes ultimately proves "but tarnishing" (492.8–10). The tarnishing breath can only be that which speaks the words of the next paragraph. Further evidence occurs at the beginning of the short seventh paragraph: "And that same day, too, gazing far down from his boat's side into that same golden sea, Starbuck lowly murmured" (492.27–28); the "too" must mean that someone else has been speaking aloud. Perhaps the error would have been noticed sooner if Melville had visualized the scene more fully (is Ahab looking over his boat's side, like Ishmael and Starbuck, and presumably Stubb, or over the ship's side?). In its consequences this emendation, though simple, is one of the more significant made in NN (critics have used the paragraph to characterize Ishmael, the presumed speaker).

497.17 striveth . . . jetteth] See the NOTE ON THE TEXT, p. 793, footnote 39.

500.3 for] This word in A and E is very likely corrupt: "Season-on-the-Line" is called a "technical phrase" at 200.30 and is repeated at 201.5; also "on the Line . . . season" occurs twice (392.3–4, 437.39) and "on" or "upon the Line" five times (301.13, 381.22–23, 429.3–4, 438.5, 439.32); but "for the Line" does not occur elsewhere in *Moby-Dick*.

500.5 spokes] See the discussion at 283.18–19.

500.12   sometimes,]   See the NOTE ON THE TEXT, p. 791.

501.3   earthly]   See the discussion of "clerical" at 38.16.

504.8–19   Oh! . . . oh!]   Melville's direct source for the text of this "old song" has not been located; but Stan Hugill has reported to the NN editors that the "hoky-poky" refrain may be related to the songs "Jibber a hokey-pokey" (also called "Jefferree jee me jibber a hoy") and "Do me hokey pokey" (a Newfoundland version of "Do me Johnny Boker"). Whatever the extent to which this song in *Moby-Dick* is Melville's own creation, it obviously contains snatches from shanties he had heard.

517.32   braced]   See the NOTE ON THE TEXT, p. 791.

522.15–16   Reward . . . clay—]   Pip's derangement seems insufficient explanation for the lack of sense in the A and E reading ("One hundred pounds of clay reward for Pip;"). More likely a mix-up by Melville, or the copyist or compositor, accounts for the fact that its two main phrases have been reversed and run together improperly punctuated, so that the intended sense is lost. NN emends to reverse their order and supply the punctuation needed to make clear that in Pip's rendition of a town-crier with a bell (Pip makes him a "ship's-crier") the announcement "Reward for Pip!" is followed by an itemized description of the missing person, beginning with his weight "One hundred pounds of clay—" (with the implication that he as a man is only so much clay). Cf. the town-crier's announcement in "Little Annie's Ramble", which Melville read and marked in the copy of *Twice-Told Tales* that Hawthorne gave him in January, 1851 (Sealts 258).

523.18–19   the pagan harpooneers]   An unemendable oversight seems involved in placing all three harpooneers in Flask's watch—or having them all awake "before the dawn". Once again, Melville is using them for suggestive effect, not writing realistically, even though he has troubled to specify twice that the watch is Flask's. Also we cannot assume from the Manxman's presence that he is a member of Flask's watch; he too seems to be placed here for his gnomic remarks, just as he was in Stubb's watch in the preceding chapter (522.38). See the discussion at 179.7.

528.29   deaf]   Since the meaning is that those to be envied are those who cannot see and hear, the context clearly calls for "deaf", rather than the A and E reading "dumb", as Robert Zoellner points out in *The Salt-Sea Mastodon: A Reading of MOBY-DICK* (Berkeley: University of California Press, 1973), p. 112. The reading "dumb" may have resulted from a slip (the association of "deaf" and "dumb") or from a misreading of handwriting (in Melville's hand "deaf" could resemble "dumb").

543.17   slouched hat]   It seems an oversight on Melville's part to allow Ahab another "slouched hat" here (even if it is a necessary duplicate), diminishing the effect of the dramatically made point in Chapter 130, "The Hat," that after the wild hawk flew off with his hat it was never recovered. See the discussion at 179.7.

545.12 Is Ahab, Ahab?] The E reading, "Is it Ahab, Ahab?", offers an attractive possibility and may in fact have resulted from Melville's correction of the American proofs. In that form the question becomes parallel in structure to those before and after it: Ahab then is asking "What is it . . . ? Is it Ahab, Ahab? Is it I, God, or who . . . ?" The repetition of "Ahab" here would suggest some degree of incredulity or wonderment. There is no doubt that the question as worded in E fits well into the context of the paragraph, which poses the question of ultimate responsibility in the universe by first asking what causes Ahab to act as he does and then attempting an answer by citing various instances of principal-agent-object relationships. However, the question in A, "Is Ahab, Ahab?", is also appropriate in the context. Ahab's questioning of his own identity—suggested by this form of the question—is closely related to his concern with ultimate responsibility, for if Ahab is not responsible for his acts, he may reasonably ask in what sense he has any identity at all. His later statement—"how then can this one small heart beat; this one small brain think thoughts; unless God does that beating, does that thinking, does that living, and not I"(545.14–16)—would seem to be a development of the question as worded in A. Furthermore, the repetition of "Ahab" is perhaps more plausibly accounted for in this form of the question, for here the second "Ahab" is a required grammatical complement rather than a rhetorical embellishment. Something can thus be said in favor of both the A and E readings, and an editor must recognize that, whichever reading is adopted, it may not be the one that represents Melville's intention. Under the circumstances, the more conservative editorial choice is to retain the copy-text reading, since it does make sense in the context and since the E reading could conceivably be an editorial sophistication or a compositorial error induced by the wording at the beginning of the next question.

548.28 laving] See the NOTE ON THE TEXT, p. 789.

551.13 other drifting end] Melville apparently lost track of which end the crew were on. At 550.5–6 they tumble over each other "to gain the uttermost stern" (to which Fedallah has already gone, at 549.28–29, while Ahab goes to the bow); after Moby Dick has bitten the boat into two parts, Fedallah is placed (correctly) as watching from the stern part (551.12), but the "clinging crew" are said to be "at the other drifting end" (551.13)—i.e., at the bow part. To secure consistency, "other" might be emended to "the same"; but the emendation would violate a more important matter—the tableau as Melville visualized it, with two floating ends, Fedallah on one, the crew on the other. See the discussion at 179.7.

552.5 circumferences] See the NOTE ON THE TEXT, p. 792, footnote 36.

552.31 Moby Dick] The name is hyphenated at this point in A; there is no hyphen in E. For comments on the NN deletion of the hyphen, see the discussion of the title at v.1.

553.18–19 outright . . . outright] The first "outright" may possibly be an excrescence: the sentence should perhaps read, "If the Gods think to speak to man, they will honorably speak outright".

553.27 unset] Possibly this word in A and E is a misreading. The problem is that, although to "set the watch" (see 170.5) is to put the men on duty, to "unset" them is not to relieve them of it, as Ahab does in ordering the look-outs down, just below (553.34). If "unset" is somehow askew, perhaps, since "it was almost dark", a clipping of the word "sunset" is involved.

557.15 guiltlessness] See the NOTE ON THE TEXT, p. 792.

559.1 gunwale] Since the context suggests that the boat landed on both of its gunwales, not just one, this word (in the singular in both A and E) may well be another of the instances in which the copyist overlooked Melville's indistinct terminal s. (See the NOTE ON THE TEXT, p. 792.) Emendation, however, is not required; the possibility remains that Melville intended the singular number, either as indicating the boat's oblique position on first striking the water or as referring to its whole gunwale surface (though no other instance of that singular usage occurs in the book, among some dozen where it refers to one side only, and the plural is used when both are involved).

561.13 blistered] Possibly a corruption of "blasted" (see 77.4, 18; 79.34, of Ahab; 102.12); but "blister it" (1840) is glossed as a euphemistic colloquialism for "blast it" by Eric Partridge, *A Dictionary of Slang and Unconventional English* (New York: Macmillan, 1961).

562.5 brave, men, brave] See the NOTE ON THE TEXT, p. 803.

566.26 crew were all such tiger-yellow] I.e., all but *one*—Ishmael, who replaced Fedallah.

566.27–28 sometimes well known] NN retains this self-contradictory phrase from A and E as more likely another of Melville's occasional mix-ups than the copyist's or the compositor's transposition (which, to give the intended sense, should precede and thus modify "to affect"). As to the posited "musky" flesh of Ahab's yellow crew, the editors are advised by an eminent anthropologist that more than racist folklore is involved, since overconsumption of curry (used to preserve meat) among such East Asian populations as those here called "tiger-yellow barbarians" sometimes gives such an odor to their perspiration. An expert on sharks advises that they do indeed swarm quickly and are indeed attracted by the odor of human perspiration. So it is not clear how much Melville's scene owes to facts of experience (however he learned them) and how much to folklore and his own gothic treatment.

566.28 affect] NN does not emend this reading (in A and E) because it makes general sense. But quite possibly it is a misreading for "attract", the more precise verb called for by the context: the effect of the "musky" smell on the sharks is not merely to "affect" them but to draw ("attract") them to Ahab's boat. In *Moby-Dick* the verb is used four times in that way: compass needles "attract" crowds (4.20), Ishmael and Queequeg are "attracted" to a sleeper by his noisy breathing (100.25), Captain Sleet is "attracted" toward a bottle (158.3), and Ahab is "attracted" by the doubloon (430.16). In Melville's hand *tt*, often uncrossed, might easily be misread as *ff* if he was writing hurriedly and if the context made the misreading plausible. Cf. various examples in the manuscripts reproduced below, pp. 955–1004.

567.9 Where's the old man now?] Quite likely Starbuck's question, just after thinking of his wife and son at home, is a private authorial allusion to the nearly identical one "Where dat old man?" that was entered by Melville, away from home at sea, three times in his 1849 London journal (October 28, 30, and November 4) and later glossed by his wife as the first "baby words" of their eight-month-old first son, Malcolm.

568.1 Tashtego] An oversight on Melville's part is involved in naming Queequeg (as A and E do) at this point, since Queequeg belonged neither to Ahab's nor to Stubb's boat but to Starbuck's, which at Ahab's command had not lowered for this chase. Since Melville's intention was to name Stubb's harpooner along with Flask's Daggoo, NN emends to "Tashtego". Cf. similar emendations of oversights relating to names at 230.12 and 286.18.

569.8–11 the unpitying sharks . . . at almost every dip] The two-part vignette, beginning at 566.13–29 and concluding here, of Ahab's boat beset by sharks biting its oars—one of them Ishmael's—appears to have been suggested to Melville by a paragraph he marked in his copy of Owen Chase's *Narrative*, which he acquired in April of 1851. There a single shark "snapped at the steering-oar"—only that oar—"several times", whereas in Melville's passage "numbers of sharks . . . maliciously snapped at the blades of the oars" and "so continually bit at the plying oars, that the blades became jagged and crunched, and left small splinters in the sea, at almost every dip." In its few lines the scene blends—in the melodramatic style of gothic romance—one element from a book source with two elements of quasi-scientific folklore about the "musky" odor of "yellow boys" and about the attractive effect of that odor upon sharks (see the discussions at 566.27–28 and 566.28). Melville had picked up the last two elements perhaps by ear, perhaps in other books, perhaps both. Thomas Heffernan in *Stove by a Whale* (Middletown, Conn.: Wesleyan University Press, 1981), p. 166, points to the *Narrative* (pp. 65–66) as Melville's source (see pp. 976–77, below). However, there are hazards in reasoning about the genesis of *Moby-Dick* on the evidence of source passages in books of known acquisition date. In *Mardi*, completed by late 1848, two years before Melville got his copy of Chase's *Narrative*, he alludes in an early chapter (13) to "the good craft Essex, and others, . . . sunk by sea-monsters"; less than twenty lines later along comes a shark who "often snapped viciously at our steering oar" (NN40.5–6,19). This passage is closer to Chase's paragraph than the one just examined at the end of *Moby-Dick*. What becomes of our evidence that Melville wrote the last chapter of *Moby-Dick* after April of 1851?

569.14 "But . . . smaller!"] Since Ishmael is the only English-speaking member (or speaker of such formal English) among the crew in Ahab's boat at this point, the logical inference is that it is he who speaks these words. It seems unlikely, however, that Melville had Ishmael or any particular speaker in mind, since he assigns the speech to no one and at no other point in the book represents Ishmael as addressing Ahab. Like similar unemendable discrepancies elsewhere in the book, this one (and the associated ones at 572.12–13 and 572.18) evidently arose from Melville's greater concern for dramatic effect than for consistency in literal detail, rather than from divergent conceptions at separate points and stages of composition. See the discussion at 179.7.

572.12–13 "The ship? . . . ship?"] Again, as at 569.14 (see the discussion), no speaker among "the tranced boat's crew" is assigned and none of the four yellow crewmen left aboard could have delivered these words, nor could Ishmael, who is overboard and swimming (569.31–36 and Epilogue).

572.18 all its crew] Not all five, but only four; see the preceeding discussion.

572.32 death-grasp] See the NOTE ON THE TEXT, p. 789.

573.2 "And . . . thee."] This epigraph is an accurate quotation of the last clause of Job 1:19 in the King James Version.

# List of Emendations

I N THIS LIST of changes made in the copy-text by the present
editors, the following abbreviations are used to designate the
sources of readings:

A   American Edition (1851)
E   English Edition (1851)
H   *Harper's New Monthly Magazine* (October, 1851)
NN  Northwestern-Newberry Edition

For further comment on this list, see p. 805 above; for discussions of
the emendations marked with an asterisk (*), see the DISCUSSIONS OF
ADOPTED READINGS, pp. 809–906 (where the entries are not always
keyed to the same words as here, because several cruxes or a longer
passage are sometimes taken up in a single discussion). The wavy dash
(~) stands for the word cited in the left column and signals that only a
punctuation mark is emended. The caret (ʌ) indicates the absence of a
punctuation mark (but does not necessarily imply the presence of a
space: see, for example, the entry for 76.26). Empty brackets ([ ]) indicate space where a letter or mark of punctuation failed to print. A slash
(/) indicates a line-end break within a word in the copy-text.

| | NN READING | COPY-TEXT READING |
|---|---|---|
| *xi.29 | *Prairie* E | Praire |
| *xv.4 | [The E | ∧~ |
| *xv.8 | mortality.] E | ~.∧ |
| *xvi.1 | תן NN | הן |
| *xvi.4 | WHÆL NN | WHŒL |
| *xvi.5 | HVAL NN | HVALT |
| *xvi.8 | HVALUR NN | WHALE |
| xvii.3 | [It E | ∧~ |
| *xviii.5 | glasses!] E | ~!∧ |
| *xviii.24 | Balænæ NN | Balæne |
| xix.20 | *Ibid.* E | ~∧ |
| *xix.24 | recure NN | secure |
| *xix.26 | lovely NN | lowly |
| *xix.28 | from NN | thro' |
| *xx.2 | Hofmannus NN | Hosmannus |
| *xx.5 | iron NN | modern |
| *xx.15 | *Holy War* E | *Pilgrim's Progress* |
| *xx.21 | on NN | in |
| *xx.24 | trunk NN | breath |
| *xxi.3 | foot NN | feet |
| *xxi.18 | Hitland NN | Shetland |
| *xxi.25 | foot NN | feet |
| *xxi.26 | beside NN | besides |
| *xxi.27 | Pitfirren NN | Pitferren |
| *xxi.32 | Stafford NN | Strafford |
| *xxii.1 | these NN | those |
| *xxii.11 | stiff E | stuffed |
| *xxii.25 | brim-stone NN | lime-stone |
| *xxii.33 | 1788 NN | 1778 |
| *xxiii.9 | coasts NN | coast |
| *xxiii.16 | flew NN | blew |
| *xxiii.17 | fires NN | fire |
| *xxiii.18 | Amid NN | Around |

|  | NN READING | COPY-TEXT READING |
|---|---|---|
| *xxiv.12 | instinct   NN | instincts |
| xxiv.15 | jaw,   E | ~. |
| xxv.7 | Chase   NN | Chace |
| xxv.11 | *Ocean."*   NN | ~.ᴧ |
| xxv.11 | *Chase*   NN | *Chace* |
| *xxv.13 | on   NN | in |
| *xxv.27 | jaw   NN | jaws |
| *xxvi.7 | those   NN | these |
| xxvi.27 | *Cruise*   E | *Cruize* |
| xxvi.30 | *Mutiny,"*   NN | ~,ᴧ |
| *xxvi.31 | *Hussey,*   E | ~ᴧ |
| xxvi.36 | Bennet   NN | Bennett |
| *xxvii.9 | *as*   NN | [*not present*] |
| xxvii.14 | *the*   E | *tke* |
| *xxvii.24 | mere   E | near |
| *xxviii.5 | *Hobomock*   NN | *Hobomack* |
| *xxviii.11 | *Fishermen*   NN | *Fisherman* |
| 3.22 | Battery   E | battery |
| *5.13 | make him the   E | [*not present*] |
| 7.36 | midmost   E | mid most |
| *10.5 | out-hanging   E | [*not present*] |
| 10.38 | wrapperᴧ   NN | ~— |
| 10.38 | afterwards)—   NN | ~)ᴧ |
| 12.15 | came   NN | come |
| *13.19 | handle,   NN | ~ᴧ |
| *15.20 | four   NN | three |
| 16.34 | any   E | my |
| *18.3 | an airley   E | an early |
| 18.7 | bamboozling   NN | bamboozingly |
| 19.19 | Sal   NN | Sall |
| *20.6 | wardrobeᴧ   NN | ~, |
| *20.6 | doubt,   NN | ~ᴧ |

| | NN Reading | Copy-Text Reading |
|---|---|---|
| *20.14 | the same as   E | as you see the same |
| *27.19 | having   NN | leaving |
| 27.33 | any   E | auy |
| 31.16 | Tongatabooans   E | Tongatabooarrs |
| *41.21 | left   E | lift |
| *42.21 | 'And   E | "~ |
| 42.21 | Jonah.'   E | ~." |
| 44.4 | " 'Who's   E | ∧'~ |
| 44.18 | "Now   E | ∧~ |
| 46.20 | become   E | became |
| 46.28 | "And   E | ∧~ |
| *48.36 | remained,   NN | ~∧ |
| *56.13 | haply   E | happily |
| *59.5 | hands   NN | hand |
| 59.14–15 | Kokovoko   E | Rokovoko |
| 59.18 | Kokovoko   E | Rokovoko |
| 60.18 | bows   E | brows |
| 61.4 | bery   NN | bevy |
| *64.29 | rests   NN | riots |
| *67.2 | fishy   E | fishing |
| *67.31 | ony   E | only |
| *67.34 | a-night   E | at night |
| 69.32 | Becket   E | Beckett |
| 71.12 | Marchant   E | Merchant |
| *73.35 | virgin,   E | ~∧ |
| *73.35 | voluntary,   E | ~∧ |
| 74.16 | Bildad   E | Peleg |
| 76.26 | " 'Lay   NN | "∧~ |
| 76.27 | moth—' "   NN | ~—∧" |
| 77.7 | " 'for   NN | "∧~ |
| 77.8 | also.' "   NN | ~.∧" |
| *78.7 | Thank ye   NN | That's he |

|  | NN Reading | Copy-Text Reading |
|---|---|---|
| 78.13 | *he* E | he |
| 79.8 | that, E | ~∧ |
| 82.39 | mustard-pot NN | vinegar-cruet |
| 83.22 | knob E | knot |
| 83.39 | I E | he |
| *87.1 | 18 E | XVII |
| 87.15 | First E | first |
| *88.39 | to NN | [*not present*] |
| *89.28 | Bel E | Bell |
| 92.31 | prophecy? E | ~. |
| 93.25 | you?" E | ~?∧ |
| 96.11 | stowage E | storage |
| *96.35 | running E | hobbling |
| 100.9 | him, E | ~∧ |
| 100.10 | fashion∧ E | ~, |
| 102.6 | gifts NN | gift |
| *104.3 | ye—spring, NN | ~—~! |
| *104.3 | Quohog E | Quohag |
| 110.8 | Cooks E | Cookes |
| 110.10 | Cook E | Cooke |
| 110.13 | Cook E | Cooke |
| *115.22 | words NN | sounds |
| 116.20 | Stubb E | Stbub |
| 117.1 | bravery, NN | ~∧ |
| 117.1 | chiefly∧ E | ~, |
| 119.37 | to E | [ ]o |
| 119.38 | battering E | batter-/[ ]ng |
| *120.3 | presently NN | probably |
| *121.30 | did! Poor E | did—oh, no! he went before. Poor |
| 122.21 | warranty E | warrantry |
| 123.35 | say. E | ~, |

| | NN Reading | Copy-Text Reading |
|---|---|---|
| *132.4 | 'Slid  NN | ∧~ |
| 132.16 | 'Halloa,'  E | '~,∧ |
| *132.35 | quick  E | [not present] |
| *135.9 | Bonnaterre  NN | Bonneterre |
| *135.11 | Olmsted  NN | Olmstead |
| *135.11 | Henry  NN | [not present] |
| *136.23 | 1766  NN | 1776 |
| 137.33 | Pottfisch  NN | Pottsfich |
| 137.34 | Lamantins  NN | Lamatins |
| 138.32 | Baleine  E | Baliene |
| *138.32 | Gronlands Walfisk  NN | Growlands Walfish |
| *141.14 | Killer  NN | Thrasher |
| *141.14 | Thrasher  NN | Killer |
| 143.21 | (Duodecimo).  NN | (~.) |
| *143.29 | i.e.  E | i.e∧ |
| *148.15 | direst  E | direct |
| 153.9 | whetstones  E | whetstone |
| 155.24 | even  E | ever |
| 155.28 | however,  NN | ~∧ |
| 156.6 | pleasant—  E | ~∧ |
| *156.33 | coolish  E | cold |
| 158.14 | Southern  E | South |
| *159.21 | Wickliff's  E | Cranmer's |
| *162.1–2 | men,—a doubloon  E | men |
| 163.9 | that  E | tha[ ] |
| 165.30 | wert  E | wer't |
| 169.21 | demogorgon  E | demigorgon |
| *171.21 | loves  NN | love, |
| 173.8 | commanded∧—  E | ~.— |
| 174.35 | comes  NN | come's |
| *175.1 | AZORES  NN | AZORE |
| 175.7 | AZORES  NN | AZORE |

| | NN Reading | Copy-Text Reading |
|---|---|---|
| 175.26 | one   E | a |
| *175.26 | your   E | you |
| 176.3 | waves'   NN | ~∧ |
| 176.3 | snow-caps'   NN | snow's caps |
| 176.13 | TAHITIAN   E | TAHITAN |
| *176.16 | valed   E | veiled |
| 181.13 | fearfully   E | fearfnlly |
| *181.28 | Povelsen   NN | Povelson |
| *181.33 | terror   NN | terrors |
| 181.37 | Povelsen   NN | Povelson |
| *182.37 | Strella   NN | Strello |
| 188.22 | Cæsarian∧   E | ~, |
| 190.1 | albatross:   E | ~, |
| 191.27 | kin?   NN | ~! |
| *192.5 | much   E | much like |
| 193.14 | seas;   E | ~: |
| *199.39 | on   NN | in |
| 200.4 | in crossing   E | incrossing |
| 200.27 | and   E | or |
| *200.28 | probability   NN | possibility |
| *201.9 | covertly   E | correctly |
| *201.24 | No   NN | Yes |
| *205.1 | Jack   NN | Tom |
| 205.4 | Tom   NN | Jack |
| *205.17 | Church   NN | Butler |
| *206.3 | others,   NN | ~∧ |
| 206.32 | Chase   NN | Chace |
| 206.35 | Chase's   NN | Chace's |
| *208.4 | Ochotsk   NN | Ochotsh |
| *209.5 | over   NN | on |
| *210.15 | Commander Davies   NN | Commodore Davis |
| 212.2 | stands   E | stand |

| | NN Reading | Copy-Text Reading |
|---|---|---|
| *215.13 | modified  E | directed |
| 215.39 | steward!"  NN | ~!∧ |
| *218.20 | back!—Never  E | ~!"[¶]"~ |
| 218.22 | sir,"  E | ~,' |
| 219.31 | boys!)"  NN | ~!") |
| *220.36 | oar  E | oars |
| 221.38 | Though,  E | ~∧ |
| 221.38 | truly,  E | ~∧ |
| 222.25 | fair  NN | far |
| 222.29 | eyes,  NN | ~∧ |
| *230.12 | Archy's  NN | Cabaco's |
| 234.22 | Tormentoso  NN | Tormentoto |
| *243.17 | westward  NN | eastward |
| *244.1 | Nantucketer  NN | Vineyarder |
| 244.3–259.15 | [*82 emendations correcting errors in the use of single and double quotation marks, recorded separately in 80 entries at the end of this* List] | |
| 244.28 | birch  NN | beech |
| 246.26 | sailor's  NN | sailors' |
| *249.13 | plaza  H | plazza |
| 252.20 | now!  E | ~? |
| 253.19 | three  H | these |
| *255.13 | beneath  NN | between |
| *256.5 | rolls!∧  H, E | ~!' |
| *256.5 | whale!'  H, E | ~!∧ |
| 256.14 | up  H, E | up up |
| 256.15 | Now,  H, E | ~. |
| *259.12 | honor,  H, E | ~∧ |
| *271.6 | else—  E | ~∧ |
| *271.7 | hills—  E | hills, that |
| 271.8 | Solomon  NN | Soloma |
| 271.9 | Figueroa  NN | Figuera |

| | NN READING | COPY-TEXT READING |
|---|---|---|
| 277.11 | Pontoppidan NN | Pontoppodan |
| *279.2 | twelve NN | twenty |
| 280.22 | contortions E | contortion |
| 285.19 | bowsman; E | ~? |
| *286.18 | Tashtego NN | Daggoo |
| *295.5 | Dough E | Do |
| 295.16 | yourselbs E | yoursebls |
| *295.18 | good NN | dood |
| 298.20–21 | fastidious E | fastidions |
| *300.15 | formerly NN | formally |
| 301.10 | two, E | ~∧ |
| 301.11 | hour∧ E | ~, |
| 308.21 | vulturism E | vultureism |
| *312.15 | lives in E | lives on |
| 313.5 | stranger's E | strangers' |
| *319.21 | skirt NN | shirt |
| 322.15 | bellows E | bitters |
| *322.15 | breath E | life |
| 326.38 | lets E | let's |
| *338.11 | Sais NN | Lais |
| 340.33 | fatal E | fata[ ] |
| *345.2 | *Prairie* E | PRAIRE |
| 349.4 | brow NN | bow |
| 354.15 | Fiercely∧ NN | ~, |
| 354.15 | evenly, NN | ~∧ |
| 354.30 | diagonally E | diagonically |
| 355.12 | and, NN | ~∧ |
| *370.11 | 1850 E | 1851 |
| 371.25 | fishermen E | fishermon |
| 372.2 | necessities, NN | ~∧ |
| 376.18 | Eckermann NN | Eckerman |
| 384.25 | *gallied.** E | gallied.∧ |

| | NN Reading | Copy-Text Reading |
|---|---|---|
| *384.28–40 | *To . . . World.   E [except that Act iii. sc. 11. is restyled by NN to Act 111. sc. ii. in 384.33] | [not present] |
| *387.30 | still,   NN | ~∧ |
| 388.25 | vicissitudes   E | vicisitudes |
| *396.25 | seas,   E | seas; and when indeed |
| *396.26 | but   E | they were |
| *396.26 | were   E | [not present] |
| 397.20 | defendants   E | plaintiffs |
| *401.11 | Plowden   NN | Plowdon |
| *401.12 | Plowden   NN | Plowdon |
| 401.18 | Yᵉ   E | Ye |
| 401.18 | yᵉ   E | ye |
| 401.19 | that yᵉ   E | that ye |
| *401.19 | wardrobe   E | warbrobe |
| 401.19 | with yᵉ   E | with ye |
| *402.4 | that   E | not |
| 405.24 | augured   NN | argued |
| 407.24 | without   E | withont |
| 412.19 | effulgences   E | effulgenees |
| 413.24 | loves   NN | loved |
| *414.9 | considerateness   E | considerations |
| 416.8 | petulance   E | petulence |
| 418.6 | assistant's   NN | assistants' |
| 431.3 | flow   E | flows |
| 432.8 | old   E | ol[ ] |
| 432.32 | almanack;   E | ~[ ] |
| 432.37 | Bull;—   E | ~∧∧ |
| 432.37 | Jimini   E | Jimimi |
| 433.23 | and,   NN | ~∧ |
| 433.23 | up,   NN | ~∧ |
| 434.29 | Hark!"   NN | ~!∧ |
| *443.19 | 1788   NN | 1778 |

| | NN Reading | Copy-Text Reading |
|---|---|---|
| *444.11 | testing NN | tasting |
| *453.13 | embryo E | [not present] |
| *456.24 | antechronical E | antichronical |
| 456.36 | Dauphine NN | Dauphiné |
| 457.18 | antechronical E | antichronical |
| *457.28 | Pharaohs' E | Pharaoh's |
| *458.10 | by NN | [not present] |
| 460.3 | Cook's E | Cooke's |
| *460.4 | Swedish NN | Danish |
| *460.5 | reydar-fiskur NN | reydan-siskur |
| *462.7 | Horto NN | Harto |
| 467.14 | longs NN | longed |
| 467.14 | oar: NN | ~; |
| 471.38 | as a E | as |
| 484.15 | petulance E | petulence |
| *492.11 | "Oh NN | ∧~ |
| *492.26 | it." NN | ~.∧ |
| 493.13 | up NN | down |
| 497.16 | power! NN | ~? |
| *497.17 | striveth NN | strivest |
| *497.17 | jetteth NN | jettest |
| *500.12 | sometimes, E | [not present] |
| 502.14 | die in NN | die |
| 505.1 | "Yes E | ∧~ |
| 506.3 | sailors, E | sailors' |
| 506.7 | Tekel, E | ~∧ |
| 506.25 | to E | too |
| 510.24 | the holder E | theh older |
| *517.32 | braced E | [not present] |
| *522.15–16 | Reward for Pip! One hundred pounds of clay— NN | One hundred pounds of clay reward for Pip; |
| 522.23 | intently E | intenting |

| | NN READING | | COPY-TEXT READING |
|---|---|---|---|
| 525.27 | it's undignified | NN | its undignified |
| 527.7 | *and* | E | *aud* |
| *528.29 | deaf | NN | dumb |
| 532.10 | boats' | NN | boat's |
| 540.6 | upon | E | upom |
| 544.2 | bread, | NN | ~∧ |
| 545.8 | cozening | E | cozzening |
| 545.22 | air | E | airs |
| 548.19 | fowls | E | fowels |
| *548.28 | laving | E | leaving |
| 551.29 | prow was | E | prows were |
| *552.31 | Moby∧Dick | E | ~-~ |
| *557.15 | guiltlessness | NN | guiltiness |
| 560.27 | being. | E | ~∧ |
| 560.31 | boats' | E | boat's |
| *562.5 | brave, | E | ~∧ |
| 562.23 | set | E | sat |
| 563.18 | turn | E | turned |
| 568.1 | While | E | Whil*c* |
| *568.1 | Tashtego | NN | Queequeg |
| 570.31 | fit. | E | ~∧ |
| *572.32 | death-grasp | E | death-gasp |

*Emendations of quotation marks in "The Town-Ho's Story"*

| | | | | | | | |
|---|---|---|---|---|---|---|---|
| 244.3 | "∧Lakeman | NN | " '~ | 248.32 | North." | NN | ~.' |
| 244.3 | Buffalo?" | NN | ~?' | *248.33 | "∧Aye | H | " '~ |
| 246.24 | nose.' | H, E | ~." | 248.35 | story.∧ | H | ~.' |
| 248.25 | Canallers." | NN | ~.∧ | 249.11 | vicinities." | NN | ~.∧ |
| 248.26 | ∧"Canallers!" | NN | ' "~!' | 249.12 | "∧Is | NN | " '~ |
| 248.26 | "∧We | H | " '~ | 249.12 | passing?" | NN | ~?' |
| 248.28 | they?" | NN | ~?' | 249.14 | "∧Well | NN | " '~ |
| *248.29 | "∧Canallers | H | " '~ | 249.15 | Lima," | NN | ~,' |
| 248.30 | it." | NN | ~.' | 249.15 | "Proceed | NN | '~ |
| 248.31 | "∧Nay | NN | " '~ | 249.15 | Senor." | NN | ~.' |

| | | | | | | |
|---|---|---|---|---|---|---|
| 249.16 | "∧A NN | " '~ | | 258.9 | "As NN | ∧~ |
| 249.16 | Pardon!" NN | ~!' | | 258.10 | me!" ' NN | ~!∧' |
| 249.16 | "∧In NN | " '~ | | 258.28 | him." NN | ~.∧ |
| 249.20 | 'Corrupt NN | "~ | | 258.29 | "∧Are NN | " '~ |
| 249.20 | Lima.' NN | ~." | | 258.29 | through?" NN | ~?' |
| 249.22 | 'Corrupt NN | "~ | | 258.30 | "∧I H | " '~ |
| 249.22 | Lima.' NN | ~." | | 258.30 | Don." NN | ~.' |
| 249.24 | again." NN | ~.' | | 258.31 | "∧Then NN | " '~ |
| 250.7 | "∧I NN | " '~ | | 258.33 | press." NN | ~.' |
| 250.7 | see!" NN | ~!' | | 258.34 | ∧"Also NN | ' "~ |
| 250.8 | "No NN | '~ | | 258.35 | suit," NN | ~,' |
| 250.10 | story." NN | ~.' | | 258.36 | ∧"Is H | ' "~ |
| 250.25 | barricade.∧ E | ~." | | 258.36 | gentlemen?" NN | ~?' |
| 251.3 | men?' H | ~?" | | 258.37 | "∧Nay," NN | " '~.' |
| 254.10 | "But H, E | ∧~ | | 258.37 | "but NN | '~ |
| 255.22 | 'but H, E | "~ | | 258.39 | serious." NN | ~.' |
| 256.5 | Dick." NN | ~.∧ | | 259.1 | "∧Will NN | " '~ |
| 256.6 | Dick'!" NN | ~∧!' | | 259.1 | Don?" NN | ~?' |
| 256.6 | "St. NN | '~. | | 259.2 | "∧Though NN | " '~ |
| 256.7 | Dick?" NN | ~?' | | 259.2 | now," NN | ~,' |
| 256.8 | "∧A H | " '~ | | 259.3 | "I NN | '~ |
| 256.9 | story." NN | ~.' | | 259.4 | this." NN | ~.' |
| 256.10 | "∧How? NN | " '~? | | 259.5 | "∧Excuse H | " '~ |
| 256.10 | how?" NN | ~?' | | 259.6 | can." NN | ~.' |
| 256.11 | "∧Nay H | " '~ | | 259.8 | "∧This NN | " '~ |
| 256.12 | Sirs." NN | ~.' | | 259.8 | Evangelists," NN | ~,' |
| 256.13 | "∧The NN | " '~ | | 259.10 | "∧Let H, E | " '~ |
| 256.13 | chicha!" NN | ~!' | | 259.11 | it.∧ H | ~.' |
| 256.13 | "our NN | '~ | | 259.12 | "∧So H | " '~ |
| 256.14 | glass!" NN | ~!' | | 259.15 | Radney.∧" H | ~.' " |

# Report of Line-End Hyphenation

T HE FIRST LIST below records the forms adopted in the present edition (NN) for compound words that were hyphenated at line-ends in the copy-text (A—or, for the passage at 384.28–40, E) and that the editors had to decide whether to print as single-word compounds without hyphens or as hyphenated compounds. The second list enables one to determine the established reading (present in the copy-text or established by the editors) of compounds that happen to be hyphenated at the ends of lines in NN; any word hyphenated at the end of a line in NN should be transcribed as one unhyphenated word unless it appears in this list. Those words coincidentally hyphenated between the same elements at line-ends in both the copy-text and NN are marked with daggers (†); in the first list they are given in the forms that would have been adopted if they had fallen within a line in NN. A slash (/) indicates the line-end break in the copy-text in a word that might possibly be hyphenated in more than one place. For futher comment on these lists, see pp. 806–7 above.

I. NN *forms of compounds that were hyphenated at copy-text line-ends*

| | | | |
|---|---|---|---|
| x.24 | *Midnight* | 88.17 | everlasting |
| xii.4 | *Schoolmasters* | 90.13 | everlasting |
| xix.1 | horse-whales | 91.7 | fore-finger |
| 4.32 | landscape | 93.38 | half-apprehensions |
| 9.32 | ash-box | 95.19 | sauce-pans |
| 9.34 | Sword-Fish | 96.1 | coster-mongers |
| 12.6 | besmoked | 97.5 | downright |
| 13.37 | shelf-like | 104.2 | backbone |
| 14.1 | dark-looking | 106.8 | midwinter |
| 16.39 | table-cloth | 109.12 | interlinked |
| 23.28 | Landlord | 109.14 | all-abounding |
| 26.24 | bedside | 117.36 | war-horse |
| 27.2 | †counterpane | 118.8 | Good-humored |
| 29.21 | cannot | 118.22 | easy-going |
| 32.3 | swallow-tailed | 120.4 | headsmen |
| 32.17 | whalemen | 120.8 | boat-steerer |
| 39.7 | man-ropes | 120.33 | coal-black |
| 39.12 | sailor-like | 123.18 | forenoon |
| 39.31 | stronghold | 124.4 | sea-traditions |
| 42.24 | sea-line | 127.13 | quarter-deck |
| 42.26 | billow-like | 127.38 | overbearing |
| 42.29 | two-stranded | 128.2 | cabin-scuttle |
| 47.3 | Shipmates | 128.36 | daylight |
| 51.30 | countryman | 132.2 | †badger-haired |
| 54.23 | household | 132.9 | sea-weed |
| 54.24 | landlord's | 135.17 | right-whale |
| 56.14 | countrymen | 139.8 | Fin-Back |
| 63.17 | snow-shoes | 139.21 | gnomon-like |
| 65.17 | larboard | 140.35 | light-hearted |
| 66.2 | cross-trees | 142.19 | ice-piercer |
| 67.12 | chowder-headed | 144.20 | gentlemanlike |
| 69.13 | Devil-dam | 146.4 | †ship-board |
| 70.16 | overlook | 147.18 | whalemen |
| 70.20 | right-whale | 150.4 | †mizen-top |
| 72.21 | a-whaling | 150.30 | war-like |
| 74.19 | straight-bodied | 151.9 | shinbones |
| 74.27 | chief-mate | 152.19 | harpoon-wise |
| 77.1 | seventy-seventh | 152.26 | Dough-Boy's |
| 79.17 | Gay-head | 153.17 | fable-mongering |
| 82.17 | chamber-maid | 154.10 | mast-heads |
| 82.30 | vinegar-cruet | 154.10 | skysail-/poles |
| 84.11 | whaling-voyage | 157.3 | mast-heads |
| 84.13 | plum-puddingers | 157.5 | look-outs |

| | | | | |
|---|---|---|---|---|
| 157.11 | *crow's-nest* | 241.1 | man-of-/war |
| 157.34 | counter-acting | 241.8 | whale-boat |
| 157.38 | blacksmiths | 242.22 | mast-head |
| 158.25 | ship-owners | 248.26 | whale-ships |
| 159.1 | absent-minded | 249.1 | holy-of-/holies |
| 159.7 | opera-glasses | 250.11 | backstay |
| 160.13 | foot-prints | 251.38 | hatchway |
| 161.15 | stand-point | 253.13 | midnight |
| 162.33 | twiske-tee | 255.30 | lanyard |
| 164.27 | cannot | 257.7 | Lakeman |
| 164.30 | foremast-/hand | 257.8 | whirlpool |
| 166.6 | cup-bearers | 259.4 | moonlight |
| 168.9 | cricket-players | 263.23 | full-grown |
| 175.6 | *a-plenty* | 266.13 | oarsman |
| 176.34 | water-spout | 266.15 | half-emptied |
| 179.19 | news-telling | 266.24 | rock-slide |
| 183.3 | whaleman | 266.32 | foreground |
| 183.25 | †milky-way | 269.23 | dentistical-looking |
| 191.2 | milk-white | 270.17 | sailor-savage |
| 192.9 | milk-white | 270.30 | †weather-cocks |
| 193.13 | cathedral-toppling | 271.7 | stand-point |
| 193.36 | headlands | 272.18 | mast-heads |
| 196.8 | quarter-deck | 273.20 | everlasting |
| 205.35 | whale-line | 276.4 | helmsman |
| 206.28 | shipwrecked | 280.2 | loggerhead |
| 207.12 | thimbleful | 280.5 | gunwales |
| 214.4 | †lead-colored | 284.28 | loggerhead |
| 215.20 | Gay-Header | 285.1 | oarsman |
| 216.18 | gunwale | 286.8 | †overwrapped |
| 218.30 | brimstone | 287.4 | whale-boat |
| 219.16 | steering-oar | 287.5 | whale-killer |
| 220.30 | outstretched | 287.6 | whale-fastener |
| 221.13 | King-Post | 288.3 | blood-vessels |
| 221.14 | loggerhead | 290.8 | sharp-edged |
| 221.27 | breast-band | 293.16 | sea-fight |
| 223.14 | tiger-yellow | 293.20 | deck-table |
| 230.1 | whale-boat | 297.33 | Whale-balls |
| 231.1 | whale-boats | 299.14 | †half-jellied |
| 231.10 | half-hinted | 300.1 | meat-market |
| 234.10 | †foam-flakes | 303.18 | side-fins |
| 235.13 | floor-screwed | 304.33 | blanket-piece |
| 236.21 | look-outs | 305.21 | whale-books |
| 239.3 | seaport | 306.31 | mystic-marked |
| 239.32 | whale-hunters | 307.2 | full-grown |
| 240.25 | whaleman | 307.6 | sea-terms |
| 240.34 | *Whale-ships* | 307.8 | counterpane |

| | | | |
|---|---|---|---|
| 308.17 | sea-vultures | 393.29 | greyheaded |
| 311.18 | quarter-deck | 397.38 | Savesoul's |
| 312.5 | main-mast-/head | 405.11 | jib-booms |
| 314.11 | main-top-/sail | 409.13 | Cologne-water |
| 314.21 | cabalistically-cut | 409.38 | text-book |
| 315.4 | overboard | 412.15 | blue-veined |
| 317.12 | †fore-announced | 412.22 | after-oarsman |
| 318.11 | oarsmen | 413.2 | boat-knife |
| 320.3 | hard-scrabble | 417.18 | whalemen |
| 320.33 | overboard | 417.37 | whaling-pike |
| 322.7 | gunpowder | 421.8 | mainmast |
| 326.7 | bloody-minded | 421.15 | hatchway |
| 327.27 | thunder-heads | 423.5 | whale-ship's |
| 329.22 | greyheaded | 423.12 | sea-sofa |
| 332.28 | forty-two | 428.30 | new-leaped |
| 333.8 | galliot-toed | 431.10 | awe-striking |
| 333.15 | spout-holes | 431.16 | horns-/of-plenty |
| 333.16 | bass-viol | 432.15 | midnight |
| 340.16 | pearl-colored | 432.19 | try-works |
| 341.4 | †main-/yard-arm | 437.17 | man-ropes |
| 343.13 | buried-alive | 438.18 | good-humoredly |
| 346.36 | semi-crescentic | 438.36 | great-grand/father |
| 352.3 | lamp-feeder | 439.3 | overboard |
| 352.9 | flying-fish | 443.9 | †fish-documents |
| 352.27 | overgrowing | 448.11 | oarsman |
| 353.24 | lamp-feeder | 448.16 | roast-pig |
| 353.31 | †blood-vessel | 448.21 | dairy-rooms |
| 354.6 | lamp-feeder | 449.24 | plumage-like |
| 354.13 | Gay-head | 451.13 | †full-grown |
| 356.9 | above-ground | 452.12 | outweigh |
| 356.23 | fish-spears | 452.15 | landsman's |
| 357.1 | ice-field | 453.23 | foot-path |
| 357.19 | well-springs | 456.8 | outreaching |
| 359.9 | †timber-heads | 457.11 | rechristened |
| 363.7 | whaleman | 457.28 | schoolboy |
| 363.16 | head-waters | 457.29 | horror-struck |
| 364.12 | old-fashioned | 468.14 | screw-drivers |
| 368.20 | pitchpoling | 472.18 | hap/hazard-like |
| 377.11 | whale-boat | 472.19 | heron-built |
| 383.15 | white-elephant | 472.23 | roly-poly |
| 384.20 | white-ash | 478.3 | whalemen |
| 384.36 | self-derived | 478.19 | coffin-colored |
| 384.38 | †furthest-descended | 480.25 | half-well |
| 385.12 | sheepfold | 480.31 | sea-chest |
| 387.9 | overarched | 485.25 | blacksmith's |
| 393.14 | country-school/master | 486.11 | broken-hearted |

| 489.8 | branding-iron | 532.1 | eight-/and-forty |
| 489.21 | water-cask | 535.22 | down-hearted |
| 489.22 | death-temper | 538.23 | mainmast |
| 497.4 | water-locked | 543.6 | laughing-eyed |
| 499.5 | pall-bearers | 545.13 | errand-boy |
| 500.14 | burning-glass | 546.16 | metallic-like |
| 502.1 | half-wheeled | 547.6 | top-gallant-/sail |
| 503.16 | quarter-deck | 547.28 | top-/gallant-sails |
| 507.10 | high-flung | 548.11 | Turkish-rugged |
| 509.13 | hunchbacked | 550.5 | tiger-yellow |
| 509.14 | main-/top-sail | 550.20 | stern-wreck |
| 511.25 | overboard | 550.37 | up-and-/down |
| 513.8 | shuttle-cock | 551.1 | Eddystone |
| 513.19 | storm-tossed | 552.35 | binnacle-watch |
| 514.38 | lightning-rods | 558.16 | backstays |
| 518.9 | loadstone | 558.24 | head-/and-head |
| 518.10 | top-maul | 564.33 | main-brace |
| 519.2 | loadstone | 566.13 | cabin-window |
| 522.1 | whale-boat | 568.32 | mast-heads |
| 526.11 | Turk's-headed | 568.35 | port-holes |
| 528.12 | church-yard | 570.21 | half-wading |
| 528.28 | woodpecker | 570.23 | mast-head |
| 530.9 | Manxman | 571.33 | death-glorious |
| 530.17 | boat-hook | 572.9 | eye-splice |
| 531.8 | mast-head | 573.6 | bowsman |
| 531.38 | eight-/and-forty | | |

II. *Compounds containing line-end hyphens in* NN *that should be retained in transcription*

| xvii.19 | Sub-Subs | 81.4 | night-fall |
| xxi.13 | Jonas-in-the-Whale | 90.20 | sail-makers |
| xxi.29 | Sperma-ceti | 100.23 | tomahawk-pipe |
| 5.2 | Tiger-lilies | 102.16 | quarter-deck |
| 6.36 | quarter-deck | 105.15 | main-yard |
| 13.32 | fire-places | 112.5 | whale-ship |
| 20.37 | head-peddler | 119.34 | King-Post |
| 32.11 | bell-buttons | 132.2 | †badger-haired |
| 44.28 | travel-weary | 135.23 | sperm-whale |
| 47.25 | pilot-prophet | 137.17 | ground-plan |
| 54.15 | twelve-o'clock-at-night | 137.28 | *Hump-backed* |
| 69.12 | three-years' | 139.8 | Long-John |
| 76.33 | seventy-seventh | 140.6 | back-fin |
| 78.6 | jack-knife | 146.4 | †ship-board |

| | | | |
|---|---|---|---|
| 147.28 | quarter-deck | 291.14 | main-rigging |
| 149.3 | loaf-of-bread | 293.21 | jewel-hilted |
| 150.4 | †mizen-top | 299.14 | †half-jellied |
| 150.26 | ship-master | 306.36 | sea-coast |
| 151.37 | dinner-time | 311.21 | crutch-wise |
| 152.23 | bread-faced | 314.34 | trap-door |
| 157.31 | crow's-nest | 316.39 | Sperm-Whale |
| 157.37 | broken-down | 317.12 | †fore-announced |
| 160.5 | cabin-gangway | 318.13 | boat-knife |
| 162.8 | main-mast | 320.1 | bow-oar |
| 162.17 | top-maul | 322.6 | fire-wood |
| 174.26 | ice-floors | 323.22 | mast-head |
| 181.22 | fire-side | 326.15 | port-hole |
| 183.25 | †milky-way | 332.11 | right-angles |
| 186.38 | right-mindedness | 333.16 | sounding-board |
| 191.2 | large-eyed | 341.4 | †main-yard-arm |
| 194.5 | snow-howdahed | 341.17 | iron-bound |
| 199.30 | mast-heads | 343.5 | iron-bound |
| 201.18 | world-circle | 343.15 | boarding-sword |
| 202.21 | horror-stricken | 346.7 | jolly-boat |
| 214.4 | †lead-colored | 352.31 | white-bone |
| 217.17 | counting-room | 353.31 | †blood-vessel |
| 218.5 | off-handed | 356.12 | line-of-battle |
| 223.30 | knife-like | 357.34 | merry-makings |
| 234.10 | †foam-flakes | 359.9 | †timber-heads |
| 235.13 | half-melted | 363.31 | member-roll |
| 240.12 | free-and-easy | 369.2 | spout-hole |
| 240.19 | Whale-ships | 380.3 | south-eastward |
| 242.7 | homeward-bound | 380.9 | sally-ports |
| 244.32 | wild-ocean | 382.31 | noon-day |
| 246.17 | file-fish | 384.38 | †furthest-descended |
| 248.24 | mast-heads | 389.26 | cutting-spade |
| 248.39 | bar-room | 390.19 | air-eddy |
| 255.32 | Twenty-four | 393.26 | forty-barrel-bulls |
| 261.21 | book-binder's | 398.15 | Loose-Fish |
| 267.3 | pell-mell | 404.35 | Guernsey-man |
| 269.14 | stump-speech | 405.21 | round-house |
| 269.18 | whaling-scenes | 416.11 | co-laborers' |
| 270.29 | old-fashioned | 416.16 | ill-humor |
| 270.30 | †weather-cocks | 417.32 | blanket-pieces |
| 271.7 | re-discovery | 417.36 | pike-and-gaff-man |
| 275.20 | stiletto-like | 417.37 | boarding-weapon |
| 278.9 | rope-maker | 426.16 | try-works |
| 279.6 | cheese-shaped | 443.9 | †fish-documents |
| 279.25 | eye-splice | 448.19 | under-pinnings |
| 280.9 | box-line | 448.20 | tallow-vats |

| | | | |
|---|---|---|---|
| 450.39 | yard-sticks | 494.20 | fiddle-bows |
| 451.13 | †full-grown | 501.28 | dead-reckoning |
| 453.3 | seventy-two | 504.34 | stand-point |
| 453.7 | back-bone | 505.33 | tri-pointed |
| 456.18 | stone-mason | 513.22 | East-south-east |
| 459.14 | tape-measure | 523.13 | half-articulated |
| 460.24 | look-outs | 524.10 | semi-intelligent |
| 461.23 | so-called | 525.14 | caulking-iron |
| 463.6 | half-splintering | 527.6 | *cabin-gangway* |
| 464.9 | joy-childlessness | 527.24 | jack-of-all-trades |
| 464.19 | harvest-moons | 538.13 | children-seeking |
| 466.18 | far-distant | 538.23 | downward-reeved |
| 467.16 | ear-rings | 540.11 | half-unhinged |
| 468.15 | screw-driver | 543.28 | boy-harpooneer |
| 473.13 | pruning-hook | 543.30 | storm-time |
| 474.31 | South-Sea-men's | 545.19 | flying-fish |
| 476.15 | air-freighted | 547.6 | top-gallant-sail |
| 478.11 | sea-custom | 548.5 | noon-meadow |
| 480.7 | whale-boat | 553.4 | quarter-deck |
| 482.15 | ever-rolling | 553.31 | top-gallant |
| 487.7 | rusty-looking | 570.18 | sledge-hammering |
| 488.20 | fin-bone | 571.32 | Pole-pointed |
| 490.5 | half-bantering | | |

# List of Substantive Variants

I N THIS LIST, which is a record of the substantive variants in the
authorized editions during Melville's lifetime, the following abbreviations are used to designate the sources of readings:

A American Edition (1851–1871)
E English Edition (1851–1853)
H *Harper's New Monthly Magazine* (October, 1851)
NN Northwestern-Newberry Edition

Copy-text (A) readings are listed in the left column and readings
differing from them on the right. (In the instances of emendations
made by the present editors, the NN reading also appears in the left
column to provide a reference to the text.) Features of the styling or
design of the American edition are not necessarily followed in the
present edition, and such deviations are not recorded here (see the
NOTE ON THE TEXT, p. 805, footnote 52); thus in the entries for the
table of contents (x.9–xiii.18) no notice is taken of the fact that NN
prints these words in italics, since in each case NN is substantively in
agreement with A. For further comment on this list, see pp. 807–8
above.

| | | |
|---|---|---|
| iii.1 | Moby-Dick  NN<br>[*no half title*]  A | THE WHALE; / OR, / MOBY DICK.  E |
| v.1–2 | MOBY-DICK; / OR,  A | [*not present*]  E |
| v.4 | [*no epigraph below Melville's name*]  A | "There Leviathan,/ Hugest of living creatures, in the deep/ Stretch'd like a promontory sleeps or swims,/ And seems a moving land; and at his gills/ Draws in, and at his breath spouts out a sea."/ PARADISE LOST.  E |
| vii.3 | This Book is  A | THESE VOLUMES ARE  E |
| x.9 | Postscript  A | [*not present*]  E |
| x.20 | Ahab and all  A | [*not present*]  E |
| x.23 | Night-Watch  A | NIGHT-WATCH—FORE-TOP  E |
| x.24 | Forecastle.—Midnight  A | MIDNIGHT, FORECASTLE—HARPOONEERS AND SAILORS  E |
| xi.2 | The Pequod meets  A | [*not present*]  E |
| xi.5 | Monstrous  A | OF THE MONSTROUS  E |
| xi.6 | Less  A | OF THE LESS  E |
| xi.6 | Whales  A | WHALES, AND THE TRUE PICTURES OF WHALING SCENES  E |
| xi.7 | &c.  A | IN WOOD: IN SHEET-IRON; IN MOUNTAINS; IN STARS  E |
| xi.21 | The Pequod meets the Jeroboam. Her Story  A | THE JEROBOAM'S STORY  E |
| xi.23 | Whale  A | WHALE: AND THEN HAVE A TALK OVER HIM  E |
| xi.24 | Head  A | HEAD—CONTRASTED VIEW  E |
| xi.25 | Head  A | HEAD—CONTRASTED VIEW  E |
| xii.16 | The Pequod meets the Samuel Enderby of London  A | LEG AND ARM  E |
| xii.21 | Whale  A | WHALE'S MAGNITUDE  E |
| xii.21 | Diminish?  A | DIMINISH?—WILL HE PERISH?  E |

| | | |
|---|---|---|
| xii.24 | The Deck. Ahab and the Carpenter   A | AHAB AND THE CARPENTER. —THE DECK: FIRST NIGHT-WATCH   E |
| xii.25 | The Cabin. Ahab and Starbuck   A | AHAB AND STARBUCK IN THE CABIN   E |
| xiii.2 | Deck   A | DECK TOWARDS THE END OF THE FIRST NIGHT-WATCH   E |
| xiii.3 | on the Forecastle   A | THE FORECASTLE BULWARKS   E |
| xiii.4 | Aloft   A | ALOFT—THUNDER AND LIGHTNING   E |
| xiii.9 | Ahab and the Carpenter   A | THE DECK   E |
| xiii.11 | Ahab and Pip   A | [not present]   E |
| xiii.18 | EPILOGUE.   A | APPENDIX   E |
| xv.1 | ETYMOLOGY.   A | APPENDIX./ ETYMOLOGY.   E [occurs at end of volume III] |
| xv.9 | ETYMOLOGY   A | [not present]   E |
| xix.15 | like   A | like a   E |
| xix.24 | leach's   A | leech's   E |
| xx.15 | Holy War   NN Pilgrim's Progress   A | Holy War   E |
| xxi.8 | into   A | to   E |
| xxi.10 | huge   A | large   E |
| xxii.11 | stiff   NN stuffed   A | stiff   E |
| xxii.16 | Goldsmith   A | Goldsmith's   E |
| xxvii.24 | mere   NN near   A | mere   E |
| xxviii.19 | upon   A | [not present]   E |
| 4.3 | of   A | on   E |
| 4.20 | virtue of   A | virtue in   E |
| 5.13 | make him the   NN [not present]   A | make him the   E |
| 6.2 | some   A | [not present]   E |
| 6.14–16 | Do . . . instance?   A | [not present]   E |
| 6.16 | aint   A | is not   E |

| 6.22 | other's A | others' E |
| 6.26–29 | The . . . it? A | [not present] E |
| 7.5–8 | And . . . performances. A | [not present] E |
| 7.9 | bill A | bill, of those three mysterious ladies, E |
| 7.36 | midmost NN<br>mid most A | midmost E |
| 10.5 | out-hanging NN<br>[not present] A | out-hanging E |
| 10.21 | poor A | St. E |
| 10.32–38 | The . . . pooh! A | [not present] E |
| 11.3–15 | But . . . be. A | [not present] E |
| 13.36 | of A | on E |
| 14.5 | like . . . him), A | [not present] E |
| 14.13 | gulph A | gulp E |
| 14.32 | he A | she E |
| 15.28 | Jonah A | fellow E |
| 15.30 | Jonah A | the old fellow E |
| 15.32 | or A | [not present] E |
| 16.31–33 | was . . . it A | [not present] E |
| 16.34 | any NN<br>my A | any E |
| 17.1 | of A | [not present] E |
| 17.27 | what A | that E |
| 18.3 | an airley NN<br>an early A | an airley E |
| 20.14 | the same as NN<br>as you see the same A | the same as E |
| 20.19 | it of A | it on E |
| 20.20 | I never . . . I A | [not present] E |
| 23.12 | so long been A | been so long E |
| 25.22 | mother A | stepmother E |
| 26.7 | for a resurrection A | to get out of bed again E |
| 26.11 | down A | [not present] E |
| 26.37 | bridegroom A | [not present] E |

| | | |
|---|---|---|
| 27.8 | matrimonial  A | [*not present*]  E |
| 32.1 | came  A | come  E |
| 32.18 | howling  A | howling a  E |
| 32.31 | Can . . . that?  A | [*not present*]  E |
| 33.3 | the  A | these  E |
| 33.3 | thrown . . . day  A | [*not present*]  E |
| 36.35 | a  A | an  E |
| 37.7 | but  A | [*not present*]  E |
| 37.25 | me  A | myself  E |
| 37.26 | Jove himself cannot.  A | who can do this?  E |
| 39.5 | without a  A | without  E |
| 40.12 | is the  A | is that the  E |
| 40.12 | storm of God's  A | storm's  E |
| 40.13 | is  A | is that  E |
| 41.21 | left  NN<br>lift  A | left  E |
| 42.1 | opening  A | open  E |
| 45.27 | clattering  A | tumbling  E |
| 46.20 | become  NN<br>became  A | become  E |
| 46.27 | of  A | upon  E |
| 47.16 | God and himself  A | his God  E |
| 50.18 | night previous  A | previous night  E |
| 51.22 | then  A | there  E |
| 52.7–10 | Do . . . Impossible!  A | [*not present*]  E |
| 52.24 | in . . . honeymoon,  A | [*not present*]  E |
| 53.4–6 | and Queequeg . . . we;  A | [*not present*]  E |
| 55.6 | When  A | While yet  E |
| 56.11 | Czar  A | the Czar  E |
| 56.13 | haply  NN<br>happily  A | haply  E |
| 58.8–9 | about . . . with  A | had previously so much<br>alarmed me about him  E |
| 60.18 | bows  NN<br>brows  A | bows  E |

| 63.20 | extravaganzas  A | extravagances  E |
| 64.4 | they  A | [*not present*]  E |
| 64.32 | not  A | scarcely  E |
| 65.7 | Try  A | Twy  E |
| 65.10 | Try  A | Twy  E |
| 67.2 | fishy  NN<br>fishing  A | fishy  E |
| 67.11 | here  A | [*not present*]  E |
| 67.11 | on  A | upon  E |
| 67.14 | Try  A | Twy  E |
| 67.19 | vertebra  A | vertebræ  E |
| 67.31 | ony  NN<br>only  A | ony  E |
| 67.34 | weepons  A | weapons  E |
| 67.34 | a-night  NN<br>at night  A | a-night  E |
| 67.37 | herring  A | herrings  E |
| 68.10 | purposed  A | proposed  E |
| 69.9 | liturgies . . . Articles  A | religion  E |
| 70.7 | over  A | through  E |
| 70.12 | its  A | his  E |
| 71.12 | Marchant  NN<br>Merchant  A | Marchant  E |
| 72.4 | by  A | about  E |
| 74.1 | have  A | has  E |
| 74.16 | Bildad  NN<br>Peleg  A | Bildad  E |
| 76.19 | what  A | that  E |
| 76.20 | mighty  A | [*not present*]  E |
| 78.10 | to  A | a  E |
| 78.26 | shore  A | short  E |
| 78.27 | have  A | has  E |
| 81.3 | Ramadan . . . Humiliation,  A | Ramadan  E |
| 83.22 | knob  NN<br>knot  A | knob  E |

| | | |
|---|---|---|
| 83.25 | top  A | the top  E |
| 83.39 | I  NN<br>he  A | I  E |
| 84.8 | it's  A | its  E |
| 85.9–20 | these . . . Ramadans | fasts, voluntary or otherwise,<br>were excessively bad for the<br>digestion  E |
| 87.1 | 18  NN<br>XVII  A | XVIII  E |
| 87.15–88.19 | Church." Here . . .<br>touching  A | Church;" and I entered upon a<br>long rigmarole story,<br>touching the conversion of<br>Queequeg, and concluded<br>by saying that in  E |
| 88.19 | belief; in *that*  A | belief  E |
| 88.19 | join  A | joined  E |
| 88.31 | poising his  A | poising the  E |
| 96.11 | stowage  NN<br>storage  A | stowage  E |
| 96.35 | running  NN<br>hobbling  A | running  E |
| 99.3 | we  A | he  E |
| 99.28 | slept  A | was  E |
| 99.32 | would  A | should  E |
| 105.31–32 | If . . . fornication.  A | [*not present*]  E |
| 107.7 | God  A | the Almighty  E |
| 109.27 | ships  A | ships'  E |
| 110.23 | those  A | these  E |
| 111.20 | somehow  A | [*not present*]  E |
| 111.28 | *  A | [*not present*]  E |
| 111.31 | very  A | [*not present*]  E |
| 112.4 | properly  A | probably  E |
| 113.1–114.4 | CHAPTER . . . stuff!  A | [*not present*]  E |
| 115.5 | an  A | [*not present*]  E |
| 116.15 | was  A | is  E |
| 116.21 | other  A | [*not present*]  E |

| | | |
|---|---|---|
| 116.23 | mortally  A | [*not present*]  E |
| 117.22–24 | The . . . equality!  A | [*not present*]  E |
| 117.32 | democratic  A | [*not present*]  E |
| 118.7 | crisis  A | crises  E |
| 120.1 | prescription  A | consent  E |
| 121.30 | did! Poor  NN<br>did—oh, no! he went before.<br>    Poor  A | did! Poor  E |
| 123.18 | forenoon  A | afternoon  E |
| 123.26 | Perseus  A | of Perseus  E |
| 124.29–30 | a crucifixion  A | an apparently eternal<br>    anguish  E |
| 124.32 | in  A | into  E |
| 132.13 | eating of  A | eating  E |
| 132.35 | quick  NN<br>[*not present*]  A | quick  E |
| 136.8–9 | description . . . a  A | [*not present*]  E |
| 136.17 | swam  A | swum  E |
| 139.25 | man-haters  A | men-haters  E |
| 140.4 | afford  A | afforded  E |
| 140.4 | basis  A | bases  E |
| 140.12 | of these  A | [*not present*]  E |
| 140.17 | has  A | have  E |
| 142.17 | bill-fish  A | the bill-fish  E |
| 142.35 | bold  A | old  E |
| 142.38 | in  A | at  E |
| 143.19 | in the  A | in  E |
| 145.14 | God  A | Heaven  E |
| 147.5 | the grand distinction  A | one of the grand<br>    distinctions  E |
| 148.5 | honors  A | honour  E |
| 148.15 | direst  NN<br>direct  A | direst  E |
| 148.22 | deep  A | deeps  E |
| 150.29 | his  A | this  E |

| 150.31 | turn A | tune E |
| 151.37 | order to A | order E |
| 152.4 | order A | method E |
| 152.30 | its A | his E |
| 153.9 | whetstones NN whetstone A | whetstones E |
| 153.26 | else A | [not present] E |
| 153.32 | hereby A | thereby E |
| 155.19 | the Devil A | Napoleon E |
| 155.24 | even NN ever A | even E |
| 156.3 | mast-heads A | masts E |
| 156.33 | coolish NN cold A | coolish E |
| 157.5 | *crow's-nests* A | *crows'-nests* E |
| 157.14 | ridiculous A | ridiculously E |
| 158.14 | Southern NN South A | Southern E |
| 158.29 | can be A | are E |
| 158.30 | young A | [not present] E |
| 159.8 | a A | an E |
| 159.21 | Wickliff's NN Cranmer's A | Wickliff's E |
| 159.21 | Pantheistic A | [not present] E |
| 161.32 | while A | when E |
| 162.1–2 | men,—a doubloon NN men A | men,—a doubloon E |
| 162.26 | ye A | you E |
| 163.3 | Stubb A | Stubbs E |
| 163.11 | sob A | shout E |
| 164.13 | man A | men E |
| 164.23 | unrecking A | unreeking E |
| 164.32 | then, A | that— E |
| 164.34 | now A | [not present] E |
| 165.28 | a noble A | an old E |

| 165.30 | wert  NN<br>wer't  A | wert  E |
| 165.37 | into them  A | them into  E |
| 166.6 | yon  A | you  E |
| 167.8 | goblet's  A | goblets  E |
| 167.9 | slow  A | long  E |
| 167.15–16 | metal . . . fight!  A | metal.  E |
| 168.7 | prophesy  A | prophecy  E |
| 168.17 | unsounded  A | unsound  E |
| 170.8 | me! that  A | I! that  E |
| 171.5 | Ha! ha! ha! ha!  A | Ha! ha! ha!  E |
| 172.3 | with  A | [*not present*]  E |
| 174.11–12 | Tell . . . judgment.  A | [*not present*]  E |
| 175.10 | jinglers  A | jigglers  E |
| 175.12 | Jinglers  A | Jigglers  E |
| 175.24 | Christ  A | Lord  E |
| 175.26 | one  NN<br>a  A | one  E |
| 175.26 | your  NN<br>you  A | your  E |
| 176.12 | not . . . satiety.  A | [*not present*]  E |
| 176.16 | low valed  NN<br>low veiled  A | low-valed  E |
| 177.24 | one  A | own  E |
| 178.13 | Why . . . ring?  A | [*not present*]  E |
| 178.21 | God!  A | [*not present*]  E |
| 182.29 | as well  A | also  E |
| 183.8 | immortality  A | mortality  E |
| 183.39 | aforethought  A | forethought  E |
| 184.22–23 | to . . . worlds;  A | [*not present*]  E |
| 184.37 | but  A | [*not present*]  E |
| 185.26 | concentred  A | concentrated  E |
| 185.34 | nobler,  A | nobler, and  E |
| 186.21 | scorched  A | sore  E |
| 186.29 | one  A | [*not present*]  E |

| | | |
|---|---|---|
| 186.30 | one A | [*not present*] E |
| 186.36 | chiefly A | that chiefly E |
| 190.14 | whence A | hence E |
| 190.15 | funereal A | funeral E |
| 190.22 | archangel A | [*not present*] E |
| 190.25 | which . . . God A | not below the heavens E |
| 190.33 | our A | the E |
| 190.43–45 | But. . . cherubim! A | [*not present*] E |
| 191.12 | hunters A | hunters have E |
| 192.5 | much NN<br>much like A | much E |
| 194.29 | of distant A | of the distant E |
| 194.31 | in A | of E |
| 195.20–22 | so . . . within; A | [*not present*] E |
| 197.1 | eat A | ate E |
| 200.5 | he could A | [*not present*] E |
| 200.27 | and NN<br>or A | and E |
| 201.9 | covertly NN<br>correctly A | covertly E |
| 202.7 | or A | of E |
| 202.22 | unfathered A | unfeathered E |
| 203.7 | but A | [*not present*] E |
| 204.15 | previous A | previously E |
| 205.12 | Tom A | Jack E |
| 206.5 | that A | [*not present*] E |
| 206.8 | ashore A | on shore E |
| 206.19 | First: A | [*not present*] E |
| 206.19 | of A | of the E |
| 206.25 | has A | has ever E |
| 207.19–20 | Was . . . fright? A | [*not present*] E |
| 207.26 | before A | [*not present*] E |
| 212.2 | stands NN<br>stand A | stands E |
| 214.12 | for the A | for a E |

| 215.13 | modified  NN<br>directed  A | modified  E |
| 216.8 | swiftly swims  A | swims swiftly  E |
| 217.9 | rumpled  A | rumbled  E |
| 217.10 | wide black  A | wide  E |
| 218.23 | the  A | [*not present*]  E |
| 218.39 | ye  A | you  E |
| 220.7 | previous  A | previously  E |
| 220.33 | whales  A | whale  E |
| 220.36 | oar  NN<br>oars  A | oar  E |
| 221.13 | a  A | [*not present*]  E |
| 221.15 | me  A | me go  E |
| 222.7 | his  A | is  E |
| 222.32 | startlingly  A | startingly  E |
| 223.8 | hearts-alive  A | heart's-alive  E |
| 223.34–35 | headsmen  A | headsman  E |
| 224.22 | sprang  A | sprung  E |
| 226.11 | worryings,  A | worrying  E |
| 228.1–2 | as good . . . resurrection;  A | [*not present*]  E |
| 229.21–22 | comprises  A | compromises  E |
| 230.1 | enter a  A | enter the  E |
| 230.24 | against  A | against it  E |
| 230.26 | depression in  A | depression of  E |
| 230.28 | it  A | [*not present*]  E |
| 230.35 | waned  A | went  E |
| 230.39 | planks  A | plank  E |
| 230.39 | wreck  A | wrecks  E |
| 231.21 | asked  A | ask  E |
| 232.14 | of  A | on  E |
| 233.3 | not  A | hardly  E |
| 233.14 | yawingly  A | yawningly  E |
| 234.36 | accustomed  A | customary  E |
| 240.9 | straightway | straitway  E |

| | | |
|---|---|---|
| 240.28 | down the A | down E |
| 242.15 | particular A, H | peculiar E |
| 244.36 | yet A, H | still E |
| 247.37 | but A, H | [*not present*] E |
| 248.3 | rose A, H | arose E |
| 248.34 | ye A | you E, H |
| 248.38 | most A, H | [*not present*] E |
| 249.1 | the holy-of-holies of A, H | [*not present*] E |
| 249.28–29 | Cleopatra . . . thigh A, H | Cleopatra E |
| 250.1 | scarce A, H | scarcely E |
| 251.6 | boy's A | boys' E, H |
| 251.10 | by God, A, H | [*not present*] E |
| 252.13 | perhaps A, H | [*not present*] E |
| 252.17 | others A, H | other E |
| 253.19 | three NN<br>these A, E | three H |
| 253.31 | try-pots A, H | twy-pots E |
| 254.27 | salvation A, H | security E |
| 254.33 | leak A, H | leek E |
| 256.14 | up NN<br>up up A | up E, H |
| 256.35 | topmost A, H | topmast E |
| 257.28 | cannon A, H | cannons E |
| 258.31 | you, A, H | you to E |
| 259.5–6 | " 'Excuse . . . can.' A, H | [*not present*] E |
| 259.14 | crew; A, H | crew; and E |
| 262.28 | systemized A | systematized E |
| 263.31 | hangs for candelabra A | is preserved E |
| 267.4 | great A | [*not present*] E |
| 270.22 | Dutch A | German E |
| 271.7 | hills— NN<br>hills, that A | hills— E |
| 272.10 | fringing A | fringy E |
| 273.21 | one A | own E |

| 273.24 | waters  A | water  E |
| 276.14 | awaiting  A | waiting  E |
| 280.22 | contortions  NN<br>contortion  A | contortions  E |
| 281.4–5 | prophesies  A | prophecies  E |
| 282.10 | then were  A | were then  E |
| 283.13 | all  A | [*not present*]  E |
| 285.6 | rocking  A | rocky  E |
| 285.35 | bowsman  A | bowman  E |
| 287.11 | uttermost  A | utmost  E |
| 293.34 | of devil-worship,  A | [*not present*]  E |
| 293.35 | the expediency  A | expediency  E |
| 294.22 | Blast  A | Hang  E |
| 294.37 | why . . . eyes,  A | why  E |
| 295.5 | Dough  NN<br>Do  A | Dough  E |
| 295.24 | Christianity  A | the right sort  E |
| 295.31–32 | the benediction  A | them a blessing  E |
| 297.1 | him . . . And  A | him—and  E |
| 297.6–7 | But . . . eh?  A | [*not present*]  E |
| 297.10–13 | But . . . yet.  A | [*not present*]  E |
| 297.29 | ye  A | you  E |
| 297.35 | of  A | a  E |
| 299.17 | substance  A | substances  E |
| 299.37 | man  A | man man  E |
| 300.4–8 | I . . . paté-de-foie-gras.  A | [*not present*]  E |
| 302.1 | her  A | [*not present*]  E |
| 302.11 | marksmen  A | marksman  E |
| 302.22–24 | "Queequeg . . . Ingin."  A | [*not present*]  E |
| 302.27 | end  A | end is  E |
| 304.26 | slicings  A | slices  E |
| 309.12 | There's orthodoxy!  A | [*not present*]  E |
| 309.14 | powerless  A | powerful  E |
| 312.3–4 | O . . . thine  A | [*not present*]  E |

| | | |
|---|---|---|
| 312.15 | lives in  NN<br>lives on  A | lives in  E |
| 313.5 | stranger's  NN<br>strangers'  A | stranger's  E |
| 314.12 | some way  A | away  E |
| 314.34 | the  A | [*not present*]  E |
| 315.15 | archangel  A | maniac  E |
| 315.20 | be  A | be in  E |
| 315.22 | the archangel  A | he  E |
| 316.10 | his  A | his self-styled  E |
| 317.11 | terrible  A | [*not present*]  E |
| 318.18 | upon  A | on  E |
| 320.33 | Nor  A | How  E |
| 321.29 | men  A | [*not present*]  E |
| 321.35 | involuntarily  A | [*not present*]  E |
| 322.15 | bellows  NN<br>bitters  A | bellows  E |
| 322.15 | breath  NN<br>life  A | breath  E |
| 322.23 | bade  A | bad  E |
| 322.28 | hit  A | strike  E |
| 324.20 | fagged  A | flagged  E |
| 325.18 | Blast  A | D—n  E |
| 325.28 | and  A | and to  E |
| 326.12 | helped  A | helped to  E |
| 326.38 | lets  NN<br>let's  A | lets  E |
| 327.3 | suppose it  A | suppose  E |
| 327.5 | his  A | the  E |
| 327.9 | and  A | an  E |
| 327.33 | black bone  A | back-bone  E |
| 327.38 | Meantime  A | Meanwhile  E |
| 330.8 | can  A | can see  E |
| 331.8 | moment of  A | [*not present*]  E |
| 332.30 | into  A | in  E |

| | | |
|---|---|---|
| 334.26 | its  A | [*not present*]  E |
| 334.35 | arch  A | reach  E |
| 336.18 | were  A | was  E |
| 340.13 | irrevocably  A | irrecoverably  E |
| 341.7 | single-sheaved  A | shingle-sheaved  E |
| 341.11 | high  A | highly  E |
| 342.9 | baling  A | bailing  E |
| 342.13 | cabled  A | cable  E |
| 342.15 | to  A | [*not present*]  E |
| 343.6 | on  A | on the  E |
| 344.2 | in obstetrics  A | [*not present*]  E |
| 344.5–7 | Midwifery . . . rowing.  A | [*not present*]  E |
| 344.23–24 | undetached  A | detached  E |
| 344.25 | obstetrics  A | dexterities  E |
| 344.26 | Yes . . . was.  A | [*not present*]  E |
| 346.10 | royal beadle  A | royalty  E |
| 346.27 | mighty  A | mighty and  E |
| 351.17 | there  A | [*not present*]  E |
| 352.34 | of  A | of a  E |
| 353.2 | yaw  A | yawn  E |
| 353.28 | ye  A | you  E |
| 353.35 | and  A | and the  E |
| 354.8 | rivals'  A | rival's  E |
| 354.35 | yawed  A | yawled  E |
| 355.16 | harpooneer  A | harpooneers  E |
| 355.34 | lead-lined  A | lead-line  E |
| 356.1 | sharp  A | keen  E |
| 356.27 | Oh . . . prophets.  A | [*not present*]  E |
| 356.27 | For  A | Why,  E |
| 356.28 | had  A | has  E |
| 357.6 | ship's  A | ships'  E |
| 357.22 | new made  A | newly-made  E |
| 359.36 | go  A | goes  E |
| 363.16 | fraternity  A | paternity  E |

| | | |
|---|---|---|
| 363.19 | in   A | of   E |
| 365.20 | by the   A | by a   E |
| 367.6 | as   A | [*not present*]   E |
| 368.32 | minds   A | reminds   E |
| 368.39 | unspeakable old   A | unspeakable   E |
| 369.6 | his   A | its   E |
| 370.11 | 1850   NN<br>1851   A | 1850   E |
| 373.13 | perceived   A | perceive   E |
| 374.3 | the Devil,   A | [*not present*]   E |
| 376.22 | hermaphroditical   A | [*not present*]   E |
| 377.7 | descend   A | descends   E |
| 377.10 | water   A | waters   E |
| 377.30 | solitary   A | the solitary   E |
| 377.34 | almost   A | [*not present*]   E |
| 378.6 | heaven   A | heavens   E |
| 378.10 | of my ship   A | [*not present*]   E |
| 379.4 | but go   A | go but   E |
| 379.5 | will   A | shall   E |
| 379.7–9 | Thou . . . face.   A | [*not present*]   E |
| 380.17 | and silks,   A | [*not present*]   E |
| 381.23 | his   A | the   E |
| 383.12 | these   A | the   E |
| 383.20 | to   A | to to   E |
| 384.2 | had   A | has   E |
| 384.18 | flashing   A | fishing   E |
| 384.25 | *   NN<br>[*not present*]   A | *   E |
| 384.28–40 | *To . . . World.   NN<br>[*not present*]   A | *To . . . World.   E |
| 385.13 | for   A | from   E |
| 386.26 | overboard   A | over   E |
| 387.31 | snuffling   A | snuffing   E |
| 388.11 | yet   A | [*not present*]   E |

| | | |
|---|---|---|
| 388.28 | We . . . deep.  A | [*not present*]  E |
| 388.39–40 | man . . . *hominum*  A | man  E |
| 392.14 | times  A | time  E |
| 392.17 | keep  A | always frustrate  E |
| 392.17 | out of his bed  A | [*not present*]  E |
| 392.17–18 | bed in common  A | have very vague ideas of the connubial tie  E |
| 392.28–29 | Lothario . . . concubines  A | Lothario  E |
| 392.30–32 | Turks; . . . small  A | Turks  E |
| 393.2 | impotent,  A | [*not present*]  E |
| 393.5 | amorous  A | own juvenile  E |
| 393.6 | fishermen  A | fisherman  E |
| 395.20 | fishermen  A | fisherman  E |
| 396.25 | seas,  NN<br>seas; and when indeed  A | seas,  E |
| 396.26 | but  NN<br>they were  A | but  E |
| 396.26 | were  NN<br>[*not present*]  A | were  E |
| 396.27 | itself. Ultimately  A | itself,—Furthermore: ultimately  E |
| 396.29 | plaintiffs. And  A | plaintiffs;—Yet again:—and  E |
| 396.31 | plaintiffs'  A | plaintiff's  E |
| 396.31 | by  A | by the  E |
| 396.32 | boat,  A | boat, all of  E |
| 397.2–3 | Erskine was on the other side; and he  A | He  E |
| 397.3 | supported it by saying,  A | proceeded to say  E |
| 397.20 | defendants  NN<br>plaintiffs  A | defendants  E |
| 398.1–2 | laborers (all . . . help)  A | labourers;  E |
| 398.2 | 100,000  A | 100,000*l.*  E |
| 398.17 | them  A | many of us  E |
| 401.5–7 | Is . . . beggars?  A | [*not present*]  E |
| 401.28 | of  A | at  E |

| | | |
|---|---|---|
| 402.4 | *that*  NN<br>not  A | that  E |
| 402.6 | vapory  A | vapour  E |
| 405.10 | a  A | [*not present*]  E |
| 406.38 | it's  A | its  E |
| 409.15 | conclude the  A | conclude this  E |
| 410.3 | forth  A | [*not present*]  E |
| 411.12 | boats'  A | boat's  E |
| 411.16 | heard of  A | head  E |
| 413.20 | wont  A | won't  E |
| 413.25 | interferes  A | interfered  E |
| 414.9 | considerateness  NN<br>considerations  A | considerateness  E |
| 414.30–31 | uncompromised . . . God  A | uncompromised  E |
| 416.2 | snuffed  A | sniffed  E |
| 417.11 | and  A | [*not present*]  E |
| 417.15 | the  A | [*not present*]  E |
| 418.3 | This  A | The  E |
| 420.18 | out  A | [*not present*]  E |
| 421.8 | foremast  A | fore-  E |
| 422.25 | a . . . or  A | [*not present*]  E |
| 422.27 | he  A | he had  E |
| 422.30–32 | It . . . pit.  A | [*not present*]  E |
| 422.34 | carcase  A | case  E |
| 423.2 | conflagrations  A | conflagration  E |
| 424.2 | But,  A | But, in  E |
| 427.9–10 | and . . . Abednego,  A | and how  E |
| 428.30 | aglow . . . Holland  A | aglow  E |
| 431.3 | flow  NN<br>flows  A | flow  E |
| 431.27 | on the  A | on a  E |
| 432.32 | I have  A | I've  E |
| 433.9–10 | lecherous dog,  A | [*not present*]  E |
| 433.18 | in  A | in the  E |

| 433.34 | wont A | won't E |
|---|---|---|
| 434.10 | it is A | is it E |
| 434.22 | that A | that old E |
| 435.13 | in the resurrection A | one day E |
| 435.16–18 | Hish . . . done! A | [not present] E |
| 437.24 | blubber-hook A | blubber-book E |
| 438.10 | from the A | from E |
| 438.16 | were A | are E |
| 438.26 | on to A | on E |
| 439.12 | when, when A | when E |
| 440.1 | you're A | you are E |
| 440.15 | wound A | a wound E |
| 440.22 | ye A | you E |
| 441.15 | swallow A | to swallow E |
| 441.31 | thou saw'st A | ye saw E |
| 443.21 | a A | a a E |
| 444.5 | Sons . . . knows— A | Sons, E |
| 445.14 | eating, and A | eating, E |
| 448.7 | untagging A | untrussing E |
| 448.19 | upon the A | upon E |
| 449.8 | And as A | As E |
| 449.33 | hair-hung A | air-hung E |
| 449.39 | with all A | with E |
| 450.8 | is he A | he is E |
| 451.16 | upon A | on E |
| 451.23–26 | Sir . . . forehead. A | [not present] E |
| 451.30 | wished A | wished all E |
| 453.13 | embryo NN<br>[not present] A | embryo E |
| 453.35 | weighty A | mighty E |
| 454.8 | knobbed A | knobbled E |
| 454.14 | the priest's children, A | [not present] E |
| 455.21 | edition A | [not present] E |
| 456.12 | universe . . . suburbs A | universe E |

| | | |
|---|---|---|
| 456.24 | antechronical NN<br>antichronical A | ante-chronical E |
| 457.9 | of the whale A | [*not present*] E |
| 457.18 | antechronical NN<br>antichronical A | ante-chronical E |
| 457.27 | like A | like the E |
| 457.28 | Pharaohs' NN<br>Pharaoh's A | Pharaohs' E |
| 457.31 | humane A | human E |
| 458.15–16 | (says John Leo) A | [*not present*] E |
| 460.11 | these A | the E |
| 461.11 | horse A | horses E |
| 464.7 | canonic A | canonical E |
| 464.22 | signers A | singers E |
| 468.16 | to do A | [*not present*] E |
| 468.19 | did not have A | had not E |
| 471.38 | as a NN<br>as A | as a E |
| 472.6 | vertebra A | vertebræ E |
| 472.26–28 | before . . . again A | [*not present*] E |
| 473.6 | into A | in E |
| 477.18 | seemed but A | seemed E |
| 477.29 | all, alike A | all, E |
| 478.10 | way. He A | way—after saying this he E |
| 478.29 | convenience A | convenience' E |
| 478.31 | be A | be made E |
| 479.19 | near A | [*not present*] E |
| 480.6 | once more A | [*not present*] E |
| 480.7 | them A | 'em E |
| 480.7 | drown A | down E |
| 482.9 | gently A | gentle E |
| 482.11 | watery A | water E |
| 482.11–12 | and Potters' Fields A | [*not present*] E |
| 483.3 | whole A | own E |
| 484.19 | painful A | painfully E |

| | | |
|---|---|---|
| 485.24 | iron A | [*not present*] E |
| 489.25 | nods A | nobs E |
| 494.2 | officers' A | officer's E |
| 494.10 | pantaloons A | pantaloon E |
| 494.14 | nearer A | near E |
| 494.24 | cursed A | accursed E |
| 497.20 | unnamable A | nameless E |
| 500.5 | and the A | and E |
| 500.12 | sometimes, NN<br>[*not present*] A | sometimes, E |
| 500.21 | its A | the E |
| 501.3 | earthly A | unearthly E |
| 501.20 | drop of A | drop E |
| 503.22 | reeling A | reelish E |
| 503.22 | tetering A | tottering E |
| 504.16 | ships A | ship E |
| 504.17 | lips A | lip E |
| 505.17 | to A | to a E |
| 506.3 | sailors, NN<br>sailors' A | sailors, E |
| 506.25 | to NN<br>too A | to E |
| 506.29 | yet A | [*not present*] E |
| 507.11 | tri-pointed A | try-pointed E |
| 507.11 | trinity of A | [*not present*] E |
| 507.28 | *lengthwise* A | [*not present*] E |
| 508.6 | omnipotent A | omniscient E |
| 508.21 | t' is A | It's E |
| 508.24 | ran A | run E |
| 511.19 | skirts A | shirts E |
| 512.2 | THUNDER AND LIGHTNING A | LIGHTNING AND THUNDER E |
| 513.10 | Pequod's A | *Pequod* E |
| 513.16 | shivered A | shivering E |
| 514.7 | *oh-he-yo* A | *ho-he-ho* E |

| | | |
|---|---|---|
| 514.9 | order  A | orders  E |
| 515.2 | come  A | comes  E |
| 515.22 | stealthily  A | steadily  E |
| 517.32 | braced  NN<br>[not present]  A | braced  E |
| 517.36 | he  A | [not present]  E |
| 518.3 | from  A | from the  E |
| 518.8 | feign  A | fain  E |
| 521.21 | hey  A | eh  E |
| 521.36 | nothing's  A | nothing  E |
| 522.4 | a hatchet!  A | [not present]  E |
| 522.21 | my  A | mine  E |
| 522.23 | What's  A | Who's  E |
| 522.23 | intently  NN<br>intenting  A | intently  E |
| 524.2 | He  A | He then  E |
| 524.25 | long beat  A | beaten  E |
| 525.23 | wont  A | won't  E |
| 527.6 | *from the*  A | *from*  E |
| 527.8 | I will  A | I'll  E |
| 528.11 | carry  A | to carry  E |
| 528.19 | of  A | of my  E |
| 528.37 | of  A | of the  E |
| 531.4 | up  A | [not present]  E |
| 531.6 | lowered  A | [not present]  E |
| 533.9 | yaw  A | yawl  E |
| 533.12 | it; while  A | it; yet  E |
| 534.19 | living  A | [not present]  E |
| 536.8 | preceding  A | preceding that  E |
| 537.11–12 | did plainly say  A | plainly said  E |
| 537.28 | two only  A | only two  E |
| 538.7 | yoked  A | yolked  E |
| 538.14 | yet  A | [not present]  E |
| 538.29 | mate,  A | mate, he  E |

| 539.16 | close  A | [*not present*]  E |
| 539.18 | Then  A | Now  E |
| 539.32–38 | An . . . sea.  A | [*not present*]  E |
| 541.7 | ye  A | you  E |
| 542.16–20 | Aloft . . . away.  A | [*not present*]  E |
| 543.1 | morn  A | moon  E |
| 543.3–8 | Oh . . . brain.  A | [*not present*]  E |
| 543.16 | wilful and  A | [*not present*]  E |
| 543.29 | forty—forty  A | forty  E |
| 543.36 | without  A | throughout  E |
| 544.16 | humped,  A | humped, and  E |
| 544.21 | sea  A | the sea  E |
| 544.22 | gaze  A | look  E |
| 544.31 | child  A | children  E |
| 545.12 | Is Ahab  A | Is it Ahab  E |
| 545.22 | air  NN<br>airs  A | air  E |
| 548.14 | of  A | off  E |
| 548.26 | not that . . . Supreme!  A | [*not present*]  E |
| 548.28 | laving  NN<br>leaving  A | laving  E |
| 548.31 | this  A | that  E |
| 548.39 | wrenched  A | wretched  E |
| 549.18 | discover  A | perceive  E |
| 550.15 | its  A | his  E |
| 550.26 | tilting  A | tilting it  E |
| 551.29 | prow was  NN<br>prows were  A | prow was  E |
| 551.33–34 | did crack  A | cracked  E |
| 552.5 | circumferences  A | circumference  E |
| 552.29 | canvas  A | canvass  E |
| 553.13 | this  A | that  E |
| 553.20 | wives'  A | wife's  E |
| 556.28 | spine's  A | spin's  E |

| | | |
|---|---|---|
| 557.17 | did point A | pointed E |
| 558.32 | those A | these E |
| 559.12 | rope A | ropes E |
| 560.11 | grimly A | [*not present*] E |
| 560.20 | not A | not not E |
| 560.31 | boats' NN | boats' E |
| | boat's A | |
| 562.13 | of the A | of all the E |
| 562.23 | set NN | set E |
| | sat A | |
| 563.18 | turn NN | turn E |
| | turned A | |
| 563.21 | Vesuvius A | Vesuvius' E |
| 564.9 | but had A | had but E |
| 564.17 | swift A | shift E |
| 565.24 | Will A | Shall E |
| 567.3 | sweep A | step E |
| 567.20 | waters A | waves E |
| 568.23 | own A | [*not present*] E |
| 569.35 | again A | [*not present*] E |
| 569.37 | simultaneously A | instantaneously E |
| 570.13 | night A | nigh E |
| 571.3 | ye A | thee E |
| 571.4 | oh, oh! A | oh, ho! E |
| 571.32 | and . . . hull; A | [*not present*] E |
| 572.21 | intermixingly A | intermixedly E |
| 572.32 | death-grasp NN | death-grasp E |
| | death-gasp A | |
| 572.33 | archangelic A | unearthly E |
| 573.1–22 | EPILOGUE . . . FINIS. A | [*not present*] E |

# Melville's Notes (1849–51) in a Shakespeare Volume

A T UNDETERMINED times between February of 1849 and July of 1851 Melville wrote the notes reproduced, transcribed, and commented upon here. He wrote the notes in pencil, on both sides of the last blank leaf (pages [523] and [524]) of Volume VII of *The Dramatic Works of William Shakspeare* (Boston: Hilliard, Gray, 1837, 7 volumes).[1] The relevance to *Moby-Dick* of the note with the

---

This RELATED DOCUMENT was prepared by Harrison Hayford and Lynn Horth.

1. The provenance of this set is clear. Although Melville did not write his name in any of its volumes, or the place and date of its acquisition, he wrote these notes and the penciled marginalia throughout. After his death in 1891 the set passed to his widow, to their daughter Frances Thomas, and then to her daughter Frances Osborne, who sold it in 1934 to the Harvard College Library. It is now in the Melville Collection of the Houghton Library with the call number *AC85M4977Zz83s. (Sealts 460, Bercaw 634.) The notes are reproduced here (at 80 percent of the original size) by permission of the Houghton Library, Harvard University. The present transcription was made and several times independently verified from the manuscript by Harrison Hayford, Lynn Horth, and Robert C. Ryan.

inverted Latin baptismal formula "in nomine diaboli," which Ahab uses, is obvious; that of various others has been suggested.

This Shakespeare set (with the spelling "Shakspeare" in its title and throughout) is now at Harvard; it is in all likelihood the same one Melville described in a letter to Evert A. Duyckinck from Boston on February 24, 1849:

> It is an edition in glorious great type, every letter whereof is a soldier, & the top of every "t" like a musket barrel. Dolt & ass that I am I have lived more than 29 years, & until a few days ago, never made close acquaintance with the divine William. Ah, he's full of sermons-on-the-mount, and gentle, aye, almost as Jesus. I take such men to be inspired. I fancy that this moment Shakspeare in heaven ranks with Gabriel Raphael and Michael. And if another Messiah ever comes twill be in Shakesper's person.—I am mad to think how minute a cause has prevented me hitherto from reading Shakspeare. But until now, every copy that was come-atable to me, happened to be in a vile small print unendurable to my eyes which are tender as young sparrows. But chancing to fall in with this glorious edition, I now exult over it, page after page.

In its typography the handsome Harvard set matches very well the "edition" Melville had at hand for this description. The two were treated as the same by Charles Olson, who first examined the Harvard set, quoted this description, and used the note with the inverted baptismal formula in his pioneer essay *"Lear and Moby-Dick"* (*Twice a Year*, I [Fall–Winter, 1938], 165–89). Later scholars have accepted the identification, influenced primarily by Jay Leyda's dating and placements (in *The Melville Log* [New York: Harcourt, Brace, 1951], I, 289, 297) of the notes in Volume VII in relation to Melville's February 24 description and also by Luther S. Mansfield and Howard P. Vincent's treatment in their Hendricks House edition of *Moby-Dick* (New York, 1952), p. 643. No one has doubted that Melville's letter describes the Harvard set, but the identity of the two is not beyond question. Arguably, since the Harvard set does not carry Melville's acquisition date—either a date "a few days" before his February 24 letter that would prove their identity, or a later one that would disprove it—his description could conjecturally be of some other set. It could describe not a set he had bought but, as his letter puts it, one he had chanced "to fall in with"—perhaps in the home of his father-in-law, Judge Lemuel Shaw, where he had already spent the month of

February and was to stay on until April 10. But if the Shakespeare "edition" he described really was a different set, what happened next must be that his delight in it soon moved him to buy and begin marking his own copy of it—or of a similarly "glorious edition," the one now at Harvard.[2]

Given the strong influence on *Moby-Dick* of both Shakespeare and Milton, it is not a digression to record here that Melville was so delighted with his "glorious" Shakespeare set that he soon found for himself the exactly matching two-volume "Boston Edition" of *The Poetical Works of John Milton*, published by the same Boston firm, Hilliard, Gray, in the previous year (1836). It was in the same imperial octavo format (25.3 x 16 cm), with large pages and ample margins, the same typography, the same blue cloth binding, and the same dolphin-and-anchor device printed on the title pages and stamped in gold at the foot of the spines. Melville's heavily read and annotated copy survives. In it his penciled signature "H. Melville" with "N.Y. 1849" on the front free endpaper of each volume suggests that he hunted up this Milton set in New York after his return home from Boston on April 10. However, since this set (unlike his Shakespeare set) is from the original Hilliard, Gray 1836 printing though later ones had been issued both by that publisher (e.g., 1839, 1841) and by Phillips, Sampson (e.g., 1849), it is possible that Melville found it in a Boston used book shop and then or later wrote "N.Y." in it not as the place of its acquisition but of his residence.[3]

2. Among other conjectural "glorious" sets he may first have fallen in with and described, there were, for example, other Boston issues or printings from the same plates as the Harvard set: by Hilliard, Gray in 1836 and 1841; by Little & Brown in 1844; and by Phillips, Sampson in 1846 and 1848 (too late, as well, in 1849, 1850, 1851, 1852, 1854). The decorated front endpapers of the Phillips, Sampson 1849 printing listed the set in the publisher's Library Edition of Standard Poetical Works, in uniform style, and described it as "complete in seven volumes, imperial octavo, of nearly 550 pages each; forming in all nearly 4000 pages. The above edition of the great dramatist is known as 'the magnificent Boston edition,' being celebrated for its transcendent beauty of typography; and in this regard, altogether the finest American edition extant." (Sets from those plates would have been easy to come by in Boston and are still occasionally to be found in used book shops in the region.) For editorial details about the Hilliard, Gray edition see Jane Sherzer, "American Editions of Shakespeare: 1753–1866," *PMLA*, XXII (December, 1907), 657–59.

3. This Milton set (Sealts 358b, Bercaw 499), its existence previously unknown to scholars, was consigned by an unidentified owner and purchased at auction for $100,000 by a dealer for a private collector on March 27, 1984. In the auction cata-

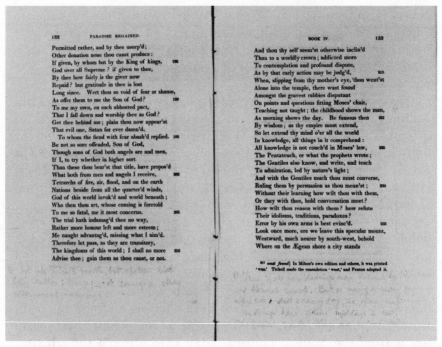

Fig. 1.   Melville's marginalia in his copy of Milton, *Paradise Regained*, Book IV, lines 197 and 220–21 (Boston: Hilliard, Gray, 1836), II, 132–33; reproduced from *Autograph Letters, Documents and Manuscripts . . .* (New York: Phillips, Son & Neale, 1984), p. 14.

[*annotation for line 197: "Though sons of God both angels are and men"*]
*Put into Satan's mouth, but spoken with / John Milton's tongue;—it conveys a strong controversial meaning.

[*annotation for lines 220–21: "the childhood shows the man, / As morning shows the day."*]
*True, if all fair dawnings were followed by high noons / & blazoned sunsets. But as many a merry morn / preceeds a dull & rainy day; so, often, unpromising / mornings have glorious middays & eves. / The greatest, grandest things are unpredicted.

To return to Melville's notes in the seventh Shakespeare volume, it must be reported that at some unrecorded time between 1954 and 1966 this volume was rebacked, recased, and supplied with new endpapers. Therefore there is now a new free endpaper following Melville's inscribed page [524], and its conjugate leaf is the new rear pastedown. Unfortunately, this pastedown covers two brief penciled notations by Melville, one above the other near the top of the original pastedown. Before this catastrophe in recasing, the lower notation was transcribed as "Eschylus' *Tragedies*" by F. O. Matthiessen (*American Renaissance* [New York: Oxford University Press, 1941], p. 448), and variantly as "Eschylus Tragedies" by Charles Olson (*Call Me Ishmael* [New York: Reynal & Hitchcock, 1947], p. 58). The two notations were transcribed by Mansfield and Vincent as "Goethe's Autobiography" just above "Eschylus Tragedies" (in their Hendricks House edition of *Moby-Dick*, 1952, p. 644). Before the recasing Harrison Hayford also transcribed in the same way as Mansfield and Vincent both notations at the corresponding point in a set of the *Dramatic Works* printed from the Hilliard, Gray plates (Boston: Little & Brown, 1844) now in the Melville Collection of The Newberry Library (67–722–193).

The dating of Melville's notes, as a group, is not difficult. Of course, he must have made them all at some time, or times, after he

---

logue, *Autograph Letters, Documents and Manuscripts* . . . (New York: Phillips, Son & Neale, 1984), p. 14, there is a reproduction of pages 132–33 of *Paradise Regained* with Melville's annotations of Book IV, lines 197 and 220–21 (see fig. 1, from the catalogue); there is also a reproduction of his signature, "H. Melville / N.Y. 1849", on the front free endpaper (verso) of Volume II, where he also wrote "Pacific Ocean / N. L. 15°— / Sep. 21st 1860". The catalogue description states: "The volumes contain 41 readable annotations in Melville's hand, varying in length from one word to several sentences. The volumes are extensively underlined, checked and marked on many other pages. Two additional annotations have been cut away and many (ten or more) lengthy annotations have been erased. . . . The first volume is also dated 1868. The front board paper of each volume is inscribed 'C. Horn 1860' (presumably Cape Horn)." Pending the auction, the volumes were inspected by several Melville scholars, who were allowed to take notes. For a further account, see *Melville Society Extracts*, Nos. 57 and 58 (February and May, 1984), 7 and 16 (with reproductions of Melville's annotated page 133 and his signature and place datings in Volume II). In these volumes, as in those of the Shakespeare set, it may prove difficult to distinguish any marginalia and markings Melville made in 1849 from any he made in 1850–51 while writing *Moby-Dick* or made in later years, including any undated ones made on his *Meteor* voyage to California in 1860.

acquired the Shakespeare set (presumably in February of 1849). It happens that two of the notes, because he used each in a later book, provide terminal dates for them all. The note about a seaman (i.e., the Shipman) in *The Canterbury Tales*, which he used in *White-Jacket* (NN363.33), must have been written before September of 1849 when he was through writing that book. The note including the blasphemous baptismal formula Ahab deliriously howls in Chapter 113 of *Moby-Dick* (489.27) must have been written before June 29, 1851, when Melville cited it in a letter to Hawthorne as the book's secret motto. None of the individual notes can now be dated more exactly, but the remaining ones must all have been written at one or more times between those two notes because on the two pages they all come after the one about the seaman in *The Canterbury Tales* and before the one with the baptismal formula.

The order in which Melville jotted his penciled notes is clear from their position on the two pages. Since the top note on page [523] continues the topic of thought (devilish "*Arguments* to persuade") in the one at the foot of page [524], it is obvious that he used page [524] first, then turned back to use page [523]. And since notes that are linked with the devil begin at least halfway down page [524], it is equally obvious that the notes on the top half above those were already there, written earlier, and that the topmost of them, about the seaman, is the earliest of all. By the same evidence of page position, the final note, one third of the way down on page [523], with the Latin baptismal formula, is the latest of them. In the present NN transcription and commentary, therefore, the notes are given in the order in which Melville made them—that is, the order in which they occur on page [524] and then on page [523]. For convenient reference, the lines are numbered here in that order; individual words are referred to by both line and word count—e.g., 9.7 is "eagles". (For symbols used in the transcription, see p. 967.)

As in other volumes of the Northwestern-Newberry Edition, words are transcribed in standard spelling except when they are clearly misspelled, even if Melville did not form all their letters distinctly. Usually the word he intended can be made out (even if it was dashed off in rough approximation of the shape and number of letters), but often only by aid of the context. It is not accurate to call such words "misspelled": Melville's inscriptions "represent" rather than "spell" the words, and it is usually pointless to try to determine and report what letters are present or absent (just as it is in reading a scrawled signature). In these notes the only two words the editors cannot yet decipher, or even conjecture from their context, are the successive ones transcribed as "?making ?almxxxx" (24.1,2); these words are discussed in the commentary below.

Transcribed as clearly misspelled words are: "pulpet" (8.5); "Micheal" (21.6); "Raphel" (21b.1); "beleive" (25.5); "nonsence" (26.1); "nominee" (34.6). Transcribed in standard spelling are many words that are only approximately represented: for example, "grief" (3.6); "would" (6.5); "impious" (14.2); "children" (14.3); "Gabriel" (21.5); "Receives" (28.1). The word "over" (11.1), though it is clearly written "ovre" by metathesis, is transcribed in standard spelling; it belongs in the category of "miswritten" (as distinguished from misspelled) words (see also "tongue" miswritten "tonuge" in the notes in the Milton volume reproduced on p. 958). A word is defined as miswritten if Melville wrote it with one or more letters clearly amiss, but obviously inadvertently so, and not as he can have meant to spell it (in the manner of such typographical errors as "hte" for "the").

These Melville notes require and will reward further study. Here only brief commentary (and no interpretation) can be offered. Most usefully, three warnings must be sounded. First, the NN editors cannot tell whether the notes were written all at one time (as seems unlikely), or at short intervals, or at long ones. The editors cannot answer this question either by inferences from kinds of pencils and placements on the pages or by sufficiently objective thematic links between the notes. Even so, two segments are distinguishable by their topics: lines 1–11 (segment A) are miscellaneous, while lines 12–40 (segment B) are devil-related. Within these two segments, there are subdivisions: within A, there are lines 1.1–3.1; 3.2–4.6; 5.1–7.3; and 8.1–5. Within B, there are lines 9.1–11.3, 12.1–14.3, intermediate lines 14.4–7 "(Devil as a Quaker)", which may belong with lines 12.1–14.3 or may be a later insertion belonging with some or all of the following lines, 15.1–40.1, from which, however, the phrase is separated by a long dividing mark before line 15.

The editors' second warning is directed at the various applications that have been made of the phrase "(Devil as a Quaker)". Jay Leyda was the first to suggest that all the notes after line 8 are tentative jottings for "a parable" with "Devil as a Quaker" as its title, "just before the action is outlined." He remarked that the story "may or may not have been written" or published, but that "an element had been isolated" that expanded into *Moby-Dick*, while the topic of "the temptation on the hill" (17.5–18.1) went beyond into *Clarel*. Leyda also presented the fullest earlier transcription, leaving out only the opening notes (1.1–7.3), with remarkable accuracy. (See Leyda's introduction to *The Complete Stories of Herman Melville* [New York: Random House, 1949], pp. x–xii.) Two years later, in *The Melville Log* (I, 297), Leyda included an entry that has shaped the received idea about these notes. In this entry Melville *"sketches a satirical story . . . (Devil as a Quaker)"*, under Leyda's dating "Before April 10?"—that is, before Melville left Boston for New York on that date. Under that phrase as a title, Leyda gave the seven lines that follow it (15–21) and three later ones (28–30), all accurately transcribed. Next, Mansfield and Vincent, carrying further Olson's linkage of the inverted baptismal formula to Ahab, and, with no reference to Leyda's suggestion that "Devil as a Quaker" was intended as a story title, developed their idea that the phrase "may have been an early hint for the character of Ahab," as indicated by the Faustian echo in the notes from "formal compact" through " 'Hellites' " (15.1–22.3). They further pointed out anticipations of *Redburn*, *White-Jacket*, and *Pierre*, with its "Society of Apostles." Their transcription of the notes was inconsecutive, incomplete, and somewhat inaccurate (see their edition of *Moby-Dick*, pp. 643–44, 667). In her notes to the Hendricks House edition of *The Confidence-Man* (New York, 1954, pp. 296–97), Elizabeth S. Foster, while conceding that some of Melville's jotted "ideas for a comic story about devils circulating in human society . . . may have found their way into *Moby-Dick* and *Pierre*," argued that "the tone of comedy, the method of parody, and the idea of the Devil disguised as a Quaker were an adumbration of *The Confidence-Man*." Foster's tentative and somewhat inaccurate transcription of the notes she took up as relevant embraced lines 12–30. Thus she included lines 12–14, which come before "(Devil as a Quaker)", but for some reason omitted lines 31–33, which are clearly devil-related, as well as lines 34–40, upon which Olson, then Mansfield and Vincent, had focused as notes for the character of Ahab—Olson even characterizing them as "a *Moby-Dick* manuscript" (1947, p. 52). On the other hand, Merrell R. Davis and William H. Gilman, in their 1960 edition of Melville's *Letters* (New Haven: Yale University Press), p. 133n., gave an accurate transcription of lines 34–40 and took them as part of "a sketch labeled 'Devil as Quaker'."

Still other writers have assumed that Melville intended "Devil as a Quaker" to be the title of a story for which the notes that follow are jottings (lines 15–40, perhaps lines 12.1–14.3, and also even some or all the preceding lines except 1.1–3.1). Such writers have not examined the manuscript critically (no reproduction and no complete and consecutive transcription has been in print); they echo earlier assertions in good faith. The fact, however, is that the placing of the parenthesized phrase "Devil as a Quaker" (see the reproduction) does not justify confident assertion that Melville intended it as the title for such a story. On the other hand, its "Devil" reference to what follows does justify assertion of that possibility. Yet its "Quaker" reference appears later in the notes only in the phrase "*Society of D's*" (19.4–6), almost certainly a parodic reference to the Quaker "Society of Friends," though other organizations used the formula (the Shakers, for example, were the United Society of Believers). Further, no one has distinguished, or perhaps can unarguably distinguish, between the Devil and "the hero" (18.11, 13–14) in the notes that follow, with sometimes indefinite references of pronouns (e.g., "him" 22.8) and subjectless verbs (e.g., "takes" 23.7). Especially unclear is which of them is meant when someone (who?) is to "find him" (whom?) performing some thus far undeciphered operation (23.1–2) "At the Astor" (22.4–6).

The only previous complete reproduction and complete transcription of Melville's notes were included by Wilson Walker Cowen in his unpublished 1965 Harvard dissertation, "Melville's Marginalia" (I, viii–ix and IX, 523–24). This heroic work is a major resource for Melville scholars, since it is the only attempt at a complete transcription of his marginalia, with typed texts of the passages he marked. Hence, the present editors must here unhappily sound their third warning: Cowen's transcription of these notes is so inaccurate in both words and mechanical details that doubt is cast on the reliability of his other transcriptions. His following misreadings are cited to support this point: "evil" (NN "over", miswritten "ovre") at 11.1; "May" (NN "Many") at 13.6; "mighty" (NN "weighty") at 19.11; "waking alone cps" (NN "?making ?almxxxx") at 23.1–2; "reverence" (NN "nonsense") at 26.1; "new" (NN "never") at 26.5; "warm" (NN "warmed") at 33.5; "reason" (NN "reasons") at 37.4.

Several of Melville's notes may be commented upon briefly.

(1) "seaman" (1.2): in Chapter 86 of *White-Jacket* (NN363.29–33) five lines about "old Chaucer's shipman" are quoted from the Prologue, including "With many a tempest hadde his berd be shake." No edition of *The Canterbury Tales* owned or borrowed by Melville in 1849 is known; but the quoted lines correspond, except for minor changes, to Thomas Tyrwhitt's 1775 text, available to him in various editions, e.g., the London editions of Pickering, 1822 and 1845.

(2) "*Bacon*" (4.6): The note is Melville's paraphrase of a passage in the essay "Of Friendship": "The parable of Pythagoras is dark, but true, *Cor ne edito*: Eat not the heart. Certainly, if a man would give it a hard phrase, those that want friends to open themselves unto are cannibals of their own hearts."

(3) "*Claudia*" (5.1): Claudia's arrogant speech is reported by Suetonius to illustrate the notorious patrician pride of the Appian family in contempt of the plebeians, in his life of Tiberius in *The Lives of the Twelve Caesars*. Melville's direct source is not known, but Robert Graves freely translates the passage: "Claudius the Fair's sister . . . was riding through the crowded streets in a carriage, and making such slow progress that she shouted: 'If only my brother were alive to lose another fleet! That would thin out the population a little!' " (*The Twelve Caesars* [Harmondsworth, Middlesex: Penguin, 1957], p. 110). No reference to Claudia's wishing for a pestilence is included in her speech as reported by Suetonius, Livy (bk. 19), or Aulus Gellius. The latter, however, does attribute the speech and her punishment for it (246 B.C.) to her speaking "too arrogantly" ("quod locuta esset petulantius"):

> Public punishment was formerly inflicted, not only upon crimes, but even upon arrogant language; so necessary did men think it to maintain the dignity of Roman conduct inviolable. For the daughter of the celebrated Appius Caecus, when leaving the plays of which she had been a spectator, was jostled by the crowd of people that surrounded her, flocking together from all sides. When she had extricated herself, complaining that she had been roughly handled, she added: "What, pray, would have become of me, and how much more should I have been crowded and pressed upon, had not my brother Publius Claudius lost his fleet in the sea-fight and with it a vast number of citizens? Surely, I should have lost my life, overwhelmed by a still greater mass of people. How I wish," said she, "that my brother might come to life

again, take another fleet to Sicily, and destroy that crowd which has just knocked poor me about." Because of such wicked and arrogant words, Gaius Fundanius and Tiberius Sempronius, the plebeian aediles, imposed a fine upon the woman of twenty-five thousand pounds of full-weight bronze. (*Attic Nights*, trans. J. C. Rolfe, Loeb Classical Library, II, 230–32).

(4) "*Roast beef*. . . over spiritual man" (8.1–11.3): This passage foreshadows Melville's comment about Hawthorne in a letter to Evert A. Duyckinck, February 12, 1851: "there is something lacking . . . to the plump sphericity of the man. . . . He doesn't patronise the butcher— he needs roast-beef, done rare."

(5) "the Astor" (22.5–6): This fashionable hotel was evidently an ironically appropriate place for whatever undeciphered operation "the hero" (or the Devil?) was to be found carrying on. Leyda (1949) plausibly read the words (23.1–2) as "making almanacks"; Elizabeth Foster (1954) as "making [illegible word]"; Cowen (1965) as "waking alone cps"; the NN editors considered such disparate readings as "making alms cups", "working at masks", "smoking alone", "waking alone", but found no satisfactory one.

(6) "Brought . . . fire" (33.1–9): This line may have been inserted later.

(7) "Ego . . . Diaboli" (34.1–36.1): Melville's direct source has not been convincingly located.

(8) "right reasons" (37.3–4): See the HISTORICAL NOTE, p. 650, footnote 33.

(9) "Goetic . . . Theurgic" (38.5–7): These terms for black and white magic have been applied to interpretations of Ahab and other characters by various critics since Olson (1938, 1947). Leon Howard (*Herman Melville* [Berkeley: University of California Press, 1951], p. 171) suggested Bulwer-Lytton's *The Last Days of Pompeii* as Melville's source, but the terms were in common use. (Cf. Bercaw 91.)

An interesting fact, in light of Melville's presumably acquiring the Shakespeare set no earlier than February of 1849, and only subsequently writing these notes in it, is that some of the topics of the earlier notes were already closely approximated in *Mardi*, which was off his hands by late January. In Chapter 85 kings "like eagles opened their right royal eyes . . . full upon the golden rays of the sun"

(NN260.14–16). In Chapter 138, the rulers of Diranda hold warlike games to keep the population down, and one of King Piko's "sagacious Ahithophels" [cf. the allusion to Absalom at 13.5, also II Samuel 15–17] advises him that "haply a pestilence may decimate the people," while Babbalanja inquires how the people "fancied being coolly thinned out" by the war games (NN440.13–14, 441.5–7). In Chapter 180 these sentences occur: "Few grand poets have good eyes; for they needs blind must be, who ever gaze upon the sun" (NN591.22–23); "Cerebrum must not overbalance cerebellum; our brains should be round as globes; and planted on capacious chests . . . " (NN593.15–16); "The way to heaven is through hell. We need fiery baptisms in the fiercest flames of our own bosoms. . . . Oh! there is a fierce, a cannibal delight, in the grief that shrieks to multiply itself. That grief is miserly of its own; it pities all the happy. Some damned spirits would not be otherwise, could they" (NN594.7–8, 16–19); and in comments on Babbalanja, who speaks the foregoing sentences, "Pray, my lord, is this good gentleman a devil?" "No, my lord; but he's possessed by one" (NN594.20–22).

## SYMBOLS USED

| | |
|---|---|
| [ . . . ] | revision or insertion enclosed in square brackets was made later than initial inscription of leaf |
| < . . . > | letters or words enclosed in diamond brackets were canceled by lining out |
| < . . . >word | letter(s) or word(s) written over are enclosed in diamond brackets closed up to the following word or letter that was superimposed |
| ?word | prefixed question mark indicates conjectural reading |
| xxxx | undeciphered letters (number of x's approximates numbers of letters involved) |
| | all words in roman are Melville's |
| | all words in italics *outside brackets* are words Melville underlined |
| | all words in italics *inside brackets* are editorial |

A seaman figures in the Canterbury Tales.

With ... a tempest has his beard been shook. — ... Secret grief is ... careful of its own head. — Bacon.

Claudia of the Appian family. "I wish some ... plight or pestilence would bring out this mind ..."

... the pulpit.

An animal of a man — "do eagles wear ... obstacles? — Health. — Contrast: an ... spiritual man.

"... madam, Cain was a ... furious boy, &

Reuben (Gen: 49) & Absalom ... many ... men have impeach'd — (Devil as a Quaker)

A formal compact — Imprimis — First — Second. Thirdly — ... soul ... — Duplicates —

"How was it about the Lieutenant ...

... help the hero to form one of a "Society of D's" — his name would be ...

... leaves a letter to the ... — "My Dear D" — Conversation upon Gabriel, Michael &c

Raphael — Gentlemen &c

"Terra Oblivionis" Hellebore — ...

... "Do you believe all that stuff? "But it's not nonsense. The world was never made.

... you mention there ... in the ...?"

... — Gentlemen's argument to persuade — "would you not rather ... with King, than a mere fool?"

*[on verso of last leaf of Volume VII, page [524]]*

1 A seaman figures in The Canterbury Tales.
2 With <a>many a tempest had his beard been
3 shook. — <S><Deep g> Secret grief is a
4 cannibal of its own heart — *Bacon.*
5 | *Claudia* of the *Appian* family, "I wish
6 | some fight or pestilence would thin out
7 | this crowd." *Arrogance.*
8 *Roast beef in the pulpet.*

9 An animal of a man — "do eagles wear
10 spectacles?"— Health. — *Contrast*: an
11 over spiritual man.

———

12 "Yes, Madam, Cain was a godless froward boy, &
13 Reuben (Gen:49) & Absalom" Many pious men
14 have impious children — (Devil as a Quaker)

———

15 A formal compact — Imprimis — First —Second.
16 The aforesaid soul. said soul &c —Duplicates —
17 ="How was it about the temptation on the
18 hill?" &c [*inserted later below in lines 21–21b after* Dear D" — *and circled*
*with guideline to caret here* Conversation upon Gabriel, Micheal & /
Raphel — gentlemanly &c] — D begs the hero to form
19 one of a *"Society of D's"* — his name would be weighty
20 &c — Leaves a letter to the D— "My
21 Dear D" — [*later insertion in lines 21–21b, reported in line 18*]

———

22 "Terra Oblivionis" "Hellites" — At the Astor find him
23 ?making ?almxxxx — going to a ball takes a long
24 time making toilette. — The Doctor's coach stops
25 the way. — "Do you beleive all that stuff?
26 nonsense — the world was never made. — [*add* "But] Is not
27 this you mentioned *here* — in the scriptures?"
28 Receives visits from the principal d's — "Gentlemen" &c.
29 *Arguments* to persuade — "Would you not rather
30 be below with kings than above with fools?"

[*on recto of last blank leaf of Volume VII, page* [523]]

31   It is better to laugh & not sin than to <be> weep & be
32   wicked. — Ten loads of coal to burn him. —
33   Brought to the stake — warmed himself by the fire.

34   Ego non baptizo te in nominee Patris et
35   Filii et Spiritus Sancti — sed in nomine
36   Diaboli. — Madness is undefinable —
37   It & right reasons extremes of one.
38   —Not the [*inserted later above line with caret below* (black art)] Goetic
     but Theurgic magic —
39   seeks converse with the Intelligence, Power, the
40   Angel.

# Melville's Memoranda in Chase's Narrative of the Essex

B Y MELVILLE'S account in these memoranda it was on his Pacific voyage aboard the *Acushnet* [1841–42] that he first heard the story of the *Essex* sunk by a whale and then read it in Chase's *Narrative*. In 1850 when he came to write his own whaling narrative that catastrophe was still fresh in his mind, whether or not he had already (or only later—scholars disagree) planned the same catastrophe to end his book. Well along in its composition, evidently in April of 1850, he again laid hands on a copy—his own—of Owen Chase's *Narrative of the Most Extraordinary and Distressing Shipwreck of the Whale-Ship Essex, of Nantucket; Which Was Attacked and Finally Destroyed by a Large Spermaceti-Whale* . . . (New York: W. B. Gilley, 1821). Melville's memoranda are bound into that copy.[1]

This RELATED DOCUMENT was prepared by Harrison Hayford and Lynn Horth.

1. At Melville's death in 1891 this volume passed to his widow, to their daughter Frances Thomas, then to her daughter Frances Osborne, and from her (1932) into the hands of successive collectors: Cortlandt F. Bishop, Frank J. Hogan, then (with the Bishop and Hogan bookplates in it) Perc S. Brown, and then Alfred C. Berol, who donated it, along with Melville's copy of Thomas Beale's *The Natural History of the Sperm Whale,* to the Harvard College Library in December, 1960. It is now preserved in the Melville Collection of the Houghton Library with the call number

According to his memoranda Melville had discussed with his father-in-law, Judge Lemuel Shaw, and others whether it was credible that a whale sank the *Essex*. Sometime before New Year's Day of 1850, Shaw undertook to find Melville a copy of Chase's *Narrative* and also one of William Lay and Cyrus M. Hussey's *A Narrative of the Mutiny, on Board the Ship Globe* . . . (New London: Lay & Hussey, 1828).[2] Melville's surviving copies of the two books reveal this background and how the judge procured them: he asked help from a Nantucket friend, T. C. Coffin, who turned to another Nantucketer, Thomas Macy. Macy supplied Shaw with both books as gifts, in January with Lay and Hussey's *Narrative* but not until April with Chase's. Melville wrote (then or later) in the Lay and Hussey volume (Sealts 323): "Herman Melville from Chief Justice Shaw 1851". Tipped to its front free endpaper is Macy's letter to Coffin, January 9, 1851, sending him the book as a present to Judge Shaw but reporting that "after the most diligent search" he had not yet found a copy of Chase's *Narrative* and promising if successful to forward it to Coffin. In April, 1850, when Melville was already well along with his own book, Macy sent Shaw, directly, the long-sought Chase *Narrative*, with a letter dated April, 1851 (now bound into it):

> Hon. Lemuel Shaw
> Herewith I send thee a mutilated copy of the Narrative of the loss of Ship Essex of Nantucket. I should not have sent this imperfect copy, <for> but for the fact, that this is the only copy that I have been able to procure—
>
> > Respectfully thy friend
> > Tho.ˢ Macy
>
> Nantucket 4 ṁ 1851

---

*AC85M4977R821c(B). (Sealts 134, Bercaw 130.) The memoranda are reproduced here (at 78 percent of the original size) by permission of the Houghton Library, Harvard University. The present transcription was made and several times verified from the manuscript by Harrison Hayford and verified from photocopy by Alma A. MacDougall.

2. See pp. 625–26 and 659 above for disproof of the long-standing speculation that Melville was in Boston with his wife during the 1850 year-end holiday season and had access then through Judge Shaw to source-books for *Moby-Dick*.

Shaw passed the book along to Melville, who read and marked it, and later had it bound, along with this letter and extra leaves of blue paper, as detailed below.[3]

Not when he got the "imperfect copy" but sometime after having

3. Macy dated both of his letters by month in a Quaker fashion, the first "I m̊ 1851", the second as shown in the illustration (a dating that in the Bishop and Hogan sale catalogues, cited below, and in *Log*, I, 407, was misread as March 4, i.e., fourth day of M[arch]). He inscribed the Lay and Hussey *Narrative* to Lemuel Shaw "I m̊ 1851". In July, 1852 (when Melville was visiting Nantucket with Judge Shaw), Macy likewise inscribed and dated the title page of a copy of Obed Macy's *The History of Nantucket* (Boston: Hilliard, Gray, 1835): "Herman Melville from his friend Tho.ˢ

it bound, Melville wrote in ink on the recto of the binder's leaf following the front free endpaper: "Herman Melville from Judge Shaw April. 1851." Perhaps Melville named the month as April from his own recollection but perhaps from the date of Macy's letter, so that April, 1851, is the earliest but (if it in fact reached Melville from Shaw later) not certainly the latest time that the *Narrative* could have come to hand for his direct use in writing *Moby-Dick*.

When Melville received it, the *Narrative* lacked the leaves that contained the last six of its 128 pages and probably also (as now) its original end leaves and whatever original binding it had. This condition moved him before long to have it bound, which he did sometime before July 6–8, 1852, when he first visited Nantucket—to judge the binding date from memoranda about Captain Pollard (pages 2, 23) already written before Melville met him there on July 8. As bound, the narrative made a neat duodecimo volume (17 x 11 cm) in half red morocco leather with marbled boards, its extant original leaves and the thirty-two added blue ones trimmed (with sprinkled edges) by the binder (16.5 x 10 cm). Stamped in small gold capitals down its narrow (1.5 cm) spine, one word to a line, is the title "LOSS OF THE WHALE SHIP ESSEX STOVE BY A WHALE 1821." The idiomatic words "LOSS" and "STOVE" in this epitome of the original verbose title suggest that Melville himself supplied it; "1821" refers to the year of publication not to that of the loss, given incorrectly on the title page as 1819 but correctly in *Moby-Dick* (206.19) and in one of Melville's memoranda (page 25) as 1820. We have not determined the source of the added paper (which is like that of some Melville manuscripts of the 1850's), or conjectured any reason for the number and the unevenly divided arrangement of its lightly-lined folded blue sheets. Whether or not at Melville's direction, ten of the thirty-two added leaves were gathered at the front (after the white endpaper and binder's leaf) and were followed by Macy's single-page April, 1851, letter (see above), placed so that its verso faced the title page; the remaining twenty-two leaves were gathered at the back following the last extant page (122) of the incomplete book and before the white binder's leaf and free endpaper.

Probably (but not certainly) it was after the blue leaves were

---

Macy 7 m 1852" (the dating has been misread as 7 January 1852—i.e., seventh day of the first month; cf. Sealts 345 and his discussion on p. 20).

bound with the book (whether before or after the ink memoranda were written) that Melville numbered some but not all of the sixty-four pages with the consecutive penciled numbers cited in the present discussion: at the front, 1–18 (19–20, presumably numbered, are now cut out, but leaving ink marks on the stub verso); at the back (after the book's page 122), 21–30, leaving seventeen more leaves of un-numbered pages [31–64]. His memoranda, titled and untitled, are present on these eighteen pages: at the front, "General Evidences", page 2; "What I know of Owen Chace &c", 3–7; "Authorship of the Book", 14; "Another Narrative of the Adventure", 15; "Note", 16; an untitled note in green pencil, 17–18; and at the rear, "Sequel", 21–25; "Further Concerning Owen Chace", 26–27. Judging from the neatly placed writing on these pages (some of it very likely copied from earlier drafts) with no lines cropped by the binder, it appears that Melville inscribed all these memoranda, at different times, after the leaves were bound into the book. The contents and ink identify most of the pages as written before July of 1852, when he visited Nantucket, where he met and conversed with Captain Pollard. Clearly later are the "Note" on page 16, and the pencil notation about Pollard ("A Night-Watchman") on page 23; many years later is the memorandum in green pencil on pages 17–18 about meeting with Pollard—so many years later that Melville could not place that 1852 meeting closer than "somewhere about 1850 – 3."[4]

For the principles guiding the report of Melville's handwriting and the symbols used in the transcription, see above, pp. 960, 967. References to words in Melville's memoranda are given by his page number (see the reproductions) and by line (e.g., "Sequel" at 21.1). In this transcription only three words are reported as conjectural: "pleasurably", possibly "pleasantly" miswritten "pleasnatly" (5.13); "missionaries", possibly "missions" (25.1); and "mariners", possibly

4. Pasted to page [64] (the verso of the last blue leaf) and to both sides of the immediately following white free binder's leaf is a clipping, dated in pencil "1851" (identified by the present editors as from the New York *Daily Tribune*, November 3, 1851), with a report headlined "Destruction of a Whale Ship by a Sperm Whale . . . ," credited to the *Panama Herald*, October 16, [1851]; the ship was the *Ann Alexander*. Evert A. Duyckinck sent Melville an unidentified clipping with the story; see Melville's letter to him, November 7, 1851 (*Letters*, ed. Merrell R. Davis and William H. Gilman [New Haven: Yale University Press, 1960], pp. 139–40); see also p. 1040, footnote 35, below.

"mariner" or another word (25.5). Transcribed as clearly misspelled words are: "stupedly" (2.3); "landsman" for "landsmen", perhaps better classified as miswritten (2.11); "Chace" (3.1 and throughout); "berth" (4.3); "mear" (5.16); "peaces" (22.16); "beleive" (23.14); and "*Carrol*" (27.1). Transcribed in standard spelling are many words that are only approximately represented: for example, "appearances" (5.7); "expressive" (5.9); "unostentatious" (5.11), and other words ending in (or including) *-ious* throughout; "prepossessing" (5.14); "opportunity" (5.18); "beginning" (21.13); "Concerning" (23.15); and "disastrous" (26.6). A number of marginal words in ink in the book (none written by Melville) have not been reported (see Heffernan, cited below, p. 35). The penciled "(6)" after "pages" (21.3) is the Harvard cataloguer's notation of the number of book pages missing.

Melville's memoranda are not annotated here, but attention must be called to two serious errors of fact in them. Melville was somehow mistaken in supposing he had met Owen Chase at sea in 1841: in 1840 Chase had retired and in that year been granted a divorce in Nantucket from his unfaithful wife—by Judge Lemuel Shaw (with whom Melville had evidently not discussed the matter). Melville was also mistaken in identifying that wife (actually Chase's third) as the mother of several of his children, including the son (William Henry Chase) who lent Melville the *Narrative*. See Heffernan, cited below, pp. 125–35 and *passim*.

For Melville's knowledge of Chase and use of his *Narrative* in *Moby-Dick*, see the HISTORICAL NOTE, p. 638, and the discussions at xxv.10, 206.31–32, 206.35–39, and 569.8–11. His use of it there and in *Clarel* is discussed by Henry F. Pommer in "Herman Melville and the Wake of the *Essex*," *American Literature*, XX (November, 1948), 290–304. Thomas F. Heffernan's *Stove by a Whale: Owen Chase and the "Essex"* (Middletown, Conn.: Wesleyan University Press, 1981) includes the complete *Narrative* itself and gives the fullest treatment of the whole *Essex* affair and of all the persons, topics, and other accounts mentioned in Melville's memoranda. Heffernan also prints from the *Narrative* about twenty passages that Melville marked in its margins in pencil. Melville underlined only one phrase: Chase describes his crew's attempts to fight off the repeated attacks of a "ravenous" shark who several times "snapped at the steering oar". At the end of this passage Chase relates that their only hope—after months at sea in a lone boat after the whale sank the ship—"was derived from a sense of the mercies of our Creator." In pencil Melville underlined the last four words, adding a parenthesized question mark (*Narrative*, pp. 65–66). (From this passage may have come the sharks who bite Ahab's oars on the third day of the chase; but see the discussion at 569.8–11; cf. 302.22–24).

The *Narrative* was included in *Narratives of the Wreck of the Whale-Ship Essex* (London: Golden Cockerel Press, 1935), with an introduction and twelve wood engravings by Robert Gibbings. Quotations from the memoranda and a reproduction of pages 14 and 15 were published in *Books, Autographs, Manuscripts . . .* (New York: American Art Association—Anderson Galleries, 1932), pp. 30–31. Quotations and a reproduction of page 3 were published in *The Cortlandt F. Bishop Library, Part Two* (New York: American Art Association—Anderson Galleries, 1938) pp. 504–6, and the same ones were published in *The Frank J. Hogan Library, Part One* (New York: Parke-Bernet Galleries, 1945), pp. 114–15. The memoranda were also prominently included, out of order, incomplete, somewhat edited, and with several misreadings, by Charles Olson in *Call Me Ishmael* (New York: Reynal & Hitchcock, 1947); see p. 653, above. Two earlier complete reproductions of the memoranda have been published. The most recent is in Heffernan's book, just cited; his accompanying transcription differs from the present one in a few details of punctuation, capitalization, and spelling. It also differs in five words: "pleasantly" (NN "?pleasurably") at 5.13; "sometime" (NN "somewhere") at 17.2; "now" (NN "more") at 21.5; "missions" (NN "?missionaries") at 25.1; and "Mariner" (NN "?mariners") at 25.5. The earlier reproduction is included in the edition of the *Narrative* (with an introduction by B. R. McElderry, Jr.) in the American Heritage series (New York: Corinth Books, 1963). In the accompanying transcription, "misspellings and some abbreviated words are silently altered," punctuation is unreliable, and there is one serious misreading, "Legend" for "Sequel" (21.1)—the similarity of Melville's capital *L* and *S* has sometimes caused similar misreadings (see the discussion at 338.11).

2

General Evidences
—— ‖ ——

This thing of the Essex is found / (stupedly abbreviated) in many / compilations
of nautical adventure / made within the last 15 or 20 / years. ¶. The Englishman
Bennett / in his exact work ("Whaling Voyage / round the Globe") quotes the
thing as / an acknowledged fact. /

¶. Besides seamen, several / landsman ( Judge Shaw & others) / acquainted with
Nantucket, have / evinced to me their unquestioning / faith in the thing; having
seen / Captain Pollard himself, & being / conversant with his situation / in
Nantucket since the disaster./

3

What I know of Owen Chace
&c
———— " ————

When I was on board / the ship Acushnet of Fairhaven, / on the passage to the Pacific / cruising-grounds, among other / matters of forecastle con- / versation at times was / the story of the Essex. It / was then that I first / became acquainted / with her history and her / truly astounding fate. /

But what then / served to specialize my / interest at the time was / the circumstance that the /

**4**
Second mate of our ship, / Mʳ Hall, an Englishman / & Londoner by berth, had / for two three-years voyages / sailed with Owen Chace (then / \<f> in command of the whale- / ship "William [*stylized asterisk inserted above later*] Wirt" (I think / it was) of Nantucket.) This / Hall always spoke of Chace / with much interest & sincere / regard — but he did not / seem to know anything / more about him or the / Essex affair than any body / else. [*Inserted later, boxed, with stylized asterisk keyed to asterisks above and on next page* See p. 19. of M.S.] /

    Somewhere about the / latter part of A. D. 1841, / in this same ship the / Acushnet, we spoke the /

5

"W$^{\underline{m}}$ Wirt [*stylized asterisk inserted above later*]" of Nantucket, & / Owen Chace was the Captain, / & so it came to pass that I / saw him. He was a / large, powerful well-made / man; rather tall; to all / appearances something past forty- / -five or so; with a handsome / face for a Yankee, & expressive / of great uprightness & calm / unostentatious courage. His / whole appearance impressed me / ?pleasurably. He was the most / prepossessing-looking whale- / hunter I think I ever saw. /

—— Being a mear / foremast-hand I had / no opportunity of conversing / with Owen (tho' he was /

6

on board our ship for two / hours at a time) nor have / I ever seen him since. /

But I should have / before mentioned, that before / seeing Chace's ship, we / spoke another Nantucket / craft & *gammed* with her. / In the forecastle I made / the acquaintance of a fine / lad of sixteen or / thereabouts, a son of / Owen Chace. I questioned / him concerning his father's / adventure; and when I / left his ship to return / again the next morning (for / the two vessels were to sail / in company for a few days) /

7

he went to his chest & / handed me a complete / copy (same edition as this / one) of the *Narrative*. / This was the first printed / account of it I had ever / seen, & the only copy of / Chace's Narrative (regular & / authentic) except the present / one. The reading of this / wondrous story upon the / landless sea, & close to the / very latitude of the shipwreck / had a surprising effect upon me. /

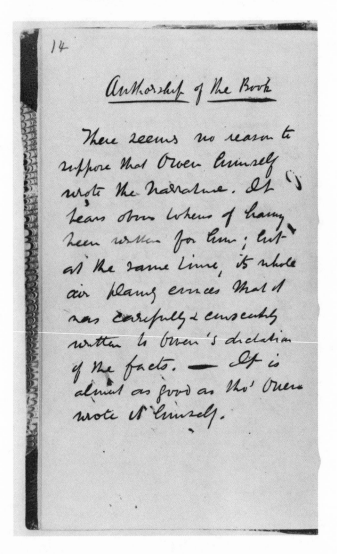

14

Authorship of the Book

There seems no reason to / suppose that Owen himself / wrote the Narrative. It / bears obvious tokens of having / been written for him; but / at the same time, its whole / air plainly evinces that it / was carefully & conscientiously / written to Owen's dictation / of the facts. ——— It is / almost as good as tho' Owen / wrote it himself. /

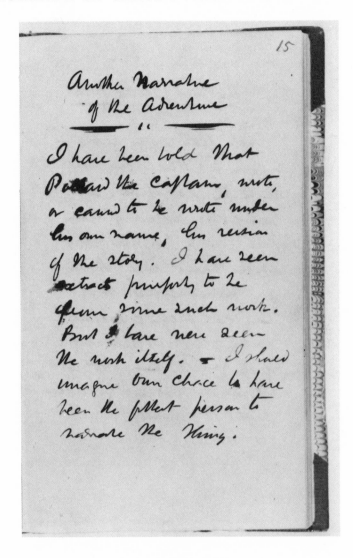

Another Narrative
of the Adventure
———— " ————

I have been told that / Pollard the Captain, wrote, / or caused to be wrote under / his own name, his version / of the story. I have seen / extracts purporting to be / from some such work. / But I have never seen / the work itself. — I should / imagine Owen Chace to have / been the fittest person to / narrate the thing. /

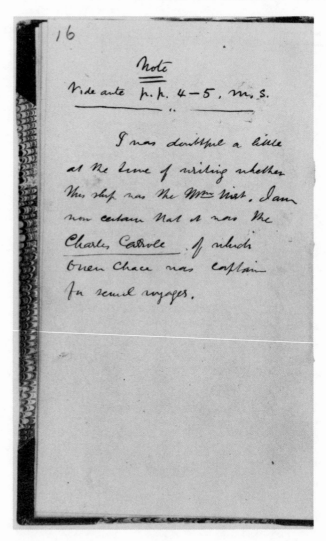

16

<u>Note</u>

Vide ante p.p. 4–5. M.S.

——— ‖ ———

I was doubtful a little / at the time of writing whether / this ship was the W<u>m</u> Wirt. I am / now certain that it was the / *Charles Carroll* of which / Owen Chace was captain / for several voyages. /

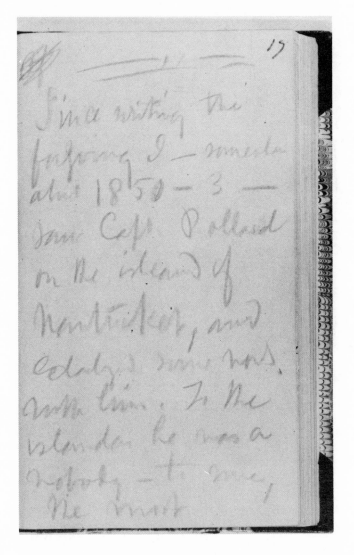

17

<Af>

———— ‖ ————

Since writing the / foregoing I — somewhere / about 1850 – 3 — / saw Capt. Pollard / on the island of / Nantucket, and / exchanged some words / with him. To the / islanders he was a / nobody — to me, / the most /

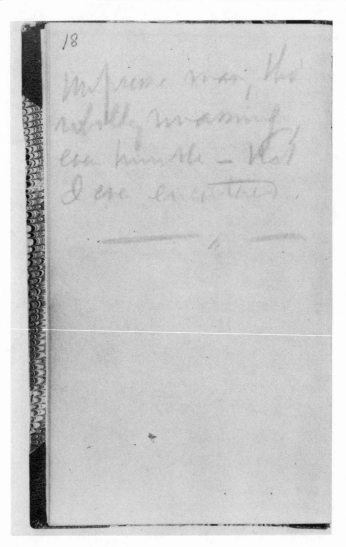

18
impressive man, tho' / wholly unassuming, / even humble — that / I ever
encountered.

———— **‖** ————

Sequel
—— ‖ ——

———————— I can not tell / exactly how many more pages the / complete narrative contains — but / at any rate, very little more remains / to be related. — The boat was / picked up by the ship, & the / poor fellows were landed in Chili. / & in time sailed for home. / Owen Chace returned to his / business of whaling, & in due / time became a Captain, / as related in the / beginning. /

Captain Pollard's boat / (from which Chace's had become / separated) was also after / a miserable time, picked / up by a ship, but not /

22

until two of its crew had / died delirious, & furnished / food for the survivors. /

The third boat, it does / not appear, that it was ever / heard of, after its sub-separation / from Pollard's. /

Pollard himself / returned to Nantucket, & / subsequently sailed on another / whaling voyage to the Pacific, / but he had not been / in the Pacific long, when / one night, his ship went / ashore on unknown rocks, / & was dashed to peaces. / The crew, with Pollard, / put off in their boats, & / were soon picked up by /

23

another whale-ship, with which, / the day previous, they had sailed / in company.
—— I got this / from Hall, Second Mate of / the Acushnet. — /

Pollard, it seems, / now took the hint, & after / reaching home from this
second / shipwreck, vowed to abide / ashore. He has ever / since lived in
Nantucket. / Hall told me that he / became a butcher there. / I beleive he is still
living. /

[*Inserted in pencil, with triple underscoring* A Night-Watchman]

Concerning the three / men left on the island;— / they were taken off at last /
(in a sad state <engh> / enough) by a ship, which /

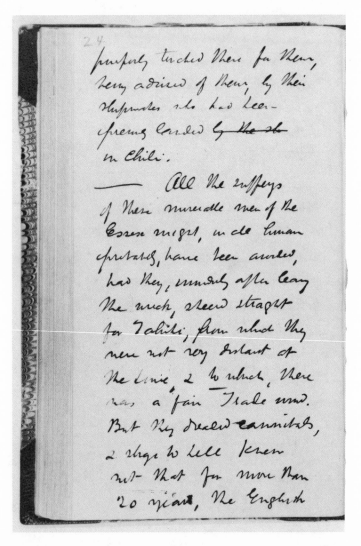

24

purposely touched there for them, / being advised of them, by their / shipmates who had been / previously landed <by the sh> / in Chili. /
—————— All the sufferings / of these miserable men of the / Essex might, in all human / probability, have been avoided, / had they, immediately after leaving / the wreck, steered straight / for Tahiti, from which they / were not very distant at / the time, & *to* which, there / was a fair Trade wind. / But they dreaded cannibals, / & strange to tell knew / not that for more than / 20 years, the English /

25

?missionaries had been resident in / Tahiti, & that in the same / year of their shipwreck —1820— / it was entirely safe for the / ?mariners to touch at Tahiti. / —— But they chose to / stem a head wind, & make / a passage of several thousand / miles (an unavoidably / roundabout one, too) in order / to gain a civilized harbor / on the coast of South America. /

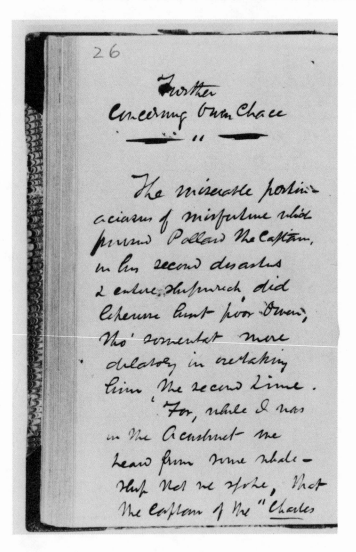

26

### Further
### Concerning Owen Chace
———— ͋ ————

The miserable pertin- / aciousness of misfortune which / pursued Pollard the Captain, / in his second disastrous / & entire shipwreck, did / likewise hunt poor Owen, / tho' somewhat more / dilatory in overtaking / him, the second time. /

For, while I was / in the Acushnet we / heard from some whale- / ship that we spoke, that / the Captain of the *"Charles* /

27

*Carrol"* — that is Owen Chace — / had recently received letters / from home, informing him of / the certain infidelity of his / wife, the mother of several / children, one of them being the / lad of sixteen, whom I / alluded to as giving me / a copy of his father's / narrative to read. We also heard that this receipt / of this news had told / most heavily upon Chace, / & that he was a prey to / the deepest gloom. /

# Melville's Acushnet Crew Memorandum

I N THE MELVILLE COLLECTION of the Houghton Library of Harvard University there is a memorandum in Melville's hand with the heading "What became of the ship's company of the whale-ship 'Acushnet,' according to Hubbard who came home in her (more than a four years' voyage) and who visited me at Pittsfield." At the end of the heading he later added "in 1850", a dating that appears to be erroneous. The possible relation of the memorandum to the composition of *Moby-Dick* is discussed below (pp. 1013–20), along with the date of Hubbard's visit, his account of the ship's company, and the copy of *The Whale* inscribed to him by Melville. The memorandum itself is reproduced (at 80 percent of the original size) and transcribed here, with textual commentary, by permission of the Houghton Library, Harvard University. For the principles guiding the report of Melville's difficult handwriting and the symbols used in the presentation, see above, pp. 960, 967. Words incompletely underlined in the memorandum are rendered completely in italics in the transcription. References are by line and word (e.g., "disease" at 15.1).[1]

This RELATED DOCUMENT was prepared by Harrison Hayford and Lynn Horth.

1. The memorandum was among manuscripts that at Melville's death in 1891 passed to his widow, then to their daughter Frances Thomas, then to her daughter

Melville wrote the memorandum in a uniform black ink on both sides of a single sheet of faintly lined blue paper, with no watermark, measuring approximately 24.6 × 19.7 cm. To judge from his use of a pen rather than a pencil, and from the neat flow of its phrasing (uninterrupted by the running cancellations, revisions, and transpositions characteristic of his tortuous first-draft manuscripts), the document could be a copy from some earlier one. Its hurried handwriting, however, shows no concern to make its words readily legible by other readers. (For a full range of Melville's handwriting, see the reproductions of manuscript fragments from successive composition stages of Chapter 14 of *The Confidence-Man*, in the Northwestern-Newberry edition, pp. 413–68.) Throughout this *Acushnet* memorandum words were carefully mended in ink after his death by his wife Elizabeth Shaw Melville, just as in others left in her care at his death, and earlier in manuscripts she was preparing to copy for him.[2]

These physical characteristics of the manuscript suggest that Melville inscribed it some while (not very soon) after Hubbard's visit, and not during it (when he would more likely have made rough pencil notes). The wording at two points carries the same suggestion. First, the double phrase "who visited me at Pittsfield" (3.8–12) suggests a double remoteness: by "who visited me", Hubbard and his visit are placed some time back, and by "at Pittsfield" Melville himself is perhaps placed somewhere else at the time of his writing. Second, while the pen and ink used do not distinguish the phrase "in 1850" from the other writing on the page, the evidence for the later

---

Eleanor Melville Metcalf, by whom they were conveyed to the Harvard College Library in 1937. It is designated by the call number MS Am 188 (360). The memorandum was reproduced (apparently for the first time), without a transcription but with reference to earlier ones, in the article by G. Thomas Tanselle cited in the unnumbered footnote on p. 1005 below. The present independent transcription by Robert C. Ryan from the manuscript was verified from the original by Harrison Hayford, from photocopy by Lynn Horth and by Harrison Hayford, and from collations with the earlier ones by G. Thomas Tanselle.

2. After Melville's death his widow added, at the bottom of the verso of the memorandum, a sixteen-line note on identifications of real-life prototypes of characters in *White-Jacket*, supplied by Samuel Rhoades Franklin in his *Memories of a Rear-Admiral* (New York: Harper & Brothers, 1898). The purpose of Melville's own marginal check marks at the left of lines 4, 5, 7, 13, 19, 22, 26 (two), 27, and 29 is conjectural, but they may attach to the names, since he made two at line 26, which lists two names.

inscription of that phrase is the presence of the period before it, the absence of a period after it, and its non-inclusion in the original underlining. For its dating from external evidence see pp. 1013–20, below.

The full text of this document has been printed several times with varying degrees of accuracy. No transcription questions "shunning" (33.4) or correctly deciphers two words here first reported: "run" not "ran" (four times, 9.5, 20.2, 24.3, 28.2), and "Hayner" not "Haynes" (28.1). In the earliest transcription, Raymond Weaver (in *Herman Melville: Mariner and Mystic* [New York: Doran, 1921], pp. 160–61) misreads eighteen words, omits five, adds one, misspells two, and does not attempt to reproduce the punctuation. Charles R. Anderson (in *Melville in the South Seas* [New York: Columbia University Press, 1939], pp. 33–34) repeats Weaver's text, omits one additional word, and reverses the order of lines 16 and 17. Charles Olson (in *Call Me Ishmael* [New York: Reynal & Hitchcock, 1947], pp. 22–23) is accurate in wording (except for "ran" and "Haynes") though not in punctuation. Jay Leyda (in *The Melville Log* [New York: Harcourt, Brace, 1951], pp. 399–400) is accurate in wording (again except for "ran" and "Haynes") and in all but two marks of punctuation, placing a comma after "Salango" (24.6) and omitting a period after "home" two lines later.

Anderson supplies the full names of some of the men listed, and Leyda offers identifications for all of them. The names of the ship's company corresponding to those on Melville's memorandum are listed here as reported by Wilson L. Heflin, in "Herman Melville's Whaling Years" (Ph.D. dissertation, Vanderbilt University, 1952), pp. 61–76, 238, 346, 428–31, which also gives brief descriptions of the men at this time. Leyda suggests different identifications (*Log*, I, 399–400) in four cases: Henry Harmer (14.1); James Rosman (24.1–2); J. Warren Steadman (29.1–2); Joseph Broadnick (34.1–2). Heflin's canvass of the crew brings together information, including variant spellings of their names, from the "Whalemen's Shipping Paper," two crew lists (the official crew list and the "Master's Crew List"), and appended certificates.[3]

3. A certified copy of the "Whalemen's Shipping Paper" of the *Acushnet* is in the New Bedford Free Public Library; the official crew list is in the Old Dartmouth Historical Society, New Bedford; and the "Master's Crew List" is in the Treasury Department Records, National Archives.

The accuracy of Hubbard's information is suggested by the fact that it is confirmed by all other documents Heflin reports (but see items 7 and 9 below). By Heflin's account, out of the twenty-three officers and men included in Melville's memorandum, twenty (plus himself, Hubbard, and Richard Tobias Greene) were among the twenty-six original members (counting Captain Pease) of the *Acushnet*'s company. (Of the three he did not list, two deserted before the ship sailed; hence, only one—George Eliot—who sailed with him is not listed.) The three men he listed who were not original crew members were James Rosman, Henry Hayner, and—most interestingly—John Backus, since he was the original of Pip (see the discussions at 121.30 and pp. 1012–13 below). Among the twenty-nine replacements Captain Pease was obliged to recruit during the whole voyage, these three were the only ones while Melville was aboard, before his own desertion. Of the original twenty-six in the company, only eleven completed the voyage. Heflin remarks (p. 72) that two of Melville's friendships with green hands would "outlast the voyage"—those with Hubbard and Richard Tobias Greene.

Crew names from Heflin's canvass, by NN lines, are: Henry F. Hubbard (2.4); Valentine Pease, Jr. (4.1–2); Frederick Raymond (5.1); John Hall (7.1); George W. Galvan (8.1–2); Martin Brown (9.2); David Smith (11.1); Wilson Barnet (13.1); David M. White (14.1); Thomas Johnson (17.1–2); Enoch Read (19.1); Ephraim Walcut (20.1); John Backus (21.1); Carlos W. Greene (22.1–2); [unidentified by Heflin—see item 7 below] (24.1–2); John Wright (25.1); John Adams (26.1–2); Joseph Luis (26.4); William Maiden (27.1–3); [unidentified by Heflin—see item 9 below] (28.1); Joseph Broadrick (29.1–2); Henry Grant (31.1); Robert Mury (33.1); Joseph Waren Stedman (34.1–2).

Several readings in the present transcription need commentary.

(1) "retired" (4.3): This word as written is a good example of others in the memorandum (and throughout Melville's manuscripts) that can be made out only from their context, and even then not unquestionably. Here Weaver's reading "returned" (paralleling "came back" in several other entries) fits the indeterminate letter strokes as well as "retired" (Olson, Leyda, NN), and one must rely on contextual arguments to justify preferring the latter.

(2) "run" (9.5, 20.2, 24.3, 28.2): The established misreading "ran" is

induced by expectation of the standard preterite form; but the letter shape in all four instances is that of the open *u* not the closed *a*, and "run", a common nonstandard form, sounds idiomatically authentic in this rough sailor world. Cf. "The carpenter run away" in the mate's deposition among the *Lucy Ann* revolt documents, in the Hendricks House edition of *Omoo* (New York, 1969), p. 322. R. D. Madison reports that "run was frequently used as the simple past tense" in such naval works as James Fenimore Cooper's *History of the Navy of the United States of America* (Philadelphia, 1839).

(3) "Ropo" (9.10): In *Typee* (NN11.3–8) Melville lists "Ruhooka, Ropo, and Nukuheva" among the Marquesas Islands; the frontispiece map in the first English and American editions labels it "Roa-Poua, or Adams I.". At Nuku Hiva Melville himself and Richard Tobias ("Toby") Greene (neither included among the crew in his memorandum) deserted the *Acushnet* on July 9, 1842.

(4) "*Crew*" (16.2): Transcribed "Czar" by Weaver, who was apparently baffled by the indistinct letter formation and incomplete terminal *w* as well as misled by its parallel listing, and seems to have taken it as a crewman's nickname. Weaver's other bizarre misreading (induced by Elizabeth Shaw Melville's *y*-like mending) placed Captain Pease "in asylum" not "ashore" (4.6) at Martha's Vineyard, as if driven into deserved insanity or religious retreat (like Benito Cereno) by the evils that had befallen his crew, as Melville lists them "according to Hubbard".

(5) "Mowee" (14.5, 17.8): Maui, second largest island of the Hawaii group. Melville uses the same spelling several times in *Typee* and refers to having been there (i.e., when discharged at Lahaina from his third whaler, the *Charles and Henry,* on May 2, 1843). See Chapter 25 (NN186.11–19), Chapter 30 (NN225.3–8), and the discussion at 225.4 in the Northwestern-Newberry edition.

(6) "various attempts at running away" (22.4–8): Out of their context in the whole memorandum, each of these words (except "at"), taken by itself or even in the phrase, might well defy deciphering. They offer an excellent example of what Melville called the "chirographical incoherencies" of his hero's manuscript in *Pierre* (bk. 21.i, NN282.12).

(7) "*The Irishman*" (24.1–2): Not identified by Heflin; James Rosman

What became of the ship's company of the whale-ship
"Acushnet" according to Hubbard who came home in her
(more than a four years' voyage) and who visited me at Pittsfield in 1850

✓ Captain Pease — retired & lives ashore at the Vineyard

Raymond 1st Mate — had a fight with the Captain & went ashore at
Payta

Hall 2d Mate came home & went to California.

3d Mate Portuguese, went ashore at Payta

Broadsteen Born Portugee, either run away or killed at Ropo
one of the Marquesas

Smith went ashore at Santa coast of Peru, afterwards committed
suicide at Mobile

✓ Barney boatsteerer came home

Carpenter went ashore at Mowee half dead with disease
Died.

The Crew

Tom Johnson black, went ashore at Mowee half dead (rotten)
& died at the hospital

✓ Reed — mulatto — came home.

Blacksmith — run away at St: Francisco.

Backus — little black — Do

✓ Bill Green — after various attempts at running away, came
home in the end.

The Irishman run away at Salango coast of Columbia

Wright went ashore half dead at the Marquesas.

✓✓ John Adams & Do Portugee came home.

✓ The old cook came home.

Haynes run away aboard of a Sydney ship.

⟨ Little Jack — came home.

(Over)

1 *What became of the ship's company of the whale-ship*
2 *"Acushnet," according to Hubbard who came home in her*
3 *(more than a four years' voyage) and who visited me at Pittsfield.* [add in 1850]

4 *Captain Pease* — retired & lives ?ashore at the Vineyard
5 *Raymond* 1st mate — had a fight with the Captain & went ashore at
6 Payta
7 *Hall* 2d Mate came home & went to California.
8 *3d Mate*, Portuguese, went ashore at Payta
9 *Boatsteerer* Brown Portuguese, either run away or killed at Ropo
10 one of the Marquesas
11 *Smith* went ashore at Santa coast of Peru, afterwards committed
12 suicide at Mobile
13 Barney boatsteerer came home
14 *Carpenter* went ashore at Mowee half dead with disreputable
15 disease
16 *The Crew*
17 *Tom Johnson*, black, went ashore at Mowee half dead (ditto)
18 & died at the hospital
19 *Reed* — mullatto — came home.
20 *Blacksmith* — run away at St: Francisco.
21 *Backus* — little black — Do
22 *Bill Green* — after various attempts at running away, came
23 home in the end.
24 *The Irishman* run away at Salango coast of Columbia
25 *Wright* went ashore half dead at the Marquesas.
26 *John Adams & Jo Portuguese* came home.
27 *The old cook* came home.
28 *Hayner* run away aboard of a Sydney ship.
29 Little Jack — came home.
30                                        (Over)

31 *Grant* — young fellow — went ashore half dead, spitting blood,
32 at Oahu
33 *Murray* went ashore, ?shunning fight, at Rio Janeiro.

34 The Cooper — came home.

is suggested by Leyda (*Log*, I, 400). Possibly this was George Eliot, the only man who sailed in the original crew not otherwise listed by Melville or accounted for by Heflin, who reports that according to Captain Pease he "deserted on the voyage" (pp. 67, 74)—which is compatible with Hubbard's report "run away at Salango" (24.3–6).

(8) "Salango" (24.6): An island off the coast of Ecuador, not of Colombia at this period. From 1822 to 1830, however, Ecuador along with Venezuela and Colombia had been subsumed within the confederation "Gran Colombia."

(9) "*Hayner*" (28.1): Misread as "Haynes" in all earlier transcriptions; Melville's weak terminal *r* looks like *s*, as it also does in "four" (3.4), "*Carpenter*" (14.1), and "Cooper" (34.2). Although Heflin reports (p. 75) that no "Hayner" or "Haynor" appears in records of the ship, he cites a letter to Melville from Richard Tobias Greene, June 16, 1856, with the spelling "Haynor". It seems likely that this man was the "Henry Harmer" whose name Heflin includes on the original crew list and cites as spelled variantly "Hamer", "Harmer", "Hermer" (p. 67). For some reason Heflin does not make the identification and concludes, "Henry Harmer was not on Melville's memorandum" (pp. 71–72). Greene's letter to Melville said: "By the way do you remember Haynor, the steward? Well I found him in New Orleans last winter keeping a Hotel! He wished to be remembered to you, should I write you . . . " (*Log*, II, 516).

(10) "?shunning" (33.4): This is Weaver's reading of this indeterminate word, followed in all later transcriptions; it makes good sense but seems enough more "literary" than any others in the memorandum to be a third one of his overdramatic misreadings (see item 4 above). Yet possible alternative readings such as "shoving", "sharing", "shamming", and even "showing" do not fit the context more convincingly.

# The Hubbard Copy of
# The Whale

ON JANUARY 26, 1977, the afternoon session of the sale at Sotheby Parke Bernet in New York included, as lot 282, a copy of *The Whale* identified as "Property of The Estate of Henry Hubbard Middlecoff."[1] This copy, as the catalogue[2] pointed out, was "an unusually clean and fresh copy," despite small tears at the heads of the backstrips of the first and third volumes (clearly shown in the catalogue photograph of the famous backstrips of that three-decker).[3] What made this copy remarkable, however, was not

This essay has been slightly revised from its original publication as Part I of G. Thomas Tanselle's "Two Melville Association Copies: The Hubbard *Whale* and the Jones *Moby-Dick*," *Book Collector*, XXXI (Summer, 1982), 171–86.

1. For assistance with this account I am indebted to Esther Bonta (and other members of the San Joaquin Genealogical Society), Clara Belle Carter, Peggy Christian, Mitchel J. Ezer, Wilson L. Heflin, Sidney Huttner, H. Bradley Martin, Lois C. Menzies, Robert Rosenthal, and Roger E. Stoddard.

2. Sale no. 3946, *Fine Books & Autograph Letters . . . the Property of Dr. Howard Mahorner of New Orleans and Other Owners.*

3. The casings, especially the one on the first volume, are also somewhat loose, and some leaves (as at I, 93–96, and II, 3–6) are carelessly opened. There is occasional foxing; there are some yellowish (e.g., I, 202) and blackish (e.g., I, 65) smudges; and stains from inserted acid paper occur at I, 6–7, and I, 74–75.

its condition but two handwritten notes that it contained. The first of these is a ten-line presentation inscription in ink on the front free endpaper of the first volume: "Henry Hubbard / from his old Shipmate / and Watchmate / On board the good ship / Achushnet / (Alas, wrecked at last / on the Nor' West) / Herman Melville / March 23$^d$ 1853 / Pittsfield. —" (See fig. 1.) Very few presentation inscriptions could be more desirable to have in this book[4] than one to a former shipmate on the whaling voyage that provided Melville with many of the experiences underlying the book—especially when the inscription alludes to the two men's association on that voyage. The second manuscript addition is a pencil note made by the recipient, Henry Hubbard, in the lower margin (lightly ruled in pencil for the purpose) of page 58 of the third volume, the page in "The Castaway" chapter describing Pip's rescue after his first jump overboard: "Pip — Backus — his real name. I was / in the boat at the time he made / the leap overboard — Stubs = J Hall / real name [space] Hubbard". (See fig. 2.) Such a note, associating two characters and one event in the book with their counterparts on board the *Acushnet,* makes one wish that Hubbard had annotated his copy more freely, but he did not mark it elsewhere.

How this set of *The Whale* came to be part of the Middlecoff estate in Los Angeles in 1976 can easily be guessed from the fact that Middlecoff's first two names were "Henry Hubbard": Middlecoff was the grandson of the man to whom Melville had presented the volumes in 1853, and they had remained in the family from then on. That they were passed down as a prized family possession, however, seems far from the truth, and their survival appears more likely to have been a mere matter of chance. Middlecoff's mother was Eliza Fitch Hubbard, the younger of Henry Hubbard's two daughters. Why she, rather than her elder sister (Maria), took possession of *The Whale* is unknown; but presumably she might have moved it from Stockton, California (where Henry Hubbard settled in 1850), to Los Angeles at any time between 1900, when she married Walter W.

---

4. One would of course be an inscription to Nathaniel Hawthorne, to whom the book is dedicated. Another presentation copy of *The Whale* that has been discussed in print is the copy (now in the Berg Collection of The New York Public Library) presented on January 6, 1853, to John C. Hoadley, who eight months later (September 15, 1853) was to marry Melville's sister Catherine. See David A. Randall, *Dukedom Large Enough* (New York: Random House, 1969), p. 207 (cf. p. 209).

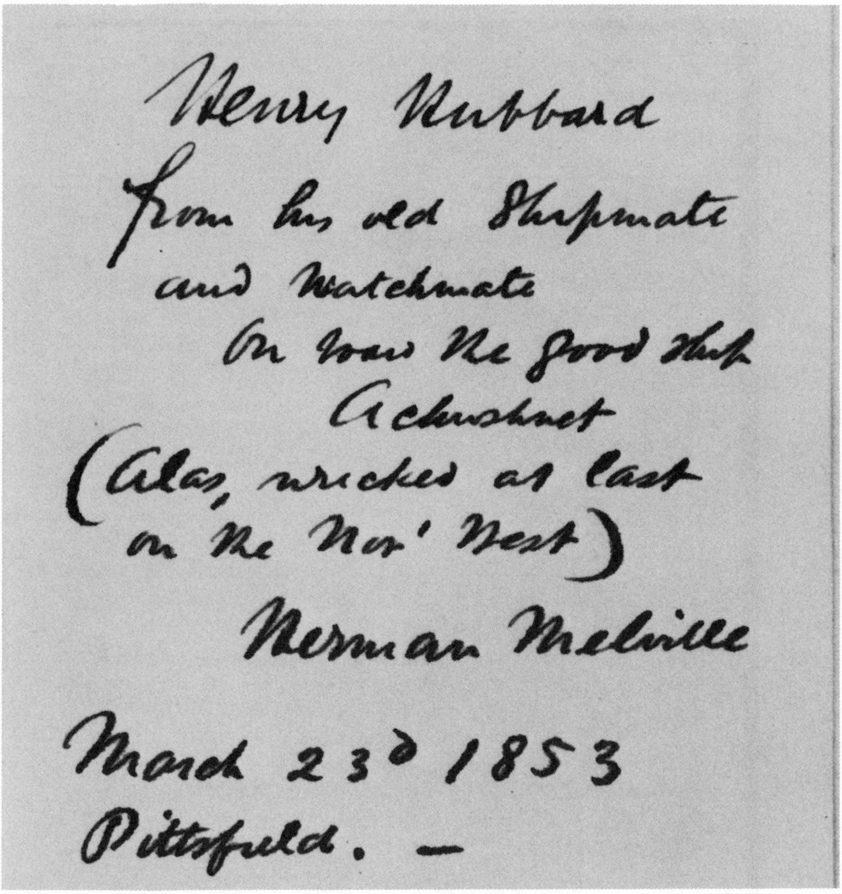

Fig. 1.   Presentation inscription from Melville to Henry Hubbard in *The Whale*. By permission of the University of Chicago Library.

Middlecoff, a prominent Los Angeles attorney, and 1917, when her mother (widowed for thirty years) died.[5] There is some evidence of an interest in the book just after this time, because a newspaper clipping dated (in pencil) December, 1919, telling about killer whales eating the carcasses of other whales, was laid into the first volume (leaving a stain on pages 74–75). There is no way to know who placed

5. A biographical sketch of Walter W. Middlecoff appears in *Who's Who in California: A Biographical Directory, 1928–29*, ed. Justice B. Detweiler et al. (San Francisco: Who's Who Publishing Co., 1929), p. 604. The burial of Hubbard's widow Maria

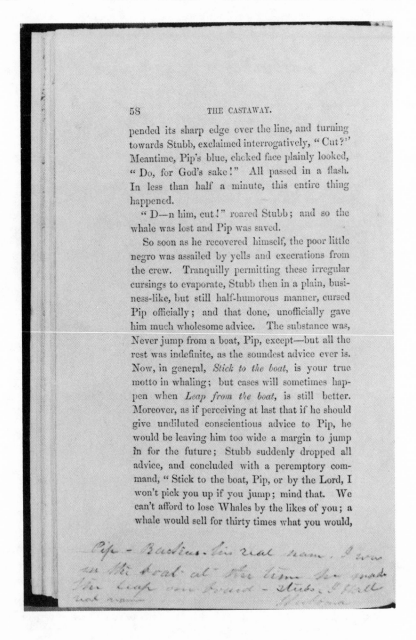

Fig. 2.   Henry Hubbard's annotation in *The Whale*, III, 58.
By permission of the University of Chicago Library.

it there; but at least one can conjecture that the presence of the book in the Walter W. Middlecoff household might suggest some interest in the book, and its association with her father, on Eliza Hubbard's part.

If so, the interest apparently diminished with the years, despite the growing recognition of Melville, for the book did not seem to have much significance for her son, Henry Hubbard Middlecoff. A friend of his, Dr. Lois C. Menzies, has recently recalled that Middlecoff telephoned her, on some evening between March, 1960, and May, 1962, to ask whether she had heard of "a Henry Something-or-other" who had written "something about a whale." Middlecoff had come across *The Whale* in the bookcase containing books that had belonged to his grandmother; the fact that neither Melville's name nor the book was familiar to him indicates that the book had not been regarded in the family—at least for the previous quarter-century or so—as anything unusual and that no family traditions about his grandfather's association with Melville had been transmitted to him. Dr. Menzies identified Melville for him, and he took the volumes with him the next time he visited her. She records that she proceeded to read *The Whale* from this copy: "Can you imagine my feeling," she adds, "when I came upon Capt. Hubbard's notation in the margin? I felt as though the old gentleman had put his hand on my shoulder and spoken directly to me, sailor to sailor. . . . I will never forget the thrill of finding that pencilled note in the margin. Think of all the years it had been there, waiting for someone to find it." Recognizing the interest of this copy, she pointed out to Middlecoff that it must be valuable. He apparently checked with someone at the Huntington Library, without taking the book there or perhaps even mentioning that it was a presentation copy, and learned that its value was about $1,500 or $2,000. The volumes remained in Dr. Menzies's possession until 1968, when she returned them to Middlecoff.[6]

A similar picture of the family's lack of interest in the set comes from Mitchel J. Ezer, counsel for the Middlecoff estate. He remembers visiting the Middlecoff apartment on one occasion when Middlecoff showed him *The Whale* in passing but expressed much

on September 6, 1917, at the age of seventy-four is recorded in vol. 2 of *Old Cemeteries of San Joaquin County, California* (Stockton: San Joaquin Genealogical Society, 1960–64).

6. Information from a letter from Lois C. Menzies to me on April 11, 1977; quoted by kind permission of Dr. Menzies.

greater interest in another of his grandfather's possessions, an oriental vase that his grandfather had brought back from one of his voyages. Although Middlecoff imagined the vase to be much more valuable than *The Whale,* it was appraised after his death at $300. At Middlecoff's death in June, 1976, his copy of *The Whale* found itself in an odd lot of five or six dozen miscellaneous books, none of the others being of interest or value except for his copy of George H. Tinkham's *Biographical* volume on San Joaquin County (Los Angeles: Historic Record Co., 1909), containing a sketch of Henry Hubbard; there were reprints of Elizabeth Barrett Browning, Emerson, Bryant, Burns, Goldsmith, Longfellow, Thomas Moore, and Whittier, the ubiquitous *Lucile,* sets of Hawthorne and Robert Louis Stevenson, a partial set of Scott, some stray volumes of Shakespeare, several of Balzac's novels, and so on. Middlecoff's widow intended to discard all the books, but when Mr. Ezer expressed an interest in *The Whale,* she presented it to him. He took possession of it, but on behalf of the estate, in case it should prove to be valuable.[7]

He then asked the Los Angeles Public Library for the names of book dealers and was apparently supplied alphabetically from the classified telephone directory those of the Caravan Bookstore, Peggy Christian, and Dawson's. The first made an outright offer and the third agreed to appraise the set if requested to, but the second, Peggy Christian, is the dealer who was actually asked (in a letter of July 15, 1976) to examine and appraise it. After her meticulous examination of it in the offices of Rich & Ezer and her thorough research (which included contacting Richard Colles Johnson of The Newberry Library[8] for verification of Melville's handwriting), she submitted on August 13, 1976, an exemplary report containing a detailed description of the volumes and an appraisal of the fair market value at

7. Information from a letter from Mitchel J. Ezer to me on March 29, 1977, and from the list of books which he sent me on April 8.

8. The Newberry's Melville Collection is the largest collection of printed primary and secondary material, and it is the headquarters for editorial work on the Northwestern-Newberry Edition. Some idea of its holdings of *Moby-Dick* editions can be gathered from *A Checklist of Editions of MOBY-DICK, 1851–1976* (Evanston and Chicago: Northwestern University Press and The Newberry Library, 1976), prepared by G. T. Tanselle on the occasion of an exhibition at the Newberry in November and December, 1976, to commemorate the 125th anniversary of the original publication of the book.

$25,000. Her estimate was an extremely sensible one, based on the fact that this copy was more desirable than the uninscribed one in the Stockhausen sale twenty-one months earlier, which brought $17,000 (having been estimated at $4,000 to $8,000),[9] and based as well on the belief that Stockhausen prices were generally inflated. Although Mr. Ezer authorized her, on August 19, 1976, to seek a buyer for the Hubbard *Whale,* the authorization was nonexclusive, and he soon concluded, from the interest that was being shown in this copy, that the estate might stand to gain if it were sent to New York for auction.

Accordingly it appeared in the sale of properties from various owners on the following January 26, with nearly an entire two-page spread in the catalogue devoted to it: there were two photographs, one of the presentation inscription (full-page) and one of the back-strips (half-page), with transcriptions both of that inscription and of Hubbard's annotation. In the list of pre-sale estimates printed at the back of the catalogue, the estimate for lot 282 was in agreement with Mrs. Christian's appraisal, for it read "25,000/30,000." What a unique item will bring, however, is impossible to predict, and as matters turned out, this estimate was considerably low. Bidding was heated, and not merely because the small and overcrowded sale room, even with windows open and an electric fan going, was uncomfortably warm. The Hubbard *Whale* was finally knocked down for $53,000 to John Fleming, acting on behalf of Mrs. Joseph Regenstein, who presented it to the University of Chicago Library. As might be expected, the sale of this book was a standard topic of conversation at bookish parties during the following three days: there were many of them, for this was the weekend of the Grolier Club dinner and the annual meeting of the Bibliographical Society of America. And the discussion continued into print, with Sotheby Parke Bernet's *Newsletter* for March–April, 1977, in its "Auction Record Update," reporting that this "superb presentation copy" had set "a new record for any work of fiction." The auction surveys in the journals have naturally paid attention to this sale: Nicolas Barker, for instance, commented that "the startled auctioneer caricatured on the cover of the 26 January sale" has evidently just sold this *Whale*—"a perfect example of an exceptional copy (it had a wonderful evocative

---

9. Sotheby Parke Bernet sale no. 3694, *The William E. Stockhausen Collection of English & American Literature,* Part I, November 19–20, 1974, lot 342.

presentation inscription from the author) making an exceptional price."¹⁰

The Hubbard *Whale* is certainly one of the great association copies in American literature. Beyond the obvious interest in a copy of Melville's most important book presented by the author to a former shipmate, and then annotated by that shipmate, there is the importance of the inscriptions themselves and the biographical and critical questions they raise. The new piece of information provided by Hubbard's note is the fact that at least one of Pip's two leaps overboard was based on an actual occurrence. Anyone familiar with Melville's way of working knows that many of the events in *Moby-Dick* must have been inspired by his own experiences on board the *Acushnet,* but this is the first time that eyewitness testimony from another member of the crew has been available. Hubbard was in a good position to know about Pip's leap, because, according to his statement, he had been lowered in the same boat as Pip—that is, the boat under the charge of the second mate, called Stubb in the book. Hubbard's comment refers only to a single leap and perhaps implies that there was only one ("I was in the boat at the time he made the leap overboard"); but it is not clear from the placement of his note whether he is referring to Pip's first or second leap as the one corresponding to the event he witnessed. The note comes at the foot of the page largely occupied with Stubb's lecture to Pip following the first leap; the facing page, beginning with the sixth line, takes up Pip's second leap. Thus the note could refer to either leap but seems somewhat more likely to refer to the first; if it had referred to the second, Hubbard would probably have entered it at the foot of the next page, which in fact offers a better surface for writing (a recto at such an early point in a volume has less curvature at the gutter than a verso). In any case, Hubbard's note testifies that a black crew member named Backus did jump from the second mate's boat, even if it does not permit one to know just which details of the episode in *Moby-Dick* are Melville's invention.

10. *Book Collector,* XXVI (Summer, 1977), 244. Robert Wilson also writes on this sale in *Book Collector's Market,* III (March–June, 1977), 25–26, including a reproduction of the inscription and the opinion that Hubbard's annotation is "Possibly the most exciting part of the book." And Sotheby Parke Bernet's *Art at Auction, 1976–77* devotes a full page (p. 215) to the Hubbard copy, providing an illustration of the backstrips and commenting briefly on the significance of the copy.

The other information provided by the note—the identification of Stubb and Pip as J. Hall and Backus—is of less moment, because the names of the crew members were already known. If Hubbard's equation of the real and the fictional names could be taken to suggest some degree of resemblance between the real and fictional personages, the information would mark some advance over knowing simply that Stubb occupies the same position that Hall held on the *Acushnet;* but it is difficult to say whether Hubbard's statement was meant to imply so much. In any event, the principal source of knowledge about the crew of the *Acushnet* besides the official crew list and associated documents comes indirectly from Hubbard himself, in a revealing memorandum written in Melville's hand that has long been known to scholars.[11] The memorandum lists twenty-three officers and crew members, briefly indicating what happened to each. The third entry is *"Hall* 2$^\text{d}$ Mate came home & went to California.", and the twelfth entry is *"Backus* — little black — Do", the "ditto" referring to the blacksmith's fate in the line above, "run away at St: Francisco." Hubbard's note in his copy of *The Whale* at least serves as corroboration of these two names in Melville's memorandum, and it makes explicit their association with Stubb and Pip.

When this memorandum is viewed in the light of the Hubbard copy of *The Whale,* an interesting biographical question arises—the answer to which, if it could be established, would perhaps be the most important fact to emerge as a result of the appearance of this presentation copy. Because Melville's memorandum dates Hubbard's visit in 1850 and his presentation inscription to Hubbard is dated 1853, the question is whether Hubbard visited Melville twice or whether the 1850 date—which was added to the memorandum at some time after the rest of it had been written—is an error for 1853. The significance of this question results from the bearing it has on understanding Melville's process of composition. Students of Melville have assumed, on the basis of the 1850 date, that Hubbard's visit served to refresh Melville's memory of various shipmates and thus may have affected his treatment of them in *Moby-Dick.* Leon Howard describes Melville's mind in the autumn of 1850 as "swirling with new ideas and old memories," stimulated in part by an "early fall"

11. See the reproduction and NN transcription of the memorandum, pp. 1002–3 above.

letter from "Long Ghost" and a "somewhat later" visit from Hubbard.[12] If, as Jay Leyda conjectures *(Log,* I, 399), the visit occurred in early November of 1850, Melville would have been engaged in writing *Moby-Dick* at the time; or if the visit came earlier in the year, it could equally well have influenced his thinking about the book. However, if Hubbard made only one visit, in 1853, and Melville simply failed to remember the precise year when adding "in 1850" to the memorandum, the visit could have played no role in the composition of the book. The Hubbard copy of *The Whale* does not rule out the possibility of an 1850 visit, but—taken in conjunction with the fact that the 1850 date was Melville's later addition—it does for the first time raise a question about whether a visit from Hubbard actually took place in that year.

The 1853 date, it would seem, is beyond question. There is no reason to believe that Melville might have falsified the date of his inscription. Furthermore, if he sent the volumes to Hubbard, rather than presenting them in person, it is difficult to explain why he waited sixteen months after the American publication of the book and why he chose the bulky three-volume English edition instead of the one-volume American. It is much more reasonable to suppose that Melville presented *The Whale* to Hubbard on the occasion of an unexpected visit, when a copy of the English edition in the original (not the remainder) binding was the only copy he had on hand (or, if not the only copy, the one he chose to present, as perhaps a more generous or elegant token of friendship than a copy of the American edition). The Hubbard *Whale,* therefore, almost certainly establishes Hubbard's presence in Pittsfield on March 23, 1853.

What brought him there and what other travel he may have engaged in during the 1850–53 period can be better speculated about with some knowledge of his biography. Henry Fitch Hubbard was born in Charlestown, New Hampshire, on October 26, 1820, the eldest of the three children of Jennison J. and Eliza Fitch Hubbard. The Hubbards were an old family in Charlestown, Jennison's grandfather, Jonathan (1719–59), having been one of the original grantees of Charlestown in 1757.[13] On December 28, 1840, Henry Hubbard

12. *Herman Melville* (Berkeley: University of California Press, 1951), pp. 173–74.

13. See Edward Warren Day, *One Thousand Years of Hubbard History* (New York, 1895), p. 354; Irvin W. Hubbard, *Record of the Descendants of George Hubbard, One of the Founders of Wethersfield, Milford, and Guilford, Connecticut* (Stockton, Calif., 1961),

signed the articles as a "green hand" on the whaleship *Acushnet,* three days after Melville had signed them.[14] But whereas Melville (in company with Richard Tobias Greene) deserted the *Acushnet* at Nuku Hiva in the Marquesas on July 9, 1842, Hubbard stayed with the ship to the end of its voyage on May 13, 1845. His first acquaintance with the California coast, according to his obituary, came in 1844 on that return voyage. Then he is said to have visited California again in 1848, following a voyage to the Sandwich Islands, and "was one of the first to enter the State after the discovery of gold." It was apparently this visit that persuaded him to try his fortune in California, and in 1850 he made his move to settle there.[15] He is reported to have worked for a time in 1850 as a cook in the "half-way house" on the Isthmus of Panama, and then to have tried his luck in the California mines, before moving, in August of 1850, into Stockton, then a mining boom-town, where money was to be made in many ways other than mining.[16] Hubbard first made a success as a drayman and then

---

pp. 23, 40, 67; Leslie S. Hubbard, *Hubbards History and Genealogy* (Lompoc, Calif., 1974), pp. 153, 166, 173. Although the birth date of Henry Fitch Hubbard is reported as 1821 in these sources, the correct date would seem to be October 26, 1820, as stated in Henry H. Saunderson, *History of Charlestown, New-Hampshire, the Old No. 4* . . . (Claremont, N.H.: Claremont Manufacturing Co., 1876), p. 418; this date fits various contemporary references (it would, for instance, make Hubbard twenty, as claimed, when he signed on the *Acushnet* at the end of 1840 and would make him thirty, as claimed, at the time of the census in December of 1850). (The year 1820 is also given in Tinkham—see note 19 below.)

14. Wilson L. Heflin, "Herman Melville's Whaling Years" (Ph.D. dissertation, Vanderbilt University, 1952), p. 69 (which also includes a brief physical description of the men at this time). See also pp. 999–1000, above.

15. Family tradition regarding this part of Hubbard's life is represented by Lois C. Menzies's recollection (in the letter to me of April 11, 1977) of what Henry Hubbard Middlecoff had told her: "Hubbard told me many times that his grandfather, Henry Hubbard, was a sea Captain in the 'China Trade' out of the east coast (Mass. ?). This was borne out by the many Chinese artifacts inherited by Hub from his grandmother. On one return trip from the Orient, the Capt. put in to San Francisco for repairs—just in time to become involved in the Gold Rush. He had aboard some picks and shovels which he promptly sold to the would be prospectors, then sailed back to the east coast, returning some time later with enough hardware to set up a store. This time he stayed in California."

16. He still listed himself as a miner, however, on December 4, 1850, when his name was entered on the books of the 1850 federal census (San Joaquin County, leaf 314 recto, line 38). Information from the 1850 census has been transcribed in *1850 Census, San Joaquin County* (Stockton: San Joaquin Genealogical Society, 1959), no.

went into partnership with a Mr. Luschinger in a furniture store. After a few years in this business, he made a brief trip to New England and shortly afterward set himself up as a money-lender, or "capitalist."[17] He prospered in this business, married Maria Slater Debnam in 1867 (by whom he had two daughters, Maria and Eliza),[18] and became, as his obituary indicated, "One of Stockton's Wealthiest Men": at the time of his death on March 25, 1887, his estate was assessed at $195,000 in personal property and $150,000 in real estate.[19]

Allusions to a trip in 1853 or 1854 occur in some of the biographical sketches of Hubbard. One (G. H. Tinkham's) says that the partnership with Luschinger "lasted for four years, when the business

---

632, and in Alan P. Bowman, *Index to the 1850 Census of the State of California* (Baltimore, 1972).

17. The exact chronology of these events is not established. Hubbard is still listed as "drayman" in the 1852 *Stockton Directory;* and the Luschinger & Hubbard firm is entered in both the 1856 *Stockton City Directory* and the 1859 *San Francisco Almanac* (which contain no entries for Henry F. Hubbard). The continuing use of this firm name does not of course necessarily mean that Hubbard was still connected with the business. In later years he is entered in the directories as "capitalist"—as in *Bishop's Stockton Directory* for 1876–77, or in the business directory included in Frank T. Gilbert's *History of San Joaquin County, California* (Oakland: Thompson & West, 1879), p. 140 (which records a few other biographical details). He is also designated "Capitalist" in the 1870 federal census (San Joaquin County, p. 80, line 8), where the value of his real estate is reported at $100,000 and of his personal effects as $10,000. (I have been unable to locate his name in the 1860 census; for the 1880 census, see Calif. vol. 13, e.d. 98, sheet 9, line 7.)

18. Hubbard's wife was twenty-three years his junior: she was born in Tennessee in late August or early September, 1843, for her age is reported as twenty-six in the 1870 census on August 11, 1870, as thirty-six in the 1880 census on June 1, 1880, and as seventy-four at the time of her burial on September 6, 1917 (see note 5 above). Their daughter Maria was one year old at the time of the 1870 census, and Eliza was eight at the time of the 1880 census.

19. This brief sketch is based principally on two biographical accounts: Hubbard's obituary in the Stockton *Evening Mail,* March 26, 1887; and Tinkham's sketch in J. M. Guinn and George H. Tinkham, *History of the State of California and Biographical Record of San Joaquin County* (Los Angeles: Historic Record Co., 1909), II, 320–21. Hubbard's burial on March 25, 1887, at the age of sixty-six is recorded in vol. 2 of *Old Cemeteries of San Joaquin County* (see note 5 above). That Hubbard may have been proud of his early association with California and interested in early California history is suggested by the fact that on November 23, 1868, he was one of nine persons who formed a committee to plan a San Joaquin Society of California Pioneers (that is, pre-1851 residents); see *An Illustrated History of San Joaquin County, California* (Chicago, 1890), p. 42.

was sold and Mr. Hubbard returned to the east. He came back to California the same year, however." By this reckoning the trip would apparently have been in 1854; but Hubbard's obituary speaks of a trip east "in 1853 or 1854," and it clearly implies that Hubbard made only one trip east during his early years[20] in Stockton:

> In 1851 Hubbard had only about $2,000. He was anxious to get some of his relatives out from the East, and on one occasion sent $300 back to them to pay their passage hither. He sent the money by a friend who very considerately pocketed it.
>
> It was in 1853 or 1854 that Mr. Hubbard returned East to see his folks. In the meantime some property had been left him there, and he was then worth about $15,000.

This trip is surely the one during which he visited Melville on March 23, 1853—and from which he returned shortly after that date: the *San Joaquin Republican* for June 28, 1853, reports Hubbard's arrival at the Magnolia House Hotel in Stockton on June 26.[21] The possibility that Hubbard paid Melville an earlier visit in Pittsfield, in 1850, can now be seen as extremely unlikely. In the first place, Hubbard probably did not make a trip back from California so soon after arriving there: not only does the obituary suggest that the 1853 trip was Hubbard's first trip east after moving to California in 1850, but some knowledge

20. He certainly made trips in his later years: for instance, Louis J. Rasmussen's *Railway Passenger Lists of Overland Trains to San Francisco and the West,* vol. I (Colma, Calif.: San Francisco Historic Records, 1966), records the arrival of Hubbard and his wife at Oakland on a westbound overland train on September 28, 1871 (p. 209; the September, 1870, reference on p. 39 is also possibly to this Hubbard). Rasmussen's *San Francisco Ship Passenger Lists* (Colma: San Francisco Historic Records, 1965– ), thus far covering the period from 1850 through January 6, 1853, does not list any Hubbard that can unequivocally be identified with Henry F. Hubbard. It records (in vol. 3) a "Mr. Hubbard" arriving April 11, 1852, on the steamer *Sea Bird* from San Diego and (in vol. 4) an "H. Hubbard" arriving October 5, 1852, on the steamer *Brother Jonathan* from New York via Valparaiso, Panama, and San Juan del Sur. These entries, taken in the context of other evidence, do not seem likely to refer to Henry F. Hubbard (it seems more likely that they could refer to the "H. P. Hubbard" recorded in vol. 2 as arriving from Panama on June 20, 1850, and from San Juan del Sur on October 16, 1851).

21. This reference to Hubbard is the only one I have been able to locate in the Stockton newspapers for the periods I have checked: March 16, 1850, through April 26, 1851 (Stockton *Times);* January through October, 1853 *(San Joaquin Republican).* His name does appear on a poll list for the election of October 17, 1852: see Gilbert's *History* (note 17 above), p. 29.

of Hubbard's life in 1850 also makes it inherently unlikely that he would have had the time, means, or inclination to return east at that point. Furthermore, the likelihood of his seeing Melville in Pittsfield before he left New England is equally slim: although the date of his departure for California is not known, he had surely left by the time Melville took his family to Pittsfield in mid-summer of 1850, if indeed he was in Stockton by late August, having in the meantime spent several weeks as a cook in Panama and some further time at the California mines.[22]

It would seem, then, that Hubbard probably paid Melville only a single visit, the one in 1853 documented by Melville's presentation inscription in *The Whale*, and that Hubbard's account of the other crew members thus occurred considerably after—and not before or during—the composition of *Moby-Dick*. On the other hand, it is a difficult question whether one should put more faith in the recollections on which Hubbard's obituary is based than in the addition of the date 1850 to Melville's memorandum. If the obituary is faulty and if Hubbard's arrival in Stockton was actually much later in 1850, it is conceivable that he could have visited Melville in Pittsfield before he left for California. On the basis of present evidence, it is impossible to rule out conclusively a summer 1850 meeting between the two.[23] But at least one can say that the Hubbard copy of *The Whale* and the investigation it has prompted have served to call into serious question the previously accepted date of 1850 on Melville's memorandum about the *Acushnet* crew.

One further detail of Hubbard family history clarifies the circumstances of Hubbard's visit to Pittsfield: his sister, Sarah Delano Hubbard (b. 1823), was the wife of Amasa Rice, a prosperous farmer of Pittsfield.[24] It seems reasonable to suppose, therefore, that Henry

22. The obituary reads as follows: "In 1850 [John] Fairbanks was taken sick on the Isthmus of Panama. He stayed there six weeks, and during that time became acquainted with Hubbard, who was then cook in the Half-way house on the Isthmus. He and Fairbanks agreed to come to California, and Hubbard shipped on a vessel and received $10 for his work. On arriving in this State they both went up into the mountains. Fairbanks returned to the valley in the middle of August, 1850, and came to Stockton. Hubbard arrived ten days afterward."

23. Leyda, in *The Melville Log,* conjecturally dates Hubbard's visit as "Early November?" (I, 399), but such a late visit in 1850 can now almost certainly be ruled out.

24. They were married on April 6, 1848, at Charlestown, N.H. (marriage record in the New Hampshire Bureau of Vital Records). Rice was entered on October 14,

Hubbard went to Pittsfield to visit his sister, not Melville; and perhaps only after he was there did he learn that his former shipmate resided in the same town. The fact that the middle name of Hubbard's sister was "Delano" is enough to make any student of Melville wonder whether there is a connection between the Hubbards and Captain Amasa Delano, whose *A Narrative of Voyages and Travels in the Northern and Southern Hemispheres* (Boston, 1817) was Melville's principal source for "Benito Cereno" and one of his sources for "The Encantadas."[25] Indeed there is: Henry and Sarah Hubbard's mother, Eliza Fitch, was a fourth cousin of Amasa Delano. (She was a great-great-granddaughter of Jonathan Delano [1647–1720]; and Amasa Delano was a great-great-grandson of Thomas Delano [1641–1723], a brother of Jonathan.)[26] Henry Hubbard may have heard his mother speak of the exploits of her fourth cousin and may have been aware of Amasa Delano's *Narrative;* and it is tempting to believe that, some time during the eighteen months Hubbard and Melville spent together on the *Acushnet,*[27] Hubbard was the one who first called Delano's story to Melville's attention.[28] This possibility gives an added interest

1850, in the Berkshire County census (p. 562, line 12), where his age is given as forty and the value of his real estate as $9,000.

25. For identification and a reprinting of Delano's *Narrative* as a source for these two pieces, see the NN *Piazza Tales* volume, pp. 581–82, 602, 809–47.

26. See Joel Andrew Delano, *The Genealogy, History, and Alliances of the American House of Delano 1621 to 1899* (New York, 1899). The descendants of Thomas (second son of Philippe De La Noye, founder of the American family) are taken up on pp. 153ff.; and those of Jonathan (fourth son of Philippe De La Noye) on pp. 293ff. Amasa Delano is treated on pp. 210–23; Eliza Fitch's place in the genealogy (as the second child of Sally Delano and Beriah Fitch, marrying Jennison J. Hubbard in April, 1817) is recorded on p. 493 (it is also repeated in the genealogy column of the Boston *Evening Transcript,* August 28 and September 5, 1911). (The Hubbard-Fitch marriage is dated October 27, 1818, in Albert Gallatin Wheeler, *The Genealogical and Encyclopedic History of the Wheeler Family in America* [Boston: American College of Genealogy, 1914], p. 551.)

27. The fullest account of this period is the section of Heflin's dissertation (see note 14 above) entitled "The *Acushnet* Outward-Bound," pp. 36–281 (see also his description of Matthew Fontaine Maury's abstract log of the *Acushnet,* pp. 465–70).

28. This would not be the only instance of Melville's learning about a book, later to be an important source for him, on the *Acushnet:* see pp. 971–95 above, about his copy of Owen Chase's *Narrative of the . . . Shipwreck of the Whale-Ship Essex . . .* (with his note saying that he "first became acquainted" with the *Essex* story in conversation with Chase's son aboard the *Acushnet).*

to the connections between Hubbard and Melville. And while it could have been uncovered without the appearance of the Hubbard copy of *The Whale*, important association copies have a way of stimulating investigation that leads to still further associations.

# The Jones Copy of
# Moby-Dick *and the*
# Harper Whale *Title Page*

O N NOVEMBER 15, 1974, an exhibition opened in the Rare Book Room of the University of Illinois Library at Urbana displaying books and manuscripts from the collection of Samuel Arthur Jones.[1] On view, in addition to materials relating to Jones's medical career and some of his own publications, were several early medical books, first editions by Addison, Goldsmith, Hawthorne, Melville, Emerson, and Holmes, some manuscripts by the latter two, and a number of significant letters to or from Jones. This material had not been seen publicly before and indeed was on loan to the library from the estate of Frida Haller Jones, daughter-in-law of Samuel Arthur Jones. Part of the collection was at that time temporarily housed in the library, but a substantial part remained in the Jones house in Urbana, where it had been for over half a century. The exhibition contained two Melville items, the first American editions

This essay has been slightly revised from its original publication as Part II of G. Thomas Tanselle's "Two Melville Association Copies: The Hubbard *Whale* and the Jones *Moby-Dick*," Book Collector, XXXI (Autumn, 1982), 309–30.

1. For assistance with this account, I am indebted to Mary Ceibert, George Hendrick, Harriet C. Jameson, Paul Haller Jones, Frederick James Kennedy, N. Frederick Nash, Merton M. Sealts, Jr., and Donald Yannella.

of *White-Jacket* and *Moby-Dick*, each rebound in half-calf bindings (the latter bound in two volumes). There was nothing in the exhibition captions or the accompanying printed catalogue to suggest that these copies were out of the ordinary,[2] and in fact one might have assumed that, being rebound, they were of less than average interest. Upon examination, however, the *Moby-Dick* proves to be a significant copy for two reasons.

The most important special feature of this copy is a printed piece of paper stuck to the recto of the third of three binder's leaves at the front of the first volume. (See fig. 1.) In the upper part of this piece of paper (beginning 31 mm from the top) appears the title "THE WHALE.", rather unattractively laid out with type measuring 2 mm in the first line and large heavy letters measuring 19 mm in the second, 10 mm below (and with part of the spacing material before and after the final "E" having worked up and printed). At the foot of the page, 83 mm below this title, is a publisher's imprint: "NEW YORK: / HARPER & BROTHERS, PUBLISHERS. / LONDON: RICHARD BENTLEY. / [rule, 5 1/3 mm] / 1851." The piece of paper thus printed appears to have been a scrap, for the blind impressions of seven other lines of type are visible on it: above the title there is one line, and below the title there are three lines, a wavy rule, and three more lines, but all these lines of type are merely rows of letters that do not form any words. Someone has apparently trimmed this piece of paper, rather unevenly, to make it fit the leaf it is now mounted on; at present it measures 168–70 x 106–7 mm and allows a border of 1–3 mm of the binder's leaf to show at the edges. It also seems to have been folded in half (across the longer dimension) sometime before it was pasted in this volume.

2. *An Exhibition from the Collection of Dr. Samuel Arthur Jones, University of Illinois Library Rare Book Room* (Urbana-Champaign: Friends of the University of Illinois Library, [1974]), with introduction and notes by George Hendrick and Fritz Oehlschlaeger. (This catalogue has been reprinted in *American Transcendental Quarterly*, No. 31 [Summer, 1976], supp. 2, pp. 30–37.) The Melville books are items 30 *(White-Jacket)* and 31 *(Moby-Dick);* the note on item 31 calls attention to two newspaper clippings about whales inserted into the volumes. That no mention is made of the more interesting insertion does not mean that it went unnoticed by those preparing the catalogue: working under pressure to get the catalogue printed and the exhibition mounted, they understandably did not have the opportunity to conduct an investigation of it and sensibly did not wish to make unsubstantiated claims about it.

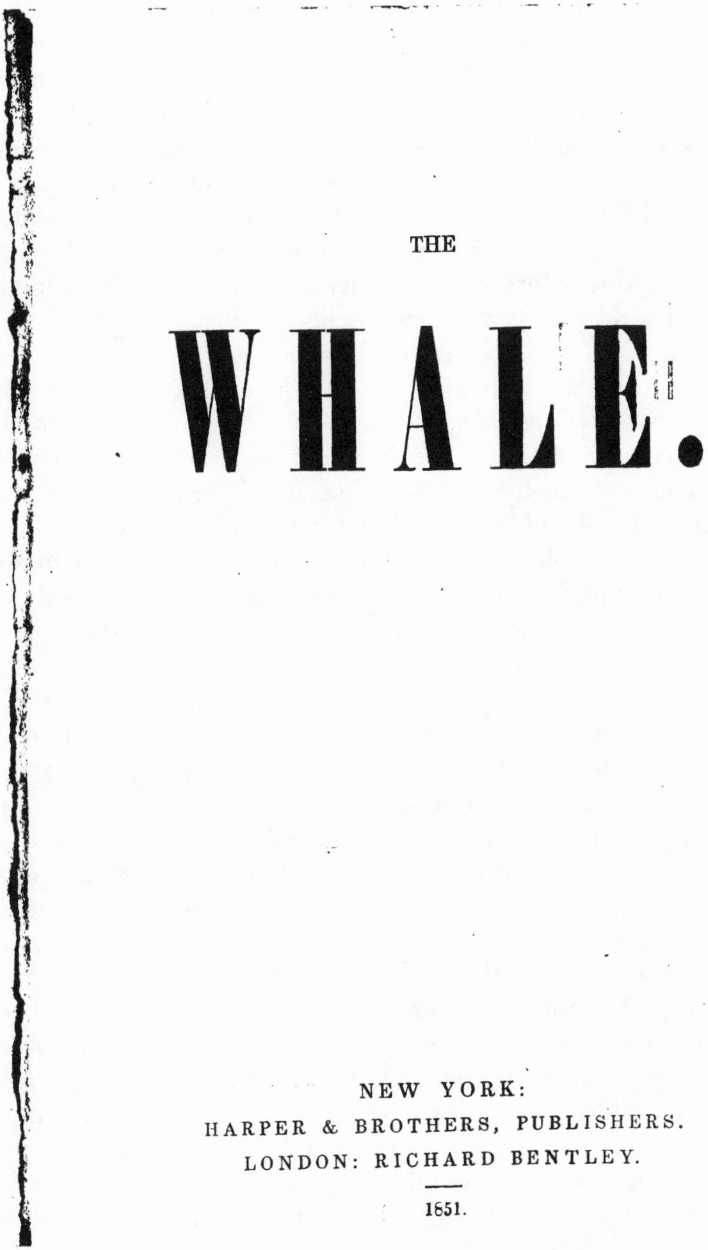

THE

# WHALE.

NEW YORK:
HARPER & BROTHERS, PUBLISHERS.
LONDON: RICHARD BENTLEY.

1851.

Fig. 1. "Trial" title page  pasted into Samuel Arthur Jones's
copy of *Moby-Dick*. By permission of the University of Illinois
Library, Urbana–Champaign.

The chief point of interest in the document is the fact that it combines in printed form the English title of the book, *The Whale,* with the American publisher's imprint. The combination is not in itself startling, for it is well established that *The Whale* was the original title of the book and that the change to *Moby-Dick* came after the American proof sheets had been sent to the English publisher and after the Harpers had accepted the book for American publication. Melville had the book set in type in New York by Robert Craighead in the summer of 1851, before arrangements for American publication had been made, and proofs were dispatched to Bentley in London on September 10. Two days later a contract with the Harpers was signed, referring to the book as "The Whale"; and in the October, 1851, number of *Harper's New Monthly Magazine* an excerpt from the book ("The Town-Ho's Story") was credited to " 'THE WHALE.' The title of a new work by Mr. Melville, in the press of Harper and Brothers, and now publishing in London by Mr. Bentley." Although this excerpt was probably planned for inclusion even before the signing of the contract for the book, since the latest news contained in the October number appears to be September 14, just two days after the date of the contract, one would expect references to Harper books in this magazine to be up-to-date; thus the title was apparently not changed before about mid-September. Exactly when the change was made is unknown, because the letter that Melville's brother Allan sent to Bentley informing him of the change is known only from an undated draft. Allan reports, "It is thought here that the new title will be a better *selling* title" (perhaps it was suggested by the Harpers); and he hopes that his letter will reach Bentley "before it is too late" to adopt the change ("I will add that the earliest opportunity has been taken to acquaint you with this change the proof was only rec$^d$ by me yesterday").[3] Even if Allan had sent this letter in mid-September, it would not have reached Bentley until early October, when some of Bentley's advertisements for *"The Whale"* were already appearing; and if it arrived much later, production would have been far enough advanced to make an alteration in three title pages and three opening text pages impractical, for Bentley's edition was published on October 18. At any rate, the change was not made in the English edition,

---

3. This draft, in the Melville collection at Harvard, is quoted in full above, p. 671.

and only the American edition (published probably on November 14) finally carried the revised title.[4]

Anyone acquainted with these facts, therefore, would not be surprised by a document combining the original title and the American imprint. What is important about the piece in the Jones *Moby-Dick,* aside from its corroboration of previously known information, is its indication that *"The Whale"* was retained as the title long enough for the Harpers to use it in what appears to be a "trial" title page. It does not otherwise help to date the change in title; and it can itself be dated, by reference to what was already known, only as falling somewhere between September 12 (or a few days thereafter) and October 15 (when a title page with the *"Moby-Dick"* title was deposited for copyright)[5]—though the change in title must certainly have taken place nearer the former date, for Allan could not otherwise have expected his letter announcing the change to reach London in time for it to be made. Whether this printed piece of paper is in fact a "trial" title page cannot at present be definitely stated. If it was intended as an experiment with the layout of the title page, the absence of Melville's name is peculiar.[6] Or if it was intended to serve simply as a covering sheet for the proofs, the omission of Melville's name is equally strange, when a full imprint, not necessary for that purpose, was included. The document is a puzzling one and its function not clear, but it certainly resembles a title page and can perhaps best be thought of (unless better information becomes available) as a "trial" title page— maybe one of several proofs that were pulled to check on spacing, some of the others presumably containing Melville's name. Its imprint is identical in wording and punctuation to the one in the published volume, but the spacing and the type sizes differ, and it in-

4. For a fuller discussion of the circumstances surrounding the publication of the two editions, see the HISTORICAL NOTE, pp. 659–81.

5. The printed title page cannot at present be located among the title-page deposits at the Library of Congress, but the wording of the deposited title page is known from its transcription in the copyright record book (entry no. 7024, Southern District of New York). Although the transcription does not include the imprint, it does follow exactly the wording and punctuation (but does not attempt to reproduce the lineation) of the first seven lines of the title page as finally published.

6. There is no evidence that Melville considered publishing the book anonymously, though he did later (in a letter to Bentley on April 16, 1852) suggest the possibility of publishing *Pierre* anonymously.

cludes a rule, above the date, not present in the published form. (See fig. 2.) The typography of this imprint, judged in the light of other mid-century Harper imprints, does nothing to arouse one's suspicions that this "trial" title page is not genuine. However peculiar it appears to be, there would seem to be no reason not to accept it, at least provisionally, as a surviving piece of the Harpers' pre-publication material for *Moby-Dick*.

Some support for its authenticity comes from a study of the history of the copy: indeed, the provenance of this copy is the second reason for its significance. The two-volume binding of Jones's *Moby-Dick*—an undistinguished nineteenth-century half-leather binding, with nonpareil marbled paper on the sides and dark red labels lettered in gold on the backstrips—is identical with the bindings on several other Melville volumes in his collection. The *Typee* volume (a copy of the Harper 1849 impression) contains, on the recto of the first of three binder's leaves at the front, the signature of Melville's brother Allan, a small clipping from a dealer's catalogue, and the notation in Jones's hand, "H. Melvilles own copies. / Sam'l A. Jones". (See fig. 3.) The excerpt from the catalogue lists the American editions of seven Melville titles, all described as in "half calf": *Mardi* in two volumes at $4, *Moby-Dick* in two volumes at $3.50, and *Omoo* (with the 1850 title page), *Pierre, Redburn, Typee* (the 1849 impression), and *White-Jacket* at $2 each. Following the entry for *Pierre* occurs an arresting statement: "All of the books of Melville that I offer came from the library of the author." There would seem to be no doubt that Jones's copies of *Typee,* the 1850 *Omoo, White-Jacket,* and *Moby-Dick* are the ones described in this clipping and little doubt that Jones was the one who, after purchasing them, pasted the catalogue entries into the *Typee* volume. It was Jones's custom, observable in other volumes, to paste catalogue entries into the copies they referred to, after he had been successful in purchasing those copies. Furthermore, his copies of these Melville titles are in half-calf, as specified in the catalogue, and those that are not first impressions—the 1849 *Typee* and the 1850 *Omoo*—correspond to the dates cited in the catalogue. And his note under the clipping refers to "H. Melvilles own copies", the plural indicating that he was thinking of other volumes in addition to the *Typee* in which he was writing. The conclusion seems inescapable that these half-calf volumes now at Illinois were

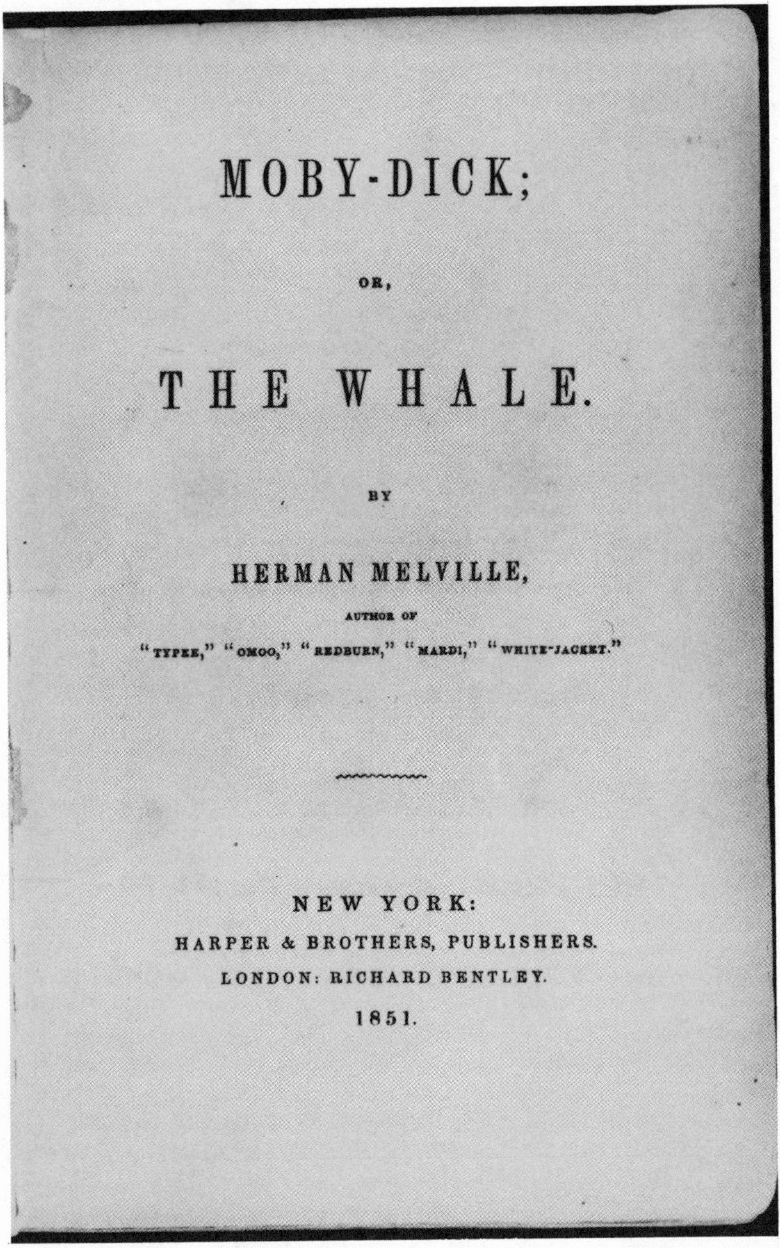

# MOBY-DICK;

OR,

# THE WHALE.

BY

## HERMAN MELVILLE,

AUTHOR OF

"TYPEE," "OMOO," "REDBURN," "MARDI," "WHITE-JACKET."

NEW YORK:

HARPER & BROTHERS, PUBLISHERS.

LONDON: RICHARD BENTLEY.

1851.

Fig. 2.   Title page of the American edition of *Moby-Dick* as published.
By permission of The Newberry Library.

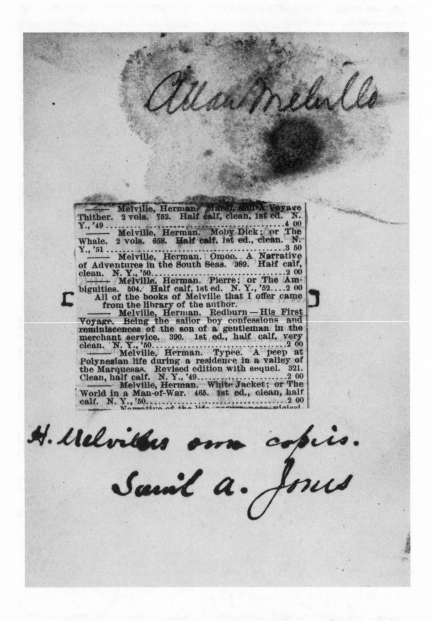

Fig. 3.   Inscriptions and clipping in Samuel Arthur Jones's copy of *Typee*. By permission of the University of Illinois Library, Urbana-Champaign.

purchased as a group by Jones from a dealer billing them as Melville's own copies.

The name of the dealer and the date of the catalogue do not appear on the face of the clipping. But its reverse, visible by holding the leaf to the light, fortunately proves to be part of the front of the catalogue and exhibits the large letters "LARK" and the address "34 Park Row"—enabling one to turn to the New York directories and identify the dealer as Anna S. Clark, who operated a bookshop at 34 Park Row in the 1880's and early 1890's, before moving to 174 Fulton Street in 1895.[7] The American Antiquarian Society has an excellent run of forty-three A. S. Clark catalogues, including the one with the seven Melville titles, which turns out to be No. 43, dated 1896. (The reason the clipping shows the pre-1895 address is that beneath the Fulton Street address on the front of the catalogue is the statement "For Fourteen Years at 34 Park Row.") Anna Clark, it seems, had a special interest in Melville, for his books turn up in her catalogues much more frequently than one would expect at this time (when his public reputation was at one of its low points), and she occasionally goes out of her way to comment on them. She was acquainted with his writings before she catalogued the lot purportedly from his library, because in No. 32 (ca. 1891) she appends to her entry for *Pierre* the statement, "I think this author wrote no better book" (p. 18). Later (in No. 54, dated 1902) she labels *Pierre* "The story of his own life", and (in No. 55) she adds to an entry for *Typee,* "Thoreau said 'Melville could more readily turn his hand to all forms of writing than any other person he ever saw' "—a sentiment that reappears (sometimes attributed to Hawthorne) in different forms in other cata-

---

7. From 1876 to 1880 the shop was located at 66 Nassau Street; in 1904 it moved to Peekskill, N.Y., where it was managed from 1916 by E. F. Hanaburgh (see catalogue No. 67). Because the New York directories beginning in 1876 generally list "Anna S. Clark" as the bookseller, I have used her name (and the feminine pronoun) here, though in fact other members of the A. S. Clark firm may have been responsible for the comments on Melville in the firm's catalogues. ("Mr. Clark" is referred to as having been in the book business for twenty-six years in newspaper accounts in 1891 of a man, identifying himself as Thomas Chancellor, who sold forged autographs of "Stonewall" Jackson in several New York shops, including the A. S. Clark shop. See "Not Jackson's Autograph," New York *Evening Sun,* October 10, 1891, and the retelling in Charles Hamilton, *Great Forgers and Famous Fakes* [New York: Crown, 1980], pp. 38–40.)

logues (e.g., Nos. 58, 62). Comments of this sort are not common in her catalogues; she may have been characteristic of her time in entering Melville under "Adventure," whereas Hawthorne rated listings under "First Editions,"[8] but she clearly took a particular interest in Melville.

Her catalogue No. 43 appeared only a few years after Jones's interest in Melville had been aroused by Henry S. Salt, an enthusiastic English champion of Melville's work, with whom Jones had carried on an extensive correspondence about Thoreau.[9] Four years after the catalogue, on January 7, 1900, Jones recalled his Melville collecting in a fascinating letter to Professor Archibald MacMechan of Dalhousie University:[10]

> Curiously, enough, I learned of Melville from Mr. Salt, Thoreau's best biographer. Just then Arthur Stedman was editing *Typee, Omoo, White Jacket,* and *Moby Dick.* These I got and read seriatim, and I too

8. If Melville had not been listed under "Adventure," entries for his books would not have been on the second page of the catalogues, and the reverse of the Jones clipping would not then have shown part of a front cover, with its clues for identification.

9. Salt's correspondence with Jones and his 1893 introduction to *Typee* and *Omoo* are discussed briefly by George Hendrick in *Henry Salt: Humanitarian Reformer and Man of Letters* (Urbana: University of Illinois Press, 1977), pp. 163–64. The texts of the letters appear in *Toward the Making of Thoreau's Modern Reputation: Selected Correspondence of S. A. Jones, A. W. Hosmer, H. S. Salt, H. G. O. Blake, and D. Ricketson,* ed. Fritz Oehlschlaeger and George Hendrick (Urbana: University of Illinois Press, 1979), esp. pp. 140, 158–59, 166, 251. See, for instance, Salt's letter of June 9, 1892, which asks Jones, "I wonder whether you are a Melville enthusiast? You *ought* to be. He was one of the very greatest of American writers" (p. 158). Jones's letters to Salt, which may contain details about his purchases of Melville's books, are presumably part of Salt's Thoreau material, now in private hands and unavailable for study (see Salt's *Company I Have Kept* [London: Allen & Unwin, 1930], pp. 103–4). On Salt's admiration for Melville, see also the HISTORICAL NOTE, pp. 739-41.

10. This letter was uncovered by Frederick James Kennedy in the Dalhousie University Archives and published, with helpful commentary, in "Dr. Samuel Arthur Jones and Herman Melville," *Melville Society Extracts,* No. 32 (November, 1977), 3–7. Jones and MacMechan were acquainted through their mutual interest in Carlyle, but Melville provided the occasion for the present letter: MacMechan had sent Jones a copy of his essay on *Moby-Dick,* "The Best Sea Story Ever Written" (*Queen's Quarterly,* VII [October, 1899], 120–30), and Jones was writing in reply, beginning, "Your Melville enthusiasm revived a spent enthusiasm of my own anent the same writer."

felt as if a new planet had swam into my ken. Of course, when I got the chance to buy the *very copies of these books that Melville himself had owned,* I went in for them *bald-headed,* as Lowell has it. Melville is very dear to me—some forty odd dollars worth!

Stedman's editions of Melville's books were published by the United States Book Company in 1892; thus Jones's initial acquaintance with Melville's work came within the four years preceding the Clark catalogue. It is easy to believe that Jones's purchases of Melville had cost more than forty dollars by 1900: the seven items in the Clark catalogue come to $17.50 (his letter leaves no doubt that he ordered all of them, though only four are now present among his books), and the four volumes of Stedman's edition would account for another $6 (if he bought the cloth copies at $1.50) or $12 (if he bought the half-calf copies at $3); in addition, he may have purchased the 1893 Murray impressions of *Typee* and *Omoo* because of the memoir by Salt that they contained, and he would have had the opportunity to buy from Anna Clark's catalogues of the 1890's—not to mention other sources—most Melville first printings at prices ranging from $1.50 to $3.

If Jones did not read Melville's work until after Melville's death, he had actually encountered Melville in person, without knowing it, during his earlier years of bookhunting in New York. In the same 1900 letter to MacMechan, he describes his discovery that Melville was one of the men he had seen in a bookshop years before:

> Imagine my astonishment when, on looking at Melville's portrait in the 1892 edition of *Typee,* I recognized a man whom I had met and whom I could easily have known by asking the bookseller in whose shop I met Melville to introduce me. Alas, I knew nothing of Melville as an author then nor as a man, so my bookselling friend is not to blame.

Whereas MacMechan in his 1899 article on *Moby-Dick* (see note 10) had described Melville from the portrait as showing "great but undisciplined strength," Jones's recollections lead him to a different conclusion.[11] "I am sure," he says, "you misinterpret his character and disposition":

11. The likeness that Jones saw in the 1892 edition was the October, 1885, photograph by Rockwood (reprinted in the *Log,* Plate xv)—Melville's last photograph,

In the flesh he did not show either strength or determination; on the contrary, he was the quietest, meekest, modestest, retiringingest [*sic*] man you can imagine. He moved from shelf to shelf so quietly—I never saw him speak to anyone—and his air was that of shrinking timidity: by no stretch of the imagination would one have thought him an author of any repute.

The time of this meeting can be roughly established by what Jones goes on to say:

At this time Melville had a berth in the Custom House, and it was after hours that both he and Richard Grant White would drop in at Luyster Brothers' bookshop before going to their up-town homes. There did not appear to be any intimacy between Melville and White; at least I never saw then [*i.e.,* them] conversing.

Richard Grant White (1821–85), a prominent New York critic and Shakespearean editor,[12] became Chief Clerk of the Marine Revenue Bureau of the New York Custom House in 1861; five years later, on December 5, 1866, Melville assumed the position of Inspector at the Custom House. The *terminus a quo* can be moved somewhat later, however, by Jones's reference to "up-town homes," for before 1870 White's residence was on Long Island.[13] And although White remained in the Custom House until 1878 and Melville until 1885, the *terminus ante quem* would probably be 1875, when Jones moved to Michigan; Jones could of course have traveled to New York and made occasional visits to New York bookshops after that time, but the description in his letter suggests habitual activity (Melville and White "would drop in," and Jones "never" saw them conversing). It was probably during the early 1870's, then, that Jones encountered Melville.[14]

At this time the bookshop of Albert L. and Samuel B. Luyster was

taken at the age of sixty-six (see Morris Star, "A Checklist of Portraits of Herman Melville," *Bulletin of the New York Public Library,* LXXI [September, 1967], 468–73). Kennedy points out that this photograph was the basis for the 1891 line drawing (in *Appleton's Annual Cyclopædia*) used by MacMechan.

12. He had also been one of the original editors of *Yankee Doodle,* to which Melville contributed several pieces in 1847.

13. Kennedy, in his *Extracts* article, points out that White moved to East Tenth Street in 1870 (an address "up-town" from the bookshop). The New York directories as of 1871 (copyrighted 1870) place him at 118 East Tenth Street.

14. At least ten years, in other words, before the date of the portrait (1885) that Jones recognized roughly twenty years later (1892 or shortly thereafter).

located at 138 Fulton Street, just down the street from where Anna Clark's shop was to be twenty years later. Melville is known to have frequented the New York bookshops, but the other recollections of such occasions refer to later years. A columnist in the *Literary World* for November 28, 1885, mentions seeing Melville in a bookstore "the other day";[15] and the firm of Francis P. & Lathrop C. Harper, founded a few years earlier, was a place where Melville "used to drop in, look over the books, and occasionally buy an unimportant title for which he paid cash without leaving his name." Like Jones, Lathrop Harper observed[16] that Melville "was a very quiet man and seldom if ever entered into conversation. If he talked at all it was never about his own writing, or about authors or literature at all." During the last year of his life, Melville frequently visited the shop of John Anderson, Jr.; Oscar Wegelin, who worked in the shop at the time, recalls the afternoon in the autumn of 1890 when Melville and Anderson had a conversation about "the sea and sailors," which marked the beginning of "a brief but pleasant friendship between the pair" (Anderson even visited the Melvilles at home). Melville's attraction to browsing in bookstores is confirmed by Wegelin, who recalls, "There was a report current in the booktrade at the time that he spent more of his slender income on books than his family liked."[17] Anderson's shop when Melville went to it was at 99 Nassau Street, near the place where the Luyster Brothers had moved in 1880 (98 Nassau). A. S. Clark's shop at 34 Park Row was about two blocks from there and would scarcely have been out of the way on a walk between Melville's house at 104 East Twenty-sixth Street and the Nassau Street shops. In his bookstore-browsing in this neighborhood, Melville may well have visited the Clark shop, perhaps becoming acquainted with its proprietor, as he did with Anderson. Conceivably Anna Clark's interest in Melville, reflected in her cata-

15. Reprinted in the *Log,* II, 794.

16. According to Douglas G. Parsonage, who wrote on behalf of Lathrop C. Harper to Merton M. Sealts, Jr., on December 26, 1947; quoted by Sealts in *Melville's Reading: A Check-List of Books Owned and Borrowed* (Madison: University of Wisconsin Press, 1966), pp. 122–23.

17. Oscar Wegelin, "Herman Melville as I Recall Him," *Colophon,* n.s., I (Summer, 1935), 21–24. Wegelin also recalled, when interviewed by Charles Olson in 1934, that Melville's purchases from Anderson would have numbered five hundred or more; see Sealts, p. 5. Melville's wife allowed him $25 a month for books and pictures after receiving an inheritance from her brother in 1884 (Sealts, p. 24).

logues, grew out of personal acquaintance. Melville would certainly have been known—if not always by name—to many of the dealers in the New York bookshop area, but Anna Clark is the only one so far discovered who paid particular attention to his books in printed catalogues.

It was fortunate that Anna Clark's catalogue No. 43 fell into the hands of Jones: for if there were few dealers in 1896 who would have cared about copies of Melville's books "from the library of the author," there were an equally small number of collectors interested in acquiring Melville's books, and Jones was one of them. Samuel Arthur Jones (1834–1912), a prominent homeopathic physician and author of numerous medical papers and *The Grounds of a Homeopath's Faith* (New York, 1880), carried on a private medical practice in Englewood, New Jersey, from 1863 to 1875 and during the last five years of that period was also professor of histology and pathology at the New York Homeopathic Medical College. In 1875 he moved to Ann Arbor to become dean and professor at the Homeopathic Medical College of the University of Michigan. Although he did not keep his deanship after 1878 or his professorship after 1880, he remained in Ann Arbor to the end of his life pursuing his private practice. His other principal interest, book collecting, was also a long-standing one, for he was acquiring first editions even before he received his first medical degree in 1860: he is known to have purchased some eighteenth-century English literature on a visit to London in 1857. His collecting encompassed three fields: medical books of the sixteenth, seventeenth, and eighteenth centuries (this collection had reached thirteen hundred volumes by 1879); eighteenth-century English literature; and books and manuscripts by a group of nineteenth-century authors, particularly Carlyle, Thoreau and the American Transcendentalists, and other American writers of the period, including Hawthorne and Melville. He concentrated on the nineteenth-century segment of his library in his later years and was best known for the Carlyle and Thoreau collections. He edited *Collectanea Thomas Carlyle, 1821–1855* in 1903, and a catalogue of his outstanding Carlyle holdings, which went to the University of Michigan in 1912, was published by the university in 1919;[18] Thoreau he promoted even

18. *A Catalogue of The Dr. Samuel A. Jones Carlyle Collection* (Ann Arbor, 1919), compiled by Mary Eunice Wead.

more intensively in a series of publications, including the first substantial bibliography of Thoreau, issued by the Rowfant Club of
Cleveland in 1894. A more detailed history of his purchases could be
constructed from the information he preserved in his copies; as Isaac
N. Demmon has remarked, "The fly leaves of his books contain
many valuable bibliographical notes on the history of these
'finds' "—and the *Moby-Dick* is a perfect illustration.[19] After Jones's
death in 1912, the books that were not purchased by the University of
Michigan[20] were eventually moved (along with papers and letters) to
Urbana by Jones's son, Paul Van Brunt Jones, who was a professor of
history at the University of Illinois from 1914 to 1950. Most of this
material remained in his house there until, after his death (1969) and
that of his wife (1974), Professor George Hendrick of the English
department came upon the books and papers and was instrumental in
arranging their purchase by the University of Illinois Library in
1975.[21] Four of the Melville books from Anna Clark's forty-third
catalogue thus stood on the shelves of the Jones collection, first in
Ann Arbor and then in Urbana, from 1896 until their transfer, nearly
eighty years later, to the Rare Book Room at Illinois.

If there is no mystery about Jones's purchase of these Melville
books or their whereabouts since that time, what remains to be dis-

19. Further information about Jones's collecting can be found in Demmon's
"Prefatory Note" to the 1919 Michigan catalogue, in the 1974 Illinois catalogue (see
note 2 above), esp. pp. 7–8, 15, in the introduction to the Hosmer letters (see note 21
below), pp. xv–xxvi, and in *Toward the Making of Thoreau's Modern Reputation* (see
note 9 above), esp. pp. 2–5, 159.

20. In September, 1912, the University of Michigan purchased for one thousand
dollars Jones's five-hundred-volume Carlyle collection and two hundred volumes of
American literature selected by Demmon. The only Melville item was apparently a
copy of *The Refugee* (the 1865 piracy, by T. B. Peterson of Philadelphia, of *Israel
Potter);* the pastedown at the back contains Jones's coded price and the date April 14,
1902, as well as some unidentified pencil notes (tabulating American states) and a
sketch (labeled "Sunday in the Backwoods").

21. Some were acquired by the University of Illinois earlier: four Melville
volumes—*Omoo, Pierre, Israel Potter,* and *The Piazza Tales*—are known to have been
acquired by the library on February 12, 1918. This *Pierre,* however, is apparently not
the one listed in Anna Clark's catalogue. For some further account of George Hendrick's locating the Jones collection and Paul Haller Jones's settling the estate, see
*Remembrances of Concord and the Thoreaus: Letters of Horace Hosmer to Dr. S. A. Jones,*
ed. George Hendrick (Urbana: University of Illinois Press, 1977), pp. ix–xiii.

covered is how the books found their way to the Clark shop and whether they were indeed "from the library of the author." Following Melville's death on September 28, 1891, his widow kept his books (estimated by the appraisers to be "about 1,000 volumes" worth $600)[22] for a short while, but a move to a smaller place the following April necessitated her disposing of some of the books. Apparently she turned first, not unexpectedly, to John Anderson, who bought a few volumes but did not wish to take the entire lot.[23] He then, according to Wegelin, called in other dealers, first Thomas E. Keane of 25 Ann Street (who offered $100), then A. F. Farnell of 42 Court Street, Brooklyn—whose offer of $120 was accepted.[24] Just how large the lot was or of what it consisted is not known, but one customer of Farnell's (who bought some of Melville's books) has remembered being told that the great number of "theological" works in it deterred some dealers from making offers and that even Farnell discarded many such volumes after his purchase.[25] Nevertheless, he later regarded the purchase, Wegelin says, "as one of the best buys of his career because the books sold with what, in the booktrade, passes for rapidity"; and Keane is said to have regretted not getting the collection. Still other dealers were involved at one point or another: Bangs & Co. examined the library, according to Farnell's son; and Francis P. Harper purchased some volumes from Mrs. Melville, volumes remembered by his brother Lathrop C. Harper as "an ordinary miscellaneous lot of books such as any reader might collect

22. This appraisal was made on March 28, 1892, and filed on May 3, according to William Charvat, "Melville's Income," *American Literature,* XV (November, 1943), 251–61.

23. Of those he did take, some were sold to Thomas J. McKee and reappeared in 1902 in the auction catalogue of McKee's library prepared by Anderson's firm: lot 5488, Southey's *Oliver Newman* (1845), is designated by Sealts in *Melville's Reading* as "apparently the first Melville association volume to be so catalogued by a dealer" (p. 5).

24. Farnell's diary of February 25, 1892, records the $120 purchase: this information was secured by Charles Olson in 1934 from Farnell's son Henry (who then ran the shop) and has been reported by Sealts in *Melville's Reading,* p. 6. Sealts's account of the dispersal of Melville's library (pp. 3–7) is basic: it not only draws together what can be learned from published sources but also records information uncovered by his own interviews and inquiries in 1947–48 and those of Charles Olson earlier.

25. Sealts's interview with Carol V. Wight in 1948; see Sealts, p. 6.

around him, on all sorts of subjects."²⁶ It is clear, as Harper recalled, that Melville's books were disposed of through several dealers—and although Anna S. Clark has never been mentioned as one of them, it is conceivable that she could have been, particularly if her shop was one that Melville visited and mentioned to his wife. However, if the seven Melville titles in catalogue 43 had been bought from Mrs. Melville in 1892, it does not seem reasonable to suppose that Anna Clark would have waited until 1896 to list them in her catalogue: if these books derived "from the library of the author," Anna Clark probably bought them from another dealer, or else from Mrs. Melville at the time of some later dispersal of books, perhaps in 1895 or early 1896.

It is certainly possible, in other words, for books from Melville's library to have turned up in Anna Clark's catalogue in 1896. (That catalogue intriguingly contains at least two other books that Melville once owned or used, including Amasa Delano's *Narrative*).²⁷ The next question is whether these particular copies of seven books by Melville are likely to have been among the books that Elizabeth Melville sold between 1892 and 1896. She certainly did not sell all the books (for part of Melville's library remained intact at her death in 1906, passing to the family and thence to Harvard); and it would seem natural that Melville's own writings, especially a matched set, would be among the items she would have kept. Whether in fact any of Melville's earlier books were a part of the collection at the time of his death is itself an issue. Oliver G. Hillard, shortly after Melville's death, remembered Melville saying (perhaps in the mid-1880's) that he did not own copies of any of his books;²⁸ but Wegelin recalls

26. Parsonage to Sealts (see note 16 above). David Randall recalls that volumes from Melville's library also turned up in Max Harzof's shop and later at Scribner's and in various shops in Brooklyn; see *Dukedom Large Enough* (New York: Random House, 1969), pp. 207–9.

27. The other book, besides Delano (Clark, p. 29) is one known to have been purchased by Allan Melville: Waddy Thompson's *Recollections of Mexico* (Clark, p. 16; Sealts 514 and Plate II). In addition, at least two books in the Clark catalogue appear in Sealts in different editions: *A Summary View of the Millennial Church* (Clark, p. 26; Sealts 459a is a later edition), and William Leete Stone's *Life of Joseph Brant* (Clark, p. 14; Sealts 491a is an earlier edition).

28. In a letter to the New York *Times* (headed "The Late Henry Melville"), October 6, 1891, quoted in the *Log*, II, 787–88: "I once asked the loan of some of his books, which early in life had given me such pleasure, and was surprised when he said that he didn't own a single copy of them."

delivering to his house in 1890–91 books purchased at Anderson's shop and says that "some of them were copies of his own sea tales, of which, oddly enough, he seemed to have had virtually no copies until Mr. Anderson supplied him" (p. 22).[29] It would seem, then, that Melville probably did have copies of his early books at the time of his death. The fact that his widow sold some of the remaining supply of *John Marr* and *Timoleon*[30] cannot be taken to suggest that she would also have sold copies of the earlier books, but if there were duplicate copies of some of them she might well have done so.

The presence of Allan Melville's signature in the *Typee* volume[31] increases the possibilities for speculation, particularly in light of the fact that several notes in the first of the *Moby-Dick* volumes also appear to be in his hand:[32] an excerpt from the review in the London *Leader,* copied onto page 207 at the beginning of the chapter on "The Whiteness of the Whale," to which the excerpt refers (see fig. 4); the date "Feby or Mch / 1871" written beside a clipping[33] pasted on the verso of the second binder's leaf at the back; and the name "Capt John Deblois / New Port" written on the verso of the third binder's leaf at the back.[34] It would seem, therefore, that the *Typee* and the *Moby-Dick* at any rate were Allan Melville's copies; and because all the located volumes are identically bound and Anna Clark indicated a common source for them all, it seems reasonable to think that all

29. Furthermore, as Sealts points out (p. 6), there are "apparent verbal echoes" in *Billy Budd* (on which Melville was working at the time of his death) that "may suggest a recent rereading" of some of his earlier books.

30. Wegelin, p. 23; cf. Sealts, p. 5.

31. This signature, when compared with other signatures of Allan Melville, appears to be authentic. And there is no reason to question its authenticity: the idea that anyone in 1896 or earlier would have wished to create the evidence for associating this volume (or these volumes) with Allan Melville seems remote indeed.

32. A convenient place for examining a sample of Allan Melville's handwriting is in Merton M. Sealts, Jr., *The Early Lives of Melville* (Madison: University of Wisconsin Press, 1974), pp. 192–93.

33. The clipping, entitled "Reminiscences of Hawthorne," prints from "advance sheets of the *Atlantic Monthly*" for February of 1871 J. T. Fields's account of the famous Monument Mountain picnic of August 5, 1850, where Melville and Hawthorne first met; one sentence is devoted to Melville.

34. Deblois was the captain of the *Ann Alexander,* which was destroyed by a whale on August 20, 1851, shortly before the publication of *Moby-Dick.* (The episode is the subject of a newspaper clipping at the front of the volume; see note 35.)

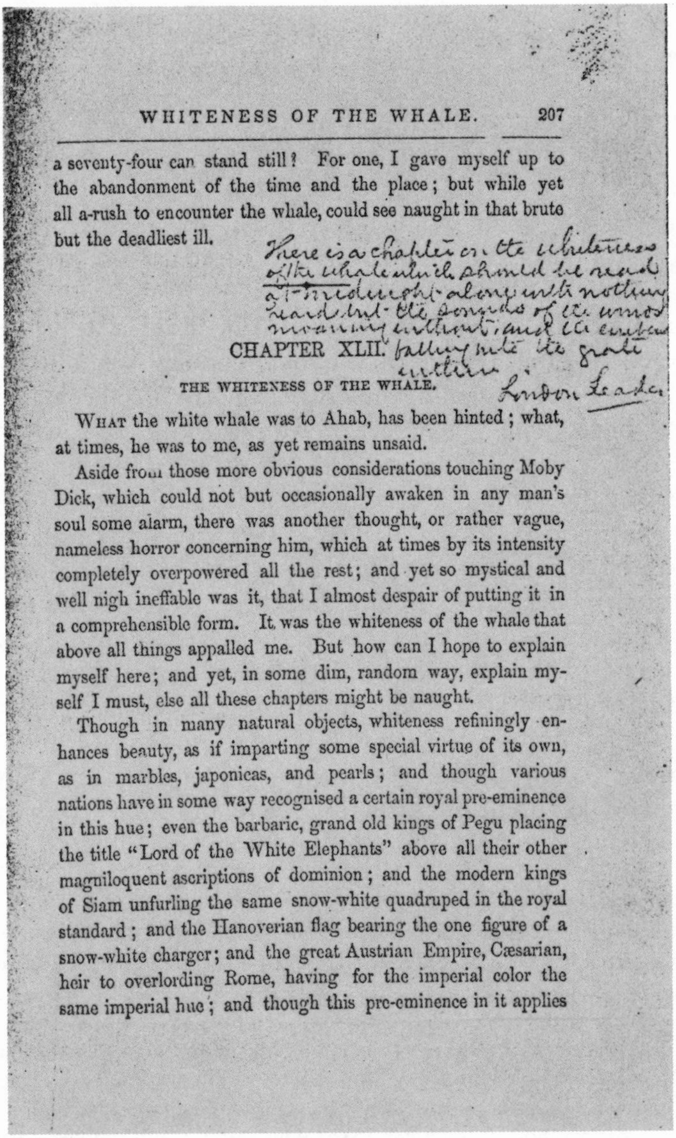

WHITENESS OF THE WHALE. 207

a seventy-four can stand still? For one, I gave myself up to the abandonment of the time and the place; but while yet all a-rush to encounter the whale, could see naught in that brute but the deadliest ill.

There is a chapter on the whiteness of the whale which should be read at midnight along with nothing heard but the sounds of the winds moaning without, and the embers falling into the grate within. London Leader.

CHAPTER XLII.

THE WHITENESS OF THE WHALE.

WHAT the white whale was to Ahab, has been hinted; what, at times, he was to me, as yet remains unsaid.

Aside from those more obvious considerations touching Moby Dick, which could not but occasionally awaken in any man's soul some alarm, there was another thought, or rather vague, nameless horror concerning him, which at times by its intensity completely overpowered all the rest; and yet so mystical and well nigh ineffable was it, that I almost despair of putting it in a comprehensible form. It was the whiteness of the whale that above all things appalled me. But how can I hope to explain myself here; and yet, in some dim, random way, explain myself I must, else all these chapters might be naught.

Though in many natural objects, whiteness refiningly enhances beauty, as if imparting some special virtue of its own, as in marbles, japonicas, and pearls; and though various nations have in some way recognised a certain royal pre-eminence in this hue; even the barbaric, grand old kings of Pegu placing the title "Lord of the White Elephants" above all their other magniloquent ascriptions of dominion; and the modern kings of Siam unfurling the same snow-white quadruped in the royal standard; and the Hanoverian flag bearing the one figure of a snow-white charger; and the great Austrian Empire, Cæsarian, heir to overlording Rome, having for the imperial color the same imperial hue; and though this pre-eminence in it applies

Fig. 4. Annotation, apparently in Allan Melville's hand, in Samuel Arthur Jones's copy of *Moby-Dick*. By permission of the University of Illinois Library, Urbana-Champaign.

belonged to him at one time. As his brother's business agent, he played an important role in the pre-publication history of Melville's books—in the case of *Moby-Dick,* he handled, among other details, the shipping of the proofs to England, and he wrote to Bentley notifying him of the change of title. He would have been in a position for pre-publication materials—like the "trial" title page—to pass through his hands, and it would not seem out of place for him to have saved certain items. The annotations and clippings that he placed in the *Moby-Dick* testify to his interest in the work,[35] and the "trial" title page could well be another memento that he decided to preserve in his copy of the book. Having the books rebound in a uniform and more elegant binding would similarly not be an unexpected gesture for him to have made. His quotation from the London *Leader* seems to have been copied before the *Moby-Dick* was rebound (judging from the way the writing meets the edge of the leaf), but the clippings pasted to the binder's leaves, as well as the "trial" title page (which appears to have been trimmed to fit), were of course added to the volume after rebinding. Assuming that the unlocated volumes from the Clark catalogue match those that have been examined, the date of the rebinding of the seven books listed there (nine volumes, with *Mardi* and *Moby-Dick* each bound in two) might perhaps be the period between the publication of *Pierre* in July, 1852, and that of *Israel Potter* in March, 1855, because the seven titles listed by Clark are Melville's first seven books, up to and including *Pierre;* of course, the set could originally have contained more volumes and the time of binding

35. Other clippings besides the one about the Monument Mountain outing may have been inserted by Allan Melville: e.g., one from the New York *Herald* of November 6, 1851, reporting the destruction of the *Ann Alexander* (a clipping on this subject had been sent to Melville in early November, 1851, by Evert A. Duyckinck—see *The Letters of Herman Melville,* ed. Merrell R. Davis and William H. Gilman [New Haven: Yale University Press, 1960], p. 139, n. 9, and p. 632, above.). Whereas the 1902 clipping about a white whale was obviously pasted in by Jones, and the one about the price of *Moby-Dick* in 1945 by his son, it seems unlikely that either of the Joneses had at hand a clipping from a newspaper of 1851. On the verso of the dedication leaf there is an undated (but probably 1853) clipping about the serialization of a French translation of parts of *Moby-Dick* in the *Courrier des Etats-Unis,* with comments by E. D. Forgues, the translator. (The *Typee* volume also contains a clipping, pasted to the inside of the front cover, regarding Toby's lecture [1855] on the Marquesas.)

could have been correspondingly later.[36] At any rate, it does not seem far-fetched to imagine Allan Melville, with his interest in *Moby-Dick*, taking a "trial" title page that he had saved, folding it across the middle, laying it—along with a newspaper clipping or two—in his copy of the book, and then, some years later, having a set of his brother's works uniformly bound and pasting these items into the *Moby-Dick* at that time. Obviously this may not have been precisely what happened, but it seems entirely reasonable to believe that Allan Melville would have had access to such a document as the "trial" title page and that the presence of such an item in a copy of *Moby-Dick* once in his possession lends support to its authenticity.

That the volumes listed by Anna Clark are actually Allan Melville's copies does not necessarily mean that she was incorrect in labeling them "from the library of the author": it is conceivable that they passed into Herman Melville's possession upon the death of Allan in 1872 or, more likely, upon the death of Allan's second wife, Jane, in 1890. If so, it is hard to know how Elizabeth Melville would have felt about disposing of them after her husband's death in 1891. She might have felt less attachment to them than to other copies (if there were any) that her husband himself had bought and perhaps reread; on the other hand, the family connection and the uniform binding might have made these volumes seem particularly desirable to her. In any case, there is a considerable question whether the volumes were ever in Melville's possession. If they had come to him in 1872 after Allan's death, he would have had to dispose of them subsequently, if it is true that late in life he had no copies of his earlier books—and dispose of them as a group, or they would not have been together in an 1896 catalogue. And the idea that they might have come to him after Jane's death in March of 1890 does not fit with Oscar Wegelin's recollection that Melville had "virtually no copies" of his books when his acquaintance with John Anderson began in the autumn of 1890.[37] Under the circumstances, it may well be that the

36. On the verso of the front free endpaper in the first volume of the *Moby-Dick* there is a pencil notation that resembles a bookseller's code and below it the indication "9 vols". Whether this notation is Anna Clark's or that of a dealer from whom she acquired the books, the nine volumes she listed presumably constituted the entire set as she received it.

37. It is of course theoretically possible that Anderson purchased books from the estate of Allan's widow and that Melville bought Allan's set from Anderson.

books reached Anna Clark by a different route—from Allan's (or his second wife's) family directly or from another dealer. It is possible that they left the family as early as 1872, if Allan's widow sold them after his death;[38] and it is easy to see how these volumes, with their clear family association, could have given rise to the story that they were once Melville's own. There is no reason to question Anna Clark's veracity; if she did not purchase the books from Melville's widow, then she probably got them from someone (whom she had reason to believe) who told her that they came "from the library of the author."

Even if these volumes were indeed a part of his library for a time, it is clear that they must be regarded primarily as Allan Melville's copies. As such, they are of interest in their own right. And what can be reconstructed of their history gives one little reason to doubt the authenticity of the "trial" title page in the Moby-Dick. The only period during which the whereabouts of this volume seem uncertain is between 1871 or 1872 and 1896. Before 1871 (when Allan apparently wrote that year on one of the binder's leaves) or 1872 (when he died), it was presumably in his possession; since 1896 (when Jones purchased it from Anna Clark), it has been on the shelves of the Jones family or of the University of Illinois Library. During that interval Melville was little enough known and his books so lacking in value on the secondhand book market that no one would have had any incentive to fabricate a pre-publication title page—or, for that matter, would have been likely to understand the significance of combining "The Whale" as title with the American imprint.[39] In the absence of additional evidence, then, this "trial" title page can be accepted as a genuine artifact from the production of Moby-Dick, preserved by Allan Melville. It tells us little that is new (only that the Harpers actually had the earlier title set in type) and indeed raises questions of its own. But it remains of great interest, being apparently the only surviving scrap from the proof stage of Moby-Dick.

The Jones Moby-Dick demonstrates the uses of association copies,

38. They were probably not sold earlier, because the 1871 date written beside one of the clippings seems to be in Allan's hand.

39. It is similarly difficult to imagine the circumstances under which anyone—either before or during that 1871–96 period—would have had this title page set up as a joke, without fraudulent intent.

as well as the byways into which they can lead. Melville association copies are now searched for as assiduously as the Sub-Sub-Librarian looked for references to whales. And the recent surfacing of this book, the Hubbard *Whale*, the annotated Milton, the Augusta Melville papers, and other documents provides welcome reassurrance that "the long Vaticans and street-stalls of the earth" have not yielded up all that they contain.

# COLOPHON

THE TEXT *of the Northwestern–Newberry Edition of* THE WRITINGS OF HER-
MAN MELVILLE *is set in eleven-point Bembo, two points leaded. This exceptionally
handsome type face is a modern rendering of designs made by Francesco Griffo for the
office of Aldus Manutius in Venice and first used for printing, in 1495, of the tract* De
Aetna *by Cardinal Pietro Bembo. The display face is Bruce Rogers's Centaur, a
twentieth-century design based on and reflective of the late-fifteenth-century Venetian
models of Nicolas Jenson.*

*The text of* Moby-Dick *in this volume was composed by William Clowes &
Sons, Ltd., of Beccles, Suffolk, England; the Editorial Appendix by Alexander
Typesetting, Inc., of Indianapolis, Indiana. It was printed and bound in paper by
Braun-Brumfield, Inc., of Ann Arbor, Michigan, and bound in cloth by John H.
Dekker & Sons, Inc., of Grand Rapids, Michigan. The typography and binding
design of the edition are by Paul Randall Mize.*